Alexander Thom und Co.

Fourth volume of minutes of evidence

Final Report

Alexander Thom und Co.

Fourth volume of minutes of evidence
Final Report

ISBN/EAN: 9783742805386

Manufactured in Europe, USA, Canada, Australia, Japa

Cover: Foto ©Andreas Hilbeck / pixelio.de

Manufactured and distributed by brebook publishing software
(www.brebook.com)

Alexander Thom und Co.

Fourth volume of minutes of evidence

COMMISSION ON MANUAL AND PRACTICAL INSTRUCTION

IN

PRIMARY SCHOOLS UNDER THE BOARD OF NATIONAL EDUCATION IN IRELAND.

FOURTH VOLUME

OF

MINUTES OF EVIDENCE,

Comprising that taken between September 29 and December 17, 1897,

BEING A SUPPLEMENT TO THE

FINAL REPORT

OF

THE COMMISSIONERS.

Presented to Parliament by Command of Her Majesty.

DUBLIN:

PRINTED FOR HER MAJESTY'S STATIONERY OFFICE,
BY ALEXANDER THOM & CO. (LIMITED).

And to be purchased, either directly or through any Bookseller, from
HODGES, FIGGIS, and Co. (Limited), 104, Grafton-street, Dublin; or
EYRE and SPOTTISWOODE, East Harding-street, Fleet-street, E.C., and
32, Abingdon-street, Westminster, S.W.; or
JOHN MENZIES and Co., 12, Hanover-street, Edinburgh, and 90, West Nile-street, Glasgow.

1898.

[C.—8924.] *Price 3s. 7d.*

TABLE OF CONTENTS.

INDEX TO WITNESSES EXAMINED BETWEEN SEPTEMBER 29 AND DECEMBER 17, 1897.

INDEX TO WITNESSES—*continued.*

COMMISSION ON MANUAL AND PRACTICAL INSTRUCTION.

MINUTES OF EVIDENCE.

THIRTY-SECOND PUBLIC SITTING—WEDNESDAY, SEPTEMBER 29TH, 1897,

AT 2 O'CLOCK P.M.,

At the Imperial Hotel, Waterford.

Present:—The Right Hon. THE EARL OF BELMORE, G.C.M.G., in the Chair; The Right Hon. C. T. REDINGTON, M.A.; Rev. HENRY EVANS, D.D.; Rev. HAMILTON WILSON, D.D.; W. R. J. MOLLOY, Esq.; and Captain T. B. SHAW;

with J. D. DALY, Esq., B.A., Secretary.

Rev. Brother THOMAS, B.A., Principal of De La Salle Training College, Waterford, examined.

14249. CHAIRMAN.—I believe you are the Principal of the De La Salle Training College, Waterford?—Yes.

14250. Will you kindly tell the Commission what are the subjects of instruction in the Training College, particularly as bearing upon the matter of our inquiry?—The principal subject bearing on the matter of the inquiry is drawing; this we make obligatory on all the students; every student must take up the course of drawing prescribed in the College.

14251. Perhaps you would tell us, as you come to the different heads, in your own words, anything that may occur to you that is likely to be useful to us?—The subject of drawing we make compulsory on all the teachers, because of its great utility in the schools. We consider, from experience of different countries, that a great deal of the prosperity of the people in the arts depends on the training they get in elementary drawing. We make it compulsory—we are most anxious to try and bring it into all the schools. Of course it is principally the ordinary freehand drawing, and, for the sake of the teachers, we have what they call "blackboard drawing," by which the teachers are trained to draw on the blackboard a design which they wish to exhibit to their classes.

14252. Have you been able to follow teachers after they have left you and gone back to their schools, and ascertain whether they have been successful or otherwise in the teaching of drawing?—To some extent, yes; and we have found that the subject of drawing is now much more taught by managers of schools. It is a great additional help to a teacher to get a school, and as a rule it is taught with success.

14253. Do you think the children take an interest in drawing?—If it is well taught, they will; but as it has been principally taught in the National schools, simply placing a model before the boys, and compelling them to copy that, without any help or any lesson to explain how they were to go about it—that kind of drawing they never take an interest in. If drawing is well taught, they always take an interest in it; some of course more than others, on account of natural aptitude and taste.

14254. Have you in your own mind any instances where teachers who have qualified for teaching drawing, owing to circumstances, have not taught drawing; and therefore their knowledge has remained useless for a number of years, say, fifteen or twenty years?—No particular cases; but I know there are some schools in which some of our own teachers have been qualified for drawing, but for some reason or other the manager does not care about introducing it.

14255. In a case of that sort, would you think that a teacher who had let his talent lie dormant for fifteen or twenty years, would be able to take the thing up again in case circumstances, either a change

Waterford. — April [illegible]. — Rev. Brother Thomas, B.A.

of school or some other reason, made it necessary for him to teach drawing?—I think so. I think it does not militate against him.

14666. You think not having practised the teaching of drawing would not militate against him?—His hand may have been out of practice a little, but nothing to signify.

14667. Coming to the subject of agriculture, what would you say to that?—Well, as far as my knowledge of the teaching of agriculture goes in the schools, I consider it a great failure, a very great failure.

14668. Why?—Because, ordinarily speaking, it is taught simply by committing the text book for the sake of results fees, and there is no intelligent work, ordinarily, the teachers are not instructed in the way of agriculture.

14669. I understand that there are only a very limited number of school gardens or school plots in this part of the country?—Very few, very limited.

14670. Do you think that if there were some small plots of a rood or half an acre attached to every school it would be an advantage—I mean for the purpose of the children being taught the principles of gardening or of agriculture?—I am afraid it would not be of general advantage, because the teachers, generally, I think, have not a taste for that. I think if teachers had a taste, generally speaking, for agriculture, they would not have become teachers at all.

14671. Do you think that if it were made worth a teacher's while to take that subject as an extra subject, and he were to receive in some way a grant in the same way as the Science and Art Department gives grants for certain subjects, that would encourage him to learn the subject?—It would encourage and assist; but what I fear is that it would not give the teachers sufficient natural taste for agriculture, which is so necessary to inform the same thing into the pupils.

14672. Then you have no means in connexion with primary education in Ireland that you could suggest by which, not the trade of agriculture, but what you might call the principles of agriculture, could be taught in a practical way, in addition to learning it out of books?—I would be inclined to suggest and recommend that those principles which you speak of should be taught in the primary schools, not as agriculture, but as the elementary principles of the natural and physical sciences. I consider that this is a way in which the teachers would all, generally, have a decided taste for it, and the boys would take to it very well. Take the case of two boys, say of fourteen years of age each, both sons of farmers, and who, as such, have worked more or less on the farms at different times, and will work after they leave school; but one of them has learned farming in the school from the text book, as is done at present, and the other has not; but instead of that, he has learned some of the fundamental principles, a little bit of agricultural chemistry, the principles of botany, how plants grow, and what they require for their food, and some principles regarding geology and other natural and physical sciences. That boy, when he goes into the farm under his father, after leaving the National school, will be far ahead, as a farmer, of the other; he will have an intelligent conception of how to carry on the farming business.

14673. Do you think he would be able to apply what he had learned in the school in that way, in a practical manner on the farm, without having had any actual instruction in the shape of work upon school gardens or plots?—I think he would, because he has enough of practical work at home. Of course, for a regular agricultural system, thoroughly scientifically carried out—you cannot do without an agricultural school, which is beyond the National school, and for which there are only a few pupils.

14674. Have you had any experience in the subject of kindergarten and hand and eye training?—Not except through teachers. Wherever it is well practised, it certainly is most successful and most useful for little children in the school; and in all the schools that we can exercise any influence over we require kindergarten, in some modification or other, to be carried out through all the classes.

14675. You don't approve of the plan, which seems very general in Ireland, of their teaching it to the infants, and then discontinuing it for a year or two, and taking up something of the same sort again afterwards?—No, I do not; but what I refer to by carrying on kindergarten in some form or another, is the giving of object lessons—on some of the natural and physical sciences—carrying them up through the classes; and of course, manual instruction and training of the eye and hand, drawing—all that is the principle of kindergarten carried on. We oblige our teachers, when they go to any of the practising schools, to give object lessons, so as to try and bring this system into the schools.

14676. Have you considered the question of manual work in wood?—I have considered the question since it was raised, but I don't exactly see how it can be carried on, under the present conditions of schools, without a decided modification, and without some provision being made for the necessary expense; but if it can be done it certainly attaches a great interest to the school.

14677. With regard to experimental science, what are your views on that subject?—Very much what I have said, that every elementary school ought, if possible, to have a little course of natural and experimental science as a foundation for technical instruction—either technical instruction in farming, or technical instruction in any other art.

14678. Would you approve of the children making experiments themselves, as we saw done, in some cases, in the English schools?—As far as it can be done, yes.

14679. Because it would be easier to do that in a large town school than in a country school?—Very much easier; of course, a good deal depends on the teacher; but it is very feasible. I have known boys, myself, taking much delight in making up little simple apparatus for chemical experiments with bottles and little things like that, using things that might be thrown away, and yet by their ingenuity they made little apparatus that would be very serviceable for the little experiments wanted.

14680. I see on your examination you have the subject of object-lessons; would you explain what you have in your mind by that term?—Well, I will take one illustration, an object-lesson on a plant; teaching them a regular lesson, or a little course of three or four lessons, as the case might be, on the plant; how it grows; how it receives its nourishment; and how it develops; and the uses that might be drawn from that particular plant, or that particular class of plants of which this one was a type. And I have shown some of the teachers myself how that could be illustrated with a large seed, a bean for example, showing three stages of development: the first stage, when it germinated; the second stage, when the leaves were thrown out; the third stage, when perhaps it flowered. Here they would have the principle of the growth of nearly all agricultural plants.

14681. That would be something in the way of teaching the principles of agriculture; suppose you applied that to a potato, for instance?—To a certain extent you can; but in the development of a plant you could not conveniently have the conditions of soil, and so forth; in a class-room you must have some other simpler thing. For object-lessons it is necessary to take things that can be handled easily in a class-room. If there were a little garden, that could be done by planting specimens at different times, and showing them the development.

14282. Rev. Dr. Evans.—Brother Thomas, have you any provision for teaching agriculture in connection with the College?—Is it here in our College?

14283. Yes, in connection with your College?—We have. We have a small farm about three miles outside of Waterford, to which our students go to see in the course of the year the different farming operations. The Professor of Agriculture gives his lessons in the College, and then he notes certain points, 1, 2, 3, as the case may be, which he wishes them to attend to in the fields, and they go out every week.

14284. And you believe they profit by that?—Well, they do, to some extent.

14285. Do your students come from families engaged in agriculture?—Largely, perhaps—yes.

14286. Then do they have a knowledge, to any extent, of agriculture before they come?—They have the rough knowledge of agriculture which one naturally acquires in the country among boys, but they have no systematic or intelligent knowledge of the subject when they come here, so much so that we have to begin at the beginning, and go through with the instruction, like the growth of a plant.

14287. Do you believe that they will be capable of teaching agriculture in the schools when they get their appointments?—I do; but I believe that the greater number of them won't care enough for it to do so; they won't have interest or enthusiasm enough, and if they have not that, they won't do it; they will simply take the book, as long as it is part of the course, and there are result fees for it, and make the boys memorise it, and nothing more.

14288. Referring to what you said in answer to the Chairman, about drawing, would you indicate, Brother Thomas, what you consider defective or faulty in the mode of teaching drawing in the National schools?—The ordinary mode of teaching drawing is this: a model is placed before a boy, and he is told to draw away; he is not shown how to begin or go about it. The same system to a great extent was prevalent, and is prevalent still, in regard to penmanship. You get a copy-book, there is the headline, and you are told to imitate it; but an intelligent explanation of how the letters are formed, and how the boy ought to begin to form them, and hold the pen, as a rule is not given. These are two points we are trying to urge into the schools as much as possible.

14289. Chairman.—Whose fault is it that the teacher takes so little pains—is it the fault of the manager?—It is simply defective training.

14290. Defective training of the teachers?—Well, up to this the teaching staff has been mainly supplied from monitors, and these monitors were trained by the previous teachers, and they imitated the teacher; they know no more than he does, and just the way he taught writing and drawing, they teach them.

14291. Rev. Dr. Evans.—I see what Brother Thomas means: you do not apply those remarks so much to those that were trained in the Training Colleges?—Oh, no.

14292. But to monitors and pupil teachers who became principal teachers without having passed through a Training College?—Yes.

14293. Do you give instruction in horticulture?—Nothing distinct from the farming.

14294. Do you happen to know whether there are school gardens in connection with National schools in this locality?—I do not know of any in this locality connected with National schools.

Waterford.

Sept. 22, 1897.

Rev. Brother Thomas, M.A.

14295. Mr. Molloy.—Brother Thomas, are you not aware of the Board's rule, to the following effect: "The Commissioners require that in all Training Colleges, and in the practising schools connected therewith, satisfactory provision be made for instruction in drawing and vocal music"?—Yes.

14296. A while ago, when you said drawing ought to be made compulsory, I did not know whether you meant in the colleges or in the schools. Which do you refer to, because that is a strong recommendation almost equivalent to an order? It is expected that in all training colleges satisfactory provision will be made?—Yes, but up to the present programme it was not compulsory in the Training Colleges; it was an extra; it was given to students who wished to take it.

14297. As a matter of fact these rules of 1890, (prior to the issue of the new programme), conveyed that as a recommendation, almost equivalent to an order, so far as the training colleges were concerned. Is drawing to scale taught in your schools?—Yes.

14298. Is construction a special subject, and the application of practical geometry to drawing?—It is connected with geometrical drawing and plan drawing.

14299. Then probably your teachers hereafter will look for certificates in that particular branch?—In that particular branch.

14300. And it is to be hoped that, getting charge of schools later on, they will introduce the subject?—It is to be hoped, especially for the benefit of those boys who will be anxious to turn to the direction of carpentry or building, where they will have a use for it in drawing their own plans and making their own designs.

14301. What is your view with regard to making drawing compulsory in the ordinary National schools, both rural and town?—I think, so far as possible, it ought to be.

14302. In both classes of schools?—In both classes.

14303. That is, in fact, wherever the teacher holds a certificate in drawing—in that I include drawing to scale—he ought to be compelled to introduce the subject?—I think he ought; there are few things more necessary and useful to children than drawing.

14304. Coming to agriculture, what is the size of your farm?—About fifty acres.

14305. That is not connected with the National Board in any way?—No.

14306. But it is utilised for the benefit of the teachers; they are brought out there?—It is used for illustrating the professor's lectures.

14307. Does the Professor of Agriculture accompany the students in training to your farm?—Yes, he is there with them.

14308. How often do they go to your farm?—Once a week.

14309. They don't take any practical part in working on the farm?—No.

14310. Chairman.—Do you think they take any interest in it, or merely go because they are obliged?—Well, not much; if they were left perfectly free the majority of them would not go there.

14311. Mr. Molloy.—Did you ever think of creating an interest by giving individual teachers small plots to work at on a regular system of rotation of crops?—That has often been spoken of, but then it takes a good deal of time, and we are anxious about other subjects on the programme.

14312. Agriculture is a very important subject on the programme, and a very high fee is paid for the instruction of pupils in that particular subject

[illegible]

theoretically, and also a special fee paid in connection with the National Board, if they work one on the farm; would you think of connecting your farm with the National Board, and identifying the College more closely in its agricultural instruction in that way?—The chief difficulty is that the students have not sufficient enthusiasm or taste for the subject to do anything.

14313. Why not try to create a taste in those students who come to you, most of them being, I presume, farmers' sons?—I am afraid it is those ones who do come, who have not got the taste for farming; if they had a taste for farming they would remain at farming.

14314. The third subject you referred to was kindergarten; have you thought out any scheme by which the principles of kindergarten could be extended regularly from, say, Classes III. to IV., V., and VI., and not confined exclusively to infants and Classes I. and II.?—Nothing more definitely than the general scheme which we do carry out, as far as our opportunities allow us, of carrying the kindergarten on in the form of object lessons and little scientific lessons.

14315. There is a museum connected with your College?—There is a small museum of objects for the object lessons I spoke of.

14316. Then your students have access to that, and receive instruction regularly from one of the professors?—As a rule the professor brings the objects into the class, just in the way that we expect the teacher himself should bring his little objects into his class. If it is a lesson on some of the ores of that particular locality he takes a few samples of the ores into the class with him, and with the blackboard gives a little instruction.

14317. Have you any chemical laboratory in your College?—We have a small commencement of a laboratory for the same purpose.

14318. Do the students themselves experiment?—No, they do not, except so far as the teacher may ask them to help.

14319. Is your College connected with the Science and Art Department for any subjects?—It is.

14320. What are the subjects in connection with the Science and Art Department?—The art subjects, drawing; and secondly, the science subjects, mathematics, and natural science, that we may be doing that particular year; natural philosophy, the present year, under what is commonly called physiography, and physiology and hygiene.

14321. An examination was held in May?—Yes.

14322. Were your students successful?—Well, fairly successful.

14323. Of course you are aware now that the National Board will recognise satisfactory proficiency at the Science and Art examinations and not oblige the student to be examined on the Board's paper, as in the past?—That is part of their new programme.

14324. You said you thought there would be no interest taken in manual working in wood; do you think the difficulty arose in regard to expense?—I think a great deal of interest would be taken in it, if it could be made feasible; the difficulty in bringing it into practice arises from the probable expense, and the difficulty of meeting that expense. I think there has been a pretty good illustration of that in the girls' industrial scheme, the alternative scheme of work for girls, which is a comparative failure in the country, and mainly because of the difficulty of meeting the expense.

14325. As a matter of fact we visited two very large Convent schools yesterday, and the nuns informed us that the alternative scheme was a complete success, and they liked it very much; but, generally speaking, it has not been carried out?—No; it is in Convent schools it has been principally carried out.

14326. No attempt has been made in connection with your College to introduce working in wood?—No regular attempt; I did make an attempt so far as to try and get a teacher trained in Sloyd and manual training from the continent, but the answer in every case was that he could not be spared—they would have to stop a course if he went.

14327. If you had been successful in getting a skilled continentalist, you would have introduced it here?—That was my intention, to have commenced it this September.

14328. You may be able at a later period, and then you intend to introduce it?—I intend to introduce it as soon as it is feasible.

14329. Rev. Dr. EVANS.—How many Queen's scholars have you?—We have at present 150.

14330. How many other students have you in training, in addition to the Queen's scholars?—That is the entire number.

14331. I thought there was another class besides, of your own order?—The members of our own order are included in that 150.

14332. Mr. MOLLOY.—For what number is the college licensed by the National Board?—For 150.

14333. Rev. Dr. EVANS.—And you have the full number?—The full number.

14334. Captain SHAW.—You teach drawing to all your students; has it been your experience that any of them are incapable of becoming teachers of drawing?—No; we find that everyone of them can qualify perfectly well for the ordinary drawing required in National schools.

14335. Would you feel confident of giving them certificates as teachers in drawing after they have gone through a course in drawing?—I would; some of them have failed to get certificates for some reason or other—accidental reasons.

14336. But you think the College authorities could give certificates?—They could; but I think it is preferable for outside parties to give the certificates.

14337. Then as to the sort of drawing which should be taught in elementary schools, you think that should be confined to freehand and scale drawing?—I think that would be quite sufficient.

14338. And, perhaps, model drawing for more advanced classes?—Yes, more advanced.

14339. In talking of models, you said a model was put before students—that meant a flat example—in elementary schools?—Up to this it was only flat in elementary schools.

14340. Then, with regard to agriculture, you think that might with advantage be dropped as a subject in elementary schools, and replaced by a course of experimental science?—I think it would be an advantage in primary schools; fifty per cent. of these children will never be farming at all; the large number of them will be mere labourers and simply have to do what the farmer tells them.

14341. Then you contemplate of course that this experimental science should be taught practically, that the apparatus should be present in the school and used by the teachers in giving instruction?—It should be, certainly.

14342. Otherwise it might be learned out of a book—the same as agriculture?—The same as agriculture, but it will be attended to with great interest, while agriculture will not, it appears to me.

14343. Is it not very important that the teachers should learn the use of apparatus under those conditions?—It would be very useful that he would be able to make up little things for himself.

14344. Is not the training college the place for him to learn that, rather?—It is to a great extent.

14345. Would you approve of laboratories for teachers in the training colleges, where they should go through a regular course for themselves?—I would, but our time unfortunately cannot be given to it; we have a very stiff programme to go through in other subjects, and it is very hard to give much time to any one subject. As things are at present with us, we are taking the natural and physical sciences, but teachers know that such subjects are not part of the school programme, and that they are not required to study them by the National Board; so that the College is handicapped in this way, that the teachers would say: "Oh, that subject is not necessary. Why should I give much time to it—why should I give much care and attention to it?"

14346. You think if it was made a subject in the syllabus for teachers they would give more care and time to it?—Certainly; and if it were brought into the curriculum of the school, they would see there was practical utility in it, and they would give a great deal more care to it.

14347. With regard to object lessons: do you think that they should learn one subject consecutively, say on a course leading up to science or leading up to agriculture, or that they should be haphazard, or taken anyhow—one day you get a flower, another day a steam engine, and another day something else?—They should follow a definite course of subjects. In England they have marked down for primary schools a definite course of object lessons that the teacher is to go through, and that course varies according to the standard.

14348. Of course it is a sine qua non of an object lesson that the object should be present?—Yes.

14349. Do you approve of having only pictures of the object?—If you cannot get the object, the nearest thing is to have the picture.

14350. But there are sufficient objects without going to pictures?—There are sufficient objects.

14351. CHAIRMAN.—Do your Queen's scholars do anything, when they are having a lecture in experimental science, in the way of measuring and weighing objects themselves?—Not much; we have not done much really in the way of experimental science for the students.

14352. It is more a lecture by the professor?—It is more a lecture.

14353. And they don't try to give effect to that themselves?—No; because it consumes relatively too much time.

14354. REV. DR. WILSON.—Could you give any idea of the probable proportion of students that have a special aptitude for drawing?—I think at least 30 per cent. have a very good aptitude.

14355. I am sure we are all agreed with you as to the importance of drawing as a fundamental subject?—At least 30 per cent. show a very good aptitude out there for drawing.

14356. Do you think is the appreciation of drawing increasing generally among the students?—I think it is, because it counts more towards a school than it used.

14357. As to chemistry: do many take an interest in that?—Everyone takes an interest in that, to some extent. The chemistry which we have covered this year is strictly agricultural chemistry, for the sake of giving a good foundation to the agriculture which they have to learn.

14358. I think it is very important that you have such a very large farm as fifty acres: do you keep any cattle at all?—Yes.

14359. Because rearing cattle in this district is an important part of the agricultural industry, and to know the different kinds of cattle there are here, and how to rear them?—Of course that is a point that the Professor of Agriculture calls special attention to in the course of his instruction.

14360. In your programme of studies could that you could re-arrange it to find room for manual training, if it was considered important to do so?—I think so—I think it could be done.

14361. You say they don't show much desire for wood or metal work; in England we found testimony borne freely that whenever they had commenced it they took a great interest in it, and I believe it would be the same with you?—I believe myself that, firstly, the boys in schools, everywhere where it is done—we have many schools in which it is done—take a very great interest in it, and it improves the school and makes them more in earnest. Now, with regard to teachers, as long as it requires much time, and tends to take them away from other subjects in which they require to get certificates, there will be a certain feeling against it; but such would not be the case if it were part of the school programme.

14362. I think there is a reasonable prejudice in the minds of many against manual training, against woodwork and metalwork, but the testimony borne to us was that really the time spent on this did not interfere with their literary studies, for they come back with more zest to them?—I believe that whatever we have any of that instruction, it does not interfere in the slightest degree with the literary instruction.

14363. MR. REDINGTON.—Do I understand you to say that you would wish the present mode of teaching agriculture entirely changed?—It seems to me that it would be beneficial to the school to do so.

14364. And you would substitute for it the elementary principles of natural and physical science?—I would.

14365. Then, what would be the use of school farms?—In that case they would not be much use at all.

14366. Would a small garden be sufficient for teaching the elements of botany?—Quite sufficient.

14367. From your knowledge of the schools of the country, would it be possible to have sufficiently large gardens attached to every school in which the principles of botany could be practically taught?—Perfectly easy; I have seen cases where boys had a little flower bed, varying from half the size of this table to the full size, where they would plant flowers, and follow them up through the whole course of the year.

14368. Have you any experience of the mode in which agriculture is taught in other countries, say France or Belgium?—No, except in the Ravenet Agricultural school.

14369. You don't know whether it is taught in the ordinary primary schools in France?—Generally speaking, as far as I am aware, it is not taught; but the principles of the natural and physical sciences are taught instead.

14370. Are you familiar with the science programmes that are contained in our rules?—I am fairly familiar with them.

14371. Do you think them suitable or not?—In some cases they are too extensive.

14372. Do you think that a science programme might be devised which could be taken up by boys in the fourth class?—I think so, certainly, beginning in the fourth and ending in the sixth.

14373. Then about drawing: do you teach the Queen's scholars in De la Salle Training College both model drawing and drawing from the flat?—Yes, we do.

14374. Would you give a certificate to a teacher for one kind of drawing only?—Well, I think it would be reasonable for him to get a certificate for one kind of drawing.

14375. Would you encourage him to take up two kinds?—I would encourage him to take up two.

Wexford.
June [illegible]
Rev. Brother Thomas, [illegible]

14376. Do you think that the study of geometrical drawing ought to be more encouraged than it has been?—I think it should; it is indispensable for all the boys who have any tendency to go to carpentering or building work; they require geometrical drawing.

14377. Do you think that heretofore we have asked too high a percentage of marks for our certificates in drawing?—If you consider the subject itself, I would say not; but considering the question of getting it spread as much as possible in the schools, I say yes; a large number of teachers at present could not get that percentage.

14378. Do you think a certificate gained by examination only is any proof that a teacher can teach drawing?—No, not exactly; because, as I said, he might not know the first thing about how to teach it.

14379. What would you say to allowing a teacher to teach without a certificate if the result of his instruction is that the pupils know how to draw?—I think that would be an advantage for a very large number of schools at present.

14380. CHAIRMAN.—With reference to school plots: I gather from what you said that you think the want of taste in that direction would lie rather with the teachers than the children?—I think it would, because, as a rule, the boys in a school will be just what the teacher is. They take to everything, and do well everything that he has a taste for, and throw enthusiasm for.

14381. But you think that, on the whole, the teachers being persons who, if they had any taste in that direction, would not become teachers, would not take an interest in it, but, on the other hand, a great many of the children, who probably would be farmers hereafter, would take an interest in it?—They would take an interest in it if the teacher had an interest in it.

14382. Do you think that the system promoted by the National Board should not look to the interest and advantage of the children, and what would be useful to the children afterwards, rather than to what would be to the taste of the teacher?—The primary thing is to look to the benefit of the children; but the question is how are you to reach the children? It would appear that if it be desirable to give the children a good course of agriculture for the benefit of the country—all the teachers are not farmers, all the boys will not be farmers—it ought to be in special schools.

14383. Special schools should be established through the country?—For that purpose.

14384. So, do you think, on the other hand, that special teachers, peripatetic teachers, going round a number of schools would be an advantage, giving a lesson once a week, or once a month, or once a fortnight, in each school?—That would do very well, but I do not think it would be at all so efficacious as having special schools directed by a teacher who had a special aptitude and taste for it; and the pupils who would go to that school would be those who had finished in the National school, having got a preliminary preparation for it in physical and natural science, and who showed they had a taste for it.

14385. Do you think that it would be possible in Ireland to establish a sufficient number of schools of that sort to be within the reach of the population generally?—I think so; say in a certain locality one of the National schools might be selected for that purpose.

14386. And there should be a plot attached to that one school at which children who lived within range should attend, after they had finished their ordinary education?—Yes.

14387. Captain SHAW.—Have you noticed the effect of science teaching on the children in other subjects in the school—do you think it has a beneficial effect on the other subjects?—It has a very great benefit, partly I think on account of the recreative effect and rest and change of mind which it gives, just as the little woodwork would do. It is a complete change from the dry book work of other subjects.

14388. It calls in the observation and reasoning powers if properly treated, more than other subjects which may be learned off by heart?—That is one way in which the children will be improved, by having their little powers of observation developed.

14389. Then it encourages the teachers of other subjects to teach those more rationally?—It does.

14390. Well, as to the framing of a syllabus, do you think it desirable that a strict syllabus should be laid down for each subject?—In the schools I think it would be necessary to lay down a strict syllabus on easy lines, or otherwise the teachers will, many of them, ramble too much out of it; they won't follow the course but will take up things at haphazard.

14391. Mr. MALLOY.—Assuming that these special agricultural schools, to which you have referred, were established in Ireland, at what age would you expect boys to go to these schools?—As soon as they finished in the ordinary National schools.

14392. Would you say fifteen?—Fourteen or fifteen.

14393. And how long would you contemplate their remaining in these schools?—I think a year would be quite sufficient to go through a complete course of agriculture as illustrated on a farm.

14394. CHAIRMAN.—An individual pupil attending, say, once a week?—Oftener.

14395. Your idea is that they should still remain as school boys in fact?—Yes.

14396. Not merely that there should be classes given for a group of schools taking the children of a part of the district one day and another group another day?—It would appear to me that they should be regular school boys; but the main subject taught in the school, both theoretically and practically, would be agriculture, and if they had only two hours theoretical, they would have two or three hours a day in the field or garden as the case might be.

14397. Do you think the parents would spare them from the work of the farm for a year after finishing their ordinary school work?—That raises the question again about the attendance.

14398. That would be a practical question?—It would.

Dr. J. B. S[illegible], District Inspector of National Schools, examined.

14399. CHAIRMAN.—You are the Inspector of schools for the Waterford district?—Yes, my lord.

14400. Will you tell us how far your district extends?—It extends sixty-five miles in length, about thirty miles to the north of this, to the county Carlow, and thirty-six miles to the south-west, beyond Dungarvan. It includes portions of four counties, Carlow, Kilkenny, Wexford, and a large part of Waterford.

14401. You are aware that the scope of our inquiry is limited, and, therefore, questions must be confined to matters within it; we won't go into the ordinary literary subjects. Perhaps you would begin by giving us your views upon the subject of needle-work?—The industrial scheme was largely taken up in this district and the county Kilkenny, amongst almost all the schools in Kilkenny and a large number of schools all through this district, but many of them have now given it up. All the convent schools in Waterford, for instance, have now given it up, and there are four within the city.

14402. I should like to get the distinction between ordinary and industrial needlework?—Ordinary needlework is taught in every school where there is a workmistress or a teacher of needlework, for an hour in the day.

14403. That is compulsory?—That is compulsory. The industrial scheme was, that the girls of the sixth class should spend most of the day also at various branches of needlework, that has been limited latterly to two hours in the day altogether under the industrial scheme, but even two hours in the day was considered too much, certainly by all the teachers, they would all be glad to get rid of it for the two hours, they think one hour is enough, and, practically, it has been got rid of in a great many schools for the two hours, but all retain it for one hour. In Dungarvan there are two convents, one convent has given it up, the other still retains it. In New Ross both the convents still retain it. In Mooncoin they still retain it.

14404. *Do you include sewing machines and dressmaking under the head of industrial instruction?*—Dressmaking is one branch of the industrial programme. There are fourteen or sixteen subjects included in the industrial scheme, dressmaking is one of the special subjects, sewing machine is not. It is an extra, and now, united with dressmaking, may be taken in any school as an extra branch, sewing machine and dressmaking.

14405. Is there a special fee?—Oh, yes.

14406. *Is that popular with the teachers?*—To a considerable extent it is, but not so much now, when dressmaking is combined with sewing machine; formerly sewing machine was a special extra, but it was considered it was too easy for a girl to spend the year at, and now sewing machine and dressmaking has been combined as one extra, and since then sewing machine has not been so much taken up; but it is still to a large extent taken up in the convent schools where they have the ordinary needlework scheme without the industrial; they do take up largely sewing machine and dressmaking. I may say that it is thought that in an hour of the day they can do enough needlework.

14407. Will you now give us your observations on the subject of kindergarten?—I think that all teachers should know and apply the principles of kindergarten; it is at present taken up chiefly in the convent schools—very few others, because it requires a special room and special teacher—and even in these it generally extends only through the infant and first classes on account of the fact that it requires a special room, because the second class have generally left that room, and the third class have mostly always, so that at present it is almost confined to infants and first class.

14408. I don't quite understand the matter about the rooms?—Kindergarten cannot be carried on, at least it may be carried on, but it won't be recognised as a special branch and paid for unless there is a special room set apart for infants.

14409. For instance, take the Model School we were in to-day, which does not appear to be full; why could not a room be set apart there?—But that room is occupied by the infants and first-class children.

14410. Could not another room be set apart for more advanced children?—It could not well be called an infant department, the kindergarten is carried on at present only in infant departments.

14411. In England I understand it is carried on beyond the infants; why should it not here?—Certainly it should be carried on.

14412. Is it anything more than a want of room?—Teachers believe it would not be paid for as a special branch.

14413. *Supposing* it was paid for?—Then there would be no difficulty about it, because a great many parts of kindergarten don't require special rooms and special desks.

14414. What do you say about object lessons, drill, marching, and so on?—Those are parts of kindergarten that don't require special rooms and desks. Object lessons could go through the school, in all classes, various kinds of objects from the simple cube up to the chair or table or machinery, and parts of machinery more difficult for the sixth class.

14415. Is there any paperfolding such as we saw in some of the schools in English towns, and wire-work and things of that sort?—You see it is limited to the first class, and there is a certain programme for each class, and the teachers don't go beyond the programme laid down. There is a little paper weaving, making little basket work.

14416. What they call cardboard work?—Yes, there is a little of that, pricking and stitching of patterns on cards.

14417. Making some objects on cards and cutting them out?—No, I don't know that they do, they fold the paper.

14418. Do they fold the paper pursuant to instructions given at the blackboard when a certain line is given by the teacher?—No, it is more after the teacher's example.

14419. He does not show it on the blackboard, first make a mark and then tell them to do it?—No, I don't think so, I don't think they do much paper-folding, I have seen very little.

14420. Is there any in Waterford?—I cannot recollect that I have seen much of it, I did see it in one school, but not here.

14421. What do you say with regard to drawing?—Drawing is a branch of kindergarten too, it should follow all through the schools from the infants up; the first class should draw on chequered slates, the second class on chequered paper, and the third class on plain paper.

14422. Do any of them draw on boards with chalk?—The teachers draw on the kindergarten board in the kindergarten school, and the children draw on kindergarten slates.

14423. The children don't draw on the board themselves?—I don't think they do.

14424. We saw that in one of the London schools, not small children, but advanced children drawing on the board themselves?—I don't think they do it here.

14425. To come to a subject we have heard a great deal about, agricultural farms and school garden?—Agriculture is taught from books, of course, in nearly all the rural schools under masters, all in fact. My opinion differs from the opinions of some others on that point, I think it is useful to teach it from books in country schools, because the country boys know the subject matter, they are accustomed from their childhood almost to planting potatoes, and weeding turnips, therefore it is not blank work to them, it is instruction about what they already know, and it can scarcely be otherwise than very useful when properly taught by an intelligent teacher. What they want to know are the principles of and the reasons for, what they have been doing all their lives; they can get that from books and teachers, and I think the book teaching must necessarily be useful with boys who know the matter already, not with town boys of course who may attend the schools.

Waterford.
Sept. [illegible]
Dr. J. F. [illegible]

14426. Do you think there would be any advantage in having a school garden attached to each rural school?—Yes, I do, there are three school gardens in this district, and the teacher of one of them told me that a good many of the boys have got gardens, and introduced vegetables that were almost unknown in the country before, and the nuns at Stradbally have got a garden lately to teach the girls, and they told me that the girls were asking the seeds of flowers from them, and beginning to have gardens of their own at home. I find there are very few gardens in the country, in four schools in one parish I found by asking the children to put up their hands, that only four of them had gardens at home.

14427. That is attached to their own houses?—Yes, these were all the children of one parish; in these gardens they had only cabbages and potatoes. I think it would be useful to teach them to grow peas and cabbages and lettuce and useful vegetables, and fruits.

14428. Would you limit a school garden to one rood or half acre?—I would not like very much more than half an acre, a garden can illustrate a great many of the principles of agriculture, the training and the pruning of trees, and even a four course rotation, they can be made experimental plots for raising new varieties of potatoes. In fact I know one place in which a teacher, out of half an acre of almost barren soil, sold £130 worth of produce in one year, with only twelve days' labour paid, that was near Belfast; he brought out a new variety of potato, and the Educational Board took three or four tons from him, Wesley Forbes, of Tullycarnet. He tells me he has a new variety this year, and also a new variety of tomato, which he thinks will make him famous.

14429. Do you think it would be useful if Parliament enabled managers of schools to borrow sums of money to provide gardens?—Most useful. I think there should be attached to every school a garden, and there should be prizes for these just as for the railway plots in the North; they have beautiful plots there with the names of the stations worked in flowers.

14430. And in shrubs?—And some of them in flowers, and if a system of prizes were given in schools to the teachers who kept the neatest gardens and plots, I think it would be of great use.

14431. Now, with regard to cookery and handicraft?—Cookery was taught in this district during the past year in three schools by Miss Dickson and Miss Pring, both from the Royal Irish Association for the Technical Training and Employment of Women: a large class of 120 girls in the Ursuline Convent was taught, and eighty were examined; and in the Dungarvan Convent of Mercy Miss Pring taught a large class, and in the model school also. The pupils were very enthusiastic, and showed great pleasure in the work of cookery.

14432. Is the convent we saw at Kilkenny yesterday in your district?—No, I don't go so far up, I only go to Thomastown.

14433. We saw cookery there?—The little girls certainly take great interest in the matter, the objection is that it is a little expensive, in fact the nuns lose by it here in town.

14434. What system is adopted? Do they find the materials?—They find the materials and the apparatus. The lecturer gave the lessons, demonstrations, and had the children in classes of sixteen each, working at the cooking for two hours in the day, generally two classes in the day, one in the morning, and one in the evening, two hours each, they had to give twenty lessons, and each pupil should attend sixteen of these to be examined.

14435. What became of the articles after they were cooked?—The Ursulines gave them to the pupils. In the Dungarvan Convent the pupils bought some, and I suppose they were able to make some use of the others; in the Model school here the pupils bought a good many of the dishes made.

14436. Was that done at a loss?—I have the figures. In the Model school there were thirty-one taught from 9th of March to 4th of May, two days a week, the cost was £4 6s. 4d., including £3 for a stove, which is still there, and will be utilized this year again; receipts fees, £1 17s. 6d., sales, £1 5s. 10d., there was a loss of £1 2s. 4d. about.

14437. That would include the stove?—Yes.

14438. But if you take the stove as capital expenditure?—Yes, there would be little loss, it was a secondhand stove, we got it from the Department in Dublin.

14439. How many years' life would that stove have?—It might last 4 or 5 years.

14440. If you took the fifth part of 40*l*, that would be a fair depreciation?—Well, the girls at the Model school took very much interest in it and purchased the dishes; it is not every school in which the children would be able to purchase the dishes made; I am not quite sure it was the children purchased all these, but they were sold. I know that a number of convents are anxious to take it up, one has applied for an instructress and has not been able to get one. About handicraft there is one school in which that is taken up, the most southerly school in the district, at Ring, 6 miles below Dungarvan, there is a very energetic teacher who has a small farm, he went up to Dublin and got a certificate, and teaches handicraft, teaches in a disused building. I examined 9 boys and others had previously passed. He provided tools and they had benches in this building. They had sharpening of tools, sharpening a chisel or knife on a grindstone or oil stone, marking and sawing off pieces of wood of given dimensions, driving in screws, putting on hinges and planing, that was the first year's course, and the boys were very eager and anxious about it, and the teacher told me that there is no subject in which they take so much interest or which they are more delighted with.

14441. Do you think that they take an interest because of the fact that they have to do things by measuring and thinking what they have to do first?—The chief interest to them is the activity, it is just like kindergarten in the upper classes, children like motion, but boys like more vigorous motion; they like activity and the doing of it and the accuracy of the measurement.

14442. Do you think that this subject is a good deal misunderstood in Ireland?—I do, certainly.

14443. I have seen it more than once described as chipping wood; as far as my experience goes there is no chipping of wood as a matter of fact?—No, there was no chipping at all by these boys.

14444. The use of the axe is very rare?—I did not go into that part of it, the teacher told me that they made little boxes and birdcages.

14445. That requires thought and mensuration?—It does of course to be able to measure off lathes and parts.

14446. And a certain amount of drawing?—They have to draw lines first, of course. Of course this is only in a rudimentary way, and I may say the teacher would have had more pupils present if he could have presented them according to their age and size, and not by their classes; he had a number of big boys who were not in the class to be able to be presented, 20 boys had worked during the year but only 9 were examined.

14447. Why were not more examined?—Because these were all that were eligible according to the rules to earn result fees.

14448. Mr Ramsterson.—They should be in the

6th class?—Yes, some of these boys were 3rd, and some 4th, big country boys.

14449. CHAIRMAN.—Then their proficiency in this manual or handicraft work is to be judged by their proficiency in literary work, because they are classed according to the literary work?—That is so according to the present arrangement.

14450. That is not a good plan?—I don't think it is.

14451. It is like a system that formerly prevailed at Cambridge, of not allowing a person to go in for classical honours unless he had attained a certain degree in mathematics?—Yes, it is something analogous to that.

14452. Rev. Dr. EVANS.—How long are you in this district?—I am only from the 1st of January.

14453. Have you been round all the schools?—I believe I have visited all except one; I believe there is one school I have not caught up yet.

14454. What proportion of teachers in this district are untrained?—I am not able to answer that question, but I could find out for you if you wished.

14455. You have told us that the industrial programme is being given up, and I want to know whether it has been given up in any school under a trained teacher?—Yes, I think so, but I don't think that makes any difference, I think they are all eager to give it up, that is the two hours.

14456. Do you think it is a want of aptitude to teach on the part of the teacher that has to do with that?—I don't think so, because the idea is, that in an hour in the day they can do good enough work; and they can and they do, where they don't take it up; indeed I have seen quite as great a variety and quantity of needlework of various kinds as in those schools where it is taken up.

14457. You have experience in Ulster?—Largely; I am nearly twenty-three years inspecting in all parts of Ireland.

14458. Do you know why the industrial programme was not taken up in Belfast?—I do, it was thought the needlework was very well taught, and I know it was, I have specimens of needlework before the industrial programme came out, quite as good as any I have seen since; they thought it was a waste of time to take it up; the cost of materials was one objection, and the want of a market; and it gave dawdling habits to girls, sitting for two hours over work.

14459. You said there were three places where there were school gardens?—Yes, Inistioge, near Kilkenny, Kilmacow and [illegible] convents, these last two are only recently connected.

14460. In these three school gardens what do they principally do?—They grow the ordinary vegetables of course, they grow some potatoes, cabbages, lettuce, beans, small fruits, and some large fruits.

14461. How does the teacher of the school garden get manure?—In Inistioge he keeps fowl and a pig, and I suppose he buys artificial manure; I think he has a cow, that was.

14462. Do you know whether in any of these they try experiments with artificial manures?—I do not know it as a matter of fact, but I have no doubt this man in Inistioge uses artificial manures, he also keeps bees, and has introduced the bar frame system.

14463. Do these schools, where the school gardens are, attain as high proficiency in other subjects as those that have not school gardens?—Oh, yes, I think so, quite so, there is only one, it is a very small school, it is a sort of exceptional school, the other two are not long enough under the system to judge, but I have no doubt that they will do quite as well, if not better, because it is a recreation for the children.

14464. By parity of reasoning you would come to the conclusion that manual instruction should rather accelerate proficiency in literary subjects than retard it?—It would have a good effect, it would be a change from the eyestrain on the mind, it would be a rest to the mind to give the body exercise.

Waterford.

Sept. 23, 1897.

Dr. J. D. [illegible].

14465. Provided we were able to introduce manual instruction, would it require any change in our inspectorial staff, or additions to it, or a new element in their qualification?—Well, I think the Inspectors would very soon learn enough, especially if they got some little training in the Training Colleges in Dublin; they would soon learn enough to judge what was being done and how it was done; there are some very nice books about it, and if they saw it done in the Training Colleges or here, and got three months or so at it, I think they would be very well able to inspect it.

14466. Is there any observation bearing on this manual instruction, that has not been touched on by any question, that you would like to make?—Well, I have a good deal down on my notes, but they would be rather long. I think teachers differ a good deal in their tastes. I know one teacher in the county Town, first of first; he did all the repairs himself, remodelled the desks, and had a special garden made out of a piece of bare soil. I knew one in the West, a third class teacher, and when I pointed out a desk as wanting repair, he asked me would I want a teacher to be a carpenter. I knew another, in Cavan, first of first, who boasted that he made the desks with his own hands, and did a good deal in building a house for himself. I knew Wesley Forbes, who says he is an expert in cabinet-making, French polishing, mechanics, photography, gardening, fowl-keeping, farming; he says, he "will be ready for anything the Manual Commission may be the means of introducing," so teachers differ very much. I think if the teachers took it as an advanced kind of kindergarten, and took the scientific aspects, as applied to science, the making of scientific apparatus, they would take an interest in it gradually.

14467. Mr. MOLLOY.—A great deal of confusion arises from the term "Industrial schools," you used it here, but it is not perhaps what you mean to convey. There is needlework instruction in the ordinary schools for an hour a day; there are also industrial departments in which needlework is taught?—Yes; that is different.

14468. You don't mean those?—No.

14469. I want to come at what you do mean; is it the alternative scheme for sixth class girls?—That is the case.

14470. By the word alternative is meant alternative literary and industrial, not altogether industrial?—No.

14471. Is it not largely literary?—It is not; where the industrial is taken up it is half and half. It was intended to be more industrial, and at first it was more; it has been reduced now in consequence of the complaints of the teachers that the whole day was nearly given up—it has been reduced now to two hours.

14472. Is it a matter of fact that three hours were ever prescribed by the National Board to carry out the alternative industrial scheme for sixth class girls?—It was not laid down in words, but it was understood to be so; but when exception was taken it was reduced under pressure from managers and teachers—I think it was intended to be three hours at first.

14473. Was it actually prescribed?—I don't think it was mentioned exactly in figures, three hours.

14474. As a matter of fact it was not, and now two hours would suffice?—Two hours—forty minutes for each of the three branches.

14475. Is it believed in schools where senior girls are in attendance that two hours is too much to devote to needlework?—Decidedly. The nuns of the Ursuline convent object in consequence of the do willing habits it created, and the nuns in St. Joseph's have given it up, and the convent at Ferrybank has given it up.

14476. A moment ago you mentioned two hours; it is not necessary that these hours should be continuous?—I am not sure that I said continuous, but it may be an hour in the morning and an hour in the evening.

14477. And that is believed to be too much?—It is. With an hour a day they can do quite as much. I had far better sewing in the North, where there was an hour a day, than I got in the county Kilkenny, where the industrial scheme was in almost every school in it, and I could show you the work.

14478. What I want to have emphatically from your evidence is that the alternative scheme was not exclusively industrial, it had a large literary element?—At first it was about one-quarter literary; it has now come to about one-half.

14479. The literary portion included reading text books on suitable industrial subjects, domestic economy, with a knowledge of the subject matter, English composition, letter writing, that might embrace exercises in geography and grammar, and also exercises in short accounts; so that virtually no important literary subject was disestablished, so to say, by the introduction of the alternative industrial scheme?—I beg your pardon, practically there were, arithmetic was disestablished, and grammar and geography were practically disestablished; it was said you might do this or that, but you might teach anything you like, provided you taught what was required by the rules; practically the teachers taught reading and those books you refer to.

14480. CHAIRMAN.—While you are on the subject of reading, do you think the reading of the sixth class is, on the whole, satisfactory or not?—I think the sixth class book——

14481. I am not talking of the book, but of the personal reading?—On the whole it is very fair indeed.

14482. The reason I ask you is that I have been in the last few days in two schools, and I really could not follow the reading from their not raising their voices and speaking distinctly?—That may be, but really after all, reading is to understand the sense of what is read, and as one inspector said, most people read quietly. Of course reading out, elocution, for the benefit of a listener, is a different matter, and they may be taught that in various degrees.

14483. MR. MALLOY.—Would you attribute the want of popularity of the alternative industrial scheme to want of skill in needlework on the part of the ordinary teachers?—Certainly not, because the same branches that come under industrial were and are taught by the teachers without being specially industrial at all, for instance, crochet and knitting socks, and that. I saw several schools in the county Down, Dromore was one; they never took up the industrial scheme, but they had the school hung round with articles of various kinds most beautifully, all the articles mentioned in the industrial programme.

14484. Am I to understand that the whole objection to the alternative literary and industrial scheme is that two hours a day devoted to it is too much?—No, that is not all, but the fact that the two hours left too little for the literary part; the fact that the things made were too many, there was no market for them, they were too costly to produce, and the children did not want them; there were half a dozen reasons. And I heard the other day in a convent school that still has the industrial scheme, that they found it difficult to obtain monitresses; when a monitress had been two years in the industrial they found it very difficult to bring them up in arithmetic and grammar.

14485. Of course you are aware that half of the sixth class may continue exclusively at literary work, with one hour at industrial work daily?—That is when they are monitresses.

14486. Yes, and senior pupils who desire to go off to any other branch?—They have to get exemption in all those cases.

14487. But it is possible to get it?—It is now, but one time it was very difficult.

14488. Am I right in saying that your experience is that the alternative literary and industrial scheme when adopted in convent schools was successful, but not equally so, or equally popular in ordinary schools? —It was more successful in convent schools, and certainly is where they still hold to it.

14489. I believe you said that one difficulty along the extension of the kindergarten system was the fact that the separate room for kindergarten was obligatory?—Yes, a separate room for the infant department and kindergarten is only recognised in the infant department of school.

14490. You referred also to special desks, surely those are not necessary?—Not at all, but it is thought they are; my view is that an ordinary desk, if painted with little squares, would do.

14491. Well, strictly speaking, kindergarten might be taught *al fresco* without any reference to a special room?—Certainly. I think we want to get analogous exercises for the upper classes suitable to the strength and age of the children.

14492. You expressed your opinion that agriculture as taught from books without any instruction in the practice of it was of use?—Certainly, if the pupils are already acquainted with the subject matter, because it gives them the scientific aspect of the question.

14493. In your district here you have got special agricultural schools—Mullinahone, Clonmore, Woodstock, and Inistioge?—Yes, one school garden; there are three model farms.

14494. Besides Inistioge there is Woodstock?—Inistioge is the name of the school and the village, Woodstock is the name of the demesne.

14495. Is it not called the Woodstock agricultural school?—That is a different one; that is a model farm. The model farms are Woodstock; one in Mullinahone; and Clonmore.

14496. Are there ordinary literary schools in connection with those schools?—There are.

14497. Is it found that the instruction in agriculture interferes with the literary work of the pupils? —It does not; the schools are, I don't think, either better or worse than they would be without them.

14498. In the three other schools, where there are only school gardens, is the literary work at all interfered with?—It is not.

14499. You mentioned that special teachers were sent from Kildare street, in cookery; of course you understand that they were sent by the National Board?—I understand they were paid by the National Board, and were then paid by the National Board.

14500. They simply had been trained in connection with the institution in Kildare-street?—Yes.

14501. And the National Board select the places to which they may be sent?—Yes, a scheme is prepared for a number of schools, and this teacher generally endeavours to have two or three, or half a dozen schools going on at once, and goes from one to another. At the [illegible] convent they applied for a teacher the other day and could not get one.

14502. The last subject I have to ask you about is that very interesting school at [illegible], where the master is very highly qualified, teaches an ordinary National school and carried on instruction in handicraft or manual work, and also farms; you have inspected the school, have you?—Yes.

14503. Did you find the literary work very efficient; is he a highly classed teacher?—Yes, I am not quite sure whether he is First of 2nd, or Second of 1st; he is pretty highly classed; the school was very fairly on, considering it is a very remote school and in an isolated

pensionnaire, and the children, I suppose, don't attend very regularly.

14504. Might I ask how he contrives within the school day to give instruction in literary work, farming work, and manual work?—He has an assistant teacher.

14505. Has he extended the ordinary school hours?—Not much; they can be at the farm work for three hours on Saturday now; I think he has the handicraft in the morning before school hours.

14506. And has he conveyed to you that the children take great interest in these extra branches?—He has stated distinctly there was no subject they were so eager for or took such delight in.

14507. Captain Shaw.—Do you find there is any difference in the literary efficiency of the girls and boys, age for age?—Well, abstractedly no, but if you take particular cases there are.

14508. I mean as a general rule?—I don't like to say there is.

14509. Don't the girls have six hours in the week sewing, while the boys have no corresponding occupation?—No, they have only five hours; of course if you take the boys and girls in the same school, the boys have agriculture while the girls have needlework, and the boys have a very difficult programme in arithmetic, and often learn geometry and algebra, so the work is about equal.

14510. Do you consider an hour a day too much for needlework for girls?—I think it is too much for the second class who have only to learn hemming and knitting; I think half an hour would be enough for second and third class.

14511. Chairman.—They are quite small girls?—Eight years of [illegible].

14512. Captain Shaw.—Is there any difficulty in providing needlework for so many hours?—Practically now there is not, material has become so cheap, and the Board have such a system on that line, and they can get materials in shops, so that I think there is not now such difficulty in ordinary needlework as there used to be. At some seasons of the year you might find materials scarce, but now they work up materials so, they can work on a scrap of cloth the size of a sheet of paper, rounding up a bit of hem with stitches on it.

14513. Could they not get it into a smaller time?—When they sit down and give out the work, it is a tedious business; I think for the upper classes an hour in the day is not too much, considering the time lost in giving it out, I think an hour in the day would do very well.

14514. Rev. Dr. Wilson.—When you said that needlework had been given up by many of the schools, I suppose you mean the two hours?—I did not say that needle work was given up, exactly; I meant the industrial scheme of needlework for each class, the second hour, not the first.

14515. Is it kept up for one hour?—Most is.

14516. As regards book teaching of agriculture I quite agree with you that it is most useful for boys that are drawn from the farming classes?—Yes, and those who know what they are talking about.

14517. As to cookery, would you think it a great advantage if that was extended much more widely?—I would indeed think it a very great advantage; I think it is very badly done, and I think it would be very useful to have it well done; it would make workmen and labourers avoid the public-house a good deal; I would like to see good cookery of plain food extended very much.

14518. And if the Board were to do more in that direction you think it would be of great advantage?—I do indeed, and I think it could be done in the ordinary schools in a simple way. I had an idea that without much expense a teacher might cook a simple plain dish, say for herself, on the ordinary school fire, the girls would take notes when she gave the instruction, and the next day she could ask one of them to cook the same from the notes, the others observing and criticising, so that it does not require any very elaborate machinery.

Waterford, [illegible]. Aug. 21, [illegible].
Dr. J. B. Skeffington.

14519. Is there instruction given in laundrying in any of the schools under you?—I have not come across that at all.

14520. Do you think that important?—It would of course, but somehow or other I don't think it is so important generally as the cooking. There are laundries for doing up clothes here, and in nearly all the towns.

14521. In the towns, but not in the country?—In the country places they do washing very well, they have the hedges for [illegible]; but cooking is universal, it has to be done everywhere.

14522. In regard to the proposal for lessening the time for grammar and geography, do you agree with that?—In second and third classes I would leave it optional, and do it a good deal by well written lessons in ordinary reading books, which should be prepared by first class teachers, and would be better than the instructions given by third-class teachers. In the senior classes I would not give up grammar and geography; it would injure schools if the fifth and sixth who remained to complete their education did not get grammar and geography, for schools would be starting up to supply these things, and they would injure the National Schools.

14523. Mr. Redington.—With reference to the teaching of cookery in small rural schools, how would the teachers get the materials, would there not be great difficulty?—Not in the way I speak of, the teacher would always have to cook for herself, if it was only in the way of boiling or poaching eggs, if it were only a herring, the simplest dish. The cookery they did at the Ursuline Convent and the Model School, they did very nicely without burning it or blackening it.

14524. How would you get the ordinary teachers taught cookery?—They can already learn that, teachers could go around to give lessons in the towns, or hold classes on Saturdays, and the country teachers could come in to them; for instance, here and in Dungarvan and New Ross, the teachers within a circle could come in.

14525. You look forward to the ordinary school teacher as the permanent teacher of cookery?—Oh, yes.

14526. You look on the present instructors we send round as temporary?—Yes, introductory.

14527. As regards kindergarten, do I understand you to say that kindergarten could be well taught in all schools, even where there is only one room?—I think so.

14528. Is it merely the regulations that prevent it being taught?—The teachers would need to be able to teach it.

14529. At present they are not paid the results fee unless there is an organised infants' department; if that rule was abolished, would it be well taught?—It might not be quite so extensively taught, as where there was a separate room, but it would be taught to a considerable extent.

14530. It would not interfere with the work of other classes?—I don't think it would, that is where you had a second teacher, or a good monitress. Of course if you had a second teacher it would not interfere at all; if you had a good monitress in third or fourth year, if trained in a school where it had been taught, she would know a good deal about it, and in a couple of years would be able to take the teacher's place.

14531. I think you had something to say about the certificates for kindergarten teaching?—Yes, I think that every teacher should know the principles of kindergarten, that is, the real principles that underlie it, which are the development of the faculties and members by exercise, and making use of the child's natural curiosity, and the inquiries it will make to obtain knowledge—these are the real points.

14532. Mr. Molloy.—And male teachers as well as female teachers?—Yes, every teacher should, I hold, because at present the fact of teaching is the main point; whereas the fact of development should be the main point.

14533. Mr. Redington.—How would you provide for the instruction of teachers who don't know how to teach kindergarten?—The training colleges now will enable all who pass through them to learn it, and those who have already passed through could come into the convent schools on Saturdays, and there could generally be a number found there who would teach the teachers, at least I mean in this part of the country; in other parts of the country you will generally find some good teacher of a large school.

14534. Then as regards drawing, how would you extend the knowledge of drawing among the teachers?—Somewhat similarly, the training colleges, of course, will teach the new teachers, and here, in Waterford, there is an art school where the teachers could come in on Saturdays.

14535. Would they come in?—I think they would. I may say, however, that drawing is not taught to the extent to which it ought to be; there are fourteen teachers here who have certificates who don't teach drawing.

14536. Would you make them teach drawing or forfeit their certificates?—I think it would be well, but the difficulty is that it is not commenced early enough. It is commenced in 3rd class; if it was commenced in 1st class, teachers would take it up.

14537. Chairman.—Who decides whether drawing is to be taught; the teacher or the manager?—Well, theoretically, the manager, but practically it is the teacher. Unless the manager is very zealous and energetic, and makes it a *sine qua non*, which he seldom does, the teacher generally succeeds in teaching it, or not, as he pleases.

14538. Teaching what he likes?—Not what he likes—the rules of the Board are there.

14539. Yes, but I mean of the optional subjects?—He generally can; but if a manager applies for a teacher who can teach drawing, and takes him on that understanding, and makes it a condition that he should teach it; then, of course, he should do so.

14540. Mr. Redington.—Would it be equally feasible to get the teachers to learn the principles of science?—I think they should learn the principles of science in training college.

14541. I am talking of teachers who are already in charge of schools?—If they came into the Training College here on Saturdays—I don't know whether they could find time for them or not—or possibly in the vacation they might bring them in; of course about Belfast there would be no difficulty at all.

14542. If it were determined to make the teaching of elementary science and drawing compulsory in all schools, and a certain number of years were laid down as the limit within which it should be introduced, do you think there would be any great difficulty in the way of teachers learning how to teach these subjects?—I am sure there would not; teachers know a lot of geometry and could learn geometrical drawing very easily, and elementary mechanics, I am sure they would soon pick it up.

14543. They would require some help, I suppose from books?—They would require, in teaching it, of course, little manuals. I should say, with regard to agriculture, I think experiments in chemistry should be taught to sixth class boys, such as are in "Johnson's Catechism of Agricultural Chemistry," and "Hodge's Principles of Agricultural Chemistry."

14544. I believe there are many books that treat of elementary physics?—There are plenty, some very nice little books; and for wood construction there is a very nice little book by George St. John,* showing the different sort of joints. Then there is a very nice little book on "Practical Physics," by Lenger (George Gill & Sons, London), and on "Physical Measurements and Experimental Mechanics," by Worden (George Gill & Sons, London), and if you take the syllabus of the Science and Art Department, there are eleven branches there, the experiments very fully gone into, and very nice experiments; there is one on Alternative Chemistry, and one on Physiography, and one on Agriculture, those are very good experiments.

14545. Supposing the teacher was able to teach, and it was made compulsory, would there be any such great expense in getting apparatus to teach chemistry and science?—There would be some, but not great.

14546. That would be no serious obstacle?—I don't think it should be.

14547. Supposing any new subjects were made compulsory, and you were asked what subjects you would exclude from the present compulsory curriculum, what answer would you give?—I would modify the present programme a great deal. I would omit oral spelling altogether, I would teach spelling by writing, as it is always used; no one has to spell orally that I know; writing is the counterpart of reading; I would teach writing and spelling altogether by transcription, and examine it in the same way.

14548. Chairman.—You give spelling as a thing you would exclude in favour of manual work. Spelling is taught, of course, at the very beginning of the education of a child; some of these things that are proposed to be taken in would be taught at the end?—The point is that time would be saved by economising the energies of the child and of his teacher in these junior classes, and they would have more time to spare for the upper classes; the teacher would have more time to spare, and the pupil also.

14550. Then is there any other modification you would make?—Well, there is a loss of time in writing, the first class learn to write on slates, the second class write on paper, going back to books. I would have the second class write with lead pencil, and I would introduce the pen in the third class. The first class can often write well on slates, but when they go to the second class they are just back to make scrawls with pen and ink, and go back to books and letters, and learn writing *de novo*.

14551. Chairman.—Do they spend much time over that?—Yes.

14552. What is to prevent a child, after a day or two, taking up his writing at the point at which he left off on the slate?—A great deal, the using of the pen, which is quite different has to be learned. Then grammar or geography might be optional in third and fourth classes, and might be taught by lessons in the reading books. I would have those lessons from the second up on the reading books; and in the geography in the other classes, I would have fewer facts and figures. In fact geographies now are bristling with facts and figures, most repulsive books they are.

14553. Mr. Redington.—Is it your opinion that too many optional subjects are taken up at present? I mean to say that instead of those optional subjects that are now taken up some practical branches could be taught—for instance, I see in one time-table provision for five optional subjects.

14554. Do you approve of that?—Well, this teacher manages to do the work well, and the time-table is 9.30 to 3, and I have another time-table for six optional subjects, from 10 to 3 in an excellent

* "Manual Instruction—Woodwork," by George St. John (Illustrated).

Waterford. Sept. [illegible], 1897. Dr. J. B. Skeffington.

school; one of your new subjects could take the place of those.

14555. Tell us the names of the six optional subjects?—Book-keeping, singing, drawing, geometry, algebra, and botany, and well taught, too.

14556. Is that geometry and mensuration?—Yes.

14557. I think you have an opinion that mensuration ought to be separated from geometry?—Certainly; and the rules of mensuration can be explained without geometry; there is a nice book on the Board's list—"Chalmers' *Elements of Geometry*"—which explains the thing very nicely to boys.

14558. That teacher whose time-table you are quoting has taken up some of the subjects we are discussing?—Yes.

14559. Could any time be gained on Saturdays?—Yes, I think so. I don't see why 10 to 12 could not be taken on Saturdays, it used to be.

14560. Would it count as a school-day?—Yes, it used to be, it has been dropped out of late years.

14561. They can now have the agricultural instruction on Saturday?—Yes, they have that in Woodstock.

14562. I suppose you would make the Saturday instruction optional?—I think there would be no great hardship in making 10 to 12 compulsory, of course the subjects taught would be paid for also. As a matter of fact, the hours are practically extended now in some of the places, at least for some months before the results examinations they are kept in late in many places.

14563. Longer than from 10 to 3?—Oh, yes, the hours in this part of the country are very often to 3.30, and in some places in summer to 4.30.

14564. Do you think school farms, as opposed to school gardens, are to be encouraged?—No, I don't think so at all; the schoolmaster cannot teach the farmer his business, and school masters who have farms admit that this is so; they can teach the theory of the subject, the reasons for it, and the scientific aspects, but they cannot go in and work a farm, it would require too much of the time of the teacher to work a farm as a farmer would.

14565. But you are in favour of school gardens?—Certainly.

14566. What is the smallest size of a school garden that you would recommend?—I think half a rood might be made a garden.

14567. Mr. Molloy.—Have you worked out any scheme by which the kindergarten could be carried on to the higher classes?—I have thought over it a little; I have a graduated scheme here, but probably it would not stand examination.

14568. Perhaps you would hand it in to the Secretary. (*Scheme handed in*). Apropos of your statement that you would abandon oral spelling, would you extend that statement to the junior standards?—Not to the infants who cannot write.

14569. Mr. [illegible].—Do you think in small schools there ought to be fewer classes?—Certainly, I do; where a man has only forty pupils and ten classes it is very difficult. They should be grouped decidedly; they have a grouping system in England.

Dr. Evans.—How long are you in school?—A little over seven years, of iddle class school.

you any of this industrial work in that school?—Well, I have not, as al curriculum, but I, myself, personally d in wood-work that I have a few of come over to the schoolroom to me after wn free will, but by the wish of their a little work with me, whilst I am further than that it is no part of the

r as you know, is there any of this in connection with any school of the he school you have charge of?—Yes; rstown School in Waterford, managed of Friends, and there they have gone expense in providing apparatus for ual work, and the boys there do a have seen some of it; it is very good; good deal of their recreation hours

gives the manual instruction there?—Is eacher or a special teacher?—I believe d men visiting there from the town.

rman.—What they call artisans?—woodwork, and basket-making, and turning, and carving; and I believe are allowed there from the town, the n, but I don't think they do all.

Dr. Evans.—Does the programme of pretty much on all fours with the d programme?—No, it does not; the ool is partly Intermediate and partly t.

ppose you send pupils to the Intermations?—I send pupils to every year. any, sometimes as few as five, some-); it is not popular in the Diocese

your work differ much from the p Foy's school?—Bishop Foy's is more re are no classics or French taught in hool.

they have no manual work there?—s I am acquainted with it.

Molloy.—Is not your school rather a ool for Trinity College?—It is.

s started mainly with that view?—I ose the work done there has been r less on University lines—matricula- Universities.

school was formerly taught by Mr. e, some years ago.

you Physical Science taught there?—Physical Science; we take up Natural

has taught theoretically. Have you l of any kind?—I have, if necessary; do the practical part continuous.

hanics, of course, would form part of ?—Elementary mechanics.

merely from books?—We teach together from books.

you recommend that in rural National ture and lace-making should be taught introduce lace-making?—At the pre-making is altogether confined to the he country, where they do excellent ould be a union of the two by the lecturer by nuns in the district, if that und as all feasible, because they seem poly of the lace teaching.

pupils of rural schools would attend convents?—Yes; let the nuns teach

14600. But as regards the subject itself, you prefer lace-making rather than any other subject?—I think so.

14601. Have you any special reason for that?—No. I think what Dr. Starkington said about cookery was very desirable, but that is so prominent I did not mention that.

14602. You would not confine it to lace-making?—No.

14603. Rev. Dr. Wilson.—You have been in Switzerland?—I have, on a visit of six or seven weeks, during which time I tried to see what I could of the educational system.

14604. What kind of woodwork did you see there?—Chiefly carving of figures and of animals for the English markets and for tourists.

14605. Was that taught in the public schools?—It was, and also more advanced woodwork for the advanced pupils.

14606. Did you see any metalwork?—No, not much metal work. I visited a woodwork school at Berne, and the system there was very good; they had different rooms for different grades of proficiency in the woodwork, and a large staff of teachers, and the work turned out was very good indeed; between sale of the work and the pupils' fees, which were very small, it made nearly a third of the whole expense.

14607. Is it your opinion that it would be expedient to introduce something of that sort in connection with our National system?—I think so, in largely populated districts; it would not be practicable in districts where the population is not large, but in the immediate vicinity of our large cities, and in the cities themselves, it would be highly desirable to found such schools as these.

14608. As far as you know is the teaching in wood by the Society of Friends popular with the pupils?—It is very popular with the pupils, and I am well aware that many of the pupils spend their whole recreation time in the workshops.

14609. Chairman. How many pupils are there there?—I think there are about thirty-five residents, sometimes I think forty.

14610. Is it a school where they board?—It was, formerly, altogether for resident pupils, a boarding school, but I think within the last twelve months they have opened it to all comers.

14611. Mr. Redington.—Do you know what kind of woodwork they do in the Friends' School here?—All kinds of fancy work; they do boat building and make boxes.

14612. Do they follow any of the systems in operation in some of the large board schools in England?—No; I think they allow each boy to go more or less according to his own taste, and the work is superintended.

14613. They have not a graduated system of lessons?—No.

14614. Chairman.—This is not a primary school at all, but a secondary school?—It is a secondary school. If a boy wishes to take up a certain article of woodwork or ironwork he has permission.

14615. Mr. Redington.—Are you acquainted with the systems in operation in Liverpool or Birmingham?—I am not.

14616. You cannot compare them, therefore, with the Swiss system?—No.

14617. Chairman.—Perhaps you are not aware that there is a difference between what they do in Liverpool and Birmingham, in woodwork; in Birmingham they don't complete any article, they make joints, but not a whole box, but in Liverpool that is not so?—I think the work ought to be limited to that.

14618. Mr. Redington.—What makes the Swiss take such an interest in this woodwork?—I think

Mr. Edward Lanigan, Teacher, [illegible] National School, Dungarvan, examined.

Mr. Edward Lanigan.

14621. Chairman.—You are teacher of the [illegible] National School in the county Waterford?—I am.

14622. Is that a rural school?—A rural school.

14623. What number of pupils have you?—Well, 104 on the rolls at present.

14624. Boys and girls?—Boys only.

14625. You have an assistant?—No.

14626. Mr. Redington.—What is the average attendance at your school?—Year in and year out, it would be perhaps fifty-four or fifty-five; for this year it is fifty-six, but some quarters I will have seventy or eighty for two successive quarters, and then for two quarters it is down. I managed to keep an assistant only for two years, and that is all.

14627. Mr. Molloy.—Why don't you apply for an assistant when you get two consecutive quarters with the required numbers?—I don't think I could manage that, if I had the average on alternate quarters I could retain the services of an assistant.

14628. Chairman.—You have given some attention to the question of manual instruction in rural National schools; do you confine what you say to rural National schools?—My experience is rural, but I would have no objection to give my opinion with regard to schools in large centres.

14629. Have you derived your views from reading principally; or have you seen any manual work?—I worked at a trade, served my time to the business; I am a bit of an amateur carpenter, and have a portable forge and turning lathe of my own. I used to do more at it in my earlier days than now. I was in the training college in 1862, and it was foreshadowed, intimated by one of the professors that probably this thing would be introduced in the near future. I tried it after coming home and it was only a partial success. I was a bit enthusiastic then, more than I am at present. I made a little gallery, and afterwards a convertible gallery; it lifts up when I want to use it as an ordinary bench, and drops down when I want to use it as a gallery. I did a little school work that way and tried the young chaps at it, and perhaps it was one out of ten I got to care for it. I had to do the work in play hour or after school.

14630. How long did you persevere trying to teach it?—I don't think it continued for a year, perhaps six months; not continuous. I got ordinary pulling round the school place, got them to help me making it, and then I gave it up. I had my own opinion. Perhaps these boys work six hours at present. I have not six per cent. of my pupils children of artizans or labourers; they are the children of exceedingly small farmers, and have to work at home.

14631. You mean besides doing literary work at school they have to work at home?—Yes. Children of my ten, often work six hours a day at home.

14632. Mr. Redington.—By work, do you mean driving cattle?—That is, for some; but according to the season, they weed potatoes, mangolds, and turnips, and attend to crops, and do carting, and follow donkeys or perhaps jennets, and do the ordinary farm work; there is practically no paid labour in my district.

14633. Chairman.—Is that, do you think, common in the South of Ireland?—Not to the same extent as in my particular district, but it is pretty general.

14634. Apart from that special reason, what would be your views on manual work?—The ordinary school programme at present is top heavy; I could not make room for it at present, even if I could teach it successfully, and if the children took to it kindly, I could not possibly make room for it, on account of the conditions of life in the locality that supplies the school. If I want to add something, the children tell me "I must go home, I have to see after the sheep," or something.

14635. We will take a supposititious case; suppose you were in a part of Ireland where that was not the case, where the children were not expected by their parents to do ordinary farm in addition to school work, and supposing that Parliament had provided funds for finding appliances and giving suitable rewards to the teachers for teaching manual work, like they would for any other extra subject, would that modify your views?—Speaking generally, I would be an advocate for manual training in large centres of population, but not certainly for rural National schools, even if you have a qualified teacher, and within my acquaintance I could not perhaps pick out three even who are doing it: in my opinion I think the children could be at more useful work.

14636. Are there any teachers doing it?—Yes, there is the one Dr. Skeffington alluded to. He lives on one side of Dungarvan bay and I live at the opposite side. I may mention, too, that in 1862 it was first introduced in the Marlborough-street training college, and perhaps I should state that Mr. Rawlins, who was connected with the Board of Works, teaching there, told me he had more trouble to get me to unlearn a bad system of holding tools than he had with those who had never handled one.

14637. Had you learned to handle tools by practising a trade?—I learned the silk business; it was in Patterson, New Jersey, U.S. I may say I earned more there than I could under the National Board. I made 50s. 6d. a week at it, when I was only seventeen years of age.

14638. Mr. Redington.—Why did you leave it?—My health broke down.

14639. Chairman.—You put down as one reason why it is not taught "the inability of the majority of teachers to impart such general instruction as would be likely to prove useful?"—Out of 108 men in 1862 in the class, I believe there were only about four that came away with any useful knowledge of it.

14640. Was that because they were incapable of learning?—I don't think the taste existed. I don't mean to say it was through want of ability.

14641. You think that another reason is that the destination of pupils in rural schools is mainly agricultural and not very often mechanical?—Yes.

14642. That would be a good reason where it was a question of teaching a trade; do you think that would be an advantage to a boy in a rural district, who was only going to agricultural work, that he should know how to mend a window or a door?—There is no farm on which there is not plenty of occupation for a skilled agriculturist, and I think he would be better employed at effecting these improvements and working the business he was brought up at and paying an ordinary carpenter for mending work; he can get him for 2s. a day.

14643. You think it would be better to pay the 2s. a day to the carpenter than to do the work himself?—Yes, in a place where there is plenty of work to be done in fencing and draining, at least in my locality.

14644. Do the farmers in your locality work from morning to night, or take things easily?—They are, perhaps, the most industrious class of farmers in Ireland, as I had occasion to mention to their landlord not many years ago, they work perhaps sixteen hours a day in certain seasons, and from light to dark on short days.

14645. You have some remarks to make on the

subject of agriculture with regard to the method of inspection?—My own personal experience is that I think the cause for the general break down, as is sometimes supposed, in the teaching of agriculture in National Schools is not attributable to the teaching of it. I reason like this, I have had an opportunity like every country-reared young man of observing agricultural operations since I was able to discern what they were doing at every season of the year; I had a fairly good taste for it, I went up to Glasnevin, and earned my time there and acquired a certain knowledge of it. I farmed three acres of land myself for nineteen years, gardening; I grew the different kinds of vegetables, although not in connexion with the Board—celery, parsnips, onions, rhubarb, parsley, and so on, and followed the usual course of cropping the soil, and still, with all that acquired knowledge, an Inspector comes round and examines my school and gives me 10 per cent. of passes in agriculture, next year he comes round and gives me 60.

14646. Mr. Molloy.—The same inspector?—Yes. Well, I say there must be something wrong. I often put the question to myself, can it be possible that I am entirely at fault or those children?

14647. Not with 60 per cent. higher?—It is a difference of 50 per cent. I never can work out the problem what does it arise from. The question arose a while ago that I would not be a teacher if I could be a farmer. I have a decided taste, I think, myself—and I know myself—for farming, yet I am a teacher of my present school for the last nineteen years.

14648. Mr. Redington.—What is your explanation of the difference between the verdicts of the Inspector on those two occasions?—It is a very human and natural one that I was not entirely at fault.

14649. Rev. Dr. Evans.—You were trained in 1882?—In 1882 and 1883.

14650. That is one year's training: you were a teacher before and you can only speak from the experience of one year's training, of what is done in the manual instruction in Marlborough-street?—That is all.

14651. Were the other men of 1882 in for one or two year's training?—One; there was no such thing as two years' training at the time except in the case of what they called a special class, twelve selected teachers.

14652. You are forming your opinion of the work done there from the experience of one year's training?—But I had a lot of experience in handiwork—manual work—before ever I went there.

14653. The question is not as to your own attainments at all, but as to what your experience would lead you to believe they can do in the way of training people in this manual work in Marlborough-street. Would young men there for two years not be able to acquire some information and some capacity?—Unless in the case of young men having a very decided taste for it I don't think so; it is only an hour a week in the first place.

14654. Don't you think two years' training would equip them better than one?—Another year's extension of time, with more than half the number that were there in my time, would not make the slightest difference to them, or three, considering their want of interest in the subject.

14655. Do the reports on your school show satisfactory results in the other subjects?—Yes, sir; in drawing, for instance. I teach drawing, and I can tell within one per cent. the number of passes I will get; I won't vary two per cent. from the Inspector. I won't vary two-and-a-half to five per cent. in any of the other subjects.

14656. Chairman.—Except agriculture?—Except agriculture.

14657. What test does the Inspector apply in his examination of agriculture?—It is a thing I don't care to enter much upon; I think, at the same time, the questions are rather scientific; they would imply a knowledge of elementary science, elementary chemistry, such as explaining how the lactometer, in conjunction with the hydrometer, would enable a farmer to judge of the quality of his milk. I think the application of the hydrometer to the testing of anything implies a knowledge of elementary science.

14658. Rev. Dr. Evans.—Do you think it is possible generally to teach all the subjects that you teach?—I teach the ordinary subjects with a few extras—drawing, algebra, and geometry.

14659. Does the teaching of agriculture which you give, interfere with the proficiency of your pupils in other subjects?—It interferes to this extent that, having the uncertainty on my mind of how those pupils will acquit themselves from the uncertainty of the examinations, I have to keep them in half an hour extra in the morning, and actually add to the time for giving instruction in the morning in the time table, add 50 per cent. for certain parts of the year; it interferes to that extent.

14660. Mr. Molloy.—What is the time that you devote, according to your time table, to agriculture?—An hour on three days of the week, but it was three-quarters of an hour formerly.

14661. Do you ever bring your boys out to your three acre farm?—Very frequently.

14662. Why would you not connect that with the Board?—The question arose last year, but the patron of the school, Sir Richard Musgrave, was away travelling in America or British Columbia, and the agent did not wish to move.

14663. Kindly mention the post town of your school?—Dungarvan, four miles to the north.

14664. You have 104 on your rolls, but only fifty-four in attendance?—I won't be certain to one or two, fifty-four or fifty-five. I have not thirty in attendance at present.

14665. How do you account for that low attendance?—From the middle of August until the 1st of November every boy over ten years of age is employed at farm work; a great many under ten will stay away because their grown brothers are not attending. I might have the senior half of the school closed. And from Patrick's Day, when the spring work begins, to the middle of May, it is in like manner. I have a good attendance in May, June, July, and August.

14666. Would you say manual work was suitable for town schools?—Certainly not.

14667. And in connexion with the rural schools, do you think that some elementary science bearing on the processes of agriculture ought to be introduced?—I think so.

14668. You mentioned that the Board's present course is too heavy. You would not advocate the propriety of having grammar and geography in second class?—No; I would rather cut it off in third.

14669. Is drawing to scale taught in your school?—I was taught it myself by an uncertificated teacher, but I do not teach it much, except to monitors and boys who learn geometry.

14670. Is mensuration taught as a special subject?—I did teach it when specially requested by a few parents, but I teach it in connexion with geometry.

14671. And the first thirty-two propositions of the first book?—Yes.

14672. Captain Shaw.—Do I understand you to say that it would be an improvement to the teaching of agriculture if it was preceded by the teaching of elementary science?—I do, decidedly; elementary chemistry, and what you may call a general course of elementary science.

14673. Do you think you would have room for that as well as agriculture as now taught?—Not according to the present arrangement of the programme.

14674. You think the present programme should be modified?—To make room for more. In a good many rural schools you may have seventy in attendance in the first half of your result year, and in the second half you may have forty only.

14675. Do you think it is necessary to cultivate the powers of observation of children by any special instruction, which they don't get now?—I think there would be nothing that could be more desirable; that is one of the chief objects of education.

14676. You think it is fully accomplished under the present system?—Not as fully as it might be.

14677. In the instruction which you gave in handicraft you tried apparently to get the boys at once to come and help you in advanced work?—Certainly not.

14678. Did you show them how to use tools before you commenced to make palings?—Not very systematically; I made experiments to satisfy myself could I manage to take it up as an extra subject, because it had been intimated by one of the Professors in the College that it was likely to be a subject in the near future. I went as far as to satisfy myself that I could take it up as a subject.

14679. Do you think the reason of the failure may have been that you did not take it up systematically?—I was not able to take it up systematically.

14680. Mr. Redington.—You say there would be no time for the introduction of manual work into the curriculum, it is already overloaded?—Not in the generality of rural schools.

14681. Why could you not exclude some of the extras you teach and substitute manual work?—I could come at it in other ways if they attended regularly.

14682. You at present teach drawing, algebra, and chemistry?—Algebra and chemistry are taught out of ordinary school hours.

14683. But whenever taught, you find it worth your while to teach algebra and chemistry out of school?—I do not find it worth my while.

14684. But you do it at any rate?—I do it in the case of monitors or prospective monitors—I say, "I will begin and lay out a little foundation for him, not leave it to the last day," but it does not pay me a penny a day.

14685. Five shillings a pass for each of them?—And in the case of two or three that is like a year.

14686. You have, as it were, hindered your curriculum, very likely quite properly, with three extra subjects, at the same time you are saying the curriculum would not stand the introduction of one extra subject?—I don't burden the ordinary school day except by drawing alone; the ordinary four hours, I only put one extra into that. I teach the others altogether outside school hours, and I would not teach them only in order to keep up the supply of monitors in the school.

Wexford.
Sept. 29, 1897.
Mr. Edmund Lalor.

14687. If instead of agriculture the sciences underlying agriculture were taught, that would not be any addition to the labour of the school?—No; I should desire it very much myself.

14688. I only put that one as a possible solution of the difficulty you brought before us?—I take more or less a utilitarian view of it; I say if you want to extend the programme you could do it more usefully in the case of country schools than with this manual work or manual instruction, for children are using their hands for perhaps four hours before they come to school that day.

14689. You keep them at algebra and geometry?—That is not manual instruction.

14690. Would they not rather have manual instruction than algebra?—I think not; because they have perhaps had three or four hours' work before they come to school in the morning.

14691.—Chairman.—Manual work may be done without thinking what you are doing in an involuntary way, or it may be done in carrying out something you have thought out, like applying mensuration?—Yes, sir; the body and mind re-act on each other; if you have a fatigued and worn out boy coming into school in the morning his mind will not be as active as that of the boy who has not gone through a certain amount of exhaustive work.

14692. Don't you think that a certain amount of physical work rather helps the mind?—Not where there is fatigue.

14693. Capt. Shaw.—Do they work before they come to school?—Certainly. I have known boys when they went to their writing lesson to go off to sleep—children up at four in the morning—it is a grazing country, and there were sheep out on the mountain which they had to go after.

THIRTY-THIRD PUBLIC SITTING.—THURSDAY, SEPTEMBER 30th, 1897,

Limerick.
Sept. 30, 1897.

AT 12 O'CLOCK, NOON,

At the Christian Brothers' Schools, Limerick.

Present:—The Right Hon. the Earl of Belmore, G.C.M.G., in the Chair; The Right Hon. C. T. Redington, M.A.; Rev. Henry Evans, D.D.; Rev. Hamilton Wilson, D.D.; Stanley Harrington, Esq., B.A.; W. R. J. Molloy, Esq.; and Captain T. B. Shaw,

with J. D. Daly, Esq., M.A., Secretary.

work first, and then
neatly; but he passes

-No; he would make
pass to the bench to

14752. But you do begin at a particular place or part of the subject, and lead the pupils on gradually?—It is graduated with care from sawing to the more difficult exercises.

14753. Another thing you would never see in Sweden is the tools left upon the benches?—The tools are never left after the exercises on the bench; they have little boxes, and they put them in the lower press. Each is accountable for the tools he was using, and he puts them safely in the press. There are twelve sets of tools, and twelve places for them.

14754. When the articles—the models—are made, what is done with them?—They are kept until after the examination, then the boys may take them home.

14755. Mr. Harrington.—I observe that you have an artisan to help you here; is that necessary?—It is necessary, because my knowledge of the mechanical part of the work is not sufficient.

14756. How could this manual work be introduced into the rural schools, where the teacher would not have the services of an artisan at his disposal?—The exercises are simple, and I think he should go through a course of them.

14757. You think that he could learn sufficient to make the presence of an artisan unnecessary?—I believe so.

14758. In what way would you suggest that the teacher should learn this manual work?—I cannot very well answer, except by taking courses in manual work.

14759. How long ought the course be?—I think an intelligent man would have it in about two months, by continuous lessons, but I am not very capable of giving an opinion on that.

14760. I thought, perhaps, you might be able to tell us from your own experience?—Well, I am not an apt scholar in that way.

14761. Do you know whether the money you get from the Science and Art Department covers the cost? Not at all. It does not cover it.

14762. There is a loss then?—The money got would not be at all sufficient.

14763. I suppose the reason of that is that you have to employ an artisan, but if you leave his wages out, would the money received from the Department cover the cost of the wood, the repair of the tools, and so on?—It would do that, but it would leave little or nothing to pay for the services of whoever would be teaching it.

14764. Is not that a difficulty in regard to the introduction of this into schools generally?—I think it ought to be a good deal more liberally supported by South Kensington, in order to make it a properly paid subject.

14765. I observed that there was one little boy of nine years of age here. You don't object to boys so young being taught this work?—Not if he is sufficiently strong.

14766. You find that it is safe to entrust him with a chisel and other tools?—Since we began to work a single accident has not happened.

14767. How long has the work been going on?—Four years. They are prevented leaving the bench with the tools, and going through the school; precautions are taken to prevent accidents.

14768. Captain Shaw.—You only use your workshop [illegible]

them, as also to induce habits of perseverance, love of work, and self reliance.

14771. And also you teach your boys drawing here. They learn some solid geometry in the course of South Kensington; do you find it an advantage that way?—We are not in connection with South Kensington in solid geometry.

14772. But you could take it in the 7th standard boys?—Yes, you could take it; we don't take it.

14773. But at any rate it gives them some idea of plans and elevations, and the use of drawings?—Yes, and the models would be useful; but I consider it a secondary matter.

14775. It helps the education to that extent?—It does.

14776. Mr. Harrington.—Am I correct in saying that your school is the first in Ireland that has adopted the system of manual instruction?—Well, I don't know if that is quite correct, because we have a place in Dublin that commenced it about the same time, and which was first I cannot say.

14777. Is it working well?—I think so.

14778. What school is that?—Glasnevin Orphanage.

14779. Anyway, it is very creditable to a small place like Lismore to be so well in the front in this movement. We had no evidence, I think, as to the cost of the building here: was this building erected by your own brotherhood?—No, it was erected by a gentleman who was a native of near Lismore. He is living in Germany now—a Mr. Walsh.

14780. An enthusiast in this subject?—An advocate of it.

14781. How are the tools provided and the wood for the boys?—They are provided partly from the Munality, and partly from a subscription given by the Duke of Devonshire of £10.

14782. Is the grant you get from the South Kensington Department sufficient to maintain the school in an efficient condition, without trespassing on your own private funds here?—You speak of the grant in addition to these other sources?

14783. Yes?—It is.

14784. Without outside help, the grant you get from the State, that is from the South Kensington Department, would not be sufficient to maintain the school in a proper state of efficiency?—Not at all.

14785. I think you told us that drawing is compulsory in the whole school here?—It is.

14786. I suppose I am right in assuming that, without it you could not possibly teach the woodwork properly?—Well, you could not have connexion with South Kensington in manual work if you hadn't drawing compulsory; although the two are distinct, they make that a condition. Of course, the fact of drawing being taught to all makes it more easy for the class to learn, but it would not be impossible, even though it was not taught at all, that a class should learn the Scale drawing required.

14787. Would you be in favour of the introduction of drawing into all the primary schools?—Decidedly.

14788. Could you give us any idea of the relative merits, from an educational point of view, of this manual instruction, and of instruction in elementary science, such as you have been alluding to. In places where you could not introduce both subjects, which would you advocate the introduction of?—I could [illegible]

14794. Rev. Dr. Evans.—Are there any models of benches or tools in that book you referred to?—Which book?

14795. You mentioned some book?—There are models I think in different books.

14796. Because your benches differ most materially from those in Sweden?—Well, I don't think that the benches are taken exactly from the models in any book, but are intended to suit the circumstances.

14797. The mode of holding the timber when planing and sawing is wholly different from what I saw in Sweden, and the mode of dealing with the tools also. When a boy is done with his tools he does not drop them on his bench; if it be a double bench he puts them in a place in the centre—between the two boys—for they are never allowed to be left on the place where he works?—Nothing objectionable arises from its being on the bench, and if the bench was raised in the centre it would obstruct the view.

14798. No, but it is lowered; there is a kind of receptacle between the two?—As a matter of fact, I see nothing objectionable in their being left on the bench.

14799. Mr. Harrington.—Have you, since you introduced this subject, noticed it has had any marked effect on the boys when they go into occupations afterwards; you have hardly had time yet, perhaps?—I cannot say that it has affected their future in a marked way; it certainly has not had the effect that some thought it would of making them all carpenters, for of all that passed through only two became carpenters, six went to other trades, ten are still at advanced schools, and the remainder went to various occupations, so that I think it had the effect that I thought it would, of not at all making them become tradesmen, or carpenters especially, as was thought, but that it had clearly an educational effect.

14800. Mr. Molloy.—During the four years since the establishment of this manual instruction class in wood, how many boys have gone through the process?—About 50.

14801. Have you been able to follow their career subsequently?—Two became carpenters, about six became tradesmen, ten, about, are still pursuing a higher course, and the remainder are at various occupations—some the church, some the army, some farmers, some in shops.

14802. The course marked down on your Time Table is a three years' course, and you have been kind enough to promise to let us have a copy of it?—Yes.

14803. Is that course based largely on any special text-book?—No special text-book, but it is taken from various text-books.

14804. The drawing exercises for the boys who come here are carried on exclusively in this room—do they also receive instruction in drawing in the outer school?—They do, but not in connection with this; all the boys have a course of drawing in the several standards, and when they pass the 4th standard in the ordinary course, they are eligible for this, and they have a special drawing for this, part of the two hours.

14805. Had your special instructor in manual work been at all engaged in teaching before he came here?—He was a carpenter, his business is only carpentry, and he merely sees that they go through the work properly.

14806. He gives no instruction in drawing to scale?—No instruction.

14807. And that instruction is carried on in a room under your direction?—Under my direction.

14808. You may have heard from Mr. Walsh, or his friends, even approximately, what the cost of the erection of this building was?—The cost was about £275.

14809. That is the building alone, and then the furnishing?—And wages of the furnishing, then different things were added.

14810. Are all your pupils free; do they pay any fee?—There is no fee of obligation; some pay a very small thing, but they are all free in the sense that nothing is obligatory.

14811. And it is optional with the pupil to attend this class?—Quite optional, except that as a matter of course they fall into it willingly.

14812. Did I catch your meaning rightly, that you think a good knowledge of drawing ought to be compulsory on every teacher, and also a knowledge of manual work?—That both drawing and manual work should be compulsory.

14813. On every teacher?—Yes.

14814. And in order to acquire a knowledge of manual work he would have to go through a course?—I imagine he would.

14815. No injurious effect arises from shortening the school course in certain subjects, grammar and geography, with a view to introduce manual instruction?—I think none at all.

THIRTY-FOURTH PUBLIC SITTING.—FRIDAY, OCTOBER 1st, 1897,

AT 3 O'CLOCK, P.M.,

At the Munster Dairy School, Cork.

Present:—The Right Hon. the Earl of Belmore, G.C.M.G., in the Chair; The Right Hon. C. T. Redington, M.A.; Rev. Henry Evans, D.D.; Rev. Hamilton Wilson, D.D.; Stanley Harrington, Esq., M.A.; W. R. J. Molloy, Esq.; Captain T. B. Shaw; and J. Struthers, Esq., M.A.;

with J. D. Daly, Esq., M.A., Secretary.

£50 in order that a thoroughly good superintendent should be obtained for the school. On the 5th of May it was proposed that there should be two sessions for resident dairy pupils. On the 16th May the committee received a report from the Commissioners, in which they declined to accede to the admission of resident female pupils. On the 25th May it was decided that a deputation should wait on Mr. Keenan; and Mr. Barry, who is present, Captain Sarsfield, who has gone, and myself, waited on Mr. Keenan. We had an interview with him, which lasted an hour and a half, and as the result of that interview we wrote him the following letter:—

14818. Rev. Dr. Evans.—I suppose you refer to Sir Patrick Keenan?—Yes, Mr. Keenan he was then. This is after our interview with him, he having said that under no circumstances could we have resident female pupils, because the school had been used as a lodging-house for the male pupil teachers who were taught in Anglesea street, at Cork, and therefore he had no means of putting up these male teachers except at the Munster Agricultural School. This is the letter:—

"Dear Sir,—Our committee feeling that the admission of female pupils as boarders is indispensably necessary for the success of the school, and being most anxious to co-operate with the Commissioners in removing any difficulties there may be, we make the following proposals, hoping they may meet with your approval:—First; that the pupil teachers should be altogether removed from the establishment, and that the school be kept, as its name implies, as a purely agricultural one. For that purpose we the local committee guarantee a sum of £100 a year for three years, to assist in providing the necessary accommodation for them."

14819. Chairman.—For whom?—The pupil teachers elsewhere.

"Second; that resident female pupils be admitted for the months of January to July, and that we guarantee their board and undertake their moral and religious supervision during their residence, the Board placing at our disposal all the resources of the establishment."

On the 1st of June we received then a letter from Mr. Sheridan, who was then Secretary to the Commissioners of National Education:—

"Sir,—I am directed by the Commissioners of National Education to acquaint you for the information of the local committee connected with the Munster Model Farm, that the proposal made in your letter of the 17th ultimo has been accepted by the Commissioners of National Education, subject to the approval of the Lords of Her Majesty's Treasury, to whom a communication on the subject will be addressed without delay.

"I am, sir,

"Your obedient servant, &c.

And then they inserted it. All we asked to have inserted was: "The local committee has intimated to the Commissioners that the arrangement for separate religious instruction of the pupils has the approval of the Most Rev. Dr. Delany, the Right Rev. Dr. Gregg, and the heads of the different denominations". After Mr. Carroll left, in 1881, he was succeeded by Mr. Smith, and the work of the school went on. We had previously extended the time from a month to six weeks. In March, 1883, we proposed that the time devoted to the dairymaids should be extended to six months—three terms of two months each; they acceded to that in May; and in 1884 we started one of two presentary terms of three terms of two months each for the dairymaids, and we have always more applications than we can fill. I only propose to take you up to 1884, and the rest of the evidence can be given by Mr. Barter or Mr. Bennick.

14622. Rev. Dr. Evans.—I should like to know what exactly is the meaning of the statement that the Commissioners would not put something into a prospectus?—This is the prospectus you see that was sent up. In the prospectus we inserted: "The local committee has intimated to the Commissioners that the arrangement for separate religious instruction of the pupils has the approval of the Most Rev. Dr. Delany, the Right Rev. Dr. Gregg, and the heads of the religious denominations." The Commissioners refused to put that into the prospectus; it was sent back to us twice, and on my finally threatening to resign, it was put in.

14623. Mr. Molloy.—May I ask you about the time of the establishment of this place; does it not go back to 1846?—Yes.

14624. And at the time one of the objects stated by the Commissioners in having model farm establishments was that they should be residential places for the male pupil teachers in the model schools. Later on a model school came to be established in Cork, and the pupil teachers were in residence, but the Commissioners never had females in residence simultaneously with the young men?—No.

14625. I would give that as a reason why they objected to the proposal in the first instance?—Yes, but this was a school that was started for agriculture, and instead of being used for agricultural students it was used as a lodging-house for pupil teachers who were teaching in Anglesea-street, in Cork, and therefore it is not unnatural that the Treasury should object to waste a sum of money in carrying out a scheme of education which did not exist.

14626. As a matter of fact, every model school had the residence for these male pupil teachers in the agricultural school; I will take for instance, Belfast, Athy, Kilkenny; as a rule the pupil teachers of the school resided on the farm, and one of the objects of the Commissioners was that these lads should receive agricultural instruction?—The result was that they did not get it.

14627. Your committee very generously offered to take that expense off the Commissioners' hands?—It was the only terms on which we could get the admission of female pupils.

14628. Mr. Harrington.—I believe that this is the only institution in Munster in which agriculture is taught to boys or girls?—The only one I know of.

14629. And if this had not been taken in hands by the local committee, Munster would be absolutely without a place for purely agricultural instruction?—It is the only one that has been kept up; the other one, Munegret, in Limerick, was given up.

14630. Mr. Molloy.—What is the size of the farm?—126 acres.

14631. And the number of the students?—You will get that from the Secretary.

Mr. Richard Barter, J.P., Vice-President of the Governors of the Munster Dairy School, examined.

14632. Chairman.—You were formerly hon. secretary of the Munster Dairy School?—Yes, my lord; I was hon. secretary for the whole time—except for two years that I was ill—that the Munster Dairy School existed under the committee before the charter was obtained.

14633. You have heard the points to which Sir George Colthurst referred, and I see from a marked copy of the evidence that you wish to refer to some of the evidence that Sir George did not refer to; perhaps I might read it to you. The Most Rev. Dr. Walsh asked Mr. Carroll, in cross-examination, as follows:— one of the most hard-working, and aided by the wonderful ability of Dr. Sullivan, this school would never be the success it is to-day. For the first two years the whole responsibility was thrown on us; we had to give all the instruction, in writing, to Mr. Carroll of what was to be carried out, in the feeding of the cows, the whole management of the cows, and everything. There was a direct rule by Professor Baldwin that everything was to be given in writing that was decided by the committee, which I invariably did as hon. secretary, after first consulting Dr. Sullivan.

14634. Then your point is that Mr. Carroll simply

told me frequently that his opinion was that it had graded up the butter in the Cork market £10,000 a year, the instruction conveyed by this school, and he could tell the hand of the Dairy School on every firkin from a pupil.

14874. They are able to make butter that fetches a higher price in the market?—Yes, £10,000 a year in that market alone, without the fresh butter and butter sold elsewhere.

14875. Rev. Dr. Evans.—Do you acknowledge any indebtedness to Mr. Carroll at all?—Certainly, he is most able, and Mrs. Carroll also.

14876. Will you kindly put in a brief form what you think you do owe him?—I think his instructions to the people has been as good as it could be, and we were extremely lucky in Mr. and Mrs. Carroll and Mr. and Mrs. Walsh who followed him, they most ably carried out the instruction in the school.

14877. Mr. [illegible]. I see by the report of the Commissioners for 1896, that during the course of last year there were eighteen male agricultural students resident here; there were thirty-seven female dairy students in the first session, thirty-six the second, and thirty-seven the third; and there were twelve creamery managers. Would more than thirty-seven female students be willing to attend if you had room for them?—I think it is a mistake to admit more than you can give practical instruction to, and I think thirty-six is a larger number than the number of cows and capacity we have here for giving instruction. I would much rather see only twenty-six or twenty-eight. We at first limited it under thirty, but under the great pressure brought on us we extended it to thirty-six, and I don't think we can do full justice to thirty-six.

14878. Is it the farm or the buildings that are too small?—For practical work, we want a lot more cows and a lot more expansion in every part of the dairy.

14879. Chairman.—In fact you want more material?—More material. Mr. Carroll has done a great deal lately, because he bought all the milk he could about the country, and also he gets a large quantity of cream twice a week from Limerick, Mr. Carroll gets that for Mr. Smith, and that has been a great boon. We have instituted a very good course of instruction lately, we give each girl five cows for two days, they have to milk them and set the milk and do all the practical work, they look after their feeding, and the butter is tested, and inspected by the Head Inspector, and they get marks accordingly. And they each get an assistant, and that assistant is next time the head herself, and the assistant learns from the one over her. Lately the Commissioners of Education have granted us a new dairy, for more fully carrying out that experiment, but still the number of cows at our disposal is not sufficient. Another thing is, we have never been able to keep on our calves, we would like to teach the farmers of the country how to breed and keep the best dairy cattle, and to give them bulls at a cheap rate from the best milking strains, but really the school is so limited, and we want such a supply of milk that we have only been able to buy from hand to mouth in Cork market.

14880. What number of cows is the maximum?—Thirty-five.

14881. Then the way you work it is this, you have thirty-six dairymaids, and thirty-five cows, and you give an individual dairymaid five cows for a certain number of days, and then other days another person has them, and then a third and so on?—We divide the girls into three divisions, one class at practical dairy work, No. 2 class is at needlework and ironing, and the third class at technical instruction and cookery, all attending daily lectures and demonstrations.

14882. They do cookery?—Yes, the ladies' committee is most careful about that, it has been one of the greatest boons, the laundry work and tidyness is very little second to the instruction they get in dairy work, thanks to the ladies committee.

14883. How many days consecutively are the girls kept at one occupation?—They rotate about daily for the eight weeks they are here.

Mr. Ludlow A. Beamish, J.P., Hon. Secretary, Munster Dairy School, examined.

14884. Chairman.—You propose to give evidence as to the want of suitable education at the Munster Dairy School for male pupils. But before we go into that perhaps you would give us a little more fully what the female pupils do; the nature of the instruction they get?—They are divided into classes; a certain number of them milk cows. Mr. Barter has told you of the recent alteration by which each girl gets five cows for two days; the others take their share of the milking of the rest of the herd, and a certain number are told off to dairy work, a certain number to laundry, and a certain number to cooking, and then they get theoretical instruction in dairying.

14885. There are thirty-five cows; one girl milks five, therefore there is employment for seven girls each day, and she takes it a second day?—Yes.

14886. Then on the next two days you have another set of seven girls?—There are only five cows exactly under the charge of one girl, because there is only one dairy; the milk from these cows is kept in a separate dairy which can only be used for one set of cows at a time.

14887. Then you have seven sets of five cows?—No, the cows are not divided into sets. The superintendent reported that he found as the result of the work that very often a sharp clever girl, great at picking up the theory of dairying, when she came to the examination came out higher than a girl who was a more practical dairymaid. He reported that to the committee, and we had a consultation, and this plan was devised to test the practical as well as the theoretical work; and, therefore, five cows are taken, in as nearly the same state of milk as we can get them, and each girl has five cows for two days; she takes the milk, keeps it in a separate dairy, is allowed to manipulate it as she pleases, the superintendent watching it carefully and seeing how she treats it. The butter so made is put apart, and a sample sent to the head inspector of the Cork butter market, who awards it a mark; that mark in conjunction with the mark the superintendent has given her for practical work in the dairy during the two days, constitutes her score for practical dairy work; to this is added her score for theoretical dairy work, and the result establishes her place in the class.

14888. Then if a girl comes for only one term, she only milks?—She may milk the cows, but she has also the treatment of five cows for two days, for the remainder of the term she is taking her portion of the ordinary dairy work of the school.

14889. Now, perhaps, you will pass on to what you intend to tell us?—I wanted shortly to sketch the development or rather retrogression of the agricultural education for male pupils. When the dairy school was started, the first session for male pupils was in 1881, and was for four months' duration; in 1882–83 there were two sessions of four months each; that was eight months; but from 1884 to 1894, in consequence of the development of the dairy classes, the increase in the number and the lengthening of the session, it was only possible to give the boys four months, and these four months were given at the end of the year, from 20th of August to 20th of December. That went on to 1895, when an additional month was added from 20th of July to 20th of December. The moment that became the rule of the institution the local committee began to object; it struck them as it must I think strike anybody, that to teach boys agriculture, bringing them in in July and sending them out in December, was very little better than a farce; the whole seed time, which is probably

Cork.
—
Oct. 1, 1896.
—
Mr. Richard Barter, J.P.

Mr. Ludlow A. Beamish, J.P.

Cork. — Oct. 1, 1897. — Mr. Ludlow A. Beamish, J.P.

one of the most important parts of agricultural work was omitted from the pupils' education, the computer work was omitted, and they could only see the results. It was very much like putting a person in charge of a drawing machine in a wool mill, and telling him he had been taught how to make tweeds. Even in a short visit here, Mr. Jenkins, the former Secretary of the Royal Agricultural Society of England, although he was very much taken by Sir Patrick Keenan's work and that of the Commissioners, in reporting on this school, stated that "four months in the year cannot be considered as of much practical use, and can be only looked upon as a stepping stone for clever boys to get free scholarships at Glasnevin." It would, perhaps, weary you to go through the various steps the committee have taken from time to time to bring this fact under the notice of the authorities. In May, 1886, we sent forward a strong resolution, pointing out the inadequacy of the education. We think it does to a certain extent harm, because it produces a superficial habit of mind. You teach a boy a good deal of the theory of agriculture, and he may be practically grossly ignorant, or he may have come with an erroneous impression as to certain details of practice, which he goes away with because he does not go through the whole work of the farm year.

14590. Will you tell us what you think would be a satisfactory course, both satisfactory and practicable, assuming you had money to carry it out?—After applying to the Commissioners on several occasions, we applied to Mr. Arthur Balfour, then we went to Mr. Morley, and Mr. Morley pointed out the great fault in Ireland was that people asked him for various things without having thought out a definite plan as to how their wishes could be carried out. We sent up a definite plan, which we repeated next year to Mr. Gerald Balfour, slightly modified. We suggested that a farm of 150 acres should be taken for the boys, and accommodation put up on it for thirty male pupils, that the existing dairy school farm should be handed over to us, and maintained as a dairy farm, and managed by the local committee, subject to central control. We estimated the cost of the farm would be £3,000 in capital and £2,250 a year, including the amount already spent on this school, that would cover the cost of the agricultural farm, and the present dairy farm.

14591. Do I rightly understand you to suggest that you should have another farm of 150 acres in addition to this one?—Yes, keep this as a dairy school.

14592. Entirely for the girls?—Either for the girls or for dairy factory instruction in the summer, but principally for the girls altogether, keeping it at all events as a dairy farm for dairy instruction.

14593. With regard to the farm for males, was that to be a dairy farm?—No, a general farm.

14594. But with dairy work included?—That might be a detail, the principle idea was that the 150 acres was to be a general agricultural farm, on which experiments of a useful character could be carried out, which, of course, it is impossible to do with the appliances at our disposal here.

14595. Do you think you could get a farm with suitable buildings on it already erected?—We contemplated getting a farm with a certain number of buildings on it, and making additions to it in galvanised iron and wood, as I happen to know has been done at the Colonial College at Hollesley Bay, where young men are educated for the Colonies. We went so far that we got estimates from one of the leading people in Dublin for putting these things up, and it was on those estimates we calculated the sum we thought was required. What among other things we found a great want of here, even for the smaller experiments that we have attempted, is that of a competent bailiff and a competent foreman. Mr. Smith has to undertake the whole supervision of the place, and do most of the theoretical education, except the lectures in veterinary science and chemistry, and it is impossible for him to be continually in the byre or field. If an experiment is to be of any value it must be done accurately, and to do that accurately you must have one of a certain type trained to carry out instructions, and attach importance to the slightest difference in weight or measure. We have applied for such a man on several occasions, at present we have only got the ordinary farmman, and a very ordinary herdsman, so the whole onus rests on Mr. Smith, and it is impossible for him to carry it out properly.

14596. Rev. Dr. Evans.—To whom did you apply?—The Commissioners. Recently we have sent up an application again. Mr. Barter alluded to the experiments carried on in reference to water in butter, that was one experiment we were able to carry out. The attention of the committee was first drawn to the subject by the Manchester prosecutions, and they thought it would be very advisable, as the State had not thought fit to establish what should be the quantity of water in good butter, that somebody should try to do it, and although our resources are limited, we spent £40 on this investigation, with the result, as I understand, that in the Cork butter market at present they are endeavouring to get the water in butter down to the standard fixed in the report of our committee. There was another question about the same time that created considerable interest in this district, and in Ireland generally, that is whether pigs could be fed at a profit at existing prices; we submitted a plan to the Commissioners of National Education by which we thought that question could be fairly well solved; we suggested it should be carried out upon 200 pigs, and the period should be for two years; the estimated cost was about £450. Of course that was entirely outside the power of our committee. I regret to say the Commissioners did not see their way to take it up. It was to be an experiment on the relative merits of various breeds and of various feedings, and that, of course, would involve additional buildings, about £200 of the sum asked for would be for buildings.

14597. Chairman.—That was a capital sum?—Yes, £450 would have been required in addition for the two years. There was another point I should like to mention; it bears on the influence of local committees, and it goes to show that not only is a local committee desirable, but that their help should continue to be given, if it is desired to produce good results. The Commissioners appointed itinerant instructors in 1891, and in such a form that it cost practically nothing to the districts applying for them; all the district had to do was to supply an assistant and show some interest. In 1891 we communicated with one of our governing body near Dunmanway, and the instruction was successful on the whole. The next year some members of our committee went to Clonakilty and Waterville, with the result that the lectures were fairly attended. The following year we thought that sending out circulars would be sufficient. In 1893 we got no application. In 1894 Lady Mary Aldworth interested herself in her district and introduced an instructor, with excellent results. In 1895 and 1896 there were no applications. In 1897 special efforts were again made to draw the attention of farmers to the advantages offered, with the result that we have had two instructors steadily employed since April and May.

14598. Mr. Molloy.—If you had your new establishment in operation to-morrow would you not still labour under the great disadvantage of not having the proper foundation that Mr. Barter referred to?—I cannot agree with Mr. Barter at all in that.

14599. In connection with primary schools?—No, my notion is if the children come thoroughly well grounded in their arithmetic, and perhaps having been taught geometrical drawing to inculcate accuracy, they are much more likely to pick up the exact technical education they would receive at a properly equipped agricultural school than if they spent their time learning a smattering of agriculture in a primary school.

14600. In addition to dairying, needlework and cookery and laundry also is taught?—These are taken by the ladies committee.

14901. Are they found to be successful?—Cookery is particularly successful. The work done in the laundry is excellent, but the pupils don't take such an interest in it.

14902. The girls who come for dairy instruction here have been, I suppose, in the main National School pupils?—I should imagine so; they are in the main farmers' daughters. I have a return here of what became of them when they left us; seventy-three per cent. of them go into places as dairy maids and to factories.

14903. Captain Shaw.—What length of course do you consider necessary to give a boy?—Two years.

14904. If you had this farm established, what extent of country do you think it would supply?—It would deal with the whole of Munster.

14905. Do you think that thirty pupils in two years would be sufficient for the whole of Munster?—I fancy so, because remember there are only a certain number of farmers who would be able to bear the cost of the fare and the loss of their children's labour.

14906. Would you not think it expedient they should learn some experimental science for themselves at school. Might they not be taught with advantage weighing and specific gravity?—They might be taught anything that would teach them accuracy. I mentioned geometrical drawing as an extension of drawing.

14907. Mr. [illegible].—Take woodwork, where they have to make accurate measurements?—Yes, accuracy is one of the greatest wants in this country.

14908. Captain Shaw.—Do you think the agriculture they are taught at present in schools is any use to them?—I should think very little. The other day I was at a place where one of our lecturers was lecturing; the clever girl of the school was put forward; she evidently had learned a good deal, but the habit of repeating everything by heart was so strongly impressed on her that when she had forgotten the actual words of the teacher, although she knew the subject, she was at a loss, she was trying to remember the exact words in which the lesson had been last taught to her, and the girl was distinctly much above the average of intelligence.

14909. We had it in evidence a few days ago that the agricultural instruction was useful because the boys saw the work on their farms and got the reasons from the book, do you think the book reasons are satisfactory as a rule?—I think if you taught them to work accurately to two places of decimals, or to be able to measure to a thousandth of an inch with exactness, as the case might be, you would do more good.

14910. Mr. [illegible].—You did not mention that the scheme you have put before the Government has been rejected, has it not been rejected?—It has not been rejected. Mr. Gerald Balfour's answer to us was that he sympathised with our movement, but that our strength was our weakness, as, if we were correct, it would involve similar schools for the whole of Ireland.

14911. Was it suggested it should be placed under the new Agricultural Board?—We were told to wait for the new Agricultural Board, that the question of agricultural education would be dealt with as a whole.

Cork.

Oct. 1, 1897.

Mr. [illegible]

Mr. Edward H. [illegible], One of the Governors of the Munster Dairy School, examined.

14926. Chairman.—I believe you wish to contrast agricultural instruction at present in vogue in Ireland with that which is in vogue in Sweden?—I think your Commission has been over there, and probably knows something about it.

Chairman.—We have been there, but only inquired into manual work; not into this class of subject at all; I don't think we either saw or heard anything of it.

14927. Mr. Struthers.—There is no instruction in agriculture in the primary schools in Sweden or Norway?—No.

14928. Chairman.—Have you any suggestions as to how that can be introduced?—I think so; I think if we take the programme of instruction, as issued to National schools, and go through it, I might point out differences in the methods in which they go to work.

14929. You say there is no instruction in Sweden in primary schools, and we are dealing only with primary schools here. I understand there is a certain amount of instruction given in the shape of school gardens, and to a lesser extent in school farms in Ireland—starting with that, tell us what you wish to say?—If I might go through the programme of the Irish Agricultural Instruction and point out what the instruction is in Ireland, and how it is that it practically does no good whatever. I notice here that the very first thing they state is that "the pupil should be able to explain intelligently on the farm the preparation of the ground, tillage, sowing, thinning" and so on. I am afraid they are not able to do it at all, they may be very intelligent pupils, but I don't see how they are able in anyway to do that intelligently. Because if the teachers have not the necessary instruction—as the teachers have abroad—how can the pupils learn?—As a rule, abroad you see the result of no teaching whatever, you see the result of system, the older boys work on all the farms, and that goes down to the smaller children. If you examine the farms here you will find that corn is marketed in a more dirty condition than it is in Sweden, Norway or Denmark. We, in this district, are interested in barley, but the stacking of barley is not understood in this country at all, the consequence is that the barley comes to market in not so good a state as it might do otherwise, and, therefore, does not fetch so high a sum of money. The yield in the potato crops is not so great in Ireland certainly as it is in England or Wales. If the agricultural instruction is to do any good, the pupils should not learn things by rote, but so as to carry them in their minds even after they become farmers. They say in addition to the foregoing, "the pupils in the second fifth class should know the points of live stock, the indications of milking qualities in cows, &c., all that is necessary for farming purposes."

14930. Do you think that can be taught in primary schools?—I am quite sure it cannot.

14931. Is your point that it is no use trying to teach children in primary schools these things, but that some system should be introduced after they leave the primary school to teach it practically?—Yes, I mean that, and I mean another thing; comparing this country with Sweden, where I have been for seven years, farming the whole time, I don't see how the children can be taught when the teachers have not been brought up to that state of knowledge they have abroad.

14932. You say the teachers have got it abroad. But they don't teach the children in the primary schools; where do they teach them?—At the continuation of ordinary school work.

14933. Mr. Struthers.—Agricultural colleges?—They have more than that; they have two agricultural institutions, they have fourteen rural schools, with a six month's course, then twenty-four agricultural schools throughout the country with a two years' course, and then they have four dairy schools, and sixteen dairy stations. That means to say they endeavour to educate the child in fewer subjects up to a certain period, and keep him concentrated on those subjects. Some of the pupils are twenty-three when they go to these schools, I don't think they take them under seventeen or eighteen, but from seventeen or eighteen up to twenty-four. They take them considerably older than we do, and then they have already acquired an accurate standard of work. When I came over here from Sweden we carried out a certain number of experiments; but I found there was absolutely no knowledge of what accuracy meant. An experiment is of no use unless one goes into it with minute accuracy. That want of accuracy runs through the whole system, it has been one of our distinct failures in this country. I can give you an instance outside agriculture altogether, because we employ a great many clerks and people, and the boys are the same way. At the schools in [illegible] they bring them up to a certain point, and then they put them into a school for book-keeping, and the boys you get from there can close books, and make out balance sheets, and even buy and sell stocks, they are consequently accurate. An ordinary boy coming from school here has a certain amount of knowledge, but it is not that form of knowledge, and one has to commence teaching him accuracy.

14934. Chairman.—What is it you propose should be done in this country to give effect to your ideas?—To remove agricultural education altogether from the primary schools, and to teach them accuracy in other forms, by Sloyd or whatever is suitable.

14935. Then, your evidence tends to this, that the teaching of agriculture in primary schools in Ireland is practically useless?—Practically useless.

14936. And you would prefer that they should turn their attention to other subjects which would teach them accuracy?—And concentration of thought.

14937. And should only begin to learn agriculture in some continuation school after their ordinary education is completed?—Perfectly so, but in order to do that we must get the schools, we are behind hand in our agricultural schools, we have not carried out experiments, we have not come up nearly to the point of the Danes and Swedes. Personally, I believe, that if we came up to it we could easily get the people to follow. We carried out certain experiments here which were very useful. Mr. Carroll said they were good experiments, but that they were more to report to the Royal Society of England than for our dairy school. I said I thought it was a good thing to raise such questions here. There was a large farmer near me and he said:—"Look here, if you like to do it I will give you the whole of my cowhouses and let you carry out on the farm what you said at the Dairy school were correct principles, and if you agree to do it, I am ready to bear the expense." So it shows they are ready to accept knowledge. Take forty pigs going to be experimented upon, each pig is an individual in himself just like a human being, and although you may separate them and feed them all on the exact kind of food these pigs will give you absolutely totally different results, and therefore, as they do in Denmark, we have to feed them together and find out the variation which result before you commence your experiment. All that is not done here. As regards dairying they have no knowledge of ripening their cream or how to use cold.

14938. Mr. Struthers.—Where do you mean?—Here in Ireland, they have no knowledge of whether it is a feasible thing to keep ice. We have proposed experiments several times but we are always refused.

14939. Refused by whom?—I cannot tell you; we suggest things to Mr. Carroll, he says he will do his best with the Commissioners of National Education, but of course they have their difficulties with the Treasury. The practical result is that what we want to do, to try and improve the country here and do what is successful in other countries, we are barred from doing. Glasnevin and the Munster Dairy School are the only two places where pupils can be taught a certain amount of practical agriculture, and if we cannot reach our own standard how can the teachers teach it, and if the teachers cannot teach it how can the children reach it. What is the good of a long list of subjects which cannot be done practically.

14940. CHAIRMAN.—We had a witness before us the day before yesterday who was objecting to certain things; but he said he thought the good of agricultural education as given in the schools at present was this, that the children came with a certain amount of practical knowledge that they had picked up at home, and what they learned out of books put that into words, and gave them the theory of what they had picked up in practice, without knowing what the practice meant. Do you agree with that?—No, not on the text-book, I have read it very carefully, it gives you a certain amount of knowledge, but a person would pick all that information up in a very short time in a properly organised and constituted establishment of any kind: it is so much waste of time to know that a cock is a cock and a hen is a hen. It gives no accurate information as regards the importance of feeding, how to feed, that certain artificial foods and manures are to be used, and so on. We know nothing of that because we have not entered on the subject.

14941. MR. STEPHENS.—And these things cannot be taught in a primary school?—They cannot, and if we could concentrate a child to more accuracy of thought and accuracy of work, people like ourselves would have greater facility in a shorter time in teaching them the real knowledge that they require, and if we ourselves were only allowed to carry out what we know to be necessary and have seen in other countries to be necessary, we would be to a certain extent prepared to undertake that instruction ourselves, but we have been barred and cannot do it under existing conditions.

14942. CHAIRMAN.—I think I gather that both in Sweden and in this country you have had some practical experience of trying experiments?—Yes.

14943. When we were in Cumberland we were taken to an experimental plot, in which they had been growing turnips, it was on that merry ground, and we were told it would have been economical to use less manure rather than much manure, on the ground that although if you used double the quantity of manure you got larger turnips you did not get double as large turnips; and, therefore, they thought less manure was more profitable; is that your opinion?—It is a very hard thing to say; it would depend on the soil; it is like an animal; if you have got a cow you must milk the cow up to a certain point, beyond that point it won't pay you, you may feed too heavily, or not feed sufficiently.

14944. Don't you think it would depend on the quality of the land?—It would.

14945. I put some questions myself with regard to putting artificial manure on land that had been ploughed out of lea last year, and I was told it was a waste of money; my steward happened to try the experiment without my knowing it, and the result was that he found it exactly the reverse, at any rate on the bad land?—Quite so.

14946. MR. HARRINGTON.—I suppose we are right in assuming that you would not object to, but would rather approve of, the introduction of very elementary science into the ordinary National schools?—I should think it would concentrate their minds to a certain extent and teach them accuracy. Try anything, it does not matter what, so long as accuracy is taught.

14947. We have seen it done in some of the English schools where they are taught with simple balances to weigh accurately?—If they are taught accurately, but I have gone through a good many experiments in Ireland, and have found that the term accuracy is not exactly understood, but if it is taught it will aid us afterwards in teaching.

14948. Captain SHAW.—Does not the present system of teaching agriculture, which is to study from the examples around them, and then to receive an explanation from their text book, which analyses the apparent causes; does not that tend to stereotype the present system and prevent any improvement; the present system is to study the fields around, and then the children are to come into the school and receive an explanation of the apparent causes of those processes?—I don't think it does any good.

14949. They only go and see what is actually in existence around them?—That is got to a certain extent altered by their taking excursions, and if you were able to take those boys out to farms, and show them different kinds of farms and different kinds of crops, if that were done it would be a good thing.

14950. Mr. MOLLOY.—Did I understand you to object to this programme on the ground that it required pupils to have an intelligent knowledge of the cultivation of an ordinary farm and garden plots, the fact being that the teachers of these pupils were not sufficiently qualified?—I don't wish to say that exactly; it is somewhat of a strong statement, but I don't see how in the natural course of events they can be qualified, comparing them with what one has seen abroad.

14951. Are you aware that no teacher is allowed to carry out that instruction unless he has undergone suitable instruction himself, and has obtained a certificate of competency?—Quite so, theoretically speaking, according to book learning, yes; but that is perfectly different from practical knowledge, and it also depends upon the standard of the examination the teacher goes through, and I say that the standard of agricultural education is a very low one in this country.

14952. Then your proposition is to remove agriculture altogether from Irish National schools?—Yes, and concentrate the child's mind to think accurately.

14953. Not merely the theory but any attempt at practice?—Yes.

14954. CHAIRMAN.—Then you would be against even school plots and school gardens?—The only thing that would be of use would be as regards potato spraying; if those school plots or gardens were under the Board of Education, and careful men were sent down to examine the disease, there would be no harm in the pupils using it, but I don't think it is of very vital importance as regards furthering agricultural education afterwards, because I think they would learn such subjects very quickly if they came here with their minds prepared for it.

14955. Mr. MOLLOY.—But these school plots are under the Board of Education?—Quite so.

14956. Would you also remove dairy instruction from the primary schools in the case of girls?—Well, no, for this reason, agriculture is a very big subject, dairying is one of its smaller branches, and to a certain extent I don't think it would do the girls any harm, but if they intended to be dairymaids it is far better not to teach a subject like that at a primary school but to go in for it thoroughly, and master it in a month or two months at some properly conducted dairy school.

14957. You referred to some part of Sweden in which there were fourteen rural schools with instruction given for six months; have these schools any literary department?—Yes, they are principally literary departments.

14958. You say there is a combination of literary and agricultural instruction?—They are for much older pupils; they embrace science and the Swedish language; it is a higher course, it would be for a man who showed himself rather more intelligent than a workman, and he would go there after having been five or six years at a farm to master the subject.

14959. Rev. Dr. WILSON.—You were for some years, I believe, at a large dairy establishment in Sweden?—Yes.

14960. Were you manager?—I was, practically.

14961. Would you not then feel yourself in a

Cork.
Oct. 1, 1897.
Mr. Richard B. [illegible]

position to introduce the same system into Ireland without any experience?—No, because every country requires its own modifications. I did try, if I may say so, experiments on the feeding of cows here, and they practically have got what our experience was in Sweden, but one has to feel one's way, what one can do in Sweden one cannot do here. You come here and say "So and so is done in Sweden," as I have often done, and they say "It is a pleasant thing to hear it is done in Sweden, but Sweden is a long way off," and they hardly believe the statement. The thing to do is to prove in our own schools that such a thing can be done, not to be ashamed of the mistakes we make, and to recognise when we make mistakes, not to gloss them over for the sake of being called a successful school. And the committees of your boards of management should be careful not to do anything they don't think would be a success. The experiments we have carried out here to a certain extent have not been failures because we have been careful to go into them beforehand. We have got the water in butter down to 10 per cent. through our experiments, when we said 16 per cent. everybody said we were wrong, but we stuck to it, and we have proved it practically.

14962. You know how a cow is fed most carefully in Sweden?—Perfectly so, but you go and ask the farmers to do the same thing here, and tell them "You must divide your cows into certain sections;" you tell them that each section should have so many pounds of food; they won't weigh the food accurately, they will simply go off and get a bucket, as I have seen it done, and put a couple of handfuls of stuff in and say "That is about the amount." That is not accuracy and would not lead to success.

14963. I know it is difficult even with an ordinary Irish cook to get them to weigh things?—Yes, but it can be done. As regards agricultural education, we are in our infancy.

14964. With your knowledge and experience, if you were to embark upon [illegible] you have [illegible] to do, would Mr. Smith cooperate with you?—Certainly, but Mr. Smith requires assistance. Mr. Smith has been most kind in all our experiments, but he requires assistance.

14965. We are far below the Danes and Swedes. What main proposals would you make to bring us up to them?—It would be an excellent thing if we could have two or four agricultural institutions. In Sweden they have four, and our populations, Sweden's and Ireland's, are about the same. But even if we started with two, we have the nucleus of two, we have Glasnevin and the Munster Dairy School, and with very little alteration in both places, but with the addition of capital and income, you might do an enormous amount; to improve the agriculture of the country, but other things will develop by degrees. We could have our rural schools develop into minor dairy schools as they do in Sweden, in some of those cooperative dairies or on some of the best farms, that is where the twenty-four agricultural schools in Sweden are. They really are estates, and the Government grants them a certain subvention, and the farmer keeps one or two trained men. He then takes these poor pupils, out of 674 pupils, 53 per cent. of the pupils of the Royal and agricultural schools are free pupils—but it hardly pays them to let them waste their time; they are given a very small subvention, but then the pupils work on the farm. They are bound for two years like ordinary labourers, a certain portion of the time is given for theoretic work, and the rest to carrying out the work of the farm in a more intelligent way than it would be by ordinary labourers, that is the way of getting over the teaching part by means of utilizing the work of the boys.

14966. Mr. STRUTHERS.—I think you would not have agriculture taught in the elementary schools at all?—No.

14967. And you think the education given there should be of such a kind as to develop the accuracy of the pupils?—And concentration.

14968. And contrasting the Swedish schools with the Irish schools, you think more accuracy is developed over there?—I think so.

14969. Because of concentration of subjects, you mentioned they had fewer subjects?—There are other things as well; race forms a difference too.

14970. I think if you look at any Swedish programme you will find the number of subjects is quite as extended as here?—But then they must be taught in quite a different way.

14971. That is the point I am coming to, that the requirement of accuracy is the result of the teaching; it is not a question of subjects, but the way in which any subject is taught?—Perfectly so; but the mere fact of studying accurately means time, and you cannot embrace a whole number of subjects. If I work inaccurately I can go through a great many more subjects in a shorter time, and therefore the fewer up to a certain proportion is my argument.

14972. But you may take it from me that the number of subjects taught in an ordinary school in Sweden is not less than here. Do you think the farmers in Sweden and Denmark are more intelligent than the farmers in England and Scotland?—England and Scotland I cannot tell you so much about; yes, on certain technical subjects, they are in Sweden.

14973. You know that Denmark has a great reputation in dairying?—Certainly.

14974. But the butter that is sent from Denmark to this country does not, as a rule, come directly from farms but from creameries?—Yes.

14975. And the success of these creameries has nothing to do with the average intelligence of the farmer but with the skill of the manager of the creamery?—That has to do with the only section we are concerned with here, that is the dairymaid; the dairymaid in Denmark and in Sweden is far more intelligent than the dairymaid here.

14976. Do you mean the dairymaid at the creamery?—Yes, on the farm too.

14977. CHAIRMAN.—Have you worked in Denmark?—I have seen many farms there.

14978. You have seen the controversy in the papers about the cleanliness or non-cleanliness of the butter?—It is a sanitary question, the question of water.

14979. Do you think there is room for improvement there?—Yes, on account of the water.

14980. Do you think they could get better water here?—Yes, it is the water the cows drink and the butter is washed in.

14981. It did not occur to me that it was the water the cows drink?—Oh, yes, it was, because typhoid fever was traced to it.

14982. There is less likelihood of that in this country?—Certainly, and the best butter in the world ought to be made here.

14983. Mr. STRUTHERS.—Is that to be attained by educating every farmer up to a certain mediocre level in dairy knowledge or by providing a few highly qualified experts?—That leads to another question as to how the butter is to be worked; Mr. Carroll and I disagree on the subject; he advocates the lump system; I am afraid I am altogether in favour of well-conducted dairies.

14984. As a practical question, which is easier, to educate the whole of the farmers of a district or to get perhaps a couple of highly qualified men?—It is far easier to do the latter, and therefore I say the creamery system would be a better system than the lump butter system because that would be the less difficulty to overcome.

14985. To come to the point, why I ask these questions is this, so far as I can see, the success of the dairying in Denmark does not depend on the education given in schools?—Not now, but it used to; but I can tell you the case of Sweden; the ordinary dairymaid of the ordinary estate in Sweden

Cork.

Oct. 2, 1902.

Mr. Richard S. [illegible].

is distinctly higher than the dairymaid is in this country; she knows infinitely more of practical matters.

14986. Where has that knowledge been acquired?—It is now simply handed down from one to another; they have educated themselves.

14987. Then it is not the result of any system of instruction?—It must have come from that, but it would be perhaps partly private instruction; the owner of the estate has brought his business, and would instruct his dairymaid.

14988. That does not imply any special aid on the part of the State?—Oh, yes, you will find that a great many of the dairymaids who go out from these different schools obtain situations on these estates, some do not; the instruction must naturally come from the State if you follow me.

14989. I am afraid I do not?—Suppose a girl has been to a State school and mastered the work and comes home, then she instructs her own sisters.

14990. That shows that special knowledge is not due to anything they acquire in the ordinary schools, but to something afterwards given?—Yes, special technical instruction afterwards.

14991. So therefore you cannot hope to effect any great reform in the agriculture of the country by doing anything in the elementary schools?—Other than the introduction of accuracy, but not on special subjects.

14992. But you have no views as to how this accuracy might be obtained to a greater degree in the ordinary schools, have you?—No, I have not; you ought to know a great deal more about it than I do; I would not venture to suggest anything in that way; I only know the want is felt.

14993. At what age do you take pupils into this institution here?—They vary from seventeen upwards.

14994. I think one of the witnesses said that the majority came from National schools; that is to say they have been at no other schools through the country?—I think so.

14995. And they probably left those schools at what age?

Mr. [illegible].—From fourteen to sixteen.

14996. Mr. Stevenson.—You could not admit them earlier to your institution?—Do you refer to females or males?

14997. Take the dairymaids?—No, I think the work would be rather against them, too heavy; the great thing here is not only accuracy, but we must teach them how to work.

14998. Chairman.—I suppose strength is required in milking a cow?—Exactly so.

14999. Mr. Stevenson.—On the other hand, if you were able to take them at an earlier age you would get them direct from the school. At present there is an interval between leaving school and coming to your institution, in which the effect of any school impression that was useful might be lost?—Yes, if a girl was strong at fifteen there would be no objection. But when she comes here she should be placed under strict discipline, and ought to have heavier physical work to show her exactly what real work means.

15000. Take the practical work of milking, is it not well that they should begin at a very early age?

Mr. [illegible].—The average of the girls coming here is about twenty.

Witness.—I think the mere process of milking is not a very difficult thing to learn.

15001. Mr. Stevenson.—I have often heard it said by farmers that you never learn to milk unless you learn when you are under twelve?—Oh, I don't think so, I have had as many as thirty women milking in one house abroad, and some of these had been taught when they were as old as twenty-five or twenty-six.

15002. Chairman.—And never milked before?—Well, they might have milked a cow, but we had to teach them de novo.

15003. Mr. Stevenson.—And they milked to your satisfaction?—Yes.

15004. About these experiments, you said the difficulty was that you could not get sufficient support to carry them out?—Both as regards money and assistance.

15005. Could they not be carried on by people having an interest in them and subscribing?—I don't think they could.

15006. If they were going to be of any practical benefit to the country?—No, I don't think people go in voluntarily for education at present, we had at first to pay the dairy people to come here, we know now the Commissioners of Education will be only too happy to give us any assistance.

15007. In Denmark the principle of the State is not to institute a technical school or any kind of school directly, but to give it a subsidy?—Denmark was altogether under Professor Ford, who was practically the most scientific man in Europe at the time, and all his experiments were carried out by the State, he experienced all the difficulties we feel here, on a smaller scale, and the way he got his money was that certain Government officials came to visit him, and he filled his laboratory with all these things that were most disagreeable. They said "This is very terrible," and he said "Gentlemen, if you don't give me money to carry on my experiments, these things will come;" that is an absolute fact.

15008. Perhaps you would give us a memorandum on your experience of dairy and agricultural schools, in Sweden?—Certainly I could, if you give me a day or two I will send it in.

Mr. James Byrne, J.P., One of the Governors of the Munster Dairy School, examined.

Mr. James Byrne, J.P.

15009. Chairman.—The Commissioners would be very glad if you would give them your opinion as to the value of the agricultural education at present carried on in the primary schools in Ireland?—Well, I don't think it is satisfactory; I don't see how it could be satisfactory, because as a rule the teachers have no land attached to their schools, and even if they had I think the greater number of them know very little about agriculture.

15010. And you include in those the teachers who have been through the Glasnevin course?—Well, even so, I don't suppose they could become at all expert agriculturists by attending a course in Glasnevin.

15011. Do you think it is worth while continuing the system, and trying to extend the principle of garden plots, which I believe are eighty-two in number now, and the school farms, which are comparatively few in the country?—I do not see any objection to them.

15012. Do you think there would be any distinct good in doing that?—I think in some cases if the teacher had a liking for that sort of work, and took a practical interest in it, it would do good. But I think a great many of the teachers would not.

15013. Supposing the State advanced the money to buy a school farm, it may work very well as long as a particular teacher was there, but when the teacher was changed and a new one came who might not have the taste for it, the thing would be thrown away?—I remember when we had a great many model farms throughout the country, and they did not seem to be successful. I don't know whether it was that the Government of the day grudged the money for them. I am not quite sure that they were so unsuccessful, but I remember a great outcry was raised that they were not self-supporting institutions, and did not pay their way the same as ordinary farms. I don't think that could ever be expected, because the work of pupils, although you may get it gratuitously, is never so valuable as the work of paid hands, because when they are beginning to do this work they often do a great deal of damage in learning.

15014. Mr. Redington.—You live in a rural district?—I do.

15015. I suppose you are acquainted with the theoretical teaching of agriculture in the schools?—I know the school books that are taught there.

15016. Do the boys gain much advantage from the study of these books?—I think they certainly do, a share; I know my youngest child, about twelve years of age, when he reads up the school book he puts a whole lot of questions to me on agriculture, which, perhaps, he would not have got otherwise. I think the teachers, if they had gardens, could create a taste for the growth of flowers and vegetables.

15017. Would it be an advantage if the teacher illustrated the book by bringing the boys into the fields and showing them the plants they read of in the book?—I think so, provided the teacher had a taste for that sort of work. I also think little museums containing chemicals, plants, and specimens of rocks, should be supplied to primary schools.

15018. Do you think that it would be well that they should learn a little agricultural chemistry in schools?—I think so.

15019. If they have not learned it in schools would they not be unable to follow the experiments described in the agricultural papers?—Yes, and I think if they came afterwards to a school such as this they would learn much quicker.

15020. Of course the majority of children could not come to a school such as this, but the teachers could teach them in the ordinary schools the elements of botany, geology, chemistry, and physics?—Yes.

15021. You would approve of that?—I would.

15022. Are there any school gardens or school farms in your neighbourhood?—No.

15023. So you have no practical knowledge of their value?—There was a model farm not far from my place at Fermoy, but it was sold out. It was one of the Government schools.

15024. Mr. Molloy.—You said that the Glasnevin Farm Establishment, you thought, was not capable of qualifying persons in agriculture?—No; for the length of time I say they are there, and the few lessons they get there, I mean the National teachers.

15025. A master of a National school going up for six weeks, that period, in your opinion, is insufficient to qualify him for giving practical instruction on the farm?—I think it is insufficient.

15026. What period would you think suitable?—I know it is generally laid down, that a man cannot have a fair knowledge of farming without being two years engaged in practical work.

15027. Would not that mean that the master should give up his school during that time, and go into a college for agriculture, and he might later on get charge of a town school in which that education would be useless?—I don't think it would be possible that all our teachers should spend that time in getting a knowledge of agriculture, but the knowledge they derive must be very superficial.

15028. Mr. Struthers.—If they had to attend two years at Glasnevin, do you think they would be likely to continue teaching in that; they might take to some other occupation?—I don't mean they should ever be asked to do that.

THIRTY-FIFTH PUBLIC SITTING.—SATURDAY, OCTOBER 2nd, 1897,

AT 10 O'CLOCK, A.M.,

At the Imperial Hotel, Cork.

Present:—The Right Hon. The Earl of Belmore, G.C.M.G., in the Chair; The Right Rev. C. T. Redington, M.A.; Rev. Henry Evans, D.D.; Rev. Hamilton Wilson, D.D., Stanley Harrington, Esq., B.A.; W. R. J. Molloy, Esq.; and J. Struthers, Esq., LL.D.; with J. D. Daly, Esq., M.A., Secretary.

Rev. Brother Beale, Superior, Christian Brothers' Schools, North Monastery, Cork.

15029. Chairman.—You are the Superior of the Christian Brothers' School in Cork?—Yes, my lord.

15030. Will you favour the Commission with your opinion upon the advantages of drawing to children in the elementary schools?—Well, I consider drawing of the greatest possible importance to the boys in elementary schools; it is, I think, in importance next to the three R's, and may fairly be ranked with them, and I find that this opinion is entertained by all the great educationists—they are all disposed to rank drawing with the three R's, and to make it compulsory in all primary schools. It has a wonderful effect in refining the children, cultivating their taste, and giving them accuracy of eye and precision of hand, and I think it is a very excellent manual instruction; it would rank with the Sloyd system, and must, of course, form the basis of it. There can be no Sloyd or manual instruction system without a previous knowledge of drawing, at least as far as the 5th standard, under the South Kensington; that embraces drawing to scale, and we find in the manual instruction classes that all the articles made by the pupils must be first drawn to scale before they can attempt to execute anything in woodwork by means of tools, and the effect of this knowledge of drawing, and of this accuracy in their work in the Sloyd or manual work system, must have a wonderful effect upon them altogether. Then I think also that drawing, like the manual instruction system, has a very great effect in giving children moral habits of attention, and neatness and precision, and intellectually great refinement; and I notice in our own schools where drawing is taught, that it has that effect upon them individually, and I can even find that it influences their home life also. Then we have industrial schools, in which there are some 8,000 boys—boys taken off the streets—and in all these schools we have introduced drawing in connection with South Kensington—we have Artane, in Dublin, for instance, where there are 800 boys, and I learned from the Superior there that they have got the award "excellent" for the last three years for these 800 boys, and he says the effect of the drawing upon them when they go to trades—for these boys learn trades—is very great indeed, and that it has a wonderful effect in refining them—

that, I think drawing should form a compulsory subject in all primary schools.

15031. Is it your opinion that manual work is a practical way of giving effect to the knowledge of drawing which has been previously acquired?—Yes, my lord; I think that the manual work, being dependent on the drawing, will have a very great effect in showing the practical utility of the drawing, and in giving effect to its advantages in every way.

15032. Do you attach great importance to manual and practical work?—Very great, indeed; I should like to see it introduced into all primary schools, but there are, of course, many difficulties in the way to its introduction, and at present I do not see that it can be made compulsory. Manual instruction implies the training of the teachers to the use of tools, and, of course, they must have a knowledge of tools as a preliminary. Now, there is expense attending it, too, for I cannot see how it can be carried on in the schoolroom, where the ordinary subjects of education are treated. And then you have tools and raw material to provide; all these being provided, I cannot see how a teacher—as the system at present exists, as the National system exists—can carry on manual work, even if he had a workshop for it. I think the great thing to be done is to begin on a small scale, begin in the centres of population, start schools, and let the teachers see how it can be done, and what it means, and then let them gradually undergo a training that will fit them for the carrying on of the Sloyd system, or this manual instruction; but I think the first thing is to have the teachers, as far as possible, taught drawing, and I find that it is now introduced into the Training Colleges, and manual work might follow that in those institutions and prepare the young men, who are to become teachers, to carry on the work.

15033. Would you make it compulsory in the Training Colleges for the teachers to take manual work?—I think it would not be well to make it compulsory in the beginning, even in the Training Colleges, but to introduce it gradually—there is at present a certain objection to it arising chiefly from its nature not being perfectly understood, and I think the first thing to do is to get rid of that prejudice, and I think that the seeing of the manual work carried on in the Colleges and in large centres, such as Dublin, Cork, Waterford, Limerick, Belfast, and Galway, would be of great importance, and make the teachers take an interest in it, and induce them, after getting this training, to carry on the work. Many of the young men having the prejudice will not enter into it as warmly as one would desire, but I fancy as soon as they really see the nature of it and that it can be done, it may be made compulsory. With regard to the schools, the Irish teacher is at a certain disadvantage, he differs in one respect, I think, from a teacher in England and Scotland; as far as I can understand those teachers have their salaries secured to them before they commence their year's work at all, they engage themselves, and they can enter with spirit into the programme as laid down for them by the governing body in the different places through England and Scotland; but in Ireland the teacher's salary is only partly secured to him, the remainder depends on his results, and he is of course very anxious about them, and necessarily so, and I believe that until he has such a programme laid down for him as will enable him to undertake both drawing and manual work with satisfaction to himself and security to his temporal interests, he will not enter on the teaching of these subjects as warmly as we should desire.

15034. When we were in Sweden we examined Herr Salomon, whose name is familiar to you, no doubt, and he was asked this question:—

"Do you consider it essential that the teacher should believe in Sloyd?—Certainly, better no Sloyd at all, than Sloyd taught by teachers unwillingly."

Do you agree with that?—I do; I believe no work is well done in which the teacher is not interested himself, and he will never be interested in it until he is satisfied in his own mind that he suffers nothing by its introduction and the carrying on of it, and also, until he is well prepared to carry it on. I think if you had Sloyd classes or manual instruction classes in centres, and that the pupil teachers and the young teachers generally were influenced to come and attend them, as they do, I find, in Leeds, Liverpool, Manchester, and other cities in England, that a great deal would be done towards its gradual introduction.

15035. What is your opinion with regard to the value of elementary physical science and elementary chemistry in primary schools?—Well, I cannot, I think, my lord, speak too highly of the advantages that would accrue to the boys generally by having an acquaintance with the elementary principles both of natural philosophy and of chemistry. I think it most desirable that a beginning should be made. But the introduction of these subjects too will be attended with some difficulty.

15036. Are they not introduced at present in places like Cork and the large towns?—I think not, my lord. You see you must have the teachers trained to the manipulation of both chemical and physical apparatus. It will not prepare the teacher to have learned from a professor, or to have heard his lectures and passed an examination; he must actually know how to manipulate the instruments. The experiments that would be necessary to illustrate the simple principles of either natural philosophy or chemistry would not require very great manipulative skill, and I think if a portion of the training time in the colleges was devoted to teaching students how to handle instruments that would illustrate the simple principles, that you would then be prepared to introduce it extensively into the schools of Ireland. I consider a £5 set of chemicals would do for an ordinary school; you would have both the apparatus and salts and other substances necessary for experiments, and comprising like two dozen or two and a half dozen of well-selected experiments on the nature of water, of the atmosphere, and the nature of gases and some other substances, which, when understood, would be quite sufficient to give the boys a general interest in natural science and encourage them to carry on these studies in after-life. Then to introduce physical science, I find that it would be necessary to have at least about £20 worth of apparatus to illustrate simple mechanics, hydrostatics, electricity, magnetism, and a few experiments on light and heat. So that the introduction of it requires this as a preliminary; and I think then that the great point would be to begin in the colleges and have the teachers trained to the use of instruments, and the way of explaining experiments and working the apparatus before the children, and then to have centres where those that are already engaged in the teaching profession could attend and learn. There are a few things that cannot be easily learned by teachers who are for any length of time engaged in the work of education. Drawing, if they have not got a knowledge of it in early life, is very difficult; just like music or the playing of instruments, they must have learned in early life; I think then that great allowance must be made for the teachers generally. They must be encouraged; and I think that would do more to promote the introduction of these new subjects than any other means. Compulsion, I think, cannot come on for drawing, physical science, or manual work for some time.

15037. Rev. Dr. Evans.—Brother Burke, would you make drawing necessary to all teachers from this forward in order to get their certificate?—Well, when you say to make it obligatory, I think that is going very far, because many of them may not have the taste for drawing; but by degrees, in the course of a few years, it may be made so, because you can have the pupil teachers and the young candidates previously prepared before entering into the training colleges, and then I think that it may be made compulsory.

F

15038. You, I think very properly, remarked about the indulgence that should be extended to old teachers, but would you extend that indulgence to new candidates?—I would not after a few years, but I would make some allowance for those who have not the taste developed up to the present. You have students in the colleges, perhaps, who never learned drawing, and they are now twenty-one years of age, and to begin that subject now, and make it compulsory for their certificate, I think would be very hard upon them; but I think by having drawing compulsory on the young lads going on for the profession, you may afterwards make it compulsory in the colleges.

15039. MR. HARRINGTON.—Would you tell us the number of people that are engaged in your schools that we saw yesterday?—You saw, I think, about a thousand yesterday at Our Lady's Mount; but besides these boys we have two establishments, one at Sullivan's Quay and another in Blarney Street; we have 300 in Sullivan's Quay, and 150 in Blarney Street.

15040. And your experience goes over a long period of years?—I am, I may say, forty-five years connected with education in the city.

15041. Does your school receive any State aid except what is earned by results in connection with the Science and Art Department?—Yes, what we get by results from the Intermediate. For the primary department we have nothing but what we receive for the drawing from Kensington. We passed, I think, 1,400 from the three establishments this year and got the award "good."

15042. How is your school maintained then?—We have a foundation, and a few benefactors left bequests; then we have an annual sermon and collection.

15043. Entirely voluntary?—Voluntary contributions.

15044. How did you provide the industrial museum that impressed us so much yesterday; was it from your own funds?—I may say that all you saw yesterday in the various rooms, all the articles and specimens the Commissioners saw, were the gifts of manufacturers and friends. Some ten years ago I myself went around to various manufacturers in this country and in England and many in Scotland, and I have to say that they received me most kindly and entered fully into my ideas about the giving the boys of the rising generation a knowledge of the raw materials, processes, and finished condition of articles in the various manufactures.

15045. But to provide the ordinary National schools through the country with a museum on a similar scale, what do you think would be the approximate cost?—I think it would not be much, because it could be done by the Commissioners; they could arrange to select a certain number of manufactures that they would wish to have illustrated, and to make an arrangement with the manufacturers for a supply of the raw material, specimens of the different stages, and some finished articles. I think they would get them at a very moderate price, and many of the manufacturers are manifestly disposed themselves to supply specimens showing the development of the articles they manufacture. Now, for instance, from a gentleman near Leeds, I got for 5s. a beautiful card of silk illustrating from the cocoon up to the finished article; he charged 5s., simply to cover the fitting up of it; but I think the rest must have been supplied by his own generosity from a desire to have the children get a knowledge of the growth of silk, and he supplies this, I have learned, to any school that applies and sends him that amount of money; and such card would be quite sufficient to give boys in elementary or higher schools a very good knowledge of the growth of silk and its manufacture.

15046. We, of course, saw ourselves yesterday a demonstration in connection with that museum system of yours—what do you consider is its educational value?—To what do you refer?

15047. The industrial museum?—Well, I found from conversation with the men engaged in the various trades that they had very little knowledge of any other branch of industry or manufacture outside what they were employed in themselves. And it was that first led me to collect these specimens, and I now find that the great value arising from it to the youth and the men who come there during the week and on Sundays, for we leave it open to these to come and see it at all times, is that their minds are expanded, and certain prejudices which they had in favour of their own business and trade has been done away with by seeing the wonderful work that can be produced from materials that look very clumsy and have very little attraction in them, and it expands their minds and gives them a great idea of human ingenuity and manipulative power on the part of men engaged in the trades, and that in itself is educative.

15048. I suppose the same advantage would be derived from the introduction of elementary science into the schools?—I think so. I don't believe there is anything in which boys take a livelier interest than seeing the laws of nature illustrated.

15049. Have you had experience of their careers afterwards—have you been able to observe in their careers the use of this elementary science teaching in your schools?—Yes, we have traced it all over the world, I may say, in boys who have left our schools and gone to the different nations where the English language is spoken; we find their knowledge of science and of elementary chemistry is of great importance, and this knowledge has placed many of them in better circumstances than they could otherwise have attained.

15050. In what class do you commence elementary science?—We begin at the 4th standard—we use for object lessons those cards you saw containing the raw material and the finished article. In each room we make all the children in the room acquainted with all the objects in the cases, and as they progress from hall to hall they get an extended knowledge of the whole. The children you saw in the junior school will next year be in another room, and so on. Boys in the 4th standard are about ten or eleven, and are fully capable of comprehending the fundamental principles of physical science and the simple experiments in chemistry.

15051. I think you said you had upper classes in connection with the Intermediate Board; does that science teaching extend to the upper classes?—In the schools it does. The boys that I lectured on physical science yesterday before the Commissioners were Intermediate boys in the Preparatory and Junior grades, and we give these classes lectures in the schools; but they are not examined very extensively under the Intermediate Board in these subjects for this reason. There are four grades in the Intermediate system—Preparatory, Junior, Middle, and Senior. In the Preparatory grade, which embraces boys from twelve to fourteen years, physical science or chemistry will not be allowed, they are not on the programme. There are 5,000 marks for languages, 1,800 for mathematics, 300 for drawing, while physical science and chemistry are not recognised at all.

15052. It is like bringing a horse to the stream and not allowing it to drink?—We made frequent recommendations to the Commissioners on that point, showing the importance of having a child begin at twelve to learn physical science and the elements of chemistry, but for some reason they did not see their way to introduce it. The disadvantage is this, that when they come on to the Junior grade, not having taken up Natural Philosophy or Chemistry in the Preparatory, these subjects are not taken up in the Junior, Middle, and Senior—so that I may say, not 7 per cent. of all the successful boys passed in natural philosophy, and out of [illegible] boys that passed this year in the Junior, Middle, and Senior grades only 11 per cent. passed in philosophy, and [illegible] per cent. in chemistry.

15053. Don't you consider it a great disadvantage to the country at large, that the education in elementary science existing in your primary schools is not continued into the upper schools?—I consider it a very serious matter, very serious indeed; because when you consider that the boys who are receiving Intermediate education through the country are the sons of gentlemen farmers, the sons of merchants, the sons of manufacturers, and that those boys leave their colleges and schools without a knowledge of the elements of physical science and chemistry to enable them to understand all the processes of the manufactures or businesses in which their fathers are engaged, is a very great evil indeed. Take the boys of the Preparatory grade, they are fourteen years of age before they begin the Junior; only 700 boys in the Middle grade, and 300 in the Senior were presented for examination, and only half of the Middle candidates and half of the Senior passed, so that the remaining thousands have gone to business after sixteen years of age, without ever having, I may say, got any knowledge of physical science or chemistry.

16054. Turning for a moment to the question of manual instruction; could you give us a definition as to what the difference between technical education and manual instruction is—we are rather in want of a good definition of it?—It struck me when this Commission was appointed that if the Commission was of no other advantage to the country than to make this known, and of causing importance to be attached to it, I think the Commission would have done good service. As I understand manual instruction, and as I have seen it carried out, it is an educational process, and purely educational, and the trades seem to have in many cases a misconception as to the nature of manual instruction; they fancy that it is an encroachment on their principles, but this is altogether a mistake. In manual instruction the best teacher is the teacher of the ordinary subjects in the primary school, if he be only qualified by having a knowledge of drawing, and a skill in the manipulation of the tools necessary for such instruction. He is a better teacher than an artisan or a mechanic, because the mechanic will not look at the educational advantages of it, and the teacher does. Now, in manual instruction we never look, so far as I can see, and have seen, so much to the work done, as to the effects produced upon the boy's mind. Of course if his work is well done that is an indication that his eye has been educated to precision, to exactness, and that his hand is dexterous in giving effect to what the eye requires, and that his mind has applied itself to what he is doing, and this is the great result to be obtained from manual training. Moreover it has a wonderful effect on the boy himself in developing many moral qualities, and a great many other advantages, such as the cultivation of his mind, and the physical exercises he has to go through, and it is a substitute in some way for physical drill. Then, in after-life its advantages are very great to him, because it will give him a respect for labour, training him from childhood to a love of labour, and at the same time it will indicate what business he would like to follow when he leaves school; he will see if he have a skill in constructing the little models required, whether he is fit for mechanical work or not; and many go to trades, for which they have no vocation, and never excel in those trades, and if they had had this manipulative drill, first, in this Sloyd education or manual instruction, they would have had early proof of their want of ability in this direction.

As to technical education, I take it to mean the teaching of the scientific principles which underlie any particular trade or manufacture.

16055. I think you contemplate, you told us yesterday, erecting a special building for the purpose of introducing this manual instruction into your own schools?—For many years we have had a desire to do so, but funds were not at hand; but seeing the importance of it, almost the absolute necessity of its introduction into all the schools of the British dominions, if those countries are to hold their own against other nations, we were most desirous of starting it, and our Superior-General encouraged the Brothers in the two places that have taken it up.

16056. Which are those two places?—Limerick and St. Vincent's Orphanage, Glasnevin, Dublin, which is under our Brothers. When I proposed to him to get up this school, he was, I may say, much interested about the matter, and most desirous that it should be erected. I proposed that we should erect it as a memorial school to Gerald Griffin, who was for a time a member of our Institute, and is buried in the little cemetery in our grounds. This idea was warmly taken up both by him and others, and we have now determined on doing so. We hope that throughout the world where there are admirers of Gerald Griffin and his works we will get subscriptions from them, and thus be able to erect and equip it; indeed a clergyman from America, who called to see the schools lately, when I told him about the project, told me to put him down for £100, and he also mentioned there was a friend of his in America, an old pupil of the schools, who would, probably, give the same sum, so we have made a good beginning.

16057. Mr. Harrington.—If the National Board decided on introducing this manual instruction into their schools, do you think they would have a better chance of getting funds from the public or from the Treasury?—Well, I think you might get aid from both.

16058. You might hope for it from both, and get it from one?—I think the Government would be disposed to enable the Commissioners to start the schools; and once started I think the public would take an interest in them, and by additional assistance from the Government, and subscriptions from the public, the work would be sustained; but the great thing the Commission has to do is to get both the drawing and the manual instruction introduced, and, once started, I think the project is on the fair way to success.

16059. Mr. Struthers.—We had yesterday a statement by one of our witnesses that one great difficulty in training boys in an advanced school is the want of accuracy that Irish children seem to show, according to the witness. You think that the teaching of drawing would help to train the children in habits of accuracy?—I have no doubt of it.

16060. And also that manual instruction is exceedingly valuable in that way?—I think it is the complement of the other—an extension of it.

16061. If they had that training they would not be so likely to disregard an eighth of an inch, or a quarter of a lb., and measure things by the basket instead of by scale?—I don't think such a thing would be possible if we had teaching in these two branches, that is, drawing and manual instruction.

16062. For that reason, among others, you think the introduction of these subjects very desirable?—Most desirable.

16063. So desirable that you would ultimately make them compulsory?—I think in the course of time they might be made compulsory.

16064. But at present you find certain obstacles in the way?—I do.

16065. One of them being a prejudice on the part of teachers, and the other the difficulty as to payment?—I would not lay too much stress on the prejudice. I think the teachers are intelligent enough from what I know and hear of them. There is a prejudice, but not to any very great extent. But I think, from the position that they are in with regard to their salaries and to the sources of those salaries, that some difficulty would arise. You see the teacher who is dependent on results is in a precarious condition during the year and as long as the work that he sees before him is not definite

Cork. Oct. 3, 1887. Rev. Brother Burke.

enough for him to calculate on his income, he won't take that interest in it that he otherwise would; but if the programme under the Board were so arranged that drawing and manual instruction could be introduced without disadvantage to him, then the teacher would enter into it very heartily. The subjects already in the programme of the Board are compulsory—there are a few class subjects which are not—but I take the fundamental subjects, these are compulsory, being so, of course he must apply all his energy to secure success in them; but I think there is room in those subjects for a good deal of diminution without interfering at all with the education that a boy would receive, or would have received, up to the age of thirteen, at which age, generally, he must leave school. Now, for instance, you have extensive grammar, very difficult parsing; you have intricate arithmetical operations, and you have extensive geographical memory work to be gone through, and a great deal of this could be eliminated without any disadvantage whatever—I would say with good results and great advantage both to the teacher and pupil; for instance, the lengths of rivers that a boy will never hear much about afterwards, the parsing of difficult sentences from the poets, and very difficult questions in decimals and stocks, and even in proportion—as, for instance, a train starts from Marylebone at such an hour and at such a speed, and after an hour and a half another train starts from Kingsbridge at a certain speed, where will the latter overtake the former? Well, for boys who have to go to business at thirteen years of age, I do not think that that kind of knowledge is at all necessary; but they could have a very nice equipment in reading, writing, and arithmetic, the substance of the lessons, the writing of a nice letter, and general intelligence, which would be a better outfit for their future than a knowledge of abstract or difficult matters, from which they would derive very little advantage after leaving school.

15066. Do you think that those subjects of grammar, geography, and arithmetic might be modified, you said eliminated?—Modified is what I meant, and, I think, with advantage; it would leave the teacher more free and the children would be less hampered.

15067. But you would not propose to do away with the teaching of grammar altogether?—I would not.

15068. You regard it as having a certain value in developing intelligence?—Apart from any advantage in letter writing, which the boy will have to do through life—I think the intellectual operation to be gone through in the parsing of simple sentences is of great importance to the boy.

15069. Might not the same be said about that arithmetical problem, that, although not practically useful, it is useful in developing intelligence?—I would say a great many these problems, involving not the mere element of mental labour, would be of more importance to him. Then there is another great disadvantage in primary schools, Irish, English, and Scotch; we have a very great difficulty in the complicated rule tables, all the weights and measures are very great labour to a boy and to the teacher, difficult sums in weights and measures, reducing so many millions of inches to miles, and things of that kind. On the Continent the decimal system is used, and it is of so simple a nature that the Continental boy has a very great advantage over the boys of these countries in this instruction.

15070. We have had lengths of rivers and heights of mountains given us as specimen questions of examination in geography. Do you know that such questions are actually put by the inspectors—do they ask the length of the Ganges, and of the Mississippi, and the height of Ben Nevis, and so on?—I think they do, and I would not object to a few questions on the principal rivers and mountains and other important points.

15071. I ask that question because, so far as my experience goes, I should think it exceedingly improbable that any inspector in Scotland ever asked such a question in geography, but these questions are asked here?—I think so. I suppose the inspectors are obliged to carry out the programme, and I think it is the programme that requires modification.

15072. Does the programme specify the lengths of rivers and heights of mountains?—I should think it does; the inspector must have some guide for the questions he feels himself bound to propose. I don't think he would voluntarily, or of his own inclination, propose those difficulties to the boys. The programme could be modified with great advantage.

15073. Owing to the difficulty of introducing them, and the want of knowledge of these subjects, you would have drawing and manual instruction introduced gradually?—I would have drawing introduced at once, but not compulsorily.

15074. I would quote from Herr Salomon's evidence. The Chairman asked: "To come now to Ireland, how would you propose, advise, or suggest to introduce Slöyd there, where we have about 8,000 schools?" And he replied—"I would say it would be the greatest mistake for you to introduce Slöyd into 8,000 schools all at once, say next year. This mistake was made in Norway and France, and the result has been unsuccessful." Then he says—"If the first year you train teachers in England, or here, for a year, let these teachers go into schools and practise the work, and when they have practised select the best and make them teach the other teachers. I would introduce Slöyd the first year into say twenty schools, the second year into 100, the third year into 500, and perhaps in ten years you would have it in 8,000." That is somewhat your idea?—I may say that would almost fully represent my idea about it.

15075. Do you think it desirable to have manual instruction, drawing, and experimental science taught in every school?—I think it most desirable.

15076. Each has a special value?—Each has a special educative value.

15077. You could not get the full result you wish by teaching drawing simply and science, and leaving out manual instruction, or by teaching science purely and leaving out drawing?—I think not. You cultivate the eye and hand by drawing. You cultivate the eye and hand and reflective powers by the manual work; but when you come to physical science you deal with the world around the boy, you deal with the laws that govern the universe, you deal with the phenomena that he witnesses every day, and you give him an insight into the constitution of the matter that is about him, and that he is actually handling, and I think that kind of knowledge can never be supplied by either the drawing or the Slöyd system.

15078. If you teach all these three subjects, that means a considerable addition to the present programme?—Any one of them means a great addition to the present programme.

15079. And all three combined must mean a still greater addition?—I think it would mean more than a full day's work for a teacher in addition to what he already has.

15080. So then it would be absolutely necessary that instruction in other subjects should be modified in some way?—Certainly, absolutely necessary, and I am convinced with advantage to both, the advantage to the teacher and the boys, and therefore to the country, would be very great indeed by eliminating or curtailing some of the matter already on the programme with regard to "The Three R's," and introducing the other subjects even on a small scale, it would make the education of the boy round about more harmonious—it would develop all his powers.

15081. One obstacle you mention to the introduction of manual training especially is the expense of the apparatus; it is much more considerable than in the case of drawing?—It is, because you require

n operation in a
ing, and placing

managers in your
introducing these
considerable direct
State?—I think
ry great interest
mary existence

distance would be
ensure the requi-
mental grant?—
rather poor, and a
getting money for
ople generally do
the work would
difficulty would

prove a decided
teacher being the
y the instruction
f that opinion.
ersions?—Rather
excessive ones ye
as subjects in
s in the school,
f drawing and c
carry on the work
manual over boys,
n the teacher in
advantage when

ordinary teacher
special subject in
?—I believe that

rural schools, what
you contemplate
ool, supposing, in
on of the system
r the purpose and
these matters and
bers in teaching
ired to get their
l a great deal of
one of the school-
ers, or more di-
concerned there,
ying on that work
, would you be in
ical science, going
ng apparatus with
teachers, and also
e in London, and
this country too,
could much prefer
duty themselves;
d object to them
would encourage
as the only thing
until they were

many years before
don or any other
nal Commissioners
s Dr. Clarke, who,
of his various parts
science apparatus,
qualified men to

enlightening the young men and women through the country on the new processes of making butter and doing other dairy work, making them acquainted with the nature and use of thermometers and hydrometers, and other suitable apparatus. I find the County Councils in England are using these lectures on a very extensive scale. Take Yorkshire for instance. They have a number of professors for each Riding giving lectures on agriculture and elementary science, and using the limelight lanterns, with slides prepared by the instrument-makers for the purpose of showing them the nature of plants, the growth of plants, the diseases of plants, and other matters of that kind so essential to farmers, and the same could be done in Ireland until such time as you would be prepared to erect schools in the various centres, especially in the rural districts.

Cork. Oct. 5, 1897. Rev. Brother Burke.

15090. Rev. Dr. Wilson.—Are the pupils that attend your schools chiefly residents in the city of Cork?—I may say all. We have a few pupils, perhaps not more than two dozen, who are sent in from the country, and who reside in Cork to get the advantage of the higher education which we give.

15091. What is the average time that the pupils spend at your schools?—From the age of six to sixteen, a very small percentage remains until seventeen; but I think that if the country had more advantages and were more prosperous than it is, then we would not have even so many of them up to that age.

15092. The ordinary time spent at a National school would be insufficient to teach all the literary subjects, and also what you add to them, such as manual instruction and physical science, and so on, but you have time enough for your work from six to sixteen years of age?—Yes, we have abundance of time for the introduction of all the extra subjects; but I think if they are to be done in the Board's schools a modification of the existing programme must be made, and it will then meet many of the requirements.

15093. Mr. Redington.—Are you familiar with the science programmes of the National Board?—I have some knowledge of them.

15094. Have you any criticism to make upon them?—Of course, science taught without experiment is of very little advantage; one experiment performed before the classes, before the boys, will give them a far deeper impression of what is to be conveyed to them than pages of book learning, and I think that is one of the defects in the teaching of agriculture in the Board schools. I have always been of opinion that two dozen experiments on the nature of the atmosphere, the nature of water, the nature of carbonic acid gas, and of ammonia, and a few experiments on the soils, would be of immense advantage to the agriculture of the country, and would do more for the people than volumes of book learning without the experiments. But I would not dispense with the books. I have looked over the Board's books on agriculture, and I think that by a modification of them, a simplifying, and putting the matter in a more attractive form, they could be much improved; they are very crowded at present; a book closely written has no attraction for a boy, but I would have the matter—which is excellent of its kind—modified and put in a more attractive form, together with two dozen of simple experiments; and then I think a great deal would be done for the teaching of agriculture and agricultural science through the

Cork. Oct. 8, 1897. Rev. Brother Burke.

them, but I don't think they would produce effect unless the children were of a more mature age.

15096. Do you think boys of the fourth class could be taught elementary chemistry?—I think so; but of course when you say "elementary," you must confine it to very simple experiments. If you tell a boy, for instance, the nature of the atmosphere, that it consists of oxygen and nitrogen gases in the proportion of one to four, and then if you pass air over red-hot iron in a tube you disengage the oxygen, and he gets the nitrogen in the gas receiver or vessel, then you show that this nitrogen will not support combustion, I think you give him a very good idea of that gas; then if you secure the oxygen of the air, and show him by a simple experiment that it will support combustion, he will comprehend it quite sufficiently.

15097. With regard to agriculture, you would not continue the present mode of teaching it, but would like to combine it with practical instruction in elementary science?—Yes, I should like to see experiments performed, and I think the teachers would find a very great delight themselves—I am confident they would—in performing these necessary experiments. They would not be very delicate, the apparatus is not very much or very expensive. As I mentioned, I think a £5 set would meet all the exigencies of the teaching of elementary chemistry in each school, and of agriculture in the rural districts; but I think a museum, a case of seeds, and of the soils, and of the plants to a limited extent, would, of course, be very interesting and very useful to the children.

15098. We were very much interested in what we saw in your schools yesterday in that respect?—We find the working people who visit the schools are very much interested in the specimens. I may mention that in our schools here we prepare many of the boys for commercial life to a great measure. A large number of our boys engage in commercial pursuits, merchants take them as clerks, and they are employed in the various establishments in the city in one capacity or another. Hence we find that the teaching of shorthand, and of book-keeping, and of drawing, and also of elementary science, is of great advantage to them. At the recent Intermediate examination, 70 of our boys passed in shorthand, 80 in book-keeping, and 116 in drawing; this number was independent of the 1,400 that passed in Kensington in the elementary drawing.

Rev. Canon Powell.

Rev. Canon Powell, B.A., Honorary Secretary of the City of Cork Church School Board, examined.

15099. Chairman.—Would you kindly state in what capacity you appear here?—I appear, my lord, as Honorary Secretary of the City of Cork Church School Board.

15100. Will you explain to us exactly what that Board is?—That Board was constituted some years ago under the Educational Endowments Act, and it is working under a scheme, of which I may hand in a copy (produced). It has control of certain primary schools in Cork, and of the grammar school; I come to speak more with regard to the primary schools than with regard to the grammar school.

15101. We are dealing only with primary schools here?—We have under our Board ten primary schools, three are boys' schools, two are girls' schools, one of them is an infant school, and four are mixed schools, and they are attended, roughly speaking, by about a thousand children, of whom 300 are boys and 700 are girls and infants. And I may just hand you in also a report for this year of the work of the Board, and also a summary giving a statement of the actual numbers attending (produced); there is a schedule giving the details with regard to each school, the name of the teacher, the classification of the teacher, the number on the roll, the average attendance in the school, the results of inspection by our own Diocesan Board of Education, and the results of inspection by the National Board of Education.

15102. We should be glad if you could give us a statement of the instruction given in various subjects in the schools under your Board?—In four of the schools kindergarten instruction is given; in none of the schools is advanced kindergarten given, nor do we give manual instruction in any of the schools; drawing is taught in nine schools, that is every school except the school which is exclusively an infant school, but kindergarten is taught in that school, and different class of subjects, such subjects as the process of digestion of food, more physical science—do you do that sort of thing, or is it the other sort of domestic economy, which consists of the work of the house?—I think that, my lord, is the subject of it, I don't like to speak with too great confidence. Book-keeping is taught in five schools, physical geography in three, hygiene in two, music and tonic sol-fa practically in all, two schools teaching it in one and seven in another way, and typewriting or shorthand in three or four.

15103. Would you not look upon typewriting and shorthand rather in the nature of teaching a trade than teaching something for mere educational purposes?—We teach it as fitting the boys or girls for commercial pursuits in the city, for its practical value. I may say with regard to the efforts the Board has made to carry out instruction of this kind that in 1886 we employed, ourselves, a certificated teacher from South Kensington to teach cookery in our schools; a course of lessons that extended over four or five months was given at six of the schools with very satisfactory results to the children. We also, when the National Board itself offered us the instruction of an itinerant teacher last session, did all we could to induce the managers to have these classes, and lessons were given in four of our schools by the special teacher sent by the Board. Then the teaching of shorthand and typewriting—the expense of that falls on the Board—and for nine months in the year we have a shorthand and typewriting teacher giving instruction at three of the schools, and children from any of our schools can attend them.

15104. Typewriting and shorthand are a little outside our scope; but we should like to have your opinion on manual and practical work, sewing work and things of that sort?—Well, the great

largely that that is not the object, but that the object is to cultivate habits of observation, which may be useful, not merely for a boy who is going to be a carpenter, but for a boy who is going to pursue any calling where he is going to use his brains; where habits of accuracy are desirable?—In that sense I am sorry to say that no manual instruction beyond that given in the kindergarten is given in our schools.

15109. Would you not think it desirable, if means could be found, as regards money and as regards teachers who were competent and willing to give the instruction, that it should be given not merely to boys going into trades, but to all boys passing through the primary schools?—I think it would; but I think so long as the literary programme is so very heavy, and as long as the teachers for the working hours of the day, are so much occupied themselves, and the children occupied, as they are, in preparing for results, unless something is done to lighten the programme and to give the teachers time and the children time for the learning of that, that in our primary National schools it would be very hard to put upon them the extra programme of manual work.

15110. Do you see your way to lightening the programme?—Well, I am afraid I am not capable of giving you any suggestions.

15111. We have had a great many suggestions already in that direction, and the thing has been practically done in some of the town schools in England?—What strikes me is this, that to the teaching of geography, and particularly to the teaching of grammar, is given an undue importance; they are very useful indeed as intellectual training, but I am afraid that the intellectual training that they actually do give is not of great value, practically, to the children, and I think that by reducing the programme, particularly in the matter of grammar and in the matter of geography, some time might be found for the manual instruction that is so desirable; and I think also, that in applying lessons, the loss that might arise from reducing the programme in these things might be compensated for, that by giving lessons in reading of an instructive kind, with regard particularly to geography, and in some degree also, but a lesser degree, with regard to grammar, that by giving that instruction in an enlightened way, expelling facts and dates (which force the teachers to cram hard facts into the children's minds, without any real intellectual value or any knowledge that abides in their minds), a compensation would be found for a considerable reduction of the programme as it now stands.

15112. When we were at Limerick, the day before yesterday, we visited the only manual school that we have seen in operation in Ireland, and we found there that the way that they gain time to give the manual instruction, which is given only once a week, was by shortening the lessons all round during the week, and that appeared to be quite feasible; do you think that could be done as there as well as Limerick?—In other words, would the teachers be able to work for their result fees with shorter lessons?

15113. By a somewhat shorter time being given to each subject during the week, whereby they gain a couple of spare hours on one day in the week?—I think the teachers, who are the best judges of that, are very jealous of any encroachment on the four hours of their working day. A little time ago we were obliged, in the school I am manager of, to have our cookery lesson once a week for two hours one day, and the teacher complained very much of the withdrawal of that time from the literary programme. I know some teachers were obliged to leave that instruction after school hours, because they felt that the time they had at their disposal now was little enough for the literary programme, and I think that it would be to a lightening of the programme you would have to look rather than to a reducing of the time for teaching it. I attach great importance to kindergarten, and I feel this, that to minor children, so to speak, before the heavy literary programme has come on them, and to avail of the early years for manual instruction in the way of drawing and little manual exercises when that can be given very much as play and entertainments to the children, is very important for them. And the manual advantages in the way of accuracy and quickness, and the other things that have been spoken of already to-day, all that is best given I think when the children are young; it is best begun when the children are young, and through the means of the kindergarten programme. But as the kindergarten programme is under the National Board at present, it is almost impossible to carry it out. You require a separate room and you require a separate staff—I think that is at page [illegible] of the Rules of the Board—so that if a school has a teacher and an assistant teacher, no fees can be given for kindergarten in that school, because if the second teacher is an assistant teacher, and that teacher cannot be regarded as a special teacher of the kindergarten programme, and it is not only necessary to have a special teacher for the purpose, but it is necessary also to have a special room where the instruction can be given. I don't think there is any more reason for having a special room for that than for any other part of the programme, and when you have put on the managers the obligation of providing a special room and a special teacher, you really put it beyond our reach in ninety-nine cases out of a hundred to have any kindergarten instruction given.

15114. It is admitted that a separate room is necessary; but is it necessary that there should be a separate teacher from the ordinary teacher?—It says "staff."

15115. Does that mean there should be a special person?—Oh, yes.

15116. Mr. Molloy.—Would not that teacher teach some other subjects?—I speak under the correction of the Commissioners, of course; but, as we understand the rule, an ordinary assistant teacher, who is recognised as an assistant teacher in the school cannot claim the extra fee for kindergarten unless that teacher be a special teacher for the purpose of teaching.

15117. That is specially qualified or certificated in the subject, but not confined the whole day long to the instruction in that particular branch. We were in a school yesterday in which the kindergarten was carried out both in the principal room and in a separate room, and by a teacher who taught other subjects as well as the kindergarten?—Then the interpretation of assistant-teacher——

15118. The teacher should be certified specially in that branch?—And he is able to claim the extra fee?

15119. That is my view of it?—That is not our interpretation of it, and of course that is a very important matter.

15120. I would hope that we would modify it before very long in the way of having it taught in the principal room?—As one of the ordinary subjects. The extra fee you give for that is 5s., and you require for that a very large amount of work. You require drilling exercises, and songs and drawing, and these manual exercises. It seems to me that a fee of 5s. is a very small remuneration for such a large programme; and one thing the Board might consider is, whether on account of the importance of teaching kindergarten a larger fee could not be given. With regard to the teaching of drawing, it is practically taught in all our schools, and it seems a great pity that the teaching of drawing should not be made, so far as possible, obligatory in all schools. Of course teachers have different tastes; some teachers will teach from their natural abilities more efficiently than others, but to teach drawing in all schools is a very important thing, and to use it, not as a mere piece of routine only, but also to teach it in that way that will most develop the intellectual qualities of the children, and will be of most value when they come to practical work. I am sorry to hear that type-writing is outside your programme.

Mr. Molloy.—It is part of the curriculum of the National Board.

15121. Chairman.—We have not considered it as a matter of manual instruction, but, however, if you have anything to say on it—— ?—It is a matter that is almost a necessity; it is a *sine quâ non* for boys, and indeed for girls also now, entering upon any mercantile pursuit.

15122. The objection to my mind is, that it is a matter of technical instruction, and we are not a Technical Instruction Committee, we are a Committee to inquire into something leading up to technical instruction?—If the Board saw its way to have results fees for the teaching of it, so as to assist managers in employing a teacher of typewriting, it would be well.

15123. Mr. Redington.—It has been separated from shorthand lately by a circular, so you can get a separate fee for it? And also providing instruments at cost price, you would suggest to us the best machine to use, and give it to us on favourable terms, that would not cost you anything. Would it be possible to have alternative programmes, so that, according to the locality, the children of the schools might be instructed in subjects that were most practically useful for them?—It is not very practically useful to children in Cork to learn about agriculture, and it is not practically useful for children in the middle of Ireland to learn navigation, but there is a temptation to the teachers to teach a subject because it is remunerative, and because the result fees will be easily obtained. I would think that if the National Board allowed alternative programmes, but required the teacher to adopt the programme most suitable to the locality, they would do a thing that would be of great practical advantage.

15124. Mr. Molloy.—Of course you know that the manager controls the programme largely; he has the power to say to the teacher: "I wish so and so to be taught in this locality"?—That is a power we would be slow to use.

15125. Mr. Redington.—Why do you allow teachers to teach agriculture in the city of Cork?—I put that as a hypothetical case.

15126. I think it is taught in one of your schools?—It is.

15127. Why is that so?—I am not the manager of that school.

15128. There are a certain number of extras taught in our schools, and there is a great choice of course; that choice would be exercised by the manager in the direction of one rather than of another?—I think it is not at all desirable to bring the managers and teachers into what might cause friction than is necessary, and one would like that the National Board, through its Inspectors, would control the matter. We, the managers, are all disposed to help our teachers in every way we can, and unless it was a thing that required interference, not to interfere.

15129. I understand you to say that the local people should be allowed to adopt one of various alternative programmes?—Yes.

15130. Would it not be better to leave that to the managers rather than to the Inspector?—What I want is a very large development of that, a development of the programme; I don't want to withdraw the power the managers may have, but I would have the opinion of the Inspector and of the Board brought to bear on the teaching of a suitable programme.

15131. Could you tell me why agriculture is taught in that city school; is it because the fee is very high for agriculture?—I would not take it on myself to say; I don't know anything about the circumstances; it is not my own school.

15132. At present there is no advanced kindergarten taught in your schools; would you be in favour of that being introduced?—I think to carry on the kindergarten instruction until it is in turn turned in the teaching of drawing and of handicraft as far as it could be, would be very important.

15133. Have you seen the cardboard work we have seen in England, or work of that kind?—No, I have not. The value of itinerating lecturers has been alluded to already. I think that is a very important thing. Take the case of cookery: it is quite impossible for a teacher of literary work to carry on efficiently cookery classes in a school; it is very hard to take the teacher from literary work for a couple of hours' teaching in cookery, and then for the teacher to go back. Of course it can be done; but I think it is very hard upon a teacher to do that, and I think giving the cookery or laundry work to a teacher or lecturer from outside would be of very great importance to our schools. And it would not only be of importance to our schools, but if that instruction was given to teachers and other instruction in drawing and matters of that kind, it would be of great value also; it would increase in the teachers a desire for self-improvement, it would prevent them resting upon the knowledge they have already acquired, and would give them a very great stimulus in what is of so great importance to them as teachers, in gaining fresh information and keeping their minds open for further knowledge.

15134. Chairman.—Do you see any force in this objection, that to introduce an outside teacher into the school would lower the teacher of the school in the eyes of the children, by making them think there was something he could not do?—I don't anticipate that would be the case.

15135. That was urged upon us very strongly?—I have only the observation of the teacher coming into my own school, and I think if you get a very highly qualified teacher, who has gained already the esteem of the children and their parents, and who is known to be as efficient as the teacher of a primary school ought to be, I would not be in the least afraid of that teacher losing in either the opinion of the pupils or of the parents because these extra branches were taught by another teacher; a great deal of course would depend on the manner and style of the other teacher.

15136. Supposing that now were to be generally adopted, do you think it would be possible in the case of a number of schools, such as you have under you, if manual work were established, to have one central room, like they have in Liverpool and other cities where manual work should be carried on and a special teacher should teach that work to classes coming from the various schools, instead of diverting the teacher from his proper work?—That would be after school hours.

15137. That would be a matter of arrangement?—I think there is unwillingness on the part of teachers to have their children go to another school for the purpose of any particular instruction, and there is always a difficulty in children going from a school.

15138. In Liverpool under the School Board, that is the way it is managed; they don't have manual work in every school, they make groups of schools, and have a manual room built on the premises of one of the schools which is most central and convenient?—Children sometimes take a long time to go from one place to another, and the teachers at first would not look at it very cordially, but I am quite certain if it worked for a little time the objections to it would pass away, and it would be very useful and important—the objections to it are superficial.

15139. Rev. Dr. Wilson.—You say you would make drawing compulsory in all schools; of course you would only do that gradually?—I am glad to say that in all our schools drawing is taught. There is a difficulty in the power of teachers, of course, to teach drawing, and of course in the case of older teachers who have not taught it hitherto there is an additional difficulty in having it taught, but these difficulties ought all to disappear.

15140. Because many of our teachers, especially the older ones, have not been taught drawing them-

advance, and we must do the thing very gradually?—Oh, yes; I don't mean to make it compulsory in that arbitrary manner.

15141. Mr. Molloy.—You referred to the school time being four hours a day; of course you are aware that is the minimum time prescribed?—Yes, we have got the other hour for extra subjects.

15142. In connection with kindergarten, have you thought out any scheme by which it could be worked up through the higher classes?—I have not.

15143. I am aware about the special teacher of cookery having been engaged in your schools not long since and very successfully; would you be in favour of the ordinary teacher continuing that subject when the specialist has gone away. She attends only for two months, giving the instruction for that period; but for the remainder of the year would you not be in favour of the ordinary teacher continuing the instruction?—I have not thought much about it; but the only thing that occurred to me was that there would be great difficulty in carrying it out, taking the teacher from the literary work, and stopping the whole of her work in the school for two hours, and the preparation that will be involved in the work afterwards will extend the two hours to a great deal longer time, and I think prove practically of great difficulty.

15144. Have you any instruction in ordinary subjects in your schools on Saturdays?—We have certain classes carried on on Saturday; we take Saturday for teaching French, and things of that kind.

15145. Of course that would be a suitable day to carry on the continuation of the instruction in cookery?—It is very good for a teacher to have a holiday on Saturday.

15146. You mentioned about managers having a controlling voice as regards the special subjects to be taken up in the locality, very much depends on the capabilities of the teacher in charge, and I think there would be a difficulty in having the alternative curriculum that you refer to, and I think also it would be a pity to deprive the managers of the controlling voice they have at present in connection with it. The programme of the National Board is very extensive, our experience is that teachers take up too many courses; we would desire that as a rule only two were taken up?—It is as a means of doing what is so very important, namely, giving manual instruction, and cultivating their minds by it and by science teaching.

Cork.
Oct. 1, 1897.
Bro. [illegible]

15147. Is not physical science carried out in any of the two schools?—In one, St. Luke's school.

15148. Mr. Molloy.—Have they a laboratory?—I think they have, but I don't like to speak on the subject. Might I say the instruction in the reading books is very important; I notice here that such things as home duties and cleanliness and treatment of simple illnesses and economy in the use of food and all that, that the teaching of that is part of the ordinary reading lesson, and explained by a teacher and taught intelligently, is very useful.

15149. And we have a special reading book on that subject called the Girls' Reading Book?—Two or three have told me that that was antiquated, but a book of that class brought up to date would be useful.

15150. Mr. Stevenson.—You are aware that there are many admirable text-books of that kind published in England—Domestic Economy Readers—would those not suit your purpose?—We must adhere to the programme of the National Board.

Dr. F. J. Alexander, Head Inspector of National Schools, examined.

Dr. F. J. Alexander.

15151. Chairman.—You are the Head Inspector of National Schools in Cork?—I am, my lord.

15152. In looking over your memorandum, I see you wish to say something about the results programme; I don't think we need go into the whole results system; but so far as it bears on the introduction of manual training we should like to have your opinion on the subject?—I mentioned that subject in my summary for this reason, that I think a thorough literary training within reasonable limits is a necessary preliminary to the introduction of any system of manual instruction, and that in close connection with the business of the Commission comes that other point, that is, whether our present programme will admit of modification, and also whether it is as suitable as it ought to be. Now it is to emphasise that point that I wish to raise that question first. If you kindly look at the programme you will notice that the first mistake made in drawing it up was the division into sub-heads, and as a consequence of that several portions of important subjects were practically labelled as of no financial value. As an instance of its indefiniteness I would ask you to look at the programme for second class arithmetic—the test in subtraction is "an easy exercise in subtraction." It is left undetermined whether any difficulties, and if so, which, are to be included. Necessarily the practice of inspectors and the work of the teachers is affected unfavourably by that—there is a lack of uniformity of practice.

15153. What does that arise from; is it the meaning of the word "easy"?—Yes, the precise construction of "easy" in that connection. Now look at fourth class; the programme in geography specifies "To be acquainted with the map of Ireland," and in first stage, fifth, it is "To know the map of Ireland." It has never been decided by authority where the limit is to be drawn there, each inspector is thrown on his own resources. In grammar for the second and third stages, you will notice that the test is described in precisely the same terms, "To parse a simple sentence syntactically." Our programme requires to be thoroughly overhauled as a preliminary to any change in the direction in which your Commission is proceeding, and I wish to mention these simple instances—there are more of them. The gravest fault is that it encourages inferior teaching; it did that by the division into sub-heads, and then it did it by the provisions contained in it. I would ask you to kindly look at the programme for infants and first-class reading. There is no requirement in that programme that the teacher shall explain or take any steps to make the child understand the language which he is taught to read in the book.

Mr. Molloy.—These points have been modified largely by the new programme.

15154. Chairman.—The Commissioners of National Education, who are better authorities than I am on the subject, seem to think that this is going rather too minutely into the subject?—Well, I wish to emphasise that as a preliminary to the other. To put it in a few words, the programme is very unpractical, and enlightened teaching is not only not asked for but appears to be discouraged.

15155. Now, having said that, we will be happy to hear you on the other subjects you have put down in your memorandum?—I would omit grammar from the third class and also geography. I thoroughly agree with the evidence that has been given by Brother Burke.

15156. You say you would omit grammar from the third class, how would that bear upon introducing a subject, which where it is introduced is introduced in the fifth class?—I will come to that presently.

15157. Tell me what you would introduce in the place of grammar?—To find room for manual

that in the third standard?—I would give the term a large connotation; I would introduce drawing in the fourth class; the programme in grammar could be very materially reduced, there is a portion of it I should like to see maintained, it is useful; and the same with geography, it could be largely reduced and that would leave time for the introduction of any additional subjects. In the fifth class I would reduce the grammar and structure parsing; I am satisfied that, for practical purposes, it is of little use. It affords a certain amount of intellectual training, no doubt, but I think that its omission, that is in the form of parsing, would not be much loss, while a portion of the grammar could be retained with advantage. In sixth class I would eliminate grammar as a separate subject, and include it as a part in composition, and require a teacher to teach his boys to write a letter grammatically, and to express themselves in what would be described as correct English. Then, in intimate connection with the point that was raised this morning, I would wish to say that our text-books are almost wholly unsuitable. I am speaking particularly of grammar and geography. I would wish them retained in a modified form, but in close connection with that arises the question of text books. Much of the matter contained in the text-books, especially in geographical text-books, I consider useless, and the time spent by a boy in learning this information is wasted. I refer to the lengths of rivers, populations to a certain extent, and matters of that kind—they remain hard, unassimilated, undigested facts in his mind, forgotten in a year or two. There is a considerable amount of time spent in committing them to memory, and there is no good done. Of course our examinations in that subject necessarily follow the text-book. The Commissioners have placed that on the list, and when we look at the programme and see there "Geography of Ireland," of course it is understood that the extent of knowledge laid down in the text-book is that which we have to require, and therefore our questions necessarily must follow those lines. The next point is the retention of the Result system partially. I would wish to say that the individual examination of the child is necessary in the essential branches, that is reading, writing, spelling, and arithmetic, but any other subjects which are taken might, I think, be examined by class and not individually. But I would wish to give my testimony emphatically in favour of the retention of individual examination for the essential branches, because in no other way would they receive due attention.

15159. In other things you think it ought to be modified?—Yes. Now, with regard to drawing, two points of course arise—one is how the teachers are to be trained to teach it. I am one of those who recommended it should be made compulsory, after a reasonable interval—the sooner the better—but the training of the teacher to teach it is the difficulty. Our present practice, and for years past, in examining for certificates, is, I hold, on wrong lines; we apply no test to the teacher to see whether he can instruct in the subject or not; we merely try his individual proficiency, and nothing more.

15160. And you give him a certificate that he can teach after that?—We do; there is no test applied

know any of the principles on which the subject should be taught, in teaching a class, for instance, freehand, what points are to be watched, what faults to be guarded against.

15163. Rev. Dr. Evans.—But could not all these questions be put in a paper of questions for Queen's scholars in July?—There is no paper of questions on freehand.

15164. You don't examine them in drawing?—They are examined by practical tests.

15165. Could you not test their ability to teach as well as proficiency in the subject by questions?—I am speaking of what the practice has been as directed by the Commissioners. I have been associated with Mr. Craig, and other gentlemen, in examining. I merely prescribe a copy, which is put before the candidates; they draw it as well as they can, and their work is submitted to Mr. Craig to be marked, and so that certificates are granted or refused.

15166. Mr. Redington.—What do you suggest in place of that?—My suggestion is twofold. In the training colleges the subject should not only be taught to the teacher as you teach a child, but it should also be taught so that he could teach it himself in turn; and I would require, in addition, a practical test by an expert as to whether that knowledge had been acquired by the teacher. In the country, dealing with those who are past middle age, or have been already trained, the test could be applied of course, after due instruction was given. I make the suggestion in view of one thing that has been referred to before—that is, that even if a teacher has not a certificate he may be allowed to teach. I am strongly of opinion that would be unwise, judging from the experience I have had for twenty years; I am not sure I can give the reason why, but I can state the fact, that there is hardly any subject in the programme which is more unsuccessfully taught on the whole than drawing, or has progress made for a great amount of effort, even by teachers who I know do their best. I am not certain I can give an explanation of the fact, but I am quite sure that it is so. Therefore I think it is desirable that something should be done to ensure that those who teach drawing should know how to teach it.

15167. How is a teacher who is not in a training college to get a certificate?—The way a teacher gets a certificate in music now—the teacher stands a theoretical test first, and then the Inspector is directed to visit the school and hear her sing—hear her give lessons to the class.

15168. You have just said you would not allow a teacher to teach drawing unless he had a certificate, so that this teacher would not be allowed to teach drawing, and unless he taught it he could not get a certificate?—The teacher of music would be refused a certificate the year she commenced the subject.

15169. But we allow her to go on teaching until the Inspector comes round for the practical test?—That is as short an interval as possible—a month or two.

15170. So that is what you would do for drawing; for a month or two you would relax the rule and allow him to teach it without a certificate?—Yes; I

drawing is worth nothing or very little, is ought to be taken up from the actual cast, and the principle that govern drawing in light and shade ought to be explained; without that it is worth nothing. I allude to sixth class programme, enlarged B; that programme all through requires consideration. I would commence practical geometry in fifth class—very practical geometry.

15171. Is not that the case at present?—Yes, I agree with that; I would not disturb that arrangement; and then have model drawing, but taught and examined on the lines I have suggested, that is not the copying of a figure already shaded, but an actual object put before the child. Now, in reference to needlework, the importance of the subject, of course, needs no testimony from me, but I am afraid that we have not acted quite wisely in connection with the arrangements contained in the programme. Kindly look at any class, say fourth, you will find that a great many subjects, which are very different indeed, are included there; look at first stage of fifth, you have sewing, knitting, and cutting-out, all these are included in the one mark. That puts a difficulty in the examiner's way, which has not been solved—it is this, the cutting-out is, I hold, a deeply important part of the programme—deeply important; but suppose the proficiency in it is very poor, or very indifferent—worthless—yet if the knitting is fair and the sewing fair, you give such a mark as exonerates the teacher from the consequences of the neglect in cutting-out, and I think that is a wrong principle. So long as the programme remains in that respect as it is, so long will the cutting out be, as it is in some cases, practically worthless. And then in connection with that, just in conclusion:—the subject is now compulsory in the new programme for teachers, but I think a higher percentage should be required; it is a very important subject—it is a manual training subject already introduced—has been for a great number of years; and although it does not come directly within the purview of the Commission, yet I wish to say that an impetus could be given to the proper teaching of the subject by a change in the programme for pupils, which would be incidental to the revision of the programme which I have already referred to.

15172. You are on the subject of the programme for pupils, and just now you referred to the programme for the classification of teachers?—In the programme for teachers the percentage should be raised, and the pupils' programme should be re-arranged.

15173. You know the teacher must pass in each section of the programme?—Yes, and the pupil also. With reference to agriculture, I have copied some particulars, but it may be sufficient to say that the views expressed by the gentlemen from Glasnevin are exactly what I hold myself, that is to say, that our present book-teaching by itself is worthless, but combined with an element of experiment, within reasonable limits could be made exceedingly useful and valuable, and that reform is urgently needed. I would venture to add that if the programme were so modified as to include in it the element of experiment it would tend to steady and give effectiveness to the instruction. If the Agricultural Superintendent were to draw up a short statement of suggestions it would assist to unify the instruction considerably and prevent any wide departure from the main object in view. The last point is, of course, the most important, and that is the difficulties which stand in the way of the desired extension of manual training, even to a limited extent. A certain amount of light has been thrown on the subject, that is, experience has been gained by what happened in the case of the alternative scheme, that is the enlarged scheme of industrial instruction intended for sixth class girls; that, of course, as most know, has not succeeded, rather the contrary, and in many schools where it had been taken up and tried for years it has ultimately been given up; in a great many it was never adopted, but even where it was tried it was ultimately withdrawn.

15174. CHAIRMAN.—Was not the alternative scheme a mere prolongation of the time devoted, and still devoted, to the same subject, namely, needlework?—No, my lord, it was far more than that—it was a radical change in the programme.

15175. Because the impression on my mind from what I have been told in visiting schools was, that the result of giving up the programme was to shorten the time in which instruction to the sixth class girls is given in needlework, but that is did not go beyond it?—That is, as I know the matter, hardly correct.

15176. Well, will you tell me what is correct. What is done in the case of sixth class girls in needlework where there is the alternative scheme, and tell me what the difference is where there is not the scheme?—Where there is no alternative scheme an hour is devoted to needlework, which includes cutting-out and knitting as well.

15177. That is done in every case, and is compulsory?—It is compulsory. In the case of the alternative scheme no hard and fast line was drawn; a suggestion was made, after the introduction of the scheme, owing to a misconception which arose, that forty minutes might be given to needlework, and forty minutes to each of the other two special industrial subjects.

15178. Which were——?—Plain dressmaking is one, the knitting of jerseys another.

15179. Still that was in the nature of needlework?—When I speak of needlework in the alternative scheme I include shirtmaking and cutting-out.

15180. Was not that merely an enlargement of the former programme, still given for an hour, to sixth class girls?—That was a section of the programme undoubtedly, but there was the addition of two heavy subjects, which might be chosen from a list of some sixteen, given in the rules, and it was the introduction of those two that crushed out a considerable portion of the literary programme.

15181. Did you say they were separate subjects—I should call them the same subjects only carried out to a higher stage?—Not the same. All the needlework programme up to sixth class in any school inclusive was, under the alternative programme, extended; in the ordinary programme in sixth class a girl is only required to cut out a shirt; under the alternative scheme she must cut out any part of a lady's dress, therefore the cutting-out was extended.

15182. MR. STRUTHERS.—Extended, not introducing a new subject?—Extended. Then, there was a list of subjects, dressmaking, for underclothing, knitting caps, wraps, clothwork, artificial flower making, ecclesiastical embroidery, and so on. Two of these had to be taken, and to make way for them arithmetic was done away with, dictation was done away with, also grammar and geography, and practically nothing was left but reading and writing tested by composition.

15183. CHAIRMAN.—Having received that explanation, still it comes to me that the alternative scheme is not at all parallel with woodwork, which does not exist at all. In the one case it is an enlargement of something to be done with a needle, in the other case it is the introduction of a new subject which does not exist at all?—Yes, but the fate of the alternative scheme contains some warning as to the possible fate of manual instruction. The first and greatest difficulty of all in the way of manual instruction is the cost of materials, and that is so great that I am afraid it will amount to a practical prohibition unless the State comes to the rescue, and under proper safeguards gives some financial help.

15184. MR. HARRINGTON.—That is assuming it is introduced into all the schools in Ireland or a very

Cork.
Oct. 1, 1897.
Dr. E. J. Alexander.

Cork.

Oct. 7, 1897.

Dr. E. E. Alexander.

large number?—I am speaking of what will be in force in three or four years.

15185. CHAIRMAN.—This is what has happened in England; the municipalities have come into play, instead of the State; in the big cities the municipalities have found the money; in the country districts no one has found the money, and it has not been introduced except in one or two cases?—In the case of needlework, the work was of a practical nature, and all the articles, easily made, could be used at home, and therefore there was a return for the money; but necessarily, in manual instruction I am afraid much of the material will be wasted, and whoever is to pay the money might hesitate to pay it for that.

15186. The cost of the material, as far as we could gather in England, was not a large element in the expense of the actual work?—I am speaking of portions of Ireland, remote corners, where it is very hard to get even the price of a copybook. There are sections of the country where, doubtless, public spirit will be sufficiently strong to provide the expense, but as a general subject in the country at large I am afraid that difficulty will meet you very early, and I know it was one of the difficulties that interfered with the success of the alternative scheme. In the next place, there is another difficulty which I think is well to advert to. The alternative scheme programme was too ambitious, and it ended in causing a great many of the managers to refrain from taking it up, who, I think, would have adopted it if it was expressed in simpler terms. When they read that list and saw ecclesiastical embroidery, cloth work, and artificial flower making, and so on, they hastily condemned the whole thing, and the moral I draw, for the present purpose, is that a small beginning would be safer than a larger one, and that it would be very easy to arouse prejudice that it would be very hard to overcome. So, of course, local support must be obtained if it is to succeed. Another point was, that it was optional, and that fact helped largely also to interfere with its success and kill it. Why that is so is a matter of speculation; I can speak as to the fact. In a great many cases when the scheme was first promulgated exemption was at once called for. It was not even tried, and the number of cases where it was ultimately tried was a very small proportion of the whole, so that if any scheme is introduced, the element of compulsion, of course cautiously applied, will certainly be necessary to secure the success of the scheme. The next point is the question of training teachers, and there, again, the alternative scheme speaks a message to us about it. A great many of the teachers were appointed—I am thinking of workmistresses who teach sewing only—a great many of the school teachers were appointed when cutting-out was not required at all, and necessarily they were quite unable to take up the subject—they had not the necessary technical knowledge. That will be of course provided for I presume, but I mention it for the purpose of saying that I think the training of the teacher most important. I have given the subject a great deal of thought. I say that manual training ought to be imparted by the teacher of the school. I am opposed to outside teachers, my ground of objection is absence of discipline, it is not properly maintained; the outside teacher does not know the children and cannot manage and control them, and very frequently I have found that one of the school staff had to be sent in with him to keep order. I allude to needlework in some cases, to vocal music in others, where an extern was imported by the manager, and it was found they had not due control, and I know that extern teaching of music and other subjects is often not so effective as teaching by a member of the staff. With regard to the training of the teacher, the best plan would be to have a sufficient number of experts who would meet the teachers at convenient centres, say at intervals of a week; that would give the members of the class time to ponder over what they had heard and they would be better able to profit by what they learn the next week. The alternative to that is a sustained course of six weeks at the schools; my opinion would be in favour of the former.

15187. That is the plan in Cumberland, the teachers go once a week to practise in Penrith under a trained teacher?—That would be my suggestion, that the teachers should meet an expert at centres, they in turn could carry the subject into their schools.

15188. I am afraid that they have not carried it very far into their schools?—The last point is one I have partly touched on, therefore a word or two will be enough. The success of any scheme of manual instruction will also be affected favourably or the reverse by the extent to which it interferes with the literary programme. There is an instinct among the people that a school is to teach reading, writing, and arithmetic, and so forth, and the moment you displace any of these for practical subjects you begin to arouse hostility more or less. Practical cookery has not aroused that hostility, because it does not interfere with the ordinary curriculum, but if it did you would have the same opposition that we had to the alternative scheme.

15189. MR. STRUTHERS.—Why does it not interfere—is it taken outside the ordinary school hours?—Yes.

15190. CHAIRMAN.—The only case in which we have seen the thing tried in the south of Ireland is at Lismore; and I know the objection you have just given is the one commonly urged. Do you think that arises to any extent from ignorance? We asked the question there, whether hostility was aroused, and we were told that at first people were against it rather, but that at present there is only one parent who objects out of all the parents who send boys to that school?—Yes, my lord; but I understood you to say that there was no omission from the short curriculum.

15191. They have shortened the subjects?—My point is, that if you omit them to any serious extent you arouse parental hostility—I myself would omit a portion as I have already indicated.

15192. The theory of those who advocate the subject strongly is that the observation of the children is so much improved by the manual work that they really get through the other subjects in a shorter time and more efficiently than they do now?—On that subject I have had a very curious experience several times. I am not a believer in the high mental value of woodwork so far as I have seen it, but I have noticed that the most skilful pupil with her hands in needlework is often the most stupid in class, and the girl who is exceedingly bright and smart is very often the worst needlewoman, and very often gets a cipher for her work. I think that has a good deal of meaning, and if manual instruction is carried on in a certain way it will be of very little mental benefit to pupils, and the benefit to be obtained from it could be got much more surely by a more modest programme, that is by introducing elementary science, and requiring the pupils to take part in making apparatus and conducting experiments. I would be much more in favour of that than of woodwork.

15193. REV. DR. EVANS.—Have you anything to do with the Model school here?—Yes, I am the Inspector in charge of it.

15194. Is it the fact that the alternative scheme for girls was carried on in this Model School until lately?—Yes, until last year.

15195. Why was it given up?—The opposition of parents.

15196. Could you put briefly what the nature of that opposition was to which you have yielded?—The main objection made was that they required their girls to get an extensive literary course, inasmuch as they had in view posts in the Post Office and situations of that kind; and we did not apply to the Commissioners for exemption until we tried our best to retain the girls and failed, even though we carried on to a certain extent the ordinary programme.

experience in the teaching [illegible] teacher or a [illegible]

15230. In whose schools the teaching of drawing is a very distinct success?—Quite so.

15231. Might not those men be employed to instruct a number of their fellow teachers, seeing they are successful in their own schools?—Well, no, I would hardly hold that view, and for this reason, the subject of drawing, more than any other, I mean the mode in which it is to be taught, has undergone very considerable modifications, and although these men succeed, I would wish to add they are succeeding in satisfying a test which I regard as insufficient, and their success is relative not absolute.

15232. You surely have some teachers in Ireland whom you would regard as successful absolutely, not relatively?—I have not met very many in the schools: I will give you a proof. I have examined in drawing in a great many schools in all parts of Ireland, and, except in a few instances, I don't remember ever to have seen any indication that the pupil's attention had been drawn to the necessary pre-analysis of his copy before he proceeded to outline it, he started at the top or left, and took it as it came, but made no effort to produce the leading lines.

15233. Do these men get a certificate of competency in drawing?—They do.

15234. Then do you suppose that while they were trained in the training college they were not taught the pre-analysis of drawing?—The colleges have been relatively a short time in operation, and I have not had an opportunity of expressing an opinion on that point; my remark referred to the mass of our teachers, who have come down to us from the past. I prefer that experts, those who know the subject as now taught, should come amongst our teachers and lead them.

15235. Where would you get these experts?—There are some schools in Ireland, and I presume there are more in England, in which the subject is taught. In Derry, for instance, there is a very large freehand school successfully taught by an English teacher, Mr. Hester.

15236. You would have a number of these experts sent to instruct the other teachers?—I would.

15237. On the ground that they had a thorough modern knowledge of the subject, and were competent to teach it. It would be better that these men should instruct the teachers generally throughout the country, and that these teachers, so instructed, should be induced to take up the subject in their schools from having a sufficient result fee attached to it, instead of attempting to make it compulsory all at once?—That would be my opinion.

15238. You spoke of your experience of finding girls who were extremely skilful at needlework stupid at other subjects?—I found that.

15239. I think you said they were stupid girls?—They compared unfavourably with others in the schools.

15240. How did you reach the conclusion that they were stupid; they showed intelligence in needle-

way it is taught in training colleges?—No, I have no experience. My conclusion is inferential, not from direct observation.

15241. You have never been present when a teacher of drawing gave lessons in the training colleges?—No, and my remark refers to teachers who got their certificates perhaps fifteen or twenty years ago.

15242. And who, although trained teachers, might not have got their certificates in training, but at a local examination?—They might.

15243. Have you any experience of schools in which physical science is carried on anywhere in the places in which you have been engaged as inspector?—I have had a small amount of experience, in the Model school at Omagh.

15244. Have they a physical science laboratory at Omagh?—They had a small one, but not sufficiently extensive.

15245. Was it in the boys' school?—Yes, but that was eleven years ago.

15246. Have you any personal knowledge of manual instruction in wood carried on anywhere throughout Ireland; have you seen the thing?—No, I only know it as described in books, the English system; I have not seen it.

15247. In the suggestions that you are offering, have you developed any scheme by which kindergarten could be brought up into the higher classes, from, say, second class and extended to third, fourth, and fifth?—No, I am not prepared with any suggestions of value at present. Still it is very desirable, and I would take this opportunity of adding that the suggestion of Canon Powell is one in which I thoroughly agree—that the introduction of kindergarten into schools has been prevented owing to the rule that has been referred to in the course of his examination, or at least that it will not be paid for. I agree that that block ought to be removed.

15248. With regard to the programme in grammar and geography, Mr. Struthers asked you whether it was obligatory on the part of the teacher to use text-books; did I understand you to say that it was?—Yes.

15249. Where is that laid down?—My information was gained in the first instance from the authoritative directions of those who trained me.

15250. But we have the programme here, and there is no mention of a text-book in connexion with grammar or geography. Text-books are referred to in certain other cases, but these were text-books which the Commissioners published; they were responsible for the matter of such text-books, but they were never responsible for the matter of text-books in grammar and geography, and consequently it was in the power of the teachers to use any suitable text-book, or to give a lesson on, say, the geography of Ireland without any reference to a text-book?—Yes, but then if you take writing there is no prescription there.

15251. But grammar and geography were the two subjects you mentioned. Are you in favour of individual examination of pupils for results fees?—I

tion, as I think you safely might, to all subjects, except the few I have mentioned, you would lighten the labours of Inspectors.

19255. Then you think class examination might be safely introduced?—Certainly.

19256. REV. DR. WHITAKER.—Our duty, as a Commission, is to ascertain how far, and in what form, we can introduce manual instruction into the schools of the Board. you propose to give causes which may prevent its successful adoption, would you give us a summary of those causes?—I have already done so.

19257. I want merely the heads?—Cost of materials; I may venture to say a modest programme not requiring too much made compulsory, that is after a due interval; providing adequately for the training of the teachers, and also providing that the introduction of it shall not interfere with the literary programme unduly, should succeed.

Cork. Oct. 5, 1897. Dr. T. J. Alexander.

Mr. C. SMITH, District Inspector of National Schools, examined.

Mr. C. Smith.

19258. CHAIRMAN.—You are a District Inspector of National schools?—Yes, my lord.

19259. What observations have you to make on needlework?—With reference to needlework my experience was that local exhibitions had a great effect in stimulating the children to improve in needlework. Prior to my coming to Cork, I was in Clonmel for several years; we started local exhibitions there, and up to £20 was given in prizes, and it had a wonderful effect in stimulating the children. Also, I should say, that there ought to be an advance in knitting. Knitting is practically at a standstill, from fifth class up; the programme might be altered, and I don't think crochet would be too much to ask teachers to give instruction in; it is very simple and it is easily mastered by even young children. And I think the teachers might very well be called upon to give instruction in the higher kinds of needlework. There is a good length of time given for it, an hour a day, that means a great deal of proficiency could be attained; and considering that one quarter of the school day, an hour a day, is given to needlework, I am very strongly of opinion that a higher fee should be paid for it, so as to stimulate the teachers and the children. A good deal has been said about judging needlework. I don't think there is much difficulty in judging needlework, a man can judge it almost as well as a woman, it is merely symmetry, if work is symmetrically done it is well done, if it is not symmetrically done it is ill-done.

19260. With regard to practical work in schools, will you give us your observations on that subject?—I think cookery and laundry work ought to be taught in all girls' schools, and I think the first part of the day on Saturday should be exclusively given to cookery and laundry work; every female teacher is perfectly competent to acquire a knowledge that will be useful and sufficient to teach cookery and laundry, and I think that they should give two hours each week to it. The expense of getting materials together might very well be contributed to by the Commissioners, i.e. by the Government, in the same way as the Government contribute two-thirds towards building a school and equipping it with desks, so they might grant two-thirds to equip it with utensils for cookery and laundry; and inasmuch as every female teacher could become an adept in cookery and laundry, I don't see why they should not be forced to do so.

19261. Then, with regard to dressmaking?—That is taught as an extra where the alternative scheme is not in existence.

19262. Have you anything to say with regard to the work done by unrecognised itinerant teachers in cookery and dressmaking?—There was a great difficulty when the results programme with regard to sewing machines and dressmaking was revised, with regard to the teaching of dressmaking; that difficulty was tided over, in the case of my late district, by getting a lady called Miss Walsh to aid. I, acting with some of the teachers in the district, organised a class for Saturdays, and Miss Walsh gave lessons in the Model school, and every teacher in the district acquired the knowledge of the approved system of dressmaking, and they taught this in their schools. And in every school where sewing machine was presented as an extra, dressmaking was well taught on scientific and approved principles. In the same way the teachers of the district could acquire a knowledge of cookery and laundry that would be useful in teaching their children. Classes could be formed under a diplomée of some recognised school of cookery and laundry.

19263. Have you anything to say with regard to cookery as an extra branch in schools?—Cookery is taught largely in all the convent schools at present as an extra branch. There is also an itinerant teacher of cookery in Cork, she had ten classes in the early part of this year. I examined these classes towards the end of April, and the results were very satisfactory.

19264. How is she paid?—I could not really say that; I fancy she is paid by the Commissioners and gets some results fees.

19265. She is in connection with the National Board?—In a certain sense.

19266. Does she give her lessons only to pupils of the National schools, or to anybody who likes to come?—At present she is engaged altogether with pupils in National schools. There are four courses of lessons going on at present in my district. There are lessons going on in the Youghal district; she is giving cookery lessons in Queen Powell's school, she gives twenty lessons, but they are quite insufficient, the children are beginning merely to get a taste for cookery, an inclination for it, a liking for it.

19267. You have a heading down here about the industrial department in connection with wages; explain what you mean by that?—I think in schools where you have an industrial department there is a wrong trend given to the careers of the children, they would be much better employed in being trained up as domestic servants, than being trained as weavers or stitchers. The wages paid in those departments is wretchedly small at best, and when these children have ceased to attend school they are cast upon the world without much means of earning a livelihood, whereas if they had got a bias towards becoming good, effective, well trained domestic servants, they would have a competency for their future, a safe home and better wages than the miserable pittance they get from working at weaving and such like industrial occupations. I had in my late district a weaving department in the Mercy Convent, Carrick-on-Suir, and I don't know that the girls there were earning very large wages. There is in this district at present the famous [illegible] department; there they are earning fair wages, but it is a very precarious business, at any moment their occupation may be gone, whereas if they were trained up as domestic servants and given a bias in that direction they would have a secure livelihood before them.

19268. What do you say with regard to agriculture as taught in the schools?—I have to differ considerably with the opinions that have been expressed about it. I think it is just as intelligently taught as grammar or geography.

19269. REV. DR. EVANS.—That might not be saying much?—It is not saying overmuch, but there is no reason why it should be run down, and I know from personal experience that the teachers are competent to teach it.

19270. CHAIRMAN.—What are the difficulties in the way of reducing the theoretical knowledge to practice?—For instance, when these boys go home, and suggest to their father to do this, that, or the other, their father would only smile at them.

15271. But when they become farmers themselves? —By the time they become farmers, their knowledge will have passed away.

15272. They could refresh their memories from the book?—I think the new book will do a great deal towards encouraging agriculture, it is a book of reference now; the old book was anything but that; the new book is a handy book of reference, and no doubt will be found very useful.

15273. Do you think any time could be gained for manual training without reducing the present programme?—I should not like to see the literary programme interfered with, because I think our boys have got a poor smattering of knowledge at the end of their course, the best of them. I believe Saturday morning should, and ought to, be given to manual training, particularly to lessons in physical science, the male teachers ought to be forced to teach elementary physical science. It gives a taste and trend to boys' thoughts.

15274. I suppose you think that some pay or other additional remuneration should be provided for the teachers for this Saturday work, so that they should lose nothing but rather gain?—Precisely so, my lord.

15275. Do you think that at present the National teachers, as a body, are suited to give practical effect to any scheme of manual training?—Some of the younger members might, but as a body, I am afraid those who have passed through the training colleges would not be very handy.

15276. You think their hand is out of practice?—Yes, my lord.

15277. Do you think that the introduction of elementary science and physical science in National schools would be an advantage?—It ought to be compulsory on all male teachers to teach natural science.

15278. What about kindergarten?—It is very useful.

15279. And you think it might be extended; or would you leave it as it is?—If it is taught, it can be taught to third class pupils.

15280. But it is not; there is where the difficulty comes in; why is it not?—Because the expenditure is too much, it is a question of money, and it is very laborious, it requires a skilled teacher to teach the third class programme in kindergarten, and it is rarely attempted.

15281. Mr. Redington.—How would you teach the teachers to give instruction in cookery and laundry work?—It would be easy to get classes together as I did in Clonmel, I got a class of twenty-five or thirty teachers in there on Saturdays, under a teacher, for acquiring knowledge in scientific dressmaking. That could be done under a trained teacher.

15282. But the centres you selected might be some distance from a large number of schools; would the teachers come in long distances?—They go into centres generally on Saturdays. The difficulty was not experienced in the Clonmel district.

15283. What did the teachers learn?—About twenty-five attended lessons in scientific dressmaking.

15284. Would you teach the male teachers elementary science in the same way?—They should know it; it is not a great requirement to ask elementary teachers to know a little physical science; a person is not properly educated unless he knows something of it; I don't think it would be asking too much of them to insist on their making it up.

15285. I suppose you would insist on their knowing it practically?—It would be better; but even theoretically, it is of advantage.

15286. You said twenty lessons in cookery were not sufficient?—Certainly not.

15287. Is that founded on your own observation or the opinion of experts?—From my own observation and the opinion of the expert, Miss O'Connor; she says it is not sufficient; in some cases the teachers are continuing cookery lessons.

15288. You are aware that cookery can be taught to fourth class now, and a fee got for it?—Quite so; I have examined fourth class children.

15289. So fourth class children can have two years at cookery?—Yes.

15290. Have you ever thought of the establishment of a course of housewifery, teaching the children all that a housemaid and a parlourmaid should know?—That comes in in domestic economy.

15291. But have you ever thought of teaching it practically?—No, I have not, except so far as it is connected with cookery and laundry.

15292. Would you approve then of having it taught practically by putting children through a course of cleaning rooms, lighting fires, lighting lamps, and so on?—Undoubtedly, I think the great advantage of cookery is making them neat and tidy as—one of the advantages—an advantage that often is overlooked where cookery is taught as an extra in the school, and not under the ordinary teacher, it is a corrective of the untidiness that often [illegible] up.

15293. I thought you were in favour of cookery being taught by the teacher of the school?—Certainly.

15294. You think the teaching of agriculture, as carried out at present, has been of value. Do you hear those who have been pupils of ourselves admitting that they have derived much benefit by the study of the book?—I could not say that, because I have no practical experience of them after they leave school. But in agriculture they are talking about matters that they know and have an idea about, it is not an abstract idea, a concrete idea, and it must tend to the development of intelligence.

15295. Don't you think it is essential to farmers to have a knowledge of agricultural chemistry?—It would be all the better.

15296. How can they understand all the developments of modern agriculture, without knowing some chemistry?—Undoubtedly not.

15297. Rev. Dr. Wilson.—You would propose that Saturdays should be utilised by manual instruction?—Yes.

15298. You are anxious, I see, to protect literary instruction on the other days?—By all means, I think we have too little literary instruction.

15299. Could you not afford to give any time on the other five days to this?—I fancy so, in the course of a little time. Now, owing to the change that has come into the programme since yesterday, whereby we will have explanation taught from the second class up, there will not be such a demand for grammar, it will be more easily taught and more readily understood by the pupils. I would certainly think the programme in geography might be very much curtailed, particularly as regards to sixth class.

15300. I quite agree with you that many of the girls should be taught for household service, but when they are taught cookery and laundry they have gone far in that direction. Would you propose any plan for, say, the duties of a housemaid being taught in a school?—These are practically taught at present wherever you have domestic economy, if the books for girls were drawn up with lessons like these, I think it would be teaching housewifery.

15301. That is only domestic economy taught in lessons, what I would ask is could you suggest any plan for having it practically taught?—No, I could not.

15302. Mr. Molloy.—I think you said you recommend that cookery and laundry work should be taught everywhere by the female teachers engaged? —Yes, everywhere: every female teacher ought to teach them.

15303. Would you indicate the sources from which the appliances would come?—I think two-thirds ought to be voted by the Commissioners and one-third from local sources.

15304. Is it your opinion that the local parties throughout Ireland would make up one-third of the cost in every school where a female teacher was engaged in order to have laundry and cookery taught? —Well, one-third is made up in the case of buildings, and there is no reason why it should not be made up in the case of utensils.

15305. In speaking of the industrial department, you advocate that the training there should be rather in the direction of making girls fit for domestic service than to earn wages as weavers?—Yes.

15306. But surely according to the Board's programme there is no mention whatever of teaching such a trade as domestic service or such a trade as weaving, neither "domestic service" nor "wages" occur throughout the programme?—When I say domestic service I mean to give the girls a trend in that direction, and to look down on domestic service as a thing beneath them, but to put it on a footing with weaving.

15307. You have already indicated that you think Saturday would be the proper time for the instruction in manual work and also for physical science?—Because I do not like any time to be taken away from the literary education of boys or girls, I want to save it as far as possible, and if any time is to be given let it be on Saturday.

15308. Could time not be found even during the ordinary week days?—A little time could be gained from geography, and some could be gained from grammar and some gained by leaving out useless extras that are taught at present, that pupils are forced to go through, although they are of very little use to them afterwards.

15309. CHAIRMAN.—What have you in your mind now?—Botany, physical geography beyond all others, because it is never taught intelligently, Latin, Greek, shorthand, and typewriting.

15310. Mr. STRUTHERS.—Could physical geography not be taught intelligently?—It could, by all means, but never is.

15311. Mr. MOLLOY.—You refer to Greek as one of them; I think you will find only two schools in which Greek was taught throughout Ireland?—Two in Greek and twenty-nine in Latin.

15312. Two out of 8,200 schools?—There is no reason why French should be taught.

15313. How many teach botany?—Only one; French eighty-five.

15314. While they are set forth there they really don't take up the ordinary time of the people. In the case of an extra subject, who is the judge of the introduction of the subject into the school?—The teacher principally.

15315. Has not the manager a controlling voice? —He has, but he scarcely ever exercises his power.

15316. Has not the Inspector also a very large voice?—Only with regard to the number of extras, he has something to say to that.

15317. But as to the particular one, if the teacher is qualified local parties make the selection. What objection have you to that?—I have no objection to the local parties selecting, but I do object to people who are badly educated in the ordinary literary programme being put forward in extras that are of very little value.

rural schools to make all the boys farmers?—To make them intelligent, that is the object of every subject taught in elementary schools.

15323. Why do you wish to have domestic economy taught specially?—Because it would make those persons intelligent for domestic service in after-life.

15324. The subject may be taught in a school in order to make pupils intelligent, and it may be taught in a school to prepare them for future life. These are two distinct ends?—They are practically the same.

15325. They are two distinct objects?—They are virtually the same, intelligence and preparation for a future life are practically the same.

15326. Then do you think that any subject might be introduced into a school which would prepare pupils for a future life, and tend to its giving them a good training in intelligence?—Yes.

15327. Then why do you attach such special importance to the literary subjects?—Because I want the people trained in intelligence up to the minute around us.

15328. Do the literary subjects give a special preparation for the future life of pupils?—Certainly, they make them intelligent.

15329. For instance, is the teaching of decimals very useful to the ordinary tradesman?—Unquestionably, it trains his intellect.

15330. I mean for himself, is it useful for his future life?—In so far as it makes him an intelligent being, able to utilise his powers.

15331. That may be achieved by many other subjects, why select this particular subject?—Because it is the usual way adopted everywhere.

15332. You fall back on custom?—Yes.

15333. We had it the other day that the special teaching of agriculture in the rural schools is not found to be of much advantage in preparing pupils for more advanced instruction in agriculture in special schools, such as the Munster Dairy School; would you be inclined to think it has?—I don't quite follow you.

15334. We had it stated, by some witness, at any rate, that the instruction in agriculture given in elementary schools was of no advantage to the pupils who afterwards go in for a more advanced course of agriculture in such schools as Glasnevin or the Munster Dairy school?—I would not at all accept that statement as correct. Agriculture in primary schools must necessarily be a proper introduction for higher forms of agriculture.

15335. Do you find that the children apply afterwards the knowledge of agriculture that they have learned in these schools?—I cannot answer for that, my experience does not reach to the children outside the school.

15336. Only theoretically you think they should? —Yes.

15337. Mr. HARRINGTON.—You mentioned that local exhibitions were organised in Clonmel for the purpose of giving encouragement to needlework teaching in schools?—Yes.

15338. How were those exhibitions started, I take it that there were Ladies' Committees?—A lady started them, and then ladies and gentlemen formed the committee, and the schools took it up heartily.

Cork. Oct. 3, 1887. Mr. C. Smith.

still they are as a matter of fact taught in some of the primary schools in your district?—Yes, lace-making is taught with great success in Kinsale.

15343. Is not weaving taught in some of the schools? —Not in my district.

15344. Well, lacemaking and crochet are?—Yes.

15345. Would you not consider these two branches are technical subjects of special trades?—They are.

15346. Do you think it is well for that regulation to be continued by which these subjects may be taught?—I don't think it does any harm or interferes materially with other trades.

15347. As regards laundry work, to what extent is laundry work taught in the National schools, outside the Convent schools?—I don't know anything about it; I have never seen a school in which laundry was taught; there are at present laundry classes going on in the Youghal district, I believe there is one in the Presentation Convent in Youghal.

15348. Could anything be done in the way of teaching laundry in the ordinary National schools? —It ought to be taught in all ordinary National schools.

Mr. E. J. Murray, Head-Master, Cork Model School, examined.

Mr. E. J. Murray.

15349. Chairman.—You are the Head-Master of the Model school here?—Yes.

15350. I think you have a suggestion to make as to how time may be found for manual training, if desirable, without much extension of the present school day?—With regard to that I am quite in accord with what has been said by Mr. Burke and Dr. Alexander, we might limit the time for grammar, geography, and arithmetic by modifying the programme.

15351. What is your opinion on the feasibility of its introduction into the elementary schools?—I don't think it could be introduced at present into the elementary schools; it might be introduced into the large centres in cities, but only in large schools with very capable teachers, and somewhat enthusiastic on the subject, in order that the public may take to it.

15352. Were you here all the day?—Yes.

15353. Did you hear a question that was read from Herr Salomon's evidence in Sweden as to the advantage of a gradual introduction of the subject? His opinion was that if you introduce it into a new country like Ireland, you should begin with very few schools, and gradually increase them; in fact, that is the system that was pursued in Sweden, they began gradually with a few schools, and have now increased to about half the schools in the whole country?—That would be my opinion too, that it should be introduced very slowly in that way, for the teachers have got to be educated to what it really is.

15354. At present there is not a staff of teachers; it would take time to prepare a staff of teachers?—I have had no experience of what the Sloyd system is, but I saw manual work done at South Kensington.

15355. What do you say with regard to the teaching of drawing?—I think the teaching of drawing is one of the most essential subjects that you can have in city and town schools.

15356. Of course if you are to have manual training you must have drawing as a basis for it; but independently of manual training, do you think there would be any advantage in making the teaching of drawing compulsory?—Oh, yes, my lord, in that respect I think that nothing trains the eye so well as the teaching of drawing. I felt it myself. I never was taught drawing until I was twenty-four years of age, when at the training school in Dublin. I experienced the benefits then, but, of course, that is only an individual case.

15357. Have you given any attention to the question of physical science in National schools?—Yes, I have had physical science classes in the Model school up to

science in the Model school now?—Yes, to the pupil teachers and a very few advanced pupils.

15362. Do you think it might be taught to children under the fifth class?—I would not be disposed to go lower on the programme than the junior stage of fifth class.

15363. Even if a simpler course of science was drawn up?—Even a very simple course of science, I would not be disposed to venture the fourth class on; I would give some preparatory knowledge to the fourth class, but I would not wish to present them for examination.

15364. Mr. Struthers.—You give object lessons? —I do.

15365. That would be called science?—We don't call it that.

15366. Mr. Redington.—It has been given in evidence that in some schools the fourth class are taught science?—I heard that mentioned by Mr. Burke, but I should say that his fourth class standard corresponds with our junior fifth.

15367. Is Saturday available in the Model school? —We teach on Saturday until twelve o'clock.

15368. Would it be available for manual training? —Oh, certainly.

15369. But at present you have other things?— At present we attend the literary programme.

15370. Would you be prepared to give up Saturday morning to manual work?—It is practically given up to cookery in the girls' school, and we would be prepared to give it up to manual work in the boys' school.

15371. You don't think the literary work would suffer?—No, but I have one remark to make, Saturday is usually a market day, the children are generally kept at home, and hence the teachers would have great difficulty in conducting any successful classes on Saturdays.

15372. Chairman.—Is Saturday a universal market day in county Cork?—Children don't suffer so much in that way in Cork, but in most of the towns I know, Saturday is the market day.

15373. Mr. Redington.—From your experience of teachers generally, do you think there would be any difficulty in instructing them in the elements of science, so as to enable them to teach science in every National school?—I don't think there would be much difficulty.

15374. Would you have Saturday lectures?—Yes, available for teachers only.

15375. Or would you prefer a course of six weeks

convenient for teachers to go to these courses if they were introduced?—It was during my July holidays I went.

15379. Most of the holidays are in summer?—Some of the teachers don't take their holidays until the harvest month, so three courses of lectures might be carried on for a month each.

15380. What lectures did you attend at Kensington?—Lectures on light, magnetism, and electricity.

15381. Do you think a course of three weeks would be quite sufficient to enable a teacher to obtain a good elementary knowledge of these things?—I should like him to have his text-book pretty well prepared.

15382. He could do that at home?—Yes, and then by his own practice afterwards, he would learn an immense amount in three weeks.

15383. How do you propose that the apparatus should be provided?—I think the apparatus should be very largely provided by the State, and the teachers might provide some also.

15384. Do you think the managers and teachers would be prepared to pay one-third of the cost of the apparatus?—I would not like to speak for the teachers.

15385. Would they be able to get it from the manager or from their friends?—If the subject was made attractive, the teachers would raise it somehow or other.

15386. The pupils would be much interested in a course of practical science?—Very much, they like it very much, particularly the practical illustrations, it would be useless without them.

15387. If facilities were given, first for the teaching of the teacher and then for the provision of apparatus, would you see any hardship in making the teaching of science compulsory?—Not after a certain number of years.

15388. Mr. Molloy.—I take it you are in favour of the introduction of manual instruction in the schools from the observations you made just now?—I am, in this way; I think that the more difficult kindergarten might be extended up into the higher school, continuing the more advanced drawing as a basis for it.

15389. Have you thought out any scheme by which that kindergarten can be developed into the higher classes, or would you undertake to turn your attention to it and later on hand it into the secretary?—I would prefer doing that.

15390. How long is it since your science classes ceased to be connected with South Kensington?—They have not ceased yet, though I may say they are now rather for the aid of the pupil teacher.

15391. What are the subjects?—Sound, light, heat, and magnetism.

15392. Was the physical science illustrated by experiments of any kind?—Yes, every physical science lesson is illustrated.

15393. Have you any laboratory?—I have, fitted up with water and gas.

15394. Mr. Redington.—Do you think that cookery ought to be taught by the teacher of the school or by a peripatetic teacher?—I am not in favour of square teachers as a rule; there is very often misunderstanding and friction between the teacher and the extern teacher, and, altogether, if the teacher could be qualified, it would be much better to have the work done by the teachers themselves.

15395. Mr. Struthers.—What subjects do you teach on the Saturday forenoon?—Drawing, we usually find we need an additional hour per week for it; we teach on Saturdays, as a rule, whatever subject in our programme we think most necessary.

15396. Did this reckon as one of the regular attendances of the school?—No.

15397. It was additional and voluntary work on your part?—The Board obliges us to keep school on Saturday in the Model school.

15398. Rev. Dr. Evans.—How long do you know the books that were put into use by the National Board?—For forty years.

15399. Do you know a book that has been called the "old fifth book?"—Oh, yes, I did know it.

15400. Wherein did that book differ from the modern book?—I am not prepared to answer that now.

15401. Dr. Skeffington's report says "The Board's old fifth book was excellent in its way, containing a résumé of history, and containing an introduction to various sciences treated in an interesting and popular way"?—Yes, I remember that book; there was one between that and the present book.

15402. Does it not seem that we are going back again to where we were forty years ago?—I would to a certain extent agree with Dr. Skeffington's remark. I would divide the ordinary school reader into sections, one of descriptive geography, another of natural history and such subjects, and have the lessons of each section consecutive and tending to some definite point.

15403. We would introduce elementary science into readers, and have elementary science then taught pari passu with other subjects?—Yes.

On resuming after the adjournment for lunch, the Commissioners present were:—W. R. J. Molloy, Esq., in the chair; Rev. Hamilton Wilson, D.D.; Stanley Harrington, Esq., M.A.; and J. Struthers, Esq., M.A.;

with J. D. Daly, Esq., M.A., Secretary.

Mr. John Dempsey, Teacher, Ballinlough National School, Cork, examined.

15404. Chairman.—Be good enough to state what position you occupy?—I am an ordinary rural National teacher, or rather a suburban one.

15405. What school, pray, are you in charge of?—Ballinlough, a mile-and-a-half from the city of Cork.

15406. Is there a farm attached to your school?—There is not.

15407. You undertake to give some evidence on the subject of agriculture?—Yes, sir.

15408. What is your view about instruction in theoretical agriculture in ordinary schools?—Theoretical agriculture in ordinary schools should in all cases be supplemented by agricultural chemistry, or practical work in the garden if possible. I maintain that a beginning should be made with the teacher. A great many of them have no information on the subject beyond what they have learned from a text-book in preparing for their classification certificate, and the teacher who has prepared for his profession in a town school has not even the information, or the knowledge that can be gained from observation, when he takes charge of a school in the country where he must teach agriculture.

15409. Then would you prevent all National schoolmasters from teaching agriculture theoretically?—I would not; it is better to teach theoretically than not teach it at all, for the children can observe themselves.

15410. You advocate the propriety of teaching only when it is joined with practical agriculture?—I think it is not much value otherwise.

15411. In towns you would not have it at all?—No. I used a very intelligent boy in a town, and by accident we came across the stalk of a potato; he never knew what it was. There is no use in teaching agriculture to that class of boy.

15412. What would you substitute for agriculture in towns?—I would substitute experimental science, drawing—both freehand and mechanical; I mean by mechanical drawing, drawing to scale and practical geometry, plane and solid, and perhaps isometric projection, and as far as possible some kind of manual training, but at present I cannot see how that can be obtained.

15413. What difficulty do you anticipate about the introduction of manual training—by that, I take it, you mean manual training in wood?—Sloyd. You must begin by training teachers and making them expert in it or it is a failure; then you must erect buildings, quite as large as those at present in use; for instance, I have a building that accommodates sixty pupils, that will only accommodate twelve Sloyd pupils, because the best you can do is fix it up with six double benches, and you must have walking space round, and you cannot put those benches in to-day and take them out to-morrow. Then there is the question of cost. I don't think the cost of keeping it going would be so large as supplying a great set of carpenters' tools, each set runs up to £100, and you require several sets.

15414. You don't look forward to manual instruction in wood being carried on in the schoolroom?—No, it should be in a separate building.

15415. If means were provided for the erection of a building and furnishing it properly you are in favour of the introduction of the subject itself?—Yes, and I believe a large majority of the teachers would be the same, if you gave them sufficient time and trained them properly.

15416. Would you favour us with your view on how the teachers could get that instruction?—"It is very hard to teach an old dog new tricks," but I maintain all those in the Training Colleges should be instructed in it, and those teachers already trained who have not been instructed in it, and would be willing to receive instruction, could attend at the district centres for a course of lectures. I don't believe in the itinerant teacher, but if he is to be there at all, he could attend on Saturday and train the teachers at district centres.

15417. By district centres, do you mean official district centres throughout Ireland: there are about 60?—You would want that at least. The teachers within, say, the district of Cork, could come to Cork; the teachers within, say, the district of Millstreet, could attend at Millstreet.

15418. When they attend in this neighbourhood, say in Cork, would it be in a separate building devoted to that purpose or would you select one of the schools already in existence?—A separate building would be the better of the two, but in place of that you could have a place like the Model School or the School of Art where a separate room could be provided.

15419. Speaking of the Cork School of Art, are any facilities afforded there for National schoolmasters getting certificates for drawing?—On the same basis as an ordinary child off the street could go in and pay his 10s. for a session and pass the Kensington [illegible]

when a teacher is lecturing on a soil he may make a mechanical analysis of the soil, or he may take sulphuric acid and ground bones and show the manufacture of superphosphate. If you teach a boy that way you need not tell him a second time, but you must tell him what superphosphate is a dozen times in the ordinary course. I would also suggest teachers should have specimens of plants, flowers, seeds and cattle food, where they cannot have the farm or garden.

15422. A sort of museum?—Yes, I know a great many teachers have done that.

15423. And trained the pupils to collect them?—Yes, my boys will go out in the fields and collect any one of the grasses that are named in the text-book. With regard to the question of flower gardening I think it is an utter waste of time, to talk to children about flowers if they cannot grow them. I think I have said in my summary that the teacher should be at liberty to select about a dozen of annual, or biennial, or perennial flowers, and that these should be grown wherever there is a little garden attached to the school, and the children should be examined on those plants especially, and in no case should the teacher be required to cultivate all the plants named in the text-book.

15424. When you speak of flower gardens, do you refer to cottage gardens, or gardens for flowers alone?—For the first year in the fourth class I would not go beyond flower gardening. I think an education on the growth of twenty or thirty flowering plants would be much better than the course they go through at present, which means a knowledge of farm crops where they cannot see them.

15425. Anything beyond that you think might be carried out on the school farm?—The school garden would be the next step, where I would have kitchen garden vegetables and fruit trees too, but to talk of teaching agriculture on a farm of five or six acres is absurd; for instance, you cannot have a threshing machine on such a farm.

15426. What would be the size of the farm on which you think practical agriculture should be exemplified?—Not less than twenty acres. I have also an idea with regard to the education of teachers at present, that in a place like Cork, where there is a dairy school, that the teachers should be at liberty on Saturday, or during their holidays, simply to visit the farm and see how theoretical agriculture is put in practical operation. The people in Dublin could do similarly at Glasnevin, and wherever there is a large farm. But you want something of that kind in every part of Ireland. Teachers in the south of Ireland must lecture on the growth of flax and many of them have never seen the plant. They must lecture on celery in Kerry, where there are not, perhaps, gardens within a great many miles in which it is grown.

15427. I may mention that yesterday at our visit to the Munster Farm the governors expressed a wish for the attendance of teachers and pupils out there. The next subject you refer to is bees?—That is simply absurd, there is no use in talking to the child about bees if he cannot see them at work in the hive.

15428. What are your views about dairying and poultry keeping?—They should become compulsory in girls' schools, boys won't become dairymaids.

Cork. — Oct. 5, 1897. — Mr. John Dowsley.

15445. Mr. Harrington. — Do you approve of getting off the rules by heart?—I do, there are very few of them. I approve of analysis. If a boy knows the subject and object and predicate of a sentence, he has the whole sentence in a nutshell.

15446. Chairman.—How early would you think analysis of sentences ought to be introduced into the school course?—That would very much depend upon the analysis the inspector required.

15447. But your idea of simple analysis of a sentence?—It would be quite as easy to teach analysis in the fifth as to teach syntactical parsing.

15448. With regard to the mode of giving instruction in geography you advocate in the first instance the instruction should be local?—Yes. If you drop on a boy in a school where the right geography is not taught and you ask the north, he may point to the ceiling and yet that boy might be able to tell you the height of Mount Everest, or that Mont Blanc is 15,000 feet. Boys have no conception of that height, I have to reduce it to miles, and say it is three miles. But if the height were taught by reference to the snow line, it would be admirable. I would introduce physical geography.

15449. Heights of mountains and lengths of rivers are not prescribed in the programme?—They are not, but they are pretty generally asked in the examination.

15450. Have you personal knowledge to that effect?—I have not heard any examiner in my school who did not ask it. The height of Mount Lebanon, for instance, is generally asked.

15451. I suppose that arises in this way, that the first four chapters in the geography are required, so the inspector thought it necessary to put those questions?—It is not the inspector's fault.

15452. Suppose the teacher had the class up before a map of Ireland, a long pointer in hand and examined the pupils for the inspector, would not results fees be paid and the examination escaped?—I don't think it would, but it might. I maintain that if an inspector examined in that way it would be a very good test of the school.

15453. Some are not in favour of physical geography, but you are, you think it ought to be maintained?—As an extra subject; I would not force it into the ordinary school hours. You can introduce it with regard to elementary science, you can show how the height of the barometer is affected by the height of a mountain.

15454. Would you advocate instead of using a specific text-book in geography that geographical readers, containing interesting accounts of voyages, should be used?—I omitted to put that into the summary I sent. When a lesson is told in a simple narrative with regard to a certain country it makes it very instructive. A child will follow it up in after years to know more about the country.

15455. Do you advocate map-drawing?—No, not for children, but of course it would be an excellent means for impressing the relative position of certain parts of the country in their memory, but it is a very elaborate affair.

15456. Suppose the teacher took a piece of chalk in his hand and went to a blackboard and outlined the Lee, and jotted down the different towns on its banks?—Yes, and he could also illustrate why the river went that way and not uphill, that would be teaching geography properly.

15457. You think freehand and mechanical drawing should be taught in all schools?—Yes in all places where it is possible, I would begin even with the infants' class, I would have chequered drawing slates in the infants' and first class, and chequered drawing copy books in second class and a chequered blackboard. In third class I would have the ordinary programme, but I would supplement that for elementary rules. I would get a third class boy to make a drawing on his paper with a ruler and immediately under that to draw a freehand copy of it, and he might also know what a perpendicular line would be and what a horizontal line.

15458. Is not that practically carried out at present?—It is not, a child gets something chalked on the blackboard, and makes a simple copy of that, I would suggest the introduction of the ruler to give him manipulative dexterity.

15459. With regard to the capability of a teacher to give instruction in drawing involving a knowledge of mensuration, would you not require a certificate?—I don't see the necessity for mechanical drawing, for most teachers know as far as the third book of Euclid, which embraces most of the principles of mechanical drawing; if you want teachers to teach solid geometry they must get special instruction in that, but elementary practical geometry may be taught by any qualified teacher, who has gone as far as the third book of Euclid.

15460. If the instruction in drawing in a school, however, were confined to mere freehand, would you allow a teacher without a certificate to take that?—I would—a teacher at present in the service. If you introduce a subject you must devise some means of getting it taught to the scholars. In England in 1891, every teacher who was in the school for six years before, and taught drawing successfully in his school, had got a certificate called "Special D," but the Department does not care in England, I understand, whether the teacher has a certificate, so long as it is taught in the school.

15461. They judge by the result of his work?—That is the proper thing.

15462. You are in favour of mensuration as a separate subject?—It should be separated from geometry, and could be taken at an earlier stage.

15463. Your views have been adopted by the Commissioners for the teachers, they have it as a special subject?—Yes, and they might begin with the pupils too.

15464. What is your experience about Sloyd?—I think I have nearly detailed all that already. I am very much in favour of it personally, and the teachers would be equally in favour of it if they saw the way to carry it out, there is the question of accommodation, there is the question of the training of teachers, and the cost of material, which would in many cases fall on the teachers themselves, as the cost of maps falls at present.

15465. If those objections were obviated?—You would find the great majority of the Cork teachers would be in favour of it, and from discussions I have had with them I know they would prefer to teach it to the kind of parsing we are compelled to teach.

15466. You had some observations to make on the results system?—I would do away with the results system. The results system neglects the intelligent pupil, the teacher's time is devoted to bringing the dull boy up to a standard which he, perhaps, is not capable of attaining, he perhaps attends barely the number of days, and he must answer the same questions as the intelligent child who has attended 200 days. I don't want to boast, but my results year terminated the day before yesterday. I had a boy who had ninety-nine days made before the last day, he went away to the races on the last day, and I lost him for the year. There was a temptation to me to mark

15468. Then the important thing is don't abolish payment for the subject?—Oh, don't abolish the payment.

15469. But change the form in which the money is obtained?—There is another defect, the classification of the pupils. I have got to teach agriculture, I may get a boy from the town, he is in second class and has not learned a word about agriculture, he must go through five years' course in that subject in that year. I maintain I should be at liberty to present him in the fourth class programme in agriculture and sixth in other subjects.

15470. What about the children who unfortunately do not make the minimum attendance of 100 days?—They should be compelled to do so. We have a very inactive Corporation, there are 8,000 children round the streets of Cork who do not go to any school. The grant to the school should not depend so much on the teacher's results, as on his manner of imparting knowledge. That boy of mine who made 99 days ought to be very nearly as good as the boy who made 100, and I ought to be entitled to quite as large a fee, or a very large percentage of the fee.

15471. Then, assuming that a certain number would make the minimum number of days, and that the others, who did not, would also be examined, what is your view of how payment should be made?—They might make payment on a reduced scale to those who did not make the minimum.

15472. Mr. Struthers.—Might it not do to pay on the average attendance of the whole lot?—That would be the really sensible plan.

15473. Chairman.—In connection with the annual results examination would you advocate examination by classes rather than of individual pupils?—Oh, by classes, because the teacher evidently gives the same instruction to all the class, and if eighteen pass out of twenty the inspector must come to the conclusion that that class is taught well, he is at present fined for not teaching the people he could not teach.

15474. In England there is a practice of neither examining the class nor the individual pupils, but of simply adopting a mode of inspection, that is, an inspector might go into a school two or three times in the year and form his opinion on what comes under his notice?—That is the best plan; at present we have no inspectors in Ireland, they are examiners. In the twenty-three years I have been in the service I have not been more than two hours inspected in the school. When a teacher knows that an inspector is liable to come in every day and observe his manner of imparting instruction he will take care that he will come every day prepared to impart that instruction in the very best manner. I notice in the report of the English Department it is stated that the inspector and the teacher have become much better friends, and the teacher is more at liberty to improve his methods of instruction.

15475. Mr. Harrington.—At present do you know the exact day the inspector will come?—Oh, yes, I know I will have an examination on the 28th October, and I can drive away to cram till then. I am open to have two or three visits, but I am certain he will come on that day.

15476. Are these not visits of inspection?—Yes; but that is simply to see that the teacher is an honest

15480. What good do you suppose the drawing part of kindergarten does for the children?—First of all they learn to draw a straight line, for although you have the chequered lines on the slates, you very frequently draw on the blackboard a diagonal and the child has no guiding line, and he learns freedom of action on the chequered copybook. Then there is the question of counting, you put so many squares on the blackboard and the child learns to count them.

15481. We may take it that it trains the hand and eye, produces accuracy and observation, and on the whole tends to make them intelligent?—Yes.

15482. I think if you had experience in the other ordinary subjects of kindergarten instruction you would find that that pretty much applied to them all?—I believe so.

15483. You would be in favour, on these lines, of having kindergarten instruction continued in the higher classes?—Yes, until you would be able to begin with practical instruction in manual training or experimental science.

15484. I would like to have it made quite clear that manual work in wood is in no respect different as an educational subject from kindergarten, it is a continuation of it?—Yes, that is the distinction I draw between Sloyd and technical education; I maintain technical education is training a child for a trade, Sloyd is educational, the other is utilitarian.

15485. You believe that that is often misunderstood?—Yes, people believe technical education and Sloyd are synonymous terms.

15486. You know that woodwork is really another form of drawing in kindergarten exercises?—Yes; because to do a model in Sloyd you have first of all to do a plan and elevation, and perhaps an isometrical projection.

15487. And the object is to train the hand and eye and secure accuracy and develop intelligence?—Yes.

15488. You think that all these things are desirable in the school, I don't mean that every form of manual instruction should be taught to every class in the school, but some form of manual instruction should be taught right through the school?—Yes, every case you should [illegible] the work for the child.

15489. And naturally exercises for the more advanced classes should be more difficult than for the elementary classes?—Yes.

15490. And that is the reason for introducing such a difficult subject as woodwork in the higher class?—Yes.

15491. Coming to your difficulties in the way of introducing it, one was want of knowledge on the part of the teacher, that is a difficulty that can be overcome in the course of time?—Yes.

15492. By instituting proper training classes?—Yes, and introducing it into the training colleges.

15493. Another difficulty was the want of accommodation?—That is the chief want, that will cost some money.

15494. In order to have woodwork properly taught in a school one would require a separate room with special benches and tools, that means a considerable expenditure of money?—It does, the building of the house, not to mind the cost of tools.

15495. Which a poor locality could not be expected to bear, so that in order to have manual instruction in the form of woodwork introduced into the higher classes in a rural school, there must be a considerable subvention from the State to support it?—Yes.

15496. But short of woodwork you could have drawing?—Yes, and you could have experimental science and agricultural chemistry.

15497. Don't let us go too fast, agricultural chemistry is not quite training the hand and eye like woodwork. Drawing would be a training of the hand and eye?—Certainly.

15498. Suppose we wanted to avoid the expense of tools and benches we might have cardboard work which is not expensive?—Yes, but that is only a continuation of kindergarten.

Cont. [illegible] Mr. John [illegible].

15499. It is more advanced than any of the exercises set down in your course, and probably is quite sufficient in difficulty for children of ten and eleven?—Yes, but as far as I understand the Sloyd, as practised in Sweden, they have thrown over every other material but wood.

15500. They have not thrown it over, they began with woodwork and continued with it?—If I don't mistake, in Salomon's lectures he referred to trials in other materials.

15501. They did not try cardboard, they tried to teach bookbinding and metalwork for utilitarian reasons; that was not successful, and they confined themselves to woodwork for educational purposes. Teachers cannot be expected to teach a subject that will take a considerable time and a considerable training to qualify them, unless they get a sufficient recompense for it?—Certainly.

15502. If these points were satisfied the difficulty of introducing woodwork in the higher classes would be overcome?—They would disappear.

15503. Coming to the teaching of agriculture in rural schools, its object is somewhat different from woodwork and drawing?—It is both theoretical and practical.

15504. What do you suppose is the object of teaching agriculture at present in the rural schools?—To promote the agriculture of the country.

15505. Do you think it succeeds in effecting that object?—I think it does not.

15506. You don't suppose a boy of eleven or twelve can be taught anything of value about the practice of farming?—Not a bit. In a school in which I was teaching once I drew the attention of the principal teacher to the nonsense of teaching the subject, getting off a lot of names by rote. I asked a boy when rye-grass was to be sown, and he told me in March.

15507. Then we may take it that the teaching of agriculture in the elementary school does not have much practical effect in the training of farmers?—Not in the absence of demonstration.

15508. All the children attending a rural school are not going to be agriculturists or labourers. Do you think it is fair to teach a boy who is going to be a clerk the science of agriculture?—It is wrong both to him and the teacher; that is where the results system is quite at fault; if a teacher had freedom of classification he would send that boy to the business most suitable to him in after life.

15509. There must be many rural schools in which a fourth of the boys are not going to be farmers or labourers?—At least a fourth, they cannot all be farmers. If a farmer has four sons and sends them to school, one only can be a farmer, the other three will have to take the map of Ireland or some other map for themselves.

15510. Then it is very unfair to teach these people a trade that they have no intention of following?—It is.

15511. As a matter of fact such a subject as agriculture should be taught to much older people and in special schools for the purpose?—Yes; of course flower-gardening could be taught in practice to very young children.

15512. For the practical purpose of training scientific farmers, who will improve the agriculture of the country, something is necessary which could never be obtained in the ordinary rural school?—It is absolutely impossible to improve the agricultural condition of the country by teaching the theory of agriculture to children.

15513. There is another point the teaching of agriculture might be supposed to serve, that is the training of the intelligence. Do you think the teaching at present develops the intelligence of the children?—It does not in the absence of practice.

15514. Let us put aside what profit it is to be in their future life, and come to the point whether it

[illegible]ing the intelligence of children ?—I [illegible]
[illegible].

[illegible] witnesses have told us that they think [illegible] extent ?—It is a very limited [illegible]

[illegible] are other subjects taught in school [illegible] intelligence might be developed in a [illegible] agree ?—Yes.

[illegible] teaching of drawing ?—I would put [illegible]

[illegible] teaching of construction with the [illegible]

15536. There is very great danger of [illegible] in proportion to the amount the [illegible] —because the question of supervision.

15537. Real teaching consists in gi[illegible] problem to do which he must work out [illegible] little help from the teacher as possible [illegible] should not help the pupil at all.

15538. And that applies to grammar [illegible] any other subject ?—Yes.

15539. So far thorough teaching [illegible] small class is as necessary as it is in hi[illegible]

15540. A class of [illegible] should [illegible]

Cork.

Oct. 5, 1897.

Mr. John [illegible].

dren. In a great many rural districts the children are away from the schools for days at a time, and country teachers have told me that they have often to work double the minimum time to bring up to the standard the children who have been away from school.

15556. That is done voluntarily?—It is not voluntary, he must work to get them up to the mark, for they will make the necessary attendances.

15557. You consider the minimum necessary attendances are quite insufficient?—Yes.

15558. Are these children necessarily absent such a length of time?—Yes.

15559. Could they by no means be brought to the school for a longer time?—In some cases they could, they stop at home for very trivial excuses.

15560. Have you any idea of how these children might be induced to attend more regularly at school?—You have got to force them to come to school; there [illegible] comes in.

15561. Do you think force is the only remedy?—Yes.

15562. Do you not think a more attractive programme will bring them?—It might, but force is the only remedy for the recalcitrant parent. If the parent insists on the child going to school the child will go.

15563. But there are many parents in this condition that they are indifferent?—It is the indifferent parent I would compel to send the child to school.

15564. But when we have no compulsion it would be a good thing to make the school curriculum attractive so that the child will come rather than stay away?—The really good child will come unless the teaching is very bad, the "mitcher" won't come to school whatever the attraction, for if there is a horse race or coursing, or a football match in the neighbourhood, he will be the first there.

15565. The universal evidence in England is that where manual instruction and physical science are taught the children find these things attractive, and the attendance has improved?—I have heard that is so.

15566. CHAIRMAN.—Do you say that a range was necessary for cookery?—No I say it is not; it is necessary to teach children cookery with the appliances that they would use at home.

15567. MR. HARRINGTON.—I see after your name occurs "suggested by the Cork Teachers' Association," are you authorised by the Association to give the views you have given?—Yes, I was sent here by them; but I cannot say that all the views I have expressed are theirs.

15568. You think that generally speaking the views you have expressed here represent the views of the teachers?—Yes, as far as the rural teachers: my friend, Mr. Gamble, will speak on behalf of the city teachers.

15569. It was said to us in Dublin by one of the representative teachers that the views he gave expression to were practically held by all the teachers in Ireland?—I would not go as far as that.

15570. And his views differed very much from yours as regards the manual training?—Yes, radically; and I see they would not have Kindergarten in the Dublin schools, but the Cork people are in favour of it.

15571. Then it is not correct to say of the teachers of Ireland generally that they are opposed to the introduction of this manual training?—I am instructed to say that if you train teachers, if you give them sufficient accommodation, and curtail the literary programme to give them time for manual instruction, they are in favour of it.

15572. And pay them for it of course?—And pay them for it of course.

15573. Your difficulties are only difficulties of means in carrying it out?—We don't want to turn the schools into tinkers' forges.

15574. You are in a fairly agricultural district?—Yes.

15575. It has been stated to us by many witnesses here that the education, especially in the rural schools, is altogether of too literary a character?—I believe it is.

15576. The book that is at present in use in the National schools, do you consider that is too elaborate a work?—Entirely. I notice that in the last report of the Commissioners the percentage of passes in agriculture is the lowest of all the compulsory subjects, while the [illegible] is the highest. If a smaller amount were attempted it would be much better done. I would have flower gardening for the fourth class and nothing else, and that practically; I would go for the kitchen garden in the next stage, and the cultivation of farm crops for the next. I would have analyses of soils and manures for the first sixth class, and experimental agricultural chemistry for the highest division. I would leave out altogether the question of bee-keeping, live stock, dairy management, and poultry.

15577. Don't you think the question of bee-keeping and raising poultry, and dairying, is rather outside the scope of an ordinary National school?—To be sure it is.

15578. Is it not the idea generally in Ireland that the ordinary agricultural labourer is very unhandy?—He is.

15579. Do you attribute that fact to the want of manual training in the schools throughout the country?—I believe manual training in the schools would do away with a lot of his unhandiness.

15580. With regard to the teaching of elementary science, do you think that could be carried out properly by ordinary teachers without the assistance of itinerant teachers?—You might have the itinerant teacher in the case of a teacher who knows nothing about agricultural chemistry or experimental science, but an ordinary teacher could qualify himself easily; he may make a few failures, but he could illustrate a great many things in connection with the analyses of soils and manures with very little help.

15581. Do many of the National teachers in this district go to the local School of Art?—I don't know; I have never been in the School of Art, but I know a number of us last winter rented a room in the School of Art for ourselves, and had a mutual improvement class, and many of the teachers went in for certificates; some of the teachers were over fifty years of age, that is one point that would prove the teachers are not opposed to this subject.

15582. CHAIRMAN.—Had you a professional teacher for the subject?—No, one of ourselves.

15583. MR. HARRINGTON.—How would you get over this difficulty—suppose the room could be provided, and the appliances provided by the State for the introduction of this manual work, where there is only one teacher?—It must be taught in that case by a special teacher, or if the ordinary teacher is qualified it must be done out of school hours.

15584. MR. STRUTHERS.—Saturday forenoon would be a useful time?—It would be out of the question altogether. I have seen it tried by a manager once anxious to get the children to school on a Saturday, but he had to give it up. They will come to town on Saturdays, especially if they have market tickets, and if the children don't come to town, their parents do, and the children have to stay at home.

Cork.
Jan. 8, 1887.
Mr. P. Gamble.

Mr. P. Gamble, Teacher, Trinitarian National School, Cork, examined.

15585. CHAIRMAN.—I see you state that you are Honorary Secretary of the Cork National Teachers' Association?—Yes, sir.

15586. Are we to understand, before you put forward your views, that in your evidence you represent the views of the association?—We have two associations in Cork, the Cork City National Teachers' Association, and the Cork City and County Association. We called a meeting of both of these associations together to know who would go forward before the Commission, and Mr. Dunphy and I were selected.

15587. Mr. Dunphy represents the rural parishes and you the city?—Yes.

15588. Then the expression of the views of you two gentlemen may be taken as the views of both associations?—In our direct examinations, but of course we have to fall back on our own convictions in cross-examination.

15589. You state that you think the children are too young to derive advantage from the handling or use of tools?—I am putting it that under the existing circumstances the teachers are opposed to the introduction of manual instruction in woodwork in schools; first, they think that a teacher to give instruction in it should be master of the subject, and we are not masters of it; secondly, we should have ample accommodation to give instruction, and we have not; thirdly, the amount of literary matter a child gets in the essential subjects at present before he leaves school is the least that we could expect he would go out into the world with, and the only subjects you have to draw from are grammar, geography, and in the higher classes, arithmetic. And besides, the children, when they leave the general run of National Schools in the city, leave at the age of ten or twelve, and, we think, at that time it is scarcely possible the child can derive any advantage from the use of tools.

15590. You say the children about Cork leave between ten and eleven, in what classes?—Fourth and fifth, as a rule.

15591. Have you any idea in the schools within the circumscription of your association how many pupils are in the senior division?—No; in a school of say 100 or 105 the sixth class will fall to five or six.

15592. And then fifth class, the two stages?—It will vary, especially according to the locality. In the poorer localities you will often have no child in fifth or sixth; in the better localities you will.

15593. Surely three pupils in the fifth and two stages of sixth must be older than between ten and twelve?—Yes, of course.

15594. Would not that be the class of pupils for whom manual work would come in properly enough?—We take drawing as the basis of manual work, and we think the children would be more judiciously employed in drawing.

15595. And the drawing may commence at a very early period?—At third class.

15596. The first difficulty suggested by your Association is want of acquaintance with the subject on the part of the teachers; but you have heard, I think, evidence to-day that perhaps provision may be made in training colleges, by means of itinerant teachers, and by attendance at special centres, and in that way in time, large bodies of teachers might be made acquainted with the subject. But the second difficulty is that the children leave school too young to learn any trade or occupation afterwards, and you cannot draw from the time devoted to subjects such as reading, writing, and arithmetic.

15599. You refer to grammar, geography, and higher arithmetic?—Yes; the time saved from them could be devoted to drawing.

15600. Would you confine any time saved to drawing alone?—Drawing alone, you cannot save more time, two or two and a half hours a week, and that is the least time a child should get for drawing.

15601. But you have drawing taught in many schools?—As an extra subject outside school hours.

15602. It was taught last year in 1,500 schools in Ireland under certificated teachers, consequently it is not any objection to it as to manual instruction in woodwork?—Oh, no.

15603. So that difficulty might be got over?—Yes.

15604. You are of opinion that drawing should be compulsory?—Yes, from third class in town and city schools, we think that drawing from its importance should be a compulsory subject.

15605. And would you say taught only by regularly certificated teachers?—No, the certificate the teacher gets at present is little good to him in the teaching of drawing; if a man is a student, and can make any put wash on a piece of drawing within an hour, he gets a certificate; that tends to make the teacher become a student, and he forgets that afterwards he has to teach the subject to the children. At the present time we get no credit for being able to teach the subject. We would say that part of the credit should be given to the man who is able to instruct a class, able to teach drawing, and part to the man who is able to draw also.

15606. Skill in drawing and ability to teach the subject united?—In the case of new appointments we would have an assistant qualified to teach drawing in a school of sixty; we would have an assistant for an average of sixty as amongst of the entire work, we think seventy too many. In the case of a teacher of a small school not qualified, we would have him get instruction in the shape of lectures at first, and let him prepare the third and fourth class the first year in drawing, the third, fourth, and fifth the second year, third, fourth, fifth, and sixth the third year, and if the results were satisfactory he should be entitled to teach it.

15607. Then by the operation of the training colleges and this additional adaptation locally, the subject in a short time might actually become compulsory in all schools?—Yes; but a teacher who wishes to impart his instruction to pupils derives little advantage in the schools of art or training colleges.

15608. Do I understand you to say that they are not taught how to teach the subject?—No; the drawing is placed before you, and if there is a defect in your drawing it is pointed out to you by the drawing master once or twice a week, and the same in the school of art where I got my certificate.

15609. Does not the master go to the blackboard and outline the figure?—No, I would not mind that so much in the school of art because it is students who attend there; but that was a defect we noticed in the training college: the teacher of drawing around

training of the hand and eye, and also in the after occupation of the child.

15612. What is your view of the statement that a man who can draw well can write well, and a man who can write well will draw well?—I doubt that. A man may write well and write a different hand to the hand he teaches in the school, it does not follow because a man is a good scholar he should be a good drawer.

15613. Of course in connexion with drawing you advocate chiefly drawing to scale?—Freehand drawing at first. In the second stage of sixth class we have at present shading, instead of that I would have drawing to scale.

15614. In what class would you begin the freehand?—Third class.

15615. You have drawing in connexion with kindergarten?—Yes, you have kindergarten at present in the second.

15616. The drawing would be one method of continuing kindergarten into the upper classes?—It would be one link.

15617. You are in favour of having kindergarten taught in the classes up to second; why do you break it up to second?—You get two new subjects in third at the present time, up to second you have not those subjects, and you have more time, and there is often a difficulty in keeping little children employed.

15618. Your observation has reference to schools where kindergarten comes in for ordinary pupils, not an organised infant school?—Yes.

15619. But if you had an organised infant school would you not desire a continuation of it to the higher classes?—If possible; but I think the children must leave at nine years an organised infant school.

15620. Then the continuation of the kindergarten, so far as drawing is concerned, might be carried on in the higher classes?—Yes.

15621. Have you worked out in your own mind a practical scheme of developing that kindergarten?—No, I have not.

15622. If your Association would turn their attention to that it would be advantageous?—We think of course that the teacher of an ordinary school should be allowed facilities to get a certificate in kindergarten, and that without separate class-rooms or furniture he should be allowed to teach it.

15623. If an ordinary schoolroom. If a teacher is qualified to teach kindergarten that ought to be a recognised branch of instruction, and the restriction of requiring special rooms and furniture and a special teacher for the subject should be done away with?—Yes.

15624. We all know that special furniture for kindergarten was a mere expedient—strictly speaking it was taught in the open air—the children's garden. You are in favour of having geography, grammar, and arithmetic a little curtailed?—Yes, in the higher classes.

15625. Would you agree with Mr. [illegible] in the views he expressed?—Yes, in the main I would agree with Mr. [illegible].

15626. That the intricate problems of higher arithmetic might be dispensed with largely, except in the case of persons qualifying for the teaching profession?—Certainly; you will find when the child leaves school, if you follow him afterwards, he has forgotten all these things, partly from the system and partly from the intricate subject.

15627. The time so gained you think might be devoted to letter-writing, and you agree with Mr. [illegible] as to analysis of simple sentences also?—Yes.

15628. You have introduced a very nice point here; you are strongly in favour of having local libraries and museums?—In connexion with the school.

15629. Do you know of any instance where your idea of the museum is carried out?—Except in connexion with the Christian Brothers' school.

15630. No National school?—No.

15631. Is it not in the power of the teacher to make a beginning himself by inducing the pupils to go round the country and bring in anything they are not acquainted with, and get information on it, and make a little collection?—Yes; but the way we are paid a teacher always has an eye to a bigger school, and is not so much interested in the smaller school.

Cork.
Oct. 8, 18[illegible].
Mr. P. [illegible]

15632. That is an accident; but would you advocate having something of the kind?—Yes, the more use you make of the hand and eye the better for the teacher.

15633. Would the library be a lending library for the pupils?—Yes, books of natural history and travel; a boy, say, by reading "Robinson Crusoe," would derive more advantage from it than if he were twelve months learning geography.

15634. You are in favour of introducing Science Readers; would you have that accompanied with practical work?—Decidedly. In the College I went through, the lecturer had no appliances to illustrate his lecture; one lecture in the week was illustrated, and that was at the Catholic University.

15635. At that University had you not suitable appliances?—Yes, for one lecture in the week only; we had two on magnetism and electricity, or on light and sound, every week, in the College, and the mechanics were taught there, and we had no illustrations.

15636. The last subject you say is to provide suitable Readers for the children?—Yes; we think the Readers on the Board's list are not suitable to the ages of the children. In the Sixth Book there is a lesson on the Study of Words; there are pieces brought in from Shakespeare, and the children are asked to explain these pieces, which we think impossible by the sixth class. We also think, in order to vary the thing, the Fifth and Sixth Book Readers should be divided into two parts, and, if possible, to have them published by the Commissioners, because it is cheaper, and a penny or two pence in the price of a book is a good deal to the ordinary pupil attending a National school.

15637. Do I understand you to mean that the Commissioners should undertake the publication of a variety of Readers?—No; one suitable set. The Fourth Book at present can be had for 3d., whereas if you go to other Readers they are 4½d. or 5d.

15638. Would you not think it desirable to give freedom of choice to local parties about the selection of Readers?—Decidedly; but in the poorer localities the teacher has great difficulties to make children buy books, and these difficulties don't count at the end of the year when the Inspector comes round to examine.

15639. Suppose various Readers were sanctioned of a suitable kind, and comparatively inexpensive, freedom of choice being given to local managers and teachers to make a selection, would not that be superior to having it narrowed down to one set of books, however they were cheap?—I would not narrow it down to one set; I would have that set go on the market at the same price.

15640. Would you prefer that the Commissioners should be the publishers, or leave it to local publishers and traders, large firms?—I would have both publishers.

15641. Of course, always provided that there was no objectionable matter in the school books?—Yes.

15642. Mr. STRUTHERS.—You would prefer a wider selection of reading books?—Yes, sir.

15643. Such as, you say, those published by many firms?—Blackie, Thom's, and the Commissioners, and let the teacher select the better books.

15644. Up to the present you are confined to one set of books?—Up to the present we were, but we are not in the future; there is one set by the Commissioners, another by Thom's, and another by Blackie—all the big publishers were invited to put out into the market.

15645. That arrangement is sanctioned?—It is not, I think, until the 1st November.

s you use the books of the Commis-
. get those books at a reduced price?—
price, which is often 1d. or 2d. less
of a cheap book from another firm.
(d) this suit your views, that the Com-
uld advance the extra 1d. or 2d. to
put that book if it were a suitable one?
ent price we think they could have a

our general views as to manual instruc-
with Mr. Dunmsky?—Yes.
attach great importance to instruction.
Very great.
you would have that connected with
ork?—Yes: combination of the kin-

16668. You are strong on the va
but you are not quite sure whether
visable to add to that some form of
tion in the higher classes?—I cannot
could get time for it.

16669. Suppose we got over that d
think it is desirable they should have
would be very good.

16670. For instance, if a boy copies
from a drawing, he understands that
better?—Undoubtedly.

16671. A boy may copy plan and e
have a real understanding unless he
solid object?—Yes.

16672. So that the teaching of ma

15692. What other subjects would you propose to teach after that?—Grammar and geography on a smaller scale than at present.

15693. On a different programme from at present?—Yes.

15694. Then, taking drawing before grammar and geography, you would have them to be taken in what time you could spare after you had taught drawing in addition to the essentials?—Yes.

15695. About science, you say you would have a library and museum attached to the school, in order to make the school attractive?—Yes, to the children.

15696. And I presume also to teach the children?—To make the teaching practical, as it is not at present; it does not pay to be practical under the result system.

15697. What do you suppose we secure by the teaching of science?—There is a training of the hand and eye also in science.

15698. But if you have drawing hand and eye is trained there, would it also be necessary to teach science?—I would have it after drawing.

15699. I have no doubt you consider science serves some larger purpose than training the hand and eye?—It begets accuracy also in the child.

15700. It does not beget accuracy if the teacher tells the child something he afterwards repeats to somebody else?—That is not teaching science, the child should make the experiments himself.

15701. You think it very important that the child should make the experiment himself?—Yes.

15702. And the child does not understand anything he does not do himself?—No.

15703. In order to have experiments that a child should do himself, they must be very simple?—Undoubtedly.

15704. In fact, experiments is too strong a word?—Rather.

15705. If you got a boy to take an accurate reading of the thermometer each day and record it in a book, that would be a training in accuracy and scientific training?—Yes.

15706. If in addition you sent a boy into the playground at a certain hour and made him measure the length of a shadow cast by a pole, and sent him out at the same hour a fortnight after to measure the length of it again and record that in a book, and so on for a series of observations, these are things a boy could do quite easily?—Yes.

15707. And these would be a training in accuracy?—Yes.

15708. And a teaching of science. You don't say anything about the teaching of agriculture?—I have nothing to do with it.

15709. On general principles would you favour the present method of teaching agriculture in rural schools?—I taught agriculture in the day for years, and passed children through the results examinations, but they had not an idea of what they were learning; we crammed them as you would cram fowl.

15710. It was not teaching science?—No.

15711. I have mentioned two or three very simple things that would be useful scientific teaching. Suppose for an advanced class the children have a series of pots, one which contains a sterilised earth, another with a certain proportion of manure, and a third with a different manure, and the children plant the same seeds in these pots and observe the results, that would be useful training, would it not?—Undoubtedly.

15712. That would give them a real knowledge of what the manure did?—Yes, they could see the result of their own work.

15713. And similarly the children might be made to make collections of useful plants, and of hurtful plants, and of weeds that damage crops?—They should be encouraged to do it.

15714. And they might be trained to do it systematically?—Undoubtedly.

15715. In order to carry out such a scheme of science instruction, it would be essential that the children should not be examined at large on what they know about certain things?—Of course.

15716. The essential thing would be that the inspector and examiner should have evidence from the notebooks that this work had actually been done by the teacher, and these observations actually made, and they should not be questioned about things that did not come within these observations.

15717. Rev. Dr. Wilson.—Subject to the three exceptions that you have mentioned, I presume you would be favourable to the introduction of manual instruction?—We are working under a system at present which we consider injurious, and we would gladly accept any other system for the good of the pupil.

15718. One of your exceptions is the accommodation; we would never think of asking the teacher to introduce manual instruction without providing accommodation, we would ask the Government to provide proper materials, that exception need not be entertained?—That does away with the difficulty.

15719. But the second is that the teachers are not sufficiently acquainted with the work so as to give the instruction, that would be remedied in course of time by gradually introducing the teachers to a knowledge of what they have to teach?—From our experience of the training colleges we think that a great defect, if teachers are not practically trained there at present, it is hard to think they would be trained in this work also.

15720. Your third objection is more serious, that the children have not sufficient literary knowledge when they leave school; it surprises me to hear that they leave between ten and eleven?—That depends on the locality; children in the poorer districts leave as soon as they are confirmed—receive the sacrament; they get 4s. or 5s. a week as messengers, and that is of great importance to them.

15721. Chairman.—You don't refer to factory children?—No.

15722. Rev. Dr. Wilson.—Always assuming that we, as Commissioners, would endeavour to protect the incomes of the teachers and ensure that no change would affect them injuriously, would you not think it better that we should have less literary instruction and more manual instruction for the mass of the population?—My idea of the literary instruction at the present day is that it is the least you can give a child and send him into the world afterwards.

15723. There are a great many departments of algebra and higher arithmetic, and if a man is to be a coal heaver or wagon driver, would he not be better fitted for his after-life, if, instead of learning them, he were taught the use of tools?—They are generally taught after school hours.

15724. We make a programme that contains a good many things that are useless for nine-tenths of the children of Ireland? We think so ourselves, but we get money for teaching them.

15725. As long as a teacher is largely paid by results then we cannot, in justice to him, interfere with the literary subjects. Suppose we could modify the basis on which teachers could be paid, do you not think we might have better schemes without results fees; for instance, you have the dull scholar, who may represent the masses, you have those comparatively uneducated, and you cram the others?—We consider there are three evil steps in the result system, you assume every child going to the school has an equal proportion of brains, that they will make an equal amount of attendance; and third, that they are equally equipped as regards worldly affairs. One child is quick, another is dull; the quick child is neglected, he is thrown back, he learns to be lazy—he has no self-reliance. If we find a child that is sure to excel at drawing, we have no interest in the child, we cannot give more than the half hour devoted to the subject on the programme. If we had not the result system at heart, it would be our interest to encourage that child; there are scholarships at the School of Art for National school children, it would be our interest to try and

Cork. — Oct. 2, 1897. — Mr. F. [illegible].

pass him into the School of Art; he may show some genius there and become a great painter, as [illegible] (James) did out of the School of Art. The [illegible] system kills that.

15726. Mr. Struthers.—You say the children are too young to receive any advantage from the handling or use of tools?—We think so.

15727. From practical experience?—The tool the child will use will be the ordinary tool, and we think that too heavy for a child of ten or twelve years.

15728. It is so in England, children of eleven use the ordinary joiner's tools; and in Sweden the central plan, which regulates the instruction in all the schools in the country, except in a few exceptional cases, provides for instruction in Sloyd in the first class of the folkschool, that is, for pupils in their tenth year, and there they begin with the knife only; they begin to use the saw and plane within a couple of [illegible]?—I did not know that.

15729. Mr. Harrington.—I was just going to ask practically the same question. Professor Sollas was asked with reference to the age of the children—"At what age do you think children can be taught the use of tools?"—and his reply was, that generally children can be taught the use of tools at ten years of age?—Well, a knife is a tool; a child can use a knife at ten, when he cannot use a plane.

15730. It was stated in Dublin by a teacher in a prominent position, with regard to kindergarten, that of the children who had come to his school, one half of whom had passed through the kindergarten school, the other half had not passed through any kindergarten, the latter were far more intelligent than the former—would you agree with that statement?—On the contrary; I think it is not so. We think for ourselves in Cork, just as these men think for themselves in Dublin.

15731. Your experience is quite the opposite?—Quite the contrary; that a child who has passed through a kindergarten school must necessarily be quicker to pick up things than a child who has been on the streets, and never learned anything before.

Limerick. — Oct. 4, 1897.

THIRTY-SIXTH PUBLIC SITTING.—MONDAY, OCTOBER 4th, 1897,

AT 2 O'CLOCK P.M.,

At Cruise's Hotel, Limerick.

Present:—The Right Hon. the Earl of Belmore, G.C.M.G., in the Chair; The Right Hon. C. T. Redington, M.A.; Rev. Henry Evans, D.D.; Rev. Hamilton Wilson, D.D.; Professor G. F. Fitzgerald, F.T.C.D.; Stanley Harrington, Esq., B.A.; W. R. J. Molloy, Esq.; and J. Struthers, Esq., B.A.;

with J. D. Daly, Esq., B.A., Secretary.

The Hon. Miss Spring Rice, examined.

The Hon. Miss Spring Rice, [illegible], Foynes, examined.

15732. Chairman.—You are prepared to give us some evidence upon the question of the supply of teachers; perhaps you would give in some detail, in your own way, what your views are?—The teacher for cookery and laundry—my idea is that there should be itinerant teachers in the rural schools (which are the schools that I have most acquaintance with), for the purpose of teaching cookery and laundry, and also to give opportunities to the resident teachers to qualify themselves.

15733. And do you include in your recommendation house cleaning?—Yes, I do. I think that is one of the most important things.

15734. Do you also think that classes in these subjects would be advantageous for the present schoolmistresses who wish to qualify themselves as teachers?—I think here and there there are women who would like to do it, and I think, particularly, it would be desirable to give them the chance of it, because it would make them take up the scheme more willingly, if they felt somebody would not be put into their school, if they themselves would be sufficient for the subjects.

15735. Are you speaking only of the rural districts, or including towns?—Rural districts, including large villages.

15736. And do you include in the sort of subjects that should be taught dressmaking of any kind?—Plain dressmaking I think.

15737. Can you tell me whether there is anything done in the way of teaching cookery and laundry outside the large cities and towns at present?—Isolated instances. I had classes last year in two villages, and I know a Parish Priest, Father O'Shaughnessy, near Newcastle, has held them.

15738. What do you say about the number and duration of lessons to the school girls, and over what period should they be spread?—I think it is much better to have them only once a week, going on all the year round, but if the schools were very far distant you would have to change to, I think, half the time, and have two lessons per week.

15739. When the Commission was at Borris-in-Ossory we had an inspection of one of the schools in which there was a laundry class, and the plan adopted there is not a usual plan: it was to have the classes only once a year to train the children thoroughly during whatever period was allotted to it, and then to let them practise at home only during the rest of the year; what do you say to that?—I would not deter it altogether, but I am sure the other is the better—it has a more educational effect.

15740. You see the argument that the lady who had adopted this plan used was, that by having the lesson only once a week, the same child was not there for the whole of the work, whereas under the system she adopted the person who began the article finished it off at the end of the week?—But I think beginning with them as we are all agreed at ten or eleven years old you don't want to make little laundresses of them, you want to get them into the habit of doing work properly much more.

15741. At what age do you think girls should be taught these different subjects?—I would begin at ten or eleven.

15742. How would you arrange for such subjects being taught in the National schools?—A class-room, when there is one, makes it all easy, or where there is an infant school. I had mine in the National school; there was no class-room, there was a girls' school and an infant school, and we had the use of the infant school, but I should say it was during holiday time.

15743. How did you manage about the arrangements for cooking?—We cooked upon a grate in the schoolroom; we considered that was very much like what they had in their own cottages, and we used a Portable oven, which can be put on any open fireplace, but you must use turf or wood.

15746. What do you conceive to be the main importance of teaching right methods of cleaning from the beginning?—Well, I am sorry to say that the idea of real cleanliness is almost absent amongst our children; therefore I think you cannot begin too early to put it into them, and go on knocking it into them every week of their lives, and I think that is the only way it has any permanent effect, because we have often seen older girls trained to be servants, and directly they go to their own home it all goes away again, leaves no effect.

15747. Even if they have been servants for some time and fairly good servants?—Yes.

15748. How do you account for that?—Because it was not put into them young, and their own homes were not affected by it.

15749. I suppose they thought it was something connected with the place where they were servants, and had nothing to do with home life?—Yes.

15750. What do you say about the importance of making housewifery subjects interesting and attractive to the children, and also as to making them more acceptable to the present schoolmistresses?—They hang together very much, because I believe the teachers would welcome it if they were sure it would be popular with the parents of the children; and it would be so if they were once convinced that it was useful and advantageous; we have to convince them of that. So that public lectures by the organiser who is sent down to start these things in certain centres would be very useful.

15751. Is it your experience of schoolmistresses that they keep their own rooms where they live tidy?—No, only tolerable, most of them; but I have seen very few.

15752. Is not their instinct to do it?—No. I should say it is tolerable, better than many of their neighbours, but not what we should wish it to be.

15753. What subjects of the ordinary course do you think could be curtailed or omitted to make room for this sort of education in housewifery subjects?—I think that grammar above all should be greatly curtailed.

15754. Well, how much time is given to the grammar lesson now, to grammar?—I am afraid I don't know; but I know schoolmasters, clever ones, have told me that it was very hard to get it into their heads, and they doubted if it ever reached their intelligence at all.

15755. In fact they don't put it into practice in their ordinary speech?—They don't. I should also curtail arithmetic and make it more practical, teaching simple bookkeeping and accounts would be very useful and they would appreciate that.

15756. Do you think geography could be curtailed?—Yes, if it was taught intelligently it might be useful; but it is not taught intelligently at present, it is only a string of names which conveys no idea to the children's minds.

15757. Do you think that grants should be made by the Commissioners of National Education out of funds that might be supplied to them by Parliament, towards the purchase of stoves and utensils and fuel for laundry work?—Yes, all the appliances; but I would make children bring things to be washed; I would leave that to the local authority.

15758. That would be to bring clothes?—Yes.

15759. But you would have soap and fuel and water provided?—Soap and fuel and water and brushes, and those sort of things. To supply materials for on, because where I had my classes we sold everything we made.

15760. But would the child of the ordinary peasant be able to bring the proper things for a cooking lesson?—I am not sure that they would like to have it to do; but I mean the teacher could get these things and sell them, so that she really would not want Government to give her money for it.

15761. What observations have you to make on the question of needlework, as it is at present taught in the National Schools, under the Industrial Scheme?—I think the Industrial Scheme has succeeded in the few cases where it has been taken up, and I attribute it to the character and capacity of the schoolmistresses largely.

15762. You are aware that some witnesses say it has failed?—It has failed in that so few classes have taken it up.

15763. But you don't think it has failed where it has been taken up?—No.

15764. Mr. Redington.—You have had experience of the teaching of cookery in two schools in the country?—Yes.

15765. Would you kindly give us your impressions in regard to it?—Well, the children seemed interested and attended fairly well in both schools. In the more rural, Shanagolden, attendance was rather the best; the other was Foynes.

15766. First of all, of what class are these schools?—I don't know how many there are on the rolls. I had 22 girls in Shanagolden attending, and in Foynes rather fewer, 18.

15767. Who supplied the materials?—I supplied the materials and sold what was cooked.

15768. Was there a great loss?—No, no loss at all.

15769. Who supplied the utensils?—We bought the utensils. I may have used a few out of my own house, but I bought what the teacher said should be bought. The cost was £3 5s. for cookery and laundry, the utensils were of a very simple and elementary sort; but my teacher said that I should have to get cookery utensils, &c., for £2, and laundry for £1 11s.

15770. Might I ask how you disposed of the cooked dishes?—The scholars bought them, I think, in every case.

15771. But of course they sometimes failed in cooking a dish—who would buy that dish?—I don't think they did. I think it turned out what they thought nice.

15772. Did you confine yourself to simple dishes?—Yes, extremely simple; Irish stew and potatoes, and [illegible] bread and soup, which latter we made for about 1½d.

15773. And boiling potatoes?—Boiling potatoes.

15774. I take it that these two schools might be called rural schools?—Certainly.

15775. And what was done in these schools might be done in others throughout the country?—Certainly.

15776. Did the lessons last during the whole school year?—No; I had the teacher for three months—twelve weeks.

15777. How many hours a week?—I think I had two lessons for each class. I had to put it in to shorter time than I would advocate, because I only had the teacher with me for a certain time.

15778. Was this a teacher from the Kildare Street Society?—No, she was English, trained up in the North—Newcastle-on-Tyne.

15779. Had she a diploma from the National Union?—I don't know; she earned first class at

be devoted to embroidery and any other industrial work?—Certainly.

13614. And, if I mistake not, your view also is that the class of needlework taught should be of a comparatively humble and useful kind, not at all ambitious? —No.

13615. And should include the repairing of garments?—By all means, most important.

13616. In addition to visiting these schools, do you encourage the teachers in any way by prizes?—Yes; our lady visitors are given money sometimes by the Association, and they also supply prizes out of their own pockets, and that has had a very beneficial and stimulative effect upon the scholars.

13617. Do the girls of the National schools participate in any of these prizes?—It is prizes to the scholars not to the teacher.

13618. The teachers, beyond the honour and glory, and pleasing the Ladies' Committee, I presume don't get any formal certificate?—No, so far we have not done that.

13619. And how do you find that prize system encourage the pupils to work?—Very well; they tell us it stimulates attendance, as well as stimulating the improvement of the needlework itself.

13620. As a matter of fact when you constituted that Committee did you find the needlework in a very backward state?—In many places.

13621. The Committee has been in existence three or four years?—Just three years.

13622. And the present condition of needlework? —Is improved and improving slowly, but of course the subject has not been properly worked up with the teachers; they are often behind-hand themselves in that subject, and therefore they cannot bring their pupils on, but I find a laudable desire to improve them; and I should say that on our visits we have been welcomed and they have responded to our efforts.

13623. Have you and the Ladies' Committee devised any plan by which teachers trained, say, many years ago, when needlework was not so very essential under the National Board as it is now, could be brought up to the requirements of the Board?—Yes, we are very anxious that the Board should supply the means of their attending classes. Several teachers have said to me: "Oh, if there were such classes we should be so glad to improve ourselves," in dressmaking for instance.

13624. Then I presume you would be in favour of classes assembling, say, here in Limerick and at certain centres?—Yes, at certain centres.

13625. And those classes to be conducted by highly qualified persons?—It would be most beneficial and would tell on the whole neighbourhood, not only on the teachers themselves, but would raise the position of needlework, and these industrial subjects altogether.

13626. With regard to the subject of cookery, in which you brought the special teacher to your school, was the subject carried on, when that teacher left, by the ordinary teacher of the school?—No, she has as much as she can do, especially as she has the industrial programme.

13627. Then you contemplate the necessity of the specialist coming again?—Decidedly so. Before I started these cookery and laundry classes I had clothes-cleaning classes, pure and simple, in my own

give five, and I have seen the English results, and I consider they are superior to ours, except the convents; some of our convent classes are as good as the English ones, because they have a superior method and a greater number of teachers.

13629. CHAIRMAN.—Have they shorter time?—No; they have as much time as they like, I think, in the convent schools.

13630. Mr. MOLLOY.—We are not very experienced in the question of needle-drill; perhaps you would favour us with an account of it?—It is writing down the exact motions that a person has to go through in the use of the needle, it is given out to the children, and, like soldiers, at a given moment, they all put on a thimble, at a given moment they all take up the needle, and at a given moment push the needle.

13631. You are pretty confident that good results come from the organization of the Ladies' Committee? —Decidedly so; I think the teachers all like it, and there are many openings for the lady to make herself useful. And the managers like it: we have always asked the approval of the manager before going to the school; that is essential of course, because he is responsible for the whole thing.

13632. The house cleaning that you referred to might come in, I think, as portion of the extra time now devoted to the alternative scheme?—Yes.

13633. And to reduce our ambitious scale of needlework requirements under it?—Yes; but I think it could also be taken out of the programme as it stands, without the industrial programme.

13634. Without interfering with that?—Without interfering with that.

13635. Such as a reduction in grammar that you referred to?—A reduction in grammar.

13636. Would you be in favour of extending the school hours?—Half an hour, you might, or even an hour on special days. The children attending my classes thought it no hardship to attend later on those days.

13637. Professor FITZGERALD.—Did they come on Saturdays?—I think Saturdays ought to be reserved for teaching the teachers if possible, or holding classes for the older girls, because in the rural districts you cannot have evening classes; they cannot go wandering about at night, but you could hold classes on Saturday for older girls and grown women if necessary.

13638. Mr. MOLLOY.—At what time of the day did your special teacher in cookery give lessons?—They came half an hour earlier, I think, and stayed as late as was necessary to finish the work.

13639. Mr. HARRINGTON.—We found that in England they had divided the school day in many of the schools into two portions, one up to twelve o'clock, when the children get an interval of two hours, so that they can go home to their parents for dinner, and they resume there again at two o'clock and remain until four; do you think that would be an improvement in Ireland?—I should hardly think so, but I have not talked to the mistresses about it; it is a new idea to me.

13640. I think you said with regard to laundry work that if the State provided the means for teaching this laundry work the landlord might be

15846. Were these classes attended by older girls who had left school?—I had a separate cookery course for the older girls who had left school.

15847. Not one of these two you referred to?—No, a separate one.

15848. And these classes you referred to were not attended by any except those children from eleven to thirteen?—Yes, or I think I had a few up to fifteen.

15849. But still attending school?—Yes.

15850. The class lasted about six weeks?—Yes.

15851. Did you find that they had made appreciable progress in that time?—They did.

15852. And it would be better to have the course repeated for the same girls another year?—Certainly.

15853. Perhaps two years?—Certainly; but if it was spread over the whole year you would get the same amount of instruction as in two years, because this was all crammed into such a short space of time.

15854. Your idea is that instead of having the course condensed into six weeks you would have the same number of lessons, or rather more, spread over the whole year?—Yes.

15855. But to be given by a special teacher?—Yes, unless the resident teacher would qualify herself for it.

15856. But you would expect a better knowledge of cookery from the special teacher?—Much better.

15857. CHAIRMAN.—Would you call the special teacher a cook, as far as qualifications go?—Oh, yes, the one I had decidedly.

15858. You could hardly expect a teacher to become as highly qualified as a regular cook?—Yes.

15859. Professor FITZGERALD.—Which was she, a cook that had been trained to teach or a teacher who had been trained to cook?—She was a teacher who had been trained to cook; she had gone through the Newcastle-on-Tyne training college.

15860. But her first idea was as a teacher?—Yes.

15861. Mr. STRUTHERS.—Was she a teacher of other subjects as well?—Yes.

15862. Suppose you had a special teacher of this kind, you would require to combine two or three classes in order to find employment for her?—Yes.

15863. That would be your idea?—Yes.

15864. You would utilise such an agency as the Ladies' Association that you spoke of to combine classes for instruction in cookery?—Yes; I think the managers would be glad of an aide-de-camp.

15865. Is that instruction not more profitably given to girls of fourteen or fifteen than to girls of eleven or twelve?—I think they would require an advanced teaching, but I think you should lay the foundation when they are young.

15866. But you don't think the early beginning of cookery or laundry work is so urgent as the early beginning of needlework?—Not so early; but I call it as urgent at ten or eleven as it is urgent to begin needlework at five.

15867. You said they must begin needlework early, otherwise they lose a certain power of hand and cannot be taught to do it so skilfully later?—Yes.

15868. Do you think the same argument applies to cookery and laundry work?—It is more educational. I think it has more effect upon their habits and turn of mind than skill of hand.

who would benefit by it most, and require it most, would not come, because there is not that feeling in the country of the desirability; it is really a few of the better sort that desire it at present.

15871. Don't you think, in course of time, the benefit that these better girls receive from this instruction would affect opinion about them in the district and more would come?—It would take a very long time, because we have not good traditions in the country such as they have in other countries.

15872. But this would be a means of forming good traditions?—Yes; but then you would have to wait a whole generation, and by catching hold of these little girls of ten or eleven we could influence a dozen generations.

15873. Supposing it was possible to have these classes entirely dissociated from the literary school, and made available for girls of the district generally after they left school, one could confine the literary school to fewer subjects with better instruction?—Yes.

15874. Is there not a danger at present of weakening instruction in the school by spreading it over too many subjects?—I should not say so, because I think the new methods of teaching make it so much easier that we should be able to do the literary instruction full justice in the same time.

15875. Would it not be better to begin with the new methods and see how they affect the school work before we take any steps?—I am very strong about starting manual training, make it very simple, but start it now and catch girls when they are young, because I have noticed everywhere that the little girls take a pride in it; they think it shows they are womanly, and the big girls don't take a pride in it unless they are pushed into it.

15876. Then, in your view, it is quite essential that these classes should be for the children who are receiving elementary literary instruction in the schools?—Yes.

15877. Then, about the needlework; that of course must be taken early in order that their hand may be accustomed to the proper operations?—Yes.

15878. I think you advocate beginning by needle-drill as they do in England. At what age would you propose to introduce needle-drill?—I think as soon as little girls begin to hold the needle. I suppose four or five, in the first class.

15879. Why I ask the question is, that I have had it frequently stated to me by lady teachers, who are teaching needlework in England and Scotland, where this needle-drill for children of five is the rule, that they think it bad for the children, because they are forced to do things at an early age that their hands are not really capable of doing, and this early needle-drill induces to habits which are difficult to eradicate afterwards, and they advocate beginning at seven?—I have not heard that expressed, but I have seen very good results in London of the needle-drill; and on the other hand over here I have seen the children holding the needle all wrong, and I have heard teachers say it is exceedingly difficult beginning with them—they waste a good deal of time.

15880. The first thing is to get systematic instruction in a subject, and we may consider afterwards the proper stage to begin?—Yes.

15918. CHAIRMAN.—Which do you value at almost nothing?—The domestic economy taught from a book.

15919. When we were in England we found what was called domestic economy was not exactly what is learned in a book, because we saw a demonstration—it was more economy in the use of materials in cookery, and also dealing with such questions as the effect of heat, and the boiling of water. And I remember seeing a class of teachers in Liverpool being lectured by a young lady upon the subject of digestion?—That might come in when they were older.

15920. REV. DR. EVANS.—Do you think that either subject could be taught in a National school properly—domestic economy or housewifery?—The scientific aspect of domestic economy?

15921. Could it be taught in a National school at all?—A few remarks could be made as she goes along, but I would not go into the subject in toto; she should point out that you should see boiling water for some things, and what is done, but I would not go into it closely, because the children could not understand it when we began them so early; I would take them to that when they were bigger.

15922. MR. MOLLOY.—With regard to the number of persons that would assemble for a class on Saturdays, you would not, I presume, confine that to teachers, you would also, perhaps, include the senior monitresses who would, in a short time, become teachers?—Yes.

15923. And in that way the class would become a very large class?—It would, and young women in the country, many of them, would be very glad of it.

15924. PROFESSOR FITZGERALD.—At present there are five hours a week given to needlework; do I understand that you think the three hours given to it in England is quite sufficient?—By the results I have seen I should say so.

15925. That they could learn in three hours, if they were well taught, as much as they do at present with our inspection teaching in five hours?—I should be inclined to keep on the five, because they can get through more work.

15926. Do you not think that some of the hours that are at present devoted to needlework might very well be devoted to housewifery?—Well, if necessary, if housewifery can't be got in otherwise; but I should say it was useful to keep the five hours, because they are making clothes for themselves if properly looked after.

PROFESSOR FITZGERALD.—I noticed that in the schools in New York they had only one hour a week needlework, and the School Board of New York was insisting on its being one and a half hours; the lady superintendent complained bitterly; she said she got quite good work out of them for the hour a week, and did not know what she should do for the hour and a half.

ment of this Commission, it would be necessary to increase the staff?—Yes, and also omit certain subjects.

15939. Mr. Redington.—Portions of certain subjects?—Yes, parts of grammar and the whole of the geography programme as it is at present, or else cut it down extensively.

15940. Chairman.—Now, what have you to say about drawing?—I consider drawing a most important subject, and I consider that in all schools in which the teachers at present possess a certificate in drawing, the subject might be made compulsory.

15941. Would you go so far as to say that in the case of all future teachers, those who are being trained at present, you would compel them to take out a certificate?—Yes.

15942. Drawing a distinction between those who are already teachers, and upon whom it might be a hardship, having perhaps passed the time of life when their hand could be trained to draw?—There are teachers who would not be able to acquire it, but in all possible cases I would require a certificate.

15943. You would not consider a person qualified to be a teacher who could not teach some one subject in the programme, such as drawing?—I would consider it desirable he should.

15944. Would you think it a hardship to make a rule, that before a person should get a certificate at all, he should be able to teach all the subjects that are in the programme, supposing drawing was a compulsory subject in the programme?—In exceptional cases it might be a hardship, but it would be most desirable in the interests of education that it should be required. Then, relative to drawing, I would recommend that drawing be introduced into the second class, both in all ordinary National schools, and also in kindergarten schools. In the kindergarten schools at present they use a chequered paper for the purpose. I think that is rather a mistake; I would prefer them not to use that chequered paper, because afterwards when they are brought into other National schools and introduced to paper without those chequered lines, they seem to draw without any definite idea of the plan set before them; it seems to me rather to impede them. In place of the kindergarten drawing being a help to them, it seems to me it is not.

15945. Have you anything more about drawing?—I would suggest that an expert be stationed in certain centres—say, at Limerick, for example—and that he could go round to schools during the week, say four days of every week, and give instruction there in cases where, at present, there is not a properly qualified teacher in drawing; then on Saturdays he might visit certain centres in the district at which teachers would attend—a centre like Castleconnell or Caherconlish—where you could get about nineteen schools in a certain distance from you; get the teachers of those places to come in to the centres; and then the expert in drawing would be able to give them instruction. I have taken my own schools and ranged them round various centres, and I found round one village, perhaps, nineteen schools might be grouped, and round another village sixteen schools might be grouped. Then if the teacher visited these centres on a Saturday the teachers could be brought into these places. Circulars might be sent to the teachers asking them what centres would be most convenient to them to attend; that would obviate the difficulty of paying their expenses into Limerick, which would, of course, in six months or twenty lessons, amount to a considerable sum. Then, in drawing, I would also recommend that there should be a test for the teachers, the same as at present in vocal music; that is, a [illegible]

done the subject. The teacher might use in the first class rulers on paper; then, in the second class, I would have a little higher, more advanced proficiency; then, in the third class, something like the patterns at present, perhaps easier; and in the fifth class I would introduce drawing according to scale, but from the very first I would be inclined to have object-drawing.

15946. You mean by object drawing, drawing from an inkstand like that?—Not for an elementary class, but a cube or rectangle, something extremely simple.

15947. But from an actual object, not copying something from a paper?—Yes.

15948. Now we will come to sewing and dressmaking?—I would take that in connection with the industrial programme we have at present, because in the subject of ordinary sewing I think we give at present ample time in our schools. But I would remodel the industrial programme in order to make it popular, and I think that could be done easily.

15949. How would you do it?—I should only require one hour's instruction in needlework in the day in place of the two hours that at present are compulsory. In the domestic economy I would prescribe for the first year, only half of the text-book; that would leave them plenty of time for other important subjects—for example, in place of the present extended course in arithmetic, I would have a practical course—I would have questions dealing with bills of parcels, with practical calculations, with addition of money, in place of the present problems we propose to our children.

15950. I don't quite see how that bears on sewing and dressmaking; I am taking the heads as you gave them in your paper?—There should be a course of two years' instruction in sewing-machine and dressmaking.

15951. Have you anything more to say about sewing?—It is very desirable that there should be a two years' course of instruction in sewing-machine and dressmaking; at present we have only got one year's course of instruction, and consequently very, very few children indeed, considering the number that pass through our schools, are examined, because the subject can be taken up in the fifth class. When the children pass through that class or any class in which the subject is taught, the subject is completed instead of being taken up year after year. Therefore I would propose that there should be a two or three years' course. For the first year's course there should be a simple programme like taking the needle out of the machine, putting it in again, threading the shuttle, winding the bobbin, arranging the work. For the second year's course I would advocate something more difficult; for instance, knowing how to use the braider and hemmer, &c. For the third year's course you might have tuck work or doing easy work and things of that kind; I have got some of the work here (producing specimens). I think it most desirable that such an important subject as that should get more than one year. Then in cookery I would also recommend that there should be a two or three years' course in place of, as at present, there being only one year's.

15952. In what schools is there cookery now?—It is principally in convent schools.

15953. If it were possible to do so, would you advocate making it universal in all schools?—Most certainly, I would. I think cookery forms an indispensable part in a girl's education, as important as needlework; therefore I would be very glad that cookery should be made universal throughout our girls' schools.

15955. You mean text-books on these subjects?—Yes.

15956. Are there any in existence now that are available?—We have a few, but they are not introduced until the sixth class, and then only in the industrial programme.

15957. Mr. Redington.—Do you mean a graduated series of readers, such as are used in English schools?—Yes. Then relative to agriculture, I consider that the present system of teaching agriculture to be practically of no use to the country; there is a large sum of money, I suppose about £12,000, paid in fees for this subject for a mere knowledge of the book work.

15958. Chairman.—We have had very different opinions on that subject; we have had some views expressed like yours, that the teaching is all a waste of time; and on the other hand we have had the view put before us that there are a great many children in Ireland who are the sons of farmers, that they have picked up a sort of practical knowledge of things without exactly understanding the why or wherefore, and that this book-learning gives them rather clearer ideas of what they have picked up in that way. Do you think there is any force in that view?—I think it does not at all pay for such a vast expenditure as £12,000. My idea, relative to agriculture, would be not to pay fees for it in this way. I would propose readers in agricultural subjects, bearing on elementary chemistry and botany, which lie at the root of agriculture. I would have these taught simply as readers, just the way that in a great number of our schools agriculture is taught. Look at the immense amount of useful work that could be done with £12,000—we could have forty or fifty experts throughout the country going about diffusing a great useful knowledge of agriculture.

15959. In what way would they diffuse it; would you have school plots?—Wherever it was available I would advocate having school plots and having practical work done.

15960. What sized plot would you consider should be sufficient?—The size should not be large, because I don't think we would be able to get it. If we had an acre it would be ample.

15961. Do you think half an acre would be enough?—It may not be enough, but it would be far better than none.

15962. Having got your half acre wherever you could, you would then advocate that a special itinerant teacher should go about to teach agriculture?—At present we would have to do that, but what I would advocate is that in training teachers special attention should be given to such subjects, because it would be extremely expensive to keep on such a work as that, having itinerant teachers going to and fro throughout the country year after year. So what I would do after a time is, I would like to change the course in the training colleges, in place of having it as it is at present, principally literary work; I would have the course in the training colleges limited to a kind of pedagogy, teaching how to give instruction in the various phases of school management, and also in practical agriculture.

15963. Would you go so far as to say that all Queen's Scholars trained at Marlborough-street should put in part of their time at Glasnevin?—I would.

15964. And make it essential that they should do so?—Yes, my lord.

15965. What do you say about grants for kindergarten desks?—I would be extremely glad that grants were given for these; grants are given for school desks in the case of vested schools at present; I don't see why grants should not be given for kindergarten desks in vested schools.

15966. What do you say about monitresses and pupil teachers?—At present the teacher is allowed by the rules to employ them for three hours in teaching; they also under the rules must get an hour's instruction in needlework; therefore, that is four hours of the school day put in. Then there is such a temptation for the monitresses to be employed in some of the literary work, in which they must pass in their annual examination, so there is a danger of their not getting full time at needlework, because they may be employed in teaching for three hours.

15967. Employed in teaching the ordinary subjects of the schools?—Yes.

15968. I don't quite know how monitors and monitresses are appointed?—They are selected by competition from the best pupils in the classes; they have to pass an examination, but my point is that there is a danger of their not getting the full hour in needlework, and as these are to be our future teachers, it is most important that this should be looked to.

15969. Are all persons who are candidates for the position of monitor those who are intended to become teachers afterwards?—Yes; that is one of the conditions.

15970. I think you did make some remarks on the alternative scheme; perhaps you would complete them if you have anything more to say?—I would recommend that the industrial programme be amended in these respects, that I would have simply one hour for instruction in needlework in place of the two hours at present, that I would allow composition subjects to be given by the inspector from some book prescribed by the Board, dealing with geographical subjects, such as the geographical readers that are in the market, that I would have a certain time given to arithmetic, as it seems to be a very favourite subject in the country, and that the course of instruction I would have in arithmetic would be an extremely practical and simple one, dealing with ordinary commercial transactions, bills of parcels, mental arithmetic, mental calculations, money bills, and questions of that nature, in place of questions true discount and alligation, and stocks and progression, and matters of that kind.

15971. Have you anything to say on the subject of physical exercise?—Yes, I would like calisthenic exercises to be taught in all female schools by teachers who had already learned these subjects in their training.

15972. To what extent are these exercises taught now?—Well, I have seen teachers coming from the training colleges, and they have simply put the children through motions with the hands.

15973. They don't carry these exercises so far in this country as I saw them do in Sweden, where little girls were taught to swing by ropes hanging from the ceiling?—No.

15974. Mr. Redington.—Is there any school in your district where manual work is taught?—Is that in the sense of Sloyd work?

15975. Yes?—No.

15976. Is there not such a school at Castlecomer?—There is a school at Abbey, in which Miss Sparks gives instruction to male pupils in woodcarving, but that is after school hours.

15977. It is not Sloyd work?—No, it is wood carving.

15978. You think that if a graduated system of woodwork were introduced it would be popular with the people; would they like to devote some hours of the week to this work?—I think it is extremely likely they would.

15979. Do you think the teachers would take to it?—That is a difficulty; there are only a minority of the teachers that would be able to give instruction in it at the present time, and only a minority of inspectors would be qualified to examine in it; therefore these things should be provided for.

15980. If facilities were given to the teachers to learn the systems of woodwork in operation in England do you think they would enter heartily into the scheme?—I think they would if they were not required to attend classes in Dublin, but

Limerick.

Mr. G.

in this matter is in the training colleges, of the future.

speaks of teaching cookery by peripatetic on Saturday afternoons, do you of that kind could be given to teachers for some time until we had our future teachers trained.

...—Would you adopt it as an teaching teachers in a locality the teaching both teachers and pupils?—Yes.

...—I did not quite understand about dressmaking, is it not sixth class now?—It is, but not taught subject. When we say dressmaking, connection with the sixth class we

... any women in the sixth class several

... that about your objection, that taught for one year only?—It was more machine and dressmaking combined that I sewing-machine is an important for girls, combined with it, that I would like to year in sewing-machine and dressmaking. they not learn the use of the sewing- year?—All we require is fifty lessons as I think it would be better to have it for year.

... laid great stress upon the necessity the average attendance for an assistant; fifty was the right number?—Sixty. your report you recommend that the average for an assistant be reduced to either forty pupils?—Yes.

... figure would you consider the right say sixty, but I would sooner have seventy.

... are aware that there can be two monitors in schools of over fifty, as well as the but there are certain circumstances that, though our Board is willing to ... teacher being third class is one, there may not be eligible pupils in the and the teacher may be inefficient and ...

... your opinion that cookery would be any rural school?—Yes, certainly, I very easy graduated course.

... to pupils of what ages, what classes?— pupils from the fifth, first stage.

... are aware that a fee is now given the fourth class, as well as the fifth?—

... would you prefer to have no fee in the —No, I would not say it was incorrect pupils in the fourth class.

... don't think them too young to learn?—

... is the age of pupils in the fourth class? considerably; I would say between ten and

... varies between town and country, per...

... the present regulations must your would only be in force where our Board arrangements with the Society for the of Women; but I would wish it to be made, even where there is not an expert. ... opinion is that in all schools there ... years' course of cookery?—Two years, ... more.

... confined to the simplest kind of cookery? ... year I would have making of bread, ... and other vegetables of that kind—

... many lessons a week?—One or two. ... the whole school year?—For part of

is a difference of opinion about that?—No, I have not given that special attention.

16005. At present the peripatetic teachers give twenty lessons?—Yes.

16006. I think it was given in evidence on Saturday that twenty lessons were not sufficient?—I would be inclined to have more than twenty lessons.

16007. Rev. Dr. Walsh.—Is there not a sufficient number of assistant teachers at present in your schools?—No, there are certain schools in my district in which I consider that the staff is insufficient to work the school efficiently, as I have mentioned in my last report.

16008. What would you specify as the most pressing need in the schools of your district?—The most pressing need I would consider, for the female schools, is cookery, one of the most pressing needs in all rural schools; then in town schools I would advocate that it would be very useful to have shorthand and type-writing, and things of that kind, if it could be done.

16009. Is drawing taught in all the schools?—No, it is not.

16010. Is it taught in a large proportion?—No, only in sixteen of the schools in my district, out of 171 in operation.

16011. Are sewing and dressmaking taught in many of them?—Sewing is compulsory in all our female schools, but there are three mixed schools in my district in which there is no workmistress, and I would like very much if something could be done to meet the want in those schools.

16012. Mr. Redington.—Do you agree with what Miss Spring Rice said, that the present average for a workmistress, twenty girls, ought to be reduced? —I would meet it in this way. I would consider it should be reduced; in all schools in which there was an average of ten we should give a grant for a workmistress. It need not be as large as the present grant, for £2 you would get it in the country.

16013. But in principle you agree with her that there should be a reduction of the average for workmistresses?—Certainly.

16014. Would you tell us how many schools there are in your district in which there ought to be a workmistress, but there is not?—Three.

16015. Mr. Strutherd.—What size are they?—Small schools—the average would range between ten and thirteen girls.

16016. Professor Fitzgerald.—And the school itself would have thirty or forty pupils?—The school itself would have thirty between male and females.

16017. Rev. Dr. Walsh.—No doubt, as to agriculture, what you say about expert teachers is very reasonable, it is very important that we should have them and expend money on them, but until we get the money for them and get them, would it not be better to teach the elements of agriculture, such as the nature of soils and the nature of manures and chemistry, and various matters connected with agriculture?—Would you be allowed to divert the £12,000 to other purposes?

16018. I think it would be far more likely to be diverted into the great gulf of the Treasury?—If that be the case I certainly would prefer that instruction would be given to them in elementary chemistry, botany and agriculture, such as we have at present.

16019. Mr. Molloy.—With regard to that average of sixty for an assistant teacher, you are aware, I presume, there was a time when an average of sixty secured the services of an assistant?—Yes.

16020. And even of fifty in a mixed school?—Yes.

16021. Perhaps you are also aware that the National Board have advocated quite lately the propriety of returning to that state of things as regards the average of sixty?—I was not aware of that.

16022. Is there a school of art in Limerick?—There is.

teachers?—I am quite sure that an arrangement could be made by which they could get instruction there on Saturdays for two hours, and I would like such a system very much and advocate it.

16024. What is the constitution of it, is it under a local committee?—Under a local committee.

16025. Mr. Harrington.—The same thing would apply to elementary science, such as chemistry?—There are science classes here in connection with the Science and Art Department.

16026. Mr. Molloy.—Is there a regular constituted committee for science classes in connection with the Science and Art Department?—Yes, I presume there is; I am not very well acquainted with the subject.

16027. Is there instruction given in the evening?—Yes.

16028. Then the National school teachers and monitors could attend such a class as that and qualify by examination, having received practical instruction in the subject?—Yes.

16029. You refer to drawing, that it ought to commence in second class, but I think you added you are not in favour of kindergarten drawing, and regarded that as a hindrance, now in what way?—The kindergarten drawing at present in the second class is on chequered paper, and then in the third class there are not chequered lines, I think it is therefore not a help to the child.

16030. Does not that observation extend very much to the ordinary writing, a junior pupil begins with lines and a more advanced pupil will be able to write without lines?—Well, it does to a certain extent, certainly, correspond with it, but I think there is a greater difference in the kindergarten.

16031. Professor Fitzgerald.—You think the child ought to be weaned off the lines in second class?—Yes.

16032. Chairman.—But you would let the child begin with lines in the kindergarten work?—Oh, certainly.

16033. Mr. Molloy.—Have you many examples of kindergarten classes in your district?—Five.

16034. They are chiefly in the city?—Yes.

16035. I presume there is one in connection with every one of the large convents?—Yes.

16036. Have you any lay schools in which kindergarten is carried out?—Not any except the model school, but I would advocate the extension of kindergarten, allow it to be taught in all schools in which there is an assistant, even if there is not an organised infant department.

16037. Would you not also advocate the extension of the kindergarten beyond the second class, let it run on through the higher classes—third and fourth?—We have it at present in the third class.

16038. Well, to a certain extent?—I would. I would wish it to be extended beyond it, and in that way you could have object lessons in elementary science subjects and geographical branches; for example, it would be a most useful thing to teach a fourth class with a globe before you, to teach them something about geography, the shape and position of the earth, and so forth.

16039. Have you worked out any plan by which that can be carried out?—Not in detail.

Professor Fitzgerald spoke, that considering a great many men go to Australia and America, it would be very useful that boys should be able to cook their own dinner?—Yes, but of course we look on cookery, like sewing, as an indispensable part of a woman's education, more her function, as it were.

16044. Mr. Molloy.—Did you say that sewing-machines required a two years' course of instruction?—In my opinion it would, for example, work like I showed here.

16045. That is sewing-machine by itself, not in connection with dressmaking?—Oh, sewing-machine by itself.

16046. Would you give a two years' course to the subject?—There are so many things in the sewing-machine, you can teach them, besides the mere adjustment of it, I would like a second year's course, and think it useful; for example, by the time you teach a girl how to put a needle in and take it out, the tension of the machine, threading the shuttle and winding the bobbin, there is no language course you might teach afterwards, such as working the treadle for a band and the working of a ... but for the mere adjustment one year would be ample.

16047. With regard to the average number required to qualify in a National school for the services of a workmistress, twenty, are you not aware that the twenty includes a large number of mere infant pupils?—Quite so.

16048. And they do not receive instruction in the needlework, therefore, practically it is limited to fifteen or even ten?—But then you may have national schools, in which the number of infants is quite limited, and the number of children in the higher classes is considerably larger.

16049. Would you leave the infants out of consideration and then say there should be an average of ten?—I think that would be a very good plan indeed.

16050. You advocate domestic economy readers, and also that the elements of science should appear in the reading books?—Yes.

16051. I don't know whether you ever met with the National School series, in which elements of science were conveyed in the fourth, fifth, and sixth books?—No, that must have been before my time as inspector.

16052. As a matter of fact there was such a series, the elements of chemistry and agriculture were taught in the ordinary "reader." With regard to the sewing, I think you made a statement that they did not get sufficient instruction in plain needlework?—Well, it was not so much that, as that I thought their time for training ought to be reduced to two hours; at present they teach for three hours. I think that too much also perhaps for girls of their tender age, considering the amount of work they have to learn.

16053. Of course you are aware now that a monitress who completes her time and comes forward to be a teacher, must qualify specially in that subject?—Quite so, a most important improvement.

16054. Therefore, if there was any likelihood in the past, there is very little in the future of an unqualified teacher, who had been a monitress, taking charge of the subject?—Quite so. But pupil teachers at present get no time during the day for work for themselves, they are employed teaching the whole day.

of grammar, and so on?—But that was one of the points which made the industrial programme not favourably received. The programme on composition or letter writing for the sixth class was a letter on a simple subject; the programme in the industrial scheme was of a much more ambitious nature. If you asked a child in the sixth class to write a letter on a simple subject, and asked the same child to write a letter describing—

16061. From Limerick to Unicorn?—Yes, there would be a considerable difference and a number of failures.

16062.—That was for sixth class, and the girls were supposed to have previously gone through a pretty complete course, it would not then be too much to expect them, if they had acquaintance with geography, to describe the progress of the vessel from one place to another?—Practically, that was one of the drawbacks in the alternative scheme.

16063. You referred to training colleges, have you personal experience of the inner life of any of the five under the National Board?—No, I have not.

16064. But you would recommend that all these subjects should be taught?—I would consider it most important that they should form an essential part of the training college course; and in place of the training college course being confined to a great extent to teachers getting a higher classification, that when these teachers come up their time should be almost wholly occupied in pedagogic studies.

16065. During the last week we visited one of the training colleges, with a farm of fifty acres attached to it, and the students are brought out and taught how to carry on agricultural operations there; of course you are aware the teachers in Marlborough-street attend classes at Glasnevin, where there are 175 acres, and the Kildare-place people have the same facility in connection with that farm, so really I think your idea is carried out?—Yes, but I would like it to be carried out still further. With the present literary programme in training colleges it seems very hard to give them sufficient time for both agricultural and also Sloyd work, which I would advocate too.

16066. Then you would propose to modify the Board's entrance curriculum for the training college, and the course through the training college?—Especially the course through the training college.

16067. Mr. Stuyvesant.—You have only three mixed schools in your district in which needlework is not taught?—Yes.

16068. It is not taught from want of a workmistress?—Yes.

16069. Do you think your district is favourably situated compared with others in Ireland in that respect?—I think it is.

16070. That is in other districts there would be a much larger number of schools in that condition?—Much larger.

16071. Do you think the number would be so great as to make it a matter of considerable cost to supply a workmistress to every school in Ireland?—I don't think it would involve a large expenditure.

16072. Supposing the other districts are much in the same position as yours, or only a little worse, then the total expenditure to supply a workmistress to every school in Ireland would not be much?—I don't think it would.

16073. Would that be a simple solution of the difficulty?—It would.

16074. Then you would send all male teachers to Glasnevin to go through a course there while they were at the training college?—Yes, or at some corresponding institution.

[illegible]

make them thoroughly qualified to teach the subject to their pupils.

16077. That would mean that these teachers should acquire an expert technical knowledge of agriculture?—Yes.

16078. But a great proportion of these teachers would be teaching afterwards in town schools, would they not?—I would not say a great proportion of them.

16079. Well you have several large towns in Ireland the teachers of which would naturally come from training colleges?—I think a considerable number of them would be teaching in rural schools; there are very few large towns in Ireland. I think the number of teachers that would be required for these large town schools would be a very small percentage of the total number trained.

16080. What is the teacher going to do in a rural school after he has acquired this knowledge of agriculture; you would have him teach the subject practically?—I would.

16081. In that case a school farm would be necessary?—Or some small school garden; even if he had half an acre of ground he would be able to explain the principles.

16082. That would be a form of technical instruction would it not, rather outside the scope of school work; you are teaching the art of practical agriculture?—Well, yes, I should say you are.

16083. Would it not suit your purpose equally well to have these teachers thoroughly instructed in the principles of science underlying agriculture, and to teach elementary science in the school instead of practical agriculture?—I think that it is most important for them to teach the elementary science that underlie agriculture, and I would prefer that to the present system; but of the two I would prefer, if it could be done, that there should be an expert to give technical instruction in agriculture.

16084. That the teacher in the rural school should be an expert, and give technical instruction in agriculture to boys of what age?—I should say to boys that would be eleven and over that.

16085. Do you think it would be any use giving technical instruction in agriculture to boys of eleven or twelve?—I think it would be most important to show them the proper way to put down potatoes and cabbages.

16086. Because we had it in evidence at the Munster Dairy School the other day that they don't think it desirable to have people enter their school under the age of sixteen?—That is expert evidence, but I would consider it an immense improvement if our teachers in training got a thorough instruction in elementary science.

16087. And that would be more in keeping with the ordinary work of an elementary school?—I think it would.

16088. And you would leave the technical instruction for more advanced institutions?—It may be better to do it.

16089. In that case your teacher would not require this course of practical training in agriculture in Glasnevin?—They would not.

16090. Would you confine the reading of the girls to these domestic economy readers?—I would not; I would make it optional with teachers to introduce them if they wished.

16091. Would you not make it compulsory that they should read something else as well?—I think it would be desirable that they should read another book, to relieve the monotony of it.

16092. I don't quite understand about the alternative scheme; if a girl takes the alternative scheme [illegible]

Limerick. Oct. 6, [illegible]. Mr. G. [illegible], LL.D.

...ate ?—Not in the present alternative

...may a girl of the sixth class presented ...rnative scheme obtain payment for ...e.

...rant can be made on account of arith... takes the alternative scheme ?—The the same as if she takes the ordinary ...her may give instruction in arithmetic, in the school in which the alternative ...ted.

...w many schools did you say you had ...n departments ?—Nine.

...you think a false impression is created ...ds by the term Kindergarten, they ...parate subject like drawing or reading ...e.

...uld it not be simpler to call them ...?"—Yes.

...let it be understood that in these ...ative the natural form of instruction ...ols ?—I see no objection to that.

...is to say that at that age the formal ...eaching and writing would be combined ...able amount of play and also exercises ...e training ?—Yes.

...referred in your report to agricultural Denmark; you say "the instruction ...d Denmark from being at the end of ...ry one of the poorest countries in ...one of the richest." Are you aware ...is not taught in any of the primary ...mark ?—No.

...dairying taught in any of the primary ...mark, and that the agricultural instruc... ...rk is given exclusively in much more ...tutions ?—Are those principles under... ...re of which you spoke taught in the ...mark ?

...—Elementary science is taught in ...ols, but it is not in the general pro... ...country.

...essor FitzGerald.—You have had ...kindergarten; do you think children ...trained in kindergarten are less able ...their school work than those that have ...d in kindergarten ?—I would say they ...better able to go on.

...experience has been that the children ...d in kindergarten are better than the ...?—I have been told by those who ...ng inspection that, as compared with ...who did not go through the kinder... those who had gone through it were

...ould have thought so, but there was ...ability to the contrary, at which I was ...l. Do you think if one in sixty was ...of teachers to children, that that ...sufficient number of teachers. One ...tion is one in seventy ?—Two in seventy. ...in seventy, I mean ?—Yes, two in sixty ...d advocate.

...you think it would be possible to in... ...occupations besides woodwork in the ...continuation of kindergarten occupa... ...ave not mentioned it here, but in a ...of schools in England we found that ...kergarten occupations children were

16111. Mr. Molloy.—Is there not a training class carried on in the Athenæum, Mr. Arnold Graves visited it ?—Oh, yes, there is in woodwork and the hand.

16112. Professor FitzGerald.—Because that would enable Limerick to act as a centre for teaching woodwork to neighbouring teachers ?—I think it is wood carving that is principally carried on there.

Most Rev. Dr. O'Dwyer.—Wood carving as an art is being taught in those classes.

16113. Professor FitzGerald.—You said that it would be desirable to make drawing compulsory ?—Yes.

16114. Would you allow teachers to teach that had no certificates ?—I would not; I would be rather inclined to train those teachers than to level down to others.

16115. Suppose a teacher were able to teach pupils sufficiently well to enable the pupils to pass, would not that be a good certificate for the teacher ?—I am very much afraid unless he was able to get a certificate in drawing he could not produce satisfactory results.

16116. If he produced satisfactory results, would you allow him to teach ?—I think if he were able to produce satisfactory results, he should be able to get a certificate in drawing.

16117. Would you compel him to go in for the certificate examination, because people who are past forty years of age don't like going in for examinations, but nevertheless they might be very well able to teach drawing ?—I think I would be inclined to make the teachers get certificates.

16118. The Board do not require the teachers in any of the convent schools to be certificated ?—No.

16119. Why should they apply any other rule to other schools ?—Because there is always a lady among the numerous ones in the convent who has got special instruction in that particular subject, and who is selected by the head of the community to teach it.

16120. But there is no test of her qualification except by finding out is she able to teach ?—The very fact of her being selected to teach the subject in the convent by the lady in charge, to my mind sufficiently proves that she is efficient to give instruction. The conductress would never select a lady to teach drawing in a convent school unless she had already given proof that she was competent.

16121. Then you think it would be desirable to compel teachers who are not at present certificated to pass some examination before they were allowed to teach drawing ?—I do, but as I said before, I would have a double test, the test of the examination; there would be a certain percentage for that, and then a certain percentage for how they taught it in the school, combining the two.

16122. Who is going to inspect the teaching in the school, do you think, the ordinary inspector, you said, or others ?—Yes.

16123. I see in your report you advocate botany to be taught in connexion with agriculture, and small fees to be paid for collections of plants, leaves, and minerals, do you think that would be a possible thing to require in all rural schools; do you think it would be possible to get the teachers to do that ?—I don't know that it would be possible in all cases, but where it was done I would certainly reward it.

16124. That is, you would encourage it, but not make it compulsory ?—I would not make it com-

16129. Rev. Dr. Evans.—We will come down, Dr. [illegible], to manual instruction; what manual instruction is given in your district?—Kindergarten, drawing, needlework, sewing [illegible], some instrumental music, if we would count all this under manual instruction.

16130. What have you included under the head of manual instruction in your report?—I only include woodcarving.

16131. Tell us, please, then, a little about it. "Apart from kindergarten," you say, "the only manual training at present in my district is the woodcarving class in connection with the boys' school at Abbeyleix." What is done there?—Miss [illegible] selects from the boys' school pupils who show some aptitude for woodcarving, and gives them instruction in a different building from the school, which belongs to Mr. [illegible], gives them instruction there twice a week; she disposes of the work done, and they get a certain proportion of the proceeds; she endeavours to stimulate and encourage them by that means.

16132. Do you examine that school?—I don't examine the woodcarving, but I examine in the National school; it is taught in a different building altogether and quite apart from the school work.

16133. Have you seen the work going on?—I have seen work going on, but the particular time I saw it there were not many engaged; it was in the evening, and when I saw it it was not exactly the time the class was being held, but there happened to be one or two working there.

16134. Have you seen the models that are in use there?—Yes, I have seen them; there would be a wardrobe or cabinet made by a cabinet maker, and there would be sent to Miss [illegible]'s school, and the panel would be carved on it and various little things of that nature.

16135. That is all the manual instruction that you refer to in your report and that you know to be done in your district?—Yes.

Limerick.
Oct. 4, 1887.
Mr. William E. Joyce, B.A.

16159. You think these object lessons should have special relation to the agricultural teaching in the country, and in the city other scientific subjects might be taken, of which local illustrations could easily be found?—Yes, my lord.

16160. You think they should be so selected as to develop the powers of observation of the children?—Precisely.

16161. And they should be illustrated by objects brought in by the children themselves?—Well, where possible.

16162. What length of course would you advocate; the course at present appears to be two years?—The sciences, such as mechanics and electricity, are at present divided into a two years' course, and are almost altogether inoperative, because they are taken in so few schools; but I would divide them more extensively, so that it would be possible to teach them in the fourth class to the end, perhaps, of a six years'

16170. And you think the requirem
and mensuration should be curtailed
year?—Yes.

16171. And you also think in the
course is much too extensive?—Yes,

16172. And the same applies to t
algebra?—Yes.

16173. What do you say about ki
should like to see kindergarten introd
school where there were two teachers
was qualified to teach it. I have be
always to introduce it into my school,
from so do so, because it would not
have not a separate organized infant de
matter of fact, I have attended lesson
convent and model school, but I did
any useful purpose, on account of thi

16174. You think that a higher
allowed to cover the expense of mater

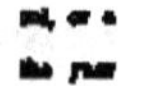

Limerick.

Oct. 4, 1886.

Mr. William B. Joyce, B.A.

of the teachers generally throughout the country?—No, sir, unfortunately I am in no way representative.

16302. Do you think the views you have put before us to-day are shared by the other teachers throughout the locality?—I cannot say that I believe they are.

16303. Your brethren differ from you, perhaps, in many points—they would not say ditto to all you have said to-day?—I am afraid they would not.

16304. Do you happen to know whether many of the pupils of National schools go on to higher schools and universities?—I could answer that for my own school. Out of 250 boys who left my school during the last two years, I find that eleven, or 4·4 per cent., went on for college, some of these would reach the university afterwards, perhaps most of them.

16305. Can you give any idea of the course which others took?—To labour, 11 per cent.; 19 per cent. went to trades; 7 per cent. went to business, that is to say, to shops; 10 per cent. went as porters and messengers; 16 per cent. went as clerks, that is to say, book-keepers; 4 per cent. went as farmers; 3 per cent. teachers, and to the civil service; 3 per cent. soldiers and sailors; 4 per cent. died; 4·4 per cent. to college; 13·2 per cent. left for other schools, and the remainder are unaccounted for or gone to America, they are a slight percentage.

16306. Would you think it right to deprive all those people of the opportunity of learning the grammar of their own language?—When boys pass in the fourth class, 79 per cent. leave our school, 21 per cent. remain; I don't see what very great good Ireland can get by teaching the remaining 21 per cent. the niceties of grammar.

16307. What would you substitute for grammar if you left it out?—I would substitute elementary science.

16308. Do you know anything of the books of the board forty years ago?—I have some of them.

16309. Do you know how largely they taught elementary science and natural history?—Yes, but I don't approve of the elementary science taught in them, I think there were some of the most silly things I ever read in my life in them. In describing the motion of the earth round the sun, a book describes the earth as coming to perihelion, and goes on to say only for the mercy of God, who is omnipotent, certain things would happen.

16310. Why was it that school books which taught science largely had to be changed for more literary readers?—Because the terminology was too difficult for children, and the teachers were not so conversant with scientific subjects as they are to-day.

16311. Then it comes to this, if we are going to do things right we should have new books to teach elementary science, and displace the whole series of readers?—I don't say we should go so far as that.

16312. Professor FitzGerald.—Did you not agree rather with Mr. Struthers in considering it undesirable that science should not be taught from books?—No, I would like to have books with oral instruction; but I would essentially have the practical teaching.

16313. So the science you propose to introduce now is quite different from the science given up?—Yes, essentially; there was no such thing as an experiment made in the former methods.

Mr. William Battle, B.Ag.

Mr. William Battle, B.Ag., Agricultural Instructor to the Trustees of the Limerick Endowment for Technical Education, examined.

16314. Chairman.—You are the agricultural instructor to the Trustees of the Limerick Endowment for Technical Education at Newcastle West in this county?—Yes, my lord.

16315. Will you tell us what faults you observed and what difficulties you encountered in your teaching?—The first fault I have to find is with the results system as a whole; throughout my teaching I am always falling across it somehow or other; first, because it tends to cram, the boys are taught the book, word for word, but when you come to ask them what is meant by the words in the book they cannot tell you at all.

16316. Will you tell us what the frequent result of the system is?—The frequent result of the system is that the clever boys that are able to quickly pick up the work are left alone because they can learn it quickly, and all the attention is paid to the dull boys to pull them up so that the teacher can pass them.

16317. That evidence applies only to the agricultural instruction?—That is as far as my experience goes.

16318. That does not involve the element of attendance in the ordinary school. I understand that if a boy has not made the requisite number of attend-

16321. Do the courses at Glasnevin commend themselves as convenient times for the teachers in this part of the country?—As far as the experience of teachers in my district, sir, I think they might be rearranged with benefit to the teachers. One of my teachers wished to go to Glasnevin, but the course did not suit him, so he did not care to go, and there he is left wanting that knowledge he otherwise would have.

16322. What do you think about the text book?—The text book is an admirable book in its way, but to teach the boys in a National school, it is one of the worst books you ever laid hold of. It is a book all consisting of practical facts, that is not the book you want, you want the principles underlying the science. You cannot learn farming out of a book. You want to teach them the science so that they will understand the practice afterwards.

16323. You don't think the illustrations in the book are sufficiently good?—Very bad indeed, and very few of them.

16324. What do you say about the gardening section?—It is far too much drawn out; there is a whole list of flowers, and the head master himself is unable to pronounce their nomenclature, and very likely the inspector cannot sometimes, such names as Bub-

Limerick.
Oct. 4, 1897.
Mr. William [illegible], B.Sc.

be certainly the more satisfactory method, because that would ensure intelligent teaching; he would not examine mechanically; he should be a man who understood agriculture thoroughly.

16343. Would it not be easy for any intelligent inspector to learn a sufficient amount of agriculture to examine children in elementary schools?—I am doubtful whether he could.

16344. Might I ask in what part of England you were teaching agriculture before you came here?—I never taught it at all, I just graduated at Durham University last year.

16345. There is an agricultural course in connection with the University?—Yes.

16346. Is it attended by elementary teachers to any extent?—Not the degree course, but there are Saturday classes for elementary teachers.

16347. And are the Professors sent on Saturdays into the rural districts of the county?—No; teachers come from the rural districts to the centre, and their expenses are paid and classes given free. That is done by the County Council.

16348. CHAIRMAN.—Have not the County Council experimental plots?—The Northumberland County Council have.

16349. Mr. REDINGTON.—Did the elementary teachers come in large numbers?—I won't say they came in large numbers, but they came in satisfactory numbers.

16350. As a result do they teach agriculture in their schools?—I am not aware that agriculture is taught in any schools, or in very few, except under the Science and Art Department.

16351. If you consider it a good thing to teach it to boys of the third and fourth class here, why is it not taught in England?—Because I think England is much more a manufacturing country, and agriculture is not so important in the schools as in Ireland.

16352. I thought agriculture was England's greatest industry?—It is, but the parents of the children who are engaged in other industries would complain if their children were taught agriculture.

16353. Mr. STRUTHERS.—There are large districts purely rural?—Yes, and I have no idea why it is not taught there.

16354. Mr. REDINGTON.—Will you kindly explain to the Commission what are your duties in connection with your present position?—I have eight schools that I teach at, and I go to each of these schools once a week, except the Newcastle school, where I go three times, and to two other schools twice. I teach one lesson a week as a rule; a class nearly as possible one an hour, or I may teach two lessons of half an hour each on agriculture to the boys. Of course I teach in conformity with the rules of the Board the subjects that the Board require.

16355. You teach in the ordinary school hours?—Yes.

16356. CHAIRMAN.—Are these National schools?—Yes.

16357. Mr. STRUTHERS.—And the pupils are examined?—They are examined by the inspector.

16358. Mr. REDINGTON.—You are working under the Trustees of the Limerick Endowment for Technical Education?—Yes.

16359. And Newcastle West is your centre?—Yes.

16360. Mr. MOLLOY.—How long are you connected with Irish agricultural schools?—Just eight months.

16361. And the extent of your experience is confined to eight schools?—Yes.

16362. On what then did you base the statement that the rural school system was all wrong; was that confined to agriculture alone?—Agriculture alone. I cannot speak as to other subjects. I don't say that it is badly taught, I don't say that it is the teacher's fault, but I think that the system tends to its being badly taught.

16363. In Newcastle West the head master is first of first, is he not?—Yes.

16364. Would you say that he teaches the subject badly?—I don't say that he teaches it badly; he teaches it intelligently as far as possible, but then the thing put before them is that they have got to earn the salary, and it does not pay them to teach the subject intelligently. You may explain everything, but it would be a waste of time, for you could not then get through all the work that has to be done. This

16365. Mr. REDINGTON.—It here it is the system you are criticising, not the individual teacher?—The system.

16366. Mr. MOLLOY.—Are there school gardens or plots attached to the eight schools you attend?—In just one, the Castlemahon school.

16367. Then your instruction is theoretical?—Exclusively theoretical, except in so far as making them collect me the grasses and a few flowers, and bringing specimens which I show to them.

16368. Have you introduced any Saturday classes for the teachers in agriculture?—No, there was no encouragement for me to do so; I suggested it, but the teachers did not seem to want it, so there was no further mention of it.

16369. In how many of the eight schools are these collections of grasses carried out?—In one of the schools there are diagrams of the grasses, but there are no actual collections of the grasses themselves in any of the schools. I made the boys collect the grasses themselves and bring them to me, but there are no dried and mounted specimens in any of the schools.

16370. Professor FITZGERALD.—Is it not much better to get the boys to collect the grasses?—It is a splendid thing, then they learn to know them.

16371. Mr. MOLLOY.—In the Durham Agricultural College there is practical agriculture taught; what is the duration of the course?—For the B.Sc. it is three years.

16372. Is it residential?—Yes; you are obliged to take classes at the college.

16373. Mr. REDINGTON.—Is it the Durham University?—It is a college under the University.

16374. CHAIRMAN.—Is it at Newcastle-on-Tyne?—Yes.

16375. Mr. MOLLOY.—Is there a large farm attached on which agriculture is carried on?—Yes.

16376. And during the three years you attended there?—Well, you go out to see the farms of the district, there are no fixed hours.

16377. The students of agriculture do not take an active and practical part in working those farms?—No; they go to see operations performed occasionally.

16378. You recommend the use of a text-book?—I do not think you can do without a text-book very well.

16379. But the present text-book you think might be improved?—It may be improved greatly.

16380. You are not quite right, I may tell you, in your statement about the inspectors under the Board, that no steps are taken to secure information in agriculture on their part before commencing to inspect schools in that subject?—I cannot find the rule.

16381. How many hours in the week would your duties extend over?—Twelve hours a week actual teaching, exclusive of travelling about.

16382. Mr. STRUTHERS.—You teach in these eight schools; have you any other form of agricultural teaching?—I give lectures to the farmers of the district.

16383. That occupies more time than the school teaching?—No, the school teaching is the larger part.

16384. Suppose you had to teach agriculture in the district, which would you think the more important, to teach classes of lads of seventeen and upwards, or to teach boys in school of eleven or twelve?—Certainly, the grown lads.

16385. Don't you think that at eleven or twelve all you can do is to give them training of the intelligence and simple observation?—That is all you can do. I agree with you.

16386. And it is rather a mistake to call the teaching at that stage agriculture?—Certainly, it is very elementary agriculture.

16387. Would it not be better to call it elementary science leading up to agriculture?—Yes, that is certainly what I should call it.

16388. Would you call agriculture a science?—Yes.

16389. Would you not rather call it the application of many sciences to farming?—Well, I have heard it called science, and I am accustomed to call it science.

16390. But might you not take that view of it, that it is the application of a great many sciences to the particular industry of farming?—It is.

16391. And the application of science to any particular industry is technical education?—Yes.

16392. So that agriculture would be more suitably taught in technical colleges?—It would as agriculture.

16393. Although in the elementary school you might have elementary science leading up to the work of the technical colleges?—Yes.

16394. As to your actual work, you teach the boys agriculture, just as the National Board teachers would?—Oh, no.

16395. I mean you teach the boys for the purpose of passing in agriculture?—Not at all.

16396. These boys you teach are put forward for grants, are they not?—Yes, but my teaching is not at all with that object, but to improve their knowledge of agriculture.

16397. But still the fact remains that these boys are put forward?—Yes.

16398. Are they taught agriculture by anybody else besides you?—By the schoolmaster.

16399. Then your teaching supplements the schoolmaster's, and is not in place of it?—Certainly not.

16400. I misunderstood you. Then you use a text-book which you mentioned?—The Downton course I use myself.

16401. Instead of the text-book of the Board?—Yes.

16402. That is allowable, is it not?—Well, I am not bound to use any text-book at all, but the way I do it is, I use this text-book, but so far as that it agrees with the programme of the Board.

16403. Must the ordinary teacher use the book?—He is compelled, I think, to take the text-book of the Board; at the examination the inspector would examine on the text-book of the Board.

16404. It comes to this—that probably these boys you are teaching from the books you use are also being taught agriculture from the text-book of the Board?—Yes.

16405. Professor FitzGerald.—Is there any way by which your teaching is tested at all?—No, I don't think there is any way by which my teaching can be tested.

16406. You think it is desirable to encourage boys to make collections?—Yes, the most desirable thing possible.

16407. Do you think that the elementary science underlying agriculture is the kind of thing a teacher could teach?—I think they are quite capable of doing it if they had the training in it.

16408. Do you think many of them would do it?—Yes, I think they would.

16409. Do you think they would come in to be taught how to do it?—Yes, I think they would.

16410. Rev. Dr. Evans.—Have you reason to believe that instruction, such as you give, really stimulates and promotes agricultural progress?—Well, I do in a certain way. I am trying to teach the boys why certain things are done, and I think they will do those things better if they know why they are done.

16411. And you believe that if such teaching were spread over the country it would help on agriculture?—I think it would; many people tell me in Ireland that there has been some result from the past teaching of the Board, and I think if it was continued there would be a similar result.

16412. Mr. Macnaghten.—I suppose you have found the boys intelligent and appreciative?—Yes, as a rule they listen very quietly to you and seem to take an interest in the work.

16413. Do you think that making the instruction practical has increased their interest in agricultural teaching?—Certainly, I think it has.

Limerick. Oct. 1, 1897. Mr. William Bartley, B.A.

Mr. J. R. Bradshaw, Teacher, Cappamore National School, Co. Limerick, examined.

16414. Chairman.—You are the principal teacher of the Cappamore Male National School?—Yes, my arithmetic, mental-arithmetic, and other useful calculations of that nature. I don't see the use of making

Mr. J. R. Bradshaw.

schools?—Practical cottage gardening, construction, and drawing.

16427. With respect to gardening, what would you advocate?—There should be a suitable plot attached to every school.

16428. How much?—Half an Irish acre, and then, of course, the present book I consider very ill-arranged altogether.

16429. What book?—The present text-book for agriculture, "Practical Farming," as it is called, especially the new edition, is entirely too extensive, especially the portion on cottage-gardening, it contains a lot of matter about flowers and growing that I consider altogether beyond the scope of children.

16430. Rev. Dr. Evans.—And you believe that is the mind of teachers generally?—Of rural teachers.

16431. Chairman.—How do you think the teaching of agriculture could be made better, more effective than it is at present?—As regards ourselves I would say that perhaps we stick too much to the book.

16432. Are you a practical man yourself?—In a way I am; I have a very small plot of ground, my garden consists of only about two perches, yet on that I contrive to grow five or six sorts of vegetables. I give some of the plants to the boys, make them sow them in their own little gardens, and bring me back plants when they are grown. I ask them did they ever eat cauliflowers, and if a boy says he did not, I say, "you should grow some." As a matter of fact I grow cauliflowers myself and give away some of the plants to the boys. With regard to flowers, there is not a window in my school in which there is not a box of geraniums; I cut slips off them for the boys, and that engenders a love of flowers. If cottage gardening was taught to the fourth class it would be a decided advantage, because only 27 per cent. of our pupils remain after passing in fourth class, and if they take away only the knowledge which is at present given of crops and other matters of that kind they can never put them into practical work; they are too young, whereas they could pretty well manage a little garden.

16433. Could you form any idea what percentage of your boys go to farm work. I don't mean mere labourers?—Between farmers and labourers I would say nearly 80 per cent.

16434. Men who are likely to own and manage a farm themselves in after-life?—I would say not more than about 30 per cent.

16435. I suppose you think there is room for improvement in the farming in your district?—Unquestionably; as a matter of fact I go to some well-skilled farmer myself to gain some knowledge. There is a very eminent gardener living not far from me who is a friend of mine, and I got him to inspect my garden the other day, and he gave me very good advice, and I have free access to the gardens which he manages. But there is one matter which has been mentioned here by men who can perhaps talk better on agriculture than I, and that is the cultivation of grasses. I do not attach much value to that; I would attach more value to a person knowing the nature of the soil and the grass seed suitable for it. I showed two rye-grasses the other day to a practical farmer's son, and he could not tell me which was which. "Which of them," I asked, "has awns on it?" He pointed it out at once. And I said, "Which does your book tell you that is?" And he said "Italian rye-grass." "Very well." I

which is three miles distant. There was a kitchen set up there in the late inspector's time, and they practically teach it there; but the great difficulty would be in teaching cookery, that when the girl goes home she cooks under different conditions, she has a range perhaps in the school and she has an open fireplace at home.

16439. Why should you not have an open fireplace, if that is the sort of thing she has to deal with afterwards?—The very same objection would apply; several cooks would prefer the range.

16440. Professor Fitzgerald.—But they can teach without a range?—It could be cooked in the same place as she has at home.

16441. Chairman.—I suppose that is one of the reasons why it is so difficult to teach grammar, because the children find at home a different way of talking to what you teach them at the school?—Unquestionably; when a boy commits an error in grammar, I always just repeat a wrong one, and he sees his error very quickly; then I will ask him why one is wrong and the other right.

16442. In what case can the cooperation of the teachers be expected?—If the subject introduced is such as they think will be suitable to their schools and if no part of the present grant—I suppose we are a little bit selfish—if no part of the grant for educational purposes would be devoted to the new matter.

16443. You think new matter should be paid for separately?—Yes, my lord.

16444. And should not be introduced in such a way as to diminish the earnings of the teacher?—No, as taking old men like myself, our position may become insecure; managers may take it into their heads to displace us, and I think it would be very hard on a man of my service to send me out, because I could not do woodwork. I don't believe there is the least danger of it with my present manager, but it may happen; if there was a change of managers to-morrow I may get a coach to deal with, who may be bicycle-mad, and run me out.

16445. From whom do you think the keenest opposition may be expected?—I would say from the parents.

16446. Why do you say so?—That is my experience.

16447. But you have not had the thing introduced?—I look at the past, and when we consider that the alternative scheme for girls' schools was one that might be considered to take specially, and I have never yet met a parent who approved of it.

16448. That is quoted to us constantly, but I do not think myself it is quite parallel. The only experience we have had of woodwork in the country parts of Ireland was at Lismore, and I put the question to the gentleman we were examining whether the parents objected; and he said before the thing was started some of them did object; but that now there are 34 pupils at this work in the school, and only one parent objected?—They actually do object; I know it as an actual fact, and as the father of children I am very sorry it was introduced into the girls' school.

16449. You are talking of sewing. I am talking of manual work?—I apprehend parents would regard the Sloyd in the very same light; they say that they send their children to our schools to be made scholars of.

is the only subject
Oh, no, [illegible]

to send them away by parcel post, and I don't think those things would be so much objected to. But when a man wants to make his son a carpenter he would send him to the proper tradesman.

16489. But the object of woodwork in a school is not to make a man a carpenter?—It would be so understood.

16490. After they had been accustomed to have cardboard work carried on in school, would not parents be willing that their children should advance and do a little woodwork?—I don't see that the two things are so akin.

16491. Woodwork is a little more advanced?—The material is very difficult; it is very easy for young children to take up a bit of cardboard and turn it when they could not take up an edged tool.

16492. But it is not the young children we ask; would it not be well for children in the fifth and sixth class to have something to do to keep up their manual dexterity, and get them into the habit of making things to scale—do you think it is desirable to get children to make things accurately to scale?—That would be going very far.

16493. Supposing you were to make a box to scale, that the child was to make a drawing of the box first, and then was to cut it out accurately, and then put it together so as to make the box of the size originally intended, do you not think that would have an educational value?—It should be a training in accuracy.

16494. And would it not be encouraging children to construct things—children at present take a pleasure in destroying things, and is it not desirable they should take a pleasure in constructing things?—Unquestionably.

16495. So that possibly parents might ultimately learn there was some educational value in this woodwork?—They may, but at the same time I don't think they would.

16496. Do you not think it is desirable to encourage children to observe what is going on around them in the fields?—On the contrary, I have said that I do.

16497. Don't you think getting them to make collections of the flowers they see in the banks, of the different kinds of grasses, will tend to make them observe what is going on around them?—I daresay it would tend to cultivate their observation.

16498. And do you not think it would be desirable to get them to observe whether injuries to plants were caused by animals or fungus?—Oh, yes, I tell them that the green fly will destroy their roses.

16499. Do you not think it would be desirable to distinguish between the injuries caused by the green fly and by red blight?—I am not so advanced in botany as that, but I know the green fly is destructive.

16500. For instance, it makes an important difference in spraying plants whether it is an animal or a fungus you are going to destroy; would it not be desirable that children's attention should be called to that sort of thing?—Undoubtedly.

16501. And would not one of the ways be to get them to make a collection of plants that were injured by fungi, and of plants that were injured by insects?—That would be a right good thing.

16502. And that would have an educational value?—I should think so.

16503. Do you think the teachers would be able to get the children to make collections in that way?—I don't see any great difficulty that could arise. As a matter of fact, I brought leaves and potato stalks into the school myself, and showed with a magnifying glass those that were blighted, and made the children look at the spores.

16504. Rev. Dr. Evans.—Do your young people understand such words as multiplier and multiplicand and product?—Certainly.

16505. Have you ever had any difficulty in making the children understand such words?—There might be some difficulty, but it is not a great difficulty.

16506. And divisor and dividend and quotient?—Yes, if you take it quietly to explain it.

16507. Is there any harder word in grammar than them? Is it harder to understand "a preposition," or the names of the tenses?—I don't see any difficulty in the matter at all. They sometimes confound two tenses, the perfect and pluperfect, and I had a very disagreeable reminiscence of that, because one of my boys of eleven got a failure in his grammar for that.

16508. I wish some of you experienced teachers would produce a book to show us how grammar should be taught?—You are not to take me at all as objecting to grammar; on the contrary, it is one of my pet subjects that I always liked intensely. I consider two of the grammars on the Board's list are excellent books—Edwards', and the other one by Mr. Strong. In Sullivan, of course, there is something very good here and there, but there is a lot of stuff in it that boys need not learn.

16509. Have you ever found it difficult to get boys to understand "plus" in algebra?—Never.

16510. Why should it be difficult to understand "pluperfect," which is simply plus added to "perfect"?—Oh, I am an advocate of grammar.

THIRTY-SEVENTH PUBLIC SITTING.—TUESDAY, OCTOBER 5TH, 1897.

Limerick. Oct. 5, 1897.

AT 2 O'CLOCK, P.M.,

At Cruise's Hotel, Limerick.

Present:—THE RIGHT HON. THE EARL OF BELMORE, G.C.M.G., in the Chair; THE RIGHT HON. C. T. REDINGTON, M.A.; REV. HENRY EVANS, D.D.; REV. HAMILTON WILSON, D.D.; PROFESSOR G. F. FITZGERALD, F.T.C.D.; STANLEY HARRINGTON, ESQ., M.A.; W. R. J. MOLLOY, ESQ.; CAPTAIN T. B. SHAW; and J. STRUTHERS, ESQ., M.A.;

with J. D. DALY, ESQ., M.A., Secretary.

The Most Rev. DR. O'DWYER, *Bishop of Limerick*, examined.

The Most Rev. Dr. O'Dwyer.

16511. CHAIRMAN.—I believe, my lord, there are a few points on which you wish to submit your views to the Commission with regard to primary schools. Will you explain why you think there is of necessity a difference between the character of the teaching in female and male schools?—So far as needlework is concerned, I think it is generally admitted that it is an essential part of the education of the working girl, and, to some extent, cookery, but I don't know of anything that is in a boy's education that corresponds precisely with those two things in a girl's education. There is no manual work which every boy is supposed to devote himself to in his life corresponding to the needlework of the girls. For that reason I think needlework might be taught in the schools generally, needlework and cookery; washing would come under domestic economy. Naturally these things would be taught girls by their own mothers, and, at first, it does not appear to be the proper function of a school to do what should be done by people in their homes. I think, though, the public estimation and the opinions of the country have put needlework on a special footing, and, I think, now, the tendency of people's minds is in favour of doing something in the schools for cookery and washing, though, theoretically, there may not be an obligation on the schools to do it.

16512. You think that these subjects you have mentioned would be sufficient to teach in the country schools?—Oh, yes, and perhaps too much; needlework, I think, should be taught in every school, town and country. Cookery might be taught in the larger country towns. There is an intermediate class of schools, between the urban schools and the ordinary rural schools. I think cookery could be very well taught in these. And then, as for washing I am not so sure about it; I think in a city, and in the larger places it might be tried. I have been asking some of the Nuns about it, and they said that if the National Board approved of it, they would be very glad to try it, and they think it could be usefully tried.

16513. Do you think anything could be added in town schools?—Yes. I just made a suggestion that possibly typewriting would be a useful thing for some of the girls in town to learn. I have heard of some girls earning their bread by typewriting, getting situations as clerks, and also shorthand might be taught. I think in some of the Convent schools, the higher Convent National schools in the city that these things might be taught, as entirely voluntary subjects.

16514. They are not taught at present?—No.

MR. REDINGTON.—They could be taught under our system; a result fee is given.

CHAIRMAN.—We saw typewriting, I think, being taught in Kilkenny in a Convent school, but not shorthand.

16515. MR. REDINGTON.—Typewriting, shorthand and laundry-work can now be taught; there is a fee of 2s. 6d. for typewriting, for shorthand, and for laundry-work?—We have no such classes here in any of our schools.

16516. CHAIRMAN.—Do you think that, as a broad principle, it should not be attempted in primary schools to teach any art?—Yes, I think that is pretty evident.

16517. And you don't include typewriting under that head?—You see I make no exception in these matters of girls' education; I merely state general principles there.

16518. But otherwise you are against technical education being given in the schools?—Quite so, that is in primary schools.

16519. You think that the teaching in primary schools should be to cultivate the faculties of the pupils?—Quite so.

16520. And to prepare them for receiving technical education after they leave school?—Yes.

16521. Do you think, my lord, that there should be any difference in the class of education given in rural and urban schools?—Oh, yes.

16522. In what way?—In an urban school the practical and manual teaching should have regard to the probable careers of the boys—urban pursuits and mechanical occupations; in the country it should be mainly agricultural.

16523. The elements of what science, would you say, would bear upon agricultural teaching?—Well, obviously botany, something about plant life and chemistry, something about manures, about the soils, geology would come in, and something about animals, I suppose, biology.

16524. Do you think there are any text-books at present on the subject simple enough for the purpose?—Well, I am not in a position to give the Commission reliable information on the text-books that are in existence. I have seen several of them; I have seen some by Dr. Tanner, and I liked the general style of them, but I cannot say any more about them; as to their accuracy or sufficiency I cannot say, but they struck me as being in general the style of book I should like to see put into the hands of children in country schools.

16525. Do you think you would confine the teaching in the boys' schools in the rural districts to the first principles of science?—Oh, entirely.

16526. And not go deeply into them?—But I should think that the text-books that were prepared, if they were prepared for the purpose and the teaching, should all get a practical turn.

16527. How would you carry that out? Would you be for having a class-room built, attached to the school?—If you were preparing a lesson, say on fungi in plants, I think that could be all explained to children in reference to the potato blight, and so with regard to other things. I would give all the illustrations that were in the text-book a practical and useful turn, so that, without formally setting about giving them information, I would give it to them.

16528. Would you be in favour of school plots or gardens?—I should not attach any great importance to them for the purpose of teaching agriculture; my idea is that if the schoolmaster knows his business, and takes an interest in it, he will be very much in-

Limerick.

Oct. 3, [illegible].

The Most Rev. Dr. O'Dwyer.

dependent of anything like a school plot. On the roadside he can teach the children all he wants to teach. On the fields about the school or in the neighbourhood he can show them everything he wants to show about agriculture without these school plots, and I think there is a danger that these would degenerate into useful places for teachers, they would be used more for the growing of vegetables for himself rather than for the instruction of his pupils.

16529. Do you think it would not be useful that the children should see how the teacher grew vegetables for himself?—I don't think so; I don't think that is the proper function of the school at all; that is what I consider technical agriculture as distinguished from the principles of agriculture; I would rather take a class of children out into the fields, where the men are digging or ploughing, or doing any other agricultural operations, and explain to the boys the use of it, and how it affected the growth of plants.

16530. I think your evidence comes to this, that while you think that the elements and the first principles of these sciences might very well be taught by the teachers, they would not be competent to teach agriculture as an art?—No, I think not.

16531. And it should not be attempted?—You see if a child comes to school and a teacher goes to teach him how to grow potatoes, and that child goes home to his father, he has been looking at his father doing the thing all his life long, and in a great many cases the teacher would be naturally laughed at by the people, and the parents would find they knew a great deal more about these practical things than the teachers.

16532. Would you carry your objection so far that if there was a teacher, as there are some few teachers, who really have a taste for this sort of thing, and have a small plot, that they should be prevented from utilising their gardens for teaching?—No, I should not put on any prohibition, but one of the great defects in general about the National Board system is that it is an absolutely uniform system all over the country, a cast iron kind of system, and there is very little room for initiative left to individual teachers. I should be very glad indeed to encourage everything of the kind on the part of individual teachers here and there, who were competent.

16533. Have you anything to say about the inspectors in regard to this matter?—Yes; I think that the inspectors have the most part to do with the whole thing. I don't think it is sufficient for a man to go into a school and examine what is done actually there and report good, bad, or indifferent, as it may be, but I think he ought to be the adviser of the teachers, he ought to direct the teaching of the people, make suggestions to the teachers, and generally do the part of the head master in his district, to cut out the work for them. And that being so, I think he ought to have an absolutely thorough knowledge of everything that is taught in the schools.

16534. Do the teachers think that the inspectors at present are capable of examining in agriculture?—Well, I will give you some little experience I have. I happen to be a member of a Board of Technical Education for the city and county, we disburse a small fund that was created here under the Educational Endowments Commission. It was originally an agricultural fund, and we thought the fairest thing to do was to employ it in promoting agricultural teaching in the county, so we formed a centre at Newcastle West, and grouped a number of schools there, and proceeded to get an agricultural teacher to teach agriculture in these rural schools. I went out there, and I met a number of the teachers, and I questioned them as to how the thing was done actually, and it was very amusing. The teachers told me that an inspector would come into the school and open the text-book. And, supposing gardening was the thing, he would say to the boys "will you tell me six hardy annuals that may be grown in a gentleman's garden?" and the children would then give out a list of flowers, about which they knew absolutely nothing. I said to the teachers:—"But why would not this gentleman ask a commonsense question about the garden himself?" "For the very best reason, because he did not know it." And the teachers all told me that was the system; here and there, of course, there are inspectors who know these things thoroughly well, but the teachers tell me that, as a rule, they don't, and the upshot of it is that there is a book of Mr. Carroll's on agriculture, and so many pages of this has to be got off by the boys in the Fourth Class, and so many pages in the Fifth Class, and they stand or fall by that. That is the whole system of examination in the teaching going on in schools. If the ordinary teachers of the schools are to teach agriculture as an art then it seems to me to be a self-evident thing that they should know it, and I think that is an impossibility. I think it is an impossibility to require all male teachers in Ireland to know agriculture as an art. Then, if they know it, they should know it in such a way as to command the respect of the locality in which they are teaching. I don't think that is possible amongst the farmers of our country, and, therefore, I think it is impossible for the teachers to teach it. I think the system of extern teachers coming in, naturally, at least into the schools, is objectionable, whatever is done in a school should be done by its own staff, and if a subject is of such a nature that any average boy is required to learn it, then every average teacher ought to be able to teach it, and every inspector ought to be able to examine it, and I don't think that ever can be true of agriculture as an art, and if you are to teach it it can only be by teaching principles.

16535. Having taught principles, you think the time for teaching it as an art is after the boys have left school, and in a different kind of school?—Yes, I think in every county there ought to be technical schools for agriculture, in certain localities; the teaching of the schools ought to be such as to lead the boys gradually up to the door of the technical school, so that they would be ready for the masters there when they left the primary school.

16536. As regards the teachers, do you think that agricultural science should be made an important part of their course of studies when they are in the training colleges?—Oh, yes.

16537. Would you make it compulsory on them to obtain a certificate?—Certainly.

16538. Then you would go so far as to say that in the case of persons coming on to be teachers, nobody should be considered a competent teacher until he had got a certificate in that subject as well as others?—Certainly, with regard to teachers. I saw it stated in the report of the Recess Committee, that they made the teaching of agriculture compulsory in all the primary schools of France some years ago, but they gave three years' notice before they brought the teaching into force, and in that time the teachers were expected to prepare themselves for teaching.

16539. As regards the inspectors, how would you deal with them in this matter?—They are chosen by examination, and I would so select the subjects of their examination as to secure that they were competent to do this work.

16540. Coming to the subject which we are now particularly inquiring into, the sort of manual teaching which is known as woodwork, what is your lordship's opinion on that subject?—I should like to see in some centres in the country an experiment tried with woodwork as an experiment. I have great doubts as to the advisability of its general introduction in our country schools. Perhaps in the larger towns in every county you might form a centre and bring the senior classes there on Saturdays or off days from the different schools and have a class of woodwork; it would be a very useful thing, extremely desirable for the people, but I have doubts as to whether it would be practicable; that is the only misgiving I have about it, that is for the country districts.

b11.—Well, you

wards the case of
vents falling in
owns I should

country schools, that is the only remark I should like to make.

16847. What has your lordship to say about practical teaching in urban male schools?—In male schools, I think the most universally useful subject

Limerick.

Oct. 6, 18[illegible].

The Most Rev. Dr. O'Dwyer.

Limerick.

Oct. 5, [illegible].

The Most Rev. Dr. O'Dwyer.

think, consult their wives before they make their purchases.

16354. Would you have male inspectors for literary work in female schools?—I don't see why you should not try a few female inspectors for everything. I don't see why an educated lady might not go into the female school and examine a child in everything.

16355. You would not introduce anything in the way of science into the female schools?—Oh, no.

16356. Then I think the summary of the principal points you wish to bring out, is, that a clear conception should be formed of the precise matter of practical instruction, which is to be taught in the schools, and then that the course of studies in the training colleges and the examination for inspectorships should be changed so as to secure in the ordinary staff of the National system competent teachers and inspectors?—Quite so.

16357. In the male schools you think there should be elementary science with a bearing on practical agriculture in the country districts, and mechanical arts in towns, together with drawing in towns. These constitute the principal part of the practical teaching?—Yes.

16358. You think also that as the Intermediate has diverted the best boys and the best teachers of the Christian Brothers from such practical work, it is important to supply it in the National schools?—Yes, with regard to that I should like to say that I really think it is a very great pity, and a great loss to the country that the Christian Brothers' schools have been forced into this Intermediate competition. In the cities they are the great teachers. In this city the Christian Brothers teach 1,844 boys out of a total of 3,131 going to primary schools; no reform in the primary schools will do much more for us in the cities, than touch the fringe of the thing, unless the Christian Brothers are brought into it; but, if the Christian Brothers, in order to support themselves and maintain their schools, are driven into the Intermediate system, as they have been driven, then of course they cannot do this work of practical teaching.

16359. I don't quite follow how they have been driven into the Intermediate?—In this way—the cost of education is becoming higher every year, the competition between schools is becoming keener, and the Christian Brothers, if they were to maintain the high position that they had for their schools relatively in the country must have rewards, must get money. The Government of the country will give them none through the primary system, and so they say:—"Here is this competition under the Intermediate, open to all comers, we will go in and put our boys in under this and earn plenty of results fees," and so they are doing. The Christian Brothers earn a very large proportion of all the results fees got under the Intermediate, I think they earned £13,000 or £14,000 last year. In that way they are able to support themselves and maintain their schools on a very high level of the style of education that they are giving. In that way the Christian Brothers are driven into the Intermediate and diverted from their own legitimate work as primary teachers.

ruined that child's career, he is nothing, he has got no education of any kind, intermediate or primary, and that is what is happening, and the people don't seem to observe it. In the Intermediate last year I saw the figures a while ago, 236 boys passed the senior grade, though 4,050 boys stood the examinations in all the grades, which simply means this, that about 2,500 boys were presented in the preparatory grade, and only about one-tenth of these ever finished the Intermediate course. They are put into the Intermediate as little money-making machines for the schools in the preparatory and in the junior grade, and not for any legitimate purpose of educating them, or bringing them to anything.

16360. You are speaking only of the Christian Brothers' Schools.—It applies to all the schools in the country, or a great many of the schools, the whole mark, because the number that pass in the senior grade is out of all proportion to the number that go in for the examinations, unless the preparatory and junior grades were being used illegitimately; in this Intermediate system you should have far more boys going in for the senior grade.

16361. Have you any other remarks you wish to make?—There was just one other thing I should like to say about technical education. I think a technical education school in a city like this ought to complete the manual, practical, and scientific education of the schools; the great difficulty in that will be to find a supply of teachers for such technical schools. In that little endowment I was speaking about—agricultural endowment for the country—we had to find a teacher, and we put ourselves in communication with the National Board, and we were referred by them to Glasnevin, the Royal Albert Agricultural Institution, and we were in correspondence with the gentleman in charge of that for about six or eight months; it was a very tiresome correspondence, and we were put in communication with one person, and then with another, but the upshot of it was that there was no teacher of agriculture to be had at Glasnevin, or on the recommendation of the people who are conducting the place. Well, it seemed an extraordinary thing that in all Ireland we could not get one teacher, we were ready to pay him, and pay him very liberally, but we had to go to England, and through Lord Monteagle we got a young Englishman, who was examined here yesterday, Mr. Berkins. Lately they set going some technical classes in the city, and they wanted a science teacher for the city, and we found it rather hard to get one. I saw some of the correspondence between the committee here and some gentlemen who interested themselves in Dublin. I saw where they went, here and there, and everywhere, and at last one gentleman was got, Mr. Jenkins, a young English mechanic, that came over to study in the College of Science in Dublin. That would point, I think, to the conclusion that you have not got, for technical education in the country, a sufficient body of teachers, and I don't believe that you ever will have a sufficient body of teachers for that or any other higher course, until there is a University education given, that the great body of the people, particularly we Catholics, can avail of. It is a curious thing that we have these two young English men teaching our Catholic children in this city and

16564. How many Christian Brothers' schools are there in your diocese?—Sexton-street, St. John's, St. Mary's, St. Munchin's, Bruff, and Adare—six.

16565. How many Convent schools?—I can give you those figures afterwards.

16566. Is there any manual instruction in any of those schools in your diocese?—The girls have lots of it in cutting and needlework; but for the boys, I don't know of any manual instruction in any of the schools.

16567. Nothing like what there is at Limerick?—No, I read about that in the paper, there is nothing of that kind that I know of.

16568. Do you think it is desirable to introduce this special manual instruction into your schools?—I should like to see it tried, in the first place I should like to see the thing in the concrete, the actual thing, and see what it led up to, then it might be useful. I should like to see it tried as an experiment, but I think it is not at all likely to be as popular here as I believe it is in a place like Birmingham. Out of our population of 37,000 people, I don't suppose you have more than 1,000 employed in mechanical arts. A considerable number of the boys of our National schools go to the Civil Service.

16569. And the manual instruction would not help them?—It would not help them so much, but if it were tried as an experiment, and were optional in the schools it would do no harm.

16570. Has your lordship thought of any plan by which it might be done?—You see, I think drawing is a very important part of it, I think the drawing in the school might be very much advanced. I think drawing ought to be done far better than it is done. Then I think that if the teachers themselves are made thoroughly masters of this manual instruction at the training colleges that they then will devise means of working it in the schools and making it popular.

16571. So that you would be in favour of introducing it gradually?—Gradually.

16572. And if, as a result of this Commission's inquiries, a proposal were made to introduce it you would be favourable to it?—Oh, decidedly.

16573. Professor FITZGERALD.—You thought there was nothing in a boy's life that corresponded to needlework in a girl's, would it not be very useful, and does not each head of a family occasionally, mend furniture and do painting and white-washing, and other manual occupations?—I don't think so.

16574. Would it not be well if they did?—That may be, but as a matter of fact the two things are on a totally different footing at present and in public estimation, a woman that was not able to stitch would be considered a fool, but a man who could not put a leg on a table would not be considered the same.

16575. Would it not be well to encourage them?—Yes, but you have to take things as you have them. The teaching of useful carpentry work, I don't think would be popular in the town schools or a desirable thing for the schools to undertake.

16576. Do you not think it would be a desirable thing, not for the sake of teaching carpentry, but for the sake of making people handy?—That is the Sloyd system of woodwork, that is a totally different thing, and even when you have that taught to a person it is not on all fours with needlework, because needlework is extremely useful and practical.

16577. Is not that a great use of needlework the fact that it trains people to be handy and to construct things?—Not at all, I think the great use of needlework is to make a shirt and do things of that kind, I think the use of needlework is its usefulness, I don't think people are taught needlework for any theoretical purpose at all.

16578. That may be the reason, but don't you think a good reason for doing it is to make them [illegible]

16579. I think a large part of its usefulness as a school subject is in order to make people handy and neat?—I can only give you my own opinion about it, I believe needlework is taught for its practical utility and not for intellectual training.

16580. You said it would be undesirable to teach an art, I presume you mean mechanical art, not in its artistic sense?—I mean a mechanical art, carpentry.

16581. Do you think it is desirable to have free-hand drawing, which trains to a certain extent the artistic art?—It is most desirable, I think.

16582. Would the managers of this district, do you think, encourage the teachers to learn how to teach elementary science, if there were inspectors sent round?—I am sure they would. And would you allow me to interpose a remark in reference to the managers, I think it would be important if managers were encouraged to group themselves into associations by districts, and they were recognised as associations by the National Board. I think a body of managers coming together, putting their heads together on school business, would strike out a great lot of useful things, that might be tried in the schools that individual managers would not attempt, and amongst other things I have no doubt, they would encourage the teaching of elementary science.

16583. Mr. STRUTHERS.—Is there anything at present to prevent the formation of such an association?—I don't know. I don't know whether they would have any status before the Board.

16584. Might they not be recognised by the Board under its present regulations?—I cannot tell you, Mr. Redington could tell you that, I don't know of any such thing. I rather think the Board deals only with individual managers.

16585. But you don't know of any rule that prevents your forming associations here?—No, but I rather doubt it, I have not seen it done, and I know nothing in the Board's rules giving any status whatsoever to anyone except a patron, or manager, of a school, and that in relation to his own school.

16586. But the patron or manager might be an association?—Oh, yes, but I don't know there is anything in the rules that gives them any status.

16587. Professor FITZGERALD.—Of course it would be possible to arrange a committee of managers at present, and put a number of schools under that one committee?—Yes.

16588. But that would be quite in accordance with our present rules?—Would it?

16589. Oh, certainly, because at present there are a number of incorporated bodies that manage schools. Several of the dioceses in the Protestant Episcopal Church in Ireland have got the Diocesan Council, or a committee of the Diocesan Council, incorporated for the purpose of managing schools in the diocese?—That committee is the manager of several schools; I might be the manager now of half a dozen schools at this minute.

16590. You might arrange that all the parish priests in Limerick were a committee for the management of the schools in Limerick?—Oh, no; that is not what I want; my idea is that each independent manager of his own school might associate with any number of managers in the locality for a common purpose.

16591. Do the teachers, as a matter of fact, like expert inspectors coming in; do they not prefer having all the inspection done by a single inspector?—I should suppose they do. What the teachers look to most now are the results fees.

16592. In any case, is it desirable to supersede the inspectors by expert inspectors?—The only necessity for that is either that you have a subject that the ordinary inspector is incapable of examining in, or that it is a subject that the ordinary inspector ought to be able to examine in, but does not.

sent round to advise the teachers?—Oh, taught in all the boys' schools?—Even than ordinary lordship made about this woodwork. You said in

. . . towns it should be ornamental, but in the country it

Limerick.

Oct. 6, 1886.

The Most Rev. Dr. O'Dwyer.

rural National school, and a very large proportion of the teachers would tell you this: that they know absolutely nothing about it, and they say that it seems a most unreasonable thing to require them to teach what they don't know.

16656. You remark that every county should have special technical schools for agriculture?—I think so.

16657. Do you think more than one agricultural school would be necessary in a county?—Oh, yes, I should say so. If you have not more than one it will have to be a boarding school. They will have to live in it as in a college. I think it would be a very desirable thing to have technical schools where the people living in their own homes could come and get instruction.

16658. Do you think they can be taught agriculture without residing for some years or more in a school?—I should think so.

16659. With regard to the two teachers whom you got, had they received a University education, do you know?—I should say not—I am pretty sure not.

16660. Could not teachers be trained at the School of Science in Dublin now?—I don't know much about that School of Science, but my remark is directed to this principle generally that the great body of the Catholics of Ireland now are cut off actually from university education, and unless you open that to them you will not have a sufficient body of highly educated men to conduct these studies.

16661. Mr. Harrington.—How do you think the parents of the children would regard a change from the present rather literary programme of our National schools to the introduction of elementary science and manual instruction, do you think it would be a change that would be approved of?—I think they would like it.

16662. You mentioned, I think, that in the results of the Intermediate examinations some of the statistics showed that a very small percentage of boys went up for practical science?—I may mention to you that in 1886 only eleven boys passed in chemistry in the senior grade in all Ireland.

16663. Is it not a fact that the reason of that is that the Intermediate Board has rather discouraged the teaching of practical science?—I should rather think that it is because practical science is not easily crammed. The whole Intermediate system is a system of the worst cram that was ever introduced into a country. I think it is doing more harm to the intellect of Ireland than any other thing in it.

16664. Don't you think it would help very much the introduction of practical science into the secondary schools if it were taken up on a more general scale by the National Board?—Oh, yes; you know you never can thoroughly reform any one branch of education without affecting the whole of it, you cannot settle the primary unless you co-ordinate it with the secondary education. The secondary education in Ireland now is about the most pernicious thing I ever heard of, it is the worst conceived system that was ever forced on the country, and why the people stand it I cannot understand at all.

16665. Mr. Molloy.—I think, my lord, you stated that you were in favour of local committees or associations of managers to advise, so to say, the National Board?—Yes.

16666. And also the heads of [illegible]

16669. Including the course of studies for girls?—Quite so.

16670. In connection with the Intermediate Board, in the early years of that Board I believe there were assemblages of schoolmasters and schoolmistresses as advising bodies for the Board?—Whether they had any local status I don't know, but I think the head-masters of schools used to meet.

16671. And so they do still—those two bodies continue. Of course your lordship is aware that already in some of the dioceses in Ireland there are committees of managers [illegible]?—No, I am not aware of it. Of course any number of managers can come together and consult, but my point is this—that as a committee of managers they should have a recognition from the National Board, so that one could write up and say he is directed by the committee of managers of such a place to put such a view before the Board, and that the Board would recognise them as a committee.

16672. If I [illegible], some communication like that has already been received. Your lordship a while ago referred to the propriety of having ladies to inspect the schools?—I merely threw it out that the experiment might be usefully tried.

16673. Of course your lordship is aware that already there is a lady at the head of the needlework department?—Yes; an organiser, I think.

16674. A directress of needlework, and there are two lady organisers, so you would be in favour of the development of that?—Quite so.

16675. As to the difficulty of getting a person from Glasnevin Farm Establishment to instruct in agriculture in Limerick schools, was the reason stated the inadequacy of remuneration?—Not the slightest reference to it.

16676. As a matter of fact under the Royal Dublin Society and under the Congested Districts Board ex-National teachers are at this moment employed in giving practical instruction in agriculture, so I am surprised that Glasnevin was not able to supply you?—If you should like to see the correspondence, and have time to read it, I should be happy to put it at the disposal of the commission.

16677. Mr. Harrington.—You made a valuable suggestion about associations of managers. Would your lordship give those associations the power of modifying the course of instruction in their district with the consent of the National Board?—Quite so.

16678. That would to a large extent lessen the rigidity of the cast-iron system?—Quite so.

16679. With reference to the expert inspectors, do you not think that it would be an advantage that there should be an expert inspector in music, as a certain number of inspectors, at least, must necessarily have no taste for music?—Yes, I think you might fairly make an exception in that.

16680. You would not extend the exception to drawing?—Perhaps so. I think within the ordinary staff of inspectors there ought to be a sufficient number of men thoroughly competent to inspect.

16681. But each inspector looks after his own district. What I was suggesting was, that if there were a certain number of [illegible]

learning to use their hands, and then there is not so important in country schools—special manual training—as it is in towns. To come a little more to detail, it appears to me that the kind of practical training you want should be specially directed—taking it that it is to have a bearing on agriculture—to train the boys to habits of observation, especially with regard to all the natural objects around them in their daily life; and should be conducted, as far as possible, not by text-books, but by object lessons. The Right Hon. Lord Monteagle.

16691. Do you think school plots would be advantageous, or would you be of the opinion that was expressed by the Bishop of Limerick that teaching the principles without any school plots would be the best plan?—I should like to have a certain amount of teaching in the schools which would bring the principles under the notice of the children, and also to have a certain amount of practical teaching that would show them the application of these principles. I don't think that a farm attached to a school or the growing of farm crops can be of any great advantage, but that school gardens and small school plots, especially if conducted in a way that each boy should work a plot for himself, and should in that way learn by experience how plants are raised, would be of more advantage than a school farm.

16692. Would you allow him to earn his experience of a garden on a small plot of half an acre?—I mean a plot more like the size of this table, raising vegetables on the smallest possible space, you would have one acre attached to the school, and have that divided up in the way explained to the Commission by an English inspector, Mr. Rooper.

16693. The Commission saw it done in Sweden in one place, where a master had laid out his garden in little plots and given each boy a plot; is that the sort of thing?—That is the sort of thing I had in my mind. I have not seen it tried; it was from the evidence of Mr. Rooper that I got the idea, and it seemed to me a very good one.

16694. You would not have agriculture, then, taught as an art?—Not the practice of agriculture; but I think what they learn in the schools in the way of teaching elementary science can be given a practical application in these little plots.

16695. Now, with regard to existing teachers, I suppose you think that many of them could not be expected to give this instruction, because they have not been trained in it?—Exactly.

16696. But in the case of future teachers, do you think that every teacher, before he receives a certificate, should be obliged to earn a certificate that he could teach this sort of scientific agriculture?—Yes, I think that the teachers should all qualify themselves to teach the elementary science bearing on agriculture.

16697. What will you do in the meanwhile until a new generation of teachers is formed?—I think in the meantime, although I agree with Dr. O'Dwyer that it is very undesirable to bring in extern teachers—it is much better that the teacher should be responsible for all the teaching that is given—I think until you can train teachers to teach in these new subjects that itinerant teachers might very well be employed.

16698. How would you pay teachers for the instruction they give in scientific agriculture?—I think that it should not be based upon actual passes, the answering of children to questions put out of a

ppears to me to be very difficult indeed

nder a system of examinations and pay-

eaching of these practical subjects; it

rather by way of general inspection,

s is the custom in England.

would you think that room could be

hing these practical subjects, with

resent curriculum.—In what way could

curtailed?—I don't imagine that any

gth of time would be required for the

ges what is the exact amount of time

given for agriculture now in fifth and

it is three hours a week. I should

it to be sufficient.

Is there already?—Yes, that is. I

the time that is considered necessary

ere they have given special attention

[illegible]

your opinion that in cities such as

ould be better to teach Sloyd than to

ure?—I don't profess to judge of the

ould not propose to teach agriculture

and I should think Sloyd would be

[illegible]

Rathwottom.—With regard to the

re not at present able to teach agricul-

lly, in what way do you think they

be taught this elementary science—

at Saturday lectures at local centres or

gh a course at Glasnevin?—I think for

ight to be given as a special course in

of the training colleges; but I think in

t might be very well to form classes at

fferent localities, as has been done in

Scotland. Whether you could get the

nd them is another matter.

might refuse to pay fees for agriculture

at through these classes?—I am not

be quite fair to make local classes of

al lectures—of such paramount impor-

know that you could ensure that the

be sufficiently efficient.

then would you introduce your new

ching agriculture into the country

ould propose, after a certain time,

s Dr. O'Dwyer suggested was done in

three years' notice, and after that

ers would be required to qualify them-

these subjects.

what means ought they qualify them-

ing through a course of training.

al course of training or not?—I have

ny opinion as to how many schools

red for the purpose; I should think the

would not be sufficient.

you find that the boys who attended Mr.

es were more interested in agriculture

I am not resident in the district, where

m sorry to say I have not been able to

ese schools when the instruction was

[illegible]

ought you were present at some

r lectures given by Mr. Burkitt?—

came down at my invitation to give

alts in two of my villages, and I

t him to talk to the boys about making

grasses and so forth.

he give any practical experiments as

es?—The lecture was illustrated by

O'Dwyer did not quite understand Mr. Molloy's question in one respect; you went on to say that teachers had been sent from there to the Congested Districts Board.

16711. Mr. Molloy.—And also in connection with the Royal Dublin Society, they were chiefly ex-teachers?—But I understand it was as practical agriculturists.

16712. As practical agriculturists?—But that was not our object. We did not profess to teach practical agriculture; our teacher was to turn the text-book of the National Board, now in use, to the best account he could, and to teach that as well as he could.

16713. Mr. Rathwottom.—You are aware that the course at Glasnevin lasts only eight months, and could not last longer without interfering with the dairy classes. I understand that the gentleman you have employed has got a degree from the Durham University, and has spent at least two years in the study of agriculture; is that the case?—Yes, I believe that is so.

16714. Rev. Dr. Wilson.—Does any portion of this Mongret endowment still remain?—It is all vested in one body.

16715. What is the annual sum available?—I think it is £130 a year about.

16716. Is that applicable to agricultural purposes in the County Limerick, or to a wider extent?—It was applicable I think to technical education generally, including agriculture. I think agriculture was specially mentioned in the scheme, but it might have been applied, I believe, to other technical education. The sum was so small we thought it could hardly be broken up.

16717. I suppose it is limited chiefly to the county Limerick?—Yes to the county and city of Limerick.

16718. Mr. Molloy.—Is there a farm or school garden in connection with the schools of which your lordship is patron?—No.

16719. Have you any acquaintance with how practical farming is carried on where there is a farm or school-garden in connection with a National school?—No, there is none in my neighbourhood.

16720. What superiority is it expected that Mr. Burkitt would have over a National school teacher, when he is confined almost entirely to the elucidation of a text-book?—The text-book was not of our choosing—we found the text-book there. The text-book had to be taught, it was a compulsory subject. We should much prefer to set him entirely free of the text-book, and let him give agricultural teaching on his own lines, but the teachers are bound to teach this book—it is an important subject in the results examination, and the inspector will examine out of that book and nothing else; so if we had thrown the book aside it would have probably taken a substantial sum out of the teachers' pockets, but we thought it was worth trying the experiment whether anything could be made of the text-book, and I am afraid from what Mr. Burkitt will have probably told you yesterday that his evidence was conclusive.

16721. He also uses a text-book as well as the National school teacher; he gives a decided preference to a certain text-book, he mentioned it yesterday?—Dr. Fream's book, I suppose. I suppose every teacher must have a text-book to go by. I think it is rather in the suggestion the point comes in whether the examination is to be conducted entirely out of that text-book.

16722. He has been only a comparatively short

Limerick.

Oct. 2, 1897.

The Right Hon. Lord Monteagle.

year in his present post?—Do you mean that Mr. Carroll's opinion of the present system in vogue or of any system of agricultural instruction is worth more than Mr. Burkitt's?

16748. I do?—Well, of course, Mr. Carroll's experience of the system gives him an enormous advantage, to my thinking of his experience in other ways, but, at the same time, of course, Mr. Carroll has been for a very long time connected with this system, and, perhaps we consider, even though he may be young and inexperienced, if he has had actual practical experience of teaching in schools, his evidence may be of value.

16749. Some of the most eminent scientific men in Dublin lecture and carry out experiments in connection with the Model Farm under the superintendence of Mr. Carroll; he knows what is done and knows the results, so that neither as regards the theory nor the practice is Mr. Carroll likely to be misinformed?—Dr. Evans, if I may stop you for one moment, my point was that Mr. Burkitt, I think, has had a unique experience. He has been in a position, coming in as an outsider, not knowing this system, he has come in to try and conduct the teaching and see how it is possible to do that on the existing lines. I don't go higher than that; of course he is a young man, and I don't think he is a presumptuous young man so far as I have seen.

16750. I don't say he is?—But I think the fact of his having actually given instruction in primary schools and come in contact with the children gives his opinion a special value quite apart from Mr. Carroll's wider experience.

16751. As a member of the National Board, in whose schools Mr. Carroll's books are used, I am somewhat sensitive lest through the medium of the Commission they should be in any way lowered in the opinion of the teachers, or considered in any way deficient in value?—I was not criticising Professor Carroll's book or comparing it unfavourably with Dr. Fream's or anybody else's.

16752. Is there anything you could suggest to us by which we might be aided in introducing and carrying out manual instruction?—I have not given so much special attention to manual instruction, because I regard that as more specially adapted for the town.

Venerable Archdeacon Hamilton, Limerick, examined.

Venerable Archdeacon Hamilton.

16753. CHAIRMAN.—You are the Manager of St. Michael's mixed school?—Yes.

16754. Have you given any attention to the subject of introducing manual instruction not as a technical subject, but as a subject which tends to increase the powers of observation of children in schools?—I have; I have thought over it very often and read about it, and heard evidence given on the subject.

16755. Have you seen anything of it?—No, I am not aware of a school in which the subject has been introduced. My own idea is that we ought to bear in mind the broad distinction between subjects that are essentially necessary for every boy and for every girl to lay the foundation of general education, from which they hope to get benefit in after life, and, therefore, I think reading, writing, arithmetic, spelling, grammar and geography are essential, and it is rather dangerous, if not unwise, to try to disparage those subjects as it were, and to diminish the time that should be given to them, which are necessary for all children, both boys and girls, by introducing such subjects as I have been hearing about for the last few days. Typewriting, shorthand, drawing, and so forth, a few might benefit in after life by them, but it would be at the loss of a great many whose time in the school would be shortened by the introduction of these subjects, which may or may not be useful to them.

16756. That is assuming it would be compulsory on all children, whether their parents wished it or not, to learn these subjects?—Well, of course, the difficulty would then arise of setting apart time in the day for such subjects as these for a few of the boys; almost every boy would like to learn something new-fangled like this.

16757. The way this is carried out in England is this; it is necessary not only to set apart a time but a separate place in which it can be done?—That would make all the difference in the world.

16758. It cannot be done, and is not done in England in the ordinary schools?—My school is in one large room, with a curtain across, with one master, one workmistress, and two monitors.

16759. One of the difficulties in introducing the subject in country places in England that has not been overcome, is the necessity of providing a separate room?—For that reason I think these subjects could be better and more usefully learned in other places after school hours, just as other special subjects are. I think the boys would be more likely to learn them in that way, and to learn them well.

16760. I think you don't quite understand the object that those who advocate this system have in view; they don't wish to teach woodwork for instance as a trade; their object is this; they see that the children in the ordinary literary subjects are too apt to commit things to memory, and not to think about what they are learning or to reason about it; and the particular sort of work which is called sloyd work has made it necessary for the person who has to practise that system to think and to measure and, in the case of elementary science, which is more or less connected with chemistry, to weigh; and therefore, they must use their reasoning powers; and they think that having to learn to use their reasoning powers in connection with these subjects, they will also do so in connection with their literary subjects? Suppose we began by carrying that out in connection with these literary subjects, and allow more time to explain what they are reading, and brighten them up. I spoke to my master, and he says they have a certain number of pages to read in a certain time, and if they were to ask questions of the first boy, "What is the meaning of this," or "Of that?" they would not be able to get half through the lesson.

16761. Do you think that a good system?—No, a very bad system.

16762. Do you think some alteration in that system would be desirable?—I do. I would allow more time to the explaining of their lessons. I have heard some of our boys one day, and I think the inspector was present, Dr. Hamilton, and they repeated the poem called "The Irish Emigrant;" they said it very nicely, indeed, and when he asked what was the meaning of the word "emigrant" they did not know. There is not enough time allowed for explaining or using their reasoning powers, and instead of strengthening their reasoning powers by woodcarving, I would insist on their using their reasoning powers by reading. The other subjects are very important, but they may be taken up after they leave school. There are such classes being formed, or ought to be formed in every town.

16763. REV. DR. EVANS.—Are you in favour of making the readers in schools much more simple and interesting than they used to be?—I think you might, with great advantage, have more interesting reading books, for I think the children like to be talked to about their reading. I know in the Scripture lesson they are quite glad that I should not merely ask them to read or repeat, but to try to show the arrangement of the words, and in that way they are taught grammar and composition, they are taught the

English language, and then they are taught to speak up, to use their own words, and hear their own voices. They are afraid to hear the sound of their own voices, for fear the other children would laugh at them if they made a mistake, but they never get a chance now, they read and read.

16764. You are aware that it was objected against the old system of teaching that interrupting children so much for explanation, and to make them acquainted with the subject matter, interfered with the teaching of reading, and, hence to redress that the tendency was to produce readers that were interesting, like story books, that would need no explanation, that the children could be taught reading by, and then if you want to give them instruction in science or anything else, have their science manuals?—I would rather they read badly and understood what they read than to read well and not to understand it, if that is the alternative; but I should hope, by not teaching so much grammar rules, those in favour of manual instruction wish to diminish the literary part to find time for manual instruction; therefore, it is plain there could be time found for learning the meaning of what they are reading about.

16765. Would you be in favour of introducing elementary science?—Well, so many of my children are so young, the average attendance was 70 last quarter, and the average age is ten, half the school is too young, and the other half would be only very small boys still, and the town boys look forward to getting into some of these large establishments; the girls are all used to be dressmakers; they would like to read and write, or otherwise they could not be taken in as apprentices in any shape. They go to shops or to the railway, they don't go into the country as farmers. I have been listening to Lord Monteagle's evidence, but the schools he spoke of and schools in town are quite different.

16766. I take it you would be in favour of retaining our present programme?—I am.

16767. And not in favour of disturbing it by the introduction of any other course of instruction?—There might be reasons where you have schools with two or three rooms and two or three teachers, but in an ordinary school with one master and a workmistress and two monitors, and about 70 children in attendance, I don't see how manual instruction could be introduced. But I would be very glad to encourage boys to learn other things afterwards. If a girl wants to learn music she goes directly she has left school, and the same with drawing. If a boy has a taste for drawing he will learn it himself.

16768. Professor FITZGERALD.—I would like to know why you consider that geography is so much more important for children to learn than drawing or elementary science?—Because they read in books—I think the chief enjoyment of our life is reading—these children when they grow up are mad to get books; we have a parish library, and distribute books every week. If they read, and never learn any geography, the interest in their reading would be very much lessened.

16769. Don't you think the interest in their reading would be very much increased if they knew a little elementary science?—I don't think they would be inclined to read scientific books.

16770. Would not elementary science enable them

schools in London with that of children in Irish National schools, as to which is the most efficient in literary work?—The Irish boys, as a rule, are very sharp, but I have been here so many years in this one city, I have not come across many English boys; do you mean to compare the boys taught in England with the boys here?

16785. Yes, a boy of thirteen or fourteen, whether the boy taught under the English or under the Irish National system has the better literary education?—I would not like to give an opinion on that subject; I know something about the boys here, they all do very well; the boys from schools like mine go into shops or the railway; they like to call themselves clerks; they go into foundries and large establishments; as a rule they don't go to a trade; I can only think of one or two, that were hopeless at school about books and went into trades, and are doing very well indeed.

16786. Is your attendance at the school regular?—The average now is seventy; the attendance, I think, is very good indeed—very regular indeed on the whole.

16787. Would you consider that any form of instruction which tended to induce the children to attend school would be useful?—After hours do you mean?

16788. No, during school hours; a large number of Irish schools complain of the irregular attendance of children when there is no compulsion?—There are so many schools here in the city, I don't think there are any children kept out in the cold as it were; I think their parents send them all to school.

16789. You think the attendance at school is sufficiently regular in Ireland?—I do; as far as my experience goes the attendance is very good.

16790. Mr. Molloy.—Have you many pupils in your fourth, fifth, or sixth classes, which constitute your senior division of the school?—Yes, we have a good many boys; two or three have just gone up to Dublin to the training college there for schoolmasters.

16791. I mean out of the average of seventy how many would constitute your senior division?—I don't think there are more than four or five boys over fourteen or fifteen; they are very anxious to get out into the world, and in a town there are so many competitions in the shops.

16792. Would you advocate, Archdeacon, the propriety of increasing the school hours each day; you referred a while ago to the fact that the pupils come in sometimes after half-past ten; is not that very late for city boys?—They ought not to be marked if they do; the school is from ten to three, and there is half an hour recreation and half an hour's religious instruction.

16793. If the school-roll was marked at ten o'clock, do you think there would be a better attendance, and the children get more instruction; they come in at half-past ten chiefly because they know the roll will not be called until eleven?—I think myself that the roll ought to be called earlier than that. I was under the impression the roll was called at half-past ten. I think the strain on the boys is enough.

16794. Of course the roll call is not later than eleven, but, as a matter of fact, it might be called at ten o'clock or a quarter past?—I think it ought to be called. I know that at the school I was at myself if you came in a quarter of an hour late you would not get a good mark.

16795. You referred to reading as being very badly taught—mere reading, the repetition of the words before the eyes, and no intelligence?—Yes; of course one must make allowances. We know the children know more than they are willing to express; there is great shyness, and that may be overcome if they were encouraged to talk about the thing, and the teacher drew them out; but at present I think there is too much mere reading, and no opportunity given to the child to explain what he knows.

16796. How do you account for no time being given to the child?—The time comes to an end, and they have to go to something else: there is a fixed programme.

16797. Reading for every class includes under the Commissioners' distinct acquaintance with the meaning of words and phrases, and with the subject matter of the lesson read, and it is expected the teacher will explain the meaning?—Children will not speak. I have got big boys up at the barracks, good big drummers, and others—I have to go to them every week—they are almost dumb, too; but I think they ought to be encouraged and made to understand what they are reading.

16798. If it was something more than an encouragement—I am not advocating the propriety of results fees—but supposing in the fee for reading were included the obligation to explain the matter read, would not that be important?—It would.

16799. I am happy to say that is the regulation in force just now. Henceforward the fee for reading will involve the necessity of careful explanation?—I know if I was asked to examine a class in reading I certainly would pause now and then to find out did they know the meaning of a word now and again.

16800. You do not approve of the National Board series of readers at present?—I don't wish to be understood as finding fault, but I think there might be some freshening up of them, or they might read some books not on the list at all.

16801. Of course you are aware as an experienced manager that it is quite open to you to submit any series of books, and, if these were found not to contain objectionable matter, they would be recognised for use in your school?—I was not aware of that. I had schools in other parishes in the city that were not under the National Board. I thought it was all fixed, and nothing could be altered.

16802. You are absolutely Lord Paramount, provided there is no objectionable matter in the series you select?—I am much obliged to you.

16803. Rev. Dr. Wilson.—How many schools in Limerick have you?—You mean under the National Board, only three—Villiers' School and my own and St. Munchin's.

16804. What other schools are there in Limerick that are not under the National Board?—There is one school in St. John's parish.

16805. Is that a Church Education School?—No, it is not under any system; it was endowed by a Mrs. Westropp; it is the Parochial School of St. John's. I had it for fourteen years under my management—a small school.

---

and I believe the power of observation would be increased if the kindergarten system was taught.

16809. You have some opinions with regard to the mode of examination in agriculture; what are they?—The work we use is called "Practical Farming," but every examination that has been conducted in my school has been one in theory. I never saw a practical examination in agriculture but once, and that was by a gentleman connected with some technical institute in this city. Lord Monteagle described for you the manner in which the examination was conducted, and I believe it had a very good effect in this way: that it made the boys actually go through the fields since and gather new specimens of grasses.

16810. You think the present system of examination in agriculture is not suited to this district?—I do not think it is at all; a boy has to answer in the words of another man actually what he does himself. For instance, a little boy—85 per cent. of the boys attending my school are either the sons of farmers or labourers, or of parents in some way connected with land or cattle—well, since the introduction of the creamery or co-operative movement in Limerick the boys of the fourth, fifth, and sixth classes can milk cows very well, they can do the work in the fields for their parents, they can weed and thin out the turnip plants; in fact they do most of the after-cultivation of the drills for their parents, and the farmers of Shanagolden are very respectable, intelligent, honest, hard-working men. When I tell you that the pupils come from two divisions of the Rathkeale Union, Dunaid, and Shanagolden, and the valuation of these two divisions is £5,909, the poor rate and county cess amounts to 4s. 6d. in the pound, and with these burdens on them they are most intelligent, industrious, hard-working men, and they could not be what they are if they were not intelligent. The children assist the parents in performing these operations. But I find when they are examined by the inspector they cannot describe in the words of the late Mr. Baldwin's book or of Professor Carroll's book, they cannot describe what they are doing. I have never seen them practically examined. May I give an instance to this Commission? Some years ago the inspector of the district was examining a class of boys in second stage of fifth, and he asked a boy to tell him how a firkin of butter should be salted and packed, and fitted out for the market; the boy was unable to answer, and I, in a very humble manner, interposed, and said, "I assure you, sir, that the best butter entering the *Limerick* market is made in that boy's father's dairy, and although he knows all about it he cannot answer." The boy in that case got a cypher in agriculture. Another instance, I was going through the fields in the summer time of this year, and I saw a boy sixteen years old, who had left school, perhaps, two years before that; he was working on his father's land, with a plough and a pair of horses. He had turned the furrow with the accuracy of a skilled workman, I mean the dividing line between two furrows of land. I was glad to see the boy such a good labourer, but on referring to his school history, I found by the register that although he had gone through all the classes, from fourth up, he never yet got a mark in agriculture. They may be good practical farmers, and assist their parents, but they very often fail in theory.

16811. How would you suggest an examination in agriculture should be conducted?—That a school-garden or little farm be attached to every school, and make the boys perform exactly the operations with their spade and plough, or to weed out the plants in the presence of the inspector.

16812. You think in large towns and cities the pupils should receive some manual instruction; why there, rather than in the country?—I believe, with the country boys, 85 per cent. are engaged in agricultural operations where their hands are employed for the greater part of the day, whereas in large towns I believe there is a great deal of idleness in the evenings. If you pass through a town or a village in Ireland in the evenings you will find a great deal of idleness, and I think that evening schools should be established, in order to give them an opportunity of being taught some sort of manual work.

16813. Will you briefly indicate the good work that is being done in the Glin school?—I visited that school on two or three occasions; the children there attend school, perhaps, 300 days in the year; they go to school in the forenoon and afternoon, and they are divided into sections. Each section is employed at something useful; that was my observation.

16814. What is your opinion of the results system of examination?—The results system of examination in my opinion is only suited to schools where education is compulsory. The results year in my school ended on the 31st of May of this year; of the number of pupils on the rolls 40 per cent. made less than 100 attendances, 46 per cent. made less than 150 attendances, and only 14 per cent. made between 150 and 200 attendances. I should say that there was a special difficulty, because owing to an epidemic or some kind of intermittent form of illness, the percentage of attendances to the number on the rolls did not reach 60 during four months previous to the results examinations, but it made no difference; the examination was as critical. The sickly or delicate boy who came to school after he was 12, and attended only 100 or 101 days, had to stand the same examination as the boy who attended 200 days.

16815. You think the course in grammar is too extended?—Decidedly.

16816. Whether would you shorten the course or modify the teaching?—It is impossible, or at all events, it is difficult and painful for children of eight or nine to remember the parts of speech. In the fourth class the conjugation in the simple tenses of the irregular verbs is very difficult, the parsing in the fifth, 2nd stage, is very difficult, but I think the examination of a boy in the sixth class is more difficult than it ought to be. I think if a boy can write a letter correctly, grammatically, and intelligently, that the examination that he is put to is too severe. And if the Commission have no objection I will give the questions the boys in the sixth class got at the last examination. It certainly is a very difficult one, I mean words detached from the sentences, the most difficult perhaps in the lesson-book.

16817. Rev. Dr. Wilson.—With regard to these evening schools that you would recommend in country places, would it not be very difficult to get young children to come on dark nights?—I did not intend that children of a young age should come, it is my opinion that the Legislature should compel children to attend school in the daytime, but there are some—there are many, for instance, in my own locality—where, if you made education compulsory, the Compulsory Act would press very severely on small farmers and labourers, but if you made some sort of a sliding scale, by which you could compel them at least to attend 100 days, and then the grown boys, when they go to work, to bring them to an evening school, as we had long ago. I remember twenty-five years ago, when I was teaching in another county, the grown boys who had left school came back to the evening school again.

16818. As to results fees, I sympathise with an inspector when he is examining a school. Can he alter his questions to suit children that have been 100 days in attendance from questions to suit those who have been 200 or 180; must he not put the same questions to all?—I say nothing about the inspector, it is the system I find fault with. The inspector's duty is laid out for him, and very honourable and upright gentlemen they are. I presume they have no option but to examine all the boys in the same manner.

16819. I don't see how results fees can be awarded except by the same questions to all in the school, and if less than 100 days in attendance, they should try to make up for that by private study?—I think it is impossible to make a boy learn as much in 100 days as he would in 200 days, and I think it is very bad to punish a teacher, and deprive him of his results fees, because he cannot cram the same quantity of knowledge into a boy.

16620. The only remedy for that, I think, is to alter the whole system about the result fees, because you must always calculate for sickness and epidemics, would you not be in favour of any modification of result fees, or the doing away with them altogether?—Well, I would not, as a teacher, like to give an opinion; all I know is, that I find it is not a just mode of payment for the services which we perform, but the question is too much for me.

16621. Mr. Struthers.—You have not formed any opinion as to how the system may be improved?—No.

16622. Mr. Molloy.—Would you kindly describe the school in which you are head teacher; I mean, as regards its attendance, and where it is situated?—Shanagolden is a village of about 400 inhabitants, purely agricultural, very much adapted to the dairy industry; in fact, we have one of the largest creameries in Limerick in the village. The industry is confined principally to dairy business, the land was, at one time, wheat-growing, but now the dairy industry is the principal industry of the people.

16623. And that you describe as eminently successful?—Oh, very.

16624. By whom is that carried out?—It is a co-operative creamery.

16625. A good many young persons connected with it, I presume?—Oh, yes. I may tell you that it has given employment to some of the young people.

16626. Where did those young people, who are now so successful at work in the creamery, receive their primary education?—In Shanagolden.

16627. Then the course must have been efficient?—Two of the boys have turned out successful creamery managers already, and others are in preparation; one is in Tipperary and the other in Londonderry.

16628. There is no school garden attached to your school?—No. I have a little farm myself, but it is attached to my residence, and it is not in the same townland as the school.

16629. How many school hours have you?—Five.

16630. That includes religious instruction and time for recreation?—Yes.

16631. That leaves the minimum of four hours net?—Yes.

16632. Was it not the custom some years ago, especially in rural parts of Limerick, to have the school hours much longer than that?—I assure you there are times, particularly when young people are harvesting, that no teacher can do his duty without keeping the children a little longer than the specified time; we often have to do that.

16633. You are in favour of night schools, and a member of the Commission pointed out the difficulty of attending night schools. Would you favour continuation schools, that is, after the ordinary school hours, from four to six?—I don't think you could keep the children in; what I advocate is, that boys who go to work, farmers' and labourers' sons, who do not attend school at all in the day time, should be brought in and receive instruction in the evening schools.

16634. Why is there not a night school in Shanagolden?—I don't know. There was a night school before I came there, I am eighteen years there, but I think the grant for night schools was withdrawn by the Commissioners a great many years ago. I think there was a small grant of £5, or something—it is a great many years ago.

16635. If the grants were financially of a satisfactory kind would you advocate the establishment of a great many night schools?—Yes.

16636. I am sorry to say we have very few of them, and the number is decreasing instead of increasing. Many years ago there were more. In one district I had at present. You are in favour of elementary science in rural as well as in town schools?—Yes.

16637. What subjects of science have you under instruction?—Euclid and algebra.

16638. No experimental science?—No.

16639. In connection with the dairy, where did the boys who are now so successful in working it get the practical instruction?—Of course their farms are good dairy farms, and any of the boys who intend to follow up the office of creamery managers serve into the creamery, and acquire a practical knowledge of it, then, of course, they are sent away to Glasnevin under Professor Carroll, to be trained.

16640. Have you thought out any particular subjects that might be curtailed in the present school curriculum with a view to the introduction of others?—I believe the arithmetic in the higher classes certainly might be curtailed, and instead of those extravagant sums that are given to boys in the sixth class, there are six standards in what the little boys call a card of sums, and we often find in those "insert two geometrical means between two numbers" and the transfer of stocks.

16641. Complicated problems in arithmetic, what would you substitute for them?—Exercises in mensuration, plain figures, or simple solids. I believe farmers' sons require to measure every inch of their life, from a rick of turf to a heap of stones, they would require a knowledge of mensuration. I can remember forty years ago old Thompson's Arithmetic had a valuable chapter on mensuration.

16642. Is drawing taught in your school?—I have a certificate for drawing and I intend to introduce it. I am doing it in a tentative way at home, the school furniture is not very well adapted for it, and I give some of the boys who have a taste for it a lesson in my own house.

16643. Then may I summarise your views as this that you advocate the propriety of introducing drawing, elementary science, and some approach to manual instruction, at least allowing it to be optional in such a school as yours?—Something practical. I could not say what would suit my locality, but something tending to make good labourers or to tilling the land better.

16644. A near approach to a school farm?—Precisely.

16645. Mr. Struthers.—I suppose you think that anything in the way of practical instruction had better be given in these evening schools, if you had evening schools?—I think that would be the time and place to give it.

16646. When pupils had gone through their school day?—Yes.

16647. So that the day programme should not be overloaded and the children's minds distracted?—They have too much to do.

16648. Such subjects as typewriting and so on you would have in the evening classes?—Yes.

16649. More advanced arithmetic possibly?—Yes.

16650. But you would still retain in the day schools such a subject as needlework for the girls, if it were a mixed school?—Certainly.

16651. And also drawing?—Yes.

16652. For what purpose would you teach drawing in a day school?—That if the boys became workmen they would turn out good ones, and it would be very well for a boy to be able with his fingers to indicate what he has in his mind, the distinction between the Bates' and the Booth's shorthorn, Mr. Carroll gives a description of these breeds of cattle, and one of the questions that might be put by an inspector in such a locality as Shanagolden is what is the distinction between a Bates' and a Booth's shorthorn. I found a difficulty in making a small boy understand that unless I drew them on a board with chalk.

16653. What advantage do you think drawing would be to the pupil?—It would make him a better workman and a better mechanic.

16655. That would depend on the kind of drawing taught?—Yes.

16656. Do you think freehand drawing—copying an example from the flat—has much effect in that direction?—I believe it has, because if a boy can copy from the flat I believe in after-life, when the copy is taken away, if he sees an object he is better able to comprehend its size, shape and dimensions.

16657. The examples he copies are generally very elaborate ornaments, such as he may never see in life afterwards; would it not be better to have a drawing more distinctly relating to objects than that?—Yes.

16658. Would it not be more useful to teach a boy if he is going into a trade, so that he should be able to draw from plan and elevation?—I cannot go so far.

16659. Perhaps you have no knowledge of that kind of drawing yourself?—No, freehand drawing only; I cannot give you an opinion on that.

16660. Do you say you are in favour of some manual instruction in the schools?—Certainly.

16661. With what object again?—First, to keep the boys employed, and, secondly, to fit them for the battle of life.

16662. Do you think that would make them more handy and intelligent?—Certainly.

16663. You spoke about examining in practical subjects, such as gardening, you thought that the inspector ought to see the boy dig in the garden, and see that he handled the spade properly?—Certainly. If I go through any portion of the County Limerick and I want to know in the springtime of the year whether a farmer is successful or not, I see if his first ploughing of the land is good and deep, because good deep ploughing is the foundation of tillage husbandry. If he does that well I come to the conclusion he is a good farmer.

16664. Would you teach the boy to dig in the school garden?—Certainly. Boys that are intended to be farmers, from the constant practice of assisting their parents, become skilful workmen.

16665. Then why teach them to dig in the school garden?—There are many boys that are not going to be farmers, and I think it would be a healthy exercise for them.

16666. Then it is for the benefit of those who are not going to be farmers you would have them digging in the school garden?—Certainly, at the present moment the country is studded with labourers' cottages, and when the labourers have to walk long distances to work for farmers it would be very well for the little boys, if they could in the evenings, or say, on Saturdays, use a spade on their father's land, and save the hire of a man.

16667. But I thought you said the majority of these boys are taught by their parents at home to dig?—I really believe they acquire it without being taught.

16668. If that is the case what is the use of providing a school garden to teach boys something they can do already?—I think it would be a most healthy occupation, in the first place, and I believe it could be made a model to all the other gardens in the district.

16669. Would it be more healthy than playing?—It may or may not.

Limerick. [illegible] Mr. William [illegible]

16670. Do you think it would be advisable to spend large sums of money for the instruction of these children in school gardens in something they could learn at home perfectly well?—No, I do not think it would. The expenditure of money on a school garden could not be very great—an acre of land.

16671. Not on one school garden, but on many throughout Ireland, it may come to a considerable sum, and it would be paying for instructing boys in a thing they can already do, at least, learn from their parents?—I think it would pay still; if those boys emigrated, they would be better workmen.

16672. You mentioned about the case of a boy who could not answer about the proper making of butter, though he knew it practically already?—Possibly the boy had read exactly the words of Mr. Baldwin's book, but could not repeat them again. If an inspector is examining little girls in the industrial programme, he does not ask them how to cut out an article of dress, or darn a stocking, but they have to do the work in his presence.

16673. You would not propose that the inspector should bring a firkin of butter into the school, and get the boy to pack it for him?—No.

16674. Then how is the inspector to ascertain whether the boy knew?—My point is that the boy did know, but could not repeat it.

16675. Then how is the inspector to know that?—Quite right; and then judgment goes by default. A boy often fails in agriculture in my school, and I know he can actually do the thing, but he cannot describe it in words.

16676. How is the inspector to know that this boy can actually do it, except he tells him?—Certainly not.

16677. Then do you not think that there is a want of intelligence in the boy who is not able to describe some simple occupation that he actually has done. If a boy is able to pack a firkin of butter an intelligent boy can tell how he did it?—There may be a want of intelligence, but there is also nervousness that would prevent a boy from answering.

16678. That would apply to any other subject just as well as agriculture?—Yes.

16679. Rev. Dr. Whelan.—You say the percentage and county cess are 5s. 6d. in the £. How much of that would be poor-rate?—6s.

16680. Would that be an average poor-rate?—In our division at all events it is 6s.; it was 6s. 6d. last year. I only used it for the purpose of showing that the farmers must be an intelligent body of men; they have to make the most of their opportunities, in order to live and support their families.

16681. Mr. Redington.—Those boys who afterwards became creamery managers, did they receive instruction in the Munster Dairy School, or Glasnevin?—Glasnevin; but they had a good practical knowledge of the matter before they went there.

THIRTY-EIGHTH PUBLIC SITTING.—WEDNESDAY, OCTOBER 5TH, 1887.

AT 2.30 O'CLOCK, P.M.,

At the Railway Hotel, Galway.

PRESENT:—THE RIGHT HON. THE EARL OF BELMORE, G.C.M.G., in the Chair; THE RIGHT HON. C. T. REDINGTON, M.A.; THE MOST REV. MONSIGNOR MOLLOY, D.D., D.SC.; REV. HENRY EVANS, D.D.; REV. HAMILTON WILSON, D.D.; PROFESSOR G. F. FITZGERALD, F.T.C.D.; STANLEY HARRINGTON, ESQ., B.A.; W. R. J. MOLLOY, ESQ.; CAPTAIN T. B. SHAW; and J. STRUTHERS, ESQ., B.A.;

with J. D. DALY, ESQ., M.A., Secretary.

REV. P. LALLY, P.P., Hon. Secretary, Galway Technical School, examined.

16832. CHAIRMAN.—Father Lally, I believe that you have started a technical school in Galway?—Well, I have acted as honorary secretary of the committee that has started a technical school in Galway since January, 1883.

16833. And you have given considerable attention to the question of manual work and what is called Sloyd work?—A good deal of attention.

16834. Will you give the Commission your ideas as to the best means of introducing that sort of teaching into National schools?—Well to begin with it would be necessary to get trained or efficient teachers. I

168[illegible]. If you had one in Galway, that would involve having one in every county in Ireland?—No, I say Galway as a centre for the province of Connaught.

168[illegible]. With regard to providing appliances, benches, and a building in which to carry on the work, because I suppose we may take it for granted that, as in England, it would be necessary to have the work carried on in a separate building. What scheme would you suggest for that?—My notion is that in a place like Galway the proper thing would be to have a centre where the children could come after the

16903. You would not suggest that there should be practical classes attached to every school?—I would have a centre, at all events, where the teachers would be trained.

16904. I am talking of the children?—They would be taken to a small centre in other towns, and used as peripatetics in the same way as I suggest in Galway.

16905. You would confine that to towns?—Yes, and to National schools within a radius of five miles from the town.

16906. Would a good many of the National schools be near enough to a town of some sort large enough to be a centre?—I think they would in most cases. Our committees, then, for cookery and laundry and other subjects supply all the materials, and we have all the proper appliances for imparting the knowledge.

16907. How would you provide those appliances and materials in small schools?—I think if the local authority in small places act as the local authority in Galway have acted, and levy a rate under the Technical Education Act, and be well subsidised by the Commissioners of National Education, the matter would work well.

16908. Do you think there would be much opposition to that on the part of the ratepayers?—The ratepayers, of course, oppose it; but their opposition is mild. They are always in hope that some legislation will come to relieve them of the burden; but still, at a sacrifice to themselves, they have done it for five years in Galway.

16909. To what do you ascribe the comparative failure of the industrial programme in the schools?—To the inefficiency of the teachers. They have never been trained themselves.

16910. To what subjects do you allude?—I allude to cookery, dressmaking, and needlework.

16911. Do you think that where it has been taken up it has failed?—I think the knowledge imparted would not amount to much. I think it is all important that the teacher of cookery would be well qualified, and have passed through the necessary training and have the necessary certificates.

16912. Are there many places in the County Galway, to your knowledge, where it has been attempted to teach cookery?—Well, there are a good many places.

16913. You think it has not been successful?—I don't think it has been successful at all; for instance, the National Board appointed four very competent teachers, and one actually worked in Galway for a considerable time, and her experience was that she was not supplied with the proper materials, and, secondly, had not the appliances.

16914. Whose fault was that?—I suppose the managers did not provide the materials. The whole burden rested on them, except in the case of the Model School, where the Commissioners provided it all.

16915. Mr. Redington.—The rate that you speak of is levied off the whole union?—It is levied off the union at large.

16916. Is any technical instruction given in the rural parts of the union?—Well, it is not given as yet, but we made an attempt to give it. We were teaching woollen weaving here, and our instructor in weaving was supposed to go as a peripatetic to the country villages, and we took a great deal of trouble

Galway.

Oct. 7, 1896.

Rev. F. Lally, P.P.

16937. You don't think a course of six weeks at some centre would be sufficient?—I don't believe it would be sufficient to qualify a teacher.

16938. For the merely elementary cookery necessary in rural schools?—It would be a good thing, but I think it would be better to have a fully qualified teacher.

16939. Have you considered the immense expense of having fully qualified teachers all over the country?—I suggest each teacher from the school should go in a radius of five miles.

16940. What would happen the schools beyond the five miles radius?—Well, make some larger provision for that or say ten miles. If the matter is to be taught at all I would have it taught well and efficiently.

16941. CHAIRMAN.—It was suggested to us yesterday, I think by the Bishop of Limerick, that what was desirable was not that the children should be taught to be cooks, but that they should be taught the principles of cooking, so as to be able to cook food for their husbands when they become wives?—I think that is quite fair enough. Of course those who wish to qualify for being cooks can go further, but for the teaching of the National system that is quite enough.

16942. MR. RICHARDSON.—Is it necessary for that purpose to have such highly qualified teachers of cookery as those now employed by the Board?—I think some way or another they understand best how to teach it and proceed about it.

16943. Now, as regards woodwork. Woodwork is not taught in any National school in this city?—Not in this city. The only place outside Galway where it is taught is Cashel.

16944. Have you any classes in woodwork at the Technical Institute?—We have.

16945. Could you tell us what kind of woodwork they do?—They have prepared models.

16946. With a view to become carpenters?—Well, some did become carpenters actually from our school. And then there is the panelling of doors.

16947. Are you acquainted with the system of woodwork that is in operation in some large English cities?—Well, I visited all the polytechnical institutes in London.

16948. But you have not seen any of the woodwork centres in connexion with the board schools in Liverpool or London?—No, I have not seen those schools.

16949. Of course you know that the kind of woodwork introduced into the English elementary schools is much simpler than you have been outlining?—They commence with us with very simple things—to make knifeboards, and small panels, and brackets, and chimney boards, and they advance to the other work.

16950. Is there any subject which you think ought to be omitted from the present programme in order to introduce manual work? I would not like to interfere with the present literary programme in the National schools at all. My notion would be that after the school work and the literary work of the day would be the time for practical training.

16951. And would not the children be tired after the school?—After an hour or two. Two hours after the school had been over.

16952. How would you carry that out in rural districts, particularly in winter?—I would make special provision for the rural districts. After school they might remain for another hour.

16953. CHAIRMAN.—Would not that interfere with their getting food. They don't get dinner in rural schools?—In some of the rural schools, especially preparing for examination, they work from three to four in the afternoon.

16954. Then you would shorten some of that extra work?—I think the time allowed by the Board's rules is up to 3 o'clock.

16955. MONSIGNOR MOLLOY.—I think it would help us, Father Lally, if you gave us a short account of the first foundation of your school, and its history up to the present time. When was it founded?—In January, 189[illegible].

16956. What was the object in view of those who founded it?—The object in view was to impart the practical and manual training.

16957. To what class of people?—To all who should come within our reach. We were anxious that the children of the advanced classes in the National schools would benefit as much as possible by our teaching.

16958. Did you propose to teach adults?—We did, and we have.

16959. Then your pupils would consist to some extent of adults, and to some extent of the advanced pupils of the National schools?—What we proposed last year to do was to have a class in the evening at 6 o'clock for the children in the sixth class of the National schools. We did form a class, and it was largely attended for some time, but my experience afterwards was that the teachers were all in opposition against us, because they thought the children coming there interfered with the preparation for the results examination—the home lessons.

16960. What subjects did you propose to teach?—For girls, cookery, and laundry, and dressmaking, and for boys manual woodwork, and girls and boys, typewriting and shorthand.

16961. And not agriculture?—No, but our anxiety is to get a fully-qualified teacher of agriculture, whom we would send as a peripatetic to country villages, and to teach in the town as well.

16962. Did you propose to teach elementary science?—We have been teaching elementary science in connection with the Department of Science and Art.

16963. Then, practically, your purpose was to establish a school in which you would teach the whole range of what are usually called technical subjects?—Yes, that was our purpose and anxiety.

16964. For boys, woodwork, agriculture, and elementary science; would you teach drawing?—Oh, yes, we have had a fully qualified teacher of drawing.

16965. And for girls, needlework, dressmaking, laundry, and cooking?—Yes.

16966. Will you give us an idea of how far your purpose has been carried out, up to the present day—first, how many pupils have you actually in the school at present?—We are only just after opening, I could not say.

16967. How many had you last year?—About 1[illegible].

16968. Of these how many were males and how many females?—I would say nearly ninety girls, and the rest were boys.

16969. What were the ages of those pupils that actually came to you?—I suppose the youngest amongst them would be twelve or fourteen, and then they went up to twenty-five.

16970. And what subjects were actually taught last year in the school?—The subjects actually taught last year were cookery and laundry, dressmaking, and cutting out, typewriting, and shorthand.

16971. Drawing?—Drawing, model drawing, freehand, and perspective drawing, and there was watercolour and painting in oils for advanced students.

16972. Are you satisfied with the success that you have achieved; does it show, do you think, that there was a want of the kind of education that you are providing?—It shows there was decidedly a want, and the only difficulty I have about the matter is that the teachers of the National schools found a difficulty in allowing the advanced children to go to us.

16973. Did that difficulty arise from the hour at which they had to come, or from the unwillingness of the teachers that the children should be taught these subjects?—They were very anxious they should be taught these subjects, but they were afraid they would neglect their home lessons in consequence of coming to our schools at night, at least that was the reason alleged.

16974. CHAIRMAN.—How often was it proposed they should go to you?—For cooking, three times a week and laundry twice, that is the girls, that was the only difficulty we found at all.

16975. Monsignor MOLLOY.—Are you of opinion that some of these subjects, at least, might be taught in the ordinary National schools, or do you think it better they should be all taught apart from the National schools, in institutions such as yours?—I think it would be the best, because we would have the highly efficient teachers there. We have a good deal of money at our disposal in consequence of the grant from the rates and the Department of Science and Art, and that enables us to have highly qualified teachers.

16976. What is the rate?—1d. in the £, and that yields £316 annually; that is collected on the entire town.

16977. Suppose your school were firmly and permanently established, would it meet your object if it were reserved for those who have already finished their National school course?—Of course, it would.

16978. And in that case a preparation might be made for the training you give, by teaching the first elements of these subjects in the National schools?—Yes.

16979. You would then have no opposition from the National school teachers?—No.

16980. You have heard I daresay that in other countries they have what they call continuation schools?—Yes.

16981. That is to say, schools which are attended by pupils who have already left the ordinary primary schools?—Ours is a school of that nature, but we were very anxious to benefit the children as long as they were not taught these subjects in the National schools.

16982. Can you tell us whether the teaching given in your institution has been accepted as satisfactory by the people—whether they appreciate the kind of teaching you give?—The best evidence of that is they are continuing the rate.

16983. So that the ratepayers are with you. Are the pupils of your school chiefly the children of ratepayers?—Oh, they are the children of ratepayers.

16984. Then we may take it that the parents of those children desire that education?—Yes.

16985. And you think is important that this kind of education should be superadded to what the children learn in the National schools?—I think it is of interest at present because the great proportion of children, as far as I have come in contact with them, after leaving the National schools, don't seem to know the elements of cookery, or laundry, or dressmaking.

16986. Do you think that the children, when they leave the National schools, are not properly fitted for the work before them in life?—There is abundant evidence of that—I have known a number of girls to leave the National schools and afterwards to get married, and they were very ignorant of how to conduct housework; they got their husband's wages at the end of the week, but were unable to conduct the household work. They could play the piano, and had accomplishments of that kind, but were wanting in practical knowledge.

16987. The children who learn dressmaking from you, do they afterwards apply that knowledge at home to practical purposes, in the way of making and mending their own clothes?—I know they do, and they prepare the dinners for their families at home.

16988. So with regard to dressmaking and cookery, they apply what they learn practically at home?—Yes, and with the best of results. I have known from their parents that.

16989. You were asked whether you thought it would be sufficient to teach the principles of cooking without teaching the art of cooking. I should like you to explain your views on that point more fully?—For young children it would be very good to begin with the principles of cooking, it would be something gained, afterwards the knowledge might be extended.

16990. But do you not think that, before you are done with them, they ought to learn the art of cooking as well as the principles?—I think so.

16991. Do you think they could ever apply the principles usefully in practice if they had not been taught the art as well as the principles?—Some clever people might, but it would be no burden to them, the knowledge would be very useful. In a great many National schools where the qualified teacher went the great difficulty was in getting proper materials to use in the cooking.

16992. How was the difficulty met in your institution?—Our committee supply everything, materials of the very first and best order, and then we have all the appliances that are needful.

16993. What do you do with the things that are cooked?—We manage to sell them immediately after the lesson.

16994. You find no difficulty in disposing of them?—Very little.

16995. Does the sale of them pay the first cost of raw material?—It goes very largely to pay the first cost of the raw material.

16996. Mr. MOLLOY.—Have you published any annual report of your institute?—We have.

16997. And the latest one is for 1896?—For the session of 1896-97.

16998. Would you have any objection to hand it in to the secretary later on?—With pleasure.

16999. What science subjects are taken up in connexion with the Science and Art Department?—Last year mathematics, building construction, practical, plane and solid geometry, and we were teaching also the principles of agriculture.

17000. And in connexion with the City and Guilds of London?—We had wood work, carpentry and joinery, and dressmaking and cutting out.

17001. What attendances are required in connexion with South Kensington and with the City and Guilds of London Institute?—I think twenty.

17002. Now in the twenty lessons did the ordinary ex-National school pupils acquire sufficient knowledge of these subjects, do you think?—Of course twenty attendances are the minimum, but there they are every night; they must qualify by twenty attendances for examination but they come regularly every night during the session.

17003. What is the state of information on these subjects that you find the National teachers have?—I think they were very well up in these sciences when they came to us even, but their knowledge was perfected at our place, so far that they passed very creditably the Department of Science and Art.

17004. Had there been a Science and Art Class in Galway before the establishment of your institute?—I believe there was, there were two or three pupils in it. There was a science and art class, also, conducted by the Jesuits for some years, but they gave it up before we began.

17005. CHAIRMAN.—Where did they get their previous knowledge?—At the different schools of the town.

17006. The National schools?—Yes, but they were anxious to get certificates under the Science and Art Department.

17007. But who taught them there?—The National teachers.

17008. Then the National teachers do teach cooking?—No, these were the scientific subjects under the Science and Art Department.

17009. Mr. MOLLOY.—The other subjects were electricity, magnetism, acoustics, light and heat?—Yes, we had these last year taught by a graduate of the University.

17010. The pupils who come forward from the National schools to receive instruction in these branches in your institute, how were they prepared previously?—They were not prepared at all, they had to commence at the beginning.

Galway.
Oct. 8, 1897.
Rev. P. Lally, P.P.

17011. Then their success, as tested by these certificates, is due to your instruction?—Yes, in technological subjects.

17012. Have you any minimum age for admission?—We have specified no minimum, but we scarcely receive any one under fourteen.

17013. And the range is from fourteen up?—Yes, we often take tradesmen in to learn the sciences that apply to their trade. My idea always was to have a man who understands building construction and plane and solid geometry, and understands the application of these subjects to trades.

17014. Of course drawing to scale is taught very carefully in your institute?—Yes.

17015. In what state were the pupils in drawing who came to you?—Except those who came from an advanced school where drawing was taught occasionally, the pupils from the ordinary National schools were innocent of it.

17016. You mentioned you were in favour of continuation schools?—Yes.

17017. At what hour would you expect them to open?—Our hours are from 7 to 9. But some classes might be carried on earlier in the evening; we have had earlier classes at 5 o'clock; we had a class working occasionally at 5 o'clock for the children of the advanced classes of the National schools.

17018. What was your average number under instruction last year?—150.

17019. What accommodation, pray, had you for the 150?—We have a large house in *Prospect Hill*, with a good many large rooms, and we pay £40 for that. And then we had three rooms, the Commissioners gave us, in the Model School; in the largest carpentry was taught, building construction, machine construction, and practical plane and solid geometry; and in another room the headmaster of the Model School was teaching science, mathematics, and the principles of agriculture in connexion with the Department of Science and Art.

17020. How many rooms have you in Prospect Hill?—We have five or six big rooms; we were teaching there cookery, laundry, and dressmaking and cutting out, typewriting and shorthand, and different branches of art.

17021. Do you find it convenient to have your school in two portions?—Exceedingly inconvenient, and it was my anxiety to have one good centre to teach all the subjects, and it was for that reason I hoped, if the Commissioners were disposing of the Model School, they would give it to us for that

17027. You have already answered this question, that you find the ratepayers are decidedly in favour of the work done, and desire a certain amount of it?—The best evidence is that they are continuing the rate.

17028. Mr. Harrington.—Where did you get the teachers for the woodwork from?—Well, I had a very great difficulty in getting a teacher of woodwork. I think we spent about £10 in advertising in Ireland, and we could not get a highly-qualified man, because my desire from the start was to have a man qualified in building construction and plane and solid geometry, and to apply these to trades, and we could not get a man so qualified in Ireland, so that it was through the agency of the principal of the Polytechnic at Borough-road I was able to get a man from London, and he worked with us for three years.

17029. So most of your teachers are drawn from England?—We had three teachers from England, one from London, and two from Leeds, but the teacher for cookery this year is drawn from the Royal Association, and she is a highly qualified lady, and teaches very efficiently indeed.

17030. Mr. Struthers.—Your school is practically an evening continuation school?—Practically a continuation school.

17031. The schools are held in the evening?—From seven to nine.

17032. All the year round?—No; during the session commencing the first Monday in October, and terminating with the May examinations conducted by the Science and Art Department and the City and Guilds Institute.

17033. You have no classes in summer?—Not at present.

17034. Would you think it useful to have classes carried on all the year round?—Exceedingly useful; but for evening classes it is scarcely practicable to have them in summer, because in the fine evenings there are so many amusements it is impossible to keep the children at school.

17035. The subjects you teach in your school are mostly of the kind that could not be taught to young children in elementary schools?—The pupils would require to be of an advanced age to be able to appreciate the information, accordingly we don't take them earlier than fourteen.

17036. They are also subjects of such a kind that they would require teachers of a special knowledge to teach thoroughly?—Yes.

17037. Such that you could not expect the ord

could be carried on in more remote districts?—I only considered the matter so far as Galway was concerned, and a radius of seven or eight miles outside of Galway. I would have all the schools within that radius served by the peripatetic teachers from our centre.

17044. You spoke of the teaching of woodwork in the town of Galway, and your idea was that the elder children should come from the National schools to your centre to be instructed there?—Yes, and that is what a good many of them have done.

17045. Then would you expect to be paid a grant for the instruction so given by the National Board?—Yes.

17046. You would wish that?—I would wish that.

17047. Professor FITZGERALD.—There is a point that I have not been able to make out—that question of time has been raised, and the instruction of boys in country schools in agriculture. What do boys in town schools do at the time the boys in country schools are taught agriculture in the elementary schools? In the elementary town schools children need not be taught agriculture; what are they taught at the hour at which agriculture is taught in the country schools?—I cannot say straight off.

17048. There is no other subject that they are generally taught in town schools corresponding to agriculture?—In a great many of the town schools I think they are taught elementary drawing; I don't think that is taught in country schools as a rule.

17049. Boys are not taught drawing in all schools now, but they are in some schools?—No; it is a great pity they would not be taught in all.

17050. Would there be time in the present programme?—In the Convent schools drawing is taught.

17051. Without interfering with the literary programme?—Oh, yes; it can be worked into the programme. It is taught in the two Convent town schools.

17052. So it could be introduced in all schools without seriously interfering with the literary training?—I think it could.

17053. Do you think the managers about this district would be willing to introduce, or anxious to encourage the introduction of drawing and elementary science into the schools?—I never knew a man to be opposed to it. I think they would be very glad of it; it would be so useful to the children.

17054. From your knowledge of the other managers about?—All the managers I ever heard expressed themselves satisfied with the children learning drawing.

17055. Do you think they would like to encourage them to do some elementary manual instruction, cardboard work, and elementary woodwork?—I would not like to speak for any other manager, but I would myself. I never heard them discuss it.

17056. It was suggested by the Bishop of Limerick that it would be desirable that the managers should combine together to arrange in a particular district what manual instruction or what general instruction in the schools would suit their particular district?—Yes; I was reading that in the newspapers this morning. I think it was a very good suggestion, and that it would work very fairly.

17057. Do you think it would be possible to work it amongst the managers of this district?—I think it would.

17058. The question has been raised as to whether it would be better to introduce elementary science and object lessons, and that class of subject, in the town schools, or to introduce manual instruction and elementary constructive work, like cardwork, and wirework, and a number of other things like that, as an introduction to woodwork that can be introduced into schools; and in opposition to that there are object lessons and elementary science; have you ever thought of which of these would be better?—I think object lessons and elementary science would be very useful for children.

17059. You think they would be more popular with the teachers?—They would be very popular with the teachers.

17060. And the parents?—The parents would be very glad of them.

17061. Do you think they would prefer them to the constructive work?—The constructive work to go on later on.

17062. Do you think the parents about this district would object to their children being made carpenters of?—Some children I have been recently speaking to say that the parents would.

17063. You have not found the parents object to the girls being taught laundry, for instance?—On the contrary, they have been delighted at it; in the beginning they did not see how they would want that knowledge, but when they commenced to learn and show their proficiency in washing the parents were delighted.

17064. Then, as a matter of fact, the parents in Galway have seen the value of it?—They have seen the value of it, both of laundry and of cookery.

17065. Then you think from that they would be likely to be willing that the other subjects should be introduced into the elementary schools?—I think they would; when it commenced they did not see the necessity of it, but after the children acquired the knowledge they saw the utility of it, and the benefit of it to their own households; they told me so.

17066. You don't think the parents would object to those subjects being introduced into our schools?—I don't see why Irish parents should object when English parents do not.

17067. There was some opposition at first?—And it was overcome, and I think it would be overcome.

17068. Rev. Dr. EVANS.—The Commissioners of National Education have granted you the use of a portion of the Model School for your technical school?—Yes, sir.

17069. How long is that ago?—About a year and a half ago.

17070. Are you the manager of the technical school in Galway?—I am not the manager, but I am honorary secretary, and have so acted since 1892.

17071. Is there a manager at all?—The Lord Bishop is chairman of the committee.

17072. There is a committee?—Yes.

17073. How many pupils have you in the school?—I have [illegible] in summer and winter, and the average was 150 last year.

17074. Where did you obtain your teachers?—I had one from London, whom I got through the agency of the principal of the Polytechnic; he was a teacher of carpentry and building construction, and practical plane and solid geometry, and I got two teachers from Leeds—the teacher of cookery and the teacher of dressmaking and cutting-out.

17075. Is there any inspection of the school?—Mr. Preston inspects on behalf of the Department of Science and Art.

17076. Do the inspectors of the National Board come into it?—The District Inspector superintended the examinations last year on behalf of the Department of Science and Art.

17077. But the Commissioners of National Education as such?—Exercise no official authority over it.

17078. Do they charge fees?—Yes.

17079. Could you give an indication, Father Lally, of what these fees are?—The rule is very elastic, because the committee, in order to put no embargo on the children using the schools, allowed me to use a discretionary power in fixing the fee, and where I saw a deserving case the fee was reduced, and sometimes remitted entirely.

17080. You reserve a discretion to yourself?—No, but the committee have allowed me a discretion in the matter.

17081. Do you send out peripatetic teachers?—We have sent out a peripatetic teacher of weaving of wool, but we found his services were not much used in the country.

17082. The services of the teacher did not quite satisfy the people?—No, the people did not want him.

17083. Have you any objection to say what you pay the teachers?—We pay to the teacher of practical instruction in wood £150 for the year, practically it was for the session, and the teacher of cookery last year from Leeds was paid £80 a year, and the teacher of dressmaking £70.

17084. Is there a Christian Brothers' school in Galway?—The Christian Brothers conduct the Industrial School; that was the only one.

17085. Is there any teaching there?—There is the teaching of woodwork.

17086. Similar to yours?—Not similar to mine; their teacher has no scientific knowledge.

17087. CHAIRMAN.—Is he an ordinary teacher?—He is an ordinary carpenter, but then he has no idea of the scientific subjects.

17088. REV DR. EVANS.—Yours is of a higher order and much more educational?—Yes, in the highest degree educational.

17089. CHAIRMAN.—You are aware that in some quarters there is an objection taken to introducing an artisan into a school, on account of the discipline of the school?—Into a National school?

17090. Well, into an elementary school?—That would be overcome by my proposal that the manual instruction would be imparted after the literary work.

17091. That the teacher, in fact, should have nothing to do with it, and, therefore, his authority would not be undermined in the eyes of the children by an outsider being brought in?—Not the slightest: he would stand as he was before.

17092. REV. DR. EVANS.—Can you put in, before we leave, a statement to show how much more you would do if you had better accommodation in the Model School?—I would tell you at once, if we had the Model School entirely as a technical school, we would acquire the land around it for practical farming and teaching of agriculture, and there are a good many more classes we could support; all we want is money and room.

17093. *Professor* FITZGERALD.—Then it would cease to be a primary school?—It would cease to be a [illegible] school.

17094. MR STRUTHERS.—It would still be available in the day time?—No, we would have our classes there; at present the difficulty is, we have two houses divided.

17095. REV. DR. WILSON.—Are you able at present to accommodate all that apply to be admitted?—We are, but the expense is large; we have to pay £7[illegible] this year for our house, and a large proportion of [illegible] and lease as well.

17096. Do you admit all denominations?—Oh, certainly; we are working under the Technical Instruction Act of 1889.

17097. Have you many not connected with your own church?—We have; in fact, I think the greater proportion are Protestants and Presbyterians.

17098. Captain SHAW.—Was the peripatetic teacher for weaving?—Yes, a teacher of woollen weaving.

17099. Would it not necessitate there being looms wherever he went?—It would not; our anxiety was that he would teach the people how to construct looms according to the latest models.

17100. Teach them to construct looms?—Teach the village carpenter how to get up a loom for the people themselves.

17101. That expense would fall on the locality?—It would come on the parties who were anxious to go on with the weaving industry themselves.

Galway. — Oct. 6, 1897. — Very Rev. Canon Lynskey, P.P.

Councils have adopted in some places in England?—I think so.

17121. What you would advocate is, that the managers of the schools should have power to make arrangements with the farmers?—To make arrangements to procure the plots.

17122. How large a plot would you think necessary?—Not more than five or six perches in some instances.

17123. That, you think, would be sufficient?—Quite enough for turnip sowing, and potato sowing, and other agricultural problems that there might be in the district.

17124. And you think that that plan would be better than the present practice of teaching agriculture, by merely getting up a text-book, or than another plan that the Bishop of Limerick suggested yesterday, of teaching the principles underlying agriculture without the use of plots?—Well, I would the instruction, such as it is given now, is very useless.

17125. The course the Bishop suggested was an intermediate course between the two, he was against the text-book and against the plot; but he thought the general principles of agriculture might be explained to the children, the use of manures, and the properties of manures; you think plots would be preferable?—I think, unless you have the manures there, and then to point out to them the value of them, it would be perfectly useless, because the children would forget the oral instruction after they leave the school.

17126. Do you think, for children living on the seaboard, it would be advisable to teach them something with regard to fish curing and the value of seaweed?—Certainly, these are the industries of the locality; it would be useless to teach them manual instruction if you did not teach them the instruction useful to them in their daily avocations.

17127. I see you have some remarks upon the subject of results examinations, what would you say upon that subject?—The examination by results, such as it is at present, is not fair to the teacher or to the pupils; it is extremely unfair to deprive the teacher of his salary, because it is part of his salary, if a child has got 100 days made, and then I think it is also unjust if seventy-five of a class pass, and there are fifteen who have not passed. I think the seventy-five ought to carry with them the other fifteen, because what the Board, I take it, desire to have, is an indication that the teacher has been doing his duty, and I think the seventy-five amply give testimony that the teacher has been doing his duty, and if, therefore, fifteen or less, three, or four, or five, or six, have not been successful, and have not brains enough to pass, it is hard to deprive the teacher of his salary on their account.

17128. What would you say with regard to the examination of Inspectors?—I think the Inspector ought to confine himself exclusively and entirely to the book, and ought not to adopt words that are not to be found out in the book; he ought to examine, and not to desire to puzzle. I heard of a question such as this:—"What are the waters about Alaska?" asked of a little child.

17129. I believe you think that no Inspector ought to be permitted to hold results examinations, until he has some trained experience in the discharge of the duty of examinations?—I think that, certainly. Suppose, for instance, a student from Trinity College became an Inspector——

17130. How would he get experience without examining?—He ought to accompany the Inspectors who go to examine for results, and see how experienced Inspectors examine, and then to take, as it were, his lesson from them.

17131. And do some trial examination himself in their presence?—Certainly. You have the training of teachers; and the training of Inspectors, I think, would be of far more importance so far as results are concerned, and the fees to be paid to the teacher.

17132. Then you think it would be better that the Inspector should earn his position by practical training in the art of inspection rather than by passing an examination in a paper?—I think so, certainly; I think it is a great encouragement to a teacher to know that he is likely, after a little time, to come to an inspectorship.

17133. Mr. Redington.—Do you think it would be fair to the children to deprive them of their play-time?—I think the manual instruction would be play, it would be very easy to make it play-time.

17134. They would enjoy it as much as running about in the play-ground?—I think so, remaining about in the cold in the play-ground. If they had this instruction in a room, although instruction, it would be amusement to them.

17135. If, by some modification of the programme, we could get time for the manual instruction without interfering with the play-time would it not be better?—It would, but it would be very hard to find it; it would be very hard to modify the programme unless you extended the time. For instance, I was in England lately, and saw the children coming from school at four o'clock or a little after (half-past four); we have our schools closed at three. I cannot understand why we would not at least have the energy of the English children.

17136. But you know that they have a two hours' break in the middle of the day in England?—That would not be of utility in my district.

17137. I don't say it would, but the English children get lots of play-time. It has been given in evidence that grammar, and possibly geography, might be made optional subjects for certain classes, would you be in favour of that?—No. I think the little grammar they have ought to be continued, and geography too.

17138. Chairman.—But the sort of geography they have, the learning of the heights of mountains, and the lengths of rivers?

Monsignor Molloy.—And the waters around Alaska?—Yes; I think it would be well to continue the teaching of geography, because, if boys or girls don't know the expansion of the globe, what else do they know?

17139. Mr. Redington.—I think you said that it would be very difficult to provide materials for cookery in rural schools?—Certainly.

17140. It was stated to us that it might be possible for a teacher to cook her dinner before the pupils, and so get over the difficulty about the provision of materials. What do you think of that?—I think it is not possible, the children would be only all laughing at her.

17141. Why should they laugh at seeing a good Irish stew cooked?—I don't think it is practicable. If you want to introduce a thing of that kind you might go about it in such a way that the children will not make a burlesque of it, and you must have a distinct room from the ordinary schoolroom.

17142. If the cooking were done at the end of the day's lesson, and the dinner were to form part of the teacher's dinner, would there not be a reality about the cookery lesson that there is not, perhaps, under other circumstances?—I don't think it is feasible in that way.

17143. Are any of the science programmes of the Board taken up in any of your schools?—Yes, Euclid and algebra.

17144. Is any chemistry taken up?—Not yet.

17145. I think you said that the study of a little chemistry might be of use with regard to the kelp industry?—Decidedly, and it would be useful in agriculture also.

17146. Why is not chemistry taught?—I suppose the teachers cannot come to that, the children have not arrived at that perfection that we would recommend them to learn chemistry.

Galway. — Oct. 1, 1887. — Very Rev. Canon Lynskey, P.P.

17147. Can the pupils of the fifth class not be taught it if the teachers are competent?—I am sure the teachers would easily learn and become competent.

17148. Would you be in favour of making some elementary science compulsory?—I would chemistry.

17149. Is not cottage-gardening taught in some of your schools?—It is.

17150. Do you think that a desirable subject to teach in elementary schools?—Very much so, it has been a great success.

17151. Does it interfere with the teaching of literary subjects?—Not at all.

17152. At what hour is it taught?—Generally after school.

17153. Monsignor Molloy.—Are the eighteen schools of which you are manager, all in the parish of Clifden?—They are all in the parish of Clifden.

17154. The greater number of them, I suppose, are rural schools?—All, except the Convent school.

17155. Could you say generally what is the number of the school-going children in the parish?—I think the number on the rolls would be about 1,800, and the average number about 700 irrespective of the Convent school.

17156. Including boys and girls?—Yes.

17157. You said, I think, that the manual training would be a kind of recreation?—I think so.

17158. A relief from the literary work?—Yes.

17159. And you think the hours of attendance at school, if manual instruction were given, might be extended a little?—I think so.

17160. Say half-an-hour a day?—Quite so.

17161. I think also you said that half-an-hour might be gained from other subjects?—Quite so, in the middle of the day.

17162. That would give an hour a day, which would be five hours a week?—That would be quite sufficient.

17163. That would leave abundance of time not only for manual teaching, but also for the elements of science?—Quite so.

17164. Do you think it desirable the elements of science should be taught as well as the literary subjects?—I think it is a very great advantage in the different countries where it is taught.

17165. Would the parents in your parish be glad to see subjects of this kind introduced of a practical character?—I think so; I don't see why there should be any objections at all. It would be the desire of a parent to advance his child and I take it the parents would be very pleased with anything that contributes to that.

17166. Do you think the education at present given in the schools of the National Board is too strictly of a literary character?—I really don't think it is at all too literary, we are advancing very rapidly—education is advancing, and with the little time that a child is able to go to school, I think in the end when he has acquired such information as he can get in a National school, he has not acquired too much.

17167. You would not desire to see that reduced in amount?—It would be a retrograde motion.

17168. But you think it desirable that something in the way of practical and manual teaching should be added?—Yes.

17169. In order to prepare the children more directly for their work in life?—Yes.

17170. Mr. Molloy.—You referred to the results examination which you characterised as unfair to the teacher?—I think so.

17171. If I understand your answer aright you would prefer having a class examination of pupils?—I would have an individual examination but class as a result.

17172. In that individual examination would you include those who had not, as they technically call it, made the minimum number of days—100?—I certainly think the number of days ought to be shortened, 100 days are too many. I think for the purpose of results 60 days ought to be quite sufficient. If the information be there, because after all if you come to the same end by 60 days, if you have the child taught in that time, I think it would be the same thing, so far as education is concerned, as if the child were there 100 days.

17173. In view of the very large number of children who do not attend the minimum number of days, would you not think it desirable on the occasion of the inspector's annual visit that there would come regular examination by him?—I do, I think it would be very proper.

17174. So practically your idea is that all the children on the school roll should be examined?—If possible.

17175. But you are in favour of individual examination?—Individual examination, at the same time that class would be taken as a result.

17176. You deem it desirable that a newly-appointed inspector should accompany an experienced one for a little while?—I think it is very important.

17177. Perhaps you are not aware that for the last forty years that has been the case?—More or less, I am aware of it. I made inquiries, but I still think it has not been sufficiently careful, or tend to bring home to the young inspector the best method of examination.

17178. Would you indicate any period that you think he ought to be, as it were, in training before commencing to examine, with a view to award results?—That would depend also on the results. If the gentleman learned quickly, and fell into harness quickly, the time could be shortened, but it is very hard often to conduct an examination of little children.

17179. In reference to your eighteen schools—which, by the way, is an unprecedented number to be under one manager—how many of them are exclusively under masters, and how many under mistresses, and how many are mixed schools?—The girls' are fewer than the boys'; I suppose about seven schools would be girls', and the others would be boys', and there are two mixed schools.

17180. Are these conducted by female teachers?—By a master and female teacher.

17181. In the eight schools for boys have you any special instruction suitable for boys?—There is no special instruction except the cot-gardening; agriculture, of course, is common.

17182. Is drawing taught in these eighteen schools?—I don't think it is taught in any of the schools, and I think it would be most valuable.

17183. Surely amongst the number of assistant teachers of the eighteen schools there must be persons who have been trained and have obtained certificates in that important subject, and thereby qualified themselves to earn results fees and introduce the subject?—I think there is only one or two who have a certificate for teaching in drawing.

17184. How many of your eighteen principal teachers are trained teachers?—I think they are nearly all trained except a few, three or four, I think.

17185. Has cookery been carried out in any of the girls' schools?—No, except in the Convent school.

17186. In the case of the girls is it plain needlework and knitting?—Yes. I am not manager of the Convent school at Clifden.

17187. Is cookery not carried out there?—It is; it is taught, but not extensively; they found it very difficult to find material.

17188. Chairman.—What sort of things do they cook?—Chops and fish, legs of mutton, hams, anything that turns up just there.

17189. Do they always buy legs of mutton?—Yes; it is useful for the nuns for the purpose of teaching as well as for their own use.

17190. Monsignor Molloy.—Can you say what is

o go to school
us have to go

kwis ?—I think

the evidence given in the class rather than by individuals here and there.

17204. Yes, but if you take away play-time and school-rate [illegible] instruction, you still [illegible] the school day ?—Not very much, only half an hour

Galway.

Oct. 8, 1898.

Very Rev. [illegible]

Galway. — Oct. 8, 1897. — Very Rev. [illegible] Lyndsey, P.P.

owned by the farmers?—Certainly; it would be very hard to get them otherwise.

17229. Would it not be well to show the children experiments illustrating the growth of plants; for instance, in their present agricultural handbook it is said that if you do such a thing with a seed it will grow. Would it not be better to show them experiments with seeds growing?—I think so, as an object lesson; nothing better.

17230. Could you not grow seeds in sand, and show them that the seeds would grow a great deal better if you put a little manure in it?—Quite so.

17231. And experiments of that kind to illustrate the principles of the growth of plants?—That would be entirely my idea.

17232. Do you think children would be willing to go into schools to learn that?—I think so.

17233. If it were substituted for their present mode of teaching agriculture?—Yes.

17234. Rev. Dr. Evans.—If three-fourths of the pupils of a school pass the examination you think it affords evidence of the teacher's fidelity and efficiency?—I think so, certainly.

17235. And that he should be paid the full fees for the teaching?—That is my view of the situation.

17236. You would not omit any part of the literary programme?—I would not. I think it is little enough as it is.

17237. You have evidence that the literary instruction is of such value to the people that you would not, on their part, feel justified in omitting any portion of it?—I don't think it would be wise.

17238. Would you be in favour of modifying it if a better method of teaching were devised?—Yes; I would like to have the best method.

17239. And if a better method of teaching grammar were devised you would be in favour of it?—Yes.

17240. Captain Shaw.—Do you think the Sixth Class Reading Book is not too difficult?—No, I do not.

17241. Do you find they understand it intelligently?—The Sixth Class child will answer intelligently from the Sixth Book.

17242. Rev. Dr. Walsh.—You are manager of eighteen schools. Assuming you do that work conscientiously, as I am sure you do, from all you have stated, have you really any time for other school work?—Oh, lots of time. I can visit six schools on any day that I go out and be back at four o'clock, and I have often done it; and go out the other side and visit six more the next day—leave at ten o'clock and be back at four o'clock.

17243. With regard to results fees, you have been speaking about them from the standpoint of the teacher; from your wide experience—and it is very wide—of the National system, are you in favour of it at all?—I am thoroughly. I think it fits a child afterwards for the battle of life. If he has to become a civil servant, it is a capital preparation for the Civil Service or any other examination.

17244. You don't think it lies open to the objection that it is a system of cramming instead of teaching?—I don't think so. I think those who say it is a system of cramming object to it on other grounds. I think it is a capital system for imparting instruction and information.

17245. Well, many have said it to us, but they have not had your experience?—Besides that I have had experience as a boy of the National school. The results system did not exist at the time, but I say the system existing now is much better than the system that was when I was a boy going to the National school.

17246. You say the inspectors should confine themselves to the book?—Most certainly.

17247. From your experience is the book often departed from in the examination?—Well, I don't think it is often departed from, but, at the same time, if difficult words be sought out in the book I think the book is more or less departed from, because the book generally is taken as the foundation, the difficult words are incidents. They must be in the course of reading, but, at the same time, the child would not, perhaps, catch that difficult word. He might go to what is the general tone of the book.

17248. Suppose the Treasury could be induced to expend the necessary money on fish curing and things of that sort, do you think it would be a judicious expenditure of public money?—Decidedly; as a matter of fact it has so proved itself already.

Galway.

Oct. 5, 1897.

Mr. James Perry, M.A.I.

mainly leniency, but my feeling is that it is only a temporary expedient. I think there ought to be some sort of test of value being given for the money, but I think the payment by results is a very rough and ready plan.

17264. As at present carried out?—As at present carried out.

17265.—Would you pay a diligent teacher more than a teacher who is lazy and idle?—Certainly, I would rather have an examination of the school than an examination of the children. I think if I was planning the thing I would send one inspector on the basis of averages, I would not let it all depend on a single inspector, not that I have any doubt about the fairness of an inspector, but inspectors have little peculiarities, and it would equalise matters if one inspector was sent after another.

17266. That would greatly increase the cost of inspection?—It would, but I would go in for a change all over, inspectors are now of pretty much the same standing, and you may have a graduated force of inspectors and assistant inspectors.

17267. You are acquainted with the agriculture of this county; do you think it might be benefited by an improvement in the system of teaching it in schools?—Certainly, my experience of the teaching of agriculture in schools is that it was not taught at all. I attended a rural school.

17268. It was taught out of a book?—It was scarcely taught at all.

17269. How were you taught?—The book was there, we knew it was in the school, but I don't remember ever reading that book in school.

17270. Did the teacher explain what was in the book?—He did not at all, he did not teach us any agriculture.

17271. Chairman.—Then he got no fees?—This was before the results system.

17272. Mr. Redington.—Do you think agriculture ought to be taught to children of the age of those who go to National schools?—I do.

17273. Do you think a school plot attached to each school would facilitate the practical teaching of agriculture?—I do.

17274. What size do you think it ought to be?—I would have it a good size, half an acre, it depends on what you could get.

17275. Could you not teach the principles of agriculture on a much smaller area?—I would rather have it taught in a more clear way, so that there would be apparently some real use in what was done; it would be more like a child's garden if you had it much smaller than that. If you have a mere small plot of 4 or 5 perches, as Father Lynskey spoke of, I think it would be too small.

17276. Could you not show the pupil all the operations of agriculture on that small plot?—You could, you could do it on a blackboard or in little boxes with sand.

17277. Could you not teach how a plant grows and how manure affects a plant in a box of sand?—You could, but I would prefer the larger operation.

17278. Is there any danger that if the plot were too large the teacher would make it a source of profit?—I don't see that there should be any objection to that.

17279. Ought it not rather to be a place for experiments, and experiments are not always profitable?—I think I would experiment in a profitable way if possible, and that is why I would go in for a larger plot. The schoolmaster who taught me had a plot in connection with the school.

17280. If you show a pupil how manure improves some vegetables and the absence of manure prevents others from growing equally well, that is not a very profitable way of carrying on agricultural operations, yet it is very useful?—Yes, but you see, to have teaching of that kind effective it would need to be continued for a considerable length of time; if you grow a crop it takes some time.

17281. Are not the children there all the year round?—They are, but I would do it on a small scale.

17282. If manual instruction were brought into the schools what kind of instruction would be most useful?—The Chairman has not allowed me to say anything about technical instruction.

17283. If you had a child ten or twelve years old of your own, and wanted to give him a little manual instruction, what would you teach him?—I would teach him to plane wood.

17284. Chairman.—You are aware that in Denmark the early lessons are exercises in sawing and planing and working with the chisel?—That is Sloyd.

17285. Professor FitzGerald.—Do you call that technical instruction?—I call every kind of instruction technical instruction.

17286. What the Chairman meant by saying that we excluded technical instruction was instruction in trades as distinguished from handiwork; the manual instruction that can be given in schools is all very well, but we are not inquiring into technical instruction in carpentry?—I call every kind of instruction to myself technical instruction from start to finish.

17287. Chairman.—I am afraid our Commission is not allowed to inquire into technical instruction so far as it is the art of learning a trade; we are only to inquire into that sort of instruction which would give elementary knowledge which would enable a pupil after he left school to learn a trade with more facility and to be handier than he otherwise would be?—In my little slip that I sent to your secretary I confined it to that.

17288. I understood you to go into a great deal more than we are inquiring into?—I said it would be good for a boy to be put to point a piece of mild rod, it is a very difficult thing for a beginner to do, and to weld two pieces of said rod. I would not call that instruction for a trade, it would teach him the properties of iron in a way he could not pick up otherwise, and then there would be the question of working with wood planing, and so on.

17289. And making simple models?—Making simple models and making the drawings of things.

17290. I don't know whether you have read the evidence that was given before us in England, but if so you will see that in Birmingham they carry the distinction so far as not to allow the pupils of the board schools to finish anything; they are allowed to make joints, but not to make a complete box?—I think we will get beyond that in time.

17291. Monsignor Molloy.—You have practical experience of the working of the present system of National Education in this country?—I think fairly.

17292. Do you think that the present system affords a good and solid groundwork for a subsequent course of technical education?—I do not.

17293. Do you think it desirable that it should afford such a groundwork?—I do.

17294. How do you think it could be modified, so as to constitute a good groundwork for technical education to be afterwards added?—The great difficulty is in rural schools, where you have a single teacher to teach a great number of subjects. I think it is an impossible task for one teacher, and there ought to be peripatetic teachers.

17295. Do you think it desirable that all pupils in the National schools should be taught to use their eyes and hands and other senses?—I do, certainly.

17296. Not merely in reading and writing, but in doing things?—Certainly.

17297. With regard to things they ought to be taught to do, would woodwork be a suitable kind of manual training for children in National schools?—It would.

17298. Do you think it desirable it should be instructed?—I do.

17299. And in connection with woodwork should they be taught drawing?—They should.

G 2

17300. And they should be shown how to work out their drawings in the wood?—They should.

17301. Ought they to be taught, do you think, the elementary principles of science?—They should.

17302. In order to teach these subjects there must be a trained body of men fit to teach them?—I think so.

17304. And, therefore, do you think that these subjects ought to be taught to the teachers in the training colleges? Well, you can't get one man to know everything well; I think I would give them all an opportunity.

17305. All the teachers in the training colleges should have an opportunity of learning some one or more of these subjects?—Yes; and the men who are specially good at these subjects I would make teachers of these subjects, and send them round the schools as peripatetic teachers.

17306. You don't think, then, that the ordinary schoolmaster, even if well trained, would be able to teach these subjects himself in addition to the ordinary literary course?—I don't think it. I think he has too much to do already. I think that is the great difficulty. I have compared the pupils at National schools with the pupils in well-organised schools attended by children whose parents are able to pay for a higher class of education. Here you have got different men having separate subjects to teach, and you find a child at one of these schools done a great deal more in the time than a child in the National schools—incomparably more.

17307. Let us take a large school with several teachers. Do you not think it would be possible so to select these teachers that amongst them they could teach the various subjects?—Yes, there are some schools where that might be done, but they are comparatively few.

17308. Where there is only one teacher, you think he ought to get assistance from peripatetic teachers for the extra subjects, such as elementary science, manual training, and drawing?—I think so.

17309. CHAIRMAN.—You are aware that some witnesses have made very great objection to that system upon the ground that it would lower the ordinary teacher in the eyes of his pupils, and then he would object very strongly to the peripatetic teacher coming in. Do you see any force in that objection?—I do not; I would make the ordinary teacher the administrator of the school, and these other men, some of them might come in as special instructors only, and some of them might be connected with the inspection, and might be really superior to him in standing, but I don't see that it would interfere with him at all.

17310. Monsignor MOLLOY.—In large towns could not the difficulty be got over by having centres to which the pupils would come from the schools around about, to learn the special subjects, such as science, woodwork, cookery, and botany?—Yes, that could be done, but there is the difficulty in the waste of time going from one place to another and one school to another.

17316. In what part of Ireland?—County Derry.

17317. Are you able to contrast the system then in force with the present system of results fees?—My knowledge of the present system is very largely hearsay, but you can hardly live in the country without knowing a great deal about it, and I sometimes do go into a school and see what is going on.

17318. You attended a National school in the County Derry?—Yes, Ballynagan, near Garvagh.

17319. Were the elements of science taught in that school?—No, I learned nothing higher than Euclid there.

17320. And algebra?—No, very little.

17321. Mensuration?—Slightly; Euclid was really the strong point beyond the ordinary things.

17322. Book-keeping?—Yes, slightly.

17323. You are in favour distinctly of the introduction of manual instruction in some rate National schools at present?—Yes, distinctly.

17324. And on the other hand you would not interfere with the existing course?—No, I would add to it. I say you have plenty of time. We really did not work at the National schools in my time; I don't know what they do now, they may be very much more industrious than we were, but I don't think we did an hour's work in the day.

17325. CHAIRMAN.—An objection was raised in Waterford by a National school teacher, who had tried and given up manual instruction that the children were so tired from the work they had to do before they came to school in the morning and after they got home in the evening, on their parents' farms, that it would be impossible to add to the amount of work they did in the school?—I really don't think there is any strength in that objection.

17326. Monsignor MOLLOY.—Change of work is as good as a rest?—Yes, I speak for myself, but we really idled in the National schools.

17327. Captain SHAW.—What time do you get to the National schools in the morning?—Ten o'clock.

17328. Nominally or really?—Oh, really.

17329. The roll is not closed until a quarter to eleven?—I really don't remember when the roll was called in my school, it is a long time ago, but I know I attended very regularly.

17330. From the conditions of the country do you think there is anything to prevent the schools from commencing earlier?—Ten is a fair time to begin. The point I want to insist upon is this, that really the children do not work during the hours they are there, and under the present system it cannot be otherwise, because one teacher is not able to manage a school, as many of them have to do.

17331. Mr. STRUTHERS. — You would have agriculture taught to the children in the National schools, I think you said?—Yes.

17332. At what age?—I think instruction of that kind might be begin about ten.

17333. You think that children from ten to eleven can usefully be taught agriculture?—I think they

ing into the National schools?—It would improve them and probably would increase their price.

17339. Do you think it would be desirable?—Certainly.

17340. Do you think that introducing more manual training, such as elementary woodwork into the schools would make them better workmen?—It would.

17341. Do you think there is room for more carpenters?—Certainly. There is plenty of room for workmen in Galway just now, we have a great difficulty in getting men here.

17342. And any way there is room for better ones?—I want to say nothing against the Galwaymen, but the difficulty in a place like this, and there is a difficulty, is produced in this way, that the good men go somewhere else. We produce plenty of good men in Galway, but they emigrate from Galway, leaving the worst ones behind.

17343. But the worst men would be improved if we had manual instruction in the schools?—They will, because you will produce a greater number for selection.

17344. The agriculture that you teach to children of ten years old, do you think it would be better to have it in the nature of object lessons or to learn it out of a text-book?—I think I would give them the real work that they have at home, and when you talk to them about agriculture in the right way you talk about things that they understand perfectly well, because they see the whole farming operations with their parents at home.

17345. What is the use of talking to them about things they know perfectly well?—I would show them a better way. If they had a plot of ground and you showed them how to cultivate it, they would compare it with what they do at home and see the difference.

17346. You think you would have the teachers to be trained to be good teachers of agriculture?—Yes, but I would not train every teacher of a National school to be a farmer. I would try to reproduce in the National schools that the children attend, as economically as possible, the conditions in the higher schools, where you have got a separate teacher for each subject. I would try to go as near to that as possible.

17347. Then you think Father Lynskey's proposal to have example plots attached to the schools would be good?—Certainly.

17348. That is to say plots that were examples of good farming?—I would have the schoolmaster's garden.

17349. His proposal was that there should be example plots owned by farmers in the district?—We are building a good many teachers' houses there, and I would have a plot like that in connection with the teacher's house and give him fixity in it, and I would let him have the crop.

17350. Would that teacher manage the farm in connection with the peripatetic teacher?—The peripatetic teacher would show the boys what to do, and the boys would do the farming.

17351. But would the teacher who owned the residence and plot be willing that a teacher should come from the neighbourhood and manage his plot for him?—I would not give him an option, if it was managed by the Department the teacher would come, and the resident teacher would not think any more of it than of an inspector coming.

Galway. Oct. 6, 1897. Mr. James Perry, M.A., C.E.

THIRTY-NINTH PUBLIC SITTING.—THURSDAY, OCTOBER 7th, 1897.

AT 2 O'CLOCK, P.M.,

At the Railway Hotel, Galway.

Galway. Oct. 7, 1897.

Present:—The Right Hon. the Earl of Belmore, G.C.M.G., in the Chair; The Right Hon. C. T. Redington, M.A.; The Most Rev. Monsignor Molloy, D.D., D.Sc.; Rev. Henry Evans, D.D.; Rev. Hamilton Wilson, D.D.; Professor G. F. Fitzgerald, F.T.C.D.; Stanley Harrington, Esq., B.A.; W. R. J. Molloy, Esq.; Captain T. B. Shaw; and J. Struthers, Esq., B.A.;

with J. D. Daly, Esq., M.A., Secretary.

Rev. J. Courtenay Clarke, B.A., Presbyterian Minister, Galway, examined.

Rev. J. Courtenay Clarke, B.A.

17358. Chairman.—You are, I believe, the Presbyterian Minister in Galway?—Yes, my lord.

17359. And you have paid some attention to the subject of our inquiry?—Yes, I have given some attention in various ways. I was taught in a National school to begin with, I was brought in contact with it as a minister, and then I have had—not just recently—but I have had some experience of the work of the technical school here, and I know something of the North and something of the West.

17360. And do you think that such changes should be made in the present educational system as would make it more effective in fitting boys and girls for their life work?—Yes, I would think that that is really the first thing that should be looked into. Could we not make the present programme more effective for that purpose? For instance, take reading. I think that very easily a wider course might be introduced, say for senior boys and girls, and that they should be brought intelligently into contact with the literature of their country, and put in the way to follow up this reading in after life. I think the course in reading is too narrow to produce boys that will follow up that as a matter of study and interest in after life. Then in grammar and geography, for instance, I see that it is mentioned that these should be dropped out, at any rate dropped out as compulsory subjects. I think that would be a sad mistake.

17361. Even in their present form of being taught?—Well, their present form is certainly not the best by any means.

17362. I think that the suggestions that have been made to us, are not that grammar and geography should not be taught at all, but that they should be taught in a more intelligent way; for instance, instead of learning lists of names of towns and villages, that geography should be taught more by the maps; that people should know the maps; and as regards grammar, that grammar should be taught incidentally in writing and in English composition, but not in the form in which it is taught now?—In regard to grammar I would not agree with that; for instance, take the definitions of grammar that come pretty hard on boys or girls, they come in very useful as they proceed with their studies, and it is just at the time when they learn them easily, and afterwards they would learn them with great difficulty and be very unwilling to learn those definitions.

17363. Do you find that notwithstanding the definitions of grammar being taught in the schools, that in practice that is counteracted by the way of talking that they are accustomed to hear at home, and that even the teachers themselves out of the school talk in an ungrammatical way?—Yes, that is quite true, but then you have the difficulty there that the school only lasts 4 or 4½ hours and the boys are in their homes and in their surroundings, and of course, that is the prevailing element, and you will have to deal with that. It will take you a long time before you make much progress in that direction. Besides a boy may know grammar fairly well, and yet when he gets into the home circle he may drop back into the old lines.

17364. How would you suggest that should be corrected?—It must be a matter of time, but in regard to grammar, of course I would have changes in the method of teaching. My own impression is that if a teacher learned a little Latin, and saw the course that is pursued in acquiring a grammatical knowledge of Latin, that he would be in a position to teach grammar much better than he is.

17365. In addition to matters of that sort do you think that where it is practicable, some form of manual and practical instruction should be introduced, such as—for boys, wood work or else experimental science, and for girls, laundry work, and cookery work, and domestic economy?—Yes, I am very favourable to something of that kind being introduced where it is practicable at all.

17366. Where do you think it would be practicable, taking town and country?—First of all I think that one element of the subject is comparatively easy. I think a great deal could be done for girls with your present machinery, with comparatively little change. I think that side of it is comparatively easy, both in town and country. Then I think that if we are ready to spend a fair sum of money it would be easy to deal with towns; I think that could be arranged for. The difficulty seems to me how you are to arrange to deal with the country districts in manual instruction for boys.

17367. On account of the expense?—On account of the expense. Of course there are two ways; I would be in the meantime favourable to the central teacher going out and visiting schools.

17368. Before you come to the teacher you must come to the building; you agree that the English system would have to be introduced, of having a separate room?—Oh, for instance, you could not teach wood work in the present schools as far as I know; you are bound to have a separate building, or at any rate a separate room.

17368a. Sometimes a room may be procured, as it is the case in Sweden, where they have not funds to build a new building, in some house adjoining?—Of course.

17369. Having got the room, do you think that you would require to have a separate teacher, or could the ordinary teacher be trained, as is done in the large towns in England, to teach manual work in addition to the ordinary work of the school?—I would prefer the skilled teacher if he could be got.

17370. What do you mean by the skilled teacher,—distinguishing the artisan from the teacher?—I mean such a man as they brought to the technical school here, and that Father Lilly described yesterday; that is a man who has studied something of the science of the subject, as well as being well up in the practical manipulation.

17371. You think that to take an ordinary artisan in a village to teach in a school, would be a failure unless he had been trained to teach as a teacher?—I am not quite prepared to say that it would be a failure in all cases, but with a good many of the ordinary I think it would not be desirable to bring them into close contact with the life of boys.

17372. And do you think, also, with other people, that they would not understand how to maintain discipline, and would not understand the methods of imparting even what they knew themselves?—You might get an odd man who could, but taking them as a rule, I would be afraid of that.

17373. How would you suggest that fully-qualified and experienced teachers should be provided, of course, by degrees; because we admit it cannot be done all at once?—I listened to the evidence yesterday; there was a suggestion about teaching on Saturday, bringing teachers into centres, teaching them on Saturday. I have not much faith in that. I think you just get a little smattering of the subject, and it would not leave in very much.

17374. We saw a class of that sort in Penrith in Cumberland, but it is fair to say that the actual teaching had made no progress in the county. I believe there was only one of those teachers who was really applying his knowledge so far, whatever might be done in the future when funds were provided for procuring rooms and materials?—I think you are under the necessity of looking to the coming teacher rather than to those already in the field; of course, there are some of them who would acquire sufficient skill and knowledge, but take it as a rule, I would not rely much on the teacher who is formed from these Saturday lessons, acquiring such skill as would be worth very much. And then there was yesterday the suggestion of a central school, say, here in Galway; the idea was to detach, say, the Model School from primary education, and to start a central school there. Well, I did not quite follow all that was involved. For instance, it was said that it would be a good place to teach agriculture, and have an agricultural farm. That would mean that you would have a residential institution, a non-sectarian institution, and I think if there is any plan of that kind to be pursued, the much better way would be to re-organise the Model School, and begin with your pupil teachers.

17375. I am not familiar quite with the system, if you would explain it a little more fully?—For instance, take a model school in the North of Ireland; they have about ten pupil teachers on the boys' side, they live in the school there for two years as a rule; now they have the whole afternoon, it would be very easy to get instruction for them, and they are just at an age when there is not special pressure, and I believe a good deal could be done in making them efficient teachers by and by.

17376. Is that the case in all the model schools?—I would not like to answer very decidedly in the presence of these gentlemen, but I think it is in the Northern model schools. I think, in that way, you would come at —I don't know the numbers exactly—but in a short time you would have a considerable number of teachers who could do good work in this matter of manual instruction; then, of course, it could be followed up when they go to train at Marlborough-street. My feeling about Marlborough-street is—I don't know enough of it to state very decidedly—but the teachers are under pressure there for their classification, and I don't think they could give the same time to it that a pupil teacher could.

17377. You think it would be better that a pupil teacher should be what you call half-trained in the model school in his county, and then begin in Marlborough-street, with a certain amount of the knowledge he has to acquire already acquired?—Largely in that direction.

17378. Coming to another matter, do you agree with the suggestion that was made yesterday, I think by Canon Lynskey, that in one district, manual instruction might be useful, but in a district like his, net-mending and basket-making help would be more useful?—Yes, I think subjects appropriate to the neighbourhood should be taught. Woodwork might be very largely taught, because it is very generally useful;

for instance, to set up a school for agriculture here in Galway for the people of the town would be, to my mind, most absurd; what you might do in Galway is—and I fancy that the gentlemen to-day, as they went around, would see that there is a necessity for it—you might give an example of cottage gardening, and that would be very useful, and serve a splendid purpose, if you could induce the people to give attention to cottage gardening. But in agriculture we have not those who need it in Galway.

17379. Rev. Dr. Evans.—You would be, Mr. Curtin, in favour of the introduction of manual instruction into the primary schools?—Yes, using that in a very wide way to include dressmaking, or sewing, or cookery, or woodwork, and so on, according to the needs of the neighbourhood.

17380. You would not be in favour, in order to make way for it, of the exclusion of English grammar?—Oh, certainly not.

17381. And in giving that opinion, you are speaking from the whole experience of your life, including early education?—Yes, I am strongly in favour of English grammar being better taught, but even as it is taught now, I believe it serves a very useful purpose.

17382. Well, no doubt, we shall come to teach English grammar better and geography better: it is not a question of improved methods, but a question of retaining the subject; you would not allow it to be abandoned in any English school?—It would be a step backward.

17383. Do you know anything of the work that was described to us yesterday by Father Lally?—Oh, yes, I know something of it—at least I knew it pretty well about a year ago.

17384. Is that work, do you think, the kind that we could spread generally through the schools and through the country?—Well, you would require to be prepared to spend a great deal of money; that school has an income of, say, £400 a year, and you can easily see that to spread that through the country, means a good deal of money.

17385. But you believe such instruction as is given there would be useful throughout Ireland, if it could be had?—Oh, yes, it would be very useful indeed.

17386. However, of course you could only have a school of that kind in a large town?—I don't think it would be possible to have it anywhere else.

17387. If manual instruction were introduced, do you think it could be taught by anybody but the teachers?—Well, I don't think that we would be prepared to spend the money, but, if you are prepared to spend the money, it would be better taught by others.

17388. You say that school costs £400 a year. If you were to provide one such school in each county in Ireland it would come to about £32,000 a year. Do you think that one school would be enough in each county?—Take that one school here, it simply benefits the town of Galway.

17389. Then you don't see your way to having more schools in a county like Galway, which has only one or two other big towns?—I think unless there is Imperial aid, apart from the £250 given by the Science and Art Department, there would be a great difficulty about the expenditure here. For instance, if you take Enniskillen, and if over the union there, there is a rate, which is spent entirely for the benefit of Enniskillen, I fancy that there would be an outcry very soon on the part of the rural districts, that they were giving money and getting no value for it.

Chairman.—I can quite agree with you there, partly because a great part of the Union of Enniskillen, of which I am Chairman, is not in the county Fermanagh at all; a large part is in Cavan.

17390. Rev. Dr. Evans.—You think, at present at all events, that the town of Galway is especially benefited, but will not this influence overflow more or less gradually to all the localities about?—Well, the overflow will be very slow; the tendency is the other way—from the country to the town. There is very little tendency from the town to the country.

Galway.

Oct. 2, 1897.

Rev. J. Greaney Curtin, P.A.

17391. But could we not have teachers trained here; would not occasional teachers come in here and get instruction, and take it with them?—As I was indicating, I would not lay much stress upon that. I think if a man is to know anything about the subject worth talking of, he must give considerable attention and time, and he must really begin young.

17392. Rev. Dr. Wilson.—Is the general intelligence of National school children as great as you would expect from the instruction they have been given?—I don't know that I could answer the question in that form. I don't think it is so great as I would like, and I am decidedly under the impression that their education should be broader.

17393. You would mean by that a modification of the school books?—I would certainly bring them into contact with literature generally, and let them see something of the fields that lie beyond.

17394. Not confine them to school books?—Certainly not; school books are very good in their way, but not enough.

17395. You heard the evidence about the Model School yesterday; do you agree with Father Lally in his testimony?—Well, I think Father Lally proved yesterday that I was rather a wise man, because I opposed the giving of a portion of the Model School to the Technical School, because I said it was the thin edge of the wedge, and here you had yesterday a broad request for the whole building, without any indication that there were children there that would have to be educated on the roadside if that were carried out. The work done by the Model School is very superior. I will give you this fact: the science results in connection with the Technical school is Model School teaching—I mean by it that it is Model School pupils. I have not seen the reports, because I am not on the committee; but I think I am warranted in saying that.

17396. What do you mean by that?—I mean, for instance, in connection with the Science and Art scientific returns, that those who passed were Model School pupils.

17397. Mr. Struthers.—In such a subject as mathematics?—Mathematics is the main subject; they had previously been taught mathematics in the Model School.

17398. Before they entered on the several classes in the Technical School?—Yes.

17399. Captain Shaw.—They have the same teachers, have they not?—They have the same teacher. Then I was glad to hear yesterday that a great many of the children attending the Technical School were Protestants; these, as a rule, are educated at the Model Schools, and it only proves that the education at the Model School is of such a character that it induces them to enter into these wider fields.

17400. Is there sufficient provision for the education of Protestant children in Galway without the Model School?—Well, there is practically none.

17401. Professor FitzGerald.—Do you think that the teachers would be favourable to the introduction of manual training and such like things into the schools here?—Well, I don't think I could give you an answer to that that would be worth much.

17402. Do you think the managers about here would generally be favourable to it?—I think the managers would be.

17403. Which do you think they would be more favourable to—the introduction of manual work or of science and object lessons and things of that kind?—Well, I don't think that my answer to that would be worth much; I have not gone into it sufficiently.

17404. Do you think there would be time for introducing some more subjects than at present are taught in the schools?—I think that if the Commissioners of National Education gave more teachers, that there would be plenty of time; I think that the time is sufficient if the teaching power was such as is required, but I don't think it is at the present time.

[illegible] collections of [illegible] and
[illegible] and [illegible]—it would be

Galway.
Oct. 1, 1897.
Rev. J. Courtenay Clarke, P.P.

17437. What you wish to produce is general common sense in the pupil rather than special knowledge?—But at the same time, whilst I would begin with that, I would give them, if the opportunity at all arose, I would give them the special knowledge.

17438. But the special knowledge acquired by one pupil is very different to the special knowledge acquired by another, according to the trade or occupation he is going to fill?—Yes.

17439. Is it not a pity to introduce a uniform programme for all the higher pupils in the school?—I say the subject should be appropriate to the neighbourhood, should look to the neighbourhood.

17440. Take a neighbourhood in which there is wood-carving, there are many people in that district who are not going to be fishermen; you would not insist on all the pupils learning that?—Certainly not, I would not insist on all the pupils learning any of this manual work.

17441. Would it not be better to have that instruction dissociated from the instruction in an ordinary elementary school, and taught specially to those who want it in a special school?—Yes, but if you want to get at the youth of the neighbourhood, you must reach them in connection with the National school.

17442. Could you not teach them in the evening, the pupils who have left school?—Oh no, you could not do much in that direction.

17443. What would be the difficulty in getting pupils to attend in the evening to learn net-making?—For instance they might be living in the country, and have to come three or four miles to get to a centre.

17444. Would not that be an extreme case?—I don't think it would be an extreme case, but I am looking at what would happen in a good many cases.

17445. But there must be a good many cases where this is not the case?—Then in addition to that, of course boys, when they get home and get into the routine of home life, have little things to do, and there is pressure in one direction or another, I am very much afraid you would not at all reach the youth of the community in that way.

17446. CHAIRMAN.—Is it not the case, in your experience, Mr. Clarke, that in the country districts, at all events in the North of Ireland, people go to bed very early?—They go to bed very early, and the young sons of farmers are under great pressure in the matter of work, and that pressure is becoming greater instead of less. I don't think you could lay much stress on getting them together in the evening.

17447. Mr. STRAHAN.—Or winter afternoons?—Oh no, labour is too costly now to get much in that direction.

17448. That applies specially to districts like Connemara, where you have a scattered population and exclusively farmers, and child labour is much used, but there must be other districts, and particularly towns where there is special instruction of the kind you refer to, that could be given in Convent schools?—I think you could do something in towns in that direction.

17449. Evening schools are not numerous in Ireland at present; have you thought of any plan by which they could be encouraged?—In this matter of manual instruction I don't know any better plan than

are introducing woodwork, and it may be that there are only two men in the whole district that have a taste for woodwork.

17452. But if the teachers have a design to learn would it not be a sufficient method of learning for them?—It may be, but my own impression is that it would not amount to much.

17453. Do you think the same remark applies to drawing?—Yes, to a large extent; drawing cannot be learned in a short time.

17454. But the drawing that would be required for an elementary school is not of a very extensive nature, it is more method than actual execution in the case of the teacher?—Still, if a man is to teach drawing effectively he would need to be beyond the elementary stage.

17455. He would require to know the method of teaching, but he would not require any great skill in execution?—I think he would require considerable skill, so far as my knowledge of drawing is concerned. I think, for instance, that the National Board did a very good work in the matter of teaching drawing when they sent down specially qualified assistants to the Model schools, the results there, so far as I know, were exceedingly good, but those were well-trained men.

17456. How long did they stay there?—Some of them stayed a considerable time.

17457. What is a considerable time?—They may have stayed three or four years; most of these men were looking forward to head-masterships: or perhaps studying for inspectorships.

17458. And you don't think the ordinary National school teacher can be instructed sufficiently in drawing to teach it in his school?—My hope is not great.

17459. Professor FITZGERALD.—Then you think it is an objection to the technical school in Galway that the rate is levied on the union?—I am not making an objection to it.

17460. You think it might be taken as an objection to it?—I think very likely that if you tried it all over Ireland the objection would be raised, and knowing something of the Northern mind, I take for instance, Enniskillen.

17461. What is the most distant point of the union from Galway?—I am not the best authority on that, but perhaps it is twenty-five miles.

CHAIRMAN.—The Enniskillen Union is about forty miles in one direction and fifteen across.

17462. Captain SHAW.—If technical schools are to be established what interval do you contemplate they should be from each other in Ireland, you cannot have them every four miles apart?—Oh, no, that was not the point with which I was dealing at the time; the point with which I was dealing was the income of the school, how it was derived, the likelihood of the income being got up in other directions in the same way, and so schools multiplied on that principle.

17463. Do you think there would be any serious difficulty for anybody living in the union to attend a certain number of classes?—I do think there would be a most serious difficulty.

17464. It would certainly serve some of the districts beyond Galway for a radius of six or seven miles, would it not?—I am afraid in the West here we have not sufficient energy and enterprise to go those six or seven miles; it would be very desirable that we had

know they are utilising the children even at an early age for these things, especially in the evening hours.

17467. They only utilise them at special times of the year?—Cattle have to be looked after the whole year for that matter.

17468. You cannot look after cattle the whole day?—Of course they cannot, but you will find, as a matter of fact, that a good many of the young people are engaged in the way I tell you.

17469. Mr. Henderson.—I suppose the children of your denomination are in considerably better circumstances than one would find in the ordinary National schools around here?—Well, yes, they are.

17470. Do you think the parents of these children would like the introduction of manual instruction?—I think they would like it very well.

17471. Because we have heard that objection in some places, that they probably would not like it?—I don't think there would be an objection to it so long as the progress of the children in other directions was not interfered with.

17472. Do you think there is too much learning by heart in the National schools, I mean learning things by rote?—I don't think so; I think that possibly, if there is anything in which they err, it is in giving too long written exercises at home. I don't think the children are burdened by committing to memory, they may not do it so intelligently as they ought.

17473. What I mean is this—do you consider they are taught to think sufficiently in the ordinary lessons?—I do not.

17474. What do you think is the cause of that, is it the fault of the inspection?—I think that the inspection could be changed a good deal for the better, at the same time I want to say that I don't know any class of men who are more conscientious or better up to their work than the inspectors I have met with in Ireland, but I think they are placed under very great difficulties. The inspection, as I knew it in olden times, was quite a different thing. An inspector came into the school; he came in unexpectedly very often, and he would say to the teacher, "Never mind, just go on;" and instead of asking questions himself, he stood there and watched the routine work of the school, sometimes for an hour and sometimes for two hours. Then I have seen him take up a class and teach a class in geography, just go through the teaching of the class; of course he would have meant to show the teacher how to teach it and various things of this kind. Then he would examine a class and pass on to another school. I think that now, owing to the system of results examination that we have, the inspector is not at all the help that he might be to the teacher. The inspector should be a helper and example to the teacher.

17475. Too much of an examiner, you think?—He is too much of an examiner.

17476. Mr. Molloy.—I did not quite catch your meaning when you said you thought the Model School might be utilised for the instruction of pupil teachers in agriculture?—Generally, I meant, for this whole manual instruction; you have teachers when they are young and not under special pressure for class examinations, and so on; they would have sufficient time in the evening, and you could likely turn out competent hands with the training that they would have in Marlborough street.

17477. But you seem to confine that practically to pupil teachers?—Oh, yes, the fact is I think our ancestors were fairly wise in establishing model schools, that is my view of it, and, if we were doing right, instead of blotting them out, we would multiply them.

17478. And your idea could not be carried out now at all events unless the residences were provided?—No, not so easily.

17480. With regard to the technical school here, you appear to me to think that the pupils who attend at mathematics, that is under the South Kensington examinations, are principally from the Model School?—Yes.

17481. Now, to-day we found that there were thirty-eight boys in attendance; there would seem somewhere about eight or ten simply in the senior classes, in which alone mathematics would be taught; consequently the number coming from the senior classes could not well constitute a large number of successes under South Kensington, and therefore they must have come also from other places?—I don't follow your reasoning in that matter, but it is a matter that can be easily settled, that is the successes in connection with the science classes. My position is that they are Model School pupils.

17482. Some years ago there was other provision for Protestant pupils in town here as well as the Model School; I recollect years ago the Erasmus Smith Schools in operation?—They are not in operation now, and have not been in operation since I came to Galway, that is sixteen years.

17483. Professor Fitzgerald.—That is the Erasmus Smith Primary School?—Yes.

17484. Mr. Molloy.—It was called the English Department; what became of the building or premises? It was a very large building and largely attended, also, exclusively by Protestant pupils?—So far as I know it is now in the hands of the Protestant Episcopalian congregation.

17485. And would you not say, therefore, available for the instruction of Protestant pupils?—Not, certainly, available for the instruction of Presbyterian pupils. I have no more interest in it than you have.

17486. May I inquire have you ever been the manager of a National school?—Well, technically I have not been, but when I was in the North of Ireland I was an assistant to a very old man, and he retained the managership, but I supervised the school, I did not want to let him feel that he was getting beyond the work.

17487. You are not in favour of the results system as at present carried out; I see you prefer the style of inspection carried on prior to the introduction of the results system?—Yes.

17488. That also of course would mean a change in the form of examination of pupils and payment of results fees?—Yes, and I am strongly in favour of some change.

17489. You would favour class examination of all the pupils on the rolls rather than a mere selection of pupils that attended a minimum number of days?—Yes, it must be in that direction that my plan would go. One thing about the results I would like to mention, I think it is very hard upon a boy who attends the full year to keep him in a class when for three months, perhaps, he should be promoted—it is occupying the best of the boys, he is not only being kept back, but he is being trained in idle habits during the last three months of his year.

17490. Of course, also, you are aware that a large number of pupils never come under examination, that is those who have not attended the minimum number of days?—Yes, and not only that, but those are the pupils who need the most attention and very likely get the least.

17491. And by a change both in the form of the inspection and of the payment these would get the benefit of instruction?—These would come under examination, and it would be the interest of the

The other school to which Mr. Molloy referred is merely a building, there is no school organization.

17493. CHAIRMAN.—It was not vested in the Erasmus Smith Board at all; I think they only gave the salaries?—I cannot tell you that.

17494. Mr. MOLLOY.—Years ago the Erasmus Smith English school at Wood-quay, as distinguished from the one on the hillside, was a primary school?—I understand so, but it was before my time.

17495. Monsignor MOLLOY.—I suppose those who go to the Erasmus Smith School go for intermediate education?—Intermediate education.

17496. And those who want primary education go chiefly to the Model School?—Yes.

17497. What number are there at present?—I really could not give you the number; we have not so many there as some time ago.

Mr. [illegible].—Number of pupils on the rolls on 31st of December, 1886, eighteen Presbyterians.

17498. Monsignor MOLLOY.—What proportion would they bear to the school-going population of Galway?—They would be a very small proportion.

17499. From the returns it appears that there are about 1,800 children in the primary schools?—There may be.

17500. Then those of your denomination would be 1 per cent. of the whole?—On that basis they would only be.

17501. I understand you to say that you are in favour generally of the introduction of manual and practical teaching into the primary schools of Ireland?—Oh, yes.

17502. And the only difficulty you seemed to apprehend was the cost of such teaching?—Yes, if certain methods were pursued.

17503. What does the education of a child cost in the present Model School?—You can easily find that out.

17504. I have found it out. Last year the total expenditure was £303, and the average attendance was 58; dividing 58 into £303 the quotient is £5 14s.; that is the average cost per child in the Model School. In the ordinary National schools in Ireland, the average cost per child is £2 2s. 8d.; therefore there is a very large excess of expenditure at present on the education per child in the Model School as compared with the National schools. It is more than double?—Yes, according to these statistics, that is so.

17505. Would not that suggest that some modification of the system is desirable, by which a larger amount of educational work should be obtained for the existing expenditure?—Yes, of course that is the general question of model schools.

17506. And the particular question of Galway?—Yes.

17507. Does not this consideration seem to justify the efforts made by Father Lally?—At the same time I think I am right in conserving the rights of the Protestant children.

involve. It is not a question I studied, but that is an element that would certainly come out.

17526. A school that is managed by the State will always cost more than a school locally managed, and for which the locality contributes part of the expense? —That is so.

17527. Mr. Molloy.—Is it not a fact, however, in the model schools that the people as a rule pay pretty high fees? —They don't pay very high fees now.

17528. Here in Galway? —I mean under the new Act. There is only a certain contribution to be made by all the people, so that the fees are greatly reduced.

Mr. Molloy.—Last week we met with a model school in which the average [illegible] fee, as it is called, was one guinea a pupil.

17529 Professor FitzGerald.—Does not the Treasury handle a large part of that? —I don't know anything of the expense [illegible] here. I know that when this Act came into operation the fees of my own two boys were reduced by one-half.

17530. Monsignor Molloy.—Then your own two boys are at the Model School? —Only one of them now.

Mr. W. H. Welply, B.A., District Inspector of National Schools, examined.

17531. Chairman.—You are the District Inspector for the Galway District? —Yes.

17532. How long have you been so? —Four years on the 1st of September.

17533. Perhaps you will give the Commissioners some views on the subject of drawing? —I think drawing is a most useful subject, and—to put it in language I have already used—I think it ought to be forced on the country; that is to say, that in every school where a teacher possesses a certificate already it ought to be taught. There are many schools at present where the teachers possess certificates, and drawing is not taught. Then of course, under the new programme for teachers drawing is practically a compulsory subject.

17534. That is, the future teachers will be compelled? —The future teachers will be compelled to take up this subject, and in that way, of course, by-and-bye we shall have all the teachers teaching that branch.

17535. What have you to say with regard to the itinerant teachers of drawing? —I think for the [illegible]

vent? —Yes, there was a special industrial teacher employed there. That grant was withdrawn a short time before I came here.

17545. Why was it withdrawn? —The number of pupils attending was not sufficient to warrant the payment of the grant.

17546. Is there any other place in your district in which there is a grant which is in danger of being withdrawn? —Yes, at Oughterard Convent there seems some danger of a withdrawal of the grant from want of a sufficient number of returns in that case.

17547. Is that on account of the unwillingness of parents to allow their children to be taught? —No, I think not; it is because the pupils are not there. I don't think there is any occasion to teach in Cong now.

17548. Do any National teachers in your district hold certificates in handicraft? —Yes, three do.

17549. Do any of them give instruction? —One.

17550. What do you think of the results in his case? —The results are very meagre judged by the number of results—there was the maximum [illegible]

17560. Is it in Mayo or Galway?—In Galway now.

17561. What is allowed to instructors in this branch?—A moiety of the salary, 12s. 6d. a week, to the instructor, and the whole of the results fees that are earned by ordinary pupils.

17562. Are you satisfied with the results that have been obtained?—Yes, especially so at Cleggan, they were very good.

17563. And you think the children have been eager to learn?—Certainly, at Cleggan.

17564. What do you say about the partial displacement of grammar and geography to make room for manual work?—Well, I have been considering that, I have analysed the time-table here and there throughout my district when opportunity offered. Suppose a school day going from ten to three with half-hour lessons and an hour out for religious instruction and recreation, that would leave four hours or eight half-hours, which would come to forty half-hour lessons in the week. I find in most cases I have analysed that grammar is taught for three of those half-hours and geography for two, or geography for three and grammar two. I think it is a very general rule throughout the country that those subjects are taken up only for that very short time, and any attempt to diminish the time I would not regard with favour.

17565. The only place in which in the South of Ireland we saw any manual work in the shape of woodwork in operation was in Lismore, and we were informed there that the time was gained, two hours in the week, not by displacing any particular subject, but by shortening the whole of the programme, ten minutes off one, and ten minutes off another?—Yes, I think so, but I would still be in favour of retaining grammar and geography.

17566. That is done there; they did not displace anything, but gained ten minutes off a variety of subjects?—Yes, I think that could be done.

17567. You would be in favour of something of that sort, and think it practicable?—I think that could be done.

17568. I think that you have some observations to make with regard to the results system; perhaps you would do so without going very fully into the matter?—I think on the whole the results system has not been such a bad system as has been maintained in certain directions. I have been a pupil of a National school myself, after that I went to an intermediate school, and afterwards to college, and graduated in the Royal University, so practically I have seen all the grades of education in the country and I cannot quite agree that the results system is so bad as it is painted. I think improvements might be made in the programme, however; for instance it was only on the 1st of October that explanation of subject matter in reading became compulsory in every class beginning with the second in the school course. I think no more important step has been taken within the last twenty years than requiring a knowledge of the words and phrases which the pupils meet in their ordinary reading lessons.

17569. Would you give us your views on the subject of the acquisition of school plots and school gardens in connection with teaching the principles of horticulture and agriculture?—I think that in certain places these plots would be useful—small plots attached to the schools.

17570. About what size?—Between ten and twenty perches.

17571. You are more in favour of that than of a two acre plot for teaching a course of farming?—I think so.

17572. Rev. Dr. Evans.—How many schools are in your district?—138.

17573. Is the alternative scheme for girls in operation in any of those schools?—Yes, it is in operation in perhaps a dozen.

17574. Was it in any other schools than the dozen?—Yes.

17575. Why was it given up?—There was a general tendency on the part of the parents to look upon it with disfavour.

17576. Then what is the reason for retaining it in the twelve?—I think it is more or less apathy, nobody has raised the question of its retention or abolition, it is just kept on.

17577. Are there any school farms in your district?—None.

17578. Are there any school-gardens at all?—No.

17579. Is there any attempt made to give instruction to the pupils in horticulture in any shape?—I don't think so, but some teachers, since instructions were issued a short time ago with regard to growing shrubs and flowers in the school plots and around the schoolhouses itself, have rather gone in for that, but I don't think it is with a view to give any instruction to the pupils.

17580. But you encourage them?—Certainly.

17581. Do you think that our agricultural class-book contains sufficient information to enable school gardens to be adopted?—I think the new book does.

17582. You have read that book?—I have.

17583. And you know the part devoted to horticulture?—Yes.

17584. Do you think there is anything in the teaching in that book that is above the capacity of National school pupils?—Well, there are a great many names of flowers, and so forth, that would offer some difficulty to them, I fancy.

17585. Anything more difficult than subtrahend and minuend?—I don't think so.

17586. And as much effort as would be needed to explain those terms in arithmetic would explain the names of flowers?—Yes.

17587. I suppose eschscholtzia is one of the hardest?—Yes.

17588. And all the rest might be easily taught?—Yes.

17589. There are from forty to forty-five half hour lessons, you told us, in the course of the school week?—Yes.

17590. And of those forty or forty-five half hour lessons only two half-hour lessons, or two and a half in the week, are given to English grammar?—That is so in the schools whose time-tables I have analysed.

17591. As an experienced educationalist yourself, do you believe it is possible in two half-hour lessons in the week to teach English grammar to any useful purpose?—I don't think it can be taught to any useful purpose in that short space of time.

17592. That the time is too little?—It is too little; of course they bring the child up to the requirements of our programme.

17593. How much time in the week is given to the teaching of needlework?—An hour a day, five hours a week.

17594. What is your impression about the results that are obtained by five hours in the week given to needlework?—The results on the whole are good.

17595. That the results in needlework are worthy of the five hours?—I think the same results might be obtained with less time, but speaking generally I think the pupils learn a good deal in the way of sewing.

17596. How much time in the week is given to the study of geography?—If grammar is taught for two half-hours in the week, geography is taken up for three.

17597. If a few of the far-away places and extraordinary unpronounceable names were left out of sight, and something more simple and practical were done in the way of teaching geography, don't you think it would be a very valuable part of National school education?—I don't think the subject, as taught at

Galway. — Oct. 7, 1887. — Mr. W. H. Welply, B.A.

gramme, is very much calculated to develop the intelligence of children.

17598. With practically 140 schools in your district, in how many of them is drawing taught?—I should say from fifteen to twenty.

17599. Why is it not taught in a larger number?—A great many of the teachers had no certificates, and having no certificates, if they teach drawing they can earn no results fees.

17600. Could you suggest, as an experienced schoolmaster, any way by which we could simplify the introduction of drawing into all these schools, or a large proportion?—I have thought of the employment, as a temporary expedient, of itinerant instructors of drawing in certain centres.

17601. Is writing sufficiently taught in this district?—I don't think so.

17602. You think if a use were made of drawing models and copies, analogous to the use made of writing copies, that drawing might be taught, not in the highest form, but usefully, in many of the schools in which it is not now taught at all?—I think so.

17603. That a teacher who can teach writing with the aid of copy-lines, who is not a good writer himself, if he attains fairly good results with a similar mode of dealing with drawing (where you cannot have a properly qualified teacher of drawing), would be better than to have no drawing?—I quite agree with that.

17604. Rev. Dr. Wilson.—You say you are favourable to the introduction of manual instruction, subject to certain restrictions; would you specify some of these restrictions?—I merely mean to say that I don't think it ought to be introduced into the country generally.

17605. Professor Fitzgerald.—Compulsorily?—Compulsorily, just as the industrial programme was sought to be introduced some years ago.

17606. Chairman.—Are you in favour of its being introduced compulsorily at all?—I would be in favour of its being introduced compulsorily at large centres.

17607. Professor Fitzgerald.—You think there is time, then, for it in the present school programme?—Yes, at present, as I say, at large centres, with that qualification; you see agriculture is not taught, and that subject might be taken in the time devoted to agriculture.

17608. What is at present done in the time devoted to agriculture?—It is simply spread over the other subjects where extra subjects are not taken up.

17609. What hour is roll-call?—The attendance for the day is supposed to be recorded not later than eleven o'clock.

17610. That is that the children need not be there before eleven?—No, a few minutes before eleven.

17611. What is the school day?—From ten to three, or half-past three, five, or five and a-half hours; the teacher is required to be present half an hour before the ordinary work of the day begins.

17612. Chairman.—To do what?—To prepare for the reception of the pupils.

17613. Professor Fitzgerald.—Is more than four hours at present required by the Board?—The minimum school day required by the Board is four.

17614. As a matter of fact, it is generally over that in the schools in this district?—Yes.

17615. Then there is an hour wasted in the beginning of the day, while the children are coming in?—I don't say that at all; in many cases they come punctually.

17616. Do you think the teachers in this district would be willing to introduce new subjects like drawing and manual training, and so on?—I don't think they would have any objection to drawing; I think there would be some objection to manual training generally.

17617. Do you think they would object to having the agricultural teaching changed from the present form of learning a book to something more practical, in the way of making collections and elementary botany, and showing plants growing from seeds?—I cannot answer that question, because I have not consulted any teachers on that point at all.

17618. Do you think the managers and parents would be willing to make these changes?—I don't think there would be any very general objection to it from them.

17619. You said there were very meagre results from the school in which manual training had been tried; was that due to want of appliances?—No, the appliances are excellent.

17620. Was it due to the course not being educational?—Perhaps I better say, with reference to the appliances, if you allow me, that all the tools were supplied by the Congested Districts Board, and the work is not carried on in the ordinary schoolroom, but in a smaller house built in the school plot, and I understand the Congested Districts Board allow £5 a year for materials.

17621. But the course in manual training in the Board's course is not an educational course, it is not graduated a bit like the courses that have been adopted in English schools for manual training?—That portion begins with the fifth class.

17622. And there is no introduction to it in the earlier classes?—No.

17623. Would not the meagre results be largely due to the course not being a well arranged course?—I think I have practically said so.

17624. Do you think the people of Ireland are particularly accurate in measurements and observation?—I don't think they are.

17625. Don't you think a training in object lessons and elementary science, and drawing to scale, would be an advantage to them?—I think that would be good if well arranged and well carried out.

17626. Then you think this practical training might be of use, even in a country like Ireland?—Oh, certainly.

17627. Because I thought you stated it would not be suitable for Ireland?—No, that was not my point of view: to use a famous expression, I have an open mind on the subject as to its application to the country generally, but at present all I would say is that it ought to be tried in large centres, and if it succeeds there it might spread to the whole country.

17628. Mr. Strangways.—Were those pupils who were taught net-mending, extern pupils, or pupils of the school?—Some externs and some pupils of the school.

17629. Which was the more successful class?—At Claggan I think they were about equal; in the Aran Islands the externs were more successful than the ordinary pupils.

17630. Those time-tables you spoke of, are they typical time-tables of your district?—I think so, I have examined a good many, and found it generally so.

17631. And you found, as a rule, two half-hours a week were given to grammar?—Two or three.

17632. And you are quite of opinion that it is impossible to impart in that time any satisfactory knowledge of grammar?—An intelligent knowledge cannot be imparted in that time.

17633. Do you know what time is given to reading in these schools?—The time varies a great deal: personally I am in favour of giving as much as possible to reading, but I think from three to four hours a week would, in some cases, be given to reading—three hours, I should think.

17634. Then you don't think it is a pity to have grammar entirely separated from reading, and considered as a separate subject?—Of course, in the time-table it is treated as a separate subject, but it perhaps very often happens that it is taken up after reading.

17635. You find in actual practice that it is taught along with reading to a certain extent?—To a certain extent.

17636. But you maintain it as a separate subject?—Yes.

17637. And it is put down officially as a separate subject, entirely disconnected from reading?—Yes.

17638. Don't you think it would be well to have both brought in connexion?—I think so; because, in order to understand the parsing of sentences, the meaning must be understood, and that comes in under the head of reading in our present programme.

17639. So if you taught grammar along with reading, you might have a more intelligent knowledge of it than you can get by only setting apart an hour a week for it?—I think so.

17640. Do you find the teachers and pupils use grammar books throughout your district?—I think almost universally; I don't think they are used in the third class, but in the fourth class they are universally used. Fourth class pupils require to know the declension of the nouns and pronouns, and the past tenses of irregular verbs, &c.

17641. And they prescribe sections to be learned off by heart?—No, I don't think so.

17642. Do you ask, if I may put this question, do you in examining them ask for any definition of parts of speech to be repeated from the books?—Oh, seldom.

17643. Is that part of the necessary examination?—No, it is not so laid down in the programme; but I suppose if a child tells me a certain word is a noun, it ought to be able to give me the reason why it is so.

17644. But you don't ask them to repeat the text of the technical definition of what the noun is?—Sometimes I do, sometimes I take it another way—ask him his reason for stating a word is a certain part of speech.

17645. If he stated his reason in the words of the definition in the book that would not be a satisfactory answer?—It would not be an intelligent reason.

17646. Do you think there is an excessive repetition in the school learning things by heart?—They learn a good many things by rote.

17647. It would tend to discourage that if the grammar were taken in connexion with the reading lesson, and no text book used at all?—Yes, I think so.

17648. Analysis does not seem to be set down in the programme for the schools?—No, analysis is not required except for monitors.

17649. You consider that really a proper introduction to parsing?—I think it would be a great advantage in sixth class, the higher forms.

17650. You would not have it introduced in the very beginning as necessary to understand the real structure of a sentence?—With the limited time given to grammar I do not see how it could be taken up.

17651. You think it would be a good thing to take the reading, grammar, and explanation of sentences in the reading-book all together as one complete subject?—I think that would be a good thing.

17652. So that one might help the other?—Particularly for explanation of particular sentences in parsing.

17653. And in that way you would probably find that the grammar teaching was done in the time now set apart for reading?—That might occur.

17654. So that there might be some time got in that way for drawing or manual work?—This time, two or three half-hours in the week must be devoted to grammar in some form.

17655. I thought you agreed it would be well not to separate the subjects, but that reading and grammar should be taken conjointly?—No deduction should be made from reading.

17656. And you still would have grammar set down as a separate subject apart from the reading, you would still retain the two half-hours for grammar?—That might be incorporated with the other time.

17657. You don't think that adding the present time for grammar to the present time for reading, you don't think that the joint time could be diminished?—No.

17658. Then five hours a week are regularly given to needlework in the schools?—Yes.

17659. And I think you said already that some of that time might be saved?—I think an hour at least of that might go to some other purpose without any serious disadvantage.

17660. You know that in England, for instance, more than three hours a week is very seldom given to needlework, and the needlework appears to be very well taught?—Yes.

17661. Which do you think is more valuable for developing intelligence—needlework or grammar?—Needlework, I should think.

17662. Do you think it is taught so as to train the intelligence?—Not in every school, it is taught in some schools so as to develop intelligence considerably.

17663. Is drawing taught to girls in your district?—Yes, certainly, where female teachers have the Board's certificates in drawing the subject is taught to their pupils.

17664. So that they take some time for drawing in addition to the time for needlework?—Yes.

17665. There would be no hardship in making drawing compulsory in the girls' schools if we had properly-qualified teachers?—None, whatever; in one of my very best schools drawing is taken up and taught very well.

17666. Might not the drawing in the girls' schools be made helpful towards teaching cutting-out?—Yes, I daresay in some of the better schools it is.

17667. Might it not be made systematically helpful to cutting out?—Certainly.

17668. Do you think any teacher uses the terms subtrahend and minuend in teaching his children?—I think very seldom.

17669. He can teach subtraction very well without using those words?—I think so.

17670. Mr. Harrington.—I suppose agriculture is taught in all the rural schools in your district?—Yes, it is a compulsory subject.

17671. Would you tell us shortly how it is taught?—The teaching of it is in some cases very unsatisfactory; it is taught as a form of reading lesson. The pupils get the text-book and read off the particular part assigned for the day's lesson, just as they read over a lesson in their readers, and sometimes questions are put to them on what they read.

17672. Do they not learn it off by heart?—In some cases they do, and in some cases catechisms of agriculture are used.

17673. As a general rule do you think the children understand at all what they are reading in this agricultural text-book?—I certainly do, because they are reading about things they see at home very often.

17674. Does the teacher explain the various expressions used in the book?—I daresay he does, I think he does in many instances, but they are reading descriptions of things they are acquainted with to a certain extent.

17675. Would you approve of shortening the text-book, epitomising it?—No, I don't think so; I don't think there is too much matter in the text-book at present.

17676. Have you anything to say about habits of cleanliness in National schools?—Nothing specially; the teachers are required to have the schoolrooms swept and dusted each evening after the ordinary business of the day, and that, as a rule, I think is carried out.

17677. I refer to the children themselves, about coming to school in a clean condition?—Some improvement certainly is desirable in parts in reference to that.

17678. How does that come under your notice—the teacher knows, does he not, that you are about to visit the school?—No, he does not; he knows when I will come for the annual examination, but he is not supposed to know when I come besides.

17679. Mr. [illegible].—Are you able to make

Galway.

Oct. 7, 18[illegible].

Mr. W. H. Welply, B.A.

Galway.

Oct. 1, 1896.

Mr. W. H. Welply, B.A.

many visits besides the annual visit?—Yes, a great many in this district; but there are other districts in which many visits cannot be made, owing to the amount of work at the annual examinations.

17680. Mr. Molloy.—In those schools where net-mending is carried on, what length of time is devoted to the subject?—It was generally taken up outside school hours—from 3 to 4 o'clock.

17681. And by a specialist?—Yes.

17682. That specialist was paid by the Congested Districts Board?—Half his salary was paid by the Congested Districts Board.

17683. And the remaining half by the National Board?—Yes.

17684. What effect had it on the children, did it interfere with their literary progress in the ordinary subjects?—Not in the least.

17685. Were they in favour of it?—Oh, decidedly.

17686. And their parents also?—Yes, their parents were most anxious; I have Cleggan particularly in my mind, which was the last place at which that was taken up—the fishing industry has been greatly developed there, and the people were most anxious to have their children taught.

17687. How many pupils under instruction?—I cannot say exactly now, but there were quite thirty or forty under instruction.

17688. What are the usual extra branches taken up in your district?—We have geometry, algebra, drawing; book-keeping is rarely taken up in this district.

17689. Mensuration?—Mensuration, of course, forms part of the programme in geometry.

17690. How do you account for the small number of schools taking up such an important subject as drawing?—Merely because not many teachers have certificates in that branch.

17691. I think you said some teachers who had certificates did not take up that subject?—Yes; only the other day I met with a case, and inquired if there was any reason why this teacher did not take up the subject, and there did not appear to be any good reason; I tried to impress on him the necessity of taking it up.

17692. Would you not bring that under the notice of the manager?—Oh, yes, and under the notice of the Department as well.

17693. You mentioned that explanation of the subject-matter of the reading lesson became compulsory from the 1st of October?—From last Friday.

17694. But is it not a fact that explanation of the subject of the lesson was at all times an essential part of the programme and of examination by the inspector?—If you will allow me to explain—explanation of the reading was always an essential part, but the marking did not depend on it—it was what was called a subhead in the programme; now, according to the new programme, this subhead forms an integral part of the marking.

17695. Prior to the 1st of October is it to be understood that if the children, merely in a mechanical way, pronounced the words and were quite unable to explain them, still it earned a results fee?—Certainly.

17696. Are you quite sure about that?—Perfectly certain, except in fifth and sixth, in which the rule was introduced about a year ago.

17697. Would you not think it your duty to call attention to the fact that there was an absolute failure of any show of intelligence as to the meaning in the other classes below the fifth and sixth?—I have done it in scores of cases.

17698. Is it to be supposed that no action was taken in these cases?—Oh, yes, action was taken always; the fees were paid, but the teacher was reprimanded for not teaching explanation.

17699. If he were fined would it not amount to a reduction in the results fees?—He was not often fined; the official censure did not go beyond a reprimand.

17700. Mr. Redington.—You gave us some returns as to the time spent in teaching grammar and geography in a certain number of schools—could you tell us how much time per week is spent in teaching the other subjects on the programme?—I cannot tell you immediately; all the other subjects had the remainder of the time, but I cannot distinguish between one subject and another.

17701. Could you put in a return with regard to those schools—the time given to reading, writing and arithmetic?—Certainly; in a few days.

17702. You say very few teachers teach drawing and a large number are not competent to teach it—how would you propose to improve their knowledge of drawing?—I have already said that, as a temporary measure, I should think that at centres itinerant teachers might be employed to give instruction in that branch.

17703. Professor FitzGerald.—To the teachers or the pupils?—To the teachers.

17704. Mr. Redington.—Would the teachers come?—I think they would in many cases.

17705. And you think that after a few years we could make drawing compulsory in all the schools?—I think so.

17706. Do you think that an inspector's knowledge of needlework is equal to that of a lady?—I don't think my knowledge of needlework is equal to that of a lady; but, at the same time, I think I am a fairly competent judge of needlework.

17707. Do you think that it would be advisable to have lady instructors, who would go about advising as to the best mode of teaching needlework, instead of leaving the matter entirely in the hands of the ordinary inspector?—I think that would be useful. I should welcome it in this way—anything that would diminish the inspectors' labours at examinations.

17708. But do you think it would be an advantage to the teacher to get the assistance of a skilled expert in needlework?—I think so.

17709. Professor FitzGerald.—Do you think children at twelve or fourteen years of age can be expected to do needlework better than you can inspect it; do you think it would be fair on the children to expect them to do work of that character, which would be of such technical excellence that you would not be competent to inspect?—No, I don't think so. I think any work done in schools the ordinary inspector is quite competent to judge.

17710. Mr. Redington.—You are aware that there is a directress of needlework?—Yes; but I understand she confined herself to specimens worked by teachers at the July examinations.

17711. Then it is found necessary in examining the teachers' work to have a lady inspector; but for the pupils the male inspector is sufficient?—I fancy so.

Mr. Joseph D. Kelly.

Mr. Joseph D. Kelly, Teacher, [illegible] National School, County Galway, examined.

have you taught?—I have been instructed to teach carpentry by the Congested Districts Board. Carpentry is my order; I sought the certificate of competency on the first introduction of handicraft, and I got it in Marlborough-street.

17716. How did you get your benches?—I taught in the school with temporary benches, for a few years, such pupils as I could have, for results. I found that very inconvenient and troublesome, great difficulty surrounding it; so I applied to the Congested Districts Board, when I had an opportunity of interviewing the late Mr Tuke, for a grant, enabling me to carry it on better. Through Mr. Tuke's influence with the Board I got a grant of £15 to build a workshop.

17717. Did you build one with that sum?—I built one with that sum, 21ft. long and 12ft. wide.

17718. How high was it?—8ft. to the eave, and 12ft. to the ridge.

17719. How was it lighted?—By five windows. Of course I did the whole work myself, with the assistance of the boys.

17720. What material was it made of?—Wood and corrugated iron.

17721. What was the floor made of?—Concrete.

17722. Were you able to do it with the £15, in addition to the labour that you yourself and your boys gave to it?—I spent a little more, and then I got an additional grant. When Mr. Tuke came the way again he was very well pleased.

17723. How much was the additional grant?—£5, and then I had a visit from Mr. Balfour and the Hon. Horace Plunkett, and I was recommended to apply for an additional grant, and I did, and I got £16, and built an addition; the workshop is 28ft. by 13ft.

17724. How many benches have you got now?—Five.

17725. What did they cost a-piece?—Something about 5s. to 7s. each.

17726. You made them yourself?—We made all ourselves.

17727. What did the material cost?—About 5s.

17728. Rev. Dr. Evans.—Are they double or single benches?—Single benches; I approve of single benches.

17729. Chairman.—You put nothing for labour?—No.

17730. But suppose you could not make them yourself, and you had to buy them, have you any idea what a bench would cost?—Something about £1 5s., and that bench would be inferior to mine, for it would be smaller.

17731. In another school, where the teacher had not your aptitude, he could not expect to get his benches under £1 5s.?—He could have them for about 7s. or 8s., for the making of the bench is not much, and a carpenter would construct five or six a day.

17732. Coming to the question of tools, how did you procure your tools?—I had a fair supply of tools of my own at the beginning, and then I got a grant of £5 for tools.

17733. What tools have you—what number could you say?—I suppose I have about £10 or £12 worth of tools altogether; it cost about 14s. to supply each bench with bench-tools.

17734. What tools do you supply at that?—Three planes, a chisel or two, a square, and ruler. These are required for each bench, and then a larger number can be laid by in process for special use.

17735. The figures you have given us are very much smaller than those we have heard of elsewhere, even in Sweden. Do you think that in a district where the teacher had no aptitude like you have, he would be able to get a school started and buildings erected, and a supply of benches and tools for anything like the figure you have mentioned?—I think he would, very near it. I supplied these figures to Dr. Joyce for a little book he has written of late, and he has adopted my figures. He held about the same view on that matter.

17736. How far do you think that in rural districts manual instruction may with advantage be made a permanent part of the curriculum in the National system?—I would be in favour of introducing a sort resembling the Swedish Sloyd system as far as possible, on account of combining so much the useful with the educational.

Galway.

Oct. 1, 18[illegible]

Mr. Joseph P. Kelly.

17737. Would you also follow the Swedish system in making it optional with the teacher to teach it?—Well, I think it might be made compulsory after a time when teachers can be got to know it.

17738. Would you encroach upon the school hours to find time for manual teaching, or would you favour the system of having an extra hour or two in the week after school hours?—After school hours would be the best, the school hours could not be well, if at all interfered with, and they don't admit of lengthening.

17739. Do you believe that you could get the pupils to remain or come after the ordinary school hours in the upper classes?—Yes, I have an evening class and it is fairly well attended, especially in winter time, with ex-pupils.

17740. Do you think that it would be advisable to introduce the system that prevails in England, of preparing for the training in fifth and sixth classes, by having such things as cardboard work and wirework in classes lower down, the third and fourth?—I think the cardboard and wirework would not meet the wishes of either teachers or parents, they don't see the benefit of it.

17741. They don't see it now, but other people have seen it elsewhere; do you think it would have any educational advantage in teaching the children habits of accuracy, and how to measure and train the eye, which would help them when they come to woodwork afterwards?—I would be entirely in favour of that, of going on with the Swedish system, which does not admit of anything but wood Sloyd.

17742. How could room be made for manual training, without diminishing the time for useful portions of literary knowledge as at present imparted?—There is a good deal in grammar, as at present taught, that is not practically useful, and that could be curtailed without detracting from its utility; the foundation is laid at present on a very large scale, and when not followed by advanced education a great deal of that becomes useless.

17743. What are the difficulties in the way of having manual instruction generally taught?—Difficulties come in the way of the room. I would not favour teaching manual instruction in the schools, for the school hours hardly admit of it and the time is too short, the place has to be brushed up, but the workshop does not require that, and then there is the difficulty of suitable teachers. I would disapprove of taking in tradesmen, if we could avoid it, they don't teach as teachers.

17744. You have been through the Marlborough-street course; do you think that the course is adequate to enable anyone that goes through it to teach woodwork properly afterwards?—I have not been through the course in manual instruction.

17745. I thought you said you had?—No, but I went for an examination in Marlborough-street.

17746. Were you trained for an artisan originally?—Oh, no, but I got practical lessons in carpentry in Mount Talbot, Roscommon, from a carpenter and clerk of works.

17747. Coming to the subject of agriculture, do you consider that it is properly taught now; or that there is any room for improvement in the teaching of it?—It is not properly taught, because it is taught in a manner not locally applicable to rural districts. There is a great deal of stereotyped rotations given in Professor Baldwin's book, on which the inspectors minutely examine, and that is all matter to be forgotten and not put into practice, or applicable to the country.

Galway.

Oct. 1, 1897.

Mr. Joseph D. Kelly.

the younger children—the first class children, the infants—dismissed rather earlier than the others?—I think it would be a great advantage; at about half-past two they ought to be let off because they become weary.

17786. When you are teaching the higher classes in grammar, or arithmetic, or agriculture, what are the younger children doing—children of about six or seven?—They are at reading exercises, writing, and spelling, and a little arithmetical calculation, in charge of unpaid monitors—more advanced school boys.

17787. That is you take some members from your highest class to assist you?—To keep them going, but it is not teaching.

17788. And it would be no loss to these children, but a great assistance to you, if they were sent home rather earlier?—It would be an advantage to the advanced classes to have these children cleared out at about half past two—the day is long enough.

17789. Or even earlier, perhaps a half-day's attendance?—Half past two I think about fair.

17790. Captain Shaw.—Your school is in a rather scattered district?—Very scattered.

17791. How far did the students come who attended at your evening classes?—Some of them came about two miles, very few came further.

17792. Would you give us a little information as to these benches of yours; what is the size of the top of the bench?—Twenty-one inches wide, and one of them is the whole length, thirteen feet, of the room across, and the five others are six feet or seven feet.

17793. What is the thickness of the bench-top?—The front of the bench-top is three inch deal, and there is what we call a bench-well, the inner part of the bench is something lower, they are at varying heights to suit the size of the boys, some are fitted with a bench-screw, others with a simple slide.

17794. Are they movable?—Oh, no, they are permanent, fixed to the side of the walls—they are along the wall.

17795. You mentioned, I think, that you supplied three planes to each bench?—I think I made a mistake in that, I don't supply three, but two; I have three planes supplied to two benches. I dispense with the trying-plane, it is too big an item. I have the jack-plane, and the smoothing-plane.

17796. Would not one plane do for ordinary manual instruction, a cross between the jack and the smoothing plane?—One plane will not do, because the edge of the plane will get done up.

17797. You get pretty rough timber to work up?—Well, the ordinary deal got from Galway.

17798. Mr. Molloy.—How many classes in your school?—Five at present; no higher than fifth.

17799. That includes the second stage of fifth, so there are virtually six classes in your school?—I had a sixth class last year.

17800. The senior division consisting of fourth, 5¹, and 5²; how many pupils in the senior division?—I include third in the senior, and that would include something about half the school.

17801. Do the pupils of the third class take part in the instruction in carpentry?—Some of them do, those who are advanced.

17802. What age are they?—Something about twelve, some might be eleven.

17803. In third class?—Those that I take into the manual instruction are from eleven to twelve.

17804. What might be the age of your senior classes?—None at present are fifteen, generally between fourteen and fifteen they drop away from school.

17805. In third, fourth, first stage of fifth, and second stage of fifth, what is the total number on the roll?—I think it is no more than twelve at present.

17806. And of the twelve on the rolls how many actually receive instruction in carpentry?—Ten pupils I have on the roll for the day class of manual instruction, and ten for the evening class.

17807. Do they get any instruction in the use of tools, or any description of them, and how to clean and sharpen them?—Oh, yes.

17808. Do they take any part in sharpening the tools themselves?—Oh, yes, they must sharpen them.

17809. Chairman.—Do you lecture to them on the subject of the different kinds of wood?—Well, I don't go largely into the different kinds of wood, for our chief wood is deal. I have three sorts—yellow pine, red, and white.

17810. Mr. Molloy.—I think you mentioned you had an evening school?—Yes, that is the evening class I refer to.

17811. At what hour does the instruction in carpentry begin?—Six to eight for evenings.

17812. And how many evenings in the week?—Three—Tuesday, Thursday, and Saturday.

17813. Chairman.—How many hours does it last?—Two hours.

17814. Mr. Molloy.—In the ordinary day school have you any science teaching?—No, sir.

17815. Any instruction in drawing?—No.

17816. The boys who learn carpentry, are they not taught drawing?—I get them usually to do little sketches, and show them the connection between the sketch and the model they are to make.

17817. I forget whether you stated you had a certificate for drawing?—I have not a certificate, except as drawing is included in the handicraft certificate, for which there is some drawing required.

17818. You would desire, in the case of infants, that they might be dismissed at an earlier hour, and you mentioned half past two; perhaps you are not aware that that is the regulation of the National Board that infants may be dismissed prior to the termination of the ordinary school time?—I am not aware of that.

17819. Monsignor Molloy.—Do the pupils who come to your evening classes pay fees?—No, sir, it is quite free.

Mr. P. J. Hannon, Organiser, Irish Agricultural Organisation Society, examined.

Mr. P. J. Hannon.

17820. Chairman.—Where do you live?—I live in Loughrea, and at the present time I am engaged for

17821. In order to earn fees?—I should think so, or to comply with the late order of the Board, making the school compulsory in rural schools.

; they are generally National school [illegible] these [illegible] for the [illegible]

all; ordinary farmers ought to be able to do these things for themselves without calling in the aid of

work, and at the same time attend to the rest of the school—it was quite impossible.

17555. Do the parents object to the alternative scheme?—Yes, they do.

17556. And it has been given up or not taken, in a great many cases?—It has not been taken up; I don't know any case where it was taken up and given up afterwards.

17557. You have some suggestion to make with regard to poultry-rearing, and egg industry, and bee-keeping?—Yes; I think if those things could be introduced into the schools in some way it would be preferable. The Irish people are very slow to take up anything out of which they cannot make a profit, and if our people could be shown some way of realizing something on what they did in school when applied at home it would be very useful.

17558. What have you to say with regard to the grouping of extra subjects?—I think in mathematics and science subjects in National schools, they could be grouped, instead of taking geometry, and algebra, and trigonometry separately, they could be grouped in three or four, copying the University plan in the Intermediate.

17559. Could drawing be made compulsory?—I think so.

17560. You think, therefore, that every teacher should be required to take it and teach it; that is every new teacher?—Yes, but I think there are many in the country quite capable of teaching drawing who have not certificates at all, and are debarred on this ground from teaching it.

17561. Why can they not obtain certificates?—Sometimes the teachers don't like to go in for certificates, I cannot tell you why.

17562. Have you given any attention to the subject of elementary practical science?—Oh, yes; I think some course of elementary practical science should be adopted in National schools; I think the mental faculties of the children would be much better brought out and developed by having some scheme of instruction of this kind, but of course the difficulty of time comes in, when you are to teach it. If it could be taken up on Saturdays or outside schooltime, such instruction would be very valuable. I would like to suggest that in National schools in Ireland the spirit of self-help ought to be impressed on the children. In this country it is very difficult to get on, people seem to want the spirit of self-help that go-ahead people have, and if the National Board took steps to infuse that spirit into the children it would be a very good thing indeed.

17563. Rev. Dr. EVANS.—Are you a school teacher yourself?—No, I never was.

17564. Do you know anything of the instruction given at the Model Farm?—Well, I have had a good many communications with Mr. Carroll, but I don't know anything directly about it.

17565. You don't know whether it is a thoroughly good place for acquiring a knowledge of agriculture?—I believe it is.

17566. And that there is a very sound system observed there, and very useful instruction in training given?—Yes, I think so.

17567. To both the teachers and farmers' sons who come up for a period?—With regard to the teachers I think the time is rather limited—the time the teachers get there.

17568. Now have you read Mr. Carroll's Manual for Instruction in agriculture in Schools?—He very kindly sent me a copy; I cannot say I read it very closely, but I am acquainted with the leading outlines.

17569. As far as you know it, do you think it is a suitable book?—Yes.

17570. CHAIRMAN.—Is it hard for children to understand?—If it is hard it is because it is so exceedingly simple; teachers complain, and say they cannot ask questions from it.

17571. Rev. Dr. EVANS.—You don't think it is a book interspersed with polysyllables and difficult words that would require an etymologist to expound?—No.

Galway. Oct. 7, 18[illegible]. Mr. P. J. [illegible]

17572. Do you teach about soils in your own work?—No, I give information when I can to farmers. I act generally in connection with the adult population.

17573. You would teach them about artificial manures?—Yes.

17574. Does it fall within your scope to teach anything about cattle keeping?—Yes, all those subjects.

17575. How do you impart that instruction?—As far as my Organisation is concerned, we generally hold public meetings; we hold meetings of intelligent farmers—I hope in a great many cases very intelligent—and I am glad to say they are carrying out our suggestions closely. We talk quietly to those farmers; from local knowledge we know what the district wants, and we put before those people the best way of utilising anything that exists in the district for the purposes of their industry. The great fundamental idea in my work is to get the Irish people to adopt the principle of self, and mutual help, and make use of it for their own benefit.

17576. I was deeply interested in what you said about the grouping of mathematical subjects, and would like to understand it a little better?—Suppose a teacher is preparing his sixth class for a results examination, I think that algebra and Euclid might be taken as one subject, and if sufficient proficiency were shown by a boy in Euclid, he ought to be allowed a pass in both. I think it should be taken as one result subject.

17577. And you would not think it serious if a teacher, at his own examination, passed in geometry, passed in trigonometry and two or three other subjects, if he failed in mensuration?—That is in the case of a teacher, but we are talking of children in National schools.

17578. Would you think it right to give that man credit for having passed in all those subjects that are embraced in the group, although he happened to fail, because he was tired?—A teacher should have a knowledge of each subject in which he was supposed to qualify, but in the case of a child in a National school certainly geometry and algebra could be grouped together, and ought to be taught as one result subject.

17579. Professor FITZGERALD.—Do you think that farming can be taught to children of about twelve years old satisfactorily?—I don't think so at all.

17580. What sort of agriculture could be taught to children of that age?—I think the taste for agriculture might be developed in children of that age; I think they ought to be taught to think about agricultural things, instead of thinking of looking for clerkships or something entirely beyond their sphere in life—they ought to be taught something that would rather turn their minds towards what they would have to deal with afterwards.

17581. You think that the teaching of agriculture might run into a practical direction, such as elements of botany and collections of plants, and so on?—I think collections would be an excellent idea, of course teaching botany technically as such I would not recommend.

17582. Showing them examples of seeds growing I would call botany?—Of course it is, but I object to taking up a text-book, as a teacher would very likely do, and take it chapter by chapter. I would object to that, but teaching it by examples would be an excellent idea.

17583. Elementary science you mentioned; do you mean the elements of chemistry?—Just a little chemistry, as much as would apply to agricultural subjects. I think a farmer ought to be able to tell, if he saw the analysis of manure, whether it was good or a bad one; an intelligent boy at a National school ought to be able to advise his father on elementary things that would involve a slight knowledge of chemistry.

17584. Do you think that the teachers in the

17902. In what locality?—County Galway and a good deal in Sligo, and some in Mayo, and recently in going over my own district, as organiser, I very often visit schools.

17903. What is the extent of your district as organiser?—It is practically the province of Connaught, but I have been so busy recently that I have not left the County Galway.

17904. Then those observations are based on the experience of casual visits to a few schools?—Not alone. I have visited a great many schools.

17905. But not in any official capacity?—Oh no.

17906. Merely calling in to the school when passing by?—Yes.

17907. And spending how much time there?—From half-an-hour, or if I was very much interested I would spend perhaps an hour. I know I spent an hour watching children under the alternative scheme doing nothing.

17908. Do you take any part in the examination?—If the teacher allows me I ask questions in agriculture.

17909. Monsignor Molloy.—Are you yourself a trained agriculturist?—Well, I am not trained.

17910. Where did you acquire your knowledge of agriculture?—I have had certificates in agriculture under the Science and Art Department. Of course you can hardly call these training, but when I was a pupil in a National school we had a model school farm attached to the school.

17911. Where was that?—In the County Sligo, and we received a certain amount of training on that. I may say I was, perhaps, one of the more intelligent pupils on the farm. I have not had any real training in agriculture as such.

17912. From your experience as an organiser do you think would the farmers generally in the district you are acquainted with be willing to allow plots on their farms for the teaching of agriculture?—I don't think they would do it voluntarily, but if some consideration was given to them I think there is no district in Ireland where you would not get a suitable plot.

17913. Such a consideration would be, perhaps, if seed and manure were provided for them?—I think so, something like what the Congested Districts Board are doing.

17914. Mr. Redington.—Why do you think agriculture should be taught outside the school hours?—I think in school hours, where five or ten minutes is lost changing from one class to another, and the teacher trying to get over the work as quickly as possible, I am afraid the full time—the full half-hour—is not given to the subject, and, perhaps, if the day's lesson could be adverted to in the afternoon it would be very useful.

17915. Would not children benefit by the lesson better if it were taught within school hours, when their minds were fresher?—I don't know.

17916. Do you think that the present book, if illustrated by practical experiments, would be a kind of agricultural teaching you would approve of?—Yes, I think you would get there a better mode of education.

17917. Have you considered the programme laid down by the *French* Minister of Public Instruction?—Yes, I have looked over that; I think it an excellent idea.

17918. That consists of experiments in elementary science?—Yes, but it set about by giving the children a taste for their work, and this was followed up by ex-

FORTIETH PUBLIC SITTING.—FRIDAY, OCTOBER 8TH, 1897,

at 3.30 o'clock, p.m.,

At the Imperial Hotel, Sligo.

Sligo. Oct. 8, 1897.

Present :—THE RIGHT HON. THE EARL OF BELMORE, G.C.M.G., in the chair; THE RIGHT HON. C. T. REDINGTON, M.A.; THE MOST REV. MONSIGNOR MOLLOY, D.D., D.SC.; REV. HENRY EVANS, D.D.; REV. HAMILTON WILSON, D.D.; PROFESSOR G. F. FITZGERALD, F.T.C.D.; STANLEY HARRINGTON, ESQ., M.A.; W. R. J. MOLLOY, ESQ.; CAPTAIN T. B. SHAW; and J. STRUTHERS, ESQ., M.A.;

with J. D. DALY, ESQ., M.A., Secretary.

Mr. THOMAS CRYAN, Teacher, Tumnabrack National School, Ballaghaderrin, examined. Mr. Thomas Cryan.

17922. CHAIRMAN.—You are the teacher of the Tumnabrack National School, Ballaghaderrin?—Yes, my lord.

17923. Do you give evidence on your own behalf or on behalf of more than yourself?—Partly on my own behalf and partly on behalf of those teachers who selected me to appear. There was a meeting of teachers held in the Town-hall on last Saturday, and they selected two teachers, and I was one of them. It was not a very representative meeting of teachers; perhaps half of them were from the town and locality around here, but there were others from other parts of the county Sligo.

17924. How far from Sligo would the district that was represented extend?—Some of the teachers who attended there live 25 miles from this place.

17925. They extend over a large area?—Over a large area.

17926. You have given some attention to the question of manual work in schools?—Well, I have thought about it, but not very much, because I have no experience in manual instruction; I never did anything that way.

17927. Do you think that there would be time—to put it in that way—that there would be time to introduce it without some alteration in the present programme?—I think there would not; my experience is that all there is in the present programme is a very heavy job for teachers and pupils to go through without adding to it, except the work would be outside school hours or on Saturdays.

17928. How long do you suppose the work would take in the week?—I have formed no opinion on that.

17929. Suppose it took two hours. Do you think it would be possible on any day in the week to secure two hours for the boys in the 5th and 6th standards?—Not if it is taught in school hours.

17930. Is there any day in the week in which there are not full school hours?—Except on Saturdays.

17931. Could it be introduced on Saturdays?—I believe it could.

17932. You are aware no doubt that there has been very little of it introduced into Ireland as yet, but the Commissioners have visited one school in the county Waterford in which it has been introduced, and the way in which the time was found for it was by somewhat shortening the time given to the lessons of those boys who were engaged in that sort of work. Do you think anything of that sort could be done generally?—I think not, except the requirements of the programme in some subjects were lessened; the amount of information required by the results examination should be made less than it is presently.

17933. Do you think that the plan adopted in this particular place, in Lismore, could be adopted generally, which I understand is by taking ten minutes off certain subjects?—I think it could not; the majority of teachers find it difficult enough to teach the existing programme within the given time.

17934. Will you give your reasons; I see that you have a number of reasons, beginning with irregularity of attendance?—I find that at certain seasons of the year a certain proportion of pupils would remain at home; they are employed at farm work. These may remain at home for three weeks or a month in succession, and the part of the programme that the teacher has in the interval gone over with the pupils those at home know nothing about, and he has to commence it again and go over it with those who stayed at home. This has to be done at different periods of the year, and the consequence is that he has to teach the same matter perhaps two or three times on account of those absent pupils, and he spends most of his time with those pupils who were absent trying to bring them up to the level of the programme; he cannot spend his time with the pupils who attend regularly—he spends his time with them, but most of his time is devoted to bringing the others up to the mark, and it frequently happens he has to teach the same subject two or three times over, owing to those absences.

17935. What other reasons have you?—The principal reason is the difficulty of teaching explanation in the lesson books, which was not insisted on before.

17936. I don't quite follow you in that—I don't know what was done before?—What was done before was that if the pupils read the lessons with due attention to pauses, and read fairly, they got a pass in reading, even without knowing the subject matter of what they read. It was a general rule that they might get passes in all classes without knowing what they read.

17937. Do you think that a good system?—I think it is a very bad system and I think it is of great importance to insist on the lessons being explained, but it means a very serious increase in the teacher's work, because the lesson books are so extensive and so many pages, and it is a difficult matter for a young child attending school.

17938. Do you think any improvement could be made in giving easier books and shorter lessons?—I examined some of the English readers and the number of pages is less, and the matter treated of in our books is suitable more for men than for children.

17939. Some alteration in that respect would gain a little time?—Yes, if the books were shortened and made easier at the same time.

17940. What do you say with regard to the revised agricultural text-book?—I think that is a very serious increase on the teacher's work and the work of the pupils, because it is a much more difficult book and more scientific than the one used before.

17941. Whose book is it?—It is on the Board's list. It is the only book on the Board's list now. That is the book [*producing Professor Carroll's book*]. That is a much larger and more difficult book than the old book that we had to teach before this.

17942. Do you think that the teaching of that book is satisfactory—the results of the teaching of the book. Do you think the pupils understand more about agriculture than they did formerly before that book came in?—Perhaps they understand more of the theory of agriculture—the scientific knowledge that underlies the theory of agriculture; but it is a far more difficult book for the pupils to get up, and the teachers to teach, and it is expected that the pupils in sixth class will have a knowledge of all the matter treated of in the preceding classes. That is a very serious matter. I don't see how it can be done; and the second-fifth class must know the knowledge that is required for the fourth and first-fifth, and the sixth must know not only the special knowledge required for their own class, but all learned in the preceding classes. It would be something like if a pupil in sixth class was examined in reading, and had to get up the reading of the fifth and fourth class, and to be liable to be examined on it.

17943. With regard to attendance many of the pupils don't make a sufficient number of attendances required for results fees?—A good many of the pupils don't make 100 attendances, and cannot be examined, and a good many of the pupils don't make many over 100—perhaps from 120 to 130.

17944. You think you are not likely to increase the attendance unless you get compulsory education?—No; I think the teachers are doing as much as at present they possibly could do.

17945. You are not sanguine of getting compulsory attendance?—I would like to get it, but I don't see how I can.

17946. You would like the present programme to be changed in some respects?—I think so. Even apart from manual work the pupils would be much better off if they were taught less and taught better.

17947. Suppose they were taught less and taught better, would you be in favour of getting a couple of hours for manual instruction?—I think that could be done if the teachers were trained to do it, and if some of the subjects were changed there might be time got.

17948. If you were to curtail the programme at all in what respects do you think it could be curtailed with advantage?—I would curtail it in grammar and geography, and I think there is far too much arithmetic required for most of the pupils attending our schools. They never have any necessity for this advanced arithmetic afterwards. They have to have a knowledge of square and cube root.

17949. Do you think too much time is given for spelling?—I do. I find spelling is a very difficult subject to teach or have a boy proficient in. There came a pupil to my school who got his leg cut off in England. He was twenty-seven years of age. He commenced at the alphabet; he went through to the fourth class. He told me he found it far harder to learn the spelling than all the other subjects put together. The books are so hard, and the lessons so long, and the words so difficult that it is hard for children to get up the knowledge required for the results examination. If the lesson book were made smaller that would be done away with to some extent.

17950. Do you think that the present system of results fees depending on individual examination of the pupils is not a good one?—I think it is a very bad one. It often happens under it that those pupils that the teacher has to spend most time and patience with, instead of bringing credit on him for the trouble, bring discredit on him, because if there are two or three stupid pupils in the class that fail, and get bad marks, it means the teacher will suffer in money and reputation; and he really deserves more credit for what they answer than for what the good ones answer, because he spends more time teaching them than he does the good ones. I think when the majority of pupils are well and sufficiently taught it proves the teacher did his duty, and he should be

17951. What do you think about the teaching of agriculture generally—do you think it would be more important for the pupils to have a practical knowledge of the best methods of cultivating crops than the theoretical knowledge they acquire at present?—I think it would be of much more importance to the majority of the pupils. They have to get up a lot of theoretical knowledge that never will be of much use to them, and they don't know the best methods of growing the crops that are grown in their localities by farmers.

17952. What scheme would you propose to give them practical knowledge?—I think it would be a good thing if there were a school garden attached to each school, and small plots of the various crops grown in the locality cultivated there to show the different varieties of seeds, and make the pupils cultivate them, and show them in the various stages of growth, and when they saw the superiority of these crops to the crops on the surrounding farms it would be a very good object lesson to them to improve their own farms when they became farmers hereafter.

17953. What sized plots would you suggest?—Half an acre would be sufficient. I think it would be a very important thing if there were some of the common vegetables grown, and perhaps that there were some flower plots, because the habits of neatness that would be shown to the pupils might have an effect on them when they go to their own homes to imitate those habits.

17954. Do you think that in the district you represent it would be easy to acquire plots?—Well, I think it would.

17955. In what way would you do it—would you follow what I understand the Congested Districts Board have begun to do, acquire plots by renting them from the farmer who happens to have land in a convenient situation?—I think they could be got that way, or bought up by the Commissioners, or the Government might advance money for buying the lands permanently.

17956. But the evidence we got yesterday in Galway showed it would be probably far easier to rent the land than buy it?—I believe it would. I believe if there was encouragement given there are many teachers in my locality that have land and don't carry on operations under the Board, as it seems the conditions for doing it are not favourable. I know many teachers who have land and don't cultivate school gardens or plots for the Board.

17957. What class of subjects would you include in manual training?—If manual training means the training of hand and eye, I think there is a great deal of manual training already given, although it is not called by that name. I think drawing is a very good training and writing an exercise, if neatly done.

17958. In any system of manual training, drawing is necessary as a foundation for it; they must draw to scale to be able to do work properly. You suggest, I suppose, that the manual training suitable to a school would not be the teaching of a trade, which is no part of our business to inquire into, but making a boy handy and observant, so that he could apply whatever knowledge he gains, by thinking of the work he has to do with his hands?—Yes; that is what I think.

17959. Do you think that the present teachers, of whom many, no doubt, have been through the Training Schools in Marlborough-street, and I suppose many have not, would be either competent, or able to make themselves in a short time competent to teach, or do you think it would be necessary to employ special teachers to teach anything in the shape of woodwork, or matters of that sort?—That would depend on the knowledge that these teachers possessed. If they were taught in a training college, and had a fair knowledge of it, they might do it, but the ordinary teacher, who did not learn it in the training college, could not do it well, and it is better not to teach

17960. What do you think about the industrial schools for girls?—The female school attached to mine, which was taught by my wife, taught it for six months, and she had a large sixth class, but most of them stopped at home, and the manager had to write to the Board and get permission to go back to the old scheme.

17961. Rev. Dr. Evans.—Could you indicate the reason the people have for doing this?—The people say if they want their children to learn a trade or dressmaking, it is better to send them to a proper place to learn the trade, and that they should not be eaten botches. They say they have the many of these in the country already. If a girl, for instance, is taught dressmaking in the school, and cannot do the business well, she will get nothing to do when she sets up for herself afterwards, whereas if she goes to a regular place, and learns the trade properly, she will.

17962. I understand that neither you nor those you represent, are opposed to any modification of the present system tending to the advantage and welfare of the pupils of the country?—We are not opposed to any scheme that is for the advantage of the children, but we think the time already given to literary instruction is scarce enough.

17963. Mr. Redington.—Do you teach many extras in your school?—I take extras for the Science and Art Department, and I teach drawing and algebra for the Board. I taught hygiene.

17964. Those are extra classes?—After school hours.

17965. Is drawing taught generally in your district?—It is not.

17966. Do you think it is important that it should be taught universally?—I think very important. I know it is very popular; in my school pupils like the subject well.

17967. Do you teach any science subject under the Board?—I taught algebra and I taught hygiene, but I generally teach the science subjects for the Science and Art Department. I taught mathematics and sound, light and heat, and hygiene for the Science and Art Department last year.

17968. Have you many pupils?—I had seventeen examined on mathematics, twenty-one on sound, light and heat, and nearly thirty on hygiene.

17969. Why do you prefer taking these subjects up under the Science and Art Department?—Because they pay more money than the National Board, they give £1 for a pass where the Board only give 4s.

17970. Mr. Struthers.—Do you also get a grant from the Board?—No, you cannot get a grant from both departments for the same subject.

17971. Mr. Redington.—Do you teach these experimentally?—I taught a little experimentally this year, and much less other years, because although I believe the experimental teaching is the best, it takes far too much time for a teacher who wants to earn results in the shortest way.

17972. Would not the pupils learn the subjects better?—They would, but the apparatus is very expensive, and beyond that it takes longer to give a lesson experimentally than a lesson out of the text-book.

17973. Perhaps it is better than a lesson out of a text-book?—As far as the examinations are a test of the knowledge acquired I did better out of the text-book.

17974. I think you said that some teachers have plots of land in your neighbourhood and yet do not go in for practical training in agriculture?—They do not.

17975. Why?—I could not say; I think they don't think the fee that is given sufficient to pay them for the trouble, because when the Agricultural Inspector comes to examine the farm he suggests a lot of improvements, improvements in out-offices, and the outlay would be too much, and the money received in results fees would not recoup them.

17976. Do you know that the fees have been increased?—Yes; I may say I was up at Glasnevin myself and intend to start this business if I think it will pay.

17977. How long were you at Glasnevin?—Six weeks.

17978. Do you think the course did you good?—I think it did me ever so much good.

17979. What lectures did you attend?—In gardening and general farm work, and how the crops are grown.

17980. Did you receive any lessons in chemistry?—No. There were lectures on zoology from Dr. M'Weeney.

17981. How many lectures in zoology did you attend?—I attended all the lectures that there were, but he went away before the six weeks were up. I did not come in for a complete series of lectures on that subject.

17982. Have you any suggestions that could help us in modifying this arrangement; do you think it would be desirable to have a complete course for those who, like you, come up from the country to study?—It would be very hard to have a complete course owing to the shortness of the time.

17983. But if there were a lecture every day?—Yes, or two lectures a day.

17984. What subjects do you think could be dealt with that way?—It is difficult to say, perhaps. An elementary knowledge of geology and botany, and those subjects that underlie agriculture, would be very useful.

17985. If you had gone through a complete course of elementary chemistry you might find it easier to give experimental lectures to the pupils in your school?—There is no doubt of that whatever.

17986. You said that you disapprove of the results system as at present carried out?—I do very much.

17987. Speaking generally, what changes would you make?—I think in some subjects that there should not be individual examination of pupils, or that the results of the teacher's work should not be judged by the individual examination.

17988. Chairman.—Are there any subjects in which you think it would be well still to retain individual examination?—In arithmetic it should be retained.

17989. It has been suggested to us by one witness that it would be desirable to retain individual examination in reading, writing, arithmetic, and drawing, but not in the others?—I was going to say so: I think in grammar and geography the work could be done as well by examining the class generally.

17990. Mr. Redington.—That is you would keep to individual examination on the subjects the Chairman has mentioned?—Yes, but I would not pay the way it is paid now. If sixty boys were taught drawing, and there were two or three boys out of the sixty that could not do the exercises well, while the rest did them well, I think the teacher should be paid for those two or three as well as for the rest.

17991. In drawing would you still have the examinations individually?—Yes; I don't see how else it could be judged.

17992. If the Inspector saw you teaching and then saw the work done by the boys?—Yes, that would be better.

17993. Is there sufficient weight given to order and discipline of the school in estimating the value of the results?—I think the order and discipline are very important factors in a school, and they are never taken into account; there is no money value attached to them, and they are more useful to boys than some of the subjects paid for, perhaps more. If a boy gets orderly habits in school it is more important than a knowledge of a lot of geography that he may never require.

17994. Monsignor Molloy.—Are you a trained teacher?—I am not; I was never trained, but I have the highest class under the Board.

17995. You are classified first of first?—First of first.

17996. Perhaps there was no training system when you were preparing to be a master?—I think there [illegible] of first in 1879, and first of first [illegible] they were in existence then.

[illegible] were selected at a meeting of your [illegible] his locality to give evidence on their [illegible] to the introduction of manual [illegible]

[illegible] many teachers attended that meeting? [illegible] the exact number, but I think [illegible] twenty.

[illegible] came, I suppose, from Sligo and the [illegible]—There were six or seven teachers [illegible] of the county.

[illegible] you said that you yourself had to [illegible] the teaching of manual work in primary [illegible]

[illegible] the other twenty any experience of [illegible] manual work?—I cannot say.

[illegible], so far as you know, you were all [illegible] in the subject here which we [illegible]?—I cannot answer for the others; I [illegible] myself, that I know nothing about [illegible]

[illegible] you said your principal reason for [illegible] introduction of manual teaching [illegible] the other subjects which are taught in [illegible] suffer?—Yes, if the requirements are [illegible] if the system of examination is not [illegible]

[illegible] these conditions were fulfilled, then [illegible] in favour of the introduction of manual [illegible] would, if it was an advantage to the [illegible]

[illegible] the question is, whether it would be an [illegible] the pupils to introduce it, and you say [illegible] an advantage if it interfered with the [illegible]?—If it diminished the time given to [illegible] at present in the school; I think the [illegible] present is little enough.

[illegible] evidence we got from those who have [illegible] teaching of manual work in schools, is [illegible] it was introduced, the proficiency of [illegible] the literary subjects was greatly [illegible], they were in a position to judge; I [illegible]

[illegible] were satisfied that this was the [illegible] to the introduction of manual [illegible] disappear?—Certainly, if it was so [illegible] think I said so in my statement.

[illegible] you also told us that the attendance [illegible] generally is very irregular and [illegible] in the rural schools.

[illegible], we have also got evidence that [illegible] work was introduced, the attend[illegible] improved; the children came more [illegible] in larger numbers, and remained at [illegible] advanced age?—That is a great [illegible] favour.

[illegible] MOLLOY.—Kindly describe your school; [illegible]?—It is a rural school.

[illegible] is your post town?—It is five miles [illegible] a wild, mountain district.

[illegible] is your average attendance?—Sixty [illegible]

[illegible] many of those in the senior division [illegible] and sixth classes?—There might be [illegible] ago twenty; sometimes the sixth class [illegible] twenty-five or thirty.

[illegible] extra branches do these pupils learn? [illegible] already I teach drawing always; I [illegible] this year for the Board. I taught [illegible] Board, but I teach for the last sixteen [illegible] connection with the Science and Art [illegible], as they pay better, I don't go in for [illegible] the Board.

[illegible] classes in connection with the Science [illegible] are taught in the evening?—Yes.

[illegible] they attended exclusively by your own [illegible] have a monitor from another school, [illegible] are my own pupils.

attending the school?—Invariably, and they wait for the Science and Art classes after the school is dis[missed].

16018. Mr. ROBERTSON.—Where do they get their dinner?—They don't get their dinner, perhaps, until night.

16019. Mr. HARRINGTON.—They live on the education you give them?—It helps them to live afterwards, perhaps.

16020. Mr. STRUTHERS.—Are classes held in the afternoon or evening?—From half-past three to half-past four o'clock, and on Saturdays.

16021. Mr. MOLLOY.—Is drawing to scale taught in your school?—No, only freehand drawing.

16022. With regard to the examination of the school, if I mistake not, you said you were in favour of all the pupils being examined. Do you mean all the pupils on the roll, or simply the pupils who have made 100 attendances alone, with a view to payment?—Oh, no; of the pupils that make the attendances.

16023. What do you propose in the case of the pupils who do not make the attendances?—I think those pupils who make the attendance in two years—fifty one year, and fifty in another—should be examined then, but it is not allowed under the present rules.

16024. Would you be in favour of having class examination in all subjects?—I would not.

16025. You prefer individual examination in certain subjects?—I do in arithmetic and writing, but, if the writing in general is good, it is only fair that all the pupils should be paid for.

16026. Your school being a rural one, have you any school garden attached?—No, I have not.

16027. What are the subjects you take up for the Science and Art Department?—I take different courses different years. I taught mathematics, agriculture, physiography, geology, sound, light and heat, hygiene, and magnetism and electricity.

16028. What are your school hours?—From nine until about five, perhaps longer preceding the examinations.

16029. And then you take up Science and Art classes?—That is inclusive, from nine to half-past three for the ordinary school; after that the Science and Art work.

16030. That is really eight hours continuous teaching?—Yes.

16031. Do the pupils bring any luncheon with them?—Of course they take luncheon at playtime; it would be very hard that they should be without luncheon.

16032. CHAIRMAN.—What do they eat at luncheon?—A piece of bread just.

16033. Mr. STRUTHERS.—Is there any interval between the afternoon attendance and the beginning of the Science and Art classes?—No, there is not; as soon as one is over the other commences.

16034. Mr. MOLLOY.—You dwell on the great importance of order and discipline, and especially that these should be recognised in some pecuniary way?—I think so.

16035. Would you think of reverting to the former practice of the National Board, viz.—giving a special premium for these—there was a time when there was a special prize of £3 in the year for order and cleanliness?—I think it was a very valuable and useful prize; the orderly habits a boy acquires are of great importance to him in after life.

16036. Mr. HARRINGTON.—Do you teach agriculture experimentally in any way in your school?—No, I do not.

16037. You received a training you say, I think, at Glasnevin?—Yes; but last July only.

16038. Did you intend, then, to introduce it?—I do intend.

16039. Bringing the boys out in the fields and showing them the crops?—Yes, after a time; that is, in anticipation that this Commission will report favourably on the business of increasing the pay-

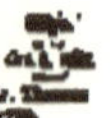

18040. What do you mean by hygiene?—A subject that relates to the general laws of health. It includes the elements of human physiology, the processes of digestion and assimilation; there is a certain elementary knowledge of that required.

18041. Is laundry work taught in any of the rural schools in your district?—It is not.

18042. Would you be in favour of its introduction into the schools?—I don't know; I have no experience to guide me in giving an opinion on that matter.

18043. Have you anything to say about kindergarten?—No, I don't know anything about it. I never saw it taught, and do not teach it.

18044. Mr. Strahan.—I think your objection to having the hours devoted to literary work shortened was that you could not get the boys to pass the examination?—Certainly.

18045. But you don't think the boys' education would suffer if the examination were modified?—I think not; it would improve them in some ways.

18046. As regards the books which they read, does that help them to read intelligently, generally, learning one book by heart?—Heretofore, when the explanation was not insisted on, they read the books mechanically, but they did not know what the books meant. If you asked them questions on the subject, very few could answer.

18047. Is the subject of the Lesson Books much more difficult to comprehend than a leading article in a newspaper?—Much more difficult, and I think it is proved by the fact that I saw in the report of the Commissioners, that with all the teachers going to be examined for training the lowest subject on which they answered was on the Lesson Books.

18048. You think if the demand for reading were modified the pupils' education would not suffer?—I think it would be improved very much.

18049. And the same applies to arithmetic?—I think there is too much arithmetic required at present; if they knew a smaller amount, and better, it would be much better.

18050. Do you regard your pupils as sources of income to a certain extent, and turn them into money making machines?—I do not. But the manager's opinion and the inspector's opinion and that of all who have control over me will be formed to a certain extent on the money I make.

18051. Do you think you would be able to give your pupils a more satisfactory education if your own salary did not depend on passing each individual one?—I think I would if the results system were modified.

18052. As regards agriculture will you tell us how many different subjects are included in that book of agriculture, it is divided roughly into divisions is it not?—I have the official paper; in fourth class should answer intelligently in the following subject as treated in Part I., "Cultivation of land &c.," that means sixty-seven pages. In the fifth class they have to answer on manuring and manures, rotation cropping, gardening, including flowers and fruits, and in addition to what is required in the fourth class, the fourth class have to get off sixty-seven pages and this class 163 pages. Then the second fifth class have to get in addition to that five how difficult it is to get that knowledge up and they have to get off a good deal about agricultural machines that they never saw, and never will see in country places; it is very hard for a teacher to get a knowledge of them from the diagrams in the book.

18053. Do you think it would be preferable to teach them the elementary science which underlies agriculture, some slight knowledge of the growth of plants and botany?—I think it would be far more interesting.

18054. Do you think as a practical teacher you would be able to make them understand the thing more thoroughly by practical demonstration?—I think so, because in teaching for the Science and Art Department, that is what you have to teach and the pupils take more interest in it than in the Board's agriculture.

18057. What is the attraction for the students to attend the Science and Art classes?—It is to give them a good education, and they are trained to write out what they know, properly.

18058. They simply attend for the purpose of being educated?—Yes, and with a view that it will help them to get posts as teachers and other positions.

18059. And with a view of being educated you find the pupils are willing to attend an extra hour a day?—They are.

18060. So there might not be any difficulty in prolonging the school hours if the instruction was satisfactory?—I think so.

18061. I suppose you have got the Science and Art Department certificate for passing the examinations?—I have.

18062. Have you ever attended any course for teachers?—I have not, with the exception of Glasnevin.

18063. Have you ever had any training in experimental work?—I never had.

18064. Then it is rather hard for you to make experiments?—I have a good deal of apparatus on some of the subjects, I have about £30 worth of apparatus, and I make a few experiments, and when the pupils see a few experiments performed, and that they agree with what they see in the book it will give them confidence in the other statements in the book.

18065. Don't you feel you would be in a better position to give instruction if you had attended a practical course yourself?—I have no doubt about it.

18066. You suggest that it was most important that children should be taught orderly habits, neatness and accuracy, would you be in favour of teaching a subject that would directly lead to these?—I think it would be an advantage to the pupil.

18067. Rev. Dr. Evans.—I think you said that you were not trained?—I did.

18068. Were you educated in a Model school originally?—I was not, I had to learn it all myself whatever I learned.

18069. Had you any training either in the position of monitor or pupil teacher?—No, I never was a monitor or pupil teacher.

18070. How many half-hour lessons have you in the day in your school?—I would have to take some time to answer.

18071. You did not think of bringing a time-table?—No.

18072. Do you teach drawing?—I do.

your schools?—For the Board it is the arithmetic on the Board's list we must use, but for the Science and Art Department we use different books.

18078. You know this book (*O'Sullivan's Principles of Arithmetic*), you believe that that is a good book?—I cannot say that, because I never studied it.

18079. What one do you use?—The Civil Service Arithmetic, and Hough's and Thom's.

18080. You, of course, send in your pupils for examination in arithmetic by the Board's Inspector?—Yes.

18081. Suppose somebody were to say of you that you did not teach your pupils to know the difference between minuend and subtrahend, would you be rightly spoken of?—I would.

18082. Do you believe that is true with regard to schools generally?—I cannot say anything for schools generally, but I know it might happen in my school, they might know it and they might not, because there is no theoretical work required.

18083. Here is Professor O'Sullivan's Arithmetic, and you know he was one of the Professors in the Board's Training College, and in the third paragraph under subtraction, he says: "In an exercise in subtraction the larger of the two given quantities is called "the minuend, the smaller of the two is called "the subtrahend, the difference when found is commonly spoken of as the remainder." Is there any difficulty in making children acquainted with that?—No, I think it is very easy if it is taught.

18084. Do you think it would be harder to teach pupils manual subjects than it is to teach that?—Well, I cannot say, I cannot give an opinion on manual subjects that I am not acquainted with.

18085. Have you commenced explanation along with reading in your school?—I have.

18086. When did that begin?—It commenced since last February in a special manner, because they were examined at the results examination in February in the explanation.

18087. Will explanation of the reading lessons, as now required, take up more time in your school?—A lot of it.

18088. Will it take up more time in the schools generally?—I think it will, because it is a difficult thing.

18089. Do you think the teaching of explanation along with reading would make it any more difficult to introduce manual instruction?—I think half an hour was sufficient for teaching them reading heretofore, and now when the explanation is insisted upon it will take more than half an hour, and if that takes more less ought to remain for the manual work.

18090. Mr. STRONGMAN.—Half an hour a day?—Yes.

18091. Rev. Dr. EVANS.—Do you think it will cause a revision of the time tables to be made?—The teacher must lengthen the lesson or give it at some other time to make them pass the results examination.

18092. Do you think you could take five minutes off each lesson in the course of the day?—Of course you could.

18093. How much would that gain you—half an hour?—It would gain five minutes for every half hour lesson.

18094. Professor FITZGERALD.—You think that in the fourth class, for example, he would read and enjoy a Fifth Reader in England much better than the Fourth Reader with us, and I think it is an easier book.

18098. That is, it would be more important to make them simpler than to make them shorter?—I think so.

18099. They would be more likely to read them themselves?—Yes, and have the matter interesting.

18100. You don't think the present books are interesting?—I don't think they are suited for young children, they are books for grown-up people.

18101. You said that the present teachers would not be able to teach manual instruction?—I mean those teachers who were not trained.

18102. Do you think the teachers would be willing to learn, for instance, drawing?—I am sure they would.

18103. Suppose there was a centre made at Sligo and a teacher was sent round to give lessons on Saturdays, do you think the teachers from neighbouring districts would come into Sligo in order to qualify?—I think so.

18104. If at the same time a teacher went round and saw them give instruction in drawing in their own schools and gave them advice about it, do you think that would help them?—They would want to have a knowledge of drawing before they could teach it in their schools.

18105. You might have a two years' course for the teachers, in the first year they might come in to be taught, and in the second year they might have the teacher going round and giving them lessons on Saturdays to improve their proficiency, and at the same time give them advice when they are then teaching in their own school?—I think that would be a good thing.

18106. Do you think other drawing besides freehand would be desirable to introduce, for instance, drawing to scale?—I think it would be very useful, because for those who wish to become artisans or tradesmen it would be very useful for them to be able to draw to scale.

18107. Perhaps more useful than freehand?—I think so.

18108. That some of the freehand drawing might be diminished and scale drawing introduced instead?—I think it would be a great advantage.

18109. And you think the teachers about here would be willing to learn it?—I think they would, anything that would tend to their own improvement or that of their children.

18110. If there was a new programme in agriculture of a more experimental kind introduced, in which the teachers were expected to make experiments, and show the pupils the growing of plants, and pull them up and show the roots growing?—That is what I say, that in the plots attached to the school gardens that could be shown.

18111. Do you think the teachers would be willing to qualify to teach that sort of agriculture?—I think there would be no qualification necessary. I think the teacher who could teach that book could teach what you say.

18112. You said you thought it is desirable that you, for instance, when you went up to be trained, should

18116. Do you think that needlework is any use for girls?—Oh, I think it is.

18117. Do you think that besides its being of practical use to teach them how to make garments for their children and husbands, and so on, do you think it makes them observant, and careful, and neat?—Oh, I believe it does, if they work neatly it should.

18118. Do you think it is desirable that boys should be trained to be dexterous, and careful, and neat, and accurate?—I think it is.

18119. Then you think some practical work similar to needlework would be useful to boys, I don't mean of the needlework kind but some other work?—I think it would.

18120. Then you think it would be desirable, educationally, for the sake of the boys that some manual training should be introduced?—I believe it would, but I can form no opinion of it, because I have no experience of the matter.

18121. Do you think it would be possible to get the teachers to encourage the boys to make collections of plants and injurious fungi?—I think that is a thing in which they take the greatest interest. I don't know about the teacher, but I know the pupils would be interested in that class of work. If there was any elementary science teaching going on in the school they would undertake such work as that very eagerly. I think it would be of the greatest importance to the children to teach them to observe things around them. I think it is of very great importance.

18122. Mr. Struthers.—Is yours a big school?—It is not; it is a small school.

18123. A mixed school, boys and girls?—No, it is separate; for the boys' school there are about 110 on the rolls; there is a girls' school adjoining.

18124. Chairman.—Have you an assistant?—I have an assistant for the boys.

18125. Mr. Struthers.—And the girls' school is close by?—It is attached to mine.

18126. Under the same management?—Under the same management and under the same roof.

18127. Who teaches in that?—My wife.

18128. Do any of the girls attend these Science and Art classes?—They do, and pass as creditably as the boys.

18129. A large proportion of the pupils who go in for the Science and Art examinations are girls?—They are.

18130. Then they are willing to attend in the afternoon to receive instruction in light, heat, and hygiene, and mathematics, in order to pass the science and art examination?—They are.

18131. Would it not be more useful for these girls to attend lessons in cookery?—Cookery is part of hygiene.

18132. They learn from a book?—They learn some of the knowledge that underlies cookery, but they don't learn practical cookery.

18133. It would improve their education to have some instruction in practical cookery?—It would.

18134. And there would be no great draft on their time apparently, seeing that they are able to take Science and Art classes?—Yes, provided it is after school hours, but then where would the material for practical cookery be got.

18135. Where did you get your apparatus for teaching for the Science and Art?—There was a grant made for that, and if we could get a grant for cookery it would be popular.

18136. Do you still teach the Science and Art classes?—Yes; anything that is well paid for, people will try to teach it.

18137. We are discussing at present the most valuable kind of education?—I think as far as girls are concerned, to teach science is a good training, because it is a written examination and they must be taught to express themselves properly and give a complete answer, and when they are instructed in one science they have a valuable training in expression and [illegible]—

18138. Professor FitzGerald.—That is that science gives them instruction in literary subjects?—Yes.

18139. Chairman.—And incidentally gives them instruction in grammar and spelling?—It does, and apart from the knowledge of science subjects, the training is very valuable.

18140. Mr. Struthers.—Does it not teach them to talk about things that they have never seen or had practical knowledge of?—Oh, they can have practical knowledge of many things that I teach.

18141. Do you present them in the advanced stage?—Yes; I presented pupils last year in geology, agriculture, and mathematics.

18142. And you got passes in those three?—I did.

18143. This book on practical farming is the basis of your teaching in agriculture?—Yes, we are commencing that now.

18144. You had a similar book before? No, that is quite a different book; if we teach the old book there is no copy of it at the Board's store.

18145. May I ask is paragraph 8 in the old book?—No, it is in the book I teach for the Science and Art Department.

18146. And a similar question on the experiments on pages 73 and 74 about weighing the ash of the plant and applying it as a manure?—None of these experiments were given in the old book; this is a much better book, but it is much more difficult for the pupils to learn, and it will take more time to teach it.

18147. But these are very useful experiments?—They are, I allow.

18148. And if you were teaching this book you would do these experiments in the school?—That would depend on the time I had. If there was no such thing as the results examination, I would make the experiments, and I think the teaching would be far better.

18149. Is it the custom to learn this book off by heart in preparing for the examination?—There must be certain parts learnt by heart; the date of sowing crops and the quantity of seeds.

18150. And it is not learned straight off page by page?—It cannot be learned straight off.

18151. Might the inspector ask such a question as "Describe the Black-faced sheep?"—He might; he is liable to ask any question; you don't know what question he will ask.

18152. You have heard such questions asked?—I have; last year, bad boys in the fifth-second; and I had one boy who had no taste at all in agriculture, he used to lose every book he got; another boy was a very good boy and both were examined in February, and the good boy got a 0, and the boy who had no book got a No. 1 pass, and the boy that got a 0 passed in the Science and Art examination afterwards in agriculture in the following May.

18153. You have not given us a specimen of the questions the inspector put?—I don't remember the questions but I know the results were disastrous to me.

18154. Would the children in examination be asked to name such things as those various flowers that are to be grown?—I suppose they will in the future; those were put in the old book. They are liable to be asked anything in the book.

18155. It says, "poor neglected land produces crops of daisies, black heads," and a number of other plants; do you show them to the children?—I do not.

18156. Are those mentioned in the old book?—They were not named in the old book.

18157. You don't teach the children to distinguish them?—I have not time, for with us such knowledge is not of use at the results examinations. If the inspector asked them to go out and gather specimens in the field I would teach it, but what I teach now is what will pass a pupil at the examinations.

18158. But as a matter of proper teaching?—I would infinitely prefer to teach it as you suggest.

Sligo. Oct. 8, 1883. Mr. Thomas Glynn.

18159. Suppose you were certain he would not ask any questions about them, would you teach them at all?—I would teach what I consider the inspector would probably ask.

18160. In fact your teaching is to teach a minimum that would secure a pass?—That is the object of all teachers in my opinion, they cannot help it.

18161. Rev. Dr. EVANS.—And that is the reason you do not explain mineral and celestial?—Certainly.

18162. Rev. Dr. WILSON.—Your opinion is that the programme as it stands fills up the school hours?—Yes.

18163. Would it be possible without diminishing the efficiency of the teaching or reducing the number of the subjects, to do less in grammar, less in arithmetic, and less in geography?—Yes, I think so.

18164. And gain time to apply to manual instruction, do you think that would be an advantage?—I don't know whether it would be an advantage or not, but I think in order to get time for the manual instruction it should be done. Those who are acquainted with the manual instruction would be better able to give an opinion than I am.

18165. Could all these subjects, in your opinion, be reduced in time?—I think they could with advantage to the pupils; I think there is far too much of them and they are all imperfectly taught; I think in general, that much less matter more efficiently taught would be of far more value to the people.

18166. With regard to this proposal to examine those who have given less than 100 attendances in the year, do you think that that would lead to great abuses?—I don't know how.

18167. Would it not come to this, that there would be attendances of 80, 60, and 70?—No, I don't think it would; there are pupils coming to my school off and on for five and six years that never make 100 attendances and they are never examined at all, they might make forty or fifty each year, it is the same pupils invariably that make the low attendances as a rule every year.

18168. Do you consider 100 attendances a very fair minimum?—It is very hard to bring the pupils up to the requirements of the results programme in time.

18169. CHAIRMAN.—What is the greatest number of attendances that a boy would make?—213 or 215.

18170. Mr. REDINGTON.—Have you taught agriculture for the Science and Art Department?—I have.

18171. Did you use a book when instructing your pupils with a view to that examination?—I did.

18172. What book?—Twelve or thirteen years ago I used Professor Tanner's book, but that would not be sufficiently extensive now. I use Professor Wallace on advanced agriculture, and I use for the elementary stage, the simplest written book on agriculture that I ever read, Lawrence's, published by Chambers; it is written in the simplest and nicest language for children I ever read.

18173. You put that book into the hands of your pupils?—Yes.

18174. And teach it in the same way that you teach "practical farming"?—Yes.

18175. Do you get them to learn anything off by heart?—No, never, but to understand the book thoroughly and to refer to matters in the locality around.

18176. And you think agriculture, as so taught, was more valuable to these boys than agriculture as taught under our system?—I think so, they understand the subject under the Science and Art Department better than they do under the Board.

18177. Mr. STRUTHERS.—But they are older children?—They must be older lately, because there was a rule that they could not be examined until they had passed second-sixth, but long ago I could put in fifth or second-sixth.

18178. But you are comparing them with fourth class children who are taught agriculture under the Board?—No, I am not.

18179. Rev. Dr. WILSON.—What steps did you take to have your pupils connected with the Science and Art Department?—I first heard I should get a certificate, and I got the certificate, and then I got a clergyman to write to the Department, asking that the school should be taken into connection, and it was, and then I went in for other certificates, until I got seven.

18180. Mr. REDINGTON.—Would Lawrence's book be too difficult for the fourth class?—It is not too difficult, but it is too extensive; I never read any book on agriculture so well written for young people.

Mr. JAMES FEEHAN, Head Master, Sligo Model School, examined.

Mr. James Feehan.

18181. CHAIRMAN.—You are the head master of the Model School?—Yes, sir.

18182. And you are willing to give the Commission whatever information you may possess upon the subject of the teaching of physical science and elementary chemistry, as formerly taught in the Board's Model Schools?—Yes, sir.

18183. Mr. MOLLOY.—At present your position is that of head master of the Sligo Model School?—Yes.

18184. And if I mistake not, you have occupied that position for a great many years?—Thirty years. Since 18[illegible].

18185. And previously had you not acted as assistant in several other Model schools?—I did, in three or four—Coleraine, Ballymoney, and Ballymena, and in addition to that, I was assistant to Dr. Clarke, who was a professor under the National Board.

18186. Was he not Professor of Physical Science and Lecturer on Physical Science to the National Board?—In the Board's Model Schools, and Central Model School.

18187. Would you briefly describe the plan adopted by Dr. Clarke in the course of his lectures; first of all, he attended a certain number of Model schools, how many of those in the country?—Nearly every one of the schools open at the time.

18188. Gave lectures to what class of pupils?—Not only to the boys and girls, but also to the senior classes of those Model schools.

18189. And he instructed also any member of the teaching staff?—He did: they afterwards were present at his lectures, and teachers from surrounding districts came in too on Saturday.

18190. Any instruction on other days of the week?—Oh, yes, every day after three o'clock.

18191. How long did it continue?—An hour.

18192. Professor FITZGERALD.—How many weeks in each course?—About six weeks at a particular Model school; for instance, he did Coleraine and Ballymoney at one time, living in Coleraine and coming to Ballymoney.

18193. Mr. MOLLOY.—When he left the Model school, was the instruction carried on by any of the staff?—He educated the assistants, I was one, there were three or four others, Mr. Morris and Mr. [illegible], who is now Head Inspector of schools, were amongst the first.

18194. You remained behind, did you, to carry on the instruction?—Yes.

18195. Would you kindly mention the particular branches of physical science that were taken up?—We were supposed to go through most of the branches in six months, giving a lecture every day. We put

nected with practical mechanics—mechanics as illustrated by Johnston's diagrams.

18196. With apparatus before you?—With apparatus; hydrostatics, and pneumatics, magnetism, heat, chemistry, the steam engine.

18197. Professor FITZGERALD.—Sound?—Yes, light and sound.

18198. Mr. MOLLOY.—Were these found in any way to interfere with the ordinary subjects of the school?—No, they were given after school hours.

18199. And continued for how long?—For an hour.

18200. Did the pupils, according to your experience, willingly attend for that extra time?—They did, and parents of the pupils came too; the experiments were very elaborate; we had splendid apparatus, both private apparatus belonging to Dr. Clarke, and those purchased by the Board.

18201. He, in the course of being an itinerant lecturer, and you, as his assistant, in that capacity, brought about some of the apparatus?—We always did.

18202. And a portion of it remained behind in the particular school for some time?—It was used in the school; but then the Board supplied each school where it had introduced the subject with a set of apparatus.

18203. What was the value of that set?—About £40 or £50. I know what they were, for I selected them.

18204. As much as that for each school?—Yes, they were very expensive.

18205. I thought about £10 to £15 was the usual amount?—More than that.

18206. And did you find so much as £50 worth of apparatus in these subjects absolutely necessary to carry on the instruction?—Well, indeed, I am sure the apparatus would cost £50.

18207. Professor FITZGERALD.—In the elaborate kind of experiments you used to do?—Yes, they were very expensive, and they were continually breaking, electrical machines, air pumps, wooden models and diagrams, were very dear—each diagram was 10s. 6d.

18208. Mr. MOLLOY.—According to the different parts of the country that Dr. Clarke was engaged in, and you were engaged in also as his assistant, did you not, both of you, accommodate your instruction to the requirements of the district?—Yes.

18209. Develop that a little—for instance, in the North of Ireland?—He taught bleaching and made experiments in it. In the West Dublin Model School, we were there for a long time, he taught——

18210. Professor FITZGERALD.—Distilling?—Yes, certainly, you are quite right.

18211. Mr. MOLLOY.—I believe at that time there was a good deal of silk manufactured in the Liberties of Dublin?—There was.

18212. And the West Dublin School is situated in the Liberties?—Yes, they were taught dyeing there, and processes connected with the manufacture of silk.

18213. These lectures, then, were illustrated?—With capital diagrams, handmade, many of them; I made several myself.

18214. Did the pupils take any part in making them?—Some did.

18215. Professor FITZGERALD.—Did they help in the experiments?—Well, sometimes they did.

18216. Did they smell chlorine and say what it was?—Oh, yes, they knew chlorine.

18217. Mr. MOLLOY.—At the Inchicore Model School—that is a railway school?—He lectured there on heat and the steam engine, and the men employed at the works there were most attentive.

18218. As well as the ordinary pupils of the school?—And there were evening lectures to the working-men.

18219. I presume the children attending were the children of the workers?—Yes, the children got their instruction in the day time, but there were night lectures.

18220. Why was that system of lectures not continued?—I think it was the results system that knocked it out; there was not time for it.

18221. The introduction of the results system interfered with the previous arrangements with regard to these itinerating lecturers?—Yes, it would take a man an hour to prepare experiments in the majority of cases; then there was no time under the results system for preparing. Supposing a man wanted to lecture on chemistry, and wanted to make oxygen, it is a thing that does not keep, and he could not do it when he had to teach up to three o'clock and give his lecture afterwards.

18222. Would you be in favour of a return to that system of itinerating lecturers?—I would, indeed; it did a great deal of good and was very interesting.

18223. Would it need a serious modification of the results programme?—I am sure it would.

18224. Have you any observations to offer on the subject of individual examination of pupils, or would you give a preference to class examination?—Oh, no, I would not make any observations at all about the results system.

18225. How do you find it working in your own school?—There is too much pressure altogether on the boys.

18226. What is the average attendance at your school at present?—About sixty-eight.

18227. How many were presented at the last results examination?—Very nearly that, between sixty and sixty-eight.

18228. Then your attendance must be very regular?—It is pretty regular; sometimes it fluctuates unaccountably.

18229. Captain SHAW.—How long were these courses of instruction carried on?—For about four or five weeks at a time, until generally they had to terminate, because Dr. Clarke had to go up to the training department to lecture there, and the teachers he left behind carried it on throughout the year.

18230. The subjects lectured on appear to be rather technical?—Yes.

18231. Do you think that is suitable instruction for young children?—It was theoretical as well as technical, but to a very large extent it was technical. Now, take mechanics, it was decidedly technical, because I don't believe in young children learning trigonometrical formulae in connection with mechanics.

18232. Would it not be more useful for children to learn elementary chemistry; it would be more within their comprehension than at once going into such a difficult subject as distilling, to understand the theory of it?—It would be suitable, but I don't know why you bring distilling in; it was just mentioned by this gentleman here.

18233. But you have been teaching a subject that necessitates a knowledge of chemistry?—It does.

18234. Would it not be better for children to learn elementary chemistry at the beginning?—I dare say it would.

18235. Do you approve of itinerating teachers in schools; would you like a teacher to come to your school and give lectures in a specific subject?—Not when I am qualified myself.

18236. Do you think the teachers would be qualified to give any instruction which the children would receive profitably?

18237. Professor FITZGERALD.—Cannot teachers learn anything that a child of twelve years old can learn?—Certainly.

18238. Captain SHAW.—You think any teacher might qualify himself to teach in his own school?—He might.

Sligo.
Oct. [illegible]
Mr. [illegible]

FORTY-FIRST PUBLIC SITTING.—SATURDAY, OCTOBER 9TH, 1897,

AT 12 O'CLOCK, NOON,

At the Imperial Hotel, Sligo.

Present:—The Right Hon. the Earl of Belmore, G.C.M.G., in the Chair; The Right Hon. C. T. Redington, M.A.; The Right Rev. Monsignor Molloy, D.D., D.Sc.; Rev. Henry Evans, D.D.; Rev. Hamilton Wilson, LL.D.; Professor G. F. Fitzgerald, F.T.C.D.; Stanley Harrington, Esq., M.A.; W. R. J. Molloy, Esq.; Captain T. B. Shaw, and J. Struthers, Esq., LL.D.;

with J. D. Daly, Esq., M.A., Secretary.

Sligo.
Oct. 5, 1897.
Mr. M. Boyle.

greater number of pages read to have a simpler set of readers in use in our schools than the present one, and also we would wish that with respect to the examination by inspectors that there would be more time given to the children, and also with respect to reading that there should be a difference made between a No. 1 and a No. 2 pass.

CHAIRMAN.—I think you are going into something rather outside our inquiry.

18249. Mr. REDINGTON.—Under what other head would you wish the programme to be modified?—A greater number of pages in the reading lessons.

CHAIRMAN.—We are not inquiring into that subject at all.

18250. Mr. STRUTHERS.—What else do you wish to have done?—We would wish also that there would be a distinction made between a No. 1 and a No. 2 pass.

18251. Is there not a distinction now?—There is no distinction. With respect to payment we say a No. 1 pass ought to carry a higher payment.

18252. Could it not be said that a No. 2 pass ought to carry a lower payment?—It might.

18253. Are you aware that in England they insist on one or three readers in every class?—I am aware of that, but you also have compulsory attendance in England.

18254. What other part of the programme do you wish to have modified?—The present standard of literary attainments I hold should be maintained, except that perhaps there might be some modification made in grammar and geography—for instance not to introduce grammar until the pupil would reach fourth class, and then grammar and geography might be taken up in alternate courses. But personally I and all the teachers I know, would not be desirous at all of leaving out either of those subjects; we say that it is impossible to teach composition or letter-writing in any general or satisfactory manner without a knowledge of grammar.

18255. Are you satisfied with the way in which grammar is taught at present?—Well, I say that there is a little too much expected of the children in the various classes.

18256. Do you teach drawing in your school?—No, sir.

18257. Rev. Dr. EVANS.—Have you a certificate for drawing?—No, sir; I was put into the drawing class in Marlborough street about this time thirty years, and we were asked, about 150 or 180 of us, to draw a circle: I made a very excellent attempt at a circle myself, by using my thumb as a centre and sweeping the pencil round, with the result that Mr. Sparrow, the drawing master, turned me, along with a number of others out of the drawing room, and that was my first and last attempt.

18258. Mr. REDINGTON.—Do you think that drawing ought to be introduced into all schools?—I believe it would do no harm to introduce it, if the teachers were taught how to draw and how to teach drawing.

18259. Would you be in favour of the establishment of centres in various localities where courses of lessons in drawing could be given to teachers?—I would be for that, but I would prefer they would be taken to a central place.

18260. For how long?—I don't think any course would be of any practical advantage for a less period than three months of the year, but I would prefer drawing to be taught in the training colleges when the Queen's Scholars enter there, and it should be made compulsory on the Queen's Scholars, and on all young teachers going up for one year's course.

18261. You are aware that it is so now?—I was not officially aware of it.

18262. As regards teachers already in charge of schools how would you teach them drawing?—I think there are very many teachers too old to make any attempt at all: for any teacher having over twenty-five years' service it should not be made compulsory, it should be optional.

18263. Do you teach any science subjects in your school?—I did some years ago, when science teaching was much more profitable than at present.

18264. How was it more profitable than now?—Well, we got in pupils under easier circumstances and there is a distinction made now by the Science and Art Department in the payments.

18265. Did you ever teach any science subjects under the Board of National Education?—Yes, I taught algebra, geometry, and physical geography.

18266. Any other?—That is all.

18267. You did not teach mechanics or anything of that kind?—No, sir.

18268. Why did you select the Science and Art system rather than ours?—They pay considerably more satisfactorily than the National Board do.

18269. And you have stopped it now because the pay has changed too?—No, but because the conditions were made heavier for the admission of pupils. For instance, the principles of agriculture was a very general subject for Irish teachers, but they imposed conditions under which we could not have sufficient material to teach a class.

18270. How did you teach the principles of agriculture for the Science and Art examinations?—Out of books.

18271. What books?—I used *Dr. Tanner's* and Wrightson's.

18272. Did you show the pupils the different plants, and give them any practical illustrations?—Well, no, not at that time; since then I got a cottage garden.

18273. Mr. STRUTHERS.—What are the conditions that prevent you going on with the Science and Art classes now?—They don't admit any pupil until he is out of the second stage of sixth class to be eligible, and a very large number of those children drop away from our schools before they reach that class.

18274. Mr. REDINGTON.—Do you think that classes for handicraft and elementary science might be held after school hours in towns and cities?—I believe so.

18275. Do you think any of the teachers of the surrounding schools would come in in the evening to attend?—I believe they would, they are so very anxious to do anything that would be for the real benefit of the education of the boys that the teachers would not hesitate.

18276. Do you teach a mixed school?—A boys' school.

18277. Have you any observations to make about the education of girls?—I know very little, except that the industrial programme is generally recognised as a failure.

18278. Why is it a failure?—The time occupied by it was too much in the opinion of the parents of the children; a very large number of those that I am acquainted with said that it was for learning the ordinary school branches they sent them to school, not to sit down in the school and gossip through the hours.

18279. Why should they gossip and not work?—The time is too long, and the teacher has to occupy herself with other classes in the school very often during this period.

18280. Would you like to see the number of classes in small rural schools reduced?—I would like to see the fifth reduced to one standard and the sixth to one standard.

18281. You think it hard for a single teacher to teach so many different classes?—Yes, and I would like those who wish for a further course should have some opportunity of encouragement given them in the evening or continuation schools.

18282. Where should these be held?—In the present schools.

18283. How could pupils in a rural district come in the evening to school?—The schools are so numerous in many parts of the country that the larger portion of the school material is within a mile or a mile and a half distance.

16294. Even in the rural districts?—Yes, the schools are very close to one another—that is one of the grievances of the teachers that the schools are so multiplied that they can only have one teacher in the school.

16295. Is it not a convenience to the pupils?—It is a convenience, but a school cannot be brought to the street of every pupil; if there were larger areas there would be better schools.

16296. Would it not be much more inconvenient for people to have to walk three miles instead of one and a half?—In some places it would be, in mountain districts, but in other places it would not be so.

16297. Professor FITZGERALD.—Would not the attendance be more irregular?—I suppose it would be.

16298. Rev. Dr. EVANS.—What is the number on the roll of your school?—110.

16299. What is your average attendance?—Something like sixty-[illegible]—in point of fact the assistant teacher has had to go round and canvass for the attendance of the children every alternate quarter, in order to come in for his salary, and that is rather a humiliating thing for him.

16300. Would compulsory attendance help you there?—I believe compulsory attendance would be

16302. Do you grow any flowers?—I do, but not very much.

16303. Any vegetables?—I grow vegetables, it is chiefly for vegetables I use the garden.

16304. Have you any experimental portion of it for working out original ideas of your own to stimulate these boys?—I have not, I have only had it three or four years.

16305. Professor FITZGERALD.—Do you know whether the children have ever made use of, in their own homes, the knowledge they acquired in the school gardens, has it produced any effect there?—I believe it has. I believe it is an impossibility [illegible] after years, when a boy gets a fair course, even though it is a book course, that it is an impossibility for that boy, if he has any intelligence, but he will apply some of the knowledge he gained [illegible] the books to operations on his farm. I am, my [illegible] in possession of sufficient experience to show [illegible] that is so.

16306. Supposing the agricultural training [illegible] changed to a certain extent to make it more practical and encourage the collections of plants and [illegible] ments in the growth of plants, do you think teachers would be willing to undertake that work rather than book-work?—I think the teachers would be [illegible]

[illegible]

[illegible] a program[illegible]
ve time could be

Sligo.
Oct. 2, 1897.
Mr. M. Doyle.

for instance, they are not asked to prune any of the gooseberry or currant trees, or to interfere with the branches of the apple tree.

18390. Or with the fruit?—We try to manage to keep them out of the fruit garden as much as possible in certain seasons of the year.

18391. How do you get these plants and vegetables supplied?—I generally get the seeds myself, sometimes from slips, but as a general rule I deal with Mr. M'Kenna, of Dublin; I found his seeds were pure and of the proper variety.

18392. Do you use any artificial manures in the growing of these plants?—Very little artificial manure. I use stable manure generally, and sometimes I mix it with common soot, which is the best artificial manure I ever came across; I sometimes mix a little guano.

18393. Mr. Molloy.—You mentioned that there were about seventy per cent. of schools under one teacher, that is spread over what area?—The Province of Connaught.

18394. Is it not a fact, however, that the single teacher is helped by a monitor in a great many of those cases, and perhaps the large majority?—Well, I am not aware of it; so far as my knowledge goes, the schools in which there are assistant teachers have very often the services of monitors.

18395. But assuming there is no assistant teacher, may there not be a monitor?—There may be.

18396. Would you not say in the great majority of those schools?—Well, within my experience I would not say that it is the great majority, or a majority at all.

18397. Well, in such schools as those in which monitors are employed, the monitor might be pretty advanced in his course, he might be in his fourth year, up to eighteen years of age, sufficiently qualified to give efficient help to the master—that is the principle of the monitorial system, not merely to be trained for the office of a teacher, but also to help in the instruction of the pupils?—Well, I believe that is the principle, but in practice we have not found the assistance of the monitors of much benefit.

18398. At present assuming there was no monitor in the school, and the master alone taught a small rural school, is there any difficulty about grouping classes; is there not a plan of grouping them by divisions, say, the whole senior division would write together and do arithmetic together?—Oh, yes, any teaching that is practically done.

18399. So that the grouping by divisions may be carried out even under the present arrangement?—Yes, to a certain extent.

18400. Mr. Struthers.—Do all the pupils of the higher division take the same arithmetic?—No, but you might commence with the lowest class, and when you have arrived at the limit of their programme, drop it, and continue with the others.

18401. Mr. Molloy.—I think you said that you would advocate the propriety of having better hours?—It is longer hours I mean.

18402. What are the usual school hours now?—From ten to half-past three.

18403. And you propose an extension?—Yes.

18404. Even in the rural schools?—Yes, I would propose an extension if possible.

18405. Are there not in this Province of Connaught a very large number of towns say like Ballymote in point of size?—Yes, there are a good number.

18406. What changes, if any, in the present programme, would you advocate, for the benefit of those pupils attending town schools, as distinct from the pupils attending the ordinary rural schools?—I make no distinction between small town schools and rural schools, because practically there are no industries carried out in the majority of the small towns in this part of the country, and most of the shopkeepers in these small towns have also farms in the country, so that their children are practically more farmers than

attend more regularly?—The children of town schools attend more regularly.

18408. Mr. MOLLOY.—Would you be in favour of the extension of knowledge of the elements of science in the town schools?—I would be for a considerable extension of that in an elementary way.

18409. Would that be carried out, do you think, properly in the evening continuation schools, or as part of the regular school course?—I think that would be better carried out in the evening schools, but I think there ought to be a little portion of time devoted to it in day schools.

18410. You complained of the irregularity of the attendance, have you any idea what is the proportion of the attendance to the number on the roll?—Oh, yes, I have. Might I take it in this way, my statement is that compulsory attendance is much more necessary in rural districts than in town districts, and for this reason, in Sligo county, the percentage is 57·6, whereas in Sligo town and its suburbs, on account of the influence exercised by the managers and by the Bishop of Sligo, and the managers of other denominations, the percentage is 69 per cent., or something like 13 per cent. over it. Then I have taken averages of eighteen schools in Galway and its surroundings; in the county Galway the percentage is 56, for the city and suburbs it is over 69.

18411. If the same influences were brought to bear on the rural schools as on the town schools would not the rate of attendance be very much improved?—It would be an utter impossibility to exercise the same influence in large districts of the county.

18412. Touching the subject of readers, of course you are aware that the managers are not compelled to use the Board's readers exclusively?—I believe that is a change that is coming on, but practically we were confined for the last thirty or forty years to the same set of readers.

18413. Chiefly because they were cheaper?—Well, because they were the only readers on the Board's list.

18414. There is a long established rule, that suitable books, that is, books free from objection, if submitted, might be used in the schools?—Yes, but practically we used only the Board's books.

18415. Monsignor MOLLOY.—With regard to the school gardens, would it remove your difficulty, if the programme of the Board fixed a certain number of hours for agricultural teaching, and left it to the discretion of the master to teach from books in the school when it was wet, and to teach in the garden when it was fine?—Yes, sir, it would admirably meet the views, but the number of hours presently insisted on by the Board is rather too much for what would be quite sufficient for the knowledge of boys in a small garden.

18416. What I suggest would remove all your difficulty?—Yes, sir.

18417. I understand you are generally in favour of the introduction of manual training, but that you think there is not at present sufficient time for it?—And that the teachers are not prepared.

18418. But the coming teachers may be prepared for it in the training colleges?—Most undoubtedly.

18419. And time could be made for it, you suggest, by an extension of the school hours?—Yes, sir.

18420. Two hours, you think, might be got upon Saturday?—Yes, in case of compulsory attendance; the children will not be got to attend on Saturdays in the absence of compulsion.

18421. The first condition then would be an extension of the hours, and the second compulsory attendance of the children?—Yes, in any case.

18422. And you think it would facilitate the introduction of manual training, if the subject were made a good paying subject for the schoolmaster?—I don't know about grafting on anything additional.

18423. I thought you said you were in favour of introducing manual instruction if the difficulties were overcome?—Yes, its gradual introduction.

18424. Then would it not remove a difficulty if it were made a good paying subject?—Well, I gave no thought to that.

18425. If it were not remunerative, that would be very much against it?—I believe it would be.

18426. Therefore to make it remunerative would remove a difficulty?—Yes.

18427. CHAIRMAN.—You stated in answer to the questions which were asked you that you thought that there was some advantage even now in agriculture, as it is taught. Now you have had long experience in this part of the country, thirty years, I think, you stated?—I am teaching thirty years.

18428. Do you think that the style of farming in the part of the country you are familiar with has improved during those thirty years in any degree, owing to the teaching that has been given in agriculture, either in your own or other schools in your neighbourhood?—I do believe it for this reason, when I was a young boy, about fifteen years of age, a larger district of the country than from here to Ballymote, while burning, just looked like Lancashire, all one sheet of smoke burning away the most valuable portions of the soil on clay land; that has been completely put an end to by the condemnation given to it in all agricultural books.

18429. You think that was the reason it was put down, not from any operation of the law?—No; the landlords had full power to prevent it at the time, but they did not. The practice was most detrimental to the soil. Then in the way of drainage, principally open drainage, you cannot go through any part of the country but there is a vast improvement, and certainly this is very largely to be attributed to the results of the teaching of agriculture. Then with respect to grain crops, I remember very well, when the general cropping in the northern parts of Mayo and the portion of Sligo adjoining it, the system was one crop of potatoes or turnips, followed by five or six crops of grain; there is nothing of the kind now; as a rule, only one grain crop follows a root crop.

18430. And is it the custom now to sow grass seed, instead of letting the grass come naturally?—Before, when the grain crop was taken off, the land used to be allowed to cover itself naturally with grass; now it is the universal custom to set grass clover.

gardens, but I have not any experience of it. I think it would be a good idea if the people were encouraged to do a little amateur gardening at home.

18434. How would you encourage them in that?—In this way—seeds and farm implements to be supplied to them at wholesale prices by some responsible authority, such as the managers of the district model farms, which I hope to see established in the country.

18435. There were district model farms at one time which have been discontinued?—Possibly from a financial point of view a district model farm would be a failure, but from a national point of view it would be a success.

18436. You would like to see them re-established?—I would, indeed; and endowed by public grants, in which pupils could be taught scientific agriculture.

18437. How far apart do you think model schools should be?—One in each district, under the present district inspectors—sixty-four in all Ireland.

18438. Have you any view with regard to the establishment of a college in Dublin, where professors could devote time to investigations in connexion with every subject which the Commission might recommend in the way of manual and physical training?—I would be decidedly in favour of it, because they could give the benefit of their knowledge and experience to the managers of district model farms, and they, in their turn, could submit it to their pupils.

18439. What do you say about drawing?—I would not be in favour of making an invidious distinction in any National school. I would be in favour of having it introduced into all schools without exception, but as the majority of teachers—I, unfortunately, among them—have not a certificate, great efficiency should not be expected for the first few years in any of these schools, and if the work was fairly done, I would say the pupils should get a pass, even though their teacher did not possess a certificate.

18440. Do you think that the Board's inspectors are the proper persons to examine in all subjects connected with manual training, rather than experts?—Yes; if a specialist was sent to examine woodwork if it was introduced into a town, and another to examine ironwork if it was a manufacturing centre, and another to examine in linen in the North of Ireland, it would be a different system of education altogether, and it would not be for the benefit of Ireland we should have two systems of education.

18441. Then you think that the ordinary inspectors are the proper persons to inspect?—I do, decidedly.

18442. How would you find time to teach new subjects?—I would not follow the last witness in saying the time should be extended; the physical strain on pupils of a tender age is very great, to keep them in school from ten to three o'clock.

18443. Would it be an advantage if the junior classes were allowed to be dismissed at half-past two?—I would say two.

Professor FITZGERALD.—Are they not allowed already?

18444. Mr. MOLLOY.—That is the regulation at present; infants may go home?—Is it in an ordinary National school? I would not like to have them go, and see an inspector driving along the road, and I am afraid the Commissioners would not stand up to defend me.

18445. REV. DR. EVANS.—Coming now to the school gardens, your experience is that parents regard the work done by the pupils in school gardens as done for the teacher?—Yes. I merely asked the parents of the locality a few days since, and they one and all objected to the pupils doing manual work for the teacher. I then suggested what would they say to doing that work at home in their own little gardens, and they would agree to that.

18446. Would it help in any way if you divided the garden into small plots, and gave a plot to each boy, allowing nobody to do anything on that but himself, so that the parents would not think he was working for you but working for himself and for his own education?—But we have no means of compelling that child to come and attend that plot on any day. I teach a small school. The number on the roll is sixty-five, and I am sorry to say the average has not reached thirty-five for the quarter ending the 30th of June, and has only barely touched it for the last quarter; and if there was a plot of ground in charge of a certain pupil, and he did not come to school for a whole month, what on earth is to become of that little plot?

18447. It might tend to lead the pupil to come, for I have seen a school garden in which each boy's name was on a label fixed in his plot, and it was a work of emulation among the boys that their plots should appear to the best advantage?—In a district model school I would like to see that, but if it was attached to an ordinary National school, boys are inclined to mischief, and if the garden was not properly protected things might look very awkward in the morning; but I would approve of it in a model farm, where the Government can pay a caretaker, who would be responsible for the safety of the plot.

18448. Do you believe if an arrangement were devised by which you were allowed to teach drawing—I mean all teachers who are not in possession of certificates—and that fees were allowed, do you believe that really good teaching would be done?—That is my opinion. I don't see why drawing could not be taught by a little more care in a school, even though the teacher does not possess the necessary certificate, any more than good handwriting.

18449. Are all the teachers good at penmanship?—I often get a letter from a teacher, and I cannot read the handwriting.

18450. And he teaches writing in the school, and obtains results fees?—Yes.

18451. With the aid of models might not a sensible teacher teach drawing?—That is my opinion, but I cannot speak from experience.

18452. Professor FITZGERALD.—Do you think it would be desirable, so far as children are concerned, that they should be taught drawing to scale?—I believe it would be the only useful drawing.

18453. And do you not believe teachers would be able to learn how to teach drawing to scale by the aid of instruments and rules?—I think they would after a little while.

18454. It would not require the dexterity necessary for freehand?—No, and I think drawing to scale would make them more accurate in drawing.

18455. If there were encouragement given to do cardboard work and some other things like that?—I could form no opinion about that. My chief concern is with agriculture, because it is at the present time, and possibly will long continue to be, the only industry in Ireland, and even our manufacturing and shipping industries at the present time depend on agriculture.

18456. You were proposing to have gardens at the children's own homes; would you now, do you think, be able to report on these home gardens?—I was thinking of that matter—it would be an exercise in drawing for each pupil at the end of the year to take to the school a plan of his garden, showing its size, drawn to scale, and the relative position of the various vegetables grown in it.

18457. But he might have got the seeds; it would be necessary for somebody to inspect the garden?—The inspector could just take two or three of them indiscriminately. I would not expect a district inspector should run round from one to another.

18458. Supposing a teacher took those indiscriminately from time to time during the year?—I doubt very much if the Commissioners would accept the opinion of the teacher; if they would, we would be only too glad to do it.

18459. You might inspect them during the year, and the inspector then inspect one or two of them?—Yes, sir.

18460. Mr. STRUTHERS.—In these model farms what pupils would you have taught?—I would have the pupils selected for a two years' course by a com-

Sligo. — Oct. 5, 1897. — Mr. Thomas Kirkpatrick.

Sligo. Oct. [illegible] 1897. Mr. Thomas McLoughlin.

competitive examination, but an essential condition to be that they have completed their school course in the National schools first, and, in addition to that, show some proficiency in mathematics, physical science, or agricultural chemistry.

18461. They would have finished their course in the National school?—Yes, according to the programme laid down, or at any future time, by the Commissioners.

18462. They would be over sixteen?—In or about; a boy that was ambitious to go to these schools would push on his education, and possibly be able to go at sixteen.

18463. You say you would require some knowledge of mathematics or physical science?—Or agricultural chemistry, according to the choice of the pupils.

18464. Where would the pupils get this instruction before they went to the model school?—In every National school, more or less, mathematics are taught.

18465. But elementary science?—They would be taught if it was made worth while.

18466. Agricultural chemistry?—Yes.

18467. Would you have that taught in a day school or an evening school?—I would not go in for evening schools in country places. A child would have to run an Irish mile or more to school, he would spend from 10 to 3 at school, get home then and take his dinner, and then, perhaps, the parents might think that they would find something for him to do besides letting him run back the same distance again.

18468. We have evidence that in country districts pupils do come to evening schools?—In certain districts they might, for instance, when Science and Art subjects were paying an Irish teacher the senior boys might come in.

18469. If you made mathematics and elementary science a paying subject again might they not find it possible to collect pupils in the evening?—In some localities they might and in others they might not. If there was a small prize given to each pupil who passed creditably at his annual examination, because if any undertaking is to be a success the workman should get his share, I would go more for giving prizes to the pupil than to the teacher.

18470. But prizes for what?—For their little gardens, each pupil who would pass creditably in his agricultural examination, and till his little garden according to the requirements of the programme, I would give him a prize.

18471. Would the pupils be boarded at these model farms?—Yes.

18472. And you would have a special staff of teachers?—Yes, men specially trained.

18473. Would you continue the literary instruction for pupils in the model farm?—That is a question that I could not form an opinion on, the knowledge of that might develop by time; after the farm had been working a little while they might be better able to know whether literary instruction would be required or not.

18474. But you think that is the way to improve agriculture in the country, and not by teaching driblets of it in the elementary school?—To continue the ordinary book in the school and to have school gardens attached to the pupils' houses.

18475. You have no certificate for drawing, I think, you said?—Yes.

18476. Would you be willing to attend at a convenient centre if classes were held there, to receive instruction in the method of drawing?—I would have no objection, but other teachers, as a rule, I believe, would have an objection.

18477. But suppose the school is not so much to teach them drawing as to give them hints how to teach drawing to their pupils?—I think every teacher should be anxious to attend that, but the risk of failing to get a certificate would deter many from going.

18478. This class is only to help the teacher?—I think that would be very beneficial.

18479. Would you like to have the junior pupils dismissed earlier in the day than at present?—I would.

18480. You mean those pupils up to the 3rd class?—Yes.

18481. Have you thought of this arrangement as a possible one, that the junior pupils should be taught in the forenoon and sent away, and the senior division taught in the afternoon exclusively?—If the Board and their officers would fall in with that idea I think it could be done, and I believe it would benefit.

18482. You would be able to devote your attention undivided to the senior pupils while you had them, and the junior pupils while you had them?—I would be for the whole of the pupils of the school coming into the school at one hour in the morning, and then I would be for the junior portion having a shorter school day than the senior.

18483. So that you might give some extra time to the senior pupils?—Yes, I find every teacher I know who is anxious to work up his school must give extra time to his pupils—more time than is on the programme; for instance, when approaching our annual examination we don't mind the time, we are there up to 5 o'clock.

18484. Can you send away the junior children?—Yes, the moment the school day ended in the time-table has expired.

18485. Rev. Dr. Wilson.—Is yours a purely agricultural district?—It is, an alluvial district, lying at the confluence of the Boyle and the Shannon.

18486. Would you support the testimony of the former witness, that in your time the mode of farming has greatly improved?—I would. I fully endorse the remarks he made about burning. I believe if the people thought burning would benefit their crops without doing irretrievable damage to the ground they would try and avoid the law, even if they had to go out at night and do it.

18487. Is it your opinion that the teaching of the National schools in agriculture has had anything to do with that improvement?—It is my opinion it has had everything to do with it.

18488. Mr. Struthers.—Has not agriculture improved in other countries in the same degree as in Ireland?—My experience of other countries is nothing; but I say in the parish in which we live, if we are to look to our own agriculture it must be improved, and if the Government does not help us our local efforts are useless.

18489. You have acquaintance of farmers?—Unfortunately not.

18490. And you trace the whole agricultural improvement to the teaching of the schools?—I do.

18491. Rev. Dr. Evans.—Not to the fear of the landlord or the fear of the law?—I could not go into that point. I look upon a farmer as protected by the law so long as he pays an honest rent, as decided by the laws of the realm, I look upon him as as independent in his farm as the Queen on the throne.

18492. Professor Fitzgerald.—Have not agricultural papers had something to do with the improvement?—Agricultural papers, as a rule, don't circulate in my district.

18493. Rev. Dr. Wilson.—Is there serious potato blight in this district?—There is in my district.

18494. Have the farmers done anything to avert it?—In some isolated cases a potato sprayer was used. That has all come out of their own pockets, no encouragement whatever. There is also a column given to agriculture in the weekly papers. I ascribe that to education because in former times people were not able to read those papers.

18495. Captain Shaw.—Have the teachers any means of becoming acquainted with contemporary educational movements in other countries?—I am not aware that they have, for this reason, our vacations are very restricted and our means do not enable us to go into other countries during our vacation in order to see what improvements are effected in those places.

18496. When the inspector comes round, has he time to enter into these subjects with you?—Between examining one section of the pupils and watching others, but they would infringe the rules, I think his work is very hard without having any conversation with the teacher, except to reprimand him for something that would go wrong; I am speaking a positive fact.

18497. Suppose that a class for manual instruction, general practical work, were established in some schools you think the teachers in the neighbourhood would be inclined to come and see the working of it?—I don't think they would; if it was established in one particular school that would create a kind of distinction, and the others would not like to fall in with that idea, and it was to remove that prejudice that I suggested the model farm.

18498. Then how are the teachers to get any acquaintance with improved methods of instruction if they won't come and see them?—I take your point to be that it would be established in one particular National school to the exclusion of the rest.

18499. Not to the exclusion of the rest, but to see whether the rest would like to adopt it?—I would not go in with that, I would go in for the Government to make a grant to establish perfect agricultural instruction.

18500. I am talking of manual instruction?—I have given no thought to that; in large cities and towns where there are commercial and manufacturing industries I am sure the teachers there would be competent to give an opinion on it, but my chief concern is agriculture.

18501. And you don't think there is any use in introducing anything else?—Not in a rural locality, but I believe it is useful in large towns like Belfast.

18502. Who do you contemplate as instructors in your model school?—Men specially trained at the Agricultural College in Dublin in future days and experts from the different agricultural colleges in the United Kingdom at present.

18503. Have you any idea what such men's opinion is as to the training that children should receive before they come to you?—No, I never met a man of them, but I am giving teachers' opinions.

18504. Would you be surprised to hear they all prefer that the children should never have been taught agriculture before they come to them, but that they should be grounded in elementary science?—I would not like to agree to that. For instance, if a boy in the higher walks of life studied in any of the diocesan colleges in Ireland and went into another to complete his education, possibly the professors there would find fault with his previous education, and I suppose it would be the same amongst us teachers.

18505. Is not the teaching of agriculture rather ambitious in the National schools, don't you try to cover all the agriculture which it is necessary for a farmer to know?—We do.

18506. Is not that an impossibility in a National school?—I don't think it an impossibility; in 1894, 1895, and 1896, under different Inspectors, I secured cent. per cent. in agriculture; in 1897 I was not so lucky; I am down to 93 per cent. Sligo. Oct. 8, 1897. Mr. Thomas McLaughlin.

18507. Were your inspectors agricultural experts?—He walked into the school with the authority of the Board, and we could not ask him, "Are you qualified to examine our school."

18508. Mr. Harrington.—Would you like to see introduced into the reading books lessons on the laws of sanitation and on temperance?—I would go in for that very much.

18509. Do you think if they were introduced into the books they would be explained by the teachers and dwelt upon by them?—I think they would, and I think it would raise the social condition of the people to a great extent.

18510. Mr. Molloy.—Is your school one of the typical rural schools that Mr. Doyle referred to, included in the seventy per cent.?—Oh, no; it is one of the worst attended. It is situated in a boggy district, where it is impossible in the winter for the children to come to school on account of the floods. The average for the year was thirty-nine, and for the last two quarters thirty-four and thirty-five.

18511. You have the aid of a monitor?—But I fear I am going to lose him on account of the average.

18512. What suggestions, if any, have you to make with regard to the programme. Would you desire changes, and if so, in what direction?—There should be more time found for teaching drawing, and I would suggest geography and grammar to be altogether omitted for third class, and the course considerably shortened for fourth and upwards. The amount of grammar required at present for high fifth should be sufficient for high sixth.

18513. Do you take up any extra subjects?—I take up algebra and book-keeping. With great difficulty I get the senior boys to finish their course. They are employed in agricultural occupations.

18514. With regard to that idea of yours that the pupils who have answered satisfactorily ought to get prizes, would you not think it right that the managers and local parties should give those prizes?—In face of the Permissive Act of 1875 and the Compulsory Act of 1892, I say any attempt to get local aid in the absence of compulsion is useless.

18515. A moment ago you said that you desired that the pupils up to third class might be able to go away. The regulation is in favour of infants only, but you generalised that up to third class. If you had it up to third class you would have very few remaining?—About half the school.

18516. And further that the time of departure for those infants would be indicated on the time-table?—Yes; from two o'clock.

Mr. Hubert J. Sweeney, Teacher, Quay-street National School, Sligo, examined. Mr. Hubert J. Sweeney.

18517. Chairman.—You are a National school teacher?—Yes; Quay-street Junior, Sligo.

18518. Will you give us your opinion upon some of the headings you have mentioned in this paper that you have handed in. What do you say with regard to the attendance of pupils at schools with a view of developing what you think are the fundamental principles of any system of primary education—namely, the developing to the highest degree the faculties of the children, the encouragement of originality or individuality, and taking cognisance of the circumstances and possible future position of the child?—*First of all*, I consider that compulsory education is absolutely necessary before any system could be effectually adopted.

18519. Do you think there would be much opposition to compulsory attendance on the part of parents?—I dare say there would; by those parents against whom it would operate, there would naturally be objection.

18520. Do you think that if a law was passed to make attendance compulsory, except for a good reason, that the parents would accept the law, and take pains to make children attend more regularly?—I think they would.

18521. In fact, any opposition which might show itself at first would soon die out?—Yes, my lord.

18522. Passing on to the payment by results, will you shortly give us your views on that subject?—I think it is a very pernicious system, the payment by results, and I will enumerate the reasons why I consider it so. First, it is organised as a system of cram by which methods have no value whatever. Secondly, all scholars, whether clever or dullards, progress at the same rate, one class per annum, and at the same rate in all subjects simul-

ardly, a degree of success in dealing capacity seems with little recognition ith success in passing a high percentage Fourth, the profession of the teacher is [illegible] and [illegible] appeals to the Teachers are tempted either to neglect [illegible] pass, or otherwise force them on Fifth, there is no encouragement under to forward the higher moral and intel- of the pupils, because it is not paid be estimated by the Inspector as an education. And, also, I believe that are passed through this system lack [illegible]. Finally it destroys all individu- [illegible], which I believe should be one of the of education to encourage.

with regard to any changes in the [illegible] would you say with regard to —I think it should be made compul- d class.

ery school?—Well, yes.

[illegible] much in rural schools, or at all —I don't know anything about rural

, with regard to town schools, is it I believe it is in the convent schools. regard to drawing, what have you to [illegible] and designing?—I think it is a subject, and if I might go into detail [illegible] wish to give you an account of [illegible] made in that respect. Some five [illegible] what I considered what might [illegible] peculiar ideas upon education. [illegible] called Leland's "Practical Educa- delighted to find that the views in that [illegible] with mine; and not only so, but carried into practical effect and proved I found also in it that there was an the purpose of starting this practical [illegible], and I communicated with the with the idea of introducing the system school. I was referred to the Irish

optional in some schools and compulsory in others?— Yes.

18530. I see you put down it should be optional in second fifth and sixth, and obligatory in third, fourth and fifth; you think it should be optional in the lowest class and two highest and compulsory in the middle of a child's education?—Yes; I consider it should be optional in the second class, so that it might be a preparation for the compulsory work in third, fourth, and fifth.

18531. Is that optional on the part of the teacher? —Optional on the part of the teacher, and it need not be carried on to the highest stages in fifth and sixth unless the children, perhaps, intend to become [illegible] or designers.

18532. Supposing that a system of manual instruction in the shape of woodwork were introduced which was not compulsory but optional, you would then be in favour of carrying on the drawing in connection with that?—Yes, my lord, I recommend that.

18533. Now, with regard to spelling do you think that the requirements should be reduced?—Yes, my lord, because they are too exacting at present, and in order to make room for other subjects that I have specified that I consider more important.

18534. How do you mean too exacting, there are only two ways of spelling, right or wrong?—The extent of it that is required in third class; it is too extensive. Some of the most difficult sentences in the book are given for children in third class to spell.

18535. But in higher classes you would have them more difficult words?—Oh, yes, but at the same time I would have it confined to a certain proportion of the book, not any part of it, like the subject matter of the reading.

18536. What would you suggest with regard to any alteration in the manner of teaching arithmetic? —That the course is too extensive at present in the senior classes; and mental arithmetic, and higher mathematics should be a distinct subject and receive a higher fee in the junior classes.

18537. As regards grammar; where would you

certain for themselves the matter out
r.
regards manual training, what do you
manual training, anything beyond
modelling in clay.
general programme than they have in
.
you are in favour of its being intro-

made compulsory?—Yes.
where would you commence with it?
m.
modelling?—Yes, where kinder-
. Kindergarten leaves off in third
modelling could be commenced in fourth.
would you begin to teach the
?—In fifth and sixth.

extensive, and the greater difficulty was the difficulty of understanding.

18361. Then, if the books were made as extensive as they are, but were made easier, and the subjects more intelligible to children, it would not require more time than at present?—No, certainly not.

18362. Mr. Strevens.—Have you actually tried the system of developing the geometry which Mr. Leland advocates?—No, I have not.

18363. Have you known any person who did it?—No. The reason I have not done it is because I have too much to do in my school, to comply with the routine system at present.

18364. When you were teaching drawing you taught it on the lines of this book?—Yes.

18365. And you consider it an easy system to teach?—Well, I don't consider it by any means an

[illegible] Oct. [illegible], 1897. Mr. Robert J. [illegible].

the size of the class, certainly two prizes in a class of, I should say, twenty or thirty.

16581. You contemplate that every child who passed should get a prize?—Not at all.

16582. Mr. Harrington.—Do you think that the managers generally—I don't want to particularise any—do you think that the managers of the schools visit them sufficiently often and exercise sufficient influence?—Well, of course, I don't know anything about any other school except my own.

16583. I don't refer to them, but I mean from your knowledge of the teachers of this district?—I am not prepared to give an opinion upon the point; I have not sufficient knowledge to express an opinion upon it.

16584. Mr. Molloy.—By your statement I observe you are a trained teacher?—Yes.

16585. And hold rank as first of first?—Yes.

16586. And you have been principal teacher for five and a-half years, and previously had been assistant?—Yes, for three and a-half.

16587. I observe that you state you are in perfect sympathy with the introduction of manual instruction into schools?—Yes.

16588. Mr. Redington.—You said that kindergarten should be made obligatory in all schools?—Yes.

16589. How could it be taught in a school with only one teacher, without a monitor?—Of course I have not considered the details of it: it is merely the principle of the thing, and looking at it from an educational point of view.

16590. Perhaps you would add "where possible"?—Yes.

16591. What has been the effect of the results system, first on the education of dull boys; and, secondly, on that of clever boys?—On dull boys it has made them duller still, if that were possible.

16592. Is it not the case, that it has induced the teacher to spend more time on the instruction of backward boys?—It is to the neglect of the clever boy.

16593. Mr. Struthers.—If they have not made their 100 attendances?—They are left aside as a rule.

16594. Mr. Redington.—It is the interest of the teacher to spend a great deal of time on the instruction of the dull boys who have made the proper number of attendances?—Yes; but, as a rule, they will not have made the proper number of attendances.

16595. There is no connexion between dulness and irregular attendance?—There is in this way: as a rule, the boy is not up in his programme who has not made his attendances, and he will be considerably backward while the others are advanced.

16596. Certainly, but where a boy who had given 100 attendances, was by nature of a duller disposition than other boys, is it not the interest of the teacher to devote considerable attention to that boy so as to enable him to pass the examination?—Yes, and it is done, but he is an exception.

16597. Then, as regards the dull boy, the system works advantageously?—Yes.

16598. Is it, in your opinion, the effect of the system that it keeps the brighter boys back?—Yes.

16599. Then it would depend on the proportion of dull to clever boys as to whether the system worked well or ill?—Yes, to a certain extent, and it depends also on the attendance of pupils.

16600. Mr. Struthers.—It would not improve the teaching of those boys who had not made their 100 attendances, I understand?—No.

16601. The present system has not the effect of making the teacher devote special attention to the dull boys who have not made their attendances?—No.

16602. And this will be a considerable proportion of the dull boys in the school?—Yes.

16603. Mr. Redington.—When will the teacher know whether they have made their 100 attendances?—He keeps a record.

16604. How does he know in the first quarter?—Not in the first quarter.

16605. Therefore, in the first quarter his interest is to look after the dull boys, and bring them up to a certain level?—Yes.

16606. And as regards the second quarter, would you not say the same?—Yes.

16607. And even the third quarter?—No, for it is very easy for him to see then.

FORTY-SECOND PUBLIC SITTING—TUESDAY, OCTOBER 12TH, 1897,

AT 2 O'CLOCK, P.M.,

At the Grand Central Hotel, Belfast.

Present:—Rev. Hamilton Wilson, B.D., in the Chair; Stanley Harrington, Esq., B.A.; W. R. J. Molloy, Esq.; Captain T. B. Shaw; and J. Struthers, Esq., B.A.; with J. D. Daly, Esq., M.A., Secretary.

John Moran, LL.D., Head Inspector of National Schools, examined.

der and would
lding Colleges:
ving a class in
who have left
until they have

me you make?
sion.
r of years you
r in Dublin?—

I mistake not,
f the National
d in Westport.

. very familiar
and also with

ment as Hand
afraid here as

the process
, are there any
rs or that you
I would, sir, in

suggestion you
arithmetic at
we prepare the
be simple and
ge is very little
a step to this
Belfast before,

ate the use of
—I think that
slasses by the

the inspector,
ation?—Not at
a secondary

pression?—They
erely incidental
the place.
penter who has
ation to hold in
also really the
as much as he

nt schools, how

ts in manual
e years?—Not

f the Belfast
the primary
was not sat-
ervey for an
a capacity of a
ly appreciable

usively in this
in Belfast.
lity?—In some

I think it would be very desirable to have it in 3rd and 4th classes. Belfast. Oct. 16, 18[illegible]. [illegible], LL.D.

18636. And even higher, perhaps?—Perhaps higher.

18637. So that it might run through the entire school course?—Through the entire school course.

18638. What is your opinion of its educational value?—I consider it of the greatest educational value to educate the eye and hand in giving the idea of form and figure and shape.

18639. Do you find drawing successfully taught here?—Drawing is very poorly taught.

18640. Is it taught in a fair number of schools?—It is taught in a large number of schools in Belfast, but with a very moderate degree of success; the children are left a good deal to themselves, and the indiarubber is too much used in rubbing out.

18641. How do you account for the want of success; one would imagine that in Belfast drawing would be regarded as a very important subject?—They take a good many extra branches in some of the schools where drawing is taught, and they are teaching those extras sometimes while the children are employed at drawing.

18642. Then you account for the inefficiency of the instruction in drawing by the fact that the teacher, who ought to be attending to the drawing, is attending really to another extra branch?—Yes.

18643. Is not that rather a departure from the arrangements of the time-table?—Of course it is, and I should feel inclined to deal very severely with it if I found it, but we cannot see them at work every day.

18644. Have you turned your attention at all to manual instruction?—I have.

18645. Have you any suggestion to offer in connection with the introduction of that into schools here; Belfast would seem to be a very suitable place for its introduction?—It would be very desirable to introduce handicraft here and in all the large towns; it would be desirable to introduce it everywhere, but unfortunately I think it would be very difficult to do so in the rural districts.

18646. But in such an important centre as Belfast you would be in favour of the introduction of manual training?—Decidedly.

18647. Not confined to handicraft or carpentry work?—Not confined to these.

18648. But to such a form of instruction as would train the hand and eye?—Yes.

18649. Have you seen the working of any manual instruction class?—I have had a good deal of experience in examining in handicraft. I examined the classes in Marlborough-street for two or three years. I had a class in handicraft at [illegible], and another at Athboy.

18650. Those were three important places; did the manual instruction extend beyond carpentry work, so to say?—Not beyond carpentry work.

18651. Was it based on the Board's present programme in handicraft?—It was.

18652. Do you approve of that programme?—I do; it might be simplified, perhaps.

18653. It has not, however, been introduced into any place in Belfast, so far as you know, up to the present?—I think there are two schools in Belfast in which it has been introduced—one of them is

16659. How did you find it working there?—Judging by the result, it did not seem to be much.

16660. By whom is it carried on?—By two of the assistants.

16661. And they hold certificates of competency in that particular branch?—I believe they do.

16662. And I presume the National Board supply the plant in the case of the Model school?—I think so.

16663. Had you any other observations to make with regard to the results programme?—No, sir, nothing particular, but cookery is a thing I would like to say a word about. I have had a good deal of experience in cookery. Two Head Inspectors, of whom I was one, examined 167 pupils in the Central Model School, Queen's Scholars, in training, and the result was remarkably good. I also had it in four Convent schools in Meath. I believe that it should be made compulsory in all the female training colleges, pretty much as handicraft in all the male training colleges.

16664. And drawing, doubtless?—And drawing.

16665. You would advocate the propriety of cookery being made compulsory in schools where teachers hold certificates?—Yes.

16666. And you would extend it to rural schools?—Extend it as much as possible.

16667. In the case of teachers already in the schools, who have been trained, say a considerable time ago, or perhaps not trained at all, have you any plan by which cookery could be established in their schools?—There was an itinerant teacher sent to Carrickfergus last autumn, and the headmistress has since qualified for a certificate, and has a class in operation in the Model school there.

16668. I presume you would advocate the propriety of the cookery instruction being carried on continuously during the year, and not confined to the short period during which the special teacher gives instruction?—Throughout the year.

16669. And then that the ordinary teacher of the school, if sufficiently qualified, would take it up and carry it on later?—Yes.

16670. Have you had experience of laundry work in any of the schools?—No.

16671. You have not touched on the subject of needlework; had you any special views to put forward with regard to needlework, say the alternative scheme?—The alternative scheme would be very desirable, but it has been a failure in this circuit; I mean it is not taken up; nearly all the schools have got exemption from its operation.

16672. I believe Belfast was the earliest place in which exemption was taken to that scheme; what was the chief ground of objection?—It was not popular with the parents. I know at Oldcastle, after it was introduced, half the sixth class girls left; then the teacher taught them a literary course in addition to the alternative scheme, and they returned again. I suggested, in my report to the Commissioners, that the needlework might be extended to one and a half hours instead of an hour, and that the boys would be engaged on handicraft or drawing, or some other manual instruction, at the time.

16673. Do I understand you now to suggest that carried on as part of the needlework instruction in the Belfast schools?—Very little, if at all; I have not met with it any where yet in Belfast.

16674. Now from your statement, Dr. Moran, needlework is in a rather low state; have you any suggestion as to how it might be improved in your circuit; are your observations exclusively applicable to Belfast?—To Belfast; it is fairly taught through most of the towns in the circuit.

16675. Has the alternative scheme been taken up largely throughout the circuit?—Very little; there are very few schools in which it is taught.

16676. I presume, except in the rural schools, agriculture is not taken up?—Agriculture is not taken up in the town schools, nor in Belfast.

16677. What is your experience of the working of it in the rural schools?—It should be made more practical, if possible; the teacher could do a good deal if he wished, either by means of the school garden or a neighbouring farm; the sole object at present is the earning of results fees by cramming them from the textbook. They are told how things are done instead of showing them how they are done, and getting them to join in doing them; that is the great fault of the teaching of agriculture in the schools.

16678. In the rural portions of your circuit are there many examples of school farms or school gardens?—There are a few, not many.

16679. Your circuit extends over a number of counties; what county in particular?—I think, in the county Armagh.

16680. How do you find these conducted?—I have not had an opportunity of examining them yet; what I should like to have extended in very much is the cottage garden; I would advocate strongly attention to cottage gardening and utilising the land at nearly all seasons of the year.

16681. In your report to the National Board you refer to the discipline of the schools, and you think it is open to great improvement; what suggestions would you offer as to carrying out that improvement?—I should say it would all depend on the teacher, it is almost impossible without the proper teacher to have proper discipline.

16682. You don't advocate any special payment for that particular branch?—I would; I think payment should be made altogether for the value of the school as a whole, and I would largely abolish the present system by having more class examinations.

16683. You advocate the propriety of having more class examination at the results examinations rather than individual examination?—Yes.

16684. And would you include the examination of pupils who perhaps did not attend the minimum number of days as well as of pupils who made those days?—I think all the children on the rolls should be examined.

16685. When your duties as Inspector commenced the results system had been only a comparatively short time in operation; the old system prevailed largely, that is, 23 or 24 years ago?—Yes, the results system commenced in 1871.

16686. Are you able to contrast the results attained under the old system and under the results system?—

I believe, under the old system to examine the whole school.

16708. Have you outlined in any way practically how that suggestion could be carried out, that is, class examination of all pupils on the rolls, and, to a certain extent, adherence to the form in use prior to the introduction of the results system?—I have not formulated anything, but I could if you considered it desirable; I would draw up some document.

16709. Mr. [illegible].—With regard to the calling of the roll, I presume that here, as in other places, the roll is called at eleven o'clock?—Before eleven o'clock; it must be entered in the daily Report Book at eleven o'clock.

16710. Would you be in favour of having that called at ten instead of eleven o'clock?—I would.

16711. You think that all the children who do come to school could be there at ten as well as at

16712. I mean in the primary schools?—Very little. Belfast.

16713. Though it would be of special importance here that hand and eye should be trained from the earliest days?—Yes. Oct. 13, [illegible]. John [illegible], LL.D.

16714. With regard to the text-books, the lesson books, do you think they are sufficiently interesting to the children?—I think they might be varied; there is a new set of alternative readers now on the Board's list which can be used instead of the old lesson books.

16715. Do you think those of an improved character?—I am not quite certain; I have not read them over yet.

16716. Would you consider that the introduction of lessons on temperance and laws regulating sanitation would be of great advantage in these schools?—It would.

16717. You think it would have a decidedly moral effect on the children in after life?—I think so; yes.

16733. You don't think it unfits children for profiting by the subsequent literary work in the more advanced classes?—Certainly not.

16734. You have seen the statement that a teacher children how to manipulate a certain type of question?—Yes.

16735. Without going into any explanation?—There is very little explanation of the principles of

Belfast.
Oct. [illegible], 1897.
John [illegible], LL.D.

a garden attached to the school that would give them a taste for a garden at home.

18781. Do you not think it could be done by plots attached to their own houses?—Not so well, the teacher could not go to every garden.

18782. At present where there is a cottage garden the teacher is bound to take out the children so many hours in the week?—Yes, usually during playtime.

18783. I believe he must bring them out every day?—It must be every day.

18784. Of course there are some days when it would be absurd to bring the children out?—Yes, you would not bring them out in bad weather.

18785. And there is a great part of the year when there is very little interest in the school garden?—Very little in winter.

18786. And if cottage gardening were retained on the programme it would be better to relax that rule so as to allow the teacher to teach them in the school?—When I say the children have to go to the garden for half an hour that does not apply to winter.

18787. Captain SHAW.—If there is a garden attached to the school is it not a rule that they are to spend half an hour every day in the school garden?—I am not aware that there is such a rule.

18788. But you think that it might be taught efficiently by taking the children out less than half an hour every day at the proper seasons of the year?—At the proper seasons of the year.

18789. Mr. STRUTHERS.—Is science taught in the schools in Belfast?—Very little.

18790. Have you any object lessons in the junior classes?—Yes, in the infant schools we insist on object lessons; I always examine on object lessons.

18791. There is no separate results fee?—They are paid 4s. for infants instead of 3s. in the ordinary national schools, and we insist that they must adopt drill and object lessons and school songs.

18792. Don't you think that object-lesson instruction might be usefully extended to the higher classes?—I think so.

18793. In the same way as kindergarten should be extended?—Yes.

18794. Do you think five hours a week absolutely necessary to obtain satisfactory results in needlework?—Yes, I think it would be necessary, especially as a good deal of the time is wasted in commencing, providing materials and giving them out to the children.

18795. You are aware that in other countries, such as England, what seem to be good results are obtained in much less time, three hours. Is there any difficulty in the way of needlework instruction in providing materials?—Yes, in some of the rural schools, very great difficulty.

18796. But not in the town schools?—Not in the town schools where the parents of the children are well-to-do.

18797. But where the parents of the children are not well-to-do?—There is some difficulty.

18798. Do you think it would be possible to have an arrangement by which the managers should provide the material?—If the managers were forced?

18799. Well, have some compensation to them from the National Board for providing materials, and then sell such things as were saleable?—Yes.

18800. Supposing the needlework to be taught efficiently, say in three hours a week, two hours of that time might be usefully devoted to cookery?—Yes.

18801. May I ask if drawing is taught to the girls as well as to the boys in Belfast town schools?—Yes.

18802. Captain SHAW.—You said that the failure in drawing was due to the teachers not teaching it, but merely allowing the pupils to work by themselves?—Of course I would modify that largely, I would say in some schools, not in all.

18803. Do you think this may be partly due to the programme of drawing which is laid down?—No, I think not.

18804. Don't you think it would be possible so to inspect drawing and lay down such a programme that the teachers would have to pay attention to the children while they were learning it?—Well, I think there would very little difference.

18805. Mr. STRUTHERS.—Is not this because general inspection of the method is better than examination of the results just as in the case of arithmetic?—Yes.

18806. Captain SHAW.—The present programme only includes freehand drawing as a necessity?—That is so.

18807. I think you said you would approve of geometrical drawing or drawing to scale, with the use of simple instruments being added to it in every case?—Yes, and model drawing in the senior classes.

18808. In the inspection do you look at the work the children have done during the year?—Yes, in some cases, for instance all the copy books the children have written during the year are to be presented to the inspector.

18809. But I am speaking of drawing?—Not in the case of drawing, but in the case of needlework, the worked articles have to be submitted to the inspector at the examinations.

18810. You said you approve of the programme of handicraft laid down by the Board?—Perhaps simplified a little.

18811. Don't you think the complicated nature of it may have led to the opposition in the giving of manual instruction?—It may have.

18812. Is it not rather a utilitarian programme than an educational?—It seems so.

18813. If you take the first year they start by having to be all expert in a number of tools, it depends on the meaning you give to "expert," but it looks as if they had to be trained carpenters at the end of the year?—Yes, there is another suggestion I have to make, for young children I believe tools specially made for children should be used; it is absurd to see a child of ten or eleven trying to work with a big saw, or to move a large jack plane along a board.

18814. Then when you get the second year's programme it is still more complicated, here they have got to be not only carpenters, but glaziers and painters?—That programme should be recast and modified considerably.

18815. Do you think there would be some opposition on the part of the teachers if they saw a course of manual instruction which was purely educational, which trained them in accuracy, taught them to appreciate the use of drawing and to apply it in practice?—Yes. I believe they would adopt it more readily than they would adopt that programme.

18816. When you say you would recommend that it should be taught in training colleges, would you prefer to have it in the training colleges or the practising schools attached to the colleges?—I would have it at both.

18817. In the training colleges students might become proficient in the use of tools themselves?—Yes, and in the practising schools that they might see how it was taught.

18818. That they might see the object of the instruction and learn that it was not to turn out carpenters or craftsmen, but assist in the general education of the child?—Yes.

18819. Is needlework taught somewhat in the same way in the school as drawing, the children are put down to sew and the teacher goes to something else?—As a rule the teacher supervises the needlework during the time.

18820. But it would be possible for her to set students down and let them work away for an hour?—It is quite possible, but I don't know that it is done, she has nothing else to do during that time, the needlework is compulsory for an hour each day.

18821. And they do nothing except the needlework?—Except the needlework.

16522. Is it your opinion that five hours is the least that can be devoted during the week to it?—I would not be very positive in that, I think three hours would do.

16523. The main reason urged for giving five hours is that it takes so long giving out the material and putting it back again, if you gave one-and-a-half hours each week you might get as much done?—You might.

16524. Perhaps one-and-a-half hours is a little too long to keep children at one occupation?—Yes.

16525. Sir Joshua Fitch told us that sewing was compatible with complete mental vacuity, do you think that is so? What do the boys in the town schools do in the place of agriculture?—Sometimes they have book-keeping, of course they have book-keeping in rural schools also, and sometimes extra branches, geometry or algebra.

16526. You say "sometimes." Is anything laid down as a necessity to replace agriculture?—No, not in town schools.

16527. Then apparently they have more time at their disposal for extra subjects in town schools than in rural schools?—Yes.

16528. Is it a common practice to give home lessons to all the students in all the schools?—Yes.

16529. Do you know how much time a day is devoted to it?—Probably one-and-a-half or two hours in the evening, they learn their lessons at home, and they are examined next morning by the teacher.

16530. That exceeds the school hours practically?—Practically it does.

16531. Don't you think they would be better employed if they were kept in school, suppose the home lesson was learned during the time for drawing and one hour put on for drawing?—I think the hours are long enough now. Probably the children themselves prefer to choose their own time at home for learning their lessons.

16532. But do they learn them as a matter of fact?—I believe they do in most cases.

16533. Then as regards extra subjects, are they generally taught?—Geometry and algebra are pretty generally taught to fifth class, first and second stages, and first stage, sixth; they are not paid any results fees for them in any lower class.

16534. Do you think the arithmetic which is taught might be modified with advantage?—I think it might.

16535. And the demands for reading in the upper classes, do you think they are excessive or unnecessary for the general education?—I think reading is extremely desirable, and I would not like to have it curtailed.

16536. But the class of reading you have in the sixth book, do you think a child could do with less of that? They are supposed to know and explain the whole of those lesson books, able to read and explain?—Yes.

16537. CHAIRMAN.—Since the Compulsory Education Act was introduced into Belfast has it been enforced really?—It has.

16538. What effect has the Act produced?—Very beneficial effects; there have been recently a good number of prosecutions under the Act.

16539. Do the parents in general show willingness to yield to this Compulsory Act?—I am not quite sure, but I think that there is no great opposition to it on the part of the parents.

16540. Captain SHAW.—At what age can children be taken into the factories here?—At the age of fourteen, or they can be taken in between thirteen and fourteen, if they have a certificate from the Inspector that they have passed into the fourth class.

16541. Mr. STRUTHERS.—But not under thirteen, not even as half-timers?—Yes, they take them in as half-timers at eleven; in a large number of our schools there are half-timers.

16542. CHAIRMAN.—Has the school accommodation in Belfast been found sufficient since compulsion was introduced?—It is amply sufficient in most cases.

16543. Mr. MOLLOY.—Has there not been an increase in the average attendance of the schools owing to the results system?—Certainly.

16544. Have you any statistics that would show that?—I have not.

schools here?—I don't know, I have no experience, I don't teach it myself.

[illegible]

18576. Captain Shaw.—You were good enough to quote from me just a minute ago, do you know that those remarks applied to organised science schools?—That may be, I don't know.

18577. Do you know that those schools are required to have thirteen hours in the week of science instruction outside literary work?—At any rate he says two hours for manual instruction must be taken off their literary instruction.

18578. Do you know that there are only eight hours left for ordinary literary work in those schools, and the remark made was that two hours deduction from those eight would diminish the literary instruction?—Any person would have prophesied that, but is manual instruction taken up much in primary schools in England?

18579. In the primary schools in all the large towns it is?—In that report we have manual instruction included with thirteen other subjects, and it says there were only 1626 pupils examined in the whole fourteen subjects.

18580. Those are specific subjects, manual instruction is not a specific subject and would not be in that return as it is examined by the Science and Art Department. There are specific subjects taught in the elementary schools, but not under the Science and Art Department?—Do I understand that manual instruction is not taught under the Science and Art Department?

18581. It is, in England, as a matter of fact, at present, and is not included in those figures?—Then it would not be included in the primary schools.

18582. But it is taught in the primary schools?—Well, but if we teach under the Science and Art Department in the primary schools the Commissioners take no notice of it. I have taught under the Science and Art Department many a year, and the Commissioners of National Education took no notice of it except to ask what money I made by it.

18583. You think then both the method of inspection and the subjects of instruction might be modified?—I think the subjects of instruction might be modified; I don't want to say anything about the method of inspection.

18584. Without the child's general education suffering?—In fact I believe the child's general education would be benefited.

18585. You make the remark that "a good general education is the best foundation for a good technical education"?—I think so.

18586. Kindly give us your views as to what would be a good general education?—I think to be well able to read, to understand what they do read, and to have a fair knowledge of commercial arithmetic and to be able to keep accounts neatly and fairly, and have a general intelligence would be what I would call a good general education. I would have drawing from the flat and drawing to scale, and I would think that a person who had done so would have a good general education.

18587. I suppose a good general education would include a certain command of the hand, quickness, accuracy and constructive ability?—But those can be

[illegible]

body by introducing the age and [illegible] into schools. What are we to do with the other children?

16889. Nobody ever contemplated that one teacher with sixty or seventy children should have manual instruction, stuck on to the top of his other duties?—I must say I am a little labouring in the dark, because I don't know what is intended by manual instruction. I don't wish to be against it, because I believe manual instruction is necessary for some people at least, who will be applying themselves to trades, but I don't see how it is to be taught in our schools without there is a revolution and there are schools built and proper teachers.

16890. You agree there is no use in teaching a subject unless you have a proper teacher and proper methods of teaching?—I think so. I am sure you will agree with me in that.

16891. I think you advocate the teaching of drawing?—Very much.

16892. But that is manual instruction to a certain extent?—It is, and so is needlework.

16893. It also, if properly taught, is a good training in observation, of which sometimes people are lacking, and after they have received their education, training in observation is also useful?—Yes.

16894. A great many people go through the world without using their eyes?—The more they can be taught to use their eyes the more generally apt they would be at anything.

16895. Would you advocate the teaching of drawing so far as it comes to for sketches for models or for practical purposes?—I don't know anything about model drawing, but certainly, for practical purposes, I would have practical geometry.

16896. Would you think it practical training if a child is taught to draw the plan and the elevation, or working drawing, of some object, and that he should carry it in some manner afterwards?—Well, if he had someone to direct him perhaps it would.

16897. You also wish a course of elementary physics?—Oh, certainly.

16898. You would advocate that being taught practically, I presume?—I would, indeed.

16899. And with experiments?—With experiments. Books are very useful, but the teaching without experiments is not very satisfactory.

16900. That is a great training in observation and also reasoning to a certain extent. If properly put before the children, would you advocate the teaching of them throughout the classes, from first class upwards?—I don't know about the first class. It takes a considerable time to teach reading mechanically, and until we have it taught mechanically explanation is no use.

16901. But you can give object lessons even to very small children?—I suppose object lessons even to the first class would be useful. They could not do any harm.

16902. And they might be made scientific without bringing in difficult words which a child cannot understand. You say Euclid and mensuration should be considered separate subjects?—Yes; I think so.

16903. Would you put mensuration in with geometry and make it part of geometrical drawing?—I would not. I would make mensuration a separate subject, because I find it is very useful in Belfast.

16904. Part of a course of accurate training in measurement, perhaps?—Well, I would use the ruler and you could measure things—everything that happened to come in your way—actually measure it and do it as practically as possible.

16905. Mr. Strutherss.—Is not that practical geometry?—Yes.

16906. Then why do you wish to make it a separate subject?—Because practical geometry sometimes takes something more in than that. Our fault is we want to make our subjects too extensive. [illegible]

16907. Do you teach agriculture in your school?—No, sir. Well, I did teach agriculture. Of course, people said I only taught it for a fee in Belfast, and I was not able to say they were wrong, and consequently I gave it up. One thing I found was I had two teachers instead of one, and I believe it was useful in making good teachers.

16908. Would you approve of reading from unseen passages?—Yes, if I could get an unseen passage that was not more difficult than the book they had been reading in, but if I got a passage from an unseen book I am afraid of it. Here is one out of my Fourth Book—"The immediate and continuous application of cold, by the employment of irrigation, will prevent much effusion into the injured joint, and also the occurrence of severe inflammation." That means the application of a wet cloth to a sprain.

16909. For pupils of what age?—Between ten and eleven.

16910. Let me see if I understand your position. You would have elementary physics taught in schools?—I would.

16911. And although you have not fully considered the question, you would begin that with object lessons in the junior classes?—That is a point I have not considered.

16912. But on the general principle you are agreed that in an ideal scheme of education you would have elementary science with experiments taught practically to the children?—Yes.

16913. For what purpose?—For the purpose of awakening their imagination and making them generally attentive.

16914. Making them more observant and training their reasoning powers?—Yes, and letting them see the reason of things.

16915. You would also teach drawing?—Yes.

16916. For a similar purpose?—Training their observation and accuracy.

16917. But at present you only teach freehand drawing, do you think that that gives all the training in accuracy that might be had?—I won't say all the training in accuracy, but I say unless we can draw freehand well, the other drawing would not be very well done.

16918. Don't you think a person can draw with scale and compasses who cannot do freehand at all?—If you give them a scale and compass, perhaps they could, but I don't consider it drawing.

16919. It is generally called drawing, but why should that form of drawing be postponed until the people are perfect in freehand?—I don't know.

16920. Don't you think it might be introduced at a comparatively early stage in the child's course?—Perhaps it might.

16921. And I think you said already that the drawing to scale and the plan and elevation might be made more intelligible to the children if they made objects from those drawings?—I said it may be so, but I did not give an opinion of my own with regard to it.

16922. Does not that seem a reasonable opinion, how are they to understand the meaning of plans and elevations, unless they make the object or see the relation of the object to it?—They draw from plan and elevation with us, and I don't see where I can take them away to build up what they have drawn.

16923. It would be a very simple thing to build up the structure of which they had drawn the plan and elevation with square cubes of brick such as they have in the kindergarten?—Where am I to have that?

16924. I am merely inquiring as to the possible scheme of education?—Oh, yes.

16925. Then both elementary instruction in science and in drawing are, in your view, parts of a good general scheme of education?—Yes.

manual instruction.

hours we received to

a making a different
developed by manual
a good idea of what
to my capacity.
recommend to you in
in Birmingham and
see that evidence at
Liverpool, where they
in connection with
lovable places where
the children.
evidence we got in

understand that
was in the primary
but that is the exact
case.
teacher that belongs
when I was making
it was taught.
are making all the
and the evidence we
I did not know of

surprised to learn
in everyone of the
schools?—It would
devoted differently,
at all.
you will find that
tion, using it in the
as in all the Board
merely in the higher
tools, of course in
in the lower stan-
ar.
are agreed that
should be part of a
you any evidence to
ortion?—I am using
one only instruction
knowing, tending to
you would be inclined
ame of education?—
rything that would

that manual instruc-
ming the age, place
done of work which
in order to get this
spoke of, you would
has?—I would.
you would teach
—Certainly, but we

have it taught in
rsonal?—I would.
ch simpler reading

such a passage as
pleasured by a child

two hours a day to
never could make it
no difference.
children at that age
A simpler book.

ciseum reading would be a very fair one, provided you are certain the passage is not more difficult than in the books from which he has been reading?—I think so.

16947. You think more time might be saved in the [illegible] of arithmetic?—Certainly, by a change in the method of teaching.

16948. You would teach it in a more practical way, teaching quickness of calculation?—Yes, quickness and accuracy.

16949. And explanation of the principles?—I would explain the principles to a certain extent.

16950. I mean so that the children did things intelligently, and you would consider that more important than questions in alligation and finding proportional means?—Yes, I don't see what use they are.

16951. If you had reading and arithmetic, the two principal subjects in an ordinary school course simplified in this way, then you would find time for the development of practical instruction?—Certainly.

16952. On the lines you have already described as part of a good general education?—Yes.

16953. You mention at the end of your memorandum that you would have boys intended for commercial pursuits instructed in a special way, they should be trained in quickness and accuracy in calculating ordinary commercial transactions, commercial geography, including the great industrial centres of the world, exports and imports, weights and measures, the money values of the different countries, commercial letter-writing are all of considerable value, would you have that taught in the ordinary day school?—The children who are going to commercial life.

16954. But then all the children are not going to commercial life, and a great many apparently leave at eleven years of age, and of those who remain after that age it does not follow that they are all going to commercial occupations?—Not all.

16955. So it would be a mistake to teach this programme to all the children of the upper classes of a day school?—It would in the same way as it would be a mistake to teach manual instruction.

16956. Excuse me, we have agreed so far as we have discussed the matter that the manual instruction contemplated was to be part of a good general education, nothing further, it is not meant to train a boy to be a carpenter or for any industrial pursuit, but merely to train his intelligence and powers of observation and sense of accuracy. This special commercial programme would not be suitable for every boy in the upper classes?—No.

16957. Would it not then be desirable to have it taught in an evening school?—It would.

16958. In fact all special subjects, which are not part of a good general education?—In continuation schools.

16959. For those who choose to benefit by them? —Yes.

16960. Have you any idea how those evening schools should be encouraged, we understand evening schools are not common in Ireland?—They are very uncommon.

16961. What is the reason for that?—I don't know, but one reason may have been that persons who did attend evening schools when they were more common, did not attend for instruction, but came for amusement, and consequently people were obliged to close them. I know that was the reason why I closed an evening school.

16962. What did you teach there?—It was a long time ago, and I taught the ordinary subjects taught

Belfast.
Oct. [illegible]
Mr. Robert [illegible]

in shape. Some people would say abolish the results system altogether, but if it is not to be abolished it must be modified in that way if we are to have any education.

18999. Has not the teacher comparative freedom of classification at present, he is under no obligation to put a boy forward from one class to another every year?—But a boy may be able to go forward in one subject and not in another, besides it is a difficult thing to keep him back if you wish to retain the child. Schools are so plenty and people think a child should not be kept back.

19000. That might be the fault of an excessive number of schools?—It is not the fault in Ballymena, for we have not school-room enough.

19001. Does your recollection extend to the state of instruction in National schools prior to the introduction of the results system?—It does, ten years before that.

19002. Then you can speak with some degree of authority on that subject. Teachers then had a very free hand as regards classification?—They had a little too free, they kept them perhaps a little too long. I think I said I would have modifications, I think that was the great fault, but I think it was a better system of education by far than we have at present only for the one thing.

19003. And in place of individual examination of which you disapprove you would prefer class examination?—I think I would like class examination, and if a fair percentage of the pupils passed then that would show how the school was taught.

19004. If the subject was shown to the examiner to be carefully taught, the salary should be paid for?—I think so.

19005. And, as far as possible, all the pupils on the rolls should participate in that examination?—There is a great fault at present; there are a great number of pupils never examined at all, for instance, I see by your report that 79,000 in 1886 who have made 100 days attendance have not been examined at all. But there will be far more than 79,000 who have been struck off during the year and won't appear on the rolls, so there must be nearly double the number. For instance, I know a teacher with 180 children and thirty-three were struck off the rolls and do not appear although they had made 100 days attendance.

19006. Mr. Struthers.—They had gone to another school?—Yes.

19007. Mr. Molloy.—Having had experience of the two kinds of programme, which would you prefer?—On the whole I would rather have the former one.

19008. But the former one did not carry with it £280,000 per annum of results fees?—Oh, no.

19009. And if the £280,000 could be retained you would prefer the former system of examination?—I think there is a difficulty, I would prefer it to be retained, but I would like to have it paid something as it is paid at present.

19010. Partly by salary, partly by the examination of the pupils; have you ever turned your attention to the propriety of having graded schools according to the degree of efficiency of the teachers?—That might be, but I would like to have uniformity among the inspectors. One inspector said he would call eighty excellent, and under sixty pay nothing; another inspector said for seventy-five, excellent, and under fifty, bad, and until you can do something with regard to uniformity I am afraid of graded schools.

19011. Mr. Struthers.—You would have the inspector pay more attention to the method of instruction as well as to the results?—Yes.

19012. Mr. Molloy.—One of the difficulties about manual instruction is the absence of proper accommodation?—Yes.

19013. Then if the thing was to be introduced at all it should be in continuation schools, and in a special department, and under specialists?—Yes, under special teachers.

19014. And the teachers at present in office would receive instruction from these itinerating specialists as well as in the training colleges?—Yes, I suppose any way at all that the teachers could receive it, but I would not have the itinerating teachers coming to the school, it would take the whole staff keeping order.

19015. And then the specialist, if at all introduced into the school, should come at an hour when the ordinary business would be over?—Yes.

19016. You were asked a question on the subject of evening or continuation schools; at one time in Belfast there were very numerous, you gave one reason?—I gave my own reason, that may not have been the original reason, but I gave the reason why I gave it up.

19017. I have personal knowledge that at one time in the Belfast district alone there were twenty-seven evening schools, unhappily we have only thirty-five in all Ireland at present?—I don't suppose there is more than one in Belfast, the Model school.

19018. You have not kindergarten in your school, what is the difficulty about introducing it?—I don't know, the greater part of the information I can get is that it is not useful.

19019. Is that based on any personal knowledge?—No personal knowledge of my own, merely reports I have got, but perhaps I have not understood those reports just as well as I ought to have done.

19020. Mr. Harrington.—This is not from the gentleman in Birkenhead?—No. Mr. E. J. Barter, I think he is one of the Head Inspectors in England, says "many teachers hold the opinion that the kindergarten drawing in the infant school rather than being an assistance to the work of the standards is a hindrance, much labour being required to eradicate the faulty method of using the pencil which has been acquired. As far as my experience warrants an opinion I am inclined to the same belief."

19021. Mr. Molloy.—Do you not see that he refers there specially to kindergarten drawing and not the general kindergarten instruction?—Yes, see I talk about kindergarten, and having no personal experience I thought kindergarten consisted principally of drawing.

19022. It is much more extensive than that. What difficulty have you about the introduction of elementary science into your school?—I don't see any except that the Commissioners don't pay for it and don't want it, and I have so much to do in the subjects that they require that I have not time.

19023. But have they not a programme for physical science subjects on a very elaborate scale?—Oh, yes; but it is so elaborate we can only look at it, we could never possibly teach it.

19024. You think it is too difficult?—It would puzzle in a University examination.

19025. Have you any recollection of the time that Dr. Clarke used to lecture to the schools in Belfast in elementary science?—Yes, I often sat under Dr. Clarke, both in Ballymena Model school and Dublin.

19026. Did you not think those lectures were particularly useful?—I think they were particularly interesting, for I remember I stayed until seven o'clock to hear them.

19027. If any revival of that system—not a very elaborate kind of science, and illustrated by experiments—if any revival of that took place would you be in favour of the introduction of it into your school?—I would, indeed. Such experiments as were conducted by him would be very useful and interesting.

19028. You think the reading books ought to be simplified—are you not aware that a manager has it in his power at present to submit, for the consideration of the Commissioners, a simpler set of books, provided there is no objectionable matter in the books?—Yes, I understand such is the case, but still, after all, getting the manager to submit them, and purchasing the books, causes us to stick by the old ones, perhaps when it is not wise to do so.

Belfast.

Oct. 22, 1887.

Mr. Robert Brown.

18029. And perhaps, also, the cheapness of the old books?—That has a good deal to do with it.

18030. And having them delivered at your doors gratis?—That is another thing.

18031. But you would be in favour of a simpler set of reading books?—Oh, yes; I intend, after my examinations, which will be next week, applying for some of them; I have not decided yet which to take.

18032. Captain Shaw.—Do you include drawing and practical physics in a literary education?—Yes, sir, I do.

18033. You call them literary?—I call them literary, in a good general education.

18034. If we called them practical, you would admit there is a necessity for a good practical education?—Yes.

Mr. Philip Ward.

Mr. Philip Ward, Teacher, St. Paul's National School, Belfast, examined.

18035. Chairman.—You are a National school teacher?—Yes, sir.

18036. Where is your school?—In the Falls district—St. Paul's.

18037. What are the numbers in attendance?—I have an average of about 560.

18038. What assistance have you in that school?—Eight assistants and seven monitors.

18039. You also, like Mr. Brown, represent the Central Committee in this case?—Yes, sir. I also take it that I represent the Belfast Teachers' Association, and in fact, I believe, two-thirds of the teachers of Belfast.

18040. I see you are opposed to manual instruction being introduced into the schools, unless there is some important modification of the present system?—Yes.

18041. What modification would you propose?—There are many modifications.

18042. So as to find time?—I don't think, after all, that the literary programme could be very largely modified; it can be modified in some particulars, but it could not be so modified as to afford considerable time for the teaching of any manual instruction in schools—any general system of manual instruction.

18043. Is yours a mixed school?—Purely a boys' school.

18044. You think there ought to be a large addition to the teaching staff before anything of the sort could be introduced?—Well, I am not so sure; I don't know that a large addition to the teaching staff would be required—there will be some addition, I daresay, required—at all events in a great number of schools.

18045. Do pupils, in your school or district, leave at so early an age as Mr. Brown has told us?—Oh, yes, about the same thing. Referring to that, I consider one of the reasons why so many children now leave school at that age, is, that, since the introduction of the compulsory system of education, they obtain a certificate when they are eleven years of age, and they can walk the streets if they like, and no person will say anything to them, provided they can produce the certificate; they will not get employment in the mills or factories, but if they have passed the standard they can walk about.

18046. Is it a fact that because children can walk about, and yet cannot get employment, that they prefer to walk about to improving their education by staying further at the school?—Yes, a great many do, and they obtain situations in shops and running messages, and so evade the Act.

18047. Do you approve of the results system?—Not as at present carried out.

18048. What changes would you make?—I would go in, as Mr. Brown has stated, for class examination, but I would not be in favour of examining all the children on the school roll; I think it would be very futile too in examining a child who had been only a fortnight or even a month at school.

18049. Have you ever seen kindergarten at work?—Well, I have not. I have read a good deal about kindergarten—yes, I did see it at work in the Infant Department of the Belfast Model school.

18050. You never have seen manual instruction given in any of the English schools?—No, sir, I have not.

18051. Mr. Molloy.—Prior to your commencing in St. Paul's school, I think you were the head master of a very large school here in town—St. Mary's?—Yes.

18052. Had you any experience, at any time, of rural schools?—No, except as a monitor.

18053. You referred, just now, to the Factory Act—is there any change in the regulations of the Factory Act from what appears in the Commissioners' report?—I don't think there is.

18054. By these the pupils ought to have attained, in order to get a certificate, a standard of proficiency in reading, writing, and arithmetic, equal to about fourth class?—Quite so.

18055. That is a pretty advanced one; you mentioned that in your school you have an average of 560, and you have eight assistants—I don't think you can complain of insufficiency of the teaching staff?—I am not complaining of it.

18056. But you refer in your statement to the insufficiency of the teaching staff in three-fourths of the National schools of Ireland; do you mean by that that you desire to see a change in the average number qualifying a school for the services of an assistant teacher?—Oh, yes.

18057. Or are you in favour of an increase in the monitorial staff?—I am not; I am in favour of a decrease of the monitorial staff.

18058. Your idea with regard to manual instruction is, that it ought not to be introduced except in continuation classes; do you mean by these the ordinary evening classes?—I don't mean the ordinary evening classes as heretofore existing, but evening classes that would be made sufficiently interesting to the children to induce them to attend, and in which such instruction could be introduced and carried on.

18059. You think the primary schools ought to lay down a safe foundation for a genuine system of technical instruction; is the Technical Education Act in force here in Belfast?—I am not sure; I think there is a technical school at all events in existence in Belfast; I think the Act does apply generally to Belfast.

18060. You say you are decidedly against the idea of introducing promiscuous handicraft employment. Where was that proposed by anyone?—I understand that there is a number of handicraft employments, a number of ways of using the hands; I object to all these ways, and, so far as I know, I don't think they could be suitably carried on in our primary schools.

18061. Ways of using the hands would hardly be expressed by "promiscuous handicraft employment;" have you not stated that a little too broadly?—It would all depend on the number of ways in which it is proposed to use the hands in the school.

18062. For girls, I suppose, needlework and cookery?—No, I refer chiefly to boys' schools. So far as girls are concerned, I never heard it asserted yet that the amount of manual instruction which girls receive as hand and eye training or handicraft made them more intelligent than they were, if they were not employed at this needlework, that it tended to make the girls smarter or more intelligent. So far as I know, I don't consider that handicraft really tends so much as is generally stated to make boys smarter or more intelligent.

19063. Well, the number of schools throughout Ireland in which handicraft is taught as a special subject happens to be only fifteen, and we were told by a previous witness that not more than two of these are in Belfast, so that the amount of experience up to the present could not be very extensive. You see no objection whatever, but rather the opposite—you say kindergarten ought to be encouraged and developed?—Yes, I hold that opinion.

19064. And particular attention paid to drawing?—Yes.

19065. Including drawing to scale?—Yes, I would add drawing to scale in the higher classes, and even perhaps drawing from easy models and the use of the ruler.

19066. And perhaps that mensuration should become a separate subject?—Oh, decidedly; it is, so far as I am aware, in the English primary schools.

19067. What are your views about the introduction of itinerant teachers into the schools of ordinary teachers, who are not themselves qualified to give instruction in special subjects?—I would be entirely against bringing itinerant teachers into the schools to teach any subjects. I think whatever is taught in the primary schools should be actually taught by the ordinary teacher.

19068. Those other subjects, then, should be taught in continuation or evening schools under special teachers?—Yes.

19069. You also advocate the propriety of teaching elementary science chiefly by experiments?—Yes.

19070. Are there many schools in Belfast where that is carried out?—I cannot say, but I don't suppose there are many at present.

19071. You heard the interesting evidence of Mr. Brown about his experience of the good effects of Dr. Clark's lectures?—Yes, they were before my time.

19072. Your idea is not that the present results system should be abolished, but that it should be greatly modified; now would you briefly indicate the lines of the modifications?—I would have, as I stated already, class examination, but I would modify the arithmetic programme considerably, and I would modify the geographical programme considerably, and also the programme in grammar, and I would make geometry and mensuration far more simple than they are, and algebra.

19073. In view of the time gained by these modifications, to which you have referred, what subject would you introduce for choice?—I am not sure whether I would advocate the introduction of any subject until I saw the amount of time at the disposal of the teacher, to find out whether he really could teach anything additional or not, because of course our schools at the present time are worked at a high pressure, we are really kept busier than we should be, and the children are kept busier than they should be.

19074. Speaking generally for Belfast and its neighbourhood, what are the hours of attendance on the part of pupils?—I presume from ten to three; in my own school we begin business at half-past nine, and continue to half-past two secular instruction, and from that to three o'clock, religious

this recent sepa
for the ordina
school, where
cannot be don
may go.

19077. You
for infants for
inmemcation of
would you also
say that teache
order to ensure
infant departm

19078. Mr.
the executive of
I am.

19079. Could
to understand
before you w
don't know of
except what is
reports and bra

19080. Migh
read?—I have
it, recently issu
name, I have
Unie, and I ha
Committee.

19081. Have
you handed
Manual Instru
not that, all
before you to
purpose, and so
great majority
far now, were
manual instru
literary departm

19082. Are
the head mast
testified to the
this manual tra
from an intelle
that is literature
in the school?
many teachers
in the literary

19083. You
to certain barg
boards?—Yes,
number of scho
report, about

19084. I thi
"Even if it
portion of hot
schools, which
of technical sub
work of the p
tically ineffecti
now be availabl
perfecting the
schools." The
duction of tech
instruction wo
—If we had to
across (or have

your view of what manual instruction is, but do you contemplate its being introduced as a compulsory subject all over the country?—Oh, yes, I had that in my mind.

19124. Have you seen a proposal by anybody to make it compulsory all over the country?—No, I have not seen a proposal as to what way it was to be introduced at all.

19125. Would you object to it being tried in selected schools?—Not at all.

19126. Would you have science teaching made compulsory all over the country?—Well, only in the schools where it would be likely to be of use, I believe in most schools it might be to a certain extent introduced.

19127. Object lessons would be of use in every school?—Certainly.

19128. And the more advanced science instruction might be followed according to the locality?—Certainly.

19129. In the country it might have a bearing on agriculture, beginning directly with objects and experiments?—Yes.

19130. You would have drawing made compulsory as soon as we get sufficient teachers, you would have kindergarten occupations extended, and you would have elementary science made compulsory, I think?—Yes.

19131. Then that is practically what we mean by manual and practical instruction?—I hope so.

19132. I think you said you had an impression that the needlework instruction did not make the girls more intelligent?—Yes, I never heard it said that it did.

19133. Do you think the girls would do as well as if they did not receive any instruction in needlework?—Yes, I think they would acquire a knowledge of the literary programme just as well.

19134. Yours is a boys' school, but, I have no doubt, you have heard the opinions of your fellow teachers; do you find the girls who devote five hours a week to needlework are any more backward in the literary programme than the boys who don't?—I don't know that they are.

19135. It is not proved, we may take it, that the girls are more backward than the boys?—It is not.

19136. Notwithstanding the fact that they give five hours a week to needlework, so that they can attain equal proficiency in the subjects that boys are examined in, in less time?—It can be looked at in another way; it is generally admitted that up to a certain age girls are more intelligent than boys. When they reach thirteen or fourteen, the boy begins to go beyond the girl.

19137. But we are dealing with children who are under thirteen or fourteen, the great majority; I think, we heard it stated that the majority of your school children leave school at eleven or twelve, so that would be at the age at which girls are more intelligent than boys?—I think so, and they apply themselves better to acquiring knowledge—to lessons at home.

19138. Don't you think needlework gives them some notion of accuracy and neatness that the boys don't have generally?—I daresay, and it is very useful for them, in fact, it is absolutely necessary for the girls to know a good deal about needlework.

19139. Don't you think exercises might be devised for boys, to give them a similar training in accuracy?—I daresay there could.

19140. It might have the effect of making boys of that young age more intelligent than at present?—I don't know that it would, but it is quite possible.

19141. You said that one objection to introducing manual instruction into elementary schools is that it is a preparation for technical education, and that the technical schools don't as yet exist?—Yes.

19142. Which is the more natural way of beginning a system of technical education, to start technical schools, and then prepare the children in the elementary schools for it, or to prepare the children in the elementary schools first and then start the technical schools?—My opinion is, that they should be started simultaneously.

19143. You think that the teaching of many of the subjects in schools might be made more practical than it is at present; you agree, the teaching of advanced arithmetic in certain forms is not profitable?—I do; I believe the higher arithmetic should be made an extra subject.

19144. Do you find the reading books too difficult for the age of the children?—The reading books that we have been using for years are far too difficult.

19145. The children might make more progress if they read a larger number of simpler books?—Yes, and I believe that instead of affording us more time in the future for teaching subjects, and especially for teaching any new subject that it might be thought well to introduce, the very fact of explanation becoming so elaborate a matter it will take a great deal more time from us than heretofore.

19146. But if the books are made simpler the explanation will be less required?—Quite so.

19147. So that a way of saving time would be, not to prescribe a small portion of a very difficult book to be explained, but to have several very easy reading books with less difficult explanation?—Yes, I would entirely agree that there should be more than one set of reading books used in the schools, because I hold that the object which should be kept in view in devising reading books is to teach reading, not to give information.

19148. So that apart from any training in observation and accuracy that we might get from the introduction of manual instruction in its various forms you think that we might make the present subjects in schools more practical?—There is no doubt about that, and more interesting.

19149. And in order to have that brought about you would think a very considerable modification of the present results system desirable?—Yes, I do.

19150. Captain Shaw.—At present, I think, grammar, writing, spelling, and reading, are held separate subjects, and are treated separately for examination?—They are.

19151. They might be all combined to a certain extent?—I don't see how.

19152. Don't you think you could teach grammar and reading and spelling at the same time?—No, I don't think it; I don't think that spelling could be taught very well with reading. To make an expert speller requires a considerable amount of time, and I don't think that it could be taught in connection with reading or grammar.

19153. Do you think it is a good system to teach children to spell by memory, rote say?—Yes, I do; I think after all it is the best system.

19154. Why do you think so, a child never has to spell a word unless he uses it in practice?—Yes, children spell very largely by sight as well as by ear.

19155. What is the advantage of teaching to spell by ear?—I don't understand you exactly.

19156. You ask a boy how he spells "geometry," and he says "g-e-o-m-e-t-r-y"; he has no assistance from his eye or written word?—He has seen it done before, and perhaps has written the spelling of it.

19157. There is one expression here of yours—"This unscientific using of tools and the ordinary legitimate work of a primary school are so incompatible, that to my mind they will never be carried on successfully together." What do you refer to there?—The use of tools in manual instruction in connection with a school.

19158. Do you contemplate that you should be asked to teach them to use their tools scientifically?—Well, as a general rule I understand that children that have been taught to use tools in primary schools acquire a very bad method of using them, and generally those methods have to be unlearnt when they go to learn trades.

Belfast.
Oct. 23, 1897.
Mr. Philip Ward.

Z 2

Belfast.
Oct. 12, 1897.
Mr. Philip Ward.

19159. Does this observation apply to Ireland or England or any particular place, or is it general?—I heard it made use of in Belfast.

19160. As a result of the handicraft teaching in Irish schools?—Yes.

19161. You object to the handicraft taught at present, and proposed, as being too extensive?—I do.

19162. As regards the length of time which the children are kept in school, do you think they learn better after they have been in school for a considerable time during the day, than if they had had an interval?—I would be in favour of an interval without the children going away, or I would have the interval very short, in the playground, for instance.

19163. Mr. Struthers.—For how long?—Half an hour.

19164. Mr. Harrington.—Don't they get an interval of that kind at present?—In some cases they do, and in some they do not.

19165. Mr. Struthers.—Have you cases in which children are actually in the schoolroom from ten in the morning to three in the afternoon?—Yes.

19166. Do you think that a reasonable proceeding?—I do not; I think we should have a sufficiently large playground attached to every school.

Belfast.
Oct. 13, 1897.

FORTY-THIRD PUBLIC SITTING.—WEDNESDAY, OCTOBER, 13th, 1897.

AT 10 O'CLOCK A.M.,

At the Grand Central Hotel, Belfast.

Present—Rev. Hamilton Wilson, D.D., in the Chair; The Right Hon. C. T. Redington, M.A.; Rev. Henry Evans, D.D.; W. R. J. Molloy, Esq.; Captain T. B. Shaw; and J. Struthers, Esq., B.A.;

with J. D. Daly, Esq., M.A., Secretary.

Rev. Thomas Quin, P.P., Rasharkin, examined.

Rev. Thomas Quin, P.P.

19167. Chairman.—You are the Parish Priest of Rasharkin?—Yes, sir.

19168. Have you been long there?—I am over fourteen years there.

19169. Have you many schools under your management?—I have five.

19170. They are pretty largely attended, I suppose?—Well, not largely, they are all single schools, some few of them able to keep a teacher.

19171. Have you any cookery or laundry in connection with the girls' schools?—No, there is no cookery or laundry.

19172. And no manual teaching for the boys either?—No.

19173. What is your opinion about the desirability of having small gardens attached to the schools?—Well, I think at the present day, as far as I have travelled and read that farming and gardening, especially gardening, are being taught in all the countries with which we are acquainted. I remember reading in France in 1889 in the debates in the Parliament about agriculture, in which of course I am specially interested, that they had made some slight mistake—before this, education went under the terms of professional or technical, as we would call it—and wanted it divided into agriculture, commercial, and industrial. One of the members said they had received a deluge of criticism because they seemed even to throw a slight on the teaching of agriculture by not having it formally mentioned. In Denmark, of which we hear so much, Mr. Poulsen at Oxford, speaking of Danish butter, of which so much is talked, stated that it was due greatly to the schools that they had for teaching how to make it. The Danes, however, I believe, hold that a good substantial foundation of general knowledge is very necessary, and that their butters are good because they are mixed with brains. Even in Egypt, I was reading something about it, but I have not been there, they are teaching agriculture. However, I don't profess to be a very high authority upon these matters, but in our National Board programme agriculture holds a very high position on the list paid on the list. It must be taught, and the only question is whether we are teaching it with as little trouble to the children and as much benefit as might be. Distinguishing between farming and gardening, a garden is a little plot, I suppose, where what might be called something like the luxuries of life are raised; of course a spade-laboured farm is five or six acres, a one horse farm, about fifteen, and a two-horse farm thirty acres. But speaking about farming as distinguished from gardening at the present time, some men hold that with the knowledge of things that children see around them in the country that farming can be taught efficiently, as it is taught. I was sometimes thinking if we had the teachers they have in Germany, if instead of keeping the boys in school the whole day the teacher were to take the boys through the country and give them a lesson, as the German teachers are so fond of doing, there might be something in that. I see you had before you my friend, Mr. Hendon, who went in very strong for the fact that you can teach it as it is. But he or anyone else would admit that it would be no harm at all events to try and teach it practically, if the thing could be done without causing any great cost or inconvenience. But whatever may be said of farming, I should think gardening at all events is an absolute necessity. In the poor districts of the country it is very difficult for children to see celery plants, even to see the simplest things, to see three sorts in the year of cabbage; they see one course of cabbage. I should think it would be far easier, in order to give a child a knowledge of the celery plant, to show him the celery plant and how it would be grown. I think sometimes it is almost cruelty to the children to ask them to learn these things without showing them. The question then arises about the time; of course some time must be expended on that, as you have it in the programme. I think there are a number of matters in connection with the general programme that might be curtailed a little any way. I am not, of course, again, a very high authority upon the matter.

19174. Well, you think some subject must be curtailed?—Yes, I think so. Take the grammar, whether you teach grammar in the third book or not I think the Inspector might be tightened a bit about the questions. The teacher should not only know but be thoroughly convinced that there would be no

Belfast.

Oct. 13, 1897.

Rev. Thomas Quin, P.P.

question in grammar in the third book asked that would require for its answering to know about the construction of the rest of the sentence. Now, words ending in "ly," little ones are generally disposed to look upon them as adverbs. The reading books are, indeed, are a little, I think, difficult to be understood by the children. There has been a change made, new things coming in this year, but I must say from the inquiries I made down in Coleraine the other day, they are not thought to be very much of an improvement. I am not much of an authority on the matter myself, but I wish there could be a selection made that would be intelligible—I know it is attended with a great deal of difficulty. Perhaps it would be no harm to say, one of your colleagues, Monsignor Molloy—he is not here—very kindly, some time ago, gave experimental lectures to the students in training in Drumcondra and also to the students at the Female College. He is looked upon as an ideal teacher. Apart altogether from the knowledge he communicates to the students, his manner of doing it was an immense advantage to persons coming out to teach. There is in the books a lesson taken from a lecture he delivered, of course to a more advanced audience, on the burning of a candle, and I am told it has caused many a candle to be burned. I merely mention this to show that there is a great deal of difficulty about it. If you had all lessons like "Whang the Miller," children would take them up. Instead of 200 pages, better 100 well understood or 150. In the two stages of fifth children often have more difficulty in plodding their way through a long sentence than they have in understanding the grammar. If a child could parse the simplest lessons on the tablets, first book, I think it would do fairly well until they go to the sixth class. In the arithmetic, too, I think it was a mistake in the alternative programme that interest was excluded, that girls were prevented from learning interest. I think at the present time, when there is so much borrowing and lending, interest is an important thing. But there are matters in the higher stages that might be reduced. Geography was not taught so well in my day as it is now, but I think if geography were made more practical, if they were asked to point out some important place on the map, and if we knew more about the geography of the United States than we do about the British possessions it would be better for us. Taking the North of Ireland, the geography of Scotland, where our kith and kin are working, and of the United States, would be important for us. This getting off names and heights of mountains, as far as I can see, in the German schools seems to be a very prohibited article. Last time I was down in Killarney a driver said, talking of a mountain, that it was 340 feet 11½ inches high, it used to be, he said, 341 feet, but an American took off the quarter inch. The knowledge that is merely acquired by committing things to memory is not of much use. At all events I think the geography might be made a little more easy and at the same time practically as good. You are very particular about needlework, an hour a day is a pretty long time for needlework, it becomes specially a trouble and inconvenience where, as in the country, you often have a workmistress and master in the school, and the girl is taken away for a full hour. It is a difficulty certainly, and I don't know that they are busy the whole time at the matter; of course it is very, very useful. Then again sometimes the inspectors object to teachers with farms. I don't know if there is such a thing as what the Board looks upon as ideal, that is of a man having his residence convenient to the school and having a farm attached; I don't know if ever an inspector has objected to that man working a farm. We have not very many of them yet, but, however, whatever may be said of a farm of 20 or 30 or 60 acres, I, for instance, have myself a married teacher, he has a large family, and, though he has no ground, he keeps a couple of cows; it is a very great luxury in the country to have your own sweet milk. He takes grass for them, and instead of buying hay he sometimes buys a field in the springtime. Instead of buying oats and straw he takes a field from a poor man at this time of the year and sows a crop, and so between odds and ends he works seven or eight acres of land anyway. And of course a garden is a thing that would be an absolute necessity in connection with a man living in the country. However, my point now—the only point remaining is about getting money to buy this. Of course there is a distinction between vested and non-vested schools. At the present time the Board of Works is empowered by Act of Parliament and the National Board, of course empowered, to advance money for the purchase of land for a farm in connection with a non-vested school, but not in connection with a vested school. They are empowered to purchase, by an Act of 1884, a farm of land, not exceeding twenty-five acres in connection with a non-vested school, and in the country at present the schools are very much vested. In the towns they are not so much. The awkwardness is there is a school within a stone's throw of me, here in Belfast, and the manager could get—at least the Act of Parliament empowers him to get—money to purchase a farm of land, where he has no use in the world for it, and I, with a vested school cannot get the money, I think that ought to be remedied.

19175. Rev. Dr. Evans.—Father Quin, you are the manager of five schools?—Yes, sir.

19176. How long is it since you began to be manager?—About fourteen years.

19177. That is a pretty long period, sufficient for you to have good experience, and to know a great deal about school work?—If I took advantage of it.

19178. What is the average age at which the pupils leave your school?—Well, indeed, I could not give you that exactly.

19179. Do any stay until they are fifteen years of age?—We have comparatively few, we have a few in all the schools of course.

19180. The most would leave probably about twelve?—I am sure they would.

19181. The agriculture that might be taught to young children, say under twelve or thirteen could not be much?—There could not be much, certainly.

19182. Have you given much attention to the subject of manual instruction in primary schools?—Not much indeed.

19183. Have you seen its working abroad on the Continent?—Well, I did not give much attention to it.

19184. Are there any school gardens in connection with your five schools?—No, there are not.

19185. Is farming well done round about you?—Well, I think it is, dairying is worst in the county Antrim; farming is pretty well done.

19186. Do you think it would be possible for the managers of schools, particularly your own clerical managers, to have anything like a committee, in which they could all meet from time to time for consultation about school affairs and to advise the Board?—It is possible, but I don't know that it is very practical.

19187. To have a body of opinion is always very important?—It is.

19188. Bodies of men consulting together are more likely to get hold of good ideas?—I know it is.

19189. But you would be in favour of school gardens, would you?—I would, certainly.

19190. What practical difficulties are there in the way of school gardens in connection with National schools?—The most practical difficulty is the land, that may appear a small thing—at least I suppose all people have their own complaints—in the county Antrim you will see from your returns that men of wealth have done less for National education than in any other county in Ireland; it is very difficult to get money.

19191. Have you been present in the schools when the inspectors conduct the results examinations?—I have.

19192. You think that to be very important?—Yes, and the inspectors like it very much.

19193. And the manager then has an opportunity of forming a very correct opinion as to how everything was going on?—Of course when I speak of finding fault with results, I would give my general opinion that it is the best conducted oral examination with which I have become acquainted in my lifetime; it is not perfect, I suppose never will be.

19194. Have you any suggestions that you could make to the Commission regarding the introduction of manual instruction into the schools?—I am afraid I would not be much use in that.

19195. As to in what class of schools we might attempt to introduce it, where the money is to come from, and how local co-operation may be secured?—They are talking about large central schools, but I am afraid in the country what you can do, must as a general rule, be done in the school.

19196. Mr. Stevenson.—I gather that you are not quite satisfied with the present agricultural teaching in the schools?—No, I am not.

19197. Where it is mainly taught from a textbook, you would like to have it more practically taught?—I would.

19198. And for that reason you would favour school gardens and school farms?—School gardens anyway, and school farms, at least on a small scale.

19199. You advocate the school gardens from two points of view, one is for the benefit of the teacher, that a teacher living in the country should have a garden as a luxury and a useful thing for him?—Yes, and another that he might be better able to teach.

19200. These are two different points of view, that the farm might be useful to the teacher as an investment or industry, but not used at all for teaching the pupils?—Both can be, of course I would have both together.

19201. Is there a difficulty in getting school gardens for the teachers. Have your schools got school gardens attached to them?—No, they have not.

19202. The teacher has no plot of ground at all?—No plot of ground at all.

19203. Then there is a difficulty in getting school gardens?—There is the main difficulty, money.

19204. But of course, as you have already said, children leaving school at eleven or twelve could not benefit very much by instruction on a school farm?—So far as they read the programme—that is a question for the National Board—whether they should bring in the agricultural programme—but certainly as far as they read the programme I think they will learn a good share.

19205. Do you think children of eleven and twelve would learn much more on a school farm than they would from the other farms round about them?—Well, you know, if a teacher were to take his children through the country and look at the crops as they grow, there would be something in that. It is a great thing when you are teaching anything as an experiment, or giving a lecture for instance, if you could bring in magic lantern views, there is a great thing in object teaching, so to speak, the general principle of object teaching, it would be a great thing, when you are explaining, for instance, the time flax should be pulled, if you were able to take the children out at the time to the fields.

19206. The children living in the district where flax is grown, would see that on the other farms?—Of course they would if they look at it carefully.

19207. You advocate permission being given to the teachers to take out the pupils for excursions in the country?—I don't exactly advocate that; I put it this way, that, if that were done there might not be the necessity for school gardens, but I don't advocate that because there may be a great many objections to it; at all events it is not done at the present time.

19208. Would it not be well to try that first before going to the expense of buying school farms?—Well, I don't know now, in the country districts our children, a great many of them, walk long distances to school.

19209. There is all the more opportunity for seeing things as they pass?—They have, but the teacher cannot be with each one of those going to school and coming home.

19210. He can ask them to bring specimens of things taught in the school?—There may be something in that. But I don't think the Irish farmer would like to see a batch of children and a teacher coming to point out the faults in his crop.

19211. Does not the teaching of any subject mean the pointing out faults to a certain extent?—It does, but there would be less objection to have that done on the teacher's own farm.

19212. You can see that buying school farms all over the country would be an enormous expense?—It would take a considerable time to do it; before you can get school farms bought all over the country there will be plenty of time to try the experiment.

19213. And so, unless we are going to get a very clear gain from these school farms, it might be started by allowing the teacher to take the children out as in Germany?—Whether you can or not I don't think you will lose. I am not wanting the money for nothing. You lend money to purchase a farm in connection with a non-vested school; my principle is if you do that, why don't you do it in connection with a vested school, you lend that at 3½ per cent., which is a very good investment. The Government lend money to public boards at 3½ per cent., and they ought to lend it to us. At all events the British Government can lend money at 3½ per cent. on good security and lose nothing by it.

19214. There are some school gardens in existence at present?—Yes; I saw one in Kilkenny. I did not see much of the teaching.

19215. It has been put to us that the children are rather made use of for weeding and enabling the teacher to make some profit out of the farm?—I am glad you mentioned that; I think at the present time that should not be done, although I suppose it would be the better way of teaching farming, still I think Irish parents would object very considerably to the children being employed at labouring in connection with the school; I think they have labour enough at home. I tried two or three gardens, but something or other turned up. I tried first a garden, and after two years on a visit from Mr. Carroll it turned out there was not ground enough. I think that is a fault in the rule; the rule should specify the minimum quantity of ground, the same as you specify the minimum attendance for a first class, second class, and third class teacher. Another time I opened a garden on the school ground and they came down heavy and tough on me from Marlborough-street, because it took away from the playground; at all events they objected to it. Under our present programme you should make the best you can of both gardening and farming without having the children to do much manual work.

19216. For that purpose a very small plot might be useful?—It would; I think I had as large a plot as would be useful; however it was against the rule; the rule does not specify the size; it was left to Mr. Carroll; I think a rood would be enough, but that was some fifteen perches.

19217. Was this lately?—Seven or eight years ago.

19218. He might possibly have changed his views now?—Perhaps so.

19219. Then you have paid some attention to the teaching of agriculture in France and Denmark?—Yes.

19220. Have you seen the new French programme for instruction in agriculture?—I have not.

19221. You don't know that that programme has made a very considerable change in the direction of substituting the teaching of certain elements of science rather than of teaching agriculture directly in the schools?—I see that is the tendency in Germany; they devote a great deal of attention to the sciences.

19222. The idea being that a good general education is a better training for after professions than beginning a special study too soon?—There is a good deal to be said in favour of it. I am sure, of course the difficulty would be about how to get experiments; on land there is a good deal to be said in favour, for instance, of an elementary knowledge of chemistry, or any of the sciences as applied to agriculture would be a desirable thing, but the difficulty is how to teach these things.

19223. You spoke of Denmark as being very much advanced in dairying; are you aware that in Denmark no instruction in agriculture is given in elementary schools?—Not in the elementary schools.

19224. And the great progress of Denmark is due to higher technical schools?—Yes, so it is.

19225. One witness has suggested to us that model farms ought to be established here and there throughout the country to which the children should go after they leave school, older children of sixteen or seventeen?—We had them before and they went down, I don't think they would be of very much use, I think with the children in the country you must try and do what you can with them in the elementary school.

19226. Do you think such institutions as Glasnevin and the Munster Dairy School are very useful?—I believe they are. We had several of them through the country before, but they seemed to be a failure.

19227. Were they not attached to schools,—school farms?—Not at all, you had what we call model farms, we had one in Belfast and one in Ballymoney.

19228. What were they?—They went down and the Munster farm was about going down too; I think the *Freeman's Journal*, if I remember, had a good deal to do with arousing local opinion, and it was continued.

19229. As any one local effort has revived it?—It has.

19230. Who attended the model farms here?—They were attended by very few, there was none of them ever near where I was in the country.

19231. Did people attending the ordinary schools receive instruction in these model farms?—I don't remember.

19232. You spoke about the reading books, that you find these rather difficult?—I think they are.

19233. Would it not be an advantage to have easier reading books?—I think it would.

19234. And instead of giving 100 pages of a difficult book, to give much more of an easier book?—You might go the length of making it more difficult still. I do think that the labour of reading is too much and I would be inclined to make the books more intelligible and not add very much to the reading.

19235. Make them more intelligible in the first place?—Yes.

19236. And then get as much reading done as possible?—The inspectors and the National Board will settle what is the best to be done.

19237. Captain Shaw.—Are you acquainted with the new book on agriculture which has been issued all that in two years?—It certainly is impossible at the present time.

Belfast.

Oct. [illegible], 1897.

Rev. Thomas Quin, P.P.

19241. Do you think even a grown man, spending three hours in the week, could learn all that?—I don't think he would.

19242. It would be more useful to have a less ambitious course, and do it more thoroughly?—I think so.

19243. Do you propose that teachers should have the management of farms if attached to schools?—Yes.

19244. How much of their time should be occupied?—As far as the children are concerned, I would not give more than about half-an-hour a day.

19245. Not to cultivate the farm?—The teacher would merely superintend the cultivation.

19246. Do you contemplate he should have assistance to work the farm?—Decidedly.

19247. That would be still more expensive?—It might, but I think he would be able to make it pay.

19248. You think the teacher should provide this assistance himself?—Most decidedly.

19249. If he is given the farm he gets no assistance towards the working of it?—I would expect him to pay interest on the money the same as he does on his house. You lend the money to the manager, as you do to build a house, and he would pay. If you would pay half the interest, as you do on the residence, it would be all the better.

19250. Do you consider that the teachers as a rule have sufficient agricultural knowledge?—I don't think they have.

19251. How would you propose they should get that?—There are teachers that have and others should be made to have. It is a drawback to the teachers in training that they don't get better opportunities, but you must begin somewhere. If a boy was a monitor in a school where there was a garden, and then went on to be a teacher and got instruction in training, it would greatly improve him. There are some more that would not have the taste for that.

19252. Do you think it would be desirable to start another course of agriculture, say in the scientific direction, and send round instructors to various centres, and let the two run side by side, have one school working the old and another the new system, and see which is the most efficient in the end for educational purposes?—The persons who would attend these teachers who go around would be grown persons.

19253. Would the teachers themselves, who would have to teach scientifically?—I think that would be a very good thing that before a teacher got charge of a school farm he should go to some place, and he is bound at the present time to do so—go to Glasnevin or to that place in Wexford; it should be part of his qualification for taking charge of his school farm that he should undergo a course of training in connection with farming, the same as he has to undergo training for anything else.

19254. Mr. Molloy.—I think, Father Quin, that prior to your taking charge of the parish of [illegible] you had extensive experience of school work in Belfast for many years?—Pretty fair.

19255. With regard to your last observation about farming, would you think it advisable that training colleges should have farms attached to them?—I think

pupils; as a matter of fact agricultural pupils resided at those places?—Yes.

19258. You are more in favour, perhaps, of school gardens attached to schools, than farms?—Certainly.

19259. And would you experience much difficulty in getting that land?—In the county Antrim, with which I am acquainted myself, there is a good deal of selling of land, that is more in the way of farms. I had several opportunities of buying land. I must say that I have been applying for ten or twelve years to the National Board on this matter. In the North of Ireland you will get land in the market, at least I got several chances to get a small portion, a rood or so; you will get that, but you will have to pay pretty well for it; a man does not like to part with a rood of land.

19260. You called attention, and properly, in my opinion, to the great difference of treatment as regards vested and non-vested schools; somewhere about 1884 an Act of Parliament was passed—I think it is dated 19th April—giving special facilities to non-vested schools to have farms attached. You would strongly advocate the great propriety of that taking place also in the case of vested schools?—Yes.

19261. In fact, of the two it seems more natural it should apply in the case of vested schools?—Yes, there is a good deal of care taken before money is advanced for a vested school, and there is a good deal of more likelihood of its continuing to exist than a non-vested school.

19262. And similarly as the Government give aid for the erection of teachers' residences, there might be a garden attached to the residence?—There should; I am inclined to think it is an absolute necessity in order that the teacher should be able to teach his pupils what he is bound to teach them at the present time.

19263. Have you ever tried any industrial work apart from the idea of the farm, and what was your experience of it?—I tried my hand at hand loom weaving one time. About 50 or 60 years ago, before the power looms started in Belfast, in the county Antrim, at all events, at that time there were three or four weaving looms in almost every house, except in the case of some very large farms. And a very comfortable thing it was, because a farm of five or ten acres at that time used to give the weaver his potatoes and corn and other things, and milk and butter at first cost, and he was, on the whole, very comfortable. There is a person in my parish, a woman, who went through all the processes of managing flax, saving the seed, and spinning. After a short time, when Belfast went ahead here, the spinning by the old wheel seemed to be done away with. But still hand loom weaving continued, dropping away gradually. There was a good share of it when I went to Rasharkin about fourteen years ago. It was in rather a depressed condition, and then it revived and went down and revived again. And I thought as it had existed forty years within forty miles of the most powerful power loom machinery in the world that there was something in it. Looking into the matter, what struck me was that the loom had made no change since the days of wooden ploughs. I applied to the National Board for money to enable the thing to be working better, it would not weave at all. The difficulty arose from the fact that the cloth we were weaving [was] heavier than the cloth they are weaving. In the ordinary hand loom the thread turns round one beam, and as it is being woven the cloth is turned round another. The hand loom weaver after he weaves up a portion had to come off and open up the whole thing in order to turn round the portion he had woven. In the power loom here they have clockwork machinery, by which the two beams are constantly turning, and I thought if that could be applied to the hand loom it would be an improvement and a great saving of time. There is another thing too, the hand loom weaver has what he calls temples, that catch in the selvage and keep it pressed out. In the power loom there is something like what you hold a bundle of papers by, clips, and these are by other machinery gradually moved on too, whereas the hand loom weaver has to keep moving them in taking off them. The loom was to be weighted to a certain extent to keep the cloth firm, and our cloth seemed to be so heavy that when the beam moved at all it was not able to keep it firm enough. I suppose I might have gone further into it, but a number of things turned up; the position of the teacher became very much improved, and every mother was sending her daughter to school to become a teacher, not to become a weaver, and sometimes the power loom was encroaching on the hand loom, which was going out of date. Indeed, I had a correspondence with the secretary of the Baroness Burdett Coutts, who has had a good deal of experience in these matters, and who seemed to think the days of hand loom weaving were numbered.

19264. At what time of the day had you instruction in this weaving?—I had not instruction at all, it never went the length of that, it never came to anything practical. I thought if I could get some loom better than the ordinary one, that was No. 1, but there were a number of other difficulties that arose, and the hand loom industry is unfortunately a thing of the past in our country now.

19265. Had you a special room for the purpose?—I intended that.

19266. Supposing it had taken practical shape would the instruction have been carried on out of ordinary school hours?—Not necessarily.

19267. Not in the continuation school?—Not necessarily.

19268. You did not expect that that would interfere with the literary instruction of pupils?—Of course it should be done in such a way that it would not.

19269. The time that you contemplated for the practical instruction in weaving, could not that be devoted to the instruction in manual training and giving more attention to elementary science?—I am sure it could.

19270. Have you ever introduced cookery?—No, I have not; I think we must have gardening before we have cookery; whatever may be the line to be drawn between theory and practice, I am afraid a theoretical dinner would be a poor thing.

19271. Mr. STRUTHERS.—Would you teach the [illegible]

complained about bringing things to market, Irish people can't do that. I tried one time an industry in Derry, you will meet it there, shirtmaking. They get the material from the Derry factories, cut out shirts, and take them to some of the convents and give them out—just as yarn used to be given—to girls to make the shirts. The programme of the sixth class would be something like the making of a shirt. Well I tried to introduce it. We have comparatively few in the sixth class, and the girls did not seem to care for it.

19275. Are any of your teachers qualified to give instruction in kindergarten?—Yes.

19276. You have some teachers trained, if I mistake not?—I have them all trained.

19277. And the female teachers, I presume, all are qualified in the kindergarten?—Yes.

19278. Have you ever thought of introducing it?—I have tried it this year, it is going on six or eight months.

19279. So far what is your experience?—Well, of course, I have only very little, I can only go on the general principle of object teaching that it ought to be beneficial, but I have not sufficient experience to enable me as yet to speak of it.

19280. It is, however, a favourite subject, is it not, with the teachers, who are trained?—Well, with some.

19281. Touching reading books, of course you are aware that if you submit to the Commissioners any series other than their own and the series happens to be free from objectionable matter, you can introduce it into your school?—Yes, I understand that.

19282. You would like a simple series?—I would, of course, but I have heard from very fine teachers that the change has not been much of an improvement in Blackie's or [illegible]'s series.

19283. By a recent regulation explanations in the subject matter has become a sine qua non in connection with reading, are you in favour of that?—Oh, I think so.

19284. That the pupils should have some intelligent comprehension of what they are reading?—I think so.

19285. Are you able to compare the state of schools now with the period prior to the introduction of results?—I could not do that. The result system came in the first year I came on the mission, 1871 or 1872.

Tralee.

Oct. [illegible]

Rev. Thomas Quin, P.P.

19286. On the whole what is your opinion of the present results system, subject to the modifications you propose?—There is one thing I have been watching, there is one thing not said about it that I think might. If it could be made a test. Take a boy on the second stage of sixth or a girl either, and the question arose that used to be discussed some years ago in the *Daily Telegraph*, what are we to do with our boys, before you make up your mind what you should do with your boy, it would be a nice thing to know what you could do with him. And if the result system were anything like a good ideal when a boy had passed in the two stages of fifth and first stage of sixth it would be a very good and useful test of what he could do. Somehow or other the gentlemen in charge of the boarding schools don't like to admit a boy because he is unfit. A boy may be fit to pass his examination, but if the parents, or if I, as a clergyman, take up his result sheet it would be a very good test and give instruction what a parent should do with the boy.

19287. Would you be in favour of giving certificates on leaving school to successful pupils?—It would be a little awkward. A teacher's character, or the character of the school, ought to be, like Cæsar's wife, held in very high esteem. A teacher may do his work very well, and yet, in some cases boys or girls did not pass well there is very great danger that the parents would throw the blame on the teacher, and thereby his influence would be impaired somewhat. I would be slow about that.

19288. One of the witnesses advocated the propriety of giving prizes to successful pupils by way of encouragement?—I think it is a great pity that has not been done, something in the nature of the intermediate and also for attendance, prizes should be given for those who make 100 days.

19289. At one time you are aware that in connection with all the model schools the National Board gave prizes to the successful answerers?—Yes.

19290. And if I mistake not you were one of those who advocated the extension of it to the ordinary schools?—I certainly think so, for poor children, and their parents make considerable sacrifices at the present time in sending them to school.

n their respective schools. The duty would be, in the first place, to give the principles of [illegible] their schools; secondly to give a fair [illegible] poultry rearing, of the qualities both [illegible] for producing eggs. With regard to [illegible] they should be able to give instruction as to the best breeds of cattle, the best [illegible] and see more particularly that they [illegible] diffuse throughout the country.—the [illegible] the necessity of spraying potatoes. I [illegible] this year it is very hard to calculate [illegible] of money has been lost by the non-[illegible] throughout the country of a system of [illegible] can speak practically on that subject, [illegible] to have observed it with more than [illegible] that those who have sprayed their [illegible] have a comparatively good crop of [illegible] with those who have not it is almost [illegible], so that there is very little share of [illegible] money lost to the country this year by [illegible] of that system. It would take [illegible] my calculations, about £20,000 yearly [illegible]. I add not only to the salaries of [illegible] I add to their travelling expenses. [illegible] about 1[illegible] teachers (leaving about five [illegible] in case of sickness) at £100 each as [illegible] would say the salary for females should [illegible] rising by £5 a year for ten years, and [illegible] males should commence by £150, [illegible] also of £5 a year for ten years, [illegible] amount to £150 and £200 respectively, [illegible] pension of £2 a year for each year's [illegible] certain number of years. That would [illegible]; travelling expenses, 10s. a day for [illegible], £12,500, making in all about [illegible] each of these district centres there [illegible] stock, with the necessary imple-[illegible] should also be taught (a training [illegible] knowledge of handicraft. I don't mean [illegible] should be able to become a carpenter [illegible], but should be able to give a knowledge [illegible] to boys, so that they might go to [illegible] own, or if they become farmers [illegible] be able to do the great bulk of the [illegible] their places. There is an amount of [illegible] very foolishly on tradesmen for [illegible] be done by the farmers themselves.

[illegible] it be your opinion, Dean, that the [illegible] school teacher, should undertake [illegible] up his literary work?—The bulk [illegible] should be done outside literary [illegible] might take an hour off the present [illegible] salary. The best time for a teacher [illegible] be in night schools, or he should [illegible] hours to four o'clock or thereabouts, [illegible] he could divide the younger [illegible] fourth class, or whatever class would [illegible] instruct in this handicraft and in another day themselves while they would be in the school.

19726. No doubt it would be very valuable instruction for the teachers?—It is not merely the pupils I would have brought into this instruction both in dairying and in handicraft, but also ex-pupils, and even the wives and daughters of surrounding farmers, because I have had a little experience of that class of training in a small way in Dungannon. We had one of the Board's dairy instructresses down there some years ago, unfortunately the area of her influence was limited, but it produced good results.

19727. You also spoke of chemistry, what have you to say on that subject?—I think it is absolutely necessary that the children should have a knowledge of the elementary principles of chemistry. First, with regard to food; I think that there is a great want at the present time of a series of lessons on the relative values of human foods. There is an immense waste, and at the same time, a very considerable injury to health, especially in large towns, by the class of food used, nothing but foreign foods, with the result that the people are losing their blood and colour and strength. I don't know where it is going to end unless there could be some lessons introduced on principles of hygiene in our schools, for if we don't commence at a proper time it is impossible to inculcate them, and if people at a certain age go on drinking tea six times a day, it is very hard to break them off it. The importance should be impressed on children of using more standard food, which would be cheaper than the present food, and far more nutritious, and better for health and strength. A slight knowledge of chemistry would be absolutely necessary for those engaged in that class of work.

19728. You also would advocate some of these branches; what time would you specify for teaching them?—Either the dairy work, poultry work, or handicraft—I say the bulk of them should be done after school hours, or you might take one hour out of the present school time, and give another hour at the part outside the present school time, either by prolonging it up to four o'clock, or in the evening.

19729. We have got the opinion of many witnesses with regard to the result system, and we would like to know yours?—I think the result system has been a great benefit to the country on the whole, it has improved the standard of education as far as my experience goes, but it is capable of improvement in one or two points. In the first place, it has led too much to a system of cram of memory, and has not given sufficient scope to the development of the intellectual faculties. The second drawback is that it has put the children too much on a dead level. In my capacity as manager of an intermediate school in Dungannon, I have had [illegible] experience of it, we have had boys competing for free places in one of these Royal schools, largely supported by Royal endowment, and we h[illegible]

18301. You heard the previous witness about school gardens, and so on; from your wide experience what would you say?—I think it is absolutely necessary that a school should have a garden or a small farm of land, in order that agriculture may be taught practically. In case one or other could not be acquired it is possible managers might make arrangements with an adjoining farmer to get a plot, in case, say for five years, so as to go through a rotation of crops. He would not like to sell that, but he might not have any objection to give it as a concern, or he might let you experiment on one portion of ground where he was putting in a crop.

18302. Mr. Molloy.—Monsignor, you advocate strongly that there should be a special male organiser, and also a female organiser in every district?—Yes.

18303. Well, we have about sixty of these districts, and of the sixty more than half happen to be town districts, such as Belfast, would you advocate that for Belfast?—Not dairy work, but I would handicraft.

18304. Even in such places as Belfast, Cork, Dublin, and leading towns?—Leave out the dairy business or poultry, but the male organiser should be there as well.

18305. These specialists should be well up in handicraft, and perhaps also in physical science?—Precisely, and in drawing too. I should say drawing is an essential.

18306. What part would you allow the ordinary teachers of the school in the instruction of pupils in these special branches?—The very same subjects that the organisers were supposed to teach themselves. They were to introduce a knowledge of practical dairywork to all their pupils of fifth and sixth class as soon as they were capable of acquiring a knowledge of it, and the duty of the organisers would be simply to go round and examine yearly, and also give some instructions themselves for a day or two in the school, because they would not have more than fifty or sixty schools to attend to in the year, and they have about 200 working days in the year, so that they could give three or four days to each.

18307. And in the absence of the special organiser would you contemplate the ordinary teacher carrying on the subject?—Unquestionably; teaching it as a part of his daily programme. I don't see in what other way it can be brought home to the people of the country.

18308. But in such places as Dublin and Belfast, you would give a decided preference to physical science?—Unquestionably. This is a place in which all the people turn to some mechanical business or profession.

18309. In rural places you would advocate the propriety of having a school garden, and if possible a small farm attached?—Yes, of five or six acres.

18310. Either attached to the school or the teacher's residence, or some way available, like that plan you advocate, the concern system?—The advantage of the farm would be that it would give an opportunity of judging the value of stock and testing the value of different feeding stuffs and manures.

18311. Do any of your teachers give instructions in handicraft?—Not in any except sewing.

18312. Drawing?—Yes; our teachers teach drawing in the ... schools ...

what they heard, and I saw afterwards an improvement in the butter myself.

18317. Did not the effect of that instruction increase the price of dairy produce?—There is one thing certain, it increased the quality, it was not sufficiently extensive to affect the price. All the townspeople said it was immensely improved, but, like everything else, unfortunately, the effect of knowledge of that kind dies away if it is not kept constantly renewed.

18318. I believe there was a local committee organised in connection with that?—Yes; Col. Burges took an active part, and the managers of schools.

18319. Would you advocate the propriety of having associations of managers acting as advising bodies, representing or calling attention to local needs, for the information of the central body of Commissioners of National Education in Dublin?—I should say it would be attended with very good results.

18320. I believe some commencement has been made in your neighbourhood?—We have a committee of managers whose business it is to make suggestions to the Commissioners of Education, and any observations on defects in the system generally.

18321. Of course such associations as these would put forward with great effect local needs?—I am not authorised by them to give evidence here, because, unfortunately, we had not time to hold a meeting since it was arranged I should come, but I think I am expressing pretty fairly the views of the managers of our diocese.

18322. And you represent the committee of managers?—Yes, but I am not here in my representative capacity. I am giving my own views, but I think they are to a great extent the views of the managers.

18323. Rev. Dr. Evans.—You mentioned Commissioners of Education, did you mean a different body from the Commissioners of National Education?—I don't remember mentioning them—it is the Commissioners of National Education I mean.

18324. Mr. Molloy.—And you would think corresponding associations advisable throughout the country generally?—I should say so.

18325. Capt. Shaw.—Have you considered what the average age of children leaving school is?—With us, unfortunately, it is rather young, because we have factories in Dungannon.

18326. But throughout the country?—Well, it is rather young.

18327. Is the average age thirteen?—It would be under that considerably.

18328. Then how long would it be before these children would have an opportunity of putting into practice the agriculture which you advocate they should be taught?—I think if the children of the county districts found this was being taught it would be a great inducement to keep them longer at school.

18329. At any rate they would not have the management of farms, or be able to work them for some considerable number of years after they got instruction?—No, nor do I mean for a moment to confine this instruction to children at the schools.

18330. Would not such instruction be much better given to persons of seventeen or twenty?—I think I mentioned that; I said that these lessons were to be given not only to pupils but also to the daughters and wives of farmers; I would say to the sons of farmers

Belfast.

Oct. 18, 1887.

Right Rev. Monsignor Byrne, P.P., V.G.

not at all particular as to what Board should have charge of this. I am not saying the Commissioners of National Education would be the best Board, I think there is some little promise of a Board of Agriculture, and it is very possible that the money would come through that Board. I am not particular what Board should take charge of it.

19333. You say they should know the best quality of cattle?—Yes.

19334. Is there any use teaching that theoretically?—It will be useful to the younger people to have a knowledge from the book itself.

19335. Do you think they would recognise a particular breed of cattle or sheep from a book description?—Certainly not, but if they got the knowledge from the book, and then bring them to a farm where the cattle would be seen.

19336. That would entail having large farms well stocked?—Oh, no, it would not be necessary at all, you could have a good breed of cattle on a small farm, one cow with one or two calves; you can see how the calves thrive and are fed as compared with some on neighbouring farms. When a man calls a calf which is of a better breed than his neighbours and gets more for it, and it has been fed on different food and has improved more in size than his neighbour's, that has an educating effect on the child.

19337. Grazing farmers generally hold a good deal of land and are in pretty good condition, would you say they are the majority in Ireland?—We have 500,000 farmers in Ireland altogether and the majority must be small farmers. Of course in Ulster they are almost all small farmers.

19338. A great number of holdings are merely used as a support of the family, in which tillage is a very important matter?—Yes.

19339. Those large farmers are generally well-to-do, don't you think they would be in a position to contribute something towards the education of their sons?—I am sorry to say that my experience with regard to the large farmers does not correspond with yours. No class in the community are suffering more than our large farmers of 70 or 80 acres in Ulster who have to pay high for labour.

19340. Don't you think they are in a position of life in which they would prefer to provide this instruction for themselves as far as they can?—No, I should say if they got instruction for nothing, they would have no objection to take it. There is no class in the community in Ulster that seem to be so little suffering from poverty and want as those who have got small farms and can cultivate them within themselves and have not to pay a shilling for hired labour. But I happen to know from friends of my own who have large farms and have to pay for anything that they can hardly make ends meet.

19341. Have you considered the system of agriculture in France, that is that the young children from eleven onwards should be taught to make careful experiments in natural science and chemistry, so that they may learn the value of experiments and be able to apply it in agriculture afterwards, and thus test how they may get the best results on their land?—I doubt very much whether it would pay in Ireland. I would advocate instruction in stock and small industries, and fruit and poultry.

19342. But will experiments are useful in such to observe increase of weight?—What I mean is that in the mere raising of crops of barley or oats no matter what amount of science you apply to it, I don't see how it would pay for the purpose of sale.

19343. If a farmer wants to find out at present whether he is doing well or not, he is not in a position to do so because he cannot make accurate experiments; if they were to make experiments so that they might each learn for themselves, don't you think that would be rather a good thing?—It would, but it might be too dearly bought.

19344. That is a training young children can get easily?—If it does not interfere with the acquisition of more useful knowledge I would see no objection to their learning it.

19345. You advocate chemistry, they would learn it in learning chemistry or in natural science?—I don't see any decided objection to it, provided it could be kept within limits and would not interfere with the acquisition of other branches of knowledge that would be more useful to them in after life. I think too many of our people have an objection to trade, I think that is objectionable.

19346. Have you considered the [illegible] course, as at present laid down?—Yes, that is what is taught at the present moment. I understand from Professor Carroll's evidence, at Glasnevin, that is about as much as you could expect in this country. In Sweden and Norway they go in for it much more largely.

19347. But they don't do nearly so extensive a course as is laid down for our children under the National Board?—I see they go in very largely there.

19348. They devote more time, but don't attempt so many subjects?—That may be. There are certain industries in which there might be instruction given in this country, such as basket-making. I think there is a great opening for that. There is a good soil for growing willows and osiers, and there is such a demand now for baskets for parcel post.

19349. Should not such a course be rather taught in a continuation school?—Yes, no doubt, but they might get some of the first principles in our primary schools.

19350. Do you know anything of the cause of the failure of model farms such as Balmoral?—I had no experience of that particular farm, but I can explain how farms of that kind would fail where you have to pay a high rate of wages for everything done on the farm.

19351. I don't mean failing to pay as a commercial concern?—Yes, it was not patronised. I think there was some kind of prejudice in the country that scientific farming would not pay, those who tried it got tired of it.

19352. But has not the science of agriculture made tremendous strides since those farms were established thirty years ago?—Well the science has made tremendous strides, I am afraid remunerative prices have not made corresponding strides for the farmer.

19353. Don't you think if you had a model farm now you could give more information which farmers generally have not than you could thirty years ago?—It is possible to give more knowledge, but I don't see that that knowledge would be of much use to the bulk of the farmers of the country, here in the North at least, because with our small farmers [illegible] machinery that might be introduced in large farms but are out of place with us unfortunately.

19354. Mr. STRUTHERS.—I think your plan is for the organisation of technical education throughout the country?—Yes.

19355. Instruction in poultry-keeping, knowledge of feeding stuffs, manures and seeds—that instruction would be better given to people already engaged in the industry?—I should say they would understand it better, but at the same time I think the children in school should be trained in the trades, and when they advance a little more they would be better able to appreciate the knowledge they acquire afterwards.

19356. You contemplate extern people coming to these classes?—Certainly but only outside school hours, in the ordinary school hours only pupils of the school should be instructed, and then over and above that I would give evening classes at which externs should attend.

19357. I thought all this instruction was to be given outside school hours?—No, I make provision that about an hour should be saved from the present programme.

19358. Your scheme is two-fold—that there should be afternoon or evening classes for grown people and then classes in the school?—Yes, in the school only principles should be taught and instruction in dairying part of class books, and in the evening get the practical instruction necessary.

19359. Which of these two do you think would be more practically useful, instruction given to children in the school or instruction given to pupils in the evening?—Of course the evening would be immediately useful, but at the same time I believe the principles are absolutely necessary to be implanted in the minds of children during school hours.

19360. But many of the children in the school might not be going to keep poultry or bees, or have anything to do with seeds or manures?—I think the general knowledge of these things has an educating effect.

19361. You would not teach these subjects specifically?—Certainly not.

19362. I suppose you would distinguish between the instruction to be given to the older pupils who are already engaged in the industry and come there to get tips, so to speak, in their special work, and the instruction to be given to the pupils in the schools?—Unquestionably.

19363. The instruction to be given in the evening would be entirely of a practical character?—I would let them go through the handicraft work with a plane and chisel in the evening.

19364. Take that first, the instruction to be given to the older pupils in the evening, that would have to be of a thoroughly practical kind?—Certainly.

19365. And would have to be taught by people who had a thorough knowledge of the subject, such as the ordinary schoolmaster could not be expected to have at present?—I don't agree with you there.

19366. At present?—Well, it is possible that at present the ordinary school teacher would not have it.

19367. Don't you contemplate giving these special instructions?—Yes.

19368. For the purpose of having the school teacher sufficiently instructed in the special subjects so as to be able to give information to the people of his district, you would institute this body of special experts who would collect the teachers in centres and instruct them?—Yes, and give occasional lessons themselves by inspecting classes and showing how the work was done.

19369. Then you want to give some instruction to the younger children, such instruction as would prepare the children to benefit by such instruction afterwards?—Certainly. I would give them technical knowledge.

19370. What we have to consider is what is the best kind of education to fit these people to profit by the more advanced lectures later on?—Get your school books arranged so as to contain ample information on the subjects in which they are to be trained practically afterwards.

19371. Do you think it is information rather than habits of study that are required?—It is information at that period, what is the best way to treat this and what is the best way to treat that.

19372. Don't you think what is wanted is rather a good general education?—I propose that to be part of his education.

19373. What do you propose as the object then of this special instruction you are giving in the schools?—In the first place with regard to those who will be required to be engaged in that class of work in after life, that will lay the foundations for perfect knowledge later on, and for those who will never require it at all, I think it is no harm to have a gentlemanly knowledge of these subjects.

19374. Might we say of all the education to be given to children in an elementary school, that it should be of a general kind such as would be profitable to the child in after life, no matter what occupation he goes to?—Yes, I would devote only an hour a day to technical work in school.

19375. Don't you think you might attain your object by modifying the present subjects instead of adding a new one?—I say some of the present subjects could be dispensed with.

19376. Might it not to be put in this way—they might be taught on better methods?—That is included in what I say. You might add on some subjects and take away others. You would make a rearrangement of the time and of the subjects.

19377. For instance, you would have more practical teaching of arithmetic?—I don't think you could add much to it at present.

19378. I don't mean add, but changing the character of the instruction so as to lay more stress on expert calculation?—Yes, I see no objection to that; but I would not like to see the present arithmetical programme enlarged.

19379. Not enlarged, but changing, making it more practical?—I agree with you.

19380. And the reading instruction made more practical, and such lessons as you allude to introduced to vary the reading?—Precisely.

19381. Would you consider drawing a necessary part of a good general education?—Absolutely.

19382. You would also consider some instruction in observation and, say, elementary science lessons, object lessons to begin with, followed by experiments later on?—Yes.

19383. That you would consider an essential part of a good general education?—Precisely.

19384. Would you consider some training of the hand in the construction of things also useful?—Yes, that is what I mean by handicraft.

19385. Some extension of what are known as kindergarten exercises of a simple character?—Yes, kindergarten is good as far as it goes; but I agree with some of the witnesses that unfortunately there is a break when a child leaves the infant school and commences in after years some of the subjects of technical education.

19386. It is a pity to think that kindergarten is to be restricted to the infant school?—Yes, it is a great mistake. I have had large experience of kindergarten and I am delighted with it.

19387. You propose having sixty organisers, sixty males and sixty females, two of them attached to each district?—It is possible that fewer might do, in the case of large city schools, where they would not be necessary.

19388. You would not propose starting all these teachers at once, you would begin gradually?—I would say the sooner they are started the better.

19389. Suppose you began by having two for each province, and see how they would succeed?—I think that has been rather a mistake in the past; we are only touching the fringe of the population in all our movements.

19390. You have been going rather on the other tack, starting things on too complete a scale, establishing model schools all over the country and then giving them up?—Model schools were established before my time.

19391. But still it is an illustration of what has been done in Ireland?—I suppose there was no Commission of Inquiry before these were established as there is at present.

19392. Is not that rather a warning to begin any new movement gradually?—This movement may be new in Ireland, but it is not new in other countries. We are behind every other country in the world in technical education.

19393. You have an admirably organised scheme, but it is much more extensive, I think you will find, than in any other country?—The difficulty of getting teachers, I think, is very slight. If the Commissioners issued a printed notice to-morrow to all the first-class teachers, and stated the requirements, you would have plenty of applicants—splendid material—who could get their training in less than twelve months.

Dublin.
Oct. [illegible], 1897.
[illegible]

19394. Do you think twelve months training would be enough?—I should say so, and with regard to dairy business, much less.

19395. That would be a matter for experiment to test. I am referring to the effect these teachers would have when they got out to the country. On the face of it, it is a very promising scheme, but it is new, and people don't quite realise what it is. Might it not be well to have its usefulness thoroughly established by experimenting in a few districts first?—As a matter of fact, we have experimented in dairy business in a small way, and the only drawback was that the classes were not sufficiently general to be appreciably felt.

19396. Did you find the dairy classes well attended?—Very well attended; at first there was some difficulty but before long they were well understood.

19397. Would you not think some local contributions should be made towards the support of these teachers?—I am afraid it would be very unpopular. Suppose we were a very rich country, I should see no objection to pay, in fact I have always felt that giving things for nothing is not a good plan in Ireland, but this would not come to anyone's door more than another's.

19398. Do you know it is a general principle of the Education Department in England and Scotland that they only contribute one penny for one penny; if one penny is contributed from the locality, they give one penny from the State funds. Perhaps it would be too much to expect such a large proportion in Ireland, but would it not be fair to make a condition that there should be some local contribution?—Unless you introduced it as a tax that can be enforced there is no possibility of raising it otherwise.

19399. Would it not be a good plan that this experiment should be started in districts where the people would be willing to contribute something?—There are very few such districts in Ireland. There is a feeling that we have not much money to spare for anything at present.

19400. Captain Shaw.—Are there any instances of rates being levied for technical education?—In a few large cities; but I would like to see you attempting to levy a rate in Cookstown or Dungannon.

19401. Mr. Struthers.—There is a technical education rate levied in Galway?—I suppose it is very trifling. It is possible we might be willing to give a trifle.

19402. Don't you think if people did give a trifle to the starting of these centres they would take a greater interest in them afterwards?—I agree with the principle that things we pay for we appreciate better.

19403. And you think it desirable that people should contribute the trifle?—I agree with you so far.

19404. Rev. Dr. Evans.—We are not a Technical Education Commission, and very much of the information with which you have favoured us, is more appropriate to technical schools than to primary schools in Ireland. What we want to ascertain is how we may introduce manual instruction into our National schools and make it a part of our primary system for educating children all over the country. Can you make any suggestion that would help us in regard to that?—Nothing further than what I have said with regard to manual instruction—that is, that I should wish to see every National teacher in Ireland trained thoroughly himself in the more elementary principles of chemistry, so that he could teach his class afterwards.

19405. Have you considered the present programme of the Board for school purposes?—Yes.

19406. Would you wish to see it altered or modified in any way?—No; I think if it were carried out universally—but you see it leaves many subjects called "extras" to the option of the teacher, and the teachers will take up whatever subjects will pay them best, as is natural enough.

19407. You said to Mr. Struthers that you would not be in favour of increasing the programme in arithmetic, but rather in favour of curtailing it. Do you think there is enough of the theory of arithmetic taught?—Unquestionably too much for the vast majority of our children.

19408. Have you looked much into the questions that are given in schools at results examinations?—Yes, we have had practical experience ourselves in that examination for our Academy.

19409. And you think these are of a practical character, and show there is a theoretical knowledge of arithmetic?—Yes.

19410. And they are not put from certain books made up of questions of all sorts and types, and the children taught to work them, while at the same time they are entirely ignorant of the principles of arithmetic, and could not reason them out?—I fully agree with you that perhaps the knowledge is not sufficiently practical.

19411. How would it be possible, do you think, to have dairying taught in connexion with our National schools at all?—I should say so.

19412. And would it be possible to have poultry management taught in our primary schools?—Certainly.

19413. How would a male teacher teach it?—In my scheme I reserve that for the female teacher.

19414. Have you seen our Agricultural Text-book—the new edition of it?—No, I have not.

19415. But it would be easier, I suppose, to teach something of the theory of arithmetic in the schools than to teach agriculture?—Yes.

Mr. Wesley Forbes, Teacher, Tullycarnet National School, Belfast, examined.

19416. Chairman.—You are a National school teacher?—Yes.

19417. Where is your school?—Four miles from here, out at Knock, county Down side.

19418. What assistance have you in the school?—I have one monitor only.

19419. Have you been teaching a long time?—Twenty-nine years.

19420. Are you favourable to manual instruction in National schools?—If the present programme was so modified and improved as to allow it, I would be.

19421. You think it would be an advantage?—Yes, I do.

19422. Would it be any advantage to the teacher himself, do you think?—My opinion is that all teachers would have an interest in it; whether it would be an advantage I don't know.

19423. With regard to the programme, would you curtail some of the subjects?—Yes, I would curtail them all very largely; I would take the useless matter out of them and keep what is useful.

19424. That answer implies, from your experience as a teacher, that there is a considerable amount of useless matter in the subjects you have to teach?—Yes, sir, I am of that opinion.

19425. You would be in favour of the introduction of science?—Yes, I would be very strong on that point.

19426. What description of science would you introduce?—The particular science would, of course, depend on the localities where it was taught, having perhaps some relation to the industries of the people in the localities.

19427. It would vary would you say with the locality?—Certainly.

19428. Rev. Dr. Evans.—How long are you a teacher?—I am twenty-nine years odd in the service of the Board.

19429. You are in the first class?—In my twenty-first year.

19430. Have you begun to give explanations of reading in your school?—I don't remember when I began to do it. I always explain reading, but I have never begun to prepare for the new examinations in reading, that is, I mean to say that I have not begun to explain every word in the reading book, word for word.

19431. Well, you know that special explanation is required now?—I do.

19432. And you have got the circular about it?—Yes.

19433. Will that take more time from you?—If I spent all my time at reading every day in the year I could not teach reading to pass one pupil if the inspector chose to take the largest view of the new programme.

19434. Well, if the programme was large enough before, and if it is enlarged now by special explanation having to be given in connection with reading, how would you suggest the introduction of manual instruction—where can you find time for it?—First I would make the programme right, and then I would introduce manual instruction afterwards.

19435. And what would you do now to lessen the programme?—I will tell you my own work. I commence at half past eight in the morning and work to four o'clock, and I have done that for the last sixteen years at any rate.

19436. What is the average attendance in your school?—For last year it was sixty-five.

19437. And you have no assistant?—No assistant.

19438. And you have to teach your sixty-five children in nine classes?—Yes.

19439. Well, you have got a pretty severe burden on your back?—I have it so severe that I cannot do it. I can only pick out the parts that will be most useful on examination day; I teach those and leave what cannot be done behind.

19440. I understand that you are in favour of manual instruction?—Certainly.

19441. What benefit will accrue to the children who receive it?—It will make them more generally useful at home in their domestic relationship; a little acquaintance with tools should enable them to dispense with tradesmen in trivial repairs in their after life.

19442. It will improve them in self use?—Yes.

19443. It will sharpen their wits as well as make them more handy with their hands?—It will.

19444. It will enable them to see more correctly—a great many people stare, they don't see?—It will make them more observant, and that is one thing we neglect altogether in our school education.

19445. Would it enlarge their capacities generally?—It would in this way, that it would make them more useful, supposing they went out as farm labourers, if they could do a little repair to a bit of machinery that got out of order. A tradesman might otherwise have to be called in for what a little handiness would repair.

19446. Would you be surprised to hear that in

as to make the education of the pupils
d ?—Yes.
nd give them a good general education
through a workshop alone would be d
had the tools lying about, they would
ives without having any instruction; in
he way I got my own interest in technical

at might be what a witness called un-
unscientific use of tools?—It might be

19503. But that is only to keep them up in the programme of the classes they have passed through. You are aware an examination goes back, so as to include the previous portion as well?—Yes.

19504. But that concentrates the time largely?—It keeps that particular class from being idle, that particular class that has passed through the lower one.

19505. You refer to the recent regulation with regard to explanation in connexion with the reading lesson?—Yes.

19506. Is there any substantial difference between the recent instruction and what was always laid down as an injunction by the National Board, namely, that pupils should be acquainted with the meaning of words and phrases and with the subject matter of the lesson read—what difference do you establish between that and the publication of the recent instruction?—It all depends on the interpretation. "Instruction" might be interpreted to mean anything.

19507. In the recent circular?—Yes, it certainly gives the liberty of asking every individual word of the lesson book.

19508. But the old programme, that you rather praise, and that you say you carried out practically, was that the pupils must be acquainted with the meaning of words and phrases, as well as the subject matter of the lesson. I am reading from the code in force for the twenty-five years?—That instruction did not refer to the pass mark at all.

19509. That is a different matter—I wanted to bring that out from you—but was it not laid down as an injunction as regards the method of teaching the subject?—Oh, yes; it was always understood that the meaning of words would be taught.

19510. And did it not form a practical part of the inspector's examination?—Yes, always, the meaning of words.

19511. And the subject matter, the general drift of the lesson?—Yes; each subject is divided into several parts, there are subheads there is the pass mark, which, of course, is the important thing in the eyes of the inspector.

19512. Would you not think the important thing, not so much the fee, as to make the subject intelligible and teach the child properly?—Yes, I think that would be carried out by a child understanding the general gist of the sentence, rather than that he should be able to go into each word and give a detailed meaning for it.

19513. My point is this, that really all along, since the establishment of the results system, explanation ought to have formed an important part of the instruction and necessarily formed a part of the examination by the inspector?—That is so.

19514. So that, strictly speaking, the publication of the recent instruction did not lead to any fundamental difference on that point?—No, only it makes a difference in what is called a pass mark; it makes it possible that we won't get any pass in reading at all.

19515. But you yourself mentioned a while ago that it was your practice all along the line for the last twenty-nine years to give instruction in the meaning of words, and especially in the drift of the passage?—Especially in the drift of the passage; but now, according to that rule rather special attention should be given to the meaning of words, and it would be more important than the meaning of the passage.

19516. I think you will find that it rather amalgamates the two; with regard to the payment of the fee, it substantially leaves the necessity for giving instruction in explanation pretty much as it was before?—Yes; it is just in the same position as I state.

Belfast. Oct. [illegible], 18[illegible]. Mr. Wesley [illegible].

Glasnevin for a short course of six or eight weeks, would you still have an objection to connect your garden with the Board and participate in those advantages?—I would have no objection; the only difficulty is about the qualification.

19540. I take it for granted that being a minister as regards the [illegible] you ought to have no difficulty about the certificate, you can come up during your vacation?—Just now I have never had time, my vacation is taken up with gardening.

Rev. George Magill, Presbyterian Minister, Belfast, examined.

Rev. George Magill.

19541. Chairman.—You are a Minister of the Presbyterian Church?—Yes.

19542. Your church is situated in Belfast?—Yes.

19543. How long have you been in Belfast?—I have been seventeen years.

19544. Are you a manager of a National school?—Yes.

19545. What are the numbers in attendance at it?—I could not say exactly, but I am sure it is above 300.

19546. Have you had any experience as a manager elsewhere?—Yes, I had some six or seven schools under my care when I was minister of First Antrim, and also I had a large school when I was a minister in the city of Cork.

19547. Would you propose any change in the subjects taught in the National schools at present, or would you leave them as they are?—I think I would rather see the subjects diminished, and I would rather see the pupils brought up to be something like experts in a few prominent branches than see them having only a moderate knowledge of a great number of subjects.

19548. Now would you specify some of those prominent subjects that you would select?—I would say, of course, the common subjects that all are agreed on almost—penmanship, arithmetic, composition, grammar, geography, especially bearing upon the great highways of commerce, illustrating our connection with our colonies and the nations of the East and West, with which we have trade—but I would not have pupils crammed with names about [illegible] and the lengths of rivers, and the heights of mountains, or matter of that kind.

19549. What modification would you make in the mode of teaching grammar, or the extent of it?—I don't see how any boy can ever understand, what I would call correct composition, except he is to a certain extent a fair grammarian, and because writing accurately the English language bulks so large in anything like an educated man's make-up, I would be anxious to see composition laid great stress upon.

19550. Would you teach shorthand and typewriting, and the like?—I would teach shorthand, but I would not teach typewriting through our schools in general. And shorthand, possibly, I would confine to our large towns and cities.

19551. Would you advise the teaching of handicraft in our ordinary schools?—It may seem strange if I should perhaps say I would not. In the first place, I think there is little enough time for boys and girls to get the literary education such as would fit them for life. I think that they could be taught handicraft better elsewhere. I have visited schools where handicraft is taught—I don't wish to give any names—but I am not prepossessed in favour of handicraft from what I have seen [illegible] handicraft the Trades Unionists would not permit you or employers to shorten the period of apprenticeship. I was hoping that something would be gained if employers would accept a shorter apprenticeship, but I find that no matter what would be the wish of the employers, the Trade Unionists would not permit it, so there must be a certain number of journeymen in proportion to the number of apprentices that would be accepted.

19552. Chairman.—As regards the present hours of the National school teaching, are you satisfied with them, or have you any change to propose?—When I take into account, Mr. Chairman, the number of hours, I must say I cannot understand how anything could be engrafted upon our present work. I find that if a pupil comes to school anytime before eleven o'clock he gets credit for four hours' instruction, half an hour in addition to that is cut off for recreation, which leaves two and a half hours for secular and moral instruction, and when I take into account, especially in a female school, that perhaps two hours in addition to this are taken off, it does not require much mental arithmetic to see what is left.

19553. Then you don't approve of not calling the roll until eleven o'clock?—I think no boy should get credit for being present a day except he is present four hours, the same applies to girls.

19554. Would he not be present four hours if he came at eleven and remained until three?—I'd require him to come at ten and leave at two.

19555. Have you anything to say with regard to domestic economy?—I think that is one thing that might be taught with great advantage to our girls, how to manage their own homes—cottages or superior houses, that they may happen to belong to—but I am not so sure that it is any advantage to the country at large for girls to be taught ornamental embroidery, and these fancy things that can only be of advantage to a very limited extent; but plain sewing and domestic economy I would approve.

19556. Cookery, I suppose?—No, I don't see how you could teach cookery in nineteen-twentieths of our schools, however desirable it might be.

19557. Mr. Molloy.—You referred a while ago to ecclesiastical embroidery as an unsuitable subject?—It only just occurred to me as an illustration, or any other handicraft that would be only of local advantage.

19558. But while there are sixteen items mentioned in that [illegible] programme, is it not a fact that the instruction is practically confined to plain dressmaking, underclothing-making, knitting, crochet, and repairing of garments?—I admit that is true, but my idea is that for the children of the peasantry—and these form the overwhelming majority—you should take into account only what would be of advantage to the great overwhelming majority—and I would say

Belfast. Oct. [illegible], 1897. Rev. George Magill.

too far?—Well, if it took much of their time from what I would call the brief precious time that they are allowed to get a literary training I think it would be a mistake.

19564. *Referring* for a moment to the industrial programme, if it were confined to those essentials I have just read out, plain dressmaking, suitable for a National school pupil, repairing garments, and making stockings, socks, petticoats, and so on, you would not think that too extensive?—It depends altogether upon whether you think that you will have sufficient time for the girls to get such a literary training as we have a right to expect—which we, the taxpayers, have a right to expect they should get.

19565. Of course you are aware, as a manager, and a manager of great experience, that it is absolutely in your power, and, under your direction or your teacher's power, to confine the instruction to such items as I have read out?—Yes, but that leaves too much to the discretion of the manager. I might, as a self-willed manager, adopt one course or another. I think the Commissioners of National Education are standing between the parent and the tax-payers, and ought not to leave such a responsibility as that in the hands of the manager.

19566. A previous witness referred to the establishment of a local association of managers as an advising body to the Commissioners of National Education in Dublin; would you approve of that?—I think it is a great pity that managers have not that intercourse referred to there. I think it would be a great advantage if managers met and compared notes, and had the advantage of each others experience.

19567. Do you think an hour a day is too much to give to needlework; we have heard in England it is confined to three hours a week?—I would confine it, perhaps, to less than that, if I had my will, simply because needlework can be learned afterwards; but when a child of the peasant class leaves school she need not hope for anything more in the way of education, and, besides, if you only get the minimum amount of knowledge with needle or any other form of handicraft that will soon be forgotten.

19568. If I mistake not, your answer a while ago, sir, was that you would not advocate the introduction of manual instruction into schools, as it might lead to trades and cause a clashing with trades union standards?—Yes, sir, I have endeavoured to understand the subject with whatever little ability I have, and I have come to the mature conviction—as far as I can say I have a matured conviction when it is my own—that it would be a mistake. There is a department in which I believe great service could be rendered by the Board, and, if you will excuse me, I will refer to it. I don't refer to scientific agriculture, because that is away from the point; but I do think a great deal could be done if the principles on which drainage should be conducted were taught boys. If they were taught that shelter from a few forest trees, such as American pine, would raise the climate, and if they were taught also to know that all the waste ground in hedgerows might be utilised by growing damsons and plums and apples and pears; and if they were taught to graft they could have the whitethorn of the country grafted with pears. You would have an enormous amount of fruit raised, you would have the climate of the country raised, you would have the land drained and then

19569. Is kindergarten taught in any of your schools?—It is being taught in my own school, but it is only lately commenced; I don't express an opinion about it; I am not very sanguine about any great advantage from kindergarten except in so far as it lures children to come to school, and that school work is not hateful to them. When it leads to that I think it is good, but I am not very sure about any great advantage gained afterwards.

19570. Would not that be a great advantage in itself?—If too much time were not taken up I think it would be a great advantage, but I think one of your own experts said that he was not aware that a child that had passed through kindergarten was a smarter boy or girl when he or she came to the fourth, fifth, or sixth—not one whit smarter than those who had not passed through kindergarten.

19571. I don't know that I would call him an "expert," I suppose one of the witnesses?—I mean a professional educationalist.

19572. Briefly, with regard to the results system, do you propose any change?—Yes, I would propose this change—I think the results system should have two grades of payment; I think for a mere pass I would allow what you allow at the present time, and by way of stimulating teachers to pay attention to clever boys I would give in a bonus, or whatever you might think was necessary to be a sufficient stimulus to make the teacher pay extra attention to boys who had extra ability.

19573. A former witness made reference to the advisability of having prizes for pupils who attended punctually; would you approve of that?—I would be strongly in favour of the inducement for the elementary system that is held out in connection with the Intermediate system. I think there are prizes given in the Model schools, and I think the other schools should not labour under any disadvantage.

19574. Almost universally prizes were given in the Model schools some years ago, but the practice has been discontinued by the Commissioners?—I was not aware of it. If you would excuse me, I think it would be a great advantage that the assistants in our ordinary schools should either get full pay for their classification, or, at any rate, pay up to the first division of second class. You want the status of teachers raised, and you want them more able to give instruction, and I think that while assistants are treated as step-bairns in ordinary schools as compared with the way they are treated in Model schools, you don't encourage these assistants to work as they otherwise would do.

19575. You would advocate the payment up to the highest division of second class?—Yes.

19576. You would not advocate the payment of first class salary, the same as to the principal teacher, because the principal teacher has the responsibility of conducting the whole school?—Yes; there are many reasons why I don't think the assistant could reasonably expect to be put on the footing with the principal, who might be first of first.

19577. You made reference to a pupil who earned a No. 1 pass, that that boy ought to get a higher fee than a boy who got an ordinary pass, what about the pupil who undergoes no examination at all, on the occasion of the Inspector's visit, not having made a

Belfast. — Oct. [illegible] — Rev. George Magill.

19579. Would you advocate any change in the present method of examination, have you turned your attention to the propriety of having class examination in certain subjects?—It is possible, but I don't see how an inspector can know whether boys have been well taught or not, except the inspector asks the boys, I must say that, and there would be room for a certain amount of smart management if each boy was not examined.

19580. But in certain subjects he might be able to say "That subject is very well taught by the instructor and I am disposed to award the full fee, although I have not examined all the pupils?"—The inspectors ought to be better judges than I would of that matter, and I would not like to commit myself.

19581. You are in favour of an individual examination?—I am in favour, but I don't mean to say that I am so much in favour. I am aware that in England they examine by classes, but we are something better than in England, we might be in advance of them.

19582. Mr. Struthers.—Perhaps you are aware that they changed the other system in England and changed their opinion?—It is quite possible that officials might have a great deal of influence in changing, and if they got the change brought about the teachers and their friends and the inspectors might not be the better of it.

19583. Mr. Molloy.—Would you be disposed to advocate the propriety of paying on the average attendance of the pupils rather than on the individual examination. Take any school of your own, what is the name of your principal school?—Avenue-street.

19584. In that school what is the average attendance?—I should say it is about 200.

19585. Would you prefer that the whole payments should be on that average attendance and a general report as to the efficiency of the school rather than on the result of an individual examination once a year?—I think that there would be great room for getting in a proper attendance, and there might be very good attendance and no very good teaching, if you adopted that method. I would be afraid of that. But the question involves an answer which might be a reflection upon the teachers, and I don't like that.

19586. Mr. Redington.—If the payment were made on the average attendance, might not the quality of the teaching be tested by constant visits on the part of the inspector?—Perhaps, but you would require to multiply your inspectors greatly if you looked into it.

19587. But if the inspectors were relieved to a large extent of the task of examining each individual child would they not have more time for visits of inspection?—Of course they would, but I don't think that payment by results of the examination of the individual pupil has got a long enough test here, and before I would make a change I would wait to see it tested a little further.

19588. You are aware that it takes up a great deal of the inspector's time, and it is very desirable he should have more time than at present for incidental visits. Could you suggest some better way of conducting the examinations?—If a man is a candidate for any public office he is tested by personal examination, and I am not sure that there is any other method by which you will know how a boy has been taught than by personal examination.

19589. And you don't think it would be safe to test the knowledge of the whole class or school by examining only a portion of it?—I think if you will examine half the class you will be fairly justified in inferring that if these answered well the class had been well taught and that the other boys would answer in like manner.

19590. Now, as regards the hours that a pupil spends in the school you said I think that it is possible for a pupil to spend only two and a half hours at literary work?—Yes.

19591. I may inform you that we have had that under consideration, and a change has been made lately in the rules in the direction that you advocate. Has your experience been in the country as well as in the city?—Yes, but it is so long ago now, it is twenty years ago, I don't think this matter of handicraft teaching was before us so strongly or so prominently as it is now, if it was at all.

19592. I am speaking generally as to the subjects that are suitable for country and for city districts, do you think there ought to be a different programme for each?—The only difference I think I would make would be that in cities I would have shorthand taught, and in large seaports I would have navigation taught, so that where a great number of boys are going to sea, if the captain was washed overboard, then with very little experience of seafaring life they might be able to bring a vessel to port.

19593. Do you think it right to allow agriculture to be taught in city schools?—I don't think it is the slightest use.

19594. Is it taken up in *Belfast* schools?—I suppose.

19595. You gave some suggestions about the mode of teaching agriculture in rural schools—did I understand you to say that you would not teach elementary chemistry or elementary physics in connection with agriculture?—Yes, sir, you understand me aright, simply because all that you would teach all you could instil at most would be so much lumber, and the time would be better occupied, I think, by teaching the things to which I referred, and they would be reduced to practice as soon and become profitable at once.

19596. Is there not a danger that what is in the agricultural text-book would be crammed into the pupil and not retained by him in an intelligent way?—My observations went in the direction rather of disapproving of anything in the nature of a training of a boy up to knowledge of agriculture.

19597. Then you don't approve of learning from a textbook without experiments?—I think that in the meantime as much theory as they could carry away and keep might be taught, we might safely trust their parents and their own instinct to acquire a great deal more than you would likely teach them by experiment.

19598. You advocate pupils being taught how to make drains and plant trees?—How to make drains and plant trees for shelter round a small farm and utilising hedges that are not being utilised at all by having damsons and plums, which will grow readily without any cultivation.

19599. Would you give up the teaching of agriculture out of a text-book?—I don't say exactly that, but I would [illegible]

Belfast.

Oct. 15, 1897.

Rev. George Magill.

and sixth classes: do not girls remain at school to attend those classes?—Not many stay in Belfast for sixth class.

19605. Do they not attend in fourth class?—Oh, yes.

19606. Under the late regulations you can get a fee for cookery in fourth class. What would be the expense in Belfast of setting aside a classroom for two days a week for that purpose?—But supposing, and that is what usually is the case, supposing all the available ground is built on round a schoolhouse.

19607. CHAIRMAN.—In the Board schools we have been in in England they have not a separate kitchen, but a stove put up in one of the classrooms and tables adapted?—I was just going to say, in that case the cookery would have to be after hours, you could not work for the edification of one class and have the young children that could take no interest in it at all sitting about.

19608. MR. REDINGTON.—Then, as to the cost, I think we have it in evidence that the London School Board makes £600 a year by the sale of cooked articles. Even assuming that could not be done here would there be a great loss in a large town on the sale of what is cooked by the pupils?—I don't know, it is a region of prophecy.

19609. Then, as to the apparatus, it is not very expensive to put up a range, and the cookery utensils are not expensive?—Yes, but the ground is so precious, and it has been so utilised, that it would be impossible to get a room set apart, the class-room would have to be so overhauled and altered.

19610. Captain SHAW.—You think that the object of elementary education should be to cultivate both the mind and body, so far as possible in the class?—They interact on each other and I think they should go part passu.

19611. And you consider that if you teach children writing, reading, composition and spelling, and arithmetic that that effects this result?—No, I did not say so, I specified those as important subjects that I thought should have great prominence given to them.

19612. I understood you would exclude all other subjects?—Oh, no, I would have in rural districts mensuration taught, in seaports I would have navigation taught, I would have shorthand taught because it is indispensable to a man going into an office now, and seeing that there are so many openings for travellers and men fit to carry on correspondence for merchants I would have in a large place like Dublin, or Cork, or Belfast, I would have French taught.

19613. Are you considering the school age of the children when you put in all those things?—They are not nearly so many subjects as are put in already. The question is whether you can render the children fit to acquire that knowledge readily afterwards if they want it, during their elementary school age in a better manner than at present.

19614. It is impossible to teach a child everything it requires in its future employment, during the school time. You cannot turn out a complete clerk from the elementary school?—That is true.

19615. And the question is how you are going to prepare him best, so that he can complete his education afterwards?—I think if a boy can write correctly, write the English language fairly well, if he can draw out an account and furnish it in a decent manner, if he can write a good hand, that that boy would be in a fair condition to accept a situation in a merchant's office.

19616. It is not a part of the training of a National school at present to draw out his powers of observation and get him to correctly describe a thing?—No, but the question is what is the best thing to do for a boy or girl up to twelve years of age.

19617. Then you wish to individualise the education of the child according to what he is going to be afterwards?—No, that is not the result; because those subjects apply to all boys, with the exception of mensuration and navigation, but the other branches refer to all children.

19618. But more especially to such children as are going to be employed in offices, or commercial life, which are in the minority in the country?—Of course if they choose to follow up those subjects afterwards I would not prohibit them.

19619. Then you made another observation that the children, after they leave the elementary school, need not hope for any further education?—I think as a rule, for example, if a girl goes into a factory or any place where she is nine or ten hours engaged, you will not likely get that fagged and jaded girl to go into a night school.

19620. If you teach that girl intelligently, can she not afterwards take up a book and complete her education, that is the way most of us do?—That may be so; you are not going to get a school for a girl, but you can get a shop where a trade is taught a girl after she leaves school.

19621. If you cultivate their powers of observation in reference to things around them, would they not be more likely after they left school to pick up information for themselves?—That I cannot say.

19622. You approve of training of the muscles so far as athletics, but do you not consider it necessary to use the muscles carefully so as to direct your hand to do what you want carefully?—Of course it is very desirable you should make a proper use of your hands; but if you have a boy with his muscles well developed by athletic exercises at the cross bar, etc., you will have a boy very well fitted to take care of himself when he takes a tool into his hands.

19623. It is much more difficult, I suppose you will allow, for any person late in life to take up any manual occupation, which requires accuracy, than if he begins early?—Yes, I admit that freely.

19624. Therefore it may be desirable to teach children at an early age to control their muscles and habits of accuracy?—I suppose so, but still is the little you can give them in that way the best way of occupying their time at school?

19625. If you find it in evidence that you can do this, and at the same time you can attain better results in their literary training, would you agree that it might be at least tried as an experiment?—I hope I would be convinced by evidence and allow evidence to weigh with me, but in the absence of evidence I am only talking of what would occur to me as an observer, that we should all aim at making the best use of the time, and it is not the best use of the time.

19626. You say the result system has not had a fair trial; it was established in 1872, that is twenty-five years ago, is not that almost long enough for an experiment in education?—Well, but I don't think it has failed; I think it has been very advantageous.

19627. You would not think it necessary to have at least twenty-five years' experience of any system before you could depend upon it?—Oh, no; sometimes a year is enough to make you know it is a bad thing.

19628. MR. STRUTHERS.—I think your strong point, Mr. Magill, is that you are afraid of overloading the school course?—Yes.

19629. You attach great importance to thorough instruction in elementary subjects?—Yes.

19630. And you would be afraid of admitting other subjects which might leave less time to be given to these?—All my views in relation to this matter gather round those points.

19631. You would exclude typewriting?—Certainly.

19632. But I think I gathered you would teach shorthand in every ordinary day school in the large towns?—In the large towns or cities where it would be likely to be of some benefit, but it would be useless teaching it to the son of a peasant in Connaught.

19633. Take a large town, you would teach shorthand in all the highest classes?—Just as I would teach penmanship.

19634. And you consider shorthand would be useful to all the boys when they leave?—I wish I could write it; I know no person advanced in life but would be thankful if he had been taught shorthand.

19635. Do you think a labouring man is going to profit by the knowledge of shorthand?—No.

19636. Or a girl in a factory?—I think not.

19637. Don't these form the majority of the people in the towns after all?—Yes, but I would not make it compulsory on them.

19638. Then would it not be better to have it taught outside the school, and let those who wish to learn it acquire it for themselves?—No, that would take up their time after school hours, and they would perhaps not be at liberty to spend an hour a day learning shorthand.

19639. Of course you are aware that evening schools have been very successful both in England and in Scotland, great numbers of pupils, apparently engaged throughout the day, attend them and acquire such subjects as shorthand and typewriting in the evening. Don't you think such a thing would be possible in Ireland in the evening?—If it would be legitimate to have shorthand and typewriting taught in the evening, then I would turn round and say *a fortiori* let the handicraft be taught after school hours.

19640. What is your conception of the handicraft introduced into schools?—What I have seen has reference to carpentry work, and joinery and plumbing to a limited extent.

19641. That is more or less in the nature of teaching a trade?—I would say so.

19642. And as is not a suitable subject for any ordinary school?—If a boy does not like it it is no use to him at all, and if he does like it it is an advantage to him when he goes to serve his apprenticeship.

19643. I think it is generally agreed that the teaching of a trade is not part of the instruction of an elementary school, and I don't think it is proposed to teach handicraft in that sense in the schools?—Suppose you did not call it the teaching of a trade, it would not be the less teaching of a trade giving it another name.

19644. What is aimed at by teaching the use of tools in schools is training in accuracy of observation and measuring power of hand and eye; is not that a valuable quality?—There is no doubt it is.

19645. And it may be attained by other things besides the use of tools, for instance, drawing. Would you not consider that a desirable part of any elementary school course?—If you were satisfied that the best use you could make of that boy's time was to teach him drawing, if you are satisfied of that I would say by all means teach him drawing.

19646. It is a point we are making inquiry into: drawing has been compared with navigation for a large seaport town; which do you think is the most useful to be taught to the great mass of the children?—In a large town such as Belfast I certainly would not exclude drawing, but I would never think of having it generally taught, where all probability is that it would never be any use afterwards.

19647. But drawing is taught, not with a view to make them tradesmen in after-life, but to make them more observant?—I would rather have the time spent in teaching him to write a hand that could be read than make him a tradesman who would draw a figure you could not understand.

19648. Would it not be possible to do them both?—It is not possible to make them good writers, except in some schools.

19649. I think you propose in large towns to teach them both shorthand and typewriting?—Shorthand in all the large towns and writing everywhere.

19650. But in addition to the writing you would also have shorthand in the large towns?—I would.

19651. Would it not be more desirable to have drawing instead of shorthand?—I don't object to drawing in large towns, because I believe it may be turned to account.

19652. At any rate in the elementary schools what should be given is a good general education—a good general education, and if either shorthand or drawing can be turned to account I would have these both taught, but I would not have them taught simply because you say they teach a boy smartness and cleverness, and so on.

19653. Quite so, but you would have a good general education which trained all a boy's faculties, would you not?—I would.

19654. You advocate, for instance, some form of physical exercise, gymnastics, and would not there be a form of training of the boy which would be very desirable for everybody. I am not taking any particular form of exercise, but some training which would develop the sense of accuracy and power of control over the muscles of the hand?—That would not be in the direction of what I call athletic exercise, I don't know that that would develop the muscle at all.

19655. *No*, but it gives control both of hand and eye, and makes a person more generally useful?—Yes.

19656. If that was part of the system of general education, if you found from experts that the teaching of drawing and of simple manual occupations had that effect, you would be disposed to consider the advisability of introducing it into a school?—I would be bound to be influenced by evidence; I would be very unreasonable if I would not.

19657. We are agreed that what should be given in elementary schools is a good all-round education, meaning an education which develops all the faculties of the pupils, and you said I mean leave it to experts who have investigated the question and tried it by experiment, to say what is the best form in which this education could be given?—If that would be your opinion that we should be guided by experts, I don't see why I or anyone like me should give evidence, because if you have the evidence of experts to settle the matter we need not bring our little common sense to bear upon it.

19658. We want the opinion of everybody on the matter, especially of those who have anything to do with the management of schools?—Well, I will put it in this shape—I would not advocate a fancy programme to catch the public eye, I would like a programme carried out that would benefit the peasantry of the country, and whether it was a flash programme or a simple modest one, if I believed it would best fit the peasantry for the battle of life, that is the programme I would carry out. I should think that would be the general aim of anyone who intended to benefit general education.

Belfast.

Oct. [illegible], 1897.

Rev. S. E. Busby, LL.D.

On resuming after lunch, the Commissioners present were:—The Right Hon. the Earl of Belmore, G.C.M.G., in the Chair; The Right Hon. C. T. Redington, M.A.; Rev. Henry Evans, D.D.; Rev. Hamilton Wilson, D.D.; W. J. M. Molloy, Esq.; Captain T. B. Shaw; and J. Struthers, Esq., M.A.

with J. D. Daly, Esq., M.A., Secretary.

Rev. S. E. Busby, LL.D., Rector of St. Andrew's, Belfast, examined.

19658. Chairman.—You are the Rector of St. Andrew's, Belfast?—Yes, my lord.

19659. And Hon. Secretary of the Church of Ireland Association of Patrons and Managers of National Schools in the united dioceses of Down, Connor, and Dromore?—Yes.

19660. Can you tell us what the effect of the Compulsory Education Act has been in Belfast?—I can tell you something about it. Do you refer to the figures or the state of education generally? I may mention that I am one of the members of the School Attendance Committee of Belfast, and that I have been a member from the beginning. It began its work in January, 1894. The effect of the Compulsory Education Act in regard to numbers is this, that in January, 1893, some little time before we began our work, there were 45,072 children on the rolls of the National schools of Belfast, and the average attendance was 30,303.

19661. That is about two in three?—Quite so. In December 1896, after three years nearly of our work we found we had got 53,676 on the rolls, with an average attendance of 37,573, showing an increase on the rolls of 8,604, and on the average attendance an increase of 7,270. I wish to remark that the National Commissioners told us to estimate the number of children by dividing six into the total population, and if we acted on these figures we would have 5,000 more in the schools of Belfast than, that dividing would give us, as then five into the total number of the people of Belfast would rather give us the number of children of school age between seven and fourteen. It would only give us 48,133, divided by six. I have also to say that a very important fact is brought out by the figures, i.e., that there are 15,000 children on the rolls of the schools that are absent from school every day in Belfast. This is one of the defects in the Compulsory Education Act.

19662. How do you account for that?—I can hardly account for it except in this way, that, when a child's parents are warned, they send the child for two or three days, so as to get rid of any further proceedings; as soon as the first proceedings have lapsed, the child absents himself again, and so it goes on fluctuating until this large average of absentees is reached.

19663. You find it is a continual battle with certain children to get them to school?—It is, and with nearly all it is a battle to get them every day to school; the Attendance Act requires some amendment made in it that would do something towards overtaking this fault.

19664. Your experience, I think, lies in the direction of the subjects of drawing, music, cookery, drill, and needlework?—Yes.

19665. Perhaps you will tell us what you consider the true object of manual and practical instruction?—I think that the manual and practical instruction should have for its object the education of the eye and hand of the children, and that it would be utterly out of the question to try and teach them trades.

19666. That is taken for granted by our Commission?—I did not know that.

19667. The reference was very carefully drafted to give effect to that idea?—I am happy to hear that.

19668. Are you in favour of some manual and practical instruction?—I am much in favour of it under certain conditions and limitations.

19669. Perhaps you would specify the sort of manual instruction you think would be advantageous?—In the first place we cannot do anything in manual instruction, except we get some shortening and revision of the programme, and there are some directions in which I would suggest the shortening of the daily programme; the first is that the whole teaching of grammar and parsing should be shortened considerably in regard to time, as being not possible to be understood or used by the children after they leave school. The second is that there is an immensity of time spent upon learning obscure geography after this fashion:—A is the capital of B, C is the capital of D; it is a regular rhyme, and that is the only way in which we can answer the inspector.

19670. Are you against the practice that appears to prevail, of teaching the heights of mountains and things of that sort?—Yes, my lord, all such things are utterly forgotten within a week after they are taught or examined in.

19671. You think that geography would be better taught by teaching them to know a map, than by getting into their heads a long list of names?—Yes. The third thing is advanced arithmetic. I think the advanced arithmetic which is taught in our schools is, in consequence of its not being followed on, actually destructive of a knowledge of common rules, which every clerk is required to know and practise while in his situation. It may seem strange to you, but such is the fact, as I have found in experience. The higher these young people go in algebra and mathematics, the worse they are as a rule in doing a common sum or making out an invoice in a shop. I was going to say that that is one direction in which I would ask the committee to shorten the daily programme.

19672. What is your experience as regards the subject of needlework in girls' schools?—Needlework has been most useful in girls' schools; they devote five hours in the week to it in my schools. I have nearly 700 children on my rolls. And likewise five hours are given to drawing.

19673. Have you the industrial programme in the upper classes?—No, my lord, we have not got it as a whole, but we have got many parts of it.

19674. As regards drawing, are you in favour of drawing being taught to both boys and girls?—I am very much in favour of it; I have brought here what I took this morning by chance—specimens of the drawing of very small boys (produced). This is part of the education of the eye for which I regard the practical and manual system with so much favour.

19675. What do you say with regard to the present programme in handicraft?—I think it is much too long and elaborate, and the things aimed at are too much in the handicraft line, for if we attempt that, we will fail altogether. There are two years given to the handicraft programme in the National Board. What is the result of it? It is so long that it is taught in very few of the schools. With a great deal of difficulty I came upon one school in which it is taught.

19676. What exactly did you observe as taught under the head of handicraft?—Plumbing and joinery.

19677. But they are trades?—Yes; and that is one of the reasons I think it will not succeed.

Belfast.

Jan. [illegible]

Rev. [illegible] [illegible], LL.D.

19679. You are aware that the object of this Commission is the introduction of something that will not be the teaching of trades, but will make boys handy and observant, and teach principles they can apply when they go to learn trades after they leave school?—Yes, that is what I so thoroughly go in with.

19680. It is admitted there would be difficulties in starting some of these sorts of manual work; about getting rooms and tools and training teachers; have you ever thought how those difficulties could be got over?—I have not. All these things which I have introduced into our schools, such as the cookery class, the cookery class, and pianoforte music, these were all outside the schools as schools.

19681. Outside the school hours?—Yes, and outside the teachers, but in the schoolroom, and with the children of the school.

19682. You heard the difficulty the previous witness thought would arise with regard to cookery; have you found any real difficulty as regards putting a range up in the schoolroom?—The teacher who came to us got it done with very little difficulty.

19683. Can you tell us at what expense—in figures?—I could not tell you now at this distance of time, but I should think we had to make up about 30s.

19684. Who made up the rest?—The fees for instruction.

19685. I believe you think that children are too young to grapple with things like sawing and planing?—I do.

19686. At what age could they begin?—Not sooner than fourteen, which is the time we lose the children from school.

19687. You are aware that in some places, particularly Sweden, they begin this work before fourteen?—Yes, but I am speaking of the heavier work such as sawing and planing.

19688. But they do teach sawing and planing, of course it is only making small articles?—That is with reference to any attempt we may make to teach those handicraft, which, as your lordship has already informed me, is given up.

19689. Given up as a trade?—I mean given up by the Commissioners as a trade.

19690. Oh, no, it is given up by the Government in framing this Commission. We are not to inquire into technical education in the sense of teaching a trade, but we are to inquire into how and to what extent manual instruction, which would lead up to teaching a trade afterwards by having trained the hand and eye, can be introduced?—But if it goes any way far in the schools it will only succeed in inducing the workmen of the various trades to regard those young fellows who get this sort of training in our schools as [illegible], and they would rather have them fresh and without any knowledge beforehand.

19691. You think that would be the case in Belfast?—I am afraid so.

19692. It has not been the case in Birmingham?—Has it not? well that is a parallel town.

19693. Mr. MOLLOY.—You attend as a representative of a number of managers in Belfast?—Yes, sir.

19694. How many of them, might I ask?—Are you speaking of Belfast or of the diocese.

19695. Whatever body you represent?—About 110 managers in the united dioceses of Down, Connor, and Dromore.

19696. And may I inquire whether the views you have expressed in favour of the introduction of manual instruction may be said to be the views of that important body?—I am afraid I shall have to ask you to take my answer with kind consideration; it is that our managers are up to this time not very well acquainted with the scope of the practical and manual instruction of which this Commission is the object.

19697. From your knowledge of the managers and the information Lord Belmore has just given of the scope of the Commission, do you think it likely that they would entertain your views?—I think their great fear would be, not about the expediency of doing this, but the expense and time that would be necessary; and the classrooms, and perhaps the trained teacher that would have to teach these things.

19698. That is in the event of the expense devolving upon the managers?—Just so.

19699. If the expense, however, in great part did not devolve upon the managers?—I think then that they would be rather inclined to regard the practical and manual teaching with very great favour, that is to say, according to the various places in which they are.

19700. Captain SHAW.—Do you teach kindergarten in all your schools?—Not as a complete system, but in the infants' school we teach nearly the whole of it, and in the girls' and boys' school it takes the form of calisthenics.

19701. You consider it should be developed and carried through the school training?—Yes, sir, I do. I think it would be a very great advantage in infant schools, and a very great attraction to the school.

19702. But I am speaking of the classes above the infant class, perhaps you are not aware that in England there is a development of the system called hand and eye training, which is an extension of kindergarten exercises to the higher classes?—I never saw that in England, and could not answer about it, but my opinion would be that in the grown class of both boys and girls the form of kindergarten which we know as calisthenics and figures and marching and drill would amply meet the advanced kindergarten.

19703. But it is the hand and eye training in which we look more especially in the older children?—I think that is very efficiently taught by the training of the hand and eye in drawing. I have been much surprised myself to see the drawing done here by the hand from the pattern.

19704. Do you have object lessons in the school?—Certainly.

19705. You consider these very useful?—Very useful indeed.

19706. Are they not a great aid to composition, if the children are required to frame original answers?—Oh, yes, a very great aid, but that subject of composition is a great difficulty in every school.

19707. Is not that because it is not properly taught?—I really cannot answer that question. I came long ago to the conclusion that if a person could compose well after arriving at years of [illegible], it was in their nature, and that all the teaching in the world would never enable a person to write his own original thoughts in a proper way if he had it not as his natural capacity.

19708. But if children are called upon to observe and express their observations in their own words they are the more likely to learn composition than if they are set down to write an essay on some subject?—Yes, sir, but I don't think one in twenty can do it.

19709. CHAIRMAN.—Do you think that applies to persons in all ranks of life?—I do, indeed.

19710. Captain SHAW.—You say tools are no [illegible] for children under fourteen years of age?—Yes. Anyone that has ever seen a [illegible] will understand how tired the arm gets in a short time.

19711. May not that be from want of early general training?—Possibly the muscles have not been developed.

19712. Really carpenters' tools should be used with no force at all, if used properly they nearly all work themselves?—That is not a [illegible] [illegible]; sawing must be done by the motion of the teeth, and the action of drawing a saw backwards and forwards is most exhausting.

19713. He need not apply any force to it to get it through the wood?—That is what we are taught, but it is done.

19714. Mr. STRUTHERS.—You are aware that in Sweden, children ten years old use the regular carpenters' tools and find no difficulty in doing it?—I was not aware of that.

19715. In Denmark they have special tools constructed for the children, but in Sweden children from eleven years up, at all events, are trained to use the ordinary carpenters' tools and no difficulty has been found in doing it?—That answers my theory altogether; I did not know that fact, and I am much obliged to you for telling me.

19716. You consider the cultivation of hand and eye just as important a part of school training as any other?—I do indeed.

19717. And you consider it is developed by this teaching in drawing which you have shown us?—Yes.

19718. And if you found there were other exercises which still further developed that power, but did not interfere with the ordinary school work, you would be in favour of their introduction?—I would indeed, very much, but when I said the ordinary school work I carefully excluded extra refinements of the three things I mentioned, geography, grammar, and arithmetic.

19719. You have been present at an examination, I presume?—I have often.

19720. You have heard the inspectors ask the children to name the capitals of France or Spain?—Often.

19721. Did he not ask the children to point them out on the map?—Oh, yes. What I spoke of were extraordinary questions about little places on the right bank of a river, and on the left bank of a river, and all that.

19722. You have heard an inspector ask questions of that kind?—I have.

19723. To name the towns on the right bank, and was not satisfied unless he got the name of every obscure village?—I would not like to say that; it would be an accusation I could not prove.

19724. Have you heard the inspector ask for the heights of mountains in his examination?—I could not answer that question, but the deduction in my mind was that the inspectors very often were obliged to frame some exceedingly difficult and subtle questions in order to discriminate; that is to say, he had found the class so well up that I thought he was forced to go on to a higher plane.

19725. Then I presume these questions were life questions, so to speak, unnecessary parts of the examination?—I don't know, the inspector's mind is one of those things that are wrapt in mystery.

19726. But still he comes down from the clouds sometimes and asks questions?—Oh, yes.

19727. And you can only judge of the state of his mind by the questions he asks?—That is so. I also must judge of the state of his mind by the return of the results sheet.

19728. In this case in which he asked questions of a difficult character because the children knew the ordinary work so well, did he fail any of the children in geography, do you remember?—I could not answer that.

19729. Perhaps he was only inquiring how far the children could go?—Perhaps so.

19730. And if the teacher knows such questions will be asked, he will be tempted to train his children during the year to answer those obscurities. I suppose he always asked the children to point out on the map the places named?—I think so, and I would like to say it is not finding fault with the inspectors I am, but I am rather referring to the system by which they are obliged to ask such questions.

19731. Rev. Dr. Evans.—When the inspector asked these questions requiring pointing on the map, did the pupils point to the name of the place?—Is not the name and the place the same?

19732. But they are not always together?—You mean the little mark on the map; I could not answer that; the pointer the child would have would cover a piece of the map sufficiently large not to discriminate between the little dot and the name.

19733. You said you would be in favour of manual instruction subject to certain limitations; will you kindly indicate them?—We should never attempt to teach them handicraft, that is, we should not have the idea of preparing them for any special work, such as carpentry or joinery, but that the practical teaching should be confined to things which would be of everyday use; for instance, let me give you a thing I was pleased with, the soldering of a kettle. That is a simple matter, but you require to be trained to it. I know that there is great trouble often in a house with kettles, and a little bit of metal with a soldering iron, if a child knew how to do it, would give a happy ending of that difficulty with the kettle, and, at the same time, interest the child.

Belfast.

Oct. 18, 1887.

Rev. S. E. [illegible]

Colonel Ynyr Burges, D.L., Parkanaur, Castlecaulfield, examined.

19734. Chairman.—You are a Deputy Lieutenant of the county Tyrone, and you live at Parkanaur, near Castlecaulfield. You have had some experience in regard to the management of primary schools?—I have been a manager for some years, say, thirty, but of only one school.

19735. I believe you have given attention to the subject of manual and practical instruction in rural schools?—I have thought it out a good deal. Well, the practical instruction—if you would embrace in that agricultural instruction—I have been very keen on that.

19736. Before you come to that, perhaps you would give us any ideas you may have on the subject of what some people call carpentry, but we prefer to call woodwork of an elementary character?—I live in a neighbourhood where the farms average 15 acres and up towards a mountain district, where they are far away from a town. One often remarks the untidy, careless state of the cottages, and the absence of gates on the farms, and so forth. It has struck me, in connection with this Commission, that handy practical carpentry, to be taught, not by the schoolmaster, who would have to learn it himself, but by the hired carpenter, to enable youngsters of the fifth and sixth class to learn the use of ordinary tools—would be very useful to them, as they would, if they went out as colonists, to be able to mend tables and chairs, and pig troughs, to mend gates, or a cart, if necessary. That would be very useful instruction for youngsters in a district of small farmers.

Colonel Ynyr Burges, D.L.

19737. We have found in the course of our inquiry that where woodwork is taught, objection is taken to the employment of an artisan as an instructor; it is thought better that the teacher should be trained to give instruction in the elementary sort of wood work that is taught, partly on the ground that an artisan, as a rule, unless he is trained to be a teacher, is not a good teacher, and partly on the ground that it is undesirable to introduce a stranger into a school because the stranger would not be able to enforce discipline, and it also might give an idea to the children that the teacher was an incompetent person; and, on the whole, it has been found better that the teacher should be trained to give this instruction than to introduce an artisan. And in one case in London, where an artisan is employed, before he was employed he was trained to be a teacher; and, therefore, having been an artisan, and knowing the technical part of his work, he was trained in this other qualification, which enabled him to be a very effective teacher of a very large board school in London. Have you considered that question at all?—Yes, I have in my eye at this moment a man who is now a carpenter, and

[illegible]
Oct. 15, 1887.
[illegible]

who, from dearth of carpenters, was sent, when he was a comparatively young man, to learn from a carpenter of some experience. I am speaking of a country district; he is what you call still a handy man, steadily improving. He resides in close proximity to the school under my management. Another young carpenter, very young, but very able, is in close proximity to another school under the management of the parish priest, within half a mile of my school. And they are two men who could teach far more practically that sort of carpentry than any schoolmaster, sent away from his work to learn carpentry, and knowing very little of it after the short time he can devote to it.

19738. Have you been in Switzerland?—Yes.

19739. Have you observed the Government subsidies for teaching wood-carving and woodwork there?—Yes; and observe that Switzerland is the resort of the tourist. We are developing very much the tourist industry in the West. The late Viceroy wrote an article which drew great attention to this, and although he and I differ in politics, I admired very much the article he wrote on "Unvisited Ireland," which, I think, has done a great deal for Ireland. And Mr. Crossley has done a great deal. If that industry is developed, we shall have Ireland another Switzerland, and we shall have a great demand for the smaller industries, eggs, poultry, and everything else, and we shall have another industry in wood-carving. In Connemara, one sees little girls running after the cars with knitted stockings. In future, we may hope to see the little boys asking, not for "a penny to buy a school-book," but for "a shilling for something I have carved." In the tourist districts you may inaugurate wood-carving, as at Brienz, where there is a Government school of carving.

19740. There is one subject we have inquired a great deal into, and that is this question of drawing in the schools; do you think that drawing should be made compulsory in all schools, or in town schools and not in country schools?—I will not speak for myself, but I may speak for my schoolmaster, who is a man of considerable experience, and he said to me that if some of these matters, such as drawing, was taken up in one school and not in another, the parents of the children would say "these are fads," and if any time was devoted to it they would send their children to other schools, and on that account he thought they should be made more or less compulsory. I look upon drawing as very useful. Take the sixth class lads, if they want to make a gate they should be able to make a drawing of a gate they saw somewhere else. If it is a gable, or a chimney, or a chimney cowl, it is useful that they should be able to sketch such things, and, in addition to that, it teaches them observation.

19741. It has been suggested to us by teachers, that although it would be hard to compel a teacher who had been teaching for a considerable number of years, and was no longer a young man, to qualify himself to teach drawing, if he had no natural taste that way, it would be only right to put all future teachers under an obligation to acquire a certificate to teach drawing, as well as to teach anything else, before they were allowed to become teachers; and also that encouragement, at any rate, should be given to the younger teachers to go to Dublin, or some centre, if centres were created in Ireland, to learn how to draw, and by degrees, and at no very distant time, that drawing should be made a compulsory subject?—I think it would be impossible to teach an old teacher to draw; and it might be difficult to teach a young teacher, so I think you must be dependent upon men who have a taste for drawing, and that would grow up by degrees.

19742. There are two kinds of drawing we have inquired into, one is freehand, and the other is scale drawing. There would be no difficulty, I suppose, in anybody learning scale drawing, and using a compass?—I suppose not.

19743. Do you think it would be a good thing that all children should be taught to use a compass and ruler?—I have not applied my thoughts to scale drawing, but more to the handy drawing that would be useful to a small farmer who would be able to sketch a thing for himself, for they build their own houses very often.

19744. I think you have come here principally to speak on the subject of agriculture?—Yes.

19745. Do you think in country schools a plot or garden should be attached to every school, and the teacher of every school should be expected to teach, at any rate, the principles of agriculture?—I think in country schools where the farming is backward — between Dungannon and Moy the farming is advanced; in the district I live in the farming is backward; and as you go to the mountain regions the farming is more backward still—you see the most lamentable ignorance of the principles of farming. You will see them making a dunghill before the door and having all the sap of the dunghill running down into a neighbouring stream. Some of these farmers, who are most anxious for the reduction of their rents, are ignorant of the leading principles of agriculture. To teach their boys in the fifth and sixth class farming from a book is mere teaching by rote, it goes in at one ear and out at the other. I think there ought to be practical instruction in a small portion of ground attached to the school, or very near it, so that what is taught from the book can be proved by object-lessons on the ground.

19747. There are three ways in which agriculture may be taught, of which we have heard in evidence. One is the present way of merely teaching out of a book; another is teaching from object-lessons the principles of farming without teaching the whole farming operations; and the third is by having a school farm, of which I believe formerly there were a good many through the country, but some of which have been given up by the National Board. Which of these three kinds of teaching would you prefer?—Take the last, the district farm; you cannot get farmers to send their sons twenty-five or ten or five miles to a district farm. There should be a plot at each National school—there were at first but two acres attached to my school—the schoolmaster knew nothing at all about farming when he commenced, but with the theoretical help of Professor Baldwin's book and with the subsequent visits of Professor Baldwin, Mr. Brogan, and, very much so, Professor Carroll, he has become the best farmer in the district. The farmers around him jeered at him at first when he spoke of making a profit in the balance sheet which he has to draw up each year for Professor Carroll.

19748. Where is this farm?—[illegible]. And although he is a family man, out of his savings he was able to pay for the tenant-right of a farm of fourteen acres, on which he had the best opportunity of illustrating what skill could do. That farm lay between two leading roads, one to two Presbyterian churches and two mills, and the other from one market town to another, and the people of the district could not fail to see what he was doing. It was one mass of couch-grass and coltsfoot, but by ploughing he got rid of the couch-grass, and by his knowledge of farming he advanced that farm from being the most neglected farm in the district—a derelict farm—to be one of the best farms in the district. When he first went there he began to grow clover with his oats; the old-fashioned farmer who lived next him said, "There is no use in putting clover in that field, that hill never grows clover." "Well, it's going to grow clover now," said he, and I saw a most magnificent field of clover in it the other day.

19749. Perhaps you are aware that there are only two Model farms in connection with the Board, namely, the farm at Glasnevin and the Munster Dairy

Belfast, Oct. 22, 1897. Colonel Ynyr Burges, J.P.

farm. It was suggested to me the other day that it would be a very good thing to establish more farms of that sort through Ireland to which boys after leaving the National schools might be sent. Of course some arrangement would have to be made for boarding them. It would be very useful after the boys had learned the elementary part of the subject that they should go on to one of these Model farms. Supposing now, for instance, there were three in each province in Ireland in addition to those already there, do you think that would be a good thing to establish?—It would be very useful for agricultural boys. For instance, I proposed to Mr. Carroll to send a clever lad from our school. I was going to send him and pay his pension for him as a reward. However, Mr. Carroll suggested I should let him compete for a free place; but that is only one boy in a dozen—the whole countryside requires this teaching. And I might add that for some time the parents were unwilling to allow their boys to do what is really necessary for them to learn what they are about by working on the master's farm. They said they did not send them there to work, so that the National Board introduced a very good system of giving a payment of so much per hour to each boy, and it is only the other day I signed the form for the quarter during which they had received instruction. The boys like it, and they get practical knowledge; they see not only how to work on the farm, but they see all that Mr. Carroll has been teaching the master, and what comes through the master to them about grasses and diseases in potatoes, and all those interesting things that Mr. Carroll is constantly teaching, for he is not only an inspector but an instructor, as the master gratefully acknowledges.

19750. If such schools as I spoke of were established, it will be necessary to have special teachers to give instruction on such farms?—Yes.

19751. Mr. Redington.—Is this two-acre plot you spoke of recognised as a school garden or school farm?—It was recognised as a school farm. The two acres are gone now: the National Board acknowledges the farm of fourteen acres as a school farm.

19752. Chairman.—Can you give me the name of the farm in their list?—Here is the report of 1894, about that farm (*produced*)—"Parkanaur National School Farm, Co. Tyrone.—The teacher of the Parkanaur school has shown here what intelligent management can effect in the improvement of land without extravagant outlay." He says before that: "I have much pleasure in describing this as one of the best of the agricultural schools under the Commissioners."

19753. Mr. Redington.—Do you think therefore that a farm of 14 acres is useful for the instruction of the boys of the school?—It has been useful in my own neighbourhood, and so I approve its use.

19754. You find that boys who have attended that school have benefited by it?—Yes; I have one pupil I propose to send up to Glasnevin, and I have another to send when he is done—[illegible].

19755. Don't you think that it is rather an important thing in teaching the elements of agriculture that a boy should see experiments tried, and of course in a farm managed for profit no experiment is likely to fail

19757. When the boys go on the farm with the master, does he give them a little lecture or set them to carry on the operations on the farm?—He gives them his little lecture himself. "Mr. Carroll, agricultural inspector, not a mere examiner, but an instructor, frames his questions to bring out the boy's powers of observation."—(*Reading from a memorandum by the master.*)

19758. Excuse me, I mean your own teacher?—This is what the teacher says is the effect of Mr. Carroll's visits and which he carried out: "The teacher notes and teaches accordingly. The mode of examination suggests the mode of teaching."

19759. You think the teacher honestly conveys to the boys all the instructions Mr. Carroll gives?—Most honestly.

19760. You think Mr. Carroll's opinion is worth a great deal?—Oh, yes, very much so.

19761. Have you seen the new book on Practical Farming that the Board has introduced?—I have seen it, but I have not had an opportunity of reading it up.

19762. Do you think there is danger that, if you teach agriculture out of a book, the boys will get a lot of names into their heads without knowing what they represent?—I don't think book agriculture is any good unless they realise it on the ground.

19763. Would you go so far as to say you would not allow agriculture to be taught unless there was a little garden on which the teaching could be illustrated?—I think it could not be taught properly at all otherwise.

19764. Then *a fortiori* you would not allow agriculture to be taught in town schools?—There is no occasion for it.

19765. Have you any acquaintance with the French syllabus of agricultural instruction in elementary schools?—No, only I have got the report of the Recess Committee here with which I am very much impressed.

19766. You are aware that they devote a good deal of time to elementary chemistry?—For large farmers that would be very useful, but not for small farmers.

19767. If small farmers are to become good farmers should they not read books on farming, and are not such books unintelligible to those who don't know the elements of chemistry?—Many years ago I got fifty copies of Mr. Baldwin's book, and I offered them to the farmers at half what I had paid for them, and then I offered them at a quarter of what I had paid for them, and so long as they paid even 1d. for them they would not have them. You must drive it into the boys, there is no use trying it on the men. I gave the books to the boys.

19768. Will they be able to understand the papers and books written on scientific farming unless they have some scientific knowledge themselves?—I am afraid they are not up to the mark yet, whatever it may be when they become peasant proprietors, which I am looking forward to; I think they will have more energy then.

19769. In preparation for that don't you think it would be a good thing to give them a little elementary scientific instruction?—There is not much time for it with the present school work.

Belfast. [illegible] [illegible]

accordingly. The present school examination is too much of a cram. Literary inspectors don't like agriculture, because they don't understand it themselves. Some inspectors say, "don't teach girls agriculture," but women sometimes have to manage farms themselves, and always manage the calves, butter, and eggs, feed the cows and sometimes the horses."

19773. You would be in favour of an increased number of agricultural inspectors who would take charge of the agricultural teaching in schools?—Undoubtedly.

19774. And you think, from your experience of what Mr. Carroll has done, that these inspectors would greatly promote the national teaching of agriculture in schools?—I think it would promote a great improvement in the agriculture of the country.

19775. Mr. Molloy.—I think that in conjunction with some member of a local committee you started a dairy industry and took charge, so to say, not exactly of Dungannon, but some three or four miles about, would you do the Commission the favour of briefly indicating what took place in reference to it?—I am sorry to say I did not take charge of the dairy industry, but Canon M'Cartan, who was the originator of the movement; he and I worked in double harness very harmoniously. Mr. Carroll sent us at our request Miss Lehane, the principal dairymaid at Glasnevin. The thing went on very well as long as Miss Lehane was there; she went from district to district, and centre to centre. The local gentlemen provided rooms and cream, the farmer's wives and some farmers attended the lectures, and we thought we were going to have a revolution in dairying; the farmers wives were very much impressed with all they had seen as to improved dairying, but when it came to practice—when it came to selling the butter—they found that after all the pains they had taken, they could only get in the Dungannon market the top price; and when they found they could get no more than the top price, with all their pains, the whole thing fell to the ground. You will have to [illegible] dairy instruction throughout the country, as in Denmark, and then we shall have the whole of the Irish butter at a different level.

19776. Did Miss Lehane take any steps to continue the instruction?—She had to go away, her time was up.

19777. But the comparative failure arose from the fact that she had not trained specialists among the teachers?—There was not time for that, it was simply a [illegible] of a few weeks, very interesting and very instructive.

19778. I believe she was not a very long time there?—No, only two or three weeks.

19779. And if she had continued, or some one corresponding to her in point of ability had continued there for some time, would not the results be more permanent?—If we had half a dozen Miss Lehanes, as in Denmark; we are all behind in Ireland—all politics and no practice.

19780. If she was there sufficiently long that the ordinary teacher of the school could get a knowledge of the subject, would not the effect of the instruction remain permanently?—Professor Carroll begged and prayed we would get somebody to go down to Glasnevin to learn dairying, but we could not get a single girl to go down. I had hoped for the schoolmaster's daughter, but she looks forward to making more profit by being a schoolmistress.

19781. However, during the time Miss Lehane was there, the instruction was very successfully carried out?—Very successfully carried out, but simply because it did not pay they left off exerting themselves.

19782. I am inclined to think they should have given it a further trial?—We would have done it, but we thought it was rather too much to ask local people to bear the expense of it.

19783. I believe there was a very influential local committee formed who worked very harmoniously?—Very much so; we had the clergy of all denominations, and they worked like brothers together.

19784. Captain Shaw.—This school [illegible] you have been talking on, does it only supp[ly] of its own district?—Yes.

19785. Would it be possible it migh[t] by more than one school?—At this mo[ment] another school on my property where [illegible] are exclusively Roman Catholics, and [I am] anxious to establish a school garden, if [illegible] the parish priest, would take it up, but [illegible] my friend, Canon M'Cartan, he is not [illegible] and I cannot get him to take it up; [illegible] ready to give the example of the [illegible] [illegible] at present. The Board have [illegible] to help the movement on.

19786. How many of the students do [illegible] get satisfactory instruction; you have [illegible] whom you think fit to go on for further i[nstruction]? There are sixteen pupils under instructi[on] I will tell you honestly, a good many [illegible] labourers' sons, and one of these two is [illegible] the father has a little farm of his own, a[nd] is a [illegible]; this little fellow has [illegible] in accordance with what he has learned. But in order to realise the full benefit, y[ou] have to districts far away from [illegible] working on so much a week, and from [illegible] other descriptions; the thing is [illegible] but there is not so much general impro[vement] [illegible] would expect to see.

19787. Does this farm teach on [illegible] than four children; give them effective [illegible] agriculture?—I had to sign for sixteen [illegible] day, for their quarter's teaching.

19788. Are they in the 6th?—6th a[nd] [illegible]

19789. Your teacher is an enthusiast[ic] [illegible]? No, he is a very active man who [illegible] what is impressed on him by Mr. Carro[ll].

19790. But he has a particular [illegible] agriculture?—He had not when he beg[an] [illegible] now, he found it so profitable.

19791. Did he not start on a farm [illegible] [illegible]?—He had two acres, but at my [illegible] began in 1870 with two acres opposite [illegible] had no practical knowledge of farmi[ng] [illegible] learning, helped by observation and [illegible] [illegible] from the young farmers around [illegible] [illegible] their system with the book, a[nd] [illegible] [illegible] he saw reason. He is a self-[illegible] He has now 25 acres, last year he [illegible] he sold nineteen lambs off the farm a[nd] has four cows, four yearlings, two [illegible] pigs, and about forty head of [illegible] no turkeys, geese, or ducks; he [illegible] they did more harm than good. His [illegible] experience, thinks that two acres and [illegible] allowed to every National schoolmaste[r] [illegible] districts, if they have a taste that wa[y] [illegible] no taste there is no use for it.

19792. It would not do to make it [illegible] all the teachers?—No.

19793. What assistance does he get [illegible] The boys and his own son; he has [illegible] [illegible] two boys in the school and [illegible] in fact he gets his 7s. where the other[s] [illegible]

19794. Is there much of the farm [illegible] [illegible] acres are all more or less [illegible] [illegible], recently added to him, so [illegible]

19795. That must entail a good [illegible] exercise?—Oh, yes; I [illegible], [illegible] continually working on the farm, a[illegible] [illegible].

19796. What is the result of his [illegible] work?—Very good, he gets very high [illegible]

19797. Chairman.—Is he first of [illegible] of [illegible]; he is a very plodding man.

19798. Captain Shaw.—In the [illegible] they come upon such things as [illegible] other matters of this sort. Do [illegible] important they should have some [illegible] they are?—He teaches them what it [illegible]

18799. Can you do that by description?—I believe it goes into their little heads, but they don't go into chemical tests.

18800. Would not a small knowledge of chemistry to illustrate the nature of these substances be of some use to the children?—If there was time for it I am sure he would be very glad to do it, and they would be very much interested in it. I know he tells them plenty about the ammonia that escapes if they don't keep their dunghills properly covered.

18801. Mr. Struthers.—I think you agree with what that teacher suggests, that you would only provide these school gardens and farms where the teacher had a taste for it?—Yes.

18802. You could not make it a compulsory system through the country?—It would be very hard on some teachers.

18803. This farm is 35 acres?—It is now about 15 under tillage, and the rest in pasture.

18804. The statement here is that only seven pupils were examined?—That is 1894, but as a matter of fact there were sixteen the other day.

18805. Well, even taking sixteen, is it necessary to have a farm of 34 acres to teach sixteen children?—Oh, no; I asked him if he would like more land and he said he would, and he took it, but the school farm proper is 14 acres, that he first acquired.

18806. Even 14 acres would be a great deal to teach sixteen children on; they could be taught with much less?—It is not necessary. He has this farm and teaches them on it, but he taught them on 3 acres just as practically.

18807. Is this district thickly populated?—It is, with ten-acre farms.

18808. Are there any schools within two miles of this school?—There is one within half a mile, the Chapel school.

18809. Any other?—There is one at Castlecaulfield within one and a half mile, one at [illegible], one and a half mile, and one at Donaghmore. You are thinking of grouping schools.

18810. Yes. Suppose you have a number of schools within two miles of this particular farm; might not the children of these other schools in the higher classes be instructed by this particular teacher without going to the expense of providing a school garden for each particular school?—I don't see why not. I attempted to start this as an emulation—that one school should have a farm and another a school garden—a pleasant emulation between Protestant and Catholic.

18811. It might be possible to bring the children of the different schools to this particular farm?—You could hardly bring them from Donaghmore. At Castlecaulfield, Mr. M'Nally would perhaps be disposed to start a farm himself.

18812. But I mean as an economical way of teaching agriculture practically, would not that be a good suggestion?—If the children could go so far. Their regular studies are up to three o'clock in the afternoon, and if they could go after that is a matter for themselves and their parents. I would support it if they do it, and I am sure Mr. Ross would too.

18813. But if the parents realised the benefit of this instruction, as no doubt some of them must, then I should think they would be rather anxious to send their children?—I should hope so.

18814. It would be a possible thing if they were willing?—Quite possible.

18815. In that case it would be necessary to have the instruction in agriculture after the regular school hours?—Yes.

18816. In fact to make it a continuation school?—Yes, it might be done on Saturdays.

18817. How does Mr. Ross teach the boys agriculture; at present he takes them out to his farm?—They have their book learning, and then he takes them out to the farm and points out the lesson.

18818. How often?—I am not sure at this moment.

18819. Several times a week?—Yes.

18820. He explains different things to them on the farm?—Yes.

18821. And do the boys do any practical work on it?—Oh, yes.

Mr. Redington.—It is half an hour a day or three hours on Saturdays.

18822. Mr. Struthers.—In the case of its being half an hour, you can see that on certain days it would be anxious to take the boys out?—Oh, of course; I have heard a master complaining of that, that he has been obliged to have them held an hour a day, and half the week it is raining.

18823. You think there should be a reasonable relaxation?—Oh, of course.

18824. What age would those children be to whom this agriculture is practically taught?—From thirteen to sixteen years.

Mr. [illegible].—That would be rather high, you might make a minimum of fourteen.

18825. Mr. Struthers.—You would have a great many children who have left school at that age, there would only be a surviving fraction?—When I mentioned thirteen I was thinking of two boys, sons of the grocer, who has a little bit of land himself. I think one of them is not more than thirteen, they are in this agricultural class.

18826. These others are from fourteen to sixteen?—Yes.

18827. There must be comparatively few who stay on so late?—Yes.

18828. And it would be advisable to induce pupils who have left school to attend schools like this?—The difficulty would be to give them an inducement, because the great complaint of the neighbourhood is the dearness of labour, and naturally they wish to have their own sons on the farms; in fact this boy I want to send to Glasnevin, he is barely sixteen, and his father took him home to help him, but I induced him to send him back.

18829. If they realised the value of this instruction, they might possibly send their children to school on Saturdays?—Possibly.

18830. Then the dairy classes you had were for people not connected with the school at all?—They were held in the school, but not connected with the school.

18831. Were they attended by pupils of the school?—Attended by those and by outsiders.

18832. Chairman.—Boys and girls?—Only girls.

18833. Mr. Struthers.—What might be called mature pupils predominated?—Yes, chiefly mothers and big sisters.

18834. I think you said already that if these classes had been continued they might have affected the general production of butter in the country, and raised the general prices?—I think so, if the whole district had been taught dairying, and if you could only manage by hook or crook to get dairymaids who would go up and learn, and then come back and teach.

18835. Both the instruction given on this farm and the instruction given in the dairy class is for the most part given to pupils who have left school?—No, the instruction on the farm is to pupils at school.

18836. But it might be extended?—Oh, yes, if they would come. I should like to add one or two extracts from the Recess Committee's report.

18837. You spoke of the agricultural education in Denmark; you are aware that that is given chiefly in evening schools—what are called the people's high school, and that agriculture is not taught in the ordinary day school, so that that would be rather in favour of establishing continuation schools rather than introducing the teaching of direct instruction in agriculture into day schools?—Oh, yes, years ago we used to have night classes.

18838. Have you any suggestion as to how these night classes might be revived?—No, they just dropped out by degrees. I was going to read about Denmark. It says at page 113: "Denmark, at the end of the

Belfast.

Oct. 12, 1897.

Colonel [illegible], J.P.

last century was one of the poorest, and today is one of the richest, entirely through agricultural education among the small freeholders." It speaks also of agricultural experts for general instruction and advice in emergency. That is a very useful thing. "France.—The agricultural instruction began in the Second Republic in 1848. There were schools of instruction to form heads of agricultural industries. M. Tisserand, Director-General of Agriculture in France, says a education specially for agriculture has become in our days a necessity, an imperious need in all countries, old and new, because it is a struggle between agriculture and agriculture and country and country." There is an extract here bearing very much upon the point. It says, "In these schools young men of ages ranging between eighteen and thirty, spend—some five winter months, besides three summer months, as boarders, receiving an education which leans chiefly to the human side, and gives but a secondary place to the scientific and technical side, and which aims—as the headmaster of one of the largest of these schools expressed it to me—at developing the heart, mind, and will."

19539. These schools correspond more to the district model school in which the pupils board, than to anything you could attach to the day school?—True; but we want in the day school to give them the elements, and make them take an interest in improved systems.

19540. Rev. Dr. Evans.—Do you really believe it is possible to give valuable agricultural instruction in primary schools?—Oh, yes, I see it so; the boys are keen over it.

19541. Do you think the teachers can teach both agriculture and the literary programme properly?—It has of late years come in as part of the literary programme for [illegible].

19542. Do you think the ordinary literary teachers can teach agriculture?—I only speak from what I know.

19543. Do you think our inspectors who are engaged in literary subjects are proper inspectors of agriculture?—No.

19544. Would not that observation you read just now, if carried out in Ireland, be a great deal more for the good of the country—that is, that we should have an agricultural department, and allow the Board of National Education to mind its own business, and teach literary subjects?—But we should like to give the agriculture in the school. They begin the farm work when they are out so high, and why should they not begin the improved agriculture, and not the "back-of-the-hill" work.

19545. Do you think we have got any occasion to teach agriculture as a trade more than blacksmithing or anything else as a trade?—You have Ireland mainly an agricultural country; you have the children of the country brought up as backward farmer's children and backward children; you want to get them when they are malleable and young, to learn improved principles.

19546. Quite right, all the elementary instruction leading on to it—you would be in favour of that?—Yes, and as much practical instruction as you could get into them.

19547. Rev. Dr. Whitaker.—I quite agree with you in all you have said; are you able to notice any improvements as regards proper culture of their farms, and especially proper modes of preserving their manures?—I can give you one very interesting answer, given to me by one of my most advanced tenants. There was an agricultural school, which is now discontinued, kept by a cousin of his some years ago, and I asked this man, when he was a young man, "What have you learned from going to the agricultural class?" "Well, your honour, before it began we used to grow three crops of oats in succession, and now we only grow one." I was remarking to somebody, not a fortnight ago, that where twenty or twenty-five years ago I could scarcely remember seeing a crop of turnips, now you have fine green crops growing up in all directions; I don't say it is entirely from this teaching, but it is very much from it.

19548. As to district farms, you are quite confident they would not go five miles to learn?—I don't think they could do it; and then they say, "We must earn money; we cannot be going on learning things, except at night"; we may revive that.

19549. Captain Shaw.—You have been always present and taken a great interest in it?—I have taken a great interest, but I have been unfortunately very much from home, and I am not very continuous in my attention at it.

19550. But you attribute some of the success to the interest you have taken in it?—Partly so. I don't like to claim too much.

19551. But you consider, in order such an undertaking may be successful, it requires local interest outside the schoolmaster?—I should be sorry to say so, because there are whole districts of country where there is nobody except the clergy—nobody in the shape of a landlord for miles and miles, and in the most backward district. I am glad to say that some of my neighbours' tenants rather look, perhaps, to one who is a local landowner as their friend.

would not care to go in for volumes of solids, I would confine myself to area.

19559. Do you think it would be a good thing to make the children take a tape and measure the playground?—Yes, that would be a splendid thing, and they ought to draw a plan of their playground on paper reduced to scale. Then a good thing would be to teach the boys to take the proper measurements in order to find the area of the playground. Very often in mensuration we give the boys the measurements—never ask them to take it out. I think it would not be a bad idea if a teacher drew out a plan of some figure in the playground and told the boys to go out and take the proper measurements.

19560. Have you ever in the course of your examinations attempted to see whether a boy could do that?—Oh, no, I have not, my lord. It is not in the programme, and, of course, the teachers would think we were going outside the programme.

19561. What do you say about the science teaching?—I think we ought to have science taught in all our schools, and I don't mean out of books—I mean by experiments. Each teacher, I think, ought to introduce twenty or thirty simple experiments in the course of the year, making them object lessons, so that he could teach the whole school.

19562. How would you provide the apparatus in the smaller schools?—I would go in for simple apparatus. I don't think the teacher would find much difficulty in introducing the apparatus I want at first.

19563. Where would you get the funds to pay for it?—The experiments I would go in for would be simple experiments that would not want expensive apparatus. I would like boys taught to make oxygen. Not much expense connected with that. Say heat—that heat expands bodies—that could be done without much expense. I don't think there would be any difficulty in the way of expense, provided the apparatus were simple. You could never hope to have very elaborate experiments. Expense would come in there.

19564. Do you know many teachers in your district who could give simple experiments?—Most of the teachers have read so much science that with very little practice they could make up those simple experiments.

19565. Would you leave the choice to the teachers?—I think in the meantime, until the system would get established, and after that the probability is a proper course could be traced; but meantime I would leave the whole system to the teachers. Simply ask them to exercise their discretion, and teach what they thought most judicious.

19566. What do you say with regard to the teaching of agriculture?—I think we cannot do much with agriculture—that is, in a practical kind of way—until we get some school gardens or school farms. Of course it is taught in all the country schools as a theoretical subject, but I am afraid the children very often don't know what they are talking about.

19567. Are there many school gardens in your district?—About half a dozen, and I have no school farm.

19568. Would it be easy to procure school gardens, if thought desirable, and, if so, would you be in favour of renting it on a neighbouring farm, or having it purchased out and out?—I think it would be better to purchase them out and out.

19569. You are aware that the Congested Districts Board, where they have established what are analogous to school gardens, have adopted the system of renting the plots?—A great many of our teachers have residences, and attached to the residence is a quarter acre. I think that would be quite enough for school gardens.

19570. You have given attention to the subject of manual occupations?—I am afraid at the present time we could hardly see our way well to introduce very much of it. I would propose to confine it to drawing and mensuration of surfaces. I quite well understand it would be a valuable acquisition, but our time is limited.

19571. Suppose arrangements could be made by recasting the programme by which the knowledge gained in drawing could be practically applied to woodwork, do you think it would be desirable in the schools of a town to introduce it?—I am not quite sure of that, the probability is the time limit would always come in; I think we ought to aim at getting our children to observe, and if we have one good subject taught where the powers of observation will be engaged I think that would be quite enough.

19572. What subject would you suggest?—I would say drawing.

19573. Drawing is a subject, no doubt, but it is a preliminary to the woodwork. Woodwork is simply carrying out in practical results the theoretical instruction gained in drawing?—I would be inclined to leave that optional with the teachers, I would not force too much of it.

19574. I agree with you there. We found when we were in Sweden that woodwork is left optional always, and Mr. Salomon, who is the great authority there, distinctly told us that it would be very unwise to force it, or engage a person to teach woodwork who had not a taste for it, or did not understand it?—I certainly would leave it optional, and confine the tuition to experts.

19575. Could you not make the teachers or some of them experts?—You might in time.

19576. You are aware that, where manual work is introduced there appears to be always a great objection to introducing anybody in the shape of an artizan, they much prefer a trained teacher. Supposing manual work was introduced, or could be introduced to any extent, to what extent do you think the results programme should be remodelled, so as to ease the care of examination and that sort of thing?—I would be inclined to leave out grammar and geography, at least in schools taught by one teacher. I think we ought to have a division of our subjects. Where one man has to teach a school I don't think he can possibly teach so many subjects as we have hitherto asked him to teach, and hence the boys' time is not only wasted but they get into bad habits and don't know the value of time. In large schools, where you have an assistant for each division, I would continue grammar and geography, but in rural schools there ought to be a change and leave it optional with the teacher whether he would teach grammar and geography, but then I would not ask him to subdivide the division. I would allow him to take the whole school and teach geography as a special subject. I would not ask him to divide it into five or six classes.

19577. The Commission in the course of their tour in Ireland heard evidence in regard to four or five schools in which manual work was taught, two or three of which were rural schools; but they have only seen and inspected one school, and that was the Christian Brothers' School in Limerick; and the way they found time there, was not by giving up anyone subject entirely, but by shortening the time of nearly all the subjects by ten minutes, by which they gained two hours that they devoted to manual work. Do you think that would be practicable?—Yes. One morning in the week might be given to sixth class. I would not introduce manual occupation to the fourth class, and certainly not to the third, and I would hesitate about the fifth. Eighty per cent. of our children never arrive at fifth class.

19578. In England, where we found manual work in operation, it only begins with the fifth class, and it is mainly taught in the towns and not in the country; and in large towns like Birmingham, instead of having the classes in every school, they form a centre in a certain district of the town to which classes from perhaps five or six schools go on different days to be taught?—I think that would be a very good plan.

19579. Rev. Dr. Wilson.—You are favourable to

Belfast.

Oct. 22, 1897.

Mr. E. F. [illegible], M.A.

BELFAST.
Oct. [illegible], 18[illegible]
Mr. E. F. Dewar, M.A.

the teaching of science with simple experiments?—Yes.

19880. It is very little use without them?—Absolutely useless without them as far as our boys are concerned.

19881. You have been with us in the Dungannon district and you are now in the Lurgan; are there more school gardens in Lurgan district than in Dungannon district?—Yes, since I have come to Lurgan three or four school gardens have been added. I think they are very valuable.

19882. And especially you would attach them to the teachers' residences?—I would, and to the schools; if the boys have to walk much they lose time.

19883. Where there is only one teacher you would omit grammar and some other things?—I would leave it optional with the teacher; if he thought he could overtake the work let him. A great many cannot overtake the work and I think it better to leave it optional.

19884. Mr [illegible].—But you would pay a fee for them?—I would.

19885. And then I suppose the teacher would endeavour to teach them?—He may, but if he taught them I would not sub-divide them.

19886. Rev. Dr. Wilson.—It would be better to have a large school with two teachers than to have two schools with one teacher in each?—Where there is not a subdivision of labour you never can have effective work.

19887. Rev. Dr. Evans.—The tendency, Mr. Dewar, in Ireland is to the multiplication of small schools?—I am sorry to say it is.

19888. And from what you know of Ireland you believe it will be likely to grow rather than shrink?—I think so.

19889. So that for anything we might hope for from larger schools we really must wait until it would come about unless in the case of those that are large now?—Yes.

19890. You are strongly in favour of drawing?—I am.

19891. Would you make drawing compulsory in all our schools?—I think I would.

19892. How would you provide for the teaching of drawing in the case of old teachers who never learned drawing?—I would allow them to teach drawing as best they could in the meantime.

19893. But you would pay them for it?—Yes, if they produced results I would pay them. I see no reason why a man should not be able to teach the elements of drawing, it is just writing. I cannot see if a man sets himself to it why he would not be able to teach the elements.

19894. You think we should require certificates in the case of all young teachers?—Yes.

19895. And all passing through the training colleges?—Yes.

19896. But you would allow a certain relaxation, which you think would have a beneficial effect, in the case of senior teachers?—Yes.

19897. With regard to mensuration I very much sympathise with what you have said. You would curtail arithmetic a little in the advanced parts and put [in] mensuration, is that right?—Yes, I think I would. I would put a little mensuration into the arithmetic programme, not as an extra subject. If the teachers preferred to have their geometry and mensuration taught as an extra subject I would allow that to go on, but I would put a little of the elements of mensuration into the arithmetic programme.

19898. And you think the elements of mensuration would be more useful than Harmonic Progression?—Yes, for boys going to certain trades.

19899. Or than cube root?—Well, cube root is useful sometimes.

19901. Rev. Dr. Evans.—Do y
teachers would be competent to go on
tion in the way you mentioned?—O
teachers know mensuration well.

19902. The trained teachers and [illegible]
no doubt?—Yes, and even the [illegible]
class teacher, a monitor coming [illegible]

19903. In the matter of agricultur[e]
school gardens, have you seen the[m]
I have examined them.

19904. Have you been impressed
viction that they are really doing go[od]

19905. And would like to see [illegible]
Yes.

19906. And you really think that [illegible]
work is done in those school garden[s]

19907. In the case of manual [illegible]
think that it would help in dev[eloping]
telligence of boys and girls [illegible]
acquirement would help in developing
the only question I would be [illegible]
would be whether the manual [illegible]
develop it better than the ordinary [illegible]
the questions we have now to set [illegible]
plan will develop best the intellige[nce]
boys and girls, who will have [illegible]
children. I have no hesitation [illegible]
that manual instruction will develop
but I have every reason for saying
the intelligence as much as a [illegible]
or a little more. I would not put [illegible]
platform.

19908. You would not put [illegible]
the same platform as algebra?—O[illegible]

19909. Is algebra taught in you[r]
yes, it is. But our programme di[vides]
three sections, first, second and thi[rd]
year's course is very seldom taught.

19910. Don't you think the the[ory]
is better taught through algebra. [illegible]
of the theory of arithmetic [illegible]
through algebra, but a boy who [illegible]
be better able to understand the [illegible]
from the training his mind has got.

19911. In your experience as an [illegible]
find that the questions in theory a[re]
more than the practical problems?—
nearly always answered carefully.

19912. By teachers, [illegible]
teachers?—Everybody.

19913. So much so that it [illegible]
with the inspectors about making [illegible]
all?—All the teachers' examinatio[ns]
contrive to set one or two, but [illegible]
avoided. At the last examinatio[n]
questions and five gained full [illegible]
may say to himself, "I know I can [illegible]
questions fully, and I will do that; [illegible]
theoretical questions fully," and [illegible]
safe side. If we want our the[ory]
answered we must change our [illegible]

19914. Can you suggest any [illegible]
teaching the theory might be imp[roved]
the children?

19915. To the children in the [illegible]
we could improve it in this way, b[y]
cards and putting theory questio[ns]
present cards have been in operati[on]
able time, and if we made new [illegible]
questions that would do. We ca[n]
questions will pass in arithmetic [illegible]
there must be a theory question.
in theory on every card and four [illegible]
and say a child must take one th[illegible]

19916. Do you think the ex[illegible]
planation in reading will much [illegible]

I think our reading books ought to be recast a little and made more interesting.

19917. Did you read Dr. Skerlington's report?—I did.

19918. Do you know what he means by "the old fifth book?"—Yes, I think I remember it.

19919. There was a great deal of elementary science in it?—Yes.

19920. And we are now talking about elementary science, do you think if that book were brought down to date would it be suitable in our schools?—No, I don't think I would introduce that, there are so many good primers in science that would be far more useful. I would introduce "Geikie's Physical Geography," a little primer on botany and one on heat in the same series, the boys could use those as reading books.

19921. Have you ever seen it put to boys whether they would prefer to go to a literary lesson or to manual work?—I *fancy* they would go to manual work; it requires less brain power, and a boy will always shirk the use of brain power, and so will men.

19922. CHAIRMAN.—Do you think it requires less brain power to do it properly?—I think it does.

19923. You can learn a lot of literary work by memory; can you do that with manual work?—I would say the literary programme is harder.

19924. REV. DR. EVANS.—Would it not be a rest to the brain, and at the same time a mental stimulus, if a boy had a turn at manual work?—Yes, and so I would give him writing and drawing; if I were a teacher drawing up a time-table I would have a hard lesson and an easy one—a hard lesson and an easy one in rotation.

19925. Have you spoken to other Inspectors about this manual instruction?—We have discussed it individually.

19926. Is your opinion and theirs in favour of its introduction?—Well, we are not very much enamoured of it; we think to give a boy a fair chance in the world the better plan would be to train him as intellectually as we can, and I think that we ought to go a good deal on the old lines, but I certainly would introduce drawing.

19927. MR. STRUTHERS.—You are quite agreed that some development of the practical faculties of the children, powers of observation, and sense of measurement should be encouraged?—Yes, I am certain of that.

19928. And for that reason you would introduce drawing, but you have some difficulty in also taking into the school a course in the form of manual instruction, however simple?—Just on the principle that if I have one good exercise to train their observation the probability is that would be quite enough.

19929. You would have observation in your lessons on experimental science?—Yes.

19930. Then why introduce drawing?—Drawing exercises, perhaps, a different part of the mind from experimental science.

19931. It trains the observation?—Yes, so it does; and it trains the hand.

19932. And makes the children more accurate?—So it does.

19933. What sort of drawing do you have in view when you say that?—I would not confine myself to drawing from mere copies; I would try to give our drawing a practical direction, so that when the boys went to learn trades they could take a sketch of some little thing used in the trade.

19934. At present it is chiefly freehand which is taught in the schools?—Yes, we have a course which says that object drawing and shading may be taught, but it is very rarely done.

19935. Do you think there is much stimulus to the intelligence in freehand?—I am not sure that there is so much stimulus to the intelligence as there is to the observation.

19936. But you were laying stress on the fact that every form of school work should train the intelligence; do you think freehand drawing is of great value in that point of view?—Well, it makes a boy observant, and anything that tends to make a boy observant will train his intelligence.

19937. Take a simple exercise in woodwork, making that pencil out of wood—don't you think there is a great deal more exercise of the intelligence in making that with a knife than there is in copying one of those *freehand* examples?—I am not quite sure about that; I would not like to pronounce categorically on it.

19938. You have not considered the intellectual effect of doing that work?—It was never put to me that way before, but if you ask me, I don't think there is much intelligence required in making that round.

19939. He has got a piece of rough wood; he has got to make a model of the exact dimensions; he has to be very accurate in his observations?—So he has in drawing.

19940. He has to consider every step he takes, every cut he makes with the knife; if he is careless and makes a cut too deep, he has to throw away his work and begin anew—is not that a valuable training?—Yes.

19941. Whereas in the case of drawing, if he makes a mistake he takes a piece of indiarubber and wipes it out?—Yes.

19942. Then is it not quite clear that there is a more valuable training in the woodwork?—No, I won't admit that.

19943. You said there was another form of training more valuable than copying examples from the flat?—Yes, sketching objects—model drawing.

19944. Would you say the same about drawing from plan and elevation?—Well, I am not sure that I would introduce that; you might introduce it in the sixth class. I think the other would come more readily into the ordinary work of every boy's life.

19945. Which do you think is the more useful for the artisan—making a sketch of the object, or making an accurate plan and elevation of the object he is going to construct?—Well, if you give me an example.

19946. Suppose he has got to construct an object of a certain size and form; he makes the plan; he has got the elevation and the dimensions marked on it; everybody who understands drawing could make the object from that, whereas if you make a rough sketch it gives the idea, no doubt, but it has not the dimensions?—In that case I would say the accurate one is the best.

19947. Perhaps you are not aware that drawing from plan and elevation could be, and is, very successfully taught to young children of the second class?—I have never seen it.

19948. It is so in the Birmingham schools?—Would the first and second class in Birmingham correspond with our first and second?

19949. It corresponds to your lowest classes, and the system is afterwards developed; they begin with paper-folding from a plan and elevation on the board; the children construct objects in paper, and know how to interpret it—or the object is constructed before them and they draw the plan and elevation?—I have never seen that.

19950. That kind of drawing is extremely useful; would it not enhance the usefulness if the children make an object to correspond with the drawing?—It certainly would.

19951. In that we may consider some simple form of construction as almost a necessary accompaniment of the drawing if it is to be of practical use?—It would be a good thing if we could introduce it and have time.

19952. You are quite agreed about the propriety of introducing drawing?—I am.

19953. And you would introduce anything to supplement the drawing which would make the instruction more intelligent, provided you could find time for it?—Yes, and provided it would not interfere with the literary instruction in other subjects.

19954. You don't think there is any intellectual training to be got from this drawing?—Oh, yes, I do. I don't think for instance drawing would give you the same intellectual training as being able to solve a question in arithmetic or a problem in algebra, but it has distinct amount of intellectual worth.

19955. Nobody proposes to leave out arithmetic, but I think you yourself propose to leave out grammar in the case of country schools?—So I think I should.

19956. And at the same time, perhaps, to make drawing compulsory?—Yes.

19957. Which means that you thought drawing was a more valuable exercise for school purposes than grammar?—Not necessarily; I said in cases where we had one teacher who had to subdivide his attention over six or seven classes, I say his work in grammar is worthless, so it is a case of doing worthless work and work which is fairly intelligent. I think I went so far as to say in town schools I would still keep grammar.

19958. Take the case of country schools where there is one teacher, he has to teach a considerable number of classes, six or seven; in order to save his work you think it better to leave out some subjects?—Yes.

19959. And you prefer to leave out grammar rather than drawing?—Yes.

19960. Why?—Drawing is more easily taught, you can teach a whole class in drawing with much [illegible] effect than five or six classes in grammar. It is a case of making your instruction intelligent, it is a case of making your instruction effective, it is a case of giving the children some benefit from their instruction.

19961. But you think ideally grammar is more intellectual?—Yes, if well done, but if not well taught it is not, but it is still more a case of a subject per se but of the mode in which it is taught.

19962. But still you think drawing has sufficient intellectual stimulus in it to make it worth while introducing it into a school at the expense of grammar?—It trains the observation, which perhaps grammar has not done.

19963. And has a certain intellectual value thereby?—Yes.

19964. You distinguish between town schools and country schools?—Naturally.

19965. And in town schools where you have a teacher for each class there cannot be the same difficulty in introducing these extra subjects?—Not at all.

19966. Therefore you would certainly introduce drawing and elementary science?—I would.

19967. Would you continue kindergarten occupations any higher than they are at present?—I don't think I would, the drawing part of it is good, and the remaining parts are pretty good to keep little children employed; in schools where you have no kindergarten the infants are left pretty much to themselves.

19968. I am taking the case of a school where there is a teacher for every class?—Then I would have kindergarten taught there certainly.

19969. Would you have it taught in the first class?—I would.

19970. In the second, supposing there is a teacher for second class?—Well, I might.

19971. And the third?—No, I don't think I would send it up to the third class. I think the time would be better employed at something else; in the second class the children are young and require some relaxation; seven years is the age in our first class, eight years is the age in second, and nine years is the age in third.

19972. And you think between eight and nine there is a peculiar change in a child's constitution, which makes a particular change in the instruction advisable?—No. Perhaps you are not aware that many of our boys leave at eleven, and it becomes a question for a teacher and manager to see what is the best education we can give that boy.

19973. But you understand it is not possible, even though you devoted double the time at nine years of age to teach certain subjects more rapidly?—No.

19974. Take a boy at nine, you consider grammar is most intellectual, you say "this boy is going to leave at eleven, it is most important he should have a thorough knowledge of grammar before leaving school, therefore we will devote four hours a day to it." Do you think he would necessarily make more progress in grammar?—No, I think a teacher would be a fool who would do it. I don't think any man should suppose such a case.

19975. Then even if you are preparing children to leave school at eleven, it does not follow that you would make them more perfect in a few subjects by confining them to those subjects?—Oh, yes, I think so, if I wanted to teach a boy reading, writing, arithmetic, and spelling, I could make the boy more perfect by keeping him to those four subjects. Take a possible case that we can argue, not an impossible case.

19976. Take the case of the subjects you have mentioned, reading, writing, arithmetic and spelling; the children are going to leave at eleven years of age, and you think it desirable that they should read a very advanced book at the time they leave?—I think they should be well up, so that they could read any book and take a pleasure in reading.

19977. Do you think by giving extra time to reading you could make the children at nine years of age read the present fifth book?—I think so.

19978. Would you not dull the children's intelligence by confining them so much to one subject?—I am not confining them, I put in the four subjects; your argument is weak on that point.

19979. Is there any special virtue in four; take five?—The reason I took four is because those are the four pass subjects in our course.

19980. In fact it is to be determined by experience what combination of subjects will give the best intellectual development to the child?—Everybody admits a boy must be able to read, write, spell, and do some accounts, these are the elements without which a boy cannot go through life; you have taken grammar, and 99 out of every 100 never knew grammar, hence I cannot argue with you, but if you take the case of a subject that a boy cannot go through life without some knowledge of.

19981. We agree that these elementary subjects must be taught; you would apparently introduce grammar as an additional subject in preference to such a subject as manual instruction?—Yes, I would. As I understand your point, you want to find out this, will teaching grammar for four hours a day be more effective than teaching it for one hour a day.

19982. In the case of country schools, you would be in favour of a large grouping of classes?—Yes.

19983. You would not have the examination individually in those cases?—No, I think I would make it the class or division.

19984. What would you say to continuing individual examinations in the higher classes, and having only class examination for the lower?—Yes, I think that would be a very good thing, but personally I am inclined to have individual examination in the most important subjects.

19985. But chiefly in the higher classes?—I think I would continue it as it is just at present.

19986. You would have individual examination at a stage at which none or very few children had left school?—If I were remodelling the results programme, a very good plan would be to divide our schools into three sections—good, fair, and, perhaps, middling, then I would only examine my good schools once every three years.

19987. Such a system as they have in England?—Something like that.

19988. Captain SHAW.—You expressed a strong opinion as to the suitable education for a child leav-

you studied many systems except the one in operation under the National Board?—I have read some books.

19989. Have you inquired as to the result of the teaching under the London or Liverpool or Birmingham School Board, and compared the effect on the children?—I have not.

19990. In considering what a child should be taught, have you considered the result of such education in other countries?—After all a certain amount of theory must be introduced. It still goes back to the question whether the manual instruction will develop the intelligence better than the old-fashioned way.

19991. I think you are rather arguing from one side of the question, not having any experience of the other?—I have no experience, but the theory stands.

19992. Yours is an a priori argument, most of it. With regard to model drawing, do you think many elementary teachers are capable of giving instruction in model drawing?—I think any teacher ought to be able to make up as much model drawing as would enable him to teach.

19993. Are you speaking from experience now, or from what you would imagine?—Oh, I have no hesitation in saying that if any teacher puts his shoulder to the wheel he can make up as much drawing as would enable him to make a sketch of anything.

19994. Have you any idea of the number of persons who send up these drawings of models to South Kensington?—I daresay so. I say the teacher ought to have some instruction, but he could arrive at that amount of information himself. Dr. Evans asked me would I recommend that old teachers who had no certificates should teach this. I said yes, of course, for I cannot understand a man of intelligence not being able to get up as much drawing as would enable him to teach the elements of drawing.

19995. You think any teacher could see whether a model was correctly drawn?—He might not, but he could give a boy a fair idea of how he should go about it.

19996. But in model drawing it would be almost absolutely necessary that he should be able to correct a boy when he went wrong?—Well, if you want our boys to be made professors we cannot hope for that. If you ask me if a boy should have a man's head on him I say he should not, and it would be a pity he should.

19997. Then you would approve of a boy learning drawing, although he may be drawing incorrectly, and the teacher could not show him where he was wrong?—I don't think the teacher need be a professor in order to show them where they went wrong.

19998. Is not drawing from plan and elevation more easily comprehended by anybody, and one in which at once a mistake can be detected?—I think not, it is not very easy.

19999. You think it is a more difficult exercise than drawing a model?—I think so, I refer to simple models.

20000. Do you think it is more difficult to draw the plan and elevation of a cube than to draw a perspective view of it, the plan is a square, and the elevation is a square?—It all depends on how you are looking at it. I think a boy ought to be able to represent a cube on paper.

20001. There are two ways of representing it, by plan and elevation, or in perspective, and the question is which is the easiest way?—I think the perspective would be the hardest way.

20002. You talked about adding mensuration on to arithmetic, you would make that practical?—Yes.

20003. That is that the boy should actually measure the area, and then calculate from his own measurements?—Yes, I would say a boy ought to be able to take the correct measurement of some little plot.

20004. Could you not cut out a piece of paper, and make the area equally well?—Yes, or mark out a figure on the floor of the school.

20005. At present, in supplying apparatus, if a teacher wished to undertake the teaching of experimental science he would have to do it at his own expense, I presume?—Yes, except the manager supplied the money.

20006. Don't you think it would be a good plan if some money was ear-marked in some way to be spent on apparatus in schools?—I think it would be a very good plan.

20007. You think there is a defect in the present system that there is no compulsion on anybody to spend money in equipping the schools?—No, except the manager is willing to do it.

20008. Mr. Molloy.—I think you have had upwards of twenty years' experience as an inspector of National schools?—Yes.

20009. Has your experience been confined to the North of Ireland?—I was in Mullingar, the centre of Ireland, and afterwards in Dungannon and Lurgan.

20010. And prior to becoming inspector you had experience of Belfast schools?—I taught a good deal of mathematics when I was a student.

20011. Would you contrast the state of mathematics at present with the mode in which the subject was taught when you were a boy in our primary schools, is there any improvement?—I was at the Belfast model school when a boy, and the model school was remarkably good; I don't suppose you would get in any school in Ireland better taught mathematics than in this school when I was there.

20012. Would you extend that observation to the elements of physical science?—Certainly, there is no physical science in my district, and when I was at the model school we had a very extensive course.

20013. And during the twenty years since the result system have you found the elements of physical science taught?—I may say not. I have one school in connection with the Science and Art Department, in which physical science and chemistry are taught, but it has nothing to do with the National Board.

20014. The physical science which you refer to as taught so successfully was under the ordinary programme of the National Board at the time?—Yes.

20015. What changes, if any, would you propose to introduce into the result programme to bring about more successful and efficient teaching of mathematics and the introduction of the elements of physical science?—I think I would give the teachers a choice. I would be inclined to divide the schools into two or three classes, and I would allow schools which got into the good class to teach whatever subjects they liked; I would allow schools that got into the second or middle class to confine themselves to one or two subjects, and I would insist on schools in the low class confining themselves to the elements of education, what a boy would want hereafter, and I would go in for allowing the good school to be examined only once in three years.

20016. You would not have a common programme?—I would have a common programme, but I would limit the third class of schools to the ordinary four or five subjects.

20017. Have you worked out your theory on paper in any way?—I have tried to do it.

20018. Would you find it convenient to work it out and then hand it in for the information of the Commission later on?—Yes.

20019. Mr. Redington.—In your report for 1885 you refer to this matter, and so far as I can see you anticipate that even the lowest grade of schools would teach a couple of optional subjects?—So I think. I would have allowed them drawing; I had that in my mind, and singing.

20020. Could you tell us what has been in your opinion the effect of the present system of examination for results on the dull boys and on the clever boys of the school?—Well, the probability is that the dull

Belfast.
Oct. 14, [illegible]
Mr. R. F. [illegible], M.A.

3 D 2

boys have got a little more teaching to bring them up to a pass, and when the clever boys were well up to the mark, they were not hurried on to a higher class.

20022. They were rather neglected?—I won't say they were, they got the same tuition as the bad boys, and the tuition made them expert in doing their work, the dull boys were brought better on—the probability is the clever boys might have got on better under the old system.

20023. If any system were adopted by which the general merit of the school was taken into account instead of the proficiency of each individual pupil, would there be any fear that the dull boys would be neglected?—I don't think there would be if the inspector was allowed to choose the boys to examine, if I went into a school and chose eight, the teacher would not know which eight I would choose.

20024. As a matter of fact, you don't find that boys who attend irregularly and who obviously will not make the 100 days are neglected by the teacher?—Not at all, they get instruction in the schools, because a teacher may not know until the last quarter whether the boy will not make the attendance.

20025. What is the reason that the science programmes under our rules are not more taken up in the fifth and sixth classes?—The probability is our programme in science demand too much, and it is a hard programme to teach, and hence teachers find, I daresay, they really cannot teach a boy in one or two days of the week. I think the programmes are pretty high in science.

20026. Even in mathematics?—That presupposes a knowledge of mathematics, and the boys might not be able to pass in mathematics sufficiently well, but if you take the elementary programme on magnetism I think that it rather advanced for our little boys.

20027. About agriculture, could you tell us what has been the effect on the literary instruction of schools of the teacher having a school farm, has he become a less careful literary teacher?—I have only had one case of that in my experience, it was the case to which Colonel Burgess referred, and this was a very good man, his school did not certainly deteriorate owing to his farming.

20028. When the boys are brought out to the school farm what kind of instruction do they get there?—Well, I am not sure, of course, you know inspectors have not to examine on school farms, they have only to examine on school gardens. In my district at the present time the boys do part of the work.

20029. Do they get any instruction; are they used merely as labourers?—Oh, no; for instance in the garden the boys are trained practically to put in strawberries and raspberries the proper distance apart, they have practical training in addition to theoretical, then in the cultivation of cabbages they measure the distances between the rows, they have also practical work in addition to theoretical.

20030. But the practical work is very much the work a labourer would do, the reasons are not given?—The reasons might be given; I don't know exactly just what you mean.

20031. For example, the effect of manure, a highly manured plot producing much better vegetables than a less manured one?—I fancy the reason then would be given in the words of the book, the book tries to account for that, and I don't think the teacher could give anything else, that would be a part of the theory rather than the practice.

20032. Would it not be a useful thing to show the pupil that the words of the book are exemplified by what he sees before him?—Where the practice would come in would be what given manure would be best for the given crop.

20033. CHAIRMAN.—Or for this given land?—Yes, here is a land and here is a crop, what is the proper manure for this crop, the proper manure would be [illegible], I am not sure that the teachers could go into the science of it and say "This particular plant requires a given food and this manure provides it."

20034. Mr. REDINGTON.—Does he say "Owing to the constituents of the manure it is the right food for this land." Would he be able to do that?—His book would tell him.

20035. Would not a little elementary chemistry teach him that?—If he knew elementary chemistry it would be better.

20036. CHAIRMAN.—Does the teacher ever try any experiments such as we saw in connexion with the Westmorland County Council, where they divided [illegible] land into plots and tried the effect with turnips of putting on a certain quantity of manure on this plot, and another quantity on the next, and no manure on the third, and weighing the crop and testing the result of manuring and over manuring and no manuring, and whether a proportionately heavy crop was produced to pay for the extra manuring?—No, I have never seen that done.

20037. Would a teacher teach a boy that at a certain period of the season if he could get his turnips in early it would be better to plant swedes; but in a wet season it would be better to plant another sort?—I fancy they would do that, but that would be more on the farm than on the garden.

20038. Mr. STRUTHERS.—Would you tell us whether you can refuse payment for extra subjects where the ordinary subjects are not well taught?—Not now, we had the power once, if a boy did not pass in the pass subjects, he would not be paid in extras, now that only holds where the extra subject is taught inside school hours, but if taught outside school hours the payment of the fee is unconditional.

FORTY-FOURTH PUBLIC SITTING—THURSDAY, OCTOBER 14, 1897,

AT 3 O'CLOCK, P.M.

At the Grand Central Hotel, Belfast.

Present:—THE RIGHT HON. THE EARL OF BELMORE, G.C.M.G., in the Chair; THE RIGHT HON. C. T. REDINGTON, M.A.; REV. HENRY EVANS, D.D.; REV. HAMILTON WILSON, D.D.; W. R. J. MOLLOY, ESQ.; CAPTAIN T. B. SHAW, and J. STRUTHERS, ESQ., B.A.;

with J. D. DALY, ESQ., B.A., Secretary.

Mr. J. P. DALTON, M.A., District Inspector of National Schools, Belfast, examined.

Mr. J. P. Dalton.

20039. CHAIRMAN.—You are a District Inspector of National Schools in Belfast?—Yes, my lord.

20040. Perhaps you will give the Commission in your own words your views upon the subject of the need of practical education?—I consider that in many points of view it is most desirable to introduce practical education. In the first place, I consider that even as a system of education, you cannot have a complete system without the work taking a practical shape. There are many faculties that cannot be cultivated at all without practical work, and notably the faculty of observation, and I consider that in schools where practical education of some kind is not adopted those faculties are allowed to go to waste.

20041. Do you think that at present there is not sufficient practical education in the National system?—I am certain of it.

20042. Will you tell us in what way you think it fails in that direction?—I might illustrate it by reference to particular subjects. Take, for example, the subject of agriculture, which, perhaps, most cries out for reform. In agriculture the instruction is absolutely worthless, I consider, unless it is illustrated practically, unless the children are brought face to face with the objects in the fields and gardens, and know the things that they are actually talking about. Otherwise, I believe that the instruction is worse than useless. I might say the same thing with regard to, perhaps, other subjects.

20043. You say the subject is worthless; do you think that is the general opinion of inspectors and educationists in Ireland; because we have heard contrary opinions—very conflicting opinions?—I think the general opinion would be pretty much in that direction at all events. Possibly the word might be a bit strong, but it would be in that direction.

20044. Now do you think that children if they were afforded an opportunity of observing improved agricultural operations step by step, should do so under a specialist or skilled instructor; or do you think that the ordinary teacher should receive sufficient training before he becomes a teacher, to be able to carry on this part of the education?—I think we would have to begin with specialists, but I hope we will reach a stage when the ordinary teacher can take his place with proper training.

20045. You think at any rate that there are a few teachers here and there at present who could take it up?—Yes, there are some; but the majority do not know sufficient of agricultural operations to be able to teach the subject usefully.

20046. How many teachers in your district?—In my district at present I have little to do with agriculture; my district is confined principally to the large towns of Belfast and Lisburn. I have only twelve or thirteen country schools.

20047. Are there any garden plots to those schools?—Not one.

20048. How much ground do you think should be attached to a rural school?—I think at least one rood, and I think that one rood would serve all practical purposes for the teaching of gardening.

20049. Do you think that if agriculture is not to be taught as a trade, and that the principles of agriculture only are to be taught in National schools, that a rood would suffice?—I was thinking more particularly now of the part of agriculture which treats of gardening. Of course a rood would not serve for the principles of agriculture, including the treatment of live stock.

20050. No; that is not what some of our witnesses have meant by agriculture, but showing more the effect of manures; that could be done in a garden, excluding live stock; they looked upon live stock as being connected with the trade of agriculture, not with the principles?—I think we could not do much more with a rood than gardening successfully. We could hardly do anything appertaining to farming.

20051. Now in those parts of the country where labourers' cottages have been built under the Labourers Acts and gardens attached to them, do you think that it would be advisable that the children of those persons should receive in the schools such an education as would enable them at any rate to make profitable use of those gardens?—Most distinctly, I do. Those gardens are of very little use at present; people grow nothing at all in them, that ever I have seen, but potatoes, cabbages, and perhaps a few onions. They know nothing at all about the growing of vegetables.

20052. Now, turning to what we may call the indoor part of the education, what have you to say upon the subject of kindergarten?—I consider it an excellent subject. I know no subject better calculated to make a beginning for a practical system of education; but as we carry it out at present it is only a beginning; we don't develop it.

20053. Do you find that kindergarten is taught in the infant school?—Yes.

20054. But that it is not followed up in 1st and 2nd class?—Well, it may be.

20055. What, as a rule, do you find?—That depends upon the kind of infant school. An infant school may include pupils up to 2nd class. They have to leave after they have reached their sixth birthday, but they may have reached 2nd class at that time; but it is only in some infant schools they have kindergarten. Some years ago I had only five kindergartens in the district; now there are close on twenty.

20056. How is the difficulty about getting the necessary appliances got over in those schools that have come into operation lately; who finds the money for it?—The locality, the manager or the teacher.

20057. But as a rule does the teacher find it or the manager?—As a rule they help each other; they get up a concert or something of that kind among the children and put a few pounds together. The beginning is perhaps a poor, humble one, but they add to it from year to year.

20058. Is kindergarten much appreciated by the parents?—I think very much in every school where it is adopted; they tell me it has attracted children to the schools.

20059. You say that the only additional furniture needed is a press for the materials and suitable desks, you want objects used in the kindergarten instruction?—I distinguish them from furniture.

20060. But they cost money?—To be sure.

20061. Do you think the special desks are absolutely necessary?—The ordinary desks, if they are of a suitable height, might be used for the purpose, provided you have kindergarten slabs; but it is an essential item in the instruction to have desks divided into squares and spaces; a great deal of the instruction consists in drawing lines, which are guided by those squares and spaces. But there are slabs that could be put on the desks.

20062. Are you of opinion that every teacher should receive a certificate of competency to teach kindergarten?—I am afraid we would have to insist on something like that. If it were not insisted on, perhaps a teacher might be taking it up who was not competent, and did not understand the system—taking it up for results fees, and instead of benefiting the pupils might be doing the opposite. It requires a considerable amount of skill and sympathy and study, and the certificate is supposed to cover those qualifications.

20063. Do you think that a kindergarten teacher requires more than any other member of the school staff, the qualifications of intelligence and sympathy with the children?—I do, distinctly; she has to train the faculties at their very first opening, and that requires more handling than dealing with children whose faculties are further developed.

20064. How would you develop the kindergarten system?—I think the development should branch out into two directions; first, I would introduce something in the third and fourth classes that would train the powers of observation of the children; that, I think, could be done by means of object lessons, and the best object lessons of all are connected with the objects that are actually found in the locality around the school, the plants that grow there, the rocks found there, the minerals or even the natural products, the manufactures of a city like this.

20065. You would connect that with kindergarten?—That would be an extension of kindergarten.

20066. Have you got any paper-folding in your district?—No, except in the kindergarten.

20067. But following on kindergarten?—None in a consideration.

20068. In one or two places we have seen some paper-folding; but it did not appear to be done in the way it is done in England from the blackboard, the children following the lines the teacher drew on the blackboard, and being able to fold the paper from understanding the signs on the blackboard. Do you think if something of that sort were first of all learned by the teachers and then introduced into the schools it would be an advantage?—That might be, but I fancy we could find quite a number of things that would be of even greater importance.

20069. That is principally introduced in the case of the younger children between the infant kindergarten and the higher sorts of manual training?—That would be useful, especially when folded from actual drawings before them. I think that would be educational.

20070. I think you have some objection to the term manual training and hand and eye training; will you tell me what they are?—I have no objection to the terms, but I am afraid they sometimes lead to a confusion of ideas; people using the phrase "manual training" are liable to imagine it is merely giving the hand a particular deftness, whereas if properly carried out I consider it is intellectual training of a very useful kind.

20071. Making the children think?—Precisely; and an aid of eye training. Undoubtedly you cannot train the eye without training the intellect, and that feature in the training is not properly brought out, and I fancy that because that is not properly understood, is the reason why a great deal of prejudice against this training arises.

20072. You have not seen the Sloyd system in operation?—No, only to read about it.

20073. Perhaps you would agree with me that if it is not taught properly it is better not to teach it at all?—Undoubtedly; that may be taken as a general principle applying to everything.

20074. Do you think it is absolutely necessary that woodwork training should be taught in connexion with drawing?—I think to make it properly educational it is; without drawing it is merely handicraft or carpentry.

20075. And bad carpentry, perhaps?—Yes.

20076. Perhaps you would give us your views about drawing, to which we have paid a great deal of attention and which seems the most popular sort of manual training—in Ireland at any rate?—I think that as regards drawing, so far as leads on to the end of the second class, we cannot improve on the system we have at present, namely, the kindergarten system, and I think that even though we don't carry out the full course of kindergarten in ordinary schools still we could do something, we could divorce the kindergarten drawing from the regular kindergarten instruction and possibly introduce it; and it is a system that would almost teach itself, that anyone could understand. When we pass at present from the infant school to the higher school we pass away from the kindergarten system of drawing to an entirely new system. The teachers who teach the new system, freehand as it is called, know little or nothing about kindergarten and have to commence de novo.

20077. Do they teach drawing at all by the blackboard here?—Very little, I am afraid.

20078. How do they teach it?—They simply set engraved figures, made out on sheets, and put them up in front, and put the pupils in the desks, and give paper, and let them copy away.

20079. The children are teaching themselves, then?—Not quite that; the teacher goes among the children, and points out defects in their drawing, and sometimes guides a pencil.

20080. They never teach the way we saw in England—by the teacher drawing the figure on the blackboard with chalk?—I don't think I saw it three times in my life in a school; if we made more out of the kindergarten drawing, and developed it into courses suitable for the 2nd and 3rd classes; introduced, say, curved lines—a point we don't reach in kindergarten—and showed them how to combine these lines in variation of ways by the blackboard, that would lay a foundation for designing and give them a taste for it. In the 3rd and 4th classes I would introduce mathematical instruments, at all events the ruler and compasses, every child should know the use of them; and I would still keep them on as a development of the kindergarten drawing. In the higher classes, after a little preliminary practice at the drawing of those engraved figures, I would put them to drawing from simple objects.

20081. What do you call a simple object—an actual article? The actual article. The teacher would stand before the blackboard, and with chalk in his hand would show the children how the object should be first regarded, the points he should take in his eye in order to reproduce it on paper; and the teacher would actually draw it on the board, and the children would imitate him, and after a time reach such a proficiency that they could sketch simple objects themselves. I have satisfied myself that the drawing done in 3rd and 4th classes, at present is really of very little value—and that the teaching is neglected—but that it leads up to very little, and I have brought some specimens here in illustration of that; that (producing example) is the drawing in second 5th—barely passable—that is done by children who are taught in 3rd, 4th, and first stage of 5th. Now, side by side with that, I would like you to look at this (producing)—that is drawn by a child in

Belfast.

Oct. 14, [illegible]

Mr. J. P. Dalton.

second 6th, who never passed through the other classes at all.

20782. The inference you want me to draw is, that this child, who has never been taught in the lower classes, draws as well as those who have been taught? —I would like you to look at the figures yourself; but the conclusion is, that the time has been wasted, and this is in a school where it has been fairly taught. I may say, also, they are different classes of children; this second child belongs to a poorer social class; the schools are at opposite sides of a street, not three minutes from each other; one is in a slum, and the one in which drawing has been taught heretofore is situated in a better locality.

20083. You think that drill should not be dropped at the end of the kindergarten course, but that physical exercises should be continued, not merely for the purpose of drill, but for the personal deportment of the children, keeping themselves neat and tidy?—Decidedly; I find the drill most efficient in securing good discipline in the school, showing the pupils how to walk and move about gently and quietly, and improving their deportment as a whole.

20084. What is your opinion about the teaching of physical science?—I would be most anxious to see it introduced, and I think that would be the second direction in which the extension of the kindergarten should branch out in the higher classes; in object teaching, and the objects to be selected should be those we find in the actual world about us. The objects we have in schools very often are artificial objects made for a set of lessons. I think we might begin very nicely, indeed, for work of the kind if we required the children to know some of the more common flowers and plants.

20085. Rev. Dr. Wilson.—You are favourable to the introduction of manual instruction in a moderate degree?—I am.

20086. What modification in our present programme would you propose to make room for that?—I think, in a district like this, at all events, and, of course, my remarks are directed more particularly to my own district, in a district like this I do not see the use of grammar and geography in the 3rd and 4th classes; fully 60 per cent. of our pupils finish their school course at the end of the 4th class, as they are then qualified to go to work in the mills by age, and by having passed the necessary standard. And for the last two years of their course they have been subjected to a great deal of pressure for the purpose of getting the preliminary principles of grammar and geography understood by them, and even when they do understand them they never know the connexion between those principles, perhaps, and the actual language—you never reach the living concrete language at all.

20087. You would make an important modification in grammar?—I would make those optional subjects, and thus I would not shut the door to any pupil who was willing to remain in school to learn them; and by postponing the commencement of grammar and geography you would do as much work in three years as is now taken beyond five or six years to do. I must say, however, with regard to that, that I would have certain notions with regard to grammar and geography taught to all the pupils, but I would connect them with other subjects, such as the subject of the reading lessons, and so forth, and with these, and no others, and the teachers would be relieved from the necessity of forcing them on children who don't want them.

20088. What would be your idea as regards Belfast of a change in the time of the school hours, that is to say, suppose they were to meet at nine o'clock in the morning and adjourn at twelve or half-past twelve for dinner, and, after an hour meet again for a short time?—I would consider it a wonderful improvement. I consider the present system of regulating the school hours is not at all adapted to the local circumstances in Belfast; as a matter of fact they all go away here for their luncheons and it is difficult to gather them back again in the afternoon. In a great many cases, of course, they have no playground and they have to let them away. A great many of these children have to go to their fathers and mothers who are working in the factories, with their dinners, and it would be a great improvement to give them a couple of hours in the middle of the day, when they could do their home work and come back again in the afternoon, fresher.

20089. You would give them two hours?—Perhaps so.

20090. Mr Strutters.—You would mark the register again in the afternoon?—That could be done.

20091. Rev. Dr. Wilson.—Would that be necessary, it has been objected that it occupies so much time?—It would be absolutely necessary; our present system consists in recording the attendance if they do not come back.

20092. Chairman.—Then they do call the roll again?—In order to do it in a complete way they should.

20093. Rev. Dr. Wilson.—There is no formal break up in the middle of the day?—No, as far as I understand the rule, it seems to require that the children should remain on the premises, but we have to give it an elastic meaning here because they go away; you could not keep them from doing so.

20094. You approve of that, I am glad to say?—I do, distinctly. I recommended that change in a report five years ago.

20095. I see you consider that real education ought to consist in more than mere book learning?—I think so; but I am afraid we are very far behind the age in Ireland, confining it to books and nothing else. My own opinion is that a mere book, especially in an objective study, teaches nothing whatsoever.

20096. Rev. Dr. Evans.—Do we teach too much arithmetic in the schools on the average?—Well, of the kind we teach I am afraid sometimes we do.

20097. Do you agree in the opinion that it would be better if we did not teach so much advanced arithmetic and more mensuration instead of it?—I do. I have actually recommended in reply to Dr. Wilson to make the higher arithmetic an optional subject, keeping on arithmetical teaching in all classes, but of a more practical kind.

20098. Is it your experience as an Inspector that the theory of arithmetic is not sufficiently well taught? —That is my experience.

20100. Could you suggest any way by which, when we are trying to make room for manual instruction, we might do better with the theory of arithmetic?—To do better with the theory of arithmetic you must pay, not merely for the results of sums worked out, no matter how they are arrived at, as you do at present, but also for the methods of working them. For

the fact that, since this Commission started, a large number of schools that taught the industrial programme for girls are wanting to give it up?—I have not noticed it because it was not in operation here when you commenced.

20103. Would you be in favour of omitting any other portion of the literary programme?—Yes, grammar and geography. I would have grammar and geography of a certain kind, that is, the leading notions of these subjects so far as they appertain to actual use—correct speaking and writing. I would teach grammar in connection with reading and composition, and geography in connection with geographical readers and topographical maps, but I would postpone the book treatment of them to a later period.

20104. Would you put analysis of sentences into the ordinary programme?—I would, but I would postpone the book treatment of them until a later date and then make it optional.

20105. Have you any manual instruction in the sense in which this Commission contemplates that

20130. You suggest that might be done by means of flowers and plants?—Yes, for a beginning.

20131. That applies more to country schools?—No, it would apply everywhere; I don't see why we should not have it carried out here.

20132. You don't have flowers growing in the neighbourhood of towns?—No, but you could collect them on Saturdays.

20133. CHAIRMAN.—It is very easy to get out of Belfast into the country?—Precisely, and it would have a most important effect in that way.

20134. Mr. [illegible].—You think that it would be very good for the children to be brought out of town and see the flowers and plants in the country?—It would, and when they grow up to be men and women it might take them out many a time.

20135. Then you would have what they call in Germany school excursions, not that the whole school should go at once, but that each teacher should take a class out in the country?—I would, and I think it is a pity that our Saturdays are allowed to

getting children to make simple apparatus for themselves.

20137. You think that this making of objects directly improves the quality of the instruction in drawing or makes it more intelligible to children?—Yes, and shows the application of drawing, of which they have not an idea at present.

20138. It has certainly an intellectual training of its own?—Certainly.

20139. In fact in a minor way it might be compared to the intellectual training that is given by grammar?—Yes, to be sure, except that you cannot show the object of grammatical teaching until you get naturally to the language, and it will take years to do that, whereas you can in the other case.

20140. And there is this other distinction the children almost invariably find making things very interesting and take to it naturally?—Yes.

20141. Do you find as a rule that children take to grammar with a great zest?—I don't think anyone has ever found it.

20142. And if the result to be got from cardboard work was inferior to that got from grammar, still you find children take to it more readily?—Yes, it develops their inventive powers and gives them originality, which grammar will never give.

20143. But the grammar itself might be taught more intelligently, I mean to say not from any fault of the teacher, but might it not be regarded as part of the essential teaching of language?—Decidedly. I had in my mind the kind of grammar that would be adapted to children who leave school long before you could give them any idea of the structure of language; I would have a kind of conversational grammar for them.

20144. But the use of grammatical terms at an early stage is useful, the distinction between a verb and a noun?—It might, provided there were very few.

20145. And it is important to teach children that a certain word is naturally connected with another word that may appear further on in the sentence?—True, but that is an essential part of explanation.

20146. But having a grammatical name is often a shorthand method of explanation?—Yes, but with us very often they are done with thinking once they get the name.

20147. At all events you are clear that grammar teaching ought to be a help and subsidiary to the reading lesson?—Yes.

20148. CHAIRMAN.—If you were asking a child what the word "unpractical" meant would you consider that it was not practical, a sufficient answer?—I would not.

20149. Rev. Dr. EVANS.—Do you think a child ought ever to replace a word by its equivalent?—To give a proper synonym might be useful, but that would lend itself very much to tricks. I think the best thing would be for him to explain the word in his own language, or apply it in another sentence; the mere synonym never reaches what you require.

20150. Mr. STRUTHERS.—Is not the teaching of synonyms a dangerous practice?—I think so, anything that lends itself to mechanical methods.

20151. It is very much better instead of asking the meaning of a word, to ask the child the meaning of a sentence?—Yes, in connection with the context.

20152. I think you say that the present method of inspection tends to make the inspector give attention to results rather than methods?—He has nothing else before him very often; our instructions say that we should get so many answers out of so many questions; he is a mere registrar of answers.

20153. You say you have 18,000 pupils in average attendance?—More now; that was in 1895.

20154. How many of those would be examined?—I examined 16,000 in the year to which that report refers.

20155. Then you examine each one of these individually?—Yes, sometimes in thirteen different subjects.

20156. And for each of these subjects you must ask a considerable number of questions?—Six would be the regulation number.

20157. That represents an enormous amount of work?—It represents as hard as we can go from morning to night, and from year's end to year's end.

20158. Do you think it is possible for a man with that work to do to give any general consideration to the work of the school?—It is not; and in connection with that perhaps you would allow me to show a return I have here that shows the number of days that an assistant inspector and myself will be occupied during the current quarter, in fact working much harder than in the interest of the school, not to speak of our own interest, we should be required to work. You will see from that there is not a solitary day vacant, and I have any number of other official matters to work in, inquiries and other matters.

20159. In any case with all that enormous amount of individual work to be done you cannot pay much attention to the methods of teaching?—No.

20160. And is it not also the case that your judgment as to the pass or fail or first or second pass is not of absolute necessity be somewhat superficial?—I try to form my judgment as accurately as I can, so far as basing the passes upon a proper percentage in regard to the number of questions answered, and I think the judgment is right enough.

20161. You give a boy six questions in geography, it may happen that that was a part of his geography that he had studied a long time ago and, was a little rusty on, and if by accident you had asked him another portion of his geography which he had done recently he might have answered very well?—I guard against that by taking questions from different parts of the course.

20162. Can you make sure that you take questions from every part of the course in the case of every individual pupil?—I would scarcely say for every individual pupil.

20163. And therefore there is a certain element of haphazard?—Perhaps; and it is not worth while spending such length of time to determine whether this or that particular boy should get first or second or O. I would retain the right of individual examination, to be applied in cases where I have doubt, but I would not be for employing it in every school; and in the report from which you have been reading, I have made recommendations to meet that.

20164. To come back to the effect of this method of examination on the method of teaching, do you pay any attention to the proper method of holding the pen?—Yes, if I am inspecting a school. But I am rarely inspecting a school. At the Results Examination I pay attention to it, but I am afraid I would be exceeding my functions to insist upon it. We give the teachers so much money for reaching such-and-such a result, and even although we want them to take an educational way to arrive at that, they will insist on taking the lines that will arrive at it with the least expenditure of effort.

20165. In the same way with the teaching of arithmetic?—With the teaching of every subject.

20166. In your opinion the ordinary subjects in schools might be taught more practically if you had some change in the method of examination?—Certainly. There is another aspect of school work that we never see at all. Two schools may appear pretty much the same in marking papers, but in one school the children may be enjoying their work, their appetite for knowledge being steadily whetted, and they may leave school with a desire to improve themselves, and in the other school they may be disgusted—their minds in a state of mental indigestion—and anxious to escape from school. We never bring out that aspect.

20167. We saw to-day in the model school a second class reading the Second Book; one of the members of the Commission heard them read an

[illegible]

looked at the programme for
which is compulsory at 16

could be introduced into our present system?—I cannot say I have put anything on paper, but I think I could very quickly make out a provisional programme as regards elementary science.

20198. Would you kindly do so at your convenience and hand it in?—Yes.

20199. By natural science what do you mean?—The extension of object lessons.

20200. Captain Shaw.—Only applied to plants and such things?—I would apply it to minerals and the products of manufacture.

20201. Natural science is the science of nature?—Natural science would be the principal part of it; but natural science includes more than plant teaching.

20202. Natural science includes the science of nature, the whole of physics and chemistry?—Of course, in its extended sense it includes botany and zoology and biology.

20203. Mr. Molloy.—Have you thought out any plan by which teachers who are not now intimately acquainted with those branches could acquire a knowledge of them in a comparatively short time?—I suggest there that something more should be done in the training colleges; and it would also be very desirable if they could be drafted over to the Royal College of Science for laboratory work.

20204. By the Royal College of Science do you mean the Dublin one?—Yes.

20205. Even at present are there not facilities for teachers to go up there and get instruction?—No, that has practically died out; the teachers have given up teaching in connection with the Science and Art Department as they used to teach formerly.

20206. Do not the facilities exist though they are not availed of?—They don't exist for teachers except such as are actually engaged in teaching Science and Art, and none of the teachers now are. The real cause that it could not be worked is that the teachers have given up teaching for the Science and Art.

20207. But that, if I mistake not, is for another reason on account of the change in the programme?—Yes, but it would have the effect of preventing us being able to utilise these classes.

20208. But locally here have you not a very good school of art?—We have.

20209. And could not the teachers here avail themselves of the school of art, especially in connection with drawing?—They could, undoubtedly; and if a programme of instruction in these subjects was drawn up, with reasonable fees attached, I fancy the teachers would very quickly qualify themselves for taking these up and teaching them.

20210. You are in favour of having an interval of say an hour, in the middle of the day, and a rollcall twice?—Yes.

20211. Is there, in your opinion, any practical difficulty with regard to that roll call?—At present of course we have not what you might designate rollcall, but they are compared in cases where children don't come back to cancel the attendance.

20212. But if there are two attendances in the day, do you see any practical inconvenience arising?—I see no practical inconvenience; it only involves the loss of a few minutes.

20213. Would it not be possible to have the junior teachers marking the rolls while the ordinary instruction was going on, and thereby economising the time?—Certainly; there is no reality in the objection.

20214. As a matter of fact, that has been carried out in the Belfast schools; it was laid down as a regulation in the model school?—Undoubtedly.

20215. Have you many half-timers?—I have more than thirty schools having half-timers—probably about 1,000 children.

20216. What subjects do they lose?—They drop off in fourth class, as a rule.

20217. Have you any half-time school not carrying out grammar or geography?—Oh, dear no; they are

based according [illegible]
subjects; [illegible]
20218. Are [illegible]
examination [illegible]
rolls?—No, I [illegible]
tion as distinguished [illegible]
but when I have [illegible]
proficiency of [illegible]
judgment of the [illegible]
that judgment [illegible]
a number of the [illegible]
20219. You [illegible]
examination you [illegible]
opportunity, or [illegible]
I have no [illegible]
20220. Have [illegible]
manner of [illegible]
school, and in [illegible]
thing?—I have [illegible]
by cards, and [illegible]
marked, [illegible]
view. I think [illegible]
recommended [illegible]
that if he [illegible]
cards would be [illegible]
away they would [illegible]
20221. That [illegible]
the press in an [illegible]
a proper [illegible]
but two forms [illegible]
I would be [illegible]
results system [illegible]
20222. Have [illegible]
and have you [illegible]
calling attention [illegible]
to me; at least [illegible]
methods.
20223. Mr. [illegible]
opportunity of [illegible]
have. My [illegible]
always working [illegible]
20224. But [illegible]
provided by the [illegible]
in these [illegible]
science would [illegible]
from my [illegible]
attention, and [illegible]
inspectors' report [illegible]
teachers [illegible]
they find the [illegible]
to themselves.
20225. You [illegible]
of children to [illegible]
unmolested 15,[illegible]
20226. What [illegible]
children being [illegible]
20 per cent.
20227. What [illegible]
in the infants [illegible]
20228. The [illegible]
is not [illegible]
instructions in [illegible]
of pupils [illegible]
Would not that [illegible]
It does not take [illegible]
in any case the [illegible]
marking. Suppose [illegible]
each nought, [illegible]
20229. Could [illegible]
the infants in [illegible]
every member [illegible]
—Without [illegible]
20230. With [illegible]
distinctly, but [illegible]
the marking [illegible]
20231. Suppose [illegible]
"heads up" [illegible]
heard a team [illegible]
would not [illegible]
are obliged to [illegible]

20232. What conspicuous marks could you have to mark everyone one if they showed vivacity and alertness?—I have always been acting on the principle that if there is a particular child there, and I give the child a mark, that is the mark the child deserved.

20233. By your own individual examination do you really differentiate between 1 and 2 mark—do you undertake by an individual examination of infants to differentiate between 1, 2, 3, and 4?—I have always done it.

20234. Your child No. 1 may get a No. 2 pass, and No. 2 child may get a No. 1?—Precisely; and my papers are always made out in that way.

20235. The chief point I want to bring out is that, while you have 18,000, 25 per cent. are infants that may be examined in the way I indicated?—I don't know that it is 25 per cent. exactly—perhaps more or less; but not a larger percentage than there is in any other district.

20236. Mr. Redington.—You are in favour of the extension of kindergarten teaching to ordinary schools where there are no organized infant departments?—I am.

20237. Could it be carried out in a school where there was one teacher and one monitor?—Of course I would not expect it would be so efficient, but some of the exercises might be taught. They have to fill up the time of the infants now.

20238. And could it be carried out where there was no class-room?—Oh, yes; you could have a few suitable infants' desks in a part of the room by themselves, and they could be put there at the exercises.

20239. You think a single teacher with a monitor could manage the ordinary classes and teach some of the kindergarten exercises?—Yes, if they understood the system. I think kindergarten drawing could be severed from the general kindergarten programme, and introduced even in ordinary schools.

20240. As regards agriculture, would you confine the teaching of agriculture to schools where there was a small plot of ground attached for the practical exemplification of the teaching?—I don't think I would; the teaching of principles, if done intelligently, is worth something, but I would try and introduce some test to see whether the teacher has done anything to illustrate his teaching by reference to the agricultural processes going on round about him.

20241. You would not be content with teaching from the text-book only?—Oh, dear, no, it is not worth anything.

20242. It has been suggested there might be pot-gardening—the rearing of plants in pots—have you seen anything of that kind tried?—Yes, we have it in some of the schools, and it is a very nice occupation for children.

20243. They might be taught the elements of botany, and shown the value of manures?—Possibly, on a small scale.

20244. Could you not show the value of manure in the case of even one plant?—You could, to be sure.

20245. Mr. Struthers.—Would it not be a condescension in the nature of the teaching you were advocating?—Yes, but it would be on a very limited scale: you would do more systematic teaching by taking the children into the country.

20246. Mr. Redington.—Then, you would not allow agriculture to be taught in city schools?—Oh, dear, no.

20247. What are the difficulties as to the extension of the teaching of cookery?—As regards the teaching of cookery, one of the principal objections at the present time with the people among whom I principally work, that is the mill population, is that they don't seem to know the meaning or advantage of it or of anything else, except earning wages in mills.

20248. Have they not to cook their dinners at home?—I think it is in a very rudimentary way.

20249. In the country districts are they not accustomed to cook all their meals at home?—In a very elementary way.

20250. Would it not be desirable that the people of the future should cook better?—Decidedly. I am only mentioning the obstacles that we have got to surmount.

20251. Then these mill-workers don't cook their food at home, but buy it?—I believe they live on two or three staple commodities, tea, bread, and a few potatoes.

20252. Captain Shaw.—Don't they get their principal meal brought to them?—Yes.

20254. Chairman.—Who cooks the potatoes?—I think they have the uncooked overnight; and with regard to the potatoes, I don't think they take them until their day's work is over.

20255. Mr. Redington.—But your opinion is that it is advantageous to have cookery taught?—Yes.

20256. Have you any estimate as to what it would cost to start a cookery class?—I have not. I put myself in communication with some of the managers last year, with a view to start some of these cookery classes, and they all complained of the expense. I spoke to one or two managers recently, and I said I thought the Commission would be very anxious to hear an account of these things from them, and possibly they may come before the Commission. The expense, of course, will be a variable quantity. Sometimes a room will be available, and sometimes it will not.

20257. If there was a classroom in the school could not that be used after school hours?—Distinctly, and I think a continuation class would be admirable for such a thing as cookery.

20258. The appliances for artisan cookery are not very numerous or expensive?—Oh, not at all, and the cookery should be adapted to the materials they are likely to have—simple cookery. Something should be done also to show them how to keep their houses comfortable.

20259. You would be in favour of including housewifery in the subjects for which we might give a fee?—I think domestic economy, hygiene and such subjects as these for girls in the higher classes would form a suitable equivalent to the elementary science for boys.

20260. I saw that in the model school they had taught the girls how to lay a table, and clean up rooms—would you extend that, and teach the girls the duties of a housemaid?—I would, distinctly.

Mr. William Pedlow, B.A., District Inspector of National Schools, Belfast, examined.

gets a clear notion of what it is drawing before it commences to draw it at all.

20265. What is the fault you find with the drawing as taught in the senior classes?—There is no connecting link whatever between the drawing in kindergarten and the drawing in the senior classes.—In the senior classes charts are put up before the pupils either on an easel or a blackboard, the pupil gets a sheet of paper, and makes as fair a copy as he can, he gets the teaching from the teacher on the blackboard, the teacher usually goes through the pupils, from pupil to pupil, and points out any errors, and draws a little himself, and that is the way the lesson proceeds. The teacher does not use the chalk at all, which I think he should do. And he might frequently put the object before the child, say an ordinary ink-bottle, and draw the outline on the board for the child. Of course these sheets that are used are very convenient, and in the end the pupils are able to make a fair copy, and use the pencil freely, but the subject is not very interesting when dealt with in that way.

20266. What do you think about the subject of kindergarten generally?—I think it is excellent, it is really manual training so far as it goes.

20267. You would have it carried up to higher stages?—Yes, I think it should be carried on to even a greater extent in infant schools, the infant schools might, in some cases, be allowed to retain their pupils for another year, and in that way there would be an extension of kindergarten in all its details. The drill and drawing, which are excellent, might be extended to the senior classes.

20268. But there is some drill in the senior classes? —It is not universal.

20269. In the model school?—Yes, but in a great many schools in my district there is no drill.

20270. Is the model school in your district?—It is.

20271. Would you tell us what practical instruction is given in your present district?—There are three classes, two large classes in handicraft, and one small class, there is practical instruction in cookery given at the model school, but only at the model school.

20272. Do you think that the instruction given in cookery is satisfactory?—Very satisfactory, and most successful.

20273. Is the instruction given in handicraft successful?—The instruction in handicraft has not, I think, been very popular.

20274. Do you think it is well given? Is it not given in connexion with drawing?—It is not.

20275. Can you give proper instruction in woodwork unconnected with drawing?—I think not; I think there should be drawing.

20276. You agree with me that it would be practically impossible to do so; the child must trust to the eye if there is no drawing?—There should be drawing.

20277. Rev. Dr. Evans.—You are the responsible manager of the model school?—Yes.

20278. Are you satisfied with the provision for rendering the teaching of drawing efficient in the model schools?—No, I am not altogether satisfied with it.

20279. What do you think is the disadvantage there?—We should have a lot of models, but we have practically none.

20280. What models would you particularly desire? —I would first take the cube, cylinder and cone, and commence with these, and advance from stage to stage.

20281. And if you were provided with these models, you have reason to believe, as the manager of the school, and a very experienced educationist, that the teaching of drawing in the model school would be more efficient?—Yes, it would, but of course the results programme as at present drawn does not actually require model drawing, and consequently to some extent it has been neglected, whereas formerly in the model school it was taught.

20282. You have been a considerable time in this district?—Nearly five years.

20283. You have come in contact, no doubt, with the objections entertained here towards the alternative scheme for girls in the sixth class?—Oh, yes.

20284. What is the nature of the objection?—One objection is that made up materials are very cheap, and can be purchased very readily here, and the other and great objection has been made on the part of parents that they think their children should go to school for literary work, and not for this industrial training, that is one of the real objections.

20285. They think the little time that children have at the primary schools should be given to literary instruction, as they won't have, after they go to their calling in life, an opportunity of acquiring this information?—Exactly.

20286. Have you ever seen the document that the managers of schools in Belfast sent to our Board in reference to this alternative programme, asking not to have it put in force here?—I have not seen the document.

20287. You heard the evidence of your colleague with regard to a modification of the curriculum in arithmetic and mensuration, do you share those opinions?—To some extent—to a considerable extent—as regards arithmetic, I think that there should always be oral arithmetic in every school from first class up. It is quite as difficult to make a child know his tables thoroughly as it is to add. Mental arithmetic should be continued step by step, examined separately, and paid for separately, and in that way the boys would be made good calculators, and I cannot say they are now.

20288. Do you think children in the model school properly understand the reason for "carrying" in subtraction?—I don't think so, because I don't think the subject is taught. I think the theory of arithmetic is not very much taught, the questions asked at the results examination don't require much theory, nor do the cards contain many questions where a knowledge of theory is required also.

20289. Do you happen to know whether the pupil teachers would be equal to explaining the reason of "carrying" in subtraction?—I don't know, I have never seen any attempt to explain it.

20290. Are you of opinion (as one of the Inspectors reported in a special report), that the contents of Inspectors' cards in these subjects are known throughout the schools before the examination comes on?—I don't think the contents are actually known, but the nature of the questions is pretty well known.

20291. If after the examination for results conducted by an Inspector a teacher were to reassemble his classes and ask the pupils one by one "what questions did you get?" and take them down, and pass that information on to another teacher, and he did the same thing, and on to another, and he did the same thing, in three or four or five weeks, would they not be able to actually have in their possession the contents of the Inspector's cards?—It would be quite possible to have the contents of most of them if that were done.

20292. And this practice would affect the examination in results and form an argument against the results system?—It would form an argument against the results system in arithmetic.

20293. You agree with Mr. Dalton with regard to the introduction of mensuration?—Certainly.

20294. Is algebra taught to any considerable extent?—Yes, algebra is taught in a large number of my schools.

20295. Do you think the theory of arithmetic would be better taught through algebra than by arithmetic itself?—Decidedly, in more advanced arithmetic.

20296. The algebraic formulae would remain more readily in their memory; also difficult questions in

schools?—I really could not say. I know one evening school was opened a couple of years ago here, the pupils attended for a while and they gradually dropped off, would not attend.

20336. Do you think the idea of evening schools is not in favour with managers and pupils?—I know managers are in favour of them. But it has been a failure, the grown-up boys and girls won't spend their evenings at the evening school; I think if there was probably manual training introduced, it would make an evening school attractive. Literary work only to young boys and girls, not very well prepared, is tedious, and they get fatigued and leave.

20337. If the present programme of the National Board for evening classes was modified you think it would lead to an extension of the number?—I think it might be modified.

20338. Mr. Redington.—What did you think of the proposal made yesterday, that schools might be divided into three grades, and those registered as excellent might not be examined minutely each year?—There is no need to examine a school that is excellent every year, if its reputation was well-known, incidental visits would be sufficient.

20339. You lay great stress in your report on incidental visits and visits made without notice?—Yes, I think to see the school in its ordinary working state is the best way of forming an idea of how the teaching is going on.

20340. At such visits the Inspector could examine a class or the whole school if he wished?—Yes, and could observe the method.

20341. The great advantage of that system is that he could observe the method of the teacher which he cannot do at present?—Yes, the results examination day is not a good day to observe method.

20342. Would you limit the number of extra subjects to be taught in the case of badly conducted schools?—Decidedly. I think a badly conducted school should not be allowed to teach extra subjects except singing and drawing.

20343. Mr. Struthers.—Do you find extra subjects are often taken up in schools where the literary work is weak?—I do not.

20344. Mr. Redington.—I see that you say in your report that grammar and geography might be regarded as optional subjects, but that the merit grant should be such as to encourage the teaching of them, and that no highly classed or trained teacher should be allowed to omit them from his programme?—A highly classed teacher can do a great deal more work than those of medium ability.

20345. You strongly advocate class examination, and say that 50 per cent. or less of the children would be quite enough to examine?—Yes, to form an idea of the whole school.

20346. You say "It would seem ludicrous to give a child of four or five years of age a failure in kindergarten where the subject is well taught, to examine and give a failure in sums to a child who has no natural ear, if the work in general be excellent, and in a very well-taught drawing class to call out one or two, through no fault of the teacher, and give them a failure"?—Yes, it nearly always happens that the child who fails is the one that has given the teacher most trouble.

20347. Chairman.—Is there any temptation on the contrary to the teacher with the present system of working for the results examination, to give most of his attention to the clever children and neglect the stupid ones, or is it rather the other way?—I think the teacher pays most attention to the stupid boys, the clever children do with very little teaching, under the results system they are sure to pass.

20348. Is it not alleged with regard to the Intermediate examinations that the effect is exactly the other way, that it pays better to attend to the clever children and let the stupid ones alone?—The reputation of the Intermediate school profits greatly by the clever children.

20349. Mr. Redington.—I see in the same report you say "Class examination should aim at discovering and encouraging successful teaching, and discountenancing merely mechanical and cramming work, this could, I think, be best accomplished by attaching special importance to reading taken in connexion with explanation, to oral as well as written arithmetic, and writing in connexion with composition." Is that still your opinion?—It is.

20350. Mr. Struthers.—Do you often find clever children who really can read a book in half a year and are kept reading the same book for another half-year before they are advanced to a new book?—Yes.

20351. That is a bad system for the purpose of education?—Yes, to keep a child back.

20352. Rev. Dr. Evans.—Arising from the answer you gave the Chairman about the teacher devoting his attention more especially to the backward children—then these backward children do not pass?—Sometimes.

20353. Then is it that the teacher gets no pay for the children on whom he bestows most pains?—Yes.

20354. Then that is a strong argument against the results system, because he is not paid for the best work he does?—In the first place the clever children are not allowed to advance, and then the teacher's attention is taken up to a great extent with the backward children. At the results examination I have been frequently told "that child gave me more trouble than all the others in the class."

H. M. Beatty, LL.D., District Inspector of National Schools, Newtownards, examined.

20355. Chairman.—You are the District Inspector of National Schools in Newtownards?—Yes, my lord.

20356. Does your district take in any part of Belfast?—Yes, the Ballymacarrett division, east of the Lagan.

20357. I understand that you are not prepared to speak upon manual instruction generally, but there are a few subjects connected with it on which you can give your opinion. What are your views as to the system of individual marking at results examinations for determining the value of the teaching and encouraging improved methods?—I think the necessity for individual examination has passed away. When the system was introduced most of the teachers were untrained and very unskilful and very badly educated, and they were perfectly ignorant of methods, it was necessary to lay down a special rule and say "You are to teach so many hours and then we will give you so much money for it." That is a thing that appeals to the most unadvanced intelligence, but the circumstances have changed, a far larger number of teachers are trained, and they have acquired proper methods and may be allowed more liberty and therefore may be allowed to return to a system of teaching proper and not preparing for examinations. There are several objections to the results system and system of individual examination, and one is that it permits no latitude to the teacher, no choice of methods, no choice as to how he should deal with a subject. If you restrict a teacher he cannot possibly show an interest in his work and infuse an interest into the children and draw out their intelligence. For instance, if you take the case of geography, from our method of examination it seems to me almost absolutely impossible there should not be a uniform programme laid down in order to facilitate the assigning of marks, because if there is any divergence, if there is any latitude allowed to the teacher, it is difficult to co-ordinate the two programmes, and say *One* for that programme has the same value as *One* in another programme. Take the case of England, they have four or five alternative programmes, in Saxony they have ten, in Weimar there is no pro-

Belfast.
Oct. 21, 1887.
R. M. Beatty, M.A.

gramme, the teacher simply draws up his own syllabus of examination and says "I will teach it in that way during the year," and it is submitted to the Department and they approve of his teaching it in that way.

20358. Does that apply to other subjects than geography?—I take geography because I think our programme is specially unsuitable, but it does apply to others.

20359. In what way is it unsuitable?—The teaching of geography as my experience begins in this way. A teacher gets up his third class in the beginning of the year round the map; to the first child he points to the map and he says "Siberia," the child then repeats it after him, he points to another place which is painted a different colour and he says "France." The child learns that by heart, and when he has gone over it the children repeat it. He puts the pointer on the map and the child says "France." A child at that age has no conception of what France may be. Probably if he is a child in the country he knows his nearest market town; if he is a child in Belfast he knows two or three surrounding streets; he has no idea of what his own country is like, much less of what the whole country is, and a child is never told what this is; he may be told it is land or water, but he is not told anything else. Compare that with a real intelligent method of teaching geography. I have no practical acquaintance with German schools but from what I have read of them it appears they lead the children up to a hill and show them the country.

20360. They teach geography from the school-door, as it is called in Germany?—They teach geography from the actual locality. To illustrate that, I have quite commonly asked in a school: "Show me the country you live in." The child could point out Europe or the Turkey Straits. "Show me the country you live in." No answer. "What is the name of the country you live in?" "I don't know." I have asked another child—"Show me Ireland." They could not show me Ireland. The other day I asked a child what province she lived in, she said "I live in Munster." Another told me she lived in Leinster.

20361. Do you think that it is a very questionable advantage to retain grammar and geography in the list of compulsory subjects?—Yes; my idea is that a child should be taught to read and write, and so much arithmetic as will keep him from being swindled by shopkeepers, but beyond that, that he is to be wanted, and the more choice you leave to the teacher of the subjects in which he is going to give the training the better. One teacher can teach grammar with advantage, another can teach geography, another can teach drawing; let him take up any one, or the whole lot, but make none compulsory.

20362. Would you agree with a view put before us by a witness the other day—one of the inspectors of schools in the South of Ireland—who said that he would still retain individual examination for the three subjects you have mentioned, reading, writing, and arithmetic; and he also added drawing; but with regard to the other subjects he would have them all to be examined by means of class examination without individual examination?—Well, there is something to be said for that, but still the continuance of the individual examination tends to cramming.

20363. Even in those subjects?—Even for those obligatory subjects I don't think it would be

at present. I have frequently cal[illegible]
and said to him, "Can you hear wha[illegible]
"No," he said, "I cannot." I have [illegible]
with regard to a particular word and
see what the child was saying.

20365. Without the book in his [illegible]
—Yes, if he had followed the chil[illegible]
the word. But with regard to that [illegible]
opportunity I have of comparing [illegible]
England in reading with the proficien[illegible]
is that there are occasionally Englis[illegible]
in Ballymacarrett classes, and I [illegible]
is of quite a different character. [illegible]
as a rule, slides into the reading [illegible]
or those words, but it does not appe[illegible]
know what he was going to read [illegible]
boy outright has himself, and out r[illegible]
beforehand what he was going to re[illegible]
intonation and expression he should g[illegible]

20366. Would you be in favour of [illegible]
tests in reading accuracy before a te[illegible]
As part of the qualification—oh, cer[illegible]

20367. It is not the case at prese[illegible]
Such a boy can read so as to underst[illegible]
he is reading, he is bound to give hi[illegible]
not?—I think that is practically [illegible]
expected we should give a boy a [illegible]
decipher the words. My reason fo[illegible]
first point was with a view to show [illegible]
vocabulary was so limited in Ballyma[illegible]
of the schoolrooms was so great, [illegible]
interfere seriously with the introdu[illegible]
instruction.

20368. With regard to manual [illegible]
found by experience in England th[illegible]
necessary to provide special classroom[illegible]
to the rules of the Department, and [illegible]
doubt here it would be so too. W[illegible]
into that point, we have taken it fo[illegible]
in wood-work—of course cookery is [illegible]
rooms in England—but manual in[illegible]
sense of woodwork, is it the case to [illegible]
existing classrooms?—From my [illegible]
don't see where the classrooms woul[illegible]

20369. Rev. Dr. Wilson.—How [illegible]
your district?—153.

20370. Are many of the teachers [illegible]
—Yes, the number is large now, I [illegible]
thing between a third and a half ar[illegible]

20371. I suppose very few teach[illegible]
manual instruction as we underst[illegible]
think at present they could teach [illegible]
they have had no training, and I [illegible]
know what it means.

20372. I gather that you think th[illegible]
at present does not develop the intelli[illegible]
because when you ask a question out o[illegible]
he seems not to be able to give a [illegible]
Yes, that is the case. For [illegible]
class they have to add three figure c[illegible]
I gave three lines sum in which they [illegible]
and the result was that half the chi[illegible]
failed, although it was a well-taugh[illegible]
them then with carrying and they [illegible]
expected to get questions with carry[illegible]

20373. As regards Ballymacarrett[illegible]
a very crowded district, and where [illegible]
tion would be very important for the [illegible]

[illegible]

ing some of the branches so as to think the children would suffer ary attainments?—No, I don't ffer in their literary attainments as a limited number were. I ry out their literary work with d thoroughness.

all the testimony given to us hey came back with fresh zest to , and lost nothing by giving so literary instruction, that being tion. You have a Model school Yes.

prosperous condition?—Yes, taken k I can describe it as pro- departments in it are taught

ools are fairly large?—Yes, they

course.—You agree with the pro- visions of the result system on attention to results rather than ?—Yes.

ccede greater freedom for the ols course of instruction?—Yes, I dom that is left the teacher, when tain limits—absolutely necessary

to say, the teacher, instead of the programme laid down at the ear, should rather state at the end he has been able to do, and the reasons on that?—Well, I think amongst inferiors, because there ne teachers who would adopt a ; you must see beforehand.

cautions—the lines on which he ould put have it in detail.

ght be from special circumstances not able to undertake the whole for him; it would be better for thoroughly, and state reasons why the whole programme, rather than it improperly?—Yes, but I think ought to know beforehand what he plish; it would show a want of

attainments of schools differ very ossible in one school is not possible may apply to the case of a teacher rest, locality; he might come from children were very bright to a were extremely dull, but I think normal.

think it would be an advantage programmes of work for schools er, and for schools taught by many know that it would be necessary ogramme; one teacher teaching take up the whole programme.

ood you to say you favoured one of programmes?—Yes, but I would programme should be part of the ld not differ qualitatively but

the single-handed teacher would overtake so much of the work, but same lines as the other?—Yes.

the case of children not knowing untry they lived in was exceptional? nal. I have frequently in good children in your schools?—Yes, their method of beginning reading is better, and it is better all through; it was what musicians call "the attack" that struck me most; the boy did not slide into the reading.

20392. I have often heard the opinion stated in Scotland that Irish children read much better than the Scotch children?—I don't say that my remarks apply to Scotch children; I have had opportunities of examining Scotch children, and I don't think they read better than Irish children.

20393. Part of your district is agricultural?—Yes.

20394. A large part?—Taken as to the amount of space, it is very much larger than Ballymacarret, but in the actual amount of schools and children examined, the children examined in Ballymacarret are about half.

20395. Do you have many schools taking up agriculture?—All the country schools under male teachers take it up.

20396. Have you any observations to offer on the teaching of agriculture in the schools in your district?—There is a new text-book issued; the old text-book, I think, was a most unsuitable book for children, but apart from that, I don't think any text-book is very much good. But if you have a text-book at all, I think it should not go so much into detail as our old text-book. It was made up of a certain number of farmers' tips, which would be very useful to grown up farmers, as to the definite amount of manure and so on, but it was not such a thing as would enable a child to apply his knowledge to his experience afterwards.

20397. You would regard it rather as a handbook for farmers?—I should think it ought to be a very useful handbook for farmers to have at hand, and apply to occasionally.

20398. So that the parents of the children might find these books occasionally useful?—Yes, I have no doubt the farmer often took the book from his child and read it.

20399. But you don't think there is much further to be said in favour of teaching from a text-book?—No.

20400. Captain Shaw.—Has a child during his school life much opportunity of putting his ideas into words under the present system?—No, he has no opportunity, I think.

20401. Do you think it would be desirable to introduce instruction which would allow him to do so? and arrangements such as would give him conversational power?—Yes, I think it would.

20402. How would you suggest that that should be done?—I have some idea of how it is done elsewhere, as for instance, now in Germany. I think the usual mode of teaching is to call upon a child, to bring him before an object and say: "What do you see there?" Then insist that the child shall form all his words into regular complete sentences, and in that way of course he gets accustomed to conversational expression.

20403. And experimental science, where it is taught experimentally the child has to watch what is occurring and give a description of it afterwards, that is useful both in furnishing him with ideas and teaching him to give expression to them?—Yes, I believe that is the system that is carried out in Germany.

20404. As a matter of fact it is the text-book that the child always learns here?—Yes, there is too much text-book

Belfast. [illegible]

upon to form their expressions in regular and consecutive shape.

20407. Is drawing taught in any of your schools?—Yes, it is taught in more than half of them now; I should think there are 55 or 56 now.

20408. Do you find that the children have sufficient room for drawing in the schools?—No, I don't think they have. As an instance of the want of desk room I might say that I was in a school the other day where the first class alone filled all the desks in the senior school; it was divided into an infant and senior department, and the first class alone filled the desks of the school.

20409. Do you think it is possible to teach drawing properly if a child cannot throw its elbow because the next child is against it?—It is very difficult, and it may be taught under difficulties to a certain extent, but it must be very imperfectly.

20410. The same thing would apply to any form of manual instruction which was done at desks in school, children must have room to use both their arms?—Yes, to a still greater extent than in drawing.

20411. As regards the question of speaking out in reading, a great many different classes go on in the schoolroom side by side in Ireland?—Yes, there are no class-rooms practically.

20412. And it is not convenient that what one child is reading should be heard in the next circle?—No.

20413. That may account to some extent for their not speaking out?—Yes, I think it does. I was in a school where there were 272 children, there was no classroom, they were all in the one room, and I don't see how reading could be taught properly in a school under such circumstances.

20414. Mr. [illegible].—I believe there is no evening school in your district?—There was one, but it has disappeared.

20415. Can you give us the reasons why evening schools are not more popular in Ireland?—The programme of the evening school was the same as in the day school to a large extent, and therefore the necessity for it has passed away somewhat, but it seemed to me that the numbers gradually dwindled until they got to five or six for examination, and then the teacher gave it up in disgust.

20416. Do you think that if the programme was modified more boys would be attracted to evening schools?—I certainly think so, if it were made of a practical character.

20417. Perhaps the payment is not sufficient to induce a teacher to start an evening school?—He is generally a teacher in the day school, at least that is my experience, and the evening school was attached to the day school, and therefore he had not to rely on it entirely for his support, it only formed a part of his support.

20418. Are you acquainted with the English Evening School Code?—No, except in a very general way, but so far as I know it, I think an adaptation of it would be extremely useful; and it seems to me that there are many branches that could not be conveniently introduced in a day school, for instance laundry work and cookery, that might be admirably introduced into an evening school, because there is plenty of space there.

20419. You see no objection to girls going to an evening school?—I merely give that as an instance, but it does not touch the point, because it would apply equally well to the manual work which boys would learn.

20420. You think that some of the extras which are now taught in the ordinary school hours might with advantage be confined to evening schools?—The extras that are generally taught in my district are algebra and geometry; I don't think they would be of a suitable character for an evening school; the boys would not be sufficiently advanced.

20421. Do any of your schools take up French?—One or two.

20422. Might not a subject of that kind, that would be of use to boys that are going in for a commercial career, be a very suitable thing for an evening school?—Boys that want instruction in that go to different schools in Belfast where the teaching would be more conversational and more useful, and given by better teachers.

20423. Could science teaching be taken up with advantage in evening schools?—Yes, I think it could.

cookery lessons, but she thought that twenty lessons were only beginning to show them the preliminaries of cooking; and to do them any good, there should be sixty lessons?—I should say she would be a much better judge than I am, but my object is to insist on the principle that it should be introduced. About 85 or 90 per cent. of the girls attending St. Mary's schools will be going into factories and mills at from eleven to fourteen years of age, and hundred places, and in the majority of cases their mothers are working in mills and factories, and they have no opportunity, as a rule, of learning at home these things; and then instead of insisting on girls like these wasting their time, as it seems to me, in the advanced branches—advanced geography, advanced grammar, advanced arithmetic and so on—that after they can read and write and count sufficiently for practical purposes the balance of the time should be devoted to practical training in how to keep a house sanitary, how to cook, how to market, household economy, first aid in case of burns or accidents, and that sort of thing.

20441. Would you think it would be a good plan if the girls who had arrived at the age of thirteen—you say they leave at fourteen—who had arrived at the last year of their school life, should be obliged to take up a course of cookery for that year?—Yes, I am strongly of that opinion, and making a change in the way of sewing; there is too much fancy work done.

20442. How many hours a week do you have for sewing in your school?—Five hours.

20443. What would be a sufficient number?—I don't object to five hours, if the sewing is broadened out and made more practically useful.

20444. You have one hour a day and you think that is sufficient?—I think that is practically sufficient.

20445. That seems to be the general opinion of those skilled in the matter. Now, we will come to the boys: I believe you think drawing should be taught to boys?—Yes, certainly.

20446. Is drawing taught in your school?—Yes, and well taught.

20447. What is the method of teaching it?—I am not sure I can exactly tell you.

20448. Does the teacher teach by drawing the figures on the blackboard?—Yes, and also by supplying the models.

20449. He does not confine himself to giving a child a copy on one page and making him copy it on the next?—He does that, but he does not confine himself to it.

20450. Have you any hand and eye training?—No, we have not, we are hampered for want of room, we have very large schools; but still we are two teachers short for the numbers of our children, our teaching room is not sufficiently large, we have not enough accommodation or enough teachers. We are in a working class district entirely and the majority are poor people, and it is a difficult thing to raise funds. I do think that when the Government has provided compulsory education it ought to make some advance towards helping us to provide sufficient accommodation.

20451. Have you sufficient ground to build upon if you had the money?—Yes.

20452. Would you advocate the introduction of manual training in the shape of woodwork?—Within limits.

20453. Of course you understand it would be necessary to have a separate room, it could not be done in the country?—No; not at the same time as the other studies.

20454. And for other reasons?—I am strongly in favour of anything that educates a boy's eye and hand.

20455. You would not advocate that it should be taught as a trade for the sake of making a boy a carpenter, but merely that elementary part that teaches him to measure accurately and use his hand and eye?—Quite so.

20456. And you would not teach it without teaching drawing also; before a boy attempted to do anything with tools he should have a sketch which he copied in doing his work?—I think drawing is very important; there are a great many boys who don't seem to have much talent for it or taste.

20457. What are the difficulties you find with regard to the supply of teachers? Did you mean the teachers of manual work or teachers generally?—Teachers generally. Our numbers are much beyond our teaching staff, especially in our infant school. We want more accommodation, and the Board won't grant us more teachers without more accommodation. Then, again, I think the Board should be a little more generous with schools with regard to supplying teachers. Some little time ago I had great difficulty in getting a grant of the teacher's salary because we were the one-tenth part of a child short of the average number, and I think that is very hard lines.

20458. Rev. Dr. Wilson.—You are teaching cookery in the evening?—We did it some time ago. We are not teaching it at present; those were voluntary lessons.

20459. Was the teacher an expert?—Yes.

20460. How did you provide the payment for her?—By charging a certain sum to each pupil.

20461. You would be in favour of curtailing the advanced branches in literary education?—Yes, for the majority of children. The advanced branches are all right for children likely to be going forward to some profession. Children that require the advanced branches could very easily be selected.

20462. You consider it very important that they should be taught how to keep house?—All-important; a couple of days' visiting with me would prove that to any person.

20463. And also to make and mend clothing—especially to mend them?—Yes.

20464. You have no teaching of woodwork to the boys yet?—No.

20465. Have you applied for a grant to the Board for an extension of your premises?—We have not, because we are not in a position to pay what it would cost. Our schools are parish schools; not vested schools.

20466. Mr. Strutt.—Were those cookery classes you had in the evening successful?—They were.

20467. Well attended?—Well attended, but they were not attended by children, but by grown-up people.

20468. Especially girls from seventeen to twenty, perhaps?—Yes; some of them married women.

20469. And you think the instruction they received there was very useful?—Highly useful.

20470. Can you give us the reason why those classes were not continued?—There was the difficulty of organisation.

20471. Was a fee charged for attending?—Yes, 1s. a head; that covered expenses.

20472. So that it would be a very simple matter to revive those classes and continue them?—Yes; if some lady would take them in charge.

20473. May I ask whether you got a grant from the National Board for those evening classes?—No.

20474. Then would be a very considerable encouragement in starting evening cookery classes?—It would be.

20475. And you think in this way these girls who attend receive a really valuable instruction in cookery?—I have no doubt about it.

20476. Don't you think these girls coming there for the purpose of learning cookery would be much more likely to benefit by the instruction than children of eleven or twelve, who are compelled to attend?—Yes, they would; but people who come to a voluntary class are people who have a certain taste and wish to excel, and we want to reach not only those who have a wish to excel, but those who have not.

Belfast. Oct. [illegible] Rev. Dr. [illegible]

20477. Don't you think the issue you speak of might extend by experience?—It would be a very slow process, unless you began early.

20478. At any rate you are quite clear that there is a considerable advantage from this teaching in the evening?—No doubt about it.

20479. But, in addition to that, you would like to have cookery taught in schools to girls before they leave school?—Yes; very simple cookery. I don't want to go in for fine dishes, but something suitable to their position in life—to teach them to economise. No one can go among the working classes without seeing how much waste there is, and how much more the food they buy would be turned to advantage than it is.

20480. Would you have laundry work taught in the school?—I should be glad; the principles of it.

20481. There would be a difficulty about the time?—That is the difficulty; but I would make time by doing away with what I think is now practically useless.

20482. You remember there was an alternative scheme of needlework, which was meant to be of an industrial character, and that does not seem to have succeeded?—Well, you see the teacher's bread and butter is dependent upon his producing certain results in certain subjects.

20483. But there was a fee paid for certain subjects, excluding arithmetic altogether; a high fee was paid for instruction in needlework and cookery?—I cannot say exactly.

20484. It has been said to us that the reason why this scheme failed was that the people, and especially in Belfast, declined to send their children to school for anything but a literary education?—I know that there is a certain amount of feeling in that direction, but still I think that would be overcome.

20485. Suppose you reduced the amount of literary instruction to girls under eleven, suppose you excluded grammar altogether and reduce the amount of geography and arithmetic, and substitute for it cookery and laundry work, do you think the parents would be willing to send their girls?—I think if you do it in one school in all probability a number of girls would say they preferred to have the branches taught in another school, but if you do it generally that cannot hold.

20486. Then you aim at making this form of instruction compulsory in all schools?—I certainly do.

20487. Don't you think there might be a popular outcry if that were the case?—That depends on the judiciousness with which it is introduced, if it is made clear to people, and, at the same time, if you provide classes for those who wish to get on in literary instruction. In my school perhaps ten or fifteen per cent. of the girls would wish to get on for professions or clerkships; it would be easy to provide classes for them.

20488. Would you get those girls to attend a course of instruction in cookery, laundry work, and house cleaning?—I think it is quite possible; in any case you could introduce the subject generally, and at the same time have special classes for them; but I would not press on the majority in the literary subjects.

20489. That really means you would not make these subjects compulsory after all?—I would make them generally compulsory. Perhaps I have not made myself clear. I would have all the girls taught these subjects, but I would have classes provided for the girls who wished to go on—special advanced classes.

20490. You would allow girls under certain circumstances to claim special exemption?—To claim exemption in certain cases.

20491. It would be very considerable assistance to your work with the adult girls if you had grants for evening classes for such subjects as cookery and laundry work?—Yes.

20492. Your school is evidently full?—It is full, and more than full according to the numbers allowed, by the rules of the National Board, in a given space.

20493. Then it is what we might call overcrowded?—Yes.

20494. That is not a desirable state of affairs?—It is not, it is not so much overcrowded as to make it unhealthy; but it is, according to the rules of the Board, overcrowded. I don't object to the rule, I only claim that the Board should help us to provide additional accommodation.

20495. Mr. REDINGTON.—Have you applied for a loan?—We have not, because we could not afford to pay five per cent.

20496. You are aware that loans and not grants are given to non-vested schools?—Yes, we thought the matter out, but could not afford to pay the five per cent.

20497. Mr. STRUTHERS.—You only have teachers in this school for the accommodation, and not for the number of children in it, so that in addition to the disadvantage of teaching in the overcrowded room you have the additional disadvantage of an insufficient staff?—That is so.

20498. That is a very unsatisfactory state of affairs?—It is; but I would wish to say I am six years past in the parish, and we have never had a failure in the infant school, which shows our work does not suffer in consequence.

20499. That means the teachers must work very hard?—They do work very hard.

20500. Too hard?—For their own health sometimes.

20501. Captain SHAW.—Have you considered at all the question of having centres for these forms of instruction, which might be available for different schools?—I have thought of it, but I have not considered it very particularly.

20502. Do you think it would be feasible in Belfast to have centres for these forms of instruction, to have a cookery centre to which the children from various schools should come in turns so that the centre should be continuously employed, and you should have an instructor always employed in giving instruction to the various classes?—That could be worked, but I don't think it would produce the efficient result that it would if introduced into all the schools.

20503. If you have a well-fitted kitchen, and an efficient instructor at the centre, would it not produce more efficient results than if you depended on a teacher in each school?—To a certain number of children, but I don't think the mass of them could be got there.

20504. CHAIRMAN.—Why should they not be brought to that centre as in Birmingham?—Well, I have no experience; but there are local reasons why it would not work well.

20505. Captain SHAW.—To what proportion of the children would you contemplate teaching cookery?—There would be a very large number of girls.

20506. Roughly 100?—Quite that number.

20507. You would teach them in classes of twenty-five, four classes a week, that would not occupy the whole of the instructor's time, or the whole of the kitchen; you might take in another school?—Yes, at a different time.

20508. It is a question whether you have the teaching at one school or at a centre?—It is so easy now providing a gas stove in the corner of the school or class-room, that it would be very much easier doing that and having a teacher migrating, giving an hour to one school and another to the next.

20509. I meant the children should migrate, not the teacher?—It would be much easier migrating the teacher than the children.

20510. I was going to ask you the same question as regards manual instruction; it is a system most usually followed in England. I did not know whether there might be any feeling in Belfast about the children leaving their schools to go to the centres. Instead of coming to the school one morning, they start and go to a centre and spend two hours there, and then go on to the school?—I have no experience of it at all. But there are certain elements existing in Belfast which don't exist in England, and which would make it difficult, if not impossible, to migrate the children in this city.

Belfast. Oct. 11, 1897. Rev. Dr. [illegible]

20511. Mr. Malloy.—I think your school building was erected many years ago and at a very heavy cost?—It was.

20512. An unusually heavy cost?—Yes.

20513. And that has been weighing on the parish ever since?—I am happy to say it has been wiped out now.

20514. I know it when the Rev. Dr. Wright happened to be the clergyman and it rather oppressed him?—It did, and it oppressed me too, I am sorry to say, for a time.

20515. Was it connected with any association prior to the National Board; was it under the Church Education Society?—No, it never was.

20516. Was it always worked as a parish school, and in connection with the National Board?—Yes.

20517. Then the attendance has increased enormously?—Enormously, the district has increased enormously.

20518. They are chiefly mill-workers in the neighbourhood?—Chiefly.

20519. You carried on an evening school for some time?—We had an evening cookery school, we had not a laundry school in my time.

20520. What objection would you have to an ordinary literary evening school?—I have none at all.

20521. In view of the great number of adult workers would it not be of service to introduce such a school?—I am sure it would if it could be carried out.

20522. Do you think the restrictions at present in force under the National Board prevent the carrying out of that?—To some extent, but not wholly.

20523. That the remuneration is not adequate and the conditions are prohibitive?—Yes, but still I think there are other elements that enter into it—there are very few men who are capable of managing fellows of from seventeen to twenty-one, and that has a large amount to do with keeping up order in the school and keeping up a moral tone. And then again there is another reason—there is only a certain percentage, and perhaps a small percentage of young men and women that care much to pursue their studies when they leave school, and those that do care are amply provided for in schools like the Workman's Institute, where they go of their own choice.

20524. With regard to their pursuits in after-life?—Yes.

20525. Would you kindly develop a little your remark about that one-tenth of a pupil when you were not able to get an assistant recognised; was the refusal of the Commissioners to appoint an assistant on the ground of overcrowding?—No, the overcrowding is in the infant school. The senior school is not so overcrowded. When you have a staff of teachers it is hard that the retaining of one of the staff should depend on whether you will have the one-tenth or not.

20526. They don't deal, however, I believe with fractions; they rather go to the next whole number and give you the benefit of the fraction?—Possibly that is so now, but they do deal with fractions.

20527. Mr. Ramsey.—Would you point out the particular regulations governing evening classes which you think have prevented the spread of these classes?—I could not put my finger on it just now, but my impression is that the teachers have not been sufficiently encouraged by a large enough payment.

20528. Are you familiar with the English way of paying for teaching in evening schools?—I am not.

20529. Mr Struthers.—Is there not one difference between Birmingham and Belfast in the way of establishing a centre—that there is one central authority in Birmingham which has all the schools under its control and there is no central authority in Belfast?—There is no central authority in Belfast.

Rev. R. J. Clarke, Rector of Trinity Church, Belfast, examined.

Rev. R. J. Clarke.

20530. Chairman.—You are the Rector of Trinity Church, Belfast, and the manager of three large National schools?—Yes, my lord.

20531. Have you tried cookery classes?—We have tried them in the evening in connection with the young people who have left school; we found them very successful and exceedingly popular. The first year we engaged a very superior Scotch lady, the lesson cost 6s. 6d. an evening; we sold 150 tickets to the young girls at 1s. each, which meant a course of twelve lessons, 1d. a lesson. These tickets were transferable. The Town Council lent us a gas stove for six months free of cost. We found the class self-supporting, 150 tickets at 1s. each, both paid for the gas and for the services of the lady and other expenses, and left a few shillings margin.

20532. Is that going on still?—No, we tried it two winters, and it was not quite so popular, and we went on to an ambulance class.

20533. You are trying ambulance classes now?—We have tried them. We did not find them so popular as the cookery class, but a good many of our young girls obtained certificates.

20534. Have you any idea of going back to the cookery classes?—Yes, we have; I think we could easily introduce it into our schools after school hours, from 4 to 5 o'clock—a good many of the girls would come back.

20535. Would you require to get the services of a special instructor, or do you think one of your teachers would qualify?—I am afraid none of our teachers would qualify, but if certificates were given in cookery, some of our assistants would attend cookery classes and qualify, I feel certain.

20536. Supposing you were to institute another class in the school, could you obtain results fees from the National Board if you had an outside teacher?—I am not quite sure, I think we could. We obtained results fees in singing once when we employed an outside teacher.

20537. Have you tried gymnastic classes and evening drill?—We have, and also we have drill classes on Saturday for the day school pupils, which is very popular, teaching children to be alert and habits of instant obedience.

20538. Have you found that that has tended to improve the demeanour of the children and their orderliness?—Yes, I think it tends to make them more respectful and to see the beauty of orderliness.

20539. Do you think that children should be taught to use all their parts both mental, moral, and physical?—I think that should be the aim of our system of education.

20540. What do you say about reading?—I find the children read very well, and I can hear them reading distinctly in our Sunday school; I superintend a large Sunday school, and I have often to say at the beginning, "I wish to remind every boy only to read so that he can be heard in his own class." He reads sometimes so that he can be heard over the whole room.

20541. Rev. Dr. Wilson.—What would be the size of your schools?—Eight hundred children on the rolls of the three schools.

20542. Did your evening cookery class embrace pupils from the three?—More senior pupils and girls of the district generally.

20543. I am not surprised to hear from you that the second winter was not so popular; we have found it the same elsewhere; I suppose they were getting wearied of it?—We found it so.

20544. The question is—would they not get wearied of it in the school?—If it was for their good we would compel them to continue it, if the teacher got good results, the manager and teacher combining could induce children to attend.

20345. Mr. [illegible].—You could induce them, but not actually compel them?—Where the manager and teacher are in touch with the parents, the parents will do anything reasonable that is put before them.

20346. Did you get any support from the National Board for your evening class?—None whatever; we thought we could not comply with the rules and restrictions.

20347. Do you know what special rule it was that prevented you making the application?—I don't recollect. We wished the class to include anyone in the district who wished to come—members of families, occasionally men.

20348. And is there some restriction in the rules of the National Board which prevented that?—I don't quite recollect.

subject of agriculture that the farmer is out and beyond everyone the best expert in reference to the practice, and I could in no way, under no system of training, hope to equal him in practice. For instance, a farmer in order to be a successful farmer, must be a good business man. When you tell him certain characteristics of a cow, of others you say a cow must have good shape and symmetry, deep and level carcase, but he has no absolute standard to compare it with, it is only opinion, he must have the experience of the fair. The teacher is forbidden by one of his rules to attend a fair. Then, again, there are many pupils in my schools—junior pupils—who could describe every point of a cow likely to have a satisfactory supply of milk, and perhaps they would not come near to the text-book. I was experimenting with the boys, because I came from a farming district.

20561. Have you a practical knowledge acquired independently?—Yes, my best, and I thought I was taught for two months practice prior to going to school and afterwards on returning from school. There is no doubt that a child who comes from a farming district gets a good practical knowledge and a good expert knowledge. For instance, I asked a farmer's son how he would know a cow likely to give a good return of milk. He said he would examine the ear of the cow, and if the ear had a yellow colour it was a very good sign; if the dandriff of the ear was yellow it was a good sign, and also if the cow had the slightest strain of a shorthorn. He would not have a cow that had any black on the crop. Then he referred to the distinguishing marks of the udder; and at last he summed up by saying that there are external indications in the cow that an expert could recognise as readily as a man well versed in horses could point out a horse that would be well suited for speed or for drawing. So I contend that in that direction I dare not approach a farmer to teach him the practice of it. But in the matter of science he is very defective, and I think that the mission of the teacher or the text-book should be to bring the two classes of workers together, bringing the scientific worker and the practical cultivator together, so as to ensure their mutual co-operation, and in that way both parties benefit. I look on the benefit of scientific training to a farmer as lying in the power it will confer on him of adapting himself to altered conditions, or availing himself of new resources, and, therefore, I think that the sphere of the teacher should be directed more to reconciling and bringing the two into closer contact, and I believe that agriculture is well-taught as far as the teachers are concerned.

20562. You have had a good deal of experience in model schools in different counties; will you tell us what schools you have been connected with in the course of your career?—Derry Model School, No. 2 Central Model School, and Carrickmacross Model School.

20563. You were at Omagh?—Yes.

20564. A pupil and pupil teacher?—Yes.

20565. Were the subjects of mechanics, magnetism, chemistry, and agricultural chemistry taught in all these schools?—No, they were taught in Omagh.

20566. Who was the head master there?—Mr. Ferguson.

20567. Mr. Strangways.—Do you find that these experimental science lessons of yours awaken the curiosity of the children and make them of a more inquiring turn of mind?—Yes, more inventive and observant.

20568. And so they presumably make greater progress in the other subjects; have you found that to be the case?—Well, yes.

20569. At any rate you can say this, that those children who have given a certain amount of time to the science instruction are not behind the others in the literary subjects?—No.

20570. You don't suppose that anybody could give practical instruction in farming who had not a thorough knowledge of the subject himself?—No, I don't think he could.

20571. In order to be a really practical instructor in farming he would require to be a practical farmer?—Yes.

Belfast.
Oct. 18, 1897.
Mr. S. Brown.

20572. Which means years of constant study?—Yes.

20573. A sort of study which could only, in exceptional cases, be combined with that of preparing a man to be a teacher; he could not be both a practical farmer and a teacher?—I don't think he could make a teacher and a practical farmer—he might make an approach to a teacher.

20574. Do you get fees from the National Board for this science teaching?—Not from the National Board, but from the Science and Art Department.

20575. But not under the scheme of the National Board?—Not under the National Board.

20576. Captain Shaw.—Have you considered the syllabus of the National Board for science?—Yes.

20577. Do you think you could teach that advantageously to your students?—I believe I could teach the inorganic chemistry programme. There are other programmes that I should like to modify.

20578. Would you like to encourage teaching science from the youngest classes?—Not for an examination.

20579. But as a mental training?—Yes, as a mental training, preparatory to the senior division.

20580. You think it ought to be taught right through the school?—I think it should; we have deficiency of touch trained and observation.

20581. If you were allowed to teach experimental science throughout your school as you like, do you think you could devise a satisfactory course?—I would not like to introduce more experimental work than I have at present. I believe I have a satisfactory course of experimental work for the junior children.

20582. You gave us your idea of it just now. You feel it important that science should be taught by experiment?—Yes.

20583. There is no use relying on a text-book if one tells you one thing and another another?—No, but I referred to inaccuracies in the text-book to show that the science of agricultural chemistry is far from being perfect at present.

20584. But the particular instances which you have given have been experimented on, and I think one of the books might be pronounced to be wrong. But that shows the necessity of experiments instead of relying on text-books?—It scarcely goes that far. I referred to that to show that the science of agricultural chemistry is far from being perfect, the scientific part is the part the teacher should be well versed in before he comes to talk to the practical farmer, or to ask a practical farmer to change his mode of doing a thing, and try another experiment. If he will ask me to explain how it is that one field of wheat is hard, and another tender, I cannot do it. That naturally discounts my teaching, and it is not likely that he will be ready to drop his own course, a course whereby he can make money, and make himself comfortable when he can point out that I do not know my subject.

20585. But still science helps to a certain extent in the agriculture?—Oh, yes, I should say that to a farmer who was instructed in science, the part of the plant's life is understanding.

20586. And you think that is a proper introduction to agriculture in schools, the science which underlies it?—Yes, I should say a course of elementary agricultural chemistry is a necessary introduction, and it is a part of agriculture that we should be asked to take up in school. The practical part is really a part where we have to deal with experts.

20587. Do the children perform experiments for themselves in your course?—They perform experiments at home.

20588. But not actually in the school?—No, the experiment is invariably repeated at home, provided it is of such a nature that the child can have the necessary apparatus at home.

20589. Would you prefer the children should do

Belfast. Oct. [illegible], 1886. Mr. [illegible].

some experimental work for themselves?—Yes, because generally, until the child performs experiments for himself, he has not that interest which attracts his close attention.

20590. Do you think you could carry out a satisfactory series of experiments by the students in the ordinary class-room?—I believe I could.

20591. Mr. Molloy.—How long are you head master of the Carrickfergus school?—Since January, 1884.

20592. Were you the first to introduce such a subject as experimental science there?—No.

20593. I believe a predecessor of yours, Mr. Stevenson, had it for some time?—Yes.

20594. Who supplied the apparatus?—I cannot say, but it is a free stock to the school at present.

20595. Do you consider that you have suitable and sufficient apparatus?—I consider so.

20596. There are really three departments in the Carrickfergus Model School, infants', girls', and boys' school, and by your memorandum it is stated the kindergarten is carried out in the infant school, and successfully?—Yes.

20597. In the girls' school they take up cookery, and you state that the result of the examination in cookery was that sixty girls passed, out of what total number?—I think sixty presented, and sixty passed; there were no failures.

20598. And the success in cookery included even one boy?—Yes; that boy made three applications to me, and he backed up the third application by saying that on one occasion he helped to prepare a dinner for the Prince of Wales. He is the son of an hotel proprietor in Larne; he said the hotel would eventually come to him, and he wanted to study cookery.

20599. Is drawing taught to scale in any department in that school?—It is, to a certain extent, in connection with the first and second years' geometry.

20600. Which is the lowest standard or class in which drawing is taken up?—In all classes in my school, but the third class is the first class in which I can present it for results fees.

20601. I find there is a total number of 380 pupils on the rolls of the three schools, and in yours, 164 on the rolls, and of the 164, as many as eighty are learning elementary science?—Yes.

20602. Would you briefly state whether the parents approve or disapprove of that?—When a teacher is popular, and has gained the confidence of the parents, it is sufficient for that teacher to say this is a proper thing to study. The only difficulty will arise in connection with a new subject, in introducing a new subject we generally meet with three or four who cannot see eye to eye with the teacher at the time. For instance, when I proposed the introduction of elocution, and suggested we should employ Professor Millen, of Belfast, one parent objected. Since then he has come round to see the advantage of it, and his children are now attending.

20603. Did you find that the reading improved?—Yes; the inspector, at the last results examination, stated that, owing to the course in elocution, the reading was distinct and accurate.

20604. Chairman.—Who teaches elocution in your school?—I employ Professor Millen.

20605. Mr. Molloy.—I observe, by the time-table, that you commence school at nine in the morning, and terminate at three o'clock; and in consequence of having so many extra subjects, you find it necessary to take up special classes on Saturday?—Yes.

20606. Virtually, the whole of Saturday appears to be devoted from nine until three. Do you find that the pupils attend willingly for those long hours, and also on the special day, Saturday. A former witness said that Saturday was virtually lost in the schools?—Not in the Model schools, we must teach up to 12 o'clock; I had 114 boys present out of a total of 164.

20607. You don't find that the teaching staff or the pupils suffer from attending on Saturdays, and these long hours?—The average percentage in my school for the number is eighty-five, which I should say would give an indication of the health of the children.

20608. Captain Shaw.—Do they do any home lessons as well?—Yes, and overtime.

20609. Mr. Molloy.—I find that they devote from half-past nine to ten to home lessons, and I observe in addition to chemistry, geometry, mensuration, algebra, book-keeping, that Latin and French are taught. Is French taught to the girls?—Boys and girls may come together, but it is not taken up extensively.

20610. Who is the special teacher of that class?—An extern teacher on Tuesday from nine to ten, and on Saturday nine to ten, Latin.

20611. They have in the girls' department instrumental music, twenty-seven girls are learning, on what instrument?—The piano.

20612. How many boys are learning Latin?—I believe eighteen.

20613. Are these taught also by an extern?—Yes, I could not devote my time to eighteen. I should state that the pupils are generally pupils who come from Intermediate schools to the Model school, and the parents are anxious to carry on the Latin and French.

20614. Mr. Redington.—Could you tell me why the science programmes are not taken up to a larger extent in the National Schools?—The science programmes in connection with the National Board?

20615. The subjects of magnetism, electricity, and chemistry?—Where it was possible to teach these subjects, up to last year a teacher could take the class on in connection with the Science and Art Department, London. Our Board pays a results fee of 5s. per pupil, whereas the Science and Art Department pays the teacher £2, if the pupil's answering obtains 50 per cent. Then again the Science and Art Department gave until 1886 certificates, and they also gave Queen's prizes. The Queen's prize was really a handsome prize and greatly coveted, and the children worked very hard. A certificate from the Science and Art Department is very often a passport to employment in Belfast. Looking over my roll of candidates who succeeded at the last examination I find they have all succeeded in getting desirable appointments in Belfast.

20616. Captain Shaw.—What is the nature of the home lessons?—I look upon that as the sphere of the parent, and if I mark out a course that a child should study it is to save the parent trouble, and I examine the lesson again on the understanding that I am doing work for the parent, but I hold it to be the parent's function to see the child is prepared at home. In the Carrickfergus Model school home lessons are very strictly looked after, it is a school that for thirty-four years has held a good name, and the late head master, Mr. Stevenson, stated to me that many of the leading business and professional men in Belfast were trained at the Carrickfergus Model school.

20617. Do you prefer that children should learn things by heart, or have problems that they should work at home as a home lesson?—Perhaps the second fifth might be required to work five sums in arithmetic, and prepare a certain number of pages in geography, and do a little parsing.

20618. Mr. Stevenson.—What do you mean by "preparing," learning it off the book?—Yes, to be able to name the capitals in Ulster, for instance.

FORTY-FIFTH PUBLIC SITTING.—SATURDAY, OCTOBER 16TH, 1897.

Londonderry.
Oct. 16, 1897.

AT 10.30 O'CLOCK, A.M.,

At the City Hotel, Londonderry.

Present:—THE RIGHT HON. THE EARL OF BELMORE, G.C.M.G., in the Chair; THE RIGHT HON. C. T. REDINGTON, M.A.; REV. HENRY EVANS, D.D.; REV. HAMILTON WILSON, D.D.; W. R. J. MOLLOY, ESQ.; CAPTAIN T. B. SHAW; and J. STRUTHERS, ESQ., M.A.;

with J. D. DALY, ESQ., M.A., Secretary.

Mr. W. J. BROWNE, B.A., District Inspector of National Schools, examined.

Mr. W. J. Browne, B.A.

20619. CHAIRMAN.—You are a District Inspector of National Schools in the Londonderry district?—I am, my lord.

20620. How many schools are there in your district?—One hundred and sixty.

20621. How far do they extend from Derry?—The farthest on the mainland is thirty-six miles north, Malin Head in Inishowen, and I have one school eight or ten miles beyond in Inistrahull, the most northerly point of Irish ground.

20622. I see that you are prepared to speak about kindergarten; will you give the Commission your views about its uses and shortcomings?—Well, my lord, I think kindergarten is of great service in training the pupils in colour and form, and in the proportion of things they handle, and also in manipulating the various matters put into their hands, and I consider the drill connected with it of exceedingly great use in strengthening the muscles and developing the bodily structure, and also in promoting the health of the pupils.

20623. As to its shortcomings?—Well, I think its principal shortcoming is that it is not continued from the infants on to the other classes.

20624. There is a break before there is any form of manual work undertaken?—Exactly.

20625. How long is the break?—The pupil passes through first and second class, and after the two years there is no continuance of the kindergarten work, even in drawing. I think that is a great mistake, because the kindergarten leads to nothing as it is at present. Then I find, so far as my experience goes, the understanding is not equally cultivated with the senses in kindergarten; however, that is a matter of detail, a matter that might be remedied in the course of teaching.

20626. What do you think about the extent and the defects of the present instruction in drawing?—In all the schools that I have examined we have nothing but freehand drawing, and that is simply copying from copies on the flat. I think that is only the beginning of drawing. Freehand drawing of an object gives a general outline of it and that requires to be corrected by measurement.

20627. When you say that is the only sort of drawing, are there no exceptions?—I am aware of none, we have no drawing to scale and no model drawing.

20628. Have you no drawing in which instruction is given otherwise than by copies; we saw some instruction yesterday in the First Derry School, given on a blackboard?—That is one of the exceptions perhaps.

20629. Are there any others beside that?—I am not aware of any and I could not have said from my own knowledge that that was done there, because I have very little opportunity of seeing the teaching of drawing; however, I must say with regard to that school that the drawing is exceptionally good, every pupil examined there last year passed and passed well.

20630. What do you find to be the extent at present of the intelligence of pupils?—I don't think it is as well developed as it ought to be, I think there is a great deal too much rote work, and a great deal too little explanation, and, perhaps I should go further than explanation—I think a more valuable thing than explanation still is getting the pupil to find out the meaning of a thing for himself. For instance there is very little consulting of the dictionary. I go strongly for the use of the dictionary, and I find in most schools I have to introduce it myself, and even when it is introduced the pupils cannot find out the words they are looking for.

20631. REV. DR. EVANS.—Is Sullivan's you employ?—That is in the school, but I don't recommend any, I am content with any dictionary.

20632. CHAIRMAN.—How do you think the intelligence can be helped or hindered by manual instruction?—I would like to make a preliminary observation. I think a great deal of the want of intelligence displayed in our schools is not attributable to the teachers and not attributable to the system of results examination, but a good deal to the character of the reading books hitherto used, they have been very difficult and hard to explain, the consequence is the teachers have largely given up explanation. The new books will perhaps meet that, because they will be made more interesting to the pupils—all the sets I have seen. Then manual training I look upon as supplementary to the mental training and as giving an outlet for the at present wasted energies of the pupils; they have got something to do with their hands that will occupy their physical part without any great strain on their minds, they will, therefore, be able to give greater attention to other subjects, and the testimony of all who have had experience is that that really is the result.

20633. What do you say with regard to the necessity for elementary science teaching, both as regards intellectual and physical training?—I think that as regards intellectual training science to my mind means systematised knowledge as distinguished from information, and it calls into play the mental powers of the child in solving problems and overcoming difficulties.

20634. I see you include in your memorandum under the head of science, botany, mathematics, drawing, weighing, measuring, mechanics, physics and elementary geometry?—I think all these ought to be taught more or less.

20635. Is elementary chemistry taught in the schools in your district?—I have never examined in chemistry. I don't think it is taught to any extent. I think all these subjects should be taught by an extension of object lessons, which we have at present in the infant classes.

20636. These subjects were formerly taught in reading books?—They were.

20637. And when did they cease to teach them?—About thirty years ago. A great many of these subjects we had in the fourth and fifth books of the old system, we had vegetable physiology, zoology, classification

Londonderry. Oct. [illegible]. Mr. W. J. [illegible], B.A.

of animals, descriptive geography and a course of geology, which would be rather out of date now, though it was very good at the time it was written; then we had a course of history in the Fifth Book.

20638. Rev. Dr. Evans.—You refer to the very old Fifth Book?—The Fifth Book that became disused about 1884.

20639. Chairman.—With regard to manual training, will you first tell us what you include under the head of manual training?—I have no experience in the matter, I have never examined a school where manual training has been carried on.

20640. We have very often in our examination confined the expression to woodwork and modelling work, there being very little of modelling work anywhere; but there are other subjects which in some of our examinations we found witnesses included in manual training; what do you consider to be such?—The simplest form of manual training is drawing, which we have already disposed of.

20641. Drawing is the preliminary to woodwork; if properly taught, I mean. Woodwork without drawing appears to be badly done and practically useless?—I think the drawing to plan should commence first.

20642. Scale drawing?—Oh, yes.

20643. Suppose that woodwork were to be introduced first of all, how do you think time and means could be provided?—I think about the time there is very little difficulty; the woodwork would be intended only for boys.

20644. And only for a couple of hours a week?—At present girls spend an hour less at ordinary subjects than boys, yet girls almost invariably answer better than boys on the same subject. There may be various causes assigned for that, perhaps girls are more attentive to their work, but I think the accuracy they have derived through sewing and needlework gives them a superior feeling of exactness, and makes them more accurate in all their subsequent work; the time spent by the girls at needlework could easily be given by the boys.

20645. There are two ways of shortening the time devoted to literary subjects, which have been suggested to us—in fact the only woodwork that you may call in satisfactory operation, that we witnessed, was at Lismore, in the Christian Brothers' School; and there, instead of omitting any subject (as I understand), the other lessons were shortened, and they gained two hours a week, by taking ten minutes off a number of subjects?—I should not approve of that plan; without this limitation I say the time devoted by the girls to needlework could easily be given by the boys.

20646. What do the girls give up which boys do?—It varies in different schools. I think that time might be devoted by the boys to manual training, or science, or whatever else is required. I hold that the senior pupils could also remain in the evening after the others have gone away. In fact it would be a relief to the teacher to get the work done after the others had gone away, and that would obviate the necessity of having a separate room. Again, I think two hours each Saturday could be devoted to science teaching and manual training.

20647. Do you think the boys would come after hours?—I think they will if you can get them [illegible]

20648. And of course you think that in some way or other, whether by compulsion or some other way, the teaching of the subject should be well paid for?—Decidedly; you cannot enlist the sympathies of the teachers unless you affect their pockets.

20649. Coming to domestic economy for girls, what do you say about that?—I think domestic economy is equally important with sewing and needlework, in fact, more so; many of the girls trained at our schools afterwards become domestic servants, and in that service their sewing is of no practical value to them as servants, but a knowledge of domestic economy would be exceedingly valuable.

20650. Is that so, that sewing is no value to them as servants?—I think not, sometimes; very often it is of very little importance except to themselves individually, whereas a knowledge of domestic economy would be of exceedingly great use to them, and secure for them better positions and higher remuneration.

20651. Do you think time could be found for teaching such subjects as cookery and domestic economy by taking two hours off the time now given to needlework, and having three hours, as in England, instead of five?—I am decidedly of that opinion; I think we spend too much time at needlework, and there is a great difficulty in getting materials and getting the children to keep up their attention.

20652. Mr. Redington.—I see that on the whole you are not in favour of the abolition of individual examination for results?—I am not, sir.

20653. What are your objections to class examination?—Well, my objection is that a class examination will be either a superficial examination or it will be an individual examination, with a general estimate formed in the mind of the examiner.

20654. If, say, a third of the pupils taken at random answered very well, could you not fairly argue that the class as a whole was well taught?—Yes; but I think the examination is valuable, not merely for ascertaining the standing of the school, but for satisfying the parents and pupils; the pupils have a great interest in the examination, the parents have a great interest in the examination, and the managers, all these are interested in having the actual proficiency of each individual ascertained.

20655. But the main object of the results examination is to ascertain whether the teacher is doing his duty, and could not that be ascertained without examining each individual in the class?—Yes, I daresay, but in many of our schools the classes are very small, and we would require to have an individual examination in them.

20656. Take a large town like Londonderry?—Yes, the classes are very large here, and it certainly would be a great ease to the Inspector to examine schools that way.

20657. Chairman.—Would it not give him more time for inspection?—It certainly would.

20658. Mr. Redington.—You admit in your Report for 1893, that cramming is rather encouraged by the system of examination pursued?—I am not sure I have admitted that; perhaps I have.

20659. "What is known as cramming is inseparably connected with this practice; the facts of the subject are memorised and repeated without being understood [illegible]

20664. Do you think that agriculture ought to be taught to girls?—I do not, decidedly.

20665. Do you think that it ought to be taught in city schools?—I think not.

20666. Are you satisfied with the teaching of it from a text-book?—I am not.

20667. What modification would you suggest?—I am afraid my modification would be rather drastic; I would abolish it altogether. I would substitute some lessons in the reading books, as from my reports you will see I have suggested time after time—a number of simple, well-illustrated, easily worded lessons, pointing to the different processes of farming, and the functions of plant life, and that would have the effect of bringing the subject before the minds of all the pupils—boys and girls.

20668. But is still would be teaching agriculture from a book?—To a certain extent, but it would not be a special subject, it would come in with their general knowledge of the text-book, which is now, I am glad to say, compulsory.

20669. Do you think it would be well to have practical experiments in elementary science as an introduction to agricultural study?—I do; I decidedly think the two should be connected together.

20670. And the pupils should be shown the things they read of, as far as it can be done?—Certainly. As a substitute for that, I get introduced, wherever I can, pictures of the plants. I often hear pupils talking about cauliflowers, who have never seen a cauliflower. I advise the teacher to write to some of the big gardeners and get an illustrated catalogue.

20671. What is your idea about elementary science?—I would introduce it through object lessons in the junior classes.

20672. Could elementary chemistry, suitable for agriculture, be taught in the fifth class?—In the senior fifth.

20673. Why are the science programmes not more largely taken up in our schools?—I really cannot tell; I have spoken to several teachers who formerly taught science, and they have not explained the matter sufficiently to me.

20674. Do you think they are too difficult?—Well, I think, perhaps, they are.

20675. You would not teach science before the fifth class?—Not science as science, but I would lead up to it.

20676. And would not that apply to mechanics as well as chemistry?—Yes, a few of the simplest ideas of mechanics, the effect of two forces acting on a body, for instance.

20677. Do you think that there should be some encouragement given to the teachers to maintain discipline and order in their schools by awarding prizes to them?—Yes, I think a merit grant, or something of that sort, might very well be given; a small amount would be a great encouragement.

20678. Do you think that at present the teachers neglect their work in the early part of the year and put on extra pressure towards the close of the examination?—I would not say that of teachers generally, but I have known instances where I am quite sure that was done.

20679. Would you go so far as to say that the effect of having an annual examination in the school would be, that in many cases, in the early months of the year, the ordinary teaching would be rather slack?—I think in some cases, but in the majority of cases the teachers are fairly conscientious, and attend to their work all through.

20680. If it were a question of maintaining the present system, by which, it is admitted, an insufficient number of incidental visits are paid, or adopting a system of less examination and more incidental visits, which would you select?—I am afraid that puts me in a dilemma. Perhaps the system that would afford more opportunities of seeing the working of the school, I think I should approve of that.

20681. Mr. Molloy.—Have you had experience of the working of inspection prior to the introduction of the results system?—Not as inspector.

Londonderry
Oct. 21, 1897.
Mr. W. J. Browne, M.A.

20682. But you were acquainted with the mode of examination?—Yes.

20683. Would you briefly contrast that mode of inspection with the inspection that prevails at present, I mean as regards its effect on the school?—The present examination passes over nothing, passes over no pupil and no subject. The former examination seemed to me to be, of course, varying with the individual inspector, but in many cases very slipshod.

20684. How many inspectors had you experience of as regards slipshod examinations?—Five or six.

20685. You say that at present inspector's questions become known, and that is one of the disadvantages of the results system?—Yes.

20686. Is not that the fault of the inspector—why does he not alter his questions and [illegible] the [illegible], and prevent the possibility of teachers becoming too familiar with the stock questions?—That is what every inspector does, but the teachers go on the system that what questions were asked in one school will be asked in others. However, I must say, that in one or two cases I purposely ask the same questions in every school, and I am sorry to say that the teachers have not yet discovered these questions and had their pupils ready to answer them, so perhaps the former statement is rather too broad, that the inspector's questions become known.

20687. You mentioned that you would abolish agriculture altogether, both in town and rural schools?—Well, perhaps that is rather too sweeping; I would abolish it as a separate subject, and have substituted for it those lessons I spoke of in the ordinary reading books.

20688. Practically, what is the difference between the use of text-books on agriculture and the introduction of agricultural lessons in the reading book?—The special text-book is too minute, too full of details.

20689. That is the present edition?—I have not studied the present edition, but I know that is the defect of most of the books.

20690. Assuming there is a specially suitable book on agriculture, would you not think it better to use that as that than desultory lessons spread over a number of reading books?—I would not; the lessons would bring it before the minds of all the pupils, and then reduce the number of subjects; however, I should add, that in the senior classes, the highest classes, I would make agriculture a separate subject, and have it practically and scientifically studied.

20691. Then you modify your original statement largely?—I do.

20692. If these desultory lessons on agriculture were in the reading books in use in Derry what interest do you think girls would take in the subject here?—I think the girls would take just the same interest as the boys.

20693. City girls?—I think so; they would know something about the cultivation of fields, the kind of crops that grow there; they would see the illustrations—I go strongly for the illustrations to bring before their minds the kind of plants and crops.

20694. But the reading books you contemplate would contain elementary lessons?—They would.

20695. Quite a number of subjects—including history of the country, and so forth?—Yes.

20696. Some reference to [illegible], and so on?—Exactly. My idea of a text-book would be to lead the child up to the knowledge that every moderately educated person is supposed to have by the reading books, except, of course, in mathematical subjects.

20697. You offer an objection to the present reading books, but of course, you are aware, that managers may use suitable books if they contain no objectionable matter—are there any instances of that kind throughout your district?—There are, in several schools new books have been adopted; they are in use in the Model school, and I daresay in First Derry.

20698. Who is the manager of the Model school?

Londonderry.
Oct. 12, 1887.
Mr. W. J. Browne, M.A.

—Well, Mr. Eardley, for the Commissioners; I have no official connection with it.

20699. In your opening statement you mentioned that kindergarten, in your opinion, did not enhance the understanding of the children?—Equally with the senses.

20700. In what way?—I see a pupil laying tables, for instance. "How many tables are there?" He counts nine. "How many white ones?" "Five." "How many red ones?" "Four." I cover them with my hands. "How many would four and five make?" I generally don't get an answer. I think concurrently with putting the tablets together, there should be a training in number.

20701. You are in favour of extending object lessons?—Very much.

20702. But under the present system there is no difficulty in giving object lessons if the teachers are qualified, and the inspector looks after the subject?—That is true, and they are sometimes given, that is in the infant classes, but I want them extended to other classes. Most of the object lessons I hear given are lessons on pictures—not real objects. I want the real objects put before the pupils.

20703. CHAIRMAN.—Sometimes they bring in flowers and make the children describe the colour?—Yes, I have heard one example of it.

20704. Mr. MOLLOY.—We had that exemplified euphically yesterday at the first school we visited—Rev. Mr. Corgan's; there is nothing to prevent the extension of that, according to the capability of the teacher, in the present system if the inspector would encourage it?—There is this to prevent it, if the teachers are not paid for it they won't do it.

20705. Is it your theory that the teachers will not teach anything suitable for the children unless they are paid specially?—I am afraid that is the case. Sometimes when they say they are not paid for that, I say "You have the fixed salary," and that seems a new idea to many of them.

20706. I believe the results fees come to something like £888,000 in the year, and in addition to that there is a fixed salary according to the classification of the teachers?—Yes.

20707. And years ago, when no results fees were in existence, the fixed salary covered the remuneration for the entire conduct of the school?—That is so.

20708. Have you from your experience as an inspector ever thought of the working out of the graded system in schools. I mean in this way, that a third class teacher, if highly efficient, would get a first class diploma and higher remuneration for efficiency?—I have not thought of it in that way. I have always connected the higher efficiency with the higher classification; the two ought to go together, they don't always do so, but practically I think they do, as a rule.

20709. Is that by the introduction of higher subjects to the curriculum?—By a general efficiency; the more efficient men are those who look for promotion and get it, and they continue their efficiency.

20710. With regard to manual instruction, you mentioned you thought there ought to be a time devoted to that corresponding to needlework for girls; you would not think of giving five hours a week to manual instruction for boys?—Certainly not. I only say that from the time the girls take for needlework there would be taken time for manual instruction.

20711. But the girls, as a matter of fact, give five hours a week; you don't advocate all that for manual instruction?—No.

20712. Perhaps two hours a week—one hour on Saturday along with an hour on another day, and outside school hours, and optional with the teachers to carry it on?—Yes.

20713. And you are in favour of its being optional as regards city schools?—Yes, I think it should not be compulsory at first in any case.

20714. CHAIRMAN.—You are aware that Sweden is the place where this woodwork, manual training, took root first. In no case there is it other than optional, and in no case more than two hours a week?—It is better to have it optional; the mere fact of compelling people to do things sometimes raises opposition.

20715. Mr. MOLLOY.—You are in favour of the introduction of elementary science?—I am.

20716. Have you any experience of schools where that was carried on at any time during your career?—Not the plan I would advocate exactly.

20717. What is your plan?—That all the schools should have object lessons involving scientific things and leading up to the natural sciences, and in the higher classes those subjects should be taught as scientific subjects.

20718. With apparatus?—Yes.

20719. What is your view with regard to the probability of managers supplying apparatus or contributing towards it?—I am hardly prepared to answer that.

20720. You think it would devolve on the department to supply the apparatus?—Or to assist in supplying, I think so.

20721. And the corresponding assistance would come from?—Local sources of some kind; but I am afraid in many cases that means the teacher.

20722. CHAIRMAN.—Do you think in a place like Derry the Corporation would assist?—I think so. We have at present in Derry a very good School of Art, and I think there is a feeling in Derry that there ought also to be a school of science and technical work.

20723. Mr. MOLLOY.—In the Derry School of Art would it be possible for the teachers to qualify for a more advanced kind of drawing?—Oh, yes, the classes are so arranged as to meet the convenience of teachers, if they only attend.

20724. Are they availed of?—They are to a certain extent.

20725. A number of teachers in Derry and the district attend the School of Art?—Yes, but not so many as I should like.

20726. Is there any examination carried on in connection with the School of Art?—There are examinations conducted by the Science and Art Department in which the school is very successful indeed.

20727. Those certificates would hold good under the National Board?—I am afraid not; but that might be modified.

20728. Why do you say you are afraid not?—I understand our Board requires their own certificate to be taken; they may take others, but I have not known it.

20729. Beyond all doubt, if satisfactory evidence of competency be given, no matter where the certificate be obtained, the National Board will accept it, and therefore it might be desirable that there would be an extension of that attendance at the School of Art, assuming it is carried on on satisfactory and efficient lines?—Yes.

20730. Captain SHAW.—If you introduce agricultural teaching into the lesson books, would they have anything which the agricultural students don't know themselves, which they cannot observe in the country round them?—As a matter of fact, boys don't learn much intelligently about agriculture from seeing what goes on around them; they are most of their time at school, and at their homes I think they don't occupy their time in agricultural work.

20731. Is it your opinion that in the country the children don't assist on the farms?—They do to a certain extent, especially in the [illegible] season, and the seed harvest.

20732. Would you wish to include in your lesson book anything which they would not see yourself and have practical experience of?—Not much. I would wish to include the explanation of what they saw.

20733. Would not that bring you back to where you are now?—It would reduce the number of subjects. We have now agriculture as a separate subject.

20734. If you were going to explain these things, would not the book be so large as almost to bring you back to the present book?—I think not. I would leave out a good deal that might come in agriculture for future explanation. I would rather teach the pupils what would interest them and give them a general understanding.

20735. I don't see how they could get a more general understanding than what they get in the field?—I would have no objection to leave it out and let them be taught in the fields.

20736. With regard to geography, do you suggest a similar course of readers?—Oh, yes. I believe the lessons descriptive of geography that were contained in our lesson books many years ago went very far to give our children an intelligent knowledge of peoples and countries.

20737. Would you approve of geographical readers in which maps were used for explanation instead of formal geography?—Yes, instead of and supplemented perhaps by the formal geography.

20738. Do you think it necessary to inspect and examine individuals for results?—I do. I have never seen any reason why it should not be done.

20739. In kindergarten?—Yes.

20740. Are there any examinations in the schools themselves; do the teachers hold examinations?—Well a few do, but I am afraid they don't generally. I think they ought to have systematic and periodic examinations of their pupils, but I don't know that that is done.

20741. If the pupils were examined periodically, and placed in the classes according to their requirements and given marks, would not that largely satisfy you instead of an annual examination?—It would certainly meet the very much.

20742. Don't you think the teachers are almost better able to examine the students in that way than an inspector coming in who does not know the idiosyncrasies of each student?—I don't know that the idiosyncrasies count for very much; they have to be attended to by any judicious examiner of course.

20743. But he only meets the student for a short time, and much of his examination is by writing?—That would be the same whether the teacher examines or the inspector.

20744. The teacher would meet the children all the year round?—Yes; of course that would go very far to do away with inspectors altogether.

20745. If a teacher examined periodically and placed the children in the schools, would you be content with a modified inspection?—You would take certain classes and examine them, and pay more attention to the teacher's method?—I should like to pay attention to the teacher's method at a different time and not combine it with an examination.

20746. Would not that imply a large increase in the inspectorial staff?—It would imply some increase, but not much; I think by slightly reducing the programme, combining the subjects, striking off the separate examination in agriculture, and a few more combinations, the work would be decreased a little.

20747. Would you approve of a leaving certificate for the children?—Yes, I think so, that is a certificate of having passed the highest grade, I think so.

20748. If you had periodic examinations by the teachers and leaving certificates, perhaps then you would see your way to having a less formal examination by the inspector?—Perhaps I would, but I should like to have it tried experimentally first.

20749. Mr. Strangways.—You attach great importance to intelligent reading?—I do.

20750. What do you say about introducing texts in unseen reading?—I think that a very desirable thing; I think in the senior classes it should always be adopted.

20751. It is very important that children when leaving school should be able to read at sight a fairly easy passage at all events, and not merely to read a book which they had got up during the year?—I sometimes do apply that test myself, not as a test for marking, but to satisfy myself; if I am reading a particular book that seems unobjectionable, I sometimes put that into the hands of the pupil or monitor.

20752. Is it not a better test of the pupil's general power of reading than to ask them to read from a book which they may have gone over two or three times in the year?—Yes.

20753. What do you say to allowing teachers to take their children out to farms in the country, see the plants that grow there, and have lectures on them afterwards?—I think that is very desirable, and that would be introducing practical agriculture, which is the only way in which agriculture can be taught, and in one school in my district that is done; they have a school farm.

20754. It can be done under the present regulations of the Board?—There are no farms attached to give this practical agriculture.

20755. I did not mean that there should be a special school farm?—I understand—the neighbouring farms, there is nothing to prevent that being done, or the teacher drawing attention to any particular operation that may be going on in a particular field.

20756. I did not mean so much directed towards agricultural operations as to the general study of natural history, so to speak,—flowers and plants and plant life generally?—I think I have a special note on that. I think botany is a subject that ought to be taught to all our pupils more or less, the materials are everywhere, the study is a most interesting one, and nothing cultivates or sharpens the eye at any rate so much as that. Then it develops the logical faculty in the study of the classification of plants.

20757. Perhaps the children's powers of observation so begun with might help the powers of reasoning, and might not these examinations and observations be made very useful material for composition afterwards in schools?—Certainly, nothing more useful.

20758. In fact it is much better the children should write about something they have definitely seen and examined, than that they should write at large about beauty, punctuality, and things of an abstract order?—Very much better; there would be something in their letters if they wrote about things they saw and were regularly trained to do that.

20759. That would help to make the work more practical?—It would; it would help to give them a greater interest in their work.

20760. And if the drawing in the school were made of such a kind that the children were able to sketch roughly the objects they have seen, it would also tend to make it more practical?—It would; I believe that drawing should be taught not merely for its own sake, but for the sake of illustrating every other school subject.

20761. So that the whole school instruction might to a certain extent be grouped round what the children actually saw and knew?—Exactly.

20762. They might examine it, describe it, read about it, write about it, draw it?—Yes.

20763. So that everything they did would be more or less of a practical nature?—Quite so; and further than that I think the microscope might be brought into play a little to show the minute structure of the plant.

20764. For the older pupils?—Yes.

20765. Don't you think that the present methods of examination rather tend to prevent an inspector giving sufficient attention to methods of teaching?—Well, to a certain extent they do, but I think every judicious examiner knows well by his examination, to indicate in what way subjects ought to be taught; I know I spend a great deal more time in my examinations than would be sufficient to satisfy myself as to the qualifications of pupils.

20766. Suppose you have a large number of pupils to go through in a limited time, and have to examine

Londonderry.
Oct. 8, 1897.
Mr. W. J. Brown, M.A.

[illegible]

each one of these pupils individually in a great number of subjects, your attention must be concentrated on the question of whether those pupils pass or not?—That is the main point, but the examination also tests the method of teaching.

20767. Take the case of writing now: you give a class a dictation test and you examine that dictation, you say that is fairly well written or indifferently written as it may be, but that test itself gives you no indication of how the children hold a pen?—Indirectly it does, because if the letters were badly formed the pen might have been properly held, but I can carry [illegible] in a great number of my schools I find the pen very badly held; I don't merely examine the writing, I watch how they do and draw the attention of the teacher to it.

20768. You find you have leisure for that?—Oh, yes.

20769. Suppose you do draw the attention of the teacher to it, could you have any means of getting him to attend to it; it does not affect the results fees?—It is only moral suasion, or if it is very bad I can mention it in my report.

20770. In examining the arithmetic, take classes four and five, and upwards, you give them a card to do a certain number of sums on it?—Yes.

20771. Do you pay any attention whether they can do their sums quickly or not, or are expert in calculation?—Well, I confess I don't limit them strictly to time.

20772. But that is rather an important thing?—It is, and that is tested sometimes, I am sorry to say not always, by slate work in compound addition sums.

20773. But the other is the thing you must do first: the test of accuracy by means of the card is the all-important thing?—It must come first.

20774. And such a consideration as speed is only a secondary thing?—Yes, it does not enter into the mark we assign for a pass.

20775. Similarly in the lower classes you give Class I. a sum in addition; if they all do it correctly they all get a first class pass?—No, in that case I am able to test the method and satisfy the method of that class. I generally find when I give a sum in addition that the children use their fingers or nod their heads. I stop that because I insist each pupil shall do it orally. I get each child to do the question orally until I have ascertained that the subject is thoroughly taught, and subsequently I take one here and there at the examination.

20776. CHAIRMAN.—Do you mean that you ask them questions, and they do the sum on the slate?—They have the questions on the slate, and they simply go through the process of adding.

20777. Mr. [illegible].—Is not that really a class examination?—It is individual examination. I examine each individual on the subject and see that he is able to do his work.

20778. I understand you gave a sum to the whole class?—I don't give the same sum.

20779. You give each individual pupil a different sum?—I do; if there are five numbers to be added I give four numbers to all, and get each to place under them a different number.

20780. You spoke of the advisability of having prizes for order and discipline?—Yes.

20781. And I think you favour that idea?—I do.

20782. Might not this happen—that only a small number of schools thought themselves in the running for these prizes, these would really make some effort to improve their condition, while the others, who thought they had no chance of it, would not be at all influenced?—You did not quite understand me; I don't see that there should be competitive prizes, but that each school that distinguishes itself should get a prize.

20783. The word "prizes" suggested to my mind that there was a competition?—I don't mean that.

20784. Without giving up individual examination altogether, what do you say to retaining it in the fourth and higher classes, and leaving it out in the lower?—Well, I confess I find less difficulty in retaining it in the lower, because I get through most of the individual examination of the junior classes, while the upper classes are at written work.

20785. It is not a question of convenience, it is a question of which is the most effective way of examining the school?—I have given my opinion at present.

20786. You would still retain individual examination in such subjects as geography?—Yes.

20787. Examining each pupil individually?—I don't know that I examine that way; I ask one question and I pass the questions round the class, and the advantage of that, to my mind is, if there is any nervousness in a particular individual he may be affected by one question, but when the questions come round to him again he may have recovered his equanimity.

20788. That is pretty near what I would call class examination?—If that is class examination, I approve of it.

20789. REV. DR. WILSON.—The scope of the Compulsory Education Act is limited to 116 towns; would you not think it much better in the interests of the education of the country to have it embrace the whole of Ireland?—Certainly.

20790. You would have every child of school age brought to some school?—Yes.

20791. Would you not believe, looking at the character of our population, that if our education were less literary, and portion of the time was given to what would enable them to be handy in every way, it would be better for the children?—I can answer that question only in a roundabout way. I don't think the education should become in any degree less literary, but rather more literary than it is, but at the same time I believe that something that should make them handy and smart in adapting themselves to circumstances afterwards is very desirable.

20792. Would you not believe that if a boy who is to be a ploughman was taught to read well and write well and count well, but not taught the higher parts of arithmetic, or the more difficult parts of geography, and if he was also taught how to mend his plough and arrange his harness, would you not think he had received the best education for him?—I am afraid not, I want him to be an educated man, and even if he is a ploughman that won't do him any harm.

20793. Even if he got the whole of it in five years?—A boy may be likely to be a ploughman, yet how often the unlikely happens. This boy we suppose likely to be a ploughman may develop some ambition, go abroad, and turn to something quite different. We should endeavour to give every boy and every girl a sufficient education to turn to any walk in life. It is very desirable that a ploughman should know all about his plough, of course, but he should know the other also besides.

20794. It has been remarked that our boys come out from the National schools all desirous to be clergymen, all looking for situations—there are being one situation for every ten applicants—and that they are above doing work that would really support them in life. Would not our education be better if it were to train them for what will be really the work of the future?—That was one consideration that weighed with me in considering this matter and in giving my approbation to the introduction of manual training. I think it is very desirable that this should be introduced, so as to do away with this idea that manual work is degrading work.

20795. The opinion very much prevails that it is degrading work. When you train a lad in the higher mathematics he is above the work that really he must do if he is to live. As regards needlework, we saw in some places here that there was needlework for an hour; do you think it would not be better if that was for half an hour, and the other half spent in teaching plain cooking?—I would not divide the hour. I think an hour at a time is little enough for needlework, but I would say three hours a week is quite sufficient, and the other two should be devoted to cookery if only the difficulties surrounding the introduction of the subject can be overcome. I think an hour is little enough time for the needlework lesson; it takes some time to get the materials out and some time to collect them afterwards.

20796. I notice you have said, and I agree with you, that the true way to interest the teacher in teaching these additional subjects is through the pocket?—Yes.

20797. That is, you put them on the same level as the clergy?—Yes, and as most other professional men.

20798. Rev. Dr. EVANS.—Are there any evening schools in your district?—There is one.

20799. Where is it?—At Malin Head.

20800. What is taught in that evening school?—It was only opened last year, and has been in existence for only one month—reading, writing, arithmetic, and spelling—four subjects.

20801. Is drawing taught in all the schools in your district?—No.

20802. In about what proportion?—Drawing was taught in thirty-one schools out of 180 in the last official year.

20803. Are there any teachers in the balance of the 150 schools certificated to teach well?—There are.

20804. Are the managers against it?—No manager is against it. The managers are all, I believe, quite glad to see the subject taken up.

20805. Are you in favour of drawing being taught wherever it can be taught?—I am, wherever it can be taught well.

20806. Would you make it compulsory in the schools?—Yes, and teachers should have certificates.

20807. What would you do with the teachers who have not certificates, and the children in those schools where the teachers have not certificates?—In the first place I would say to those teachers: "get certificates, the way is open," we hold examinations every year. And if there be some who don't quite come up to the standard, I would say let a provisional certificate be given to them.

20808. But you are in favour of having drawing taught as widely as possible?—I am very much.

20809. Is there any manual instruction given in your district?—None.

20810. Is the alternative programme for girls in use in your district?—I think, in two schools, there is one near Malin Head, and I think a convent school in Carndonagh, I am not quite sure about that.

20811. Were there a larger number of schools that taught that programme formerly?—I think so.

Londonderry, Oct. [illegible], 1897. Mr. W. J. Browne, M.A.

20812. Why was it given up?—It was given up because the teachers were never in favour of it, so long as they were compelled to teach it of course they did, then when they saw they could get exemption from it one after the other claimed exemption; and the pupils and their parents were not in favour of it.

20813. I think you said you were in favour of elementary science being taught?—Yes, very much.

20814. I don't remember that you told us what portions of elementary science you think suitable for our National schools?—Well, I think, what the Science and Art Department call physiography would include a great deal, and perhaps more, but a great deal of what I would consider suitable for the classes, that is for the lower classes, and in the higher classes I think some chemistry should be taught and certainly some botany.

20815. Dr. Wilson asked you a question about advanced arithmetic, do you think our programme in arithmetic is too far advanced?—I do not.

20816. You would not be in favour of omitting any portion of the advanced arithmetic and substituting for it practical mensuration?—I think practical mensuration should be joined on to advanced arithmetic, but the parts that need be joined on are not so heavy as to involve an omission from the present course.

20817. But there are parts of mensuration that would be very useful to a boy in the country?—Certainly, a boy ought to be able to calculate the area of a field.

20818. And when he has a quantity of seed to put into a field of a certain size he ought to be able to go pretty accurately to work and not go by rule of thumb?—Yes.

20819. You would not omit any portion of arithmetic to introduce mensuration?—I would not. Of course arithmetic is very difficult to teach, and made heavier by our absurd system of weights and measures, but if we could get the metric system introduced it would simplify the matter.

20820. You are in favour of domestic economy, what is taught under that name in our schools?—The various ideas connected with healthy homes, the ventilation of the house, the necessity for cleanliness, the value of pure air, and the process of respiration; and cookery of course would come in.

Mr. F. Eardley, Head Inspector of National Schools, examined.

Mr. F. Eardley.

20821. CHAIRMAN.—You are the head inspector of National schools in the Londonderry district?—I am, my lord.

20822. Will you give the Commission your views on the subject of the teaching of physical and applied science in National schools?—I can go back to the period when it was first introduced, that was in the year 1852, it was taught by Dr. Clarke, and I was his assistant. Here is a syllabus (produced) of a portion of the subjects actually taught in the Galway Model School. The actual teaching was an hour a day to the pupils, and as far as possible the advanced pupils were encouraged to assist in giving experiments, and also to endeavour to construct simple forms of apparatus.

20823. To make balances?—Precisely, and also levers, a combination of lever, wheel and axle, pulleys, and see their practical effect. This instruction was also given to teachers, a class was opened in the morning, the teachers in the model school were instructed in that for an hour every morning, and then there were lectures given to which the teachers of the district were invited to attend on Saturdays.

20824. Did they come?—They did in large

20825. Then you were not confined to Galway?—No. I give this table as representing the course of instruction given in each of the model schools, this happened to be published in the report of the Galway Model School.

20826. Is that system taught in the schools now?—No, it was given up after the death of Dr. Clarke, the same enthusiasm that he devoted to it could not again be found and it died out.

20827. Do you think it would be advisable to revive it?—I do, I think that would be the proper extension on the manual side of the literary instruction that the children now receive, that would be one means; drawing with practical geometry, to include the measurement of the school, drawing to scale, making the elevation, measuring fields, laying maps; all this would be using the hand and eye. And practical geometry coupled with mensuration would then be a natural extension of the drawing lesson in the school and coupling it with kindergarten, so that it would furnish without a break the regular instruction of the hand and eye from the infant to the time he would leave school.

20828. You disapprove of the present system of

Londonderry.

Oct. 15, 1886.

Mr F. Eardley.

20529. Is kindergarten taught in the first class?—It is, it is taught in the two classes to the child while he remains in the infant school.

20530. Do you call the first and second class the infant school?—Yes, children who are under eight are infants, it is an age division.

20531. Rev. Dr. Evans.—Where is your own district, Mr. Eardley?—I have thirty-four schools, principally in the neighbourhood of Limavady, a few on the Waterside, the south side or west side of the Foyle.

20532. Your circuit is a very wide one?—It extends from Fair Head down to Mullaghmore in Sligo, goes down to Ballinamore, embraces the whole of the counties Fermanagh, Donegal, Londonderry and Tyrone, and that portion of Antrim that skirts the Bann, it has the east side of the river Bann, a strip along the east side, from Toome Bridge to Bushmills and Giants Causeway.

20533. Are there any school gardens in your district or in the circuit?—I have two school gardens in my own special district.

20534. Is the work done there useful?—Extremely useful.

20535. Would you like to see it extended?—I am very anxious that it should.

20536. Are fees paid to the teacher there for the work done in the school garden?—Yes.

20537. Does he use our agricultural text-book?—He does.

20538. The one edited by Mr. Carroll?—The new edition is introduced now.

20539. Have you read that book?—I have read it, but not to be able to speak very minutely of it.

20540. Did you examine in it?—I am not very familiar with it.

20541. Don't you examine the pupils?—Where they have been taught it, because there is a latitude allowed, they don't like to buy the new book where they have the old ones.

20542. Chairman.—It is a very long book?—No, my lord, it is divided into two.

20543. Rev. Dr. Evans.—You have no fault yourself to find with it?—No.

20544. And you think an intelligent teacher might find it a very suitable text-book for use in the schools?—He might; but there are a whole lot of technicalities and big words that convey no information to the teacher or to the child.

20545. To the teacher himself? A specimen, please?—A great many of them. Take "carbonic acid." It conveys no idea to their minds, or the use of classical language, of which they have no comprehension. If they could be taught to understand these things it would be useful.

20546. Is there a school-farm at all in all your circuit?—No.

20547. Mr. Molloy.—Eglinton, Templemoyle?—That is given up.

Mr. Strahan.—There is one at Park, in my district.

20548. Rev. Dr. Evans.—Do you find any difficulty in getting an adequate supply of boys to come forward as monitors and pupil teachers?—No difficulty, and there is rather an excessive amount of girls for girls, for boys it is fair enough. I would couple mensuration with it.

20552. You are very confident, in your opinion, that that would be a wise thing?—I am. I think I would leave out all beyond commercial arithmetic. I would let them have the square root, but I don't see the use of the cube root. It is a hard rule for them to learn, and in place of that I would put in mensuration.

20553. Is needlework well taught in your schools?—There is the time given to it that is prescribed. I cannot say it is well taught—in this way, that the children seldom or never bring garments. They bring, approaching the day of the examination, the little article prescribed by the programme, and this is made up for the day of the examination. All the rest of the time they are only working on practising specimens—little bits of calico on which they hem and stitch.

20554. You have made a very interesting observation in your report, to the effect that "Drawing is becoming a very popular subject, and instruction in it is extending every day." Is that still going on?—It is.

20555. What has rendered it more popular than formerly?—People are commencing to see it is akin to writing. It helps the writing, and is a means of occupying the children usefully and intelligently.

20556. You yourself encourage it, and would wish to see it universal?—I would.

20557. What would you do in the case of old teachers who have not certificates?—I would accept his results, and sometimes the boys by competition sharpen each other, and will really acquire skill in that way if he supervises; and these old teachers would look after it pretty keenly themselves.

20558. You think the training colleges have helped in bringing about this increased popularity in the teaching of drawing?—I do.

20559. You say it is the best introduction to hand and eye training?—Yes.

20560. Would you develop that a little?—In drawing we have to observe first the shape of the object we are going to draw; there the eye is called in; then that is reproduced by the hand. If you are using a saw or chisel, when the eye has got some training the hand is guided by the previous training the eye has received.

20561. You have found managers to co-operate heartily with you?—Without exception I can say so.

20562. You regard the managers throughout your circuit as very much interested in their work, and in the prosperity of their schools?—Some of them enthusiastically so.

20563. Do you think these managers would co-operate in the introduction of a kind of manual instruction in the schools?—I do.

20564. We should have the managers with us?—We would have the managers, and I would say the teachers.

20565. The teachers as a body?—Yes; and I would think the subject itself would be very popular with the people.

20566. Rev. Dr. Wilson.—You think it would be very important that the eye and hand should be trained?—I do. I think without training the hand

20868. As our Chairman has brought out, we have had it stated to us that the boys were all delighted with the manual instruction, and that the days on which it was given were the days of the best attendance; you think it would be equally popular in your district?—I have no reason to believe otherwise.

20869. Captain SHAW.—Was this syllabus you have handed in, all taught in the schools?—It was all taught.

20870. How many years' course does it represent?—It represents three months' instruction.

20871. Do you think all these subjects could be properly covered in that time?—They were so; the Professors of the Queen's College in Galway were invited to examine, and this syllabus was handed to them.

20872. How many hours a day were given?—I would say there was one hour in the middle of the day, and another in the afternoon, and another in the evening. One hour was compulsory during school hours, the other hours were optional.

20873. What was the class of students?—The senior students.

20874. Do you know how long the elementary course in physiography under the Science and Art Department is intended to take?—No, I do not. I am not familiar at present with the Department's course.

20875. The course is a two-years' course?—But the Science and Art Department only requires twenty lessons in the year.

20876. That is the minimum?—If you give three lessons a day for three months, you have 270, and that represents nine years of yours.

20877. Have you considered how far the children should do experimental work themselves?—Yes; there is nothing to prevent them making levers in the mechanical powers.

20878. What class would you contemplate should begin to do experimental work?—The fifth class. They would use a penknife with soft wood, and make these levers of the first, second, and third orders. Little spools could be made into pulleys, wheels and axles; they would extemporise them.

20879. Do you think they get any accurate results from apparatus they make so?—Not much, not accurate; but it would occupy the hand, and train the eye. There is nothing to prevent them utilising Florence flasks and making retorts, bending glass tubes with a Bunsen burner and gas. They can all do that.

20880. They can learn the use of the balance?—They can.

20881. And they can do a large amount of experimental work with it?—They can.

20882. They can also do a great deal in the way of measurement?—Yes.

20883. You think those would be suitable for the fifth class?—I do.

20884. And continued through the sixth?—Continued through the sixth.

20885. Then do you think the addition of mensuration to arithmetic would give greater labour in teaching it?—I think not.

20886. On the contrary, would it not rather tend to simplify it?—It would give them an interest to see one of the applications of arithmetic.

20887. Can you not take multiplication and division and all these things with a simple scale?—To let them see a room and measure it, and find out its dimensions and make a plan of it, it would give them an increased interest. They have nothing but abstract things up to this, and to get some concrete matter is what they require.

20888. That would render the teaching of arithmetic easier?—I would say it would make it easier.

20889. Mr. MOLLOY.—You are in favour of the extension of the kindergarten system throughout the schools?—I am of opinion that any training we give in manual work should be a development and extension of the kindergarten.

20890. A former witness, a practical teacher, stated to us, that he preferred to begin the instruction with pupils who had never learned kindergarten rather than with those who had received some instruction in it. Would you concur in such a statement as that?—It must have been very badly taught, the kindergarten he speaks of.

20891. Practically you say that kindergarten would be an advantage in the teaching of writing. Allow me to read a passage from your report—"A pupil who is advanced in kindergarten learns to write sooner a good hand and to be more generally apt, to get on quicker in the other branches of the school course than one not so brought up?"—That is my experience.

20892. "I mention writing first as more or less kindergarten drawing;" you also say "drawing in one form or another is practised in all the infant schools where kindergarten is taught, and the hand and eye is educated in both," and you look forward to the extension of that practice as carrying with it very valuable results?—I do.

20893. Then I take it you are in favour of the extension of the kindergarten beyond the second class?—I am.

20894. Would you desire to have it introduced into the ordinary schools generally?—I would; our infants are idle during the greater part of the day, and if we had kindergarten exercises they would not have to stay idle.

20895. Then not merely as an occupation for infants, but also for its educational value, you desire an extension of kindergarten throughout the school?—Yes.

20896. Would you think any difficulty would be experienced in carrying it on in the principal room of the school if there were no class-room attached?—It could be done.

20897. And the ordinary business of the other classes would not be thereby interfered with?—I think so.

20898. You say you agree in the statement—"It is not desirable that trades, in connection with the manual instruction idea, should be taught in schools, but we may at least ensure such a well balanced development of the faculties of the pupils as shall place them in a position of greater freedom in the choice of their life-work, when they leave school." You agree in that statement?—I do.

20899. It is made in the report of Mr. Struthers, a member of this Commission. Coming for a moment to a matter in which you were practically, and, as I happen to know, very successfully engaged some years ago, when you were assistant to the late Dr Clarke, you mentioned that his course embraced applied science, and not merely theoretical?—Yes.

20900. And it took in such subjects as chemistry, hydrostatics, pneumatics, magnetism, electricity, light and sound. Now would you kindly indicate what particular branches of those were carried on, chemistry, air and water?—Yes, the manufacture of coal gas, also the preparation of bleaching powder. I remember going with him to see how bleaching powder was manufactured near the Inchicore Railway Works. And the manufacture of sulphuric acid, commonly known as oil of vitriol, we went to see that made in Ballymacarret, there are also works in Dublin. The making of the other ordinary commercial acids. This did not extend very far, but the elementary principles were taken up, they were illustrated in these manufactures.

20901. Hydrostatics, pneumatics, the general laws of liquids and gases?—Yes, and their applications, pumps.

20902. And particular attention was paid to the subject of mechanics?—Yes.

20903. Properties of matter, mechanical power, relation of cause and effect?—The construction of a

Londonderry.
Oct. 15, 1897.
Mr. F. Kerley.

20946. Who supplied the materials?—A committee of ladies supplied it in the case of the Sunday-school, and the Nuns supplied the materials in the other place.

20947. Any inconvenience found with regard to that?—No, they were enthusiastic at first, but the interest in it died out. It is dead now.

20948. Did that unhappy effect arise from the fact of want of skill on the part of the ordinary teachers of the school or inability to conduct the classes continuously for the year on the departure of the specialist?—I take it to be unwillingness.

20949. Was it not enthusiastically worked out by the local committee?—The enthusiasm lasted but a very short time.

20950. They subscribed money?—They did, £8 or £10, and I think it cost the convent £8 or £10, but somehow or other they all told me that, while they benefited by it and were able to make their dinners more savoury, and employed materials more economically, they got tired of it.

20951. CHAIRMAN.—Perhaps they thought they had learned enough?—That is it.

20952. Mr. MOLLOY.—Do you not think if the teachers of the ordinary schools, the mistresses, were sufficiently qualified and carried that on continuously it would be a very great advantage to local parties?—In the country, no—in the towns it would have a chance—the fare in the country is very poor and requires very little cooking. For instance, meat is a thing almost unknown in their food.

20953. Was it not advantageous that other than senior pupils took part in the cookery, theoretically and practically, and listened to the demonstration lesson?—Yes, grown girls were invited to come.

20954. Did many ex-National pupils take advantage of that permission?—Not many.

20955. But there was the opportunity?—Yes, and some did, particularly in the convent school; there are mills in Carrickmacross(?), and there is a good opening for female employment in the mills.

20956. But if I mistake not, the instruction was carried on in the evening, chiefly to take in those mill hands?—It was.

20957. The cookery class in connection with the convent was an evening class?—There was also a day class.

20958. Captain SHAW.—When you and Dr. Clarke were giving these lessons in science, for which you received no fees, the results system was not in force?—No.

20959. Do you think if the teacher had to earn results, he would be pleased to have an outside teacher coming in and taking two hours a day from his school?—He would be received with the cold shoulder—teachers don't like outside teachers coming in. The plan would be to let teachers come into centres and acquire the power of giving these lectures themselves; that is the feasible way to introduce this subject.

20960. Mr. REDINGTON.—Do you think that kindergarten could be taught in a school with one teacher and a monitor?—I do; he could employ an unpaid monitor or two to assist, and they would do—there is a certain amount of willingness to assist on the part of the monitors.

[illegible]

20965. Does not this point to the necessity of teaching elementary science?—With agriculture as its crowning.

20966. But rather to teach it first before you taught agriculture?—I would teach a little elementary science as the foundation of it, agriculture should be applied with intelligence.

20967. Why are not the science programmes taken up more largely in our schools?—Because the teachers have not the aptitude to use the apparatus; their knowledge of apparatus is so scanty that very few of them can use it.

20968. You think that those programmes are fair enough?—The programmes are fair enough, but if they were taught the instruments necessary to carry out the experiments, for instance the electric telegraph, it would not take very much to let the children see how it was done. It could be done very cheaply.

20969. Do you think science could be taught in any earlier class than the fifth?—I don't think so; I think it would be injudicious. You could teach the children of the third and fourth to cut out with their penknives in soft wood; they might make little toys involving mechanical principles with soft wood and a little wire.

20970. CHAIRMAN.—You never saw any wirework done in schools?—No, never.

20971. Mr. REDINGTON.—I see in your report for 1895 you say, "The present system of examination leaves too little time for inspection proper," and you go on to say that "it is at incidental visits principally one can judge best of the discipline, tone, and methods; for at the results examination these points are in the hands of the inspector, and it is his own rather than the teacher's methods and discipline he has before him on such an occasion." Are you still of that opinion?—I am.

20972. Therefore for thorough examination of the teacher's methods you should pay incidental visits?—Incidental visits are necessary.

20973. And more than one?—More than one; there should be a forenoon visit to the school to see that the teacher and the pupils are punctual, and an afternoon visit to see that the rolls are marked and the ventilation attended to.

20974. These incidental visits should last a considerable time?—Not less than half an hour.

20975. A mere visit of a quarter of an hour on the way to a results examination would not be of value?—No, you seem to take surprise them, and they do not get over their surprise for the few minutes you remain.

20976. Do you think class examination could be substituted for individual examination in some subjects?—I do. I would persevere with the individual results examination in schools that were not doing well. For those schools that have passed well for two or three years or more I would say accept their results and pay them at the rate they were formerly paid at, have incidental visits until the three years would elapse, and then re-examine, or until a distinct change in the teaching staff occurred. A school that has been satisfactorily conducted for a number of years—you might pass that for three years, and only have incidental visits—but those schools that

[illegible] Oct. [illegible], 189[illegible]. Mr. F. [illegible]

20979. But I think you have admitted that the method of the teacher is important, and you cannot judge of that by an examination of the pupils?—No, but you can judge backwards; if he turns out good results his methods must be good.

20980. Does that follow?—I think it may; they are not actually convertible, but very nearly so.

20981. Mr. Molloy.—You may achieve some of the results in very mechanical ways?—Yes.

20982. Mr Redington.—Suppose they had learned a reading lesson by heart and you happened to hit upon that particular lesson?—We can very soon discover whether it is rote work. There are a great many things we all have to learn by rote; we must learn tables, and our vocabularies are rote work; you would not call that cramming. Where what is legitimate ends and the improper begins, that is what the experienced examiner has to distinguish.

20983. Without going into minute details could you tell us how you would lighten the programme if it were thought desirable to do so?—In the third class I would limit the knowledge to be expected in grammar to the noun, adjective and verb. I would retain his knowledge of the noun and adjective as a necessity to teach him spelling; for instance, the great stumbling-block with young children is that they cannot distinguish between the pronoun "they" and the definite article "the." If you teach him that the definite article is used before a noun, and the pronoun before a verb it is necessary he should know the noun and the verb. In the higher classes I would leave them to concord and syntax.

20984. In your report you say in one place that grammar and geography should be optional subjects; now I understand you to say you would modify the grammar and make it compulsory?—I would make it optional still.

20985. And modify it for those who chose to take it up?—Yes.

20986. In the same way with regard to geography you would make that optional, and perhaps modify the details of the programme?—Yes.

Rev. James Gaboon, B.A., Presbyterian Minister, Londonderry, examined.

20987. Chairman.—You are the Minister of the First Derry Church?—Yes.

20988. And you are prepared to give the Commissioners your views upon the additional subjects that can be taught in National schools without infringing much on the time?—Yes. In the first place, your lordship, I venture to suggest with all deference that drill should be given to both boys and girls. That, I think, could be done at recess, at the periods of changes, without infringing to any appreciable extent upon school time; my object being, your lordship, to keep the bodies of the children in the best possible health, and, in consequence, to keep their minds in the best possible condition for attending to the instructions given, in such a way as to profit both. I think, in the next place, it would be quite possible, without infringing upon school time, to introduce lessons upon natural science, such, for example, as physiology, hygiene, zoology, botany, astronomy, on the principle of a graduated scale running from the simple forms up to the higher and more intricate. These I would introduce, if I could, into the lesson books, according to the precise position the scholar had reached. I would introduce also, in the third place, domestic economy and cookery. Our Government, I think, would give us a central place, say here in this city of Derry, with all the appliances necessary, and the school girls from the various schools in the city and surrounding districts could be drafted there at specified times, to get the benefit of the instruction given without infringing very much on school hours. Saturday is a dies non with us in reference to school work; that could be utilised, and I think it would be possible to utilise an afternoon in the week, Wednesday or Thursday, by dispensing with certain lessons.

20989. What lessons would you dispense with?—I am not prepared exactly to go into details on that matter. I think, perhaps, dispensing, for example, with home lessons, such as would be given, those were the [illegible] land and Germany. Then as to the methods of teaching, my position with regard to that is this; I look upon methods of teaching as practically amounting to this, the accumulated experience of the great teachers of the world, whose teaching has been to leave in the child's mind the desire to know more. Now there are three things that it strikes me are necessary in that point of view: in the first place, talent, in the second place, training, and in the third place, experience. I would, as far as possible, educate our teachers more, so that they may be able to educate our scholars more. I mean by education—as distinguished from instruction, by way of teaching the scholars to think and see right, and I would do that as far as possible by object lessons—by cultivating their powers of observation as far as possible upon things round about us, as far as that could well be done, such as the things they see, birds and beasts, brick and coal, wind and water, and all those objects. I think in the next place, as illustrating the point I now try to make, that grammar is too much taught in our schools by analysis, and not enough by synthesis. To give an example; a young man applies to me for a situation as assistant teacher; he writes me a letter of application, and there are several mistakes in that letter. If I ask the young man to parse the letter he could parse it every word, but he does not know how to write the letter in a proper form grammatically to me. I submit there is something wrong about the conditions of education that creates that thing, and I speak not from one particular instance, but from several instances of a similar kind that have come under my knowledge as a manager of schools. I will give another instance:

"Was worth the chase, was worth the day,
That saved thy life, my gallant grey!"

There is not any of those young men or women that would not be able to parse that right through

Londonderry.

Oct. 16, [illegible]

Rev. [illegible] [illegible]

is the north from the school, they cannot tell me. I submit that this is not a condition of things that ought to exist in the last years of the nineteenth century. Your third class at present requires the outline and leading features of the map of the world. If any give the pupils' minds fair play, let them find the cardinal points of the school by setting up a pole at 12 o'clock on the floor, by sunshine and shadow, do a rough sketch of the school, placing desk, door, and fireplace in their proper positions, attach the sketch to the city or county map, explain why the proportion is so different, attach that to the map of Ireland, and explain why the proportion is abnormal, and then a map of Europe, and lastly a map of the globe we live on. Then show the globe with the orrery, and explain the position of the universe, and I submit a lesson given like that would leave an impression on the child's mind that would be healthful, strengthen its thinking powers, and do it a measure of good. In that connection I am not sure that physical descriptive geography—such, for instance, as the question of dews and fogs, and climates and products—is taught in our schools as it ought to be. If our young boys and girls are to be merchants and business people, they ought to be acquainted with the climatic conditions of the various countries of the world, with their governmental conditions, and to know exactly where they can get certain products, &c. In that way there are open doors, through which their minds may look, that would bring in large revenues of knowledge to themselves and benefit humanity. I submit, in the third place, that the word "educate" in its literary and derivative significance ought to be more emphasised. Suppose the inspector comes into my school and gives to my fourth class boys—a class that is taught by my very superior and excellent teacher in the male school, whom you saw yesterday—a lesson such as they have never seen before, and grants them ten minutes to look over that lesson, and when they have looked over the lesson silently themselves, they have never seen it before, to know it perfectly, he calls up the class and asks them all the questions he can think of out of that lesson, and questions them in regard to their capacity to receive information from it on the things taught in such lesson. I do think an exercise like that would have a very beneficial effect upon the scholars, and I can easily see how it would enable the inspector to find whether the child was crammed or taught, whether the child's intellectual faculties were properly exercised, and whether that with which their whole future lifework is to be done—I mean their mind—was cultivated to any appreciable extent. In that way I think they would see not only effects and causes, but objects and qualities and relations; they would see the flash of lightning in the drop of dew, and the crystal in the snowflake, see the structure of the daisy, and understand something of the telephone. And I think that subjects like these would be of enormous benefit to the rising generation with whom we have to deal, and would generate inquiry in those children's minds in after years that would be exceedingly healthful. The last point I wish to touch upon is this, some unfairness to the teachers. What I mean by that is this, that in these last years of the nineteenth century, when education should be as free as it is possible to make it, I think it unfair to the teacher that he should have to be paid for teaching Latin and French, that a fee of 5s. must be paid for such subjects before a child can go and learn them.

20990. You mean paid by the child?—Paid by the child. And in relation, for example, to kindergarten, if a child cannot read, and is five years of age, the teacher gets no result fee for kindergarten simply because the child has failed in reading, and the same all along the line in reference to sewing, freehand drawing, and the theory of music. I would pay every teacher [illegible] he would and I would see that he taught it well, and would not stand anything else. And I would say equalise your payment by results in the best way you can, so as to reach the maximum of benefit to the generation to which we belong. I beg pardon if I have been too long, but I will now answer any question your lordship wishes upon anything I have said.

20991. Have you given any consideration to the question of the introduction of manual work?—My conviction is this, that taking the age at which we can alone have our children here in this community, and I only speak for this community—that is to say, a child leaves us on the average about twelve years of age, and you only have the child about six years—I think it is not possible for us to do very much, if anything at all, in industrial work, and I would leave that to the various trades, as the thing may arise afterwards. But I would say discipline the hand of the child and the eye of the child and the ear of the child and the mind of the child, so that when it came to do with particular trades, whatever the trade was, the child would be able to acquire it and deal with it in the very best way.

20992. You have expressed very clearly the object of this Commission. This Commission is distinctly not one to inquire how to teach trades, but how to give that preliminary instruction you have mentioned. Do you think that children of eleven years old would benefit by having a course of instruction during their last year in woodwork?—I think probably they would, but the difficulty just there is this—no man knows to what particular trade that particular child would go.

20993. That would be quite true if you were teaching a particular trade; but the object of this manual work, as taught in England, is not to teach a trade, and without the least reference to what particular trade a child will go; but to give him that general power of observation which will enable him to adapt himself to any trade, whether woodwork or something quite different?—If the child had in his mind being a mechanic I would advocate very strongly he should have a basis of applied mechanics.

20994. In point of fact the woodwork, as taught under the Sloyd system, is connected with drawing; and it is putting into practice the knowledge the pupil has gained in drawing. Are you in favour of that?—I would, if time allowed; but you cramp the child's mind to a degree when you tie down a child of those years to that particular kind of thing, because that child may be going to work as a clerk—that child may be going, perhaps, to some profession.

20995. How do you cramp his mind—the experience gained elsewhere is exactly the reverse. Instead of cramping his mind you make it more intelligent?—If your lordship will allow me I will withdraw that phrase. But if a child's mind is directed to this particular thing the child has not the opportunity for acquiring what, in my judgment, would be a much more useful thing in after life—getting the mental instrument thoroughly whetted, that it would be able to apply itself to anything, and its power of observation made so accurate that when it came to work of that kind it would know how to do it.

20996. Rev. Dr. Evans.—You have been a long time a manager?—Yes, a few years.

20997. How many schools are you manager of?—Four schools.

20998. And, of course, have a long and large experience?—I might query that, but not to you under the circumstances.

20999. Do you think that the managers of schools might form themselves into an organisation or committee of their own for consultation and mutual instruction in the duties of managers?—Well, I think that is possible, but I see very serious difficulties in the way.

21000. Where? Might not the Presbyterian managers, for instance, in Londonderry form themselves into a committee, talk about the state of their schools, know what is taught well in one school, what

31024. CHAIRMAN.—You are the Administrator of St. Columb's parish, Londonderry?—Yes, my lord.

31025. How many National schools are you manager of?—Seven. At Long Tower we have four schools, male and female senior, male and female infants. St. Columb's Hall school, Nazareth House, and Bridge-street.

31026. Have you any on the other side of the river?—No.

31027. Will you give us your views on the subject of kindergarten.—Kindergarten I regard as a subject of very special importance in the infant departments of schools, and not only in the infant departments, but I would say it is a mistake to drop kindergarten, where it is generally dropped now, at the second class. In some schools it is only taught in first class, but in some up to second. I would say, to have the practical utility of kindergarten brought out, it should be carried up into all the classes in some modified form. For instance, carry on the system of kindergarten drawing until you bring in freehand and object drawing, and geometrical drawing and model drawing, and in that way I think that education would be very much benefited in a practical manner. It is the experience of all in charge of it that it is very beneficial to children; every faculty they possess is exercised; moreover, the physical development of the children is brought out with ease and pleasure; it interests, amuses, and instructs the children; and, besides it trains the children to accuracy of eye and hand, and methodical habits also are acquired by it.

31028. Do you agree with an opinion which was expressed to us at Belfast with regard to the present teaching of drawing, that the freehand drawing, which is taken up after an interval, has nothing to do with the kindergarten drawing, which has been taught before?—I do not; I would say that the kindergarten drawing is a great help to the freehand drawing afterwards, because under the system of kindergarten drawing the hand acquires a steadiness and accuracy which will be of great service in the freehand drawing.

31029. You don't agree with the opinion that was expressed, that a person who had never done any kindergarten could begin the freehand drawing with the same advantage as a person who had had instruction in kindergarten?—Certainly not. I would wish to give you a little local testimony to the advantages of kindergarten. In a large school in the city where kindergarten is taught up to II. standard, two divisions had to be made of the pupils of the same class, these were taught in separate rooms—in one of the rooms kindergarten was taught, in the other it was not for want of appliances. When the two divisions met in third class it was found that those taught kindergarten excelled the others much in intelligent answering on the subject-matter of the lesson-books. Their intelligence was developed and quickened. The other children, under an equally efficient and assiduous teacher, were dull and sleepy, and required much more repetition of instruction. And it is the experience, too, that children taught drawing in kindergarten methods have much greater facility in copying freehand; that is the experience of several teachers; it steadies the hand and handwriting, because they have to be particular in laying everything on exact lines. It steadies the eye. They are trained in arithmetic, having to count beads; half an hour is given to kindergarten each day, and to drill and singing once a week. A local male teacher also testifies that the children coming to his school from kindergarten schools get better marks from the Inspector for reading in some of the advanced classes. Another male teacher, examining a class, was asked by a person standing by, how it was that some of the children answered with much more readiness and intelligence on the subject matter, and he said—"These come from a kindergarten school." It is found, too, that where kindergarten children come to the fifth class, when they are asked to write letters, and say what they saw coming to school, the kindergarten children have a much wider range of observation than the children that were not taught it. When they are asked to write a letter on what they saw coming along the streets, the kindergarten children hardly miss anything, but describe it very accurately, whereas the children who have not been taught in a kindergarten school merely say they saw a cow on the street, or a dog or something of that kind, nothing more.

31030. Do you think that the teachers in the schools you manage are of the same opinion as yourself with regard to kindergarten?—Any teachers that I have applied to are in favour of it, not only those who are teaching it but those into whose schools it has not yet been introduced.

31031. Then you would not agree with the evidence of a gentleman in Dublin, a teacher put forward by the Teachers' Association, that he would rather have children straight from the gutter than children from a kindergarten school to teach literary subjects to?—I certainly would not. When I go into the kindergarten school I notice at once that the children there are bright and intelligent and observant, and when I go into a school where it is not taught, I perhaps find only a small number sitting in the front seat, sucking their fingers or longing to see the hour for getting home. I think if a larger fee were given for kindergarten the teachers would be stimulated, they would have more interest in taking up the subject; then the expense of providing the equipment, that is a difficulty in our schools; it is principally the Sisters of Mercy that have kindergarten here.

31032. Would not that be met by giving larger fees?—There should be a special grant to start with, and then a larger fee, but I think that to make the kindergarten useful as bearing upon manual instruction it should be carried up into the higher classes in the form of geometrical drawing and drawing with a rule and compass, scale drawing. I wish to say with regard to small country schools, where there would be only ten or eleven infants and only one teacher, I think the average for an assistant or monitor should be lower in those schools, and they should have a monitor or assistant there who would be trained in the kindergarten system, or where that would not be convenient, to have a workmistress in a country district in charge of three or four schools within a convenient radius, and let her go around those schools to teach the children in a mixed school under a male teacher, teach the little girls' needlework and also kindergarten, take one or two days each week, a peripatetic teacher for a radius of two or three miles.

31033. With regard to the subject of agriculture, do you think that there is too much attention given to that subject in the city schools at present?—I think there is, I think that except the general principles of agriculture, such as any educated gentleman should be expected to know, for practical purposes it is altogether useless in city schools.

31034. What do you say about the teaching of it in country schools?—I think the teaching of it in country schools as at present carried on has no practical bearing upon agriculture as practised by farmers. I would say to have it practically carried out, where a central school farm for a district could not be acquired, there should be school museums or some sort of cabinet of specimens provided in that school, say specimens of different kinds of soil, grasses and so forth, and let children be encouraged to bring those specimens with them, let their parents gather them and send them to the school, then the interest both of children and parents will be stimulated, and the parents will begin to get over the idea

Londonderry.

Oct. 19, 1897.

Rev. Hugh M'Menamin.

some of them have that they know more than any National teacher even about the theory of agriculture.

31035. Are you in favour of the plan of having school plots where possible attached to the rural schools?—I am, but I am afraid the acquisition of these plots would be attended with great difficulty. Wherever practical, by all means.

31036. There is a way in which the difficulty has been got over, where the Congested Districts Board has been at work, and that is instead of buying plots they hire the plot from somebody willing to let it?—Where that could be done I would be in favour of it, and, I think too, if the teachers somehow could approach the farmers themselves, and point out to them the utility of these principles of agriculture in a practical manner, it would have a practical effect.

31037. What do you say about the industrial programme for girls?—The industrial programme for girls was adopted in our Convent schools here for some time, but exemption from it has been obtained, for this reason, that it was only in the sixth class that the industrial programme became obligatory, and the class of children in our city here who remained up to sixth class are a class of children who are generally aspiring to be teachers or seeking higher situations, and the parents and they themselves consider that two hours a day given to sewing was not of practical utility, and, therefore, they found it was better to have it dropped.

31038. Would you be of the opinion, which has been expressed to us by some persons lately, that instead of increasing the number of hours for sewing it would be advisable to diminish them to three hours, and apply the two hours thus gained to some other kind of practical instruction?—I would, certainly.

31039. Would one of those subjects be cookery?—Yes, I should say so, but I am afraid that the introduction of cookery in connection with the school apartments is hardly practicable; I would go in for a central building where a special teacher would be and have the children from the different schools brought there in rotation and make it compulsory, because if it is left to their own option to go or stay, they will not go; the teachers should see that the children in certain classes would attend there in turn.

31040. Do you think that class of instruction would be better given in the evening?—I think it would.

31041. And you would have a special teacher?—I would have a special teacher.

31042. How would you have the teacher supported?—Well, a State salary.

31043. How would you have the materials supplied?—I think the children who were in a position or had the means to provide suitable materials should be asked to bring them with them, and then there should be some small grant given annually to assist the poorer classes in providing the materials, there should be some subsidy whereby sufficient materials could be procured.

31044. Would there be sufficient means of disposing of the materials after they were cooked, as has been done with considerable profit by the London School Board?—In course of time there might, but at first the thing might be more or less unpopular, but if it became recognised I am sure it would be of immense benefit, and become popular in a few years.

31045. Continuation schools in Londonderry would be a good thing?—I think so, but we have tried continuation schools for boys who had not acquired sufficient education or who had to leave school, or perhaps some of them had not gone to school at all on account of some domestic circumstances, but we found that although the attendance at first was very promising, it soon fell off, and I think that arises from the fact that there was nothing of an interesting nature in the school, but the mere drudgery of reading, writing and arithmetic. I think if there was something of a practical nature taught it would make the school attractive, and perhaps they would acquire the knowledge of reading, writing and arithmetic, and perhaps a little manual training as well.

31046. Would you go further and carry it on to woodwork as practised under the Sloyd system?—I would where it could be done conveniently.

31047. Could it be done in Derry?—I am afraid not, except in some central establishment.

31048. In England where the Board schools prevail it is carried on in a central school, several schools send a class on different days to the centre?—I think that is the only way.

31049. Mr. Henderson.—You are in favour of the appointment of peripatetic teachers of kindergarten?—I am.

31050. You think the workmistresses we have at present might be made peripatetic teachers of kindergarten?—If they got some training, if there was a programme laid down and these teachers were asked to attend lessons.

31051. Would it not be possible to get the female teachers to learn how to teach kindergarten, and then to teach it themselves?—What I would mean by the peripatetic teacher is that it would be her business to train local teachers in that particular branch and once they had acquired sufficient knowledge to teach it let her withdraw.

31052. Do you think there ought to be a specialist as teacher of agriculture?—I think so, to give it practical effect.

31053. Would you confine the teaching of agriculture to those schools that had school gardens attached?—I would not; school gardens are certainly preferable, but where they cannot be had let them go in for practical illustrations, gathering specimens of different kinds of soils, and seeds, and grasses.

31054. What would you think of a little elementary science?—I would be very much in favour of it.

31055. Would it be difficult to give a teacher sufficient instruction in elementary science to enable him to give simple lessons?—I don't think so at all.

31056. It would be very interesting to the pupils?—It would, and I think the teachers would readily adopt it.

31057. Do you think the teacher of an evening school ought to be the teacher of the day school?—Well, I think it would be better not if other competent teachers are to be had.

31058. Do you think that the mode of payment in evening schools does not offer sufficient inducement to teachers?—I think it is one of the principal reasons why evening schools fall through, that the salary allowed is so small that the teachers, in order to have decent remuneration for their services, have to charge too large a fee to the pupils attending the school, and because of that, then, the children withdraw.

31059. Does it not rest with the manager to determine what fees are to be charged by the teacher?—Of course, if a manager charges a fee that would not be sufficient to remunerate the teacher the teacher would not take it up; if he remunerated him out of his own pocket, or some other source, it would be different.

31060. If the results fees, or payment made by the State to the evening schools, were sufficient to remunerate the teacher, there would be no necessity to charge a school fee?—No.

31061. Have you thought over the details of the regulations for evening schools, and could you suggest any modification?—I should suggest adding them to the subjects already laid down in the programme.

31062. Perhaps you would kindly send in a paper with your ideas on the subject?—Yes, I will have pleasure in doing so.

31063. As to the teaching of cookery in rural schools, do you think that is impossible?—I don't think it is impossible; I think it should be adopted to some modified form.

31064. It was suggested to us, as a means of getting over the difficulty about the provision of materials, that the teacher, if her residence was near, might cook her own dinner before the pupils, and so give them a demonstration?—I think that would be very practical, and a step in the right direction.

31065. I refer only to simple cookery?—Simple cookery.

31066. Have you considered the question of forming associations of managers?—I have not considered it, but since I heard the thing mooted, I am inclined to be very much in favour of it. There should be an interchange of views amongst these managers, and I would say, too, that occasionally there should be a meeting, not only between the managers of the district, but between the managers and teachers, to discuss the subjects of practical importance for that particular district, and submit them then to the Inspector, and the Inspector to the Board.

31067. Then you would be in favour of this association being given liberty to modify the programme within such limits as would be approved of by the Board?—Yes—to suggest to the Board such modifications as in their judgment would be suitable for the requirements of the particular locality in which they live.

31068. And it may so happen that the Board would approve of those modifications for that locality only?—Yes.

31069. You think that would be an improvement on the present arrangements?—Very great, in certain districts; there are, perhaps, particular industries or habits of life which are peculiar to the district, and the teachers and managers could frame some system of education which would suit the requirements of the particular locality.

31070. Mr. Molloy.—You testify, very strongly, to the great importance of kindergarten instruction?—I do.

31071. I quite agree with all you have said on the subject, but there is one point I wish to advert to—how would that be carried out by the teachers who were not familiar with the instruction?—I was very much struck with an observation made before the Commissioners by an eminent educationist in England, and I would certainly take his view. Sir Joshua Fitch says:—

"We began, so far as kindergarten is concerned, by not insisting on a particular kind of training. We began by setting forth the thing we wanted to have done, and saying it should be encouraged, and dealing gently with teachers who were not quite prepared, but, at the same time, insisting on it in the training colleges." Sir Joshua Fitch adds that the "English system is not to insist upon certificates for every subject that a teacher may be called upon to teach, but to give a general certificate based on the general capacity of the teacher, and then test his capacity in special subjects by the actual results of his work."

I entirely agree with that.

31072. My question has brought out the statement that you rely very much on training colleges?—Certainly.

31073. As a matter of fact, however, in every female training college instruction in kindergarten is a sine qua non, just in the same way as drawing is a sine qua non?—Yes, but I refer to older teachers who were not trained; I would say to insist on their getting a certificate for a special subject would be, perhaps, a hardship.

31074. Are you quite clear that workmistresses would be suitable persons to carry on the ordinary instruction in needlework and kindergarten?—No; I said if this workmistress got a training from a peripatetic specialist.

31075. Would it not be better to have the ordinary teacher of the school sufficiently qualified to carry it on—it is rare to find a workmistress capable of imparting knowledge in a technical subject like kindergarten?—Of course, if you could get a male teacher to take it up in his school, by all means.

31076. Chairman.—In the case of a female teacher you would suggest that the female teacher should be qualified?—Yes, where there is a female teacher.

31077. Mr. Molloy.—You say, attention in city schools is paid at present to agriculture; surely it is not introduced into city schools except very rarely?—It is taught in a good many city schools, but it is given up, I must say, in some of them at present.

31078. But you think that book-keeping is an essential for the city schools?—I think it is, and I would have it taught on more practical lines, more in the manner in which it is done in good business houses, and accustom the boys to all the business terms of banking houses.

31079. With regard to the industrial programme, you mentioned that in Derry the shirtmaking industry is carried out—is not that a trade?—It is a trade; but I would only in the schools teach them to use their hands and fingers in such a way, that when they went to the factory, they could apply them with more skill and dexterity to actual work; I would not teach them trades.

31080. You are not in favour of having sewing classes in the classrooms?—If it could be done I would be in favour of it, but I would be more in favour of a great central establishment to which the people would come.

31081. That would be very costly: as a matter of fact we have in a number of cases sewing classes successfully carried out, and the whole plant is in the class rooms. How is it that evening schools have not flourished in Derry?—For the reason I have already given, that the salary allowed by the Board for the teacher of the evening school is very small, and the results would be small on account of the class of boys that come to these schools.

31082. Were any attempts made to introduce evening schools?—I have tried it several years—at first we would have fifty or sixty, but in the course of time they would fall off, and I think chiefly because the fee charged was such that for the poorer class of boys it was made prohibitive.

31083. Chairman.—How much was the fee?—Sometimes 6d. a week.

31084. Mr. Molloy.—Mr. Redington pointed out that the manager could make a change?—If the manager had money in his own pocket to pay, but I do not happen to be one of those.

31085. Rev. Dr. Wilson.—Do you think the fee is the main reason why evening classes are not more popular?—I think it is not the only reason; I think it is because of the dull teaching of reading, writing and arithmetic to poor boys who have been working all day—it is a drudgery, but if there was something practical introduced it would stir them up and stimulate them.

31086. Rev. Dr. Evans.—We have been over the whole programme pretty fairly now, Father McMenamin, but I think you are in favour of special examiners for kindergarten?—What I meant by that was that special peripatetic teachers should come round to organise and give special training.

Londonderry.
Oct. 21, 1897.
Rev. Hugh McMenamin.

Rev. Edward McKenna, P.P., Claudy, Londonderry, examined.

Rev. Edward McKenna, P.P.

31087. Chairman.—You are, I believe, the Parish Priest of Claudy in this county?—Yes, my lord.

31088. Is Claudy a part of the city or an outside parish?—It is an outside parish, a village of very [illegible].

Londonderry.

Oct. 8, 1887.

Rev. Edward M'Keown, P.P.

31069. Do you think that more alteration should be made in the time that is now devoted to teaching grammar?—I do, my lord.

31070. Will you tell us in what respect?—With your permission I would read my memorandum, as I cannot trust my memory much:—I think that the manner in which grammar is provided for is the great blot of the system, or one of its greatest blots, and I was astonished to find that there were in Ireland men thought worthy of coming before this Commission who could be capable of speaking so little of the study of grammar in our schools. One opinion was put before you that it should be shut out of the school till the sixth class is reached or second stage of fifth; that is to say, three fourths or more of our children, who never reach either of those classes, are to go out of school without any knowledge of grammar. Another opinion was that grammar should be made optional—that is to say, the teacher might omit grammar altogether if he chose. A few others in same strain followed suit, and no doubt with good intentions. I trust, however, for the honour of our country and the credit of our National schools, that the propounders of such doctrine will find that they have come before the wrong Commission. I look upon grammar, and so do the bulk of my more intelligent countrymen, as the cream of schooling in any spoken language in the world, because it is a precious part of it; and it is the cream of schooling in another sense, for, whether it be good or bad, it comes to the surface. Men who speak at the bar or from the pulpit, or in Parliament, may know Greek and Chaldaic; but those who hear them speak don't know or care much whether the speakers understand those languages or not; but they do know very well when they pronounce incorrectly or speak ungrammatically, and so, our boys and girls may be able to find the square root of a fraction, or to tell you that the river Kama is a tributary of the Volga, but those who converse with these young people or receive letters from them don't know or care whether they know these things or not, but they can judge very well of their grammatical blunders in conversation or on paper. Now, how has grammar been treated in our present advanced and comprehensive system of primary education? The authorities have made it unwittingly I think, the scapegoat of the school. In third class they give 2s. 6d. for a pass in arithmetic, and 1s. for a pass in grammar. They allow a time-table to be drawn up, giving a good allowance of time to every subject except grammar. The surprising statement of Mr Walpy, of Galway, in the last Report, confirms me in this. At page 180 he speaks of the way grammar is treated, not in one or two schools, but in "several" schools. His words are worth quoting, and here they are:—"Analysis of several school time-tables recently revealed the fact that, with almost unbroken uniformity, out of a school-week with five days, with forty or forty-five half-hour lessons devoted to secular instruction, two half-hour lessons were given in grammar," just as if it were an easy A B C lesson, but we all know it is far from easy. "The subject" says Mr. Smyth of Clonmel, at 248 of the 60th Report, "is generally considered one of the most difficult in the programme." Mr. Fitzpatrick of Armagh, with long literary taste, says at page 171. "No other subject shows so quickly and certainly the condition of a school as this one of grammar, of its educational value there is no room to doubt. At every step the pupil is made to think." What then are the remedies? The first remedy is, pay as high a fee for grammar as for arithmetic. The second remedy is, give as much time for it as for any other subject. I will ask no more, and, as an Irishman, and for twenty-six years manager of schools, I will never be contented with less. The third remedy is, teach syntax, or enough of it, before you begin to parse at all. For what does the present system say:—"Teach grammar in third class a whole year without one word of syntax. Teach it in fourth class a whole year without one word of syntax." In the third class year—the first year for grammar—the child is taught to define the parts of speech, and to tell that such a word is a pronoun, such another a verb, such another a noun. In the fourth class, in second year of grammar, the child is made to tell genders, numbers, cases, moods, and comparisons. They can tell you such a pronoun is in a certain number and case, and such a verb is in such a number; but they are not asked to tell you why. To go on in this way is called simple parsing, and the word "simple" is appropriate in a certain sense in which we all understand the word "simple." There is not a word about concord or government; and after these two grammar years are over a parent can come in to and say what kind of grammar-teaching have you when my boy, that is two years at it, can't correct the sentence, "The men has got their dinner?" Our answer is—the rules of the Board provide no key during these two years to unlock the mystery. I would, therefore, wipe out this simple parsing and do as Mr. M'Millan, senior, of Wexford, recommends in 53rd Report, page 310:—"In whatever part of the course English grammar is introduced the study should begin with the sentence, and not with the word." The word work has been tried, and it has failed; nine out of ten of the reports of the inspectors tell this "doleful lamentation." Let parsing, from its very beginning, be guided by syntax. Without syntax the parsing is like the pump without the handle. What the handle is to the pump syntax is to etymology; as the rudder is to the ship so is syntax to the rest of grammar. If I am told "you want to get too much into the child's head at once," I answer, no; let the time the child loses at simple parsing be saved for syntax. Keep back parsing, if you like, for the first half year of the first grammar year, and in that half year the child will know a good many things about etymology and syntax also. If I am told that syntax is the heavy end of the beam, I deny it and say it is the lightsome and joyous part of the work, for it enables the young parser to unravel his forms, and to command this or that word to change its form if it needs to be changed. Besides, syntax is brief. Sullivan has only eleven pages for it, and he has ninety-three for etymology. Of the twenty rules of syntax in Sullivan, only a few are needful or essential for starting a child with:—A verb must agree with its nominative. Transitive verbs and prepositions govern the objective case. Two or more nouns in the singular, joined by a copulative conjunction, require a plural pronoun, and the rule about the verb "to be," will enable a child to reach. These five or six, and more, could easily be got by heart, in addition to the easier part of etymology, in six months. The rest could be got off by degrees without cramming. In this plan all the grammar children could stand up together in one class—the stronger could help the weaker by their better answering; and the classes would be greatly enlivened by the amalgamation. The fourth remedy is—take five minutes each day from the school time, so as to provide, as far as you can, a grammatical atmosphere in the school. How is this to be done?—It can be done easily, by introducing what I will call "phrase grammar." Let the teacher draw up twenty ungrammatical loose phrases. Let him announce them to all the children, in globo, large and small, to those who know grammar, and those who do not. Let him say to the children—these phrases are wrong in grammar, and I will tell you how to set them right; and when I have told you that you will tell me in a clear, loud voice, the right way of saying them.

"The nights is getting longer."
"No, sir, 'the nights are getting longer.'"
"Soldiers wears red coats."
"No, sir, 'soldiers wear red coats.'"
"He gave apples to him and I."
"No, sir, 'he gave apples to him and me.'"

And so on. For sake of variety and utility there should be a new store of such phrases every new quarter. This kind of oral grammar will not, I grant, overcome the habits of home surroundings; but it will do a great deal in that line. It will even help the parsing classes, and will help the children who will never get learning book grammar at all. The right words imprinted on their tender minds will remain there in after life. I have known young gentlemen and housemaids, who were never at school, pronouncing so well, and speaking so grammatically that you could scarcely detect their errors if they were talking to you now and then for a twelvemonth. Why? Because their masters and mistresses and their children always spoke grammatically. Head-Inspector Downing, at page 188, says very truly:—"It is merely necessary to consider the value of the acquisitions of a child of the better class at seven years of age." Why did he say so? Because that child then knew not a line of grammar but heard pure English spoken, and therefore speaks pure English from imitation. The fifth remedy is—take another five minutes, not for grammatical phrases, but for correct pronunciation and for what I may call propriety of expression. Let the teacher draw up a list of one or more mispronounced words, in little sentences, such as:—

"The kettle got out of the byre."
"No, sir, 'the cattle got out of the byre.'"

He should fill out the twenty list with words or forms of impropriety, such as:—

"He learned me to play marbles."
"No, sir, 'he taught me to play marbles.'"
"I and Harry got new shoes."
"No, sir, 'Harry and I got new shoes.'"

The phrase grammar lists should show all the concords and governments, and vary in new forms as well as possible; and so should the pronunciation and propriety list vary also. These lists should be sent to the Inspectors for approval, in order to guard against anything denominationally offensive. I have now taken ten minutes off the time, but no ten minutes were ever better employed in any school. Without well-taught text book grammar, and these helpmates of grammar our children will go out from our schools in a garb that will be very uncouth. They will be like the strongly-framed mahogany table that is not smoothed by the plane or finished by the polisher—a table that nobody would like to buy. I saw this out-teaching exemplified by an Inspector. The children ignored the grammatical expression in their table-books, and said "twenty-four pence is two shillings." He set his face firmly against it, and now there is not a child, whether it knows grammar or not, will say "3 and 5 is 8," or "4 from 7 and 3 remains;" but "3 and 5 are 8"—"4 from 7 and 3 remain;" and that Inspector is Mr. Browne, of Londonderry. Mr. Codrington, of Roscommon, supports me in this. At page 194 he says:—"So long as grammar continues to be taught without reference to the language the children themselves use in speaking and writing, so long will it remain unattractive, and in a large measure unproductive of practical results." Head-Inspector Hardly, 201, says the "instruction is not sufficiently practical, as is evidenced by the circumstance that a scholar will parse both poetry and prose correctly, and yet in his composition exercises fall into the grossest mistakes." Our children and our people should be freed as soon as possible from the jibes of the English-speaking world in this grammar task of our education. Is it any wonder that the taunt should come to us from America in the dialogue between an American woman and her servant? One of our Irish girls says one day to her mistress, who has got good schooling, "Mam, these tomatoes has a bad smell." "Yes, and your grammar has a bad smell; and so has the schooling you got." "Oh, mam, I was teached lots of grammar, for I was two years at it in Ireland; but, indeed, I was never teached to speak it." "Yes, I say, you were teached grammar in Ireland, but you were never taught it. Take the children out for a walk, and if you don't speak more correctly to them than you did to me I will have to send you down to the kitchen, and try to get a housemaid that will be able to express herself a little more 'grammatically.'"

Londonderry. Oct. [illegible] Rev. Edward [illegible], P.P.

21091. Have you given any attention to the subject of manual instruction in schools?—I have given a great deal.

21092. Will you tell us your views on it?—I am afraid you will be tired of me by this time, but I will ask your leave to read again, because I cannot trust my memory.

21093. Would you hand the paper in, perhaps, and tell us the substance of it?—That would make a mess of it; it would be no use. It is too much detailed and carefully drawn up to be taken piecemeal.

21094. REV. DR. WILSON.—I am very glad to meet a champion of grammar, such as you are. We have met with any amount of evidence to go to show we should not teach such grammar?—I know that; I saw it with very great regret, and, I would say, with humiliation.

21095. Well, I largely sympathise with your views.

REV. DR. EVANS.—We were delighted in listening to the most admirable paper you have read for us; and I congratulate the people of [illegible] on having such a parish priest.

WITNESS.—There is another thing—this would take as long to read as that, and, therefore, it might not be feasible. I am now a quarter of an hour under examination. I would like to speak of the drawback of your system with regard to writing letters and making out plain accounts. I venture to say that when a child has gone out of sixth class even, that there is not one out of ten can write distinctly the form of a plain account; but, with regard to children up to fifth class they know nothing whatever about writing letters. Now, that is very painful, with such great machinery as we have. I tried yesterday at my own school what the children could do in making out a plain account of the very lowest class. And I say if they make out a plain account and write a short letter that they will be trained in a way that they can write these letters at home. There is my idea: make out a plain account, with its headings and footings, of which the poor children are absolutely ignorant when they leave school (produces specimens).

21096. CHAIRMAN.—Is this what has been done by children in your school?—That is the fourth class, and then the poor little children of the second class have done the same thing. But I would say that the National Board should make it imperative in all schools that a simple letter should be written, and a simple plain account written out by every child in third and fourth class, and I would even go so far as to say in second; and I would say also that the Board should take the trouble of writing on the left-hand side the copy of a plain account, and leave the child to write on the right-hand side a copy of that, and if they had that and got thirty plain accounts and thirty little letters in one year, even the lowest class will have done a great deal.

Londonderry. Oct. [illegible] Mr. James Brown.

represent any other teachers?—In one sense I represent other teachers, but I just speak on my own behalf as a teacher of a rural school. I believe I express the mind of a great many teachers similarly circumstanced to myself.

21100. We will begin with cottage gardening; what are your views on that subject?—I think there should be a small plot of ground attached to each school, where cottage gardening could be taught practically.

21101. What size would you suggest?—I would not limit it to any particular size, for getting a lease on a certain plot sometimes prevents a plot being got. I would say a rood would be necessary, but I would work with less if that could not be got.

21102. You would not think that two acres would be suitable?—I would think it rather too much.

21103. You think that anything exceeding half an acre would be too large?—I would limit it to half an acre.

21104. Do you think there would be much difficulty in acquiring it in the way the Congested Districts Board has done, by renting it from a neighbouring farmer?—In some circumstances that would be possible, but not in a great many.

21105. How would you acquire it in cases where that is not possible?—I think there are compulsory powers in the Act to give sites for schools and teachers' residences.

21106. But if there was no case of building a new teacher's residence, probably those powers could not be exercised; in such a case as that you would have to fall back upon renting?—Yes, but it would be very difficult to get it.

21107. Unless you got it by agreement?—Yes.

21108. Would it be equally difficult to get it by purchase?—It would be more difficult, many farmers would not like to sell a bit off their farm; they would rather add a little to their farm than sell a bit off it.

21110. Perhaps you would give us your general ideas upon the subject of the cultivation of fruit and other matters which you have in your memorandum?—I think in this plot of ground I would have attached to each school that the ordinary common vegetables that are capable of being cultivated in that neighbourhood should be grown, and the ordinary fruit trees such as are suitable to be grown in that exact locality should be grown. I think the children should be instructed in more than the names of vegetables, they should see them growing, and be trained in the time to sow them and plant them, and their treatment afterwards, and have a practical illustration of plain cottage gardening.

21111. Are you of opinion that poultry-keeping and bee-keeping should be taught?—I think where there is a garden like that attached to a school the like of that should be attempted.

21112. You would not think that poultry-keeping and bee-keeping, the teaching of the art of keeping them, are educational in the same sense as the teaching of gardening would include botany?—Not just in the same sense, but very educational, training them to thrift and carefulness in after-life.

21113. Would you say that flowers should be cultivated in connection with schools?—Certainly. I think the taste for flowers should be more widespread, that flowers should be cultivated in connection with Irish cottages, as in other countries.

21114. It has been suggested by one of our witnesses, that it would be a good thing to give pupils whose parents would allow them gardens near their own homes, prizes for the successful cultivation of flowers and plants?—I think it would be a good idea; in localities where gardening societies have given prizes, it has much encouraged horticulture among the cottagers, and flowers might be distributed by the teachers at certain seasons among the pupils.

21115. Do you teach drawing?—Not myself, it is taught in my school.

21116. Who is it taught by?—An assistant teacher.

21117. Is he certificated?—Yes.

21118. Do you think that drawing should be taught in all the schools?—I do, decidedly.

21119. How would you provide for the teaching of drawing, where there was only one teacher, and that one teacher either had not a certificate or had no practical knowledge of drawing?—I think a great many teachers have a practical knowledge of drawing, and a great many teachers can draw well and have no certificate.

21120. And you think that those who cannot at present draw, might acquire some knowledge of drawing?—A great many of them could.

21121. At any rate if they could not acquire freehand, they could acquire the art of drawing with a rule and compass?—Yes, mechanical drawing.

21122. Do you think that elementary science should be taught in rural and town schools?—Yes, your lordship.

21123. Will you explain what you mean by elementary science, what branches of education do you include under the term?—I would first, I think, begin with mechanics in connection with the drawing, and then I would certainly have a little chemistry, then I would make that a foundation for science in connection with agriculture, and also domestic science and domestic economy.

21124. Do you think that elementary chemistry could be taught unless the children were allowed to have a hand in making simple experiments?—I think it would be well to have them make simple experiments for themselves; of course it would imply a separate room, and in many country places there are no separate rooms.

21125. But if a room could be acquired?—I certainly would—that is, of course in the higher classes.

21126. What do you say about practical mensuration as a separate subject?—I think it is a great pity we cannot teach mensuration to grown boys without getting them to learn geometry. I mean that we should teach mensuration practically, that is what will be useful to them in their future life. The teachers of all rural schools are greatly troubled with farmers asking them to survey for them. Supposing they were going to sow a field with flax seed or some seed that requires a particular quantity for a particular measurement, they have to go for the teacher to lay off that amount of land. I think it is a great pity that boys could not be trained to do their own measurements. The teaching of the thirty-five propositions along with it in many cases prevents the boys being taught it, except the teacher out of generosity enabled them to get some knowledge of it.

21127. Are you in favour of household management being taught to girls of the sixth class?—Yes, your lordship.

21128. I believe you think that the present programme might be considerably lightened?—Yes, I believe it might.

21129. In what direction would you lighten it?—I would commence with arithmetic. Arithmetic, as at present taught, swallows up almost everything else, requires twice as much time and attention to be devoted to it as any other subject in the school programme, and I would give the pupils as much practical knowledge of arithmetic with half the time and half the attention, supposing that it was examined in the right manner, supposing that the questions they now give on their cards were framed in a more practical way. For instance, I would not ask them to understand circulating decimals and the theory of them. I would think it far better that they would calculate the price of so many cwts. at such a price. Of course, I would teach the higher arithmetic as an extra subject to those boys who

31159. Have you any criticism to make on our present science programme?—No; only there is a fee of 2s. attached, and that would be a difficulty in some cases.

31160. To whom?—The pupil. He has to pay a fee of 2s. to the teacher. I am not much interested in it.

31161. Under a rule of the National Board?—Yes; that was a rule of the National Board.

31162. There is no such rule now?—It may not be now; but it was at one time.

31163. If the pupils were allowed to attend without a fee—do you see any objection to the science programme from any other point of view?—No; only that it is too difficult. There is far too much science required from the children. The syllabus should be drawn up so much milder than. We do far too much, as we do in other subjects—reading, for instance.

31164. Is the Compulsory Act in operation in Londonderry?—Yes; but not in the rural districts.

31165. Mr. Molloy.—Would you briefly indicate the character of your school?—It is a rural school.

31166. How many classes in it?—Nine, of course.

31167. That includes the sub-divisions of 4th and sixth?—Yes.

31168. What is the teaching staff?—Principal, assistant, and monitress.

31169. It is a mixed school, then?—A mixed school in a purely agricultural district.

31170. How many in the senior division of the school?—At last examination forty-one were examined in the junior, and thirty-nine in the senior, but that is an extraordinary high percentage of senior pupils.

31171. What is the total number on the rolls of the school?—About 108.

31172. Then it may be characterised as a more than usually advanced rural school?—Yes; the senior division is unusual, I think.

31173. What extra subjects do you take up in your school?—Drawing, book-keeping, and then we had algebra last year.

31174. Geometry?—No.

31175. For a school of that kind would not the elements of agriculture be more important than book-keeping?—We have it, it is compulsory in our school, but book-keeping is not.

31176. You expressed the opinion that a teacher devotes a good deal of his attention to the dull pupils in connection with the results examinations?—Yes.

31177. What is your definition of a dull pupil—is it one who did not attend very well, one not likely to make the days?—No, one that has not the natural capacity to learn as quickly as the others.

31178. Is it your experience that these prevail largely?—Indeed it is, I am sorry to say.

31179. May I ask your classification?—First of first.

31180. And trained?—No, sir, untrained.

31181. Would you approve of a third-class teacher who was very efficient getting a higher rate of pay-

tion as a whole, having regard to their classification?—They do as regards their fixed salary, but not as regards result fees, they are equal to us there.

31185. In your own case, what proportion does the fixed salary bear to the result fees earned in the year?—Do you mean the result fees earned by the school, or my share of it?

31186. I would rather take it by the school.—About, I would say, as twenty-three is to eleven.

31187. In your own case personally now, apart from the school?—About as two to five.

31188. You are in favour of compulsory attendance even in rural schools?—Yes, some modified system of it.

31189. Ordinarily speaking, the National schools are open 210 days in the year, and under the Compulsory Education Act, where it is in operation, 150 attendances are expected—that is 75 one half year and 75 in the next. Do you think in rural places that is excessive to expect?—I think not, there are at present 240 school days in the year—the average for my higher class is 150 attendances, and that leaves them 110 days at home, or taking five days to the school week, that is about 22 weeks they are absent in the course of the year. I think that is amply sufficient for any farm work, such as harvest or spring work.

31190. Amongst the other subjects that you said you taught was algebra as an extra; have you any observation to offer on the advanced character of the algebra required in third year course?—I believe it is too difficult. I never teach the third year, I stop with the second year; the programme is prohibitive.

31191. You also think the arithmetic might be diminished in some respects?—It should be made more practical.

31192. What would you think of an inspector not using cards at all during the examination, and proposing questions when he arrives at the school?—So long as we are to have mechanical examinations the cards are the fairest; it ensures that each other will get the same questions, and there are a certain number of questions always given, and it is easy to check how many are done correctly, and if it is a mechanical thing it is better to have a mechanical test.

31193. Why would you call it a mechanical thing?—Because we are trying to work the school as a machine largely. It is a machine from beginning to end.

31194. A machine for what purpose—for the education of the children or to earn result fees?—To keep up the standing of the school, by earning the number of passes at the end of the year, that is how we are judged as teachers.

31195. Would you not also say it is the great ambition of the majority of teachers to work their schools from an educational standpoint?—That is what we would like.

31196. Would you not say that is the object?—I believe, with the great majority of teachers—they attend to education, as part of the machine. Any teacher of experience understands perfectly that if he neglects the education of his pupils he will never have them as they should be.

31197. But by education you mean mechanical to

21901. Believing that myself, I asked the question whether the great aim was not of an educational character?—Of course it is; we want a clear field for educational instruction.

21902. Rev. Dr. Wilson.—I suppose your observation has led you to think that the attendance is rather irregular?—Yes, decidedly, most irregular.

21903. And, therefore, you would be favourable to compulsory attendance?—If no other means could be devised.

21904. You supposed the case of a family that lived near a schoolhouse, and not one of them crossed the school door; surely there is very little of that in your experience?—Very little, but we have some cases of a family living, perhaps, within a quarter of a mile of a school who will come to school, and one member of that family will never qualify for examination, they will leave school, and be finished, as they say, without ever being examined. We have some of that, I believe, in every locality.

21905. You would agree to lighten or shorten the programme of literary instruction?—Not very much. I would not take off any subject, but I would lighten the three subjects, curtail them a little.

21906. In face of the evidence that our friend Father M'Keone has given about grammar, you would not press it to the extreme?—I would have the grammar to be explained it. For instance, we heard of a grammar exercise to-day, "Was worth the chase." I don't believe in asking boys to parse puzzles. I believe in asking them to parse an ordinary sentence, and even to analyse an ordinary sentence, but our tendency is not to teach them to parse a puzzle merely.

21907. But you would like to have the opportunity of teaching the cultivation of flowers and the cultivation of fruit?—Decidedly.

21908. You practically would go in for the form of instruction we aim at?—I would cultivate intelligence in every subject and everything.

21909. Does the National system from your experience tend to develop the intelligence of the child or to cramp it?—I would not say that it tended to cramp it. I believe in most National schools we lay the foundation; if the teacher knows his business, as the majority do, we lay a foundation that enables the child to work to educate itself. That I consider the highest type of education.

21910. Because we have had information that no matter how glibly a child is able to answer questions put to it from the book, that if you put any question outside the book there is the greatest ignorance?—Would you like my opinion on that?

21911. I would.—I have a decided opinion against that. I believe we try to cultivate their intelligence; we could not get them to answer every question on the page of the book if we did not attend to a limited extent, it may be, to the education of the child to cultivate his intelligence, or what is known by "cramming," if that word is to be used.

Londonderry.
Oct. 25, 1897.
Mr. Adam Kerr.

Mr. William Patterson, Teacher, Carlisle-road National School, Londonderry, examined.

Mr. William Patterson.

21912. Chairman.—You are the teacher of the Carlisle-road National School, Londonderry?—Yes, my lord.

21913. I understand that you were a member of the Teachers' Congress appointed to inquire into the subject of manual and practical instruction in National schools which met last Easter in Galway?—Yes, my lord.

21914. I further understand that owing to the want of evidence as to what was exactly meant by manual and practical instruction, that committee came to no definite conclusion?—Nothing definite. I might remark here that there was a wrong impression among many of them from the manual training given in the Central Training Colleges as to carpentry work; quite a number of them thought that was about to be introduced into the schools, and did not think it practicable, and seeing that some of them were inclined to oppose the matter, they finally came to the conclusion it was better to leave the matter an open question.

21915. Do you think that the teachers generally would be prepared to welcome a change if they thought it was better and for the good of the country?—I would certainly say the teachers would receive it in the best spirit and give it every trial if they can be convinced it is for the advantage of the country.

21916. First I will ask you what your opinion is upon the subject of agriculture as taught at present in the primary schools?—It is principally book work.

21917. And what do you think about it?—I think so far as the mere book work, it is of very little value except it goes into practical work.

21918. In what form would you suggest it should be done?—When I taught a country school, a good many years ago, I had half an acre of a garden; it would produce nothing, there were large oak trees growing round it and extending across the garden; I had a trench cut right round, and men to cut it in winter, and in time got it a good garden.

21919. What did you do with the oak trees?—I left them there, only cut the roots.

21920. Would it be a good plan if a school plot were attached to every rural school?—Yes.

21921. Would you say that half an acre would be a good size?—It would be a fair average size.

21922. A complaint was made to us by a teacher, I think in Sligo, as to the difficulty of complying with the Board's regulations with regard to the teaching of agriculture on account of the state of the weather. He said that last year there were a great many days on which, owing to the continued rain, it was hard to comply with the rules; and he seemed to think that if a teacher was allowed more latitude as to the days on which he should take his school out to the plot, it would be better?—I think there should be a little latitude in that. I know when I had a school garden I took the children out just as the weather answered, and my memory does not carry me back to any difficulty.

21923. Mr. Redington.—Did you ever hear of school time for practical agriculture being fixed on the ground?—No, sir, I never did.

21924. Chairman.—What are your views on the subject of the teaching of physical science in school?—I think physical science is about one of the most practical and useful things in a school; I taught it for a great number of years until the last few years.

21925. Why did you give it up?—I have not given it up, but 1892 was the last time I taught it for regular examination. There were two reasons; the Board has ruled that each child that is taught physical science must pay 5s. per quarter to the teacher; and the examinations were not on practical work.

21926. Chairman.—You were teaching under the Science and Art Department?—I am teaching under the Board the day school pupils the Physical Science programme of the National Board, but I have taught under the Science and Art Department for a great number of years. That 5s. you could not get from all the children; but now that education is free, when I have to charge the children 5s. for these subjects, while all the other subjects are free, parents cannot understand it.

21927. What do you conceive to be the main use of science teaching?—If taught properly the children used hand and eye and brain; it trains the three faculties. Last night I had a class of physical science, and the work I set them to do was to amalgamate

Londonderry.

Oct. 22, 188[illegible].

Mr. W[illegible] Patterson.

zinc and prepare for making electric batteries, mixing acid, water and zinc, to make hydrogen gas, and set fire to it—a very easy matter.

21229. I believe that there have been some changes in the rules of the Science and Art Department as regards grants for teaching science?—When I commenced to teach science first I joined a science class, and when I got certificates in 1869 and 1869 I taught science classes in Buncrana and Donegal. I taught from 1870 to 1880; then the Science and Art increased the regulations and adopted new rules, and those classes now have all dropped. In that year science grants were only made for schools whose total income amounted to less than £100 a year; then they raised it to £200, £300, and £500, and now they have abolished it. The grant of the Department is now confined to Organised Science schools in England, and the people it was originally intended for have ceased to get anything.

21230. How much do they give in England altogether?—Last year £308,000, and I think this year it is much more. In Ireland it has fallen from £5,600 to £3,600. The total science classes in Ireland last year were 160, and there are 8,106 in England. This year the science classes will probably not amount to 100. I may observe that while science instruction is rapidly increasing in England and Scotland, it is decreasing as rapidly in Ireland.

21231. What remedy would you suggest?—I think the standard of the Science and Art Department up to 1870, or from 1870 to 1880, was quite high enough for the class of boys who attend these evening science classes. Teachers saw it was practical, that they were able to teach it, and they took it up largely in the country. The first experience I had of science classes after I got certificates was in a rural school. I gathered a number of country boys about me and they almost all passed, and they were quite pleased with themselves.

21232. Did you allow them to try experiments themselves?—Yes, the experiments were not so much practised then as now. I taught it largely from books, and when I begin to look at the teaching we gave before we knew what a Leyden jar was, I don't know that I could teach it now on that system. I think it should be taught practically. I was in London this year and met teachers from all parts of England and Scotland; I think I was the only Irish National teacher there, and when I was over there in 1879 to 1880 we were in the majority; the Irish contingent was in the majority, now we are nowhere.

21233. What have you to say upon the question of needlework and the sewing machine?—The sewing machine is a very practical thing for liberty, and it was taught in a number of schools until the Board tacked on advanced dressmaking. The teachers found that they could not teach advanced dressmaking and sewing machine at the same time to the fifth class girls, and they dropped it.

21234. They kept to the sewing machine?—No; to the ordinary hour's needlework in the school, and dropped the sewing machine.

21235. Would you be in favour of keeping the present hours or reducing them?—I think the sewing might be curtailed a little, and give us two or three hours for some useful practical work.

21237. How would you suggest that the present programme could be modified, and the subjects made more practical and interesting?—I think the algebra and Euclid might be reduced considerably, and it would not be much disadvantage if they were dismissed in first stage of fifth, and something else more practical taken up instead, and with the metric system and decimal system introduced in some slight way in the junior classes, and prepare for what I expect is coming, and by these means compound rules would be largely done away with. By giving the children rulers to draw with, centimetres marked, it might be introduced a little. In fact, I am trying to introduce it a little.

21238. Do you think that mensuration should be made a separate subject?—Yes, and made practical.

21239.—Taught with the rule and tape-line and chain?—Yes; and if you want advanced arithmetic, the square and cube root should be added, as you cannot teach mensuration without the square root.

21240. Are you of opinion that there is any use in cube root?—Very little; we teach it because it is in the programme, and if you teach it, and a month has gone by, the boys don't know it, and you have to begin over again.

21241. How do you think reading-books could be made more interesting?—I have looked into that; I have had all the reading-books I could lay my hands on—got them from Blackie, Longmans and Nelson, but I have kept to the Board's. They are very objectionable—the difficult phrases in the Board's—but there are more objectionable things in others, and I stick to Board's books until we get something better.

21242. You think writing in simple language is an art?—Yes. The other day, after reading a description of Connemara, I asked a boy to pick me out a sentence he would like explained. The boy immediately picked out the sentence: "In Connemara the formation is different, for instead of the plains of granite and quartz, there extend platforms for the most part, sandstone." He wanted to know what granite, quartz, and sandstone were. I happened to have samples, and I explained them. I don't know that he understood it, but there was the thing practically. I told him where he could get quartz and granite very easily, and the sandstone was in a stoneyard close by. In the Sixth Book there is an article on casts of shells and ammonites, which seems rather difficult, but you can easily get specimens. I picked up a cast of a shell at the Causeway, and I got quite a number. I thought it was a great prize I had got, but an old man said he could show me better than that, and he produced an article from his pocket. It is one of the best ammonites I have ever seen. "What do you want for it?" said I. "I think," said he "I should get 6s. 6d. for it." I gave him the half-crown, and brought it with me. I think a school should have a small museum. I have a small one.

21243. Should reading books be illustrated by diagrams, and would it be an advantage to teach simple lessons in physiology, hygiene, health, cleanliness, &c.?—Yes, I think it would be very useful, lessons running from first to last right through the books.

21244. What do you say about the amount of grammar and geography taught?—I would not put them out of a school, but I think they could be reduced and made less formidable than at the present time.

21245. Is book-keeping a useful subject?—Very useful in a town school, if well and practically taught.

21246. Now, I should like to have your views on the subject of drawing?—I think drawing is one of the most useful subjects we teach in schools, and it can be quite practically taught if a teacher is fairly careful.

21247. Would you have drawing made compulsory in all schools?—As far as it was possible, doing no personal injustice.

21248. Is the blackboard sufficiently used in teaching drawing?—Well, I think not; I did not use it sufficiently myself at one time, but I have used it a great deal more, and I find it very useful.

21249. Do you teach drawing from the object itself for advanced children?—As far as I can I bring the object before them, but not object drawing. Object drawing, except you take great care with it with a fifth class child, injures the child. I saw a teacher giving a lesson on what he called model drawing. I know, from my standpoint, it was not the model I was looking at, and, perhaps, not two children saw the model as he drew it. I would take the ball, that is in our drawing books, and place the school ball alongside it as close as possible, and let them see what they were drawing.

Londonderry. Oct. [illegible] Mr. William [illegible]

31250. What do you think about kindergarten?—It is very nice to look at, and instructive, and if carried out properly, I think it would be very useful; but the teachers I met with in England complained of its defect in not teaching drawing properly; they had got their experience in schools where it was a system of folding. One man said they were a set of [illegible], but I suppose that is not the system itself, but the fault of the teaching as used it could be made a good thing.

31251. To come more particularly to the subject we are inquiring into—manual and practical work—what are the main objections that occur to your mind as regards the difficulty of introducing it in a more extended form?—So far as I have looked at it—

31252. Did you see it in England?—Yes, and I made inquiries carefully from the teachers.

31253. Did you see any class at work?—I did; our hours in London were from ten to three, and it was difficult to get time to see it; but I went to some of the technical schools and manual training schools.

31254. Perhaps you will tell us what your objections are in detail?—In our schools there is only one room—in some of them—and managed by one teacher, except there was some arrangement for junior classes to be dismissed, and to take an extra hour for manual training, I don't see it could be very well done.

31255. When we were in the West of Ireland a teacher came before us, who said that he put up a room himself at very little expense; and he put the price of desks and benches, and all that sort of apparatus, at a very much lower figure than we had ever heard it put anywhere else. Do you think that it would be possible to put up a low-roofed room over a schoolhouse?—It would be quite possible, but if you have only one teacher he may as well dismiss the lessons. I presume he taught it at a separate time from the regular school hours.

31256. Do you think it would be possible to erect buildings, either of corrugated iron or wood, that would be sufficiently large, at no great expense?—Yes, I think there could be, now that there are such a number of houses of corrugated iron.

31257. I see by your memorandum that you think that the greater number of children leave school before the age at which manual instruction begins in England?—If we stick up using the saw and plane; but a great amount of manual training could be carried up from the infants through all the classes.

31258. In the way of cardboard-work and wire-work?—Exactly.

31259. Did you see any wirework?—Yes.

31260. Did you consider that it was a good complex?—I rather thought cardboard-work was a nicer thing; I tried some cardboard-work for solid geometry myself some time ago, and I found it was the only way to get the regular bodies, to cut them in cardboard and set them up.

31261. Do you think a desire for a good general education is required to take advantage of manual training?—Yes, that was the general experience of the teachers; they find they have to institute in some places a preparatory or junior class; in order that the pupils may be able to take advantage of training, particularly in the Midland counties of England, they came in not knowing what a plate angle was, or how training to the second stage of fifth class?—Yes, I think it would be the very lowest grade for leaving school. A boy passing out of the fourth class and leaving school gets a very poor notion of school work. Sometimes I have applications from parents to send them a certificate, or else to say their girl has passed in fourth class, and that is often the last at school.

31262. Granting all the objections which we have heard repeated very often, what would you say supposing that they could be got over? What course or courses of manual instruction do you think could be introduced with advantage into day schools?—I think cardboard work might be introduced, brushwork in connection with drawing, and blackboard drawing and kindergarten extended to paper-folding and cutting, and something and crayon work.

31264. Perhaps you will tell us first which you would advocate—would you advocate clay modelling?—Very little, cardboard would be a nicer thing; it takes up geometry well and shows geometrical figures.

31265. I suppose you mean by bent ironwork what they call wirework?—Exactly. For any teacher that wants to teach drawing here is a book from the Birmingham School, Mr. Taylor's (*produced*.) Here is some cardboard work that was done by a pupil in the ordinary course. Here (*produced*) is a rejected model, and that (*produced*) is a passed model; that is drawn by a girl just passed her monitorship.

31266. What was wrong with it?—It appears it would not pass the teacher.

31267. Having told us what you think might be introduced with advantage, what do you think should not be introduced?—To go into the solid metals would not be practicable.

31268. There are very few instances even in Sweden where that is done; it is only in towns like Birmingham or Stockholm that we have seen it?—And these things might be introduced in any schools. I have inquired of teachers, and I find they are not generally taken up through the country schools in England.

31269. We were told that the main reason for that is the difficulty of providing the buildings and providing the appliances. At Fenwick we saw a class of teachers on one Saturday morning at work at a course, but we were told that only one of them was actually carrying out, in his own school, instruction in what he was there practising; and the reason for that appeared to be that it was only in one school had the money been found that made it possible?—I thought the money for all books and materials is found in England by the authorities.

31270. It is found in the big cities by the School Board?—I find in England they have £800,000 for practical art and science teaching, and we have nothing corresponding in Ireland.

31271. Did you not find that that was almost entirely spent in the big towns?—Yes, we have the same country, but it is not devoted to education here. We are perhaps not as practical in our day schools as might be wished, but we are more practical than even the Intermediate; it is all book work with them.

31272. There is another subject within the scope of our inquiry, and that is with regard to a special

Londonderry.

Oct. 25, 1886.

Mr. William Patterson.

21275. And do you believe as an experienced teacher that we could introduce this work about which we have been talking into our schools?—If we first prepared the teacher and found the money some modified form could be introduced.

21276. Could we not introduce it on a small scale first?—You could; the physical training would cost very little at first, and it would train the muscles and the whole activity of the child.

21277. And as it grew it would be taken up more and more extensively?—Yes, if you brought it under the teachers' notice and added a money value for it.

21278. How do you suggest that qualified teachers may be obtained?—The present teachers are able and competent men, and anxious to do the best they can.

21279. They are a noble body of workers, whose value has not been sufficiently appreciated or paid for?—We think that if the time and the accommodation and the money were provided the teachers could learn it, if it is to be introduced. I know the teachers pretty well. There are quite a number of science certificates and drawing certificates through the country that are not made use of.

21280. How many teachers have we in our National system in Ireland who could give manual instruction in woodwork?—That depends on what kind of woodwork. There is a prejudice against it at the present time, because it has been making and sawing and making stools. I know one school where it was given; so that they had a special teacher; the manager had been all over Ireland and got him at last.

21281. What is the value of a copybook when it is written?—Very little.

21282. Was there no value in the teaching which enabled the pupils to produce that book?—I don't know much about it practically. This teacher was brought, he was set to work at carpentry work, and the people flocked to the school who were going to be turned out carpenters, but for five or six years it had not been heard of in that school; the parents laughed at it and the pupils would not go.

21283. In a great many of the training colleges where woodwork is taught many of the teachers never take a saw in their hand, and the great objection at Galway was that they were going to make botches of the pupils; it was this carpentry work that they were considering. You believe manual training would be beneficial to the pupils?—It would sharpen the eye and the intelligence. Science teaching is about the best training for a teacher and for a pupil also.

21284. Rev. Dr. Wilson.—Is the Carlisle Road National school a large one?—Yes, from 160 to 200.

21285. Have you an infants' class?—We have.

21286. Do you teach kindergarten?—Not as kindergarten; we teach exercises, but we have neither the space nor the money nor the accommodation; we have plenty of accommodation if we could make use of it; we have an upper room idle.

21287. You say kindergarten is nice to look at; don't you think it has more merits than that?—I do, but it is found by a great number of teachers I have met—for instance those pupils we were told of in London who do everything for themselves; I have been in search of them and never could find them. I went to a school and found they were lectured at and

21291. And did they attend at extra hours?—They would come on Saturday for that when they would come for nothing else. I have endeavoured in the winter time to bring my advanced class in, and they would come on Saturday for that or to learn drill, when they would not come for anything else.

21292. Did you find the pupils were satisfied with giving up Saturday for that purpose?—Quite satisfied. I did not put down the Saturday work on the time-table. I would be very glad to get the senior pupils in for an hour or two hours on a Saturday.

21293. Were they schools in connection with the Science and Art Department?—No; a class of advanced day boys that I brought in for morning work.

21294. Did you hear the evidence of Head-Inspector Eardley this morning?—I did.

21295. Would you agree with him?—I would. I remember Dr. Clarke. I remember when Mr. Eardley left and was appointed inspector.

21296. Then you received instruction at the normal training college from Dr. Clarke, who was lecturing on physical science?—Yes; and I think it was a great pity that those practical lectures were done away with at the training colleges. You came back with the teachers there.

21297. It was the lectures you participated in there that led you to introduce this subject later on?—I had tried some of the experiments before I commenced to be a teacher. I had read in an old book about zinc and hydrogen, and I did it, and burst the bottle; but after I came home from Dr. Clarke's lectures and took a school, in the winter time I was idle, and I introduced lectures and gathered the people in, and I had science classes.

21298. Taking manual instruction, waiving these comparatively small points of difficulty you have raised here, and looking only to the broad principle of it, are you not in favour of its introduction optionally in leading places where the teachers are qualified to give instruction?—Yes, sir; and I believe all teachers could qualify with a little exertion, and the teachers would be satisfied if it were properly understood, and it was explained to them what was meant and wanted. They are prejudiced as to these carpentry classes, which have done more harm than good, but if they saw the nice geometrical models I think this could be done under a little supervision.

21299. In town schools what are your hours?—Our hours are from 10 to 3, but we are generally in from 9 to 3.30.

21300. With an intermission of half an hour?—Yes.

21301. Would you be in favour of a longer intermission and two roll-calls?—Calling the roll twice is a great difficulty. I remember a head-inspector coming in to check my roll, and he spent from twenty to two until ten past three.

21302. On the other hand, I had in my mind a large model school for 500 pupils, and no time was taken away from the general instruction. The rolls were marked by the junior teacher?—I do that at the present time. I stop no work, and the roll is checked.

21303. So practically a second roll-call would not be attended with any loss of time?—No; it is only

21306. But in those schools they allow an interval of two hours?—Yes.

21307. You are also in favour of kindergarten, and its development into higher classes?—If it is started at all it should be carried right through the classes, and the drawing in kindergarten should not be a lot of toys. A teacher told me last a large school, and was obliged to complain to the Board and have the whole thing remodelled, owing to idling.

21308. Mr. Redington.—What has been the effect of the Compulsory Education Act in Derry?—It has improved the attendance to a certain extent, but not nearly so much as we expected. Some people are absent a fortnight; then the officer calls, and they go to school for a few days, and then they are away again. They don't attend in a satisfactory way.

21309. Rev. Dr. Evans.—If it has not put more on the roll, has it not increased the average attendance?—I think it has made those who were irregular, perhaps, attend a little more regular, so as not to have the officers calling around.

21310. Mr. Redington.—When you were in England you spoke on the subject of manual instruction to a good many teachers?—I endeavoured to get all the information I could.

21311. What was their opinion about it?—It was not so entirely favourable as I thought. I met a man from Cambridge, and he was all for it, there was nothing like it. Another man, who taught it in Birmingham, when the Cambridge man asked "Did it not develop their intelligence?" "Well," said he, "I am at it three years, and I don't think they are any the worse." That is as far as he could go.

21312. Were you in Birmingham?—No; I only spoke to the teacher.

21313. Where did you see manual work carried on?—In one of the Board schools at Marylebone. I was through the technical schools in Chelsea and Oxford Circus, but I had not a good time to gauge the class. The science work there was all practical. They gave few lectures; they were working with gum and lampblack, &c.

21314. Would it be easy to extend the teaching of science in the rural schools in Ireland?—I believe it would be very easy. My experience is that any teacher can make the apparatus necessary, and get the children to make them, and then, with a little additional money to provide the apparatus he cannot make, would introduce science all through. And it is a pity the Science and Art Department took such a step as to kill science in Ireland.

21315. How could the Board of National Education encourage the teaching of science?—By making a fair liberal grant, and providing the teachers with facilities.

21316. Mr. Molloy.—And waiving that question of the fee from the pupils?—Yes.

21317. Mr. Redington.—Do you think that teachers could easily learn sufficient science to be able to teach it in their schools?—I am certain of it, from my knowledge of the teachers. They already have the knowledge, and only require to apply themselves, and would be quite willing to do it.

21318. If you had your choice between manual instruction and elementary science teaching, which would you think the more useful?—I would prefer science.

21319. Would you be inclined to make it a compulsory subject in schools?—I don't know that I would go so far as to make it compulsory.

21320. Even if one of the existing compulsory subjects were omitted?—If you made it optional for a time, and put a respectable fee to it, that would make it worth while taking it up.

21321. Have you any remarks to offer about grammar and geography?—I think they might be a little modified, and both made more practical.

FORTY-SIXTH PUBLIC SITTING.—TUESDAY, OCTOBER 19, 1897,

AT 10 O'CLOCK, A.M.,

At the County Buildings, Dumfries.

Present:—The Right Hon. the Earl of Belmore, G.C.M.G. in the Chair; Rev. Henry Evans, D.D.; Rev. Hamilton Wilson, D.D.; W. R. J. Molloy, Esq.; Captain Shaw; and J. Struthers, Esq., B.A.;

with J. D. Daly, Esq., M.A., Secretary.

Mr. John Malcolm Aitken, F.H.A.S., Member of the Education Committee, Dumfries, examined.

21322. Chairman.—You are, I believe, a Fellow of the Highland and Agricultural Society?—Yes, my lord.

21323. And Chairman of the Technical Instruction Committee of the County Council of Dumfriesshire prior to its amalgamation with the Secondary Education Committee in 1896?—Yes.

21324. Will you kindly explain to the Commission the constitution of the County Technical Instruction Committee?—The County Council in 1891 decided to apply the Residue Grant under the Local Taxation (Customs and Excise) Act, 1890, for the purpose of technical education, and the Council having regard to the pursuits of the great majority of the inhabitants of the county, and with a view to enlisting the sympathy and aid of those bodies more specially interested in technical instruction, resolved to entrust the administration of the funds to a committee representative of (1) the Council; (2) the School Boards in the county; and (3) the Agricultural and Dairy Associations. There was also a committee in each of the five County Council districts of the county consisting of (1) the members of the district Committee of the County Council; and (2) representatives from the district Agricultural Society and School Boards. These district committees are under the control of the county committee. The committee, in view of the facts that the importance of technical instruction was not then so generally recognised as it now is, and that little or no provision for that branch of education then existed in the county, was early convinced of the necessity of firstly, by a kind of pioneer work, awakening as widespread an interest as possible in the subject, and secondly of making such provision of a more permanent nature for the teaching of technical subjects in all the schools in the county as the funds at its command would admit of; and the following arrangements were accordingly made, viz.—1. *Pioneer Work.* (a) *Popular Lectures for farmers and others.*

Dumfries.
[illegible]
Mr. John Halliday [illegible]

—In 1891, by arrangement with the Glasgow and West of Scotland Technical College, short courses of lectures on agricultural botany (chiefly grasses) and agricultural chemistry were delivered at six centres, but the attendance, except in the case of one centre, was disappointing, and nothing further was done in this direction until 1894 when there was given a further course of lectures on such subjects as farm-yard manure and loss; purchase, valuation, and balancing of manures; feeding stuffs; "finger and toe," &c. These lectures were evidently so much appreciated that a more advanced course of six lectures on "manures and manuring" was given in the following year at three centres, and the attendance was again very good. Looking to the interest that had been aroused by these lectures, and by a series of lectures kindly delivered by Professor Wright of the above college on the results of certain manuring experiments in the county, voluntarily carried out by the college, the committee arranged with the college for the carrying out of certain further experiments, as follows, viz.—(b) *Field experiments.*—In 1893 an important set of experiments on the manuring of turnips was carried out on nine farms throughout the county with the assistance of the college staff and under the supervision of small local committees; the results, which were very instructive, were embodied in a report, and also formed the subject of a lecture delivered at a convenient centre in each of the five districts of the county, but, except in two instances, the lectures were indifferently attended. In 1894 more extensive experiments on the manuring of hay, pasture land, and turnips, were satisfactorily carried out. Lectures explanatory of the results were also delivered and were well attended.—(c) *Dairying.* (1) *Cheese making.*—In 1892 and two following years, by arrangement with the Wigtownshire Dairy Association, their instructor gave demonstrations in cheese-making at a large number of centres; the committee paid the salary of the instructor, and the county dairy association made all the other arrangements. In 1892 during twenty-four days the instructor was engaged there were 349 attendances registered as against fifty-three in the previous year when the instruction was under the Dumfriesshire Dairy Association; in 1893 (twenty-four days' instruction) the attendances numbered 175, and 180 in 1894 (eighteen days). A fee of 2s. 6d. was charged, the holder of the ticket being entitled to attend any or all of the demonstrations. The demand for the services of the instructor becoming practically confined to one district and pretty much the same people attending each season, it was considered advisable to discontinue this form of giving instruction and hold out inducements to those engaged in dairying to attend for a regular course of instruction at Kilmarnock Dairy School. As to the result of the instruction given by itinerant instructor the chairman of the Dumfriesshire Dairy Association reported that much good had been derived and that there was a marked improvement in the cheese produced in the districts where the instruction had been given.—(2) *Butter-making.*—Practically the same course was followed in regard to giving instruction in butter-making, save that in addition to demonstrations practice classes were also held—in the second and third years. In 1892 (for twenty-five weeks) the daily attendance at the various centres was from thirty-five to fifty; in 1893 (twenty-five weeks) 103 students received practical instruction, and the average attendance at the demonstrations was about fifty; in 1894 the attendance was smaller and difficulty was experienced in getting up classes in several of the districts, and the committee resolved not to continue them in 1895, but arranged for students obtaining instruction at Kilmarnock Dairy School. Very considerable interest was aroused, and it may be fairly said that there has been less bad butter in the county than before this instruction was given. Fees were charged of 2s. 6d. for a week's theoretical and practical instruction, 1s. for a week's theoretical instruction alone, and 3d. for a single attendance at the theoretical instruction. (d) *Cookery and Laundry work.*—In 1891 classes for demonstrations and practice were held in the district towns; there were two classes daily—the evening class being specially intended for the working classes. Both classes were well attended at all the towns. Classes were afterwards held in a number of the villages and were very successful. So great was the demand for the services of the instructress that a second instructress was engaged in 1894, and thirty-seven classes were held in the rural districts with gratifying attendances. In the course of the following year, however, it became evident that the ground had been overtaken, and the classes were abandoned. Small fees were charged for these classes. (e.) *Lectures on Hygiene.*—With the view of giving effect to a special resolution of the Council, the County Medical Officer, by arrangement with the Committee, kindly delivered lectures at thirteen centres in 1893-94 on such subjects as air and ventilation; water in relation to health; infection; food and digestion; dairies and milk supplies. The lectures, which were illustrated by lime-light views, proved very instructive and were well attended. Lectures were given in the following year at twenty-one centres with like results, and again in 1895-96 at thirty centres. The attendance at certain of the places that had previously been visited showed a falling off, and for the present these lectures have been discontinued. Admission to the lectures was free. (f) *Plumbers' Work.*—In 1893 the District Council of the National Society for the Registration of Plumbers applied to the Committee for aid in carrying on classes for the instruction of apprentice plumbers and others in the principles of plumbing work, and the Committee, being impressed with the importance of such instruction being given, voted £30 towards the expenses of the classes, and the grant has been continued yearly since. The Committee have been assured that the classes have been productive of good. I come now to the second branch of the Committee's work, that is, *Permanent Work.* This the Committee regarded as the most important part of their work. They felt that if permanent good was to be done it could only be by reaching the young, and they resolved to take steps, so far as the means at their disposal would admit, to put it within the reach of every child of suitable age attending the public schools in the county to obtain instruction, more or less advanced, in technical subjects, and with that object in view they made the following arrangements, viz.:—(1.) *Preparatory Classes for Teachers in Public Schools.*—In order that the teachers of all the schools, secondary and elementary alike, should have an opportunity of making themselves familiar with certain subjects which it was expected they would teach, and for which the Committee undertook to give grants, classes for agriculture, chemistry (theoretical), Sloyd, and cookery were instituted. The classes for agriculture and chemistry were conducted under the Science and Art regulations by Professors from the Glasgow and West of Scotland Technical College; the cookery class by the County Instructress, and extended to qualify for teaching under the code; and the Sloyd by Mr. James Wallace, following out a valuable report by him, which is annexed to the Committee's scheme for 1894-95.

31633. Who conducted the agriculture?—Professors from the Glasgow and West of Scotland College. The whole of these classes were very largely attended, and there has been no more gratifying feature than the hearty and self-sacrificing way in which the teachers—male and female—have thrown themselves into this movement. It had been intended to follow up the classes for theoretical chemistry by practical classes, but the idea had to be given up for the want of laboratory accommodation; now, however, with the well-equipped laboratory in the new Dumfries Academy, it has been possible to make arrangements with the managers for forty teachers of public schools receiving instruction in practical chemistry during the current session.

Dumfries-shire. — Oct. [illegible], 1897. — Mr. John [illegible], [illegible].

Over sixty applications were received, but places could not be found this year for so large a number. (2.) "Selected" or Central Schools where provision made for Technical (and also Secondary) Education.—The Committee, after carefully considering the whole situation, resolved that, if possible, there should be in each of the five districts or divisions of the county a school, or rather a secondary department attached to a school, which, while providing for the wants of the parish in which it was situated, would also be available to the more advanced pupils from the schools in the surrounding parishes, and this the Committee was able to accomplish by means of building and annual grants to the Managers of Dumfries Academy, Lockerbie Public School, Annan Academy, Wallace Hall Academy, and Langholm Academy. The building grants do not call for any special remark, but it may be noted that the annual grants from the Technical Grant consist of (1) certain fixed sums amounting in all to £[illegible], and (2) capitation grants paid in respect of pupils who, having previously passed the sixth standard, pass examination by the Science and Art Department in one or more of a comprehensive list of subjects, including agriculture, chemistry, machine construction and drawing, mathematics, magnetism and electricity, hygiene, sloyd, and cookery. These capitation grants are distributed at so much per pass, and in the aggregate are equal to the amount (£[illegible]) of the fixed grants. Where fees are charged it is a condition that these are not to exceed 5s. per pupil per subject per session, and at least one-half of the fees to be refunded to the pupils for each subject in which they pass the Science and Art Examination. (3.) Elementary Schools.—In order to encourage the teaching of technical subjects in the rural schools, and also in the junior classes in the "Selected" schools, grants at a rate not exceeding 2s. 6d. per head are given in respect of pupils passing inspection in standards V. and VI., and who (1) have been instructed in cookery by a qualified teacher, or (2) are examined in drawing or sloyd by a Science and Art Inspector, or (3) pass inspection under the Code in book-keeping, chemistry, mathematics, shorthand, or agriculture. These grants to be expended in remunerating the teachers and defraying other necessary expenses of these schools. (4) Apparatus Grants.—Grants varying in amount, according to the importance of the school, are given towards the purchase of apparatus, etc., the managers being usually required to provide at least a half of the cost.

31,826. Are they given by the County Council?—By the County Council; we give usually half, sometimes a third, the managers find the rest. (5.) Bursaries and Free Scholarships.—In order to assist promising pupils residing more than four miles from any of the central schools who desire to pursue their studies at one or other of these schools, a certain number of bursaries of £10 each (with free education in addition) tenable for three years are awarded by competition, and an equal number of scholarships, entitling the holder to free education, are awarded in the same way. The bursaries and scholarships have been keenly competed for. The committee hoped that by these arrangements the rural schools would act as feeders to the central schools, and they have the satisfaction of knowing that, thanks to the cordial co-operation of the School Boards and teachers, their highest expectations in that direction and also in respect of the work at the central schools are likely to be fully realised. (6.) Instruction in Dairying.—To meet the wishes of certain people, and in view of the possible abandonment of the dairymaking and butter-making classes conducted by the itinerant instructors, arrangements were made by means of a grant to the Kilmarnock Dairy School, for the free admission to that school of all students desiring to attend from Dumfriesshire. Those attending also receive from the authorities their train fare and an allowance towards lodging expenses. The students who have taken advantage of this arrangement have numbered in 1892, 13; in 1893, 21; in 1894, [illegible]; in 1895, [illegible]; in 1896, [illegible]; in 1897, 15. (7.) Grants to "Local Committees" providing Technical Instruction.—Grants are offered to local committees providing technical instruction under the Science and Art Department's regulations, but these have not as yet, except in the case of the "selected" schools, been taken much advantage of. It is to be hoped, however, that when the older pupils come to leave the rural schools, a fair proportion of those who may not be able to attend the secondary schools will evince a desire for further instruction in evening schools.

8. General Remarks.—The committee has always been of opinion that, however desirable popular work, such as has been described, may be for awakening the interest of the older people, the best results are more likely to be got by providing instruction for the young, both in the elementary schools, and in the higher or secondary schools. The work of the committee on its more permanent side is really only in process of development. The new academy at Dumfries was only opened the other day, and the additional buildings at Annan, Langholm, and Lockerbie were only completed very recently, and it can readily be understood that the work at these schools has been carried on under difficulties. The committee believes, however, that right lines are being followed, and that good work will be done on these lines, more especially as the administration of the grants for secondary education and technical education throughout the whole county, including the burghs, with the exception of one burgh, Sanquhar, is now under the charge of one committee representative of all the interests concerned. As an indication of the progress already made, the Commission is respectfully referred to the note on page [illegible] of the committee's report for year [illegible], from which it will be seen that there is a gratifying increase in the number of passes in technical subjects for which grants were paid to the various School Boards throughout the county.

Note referred to.

Year.	Agriculture.	Domestic Economy.	Cookery.	Chemistry.	[illegible]	Book-keeping.	[illegible]	[illegible]	Drawing and Sloyd.	Total.
To 1892, . .	340	161	116	5	–	–	–	–	–	[illegible]
To 1893, . .	436	230	97	7	64	9	–	–	–	[illegible]
To 1894, . .	610	486	180	10	83	6	19	–	–	1,[illegible]
To 1895, . .	474	496	180	3	91	16	54	5	306	1,645
To 1896, . .	[illegible]	[illegible]	100	10	[illegible]	[illegible]	81	17	*405	1,[illegible]
Grand Totals, .	2,144	1,994	[illegible]	44	[illegible]	71	164	[illegible]	713	[illegible]

* Sloyd.

Dumfries.

Oct. 22, 1897.

Mr. John [illegible] [illegible]

21327. First, with regard to the work of the committee under the head of pioneer work, you mentioned cookery and laundry work; were those lessons which you spoke of accompanied by demonstrations and also by experiments on the part of the persons who were attending those lectures?—First the demonstration, and also a practise class.

21328. A class of adults, not the school children?—Yes, adults.

21329. Then, with regard to the permanent work and the preparatory classes for teachers and pupil teachers in the public schools, was it intended by those classes to teach trades or merely to teach the principles of certain trades to be followed up after children had left the schools?—Exclusively the principles, we have never had the idea of teaching trades at all.

21330. Coming to the question of Sloyd; I understand that the teachers attend the classes with a view that they ultimately should be able to teach Sloyd themselves in the schools?—Yes.

21331. Meaning by Sloyd, woodwork?—Yes, that was the object in view.

21332. Is there any metal work in Scotland?—Not in this county.

21333. I suppose Sloyd is always connected with drawing?—Yes, the two things went together.

21334. And the opinion of your committee would be that any attempt to teach what in Ireland they call handicraft, meaning a certain amount of woodwork, without drawing would be very useless?—I think that would be the opinion of the committee.

21335. We have a term which we know very well, results fees, by which part of the salary of our Irish teachers are paid; you mentioned capitation grants?—Yes, so much per head.

21336. Those grants I suppose are very much of the nature of Irish results fees?—Yes. We had the idea we should give the managers of the selected schools certain lump or fixed sums which did not depend on the results at all, they had spent so much money or sunk capital so to speak.

21337. In a school where Sloyd is in operation, what is the method by which you pay the teacher for teaching the Sloyd; how do you ascertain the amount of passes that the children make and the amount due to the teacher?—We only pay after inspection by a Government Inspector.

21338. And not a grant similar to the Irish results fee grant, after examining each individual child's work?—That is done by the Science and Art Inspector, and we then pay on his report so much per head.

21339. Mr. Strutters.—Have you any opinion as to the reasons for the falling off in attendance at the cookery classes for older people and the classes in agricultural chemistry, they all seem to have fallen off more or less at one period?—Yes, people go with a rush to something new, others have got all the instruction which they think they can get and leave: there is only a limited number of the older people who care for this technical instruction, we look to the young.

21340. About what age would those older people be as a rule?—Twenty and upwards.

21341. But would there not be the possibility of getting a younger class of pupils, those who had left school, pupils between fourteen or eighteen to attend special classes?—Yes, I believe there would be, but we wish, if possible, to give them the instruction in the schools; we hope we will give everyone who wants that instruction the opportunity of getting it in a school somewhere, up to the age of fourteen.

21342. During the day?—Yes.

21343. Up to what age do you expect the pupils will remain in these central schools?—We hope to fifteen, possibly over, but Mr. Malcolm, Head Master of Dryfesdale School, will speak as to some of these particulars, he will give you exact information.

21344. During that time they would be devoting their whole attention to education, they would not be employed as boys in any way?—No, not at the central schools.

21345. There would be only a comparatively few who would attend to fourteen or fifteen?—Yes.

21346. Could not something be done for the sake of those pupils who must in many cases leave school at thirteen, and who nevertheless are interested in such subjects as cookery or agriculture?—My hope is that that will be done in the evening classes.

21347. Have you thought of any plan for drafting pupils out of the day schools as it were into the evening schools, keeping the two in continuous operation?—There is such a school in operation now at Lockerbie in the evening, very well attended indeed, with that object in view.

21348. But you have not thought of any machinery by which a pupil when he says he is going to leave the day school should be put in train for going to an evening school?—Under compulsion do you mean?

21349. No, by strong advice?—That has been attempted in Lockerbie.

21350. Among the special classes for training teachers you made no mention of drawing especially?—That went with Sloyd, Mr Jerome Wallace, who conducted the classes, is here and will be able to speak presently.

21351. Do you know to what extent drawing is taught in the county in elementary schools?—All over is, I think it is quite a general subject, I hoped Mr. Barrie, the Inspector, would have been here today, but he is engaged.

21352. Then about these five central schools you spoke of, has anything been done to strengthen the staff of those schools on the technical side?—Yes, it is a condition that they must have a thoroughly qualified staff before we give the grant.

21353. I don't mean adding a teacher with general qualifications, who might teach Latin or French or mathematics or English, but one who would definitely teach science, definitely teach drawing and definitely teach woodwork?—We are working to that now, it is a slow process but we have it in view that the classes should be taught by a man specially trained for the purpose.

21354. So that the technical side of education in those schools will not be lost sight of in the general secondary work?—No, it must be kept distinctly in view.

21355. I think you have amalgamated the secondary committee and the technical education committee?—That was done last year.

21356. And that scheme is now in operation?—Yes.

21357. Can you tell us whether under that scheme you can, so to speak, lump the two grants and distribute it generally or must the technical money be earmarked for technical purposes?—We put them together and that has been approved of by the Scotch Education Department.

21358. That is understood to be the meaning of the Act?—Yes, at least we read it that way, and have followed that course.

21359. Have you any doubts on that point?—None at all, we thought it the best way and adopted it, and the Education Board has approved of it.

21360. You spoke of £305 which each school might get in grants in addition to the fixed sum, does that mean £305 for each school?—No, we have set aside £410 for subsidising technical work in the selected schools, and out of that sum, we give lump grants amounting in all to £105 for these five schools; the other £305 is set aside for capitation grants, and accordingly those who make the most passes will get the most of this £305.

21361. The managers of the schools pay half or one-third of the cost of the apparatus?—Yes.

21362. Does the same apply to the expenses of building?—We are only able to give one-eighth to one-twelfth, they have spent thousands of pounds.

31363. So the local contribution is ever so much greater than the contribution of the central committee?—Undoubtedly.

31364. I suppose you regard it as indispensable in any scheme of education of this kind that the local interest should be encouraged and maintained?—Certainly, I think it is hopeless unless you get local interest.

31365. And it would not be much good by a central department to spend money in creating technical schools through the country and administering it from the capital of the country?—I think you must have both to be perfectly successful. You cannot leave it all to the local authority, that is my opinion, you must have some compelling power behind the local authority to direct it and to see that it is doing its duty.

31366. On the other hand you would not have the compelling power alone, but something to be supplied in the locality?—I think so.

31367. To what extent are the bursaries and free scholarships availed of?—We are only able to give eleven each year, but we had some sixty applications for them.

31368. Will you make it a condition in the case of these bursaries that they must complete their three years at a secondary school?—We have not made that condition yet, we don't wish to be too strict to begin with.

31369. But you will aim at that by and by?—Yes.

31370. You would not think it satisfactory that a pupil should get a scholarship of that kind, go to a secondary school for a year and go away again?—We would like that they should stay three years.

31371. It would be so much money lost?—In a great measure.

31372. Rev. Dr. Evans.—You used the word *lump* sum, I don't understand it?—A lump sum means a fixed sum not depending on anything in the way of passes or results.

31373. You said you always began with the young, now why?—We have found that the older people come and attend lectures, listen to them and go away and forget it almost all in a great many instances. But we think the young will be able to retain what they learn if they are kept at the school, and get to know what is considered the best way of doing things, they won't know how to do a thing badly when they are trained to do it right to begin with.

31374. You spoke of preparatory classes for teachers, where are they held?—In Dumfries and Lockerbie.

31375. And you have similar classes for instruction in agriculture?—We had these, but not now, we suppose the teachers have got all the instruction they wish to enable them to teach it in primary schools.

31376. And you told us that cookery was taught by the county instructress?—Yes.

31377. Now would you kindly indicate what her functions are, what she does, does she go from school to school?—No, to centres. Take a village, the cookery classes are advertised to be held in the afternoon and evening, and the people attend there. She gives so many lessons, and then moves on to the next village.

31378. She is a peripatetic teacher?—That is so; of course her services have been dispensed with now, we have been round all the villages, and she went round a second time, and even a third time, to some places, until the supply of grown up pupils was exhausted.

31379. I think you said also that you had selected or secondary schools and that secondary departments are those secondary departments in Board schools?—Yes; there is one in Dumfries, the Dumfries Academy, they have a secondary department in Lockerbie, they have a secondary department with a Board school, Langholm Academy, the district town of another division of the county that is a Board school, they are all Board schools, I should say, with the exception of Wallace Hall, which is under a body of governors.

31380. But there are elementary classes in these schools with pupils from six to seven years of age?—Yes.

31381. Rev. Dr. Evans.—About the bursaries and free scholarships, you said that there were eleven of these; does that mean that there are eleven bursaries and eleven free scholarships, or both together eleven?—eleven of each.

31382. And the bursaries are valued at £10 each?—Yes.

31383. Is the free scholarship of the same value?—No; the value depends on the fees charged. There are only two schools where fees are charged, the Dumfries Academy and Wallace Hall.

Mr. *Robson*.—For one or two subjects.

Witness.—In all the other schools the education is quite free.

31384. Captain Shaw.—Could you tell us what is the total amount you have at your disposal for technical instruction?—About £1,100 yearly; it varies a good deal, according to the swine fever in the country; if there is swine fever we get less money.

31385. Have you taken any steps for instruction in agriculture beyond what is given in these secondary schools?—Not yet.

31386. Do you contemplate doing so?—Dr. Gillespie will speak as to that point; we hope to have a college, if we can get it, for the southern counties.

31387. At present students go in for the Science and Art examination in agriculture?—In the selected schools.

31388. Do you think they get a good knowledge of agriculture from such a course, or merely book-work answering?—It is the best we have at present; if anything higher or better could be instituted, we would go in for it. What we have done is to take the best we could get for the present.

31389. You have not any classes formed for practical instruction?—Not yet; in connection with this college there is a wish that some such arrangement should be made.

31390. Mr. Stevenson.—But you have already example plots under the management of the professors of the West of Scotland College?—Yes, these are for farmers, not scholars.

31391. Captain Shaw.—They are not utilised by the boys in the secondary schools?—No.

31392. Is agriculture taught in all the elementary Scotch schools?—I think not throughout this land.

31393. Then there is one remark you made about the results of the inspecting of Boyd by the Science and Art department; they don't say that each student has passed—they merely give a general pass for the whole class?—Some of these points I cannot speak to; Mr. Barrie would have given exact information.

31393. Because I think there is a wrong impression that each boy passed, and you gave your grant on each boy that passed; you said so in your evidence?—We pay for the pupils certified by the inspector.

31394. The inspector does not pass each boy separately; he reports on the whole class?

Mr. *Robson*.—We give a grant for the total of the class—so much per head.

31395. Rev. Dr. Wilson.—From what source does the County Council derive its funds?—Government grant.

31396. What would be the amount of the grant to this county?—£1,100; we always hope for £1,000; we have sometimes got £1,100, and have had to take £800.

Dumfries.
Oct. 22, 1895.
Mr. John Robson,
[illegible]

21397. I thought it had been raised by an assessment on the county?—No; the County Council had the option of applying this money to the relief of rates or making provision for technical instruction, and we chose to give it for technical instruction.

21398. You gave public lectures for farmers; were those well attended?—They were to begin with, and then they fell off.

21399. They think they have got knowledge enough?—It looks like it, unfortunately.

21400. With field experiments, did the teachers go out and take farmers and others so as to see in the fields how the various crops were advancing?—They were only accompanied in some instances by a small band consisting of farmers, but the lectures explanatory of these experiments were well attended.

21401. As to buttermaking, have the people attained marked excellence in butter-making?—Many of those who attended have; it can be seen; even those who attended some years ago still go on making good butter.

21402. Does the article compete, do you think, with what comes from Denmark?—Only to a limited extent. In this county there is a good deal of new milk sold, and very little butter made, comparatively speaking.

21403. What proportion of the building is paid for by the public grant—this committee's grant?—From one-eighth to one-twelfth.

21404. And from what source are the other portions got?—Rates levied on the parish; that seems to be a little hard on the particular parish, the rates levied on the parish in which the school is situated.

21405. What is the value of the capitation grant you give to each pupil that passes a certain subject?—From £1, we have got £2, I think, for some of the subjects; those are in the Science and Art classes in the selected schools. In the rural schools we have only been able to give 7s. 6d., and it is too little, I think.

21406. Mr. Wallace.—Is the entire organisation as regards education in your county carried on by the County Council?—No, we have only the technical instruction and secondary education. All the elementary work is carried on entirely by School Boards, having nothing to do with the County Council.

21407. But do they not dovetail into each other, so to say, for general purposes?—They do.

21408. They work harmoniously, I presume?—They do; we have the money, and we say, in effect if you, the School Board, will make certain arrangements, we will hand this money over to you, but we do not interfere with the internal arrangements.

21409. Socially, is there any distinction between the class of people in the elementary and the secondary schools?—None whatever. By elementary I mean the rural schools where the younger children are, and we hope they will come to the secondary school, but in the secondary school there are the young of the parish in which that school is situated.

21410. In Dumfries have you elementary schools along with secondary schools?—Yes.

21411. And from the elementary they are expected to go into the secondary school?—Yes, that is the expectation.

21412. And socially there is no distinction?—None whatever.

21413. What is the average rate per head for the education of a child in the place where we are at present, counting all the items—what you get from the County Council, the Scotch Department, and the Science and Art Department?—I could not state that, but we will be pleased to send you particulars.

21414. And perhaps at the same time you will kindly let us have a copy of your statement for 1896-95?—Yes.

21415. Mr. Stevenson.—Was there any reluctance on the part of the teachers to attend these special classes you had in Sloyd and drawing and agriculture?—None whatever, they seemed very anxious to come.

21416. Did you charge them a fee?—No.

21417. Mr. Stevenson.—What was the length of the course at the Kilmarnock dairy school?—We say they must not take less than six days—some took six weeks.

21418. You are aware that in Scotland there is no distinction between the elementary and the secondary schools in the eye of the department?—None at all.

21419. The one shades off into the other—the one school may be both elementary and secondary?—Yes.

Rev. J. Gillespie, LL.D., Chairman, Highland and Agricultural Society, examined.

21420. Chairman.—You are Chairman of the Highland and Agricultural Society of Scotland?—I am.

21421. And a member of the Education Committee of the County Council of Dumfries?—Yes.

[illegible] or less directly, and these children are perfectly familiar day by day with everything that takes place on a farm so far as they can see it, and are quite able to appreciate any illustration that the teacher

we have encouraged and exhibited a course there which lasts only a month, and I am of opinion that is quite insufficient. It is, of course, better than nothing, but it would be very much better if a more systematic course would be organised and carried out. And I have long been of opinion that in such a country as Scotland it would be very desirable if in our normal schools, where a very large proportion of our normal teachers are trained, there was provision made for giving them a sufficient course, at all events in the principles of agriculture.

21429. I am not familiar with the term normal school; does that answer to training college in Ireland?—I suppose it does.

Mr. Struthers.—It is the same thing.

21430. Chairman.—Do you corroborate Mr. Aitken's evidence as to the good done by experiments of the Glasgow and West of Scotland College?—I think they have done more good than anything connected with agriculture in Scotland of recent years. The experiments themselves were valuable, but they have awakened interest in the minds of the farmers to a degree I have not seen aroused by any other movement. The farmers have been led to think on practical agricultural questions to a greater degree than they did before, and I believe, in consequence of this, are farming more economically than they did before. That is to say, they are producing perhaps fully better crops than they did, and doing it at a less cost, cheapening production. I think any such scheme as that is of the greatest practical benefit for the enlightenment of the usual farmers of the present day.

21431. How far do the teaching experiments of the Glasgow and West of Scotland College extend; to what distance from the central point?—Well, the idea has been to have three centres in Scotland, Edinburgh, Glasgow, and Aberdeen, and to make these centres the headquarters of the counties that are adjacent, lie nearest to them, and the Glasgow and Technical College is supposed to include within its area the south-west of Scotland. I believe they also experiment in Fife, but I don't know how they came to go to Fife.

21432. I believe that you attach great importance to instruction regarding live stock?—That is a part of agricultural education in this country that has been almost entirely neglected, except in such places as Cirencester or Downton in England. I am not sure whether they do it at Downton or not, but I had an opportunity of examining with great care for two days the agricultural college at Guelph, Ontario, Canada; they have a most complete and successful system there of demonstrations with live stock. They have a special class room, fitted with very steep benches, and into this class room animals of various breeds are brought, and the professor demonstrates the characteristics of the different breeds, not simply of the individual breeds, the separate breeds, but of the breeds for separate purposes, beef producers, dairy producers, what are the characteristics that ought to be aimed at in producing these breeds, and then the pupils are brought down to demonstrate one by one, and are criticised by their fellow pupils and by the professor, and I believe that that, especially in a great live-stock producing country like Ireland, would be extremely valuable, because it would help the farmers to understand the ideal at which they should aim, for whatever purpose they have in view, in producing any class of breed.

21433. Mr. Mulcahy.—Dr. Gillespie, have you mentioned that the elementary teachers bring their pupils out to see how farming was conducted on the neighbouring farmers' fields; do the farmers offer any [illegible]

21434. Would you advocate that more attention should be paid in the normal schools, or, as we call them training colleges, to agriculture. Would you think it right that farms should be attached to these colleges, and that practical agriculture should be exhibited to the students?—No, I don't think they should be attached to a training college or normal school. I am very much in favour of the establishment of several large colleges in Scotland on the same lines as the college at Guelph to which I have referred. A movement has been initiated now, an attempt to get the south western counties of Scotland to combine and establish an experimental college in the south-west of Scotland, with a teaching staff and an experimental farm attached, but I don't think it would do at an elementary or normal school.

21435. In connection with the three places you mentioned, Edinburgh, Glasgow and Aberdeen, will these colleges have farms attached to them that the students can go out and see the work carried on?—No. In the Glasgow and West of Scotland College they utilise the Saturdays, which otherwise would be holidays, to visit, sometimes at great distances, representative farms, and to see the different systems pursued on these farms. I think that is the most that is done at the present time.

21436. Is instruction in agriculture confined to rural schools, or do boys in Dumfries get instruction in agriculture?—I am not aware about Dumfries Academy, but in all the other secondary schools in Dumfriesshire they do.

21437. And you mentioned from text-books—would you favour us with a list of the textbooks?—I could ascertain. There are forty-three parishes, I think, in the county, and in these forty-three parishes there are twenty-eight boards.

21438. Rev. Dr. Wilson.—Do the farmers as a class readily accept instruction as to better modes of farming?—I think they did not use to, they don't readily yet, but I think they are gradually yielding.

21439. We look upon them, without any discredit to them, in some ways as rather immovable?—We call them very conservative in their habits.

21440. It is a more complimentary term than stolid and immovable?—Well, such work as has been done by this Glasgow and West of Scotland Technical College has done more to break down that characteristic of which you speak than anything else. You find a farmer who sneers at agricultural science and will not be moved by it; but his neighbour is influenced by it and adopts some new methods, and he follows his neighbour, and imagines he is not being influenced by agricultural science.

21441. You give him an experiment and he profits by it?—Yes.

21442. I suppose cattle-feeding and rearing is becoming the most profitable department in Scotland?—Yes, if any department can be called profitable in agriculture now.

21443. Well we can compete with foreign countries, better in cattle than we can in grain. What you tell us about that college in Canada would be most important to be taught in our country at all events, and I suppose also in Scotland?—I would very much like to see it taught extensively in Ireland, because we get an immense number of Irish cattle here; they are greatly improved from what they were, but they will have to be further improved.

21444. What do you do with them when you get them here—your grass is not better than ours to feed them?—I don't know; we rear them.

21445. Captain Shaw.—How many schools of the Guelph type do you think would be necessary for Scotland?—I should think three.

Dumfries.
Oct. [illegible]
Rev. J. Gillespie, LL.D.

Dumfries.

Oct. [illegible].

Rev. P. Gillespie, M.A.

31446. You think it should be taught?—It should if it was practicable.

31447. Do you know in what class or standards in Scotland they teach agriculture?—I should think the fifth and sixth.

31448. Then the students only get about two years instruction probably in agriculture?—Yes, that is so far as the rural schools go, but if they go to the secondary school they will get more advanced.

31449. Do they do any practical work in elementary botany or elementary chemistry at present?—Not in the rural schools.

31450. Do they learn such subjects as the amount of seed which is required to sow an acre of anything?—I don't think so.

31451. Do you think that would be useful for them to learn?—I think it would be thrown away on a child of twelve or thirteen.

31452. Do you think learning the description of various breeds of cattle from a book would be useful to children of that age?—I am not advocating the characteristics of breeds for children.

31453. You don't think a child would be likely to recognise an animal from learning in a book what its points are?—No, I don't think so.

31454. Mr. Struthers.—You would not advocate an Irish child learning off by heart a description of the black-faced sheep, which he seldom sees?—Oh, no.

31455. Captain Shaw.—You say you think experimental plots would be no use for schools?—As regards the children attending school, even if they were successfully taught, that they would be much good. I don't think a child of twelve or thirteen is in a position to appreciate the nice points that are necessarily involved in an agricultural experiment.

31456. In such plots they would never get any results which could be relied on, working themselves?—Oh, no.

31457. But still they could be shown roughly the best results by using certain manures and certain other things, and could be taught the value of experiments even if they made no valuable experiments themselves?—That might be useful if you had an object lesson around.

31458. But then they don't get object lessons in the form of lectures, which they might get in small plots of their own?—I don't think it is so important that a child of that age should be taught the subject, it is rather the principles.

31459. You think he ought to be taught the elements of botany and plant life and chemistry so that he may be able to appreciate the object of experiments later on?—I think so.

31460. Rev. Dr. Evans.—Do you teach any portion of entomology in connection with your agricultural work?—No.

31461. I mean respecting insects and pests of that kind that are injurious to crops?—I don't think it is done, but it may be done with great advantage.

31462. Have you any experimental plots or farms in Scotland for purely experimental purposes?—No, I don't think at the present moment there is any. The Highland Society, of which I have been a Director for twenty years, had an experimental station and conducted experiments on manures, on turnips and potatoes or such work as that?—Yes; experiments were conducted within a mile of here two years ago.

31463. Or hybridising in order to produce better varieties?—No, that is done by private individuals and done very successfully.

31464. Are the results of this work obtainable anywhere?—Yes; the work of the Glasgow and West of Scotland College is contained each year in the annual report.

31465. Mr. Struthers.—I think, Dr. Gillespie, you rather advocate the training of the teachers in rural schools in agriculture?—Yes.

31466. But, of course, many of those teachers are not going to be teachers of rural schools at all—they are going to teach in large towns, would it not be better to give them a course in elementary science—botany and chemistry—rather than agriculture specifically?—I include botany and chemistry—I mean agriculture and the allied sciences.

31467. But rather the allied sciences than the application to agriculture?—Yes, but there are matters in agriculture proper in addition to chemistry and botany.

31468. Such as the effect of manures, I suppose?—Yes, and the nature of soils and everything connected with soils, which is not botany or chemistry proper.

31469. It might come to under the head of geology?—Perhaps it might.

31470. You might call it a course in elementary science instead of specifically agriculture?—Yes.

31471. Might not the same be said about the children in schools that it would be better not to teach them agriculture, but rather such scientific principles that they could comprehend at twelve or thirteen as might have some bearing on agriculture?—Yes, I think so, a good deal depends on the situation of the school and the future of the children who are to attend the school.

31472. But something depends also on making the children observant, training them in habits of observation, and getting them to make experiments for themselves instead of reading a thing out of a book?—Oh, yes.

31473. I daresay you have had some experience with the teaching of agriculture in these rural schools?—Yes.

31474. Do you know to what extent it consists of learning a book by heart?—I know it only from the elementary school in my own parish, and I don't think it is done that way. The teacher is exceptionally well qualified, for he attended a course of science and art instruction in London.

31475. You would not consider learning a book off by heart satisfactory?—No use at all.

31476. I think you said that the course of a month which the teacher received at the vacation course in Edinburgh is not at all sufficient?—I don't think so.

31477. So that men who have not received a longer training in agriculture than that would not be competent teachers of agriculture?—They might teach the elements but nothing further.

31478. But for real agricultural education you would look to more advanced schools?—Certainly.

31479. Especially such schools as you spoke of after the manner of Guelph, where there would be

Council farm, where something of the kind has been done, near Penrith?—I know it by name only.

31484. They are evidently aiming at the same purpose there that you have spoken of. I suppose you think the knowledge of cattle to be obtained at these classes or schools could not be attained by cattle shows?—No, cattle shows are not at very educative.

31485. Don't you think that shows where cattle are judged, and there is a large crowd of observant farmers around criticising the judgment, don't they learn a good deal there as to the best of the breeds?—Yes, the best of the breeds.

31486. And the good points of each breed?—It is a very indirect and slow education.

Dumfries. Oct. [illegible]

Rev. J. Gillespie, LL.D.

Mr. John Hiddleston, Chairman of the Finance Committee of Dumfries County Council, examined.

31487. Chairman.—You are Chairman of the Finance Committee of Dumfries County Council, and member of the Education Committee?—I am.

31488. You have a statement there of the grant available for technical education in Scotland?—I have prepared a few statements for the use of the Commission. In the first place I may state that I began to take an interest in this thing in 1892-93, and having talked to my friend Mr. Gillespie, he used his force in the press to endeavour to persuade other counties in Scotland to devote their money to technical instruction, and not any part of it, as they were entitled to do, to the relief of the rates. I think our efforts have been very successful, or in other words that the counties have begun to appreciate the benefits of technical instruction, because while there was £4,703 of the grant applied to rates in 1892-93, next year there was £3,943, next year it rose to £3,763, from a large county applying the whole of their portion; next year it fell to £2,791 and in the year ending Whitsunday last only £1,820 1s. 10d. out of a grant of £17,099 16s. 6d. was applied to the rates in Scotland, the rest being applied to technical education. I may say that in 1892-93 the percentage of the grant spent on technical education was 47·58; next year, 70·4; next year, 89·12; next year, 107·31, and this year it was 89·[illegible], showing a gradual increase on the amount spent. As Mr. Aitken said, we suffer in Scotland from the grant not being equal every year, through having the payments connected with the swine fever in Scotland connected with the same fund. I have also prepared a statement of the income and expenditure in regard to our grant in this county, and also an abstract of the expenditure in the counties of Scotland for the year ending 15th of May.

31489. Mr. Mulley.—Is there any local rate supplementing the £17,000?—There are three counties in Scotland—three of our most important counties, Forfar, Lanark, and Perth—which each give now a subvention or grant from what is known as the local taxation relief grant; they each give a grant in aid of technical education in their own counties. These are Government grants.

Mr. John Hiddleston.

31490. Are these grants applicable to elementary schools, the £17,000 and the local aid in certain places, where you have it?—Oh, no; they are applicable to secondary schools as well. And eight of the counties of Scotland now hand their grant over to the secondary committees that have been formed, for technical education only.

31491. Rev. Dr. Wilson.—The grant made by the County Council is practically from the rates, because if they did not give it to education it would go in reduction of the rates?—They have the power to apply it for the reduction of the rates, but the first purpose aimed was for technical education.

31492. Practically, then, it comes from the rates?—It might be applied to the rates.

31493. Did swine fever do much injury in Scotland?—It pulled down our £7,000 grant in one year; in 1894-95 our grant was over £23,000, in 1895-96 it was under £16,000.

31494. Captain Shaw.—Do you receive a grant for secondary education from the Government?—We receive a grant for secondary education, £1,031 I think it is; our technical grant this year is £495 6s. 11d.

31495. And the two grants are lumped together in this county?—Yes, and administered by the county secondary education committee.

31496. Has the Scotch Education Department the general control of the expenditure of this money?—Yes, the scheme is approved of by them—that is, so far as the secondary education is concerned.

Mr. Jerome Wallace, F.E.I.S., Head Master, Harlow Public School, Cumnock, N.B., examined.

31497. Chairman.—You are Head Master of the Harlow Public School, Cumnock. Will you tell us what are the ages at which children begin to benefit by working in wood?—From ten to fourteen.

31498. They would begin as soon as ten?—Between ten and eleven.

31499. Do you find that they are able to handle the tools at ten?—Some of them even earlier.

31500. Have you special tools for small children, or do they handle the same tools as the bigger children?—The tools are slightly less than the ordinary trade size.

31501. What is the nature and the scope of the woodwork suited to the different ages at which the children are working?—The system which I have wrought in my own small school—in that scheme I have endeavoured to keep in view the central Sloyd principles, instead of adopting the scheme that has been put forward by the London City and Guilds Institute, which consists in making abstract joints instead of finishing useful articles in which the joints, of course the lighter ones, are embodied, and it consists of drawing to scale plans and solid geometrical drawings; it also touches on the arithmetic taught in the school, mensuration especially.

31502. You are of opinion, I believe, that without scale drawing you could not give very efficient instruction in woodwork?—No, certainly not; drawing, bench work, and mensuration must form part of one whole.

Mr. Jerome Wallace, F.E.I.S.

31503. And therefore it is not surprising that where, as we saw in a school in Ireland the other day, drawing was not practised in connection with the woodwork, that the woodwork was rather, what they call, a botch?—I should fancy it would be.

31504. What additional subjects are absolutely necessary for the maximum benefit to accrue?—Those I have mentioned, drawing, and not copying drawings only, but encouraging original design from the start. For example, one of the earliest models in the series that I have designed for my own school, and which at the present moment is in the press, begins with the planing up of a rectangular flower stick, and the children are required to make that from my own drawing. Afterwards they are asked to design one to different dimensions, altering the details slightly, and they are encouraged all through the course to original design, so that the drawing is not copying simply.

31505. What class of schools do you think the woodwork is suited for?—Small schools equally with large, for this reason, that from the nature of the training the classes must necessarily be smaller than for other subjects.

* * *

21506. You don't find it necessary to have a separate building?—No, because I have only seven to ten pupils taking woodwork.

21507. And you take it in another hour from the ordinary work of the school?—Yes.

21508. Therefore in schools where there is only one teacher with all the classes in the schools to attend to, if it were to be introduced, it would be necessary to have either a separate building or to take it at a different hour from the ordinary school work?—Better to have a separate building, but according to the nature of the building one part of it, as in my own case, might be used as a workroom.

21509. What is the first essential to success?—That the teacher should be trained.

21510. Mr. Molloy.—You mentioned you had from seven to ten pupils under instruction in this woodwork class. Now is admission to the woodwork class based on their position in the standard in the school, on age, or both combined?—Both, and general intelligence, usually about our 5th standard.

21511. What is the lowest standard that you admit pupils from to the woodwork?—Standard 5, but I do as a matter of fact take some of the older pupils in standard 4, in the last few months of the year that they are in standard 4.

21512. I take it your instruction is not carried out in a separate building but in the schoolroom?—In a part of the schoolroom.

21513. How many rooms are there in your school?—Only one.

21514. Do you find any practical inconvenience from the woodwork chips or shavings requiring to be swept away?—No, the woodwork lesson is carried on when the other classes are away, and that is all looked after before they come in again.

21515. What time have you for the woodwork instruction?—Twice a week, from 3 o'clock to 4.30.

21516. And what are the ordinary school hours?—From 9.30 to 4, and on these days the other classes are dismissed at 3.15.

21517. Then your hours are extremely long hours, because you have to be there?—I have to extend the time in order to get this work taken.

21518. As regards the plant, benches, tools, and so on, who supplied the funds?—The School Board.

21519. What do you say is the cost per child for the instruction in woodwork?—The cost in the case of my own school would be about 30s. or 35s. a head.

21520. Captain Shaw.—The annual cost?—No, the initial cost for benches and tools.

21521. Mr. Stevenson.—Who provided that money?—The School Board.

21522. Mr. Molloy.—Is the instruction in drawing in the case of the seven or ten pupils carried on in the workroom?—At a different time there are three hours per week devoted to drawing, according to the Science and Art regulations, and part of that time is taken for the special scale and geometrical drawing required for the woodwork.

21523. And the rest of the drawing is common to the other pupils of the school?—Quite so.

21524. And you mention you pay special attention to mensuration as a separate subject?—Yes.

21525. Captain Shaw.—Is this woodwork inspected for you under the Science and Art Department

21530. As long as the teacher understands what he has got to teach?—Yes.

21531. You think it is desirable that he should be allowed a latitude in the manner in which he teaches it?—My experience of the Science and Art Inspector has been that they have followed largely on the lines of the City and Guilds Institute, which is the only examining body for teachers in the country, and their scheme suggests that only abstract joints should be made; and I have an idea that if the Science and Art Department's Inspector would base his award on the quality of the drawing and the bench work done throughout the session, and not on his single day's test, it would be better.

21532. What has been the annual cost per pupil?—It has not amounted to 2s. per head.

21533. I suppose your schoolroom has more accommodation than is necessary for the number of students attending it?—Yes, there is accommodation for seventy or eighty, and the average barely touches fifty.

21534. Do you find any difficulty in disposing of the benches when you are not teaching woodwork?—Not the least.

21535. Mr. Stevenson.—They remain in one end of the schoolroom all the time?—All the time, and don't need to be moved at all.

21536. Captain Shaw.—Then you don't utilise them for any other purpose?—No.

21537. Rev. Dr. Evans.—You have experience in teaching literary subjects?—The ordinary school subjects.

21538. Have you found that this special manual work aids or hinders proficiency of the pupils in other subjects?—I should say it aids; it sharpens their intelligence.

21539. You would like to see the teachers all trained to do this work?—Yes.

21540. Where might they be trained?—At central classes, the same as Mr. Aitken has already spoken of.

21541. Is there any training work of this sort done in the training colleges?—None whatever.

21542. So that this Commission could not see it done in any training college in Scotland?—Not so far as I know.

21543. Mr. Stevenson.—Have you any assistant in your school?—No, only a female teacher who teaches sewing.

21544. Would it be any advantage to you to have standards 1, 2, and 3 dismissed earlier than the others?—On days on which manual work is taken they are dismissed earlier than the others, at 3.15.

21545. Mr. Aitken left it to you to explain what the arrangements are for training teachers in woodwork; you have been conducting classes for training teachers in woodwork?—Yes, for the last two and a half years, the first year we had twenty-five, and it was decided to send them in for the London City and Guilds examination. A number of these were teachers in Dumfries Academy who did not hold the Education Department's certificate, and under the City and Guilds regulations they were not allowed to sit. There were sixteen went in for the examination in the first year's work and eighteen of them got through. In the second year the attendance dropped, and number

21549. How many are actually giving instruction in their own schools?—One, Mr. Malcolm, at Lockerbie.

21550. And there is no other school in the county in which woodwork is given to the children except in your own?—I was told this morning that there are two.

21551. You yourself were trained at Nääs?—Yes.

21552. Of course you had a knowledge of woodwork before that, and you have since been instructor there?—Yes.

21553. And your teaching of the teachers here is very much on the Nääs principle?—The main principles, but the use of the knife is discarded.

21554. And you find it rather in the way of teaching that, that you cannot get a qualifying certificate from anybody but the City and Guilds Institute?—Yes.

21555. Which you don't think quite a suitable line of work for teachers in small schools?—Part of it is really good, I think. They require drawing, bench work, and a knowledge of timber and tools. There is a written examination; the drawing and written portion I think a great deal of, but the other part, the bench work, which is making simple abstract joints, I think, is no good.

21556. Could you not form an association to give a certificate of your own, on the lines you desire?—It was once considered by the Scotch Sloyd Association.

21557. You are aware there is a large movement in England for issuing a certificate on the lines you wish?—Yes, but when teaching in Sweden, I had some of the men who were on the examination committee, and I would rather have Scotchmen.

21558. Rev. Dr. Evans.—When were you at Nääs?—1888, 1891, and 1892, and in 1893 I was instructor at Nääs. Dumfries. Oct. 18, 1897.

21559. Mr. Struthers.—You attach great importance to the teaching of mensuration in a practical way?—I do. Mr. [illegible] Wallace, F.E.I.S.

21560. Not simply learning rules from a book?—There (produced) is a scheme of mensuration that I consider practical.

21561. Captain Shaw.—The City and Guilds do not give a certificate to a teacher unless he has been for twelve months actually learning?—They give two certificates, he must make twenty attendances of two hours duration, before he can be allowed to sit the first year's examination, and twelve attendances before he can be allowed to sit the final examination. The first year's examination consists of an examination in benchwork and drawing. The second year's of benchwork, drawing, and the written one of questions on timber and tools.

21562. But so far as the benchwork goes, it is only a test of the teacher's ability to use tools?—Yes, but my idea is that you create a more healthy interest in children when they are making some object they know to be useful.

21563. But as far as the teacher goes he can make these afterwards if he has got the manual dexterity?—No, for this reason, that if the Science and Art Department, or any other examining body, model their system on the lines of the City and Guilds, that will determine the direction of the teaching. It leaves a possibility of simply cramming up for that examination, and the education of the people will ultimately suffer.

Mr. John Malcolm Aitken further examined.

21564. Mr. Struthers.—Then these classes for training teachers in woodwork have been discontinued now?—They have. Mr. John Malcolm Aitken.

21565. But that is not because your committee think this woodwork training of little value, you intend to foster it still?—I do, and I think it very probable that it will be made compulsory in the selected schools, that this instruction should be given. And we hope for larger grants; whenever we can get funds that are set free from other purposes, our intention would be to devote a considerable portion of this to the fostering of manual instruction in the rural schools, and we hope to make it compulsory in the rural schools.

FORTY-SEVENTH PUBLIC SITTING.—TUESDAY, OCTOBER 19TH, 1897,

AT 2.45 O'CLOCK, P.M.

At Dryfesdale Public School, Lockerbie, N.B.

Lockerbie, N.B. Oct. 19, 1897.

Present:—The Right Hon. The Earl of Belmore, G.C.M.G., in the Chair; Rev. Henry Evans, D.D.; Rev. Hamilton Wilson, D.D.; W. R. J. Molloy, Esq.; Captain Shaw, and J. Struthers, Esq., LL.D.;

with J. D. Daly, Esq., B.A., Secretary.

[illegible] Oct. [illegible], 1887. [illegible]

mental drawing, they have special drawing for woodwork.

21569. You have freehand drawing?—We have drawing according to the Department's regulations, according to the old scheme, which required scale drawing and freehand in the fourth; model drawing, freehand, and a little geometry in the fifth standard; and now we have taken solid geometry, plan and elevation in the sixth standard instead of plane geometry.

21570. When you are beginning with a class in woodwork, what are the first exercises you put them to?—The first exercise is to plane up a piece of wood to a certain length and breadth and thickness, after having drawn it to scale full size in plan and elevation. That was the first exercise, to make a rectangular piece of wood.

21571. What was the next?—The next was to make marks on it at certain depths, and saw down to them and cut out the pieces between the saw cuts.

21572. Do you go on from that sort of work to make the finished article?—They have not got so far as any finished article yet, they have got no further than making simple joints.

21573. Do you intend to bring them on by degrees?—I hope so, some of the boys have already done such finished articles as a paper cutter and a ruler, for their own amusement.

21574. Do you find that the attendance has improved since woodwork was begun?—Oh, no, we have all the scholars in this district, we have all the scholars in the parish at this school, there are no more to be got.

21575. Is there compulsory attendance?—It is compulsory, there is nothing to improve except that perhaps we might keep them a little longer for the sake of the woodwork.

21576. Mr. Struthers.—Or they might be more regular?—We have a committee of the School Board which meets every Monday to look after the regularity, and I think they have got them screwed up to what they can do.

21577. Chairman.—What did the benches cost?—They cost about 25s. each, ten benches.

21578. How was that money provided?—The School Board provided it.

21579. And the tools?—The tools cost £25, I think; the county, I believe, pays its share, half or one-third, as Mr. Aitken informed you this morning.

21580. Mr. Mulloy.—May I ask the total number of pupils under instruction, boys and girls and infants, in the school?—650.

21581. Now, on the boy's side, what are the special subjects you take up apart from ordinary reading and explanation, apart from the purely literary subjects?—We have English grammar and geography, these are class subjects, then object lessons through the school, object lessons up to the second standard, thereafter organised science lessons, organised science lessons.

21582. In the infant department, you have kindergarten exercises, I presume?—We have kindergarten in the infant department.

21583. Where does that terminate, if at all?—It terminates in the infant department, I am sorry to say.

21584. Would you advocate the propriety of carrying that on to higher classes?—I would, if we could do it, but we cannot.

21585. How often is the workshop instruction carried on in the week?—Each boy gets two hours in the week, we have five classes at present.

21586. Do you find they attend willingly?—Yes, many of the classes meet at eight in the morning, and a number of boys who are not attached to these classes come in for extra practice.

21588. The cost of the benches and tools?—£50 would cover all the cost.

21589. On an average how much per child, of those receiving instruction?—We have eighty children, 12s. 6d. each.

21590. Are the pupils all free?—They are all free.

21591. The cost per head all round of your the pupils?—About £3 1s.

21592. Rev. Dr. Wilson.—I see you have a large number at shorthand, do the children like that?—Oh, I think so, I think they do, they only have two periods of three quarters of an hour each during the week for shorthand.

21593. Are they making reasonably good progress?—They learn to write it. They don't get up speed of course, but by the time they have been three years in it I believe they are able to take places in offices as shorthand writers, and the practice they get after a few months will enable them to do very well. Some of the older boys I notice take their notes in shorthand.

21594. I suppose the difficulty chiefly is in reading what they have written?—Principally, that is the test the inspector applies.

21595. Captain Shaw.—How many children have you got in the secondary department?—Our average for last year was sixty-two.

21596. You have five masters for them?—Yes.

21597. Exclusively?—Oh, no, I give you the wrong number, there are sixty-two beyond the sixth standard, the five masters are from fifth standard up, and fifth and sixth are partly elementary and partly secondary. We only count those scholars who are taking Latin.

21598. With fifth and sixth in the secondary department how many would you have?—I could not say what the average attendance would be, but there are 200 roughly on the roll.

21599. In the upper fifth and upper sixth do they take agriculture here?—They take agriculture.

21600. How is it taught?—Well, it is taught by the ordinary class teachers, one of them, Mr. [illegible], whom you saw in the fifth standard giving a lesson there, has attended two classes in Edinburgh, summer classes at the School of Rural Economy, and he, I believe, will teach all the agriculture next year at the same time that Mr. Wright, the teacher who is taking the woodwork, will take the woodwork of the other classes, but at present both these masters are employed in teaching agriculture.

21601. Is the agriculture practical agriculture or principles?—It is principles from a little text-book, but of course the text-book is not the only thing, the teacher knows something of the subject himself and he has experience.

21602. Rev. Dr. Evans.—Have you omitted any subject from the programme to make room for this manual work?—None whatever.

21603. What is the effect of the manual instruction on the proficiency of the pupils in the literary subjects?—I should not say that it had any effect at all that I have seen yet, it ought to tend to make them more accurate.

21604. Do you find that the manual work is popular with the parents and with the boys?—So far as I have heard it is popular with the parents, but of course any parent that it was unpopular with might not mention the subject to me.

21605. Mr. Struthers.—What children are attending the woodwork classes?—From fifth standard upwards.

21606. All the boys?—Not all the boys, a good many of the ex-sixth don't take it, a good many of those who are taking Latin and perhaps Latin and Greek, none of these take woodwork.

21607. Do all the boys in the fifth standard take

them to wash and clean up everything themselves?—Quite so.

21628. CHAIRMAN.—I don't quite understand when you say forty lessons; is that forty lessons for the whole of a Friday?—Forty hours, six hours a day for seven Fridays cover it.

21629. Rev. Dr. WILSON.—Do the children make much progress during that time?—They make soup, in fact cook a dinner in the morning, and in the afternoon they bake, and there is a great demand for the finished articles.

21630. Captain SHAW.—Do you find it better to give them a course for seven weeks and then not touch it for the rest of the year; have you ever tried the plan of teaching them during the whole of the year?—In a school I was in before this we used to have considerable trouble with children; I was an assistant in the school, and I only know from the effect on my attendance on the cookery afternoon. The plan was the scholars went for two hours to a central school for cookery, they were taken away for one hour in the afternoon from my class, and one hour they were kept beyond the school day, that is one hour of their own time and one hour of the school time was taken, and the attendance was always low on that afternoon, the parents kept them away.

21631. Mr. STRUTHERS.—That might be an exceptional case?—I think it was a pretty general cause of complaint in Edinburgh at that time.

21632. Captain SHAW.—What classes are taught cooking?—From the fifth up.

21633. You cannot teach them all in the one day?—No, they take it in turns.

21634. But during the year by devoting one day a week you teach them all?—Yes, we begin now and finish generally about the end of May.

21635. Rev. Dr. EVANS.—Where do the pupils get the materials for the cookery?—They buy them in the town.

21636. The pupils bring the materials?—Oh no, the cookery mistress buys them, she orders in the things just as a housekeeper would order them in, and distributes them among the pupils.

21637. Then the cooked articles are sold?—Yes.

21638. And I suppose the produce of the sale covers the expenditure?—Pretty nearly.

21639. Mr. STRUTHERS.—Would it be possible to get the children to buy instead of the mistress?—They do the actual buying to the extent of going messages, but of course they are simply told what to get.

21640. And they know the price of it?—I expect they are told; we have a book, as a matter of fact.

21641. Could that book not be kept by the children in turns?—The shopkeeper keeps it.

21642. But as a matter of training for children might it not be a useful thing for the children to keep the book, make the actual purchases, and enter it in proper form?—It would certainly have an educative value, but I never thought of it.

21643. Seeing we have those girls there the whole day on Friday, might it not be possible to have some practical illustrations of domestic economy lessons; I presume you teach domestic economy as a specific subject?—Yes.

21644. And in that case it is taught chiefly from a text-book?—I don't think the cooking mistress relies much on the text-book. The cookery mistress teaches domestic economy too.

21645. But the girls have a text-book?—They have a text-book.

21646. Do you know whether they are not prescribed lessons to get up from it each day?—I fancy they are.

21647. Do you know if there is any practical illustration of the various processes apart from cookery, for instance, those connected with washing or cleaning out a room?—I should not think so.

21648. Having the girls there all day on a Friday might it not be possible to associate practical work of that kind with the domestic economy lessons?—Yes, I think it would be advisable; they do clean up, but that is all beyond the actual cooking.

31649. Does the grant you receive for the cooking pay the salary of the mistress?—Oh, no, not nearly.

31650. The whole grant you get is how much?—It won't be more than £10.

31651. But that means her time is not fully occupied with the cookery classes?—No, only one day a week.

31652. Because it seems to have been found in other places where the cookery mistress is employed each day, giving continuous lessons, the grant paid her salary?—I suppose it would.

31653. Have you ever thought of utilising the buildings you have here to provide special rooms for afternoon classes or Saturday classes for pupils who have already left school?—Yes, I believe the County Council thought of that when the buildings were put up, and they were put up keeping that purpose in view, but I believe there is not much demand. We had, however, one class in the school, a dressmaking class, in the afternoons, and there is an evening class at which dressmaking and laundry work are taught.

31654. At these dressmaking classes in the afternoons were there both pupils of the day school and what might be called outside pupils?—The outside pupils were all teachers in the day school, and that has been the case in some of the classes that have been held here. In agriculture, outside the teaching profession, there were very few.

31655. So the teachers learn everything, and the other people they are supposed to teach learn nothing?—That is about it.

31656. It is quite possible the liking for this kind of instruction may grow when they have more experience of it?—I hope it may. There are some country Boards, I mean parishes, round about that have spoken of sending their children in here, on Saturdays probably, if we could manage to take them.

31657. Perhaps you could give us one or two facts about evening classes here. What are the evening classes you have here?—The evening classes are continuation classes in connection with the department, and the subjects taught are arithmetic, shorthand, and composition; I think these are the most popular subjects among the men; drawing, too; and among the women they have cookery, we call it domestic economy, but it is really cookery, and laundry work, and dressmaking. There are at present, I think, about thirty women in attendance, and about forty men on the roll.

31658. Any of these teachers again?—No, none of them.

31659. Any other class in the evening school?—No.

31660. No drawing class?—There is no drawing class in connection with the Department, there are a small number taking drawing.

31661. And no book-keeping class?—Yes, there is a book-keeping class.

31662. You said you rather approved of kindergarten work in the infant school, and would like to see it extended?—Yes, if we could.

31663. What are the obstacles in the way of extending it?—The want of time.

31664. The want of time in order to get a sufficient number of elementary subjects, or the want of time to meet the requirements of the examination?—To meet the requirements without dropping some of the other work. In woodwork we are taking them in for extra time; we could not keep the little ones in later.

31665. You don't think something could be taken off other lessons to vary the work and relieve the strain from literary subjects all day?—It might with advantage to the children, but I should not like to risk my professional reputation by doing so.

31666. It is an experiment worth making; perhaps your professional reputation might improve?—Perhaps it would from excellent to good.

31667. Rev. Dr. Evans.—You mean that the pupils would not be well taught if you took something away from the other subjects?—They might not show up so well before the inspector.

31668. Mr. Struthers.—Do you regard these two things as different?—Yes.

31669. You think it would improve the teaching?—Yes.

31670. But it would not show up so well before the inspector?—They are not things that could be examined on.

31671. That would be an argument in favour of inspection rather than examinations?—Yes. I may say in the matter of geography I have tried the experiment of taking out some of the younger scholars myself for half an hour now and again and calling their attention to the way rain ran off the road, and when I went to examine on it myself I found there was practically nothing I could examine on. Our examiner here of course we know him very well, and we could depend upon him giving us credit for what we really had done, but at the same time it is too risky I think to make the experiment.

31672. Take that one case, do you think these children benefited by being taken out and shown natural phenomena, although there was nothing to examine on?—I think they would, but they could not put it into words.

31673. That may come later on?—Yes.

31674. Captain Shaw.—You have four courses, could you give us any indication of how they take them up?—They were arranged to suit the requirements of the county, but they have not worked in practice; we have not staff enough to keep them separate. Any boy who wants to take any particular course, gets more time for the subjects required.

FORTY-EIGHTH PUBLIC SITTING.—WEDNESDAY, OCTOBER 20TH, 1897.

AT 1.30 o'clock, P.M.,

At the School Board Offices, Edinburgh.

Present:—THE RIGHT HON. THE EARL OF BELMORE, G.C.M.G., in the Chair; HIS GRACE THE MOST REV. WILLIAM J. WALSH, D.D.; THE RIGHT REV. MONSIGNOR MOLLOY, D.D., D.SC.; REV. HENRY EVANS, D.D.; REV. HAMILTON WILSON, D.D.; STANLEY HARRINGTON, ESQ., M.A.; W. R. J. MOLLOY, ESQ.; CAPTAIN T. B. SHAW; and J. STRUTHERS, ESQ., M.A.;

with J. D. DALY, ESQ., M.A., Secretary.

Mr. COLIN G. MACRAE, M.A., Chairman of the Edinburgh School Board, examined.

Edinburgh. Oct. 20, 1897. Mr. Colin G. Macrae, M.A.

31675. CHAIRMAN.—I believe you are Chairman of the Edinburgh School Board since the 15th of October, 1890?—Yes, I am; and I have been a member of the Board since 1885.

31676. And you have taken an active interest in the movement throughout the country which has resulted in the institution of technical classes and workshops?—I have.

31677. When and where did you open your first workshop?—It was opened in the Gilmore school in 1892.

31678. I suppose that that was for woodwork?—It was woodwork.

31679. Had you any teaching of woodwork before that?—Well, only in a desultory form, at the instance of one or two headmasters, who began classes for themselves, finding that the work interested the boys.

31680. When did you appoint your present chief instructor, Mr. Graham?—Mr. Graham was appointed in October, 1893.

31681. Is he a practical workman?—Yes, he was trained as a practical workman, I believe; and he afterwards qualified himself as a certificated teacher of drawing.

31682. How many schools with separate woodwork rooms have you?—Sixteen at present, but we expect within a month or so to have them also in two schools.

31683. What is your present number of day schools?—Thirty-two schools, including one that is just opened.

31684. You think it advisable to proceed gradually?—Yes, partly on account of the expense and partly because at first we regarded it as very much of an experiment, and we did not supply all our schools at once.

31685. I understand that some of your schoolrooms are arranged to take both woodwork and cookery; how many of that sort are there?—There are nine in that position, I understand. The way we arrange that is, we provide table tops for the benches, which can be put on and provide accommodation for teaching cookery after the woodwork is concluded.

31686. What do you do with the tools?—The tools are stowed away in the lockers of the benches.

31687. You find that this arrangement works well and saves multiplying the rooms?—It does.

31688. In the other cases your rooms, I believe, are preserved for woodwork alone?—Yes.

31689. How many workshops have you at present erected outside the school in the playground, and how many situated within the building?—We have seven in the playground, separated from the building, and we have nine situated within the school building.

31690. Could you give me any idea of the cost of the outside rooms, especially for the purpose of woodwork?—The one you saw this morning in Lauriston-street cost about £460, as closely as possible. There was some additional cost in consequence of having opened it on standards so as to give more accommodation for the playground.

31691. Therefore it would not be quite fair to charge all that expense to the workshop?—No. I think you could erect it cheaper if you erected it independently upon the ground.

31692. Have you any workshops that are built of wood and corrugated iron?—No, I don't think we have.

31693. To come back to my former question, you find that there are advantages in having some workshops within the school-buildings and some in the playground?—Yes.

31694. Will you tell us what they are?—When they are inside the school buildings they are more under the direction of the staff, and especially of the headmaster, and therefore the discipline is the more easily preserved. When they are outside in the yards there is the advantage that they make no noise, and I don't think it is any disadvantage to the children to move from the playground to their work.

31695. How many boys can be accommodated at the benches at a class?—We accommodate from twelve to twenty-three in the various classrooms.

31696. How many boys at a bench?—Four boys to a bench exactly.

31697. What is the cost of your benches?—They cost £5, and the vices are in addition 15s. each.

31698. What is there peculiar about your benches that make them cost so much as £5; because we have found benches elsewhere generally costing less than half that sum?—We have put up some a little cheaper recently, but the benches, as they were recently constructed, were of the very best quality.

Mr. Graham.—We have patent vices.

31699. They all accommodate four boys?—Yes.

31700. You have not any benches that accommodate only two boys?—No.

31701. You don't know, therefore, what price they would be?—No, I cannot say that.

31702. What do you consider would be the best size for a class?—The Department, I think, expect twenty in each class, and we regard twenty as about the proper number.

31703. Not more than twenty?—Not more than twenty.

31704. What are the advantages in limiting it to twenty?—It is quite a sufficiently manageable number. The teacher can overtake them all with individual attention; if there are less than that, some of the power of the teacher is lost.

31705. And you find at the same time that the class is sufficiently large to enable the whole school to be overtaken with comparative ease?—That is so.

31706. What boys are required to take woodwork?—All above the fourth standard.

31707. Is it compulsory?—With us it is compulsory; but we have no difficulty in that respect, for

Edinburgh. [illegible]

the boys regard it, not as a hardship, but as a pleasure.

21708. And you are working under the Science and Art regulations?—We have been.

21709. What is the minimum number of lessons required by the Science and Art Department for each pupil?—Fifteen lessons.

21710. How many lessons in point of fact do you give to each boy?—If they attend regularly they have from thirty-five to forty lessons in the course of the session.

21711. How many lessons does the Department require of two hours each as a minimum for each school?—Twenty-two lessons of two hours each.

21712. What is your staff?—We have one chief instructor and seven assistants under him. The chief instructor arranges the duties of the assistants.

21713. Is it the case in Edinburgh that all the teachers of woodwork are specialists, or are some of them the ordinary school teachers?—No, they are all specialists.

21714. You think that a better plan than instructing your ordinary teachers?—Yes, our ordinary teachers did take a class of instruction for one session, but we found the practical men, so long as they were able to exercise proper discipline, were more qualified to do the work.

21715. I understand that the Edinburgh School Board is not very much in favour of the central system?—No. It was once tried in connection with cookery, and it was not found very successful; the staff complained of losing portions of their classes for large portions of the day, and the distances they had to walk.

21716. You prefer to teach everything within the walls of each school?—That is so.

21717. You find the discipline is better maintained and the time-table more conveniently arranged when all the classes are taught in the same school?—Yes.

21718. How many schools has each assistant under his charge?—Each assistant has two schools, except one assistant who has four smaller schools.

21719. How many days a week does he give to each school?—From two to three days a week.

21720. And how are the classes taken?—From the senior boys in relays of eighteen or twenty at a time.

21721. Although you make the learning of woodwork compulsory on all boys in and beyond the fifth standard, it is not felt as any hardship on the student?—No; they regard it rather as a privilege.

21722. And you don't often find a boy asking to be relieved of this work?—No.

21723. In such cases as may occur it is generally from ill-health?—Or constitutional weakness; these are very rare cases.

21724. And you find all boys, irrespective of their wishing to become carpenters or joiners, are willing to take to this work?—It is a rather remarkable fact that we have ascertained on inquiry that by far the larger proportion of boys who take woodwork do not adopt that as their trade afterwards.

21725. You don't teach for the purpose of teaching trades, but your teaching is of a purely educational character?—That is so. We avoid any attempt to teach trades.

21726. Your chief instructor, as I understand, prepared a graduated series of exercises which begins with simple exercises, and leads up to more advanced work, and you adopted this system?—Yes.

21727. It is not exactly the Sloyd system?—No:

much as people imagine in this country?—We think it desirable to teach them the use of tools.

21731. That is taught, too. Their principal instruction is not so much to make articles as to indicate the principles which underlie all handwork?—Yes. We wish especially to familiarise the boys with the use of tools, and give them accuracy of observation and correctness of hand and eye, and general deftness in handiwork.

21732. And you find that it is very difficult to accomplish that without practice?—Yes.

21733. You make a great point of drawing as an essential part of the woodwork instruction?—We consider drawing absolutely essential.

21734. Every pupil, I suppose, has to draw his work first with his own hands?—Yes. Two hours are occupied out of every eight in drawing, and the other six hours in finishing the article from the drawing.

21735. The boy does not copy his own sketch, but copies from the copybook?—No; that might be faulty.

21736. But still he has drawn?—Yes; and knows exactly what he is doing.

21737. What becomes of the articles the boys make?—They are always sold to the boys at the price of the wood—a mere trifle.

21738. I think you have a table showing the number of boys who receive woodwork instruction?—I have taken a note of the number. The total number of students in the various standards are: In the ex-sixth, 164; in the sixth, 385; in the fifth, 750; that is, 1,302 in all; and 103 which we have taken out of the fourth, in cases where the boys are, perhaps, a little backward and over age, and where there is room for them. We don't get any grant for them, but we think it due to them to give them some opportunity.

21739. You don't think that teaching woodwork detracts from the results of general education on the one hand; or, on the other hand, you don't see that it makes very much difference in improving education?—No; we are quite persuaded it does not detract from the general education, but it is not very easy to prove whether it does them any great good in regard to their general education; although one is entitled to assume that the additional education which it involves does sharpen them and improve their faculties.

21740. You find that some of the boys who are not very good in literary studies are the best in handwork?—That is often the case.

21741. It stimulates them and makes them feel they are able to do something?—Yes.

21742. What are the tools you use?—We use the ordinary workman's tools, such as are used in a joiner's shop in this country—the plane, saw, and chisel.

21743. You use smaller ones?—No; they are the usual size.

21744. I did not mean that they were smaller for the boys, but the smaller tools that a workman uses?—Yes; we do.

21745. Do you regard this kind of instruction as tending to keep children longer at school?—I think it has that tendency.

21746. And among the work which you think has that effect, you include woodwork, laundry work, and cookery?—Yes. I think where the children have the impression that they are learning something that will be of value to them in afterlife they are more inclined to stay.

21747. Do you find that the weakness of the

for the purpose of practical and technical instruction, it would be of use for the industrial classes—the children of the industrial classes.

21750. You mean for children who have left the ordinary school work?—Well, for children who are willing to proceed a little further than the compulsory standards.

21751. Are the people of Edinburgh rather afraid of the expense?—Yes; we have met that difficulty sometimes in connection with matters of progress.

21752. You think if the matter were better understood they would be willing to pay a small fee?—I think many of the parents would be glad to do so.

21753. Most Rev. Dr. WALSH.—Is the tendency to enlarge the scope of woodwork teaching in the Edinburgh schools or to diminish it?—I think to enlarge it.

21754. I find by your School Board report for the year 1893–94 that twelve out of twenty-nine schools under the Board had classes of woodwork instruction. Has that number since been increased or diminished?—We have now sixteen, and we are expecting three more in a few weeks to be opened—that will make nineteen out of thirty-two schools.

21755. So that both the number of schools and the proportion of the schools having this branch of instruction is increasing?—The proportion is increasing.

21756. May I call your attention to some passages in the Edinburgh School Board Report. I find in the report of the Castle Hill School the headmaster says, "I should like again to refer to the need there is of provision being made for manual training to the boys in the three higher standards." That was a school, I take it, in which provision for woodwork had not been made at the time of the report?—That is so.

21757. So that, even in schools where provision has not yet been made for this branch, there is a desire to have the provision made?—Yes. I think that is very general.

21758. In the report of the Lothian-road School it is stated: "The woodwork class has again been attended with much success." In that school the work has been popular with the boys of the upper standards?—That is so.

21759. And that is the general state of affairs wherever woodwork is taught?—Yes.

21760. I find it stated in the report of the Milton House School that "the boys take great delight in the work, and have made very great progress"?—Yes; that is so.

21761. In another report—that of the South Bridge-street School—the headmaster says: "The manual training class, in my opinion, counteracts to some extent the tendency to leave school at the early age complained of"?—That is exactly what I am saying.

21762. You have never found that the introduction of this branch has had the effect of driving the children away from the school?—Certainly not; the reverse.

21763. The manual training never led to encounter any opposition from any mistaken notion on the part either of the children or of their parents, that what children go to school for is to learn things out of books?—I don't think that is so.

21764. The Edinburgh people have broader views of education than to fall into an error of that sort?—I should hope so.

sixth standard than remained before. You consider that this is partly due to the fact that this new branch of instruction has been introduced?—Yes; that is my opinion.

21767. I find that in 1880–81 there were just 40 per cent. of the children in or above Standard V., but last year there were 50 per cent. That is a very important increase?—Yes.

21768. Has it not also been found that the percentage of children over thirteen in the upper standards is improving?—Yes, but not quite so rapidly.

21769. I find, taking the same years, that in 1880–81 the percentage of children over thirteen in and above standard V. was 32; and it is now 43?—Yes, but the numbers were very small at that time.

21770. No doubt. But you attach great importance to this particular increase?—We do, very much.

21771. I believe you complain that there is a tendency on the part of parents to take away their children from school at too early an age?—Yes, we suffer from that very much.

21772. What is the standard of exemption from the compulsory attendance?—They can obtain a certificate of exemption after passing the V. standard.

21773. I have seen it stated that last year there were over 500 children presented and passed in the V. standard who were only eleven years of age?—Yes, the majority of children passing the V. standard were only eleven years of age.

21774. At what age do the children in the schools here begin to learn the use of tools?—I fancy the average will be at eleven years of age.

21775. The average. So that a number of them begin before that?—Many of them before it; but that will be the average age.

21776. Then you here, in Edinburgh, do not consider that it is physically impossible to teach the use of tools to a child before eleven?—No, not such work as they are called upon to do.

21777. Your experience here of course proves the contrary?—It does.

21778. And proves that it is not merely physically possible, but that it is fairly easy?—Yes, and that they take it up and understand it thoroughly.

21779. Have you any idea what this branch of school work costs in Edinburgh?—The total cost to the Board is £250, made up in this way:—salaries of instructors, £150, and the cost of materials, say 1s. per pupil on 1,400 children, £70; then we receive a grant of 6d. per thousand per week for 40 weeks on 1,400 pupils, £136, and 50 per cent. for the "excellent" grant, £70; in all we receive £206, leaving the annual net cost to the Board, £[illegible].

21780. And that is the net yearly cost of this work for all the schools under the School Board of Edinburgh?—Yes, that to some extent depends on whether the schools are fully occupied; if anything happens to prevent their being quite fully occupied there might be a slight decrease.

21781. This educational woodwork, I think you have said, is now compulsory in the Edinburgh Board Schools?—Yes.

21782. That is, the attendance at the class is compulsory in any school in which this branch has been introduced?—Yes.

21783. Was it compulsory from the time you first introduced it?—I think we have always, since we erected a workshop, insisted on the boys of the upper standard taking it up.

21784. Did you find any difficulty at first in intro

Edinburgh. — Oct. [illegible], 18[illegible]. — Mr. [illegible] & [illegible], M.A.

21787. Is there not something of a drawback in your Edinburgh system of having the teaching of woodwork in the hands of a set of teachers distinct from the ordinary teachers of the school; is it not likely to suggest to the pupils, or to the public, that this branch is something that lies outside school work properly so called, and is connected with industry or trade, rather than with education?—That may be so; but, on the other hand, the teaching I am satisfied at present is better done by special instructors who are conversant with manual work; the teachers in the normal colleges are not trained to it.

21788. But suppose the teachers were trained to it in the normal or training colleges, which kind of teacher do you think more likely to teach well in the ordinary school—a trained teacher specially and properly trained in this branch of school work—or an artisan?—Assuming they have equal capacities and practical knowledge of the woodwork, the trained teacher would have the advantage.

21789. Inasmuch as he would have a better grasp of the general principles of the art of teaching?—Yes, that is so; but at the present moment I don't think that they have the same practical acquaintance with the subject.

21790. But my question goes exclusively on the supposition that the necessary special training was provided for the ordinary school teacher?—Yes, I quite agree with you.

21791. This, however, throws no discredit on your present teachers of woodwork—at present the work is in the hands of artisan teachers, and it is done perfectly to your satisfaction?—It is.

21792. I think you said there was some difference between your Edinburgh system of school woodwork and the Sloyd system?—There is not a great difference.

21793. By the Sloyd system you probably understand that special form of instruction in wood that is practised in the schools of Sweden?—Yes, that is so.

21794. Well, I always prefer speaking of that as Swedish Sloyd. May we not call your system Scottish Sloyd?—I think that is a very good term.

21795. One of the differences between the two is, that the knife is largely used in Sweden, whereas you teach rather the use of formal tools?—Yes.

21796. You are, perhaps, aware that the reason why the Sloyd knife is used in the Swedish Sloyd system is that it is one of the ordinary Swedish tools?—Yes.

21797. So that, as to this point, there really is no difference in principle; it is only in the application of the principle: the use of tools is taught in both countries, and it is only because the Sloyd knife is a common tool in Sweden that its use is so much insisted on in the Swedish Sloyd; so far, then, you don't differ in principle from the Swedes?—No.

21798. You have said that you attach great importance to this woodwork on account of its making the children handy; has it not the further advantage of training them in habits that have a far wider range of application than mere handiness, or the sphere merely of this manual work considered in itself—habits of accurate observation, for instance?—That is very important.

21799. And a sense of the importance of accuracy even in small things, and of attention even to minute differences, and general neatness and tidiness—all of which would be of use to them, whether they afterwards became workers in wood, or workers in any other material, and even if they have nothing to do with manual work, but became members of one of the learned professions?—Yes, we feel that very much, and we are very particular about the accuracy of the work.

21802. You don't find that it tends to make the children backward?—No.

21803. You don't find that the children when they have passed through it, on to the ordinary school work, would be better prepared for that work if they had come in off the streets, without having had any preliminary education of any kind, than if they came, as they do, from the kindergarten training?—Not at all.

21804. It would surprise you, perhaps, to hear that when we were taking evidence in Dublin, a statement to the effect suggested by the question I have put to you, was made by a teacher of great experience?—Well, I certainly would not expect to hear that.

21805. Supposing the teacher was telling the truth, as we must assume he was, what conclusion would you draw from his statement—would you not infer that the kindergarten department must have been very badly managed in the school from which the children came on to his school?—Yes, it could not be the kind of kindergarten we are accustomed to.

21806. And I suppose you would infer that it would be the business of the Education Board in Ireland to look very closely after that particular school where the kindergarten training is thus publicly represented as of such a backward, and indeed harmful, kind?—I would think so.

21807. Now let me ask you about bookkeeping. Book-keeping, I see, is taken as a specific subject in only four of your schools. There is perhaps freedom on the part of the teachers to take up book-keeping as a specific subject?—Yes.

21808. It has never, of course, been proposed to make book-keeping an obligatory subject for boys in the Edinburgh Board Schools?—No, we found it a popular subject.

21809. But still it is taken up in only four schools in Edinburgh, whereas woodwork is taken up, in how many?—It will be in nineteen.

21810. Monsignor Molloy.—How long is it since manual training in woodwork was introduced into the schools under the School Board of Edinburgh?—It was in 18[illegible] we first established a workshop.

21811. And, consequently, the evidence you have given is founded upon the experience of five years?—Of five years.

21812. At first you did not introduce it into all the schools where it now exists?—No, we regarded it very much as an experiment.

21813. And the experiment, being successful, you extended it until it now reaches nineteen schools?—Yes, that is so.

21814. Is cookery taught in many of the schools under your Board?—It is taught in them all.

21815. How long is it since cookery was first introduced?—Just about twelve years ago, I think.

21816. Then, with respect to cookery, you have the experience of a period of at least ten years?—Yes.

21817. And the result of that experience is that you have been disposed rather to extend it [illegible]?—Yes.

21818. You have given us the figures of the absolute cost of the introduction of manual training, and it amounts to the net sum of £[illegible] a year, making allowance for the grants which you get?—That is so.

21819. From what body do those grants come?—The Science and Art Department.

21820. And the grants amount to considerably more than half the total annual cost?—About two thirds.

21821. At the present moment the total cost for 14,000 pupils is £[illegible] a year?—Yes.

[illegible]

money in building and providing tools?—Yes, and materials.

21624. The materials are allowed for in the sum of £70 a year?—Yes, that is so; the tools and the workshops themselves is the only additional expense.

21625. Now, with regard to the effect of the manual teaching, you said that you were quite convinced that it has not interfered in any degree with the proficiency of the pupils in the ordinary subjects of the school course?—That is our experience.

21626. But you have not distinct proof that it has contributed to improvement?—It is difficult to ascertain that.

21627. That refers to the pupils while they are in the school; but with respect to their subsequent career, do you consider that the introduction of manual training has fitted them better for their work in life?—Well, I am afraid that we must only hope, for I don't see how we can prove it very well; no doubt many of them have entered into trades, and so far as we know they are doing well in their trades, but it is not easy to follow them after they leave school.

21628. I did not mean to ask you for statistical evidence, but what is your opinion—do you think that those trained in manual work are better equipped for after life than if they were not so trained?—Undoubtedly.

21629. They have certain faculties trained which otherwise would have been left untrained, and these are faculties of great utility in their ordinary life?—Yes.

21630. You have said that the woodwork is popular with the boys—is it popular with the parents?—I think it is; I think they look at it from a practical point of view as being useful.

21631. Is the same true of cookery?—Undoubtedly, cookery is popular with the parents.

21632. Did you find there was any opposition on the part of the parents when these subjects were introduced first?—No, we had no opposition from the parents at all.

21633. Nor since?—No.

21634. And do you think that the parents are now better pleased to have manual work taught to the boys and cookery to the girls than to have them omitted?—Undoubtedly.

21635. So that your experience is, that parents when they become accustomed to these subjects are not unfavourable to them, but are favourable?—No; I am satisfied that the population of Edinburgh like to see these technical subjects extended.

21636. Most Rev. Dr. Walsh.—Still, I suppose, they would be very glad if someone else would pay for them?—That is the only question that would arise.

21637. Monsignor Molloy.—I don't think you have been asked whether the elements of physical science are taught in your schools?—Yes, elementary science is taught.

21638. In all the schools?—Yes, it is compulsory. It is a class subject; they have a choice of class subjects, and it is left to the headmaster to select.

Most Rev. Dr. Walsh.—It is taken in six schools.

21639. Monsignor Molloy.—Have you what are called continuation schools under your Board?—We have evening schools, which we call continuation schools.

21640. What class of pupils attend the evening schools?—The older lads and girls who have left school and desire to continue their education.

21641. Is woodwork taught in those evening schools?—Yes, in two of them.

21642. Mr. Strevens.—Cookery is taught in some?—Yes, four or five, I think.

21643. Monsignor Molloy.—With respect to the training in woodwork, do you think that in addition to the ordinary educational advantages of it, there are special advantages for those who afterwards go to technical schools?—Yes.

21644. That they are better prepared to profit by the teaching in technical schools?—Yes, in technical schools we think they have a great advantage.

21645. Rev. Dr. Wilson.—Is your School Board confined to primary education?—It is primary education with the specific subjects taught in the higher standards.

21646. Is Edinburgh placed under an Act for compulsory attendance?—It is.

21647. Do you find any difficulty in getting all the children to attend?—There is naturally some difficulty, but a very large proportion of the children attend without trouble; we have an average attendance of about 88 per cent.

21648. You commence Kindergarten with the younger children?—We do.

21649. How long do you continue to teach Kindergarten?—In the infant department?

21650. Mr. Strevens.—That includes standard I.?—Yes, in most of the schools.

21651. Rev. Dr. Wilson.—We found in some places a desire to extend it higher up?—I think there might be something to bridge over the gap between Kindergarten and technical education that we have been speaking of, such as wirework or clay modelling.

21652. Mr. Molloy.—Could you give us information about the hours that children receive instruction in woodwork?—Every lesson consists of two hours and they have it twice a week.

21653. At what time of the day? Is it after the ordinary school hours?—Most of the children are taught during the ordinary school hours, but there is one class extends for an hour later; you fill up the day with six hours, and necessarily they extend a little over the ordinary school hours.

21654. All the pupils in standards V., VI., and ex-VI. would not be away from the regular teachers of the school?—No.

21655. Only the relays of pupils who go to the woodwork?—I believe it is practically arranged that a child is only away once in three or four weeks from the other lessons.

21656. On the days that they receive this instruction, how much longer are they behind the other pupils?—About an hour.

21657. They attend that willingly?—Perfectly; the children are delighted to stay apparently.

21658. Are all the School Board schools mixed schools, of boys and girls?—They are, but we have infant departments separately.

21659. And you have a large staff of teachers, I see, close on 900?—Yes, including pupil teachers.

21660. £1 5s. 11d. was earned per child; is that only from the Elementary Education department, does it also include the Science and Art grant?—Yes.

21661. Are all the children free?—They are all free.

21662. Are they supplied with books and apparatus free?—Yes, we supply them with books.

21663. And their tools as well?—Yes, they get them too.

21664. Are there any voluntary schools in Edinburgh not connected with your School Board?—There are; there are two practising schools under the charge of the training colleges, and there is one elementary school under the Merchant Company, and there are one or two small sessional schools still left.

21665. Mr. Strevens.—There are those practising schools?—Yes.

21666. Mr. Molloy.—Is instruction in woodwork carried out in the practising school of the training college?—No, it is not.

21667. Your specialists then derive their information in this particular branch—where, pray?—The chief instructor has visited many of the countries of Europe and most of the cities of England.

21668. Captain Shaw.—Are your workshops fully occupied during the week?—No, many of them are used for cookery also; they are fully occupied with

to drop any of the other
These children have for a
s in which they are being

continue in society?—No.

21915. Dressmaking?—I don't know about dressmaking; we have one or two schools where it is carried out with great efficiency.

21916. Either those subjects might be confined to the evening schools, or you might have a day school with a higher department in which those various branches might form an important part of the curriculum?—That is what I would prefer to see.

21917. Such a school would be very useful practically?—Yes. I always feel that the evening schools labour under a great disadvantage in taking the children after a hard day's work, and you can make less impression on their minds at night.

21918. And there are a considerable number of children in Edinburgh from 12 to 15 who would never think of going to a secondary school, but might attend a school of this kind if satisfactory instruction were given?—I think they would.

21919. You have no statistics whether any of the boys who have been taught manual work have gone on to a technical school, such as Heriot's or the Heriot Watt College?—No, we have not.

21920. To-day I found that one boy who had two years' instruction in woodwork has now left school and become an engineer?—Yes.

21921. And I saw his drawing, which he had done for his woodwork; it was clearly of a kind that must have given him an enormous advantage on entering as an engineering apprentice?—I think it would be most interesting to follow the boys.

21922. It would be possible to get a collection of such cases?—Yes.

21923. And that would be a good proof, if it should turn out favourable, that this form of teaching was a great advantage?—Yes; I am much obliged to you for the suggestion.

21924. Drawing is a necessary part of the manual work?—Yes.

21925. It is of a different kind from the ordinary drawing taught in the day school?—Yes.

21926. Do you think it is necessary to have freehand drawing continued alongside this special woodwork drawing; might not the time be reduced that is given to these two forms of drawing by substituting this woodwork drawing to a certain extent for the ordinary school drawing?—I would think so, but perhaps I am hardly warranted in so speaking.

21927. You are quite clear that it is better to have a workshop attached to every school rather than have centres to which children are brought?—Yes. That is the feeling of the Board.

21928. You are quite clear that it is better to have special teachers who will teach this subject and nothing else?—Yes, that is my opinion.

21929. Seeing the time of those special instructors would be fully occupied. For instance, you say that a child leaves a class in arithmetic or geography or grammar on a certain day in the week for his woodwork instruction, but the class goes on as before because his teacher remains there; whereas if you took one of the ordinary standard teachers that class would have to be dismissed or taken after hours?—Yes; you would not know what to do with the remaining scholars who were not engaged in woodwork.

21930. That being clear, we come to the point as to whether it is better that special teacher should be an artisan, pure and simple, or a teacher who has become more or less skilled in handiwork?—Yes.

21931. You have [illegible] this volume of evidence?—I have glanced at it.

21932. You will find some very interesting statements on that point in it. For instance, at Birmingham, Mr. Hevis, Director of Manual Training, says: "What have you to say as regards a comparison of "trained teachers with artisan teachers?—That only "refers to Standards 5 and 6; I should prefer to take "a trained teacher and train him to the practical "work, than I would to take an artisan and train "him to the teaching. One reason is, because an "artisan, when he comes to a school, is of such an age "that you scarcely can train him to teach or to "manage children. There are exceptions." And then he goes on to name them. And Mr. Pearson, the Director of Instruction at Liverpool, is of precisely the same opinion?—We must take things as we find them at present.

21933. I thought you put it that the artisan teacher is to be preferred generally. But you are satisfied that the work, as you are carrying it on, is extremely useful?—Yes, and in the meantime, I think, we find the practical teacher is more capable to teach woodwork.

21934. You spoke of a large number of children who leave school after standard 5; I think at page 7 of your report you say that number is diminishing: "From the following statistics it will be seen that the percentage of children under 13 years of age in the fifth standard is rapidly becoming smaller"?—Yes.

21935. That is to say the children are not leaving school at 11 years of age so much as they did?—Yes.

21936. Rev. Dr. Wilson.—Are you not favourable to having centres for teaching woodwork or cookery, and schools coming to those centres?—They, no doubt, are necessary in some cases, but they are attended with a good deal of inconvenience, and we believe there is less inconvenience and more profitable instruction given where we can teach them within our own walls in each case.

21937. Where you have such large schools as you have in Edinburgh; but that is the difficulty?—Yes, I can understand that it might be inconvenient in other towns.

21938. Most Rev. Dr. Walsh.—At page 16 of your report there are some figures that it would be well to have cleared up. There is a table giving the results of the "*Leaving Certificate*" examination. It strikes me that there is a very large percentage of failures. I don't wish to go into the figures in detail. I may just put this one point to you: Does this really represent the work of the elementary schools of Edinburgh?—Well, the failures are due to the fact that the Leaving Certificate, for one thing, is a comparatively new institution, and they put forward pupils who have been in other schools, but really have very little prospect of passing.

21939. In the first place, is it not a fact that a great many of these pupils are examined from higher schools—I mean secondary schools? I will take one particular figure: 330 pupils were examined in English, and of these, two-thirds failed and only one-third passed—that is, 110 passed, 220 failed; and in arithmetic, out of 498 examined, only 233 passed and 275 failed?—I think your Grace must remember that the *Leaving Certificate*, after all, is a certificate which is foreign to a primary school—it is a secondary school certificate.

21940. That is what I suggest. Is it not also a fact that many of the better educated children of your primary schools are drawn away by some other examination; you have these fine schools, the Heriot schools?—It is quite true; they have to compete for bursaries at various parts of the year.

21941. Then, so many of the more promising class of children being taken out of this examination, it would not be at all fair to take these figures as representing the work of the elementary schools of Edinburgh?—No; that is quite so.

Edinburgh.
[illegible]

Mr. Alexander Gray, Member of the Edinburgh School Board, examined.

[CHAIRM]an.—I believe that you are a mem[ber of the School] Board of Edinburgh?—Yes, my lord.

I think, you can give us some infor[mation as to t]he cost of providing workshops and [tools] in connection with the manual work?[—I think] that I have is very much what Mr. [... said].

[There] are some points of detail which we [might ask, par]ticularly as regards the minimum cost. [Do you] think workshops could be erected [according to the] number of pupils to be taught, and [provi]ding tools, and so on?—I have got [an estimate] from our architect, and he makes out [the cost o]f a workshop is somewhere between [...]—a complete workshop, fitted up with [...]

[What] sort of a workshop?—Built of stone [wit]h benches, such as described by Mr. [...]

[We s]aw some workshops in Birmingham [not] built of stone, but built of wood with [iron] roofs, and they appear to have been [of sm]aller cost. Have you any experience [of] that kind?—We have never put up [any of] that kind. Of course, stone is the [material of the co]untry, and comparatively cheap here, [and subst]antial and economical.

[In th]e case of Ireland, where money is not [plentiful], and the schools are not large, our [object is t]o find out how cheaply a second build[ing could be erec]ted?—I don't think you could put up [a workshop for ver]y much less than £400. It might be [...]

[...], a teacher told us the other day that, [doing it with hi]s own hands as it, he put one up for [...] indeed. Perhaps that is hardly a [...] hope to do it for a smaller sum than [...]ould not want a very large one for a [...]?—Mr. Macrae has spoken upon all [these po]ints, but there was one thing I would [like to say] to you. The one great advantage of [manual training] is this, that it helps boys to choose [the work] they are best fitted for. A teacher [...] knows what occupation to choose, but [when they] have a couple of years in the work[shop he can t]ell at once whether they have got a [...] aptitude for anything with their fingers, [which, I thin]k, is a matter of considerable import[ance. Then] you spoke of a school not having a [...] I would like to mention that [...] for two years have been try[ing to get acc]ommodation for a workshop; we think [that] for that school we would do almost [...] accommodation for it, but we could not [...]. I would like also to mention that [...]-keeping is not a special subject [in ...]ny many of our schools, yet it is [...] of our schools. Many of them teach [it to a greate]r less extent. Then in some schools [manual ins]truction is carried on from kindergarten [to the] workshop. That is the aim of some [...], and we hope it will be carried out [to a greater] extent before very long.

21952. The introduction of manual instruction has the effect of putting the two views of the case before the pupils' minds?—That is so.

21953. They get a certain amount of book instruction and a certain amount of practical instruction, and their minds are thus opened to the fact that there are two lines of occupation in life?—That matter you first mentioned is accentuated by the fact that boys get bigger wages when they go as messengers or clerks. Better wages at the beginning, and very much lower at the end of their career, and children are attracted by the immediate advantage.

21954. Then it is important to have something that will give them a bend in the other direction, or that, at all events, will in some way turn their thoughts in the direction of practical work?—Yes.

21955. Chairman.—I see that Mr. Davis, the Director at Birmingham, stated that the building we had there cost about £400. He then went on to say in answer to a question by myself:—"Then there would be an initial expense in a case of that sort at any rate of £400 for the building and benches, before you began to provide either tools or materials"?—His answer was:—"If you build on to a school you will get it very much cheaper. That is entirely a separate building. It is a good building. The foundations are good. You could build one for £250. That would answer the purpose very well. It is a case where you can spend as much as you like"?—By building it up against another building, you would save money in that way.

21956. Monsignor Molloy.—Perhaps you could tell us sir, what is the cost per child, taking all your schools together, for the education which they receive?—The annual cost; I understand it was approximately about £3 per child.

21957. It would be the total cost divided by the number of children?—On the average roll, £2 6s. 4½d., and on the average attendance, £3 13s.

21958. It is £3 13s. per pupil on the average attendance?—Yes, and the average cost to the ratepayers is £1 3s. 0½d., the difference being made up of grants.

21959. Then the portion of the cost represented by the manual training is, as we had before, £225 for 1,400 pupils, which I make up to be 3s. 2d. per pupil?—Yes. I would like to mention that the cooking does not cost the ratepayers anything. The grants we earn pay for all the cost of the cookery instruction and everything.

21960. The principal cost of the cooking is the payment of the teachers?—Yes.

21961. And that is covered?—That is covered by the grants from South Kensington.

21962. So that so far as the ratepayers are concerned it costs nothing?—It costs nothing.

21963. Mr. Molloy.—May I ask you what are the various sources of income of the School Board?—We have the Government grant, the grant in aid of fees, the grant for specific subjects, and, of course, the charge on the rates.

21964. What is the charge upon the rates?—6½d.

Edinburgh.

Oct. 28, 1897.

Mr. Alexander Gray.

31968. Have you any idea what the number on the rolls is of the voluntary schools outside the operation of the School Board?—It is a very small number.

31969. In proportion to the population of Edinburgh, what number of pupils are under instruction—one in five, or six or seven of the population?—Well, I don't know that. There are 32,500 children in the Board Schools.

31970. Captain SHAW.—There is a reference in your report to a system of prize-giving. Could you explain what it is?—We instituted prizes for regular attendance. We minuted that there would be a prize given to every child who made a perfect attendance during the year, and that worked exceedingly well.

31971. It says here only as regards people who attended regularly before?—That means the people who were in the habit of coming to school regularly got regular habits, the prizes did not matter to them.

31972. I think your statement is the other way, that it is only those who came regularly before that won the prizes?—The bad ones were not much influenced by the prizes, because when they were unable to come in for one day they got discouraged at the beginning of the session and did not exert themselves.

31973. Is the prize of any value?—We began at 5s., but so many children earned it we brought it down to 2s. 6d., and there are some of them even lower.

31974. Mr. HARRINGTON.—It has been stated by a teacher in a prominent position in Ireland, that he considered one of the objections to the introduction of manual work was that it was meant for boys of a tender age, ten or eleven, and it would be physically impossible for them to handle the tools and so forth at that age; is that your opinion?—Not at all.

31975. You think that objection is quite groundless from your experience?—I think so, the tools are very light, they are not heavy. I have seen no evidence of that whatever.

31976. In no way you consider is a hardship on the children?—Not the least, they are delighted at it.

31977. Rev. Dr. EVANS.—Has the Compulsory Act added to the number on the rolls of the schools of Edinburgh?—Oh, yes, I think so.

31978. To the number on the rolls?—I think so.

31979. Has it increased the average attendance in proportion?—Well, perhaps, not in proportion, but I think it has increased the average attendance.

31980. That would necessarily follow to some extent, but has it in proportion?—That I am not prepared to say.

31981. Could you help me to understand this paragraph on page 15, "The work in each of these schools was examined by Lieut.-Colonel G. Cunningham, R.E., local Inspector of Drawing and Manual Instruction for Edinburgh and district." What does this gentleman do?

Captain SHAW.—He is temporary Inspector of the Science and Art Department.

31982. Rev. Dr. EVANS.—He is local but he is at the same time under the Science and Art Department?—That is so.

31983. And your manual work is conducted under the Science and Art Department and they pay for it?—Yes.

Edinburgh.
Oct. [illegible]
Mr. David Graham.

Board Schools?—The capacity at the present time is for 1,800, what I mean by that is that if the workshops were always filled there would be 1,800 taught every week.

22009. Are there any evening schools for the instruction of teachers in manual work, and, if so, what is your experience of them?—We have had classes for the instruction of teachers but we have not got them now, they are discontinued.

22010. They were a failure?—In point of fact they were not a failure in so far as the teachers were able to take certificates, but the teachers could see no outlet for having this work in their ordinary day schools.

22011. Why was that? Was it because you always employed artisan teachers or because of the expense?—One reason was because we always employ artisan teachers, but another reason and possibly a more important reason is that an ordinary teacher generally has a class of forty boys; now in the woodwork he is not able to take any more than twenty and the difficulty at once arises what would the other half of the class be doing while the teacher was engaged in manual work.

22012. That was assuming that the manual work was taught during school hours and not in extra hours?—Exactly so, and manual work is taught at present in school hours.

22013. What is the composition of the boys who attend the Evening School Manual Training class?—I may say, to begin with, that these evening schools are not under my charge, but I have been furnished with this information. There are classes in connection with two evening schools, Stockbridge and South Bridge. The class in Stockbridge has been increasing annually, it began in 1885 with thirty pupils, next year it increased to fifty-five, while this session the number is seventy-one. That last number includes the following trades.—Messenger boys, 13; compositors, 7; clerks, 7; joiners, 7; telegraph messengers, 4; tailors, 3; plumbers, 3; masons, 3; cabinet makers, 3; grocers, 3; brassfounders, 3; upholsterers, 2; printers, 2, and 1 each of the following, organ builder, gardener, draper, brass finisher, coach builder, engineer, bell hanger, silversmith, jeweller, golf maker, bookbinder, cabinetmaker and stereotyper.

22014. Most Rev. Dr. Walsh.—The inspector has given the mark "excellent" on each occasion that he examined the school?—On every occasion.

22015. I take it this does not necessarily mean that he would give the mark "excellent" to each individual pupil?—The examination is a class one, and the mark is given on the work done by the whole.

22016. And I suppose that it does not even imply that each individual pupil was examined?—No.

22017. All the pupils might, as a matter of fact, happen to be examined, but that is not at all implied by the fact that the mark "excellent" was given to the class?—No.

22018. What is it that determines the amount of the grant that will be paid to the school?—The number of attendances made by the pupils.

22019. But on a given number of attendances you may have a higher grant or a lower one?—No, on the boy that you claim on, you must have fifteen attendances, but you can only get one grant on that particular attendance.

children, or the standard that they have reached in the school, that should be looked to if we are deciding at what point woodwork instruction should be given?—I would say the age.

22025. In your Scotch system this branch comes in with the fifth standard; may I take it that this is so because it is thought that pupils of the average age of the fifth standard, and even the lowest age of the fifth standard, may be put to woodwork without inconvenience; in other words, it is not because they are in the fifth standard that they are put to woodwork, but because the children of the fifth standard are of an age at which woodwork may well be commenced?—Practically it amounts to that.

22026. So if you found in any other part of the country, or in another country, children of the fourth standard who were of the age that your children are in the fifth standard, you would not consider that woodwork should necessarily be deferred to the fifth standard?—No. I would begin at the fourth standard.

22027. Mr. Stephenson.—Is it not the case that some children in the fourth standard are taught?—Yes, when we have room.

22028. Most Rev. Dr. Walsh.—But of course you would not take particularly young children?—We take them indiscriminately.

22029. What is the youngest age at which children are brought into this woodwork with you?—I don't think there are any under ten.

22030. But there are some between ten and eleven?—A fair number.

22031. And you never found it physically impossible to teach these children to handle tools?—No.

22032. We saw some of these younger children in school today, and I think you told me there that some of them have done excellent work, not merely handling tools, but handling them with skill and success?—I have often found that the boy dull at ordinary work was very good at woodwork.

22033. Did it ever end by his ceasing to be dull at the other work; did you find that it had the useful effect of encouraging him, so that he came gradually to get on better with his ordinary work?—I cannot speak for the ordinary work.

22034. As we have heard that elsewhere, I may ask you would it surprise you to hear of its having that effect?—No, I should rather expect it.

22035. That is, you should expect it from the general knowledge that you have of the effect of woodwork instruction on the intelligence of the children?—I should expect it for that reason.

22036. Monsignor Molloy.—Do you find that the boys generally are interested in the work?—Very much so.

22037. Is there much diversity between them as to fitness for the work?—Some do better than others, but they all do it.

22038. Can you say that they all profit by it?—Undoubtedly.

22039. At present each boy gets two hours a week for woodwork; which should you consider it better to have that two hours together on one day of the week, or to have one hour on each two days?—I should prefer to have two hours continuous.

22040. Why?—Because there is a certain amount [illegible]

22044. With regard to this rate that you receive what local authority has the power to strike the rate in Edinburgh, is it the School Board?—The Parish Council.

22045. Mr. MOLLOY.—Is more attention given to drawing in the manual workrooms than to the pupils who do not attend there?—The pupils who come to manual work get all the drawing given in the manual work, and they get class work in the ordinary school.

22046. In the ordinary school what is the most advanced kind of drawing, does it go beyond freehand, do they draw from objects?—I am not able to speak on that matter.

22047. In one school today we found arrangements for cookery in the same room with the manual instruction work, does any inconvenience arise from that?—From my point of view I prefer that the woodwork room should be a cookery room also.

22048. Why is that?—I find that when the workshop is also used for cookery it is kept much cleaner.

22049. CHAIRMAN.—The cook cleans it up for the woodwork?—No.

22050. Mr. STRUTHERS.—Perhaps the cook objects if the room is not clean when she comes?—I don't know.

22051. Mr. MOLLOY.—You have, I presume, a detailed scheme for a three years' course in woodwork?—I have.

22052. Would you do the Commissioners the favour of letting us have a copy of it?—I will.

22053. Captain SHAW.—With regard to these artisan teachers you said they went through a course of drawing at one of the technical schools, was that after they were appointed or before?—Before.

22054. Were they selected because they were people who were paying attention to manual education?—That was one of the reasons.

22055. And in selecting them you took care that they were men who had taken pains in their own education?—Yes.

22056. Therefore you perhaps got a superior man to the village carpenter?—Decidedly.

22057. Do you think the village carpenter would be a suitable teacher?—If he took it up in the proper spirit.

22058. But then he would require training before you took him in?—Yes.

22059. With regard to this course, you have drawn it up yourself?—I have.

22060. Do you find it work satisfactorily?—Yes, as testified by the Science and Art returns.

22061. But, as judged by your own criticism, do you feel you are hampered by the regulations under which you have got to work?—To a certain extent I am.

22062. Would you let us know how?—Well, I don't believe in annual examinations. I should prefer the Department to send only at stated times their inspector to see the work being done, not to have an examination, as we have at present.

22063. You prefer to have an inspection, not to have an examination?—Yes.

22064. But as to the course of woodwork which you carry out, whether it is inspected or examined, does that affect it very much?—As long as the Science and Art Department pay grants we must to a certain extent prepare our course to earn that grant.

22065. But they don't lay down that you are to do any particular course of woodwork?—No, but they lay down a certain examination, and unless you make your course suitable you won't be able to perform that examination.

22066. Then what is objectionable in the examination?—I think the examination, as it is conducted just now, is too much on the lines of trade joints and things of that kind. I think a child in woodwork gives more attention to it, and takes a greater interest in it if he is working at an article that will afterwards be useful.

22067. They make a considerable number of articles in your course?—Yes, but they are sometimes making an object that has really no value, except an educational value, attached to it.

22068. Would you prefer they should make useful models from the beginning?—Yes, decidedly.

22069. How should the instruction be conducted?—I would instruct them just as I do now; but I would not continue to give them examination tests, as I have to do at the present time. At the present time I have to stop everything, the work in the bench for a day or two before the examination and give them test exercises.

22070. And the work which they get to do now at the inspection is not the work in your book?—Sometimes it is and sometimes it is not.

22071. Then you don't think it is a fair test of the children's ability to construct an object from a drawing which they have not seen before?—Well, it is a fair enough test of the work to construct an object, but I don't see that it is a fair test after one year's instruction.

22072. Would you prefer it after more than one year's instruction?—Yes, I believe it would be valuable after two years' instruction.

22073. Mr. HARRINGTON.—Is there any objection on the part of the trades to this manual instruction in schools?—We have not had any in Edinburgh.

22074. There is no idea that you are encouraging too many boys to become carpenters, and flooding the market in that way?—No, we have had no objection of that kind.

22075. Rev. Dr. EVANS.—Is truancy practised in the Edinburgh schools?—I have never heard anything of it—I don't know.

22076. I wanted to find out, if I could, whether manual instruction did anything to cure that vice?—As to that I cannot say.

22077. Is manual instruction taught in the voluntary schools?—The voluntary schools in the town don't take manual work so far as I know.

22078. Do the pupil teachers receive manual instruction?—No, not at present.

22079. Are pupil teachers examined one by one by the inspector?—They get no manual work, and I am not sure as to how they are examined by the inspector.

22080. Mr. STRUTHERS.—I think you said you had some children in the fourth standard taking manual work?—I have.

22081. You don't get any grant for these pupils?—No.

22082. So you teach them without any prospect of a grant?—Without any view of getting a grant.

22083. Simply because you think it is good for these children educationally?—That is so.

22084. That is a very strong proof of the value you and the Board attach to this form of instruction?—Yes.

22085. As regards the examination, you get a bonus of 20 per cent. if a class pass "excellent" from the Science and Art examiners, and, of course, if a class did very badly in a supposititious case the grant would be withdrawn or reduced?—Yes.

22086. You prefer to have inspection rather than examination you say—inspection of the classes, and the inspector coming and seeing their work going on?—Exactly.

22087. Rather than have a fixed examination at which the pupils have to come out then?—Yes.

22088. In that way the inspector would be able to give more attention to the method of instruction than he is able to do at present?—Yes.

22089. Is that point inquired into at present, the method by which you teach?—I may say that we have at present, inspection by Mr. Blair, the inspector for the district, but over and above his inspection we have the annual examination.

Edinburgh.
Oct. 23, 1897.
Mr. [illegible] Gordon.

Edinburgh.

Oct. [illegible]

Mr. David [illegible]

23090. Then the annual examination is confined chiefly to testing the pupils?—Wholly to testing the pupils.

23091. There is no notice taken of how the class is taught, the methods of work?—The Inspector sees the pupils do the work.

23092. Captain Shaw.—Has the teacher never to give demonstrations to the pupils?—He demonstrates to the class on the model that has to be made.

23093. Mr. Strutt.—That shows how he does his work?—I think you objected to the test set at the examination, from this point of view, that you more or less know the sort of test that will be set, and you feel obliged to prepare for it?—That is what it amounts to.

23094. You know pretty well the type of thing that is to be set, and, consequently, you take the pupils' time to prepare them, when you would be rather doing other work, if left a free hand?—That is so.

23095. Then as to the class of teachers, you said that there is no opportunity of receiving practical instruction in woodwork in Scotland; you yourself conducted some classes for teachers, did you not?—I did.

23096. And did they make good progress under you?—Very good, indeed.

23097. Would they be capable teachers of woodwork if they took it in hands, from your point of view, from what you know of their work?—I would not say they would be capable teachers for a whole course, but they might be capable for the first part.

23098. But they might improve?—Yes, if they applied themselves to the work.

23099. Chairman.—You would not like to say they were capable teachers until you had seen them teach?—It amounts to that.

23100. Mr. [illegible].—These were men who had considerable experience in the teaching of other subjects?—Yes, but a man ought to have a thorough knowledge of the work he professes to teach.

23101. But he may have that combined with the general education that a teacher gets before he begins to teach at all?—That is quite possible.

23102. And you gave a reason why these men could not be employed in Edinburgh, and it was that they would be taken away from their other classes?—Yes.

23103. But suppose you multiplied your present assistants—I am only putting a suppositious case—suppose you had teachers who had been trained to do these different kinds of work and devoted themselves entirely to manual work, just as your present assistants do, theoretically at all events they would be more capable teachers?—Yes, theoretically.

23104. We cannot say more except from the experience of other towns. It would be quite possible then that they might take the place of your present assistants?—If they were to devote their whole attention to it they might.

23105. Your objection was that they would necessarily be employed in taking another class and be withdrawn from that class to manual instruction?—Yes.

23106. But it is quite possible that a teacher might devote his whole time to manual work or to manual work and drawing. Would it not be a good thing to have manual work and drawing throughout taught by some one man?—I would rather devote the man's time to having a continuation of some form of manual work from where it is left at the present time in kindergarten, carrying it right up through the school. The same man might teach drawing.

23107. Have you any oversight of such work as is done at present?—No, I have no official position.

23108. But you are a sort of informal adviser?—[illegible] I am asked.

23109. Did you not conduct some classes for instruction in cardboard work?—I did.

23110. And you might conduct other classes of a similar kind if the Board found it expedient to introduce these various branches of instruction?—I should be pleased to do so.

23111. You say you would like the same man to look after both woodworking and preliminary manual exercises?—Yes.

23112. Would you not extend that and say the same man might look after all forms of manual work and drawing, seeing they are so intimately connected?—It would be advisable to do that.

23113. Are not the two things of very much the same nature?—Yes, and the training for one very similar to the training for the other.

23114. And does it not help the teaching of drawing when they see the practical application of it in the work?—Yes, the lesson is much more valuable.

23115. So that this being one consolidated piece of work, as it were, it is better it should be in the hands of one set of teachers?—Yes.

23116. Monsignor Molloy.—Suppose you had an intelligent teacher with an aptitude to learn woodwork, but without any training in it, what amount of teaching would he require to make him fit to teach it?—That to a certain extent is an unknown quantity. It depends on the man in the first place and the amount of time he could devote to it.

23117. How much time do you think he must devote to it before he is fit to teach it, supposing him to have an aptitude for learning it?—Possibly 500 or 600 hours.

23118. Say one hour a day for two years?—Yes, I should say so.

23119. Now take the case of a boy who has learned woodwork at school as you are now teaching it to your pupils, and suppose him afterwards to go to a training college, how long would he require at that college in order to fit himself for teaching woodwork?—While learning the educational theory connected with it, he would acquire additional practical skill.

23120. As regards practical knowledge, you think he has already acquired enough at school?—His practical knowledge would be much in advance of his theoretical knowledge; we don't teach the theory at all.

23121. Suppose a boy who has learned woodwork at school for two years under such a teacher as you are, what additional time would he require in a training college to fit him to teach woodwork to his pupils?—To begin with he would require 200 or 250 hours spread over a course.

23122. Mr. Strutt.—In order to acquire further practical skill?—Yes.

23123. Monsignor Molloy.—Not only to acquire practical skill in his work, but also to acquire the art of teaching the work to others?—Yes.

23124. Mr. Strutt.—From those classes you yourself conducted for teachers you said some of them in your opinion were qualified to give the instruction, how long did that course last?—About six months the first year and six months the second year.

23125. And how often did they attend per week during that time?—Once.

23126. And how long was the lesson?—Two hours.

23127. So that it was one lesson of two hours per week for six months, followed by a similar course the second year. That gives a practical test of what you consider would be sufficient instruction for men who had some capacity for this subject?—They would have got so much information on the subject as to be able to begin to teach it, but to become skilled teachers they would require much more.

22128. CHAIRMAN.—You are Head Master of the Sciennes School, Edinburgh?—That is so, my lord.

22129. You are conversant with the manual training and science work and drawing taught in that school?—Yes.

22130. When was the school opened?—March, 1892.

22131. What is the accommodation in the school?—The accommodation in the building is roughly 2,000, but for teaching purposes 1,517.

22132. What was the average attendance last year?—1,411.

22133. What does the staff include?—Twenty-six certificated teachers, eleven pupil teachers, three special teachers for sewing, special instructors for woodwork, singing, gymnastics, cookery, and swimming.

22134. Has woodwork been taught in the school since the opening of it?—Within six months after the opening of the school; it was begun in October.

22135. By whom was it taught?—By Mr. Graham, but the woodwork department was so far started by myself before Mr. Graham's appointment.

22136. Was Mr. Graham an artisan?—He was an artisan at that time who had qualified by drawing and teaching in the evening classes, and his appointment was recommended by myself because of my knowledge of him as a teacher and his skill as an artisan.

22137. Do all the boys in the fifth standard and upwards take woodwork?—Yes, that is to say about 200 boys.

22138. Only excluding those who for some physical or other reasons are not fit?—That means very few.

22139. How many days weekly is the instructor employed?—Three days a week, giving eight sections.

22140. On the other days of the week how is the room used?—It is used as a cookery room on Mondays and Fridays.

22141. Do you find any difficulty or any advantage in the combined use of the room?—The plan in the Edinburgh schools was largely due to my suggestion for the use of a room that I had in the school at that time standing empty. There was no woodwork in operation under the Board; this room was meant to be a cookery room; we could only employ the teacher for two days in the week, and I suggested the utilising of it for woodwork and giving the full five days' use for the room. I have found it fully to come up to my expectations, in so far as it puts the cookery and woodwork in the same relation to myself as head master as the other subjects in the school.

22142. What other occupations are taught in the school beginning with the infant department?—We have a more or less temporary scheme that varies from year to year according to the capabilities of the assistant teachers; we have mat-weaving, brush-drawing, pattern-making with coloured papers, designing in colours, and in some of the upper standards map-drawing of a more or less advanced kind; occasionally cardboard when we get a teacher who can take it, and clay-modelling. We have all these things going on in the various classes of the school.

22143. And you include all these under the head of kindergarten occupations?—Yes; I prefer the "Continuation of kindergarten."

22144. Are such occupations popular with the pupils?—They are very highly popular with the pupils.

22145. And the parents don't object?—There have been no objections in the six years since we have been started; it has happened that parents have asked explanations, but no objection has been taken.

22146. What do you consider the benefits derived, both direct and indirect benefits?—The indirect benefit would be in the increased interest a boy takes in all his work from having this change of occupation that this hand and eye work gives him.

22147. Do you think that it improves the physical powers of the boy?—It does, it distinctly improves his physical powers. I look upon it as part of the physical education of the school, that we give a good deal of attention to elsewhere.

22148. Do boys take more readily to a trade?—I think they do. I have this last year tabulated the trades and employments to which seventy boys who have left since last March and passed standard 6 or 7 have gone. I find of these, twenty-two had gone to trades; that is an unusually large proportion in a town where there are so many other occupations for lads of that age. Of these trades seven were connected with woodwork, five were joiners, pure and simple, one was a cabinet-maker, a very special case, and one was a golf-club maker. The lad who went to cabinet-making was a boy very far back and old when he joined me in standard 3, fourteen years of age, and hopelessly dull at his work. He stayed until past standard 5, and was then two years at woodwork, and he turned out to be capable of excellent work, at least he is turning out. Thirty have gone to shops, that is because we have a large shop-keeping element among the parents of the pupils. The rest have gone to odds and ends, such as postal telegraph and teaching.

22149. REV. DR STARK.—Have any gone on to the University?—No.

22150. CHAIRMAN.—I have a table here which embodies what you have told us, and also gives the average age of your school as compared with other Board schools?—That is so.

22151. What do you consider the indirect advantages?—I have nothing to add to what I have already stated. It improves them in their skill in drawing distinctly, especially the model drawing, that we teach from standard 5 upwards; five and six take drawing from models in connection with freehand and drawing to scale.

22152. And you find that it gives relief to their minds by change of occupation?—Yes.

22153. And also improves the regularity of attendance in the younger classes?—Yes, these several forms of employment we have in the lower standards. I have not noticed much difference in the attendance, partly because our school has a very high average. Last month about 91 per cent. was our average attendance even after the holidays, and this week we are as high as 91 per cent.

22154. What are the drawbacks to the introduction of woodwork?—The main drawback to a headmaster of a school with a number of departments in it is that we have to add it to a curriculum that is very full on account of the number of extra subjects we take in our schools, and we have [illegible]. When we take on this manual training, which takes about two hours, or one-twelfth of the ordinary time, away from those subjects it breaks up the work of the schools, and the assistant teachers rather object to that, and I think to some extent they have reason. But that is also local to Edinburgh, in so far as the lesson is two hours in length. I would rather, as a headmaster, prefer the single hour lesson; it is better for the general work of the school, although not perhaps so good for the woodwork itself.

22155. When you say that it breaks up a class I understand, from former evidence, that a certain number of boys are taken out of a particular class this week, and they are taken out of another class next week, but I suppose that next week some other boys will be taken out of the first class, and the third week different boys again?—That is so; but the arrangement that has been mentioned has been in force for six years. We were the school that started this woodwork, and that is my own arrangement of rotating the classes, beginning with A, following with

Edinburgh. [illegible]

B and C, and after that beginning with B next week.

23156. You have some observations upon the subject of science; what do you say about elementary science in connection with your school?—We have taught elementary science for the last six years. For the first four we had it as a class subject earning the 2s. grant; two years ago that was changed in the Scotch code and put under a separate article for a 1s. grant, and we still continue to teach the same subject under the same syllabus.

23157. You annex a copy of the scheme?—I annex a copy of the scheme.

23158. Perhaps you will kindly tell us what is taught under the head of science?—We teach elementary science under three divisions—elementary botany or plant life, elementary zoology or animal life, and elementary chemistry. We lead up from the infant department with specially graded object lessons, to the beginning of the science proper in standard 3; we try to make the teaching as objective as possible in the lower classes, and only begin the idea of classification as we advance to the upper.

23159. I think that you say the lessons are taught by the ordinary class teacher and given in the ordinary class-room, although the necessary preparations are made in the laboratories?—That is so.

23160. What happened when the class had to be moved into the demonstration room proper?—I found it led to a considerable waste of time, and the assistant teacher frequently omitted to take the class when he found some other lesson that was perhaps pressing.

23161. Was it optional with him?—No, but it occasionally happened he could have a temporary reason for not going.

23162. Are the lessons in all cases practical?—Yes, largely.

23163. The objects are seen and handled as far as possible?—That is so.

23164. And the aim has been to convey useful information and cultivate the powers of observation?—That is so.

23165. Is the lantern used?—We use the lantern for science and geography, especially in the winter months.

23166. Is it used in the ordinary class-room?—An ordinary class-room that can be darkened with five minutes preparation.

23167. A supply of slides illustrate the botany and zoology lessons more particularly?—Yes.

23168. What are the qualifications of the teachers?—They have the ordinary certificate of the Education Department, but they have qualified locally for this particular work by taking science classes in the Heriot Watt College.

23169. Are some of the lessons kept and submitted to Her Majesty's Inspector at his annual visit?—That is so.

23170. Are any text-books used by the pupils?—No text-books are used by the pupils.

23171. What sort of science is taught?—Elementary science.

23172. What do you think is the proper function of a public school in this kind of instruction?—To give the basis of a general scientific education that

23177. By whom is it taught?—By the ordinary staff for, roughly speaking, two hours per week.

23178. Do you think two hours a fair allowance?—A fair allowance, considering the state of our curriculum.

23179. What do you say about the sewing class?—The sewing classes go for three hours per week, they are taken in rotation, and that leaves boys free to take up drawing when the girls are at their sewing room.

23180. You have a separate staff for teaching sewing?—That is so.

23181. Mr. [illegible].—Are the girls taught drawing?—No.

23182. Chairman.—The pupils, as a rule, must take the drawing in the standard in which they are placed for ordinary subjects?—That is the rule.

23183. Why is that so?—It is impossible to have a separate classification in the Edinburgh schools that run these separate sewing rooms; in them the various standards are taken at different times of the day, and it follows from that that drawing must be taken at different times for different standards.

23184. You think that the Science and Art Department requires to give greater attention to this subject?—I do; in Scotch schools, with our complicated time-table, due allowance is not made for that; it is less applicable to English schools that do not teach specific subjects to the same extent as we do that have these separate departments.

23185. Do you find that while there is inequality in the individual papers worked in any one standard, there is even much more real power of drawing evinced by backward pupils than if they had been put back, say, from Standard V. to Standard II.?—I am speaking about the difficulty of getting higher grants of the Science and Art Department in the Scotch schools. None of the Edinburgh schools last year earned the mark "excellent" for drawing. That is unusual from the English average, the reason being that we cannot put backward pupils back to lower standards for drawing purposes.

23186. Are you of opinion that drawing to scale should be postponed from Standard IV. to Standard V.?—I am.

23187. Do you think that solid geometry should be removed from the requirements altogether, and relegated to the syllabus which has to do with the work of the specialist?—That is so.

23188. Does the same apply to geometrical drawing?—Yes, the advanced geometrical drawing as given in the 6th standard, the alternative course.

23189. With regard to the inspection of drawing, what do you say about that?—We rather object to the papers going up to the Department, and not being judged on the spot by the Inspector, who sees the methods as well as the results of the teaching.

23190. Then you think that the ordinary Inspector, resident in Edinburgh, would be the best person?—That is so.

23191. Most Rev. Dr. Walsh.—I see it suggested by one of the head masters that the rule requiring three hours sewing per week, in the case of girls, might well be relaxed; have you formed any opinion on that point?—It might be relaxed in what we call the ex-6th standard; that has a very heavy amount of work

boys solid geometry?—The broad fact that we have to have so many expedients to bring it home to the average child shows it is beyond his particular development for the time.

22356. Does not the manual instruction help you in that?—It does to some extent, not to a great extent. As a matter of fact, Mr. Graham would tell you that he prefers the teaching of geometry to precede the particular manual drawing he is giving for the year.

22357. But you think that it ought to be abolished altogether?—Yes.

22358. A difference of opinion?—Not a difference of opinion; but Mr. Graham finds the teaching by the ordinary school teachers advantageous to him in his work.

22359. Rev. Dr Wilson.—You say that religious instruction is given for half an hour, who gives that?—The ordinary class teachers.

22360. What does that instruction consist of?—We have a regular syllabus of instruction drawn up by the School Board to which we adhere, taking up the various parts of the Bible in rotation from year to year.

22361. Have you any conscience clauses?—We have, and that is taken advantage of by three classes in the day, those that don't take the Old Testament, those that don't take the New, and those that don't take the shorter catechism we teach in the schools.

22362. Have you some that don't take the Old Testament?—We have.

22363. And some that don't take the New?—Yes, we have a number of Jews in the schools.

22364. Mr. Stevenson.—You, as head-master, are impartially interested in all the school subjects?—That is so.

22365. Being in that position you still think it advisable to introduce manual occupations in the various standards?—Yes.

22366. Did you find that it introduced a complication into the time-table?—It does in a school that is already complicated.

22367. That applies particularly to the higher standards beyond standard 5?—It does.

22368. And that enters there largely because your school being a more advanced school you prepare pupils for the leaving certificate examination?—That is so.

22369. You do a great deal of special subject work

standard 3 and into standard 2 completely. I put that down to the thorough training, in arithmetic for example, that is so much improved by the counting training that comes from kindergarten work.

22278. Then in these standards you have not found it necessary to omit any part of the regular school work?—No part of the work.

22279. You would not introduce this subject in those standards unless you were satisfied that it did not do any harm to the efficiency in writing, reading, and arithmetic?—That is so.

22280. In your school, as in every other school in Scotland, you have what are called class subjects, perhaps you will explain to the Commission what those class subjects are?—We have a choice of four or five subjects that are called class subjects—English, geography, history, elementary science, and, if need be, some form of manual training. We must make a choice of two of these—at least we must not make a choice of two, but we can make a choice of two, and the examination of Her Majesty's inspector is not an individual examination but a class examination. There are standard subjects, class subjects, and specific subjects.

22281. Most Rev. Dr. Walsh.—The standard subjects being the three elementary subjects?—Yes, the standard subjects are reading, writing, and arithmetic. The class subjects are a choice among a set of five—two of the five; we take English and geography. The five are English, geography, history, some form of manual instruction, and elementary science.

22282. Rev. Dr. Evans.—What do you include in English; how much does that cover?—There is a regular course per standard, it means getting up so much of a standard poem or work—in the 5th standard "The Merchant of Venice"—part of that; then along with that would go explanation of the text and the story of the play, and essays on the characters that the pupils would read of in that play, and a short notion of the literature, of the history, and then the formal parsing and analysis to some extent, but perhaps not so much; that is what we call English. Then in addition to these class subjects come the specific subjects, which are not very numerous and are mostly literary in Scotland.

22283. Most Rev. Dr. Walsh.—We cannot have this put too plainly. Is it that there are, in the first place, three elementary subjects; then five class subjects are set down in the Code, of which some two must be taken; and then come the specific subjects?—Yes, mathematics, the language subjects are—Latin, French, German, Greek. I had one pupil in Greek last year.

22284. What about Gaelic?—That is a special subject for the Highlands. We have extra subjects, such as navigation, the principles of agriculture, and domestic economy.

22285. Cookery?—Cookery comes in under a separate article; it is not called either a class subject or a standard subject.

22286. Then it would seem to be a specific subject?—No, it counts as a specific.

22287. Mr. Stevenson.—Special arrangements as to the hours of teaching and the manner in class have to be made, and in that way it is distinguished?—Yes.

22288. So is dairy and laundry work?—Yes, but may be 6d. or 1s., also paid on the average attendance. There is a grant for organisation and discipline, which is 1s. or 1s. 6d., according to the state of the school.

22291. These are all fixed grants?—These are all preliminary grants that practically do not depend on the success or smartness of the school.

22292. Except in so far as the organisation of the school may be good, bad, or indifferent?—That is so. In addition to these, under article 19, A¹ and A², we get 1s. grant for needlework and elementary science. Then as the standard subjects, in addition to the fixed grant of 10s., there is a variable grant of 3s., 2s., or 1s., according as the school is fair, good, or excellent, for the standard subjects.

22293. Then for the class subjects?—There are three grades of payment, 4s., 3s., or 2s., for the combined class subjects, not for them separately. In addition to that, there is a payment on the specific subjects which are paid on the individual passes of the scholar.

22294. But not a grant for the class in each specific subject?—It is not for the class, but for each individual pass in each specific subject.

22295. And how many of those specific subjects can be taken?—Two by pupils under the standard, and three beyond.

22296. Mr. Stevenson.—And no grant is made for specific subjects if the ordinary work of the school is not good?—That is so.

22297. Most Rev. Dr. Walsh.—You spoke of the 10s. fixed grant in the elementary subjects: is there not a grant that depends on the average attendance of the school; as I read the code there is some provision for such a grant; here is a provision for a capitation grant of 10s. certain, but if the average attendance in the school exceeds 55 per cent., and is under 70, they get 11s.; that seems to be provided at all events for some places, probably for districts where the population is scattered, so that the schools must have only a small attendance?—That is so in the Highlands.

22298. And so, when the attendance in a Highland school is from 50 to 75, the lowest capitation runs to 11s.; with an attendance of from 75 to 80, it is 12s.; and wherever in such districts the average attendance of the school exceeds 80, that 10s. grant is turned into a 14s. grant?—That is so, but only for special districts.

22299. Mr. Stevenson.—About the class subjects, there are five of them?—Yes.

22300. And the school may take any two or three or four?—It may, but will get no extra payment beyond what you get for the two.

22301. That is to say, the grant for class subjects is not paid on the number of subjects you take up, but the way those subjects have been used for training the intelligence of the children?—That is so.

22302. So from one point of view it is immaterial what number you take up; it is the quality of the work?—Yes. We take a third—history.

22303. Under this scheme it would be quite in your power to substitute manual work for the English?—If I thought it judicious.

22304. But you don't think it judicious?—I don't think it judicious.

22305. So you would always teach English in pre-

Edinburgh. — Oct. [illegible], 18[illegible]. — Mr. [illegible].

22311. It means the understanding of the reading lesson?—Intelligence, very largely. We don't use any grammar text-book at all, only in the upper standards.

22312. Can you say that it is not usual in the Scotch schools—in the Edinburgh schools, at any rate—to use a grammar text-book?—That is so.

22313. Except when you come to very advanced classes?—Yes.

22314. About geography, do the pupils in three, four, and five standards use a geography text-book?—They use a small text-book.

22315. Are lessons set from that text-book to be learned by heart?—No; nine-tenths of the teaching is done by a map.

22316. Have you ever seen an inspector in your school take the geography or grammar manual, and ask the class questions from it?—Never; in schools in Scotland it is an unheard of thing.

22317. Thus grammar is regarded as a subordinate subject—useful so far as it leads to the intelligent interpretation of the reading lesson?—That is so. Any grammar we take is based on the lesson.

22318. Rev. Dr. Evans.—Do you include analysis in grammar?—We do.

22319. Mr. Stevenson.—Grammar, so far as it is defined, begins with analysis?—It does; we teach our parsing as secondary to analysis.

22320. So far as formal grammar is concerned analysis is the leading part of it?—Yes.

22321. Rev. Dr. Evans.—And that is universal, so far as you know?—Yes; any assistants that come to me from other schools teach much the same.

22322. Mr. Stevenson.—You have already explained the way in which these various kinds of manual occupation and drawing are useful in developing the children's intelligence, but have you any opinion as to whether ordinary school subjects—arithmetic, for instance—might be made more practical by being taught in a different way from what it is at present?—I have not considered the teaching of it in that way. Our arithmetic is taught very largely from the mental side; we don't use text-books in the school, and the first part, practically, of every lesson in the school is a mental lesson rather than a text-book lesson.

22323. But mental arithmetic is always part of the examination?—It is. In some cases, if the inspector is satisfied with the teaching, he will only judge the class by the mental arithmetic—by the oral examination.

22324. Without any card-test at all?—Without any card-test at all.

22325. But usually he has both?—Generally he has both.

22326. Do you find it is necessary to use special cards to a large extent, in order to prepare for the inspector's examination?—No; but, in order to give the pupils practice in reading from a printed card, for the last month or two we get a set, which we use, but we never think of teaching from them.

22327. Do you attach much importance to expertness in calculation—the quickness with which they can do ordinary sums?—Yes. I find the pupils who are quickest are most accurate.

22328. So, to begin with, a teacher ought to pay more attention to quickness than accuracy?—I think so; the accuracy will come.

22329. Taking arithmetic in standard I, you don't think it would be a proper way of testing the work in that class to set the children three sums, give them an indefinite time to do it, and see how many were correct?—It would be the very acme of wrong method.

22330. Would you be in favour of having one reading book in each class to be got up thoroughly by the pupils, so that they could learn it by heart?—No. We use as many as three or four books in standard I in the course of the year.

22331. And at the examinations you frequently have a test set to the various classes in unseen Readers?—In the upper classes the test is usually wholly unseen and from that day's paper.

22332. You don't object to that system of examination?—No; we rather prefer it.

22333. They are occasionally examined in the meaning of what they have read, although the passage is unseen?—That is so.

22334. But still you don't object to it?—No.

22335. You think that leads to proper teaching of reading?—Yes.

22336. You made a remark about the inspection of drawing for examination?—I beg your pardon, it was Mr. Graham.

22337. Well, would you say the same about other subjects?—I would prefer——

22338. That you should have an inspection of your school, seeing that the work you profess to do has been done, rather than set fixed tests on a certain day?—That is so. The main reason I would give for that would be that our smart classes have to mark time for the last four or five months of the school year, while the duller classes are getting over the allotted work of the standards.

22339. You cannot risk your grade being lowered from excellent to good by putting your children forward until the examination comes?—That is so.

22340. If you had not a fixed examination?—The system of classification would be much more at my disposal.

22341. You think there are children who are being kept back for a month or two under the present system who might have been advanced if there was no fixed examination?—I quite believe so.

Mr. William B. [illegible].

Mr. William B. [illegible], Treasurer, Edinburgh School Board, examined.

22353. I think about £4,000 a year?—Yes, £4,0[illegible] last year.

22354. So that the Education Department gives you in Edinburgh £4,000 for your evening Board schools in Edinburgh, and you seem to have a further grant, a small one, from the Science and Art Department for these evening schools, £20, I think?—Yes.

22355. By means of the large sum, £80,000 raised on a day rate, you are able not only to supply free education, but school books; you spend apparently over £2,000 a year supplying the children with books?—Yes; £1,[illegible] for day schools and £1[illegible] for evening schools.

22356. It comes, I think, to an average of about 1s. 2d. per child, yearly?—Yes; 1s. 3½d. for the day schools, calculated on the average roll.

22357. And I see that you spend about £3,000 a year in providing stationery and apparatus?—Yes; £2,[illegible] for day schools and £231 for evening schools.

22358. And you also give £[illegible] for prizes?—That is so; for day schools, £511, and for evening schools £[illegible].

22359. These, I believe, are mainly prizes for attendance?—Attendance prizes.

22360. I see by the regulations that these prizes are given only to children who do not miss one attendance in the whole year?—Yes.

22361. Am I right in saying that the year before last, there were over 800 children who never missed an attendance, and that last year, owing in great measure to these attendance prizes, there were 1,700 who made that extraordinary record?—Yes. These numbers apply to the day schools.

Edinburgh.
Oct. [illegible]
Mr. William [illegible]

22362. Of course, there are other charges upon your day school rate of £80,000, over and above those concerned with the mere working of the schools?—Yes.

22363. I see that the expenses of the School Board itself, including salaries of officials, office expenses, and so forth, come to between £4,000 and £5,000?—Yes, last year it was £4,700; and then I should explain that this £80,000 also provides for the repayment of money borrowed for the erection of schools.

22364. The accounts seem to show that the Edinburgh School Board borrowed, in all, for school building purposes, over half a million sterling, £51[illegible], and that it has paid off £1[illegible] of this, with the interest, of course?—Yes.

22365. Last year the Board paid off £1[illegible] of that principal, with £11,[illegible] of interest?—Yes, the total amount paid under those two heads for the year, was £2[illegible].

22366. The teachers' salaries in your Edinburgh Board schools amount to £73,[illegible]?—Yes; £6[illegible] for day schools, and £4,[illegible] for evening schools.

22367. So that if the whole £55,000 which you receive from the Education Department, and the Science and Art Department, for your day schools and your evening schools, with the fee grant of £1[illegible], went exclusively to the teachers, it would not be sufficient to pay them much more than two-thirds of the salaries they receive?—That is so.

23396. Or if a number of teachers came to a particular centre the same object would be attained?—Yes, if model lessons were given to a class of children as part of the course.

23397. What is the age usually of the children in standard I?—Eight is the average age, but seven in the whole department.

23398. Then you find for standard I two hours is sufficient to give instruction in kindergarten?—Yes.

23399. What instruction is there in drawing?—We give the Science and Art instruction in drawing, freehand and with a ruler.

23400. Is the sewing the kind that comes under the generic term of kindergarten sewing?—We have other sewing.

23401. Actual pieces of calico on which the children work?—Yes.

23402. Mr. STRUTHERS.—Do you remember the time when kindergarten work was not at all common in the schools?—Yes.

23403. When the whole time was given practically to reading, writing, and arithmetic?—Yes.

23404. Do you think the proficiency in those days was greater than it is at present?—Not nearly so great.

23405. In those days standard I was examined individually, each child was examined in reading, writing and arithmetic; certain tests were set to each child individually?—Yes.

23406. That is no longer the case?—No.

23407. Do you think there is less attention paid to the individual children now than there was when that was the rule?—No, I don't think so.

23408. You think the clever children are advanced, and those who are not smart are kept longer in the class until they are able to do the work of it?—They are.

23409. That is the classification is much better than it used to be?—It is much freer.

23410. And children make progress according to their natural capacity and not according to a fixed rule?—Yes.

23411. Are the children kept longer in the infant department than they used to be?—A little longer.

23412. Before they must leave when they were seven years of age?—Yes.

Mr. ROBERT WALLACE, Professor of Agriculture and Rural Economy in the University of Edinburgh, examined.

23413. CHAIRMAN.—You are Professor of Agriculture and Rural Economy in the University of Edinburgh?—Yes.

23414. And do you represent the Edinburgh School of Rural Economy?—Yes.

23415. And you have had experience in educational matters?—Well, probably, I had better say with regard to the experience I have had, this is my thirteenth session in Edinburgh, and I was before that fully three years a Professor of Agriculture at the Royal Agricultural College, Cirencester; and during my excursions abroad I have paid a great deal of attention to the working of all sorts of agricultural schools, in the Colonies and America, as well as Canada.

23416. Will you give a brief description of the Edinburgh School of Rural Economy?—The Edinburgh School of Rural Economy has only been instituted within the last three years. It was felt that there was a necessity for some consolidation of the work—it was done in too many centres, and under too many bodies—and a body of responsible representatives were appointed by the University Council and by the Highland Society to begin with, and they subsequently added to their number representatives from the Town Council of Edinburgh and from County Councils giving grants in support of the school, and that body is now known by the name of the Edinburgh School of Rural Economy, and it takes under its care all the different grades of agricultural instruction given in Edinburgh.

23417. Does it train teachers in agriculture?—It is not a teaching body at all, it simply receives grants from Government and other institutions, and frames a scheme of education, and among the schemes of education there is one for the teaching of schoolmasters a little in detail, in connection with this particular institution?—The instruction given, to begin with, when the men came in at first was in agriculture—forty lectures—and in chemistry twenty lectures, besides laboratory work. That was the work of the first stage of preparation for schoolmasters, and during the latter years a further development has taken place, and it is intended now to have chemistry, botany, geology, entomology, and probably other subjects taught principally in alternative years, taking perhaps two subjects each year.

23424. Do you have a system of examination of the teachers after they have been at work?—Yes, there are class examinations, and class certificates are given.

23425. I understand that agriculture is taught in Scotland in rural schools as a voluntary subject?—It is taught under the Science and Art Department, and in the Board schools as a science subject.

23426. Mr. STRUTHERS.—In evening schools?—It is taught in evening classes under the Science and Art Department, but it is taught as a science subject in the Board schools, and more so in recent years than formerly.

23427. As a specific subject, but it is not compulsory, as in the rural schools in Ireland?—It is not compulsory at all.

23428. CHAIRMAN.—How is it taught in Scotch schools—out of a book or practically?—An effort has been made to make it something better than merely book instruction. The schoolmasters when they come here have been taught methods of instruction, and they are recommended to use diagrams largely, and models, and also to take in specimens of all sorts of things that the pupils may be able to pick up in the country districts.

teach them, the work done by an ordinary labourer on the farm. I can read you one or two suggestions from my introductory address to the school masters:—

"It is intended merely that they should, by building on the foundation of a good general education, become literary experts in the subject of agriculture, and be able to direct the youthful mind in proper grooves; above all, to encourage the development of the power of observation, for which there is no finer opportunity as a training for every walk in life, and so much scope and material generally as is found in a country place."

I believe that an immense amount of useful elementary knowledge can be disseminated by schoolmasters if they will confine themselves to principles, leaving practice entirely to those who have spent their life in it.

"The employment of rural schoolmasters has many conspicuous advantages.

"To begin with, it is within the range of everybody to do so with the means at our disposal. We have at the elementary ones who are in touch, each with, and in genuine touch of, the very classes we want to influence; we have, further, men who are trained to impart instruction. All that is really needed under these circumstances is to ensure that the teachers are themselves instructed in the work laid out for them. It is possible to do this if the matter is not neglected.

"I have no hesitation in saying I am firmly convinced that if there were any elaborate attempt made to get schoolmasters to teach practical agriculture in Scotland, it would not only end in failure, but injure the chances of that success which, I feel assured, will attend their efforts in teaching scientific principles.

"It appears, from what I have said, to be clearly the work of the Government to confine their efforts to the dissemination of scientific principles, and leave to the practical agriculturalists of the country the duty, as has been the case in the past, of training their men in the practical operations which they, of all classes of the community, know best."

22431. Most Rev. Dr. Walsh.—May I take it that as regards the teaching of agriculture as an industrial occupation, you would put it on the same footing as the teaching, say, of shoemaking or tailoring?—No, you cannot put it on such a footing; agriculture in some of its different branches can be taught differently from the main subject of agriculture.

22432. I don't think you quite follow the question. Let me put it in this way. I take it that you are not in favour of teaching trades, say, the trade of a tailor or of a shoemaker, in the elementary schools in the country?—No, of course, not.

22433. My question was whether you would not, to that extent, put the teaching of agriculture or, let us call it, farming, on the same footing as the teaching of a trade; in other words, you would not be in favour of recognising the teaching of farming as a branch of elementary school work?—Certainly not.

22434. But you would favour the teaching of certain principles which would be of practical use to a boy when he afterwards goes to work on a farm?—It is so to some extent; but I believe the teaching of agriculture will do more to develop his power of observation than any information he would derive from it.

22435. I understand you to say you were opposed to the teaching of agriculture in elementary schools?—I am not opposed to the teaching of agriculture in elementary schools.

22436. Then it is better to ask what you mean by agriculture?—It is difficult to define the subject of agriculture.

22437. Suppose we take it as meaning the cultivation of land?—You can say it is the cultivation of land, but that does not embrace everything included in agriculture.

22438. Of course not. But this will bring out the point. You are not in favour of teaching the cultivation of land in the elementary school?—Certainly not.

22439. And you are in favour of teaching those principles that underlie the proper cultivation of land?—Yes.

22440. Monsignor Molloy.—I notice here you say that schoolmasters who receive instruction in agriculture in the University under yourself, and agricultural chemistry under Dr. Aitken, and agricultural entomology, qualify later on by studying those branches for the degree of B.Sc. in agriculture?—No; that is quite a different thing, the degree of B.Sc. in agriculture is apart altogether from what you see there.

22441. It has nothing at all to do with the school masters?—No.

22442. When the schoolmasters receive your instruction in theoretical agriculture are they entitled later on to a diploma or certificate?—They get a class certificate, it is not anything like a diploma.

22443. Would this certificate qualify the man to earn money in the teaching of agriculture, that he would not earn by any other means?—That does not qualify him to earn under the Science and Art Department; it is not accepted by the Science and Art Department unless he works under a local board. If there is a local board established, and they say that man is qualified, then the Science and Art Department will recognise him.

22444. Then the schoolmaster attending your lectures has this advantage, that he acquires a knowledge of the subject?—Yes, and of methods of teaching.

22445. Captain Shaw.—Have you considered the syllabus of agriculture, as laid down by the Scottish Education Department?—I don't think I have paid much attention to it.

22446. You know it is taught as a specific subject. "The principles influencing the supply of plant food in the soil, necessity for cultivation, circumstances making tillage more or less effective." That is the first stage. The second stage is, "The principles regulating the more or less perfect supply of plant food, manures and supplementary sources of plant food." Third, "Principles relating to the growth of crops and variation in their yield and quality." Is that what you would sketch as suitable instruction to be given in an elementary school?—So far as it goes it is all right, but it does not include anything like the amount I would wish to be taught. I have not studied it, but from what you have read there it is certainly not comprehensive enough; it is good enough for a beginning.

22447. You recognise the fact that the children will probably only be taught for a two years' course, and have a few hours' instruction in the week?—It would be difficult to bring in all the country labourers under that heading.

22448. It may be supplemented, perhaps, by the inspection of collections of natural history—insects and such like?—Yes, and those German models of all sorts of things ought to be brought into the teaching of agriculture; in Sweden and Denmark the schools are properly provided with magnificent sets of specimens that are of the greatest use to the young people.

22449. Mr. Strutherm.—May I ask to what sort of models you refer?—Almost anything—animals.

22450. You mean the model of a cow?—Model of a cow or a horse, the internal arrangements of them, and the implements of the farm, everything you could mention is modelled and shown in those German and Danish and Swedish schools.

22451. Captain Shaw.—Is this course now that is given on page 95 of your book for schoolmasters?—Yes, this is the course for schoolmasters this year.

22451a. And that is the style of thing which you expect them to teach to their students when they go back?—We have had somewhat of a rotation of subjects in the country places: agriculture will be taken one year, botany the next year, the principles of chemistry the third year, and physiography the fourth year. To try to get an educational rotation of subjects, because it is impossible to keep agricultural classes going consecutively, botany will be taken up one year and

Edinburgh.
Oct. [illegible]
Professor Robert Wallace.

chemistry perhaps the most, and it is not intended that chemistry and botany should be taught every year. These are the subjects taught this year, next year probably geology and entomology, or perhaps some other subject may be taken up.

22455. Does not agriculture include them all?—Yes, they have a bearing on agriculture, and agriculture cannot be taught without a knowledge of them.

22456. I don't quite follow what you would call agriculture as distinguished from these subjects?—The subject of agriculture deals with the cultivation of crops, the management generally of the farm, and you cannot exclude altogether other subjects, for they come in at all times in the learning of agriculture.

22457. Would you be in favour of the children working in the laboratory themselves?—Yes, the more practical work they can get in the laboratory the better, and the more they can use the magnifying glass when dissecting the specimens the more interest they will have in the work.

22458. And you think children from 11 to 13 will be able to do this?—Oh yes, they can do flowers, and make collections of plants and all sorts of things connected with agriculture; collections of grasses and all those subjects that come directly or indirectly in connection with agriculture.

22459. Would you consider it any use of children learning off by heart the description of various breeds of animals and cattle, and so forth?—No, I don't believe agriculture can be taught at all unless you get the children interested in the subject, and get them to know what they are studying—there is no good in teaching agriculture as a mere matter of memory.

22460. Or yet, learning how many cwt. of a particular manure you have to put into a particular field to grow a particular crop?—I think that probably is too much for a young student to know, but I think it is an exceedingly important thing that they should know what the manures are that go to the particular crops.

22461. But these details of figures you don't think are necessary?—These are subordinate things, which may come in or may not, but I should not place any importance on that kind of mental exercise.

22462. If you had trained a teacher to teach agriculture would you expect him to have recourse to a text-book with the children?—It would be best taught if he were the man who used the text-book, and instructed them by writing on the board, and by dictation and explanation. I don't think it is absolutely necessary to put a text-book in the children's hands—it is dangerous to trust too much to it.

22463. He should be cultivating the children's observations all the time by experiments?—Yes, and not use a text-book that probably is too advanced for the children.

22464. Mr. Stevenson.—Do you represent the views of the committee of management of this school; there is a committee of management of the School of Rural Economy?—I don't know that I am here to represent their views, but only facts I know; I can tell you what their views were in the past.

22465. The opinions you give are your own in the first place?—This school was established by myself; different classes that are being taught in the various schools, the Heriot-Watt and Dick colleges and the botanical gardens, and they formulated a scheme by which the teachers employed in those schools are enabled to do the work necessary for agricultural teaching.

22466. That is, they are the agency through which this grant is distributed to various special schools?—They are the educational authority of Edinburgh to receive all grants from the Government that have to go to these different schools.

22467. In addition to that work they maintain special vacation classes for teachers?—Yes, but for these they get grants from the Government, also.

22468. Besides what they get from the school of Rural Economy?—The funds of the School of Rural Economy come entirely from Government and the County and Town Councils.

22469. You contribute certain money for the conduct of these vacation classes for teachers?—Yes, that used to come from the Board of Agriculture.

22470. Does it come through the School of Rural Economy?—Yes.

22471. There is no other grant from Government?—No, but there are grants from County Councils.

22472. But that also comes through this Board?—Yes, or it may be paid to the men themselves; some of the County Councils give £5 a head to each man who attends.

22473. These vacation classes are for the purpose of enabling teachers to give satisfactory agricultural instruction to their schools?—Yes.

22474. Do you think the training for a month is sufficient for that purpose?—It is all you can give for the first year, and after going through this preliminary training a great many come back for a further course.

22475. But you have formed no opinion as to whether these men at the end of their first course of training are in a position to give really efficient agricultural training in the school?—They are indefinitely better able than they were before, and many of these were teaching under the Science and Art Department and Scottish Code.

22476. Then this is, in fact, a supplementary class?—A great many never had teaching before they began it from text-books.

22477. What sort of agriculture do you wish that these men should teach in the schools when they go back?—First of all you don't wish the practice of agriculture should be taught in any form?—Oh, no.

22478. There is a scheme for teaching of agriculture in the Code here, which has been already referred to. You said you would simplify that. Would you not change it at all?—I think I would draw up a different scheme from that. I have not taken it in fully, but it does not seem to me to cover much ground.

22479. Could you specify some of the points on which you would simplify it?—There is nothing about stock. I think children of that age if they are to learn anything about stock should learn it when they are young.

22480. Of what age are you talking?—Children begin to learn about stock when they are seven or eight, the younger they begin the better.

22481. They learn that at home?—Yes.

quite outside of it. … taught to children … ng diagrams. … always better than … ad if you could get … the usual thing?— … cotland are not the … within the reach of … d take the children … to take them out on … re?—It would be a … be useful; you could … d than taking them … weaving machine?— … ough … , and begins to be a … he will get to know … ery well, even if he … —Yes, but he will … fit by taking an in- … hough. … better to give him … ich he begins to use … ; but his case is a … Yes, if he will do so, … number of boys who … be done by outside … right have to dis- … —I thoroughly agree … words which were … ?—Yes. … collections of in- … 't think they would … in connection with … y would by making … the teachers, and … thoroughly believe in … programme issued by … uction in agriculture … ar to Major Craigie … ase, they advocate … speak of, but they … ntary experiments … the nature of air … the difference be- … known manure to an … grown in soil with … have further experi- … ent combinations of … instruction?—Yes, … call that distinctly … you should begin … elementary science … the principal branch … agricultural interest … would like to have … these things we have … demonstration. I … can be taught by … instance, that they … live stock, different … eding; if there any … ght in an elementary … ould be taught a boy … a farm and deal- … ealing with different

22501. Of course you are remembering this point—that in every rural school there are a very large number of boys who are not going to be farmers. Would it not be better to teach them elementary principles of science bearing on drainage rather than the work of drainage?—I have no objection to elementary principles of these other sciences coming in their proper place; take them in rotation—give agriculture one year, botany the next year, chemistry the next year, or vary the subjects, so that the boys never get tired of them. We had no less than 18,000 pupils taught in Scotch country districts, and I have heard from schoolmasters it was impossible to form a class of agriculture every year; they must vary the subject.

22502. If you taught the elementary principles of science rather than agriculture specifically you could have a great rotation of subjects?—Yes, but I don't think you should teach it in place of agriculture, because in what I call agriculture some things you cannot get in any other branch of science.

22503. Many of those children are not going to be farmers, therefore what is taught to those children should be what is useful for all, as elementary science would be, while agriculture would be useful for those going to be farmers only?—I don't think so; I think elementary agriculture would be quite as useful as elementary botany or elementary geology to anybody, because it is not so much the facts that he becomes possessed of as the benefit the teaching confers on him. I believe agriculture could be made more interesting than any one of these sciences, and you would do more good to a boy than by trying to teach him the bare and dry sciences.

22504. If science is taught with experiments and making collections as you yourself suggested, it can scarcely be called a bare and dry science?—You can improve it to some extent; still I don't think any are so interesting as agriculture—fascinating for the pupil.

22505. Have you seen a teacher giving a lesson in agriculture in an elementary school?—No, I don't think I have.

22506. In the course of a somewhat careful inquiry in Denmark we found that as a matter of fact agriculture was not taught in the elementary schools at all there?—No, but it is taught in a very superior way in the intermediate and higher schools.

22507. But then you spoke of certain models to be seen in the schools of Sweden and Denmark?—Those were the higher schools.

22508. Then you are of opinion that real agricultural teaching should begin in the intermediate and higher schools—I mean the teaching of agriculture thoroughly—you would not depend on the teaching given in the elementary schools?—No, I think it ought to begin in the elementary schools.

22509. But you lay stress on the teaching that comes in in the intermediate and higher schools?—I lay equal stress on the elementary work.

22510. Suppose you want to produce a class of thoroughly trained agriculturists who have a complete knowledge of the subject, and are likely to improve the agriculture of the country, you would require to have higher schools?—Undoubtedly.

22511. Have you any idea what form that higher instruction should take?—They will simply have to expand the subject and go into a little more teaching.

22512. Would you have special institutions in each county?—Not in each county.

22513. Perhaps three or four in each county in Scotland?—I don't know that special institutions would be necessary; I think sides to those institutions now in existence, sides to scientific institutions, such as the Perth Academy and higher schools.

22514. Most Rev. Dr. Walsh.—I understand from one of your pamphlets that you are totally opposed to the idea of having one great central establishment for the purpose of teaching agriculture?—Distinctly.

Edinburgh. Oct. 22, 1888. Professor Robert Wallace.

22315. Mr. Struthers.—Then attaching aside to existing higher institutions, you would practically have one in each county?—Perhaps so.

22316. Do you attach any importance to teachers going around lecturing to farmers?—No.

22317. Or to plots for experiments?—Not if the results are to be published. You cannot have experimental plots conducted on a small scale, the results of which are of any value to the public. But these small plots may be conducted for the purpose of illustrating how experiments should be conducted.

22318. Suppose you had some such plot in the county and an expert employed by the County Council to go round and give lectures, using the plot as his basis of demonstration, would not that be a useful form of instruction?—You could not gain any benefit from that to my mind.

FORTY-NINTH PUBLIC SITTING—THURSDAY, OCTOBER 21st, 1897,

AT 1.30 O'CLOCK, P.M.

At the School Board Offices, Edinburgh.

Present:—The Right Hon. The Earl of Belmore, G.C.M.G., in the Chair; His Grace The Most Rev. William J. Walsh, D.D.; The Right Rev. Monsignor Molloy, D.D., D.SC.; Rev. Henry Evans, D.D.; Rev. Hamilton Wilson, D.D.; Stanley Harrington, Esq., M.A.; W. R. J. Molloy, Esq.; Captain T. B. Shaw; and J. Struthers, Esq., M.A.;

with J. D. Daly, Esq., M.A., Secretary.

Edinburgh.

[illegible]

Mr. Andrew R. [illegible]

22539. Is that considered more advantageous than having an ordinary teacher trained?—Well, I am afraid they could not help themselves, circumstanced as they were.

22540. Suppose you had the choice, which would you prefer?—I should prefer a trained teacher who had acquired sufficient technical skill.

22541. You would prefer to train a teacher in technical skill rather than take an artisan and train him up to be a teacher?—Undoubtedly, both for the proficiency and the principle, for I consider all these things portions of the regular school work.

22542. What do you consider the place of cookery and laundry instruction in primary schools both as regards their place in the curriculum, and also as regards the staff and equipment for them?—I am a little doubtful as to these subjects in this way: they seem to me to be subjects of a kind that belongs more to practical arts than to educational lines of development, and I should be inclined to restrict the teaching of these subjects to children of a more mature age than we have to deal with in our ordinary elementary schools, that is certainly above twelve years of age. The Code says the fourth standard, but my personal opinion is that the children of the fourth standard can be better employed than by being taken to learn mere practical arts.

22543. Have you many children in the Leith schools who are learning cookery or laundry work?—The girls of standard five and six throughout the schools, and, in some cases, of standard four, learn cookery; but laundry work was taken up only for one year, and that has been abandoned within the range of the ordinary standards. It is taught at Craighall-road in what is commonly called the secondary department, which is considerably above the range of the ordinary standards.

22544. What is the position of needlework instruction in primary schools in Leith?—I can speak of it with the heartiest praise: exceedingly satisfactory.

22545. How many hours a week do they give to needlework?—They used to give more than they do now. I think that on the average, as far as I can gather, it does not amount to more than two and a half or three hours. The curriculum has been widened, and the amount of time devoted to that subject has been cut down; but I have seen no practical result of that in the way of deterioration of the work, beyond some diminution in the quantity of finished garments turned out. I may mention that the Leith schools, being large, thoroughly organised schools, some of them holding from 1,800 down to 600 children, have all special instructors in needlework distinct from the rest of the staff. The common arrangement throughout the country in the smaller schools is that one member of the ordinary female staff takes charge of the needlework, or it may be more than one member; but in the Leith schools they have a special sewing mistress who devotes her whole time during the whole of the day to needlework instruction and takes the children from the different standards in relays.

22546. Mr. Stevenson.—And in a large school she has an assistant?—She has in three of the schools.

22547. Chairman.—Do you find that any of the little girls, before they come to school, have been taught

they testified of their own accord that the hand and eye training had had a very decidedly good effect upon the quality of the drawing.

22550. Dr. Evans.—I think you said that manual instruction was introduced in Leith in 1889?—That is so.

22551. You have not, therefore, any very long experience of its utility?—Not beyond that time.

22552. But such experience as you have I presume is in its favour?—Most distinctly; and I may mention that the evidence of the teachers is unanimous in its favour.

22553. Have you yet been able to find how it bears upon the ordinary subjects of the curriculum?—Well, if you mean, Has it any deteriorating effect upon the other subjects? I can testify to the contrary decidedly.

22554. So that from its effect upon education you would not wish to see it abandoned?—Certainly not, I would rather see it developed.

22555. Is manual instruction given in all the standards?—Yes, in the Leith Board Schools; I am not aware that there is any other School Board in Scotland that has carried out the thing so systematically.

22556. What would be the models in the first standard?—There are a great variety; there are a little above the infant stage; embroidery, flower-making, basket-weaving, paper-folding, etc.

22557. That you call rather an extension of kindergarten?—An extension of kindergarten.

22558. And it was the value that accrued from the teaching of kindergarten that led you to desire the introduction of the manual work?—Certainly. I maintain that the two things are practically and educationally the same.

22559. About where would the manual instruction properly come in?—I should say that these are all manual instruction. Would you kindly define to me exactly what you mean by manual instruction?

22560. Where they would begin to use tools, I suppose is the simplest way I could put it?—They use tools to a certain extent in part of the paper-folding; they use a small paper-cutter. In the clay-modelling they use a tool to a certain extent, a sort of blunt knife for the finer work; in designing patterns and bringing out details in the cardboard work, they use an iron ruler; they use a knife and measuring instruments for extension of dimensions, and from that stage upwards they always use drawing in connection with the hand and eye work.

22561. When did you begin to teach elementary science?—It began in a tentative way in one school, where the master had a taste for it, in 1889. It grew in various schools after that. At first it was taken as a class subject, chiefly for the boys against the needlework for the girls. Time after time I got from teachers a request that they might change their time-table and curriculum in order to let girls have the benefit of elementary science as well as the boys, because they had found it so beneficial that they wished to carry it through the whole school, instead of confining it to the boys; and, in 1895, when the curriculum was finally rearranged, it was decided to give elementary science throughout the school to boys and girls.

22562. In what standard do you begin the

and, as far as I recollect, the subject was started by a book published by Longmans, on Object Lessons. That was at a time when our Scotch Code gave a tripartite division to elementary science, and allowed the teachers to take up any one of the three divisions, namely, plant life or common things, leading up to elementary knowledge of physics and mechanics and electricity and chemistry. After due consideration and conference with the teachers, and after some experience of the more limited teaching before, where they had confined themselves, as it were, to one branch in each of the schools, we came to the conclusion that it would be very much better to treat the whole thing on broad lines; and the schools now take up in the course of the year throughout all the standards the whole three divisions of the elementary science subjects, that is to say, it includes animal life, plant life, knowledge of common things, manufactures, and something of electricity, chemistry, mechanics and physics.

22565. And generally, I suppose, the scientific principles that underlie the common phenomena of nature?—Just so.

22566. Was there a special programme prepared for this course, or does the teacher follow a text-book, or is he left to his own discretion in selecting the subjects?—The staff of each school was left to its own discretion in drawing out a programme which was submitted to me for approval. They run on general lines, but there is, I am glad to say, a good deal of variety between school and school.

22567. Will you give us one or two of those programmes?—With pleasure.

22568. Probably you are acquainted with the way in which these subjects are taught in the schools of Edinburgh, for instance, in such a school as Bellevue?—I have no experience of the Edinburgh schools.

22569. You cannot say whether they follow the same lines as in your own district?—I cannot say at all.

22570. Is physical science taught generally in the Leith schools?—Yes, this subject of elementary science is taught in all the schools, throughout all the classes.

22571. Then most of the boys and girls taught in these schools learn physical science?—All the boys and girls.

22572. And, as you say, you don't aim at teaching particular branches of science, but rather at teaching the simple facts of animal and plant life, and the general principles that underlie the common phenomena of nature?—Exactly so; so that the children shall be taught to observe for themselves and draw inferences.

22573. I suppose that, in these lessons, the professor gives an exposition, and illustrates his exposition either by objects or experiments?—That is insisted upon as a part of the correct method.

22574. Are the pupils called upon to make experiments for themselves?—In all the best schools that is what one sets before one; I am afraid in some of the classes it depends very much on the teacher. Sometimes one has to check the neglect of this.

22575. When you find the teacher fit, you get him to train the pupils to make experiments themselves?—Yes, it is done to a large extent.

22576. Do you find this subject popular with the pupils?—Undoubtedly, it is a very favourite subject with them.

22577. With regard to manual training, how long is it since manual training was introduced into the schools of your district?—In the session 1895-96. We have had two sessions of it running; they are beginning the third.

22578. You speak now from the experience of two years?—Yes; and the results have been so far excellent; the authorities and teachers are strongly in favour of continuing it and developing it.

Edinburgh.
—
Oct. 22, 1897.
—
Mr Andrew E. Scougal.

22580. Is it popular with the pupils?—The most popular part of the school work probably.

22581. And how are the parents affected towards it?—Well, I really have no special information about that except a very interesting letter that I got from a member of the Leith School Board, who, I may say, is a practical engineer himself and is out of work in consequence of the strike. I heard when I was making inquiries in Leith about some of the work there for the purpose of this Commission, that he had been personally visiting the schools. He is a newly elected member of the School Board, and came in rather on the economical side,—thought there was too much attempted. He had been round the schools within the past few weeks. I heard that and wrote to him, and he wrote me a most enthusiastic letter as to what he had seen, and his conversion as to the work done. He used a good many more favourable epithets than I am generally able to use in my official reports. He was quite enthusiastic.

22582. And he is gradually ceasing to be such a rigid economist?—Quite so. He said two things: one was that the woodwork astonished him greatly; the quality of the work turned out was such that it would put to shame the actual work of many tradesmen he came in contact with; and in regard to the schools generally he said that, as compared with education in 1872, the state of things in our schools now was simply perfect.

22583. We may take it generally that you agree with the evidence we have uniformly got, that where this manual training has been introduced it has become popular both with the pupils and the parents, as well as with the teachers and the school authorities?—Most emphatically. There is one special development of manual work in Newhaven Victoria school, a fishing school; it is the only case in which I have seen what is called wirework; it seems to be attractive, and educative also.

22584. Captain Shaw.—Do the students in the senior classes, the sixth standard, work for the leaving certificate much in the Board schools?—Oh, no; it is several years beyond the sixth standard—I should say at least three—the leaving certificate. You don't mean the merit certificate?

22585. I mean the leaving certificate?—The leaving certificate is practically for a stage three years beyond the sixth standard.

22586. Mr. Struthers.—It is meant for secondary schools?—Chiefly.

22587. And for such higher departments of elementary schools as are practically on a level with secondary schools?—Yes, specially organised.

22588. Captain Shaw.—There does not appear to be any science paper in this leaving certificate?—No, there is not, as far as I am aware.

22589. Would that tend to discourage the teaching of science in the schools at all?—I think not, as science is taught on the lines I have been speaking of in our elementary schools.

22590. Do I understand from you that each teacher teaches one standard in all subjects?—Yes, that is the normal way in the elementary school.

22591. Does he follow the standard, or go on with a new lot of boys in that same standard next year?—That practice varies; it depends on the head-master's idea of organisation; it is sometimes one way and sometimes another. Of course it would only be done, on the whole, to a limited extent; no teacher is likely to follow a standard from first up to sixth because first, second, and probably third are usually taught by women teachers. It is only above that that the men are employed.

22592. And the great reason for a teacher teaching

teaching of science has
of ordinary subjects—
should be inclined to
the case; it has taught
to adopt more thorough
He is less inclined to
is thrown more in par-

member of the School

it is not officially pre-

y I inquire whether
the Scotch mode of in-
ng to the changes in
, say, in 1870 or 1871
ation, then going on
always simple inspection?
so far, but as yet we
ple inspection.
at mode?—We have an
n in a given month of
authorities have notice,
ely is that instead of
children for individual
he elementary stages to
hole, by sample. Indi-
ate in cases where the
bour certificate in stan-
, and in standard five
r exemption standard.
n as regards individual
with a view to the pay-
ation in that subject?—
our experience, that it
xaminers and teachers,
d teaching, and in the
umber for the object is
of the introduction of
e, Lord Northbrook, it
nsmuch it was thought
ntaken as regards attend-
ally; but we have con-

72607. I suppose you would be of opinion that before teaching such subjects as elementary science in secondary or technical schools it should be first introduced into the primary schools of the country?—I think what you might call the general scientific training I have been speaking of, dealing with phenomena and objects on a scientific basis and principles, would be a great help, but I should hardly be prepared to say it was an absolute *sine qua non* that work like that should be taken up in the elementary stage in order that it might be taught efficiently in higher schools.

72608. And technical institutes would be much more likely to succeed if suitable training were introduced into the elementary schools first?—I think there is little doubt of that, and I think they would be more likely to be fed by fit pupils.

72609. Mr. Shuttleworth.—There is a point about the nature of secondary schools which it might be well to make clear. These secondary schools take children from an early age—in most cases from six and seven years of age?—Yes, from practically the infant stage.

72610. And they are not to any large extent, at all events, recruited by pupils from the elementary schools?—Oh, no, that is quite an exceptional arrangement.

72611. Chairman.—They run parallel?—Yes, the differentiation is to a great extent a social one.

72612. Mr. Shuttleworth.—So any teaching of science in the primary schools would not affect, to a great extent, the teaching in secondary schools?—No, except in leading to a sort of taste for the subject, and a probable increase in the number of pupils who may wish to go on; but there is no direct connection.

72613. Rev. Dr. Wilson.—Have you a college in Edinburgh for training teachers?—Oh, yes, there are three training colleges. They are denominational at present, one connected with the Church of Scotland, another with the Free Church, and another with the Episcopal Church.

72614. And do these training colleges train the teachers of all Scotland?—Of all Scotland.

72615. Is there no training college for the Board's teachers?—Oh, no, there is no distinction in that

heard anyone there
kindergarten in those

r, heard it stated that
from going to be at school
conducted on kinder-
heard any such state-

would get on far better
had never been brought
garten system?—No, I
ever made to me.

a state of things is con-
chool in which kinder-
rted?—Certainly not.
came under your notice
n kindergarten work in
at would you consider it
ratter in that school, a
t it was better for the
a school at all, then to
kindergarten work went
ter is your duty to make
the way in which the
there?—I was going to
watch that school very

another point, speaking
in the Scotch schools,—
re under the Education
bargain,—arithmetic is
lation?—To a great ex-
ten.
y it a very satisfactory

your reports you have

headmaster.

22643. You think then that the teachers in your schools are not sufficiently alive to the advantages of the system that is within their reach?—I believe so. I don't think they really have realised their freedom and see all the advantage of it. The influence of the parents is an element that comes in there; parents have an astonishing objection to their children being "put back," as it is called, and that is a trouble to a head-master who is not very strong.

22644. So then, in Scotland, if the parents find out anything they don't like, they express their opinions freely?—They do very freely.

22645. Have you ever heard of parents here making objections to the manual or practical instruction?—No, I have never heard of it.

22646. Then may we infer that they do not object to it?—Yes. Of course the objections would have to be referred to me; but it is probable that in conference with the authorities I should have heard of any.

22647. You have never heard of their objecting to this, although you have heard of their making objections on other matters?—I have.

22648. Now, as to the best way of introducing these practical branches of school-work that this Commission has to deal with, supposing that room has to be made for them, are there any subjects of the ordinary course that you think could either be dropped, or could have less time allotted to them. First let me ask you was there anything dropped when these subjects were introduced into your schools?—Nothing was dropped. Latterly there has been what we might call the dropping of the subject of history to some extent.

22649. How is history now dealt with in your schools?—In the Leith schools it is dealt with by

Edinburgh. Oct. 12, 1897. Mr. Andrew [illegible].

23686. We learned today that they have not only woodwork but metalwork. So that in those schools they find this side of education quite compatible with a very thorough training in what used to be the strictly classical branches of education?—That is quite what I should have expected.

23687. You spoke of science being taught by the ordinary class teacher rather than a special expert. I suppose you think that it is not the amount of science that the teacher possesses that is important so much as the method by which he teaches it?—Certainly.

23688. And the amount of scientific knowledge he must possess need not be very great if it is to be taught to those children who are under twelve in the ordinary schools?—It need not be great so long as it is sound as far as it goes.

23689. The method is more important than the extent of the knowledge?—Certainly, at that stage.

23690. So that it is quite possible for the ordinary class teacher to give a satisfactory instruction in science although he is not an expert?—Quite possible, we have proved it by experience.

23691. The introduction of hand and eye training in its various forms has been largely voluntary on the part of the teachers, that is to say, the teachers have taken to it and in individual cases themselves led the way?—Yes, they began it. Of course in Leith it was the result of a conference amongst the teachers and the School Board and myself; since then you may say it has been compulsory.

23692. You are Vice-President of the Sloyd Association of Scotland?—I am.

23693. You know that that Association did a good deal of work in stimulating interest among teachers in this particular form of instruction?—I think it did.

23694. And it also conducted classes for instructing teachers in such subjects as cardboard and clay modelling?—Yes.

23695. And that association is very largely composed of teachers?—It is largely.

23696. So that it shows that of their own accord teachers appreciate the value of this form of work?—A very fair deduction, I think.

23697. Would you consider it satisfactory to have infants and children of six or seven taught by males?—No, I think not.

23698. You think that in ordinary cases the instruction is much more suitably and efficiently given by a female teacher?—Undoubtedly, at that age. I remember in Aberdeen one purely infant school that was taught by a gentleman of twenty or more years, but that was quite an exceptional experience.

23699. Does the Scotch Sloyd Association furnish a certificate after training in that branch?—They have been aiming at that.

23700. Mr. STEVENSON.—They issue a certificate of the work actually done in the class.

23700a. Mr. MOLLOY.—Does that certificate qualify the person to give instruction?—No, there is no certificate to qualify them.

23701. Rev. Dr. EVANS.—How many inspectors are there in Scotland?—Twenty-six.

23702. Do you happen to know whether their opinions on this subject of manual instruction are similar to yours?—Well, I should think there is some variety. I cannot really speak for them. It is not a subject that has come up very much among us. I know several of them whose opinions agree with my own.

23703. Monsignor MOLLOY.—In the programme for the physical science I find you have chemistry, physics, plant life, animal life, are all those subjects taught by the same teacher?—All.

23704. And you find there is no difficulty, if a teacher is properly prepared, in the same person teaching all those subjects?—No, I have not found that.

Mr. ROBERT [illegible], B.A., B.Sc., Inspector of Schools under the Science and Art Department, examined.

Mr. Robert [illegible], B.A., B.Sc.

23705. CHAIRMAN.—You are an Inspector of Schools under the Science and Art Department?—That is so.

23706. Which is your district?—"North Scotland" it is called, and it extends from Haddington in the south to Lerwick in the north, and on the other hand extending over from Aberdeen to Inverness, including the Western Islands.

23707. Perhaps you will tell us to what extent woodwork is introduced in standards five and six in your district?—In Edinburgh we have about two-thirds of the schools taking woodwork; in Leith only one, in Dundee, five or six, in Aberdeen, three or four.

23708. What general observations can you make on the subject of woodwork?—I don't know that there is anything I can say. I am satisfied with the work so far as it goes in the south, but I am not yet satisfied with the work in the North.

23709. Do you call Aberdeen the north?—I mean north of the Tay. We have only Edinburgh and Leith in the south, and then Dundee and Aberdeen in the north.

23710. Therefore you are not satisfied in Dundee and Aberdeen?—No, although the work is improving. These schools have not been so long opened as the Edinburgh schools.

23711. Coming on to drawing, first of all as to the teacher's qualifications, what do you say about that?—I think it would be quite sufficient to have from the teachers a qualification in freehand and model drawing and geometrical drawing—as distinguished from what is called solid geometry—and blackboard.

23712. Do the teachers require a certificate in drawing?—It is not necessary to have a certificate, but certificates are given.

23713. Are most of the teachers who teach drawing certificated teachers?—No, you may take it that they are certificated teachers generally but not in drawing.

23714. Have you any considerable number of teachers who have obtained certificates in drawing, but who, owing to the circumstances of their schools, have for a number of years not been in a position to practise drawing?—Most of the teachers who have any qualification whatever have had plenty of practice for the last five or six years, or as much as they cared to have.

23715. Therefore it would probably be useless to ask you the question whether you think a man who had obtained a certificate twenty years ago and never practised drawing, would be in a position to teach drawing properly?—I am afraid not. I think some who have certificates in the present year are not in a position to teach drawing properly.

23716. How did they manage to obtain a certificate if they are not competent?—The certificate is not a certificate of competency to teach, it is only of ability to draw.

23717. Then there is no system of ascertaining whether a teacher is capable of teaching drawing?—No test.

23718. What method would you suggest for assisting the teachers?—To assist teachers in getting good drawing in the schools is a question of beginning with the top; you must have an inspector who is interested in or sympathetic with the work, and he should pay occasional visits to the school without notice, he should find the teachers at their work, as most certainly he will do in most of the schools, but it would be useful for him then to take the teachers aside after the lesson and show them the faults that he had discovered in their drawing lessons or lessons, and generally give them assistance as how they should have taken up this or that.

23719. Is that the only method that you suggest. It has been suggested to us that in Ireland it would be possible, and, perhaps, advisable that centres should be formed which should be under a competent teacher, and that the teachers from the schools within a get-at-able area should come in once a week to receive a lesson in the method of teaching drawing. Do you think that would be a good plan?—I think it would, especially in the beginning of the subject; but you would have to insist on good training first in your training colleges.

23720. Supposing the teacher had not been in a training college?—To begin with, the teachers who are now coming out of the training colleges should be qualified to teach drawing.

23721. Do you think it should be made compulsory that every teacher who is now passing, or will in the future pass through a training college in Ireland, should be able to teach drawing as well as anything else?—If you are going to teach drawing in the schools.

23722. Do you think the system of a centre would be better than having a peripatetic instructor in drawing going round to the different schools, who should see what was going on, and advise the teacher?—Are you thinking of teaching children or teachers at the centres?

23723. I am thinking of a method of helping the teachers to qualify themselves. One suggestion is that there should be a centre in the county town, or some town analogous; another is that a person thoroughly competent should be stationed in the centre and go round to different schools, and should be present when the drawing lesson was being given, and if there was anything wrong should interfere and show how it was to be done?—I think the best would be a combination of the two. You would have first to insist on the teacher at the centre being qualified, and the peripatetic teacher could point out the faults in any system and how to improve it.

23724. You have a sub-head under the title of the yearly examination—what does that mean?—We hold an examination at the end of each year in the schools which offer to teach drawing. Drawing is voluntary in the schools, and you may say that only the largest schools in Scotland have taken it up—the town schools. At the end of each year we hold an examination, and I think there is room for improvement in that examination. The papers that are received from the children on the day of the examination are partly marked by the inspectors, and partly sent to South Kensington. That system is good so long as it leaves to the inspector a fair control over the result. It would not do to give him full control, but I think he ought to have considerable control over the result, so that he can take local circumstances, and whether the school is improving or not, into account.

23725. With regard to the number of inspectors; you are an inspector under the Science and Art Department; but do other inspectors, who are not under the Science and Art Department—the ordinary inspectors of elementary education—interfere in the [illegible]

write on the blackboard, and if he could not write fairly on the blackboard he would be a bad teacher of writing, so I should insist on all teachers being able to draw on the blackboard.

23729. It would be desirable, no doubt; but supposing you had not any certificated teacher in the school, and we were striving to make drawing obligatory, would it be possible to get it taught in a school of that kind?—Oh, yes. It is now taught in schools by teachers who have not certificates.

23730. And you judge of the teaching by the work done?—Yes.

23731. And on such work results are paid?—Yes.

23732. Mr. Strathern.—You say it would not do to give the inspector full control in deciding the grant—on what grounds?—The standard is so likely to drop as to rise from the inspector having full control, and you must have a guarantee that it won't drop, and the guarantee is the central system of marking.

23733. Is it necessary to send up all the papers? Would it not do to send up sample papers?—I think it would answer the same purpose if the sample was large enough.

23734. But you don't think it would be necessary to send up papers from each school?—I think I would have samples from every school. It is the tendency to drop I am afraid of.

23735. You don't think that a selection of the inspector's marking from the whole of the schools of his district would be a sufficient guarantee of the standard?—I don't think it would.

23736. Suppose the Department reserved to itself power to say, "We wish you to send up the papers of such and such a school, with your marking"—to send for three or four from his department in the course of the year?—If the Department selected the three or four that would be enough.

23737. Captain Shaw.—You think the inspector should be a qualified judge of drawing?—I think so.

23738. Don't you think every inspector would be?—I think every inspector ought to be. I don't think I can say that every inspector is or would be.

23739. For that reason it would be desirable in some cases that the papers should be marked by a central authority where they have experts in drawing?—In addition to the inspector?—Yes.

23740. Mr. Molloy.—Could you state the number of elementary schools in Scotland that are connected with the Science and Art Department?—You mean schools taking drawing?

23741. No, altogether?—900 to 1,000 schools. Of these the most of them, of course, are simply taking drawing in connection with the Department.

23742. And then, in round numbers, or approximately, the total grant earned from the Science and Art Department?—£20,000 for drawing.

23743. How many of those schools under the Science and Art Department are carried on during the day time, as part of the ordinary school work, even approximately, and how many of them in the evening continuation schools?—Do you mean drawing only?

23744. No; I want to get at the total?—According to a new regulation of the Science and Art De-

moment. It is difficult to define where we are, owing to this new regulation of the Science and Art Department, that no pupil who is on the books of the Scotch Education Department for day attendance shall be also on their books for day attendance, and an effort is being made at the present moment to get the Science and Art Department to rescind that rule—it affects a great many schools.

27747. The object is to prevent the duplication of payment?—Yes.

27748. Mr. Hammersmith.—Can you tell us why it is not thought well to have drawing made a compulsory subject in the schools?—I think it was a question for the Scotch Education Department, and I suppose as the control was not in their own hands they did not care to have it compulsory; but I am speaking my own opinion.

27749. Would you be in favour of making it compulsory?—After a time. You would have to give notice, because the country schools would not be prepared at present to teach drawing.

27750. Rev. Dr. Wilson.—Woodwork you say is taken in a certain number of schools, is that increasing?—Yes, rapidly.

27751. You don't know of any schools that had woodwork and gave it up?—I know of one school, but that is exceptional, and it was given up because it was so badly taught.

27752. The tendency is for the numbers to increase and increase rapidly?—Yes.

27753. Most Rev. Dr. Walsh.—I suppose the reports on the teaching of that school were unfavourable?—I think that was it.

27754. In the examination in drawing, I understand, some of the papers are sent up to South Kensington to be marked?—Yes.

27755. All are not sent?—All are not sent; from a third to a half.

27756. The Inspector makes the selection?—He sends all the papers, but he marks from a third to half himself, and then these may be re-marked in South Kensington.

27757. Is the distinction between those that he marks finally and those that he does not mark finally, a distinction of standards, or what is it; kindly explain to us what occurs?—It comes to this: the Inspector, when he holds the examination in the school, marks the first standard and the second and sometimes the third standards; those papers, with the fourth, fifth, and sixth, are then sent up to South Kensington.

27758. Without the Inspector's having marked the papers of the fourth, fifth, or sixth standards?—Without his having marked the fourth, fifth, and sixth.

27759. Mr. Hammersmith.—And is the work in the first standard on paper?—It is on slates. It would not be sent unless it was done on paper; it may be done on paper.

27760. Most Rev. Dr. Walsh.—The Inspector marks the first, the second, and the third standards, and does not mark the fourth, fifth, or sixth, but sends up all the exercises that are on paper, and this may include the first standard, or it may not?—It may.

27761. Chairman.—Does South Kensington look at them all?—Every paper is marked in South Kensington—the individual paper is marked.

27762. In addition to the Inspector's marking?—

to their capacity to teach drawing?—It is difficult to say whether the instructor of method would be capable of teaching them.

27753. He is an official of the Education Department?—Yes; i.e., he is an official of the Training College, working under the Education Department.

27754. The Education Department looks after the teaching of method in these branches of work with which it has to do, and does not look after the teaching of method in the case of drawing, which is altogether outside its province?—So far as I understand. I thought you would like to see what could be done by a teacher who is not working under our rules (*producing examples*). He is enthusiastic, but he is not working for the grant. This is a secondary school, but these children are about the age of primary school children.

27755. We were told that primary and secondary schools here run on somewhat parallel lines, the distinction being rather social than educational?—I only know one really secondary school, which really begins at secondary work.

27756. It is, then, that the secondary schools here are really primary schools for children of a higher social class?—And they go further than the Board schools.

Miss Guthrie Wright, Hon. Secretary, Edinburgh School of Domestic Economy, examined.

27757. Chairman.—Will you tell the Commissioners what are the arrangements for teaching cookery to teachers in the Edinburgh School of Domestic Economy, of which I think you are the Honorary Secretary?—I am. Our arrangements are on two lines, one for teachers of all branches, from the cheapest cookery up to high class dish cookery, and the other is for artisan and plain cookery. One extends to a minimum of eight months, and the other to a minimum of six months, and the details of what we give in the minimum training is stated on page 4 of our prospectus, that is the minimum, but we go far beyond that.

27758. To what class, in your opinion, should cookery be taught in public schools, and by whom, the class teacher or a special teacher?—For some time my school taught in the Edinburgh Board schools and in Leith. The Boards then formed their own staff of cookery teachers. And we then formed the opinion, which we have not seen since any ground to go back from, that very young children do not benefit adequately by it, they forget it before they turn it to any purpose, and therefore it should be thrown as far on as possible in the elementary school teaching. The Board have not control over the children after they leave school, but it would have been better even after the ordinary school years; but the arrangement then made was one which we thought desirable and a have been accompanied by a good many difficulties, and from all we have heard yet of the experiment, it appears to us, as far as we have talked over it, that the expense is probably in excess of the benefit to be gained from it. It is very difficult to give anything equivalent to a home training in any place that is not a home, it is more or less make-belief. We very strongly go in for the teaching of cookery and laundry work as being special subjects which can be well taught to children, because the knowledge can be kept in their minds until they bring it into operation. It is of value so far as it goes; but working the practical details of a house always seems to be accompanied by many difficulties, and we are rather in a waiting attitude towards that.

27759. Mr. Harrington.—Does the presence of the special teacher for cookery cause any friction in the schools with the ordinary teacher?—Friction in the sense of its being very difficult for the cookery classes to be given full justice to, for this reason, that whereas in England the boys' and girls' schools are separated, and the girls' classes can be adjusted so as to allow of cookery getting its full share of attention; in Scotland our experience was at the time we taught—I am not able to speak of the present arrangements—but our experience was that cookery rather interfered with the other subjects, and drafting children out of classes in small numbers interfered with the class arrange-

those who go in for the housewifery diploma; we at first called it book-keeping and it rather frightened them; all we teach is what young ladies have to keep in their own houses, the house-book.

22902. Rev. Dr. Whelan [illegible].—I suppose you turn your attention mainly to the artisan and plain cookery?—That is the part we have always given the greatest importance to in our school, as being the most important nationally.

22903. You prefer that the ordinary teacher of the subject should learn if she is at all competent to do so?—It is an important "if," because I have not yet known of any teachers in the schools being fully trained, and the training we at one time proposed to give as a minimum in our training school there was so much pressure put upon the teachers in training in other ways that they tried to minimise it on us.

22904. So, up to this date an expert is a necessity?—I think so.

22905. We saw in London a case where an artisan's house was taken, so many rooms, and every department connected with the house was taught, have you anything of that sort here?—We have not; one of our committee just returned yesterday from a visit to the London centres and specially saw those arrangements with a view to a consideration of the subject.

22906. You regard cookery and laundry as the essentials of housewifery?—Yes, and as practicable to teach in elementary schools.

22907. Chairman.—I think you have some observations you would like to make about kindergarten?—No. The only observation I would make is that there are a considerable variety of ways in which cookery, for example, is taught to children; our different schools have worked things out in different ways; our school, and I, individually, have always had a very strong feeling that for cookery and laundry also the classes should be small; the teacher cannot do justice to a large class at a time, and not more than two children should work together at one desk.

22908. But how many in a class?—About fourteen is a very good number; eighteen or twenty-four has been attempted, but we have rather declined the work than take it under such circumstances—the teacher cannot do justice to that number.

22909. Most Rev. Dr. Walsh.—Are there more children going in for the cookery certificate now than went in for it formerly?—I believe so, but I have not so much detailed knowledge of what takes place in the Board schools. All our schools are doing their best to work out the best methods. Our own school is at present hoping to make some alteration and development.

22910. Has any change been recently made in the Education Code that would act adversely to the teaching of cookery?—I don't think so. The last arrangements issued as to the training of teachers by our Scotch Code were not so specific; they were rather left vague to allow the schools to follow their own way in matters. But I think they will be more specific shortly, and our school has made a representation to the Scotch Education Department, both our Edinburgh school and the Glasgow school. Sir Henry Craik authorised me to mention this to-day, with a view to see if the School Board would afford us the necessary facilities for the training of teachers in teaching actual classes of children, and Sir Henry has written both to the Edinburgh and Glasgow School Boards upon this subject. We are rather at a disadvantage in Scotland as compared with England in the training of teachers in teaching, because in England so many schools are voluntary schools, and many of those work with the schools of cookery. In Scotland the system is almost entirely a Board school system, and these have their own staffs of teachers.

22911. You don't work here on the centre system—having centres for such subjects as cookery set up for a number of schools in a neighbourhood—as they do in England?—Yes; in England they work more on the centre system.

22912. Mr. Harrington [illegible].—Are there introduced into the reading books in the elementary schools here, little simple lessons on the laws of health, and the evils of strong drink, and so forth?—That I am not aware of.

22913. Would you like to see that in the reading lessons?—Yes; I think even matters of cookery could be introduced into reading lessons, and in dictation work I think cookery work might be advantageously used. I think Sir Thomas Acland, in England, at one time made an effort of that kind, and it worked advantageously, so as not to have so much writing in the cookery class, and yet to utilise the instruction from one class to the other.

Edinburgh. Oct. 2, 1897. Miss Grace Wright.

Principal Grant Ogilvie, Heriot Watt College, Edinburgh, examined.

22914. Chairman.—I believe you are the Principal of the Heriot Watt College in Edinburgh?—Yes, my lord.

22915. You have paid considerable attention to drawing and manual training in primary schools, as preparatory to technical instruction?—I think that, as a preparation for technical instruction, the first essential, and really the only essential, is a sound elementary education; putting the matter quite generally, drawing I regard as an essential part of an elementary education, manual instruction should find its place in elementary education on grounds quite distinct from those of its necessity as a preparation for technical work. A most important aspect of elementary education, from the point of view of such instruction as is given under my direction, that is instruction to adults who are engaged in technical operations, and require to prosecute their education, is that they should have a thorough knowledge of arithmetic, a practical knowledge of composition, and that they should be able to use their drawing. The tendency in teaching drawing is to teach it as a subject, which is of importance, simply for its own purposes. Now, if that be the only aspect in which a student regards it, he does not make use of it as a tool. In technical education, drawing is of advantage principally as a tool, and therefore the more in ordinary school work it can be introduced into every lesson—there are very few lessons it cannot aid—and the more it is introduced as an accompaniment of lessons, and not merely for the purpose of ornament, the better it will be for the pupil as a preparation for his technical instruction afterwards. When I speak of the application of composition, and so on, the difficulty that I find is that an adult, who, no doubt, was quite able to write an essay upon a cat, or a holiday, or honesty, in the ordinary way of a school exercise, fails when you put him down to describe some object which is placed before him, suppose it were merely a chair, or again if you ask him to give an intelligible description of that object, or of an ink bottle, anything in front of him, he does not know where to begin. Similarly he is quite at a loss when asked to describe perhaps in words, apart from writing, a simple action performed by him. That is merely a question of the method of teaching, and what is desirable is that, is rather that the attention of teachers be directed to that aspect of composition, because, after all, that is the final test in life of composition for these pupils.

22916. Do you think that in arithmetic there is too much evidence of a tendency to lose sight of reality in figures?—In testing a pupil, even an adult, who has been away from school a year or two, if one puts an arithmetical question on a blackboard, or in a paper in the ordinary form in which it appears in the text-book, say multiply 6 inches by 37, he will work it out all

Principal Grant Ogilvie.

Edinburgh.
Oct. 8, 1896.
Principal Grant Ogilvie.

right, but if you put to the same adult the question in this form: "Each flooring board in this room is 6 inches broad, there are 37 flooring boards, what is the breadth of the floor," he is in a great difficulty. Adult pupils show they have not regarded arithmetic as connected with an end, they regard it as they regard drawing and school exercises.

22517. A sort of abstraction?—Yes; I would urge that arithmetic should be worked in on every possible occasion, in the various lessons a child may have, and that questions should be set on measurements taken actually before the pupil. For instance geography; I think I am right in saying it would be an exceptional thing to find a teacher set an arithmetical question in the course of a lesson in geography, yet there would be much advantage in such an exercise as connecting the distances between towns with the times of travelling between them.

22518. Do the teachers in Scotland ever ask, as is done in Ireland, the length of rivers and heights of mountains?—I have no doubt they do; but that is an effort of memory.

22519. Most Rev. Dr. Walsh.—They might ask: "How long would you take travelling down a river going at so many miles an hour?"—Yes, an intelligent teacher would do that, and unless the subject is applied in that way throughout the whole of the child's education, he can never have a grasp of the work.

22520. Chairman.—Have you given attention to the subject of woodwork in primary schools?—But little; not very much.

22521. What do you think about it?—I think woodwork is a very excellent thing in its proper place, my own impression is that there is no doubt about its advantage in those schools in which it was first introduced in Britain—that is secondary schools—those schools where the children continue beyond fourteen years of age, and where it is necessary to keep their manual training going on, so that they may not be handicapped in entering upon an apprenticeship subsequently. At the same, I doubt whether carpentry is the best form of manual training for an elementary school. I am of opinion that there are simpler operations that would be of advantage, but I must say that my experience in that matter is not sufficient to enable me to attach any particular importance to my view.

22522. Rev. Dr. Evans.—Apart from the benefit of drawing, as applied to art and industry, I suppose you would be of opinion that it is profitable to the individual student himself?—Undoubtedly; I consider it is an essential part of the training of a pupil in a primary school, I think manual training, including drawing and other occupations of a simple kind, are essential parts of training during the elementary stages of instruction.

22523. Drawing, I suppose, teaches the pupils observation?—Certainly.

22524. And I suppose writing is a manual training?—Yes.

22525. And drawing aids in training the hand as well as writing?—Yes.

22526. So that the pupil himself is benefited apart from any application that may be made of it to particular arts; is benefited by having been taught drawing?—Very much so.

22527. Do you think that the Government Inspectors, taking the Inspectors in the average, are competent judges of drawing?—Yes.

inspectors generally, if they can judge needlework properly, might not also judge drawing properly?—I don't attach so much importance to the actual finished accuracy of the result in the drawing exercise as I do to the method in which the work is set about, and I think that any gentleman who is selected for the position of inspector of schools is necessarily a sufficiently qualified judge of the educational result which has been produced by the drawing. The average inspector of schools is able to tell when a picture is out of drawing. I think he would be much more ready to judge of simpler points raised in elementary drawing.

22531. Mr. Harrington.—I suppose a considerable number of boys from elementary schools here go into business offices?—Yes; very large numbers.

22532. Do you think the system of arithmetic as taught is sufficiently practical to be of much value to them when they go to business afterwards?—The system of arithmetic is all right itself, but they are not accustomed to apply it; but, for those going into offices, there is not so much difficulty, because the questions that occur are generally of the type of questions that are given in the arithmetic books.

22533. Don't you think a great deal could be done by the introduction of the teaching of the decimal system into schools?—Very much more. I believe that boys who go to business with a good knowledge of the decimal system, become much more valuable as clerks afterwards. As a matter of fact, the first thing we teach every pupil who comes up for technical instruction is decimal fractions, but we don't call them decimal fractions. We are careful to base them on certain units of the metric system, and take measurements before the pupils; or, if they are agricultural students, the first thing we teach them is the Chain, which is the only British decimal measure, as a concrete illustration. Personally I hold very strongly the opinion that the teaching of calculation by decimals is of the greatest importance.

22534. Do you think it is sufficiently taught in your primary schools at present?—No, I do not; otherwise we should not have to begin by teaching it.

22535. So that boys in Scotland are at a great disadvantage as compared with foreign boys?—Yes; there is a good deal of time lost.

22536. In learning arithmetic owing to our complicated system?—Yes.

22537. Rev. Dr. Wilson.—Yours is a technical school?—The main part of the institution is. It has evening classes for adults who are engaged in business or manufactures.

22538. Have you a day school as well?—We have day classes, but they are for pupils who have passed through a secondary school—sixteen to twenty years of age.

22539. How many attend that evening school?—3,700.

22540. At what time?—The average period would be two evenings a week, so that there would be about 1,500 in attendance each evening.

22541. You have accommodation for those numbers?—Yes.

22542. What will they now be chiefly occupied at?—The occupations vary just as much as the occupations in the town do. In the first place, there are

in the work of a technical school?—Yes; I consider that a case for a full and adequate training in drawing could be made out on its importance as a part of general education alone; but I consider, further, that even if that were not the case, you could show sufficient reason for its being included in school work as a part of the preparation for technical training.

22845. Does the same not apply to manual instruction?—No, I do not think that of manual instruction. I have no information which leads me to consider manual instruction in primary schools an essential part of the preparation for technical instruction. I consider, however, that it is an essential part of elementary education. That is to say, in the technical instruction of the whole, we do not build upon or make use of the manual training which has been given during the primary school years.

22846. Precisely so; that was what I wished you to explain. I was afraid your first answer might be misunderstood. You regard manual instruction as of importance in the primary school, quite apart from all consideration of its relation to technical education?—Yes.

22847. You are quite clear upon that?—Quite clear.

22848. You would, therefore, consider it a fatal mistake to say, "Let us have none of this work in the primary school; let us remove everything of that kind for those technical schools that the pupils may afterwards go to?"—I should; but may I add that, the distinction I have drawn leads to an important qualification of the nature of the work which is to be given as manual instruction.

22849. I intend to come to that afterwards, but, first taking manual instruction in itself, you consider it would be a fatal mistake to separate it from a complete system—or a system professing to be complete—in primary education, and to reserve it altogether for a technical school?—Yes.

22850. Now, as to the kind of manual instruction to be introduced into the primary school, you consider it should be something that would exercise the children in accuracy of observation?—Yes.

22851. And you also consider that it should be such as would exercise their constructive faculties?—Yes.

22852. Of course there might be an immense variety of occupations that would answer those conditions; can you give us a few examples of the kind you think best fitting for the purpose?—I think I might put it otherwise. I rather hesitate to accept the almost universal seizing upon carpentry as the one subject which is to form manual training, because I think that in carpentry there is a great deal of time spent on operations which are not necessarily educative. I prefer the simpler studies—the fixing of wires and cardboard work. In fact, you may take generally the Sloyd occupations, other than carpentry. I think carpentry occupies a needlessly long time for the educative results it produces.

22853. But you consider those exercises in cardboard folding and cutting, and folding pieces of paper, according to a prescribed plan, or according to directions given by the teacher, and measuring and cutting bits of wire, and twisting them into certain shapes, all have a useful educative purpose?—Very great.

22854. You would not consider them of more educational advantage than the Sloyd exercises in wood?—No; but they take up less time, and they are of equal educational value. For the same amount of time, I should say that they are of more.

22855. You are probably aware of the system that has been worked out so fully in places like Birmingham, where in the earlier stages the children occupy themselves with these elementary exercises—folding and cutting pieces of cardboard, and twisting pieces of wire—as a preparation for the Sloyd exercises in the fifth and sixth standards?—I have not seen the arrangement, but I understand it.

22856. Do you not think that no matter how good the arrangement might be, the time would come when the child would get tired of dealing with little bits of paper and wire?—Yes, I quite approve of that, but I don't think it is in the near future that we are to get the work carried out so thoroughly generally as it is in Birmingham.

22857. But you think that the Birmingham plan represents a desirable ideal?—Undoubtedly; that is, as to carpentry. I rather distinguish it from Sloyd, I don't wish to be misunderstood on that point.

22858. Obviously, carpentry and Sloyd are essentially different things, and also at two essentially different ends?—Yes, woodwork on the Sloyd system is different from carpentry. I deprecate carpentry training, as distinct from Sloyd exercises in wood.

22859. CHAIRMAN.—You made one remark with regard to the application and the knowledge of arithmetic that a child receives in Scotland, you said that although he could multiply six inches by fifty-seven he could not apply it when he came to measure a floor, do you think it could be said of any children who had passed through the schools you know of in Scotland as I have heard it said in a town near where I live, by a man of business, with reference to arithmetic, that it was almost impossible to get an apprentice who could do a sum correctly?—I don't mean to say that no pupil could do that, and I don't suppose your friend meant it literally, perhaps I ought to guard my own remark a little, there is a very large number of artisans who have gone through school training and undoubtedly have done it satisfactorily, who yet, from want of habit of applying their arithmetic, lose their arithmetical knowledge very quickly. Of those who retain it one makes no remark, for one expects that it will be retained; yet it is undoubted that there is the need for refreshing arithmetical knowledge, indeed it is scarcely a matter of refreshing, but of rendering the knowledge applicable to practice.

22860. Most Rev. Dr WALSH.—I dare say there are people who are able to perform the abstract sum of subtracting £1 10s. and 11½d. from £5, quite correctly on paper, and yet would blunder in giving you the change of £1 10s. and 11½d. out of a £5 note?—Yes, children regard the one question as arithmetic and the other as a problem, and say—"We cannot do problems."

Miss FLORA C. STEVENSON, Member of the Edinburgh School Board examined.

22861. CHAIRMAN.—You are a member of the Edinburgh School Board?—I am.

22862. And you have had great experience in subjects connected with education?—I have been a member of the Board for twenty-four years.

22863. With regard to cookery what are the conditions on which grants for this subject are given by the Scotch Education Department in day schools?—The conditions are that domestic economy as a theoretical subject is taught to the girls, that they shall receive forty hours of instruction in cookery, twenty of which must be spent in actual cooking with their own hands, and that no class shall contain more than twenty-four girls for this practical work, and a grant of 4s. is given for each girl in these classes. A grant of 2s. is given for classes of twelve, where there are only twelve in the same class, and they must have received altogether twenty-four hours of instruction.

22864. You think forty lessons are as little as are of any use?—I think so, but I also am of opinion that twelve hours of practical training given to twelve girls is of more value than twenty hours given to twenty-four girls under one teacher.

22865. Because they get more individual attention?

Edinburgh. O. F. [illegible] Principal [illegible]

Miss Flora C. Stevenson.

—They get much more individual attention, and I think altogether it is more valuable when the classes are small.

22566. The other day when we were making our tour in Ireland, we visited, not a primary school, but a technical school in Galway. We did not see anything going on, but we saw the instructress in cookery, and asked her opinion on the subject; and she told us that the number of lessons that was comprised in the course were, I think, only twenty, and she thought that that was a great deal too little; because the pupils or persons who were attending were only just beginning to understand the elements of the thing. To teach the matter properly she ought to be able to give sixty lessons?—I think forty lessons, of course, is very much better, and the ideal would be that they should get their forty hours of instruction, and for twenty of them they should cook with their own hands, but the number in each class under one teacher should be limited to fourteen at the outside. We, in our classes, teach twenty-four at a time, and I don't think it is at all satisfactory, they get into little slovenly ways.

22567. You think on the one hand twenty lessons would be too little and sixty lessons would be more than enough?—Rather more, I think forty would be sufficient, if the practical classes were limited in number to fourteen at the outside.

22568. Now, as regards the age of the scholars?—The Scottish Educational Code gives grants for girls from the fourth standard upwards; my opinion is that that is rather too early to begin cookery teaching. I don't think they should begin until they are thirteen years of age, and it should as far as possible be given to a girl in the last year of her school attendance. Before the Department recognised cookery at all as a subject of instruction the Edinburgh School Board gave cookery teaching to the older girls, we had no grants for it, and no conditions connected with the teaching, and I am of opinion that we did very nearly as much good as we do now with our elaborate kitchens and apparatus and the restrictions of the Education Department. We have certainly more children receiving instruction. Last year we taught between 2,000 and 3,000 girls that we got the grant for, but still I am of opinion that a great deal of the money which is given in cookery grants is wasted because of the very youthful age of the children who get the teaching, the children like it immensely, it is a great variety from their work, but I believe a good deal of the good of the teaching is lost.

22569. Do you think that any considerable number of the girls who have been taught cookery in the primary schools for a sufficient number of hours, could go home, and being provided with materials, could cook a dinner at home without any superintendence?—I think the older girls could, the girls of thirteen or fourteen, but the average age of the girls in our schools in the fifth standard is between eleven and twelve, I think that is too young, I don't think they could; I have known cases of girls who having got their preliminary instruction in the Board schools in cookery have gone and followed it up at these employments and made very good cooks indeed.

22570. I suppose in all cases a girl who had received her instruction only in school, would require to learn a great many things beyond what she had learned in school before she became a cook?—Oh, certainly, a great deal more.

22571. What is the relation between theoretical and practical instruction in cookery?—All the girls who are to receive cookery instruction receive what are called demonstration lessons, the number in classification is limited by the accommodation of the class-room, the possibility of hearing the teacher and of seeing what she does, the numbers attending these classes are not limited; but the misfortune in our teaching is that they get all their demonstration lessons at one time and the practical lessons follow afterwards, in many cases, very many weeks after the girl has received the theoretical instruction she receives the practical instruction. We can only teach twenty-four at the outside in the practice classes.

22572. To carry the thing out in a perfect way, I suppose you should limit your theoretical class to the number of the practical class, and have the practical class follow immediately on the theoretical?—Or have a sufficient number of teachers in the practical class-room to teach half as many as have received the demonstration lesson, the ideal thing would be to have the practical lesson follow on the demonstration but that would be very expensive.

22573. Unless you had to deal with a small number?—Yes.

22574. Suppose you were to establish cookery in a rural school, it would be easier to carry that out than in a large town school?—Very much easier, in a small school it would be quite practicable to give the practical lesson after the demonstration lesson. My view is that this instruction ought to be given to children after they had passed their fifth standard, and should be confined to evening schools or continuation schools.

22575. I think you have already told us that cookery was taught in the Edinburgh schools before it was recognised as a school subject by the Department, and was only given to the older girls. Can you tell us what were the grants first given under the Code of 1884?—It was given as a grant for a class subject; there was no grant given specially for practical work. Cookery was given as domestic economy, which was taught as a specific subject, before it was recognised as a grant-earning subject. A girl was obliged to take domestic economy as one of those specific subjects she was allowed to take. If a girl took specific subjects she was obliged to take domestic economy as one of them, and it was then paid at the same rate as a specific subject; I forget what the amount was prior to 1884—I think it was 4s. we got for the two subjects.

22576. Can you tell me what number of children were taught in the day schools in cookery last year?—I think we had last year altogether 3,536; the average attendance is about 37,000 at our schools, and half of those would be girls.

22577. As regards sewing, has instruction in that subject always been a primary condition of any grant being given to a school?—Yes, it has always been a primary condition on which schools are recognised as grant-earning, that sewing should be taught to the girls.

22578. There is now a code of regulations on the subject?—Yes, called the third schedule, which minutely details what is to be expected from the girls in these subjects from the infant department up to sixth.

22579. What is the number of hours that should be given to sewing?—I should like each girl to have four hours a week, certainly not less than three; in our schools we are only able to give them three.

22580. You think three is not enough?—It is better if we could have four, but I may say, and this remark applies to all the domestic subjects in our schools—our schools are mixed schools—the boys and girls, as a rule, are taught together, and of course each class of girls that is taken away for sewing or cookery disorganises the class to a certain extent.

22581. The number of hours in the ordinary schools in Ireland given to sewing is five hours, that is outside what they call the alternative subjects which is not much taken up, which was two hours; and it has been suggested to us it would be a very good thing to reduce the number to three hours, in order to gain time for other subjects, such as cookery?—I think if they get the full hours, so that no time is lost, three hours ought to do; of course four hours is better, but we have managed to produce very good results with three hours.

22582. Are you of opinion that more time should be given to mending and darning?—Much more time. The difficulty which arises under the regulations with

that after the
, the parasit

are so apt to direct the whole of their teaching with a view to satisfying the inspectors.

27898. CHAIRMAN.—You mean the teacher knows the examiner, and knows what he is likely to require, and works up to that?—That is so, and that applies specially to the examinations in our schools.

27899. That would apply, I suppose, to other subjects?—Yes, but we suffer most in reference to our sewing; with all deference to Her Majesty's Inspectors, I don't think they are the people best qualified to examine sewing.

27900. Do you think the suggestion made to us in Ireland, to have lady inspectors of sewing, is a good one?—It would be most desirable; certainly some of the inspectors know a great deal about it, and I am filled with astonishment at the amount they have learned after long experience.

27901. You have some remarks to make about kindergarten?—I wish to make one remark, because I heard a question that was put by the Archbishop in regard to its interference with the ordinary work of the school; I think this difficulty arises from a confused idea that exists in people's minds as to the *Froebel* system of kindergarten occupations. Froebel never taught children to read until they were five or six years of age, he confined the instruction to certain games and learning certain manual exercises, and they did not learn anything out of books for a good many years after they had been in the school. Now, it would be quite impossible to carry out that system in State-aided schools that had to conform to the regulations of the Code, but we have quite successfully introduced into our schools a great many of the kindergarten occupations, and these have come to be called kindergarten education. It is perfectly true that a child who had been brought up in the kindergarten, strictly on *Froebel's* principles, would be very far behind in many subjects—in reading and spelling—especially he would be very far behind a child taught in an ordinary school.

27902. MOST REV. DR. WALSH.—But plainly not behind a child who had come in from the street, and had not been put through a kindergarten course?—No; his general intelligence would have been very much quickened, and he might have a very fair knowledge of common objects; he might have a fair knowledge of certain facts of natural history, but in ordinary school subjects he undoubtedly would be behind a child who had been brought up in an ordinary infant school—an ordinary school of any kind. I think the difficulty arises from people applying the name kindergarten to the kindergarten occupations, which are merely an adjunct of the ordinary work of the infant school.

27903. REV. DR. EVANS.—I feel greatly interested in the last remark you made, because I think it really contains the explanation of the difficulty that has been mentioned and that we have more than once referred to. As to needlework, and the inspection of needlework, do you think it desirable that an examiner or inspector should be able to point out to the teacher wherein there was fault, not merely to test a thing, but if the work was not well done to be able to show how it should be done?—Certainly.

27904. And, consequently, only a lady could do

own home was not better in her performance of cookery than the other girls of a similar class of life; and thus the only way to get cookery properly introduced into our families was to begin with the children and get it into their nature as early as possible?—I would begin at an early age, but not at such an early age; I think that a girl of thirteen or fourteen might quite well learn a great deal, but I think the cookery teaching should not begin before that age.

27905. Have you found this difficulty here; the girls are taught cookery at the school, but when they go home, the practice of their mothers—who are generally the cooks in the house—is so different that the young people follow the mother rather than the teacher?—We find that a great deal of the value of the teaching given depends almost entirely on the mothers; if the mothers encourage the children to practise what they have learned in the school we find it does good. That applies to all the education in our schools, that where there is a good background of a good home, and interested parents, then the school work is valuable. In regard to cookery, there are cases, I know where it has been followed up by the parents, and the children have done good work, but it depends a great deal on the parents whether they are ready to practise at home the work they have done in the school.

27906. MR. HARRINGTON.—I suppose that what you mean is that if cookery is to be taught to girls in the last year of their school life, it would be with a view of their continuing it in the continuation school?—Possibly in the continuation school or at home, when they will have ample leisure to carry out their instruction before they have forgotten it.

27907. I suppose you hardly consider that a girl learning cookery in her last school year would have sufficient education in that branch?—I think she might learn enough to be valuable to her if she carried it on after she left school. Unfortunately I find the practice in our schools and in most of the schools of the country is to give the cookery instruction in the fifth standard. One reason adduced for that is that so many children leave school after the fifth standard, and if they don't get the teaching then, they don't get it at all. But I think the principal reason is that the girls in the sixth standard go in for so many extra subjects that it is impossible for them to make sufficient advance in them to earn grants if they are taken away for the cookery lessons. I believe it is to a very large extent a question of how the school managers can earn the most grants.

27908. You referred to the question of domestic economy, what do you understand exactly here by that?—Domestic economy in the schedule refers to questions as to food and clothing, the different constituents of food and the different kinds of clothing that are healthy, and so on. There are very many books on domestic economy. The teaching may be made valuable if the teacher is interested and knows about it, but it also may be taught in a very perfunctory manner.

27909. REV. DR. WILSON.—You prefer in regard to the forty hours' teaching that it should be one hour a week for forty weeks?—No, I think not, because [illegible]

Edinburgh.
—
Oct. 11, 1897.
—
Miss Flora C. Stevenson.

27912. It would occur to me that twenty lessons would be too few to give a girl a knowledge of cookery?—We don't profess to turn the little girls out as cooks, but to give them some lessons in the principles of cookery, and teach them to make a few simple inexpensive dishes.

27913. And you prefer to limit the numbers in the class to fourteen, or still better to twelve?—Yes.

27914. We find that to be the general opinion that a limited number is the best number?—Much better unless the teacher has assistants.

27915. Most Rev. Dr. Walsh.—You think it of great importance at all events, I suppose, to teach them that there is an art of cookery, and that there are principles underlying it?—Oh, certainly.

27916. So that there would be, at all events, that advantage in giving even a small number of cookery lessons?—Yes.

27917. May I ask whether you aim at teaching them to cook with appliances such as they are likely to have in their own homes?—To a certain extent we try to do that.

27918. Is it not very hard to expect the children to carry out in practice the lessons that they get in school, if they are taught in school to work with a range of a more or less finished kind, and if when they go home they have only the plainest and poorest kind of grate?—That is the weak point of the whole subject, that the appliances in the school are much more elaborate than the children have in their own houses.

27919. It is not that a very serious drawback to it; but the difficulty would be in teaching a class of children with the appliances you would find in an artisan's house. You might teach two children at a time.

27920. But the main point would seem to be to teach them in a way that will be of practical advantage to them afterwards, and you lose that if you don't teach them a thing that they can afterwards carry out?—They can carry it on afterwards to a certain extent, but that is one of the difficulties and disadvantages we have to contend with in giving this teaching.

27921. It is one of the drawbacks that have been found to exist when children who have been brought up in well-equipped industrial schools are sent out as domestic servants in small households of the humbler kind?—I don't think it applies to our schools so much as to large institutions, where they cook a large amount of food.

27922. I heard of one case of a child who was trained in a grand institution, where there was no light but electric light, and when the poor child went out to domestic service she did not know how to turn off the gas; but that is merely one aspect—a very important one, indeed—of a very important question?—That is a very important point, and it is a difficulty which has not yet been surmounted.

27923. We had some very interesting evidence in London from Sir Joshua Fitch in reference to needlework, and I should like to know to what extent you agree with him. He utterly condemned a system that exists to a certain extent in Ireland, of giving ten hours a week to needlework; he said it was a important point—that a great deal of what goes on in the schools under the name of needlework teaching is simply children passing their time doing over and over again some things that they already know perfectly how to do?—I don't think so, because there is a progression.

27927. Suppose that girls in a school were kept for ten hours in the week at needlework, is it not very likely that a great deal of their time would be spent in that kind of thing, and utterly wasted?—Oh, yes, ten hours would be most undesirable.

27928. Sir Joshua Fitch's idea was that in this department the elementary school should aim simply at two things; first, to give the children sufficient instruction in the art of needlework, and then to provide for them so much practice as is needful to make that instruction effective?—Yes, exactly.

27929. What he protested against was turning the schools into workshops, or treating them as places in which needlework may be practised with a view, for instance, of turning out garments for commercial purposes?—I quite agree with him.

27930. But he recognises this—and I would ask for your opinion upon the point—that it is only by the making of garments you can really secure a sufficient amount of practice, or give the children a sufficiently lively interest in their work?—By our regulations each girl is required to turn out one garment complete in the year.

27931. And that is not with a view of turning out a thing of commercial value, but as a useful means to an end, that falls strictly within educational lines, as applied even to a primary school?—Yes.

27932. You have a very high opinion, I take it, of the educational value of kindergarten?—I have a very high opinion of its educational value as an adjunct to the ordinary teaching. I don't know that I at all accept all Froebel's principles.

27933. Probably what you now refer to is Froebel's original conception, according to which the school is one thing, and the kindergarten another. He objected to children going to school, I think, before they were six years old, or thereabouts, and he said, "We must send them into the school nursery, as it were, where there is to be no book work, but where their faculties are to be developed according to certain natural principles;" is not kindergarten in that sense wholly unknown in the public educational systems of these countries?—Yes, quite unknown.

27934. The kindergarten training that we have in Ireland is just what you seem to have here; now do you think it conceivable that the result of proper teaching on kindergarten lines would be to leave the children who had gone through it in a worse condition than if they had never got any training at all, and had spent their time out in the streets?—No; certainly not; but I think there is far too great a tendency on the part of managers and teachers to elaborate kindergarten occupations. I think the highest idea of kindergarten would be that the children should be taught such exercises as would utilise inexpensive materials. Some of our teachers are exceedingly resourceful, and provide materials at a very nominal cost. In other schools we have considerable expense.

27935. Don't you think that in this matter of

Edinburgh.

Oct. [illegible], 1887.

Miss Flora C. Stevenson.

having real kindergarten work at all: now, if in any place the children really come out from the kindergarten training, or so-called kindergarten training, worse than if they had not been at school at all, is it not the obvious inference that they must have been getting, not real kindergarten training, but only the name of it, some various, or probably some harmful, attempt at it?—Exactly.

Mr. Andrew C. Tait.

Mr. Andrew C. Tait, Head Master, Science Evening School, Edinburgh, examined.

22937. Chairman.—You are the First Assistant Teacher of the Warrender Park Day School and the Head Master of the Science Evening School?—I am.

22938. What class of pupils attend in the evening schools of the Board?—The class of children who attend the evening schools are practically the same as those who attend the day schools, of course the average age is higher; in addition to that we have a small proportion of pupils who have been trained in the secondary schools in the town. I have, as far as possible, made an abstract of the occupations of the pupils for the last year. I find that, taking the males, there were 256 clerks, 340 message boys, 79 unemployed, 1,114 who were engaged in one or other branches of artisan occupations, 115 who were shopmen, and 30 engaged in professional careers.

22939. Are there several grades of schools?—Until three years ago there were two grades of schools, the higher grade of school took only those pupils who had passed the sixth standard in the day school; the lower grade of schools took those who had passed standard five. Now, all the schools are grouped together under one name, continuation schools, with the exception of one which is attended by those pupils who have not passed standard five in the day school and who are allowed by special permission of the Board to leave the day school on condition that they go to that school. One distinction, however, there is in the schools, that in four or five of these classes special facilities have always been given for the teaching of the different branches of drawing, freehand, model, geometrical drawing, shading and building construction.

22940. And physical science?—And physical science.

22941. Was machine and building construction taught until last session with a view to the May Science and Art examinations?—Yes, until that time.

22942. What was the reason for severing the connection with the Science and Art Department?—It was found there was great difficulty to make the regulations fit in with the regulations in connection with our evening schools. The minimum requirement of the Science and Art Department is an hour, and the register must be marked at the end of the lesson. If a pupil were at that is deterred so from getting him for the evening for any of our subjects of general instruction, so when our pupils had that they had to devote two entire evenings to that particular subject on the lines of the syllabus of the Science and Art Department.

22943. Is physical science taught as a specific subject according to the regulations approved by the Scotch Education Department?—Not now. Until the introduction of the new evening school Code in 1893 that was the case, but since the introduction of the new evening school Code in 1893 it comes under the head of science subjects and subjects of practical utility.

22944. I see that there is a table you have prepared here which gives these schemes; is it with reference to the old system or with reference to the new?—With reference to the new.

22945. What were the effects of the new Code of 1893?—Before 1893, in the advanced schools, that is to say, the schools which were attended by those pupils who had passed standard six in the day school, grants of 4s. could only be claimed on every individual pass, in what were then considered the specific subjects. These specific subjects were the same as were taught in the day school, or a special scheme might be submitted by the headmaster to the Department, and the examination would be made on that, but the payment was entirely made on individual passes. Now the payment is made entirely on the attendance and the quality of the work done. Two grants are paid: a fixed grant of 1d. per pupil per hour, and a variable grant of 1d. or 1½d. per pupil per hour depending on the quality of the work done. The effect of that was to give us much more freedom in the class of subjects we taught. We were thus enabled to give more of a general education even in what had been the advanced schools, that is to say, not to neglect such subjects as English, English literature, and composition and arithmetic.

22946. What subjects are taught in the various schools?—The various subjects of practical science, and in addition to these we have such subjects as shorthand, book-keeping, English, geography, French, conversation, domestic economy, needlework, cookery, drawing, manual instruction in woodwork, dressmaking, and vocal music, besides all the subjects of the ordinary day school curriculum.

22947. How long does the course extend?—The course in science extends to twenty-four lessons of one hour each.

22948. And in building and machine construction?—Two hours per week, extending over 24 weeks of

the teachers in our Edinburgh Board schools have received a certain amount of scientific instruction in the training colleges; we very rarely in our staffs are without one or more who possess certificates under the Science and Art Department to qualify them to give instruction in particular branches in which we wish instruction given; but the difficulty is sometimes this, that although they have this theoretical knowledge, as the subject is not taught generally in schools there is some difficulty in getting a man with practical experience.

22954. Mr. H[illegible].—How is the apparatus you speak of supplied, is it supplied by contract?—No, we send in our order to the School Board offices. It is supplied by a firm in town, not by contract at all; we can the articles we wish and select them; there is never any trouble about that.

22955. Rev. Dr. W[illegible].—What are the numbers that attend the school?—Last session the enrolment was over 3,000, the average attendance was 2,834.

22956. How long have these schools been in operation?—I suppose the Edinburgh Board have had evening schools open for the last twenty years, but it is only within the last eight years they really have become popular.

22957. Most Rev. Dr. Walsh.—Is there not considerable elasticity in the Scotch Code as regards the programme for elementary science work?—Oh, yes, we have perfect freedom in that matter. The Department issues a syllabus, but we are not bound down to that at all, they are always willing to accept any scheme submitted to them.

22958. Does the Code itself contain a number of alternative programmes?—No alternative programme.

22959. We found that the English Code does; but then we were told that, in addition to all the alternative courses set forth as alternatives in the Code, it was open to the manager of any school to submit a programme of his own, and if his programme was approved by the inspector, he could then go on teaching his school according to that programme?—That is the regulation here.

22960. In the English Code I think there are seven programmes in elementary science, and we were told that these were merely specimens, each of them representing a particular type, for the information of the teachers, or of the public, all the further latitude which I have described being allowed besides; have you in Scotland the same variety?—The Department themselves give a Code to be followed in connection with the practical science, but you don't need to follow it unless you like; you have perfect liberty to submit any scheme you think suitable for your district.

22961. And having made out a suitable scheme, you teach according to that scheme, and the inspector is bound to deal with you on the basis of that scheme?—Yes.

22962. Does that apply only to elementary science?—No. In the evening school we have book-keeping, shorthand, and English literature.

22963. Does it apply to the subjects in which you are in connection with the Science and Art Department?—Yes. We are not now in connection with the Science and Art Department for any subject; but we may submit schemes for any science subject we wish to teach, to the Scotch Education Department, and then, when it has been approved, we teach in accordance with it.

22964. Mr. S[illegible].—Might you not put it this way that there is no subject in which the managers may not submit what scheme they please?—There is no subject in which they may not submit a programme in evening schools.

22965. Even in elementary subjects?—Yes.

22966. Does not that apply to day schools in the case of class subjects?—Yes, in geography, history, and English.

22967. I find a note in the fifth schedule in the Code—"The class-teaching in the class subjects mentioned in this schedule will either follow one of the courses indicated in the schedule, or if the managers desire they may submit to the inspector at his annual visit some progressive scheme of lessons in this subject suited to the requirements of the school?"—That is so.

22968. In the case of an evening school as distinguished from a day school there is no fixed annual examination?—None.

22969. They have visits without notice?—We have during the course of the year two or three visits without notice from the inspector; he goes round and sees the working of the whole school, he may examine orally any class which is going on at the time. The work goes on without disarranging the time table, and towards the end of the session he is at liberty to give a written examination in any subject he thinks fit.

22970. But that would be only towards the end of the session?—Yes.

22971. And in setting the written examination, or even in the oral examination, he would be very careful to follow the lines of teaching?—Each teacher in our evening schools keeps a note of what he has done during the session; he has the scheme before him, and is able at any part of the year to tell the inspector how far he has gone, and the inspector will make his examination follow the scheme.

22972. He does not examine on a scheme arranged beforehand, which the teacher may not have been able to carry out, but examines on what the teacher has been able to do—the examination would be on what he had done?—That is so.

22973. And don't you think that that method of examination has conduced to some extent to the efficiency of the evening schools?—It has conduced very greatly to the efficiency of the evening schools.

22974. You are able to carry on your work on the lines you think best without having it disarranged for the purpose of an examination?—We simply teach as we find we are able to carry our people on through the session, and the inspector, if he is satisfied that sufficient progress has been made, is quite willing to accept what has been done.

22975. And on the other hand there is no barrier to a perfectly thorough examination towards the end of the session on the work that has been done?—Last year we had no written examination whatever, but in the previous session we had a written examination in book-keeping, shorthand, and arithmetic, almost on the same lines as what we had before individual examination was abolished.

22976. Judging from your experience of that method of examination in evening schools, you would rather argue that a similar method would have good results in a day school?—Yes, to a certain extent, only in some subjects in the day schools I don't think individual examination could be discontinued; I think you can only form a complete judgment of parts of the work by seeing individual results.

22977. My point is rather the question of a fixed date for examination versus a visit to the school at uncertain intervals and examining on the work done?—I would prefer a visit at uncertain intervals and examination on the work done even in day schools.

22978. And it would permit of more progress being made in every subject?—I think so.

22979. Is it not the case that children are kept marking time in reading and arithmetic perhaps for a month before the examination—I don't mean the whole of the school?—In very many cases it is; many of the better children have the work of their standard up two or three months before the time of the annual examination, and the rest of the time is marking time.

22980. That is an enormous waste of educational power?—Yes.

22981. And that is due to having a fixed examination?—To a very great extent it is.

Edinburgh.

Oct. [illegible]

Mr. Arthur C. [illegible]

22982. You have a great many subjects taught in the evening schools?—Yes.

22983. Very largely of a practical character?—Almost entirely.

22984. Such things as the pupils are likely to need in the occupations they are now following?—In the subjects of science we draw out we keep that in view almost entirely, and select those parts of the sciences which are likely to be useful to the pupils.

22985. You find a great many pupils taking up book-keeping because they find it useful in their occupations?—We find book-keeping most commonly taken of all the subjects.

22986. And shorthand is very commonly taken by pupils because they have found it useful in their employments?—Almost every clerk who comes to the school takes shorthand.

22987. Would it not be better to have these subjects taught as much as possible in the evening schools entirely, and relieve the day school teacher of a large amount of that work?—I think so; I think book-keeping and shorthand ought to be taught entirely after the pupil's more elementary education has been completed.

22988. That is to say book-keeping should be taught to those children who want book-keeping and find it an advantage to them, and in that case it should be taught in the evening school?—Yes, and not taught to all and sundry, as it would be if it was a subject in a day school.

22989. Nine-tenths of whom may never have any occasion for book-keeping?—It is quite possible.

22990. Most Rev. Dr. Walsh.—What would you think of a suggestion that seems to me a rather indefensible one, that in all day or town schools book-keeping should be made an obligatory subject?—I think it would be a very bad one.

FIFTIETH PUBLIC SITTING.—SATURDAY, OCTOBER 23, 1897.

AT 10 O'CLOCK, A.M.,

At the School Board Offices, Bath-street, Glasgow.

Present:—The Right Hon. The Earl of Belmore, G.C.M.G., in the Chair; His Grace The Most Rev. William J. Walsh, D.D.; The Right Rev. Monsignor Molloy, D.D., D.Sc.; Rev. Henry Evans, D.D.; Rev. Hamilton Wilson, D.D.; Stanley Harrington, Esq., M.A.; W. R. J. Molloy, Esq.; and J. Struthers, Esq., M.A.;

with J. D. Daly, Esq., B.A., Secretary.

Sir John Neilson Cuthbertson, LL.D., Chairman, School Board of Glasgow, examined.

22991. Chairman.—You are the Chairman of the School Board of Glasgow?—Yes.

22992. You have paid considerable attention to the subject of our inquiry?—Well, I should like to say, my lord, that my first desire is to welcome you to Glasgow, and these rooms, and to answer any questions of a general kind that you may have to put. I would like to refer to our clerk, Mr. Alexander, for any details, while I am quite prepared to reply to general questions.

22993. Perhaps then you would in general terms make some observations upon the instruction in woodwork that is carried on in Glasgow?—Well, I must say, my lord, that it is still on its trial with us. About six years ago it was first introduced, and we have every reason to be satisfied with it. We have at the present moment ten special workshops in different parts of the town, seven in operation, and three nearly completed. The first one that we established, five or six years ago, has been very successful; it is a centre, and the schools of the district, to the number of about nine, send their scholars there, chiefly the upper standards. As far as I can form any opinion I should say it is not desirable to send young boys to this manual instruction, in fact I should be inclined to restrict it to the sixth standard.

22994. At what age do they enter the sixth standard, as a rule?—About twelve or so. I should say that it does not lead to much advantage for younger boys than that, however, we have some of the fifth standard that are sent, and the testimony of our headmasters is entirely in favour of it. We thought at first it might take the scholars' minds off their general lessons, but it is not so; in fact I have one case in my mind at present where the headmaster, being told that a boy had attained great proficiency in the manual instruction place, said "Well, that is the dullest, stupidest boy in my school," and it was the means of rousing him and finding the way he was capable of being got at. On the other hand the same headmaster said that some of his brightest boys could make little head of this manual instruction. Our experience is that it has brightened the school, especially the slower boys, who don't take up literary studies, and I don't say that the better scholars have not profited too, but it is more marked in the case of the boys who have not taken to literary work.

22995. How did you commence and develop the system?—It began in one of our schools where we put aside one of the rooms for the purpose, and fitted it up with benches and tools, and put an instructor. I may mention that the instructor was a skilled mechanic who had resolved to follow up his studies at the University, a man of considerable acquaintance with mathematics and practical mechanics. He gave us his spare time from his university studies, and we were so pleased with the success of that one class that we next built a special building in the east end of the town, Dalmarnock school, which I am told you are likely to see on Monday, and thither we transferred that same gentleman, and he takes the scholars from the nine schools in relays and occupies all his spare time in that way.

22996. Perhaps I better leave this question of cost to Mr. Alexander, and ask you generally what you consider to be the value of the instruction?—You mean from an educational point of view? I have explained that I think it brightens the scholar and is a pleasant relief from the drudgery of the schoolroom.

22997. Do you think that it develops the powers of observation in a way to counteract the effect of the tendency to learn lessons by rote, which all children

nine laboratories, eight in the elementary schools and one in the High school; that is a matter that dates back fourteen or fifteen years when we began to have these laboratories and consulted the Science and Art Department, who gave us their advice and we have found them very useful.

Glasgow. Oct. 25, 1888. Sir John Neilson Cuthbertson, LL.D.

23009. Are the teachers of science, teachers on the ordinary staff?—Yes, we are speaking about the day schools not the evening schools.

23010. Elementary science was taken as a class subject, in eight schools, I understand?—Yes, we are trying to promote it in every school now.

Mr. Alexander.—There has been a change in the Code.

23011. CHAIRMAN.—The Board is now taking steps, I understand, under articles 19a and 19b to make the teaching better in forty-one schools?

Mr. Alexander.—It is given in forty-one; we mean to add the other twenty-seven or twenty-eight now if possible.

23012. CHAIRMAN.—What is the Board's scheme of lessons?—It is meant chiefly as a guide, and considerable scope is left to the teacher to present a scheme of his own, but it might be well that you should have this paper (produced) as a suggested syllabus of instruction.

23013. Science is taught to pupil teachers?—Oh yes, we are carrying the education of our pupil teachers to a very considerable length now. I may mention as a gratifying feature that at the preliminary entrance examination of the University just concluded, six of our pupil teachers passed that examination, which is a stiff one, and obtained bursaries.

23014. Rev. Dr. EVANS.—What difficulties had you to encounter when you started this manual work, I mean difficulties on the part of parents of children, objections on their part?—We have not had any serious objections so far as I know; one or two parents have just recently asked their children to be excused for different reasons.

23015. Did they say they did not want their boys to be carpenters or something of that kind?—They said so; they did not quite understand our object.

23016. Have these objections melted away or do they still continue?—They still continue to a certain extent on the part of parents who are ill-informed.

Mr. Alexander.—Less than two per cent. of the whole boys are withdrawn just now.

23017. Does the Glasgow School Board employ an inspector of its own?—No, our manual instruction work has not yet reached such magnitude as to require an inspector; we have only three seven centres with three in the course of formation, scarcely requiring a general inspector, but it is quite likely we shall by and by have one.

23018. Does the Science and Art Department pay you fees for this manual instruction?—A grant.

23019. Mr. HARRINGTON.—Is this scheme of object lessons and elementary science teaching compulsory by the standards?—Oh, no, it is suggested.

Mr. Alexander.—Do you mean is it made compulsory by the Code?

23020. Mr. HARRINGTON.—Are the pupils obliged to take it?

Mr. Alexander.—Oh, yes, in the schools where it is taught, but the teaching of it has been left to the option of headmasters.

23021. Is it a popular subject with the pupils?—Decidedly.

23022. And how long is it since this has been introduced?—I think about four years.

Mr. Alexander.—That particular article in the Code was introduced in 1886.

23023. Has the effect on the pupils been appreciated, do you think, by the employers of labour?—I don't know that there has been time. I don't think the nature of that instruction is such as materially to tell on the future employment of the child; it is more

23051. But, for instance, when he deals with magnetism, he will have magnets and needles?—Oh, certainly; we supply apparatus to all the teachers who teach these subjects.

23052. Is the apparatus supplied at the cost of the School Board?—Oh, certainly.

23053. Now, is there in Glasgow any system of technical education to which your children can go when their school course is finished?—Yes, sir; in the first place, there is the Allan Glen school, which I understand you are going to see on Monday, which is an organised science school of the first rank; and after that there is the Technical College, a very successful institution, which is attended by about 5,000 students, day and evening.

23054. And is there a considerable proportion of the School Board children who go to these technical colleges?—I cannot say that; the proportion of School Board children who go to higher education of any kind is only 4 per cent.

23055. Do you desire that that proportion should be increased?—Most certainly; all my effort—I have been eighteen years on this Board—has been to promote secondary education, but the temptation of wage earning is too great.

23056. Then the bulk of children go to wage earning after their School Board course is finished?—Unfortunately we cannot keep them so long as we would like.

23057. Mr. Hardcastle.—How long are they kept?—Fifth standard is the compulsory age in Scotland, and an intelligent child can pass that at eleven years of age.

23058. Monsignor Molloy.—Is there no limit of age as to the time at which they can begin to earn wages by labour?—Oh, yes, they cannot be employed full time in a factory under thirteen.

23059. Then those who go to factories may remain for two years after leaving school, loafing about?—That is quite true, they may get employment as message boys or girls.

23060. You would desire to improve that system?—Certainly; it is the defect of our system at present that we cannot keep them longer.

23061. Do you think if they could be induced to go to these technical schools, in the intermediate stage, it would be of great advantage to them?—I rather think technical schools of that kind are beyond the capacity of the great bulk of them.

23062. But suppose that 20 per cent. were fit for technical education, instead of 4 per cent.?—It would be very desirable, and observe we encourage them all we can to attend evening schools, and we have evening schools attended by about 14,000 students; they are going on now.

23063. Can you say, roughly, what proportion of the School Board children go to evening schools after their School Board course is finished?—We might say 10 to 15 per cent.

23064. Are these evening schools under the Board?—Yes; we are very pleased with the result.

23065. In the evening schools do you continue the course of manual work, and of physical science?—I think there are two classes for manual work.

Mr. *Alexander*.—It was begun this winter for the first time.

23066. What about physical science?—That is developed of course, much more largely in the evening; there are classes quite advanced for these subjects.

Mr. *Alexander*.—Under the Science and Art Department.

23067. Then, in fact, you have made provision, in your scheme, for the training of pupils in manual work, and also in the elements of physical science, from the time they begin their education, until they have completed a course in the evening schools, if they wish to go to these schools?—Yes, we have pupils going on twenty and twenty-one, and twenty-two years of age, in the evening schools.

23068. And if they choose to go farther, they have the technical schools?—Yes, and any amount of bursaries; we have no trouble in Glasgow in getting clever children educated.

23069. Do you find, practically, that these simple elements of science, which are taught in a primary school, are of great advantage to the children who wish to continue their education afterwards in evening schools and in technical schools?—Of course that is only a matter of opinion, but I give my opinion that it is of advantage.

23070. If they had not got these first elements in the primary schools, they would not be fit to begin the technical course?—I daresay you may have heard different opinions about that. I have heard professors at the University say they would far rather have a student who knew nothing, and the professor could mould him according to his own ways.

23071. Well, university professors sometimes have peculiar opinions. I suppose if the children were taught according to the particular ideas of these university professors you refer to, they would be willing to have them taught in the primary schools?—I don't know, sir, I don't think anybody supposes they will learn a great deal, but they have got their eyes sharpened; they are being got to observe nature and natural objects, and they get a taste, I think, to pursue their studies further.

23072. Then you consider the chief advantage of this teaching is that it cultivates their faculties of observation?—I do.

23073. And that they acquire some skill to use their hands and fingers?—I think that is always it.

23074. You have two training colleges, I think, under the Board?—Not under the Board, they are under the churches, they are denominational; the Roman Catholic one, I speak with deference, is entirely denominational, but the other two receive pupils without distinction.

23075. But in their administration they are denominational. They receive pupils of all denominations, but the authorities belong to particular denominations?—They do. I would like to say that the new one for Catholics is very admirably equipped.

23076. I think you said that a large proportion of the teachers in the Board schools, have been trained in these denominational training colleges?—You may say the bulk of them, because we always prefer those who have been trained.

23077. I suppose in the training colleges they give a course of physical science?—They do.

23078. And of manual work?—Not manual work, I think it might be desirable that they did give manual work, but they don't, they teach mathematics. I am chairman of one of the colleges.

23079. Could we see the actual teaching of physical science in one of these colleges?—I shall be very happy to inquire. They are open to inspection.

23080. Rev. Dr. Wilson.—You mentioned that you had a pupil teachers' institute; what is the nature of the instruction given in that institute?—Well, it is the highest professional training we can give them as teachers; it is in a measure a preparatory school for training college and university.

23081. The training colleges you say are practically denominational. From what sources are the expenses of these training colleges derived?—Chiefly by Parliamentary grant.

23082. Most Rev. Dr. Walsh.—Three-fourths of the expense comes from the Parliamentary grant?—Yes.

23083. Rev. Dr. Wilson.—You have no result fees in the Glasgow schools?—No, our schools are all free, with the exception of the upper.

23084. A fixed salary to the teacher?—It is in most cases a fixed salary.

23085. The School Board provides that salary?—Yes, out of its funds.

23086. And these funds are derived from the only rates?—First from the Government, the Parliamentary grant, and secondly by local rates and grant in relief of fees, and, to a small extent, from fees in the secondary departments.

Glasgow.
Oct. [illegible], 18[illegible].
Sir John Neilson Cuthbertson, LL.D.

Glasgow.

Oct. [illegible], 1897.

Sir John Neilson Cuthbertson, LL.D.

the least sense of competition and rivalry holds out to entice the child, at all hazards, to come to school; it seems to me a shocking thing; you here in Glasgow allow a reward for good attendance, even although the attendance is not absolutely perfect?—I think we allow eight or ten absences.

23120. You are wise. Now with reference to the Science and Art grants, you said, I think, that it was announced that these grants were to be withdrawn?—The day school grant.

23121. But in the Report of the School Education Department I see a correspondence beginning with a minute dated July, 1897, and from the minute it would appear that what is contemplated is simply a transfer of the administration of these grants from the Science and Art Department to the Education Department; it surely is not proposed to cancel the grant?—But the Science and Art Department have begun by cancelling them.

23122. Perhaps I do not take in all the bearings of this. There is an official letter here from the Education Department, in which, if I understand it rightly, they say that the grants for the present financial year, ending March, 1898, will be accounted for by the Science and Art Department. "The grants for the forthcoming Session," that is, for 1898-99, "will be transferred to this Department," that is to the Education Department?—Yes, but you will see, my lord, that they have already cancelled the grant.

23123. So far as I can see they have only announced that it is to be given in future by another body, that is, by the Education Department?—I don't know what the Scotch Education Department may do, and we are still trying to get them to alter the decision, but the decision as at present intimated is that we shall get no grants this year for these different classes.

23124. Let me read this for you:—"It has been determined that the administration of the grants to schools and classes of Science and Art in Scotland shall be transferred from the Department of Science and Art to this Department," that is, to the Education Department. "During the current financial year, ending March 31st, 1898, the grants for Science and Art Schools will be accounted for by the Science and Art Department, in the vote for which Department they have been included." Surely that money has been voted for you by Parliament?—Yes I should hope we will get it.

23125. I dare say you will, as you are Scotchmen: with us in Ireland I should not be so sure of it: Your difficulty is only for the current financial year?

Mr. *Alexander*.—I think you will find that they state this year the schools must be worked in accordance with regulations of the Science and Art Directory, and according to the new Science and Art Directory, our day classes are not recognised.

23126. I think you may be safely trusted to get your own from them. There is just one other point. Have you heard it suggested that the kindergarten departments were doing harm in your schools, instead of good?—No, not at all.

23127. I dare say it would surprise you to hear that such a notion was suggested to us in Ireland by an experienced, intelligent, and, I may say, representative teacher?—Well, you will have evidence from one of our infant mistresses, and I have no doubt she will be surprised to hear that.

Do you know to what occupations the boys who have had manual training subsequently go?—I have been making some inquiry about that recently. It is in a district where the most of them went into special trades of one kind or another, and the masters were not prepared to say that the manual training had had any influence on them, not yet had experience enough of it.

You could not give us an indication of the number that go to universities and go on professional ways of life?—I am afraid not without inquiry.

Mr. HARRINGTON.—I think you said that about the sum allowed for apparatus for elementary science?—At the maximum.

Monsignor MOLLOY.—In any one year?—

Mr. HARRINGTON.—For one school?—

How would that be divided—for instance, how much for physical apparatus and for chemical?—I am afraid I could not tell you that; the teachers ask for what is required at the time.

I suppose in some schools we may take it the teacher would teach elementary physics and elementary chemistry, and perhaps a little botany?—Yes, but the idea of the Board was not to have science taught in that way, not to have regular teaching, but more to have advanced object lessons.

But he might teach a little of either of these in an elementary way?—Yes.

So for £10 your Board considered he could get sufficient apparatus for simple illustration—£10 a year.

J. N. Cuthbertson.—He may get more than that; in the course of years get £40 or £50.

Mr. DARRINGTON.—What would be the number of pupils in any one school?—I have one or two schools where there are 300 scholars.

Would he be allowed the same amount for that as in a large school?—Probably we should make more inquiry before we granted a large sum.

CHAIRMAN.—Do you mean 300 scholars in science?—No, the size of the total school.

We have not got the average size of your schools?—From 1,000 to 1,200, the accommodation.

What are the 300 you are alluding to?—One or two small schools.

Mr. HARRINGTON.—Is this science teaching given chiefly by the ordinary teachers?—Always by the ordinary teachers.

What difficulties had you in the way of getting these subjects taught when the Board decided upon it?—You understand this Article [illegible] introduced into the Code in 1883, and it was left to the masters to introduce science or not, and they introduced it of their own option; the Board never applied any pressure.

Is this form of teaching generally in your schools under the supervision of any particular inspector?—The Government inspector; we have no inspector here.

Rev. Dr. EVANS.—No Science and Art inspector?—We have a Science and Art inspector.

Mr. HARRINGTON.—Not for the elementary schools?—No, they don't visit them except for [illegible]

Mr. MOLLOY.—What is the duration of the college course?—Two years.

23167. Then there is a special course of instruction and there are examinations for that degree?

Sir J. N. Cuthbertson.—Yes.

23168. Would you under the Glasgow School Board accept the services of a teacher or drawing who had not a certificate?—Oh, yes, we have taken on teachers who had not the full certificate, but the usual thing is that they have passed in three or four subjects, and they usually undertake to complete it, but the great majority of our teachers have some qualification under the Science and Art Department.

23169. Monsignor MOLLOY.—In your system, the headmaster superintends all the classes of the school?—That is so.

23170. Does he himself teach any of the classes?—Well, in some of the smaller schools the headmaster will teach pretty regularly, but in the larger schools he will only teach occasionally.

23171. His chief business is to superintend the school and look after the teachers in the performance of their work?—Yes.

23172. Is he generally a person who has passed through the usual stages of teaching?—As a rule, yes.

23173. So he has a practical knowledge of teaching?—Yes, he has probably been a pupil teacher, and assistant and second master as well.

23174. He is a man who has risen from below, rather than come down from above?—That is so in our system.

23175. I suppose then when application is made for money for apparatus, the application is made by the headmaster?—By the headmaster.

23176. He settles the requirements of the school according to his judgment?—Yes.

23177. Have you any list of apparatus drawn up, such as is usually published by the Science and Art Department, showing what the Board would be prepared to provide?—No, we have never drawn up a list of that kind here.

23178. Then is the headmaster quite free to apply for anything he wants?—He is quite free to apply, but it does not follow that he will get it.

23179. He knows by the experience of others what he is likely to get, and keeps his demands a little above that?—Yes.

23180. Do you think it would be useful, eventually, when you have had sufficient experience, to draw up a list of apparatus such as would be a normal equipment for any one school?—We have always gone on the principle of allowing our headmasters as much liberty and discretion in these matters as possible.

23181. I was told that the detailed programme under which the elements of science are taught, is drawn up by the masters, but I was not quite clear whether this meant the headmaster, or the master actually engaged in teaching the subject?—Well, it comes to the Board from the headmaster; he is responsible for it.

23182. He probably has drawn it up in conference with the actual teacher of the subject?—That is so.

23183. Rev. Dr. WILSON.—Your teachers are classified according to merit, for instance, under the National Board in Ireland we have first, second, and third, and first of first, and second of first, and so on; have you a similar classification?—No.

23184. Each class will have a fixed salary?—There is a scale of salaries for headmasters, second masters, third masters, infant mistresses, and assistants.

23185. What is the usual salary for your head-

Glasgow.

Oct. [illegible]

Mr. George W. Alexander, M.A.

23187. Most Rev. Dr. Walsh.—These salaries that you have now described are paid out of the general funds of the Glasgow School Board?—That is so.

23188. Not exclusively out of the Government grant?—No.

23189. The accounts of your School Board seem to show that the total expense of the Board at present is over £300,000 a year?—Yes.

23190. Of that amount a considerable sum has to be paid for the purchase of land for schools?—That is so.

23191. I see about £40,000?—Yes.

23192. A considerable portion has also to be paid in interest on loans and repayment of loans; that comes to about £90,000 more?—Yes.

Sir J. N. Cuthbertson.—Allow me to explain, that is more theoretical than actual; our outlay for buildings and interest is £60,000 a year, not more; we got them all by loan; the amount is about £25,000 interest, and £35,000 for the repayment of the loans.

Witness.—I think, roughly speaking, that is about it.

23193. Well, say £50,000 or £60,000; then the expense of administration of the School Board work in Glasgow must come to a good deal; it seems to amount to £7,000 or £8,000 a year?—That is for salaries of officials.

23194. Then I see that the amount paid in salaries, I suppose to teachers, is £130,000 a year?—Yes, that is for both day and evening schools.

23195. These are the principal items of expenditure; but I see you also spend about £11,000 or £12,000 a year on fuel and lighting for the schools?—Fuel and lighting and cleaning, that includes the salaries of the janitors.

23196. The janitors seem to be very important functionaries in the Board's town schools. Now, on the other hand, as regards income, your whole Parliamentary grant from the Education Department is only £70,000 a year?—Yes.

23197. So that it would not do much more than pay one-half of the salaries that the teachers get?—Not much more.

23198. If you spent the whole of the Parliamentary grant in paying the teachers you would be only able to pay them half their present salaries?—That is so.

23199. You also get from the Science and Art Department £4,000 a year, and the fee grant comes to about £40,000?—Yes.

23200. I see you receive about £11,000 in school fees; I suppose that includes evening schools?—Day and evening. There are only two day schools that are not free, a boys' school and a girls' school, and we charge fees in the secondary departments.

23201. How many evening schools have you?—Thirty-one.

23202. And the Parliamentary grant is available for them?—Yes.

23203. I suppose that in the evening schools special attention is paid to practical subjects?—We have all kinds of evening schools; and several give attention to the more practical subjects.

23204. The cost of maintaining the schools in your Glasgow Board Schools is £3 7s. 7d. per scholar?—That is so.

23205. Does this mean that the total cost of the education instruction you are giving in Glasgow is £3 7s. 7d. per head?

Sir J. N. Cuthbertson.—Not including buildings.

23206. Am I right in taking it that of this £3 7s. 7d. a head, £2 17s. goes in salaries for teachers, and 10s. for other expenses?—That is so.

23207. And am I also right in taking it that of this £3 7s. 7d. a head, less than half comes from the Parliamentary grant, £1 1s. 7d. a head?—Yes.

23208. And 13s. 2d. comes from school fees?—Yes, including the grant in relief of fees.

23209. I see you have expended over a million sterling in building schools—that is, between the cost of sites and buildings—£312,663 for sites, and £720,109 on buildings?—Yes.

23210. And the cost of the sites per unit of accommodation is £4 8s.?—Yes.

23211. And £10 per unit of accommodation is the cost of the erection of the buildings?—Yes.

23212. So that you allow a total cost per unit of accommodation of £14 9s. 6d.?—Yes.

23213. Of the total income of the Board a very considerable portion is derived from the School rate of the city?—That is so.

23214. The city, I think, must levy to the amount of about £100,000 a year in order to keep up its system of Board Schools?—Rather more than that.

23215. I have the figures here for the last three years. In 1894 it was £93,000; in 1895 it was £98,000; and in 1896 it was £109,000. The amount is large, and it is steadily increasing, which seems to show pretty plainly that the people are satisfied with the kind of instruction that is given, and with the results that are attained. The rate at present is, I think, over 10d. in the £?—It is 10½d.

23216. Each penny in the £ with you brings in £11,000 a year?—Yes.

23217. Monsignor Molloy.—Do they grumble at the rates?

Sir J. N. Cuthbertson.—We have been extremely well supported by the public. I never heard any serious grumbling. A rate is always grumbled at; but not the school rate more than any other.

23218. Mr. Harrington.—Monsignor Molloy asked you whether there was any printed list of the apparatus required in your school, and you said there was not; could you give us any written list of what you have in a well-organised school where elementary science is taught, and the cost of it?—Yes, I shall be very glad to give you that; we have a stock-book in each school.

23219. Rev. Dr. Evans.—I should like to know if you gave up any subject on your programme that had been previously there in order to make room for manual instruction?—Not that I am aware of.

23220. The other subjects have not been curtailed in any way?—Something must have been curtailed, but that was left to the headmaster. The majority of the classes meet from either 9 to 11 or 3 to 5, which means an extension of one hour, as the schools usually close at 4.

23221. But, practically, there has been no curtailment; they find time to get it all worked in?—Yes.

23222. And the other subjects have not suffered?—The headmaster's opinion is that the other subjects have benefited.

23223. Rev. Dr. Wilson.—What are your school hours in Glasgow?—Usually from a quarter past 9 to a quarter past 12, and from a quarter past 1 to 4 o'clock; there is an hour for dinner, and there are short intervals in the forenoon and afternoon besides, five or ten minutes.

and by practice lessons; kitchens have been fitted up by the Board in forty-eight centres for the teaching of cookery; fourteen of these kitchens are centres for thirty-three of the schools, and in the thirty-four remaining schools, the scholars of those particular schools receive their instruction.

23725. Are these kitchens used for any other purpose?—Sometimes we give permission that they should be used for other purposes when cookery is not being taught; we dislike doing so, but sometimes when there is great pressure in the school at the end of the school year permission is given. The head-master has to apply to the Board.

23727. Has there been any instance where the room in which manual woodwork is taught is used on other days for a kitchen?—Nothing of the kind exists here.

23728. Do you think that would be a good plan or an objectionable plan?—Very objectionable, indeed; a cookery centre has to be well fitted up and kept exceptionally clean and in good order; we consider the lesson in cookery should be a lesson in cleanliness and tidiness.

23729. What is the extent of the work?—The number of scholars under instruction in the school year ending 1883 was 7,781; the number of girls for whom grant was received, was 6,511. There are two courses permitted by the Scotch Code—a course of forty hours in the year, for which we receive a grant of 4s. a head. We received that grant last year for 6,367 scholars. Then it is also possible to give a course of twenty hours in the year. The scholars working in that class are a smaller number, and we received a grant of 2s for 444 scholars.

23730. What do you consider the best size for a class?—The Scotch Code permits twenty-four to be taught together in a practice class; I consider that much too large a number; twelve or fourteen, I consider, is the best number.

23731. What is the age at which girls begin to be taught?—Sometimes they are very young. We think that cookery requires to be taught to the girls in [illegible] class schools in standard 4. The Board like the girls to have two courses if possible. We leave it to the head-master to decide whether cookery will be taught in standards 4 and 5 or in 5 and 6. A great number of our girls leave school at the end of standard 5; therefore in many of our schools they receive instruction in 4 and 5. In the year for which I took these figures instruction was given in 4 and 5 in forty-two schools, and in twenty-six schools in 5 and 6.

23732. What is the length of the lesson?—Two [illegible]

[illegible] regulations for the training [illegible] the Scotch Department, too, has moved [illegible] not so definite as the English Depa[rtment] [illegible] this school of ours is worked to [illegible] the English Department. The time [illegible] training of teachers of cookery under [illegible] Department—I speak of the teachers who [illegible] schools receiving Government grants—[illegible] That is the least time accepted, and a [illegible] of that time has to be devoted to practis[ing] [illegible] children.

23736. What is the teacher before [illegible] teaching cookery—is she an ordinary [illegible] a rule not, the School Board of Glasgow [illegible] the idea that it was best to train the ordi[nary] [illegible] in cookery, but we found that cookery [illegible] ordinary teachers was not practicable [illegible] schools. Girls with a good general edu[cation] [illegible] forward to be trained as teachers.

23737. Beginning at the beginning [illegible] had any previous experience?—Yes, [illegible] one of the chief difficulties is to get them [illegible] trained in teaching; I don't think [illegible] sufficient.

23738. Is the social position of th[e] teacher under your institution that of [illegible] teach or something higher than a cook? [illegible] something higher—an ordinary cook [illegible] possibly pass the examinations. We require [illegible] have a very thorough knowledge of [illegible] thoroughly get up the processes of diges[tion], circulation and respiration, and to have [illegible] knowledge of food and its functions, [illegible] found in the human body, waste and [illegible] composition of air and water, and all the[se]. They have to pass three theoretical [illegible] and the practical examinations before [illegible] their diplomas.

23739. How are the materials provided in the schools?—The teacher draws up [illegible] order, which she sends into the office, [illegible] be provided before the first lesson, and [illegible] leaving her kitchen, she leaves an [illegible] perishables to be provided for the next [illegible] these provisions are ordered by the [illegible]

23740. After the materials have [illegible] what becomes of them?—They are [illegible] scholars or to the teachers in the school. [illegible] the teachers of cookery to encourage [illegible] teachers to take dinner in the middle [illegible] course that provides a larger quantity of [illegible] scholars to cook.

23741. [illegible]

Mr. *Alexander*.—Last year the balance-sheet shows a balance to the good of £83, but we cannot keep the account for gas, for instance, separate.

22346. But the £83 is not after paying salaries. *Mr. Alexander*.—Oh, yes.

22347. Do you count that the sale of materials pays all that.

Mr. Alexander.—That and the grants.

Witness.—The total grant we received this year was £1,317 1s. 2d.

22348. Therefore it met the grant minus about £83?—Yes, after paying the teachers' salaries and working expenses.

22349. What would be the total number of pupils taught during the year?—7,701.

22350. How much per head would that be, how much per child?

Mr. Alexander.—About 3s. 6d. a head.

22351. Mr. Stevenson.—The grant represents the total cost of the teachers' salaries and the material for cooking is recovered from the pupils?—It is, as far as possible.

22352. So that the grant pays for the teachers' salaries and gives you a small balance over, which remains against the outlay on gas?—Yes.

Mr. Alexander.—And it covers the payment to janitors' wives.

Witness.—The working expenses, we may say, but it does not cover the replacement of stoves, utensils, and gas.

22353. You don't find that forty hours in the year are quite sufficient?—I don't think it is sufficient; hence our reason for teaching in standard four in certain schools, the very poor schools where we know girls will leave in standard five.

22354. You would like to have them continued two years in cookery?—I should like to continue the domestic subjects all the year round. I think in England the girls' subjects are got in with less difficulty than here.

22355. You could not possibly have it so arranged that it would be taken after the other school work was finished?—The girls would object. Headmasters have certainly endeavoured to get us to grant them permission to have the cookery after school hours, but the people object to that.

22356. You could not get any plan to get these girls to come for the cookery lessons after they had left school?—Yes, we have made a small experiment here during the last two years; the Board opened two centres, into which we tried to induce the girls to come after they had left school. In these centres they were asked to promise to remain with us for six months. One half of the day they got industrial subjects alone, cookery, laundry work, and some instruction in dressmaking—dressmaking by a simple system of cutting out—and each girl making a dress for herself.

22357. Then at the cookery school they have a joint examination and a joint certificate?—Yes.

22358. What other school in Scotland belongs to that Union?—No other. The Edinburgh school did belong to the Union at the beginning but only remained in it for three years.

22359. Do you know what might be the reason for leaving the Union—did they regard the standard as too high?—I think they did; I think they thought the training was unnecessarily long, but I think they have now fully realised that instead of being shortened it requires to be lengthened; I think the Edinburgh school has some idea of joining one of the Unions again.

22360. You said you worked according to the scheme of the English Education Department or in such a way as to satisfy the requirements of the English Department?—We do.

22361. The Scotch Department has some requirements on the subject of the instruction of cookery teachers; you evidently don't accept these as satisfactory?—I think those requirements are insufficient. The Scotch Department requires 250 hours to be devoted to training, spread over a period of not less than four months. The English Department requires six months, and during the six months twenty hours a week must be devoted to the training.

22362. And you think 250 hours spent in training is not sufficient?—The English Department requires 520 hours—a very much longer period. Of course the great difficulty is in training these young women to teach. The cookery is comparatively easy.

22363. Might there not be a difficulty in getting a supply of teachers who had gone through such a long course as that required by the English Education Department at present?—You mean a difficulty in getting girls to come forward to be trained?

22364. Well, such a supply of cookery teachers as would supply our schools in the meantime?—We don't find any difficulty.

22365. Then, have all your cookery teachers gone through a six-months' course?—Yes; of course some of them were trained about ten years ago, and the training was shorter at that period than it is now; but I consider some of them have made up for that by experience.

22366. Might not that apply to teachers who had satisfied the smaller requirements of the Scotch Department?—These were only issued a short time ago, and I think we are all feeling—those who have to do with the training of teachers—that such teachers require more science and theoretical training than they have had up to this time, and should be encouraged to take training certificates under the Science and Art Department.

22367. But that would be a point for each cookery school to arrange for itself what the nature of its curriculum should be. What the Department insists on is simply the length of the training and the amount of practice in teaching?—Yes.

22368. Well, while it might be a very desirable thing to have the six months' training you speak of, might it not be advisable in the meantime to accept teachers with a smaller qualification until we have had time to have a class of cookery teachers trained?—I would not advise that certainly.

22369. I mean to say not to make it imperative in the meantime, but after some years?—I would not recommend that. There are plenty of teachers to be had.

22370. Do you find that the teachers in country districts who take cookery are well trained?—Perhaps not in country districts; but training is now given in normal colleges, and I believe that is accepted.

22371. While it is possible for a School Board such as yours to obtain qualified teachers, if cookery is to be taught in less favoured districts we must accept a lower qualification?—In that case I would employ a trained teacher. Some of the teachers here do qualify in cookery, and in a country district the Board often cannot afford to have a specialist.

22372. There are other schools in cookery besides yours?—Mrs. Black, also a member of the School Board, has a school.

22373. That school issues certificates on a different system of training than yours?—I understand it does.

22374. Mr. Haldane.—Do you consider that cookery should necessarily form part of an elementary education for girls?—I certainly think so. I think the girls get very little training in these subjects at home, and I think the domestic subjects are of more use to them than the specific subjects in elementary schools.

22375. What you mean to say is, if they did not get them at school, they would not get them at all?—Yes. In our schools, where we have secondary departments, the girls don't get much of that teaching, because the girls

Glasgow, Oct. 22, 1895. Miss Grace Paterson.

Glasgow.

Oct. 25, 1887.

Miss Grace Paterson.

think, and the parents think, they can get it after they leave school.

23276. I suppose it is the general opinion in the country that cooking should form part of an essential elementary education for girls?—Certainly.

23277. Is the apparatus employed of the kind that the people themselves have in their own homes, or of the rather elaborate kind that we have seen in many places?—We endeavour to make it as simple as possible; but we fit up our centres for evening teaching of adults, and, perhaps, we have been a little more extravagant on that account than if we had been teaching children alone.

23278. I refer to the heating apparatus we have seen in Edinburgh?—As a rule we have a Carron cooking range and a gas-stove.

23279. Mr. Molloy.—Are the Glasgow cookery schools associated in any way with the Liverpool National Centre?—Yes; it is the same Union.

23280. Miss Calder presides over it in Liverpool?—Yes.

23281. And, if I remember aright, the school in Dublin is associated with that Liverpool school; and, therefore, on the same lines with your Glasgow school?—Quite on the same lines. We have joint examiners, and the same examination.

23282. It is a six-months' course in your training school?—Yes; from six to nine months.

23283. Is there any payment made by those attending?—Oh, yes; the scholars pay for their instruction eighteen or twenty guineas for a full diploma. That includes high-class cookery, which is not necessary for elementary school teaching, but we think it is an additional advantage if a teacher who is to teach in the public schools takes all the branches; but she can train for fourteen guineas. Then we have a special certificate for trained teachers. The payment for that is only six guineas, because we don't have to train them in teaching.

23284. What course does the ordinary teacher of a school pursue if she desires to enter your cookery school?—We grant a special certificate to her, saying that less attendance and a less fee will be required. We don't call it a diploma, we call it a certificate, and the fee she pays is six guineas.

23285. But still it qualifies her to give the instruction?—Yes.

23286. I think you mentioned twenty lessons of two hours each, would that include the demonstration lesson?—We usually give ten demonstration lessons and ten practice lessons to each scholar.

23287. Do the same pupils receive instruction in the demonstration as in the practice lesson?—Yes; we sometimes take three practice classes together to demonstration, and then divide up those scholars into groups of twenty-four each.

23288. May I inquire with regard to your school year—is it the calendar year or the financial year?—The school year terminates at the time of the Government inspection. Each school has a different time.

23289. At the termination of the course of twenty lessons, will cookery be abandoned altogether when the visiting teacher has left?—Entirely; until the course begins next year. Sometimes they get a third course in another year; only twenty lessons in each year.

23290. Then some of the girls will not receive instruction in cookery at all. Will that happen?—[illegible] number of girls being so frequently withdrawn from the ordinary work.

23292. Who tests the proficiency in the cookery?—It is not tested except by visits of members of the School Board, or officials from their office. One great is paid on attendance, and a careful record is kept of the attendance by the cookery teacher.

23293. Monsignor Molloy.—How are the parents of the pupils disposed towards the teaching of cookery in the elementary schools?—I think very favourably, indeed; and I think the children enjoy it. Some times we find that the children attend on a Friday afternoon, (when there is apt to be a lax attendance) better on the day of cookery than on an ordinary occasion.

23294. Did you find any opposition on the part of the parents when it was first established?—I think we did not.

23295. I think you said you have no difficulty in disposing of the articles that are cooked to the pupils and the teachers?—Not quite no difficulty; but we find that, on the whole, we can make the materials cover their cost. If the teachers take dinner in school, for instance, that is a great help.

23296. If they take dinner in the school they purchase the dinner that is cooked in the school?—Yes.

23297. And if the pupils purchase the dinner do they also eat it in the school?—As a rule they do; sometimes they carry it home with them. If they purchase complete dishes, but often the food is divided into small quantities for which they pay a penny or twopence.

23298. I suppose it is cheaper and better than they would be able to get at home?—In some instances very much better.

23299. Rev. Dr. Wilson.—In the evening schools do you admit other girls than the pupils of the ordinary day schools?—The day school pupils and evening school pupils are a thing apart. We teach cookery to the ordinary scholars in the evening schools and also have public lessons which anyone can attend.

23300. You receive other girls than those in attendance at the day schools?—Yes.

Mr. Alexander.—They are quite open to all.

Witness.—I thought you meant did the day school scholars return in the evening for lessons; as a rule they do not.

23301. Are these evening classes largely attended by outsiders?—Sometimes they are more attended, and other years less; we find they come and go.

23302. Most Rev. Dr. Walsh.—What test is applied to your teachers before they are appointed to teach cookery?—We have examiners, theoretical and practical.

23303. Into what do they examine, is it as to the ability of these ladies as cooks, or as to their capacity for teaching?—First of all there is a very complete and careful examination on the theory; they have to get up the processes of digestion, nutrition, circulation and respiration, and a very thorough knowledge of physiology, and we recommend students to take certificates of the Science and Art. We don't make it compulsory, but recommend them; and also certificates for hygiene.

23304. My question is about the examination. Is it held with a view of testing the knowledge of these ladies in these various subjects, or with a view of testing their capacity as teachers of those subjects?—We have two separate examinations; theoretical papers are sent to us by the examiners who have charge of that part of the work and are returned to them and marked by them, then we have examiners

to make them for themselves?—We have not found that here at all. I don't think we give so very much choice; the teachers lay down that a certain garment must be made in the standard, and the scholars must conform to that.

23325. What are the grants for needlework?—It is paid on the average attendance of girls.

23326. What classes have you in housewifery and domestic economy?—We have not yet attempted anything which might be called housewifery, but in order to make preparation for something of the kind we have had special classes in three different centres. Into these centres we invite the girls who are leaving schools, to come, some of them in standard 6 and ex-6th, and we there give instruction in laundry work, in cookery, and in dressmaking, and making up of dresses. These classes are held in ordinary school-rooms, therefore we have been unable to teach housewifery so-called—the management of the house.

23327. Are these evening classes?—Day classes.

23328. And what do you teach under the head of domestic economy?—The Scotch Code requires that some instruction in domestic economy should be given concurrently with cookery.

23329. Yes, you have already explained that?—Yes, we ask the teachers to give the children instruction in food, its composition and uses, and to teach them generally how to spend money to the best advantage, how to market, and the prices of the different materials they work with. Domestic economy is taken as a specific in twelve schools at present, but that is merely book-teaching.

23330. Rev. Dr. Evans.—I believe your ordinary teachers are usually qualified in laundry work?—They are.

23331. And do they teach in the laundry work?—If asked to do so. The laundry teaching under the School Board is very much less than the cookery teaching, therefore we don't always require their services for that subject.

23332. But their services are valuable?—They are.

23333. The needlework is taught according to the code by the ordinary teachers?—It is.

23334. Do any other teachers give instruction in needlework but the ordinary teachers?—Not during the day, but in the evening classes there are a few who are not the day teachers.

23335. Who inspects the needlework?—Her Majesty's inspector.

23336. There are no inspectors then appointed by the School Board itself?—No.

23337. No ladies advise the School Board as to the conditions of needlework instruction?—No, Mrs. Black and I make a point of seeing the needlework very thoroughly every year, because we award prizes, and we make occasional visits all the year round.

23338. I should feel extremely obliged if you could aid us to a proper distinction between housewifery and domestic economy?—I say my housewifery is domestic economy in a practical form. I have been in London during the last two days and inspected the centres there, and I found that besides learning the theory of household matters the children are shown practically how to do housework, how to clean rooms and make a bed or air a room, and I think that is very valuable, because our book teaching just passes out of their minds immediately.

Glasgow. [illegible]

23341. Mr. STRUTHERS.—Do these girls receive instruction in any other subject besides what you call domestic subjects?—None whatever, because we are teaching in the ordinary school, in the ordinary class-room, and it is not possible to do any more than that, hence my desire for special buildings.

Mr. Alexander.—Yes, but you are giving them instruction in ordinary subjects—you are giving them revision?

Witness.—Yes, we are giving them revision. It was suggested that would be a useful experiment.

23342. Do these girls attend all day?—One attendance is for revision of the ordinary subjects, the other for domestic subjects.

23343. CHAIRMAN.—What do you call revision?—Going over the work of the standards again, perfecting their composition, writing and reading. These things more especially, I find to be very useful.

23344. Mr. STRUTHERS.—You think that giving special attention to the domestic subjects induces pupils to come to these schools, who might otherwise not continue at school?—The pupils whom we have induced to come back would certainly have left if we had not had these classes.

23345. So from the point of view of their ordinary education it is advisable to have these classes provided for them?—Yes, and they certainly would not come back for the revision of the ordinary work alone, but they get that in at the same time.

23346. You gain that in addition to giving them instruction in domestic subjects?—We do.

23347. You yourself think that is a very useful line of instruction, that might be developed with advantage?—I think most necessary.

23348. You also express great dissatisfaction with the teaching of domestic economy from books?—Certainly, but I think it is better than nothing at all.

23349. But it would be advisable, as far as possible, to replace the teaching from books by this form of practical instruction you speak of?—Certainly.

23350. And for that purpose you would have the children taking these domestic subjects after they had more or less completed their ordinary school course?—I would prefer that.

23351. After they had finished standard five?—I would prefer that if we got them back for a certain period.

23352. And if you found you were able to extend these classes, make them more general than at present, you would be able to leave domestic economy out of the ordinary school curriculum and teach domestic economy practically in these special classes?—We would aim at that.

23353. We might call the practical side of domestic economy housewifery?—Yes.

23354. You have the same teachers teaching cookery and laundry work?—As a rule we have.

23355. And they are all specially trained on the lines you have already described, having a good knowledge of physiology and kindred subjects?—They are.

23356. Even supposing you continued to teach domestic economy in schools outside these practical classes would it be possible to have the instruction given by these specially qualified teachers?—I think they would have to take some technical lessons in combined also with laundry work?—The certificates are quite separate, the training may be given concurrently or separately, and the examination of course is quite separate and the diploma quite separate.

23360. The same person may not have the two certificates, it may so happen?—Yes.

23361. Then where you have to introduce laundry work and you have a special teacher for cookery, you must get a special teacher for laundry work?—Yes, or the cookery teacher must qualify in laundry work.

23362. You mentioned out of 720 scholars examined 190 passed in laundry work, who conducted the examination, that looks like an individual examination?—We receive the grant not for examination at all but for attendance, and the scholars for whom we did not receive the grant had not made the necessary attendance.

23363. There was no test otherwise than attendance?—No.

23364. With regard to needlework what time is devoted daily to that subject?—It varies in different schools from three to five hours a week; in some schools a lesson is given every day, but as a rule four hours a week is the time.

23365. In the case of these special courses, is it for girls who have left school or are leaving school?—They have left school and been induced to return.

23366. Do these cease to be recognised pupils of the school, are their names struck off the register?—No, they continue to be recognised in the attendance roll.

23367. But they would only attend for a limited period of the day?—They attend all day, one part of the day being for revision of ordinary work and the other part being for domestic subjects.

23368. And the ordinary work being literary subjects?—The standard subjects. I think it is very necessary to work up their composition, spelling, writing, and reading.

23369. How long would that course of instruction continue?—We ask them to attend for six months, we don't insist on their attending longer, but they must promise to attend for six months before they join the classes.

23370. If they happen to be proficient in literary subjects would you divert their attention to the other practical subjects?—I certainly would.

23371. The teacher has an option?—Well, as we have small numbers and we have to make special arrangements for these children, at present, because we are teaching in an ordinary school.

23372. You find that system of instruction very valuable?—Very valuable indeed, and I would extend it to all the schools if I possibly could.

23373. Most Rev. Dr. WALSH.—You spoke of a special difficulty in the Scotch schools, that would stand in the way of the children being taken away for a whole week at a time for the laundry work?—I think the teachers would very much object to all the classes being interrupted; they would object more to that than to having them absent on one day at a particular time for ten weeks.

23374. The withdrawal of the children for laundry work always involves some difficulty, as it involves an interruption of some kind to the work of the class?—Yes.

an average [illegible] in

[illegible] are paid on the
[illegible] and [illegible] it is on

guidance here is that we have only small numbers in the higher classes of the school; we take cookery for two years and laundry only in the third year, so that is in standard sixth, and the number may be small, and there may be a corresponding number of boys in the class, the boys are left, and sometimes the whole of the girls go to that class and don't even take up [illegible].

23408. The same difficulty applies to cookery, withdrawing the girls from school subjects?—Yes.

23409. How many girls at a time are taken from a class for cookery?—Twenty-four girls for a practice class, and there may be 60 or 70 at a demonstration.

23410. So that if you had a class composed entirely of girls, there would be still a remnant of girls left with nothing to do?—Yes, but we might take half the class to laundry and half to cookery at the same time, it would dispose of the whole number of girls for practical work at the same time.

23411. Under your present arrangement the difficulty would still exist whether you had mixed classes or not?—Yes, to a measure.

Miss Jane Thomson, Infant Mistress, Gorbals Public School, Glasgow, examined.

23412. Chairman.—You are the Infant Mistress of Gorbals Public School in Glasgow?—Yes.

23413. I think you can give us some information on the subject of Kindergarten; what is the nature of the instruction you give in kindergarten?—Froebel's gifts predominate; about six gifts on an average are taught in each of the Glasgow schools, sixty-seven teach kindergarten out of sixty-eight; out of the six gifts four would be Froebel's, and the other two more modern occupations.

23414. Will you tell us what the occupations are?—Basketwork, cardboard modelling, paper-cutting, [illegible] work, and making picture frames.

23415. Is kindergarten taught by the ordinary staff?—Yes.

23416. How are the teachers trained to teach it?—In the Normal College they receive a little training, and the rest is made up by actual teaching.

23417. Are most of the teachers capable of teaching kindergarten?—At present, coming out of the Normal they do not know where they may be allocated, and it is a question of training after they have been placed in the infant department; that does not apply to the headmistresses but to the assistants.

23418. How are the materials supplied; at whose cost?—The Board managers supply the material; they encourage us to realise a little money by the sale of the articles, but they do not insist on our covering the cost.

23419. Are you in favour of kindergarten as improving the powers of observation of the children?—Very much in favour of it.

23420. You think they pay more attention to the other lessons since that instruction was established?—Very much so.

23421. Mr. Molloy.—Are you in favour of the kindergarten instruction being confined to the infant schools specially?—No, I think it is lost if it is not carried higher.

23422. Would you see any difficulty in having it in first and second classes and upwards in an ordinary school that has no infant class?—No, I think it might be carried further, ought to be, if it exists at all.

23423. Might it also be carried on in the same room, or would you desire to have a separate room?—It can be carried on quite well in the same room.

23424. I think you mentioned that the assistants were not always certificated in kindergarten?—No, they are not always certificated, they are left to find their own qualifications.

23425. But the principal teacher who gives instruction in kindergarten must have a certificate?—Not necessarily; that is, in order to do her work she is bound to get a certificate, but the Government does not require that. The grant varies according to the work done and the improvement of the department.

23426. Most Rev. Dr. Walsh.—I assume you have never thought of introducing kindergarten on the strict lines of Froebel's system, that is, of having the children attending a kindergarten, strictly so called, as distinct from being at school, or learning any of the school subjects even in an elementary form?—That has never been practicable with us.

23427. And it has never been suggested that it might be introduced with advantage?—In Glasgow, I do not know that. All the kindergarten work is taught by the ordinary teachers and in the ordinary schoolroom.

23428. In your modified kindergarten training, while the kindergarten work is going on, the children also, during the same years, learn something of reading and spelling in the ordinary way?—Oh, yes.

23429. As far as you know, is the favourable opinion which you have formed of the effect of kindergarten work, the general opinion of the teachers who have to do with it?—Yes.

23430. And the general opinion of the inspectors and school authorities in Glasgow?—Decidedly.

23431. Mr. Struthers.—When you spoke of certificates a moment ago, Miss Thomson, you said that some of the teachers in infant departments were not certificated, meaning that they had not a special certificate?—That is what I mean.

23432. But as a rule they are certificated by being in the training college, in which instruction in the principles of kindergarten and infant school teaching is part of the course?—Yes.

23433. But they have no special certificate for kindergarten?—No.

23434. And they acquire their knowledge of kindergarten by actual practice in the school, having only some of the theoretical knowledge before they entered?—Yes.

Mr. Alexander [illegible], Manual Instructor under the School Board of Glasgow, examined.

23435. Chairman.—You are a manual instructor?

23436. Has every pupil to draw the object he is

Glasgow. Oct. [illegible], 1897. Mr. Alexander [illegible].

23444. Most Rev. Dr. Walsh.—Did you receive any instruction in the art of teaching?—Before taking manual instruction I had two years teaching evening class students engineering, drawing, and [illegible].

23445. That is, you had actual experience?—Yes.

23446. You never were in a training college?—I was two years in a technical college in Glasgow.

23447. Not in a training college?—No.

23448. In the training college the pupils, in addition to learning, for instance, arithmetic, learn, or are supposed to learn, how to teach arithmetic; I wish to know whether you received any similar instruction in the art of teaching school woodwork?—No, I never received any instruction in the art of teaching.

23449. Of course you have had by this time a good deal of experience in that department, and this has fully qualified you to teach it?—Four years experience.

Mr. George F. D[illegible], Manual Instructor under the School Board of Glasgow, examined.

Mr. George F. D[illegible].

23450. Chairman.—You are a manual instructor?—Yes.

23451. And I understand that you are a trained teacher, and were not an engineer?—No, I am a trained teacher.

23452. What is the course of lessons that you give?—Well, I begin with simple planing and sawing, the only difference from some other courses being that I give small models from the commencement. I find the boy's interest is not kept up unless we give that.

23453. Were you at Nääs?—No, I was at Leipzig.

23454. Do they follow the Nääs system there?—No, they used the ordinary tools, simplified to some extent.

23455. What do you conceive to be the value of the instruction that you give, from an educational point of view?—I think it has an effect on the whole nature of the child—mental, moral and physical—and as a teacher I observe that effect. I taught the subject in my own school, as a head master, before I came to Glasgow.

23456. Was your school a country school?—Yes, in Staffordshire.

23457. Had you any difficulty in finding room for teaching it, and also with regard to meeting the cost of the benches and appliances and wood?—No, but we were under somewhat special circumstances, we simply rented the tools and benches from the County Council.

23458. You did not teach in the school-house; that, I believe, you cannot do in England, you must teach in a separate place?—No; we taught it in the school-room for three years, and gained the grant.

23459. And nobody made any objection?—No.

23460. Most Rev. Dr. Walsh.—Did you receive any grant for it?—Yes, 7s. a child.

23461. Chairman.—How many benches had you in that school?—Five double benches.

23462. You had perhaps more rooms than one?—Yes, but we only used one for that.

23463. Only used one for all purposes?—No, we had other rooms.

23464. Rev. Dr. Evans.—Was the school in which you formerly were head master, and where you introduced this valuable instruction, a Board School?—No, it was under private management.

23465. Are the private managers in favour of manual instruction, as far as you know?—I think they are; they were, decidedly.

23466. What was your experience of the effect of manual instruction on other subjects in the programme?—I found it sharpened the children all round.

23467. Did you lessen the programme in any wise in order to make room?—We did, we taught only one class subject, and in some of the other subjects we shortened the time given to them.

23468. Which were they?—In arithmetic we shortened the time, and I think in geography and history; we dropped history, after a time, altogether.

23469. Did you shorten English at all?—We did not.

23470. Would you think it advisable to do so?—I don't think it would be.

23471. Mr. Molloy.—Did you experience any inconvenience carrying on the manual instruction in the school room or class-rooms of the ordinary school?—No, we had no difficulty.

23472. Then the attendance must have been much lower than the amount of accommodation provided for the attendance?—Well, the accommodation was slightly over the average attendance.

23473. From shavings or otherwise was there no inconvenience?—It was taken the last two hours of the school day.

23474. One hour, perhaps, outside the ordinary school hours?—No, half an hour.

23475. And one and a-half of the ordinary time; how often in the week?—Once.

23476. Mr. Struthers.—You regard considerable practical skill as an indispensable qualification for the teacher of manual work?—Yes.

23477. But he should also have an understanding of what the object of the work is, that it is not merely making pupils expert in using certain tools, but that it also has a distinct object in training his intelligence?—Yes.

23478. And you think a man who was merely a skilled worker might be very apt to lose sight of that object?—I have had as assistants skilled workmen and teachers, and my idea is that the skilled workmen were generally unsuitable, they turned their attention chiefly to the models.

23479. But in an exceptional case a skilled workman, who was a workman to begin with, might develop sufficient knowledge of the educational end to be aimed at to make him an efficient instructor in this work?—Yes, and I know some men who did so.

23480. Most Rev. Dr. Walsh.—But that would be exceptional?—Yes.

23481. Monsignor Molloy.—You have had experience of teaching woodwork, both before you went to Leipzig, and after you returned?—Yes; my knowledge was not gained in Leipzig, it was more for the training in teaching that I went.

23482. Where did you gain your knowledge of woodwork?—I had a knowledge of woodwork since I remember, almost; it happened to be what I saw daily.

23483. Could you tell us, if you had an intelligent teacher skilled to teach literary subjects, but not yet trained in woodwork, how long would it take him to qualify to be a good teacher of woodwork?—The most intelligent and successful assistant I ever had was a certificated teacher, and he had only the training I gave him in one winter session, six months, for four hours a week.

23484. Suppose, now, that instead of being altogether ignorant of woodwork, he had such a knowledge of woodwork as is acquired by your pupils, he could be trained as a teacher of woodwork in a still shorter time?—Yes, very much.

23485. Perhaps six months with two hours a week?—I should think so.

23486. Most Rev. Dr. Walsh.—Or possibly even in less time?—Possibly.

COMMISSION ON MANUAL AND PRACTICAL INSTRUCTION.

Mr. John G. Kerr, M.A., Headmaster, Allan Glen's School, Glasgow, examined.

the experiment several times but was horrified to discover that the children were being introduced to steam and molecules, so I stopped that. I took the five and second sections of standard six to the physical laboratory last year, and made them do simple things. They made elementary measurements for themselves and reached ideas of mass and force. They wrote down in simple language the results they got, but of course there was no tinkering in the principles of calculation.

23511. You insist on their keeping accurate records?—Yes; we have, later on, to take advantage of the physical and scientific work in order to make up for the defect in the hours we have for English. I don't think it is quite satisfactory, but it is our solution.

23512. Then you have woodwork in your school?—From the youngest pupil onwards, for every pupil.

23513. What would be the age of the youngest class?—Ten or ten and a half.

23514. Do you find pupils of that age can use tools?—Of course they cannot use the heavy planes. Our planes however are not up to the usual weight. We start the younger pupils with the knife on the lines of Sloyd.

23515. But you don't think, so far as you have occasion to use tools, pupils have any difficulty in handling them?—None at all.

23516. For the most part they are the ordinary carpenter's tools?—Yes, with the exception of the knife, and that the planes are lighter and shorter.

23517. What is your opinion of the value of that instruction in schools—again I speak more particularly of standards four, five, and six?—It is easy to use general phrases; this I would say, however, that boys after they have been there their hour or two hours are not handicapped either as regards the time spent or the energies expended; they work just as quite as freshly and vigorously as if they had not had the two hours.

23518. So that negatively we may say there is no loss?—I feel absolutely satisfied that there is no loss to the efficiency of the other subjects; but remember the time spent is relatively small, for the very most standard six had was two hours a week.

23519. What might be the least?—One hour.

23520. From one to two hours?—Yes.

23521. Apart from the fact that it does not interfere with the efficiency of the rest of the work, do you find any positive advantage from the teaching of woodwork?—Yes, I think I do; but as my direct experience has been in a school with woodwork I can make no comparison.

23522. Let us put it this way; would you, from your knowledge of educational work generally, be inclined to dispense with it?—I would not dispense with it, I am satisfied of that for various reasons. There is a quite reason that probably the head of a school has never before his mind that one set under such a responsibility, and that is this—the workshop removes the boy from the domination of the teacher in the class room and gives him an opportunity of himself doing and himself managing that which he does; there is more of absolute individual effort, and he is not dominated by the will of the teacher, and that I think is one of the great defects in ordinary school work.

23523. That is to say, it is a means of ensuring much more effectually that the boy is making real intellectual effort?—That is exactly my opinion.

23524. Is it your experience with a teacher giving a lesson to a class of fifty or sixty, that however clear his methods or vigorous his manner, it is quite possible that a considerable portion of his pupils are practically inert?—It is absolutely certain; there is too big a strain; an hour is too long for ordinary class teaching, our system is entirely wrong in that respect. We have our children too long at school each day, and too long at a subject each lesson, and they certainly get dull. They are extremely well-behaved, and their behaviour is generally in inverse ratio to the intelligent effort they are making.

23525. CHAIRMAN.—You find that when they are making intellectual efforts they are not so well behaved?—They are more vigorous, they move about, they are not hypnotised.

MOST REV. DR. WALSH.—The maximum of good behaviour, I suppose, is reached when they are asleep.

23526. MR. STRUTHERS.—You use the word hypnotised; that would describe your experience of the effects of teaching a large class?—I have taught large classes; it is a very difficult job; the teacher is bound to adopt a method of getting absolute uniformity of drillwork; there is no great spontaneity of effort on the part of the pupils.

23527. That is to say he must endeavour to reduce his work more or less to a sort of mechanical catechism?—He cannot help it with large classes; but all that is getting improved, our classes are getting reduced.

23528. CHAIRMAN.—What is the largest class a teacher can teach properly?—A very able and energetic man, a man who can discern exactly what is going on with each boy, might manage in a fairly successful manner fifty, but not more. I would like to say our classes never exceed forty. We have had classes of eighty under one man in mathematics.

23529. MOST REV. DR. WALSH.—Fifty is the largest number allowed in the English Code?—Yes, and forty in an organised science school; that is a step in the right direction.

23530. MR. STRUTHERS.—In addition to diminishing the numbers in classes you would advocate the shortening of lessons?—I believe much could be done.

23531. A teacher can impress a few essential points in a comparatively short time, and gain more by doing that oftener than taking the lesson on the same subject too long?—I think the danger the teacher runs is this, he is too anxious to get over a certain amount of work rather than to get a certain amount of effort.

23532. Your standard of intellectual efficiency is the amount of effort the pupil is induced to make?—Certainly.

23533. In addition to these other methods of improving the efficiency of the work in a school, reducing the number in class, you think that woodwork is a valuable element in a good general education?—Yes.

23534. Of course in your school you don't teach it for the purpose that many people suppose is the object of woodwork instruction, of making tradesmen, or shortening apprenticeships?—Not at all. In fact I might quote words I used the other day to a gentleman who came with reference to his boy; the gentleman is one of the most expert merchants I know. He said: "Now, Mr Kerr, I don't want my boy to be bothered with woodwork; I can teach him all I want him to know, and teach him better than you can." I said: "My dear sir, my position is this, if I were satisfied that a boy would lose his hands immediately his course was finished, I still would insist on teaching him woodwork, or at least I would urge it strongly, for the amount of general advantage he receives from it."

23535. So, very clearly you value it for the intellectual advantage, not for the manual dexterity in after-life?—Quite so; in fact I am inclined to put to the workshop those who make the least progress in such work. I have boys of my own, and I watch them individually, and those boys for whom I would insist on a little extra work are those who are going to make no use of it afterwards, and who are practically handless.

23536. Do you find boys who are dull in other subjects are sometimes intellectually able in the workshop?—Yes.

23537. Develop an unexpected intellectual faculty when they come to work with tools?—I have seen relatively dull boys do splendid work; but I would not like to go beyond that, because all the work is done in drawing.

23538. But there is a considerable intellectual effort in interpreting a drawing and constructing it in woodwork?—I certainly cannot give evidence of having observed any boy dull in his ordinary class work who showed any special ability over his neighbour in interpreting a drawing. I have no evidence of it at all, and I don't think I could get it.

23539. Why?—It is another kind of thing; you come to the mathematical region now.

23540. Then would you in an ordinary school advocate some form of manual instruction and some form of elementary science instruction as part of the general instruction of the school?—If the time could be given, undoubtedly I would; I would introduce some form of manual work, without regard as to whether time could be had or not; but as for science, unless adequate time is given, the appliances suitable, and the course well devised, it is better to be without it.

23541. Then it is your view that if there is time to introduce only one of these subjects you would prefer woodwork rather than science?—I think that is absolutely my view.

23542. But you prefer to have both, provided time could be found?—I would not have science early.

23543. You don't attach much importance to object lessons?—I attach very little importance to object lessons as I know them.

23544. Then you distinguish between object lessons as you know them and object lessons as you would have them?—I object to the word object lessons. I would try and give them a course of practical work in elementary science; it must be well devised and well supervised.

23545. That means you would not begin with very young children?—No, the earliest with pupils is standard six. I try with standard four and five another type of training, which is not science; it is for the purpose of developing quick observation, but it is not an object lesson and it is not elementary science. I will give you an example.

23546. I was going to ask you to explain to the Commissioners some of the observations you have made in that way?—I have spent a good deal of time and thought on this matter and made many experiments, or rather, I have done a good deal of work in connection with it, and I find that wonderful things can be done to the advantage of the pupils by a little departure from the ordinary routine; and, accordingly, I introduced into the school, and it is now accepted in some schools in India and some in Glasgow, a little modification of the blackboard, a blackboard that revolves on a vertical instead of a horizontal axis. I put upon that board, perhaps, to start with, merely a row of figures; the pupil cannot see the figures until the board is turned to him, then, at a signal, the board turns round and the figures are again concealed. The business is to catch the figures and write them down. The next exercise is one in addition or any elementary operation in ordinary arithmetic. The point is, that the teacher is saying nothing, even if a child is not attending he can hear the voice of a loud-voiced teacher, but a child must be sharp if he is going to pick a thing up by his eye. You may make crosses on the board and they must say how many, or you may put on the board a picture. I use with great advantage those pictures issued about Christmas from grocers' shops; they are crude; the pupil gets a short view, and his object is to put the items down on paper, and to make a little analysis of the pictures. With map-drawing we begin with a rough outline; they have to catch that and get the proportions and reproduce it, never drawing while the object is before them. A second drawing giving a little more detail. I tested that by using maps they had never seen, such as the Treasure Island of Robert Louis Stevenson, and it was marvellous how well they did it. A day or two afterwards they could reproduce it without having it before them. I kept some of them and exhibited them in the course of an address I gave on the subject.

23547. From your experience in that way did you observe any development in the quickness of observation of pupils?—I have no doubt about it. Of course one is liable to believe that that has happened which he desires to happen, but I have no doubt about it. But I need hardly tell the Commissioners an exercise of that kind can only be for a very few minutes a day, a quarter of an hour exhausts the child, and that is the difference between that kind of work and ordinary class teaching; that is the whole matter in a nutshell.

23548. And you consider that kind of teaching more advantageous to children than an hour's ordinary teaching?—Yes; I would cut down the time devoted to arithmetic in this commercial country to one half, and know that it would be one half better.

23549. That is, you would aim at getting some quickness of calculation?—Absolutely minimum precision.

23550. These experiments you have described would really obtain the intellectual results supposed to be aimed at in object lessons and elementary science?—That is so; my feeling is that it is a very effective way, but then it is my own child.

23551. You have spoken very highly of the value of woodwork and manual instruction generally, but that does not imply that you attach little importance to the literary side of education?—I attach very great importance to the literary side of education, and I may say that side of the work of the school has undergone very considerable change since I was there, probably not merely because I attach great importance to it, but to be strictly honest because of the fact that I saw that people would very soon come to the conclusion that a purely science school was not the place at which to educate their children. I realised that, but of course that means that I was satisfied that if you cut down your literary education in a school such as ours you diminish its efficiency enormously.

23552. If you had your choice in a time table between woodwork and science on the one side as against English on the other, which would you retain on your programme?—Of what age do you speak?

23553. I speak of the age of children in an elementary school, say from seven to thirteen?—I never would dream of displacing English by woodwork, however much I thought of it.

23554. Take specifically higher ages, twelve or thirteen?—Right on to the end of our course I arrange that every boy shall have at least one hour per day of his English, boys who are doing advanced work in mathematics and physics.

23555. Would you retain geography as an element in the curriculum of every elementary school in preference to woodwork and science. Have you considered that point?—I have not. I cannot just conceive the necessity for an alternative.

23556. Rev. Dr. Evans.—Are your views such as we have just heard, on paper?—I brought with me a little statement I published before the Philosophical Society of Glasgow, a meeting consisting of business men, this last spring.

23557. Mr. Molloy.—Is the Allan Glen school to be regarded as a higher class school beyond the ordinary School Board requirements?—Yes, it is scheduled as a higher class school, and we turn out boys who go right to the university and do well.

23558. You mentioned the ages were from twelve to sixteen?—We have boys even up to seventeen.

23559. And the total number under instruction 430; of the 430 you have 200 apparently in standards corresponding to four, five, and six of the ordinary school?—And ex-sixth.

Glasgow. [illegible] Mr. John G. Kerr, M.A.

23569. Do you give any teaching in physics except what you call practical physics?—Oh, yes, there are two hours spent in the ordinary classroom in which theoretical work is done based on that done in the laboratory, and of course the work is extended.

23570. Does the master who teaches practical physics in the laboratory, give lectures as well?—Yes, one of the two men superintending a class in the laboratory is the man who does the class teaching.

23571. Does he give his class teaching under a programme drawn up by you?—A programme drawn up by me in accordance with the organised science school scheme of instruction.

23572. Does that begin at the beginning and go through the whole course?—It begins at the very beginning, and goes right through. I shall have in print in a very short time the whole of the first year's course, but I could sketch out the points of the second year, and indicate the third and fourth years' course.

23573. We should be very much obliged if you would. You seem not to recommend very strongly the teaching of elementary science in the primary schools; do you think it desirable or not to have elementary science taught in primary schools?—I am not inclined to think that it is very desirable in view of the excellent work that may be done with so many other things. Science qua science is not of sufficient consequence at that point to justify the exclusion of any of the ordinary work.

23574. But a very large proportion of the pupils will never go to any higher point?—That is quite true.

23575. Therefore if they are not taught in the primary schools they will never be taught?—That is quite true, but it would not be possible, I think, to give more than an hour or so a week.

23576. Do you consider it would be desirable to give an hour a week to it?—If that hour could be spared, and if I had a good teacher and fair appliances.

23577. I suppose you consider that the success of the teaching, especially in a primary school, will depend very largely upon the efficiency of the teacher, and his special fitness for the subject?—Yes.

23578. Can you give us some general ideas as to how such a teacher should be prepared for that work in a training college?—At the present time the student in training in a training college is not trained directly—at least in the training colleges I know—to teach elementary science at all, and it would be necessary to remodel in a considerable measure the science training in the training college to get that, which I would like.

23579. Suppose you got a training college where no such system existed, will you give us your idea as to how it should be established; there is nothing to be set aside, you have simply to introduce it?—Then I would introduce a laboratory course precisely on the lines adopted for young people, and I would make the students in training under the supervision of the teacher go through this course themselves. They should also see this lecturer, we may call him, using the course with children, and the students should themselves have frequent opportunities of conducting practical instruction.

o say you are familiar with the pro-
nical science of the Science and Art

cational ladder?—The High School
school we have in Glasgow, at a success

23611. And is it the custom of your school to do it?—Yes.

23612. The "interpretation of drawing" is referred to as one of the objects of your teaching; do the boys work from their own drawing?—From their own drawings, as a rule. Our ordinary class teachers are not workshop instructors; we have a skilled artisan assisted by another skilled artisan. The work was originally arranged by a gentleman who was a high Whitworth scholar, a man with a training as an artisan engineer. The various class teachers spend half-an-hour a week in training boys in the making of drawings, they have the block before them; supposing it is a simple joint, they teach them how to make the plan and elevation. Then the pupil goes down with that, and gets his wood and proceeds to work. We endeavour to carry that always out rigidly, but I would not say that it does, for sometimes the work is ahead of the drawing, and the drawing sometimes ahead of the work.

23613. Would you approve of a system such as we saw carried out in a certain school; the instructor made a drawing on the blackboard, the plan and elevation of a particular object, delivering at the same time a sort of general lecture to the boys as to the way in which he did this; and then, having put in the measurements of each particular part, he put the boys simply to copy down on paper that plan and elevation from the blackboard?—The last point is the important part of the question; as a matter of fact, I am afraid there is too much of that done.

23614. Then from your saying you are afraid there is too much of it, it is plain you do not consider it a good thing?—It is not a good thing that he should copy it off.

23615. Don't you think it would be much better that the pupil should draw the plan and elevation for himself, no matter how rude his attempts might be to begin with?—Very soon after my joining the school I was satisfied a mistake had been committed in the workshop. They worked from a book with plans and elevations. It so happened that the teacher of the class was one day absent. I took the class; I took out a joint from my pocket, made a measurement of it, put it back, and asked them to make the same joint as they had been looking at, and I had only three who made a fair drawing, and the book is no longer in existence.

23616. The really valuable thing would be to show them how to make plans and elevations for themselves?—Yes, and then they have to make the drawing from a description; we don't always manage to carry it out, but that is the idea.

23617. Have you any other general observations to make on the subject of drawing, that you think would be of use to us?—No, we look upon drawing as a compulsory, necessary subject.

23618. It is not compulsory under the Scotch Code?—No. There is no doubt that there is magnificent discipline in drawing. We have two hours a week at least, for every boy in the school; we are not paid for a great many of these things; we are paid for nothing in the four junior classes, so that which we do is done because we think it profitable.

23619. You pay a good deal of attention in your school to drill?—In a way I might almost claim to be, if not quite a pioneer in Glasgow, certainly a very strong advocate long ago in physical drill.

23620. I believe it is now recognised in the Scotch Code?—It is paid for.

23621. And, I think, not merely paid for, but made a condition of the giving of the highest capitation grant, so that if drill is not taught in a school, the highest grant cannot be earned by that school?—I believe so.

23622. You consider that arrangement a useful one?—It is useful in many ways, and particularly in a city school. Our arrangements, of course, are cramped with regard to our own school. We have a very limited playground, and our boys don't go home to dinner, 600 come by railway. I introduced drill into the school, and have found it extremely profitable. I am quite sure of the value of the experiment I carried on the first year I was there. I took the first couples of an advanced class myself and taught them mathematics. I would often stop in the course of the work and put these boys through physical exercises, jumping and horizontal bar, &c. We ran two hours, uninterruption, and I took nearly half an hour out of the centre of the period, and I found instead of losing time, that when our harvest came round there was a bigger return in money than I almost hoped for.

23623. Then you attach importance to the teaching of drill, not merely on account of the facility that is given the boys in going through particular evolutions, which they may never again in their lives be called upon to go through, but for the general effect it has in smartening them up?—Yes, I put it on that ground.

23624. You also mention singing?—We think it a good thing for boys to learn how to use their voices properly, and to get them familiar with melody and harmony.

23625. In the same way as you have said about drill, singing brightens them up; they are not merely learning things out of a book, but exercising their faculties?—Yes.

23626. Mr. Slagg.—I think in your memorandum you indicate an intention of saying something as to what became of these boys?—I had yesterday accidental evidence, not sought for on my part. I did not lead the conversation even, but it represents fairly well the relation of our work to the future of the boy. A gentleman, the head of a big firm, came in to place a boy with me, and in the course of some remarks he said he had engaged many boys who had gone through the training in our school, and he added that he noticed that as we trained them with a greater attention to detail they had a feeling of responsibility from the first day they entered the office that made them very serviceable. I have from business men in Glasgow—lawyers, stockbrokers and manufacturing firms—more applications for boys than I can meet, although we give no training in what is called mercantile education. The boy learns to do a little for himself, and a very little makes a great difference.

FIFTY-FIRST PUBLIC SITTING.—TUESDAY, OCTOBER 26TH, 1897,

Dundee.
Oct. 26, 1897.

AT 2 O'CLOCK, P.M.,

At the Town House, Dundee.

Present:—THE RIGHT REV. MONSIGNOR MOLLOY, D.D., D.SC., in the Chair; W. R. J. MOLLOY, Esq.; and J. STRUTHERS, Esq., M.D.;

with J. D. DALY, Esq., B.A., Secretary.

Sir James Low.

Sir JAMES LOW, ex-Lord Provost of Dundee, examined.

23427. MR. STRUTHERS.—These classes, Sir James, about which you are going to give us information, have for their object the instruction of poor lads in Dundee in manual work and in the ordinary elementary subjects of reading, writing and arithmetic?—Yes.

23428. You make the manual instruction taken on two evenings in the week an inducement for them to attend on the other two evenings to receive instruction in ordinary subjects?—That is so.

23429. Perhaps you will kindly tell us what was the origin of this movement?—I may mention, in explanation, that in 1891 the Town Council of Dundee received its first grant under the Local Taxation Inland Revenue and Excise Act, 1890, an Act which provided that Scotland should receive a certain grant from the Government annually, but which I may mention is variable, that is to say, the amount given to Scotland each year for this purpose, for the purpose of distribution amongst local authorities, Town Councils, and County Councils, is not always the same. In any case Dundee always receives a considerable sum. I may mention, also, that when this grant was given in 1891, the Chancellor of the Exchequer, then Mr. Goschen, informed the local authorities that the Government wished that this particular money should be given for the support and development of technical education in Scotland. Then it was the duty of Dundee, as of other towns and counties, to utilise this money so far as was necessary for this particular purpose.

23430. They were also warned that if it was not applied to this purpose it might be withdrawn?—Yes, Mr. Goschen intimated as much, that if the money was not so utilised the Government would consider it within their right to withdraw the allowance altogether. In 1891 the Town Council of Dundee appointed a committee, with myself as its chairman. The committee had no difficulty whatever in allocating the money to certain institutions, which were already doing good work in Dundee, such as the Technical Institute classes in connection with the Young Men's Christian Institute, the High School, and several other institutions. But the committee felt that while in giving these institutions money for this particular purpose they were doing good, yet there was a class in the community who did not at all benefit from any of these institutions, inasmuch as their social conditions prevented their attending such classes. The committee, after very careful consideration, felt that something ought to be done for what might be termed the lower class lads in Dundee—lads, that is to say, whose opportunities were very much smaller than boys born of parents who were in a better position—and the question came to be how could such boys be assisted, and after a very careful consideration of the whole matter it was resolved to recommend the Town Council cordially and unanimously agreed with the committee that this was an excellent object, and resolved to grant a maximum sum for the last year of £500 to this committee. With this sum the committee undertake to support three schools and three workshops in three different parts of the city. With this money they furnish benches and tools and other necessaries for the three manual schools, and commenced work in the years 1892-93, in the winter of 1892. Thus the schools were started with that particular object. At that time I may mention there was no suggestion to have anything other than merely manual instruction, no suggestion to have a continuation class combined with manual instruction classes. Thus the thing was started and with considerable success, so great success as the means at the committee's command was able to make.

23431. Was it not the case that the committee approached in the first place the School Board, regarding the work as more in their province, with the idea that the School Board might take it up?—Yes, that is so. The committee thought that the School Board, being the educational authority in Dundee, were the proper authority to carry out this work, and a small deputation from the committee waited upon the School Board, suggesting they should carry out this work, and the Town Council would give them a sum of money adequate to meet the expenses of this thing. But the School Board said they had already so much on their hands as they could satisfactorily perform, and that in their opinion the committee itself would have much more chance of satisfactorily carrying on the work than the School Board, and so the committee simply had to do the work itself, and has done it ever since.

23432. Perhaps you would explain to the Commissioners what the constitution of the committee was?—To begin with, a short time after it started, it was simply a committee from the Town Council and School Board, a joint committee, but it was very soon discovered that for various reasons, it would be well to make it a joint committee of the School Board, Town Council, and Trades' Council; the Trades' Council of Dundee represent the various united trades in Dundee. Every one of whom, of course, are Trades Unionists, and the Trades Council of Dundee is really representative of the Trades' Unions in Dundee, and a thoroughly representative body. The Town Council felt it was desirable that these should be associated with them in the work, especially having regard to the fact that they were going to deal with a class in which such a body as the Trades' Council is very much interested, and since then, therefore, the committee has been jointly composed of the School Board, Trades' Council, and Town Council.

23433. Can you tell what the number of representatives of each body is at present?—Three of

I have already stated
or them but the streets,
they would be doing a
ld rather be those poor
neral education on the
preparation on the other, as
, learn the use of tools
l in that way have both
and whatever they might
ey would, at all events,
lads of that sort have
I am sorry to say, do
l where they occur to the
not qualified for any work
labouring work.
articulated longer at their
perhaps, they receive the
get comparatively small
they become men they are
young lads again, and
many of these are drafted
ant, they get education,
r the rest of their days.
, indeed. Whereas, we
l continue to be labourers
labourers than they would
we give them: that was
yment feature, the initial
ational one was, in our

ake you have made apply
ple, for instance, trace any
their employment when
acquired any knowledge
occupation, and necessit-
h as with mill hands; the
was to get hold of mill
the schools to-night you
ge number of boys who
jute spinning mills.
u have observed, I pre-
nent in the behaviour of
conduct and discipline?—
when we commenced at
was quite an impossible
ult it was to discipline
after a session or two the

for the first time this year to draft a few of them into the Technical Institute. And this was really the ground of the whole idea to give these boys an equal chance in life with boys better born, so that they might have a chance of rising, if they have qualifications, and I am glad to say we have a few this year now who are prepared to take the advantages of the Technical Institute itself.

23470. That of itself would be a proof of the educational value of the work you do, the fact that after two years or three years' attendance at your school they are able to engage in the work of such a school as the Technical Institute?—Some of them, I am bound to say very few.

23471. You would rather expect that number to increase, would you not?—Well, I would rather say I should hope it would; you must remember that we are dealing with a class of boys who don't get much encouragement, at least many of them, at home to push ahead with their education; we are dealing with a class who I am afraid get very little encouragement.

23472. Of course as regards the essential subjects of reading, writing and arithmetic, I presume you employ certificated teachers, who are engaged in the day schools?—We do.

23473. But for the special subjects of manual instruction, woodwork, clay-modelling and drawing you require special teachers?—Yes.

23474. Could you tell us what qualifications you look for in these teachers?—We employ thoroughly intelligent tradesmen—men who are themselves enthusiastic educationalists, and I am glad to say there are plenty of working men in Dundee with that qualification. We have been exceedingly fortunate in that respect in obtaining thoroughly intelligent teachers—tradesmen, who are at the same time teachers in the true sense of the word—by instinct, teachers. We thought out that subject very carefully, and we came to the conclusion that a tradesman was the best man for the work we had to do.

23475. You wished to have a teacher of high practical skill in the work he is going to teach. To begin with, you think it also important that he should have some educational knowledge and, as it were, an educational enthusiasm?—Yes.

23476. To understand what is the object of the work?—Yes.

Dundee.
Oct. [illegible], 1897.
Mr. [illegible]

is reasonable with lads
beginning.
rawing as soon as you ven-
ken a drawing, and the
he drawing which the
e boys are able now to
e make, but I am bound
h the boys we have.
nt very few of these boys
school before they came

could as regards that part
ht of it.
he work of your organisation
f five years, you are led to
important influence on
al self-restraint of these
it it.
s has had considerable
y of making them more
powers of observation?—

n able in a few cases to
ange that they are able to
chnical Institute?—Yes;
es. As I have already
in numbers are only to
the material we are work-

ut how much does Dundee
uation grant; just say
ar to year?—In 1896–97

an excessively large or
hat was large. In 1895–
1,110.
varies within very wide
,160 up to about £1,100.
age be somewhere about

had expended upon educa-
don it is. I think Dundee
t by itself.
take it that the Town
date the importance of
t that grant is applied?—

nowhere about one-third is
articular school, I think
11—these years there a
ample, in 1893–94 the sum

£300 to £900?—I would

pended upon these classes
lo don't cost you much
e of £1 per pupil. Last
ber of pupils was 700, and
712?—Yes; that included

e grants earned both from
and the South Kensington
not include the South
ve only given you the
two sets of grants—one
Department in respect of
continuation classes, and
nt of the-[illegible] and
ensington Department, but
number of pupils and also
ment.
into between £415 and
on the school, since from
£415 came as grants from
artment in respect of the
e manual instruction and
£312 came from the Town
hle; I think that it must
ith the cost we have got
we have supplied all our

schools with furniture, which cost a lot of money. This committee has no power to incur debt, and we, therefore, pay every year everything it spends out of the grant it receives from the Town Council and the Education Department.

23699. With regard to the subjects taught, they are of two classes. One is manual training with a certain amount of drawing, and the other consists of the ordinary elementary subjects of a primary school?—Yes.

23700. You try to combine these two sets of subjects—teaching them upon alternate evenings?—Yes; we insist upon it.

23701. And you find the manual training is so popular with the boys that it constitutes an inducement to them to come to the other classes?—That is the inducement, otherwise I don't believe they would come to the ordinary classes.

23702. If the boys had got a good primary education before they came to you, would you be disposed to improve the literary education that is at present given?—We have three different classes in connection with the ordinary evening schools for these boys. We have a lower, medium, and higher; and, of course, those who are pretty well educated get the higher, and they get what they have not got before.

23703. Then for these boys it is really an advanced primary education that is given?—It is.

23704. But you are obliged to give also a very elementary education, to provide for these half-timers you have spoken of, who come very imperfectly prepared in the subjects of a primary school?—The great number of these have to be taught the very lowest rudiments of education.

23705. Now, with respect to the manual training, I think you made it clear that it is not your object to teach trades, but to give such an education as will make the pupils fit to learn a trade afterwards?—Yes; we want to make them handy boys, so that they may be all the better adapted to any trade they may go to, no matter what it is.

23706. And the representatives of the trades now understand that they get their boys better prepared for their work in life?—Well, tradesmen occasionally take these boys as apprentices, simply because they have received the little education we can give them in our schools.

23707. And therefore the school is beneficial both to the trades unions and to the employers?—I could not really say that; they find that the boys that come from our school are fitted to profit by their teaching on account of the manual training they previously had received. The Trades' Council is a body of operatives, those who employ the boys as apprentices are masters necessarily, and I mean to say that I know masters who prefer a boy from these schools, simply because he has already got some training in the use of tools and is therefore more adaptable when he comes to learn his business.

23708. At present there is no distrust, on the part of the Trades' Council, of your school?—No.

23709. Although, I think, you said at first there was?—At first there was an inclination on the part of some of them—it was not by any means universal; there were a few men in the Trades' Council who doubted whether we were doing a right thing from their point of view, but we satisfied the Trades' Council that we were doing nothing at all detrimental to the interests of tradesmen in these directions.

23710. Are your pupils, to any extent, the children of tradesmen?—Oh, yes, a good few of them are, but the great bulk are not; the great bulk are the children of mere labourers, who, themselves have never had an opportunity of getting education, and perhaps don't know the value of it to their children.

23711. You have spoken of the Technical Institute in Dundee; is that also supported out of the local taxation grant?—To a considerable extent, the

Dundee. [illegible]

Technical Institute receives out of the Technical Education grant £200 a year.

23712. But at present, comparatively few of the pupils of your evening school are able to go to the Technical Institute?—This is the first year that any of them have asked to be sent there.

23713. That seems to show that already the feeling is growing that they may be prepared in your school, and hoped to profit by the Technical Institute afterwards?—Yes, that was the crown of the edifice we had in view when we started this thing; we wanted to gradually raise these boys until we could take advantage of this greater institution where tradesmen's sons and sons of people of all classes go to get trained in purely technical work.

23714. And that crown is already in view?—It is on the part of one or two of them.

23715. Mr. Mellor.—Your evening school started about five years ago?—Yes.

23716. And the general result of it is very satisfactory?—I should have said six years ago, this is the sixth year.

23717. And your experience is that the outcome is of a very satisfactory character?—Yes.

23718. I notice that all along you spoke of provision for the instruction in the evening of boys, is there any corresponding instruction for girls in Dundee?—The School Board give instruction to girls in the evening, but I am afraid hardly for a class of girls analogous to the boys we are dealing with, I mean mill hands; this very committee tried something of that sort, I may tell you, and they were more or less successful, I am afraid rather less than more successful.

23719. Did that arise from indisposition on the part of the girls to attend in the evening?—It is not an easy to manage, and of course there is another difficulty and a very serious one, the committee think it is a most necessary thing to attend to the wants of the girls in that direction, but of course the training they would want would be domestic training.

23720. Quite so, cookery and laundry work?—Yes, I am afraid we have not been able to do it in such a manner as would lead to much good.

23721. Then all your efforts up to the present have been on the side of the boys?—Practically.

23722. Have you compulsory attendance in Dundee?—At the day school, yes.

23723. How many boys are on the rolls of the evening schools, how many are registered for admission to the schools?—700 is the number on whom we got grants. I have taken it in that way because at the beginning of the session there is always quite a crowd of boys, far more than we can take, but they drop off. I have taken the numbers on whom we get the actual grants, indicating that they have been there a sufficient time to warrant the Department in giving us a grant.

23724. Could you broadly indicate what the average nightly attendance is, say for the last session; what I want to come at is the ratio of the attendance to the number on the rolls, how many entered at the beginning and then, perhaps, fell away from the instruction and might have remained for a little time in a desultory manner?—You may take it that the number at the school is the number I have said, 700. I cannot say how many fall away.

23725. That 700 represents 700 individual pupils?—Oh, yes, certainly.

23726. Mr. Stevenson.—Some of whom may have attended a fortnight, or a month or three months.

23727. Chairman.—But all these 700 attended sufficiently often to get a grant?—Certainly.

23728. And the number who have attended from time to time is very much larger than 700?—You may take it that way.

23729. Is the ordinary nightly attendance about 700?—I think, so, you may take it on the whole that the number I have given is about the attendance; some nights there may be fifty fewer, but it would be very rare, some exceptional occasion would keep them away, some boys, for example, have to work at nights in their mills.

23730. Mr. Mellor.—What is the minimum number of attendances required by the Department to warrant their grant?—That I am not certain of.

23731. And the duration of the class, it opens, I suppose, in September?—It begins at the beginning of October, but that also another witness will tell you.

23732. Is there any test applied to the proficiency of the pupils at the end of the session?—No, there is no test.

23733. Are there any prizes distributed for regular attendance?—There is a test by the Inspector of schools; well, he is here and he will tell you about that, I have no doubt.

23734. But your contribution does not apply any test?—Oh, no, it does not.

23735. Along with the ordinary subjects such as reading, writing, and arithmetic, you have manual instruction on two nights, the other subjects on two other nights, you have drawing also; is there any elementary science taught?—I believe there is, I cannot give you details as to what it is, but we have asked one of the teachers to be here today just to tell you these things.

23736. Would you be able to say whether music is taught also?—No, we do not teach singing.

23737. Chairman.—You mentioned that the rate per head of cost for all this instruction was about £1?—Yes.

23738. And out of the sum total your Town Council contributed £610 for the last session?—Yes, that is it.

23739. What is the local education rate in Dundee on the valuation of property?—1s. 1d. in the £ this year.

23740. That is high, is it not?—We ratepayers consider it very high.

23741. But I hope the ratepayers also think they get very good value?—I have no doubt they do.

23742. If they get as good value in the day time as they do in the evening they ought to be content?—I think they get good work for the money.

23743. I would like to emphasise this, that your expression was that the great object of the manual instruction was to teach the boys how to use tools and handle tools, not at all to teach trades, and as a subsidiary thing that they may be led up to enter at the institute?—Yes.

23744. Have any objections been offered by the parents?—Far from that.

23745. Parents and boys co-operate enthusiastically with you about this manual instruction in the evening?—Yes, the parents are delighted that the boys should attend.

23746. And from a commencement of 270, when there was a novelty about it, you have brought it up to 700?—Yes.

23747. Mr. Stevenson.—And your impression is that if you had more accommodation you might have a larger number?—I believe if we had accommodation and schools in suitable districts, and money to carry them on with, that this system would be far more extensively taken advantage of by boys than it is in Dundee.

23748. Could you give us any information about the plant?—The figures I have given you include the cost of the plant that we paid out of the money we received from the Town Council, because as I understand it, the Department will not give grants in respect of putting down plant such as we require in these schools.

23749. Chairman.—You mentioned that in the first year you spent £800, and that a large part of that sum went in the equipment of the schools; afterwards your expenditure on equipment went up to £410 one year, and £490 another year?—That is so.

Councillor Elliot, Chairman of Manual Instruction Committee, Dundee, examined.

23750. Chairman.—You are a member of the Town Council of Dundee.—Yes.

23751. And you are also a member of the joint committee which manage the evening schools?—Yes.

23752. And you are Chairman of the Manual Instruction Committee which, I suppose, is a sub-committee of that body?—No, the whole committee work simultaneously; there is no sub-committee.

23753. Then the Manual Instruction Committee is the whole committee?—Yes.

23754. You have heard the evidence given us by Sir James Low. Do you agree substantially with the opinions he has expressed?—Substantially, in every respect, so far as the material details are concerned, but I might give you some information with regard to the boys themselves. The object of these classes has been explained to some extent, but I may tell you that the lads who attend these classes are principally mill lads. If I mistake not, sir, you made the inquiry as to whether any of these lads were the sons of tradesmen; I might say very few of them are the sons of tradesmen; the big majority, at least 90 per cent., belong to the very poorest of Dundee, the residuum, the lowest grade boys; a large proportion of them are destitute of father or mother, either one or the other; a very considerable number are orphans. During the past five years I might say that the aggregate numbers who passed through our hands in the session have been close upon a thousand; I wish to explain that, although 700 has been the average attendance so last year, we have always a pretty large number upon our list, and as soon as there is a vacancy they are ready to come in. I will give you an instance: one individual school, the headmaster of which is a witness here, enrolled this year somewhere about 600 lads. We could only accommodate probably less than half that number in our manual school; consequently, while our manual or workshop school was filled, we had this large proportion in our continuation school. Of course they dropped off bit by bit from the workshop. We then have recourse to the continuation school and fill up the vacancies there, but in the course of the session, even in these continuation schools, the attendance drops off.

23755. The substantial and important fact for us is that you have about 700 whose attendances are sufficient to earn the grants?—Always. Between five and six years ago when these classes were started, as the last witness stated, we thought we could never manage these boys, but we were exceedingly careful as to the class of men who were to teach them. In the first place, in the workshops or manual school the teachers that were selected we knew the work of them, their characters and their abilities, and we were careful to select good tradesmen, and men, if possible, who had taken certificates in Ornamental Art from South Kensington; some of these had and some of them had not, but apart from that we took care these in addition to being good tradesmen, they had also an idea of imparting knowledge as teachers, and then that their moral and social characters were such as to have a moral effect upon lads. The consequence has been that at the end of each session the lad who comes in a wild rowdy boy goes away altogether changed. To supplement that, I have been told by mill managers and overseers long after them that lads who spend a short time in our classes, say a single session, are not only better boys but handier at their occupations.

23756. Mr. Mollet.—You say you employ good tradesmen, and you also take pains that they should be qualified in teaching?—Yes, in the art of imparting knowledge.

23757. Not merely that they should know the subject themselves, but know how to teach the subject?—Yes, and how to handle the boys.

23758. What steps are taken to ascertain that?—Most of the men belong to the city here, and we know them by repute. Take, for instance, the headmasters; the headmasters are all highly qualified men in their different professions; we knew them perfectly well before we took them. Then, with regard to the subordinates, a number of those we did not know, but our headmasters knew them and knew what they wanted.

23759. Mr. Struthers.—Do you teach elementary science at all?—Physiography.

23760. That is on the evening devoted to continuation subjects?—Yes.

23761. And to the most advanced of the three groups into which the evening school is divided?—The most advanced only.

23762. I suppose that while you lay great stress on the teacher having a practical knowledge of the work he was going to teach, you think he should also have skill in imparting his knowledge and if possible some enthusiasm in his work?—Undoubtedly, the success of the schools has lain a great deal in the enthusiasm of these teachers.

23763. And if you found these qualities united in a certificated teacher you would have no difficulty in engaging him?—Do you refer to continuation teachers or workshop teachers?

23764. I refer to the workshop teachers; if by chance you found a certificated teacher in the ordinary schools who had really a practical command of woodwork and was enthusiastic about its educational benefits, you would have no hesitation in employing him?—No, I have explained to you that the mass of these boys are employed in mills and factories.

23765. Mr. Mollet.—With regard to hours of attendance?—We commence at a quarter past seven and stop at a quarter past nine, four nights every week.

23766. That does not include any time for religious instruction?—We give no religious instruction whatever.

Bailie Macdonald, Member of the School Board, Dundee, examined.

23767. Chairman.—You were formerly Chairman of the School Board of Dundee?—I was during the last School Board.

of the boys is wonderful. Indeed one who visited one of our schools six years ago, and again one of our schools now, could not conceive that the pupils were

found some. Indeed we found on some that one occasion very poor little boys so anxious to attend, that I have seen them coming in the stormy, snowy winter nights barefooted.

23774. These are boys whose primary education had been imperfect in many cases?—Very imperfect.

23775. How was it that they did not profit of the opportunities offered by the Board Schools?—Well, it is very difficult to explain that, but there is a residuum of boys and girls that it is impossible for the Board School to draw in within their net. A very large number of these poorer classes come from different parts of the country and other towns. We have found boys of fifteen and sixteen years of age in these schools that did not know the alphabet, but in every case we found that they were only a year or two, or perhaps a few months, in Dundee.

23776. Then in many cases their backwardness has arisen from the fact that they were not natives of Dundee, but of some other district, where perhaps they had not the same opportunities as exist in Dundee?—Well, they are very much of a migratory habit. A great many of them are low mill workers; and although one School Board may get hold of them, it is only for a week or two when they are off.

23777. You seemed to say that the pupils coming to these evening classes have a great desire to profit of the opportunities which they offer; and that suggests a question, how is it that they did not profit of the opportunities which the School Boards now generally afford in Scotland?—A great many of these boys had not the opportunity, they were wandering from place to place; but there is not so much desire on the part of the low class of boys to attend the ordinary continuation class as to attend the manual, and it is as a bait to them to attend the ordinary class, that the first year, as Sir James Low explained to you, we did not insist upon their attending other classes. That was not my wish; I was anxious that it should be made a condition from the first, but the majority of the committee thought they would begin with manual instruction alone; but by-and-by we saw that it was necessary to combine with the ordinary manual instruction the regular branches of ordinary education.

23778. And the manual instruction is so attractive that, for the sake of it, they will come to the other classes?—They will; we make it a condition that if they don't attend the ordinary classes regularly they are not allowed to go to the other.

23779. Then with respect to the general statements and views expressed by Sir James Low, I gather that you concur entirely in what he has told us?—Entirely. I might mention that, in addition to these classes of which Sir James and Mr. Elliott spoke, we have in connexion with the School Board very large classes for ordinary education.

23780. I was going to ask you if you could give us a short account of the education given under the School Board in Dundee?—I spoke only generally just now, because I was not aware until this morning that I was expected to be here, and the School Board has up to this moment no official knowledge of this inquiry. If we had known of it we would have been prepared to lay the figures before you, but I shall be delighted to give you information generally.

23781. We should like to know whether any manual training is given in the Board Schools?—Yes, to some extent. We have in connection with one of our academies a workshop, but the boys are accustomed to pay for that in addition to the ordinary fee. Then, again, we have one central school to which pupils in the sixth standard are drafted from the surrounding schools, and we have a teacher employed for that purpose—that is merely experimental.

23782. How long has the experiment been going on?—Well, I am not quite in a position to speak to that. I may mention that I do not attach, myself, very much importance to these classes in connexion with day schools; but I attach the greatest importance to this work after the boys have left school, but not during school hours.

23783. You approve of it, I understand, in what are called continuation schools?—Thoroughly.

23784. Have you any such continuation schools under the School Board?—Oh, yes, for both boys and girls. We have just now in regular attendance about 2,000 pupils, boys and girls, attending our ordinary evening continuation schools over and above those of which Sir James Low and Mr. Elliott spoke.

23785. In these evening continuation schools, you teach the ordinary subjects of primary education?—Yes.

23786. Is that education somewhat more advanced than what is taught in the day schools?—Yes, more advanced in several of our schools. I may state that when we opened these schools a number of years ago we were obliged to have classes for boys and girls in standard two and three, but we find now that there are very few attending who are not able to begin with standard four or five.

23787. Then the bulk of the pupils in the evening continuation schools have already reached standard four or five in the primary school?—The great bulk, we find, however, a very sad feature in connection with our evening schools; we find that boys and girls who have passed, say standard five, and have absented themselves from school there, during, say, two years, are not fit to go into standard five, so quickly do they forget what they have learned in the day schools.

23788. You think it would be desirable that they should go at once to the continuation school as soon as they leave the ordinary one?—That is what we press very strongly.

23789. In the evening continuation school is there manual training?—No, except for girls, in laundry, sewing, and cookery.

23790. That is a good deal for girls; but you don't teach any manual work to the boys?—No; I may supplement what Sir James said about our having at a several committees done nothing for girls, that in three sessions for 1883–84–85 we employed a special teacher of cookery for the benefit of these poorer girls attending no evening class. We employed a lady very highly competent for the work to teach them cookery and the elements of domestic economy.

23791. You said that in the evening continuation schools there are about 2,000 pupils; what would be the total number of pupils in the day schools roughly?—About 20,000.

23792. The numbers in the evening schools are about 10 per cent. of those in the day schools?—Rather more if you count 700 or so attending the manual classes; the 2,000 I give you are over and above.

23793. I mean the evening schools under the Board?—Under the Board entirely, having no connection with the Manual Committee.

23794. Are the elements of science taught in any of your schools—day schools or evening schools?—In all our day schools, and now in several of our evening schools. We have two of our evening schools specially set apart for the higher education—that is education above the sixth standard—in which we teach physiography and chemistry and several other such branches.

23795. Is the teaching of the subjects conducted under the programme of the Science and Art Department?—Yes.

23796. And do you get grants according to the results examination?—We have hitherto done so.

23797. Mr. Mallock.—Do you publish any School

Dundee.
Oct. [illegible]
Bailie Macdonald.

23799. What was the date of the last publication? —In April of this year.

23800. Would you do us the favour of letting us have a copy of the report?—I shall be delighted.

23801. How many schools are there under the Dundee School Board?—Twenty-two.

23802. And how many pupils in the twenty-two schools?—Close upon 20,000.

23803. And over and above the 20,000 you have pupils also attending evening schools quite distinct from the manual instruction schools?—About 2,000.

23804. Do many pupils attend both day and evening schools?—No.

23805. Do you prohibit that?—We do; we have found in going round our evening schools perhaps half a dozen out of the whole number, very exceptional cases; but we don't allow it, and we get no grant. I might say that the grants Sir James Low spoke of as earned were the grants paid. We earn a great deal more, but I am sorry to say that the Department manage to slip off sometimes for our evening schools about upon 50 per cent. of the grant earned; we know what we have earned, but we don't know what we will get, and in some schools the grant earned is very close upon double the grant paid, and in every case very much larger.

23806. CHAIRMAN.—Then they must owe you a great deal after so many years?—I am afraid we may let it pass as irrecoverable.

23807. Mr. MOLLOY.—In addition to the ordinary literary subjects, what special subjects are taken up by boys in the ordinary day schools?—We have mathematics, chemistry, physics, physiography, shorthand, book-keeping, and so on. I am speaking of the ordinary schools in connection with two of our academies; we have all the advanced branches of a liberal education.

23808. Where does the money come from for the instruction in these higher branches—Latin, French, Greek—if you have any?—Well, we get a grant from the Burgh Committee, and by means of it we are able to give free scholarships just now to 570 pupils in the higher branches of education. Without this grant we would not be able to do it.

23809. Is that included in the 13d. in the £ rate? —We are not entitled to take it out of the 13d. rate. We are not entitled to the rate for secondary education.

23810. But you have money at your disposal? —Yes.

23811. On the side of the girls you mentioned cookery, laundry work, and, in a general way, domestic economy?—Yes.

23812. May I inquire is book-keeping taught to your boys?—Yes.

23813. Is kindergarten taught in your infant schools and other schools?—In every case.

23814. Not confined to mere infant schools?—We have no infant schools apart from ordinary schools; we have infant departments, and in every one of these we have kindergarten work.

23815. And if I mistake not, the infant department comprises mere infants, and those in standard 1; would kindergarten instruction extend beyond standard 1?—No.

23816. Is your committee in favour of extending it into the higher standards?—That has not been discussed; I am not in favour of it.

23817. We have heard a good deal of evidence on the other side. Would you let us know why you object to the extension of kindergarten?—I don't attach the importance to it at all that is attached to it now-a-days. I am an old retired teacher; I have been engaged in teaching from my youth upwards until I became a member of the School Board. I quite approve of kindergarten for infants.

23818. CHAIRMAN.—Have you object lessons in your system?—Invariably in all schools.

23819. How far do the object lessons extend in the standards?—To the very highest.

23820. Many persons look upon object lessons as a kind of advanced kindergarten?—If that is so I approve of that thoroughly.

23821. Mr. MOLLOY.—I presume also you have music and drawing?—In every school.

23822.—Drawing is compulsory on boys; do girls participate in the instruction?—It is compulsory on boys, but not on girls; we have also cookery lessons given in all our schools; we have four teachers specially qualified for the teaching of cookery, and they give a course of lessons in one school and then in another, so that all the girls of standard 4 and upwards get lessons in cookery.

23823. Are all the pupils of the ordinary day school free as regards fees?—All except the two academies; in the two academies the highest fee is £1 per quarter, and for that they are entitled to all the branches of a liberal education.

23824. Preparatory to a university?—Yes; many of our boys go direct from these to a university.

23825. Having previously graduated in an ordinary day school?—Yes.

23826. Mr. STRUTHERS.—You spoke, Bailie Macdonald, in the highest terms of the manual evening classes; you found these work very successfully?—Yes, I attach the very greatest importance to them.

23827. And you don't think the pupils who attend these classes would have attended the ordinary evening classes in such large numbers?—I do not think so.

23828. You spoke of the manual work as being a bait which attracted them to the ordinary evening school?—Yes, in a great measure.

23829. And you think the bait has been taken?—No doubt of that.

23830. Would not the same thing apply to the day schools?—No.

23831. You might hold out a bait to get children to the day schools?—Well, the attendance at the day school is compulsory.

23832. I thought you said you found compulsion does not reach a certain class of the population?—It is the younger children, who would not be fit for manual work.

23833. By manual work one does not mean exclusively woodwork; it may comprehend everything from kindergarten up to woodwork. There are various forms, which all have for one of their objects, holding out a bait to children to come to school?—That may be so; we try to attract them in every possible way.

23834. Except this?—I am afraid that would not be successful at all.

23835. It might be worth trying in the case of the schools in the poorer districts, where the children were difficult to get at?—I would have no objection to try it in one or two of our poorer schools.

23836. Turning to the case of Ireland, where there is no compulsion, in many districts would it not be a good thing to make the schools attractive in every possible way?—Oh, certainly.

23837. If you get the children to school by something that attracts them, you may be able to teach them something else that is useful?—Yes.

23838. Putting aside what educational value there may be in the attraction?—I thoroughly agree with that view.

23839. So, in the case of schools in poor districts where compulsion is not in operation, a considerable development of manual work on the lines of your evening schools here would be desirable?—I have no doubt it would be a strong incentive to children to attend.

23840. Then you said you approved of kindergarten in the infant departments?—Yes.

23841. Then you would not have it in standard 1? —I would not object to standard 1.

23842. In standard 2 would you object to it?—I think standard 1 is quite enough.

Dundee,
Oct. [illegible]
Bailie Macdonald.

23877. Mr. Mulloy.—The assistant teachers of the day schools are the principal teachers of the night schools?—They are.

23878. And of course they have a separate salary for their work done at night?—They have.

23879. Might I inquire the rate of salary?—The salary for three nights of the head assistants just now is 60s. and 15s. for assistants—this is the first year that we have had them for three nights only. Up to that time they were teaching four nights, this year an experiment has been made, following the example of some other towns to have them for only three nights.

23880. That rate of remuneration is independent altogether of the number under instruction?—Wholly independent.

23881. Chairman.—You have spoken of two academies under the Board; I should like to know in what respect exactly do these academies differ from ordinary Board Schools?—In the first place, they are fee-paying schools, and then they are divided into two departments—an elementary, the same as the ordinary day schools, and then a senior or secondary department, in which Latin, Greek, mathematics, chemistry, and such other branches are taught.

23882. And do all the children of the academies pay fees?—Except those who have free scholarships from the grant to which I alluded. We make that a competitive examination.

23883. Do many of the pupils of the ordinary schools come afterwards to the academies?—They do; we hold an examination every year about the middle of June, to which pupils from all the schools are invited to attend, and those who make a certain percentage—this year I think it was 50 per cent. of marks—are entitled to free scholarships, so far as we can give it to the academies. This year the number is 271.

23884. Then these academies afford an opportunity to all the pupils in Dundee of obtaining a higher education if they qualify themselves for it?—Yes.

23885. And those who gain scholarships can obtain that higher education free?—That is so. These two academies are the schools or academies under the School Board. In addition to that there is a very excellent institution—the Dundee High School—of which I have the honour of being a director, but it is not under the School Board.

23886. Is that a secondary school?—It is elementary as well as secondary; all the branches of the elementary education are taught as well as the higher, but that is independent altogether of the School Board.

23887. Mr. Stevenson.—It teaches such subjects as you have already mentioned, Latin, French, mathematics, Greek, and so on, and you also teach woodwork in it?—Yes.

23888. Do you consider that on a level with the other subjects you have mentioned as a subject of secondary education?—It is optional.

23889. Do many attend?—A good many do, but only a comparatively small number of the whole of the pupils.

23890. Pupils who are preparing for engineering or some such occupation?—I should think so, and also pupils who wish to have some little handicraft.

23891. Do you think it is taken with a view of preparing for a future occupation, or with a view of giving them a more all-round education?—I think more of an all-round education. I may mention we had a very great difficulty at first with the Department with regard to our grants for manual work. According to the Code we are obliged to take manual instruction concurrently with the ordinary subjects, that is on the same night, and, indeed, according to the regulations of the Department, in the same building; but I think we, in Dundee, managed to convince the Department that that was not practicable. In the first place, it was impossible to teach them manual work, I mean joinery work, in an ordinary day school; and then, in the next place, we convinced the Department, too, that to teach them manual work, and also the ordinary branches on the same night, consisting of only two hours, was not a very satisfactory way. For instance, boys working with tools or saws from seven to eight, were not in the best position to go to drawing, and also sums, and the Department yielded on that point, and allow us now to have the Schools in separate buildings and on separate nights.

23892. So you found the Department open to conviction?—On this occasion they were.

Mr. Robert Calder, One of Her Majesty's Inspectors of Schools in Scotland, examined.

Mr. Robert Calder.

23893. Mr. Stevenson.—You are Inspector of schools for the Dundee district?—I am.

23894. And you have inspected the manual instruction classes, about which we have already had evidence, since they were opened—the manual instruction classes, of course, being taken in connection with classes for elementary subjects?—Yes.

23895. You concur generally in the evidence you have heard as to the influence of these manual classes?—I do; I consider them an important social movement in the city, getting hold of young lads who would not be got to the ordinary evening schools before.

23896. You find the discipline in these evening schools quite satisfactory?—The first year, at the beginning of the session, it was not; but as the session went on it became satisfactory, and in the succeeding session it was quite satisfactory.

23897. In fact more satisfactory than you would expect from the class of lads who attend?—Quite so.

23898. And do you find instruction in the ordinary subjects also satisfactory?—Standards four, five, and six make satisfactory progress.

23899. Have you paid attention specially to the manual work that is carried on?—I have, a good deal.

23900. Do you think it has any educational ad- [illegible] telligence as well as making them handy in the management of tools.

23901. They have got to be reasonably accurate?—They have to be reasonably accurate and take great pains, and to think out what they are about, which is an important matter.

23902. So that generally tends to an increase of intelligence?—I think it does.

23903. It might have a marked effect in that way in the case of pupils who would not profit by the ordinary subjects?—Yes, to a certain extent, it would.

23904. That is to say, as one finds in ordinary school work, pupils profit by one subject more than another, and we have to provide a certain diversity of subjects, in order to bring out the best powers of the pupils?—Certainly; there are some that would take to manual work more readily, and get more benefit from it.

23905. You have, also, experience of the other evening schools in Dundee. We have heard it stated that there are 2,000 children attending evening continuation schools?—There are about 2,000 attending ordinary Board schools, but there is a considerable number of evening scholars in Dundee besides Board scholars.

are schools for girls, and there are a good many schools for girls outside the Board system.

23907. Who conduct these other schools?—Principally church organisations.

23908. They are purely voluntary schools?—Purely voluntary schools.

23909. In these schools do you find that much attention is given to instructing the girls in cookery and laundry work?—That is the main object. The schools conducted by the churches take up a corresponding class of girls to those who go to the manual instruction classes; they teach them needlework one evening in the week, and in addition, laundry and cookery, and in some instances dressmaking and one or two other useful branches.

23910. Then these classes do for the girls somewhat the same work that the special manual schools we have heard about, do for the boys?—So far as regards manual training, they do, but there is no continuation school for ordinary literary work in connection with them.

23911. They are not held out as a bait to induce the children to attend instruction in ordinary subjects?—No. The Board tried evening schools corresponding to the manual classes for boys, and found it very difficult to get girls induced to take ordinary instruction in order to get cookery or laundry work. They will come to cookery, dressmaking, or laundry work, but they don't like to be tied up to attend other classes.

23912. But they can be brought to attend other classes by making it a condition that they can only get cookery and laundry work by attending?—Not successfully.

23913. Then cookery and laundry has not the same attraction for them that manual work has for boys?—I would not say that, they are very anxious to get cookery and laundry work.

23914. But they are not prepared to pay for this instruction by attending classes in ordinary subjects as boys are?—That has been the experience; they seem to think cookery, laundry, and dressmaking are subjects they would like to acquire, but ordinary reading lessons, arithmetic, and such like subjects they think they can do without: it is very difficult to get them to go to such classes.

23915. Have you considered the method in which cookery and laundry work are taught in these schools?—Yes.

23916. Do you think it is made as attractive as it might be?—I think so.

23917. So that it is not for that reason that the girls cannot be induced to attend on the condition of taking the ordinary subjects as well?—No, it is not for that reason; the girls are quite attracted by the cookery and laundry as taught them.

23918. There is not the provision for the practical instruction of girls corresponding to what there is for boys?—There are four schools conducted by churches under inspection, with at least 300 girls in attendance, young women, many of them, from 20 to 25 years of age. Then there is the Young Men's Christian Association and the Young Women's Christian Association—they have large classes, the Young Men's have 400 in attendance; it is under inspection. The Young Women's Christian Association is not under-

23920. It seems more natural, does it not, that these subjects, which are of use to certain people and not to others, should be taught in continuation schools when the attendance is voluntary rather than in the ordinary day schools?—I think so, book-keeping at all events.

23921. You have kindergarten departments in all the Board schools in the town?—In the infant department of nearly all the schools in the district we have kindergarten.

23922. And you find it does not interfere with the progress in the ordinary subjects?—Not in the least, I think at that stage of the scholar's career it is a great awakener of the intelligence and enables him to get on quicker.

23923. Have you anything corresponding to kindergarten in standard one and two?—A good many of the schools carry on kindergarten to standard one, but there is nothing beyond that, in many of the schools standard one is considered part of the infant department.

23924. Is woodwork taught in the higher departments in any of the Board schools outside Dundee?—No. In the High School (that is not an inspected school, but I know the workshop well. It is one of the best workshops in Scotland, almost all the boys from the sixth form get an opportunity of getting instruction in woodwork.

23925. Do you know whether a large portion take advantage of the opportunity?—I believe a considerable portion, about one half, take advantage of the opportunity given, and they have a regular course of instruction given, the teachers there are on the staff of the school and are engaged in teaching geometrical and other drawing, and so arrange the work that drawing dovetails into the woodwork.

23926. I suppose it is taken up in the High School because it is found to have a useful educational effect?—I think so.

23927. There is no intention of preparing them for a profession or trade which involves knowledge of woodwork?—Not in the least. But the boys are very fond of it.

23928. Might it not be said about woodwork in the ordinary elementary school that it has an educational effect?—If it could be provided in a similar way my impression is that it might be very useful in the higher classes, especially in Dundee. I have often thought it might be good as a bait—the word has been used by a previous witness—a bait to boys to remain at school longer than they do. In Dundee there is great falling off in the fourth and fifth standards, and in the sixth there is seldom one-third of the number in the fifth. As soon as they get through the labour certificate examination, they are away from school, and very often run about the streets for a year or more before coming to the evening continuation school, by which time they have forgotten a great deal that they learned before.

23929. Short of the compulsion that Bailie M'Leod spoke of, don't you think that everything should be done to make the attendance in the higher classes of the day school attractive?—I do.

23930. And if it was found by actual experience in other districts that woodwork was an attractive subject, it would be a subject the School Board might naturally introduce?—I think it would be very desirable to introduce it if it was found by experience

Dundee. [illegible]

27936. CHAIRMAN.—I think you have said that the elements of science are taught in all the Board schools in Dundee; are they taught from a specific programme or is it left to each master to teach according to his own ideas?—There is a specific programme, which is submitted to me and approved of at the beginning of the year, but the same programme suits the whole of the schools under the Board.

27937. That programme is only, I suppose, a skeleton programme?—It is pretty detailed as to the work to be taken up during the year, providing a sufficient amount of work for each standard.

27938. By whom was that drawn up originally?—By the head teachers in Dundee in consultation with myself.

27939. Mr. MOLLOY.—You referred to the labour certificate; who conducts the examination?—I do, with my assistants.

27940. It is an individual examination?—An individual in all cases.

27941. And it takes in reading, writing, spelling, and arithmetic?—Yes, there are two labour certificates, there is the labour certificate for half time employment in this district, and then the labour certificate for full time employment, which can only be earned after they are thirteen years of age.

27942. And for the half-timers?—Eleven years of age.

27943. Is there a substantial difference in the requirements of the two certificates?—Yes, for the half-timers, standard three, reading, writing, and arithmetic—with dictation; for full timers in the fifth standard, reading with intelligence, composition, spelling, and arithmetic of a higher grade.

27944. These certificates are not given on easy terms?—Certainly not, they must come up to the standard three for half time, and to standard five for the time full certificate.

27945. In the case of a full certificate at the age of thirteen the child need not attend school any more?—It is not required to attend at school any more.

27946. And that is where the gap occurs. After two years the child, perhaps not attending school at all, gets rusty, and when it comes to the evening school does not come up to the fourth standard?—That accounts for it, but there are a great many others that leave school without obtaining this certificate; their parents allow them to run about the streets as message boys or in various other occupations.

27947. What special advantage does the labour certificate in the fifth standard give the children?—Those who have been working half time are allowed, as soon as they become thirteen, to work full time, and get full wages. If they have not the fifth standard certificate they are not allowed full time until they are fourteen years of age. In Dundee we have between 3,000 and 4,000 children as half timers.

27948. The examination for the labour certificate may be regarded as the only instance of an individual examination conducted by you?—Except in specific subjects. Where pupils take mathematics, Latin, French, or German the grant is paid on individual examination, but for a general certificate the examination in the third standard for the half time certificate, and in the fifth for the full labour certificate, are the only individual examinations.

27949. Then at your annual examinations there are some subjects involving individual examination?—In every school. But there are higher people taking specific subjects in the upper classes; they begin with standard five, and go through six and ex-sixth.

27950. And special grants are given on the individual passes?—Yes; so a head.

27951. And in all other branches of the inspection?—It is class inspection.

27952. It is a general view of what comes under your notice?—A general view of the average attainments of the class.

27953. Is the examination by class or by sample?—By class, invariably.

27954. You may select any number out of a class and examine them?—We may, but we never do; we find it just as well to take a whole class.

27955. Is there an obligation to take a class?—No; we may take a sample if we thought it convenient.

27956. Or, as we heard of in England, by mere inspection, after a conference with the local managers and head teacher?—We never do that in Scotland.

FIFTY-SECOND PUBLIC SITTING.—WEDNESDAY, NOVEMBER 17TH, 1897,

AT 11 O'CLOCK, A.M.

At the Antient Concert Rooms, Dublin.

Present:—THE RIGHT HON. THE EARL OF BELMORE, G.C.M.G., in the Chair; HIS GRACE THE MOST REV. WILLIAM J. WALSH, D.D.; THE RIGHT HON. C. T. REDINGTON, M.A.; THE RIGHT REV. MONSIGNOR MOLLOY, D.D., D.SC.; REV. HENRY EVANS, D.D.; REV. HAMILTON WILSON, D.D.; and W. R. J. MOLLOY, ESQ.;

science for women; I think these subjects should be specially taught, with reference to horticulture, in their relation to horticulture, and, so far as possible, agriculture. I jotted down here a few of the heads of such a course. I don't know whether it would be material to mention them. In physical science, for instance—this is merely an outline, and it is not to be taken as a programme by any means—in physical science, I., the different states of matter, simple and compound bodies, general properties of matter; II., weight, equilibrium, centre of gravity; III., water: its composition, dissolving properties, pure, impure, and distilled, evaporation, clouds, rain, &c.; IV., expansion, thermometer, and so on; V., the atmosphere: its properties, pressure, ventilation, the barometer; VI., elementary magnetism and electricity, which should be very elementary; VII., light, luminous and opaque bodies, reflection, shadows, twilight, rainbow, plain and convex mirrors, elementary principles of sound. In natural science the first head would be the three kingdoms of nature, vegetable life, living and non-living things, difference between plants and animals, minerals; structure and organisation of plants, life of plants, roots, stems, buds, foliage, insects injurious to plants; flowers, general description, receptacles, relation of parts, essential parts of flowers, protection, respiration, propagation and fertilisation; the properties of soils. That is the course I should recommend for women—that is, that there should be a special course of instruction given on these subjects, and that that instruction should be practical. There should be experiments in physical science, in horticulture, in agriculture, and that course should include teaching object lessons on these subjects. The examination at the end of the course should be practical and oral, and, perhaps, to a less extent, a written examination, which I think should be very short in subjects of that class. In order to carry that out, there would be several courses open but I think the best might be to extend the present course of training, which consists of two sessions of ten months, to a third session. At the end of the second session the instruction in literature and mathematics should cease and the third session should be entirely devoted to training in those branches which I have indicated, an examination should be held at the end of the course in those branches and until the teachers satisfied the examiners at that examination, certificates, which they had obtained in the preceding year might be withheld. There are other courses, other means by which it might be done, but I think myself that the course I have indicated would be the most effective.

22984. Now we will come to the course of practical instruction for men; I suppose there are some things which may be taken in common?—Yes, my lord.

22985. Will you supplement what you have said for women with what you think might be further introduced as regards men?—Subjects such as practical cookery, domestic science, dairying and practical kindergarten are hardly subjects for men. But for men I should say, practical geometry, drawing and their application to handicrafts, practical agriculture and horticulture, physical and natural science, the course in physical and natural science might be a little more extensive for men than for women. What I have stated with reference to the course of examination would apply to men equally as to women.

22986. I think you are of opinion that training colleges can deal only with future teachers?—Yes, my lord.

22987. What course do you think could be adopted with advantage to introduce practical training among the present teachers?—For instance there is hand and eye training, and the course I would suggest would be this, that a number of teachers who have certificates in drawing and who are known to be expert at drawing and in handicraft, should be selected by the Commissioners and a few of these should be attached to each inspector's district in Ireland, such a number as would be decided on after careful consideration by the Board; that these should commence in the large centres of population, in the towns for instance, and in those towns assemble the teachers together, the teachers of the town and of the immediate neighbourhood and instruct them in drawing. First instruct them thoroughly in drawing, a very high course I don't think would be necessary for a beginning, then they should instruct them in the use of tools, a very short course, and then the application of drawing to handicraft, the one going hand in hand with the other, the application of drawing to handicraft and the actual work. Then when these teachers are so trained, these superintendents or assistant inspectors, or whatever they may be called, should superintend the introduction of drawing and handicraft into the schools of these teachers, and when the teachers are trained in the centres of population they should then hold centres of teachers all over the inspector's district and assemble them for a similar course of instruction and extend it through the towns to the country districts.

Dublin. — Jan. 22, 1897. — Professor T. W. Tugan.

22988. Have you seen the system in operation anywhere abroad?—Well, not that system exactly; a system has sprung up in Switzerland, which is not precisely that system, it would be a little too slow for us; that is during the summer vacation courses of instruction in drawing and handicraft are held from time to time in such places as Bienne, Geneva, Lausanne, Berne, and other places. The teachers are invited to attend this course of instruction, the Government authorities, and sometimes the authorities of the Canton, bear a certain amount of expense in connection with these courses, and the only expense the teacher has to undergo is that of his living in the town during the course. These courses are sometimes a month, sometimes six weeks. I think thirteen or fourteen of these courses have been held already in various towns in Switzerland, and a considerable number of teachers have received instruction, but I might point out that in general, a teacher in Switzerland has received a better training to enable him to profit by such a course of training than a teacher has in Ireland, because manual arts are to a certain extent essential in the pursuits of the country, and you find people up in the mountains who are very expert at these manual arts. I think that would be a very slow process in Ireland, and I would hardly recommend it for the present. Afterwards in order to maintain the standard, some course like that could be adopted. I have here a programme of one of the best training colleges in Switzerland, that at Lausanne, for male and female teachers, and the Professor of Physical and Natural Science there gives nineteen hours instruction in the week, the Professor of Drawing gives eleven, the Professor of Handicraft gives four, that is four hours for wood-work and eight hours for modelling, and then for bookbinding and things like that, six hours, two hours instruction in domestic economy are given for females and fourteen hours for needlework.

22989. Most Rev. Dr. Walsh.—What do you consider the main purpose of a training college to be?—Principally to train teachers in the art of teaching, your Grace, and to a certain extent, of course, to improve their general education.

22990. But I take it that the improvement of their general education ought to come in only as a means to an end?—Precisely.

22991. The primary object of the establishment and maintenance of the college being to train them in the art of teaching?—Quite so.

22992. Now do you think that in our present system sufficient prominence is given to that main object of the training colleges?—Do you mean with

Dublin. [illegible]

reference to the hand and eye training, or the whole course?

23993. I have said nothing about hand and eye training. My question was a general one. Do you think that in our present system of working the training colleges, the main object of a training college is kept sufficiently in view?—No, I don't think so.

23994. Do you think that we can set up a proper system of training in reference to manual instruction, or hand and eye training, without considering the general system of the training colleges, considering it as a whole, and to a certain extent re-casting it?—I certainly think you cannot.

23995. Then I have to ask you in what way do you think that more prominence could be given to the main object of the training colleges than is at present given?—Well, I have indicated one course, by extending the course for an additional year.

23996. My reason for putting the question was that you said there were several ways; you have indicated the one which you prefer; it may be a help to us to have a variety of courses to choose from; the first plan, you say, is an extension of the course, that is a prolongation of it?—To another year.

23997. In answer to Lord Belmore you said another session; I take it that by a session you mean a College year?—Yes, ten months.

23998. So then in your plan of reform, the training course should be extended into a course of three years, instead of two?—Quite so.

23999. You are of course aware that there is no such training course recognised, at all events as a general thing, anywhere in these countries?—Not in Ireland.

24000. Nor in England or Scotland?—Not many-

[illegible]

second portion of the course, long or sh[illegible]
be, should be given up to training the[illegible]
teaching what they have learned?—[illegible]
I do not; what I suggest is this, that [illegible]
of the course, the two sessions, should [illegible]
given up to literature and mathematic[illegible]
practical teaching should go on at the [illegible]
these subjects.

24007. By practical teaching, you m[illegible]
teaching them how to teach?—Practical[illegible]
teaching is training the teachers how [illegible]
special subjects should go on during the [illegible]

24008. I am afraid we have not yet [illegible]
[illegible] matter thoroughly cleared up. [illegible]
a distinction between two classes of su[illegible]
one hand there are, what we may call [illegible]
[illegible], and, on the other hand, the pra[illegible]
hand and eye training, and so on?—Q[illegible]

24009. There is also an equally imp[illegible]
tion between two other things which a[illegible]
quite a different line; first, teaching a s[illegible]
subject, to the students of the traini[illegible]
secondly, training those students in the [illegible]
that subject, so that they may afterw[illegible]
teach it efficiently in their schools. [illegible]
kindly explain your view clearly u[illegible]
question, bearing in mind these two dis[illegible]
I have pointed out?—In the first cours[illegible]
I would have the art of teaching, as we[illegible]
in the subjects themselves, but I wou[illegible]
almost entirely to teaching these lit[illegible]
literary and mathematical subjects.

24010. In other words, you wan[illegible]
work of the training college student[illegible]
the book subjects as distinct from wha[illegible]
the practical subjects?—Quite so.

of us in that matter?—These subjects you have read out there, pedagogy, French, German, and so on, that is very much in advance of ours.

24058. Do you think it right to give only six hours a week in all the classes to the study of method?—I think it is not so bad; they have four years there, remember, in the training colleges.

24059. CHAIRMAN.—Do they go at a younger age?—Yes, they are sixteen.

24060. In Germany, they go for six years to the training colleges?—Yes. Three years in France, but females have only two years in Switzerland in some of the colleges.

24061. Mr. NEWPORT.—I see they give eighteen hours a week for the study of the violin?—Yes, music is a great subject there, they are brought from the preparatory schools, and teachers and pupils meet together at these instruments.

24062. They only give two hours a week for the study of domestic economy?—But look at the fourteen hours after that for work peculiar to women, two hours a week is not bad for domestic economy, for they give fourteen hours for needlework, household duties, and things of that class. What I would wish to point out is that handicraft, physical and manual science, are compulsory subjects, and have to be taught as part of the college curriculum. I think that is more important than geography, quadratic equations, or the binomial theorem. I don't see the good of giving a high course of instruction to teachers in geometry and algebra. I don't see what benefit it will be to the country afterwards.

24063. But they teach geometry, and yet you say it is no use?—I don't wish to say it is no use. It's too high a course, and should not usurp the place of more useful instruction; the programme is not high, but the actual examination in geometry is so high that a great deal of valuable time is lost in preparing for it.

24064. Would you leave out any of the ordinary subjects of our training college course?—I don't think you could. I would alter the teaching of geography considerably; we have too much bad geography; I don't see what advantage it is to people to learn by rote the heights of the peaks of the Alps. I was on every one of them, but never got any idea of their heights until I got near them. The populations of little towns and the lengths of rivers—I had to learn them, but I don't know them now. I would cut all that class of work, and I think it would be very much better that a teacher going through a training college should be able to make experiments in horticulture, agriculture, and physical science, to take up his leisure hours, even if he were never to teach these subjects in the school, than to be able to call out heights of mountains and the lengths of rivers.

24065. Is it necessary to know the lengths of rivers?—If you look into the examinations for some years you will find it will be necessary to know the heights of mountains, lengths of rivers, and populations of towns and districts.

24066. I see in an examination paper now before me, "Draw an outline map of Ireland, to show the principal rivers and mountains." It does not say heights and lengths?—You have reduced that very much, and the programme is greatly improved.

24067. And geography is optional in the third year?—Yes.

24068. Monsignor MOLLOY.—Is experimental physics taught at present in the training college of which you are the principal?—No, sir; it is not.

24069. Has it been taught in the past?—Yes, Dr. Delany used to teach it.

24070. How long is it since it was given up?—Last year under the new programme; Dr. Delany will be here immediately.

24072. Is elementary science taught in the female department?—Oh, never taught in the female department.

24073. I find in the programme under which you teach at present, that the various branches of science are put down as alternatives to one another?—Optional.

24074. They are optional in this sense that a pupil wanting to get first division of first class may take any one of twelve subjects?—Yes.

24075. And among those twelve occur seven scientific subjects?—You are speaking of first division of first, but that hardly counts, there are so very few in the training colleges.

24076. That is the highest standard of classification to which a teacher can attain?—Yes.

24077. An option is allowed between twelve different subjects?—Quite so.

24078. Amongst them, there are seven science subjects, namely, mathematics, mechanical physics, experimental physics, chemistry, physiology, geology, and botany; and of these seven subjects together with the other five, he can only choose one?—Yes.

24079. A teacher may be prepared to teach one of these subjects, but he cannot be prepared to teach any of the others; and it is optional for him to choose. Therefore your teachers will go out, some of them qualified to teach botany, some to teach geology, some to teach chemistry, some to teach physics, and some to teach mathematics?—As a matter of fact it hardly comes to that, there are very few first of first candidates in training colleges; if you look at column 3 of the new programme you will find a teacher can only take one of these optional subjects.

24080. That is what I say?—It is optional with him to a certain extent to select a subject, but as a matter of fact, he will consult with the professor who is in charge of these subjects, and all the students will likely take the same.

24081. Then all the students will be prepared to teach the same subject?—As a rule they will.

24082. That one may be geology?—It may be anyone.

24083. It may be botany or mathematical physics, according to the judgment of the professor who teaches them or of the principal of the college?—Yes.

24084. But he would be quite unprepared to teach the general principles of science?—Quite so.

24085. Do you consider that a good system?—No, I have just been finding fault with it.

24086. The system you propose is entirely different from that; it is that certain general principles underlying science should be set forth in the programme, and that these should be taught to all, and all required to learn them?—That is my opinion.

24087. Is not that a very much better system?—That is the system I have suggested; I think it is only right to state that I don't know whether the professors or my colleagues, Dr. Doherty, share my views in this matter, I have consulted no one, these are entirely my own views, and none of my colleagues are responsible.

24088. At all events your views are quite at variance with this alternative system, by which one only out of twelve subjects can be chosen by the pupil; and you are in favour of a system under which all should be taught certain general principles of science, and be prepared to teach them?—Yes, I would do away with the selection of optional subjects altogether.

24090. Mr. MOLLOY.—You have not given us up to the present any information as to the students who attend Marlborough-street College, if I mistake not they may be classed teachers already in charge of schools or persons qualifying themselves to become teachers?—We have fourteen: the vast majority are students who come in for the two years' course, but the fourteen females at present are either assistants or principals in charge of schools. And there are 150 students in the college altogether, that is 136 for the two years' course, and fourteen for the one year's course. I have not said anything about the one year's course, because I think the number attending that course will decrease from year to year.

24091. What proposal do you make in the case of those fourteen?—I should be in favour of extending their course for another year, it would be difficult to break up their year into two courses, and I don't see any course I would recommend except to extend their course to two years.

24092. In the said a very important element in the training college history, namely, persons who come in, already in charge of schools, and want to improve their system of teaching?—Yes, but these are falling away, and in the future years we will hardly have any.

24093. How many untrained teachers are in charge of National schools?—I never made up those statistics, there are a large number, but I understand from the authorities of other colleges that the number of such teachers claiming admission to colleges is decreasing from year to year.

24094. Have you heard there are upwards of 2,000 untrained teachers suitable by age and otherwise for training?—I have no doubt there are, but a great many, I daresay, are old teachers.

24095. What provision do you make for the training of those people?—I would add a year to their course.

24096. Do you give them an opportunity of coming up to Marlborough-street?—Oh, certainly.

24097. But still you find that last session there were only fourteen out of 150?—Yes, and thirty the year before.

24098. Had you a greater number of applications from people of that kind?—There were a number who applied this year, who were subjected to a test examination at the local centres, and some of them failed, some failed to come to the examination and others failed at the examination.

24099. Would you not think it desirable to make some provision for instruction in the art of teaching of persons already in charge of schools?—Yes, we give them an opportunity; there is a course of ten months open to them.

24100. You started by saying that you proposed to give a two years' course; how would you expect those people to be away from their own schools for two years?—I cannot help that; I did not touch on the one year's course people; but I say if you want to train these one year's people in those subjects of practical education, which I have already read out, you cannot do it within the one year, and the only course is to extend it.

24101. Then it practically comes to this that upwards of 2,000 untrained teachers, in many respects eligible for training, must remain out in the cold?—There is a training college open to them.

24102. Coming up for two years?—It is open to them at present. They may come or not as they please; but if you want to introduce those subjects of practical education for these one year's students you must give them a longer course.

24103. CHAIRMAN.—I think you said that a great many of these 2,000 teachers are old teachers?—Yes.

24104. And they are not likely to take up any new subject or come to the training college at their—people past middle age?—A great many of them must be.

24105. Monsignor MOLLOY.—You say it would require two years to carry out an ideal system of training?—I said three.

24106. But second students obtain some kind of

24107. Then you agree that if it be found practically impossible to get the teachers up for a two years' course, it may still be a good thing to get them up for one year?—Certainly; but if you adopt the system of hand and eye training in local centres, you can bring teachers of that class and train them.

24108. Mr. Molloy.—Do you mean to convey practically that the 2,000 teachers are old teachers?—I have not the slightest idea of their age, but I should think a great many of them must be.

24109. Is it not a fact that a monitor on the completion of the monitorial course can become a principal teacher of the third class, and on the conclusion of the July examinations last year a number of those were appointed, some being even eighteen years of age?—Quite possible. A monitor who is appointed a teacher from being a monitor ought not to be brought into a training college for a one year's course, because he chooses to be principal or assistant. I think he ought to be brought in for the existing course.

24110. What was the highest classification that any of your teachers last year aimed at by coming up to the college?—Column 3 of the new programme; all want it except one man; that would entitle them under certain conditions to second of first.

24111. Had you any applications for first class among those candidates for training?—Yes; all the senior division were applicants for first class under the new programme.

24112. Well, first of first?—One only.

24113. There were 257 in training, and only one was a candidate for first of first?—Yes; I had no girls.

24114. Had you any for second of first?—Yes; all the senior division, both men and women. Column 3 of the new programme would entitle them to second of first at the last examination provided they made 65 per cent.

24115. I take it now, having disposed of the actual teachers, your general body of students are ex-monitors, ex-pupil teachers, or senior pupils who have passed a preliminary examination?—Yes.

24116. And for that class you advocate at least two years' and perhaps a three years' course?—Yes.

24117. How are those people selected?—By competitive examination according to denomination. Our college admits all denominations; we decide on the number of each to be brought in. We take the Presbyterians in order of merit and the Catholics in order of merit. We take all denominations equally.

24118. Nearly all the pupil teachers or ex-pupil teachers already classified attend Marlborough-street College, I think, for training?—I think so.

24119. Now these people had undergone a preliminary course of training for two years, and some of them may have been monitors for five years?—I don't

for Marlborough-street?—He generally sends up a list of those who apply to him.

24124. But he does not send a corresponding list for any other college?—I do not know, nor do I care very much whether he sends it to me either. I should be just as glad he did not.

24125. Coming to your own subjects, arithmetic, algebra, and book-keeping, along with teaching these subjects do you not bring up a class of pupils and show the teacher how to teach the particular subject?—Frequently; but that is the distinctive duty of the teacher of method. I sometimes take a set of students and form a class and sometimes a set of pupils; the the professor of method sees that they actually teach the class.

24126. Is it to be understood that he duplicates your work?—Certainly, he sees lessons taught in these subjects as well as in every other.

24127. Speaking of the examinations in music, is there anything to prevent Mr. Goodman applying practical tests by bringing up a number of students and asking the particular candidate for a certificate to give a lesson in music to them?—Well, that is not included in the programme. I don't know what Mr. Goodman is empowered to do, but I doubt whether he is entitled to test the student by asking her to teach the subject to pupils. I think he is not. I am certain Mr. Goodman does what he is entitled to and no more.

24128. I think you mentioned in reply to Monsignor Molloy that no physical science is taught to girls in Marlborough-street?—The principles of hygiene and domestic economy. I took them as distinct subjects. I don't call them physical science.

24129. What is to prevent you in view of the fact that for many years you had a programme published in those subjects?—To prepare for your examinations at the end of the course is our first duty.

24130. Monsignor Molloy. And in selecting from the optional subjects you select those which are the easiest for the pupils to pass in?—Those optional subjects have come in for the first time under that programme, but Mr. Molloy is speaking of years back.

24131. And under this programme, physical science is not a remunerative subject?—No, and under the old programme it was the same for girls, it could not enter into classification, it could be taken as a special subject for which there was a special certificate, but nothing more.

24132. Mr. Molloy.—In view of the fact that they had the elements of physical science taught in some of the model schools, do you not think it is a drawback to the Marlborough-street Training College not to have it introduced?—Certainly, but I say means should be introduced for dealing with it.

24133. And that shortcoming has existed for a

the question, a student who is two years in the college, will get twenty-two hours instruction. They are able, I should say, to make homes very fairly.

24162. Rev. Dr. Evans.—As to the amount of teaching and training, I quite agree with your view; the very name of training college means you have those under you to train them how to teach; of course there must be a substratum of knowledge on which to act, but the important part is the art of conveying that knowledge, teaching it to pupils, and that you bear in mind?—We do, certainly; Dr. Doherty, who has charge of that, was, and is, a distinguished teacher, and since he got charge of the subject in 1883 or 1884, it has been a very great success indeed.

24163. Has Dr. Doherty the training of the females as well as the males?—Yes, I think; of course he is responsible.

24164. Most Rev. Dr. Walsh.—There were some questions put to you about the number of untrained teachers in Ireland, with a view of seeing whether something could not be done for those teachers in the way of training; I think 3,000 was mentioned as the present number of untrained teachers?—Yes.

24165. Kindly look at this official Report of the Commissioners of National Education. Look at that table in the Commissioners' Report, page 30 of the Report for last year—can you tell me, from it, what is the present number of untrained teachers in the service of the National Education Board in Ireland?—It comes here to be 6,619.

24166. That is the number. Now, you spoke, I think, of the untrained teachers as probably old teachers?—Well, I should say a fair proportion.

24167. Now, let me ask you to look at another part of the Report, at page 29, the table which gives the number of vacancies in the office of teacher, occurring from year to year. This table also gives the number of trained teachers coming out each year from the training colleges. If you look at the bottom of the columns in that table, where the figures are totted up, you will see that, during the last ten years, the training colleges turned out, as trained teachers, 2,286 students not previously employed as teachers?—Yes.

24168. Do you not also see that during the same ten years, the number of vacancies that had to be filled was 6,021, so that within those ten years, 3,735 untrained teachers had to be appointed?—Yes.

24169. Then, as so many as 3,735 untrained teachers have had to be appointed even within the last ten years, we are not at all to assume that a very large proportion of the total number of 6,619 untrained teachers in Ireland, may not be comparatively young?—Quite so; but I should say all those young teachers ought to undergo a three years' course.

24170. Let us be practical. The training colleges at present are as full as they can be; but, nevertheless, during the last ten years, the supply has fallen short of the demand, to the extent of 3,735 teachers?—Yes, we are not training enough teachers for the demand.

24171. Plainly we are not. That is what I want to bring out. Every year there are hundreds of untrained teachers being placed over the schools?—Yes.

24172. It is plain then, that a fair proportion of the existing untrained teachers may be comparatively young?—I should say a number would be.

24173. Taking them all, young and old as they may be, would it not be desirable if something could be done to give them the benefit of some kind of training?—Undoubtedly.

24174. Suppose we distinguish between the two functions of the training colleges, as at present worked, one, under which a great deal of time is given to teaching certain subjects, the other, under which a comparatively small time is given to instructing and training the students of the college in the art of teaching those subjects afterwards in their schools, suppose—as we cannot do everything for those untrained teachers that we should wish to do—that a system was established in which we could give them, at all events, the main thing, a course of instruction, even a short course, in the art of teaching, would not that be a great advantage?—It would be a decided advantage.

J. J. Doherty, ll.d., Principal, Marlborough-street Training College, Dublin, examined.

24175. Chairman.—You are the Principal of the Marlborough-street Training College?—The male department.

24176. And you have come here to speak on certain matters which are in the memorandum you have handed in, with regard to what we may call hand and eye training, and things in that connection?—Yes.

24177. First of all, with regard to hand and eye training, what do you say with regard to the extension of it?—Well, as my colleague has pointed out, all our female students receive instruction in kindergarten at the present time, in our college, and I would like to see the extension of kindergarten exercises forming what we may call elementary manual instruction—what is called in English schools, hand and eye training—introduced into our college; and all our students, male and female, should be required to go through a course of this hand and eye training.

24178. How do you distinguish between the alternatives of hand and eye training and object lessons?—This hand and eye training is, no doubt, familiar to the Commissioners as they have seen it in a number of schools that I understand they have visited. Object lessons form an elementary science teaching of various natural objects and ordinary phenomena. With regard to this object teaching, I would like to see it introduced into all our schools, indeed, made compulsory, both for boys and girls. With regard to this elementary course of manual instruction I would

24179. I want to ask you how far, taking manual instruction to consist, first of all, of drawing, then easy cardboard work, and then coming up higher to woodwork, only taking these as specimens, how far would you make any or all of these compulsory?—I would not take woodwork at all in this elementary hand and eye training. I would confine this elementary course of the hand and eye training to simple geometrical drawing, scale drawing, construction of simple geometrical figures, paper folding, stick laying, paper cutting, designing, and, perhaps, as the farthest extension of that, cardboard modelling; but I would reserve woodwork for what I would call manual instruction proper, and confine it to the senior classes, and I would not make it obligatory in our schools.

24180. In any case?—In every case I would make it optional.

24181. Would you make cardboard work obligatory in its proper class?—I think it is a very useful exercise, and I would regard it as a portion of the elementary manual training that should be made compulsory.

24182. And that is a thing that could be done without any expensive apparatus?—Yes; that is one of the reasons why I would like to see it made compulsory, because the expense would be trifling, and in the case of extended manual instruction, such as woodwork, the expense would be considerable.

Dublin.

[illegible]

24190. What subjects do you suggest for boys?—If they do not take up manual instruction, which in my opinion might be regarded as sufficient—that is advanced manual instruction—and in my opinion this will be taken up in only a few schools.—

24191. Most Rev. Dr. Walsh.—We are getting, I fear, into confusion about some of the terms that have to be used; manual instruction is one of them: as you now use it, you refer, I think, to woodwork?—Yes; I would say that boys and girls might take up such subjects as gardening, mechanics—meaning the mechanical laws of solids and fluids—one or more of the experimental sciences, and one or more of the natural sciences; and for girls only such as needlework, cookery, and domestic science.

24192. Chairman.—What mode of examination do you suggest in these subjects?—In all of these cases I would strongly recommend that the examination should not be a results examination, but an examination by inspection. I don't condemn results examination in all cases, but I think in the case of such subjects where it is not so much the amount of information that the pupils obtain, but the mode of gaining that information, which is the all-important matter, that then the examination should be an inspection by the officers of the Board seeing the work done, questioning the pupils to some extent to see how they have followed the teacher; and that then the payment should be based, not on a result examination, but on the inspector's opinion with regard to the ability and energy with which the lessons had been taught to the pupils.

24193. What do you consider to be the relative advantages of manual instruction and science as school subjects?—I prefer, on the whole, science training, which has special advantages. The science training would develop the intellectual powers to a very much greater extent in my opinion than the manual instruction would do, and also it may be made to afford a considerable amount of manual instruction. If a pupil is engaged in any of the physical sciences, say magnetism or electricity, he can contrive little experiments, and the teacher ought to show them how to contrive these experiments. A very considerable amount of manual work can thus be carried on by the pupils themselves, aided by the teacher in the actual work of science instruction. But comparing manual instruction with science instruction, there is a less strain placed on both teachers and pupils in manual instruction, it is easier to get the pupils to join in it, and it is easier to keep it going; it gives practice in manual work, cultivates power of hand and eye, teaches accuracy and perseverance, and therefore I consider it an extremely valuable aid to the teacher's work.

24194. With regard to gardening, the male students of your college now receive instruction in agriculture and gardening at Glasnevin?—Yes.

24195. Do you think that the work in gardening might be extended and made a separate subject?—I would like to see it made a separate subject; it is at present taught as a portion of a much wider subject, agriculture. A comparatively small amount of time and attention is given to the subject of gardening. I think that gardening might be made a separate subject by itself. I think it might be introduced, not alone into the training colleges, but into our rural schools throughout the country. Agriculture, in my opinion, cannot be taught very efficiently in a National school; but as every teacher has a garden associated with his school or near it, I think a practical knowledge of gardening might be very readily given to pupils of National schools.

24196. And you think that female students should receive instruction in gardening during their residence at Glasnevin?—Yes, and this subject might also be introduced into female schools.

24197. What do you say with regard to the programme for the junior classes, 1, 2 and 3, as regards object lessons; and what time do you think should be

Dublin.

Professor [illegible]

given to the subject?—The subject of gardening in I, 2 and 3 class should be treated in the form of object lessons, the pupils collecting flowers and grasses, and plants of various kinds and vegetables. The lesson should deal with each particular object as an object lesson, and be given by the teacher, the pupils writing out their notes upon the lesson, and preserving them for the inspector. Similar lessons should be given upon the function of the root, leaf, and so on. If such a lesson were given once a week, another lesson, or a repetition once a week, might be given where the teacher might have a conversation with his pupils over the objects that had been treated of in the previous lesson, and then get them to write down everything they had learned upon the subject.

34198. What time would be found for this class of teaching?—I think either half or three-quarters of an hour, twice a week, for that subject in the junior classes. These would be object lessons; and there might be also object lessons taken up in connection with other subjects upon elementary natural phenomena, and in that case I would allow in the school about two half hours a week for object lessons in elementary gardening.

34199. How would you conduct the examination?—In all these cases I would like to see the examination conducted by inspection, the inspector listening to the teacher giving the lesson, seeing how the lesson is given, looking at the result of the work for the past session, and reporting whether, in his opinion, the instruction was good and worth the payment.

34200. With regard to the senior classes, would you extend this rather?—I would make an extension of it into gardening proper, treating of the functions of the various parts of plants, culture of plants, formation and care of flower-beds; and the subject of window-gardening should be taken up, and in the more advanced classes the culture of roses, and fruits, and grafting.

34201. Would you give the same amount of time, or more?—I should say a three-quarter hour lesson twice a week would be sufficient.

34202. And you would conduct the examination on the same principle?—In the same way, and that would be of a practical character; I would require that the pupils should actually work in the garden, the whole class taking charge of one particular bed or portion of a bed.

34203. Would you make this compulsory or optional?—Optional; I would leave it optional with the teacher to select some one science subject or advanced manual instruction, but I would make some one subject that would develop the thinking and observing powers obligatory upon all teachers.

34204. Do you think that an elementary course of mechanics of solids and fluids should be obligatory for the male students in the training colleges, and should form a part of the course for examination?—I do. I consider that is so important a subject that it ought to be made obligatory upon our male students. I would make obligatory some one or more of the science subjects to be selected by them.

34205. But in the case of teaching in National schools, would you leave it optional?—I would regard it as one of the subjects that might be chosen by the teachers. In the junior classes it might be treated as a series of object lessons upon familiar tools and instruments, and the application of them; and in the senior classes I would like to see it treated in the regular course—the mechanical laws of solids and fluids.

in the same way?—I would continue in the same way.

34208. With regard to the experi[illegible] would you deal with them in much [illegible] In much the same way.

34209. First, as regards the traini[illegible] generally, as regards the schools?—T[illegible] the mechanics I would recommend t[illegible] the experimental or natural science[illegible] We cannot take the whole of them[illegible] will be chosen will depend upon the[illegible] able to undertake the subject in the[illegible] but some one of the experimental sc[illegible] should, in my opinion, be taken up[illegible] colleges.

34210. Meaning by that magne[illegible] sound, light, heat, and chemistry?—[illegible]

34211. In the National schools yo[illegible] the study should be confined to the[illegible] In the case of some of these subjects[illegible] it would be better to confine their s[illegible] classes; there is no difficulty at all[illegible] series of object lessons for the junio[illegible] secure some of these object lessons[illegible] some of the subjects of magnetism or[illegible]

34212. Do you think that the teach[illegible] be by experiment?—Entirely experim[illegible] subject should be treated experiment[illegible] students of the training college, and [illegible] experimentally before the pupils i[illegible] the National school.

34213. You hold the same views [illegible] teaching of botany, zoology, and [illegible] same.

34214. Turning to girls in Nation[illegible] research do you make on needlew[illegible] domestic economy?—In our training[illegible] up all these subjects. I should like t[illegible] much in the same way in the femal[illegible] the case of a girls' school any one of the[illegible] be made the science subject, obligato[illegible] of National schools.

34215. Do you think, as regards[illegible] drawing, simple geometrical drawin[illegible] freehand or object drawing, should [illegible] all students, male and female, in [illegible] colleges, and also in the National sch[illegible] both boys and girls?—Yes, I am str[illegible] of introducing elementary geometrica[illegible] our students and for all pupils in sch[illegible]

34216. Most Rev. Dr. Walsh.[illegible] Delaney, we may take it from your [illegible] have read some of the evidence t[illegible] England?—Portions of it.

34217. And I see that you are fa[illegible] the branches of school work that go[illegible] and probably in other English town[illegible] of hand and eye training?—Yes, I [illegible] schools in operation.

34218. Amongst the exercises i[illegible] training that go on there, you would[illegible] ing and cardboard work; you did n[illegible] work, I think, but I am sure you ha[illegible] of the system of hand and eye train[illegible] highly approved of. You approve of[illegible] of these branches of school work b[illegible] schools of Ireland?—I do.

34219. Do you not think that i[illegible] these exercises in paper-folding and [illegible] so forth, a great many ill-informed[illegible] people, to put it plainly—would not [illegible] whole thing into ridicule?—No doubt[illegible]

[illegible]

34222. You are aware of the important distinction that is made in Birmingham and other such places between what is termed "Hand and Eye Training" on the one hand, and what is termed "Manual Instruction" on the other?—Yes.

34223. By "Hand and Eye Training" they mean those branches of practical instruction that go on in the junior classes?—Quite so.

34224. And by manual instruction, as distinct from hand and eye training, they mean educational woodwork and metal work?—Yes.

34225. The former of these you would wish to see made obligatory?—Quite so.

34226. And the latter you would not?—I would not.

34227. And this is because you see it to be obviously impossible to introduce the subject into many of our schools?—Quite so.

34228. Of course: it would be impossible, for instance, except in extremely exceptional cases, in a country school where there is only one teacher?—I would not say impossible.

34229. Well, I mean, practically impossible?—With regard to our country schools if there was a master——

34230. I think we are agreed. You recognise that it would be exceedingly difficult?—It would.

34231. And the case would be exceptional where it could be done at all: it would require a very enterprising and industrious teacher?—I was going to say he should be an enthusiast.

34232. CHAIRMAN.—Do you know that as a matter of fact there are one or two such teachers?—I was not aware.

34233. MOST REV. DR. WALSH.—But these are plainly exceptional cases. However, as to larger centres of population, towns and cities where the schools are larger, no such difficulty would exist?—No.

34234. You consider that it would be an advantage if the introduction of woodwork, for instance, was encouraged, without having it made compulsory, in city schools?—Decidedly.

34235. I am aware, Dr. Doherty, that you have a very wide experience of school work under our existing programme?—A large experience.

34236. Now, taking the "Handicraft" programme, do you approve of it?—Well, as it is drafted in the revised programme of the Board I approve of it, because it was myself drew it up.

34237. You are speaking now of the revised programme recently issued by the Commissioners of National Education for the examination and classification of teachers. That is a totally new thing. My question had reference to the school programme, the programme that was drawn up when the new subject of handicraft was introduced, I think it was in 1885. What do you think of that programme; surely you do not approve of it?—I do not; it was not educational.

34238. It seems that under this programme, as we are aware, woodwork is taught without any reference to drawing?—That is a mistake.

34239. Of course it is a fundamental mistake. But it appears that, under that programme, there is nothing to hinder a teacher from getting a certificate authorising him to teach handicraft under the rules of the Commissioners of National Education, even though unfortunately he knows nothing whatever of drawing: that was possible under the state of affairs that has hitherto existed?—Yes.

34240. I understand that fully. But the handicraft system, as you have it, was not constructed on scientific lines, as any system now introduced would be. In the new programme for the examination and classification of teachers, full provision is made for drawing in connection with woodwork?—Quite so.

34241. CHAIRMAN.—Is it a necessary provision?—Yes. It is expressed that the models are all to be made from previous drawings made by the pupils.

34242. MOST REV. DR. WALSH.—We are now speaking of the new programme for teachers recently issued by the National Education Board; that programme is all right, at least in this respect?—Yes.

34243. Now, Dr. Doherty, in reference to another matter. I think you said that you could rearrange the school time-table so as to provide for the introduction of the new branches of manual and practical instruction, without sacrificing anything in the line of mere book work, that was really of importance?—I think so.

34244. I think you said that without sacrificing anything that was really of importance on the book-work side, you could provide 5½ hours a week for this manual and practical instruction?—Quite so.

34245. You may take it that in England two hours a week is considered sufficient for this special work?—Does that mean manual instruction only?

34246. Here again we are getting into some confusion about words; in England they use the words hand and eye training for what goes on in the lower classes, up to the point where woodwork comes in, then they begin to speak of manual instruction. Now as to the hand and eye training?—I am only allowing 1½ hours for that.

34247. And that time can be given to it without sacrificing anything that is really of importance in the book-work, or "literary instruction" as we usually hear it called?—Yes.

34248. In giving that answer you have, of course, considered the matter in all its bearings?—I have.

34249. You are a teacher of long standing?—I am.

34250. And you are the Professor of Method in the Training College of the National Education Board?—Quite so.

34251. Well, so much for these points. I think, Dr. Doherty, you said that, as regards the higher classes in the National schools, while you would not make woodwork obligatory in the schools generally, you would insist upon their having either woodwork or some other subject of a practical character?—Quite so.

34252. In connection with that, you spoke of elementary science, and you said, I think, that as regards the teachers, some specific branch of natural science should be taught to them?—Some branch of experimental or natural science.

34253. Let us take the science that is to be taught in the schools: kindly look at this programme; it is the English code for 1897?—I know it.

34254. You will find there, on page 64, a number of alternative courses assigned for elementary science in the schools; if you look through them I think you will find that nearly all of them are courses in specific subjects?—Quite so.

34255. There is one in mechanics, one in electricity and magnetism, and so on. But now look at course III in that section; what is the character of that course; does it deal with any specific branch of science, and

Dublin. Jan. [illegible] 1897. Professor Doherty, LL.D.

sure, what he was hinting at was the method of carrying grants?—That is a low view of the subject that we never take in our training college.

24284. Then you resist a strong temptation. Now as to method, as I understand it, it comprises two things. There is the method of teaching a school; and the method of conducting a school, in the sense of keeping records, and filling the school rolls, and so forth; all this book-keeping as I may call it—is a very complicated and difficult thing: you have to teach all that?—Yes.

24285. So that, although you are professor of method, a great deal of your time has to be given to something outside the really important work of instructing the students in the art of teaching?—In our college we have a very good arrangement in that respect; the head teachers connected with our model schools relieve me practically of the greater portion of this merely mechanical work of telling the students how to keep the rolls and the registers.

24286. Coming now to the teaching of method in what I regard as the really essential sense, is the capacity of the Queen's scholar to teach the different subjects in which they are themselves instructed in the training college really tested under the present system?—Yes, I would say so.

24287. Who tests it?—A head inspector is appointed by the Board to come at the end of each training session, and he tests every individual student.

24288. In every individual subject?—Not in every individual subject.

24289. Then in what subjects are they not tested in this vitally important matter?—Each individual student would not be tested in all the subjects.

24290. I am not putting it in that way. The main point is whether every subject is provided for in any really effective sense in the present system. Who tests them, for instance, in drawing?—The only test that is actually applied in drawing, is merely an examination which tests the students' powers to make a drawing.

24291. But you see that my question is upon a totally different matter. I am speaking not of their capacity for drawing, but of their capacity to teach drawing. In the interests of practical instruction, drawing is one of the most important subjects we have to provide for. Now who tests their capacity of teaching, for instance, in this important subject of drawing?—There is no test applied by an inspector at the end of the course, but the principals of the college see that the subject of drawing is not alone taught to the students during their two years' residence with us, but that they are taught by the professor of drawing how to teach the subject.

24292. Am I right then in inferring that it is no part of your business as professor of method to deal with this important branch, and to see whether the students trained in the training college are fit or unfit to teach drawing?—But it is my province as principal of the college.

24293. I am speaking of your business as professor of method?—It is. My students have to teach before me.

24294. To teach drawing?—They have and do so.

24295. But, Dr. Doherty, is their power of teaching drawing really taken into account in giving them their final teaching certificate?—Their certificate for teaching drawing—no.

24296. But surely you recognise that it ought to be?—Undoubtedly.

24297. I need not say that no one can consider that you are to blame for what is wrong in the present system?—Well, I would like to point out that even with regard to the subject of drawing, the method of teaching the subject is not neglected in our college.

24298. But you will agree with me that sufficient importance is not attached to it, in the giving of the teacher's certificate; I mean that it seems an extraordinary thing to require a certificate before a teacher is allowed to teach drawing, and at the same time to give people certificates to teach drawing without doing anything whatever to ascertain whether they have any power of teaching it or not?—Certainly.

24299. Now there are a few other matters I should wish to ask you about. First, do you think it advisable in the training colleges to give so much time as they seem to be given to the teaching of geography; am I not right in saying that geography is taught as a subject in your college, as I suppose it is in all the training colleges?—It is.

24300. That is, not merely the most approved methods of teaching geography, but geography itself as a branch of knowledge, just as it is learned at school?—Quite so.

24301. Don't you think that geography is a subject that might be to a large extent dispensed with?—I think that for the Training Colleges it is now fully enough dispensed with by the new programme issued for the examination and classification of teachers last year by the National Education Board. These regulations provide that if the first year's students distinguish themselves at the examination in geography at the end of their year, they will not be required to take it up at all in the next year.

24302. In column 8 of the new programme the examination in geography consists of these sections. Take only two of them—"The British Empire (Political and Descriptive"), also its commercial aspect, and then "Physical Geography—mountains, plains, rivers, deserts, winds, climate, tides, and currents," that seems to cover an enormous range of matter?—Yes, but very important.

24303. Important, no doubt; but is it of such importance that it should occupy all the time that it must occupy in a Training College?—There is one great advantage in it: it is taught to our female students as well as to our male students; and mathematical and physical geography is really a science subject.

24304. But a great deal of what they are taught is what is already printed in books?—No doubt.

24305. Lists of mountains?—Not in physical geography.

24306. But there are a great many mountains in the British Empire. In the course on Physical Geography, it is merely the names of the mountains, their elevation, and so on?—Yes.

24307. Take the descriptive geography: is it not open to examiners to ask the height of some particular mountain?—No examiner would now, I think, give such a question.

24308. But is it open to an examiner to ask the question: if it is open to him to do so, the unfortunate students must be prepared for it?—Beyond doubt it is open to the examiner.

24309. Now do you think it advisable that the students should be left in that position, that they are not really safe in going into an examination unless they know the heights of ever so many mountains, and the lengths of ever so many rivers?—That is fairly provided for in our examination papers; all the questions are not obligatory on the candidate.

24310. At all events, in so far as geography has been cut down in the new programme for teachers, you think that an improvement?—I do.

24311. Some reference, I think, was made to the programme known as "the industrial programme," as your Training College or in the practising schools attached to it, that is to say, the Central Model Schools in Marlborough street; I believe that so far as that college and those schools are concerned, that programme is now abandoned?—It is now abandoned.

24312. Lest there should be any mistake on the point, as it will go to the public, it might be well to clear this up. When you say that the "industrial programme" is abandoned, you don't mean that the teaching of needlework, for instance, is given up in those schools?—By no means.

hat sense then do you speak of the
[illegible] than industrial work?—The industrial
, technical sense we apply to a special
rndment for the 5th class girls.
that is a course in which two hours a
given to needlework—in other words,
rk?—Quite so.
is now found by experience to be a
allowance?—Yes; it is too large. We
the hour which is still compulsory

giving only one hour a day to it, you
at the work of that department is still
to a quite sufficient extent?—Yes.
ough what is technically known as the
rogramme is abandoned?—Yes; in fact in
ere is a little too much needlework,
sent time.
Joshua Fitch, in answering some ques-
t to him in London, told us that he be-
e a great mistake made in schools in the
ework was dealt with; it is dealt with,
as a means of occupation than as an
ject. Now, would you go the length that
this point; he said that perhaps two
ek would be quite as much as could
ven to needlework, from the educational
—I would perhaps give three hours a

at all events, not more than three
ore than three hours; I think it
s entirely mechanical after a little

Joshua Fitch put it in this way, or at
ard to this way of putting it, that as
ework that the work of the elementary
fold: first, to teach the art of needle-
ently, to give a sufficient amount of
tice in the art, just as much practice as
ake that teaching effective; does that
ew?—Quite so.
Robertson.—At present needlework
for girls in National schools; would
other subject of a practical character
them?—I would; in addition to needle-
ould some such subject as cookery or
e.
ld it be possible to make cookery
a large number of schools?—I have
amount of attention to the subject of
I think there is no difficulty in intro-
aching of cookery if it only received
into any of our National schools
country.
t about the difficulty of providing
'e school that at Marlborough-street;
fficulty; the classes in Marlborough-
re self-paying, so far as the girls are
ere was no difficulty at all. The
ent was, the lecturer in cookery pur-
terials, the children themselves perform-
onstrations, and cooking the different
en these dishes were sold to the pupils
cost of the materials, and there were
ular demands for particular dishes than
ed.
not the pupils sometimes cook the
pupils always cook the dishes.
you got sale for dishes cooked by
pupils themselves were willing to buy
ould be glad to buy them and bring
their parents to show their handiwork.
the first dish cooked by a girl cannot
atory?—Of course in some cases there
fure.
you think the teaching of cookery

24328. Would you find people willing to buy what is cooked in the same way as you can in towns?—I think so.

24329. It was suggested to us that the teacher might cook her dinner before the pupils, and in that way might get over the difficulty of providing materials?—That never occurred to me, and I think that would not be a bad arrangement. But, as a matter of fact, in our schools—I made special inquiry into that matter—there was no difficulty in getting the pupils to purchase the dishes that were cooked, except perhaps in one or two instances, and the classes were thereby self-supporting.

24330. Can you mention some other subject as an alternative to cookery?—Domestic science.

24331. What is domestic science?—It covers a wide range; it would take up of course everything about washing the tea things, arranging the table, making beds, some small amount of cookery, not going into it very extensively; some small amount of subjects dealing with ventilation.

24332. Would it be taught from a text book?—Taught almost entirely by the lectures of the teachers. The difficulty with domestic science has always been to make the whole lesson a practical one as we can do in cookery. But although the making of beds cannot be taught practically in a school, yet, since the children would have the experience at home, and since their attention would be directed to this experience, and since they would be asked by the teachers to make the beds and carry out all the instructions in their homes, the practical instruction would thus be carried on at home, while a great part of the theoretical instruction would be given in the schools.

24333. Do you think that theoretical instruction ought always to be illustrated by practical experiments?—Yes, so far as possible.

24334. Then, as to the boys, you think that for the senior classes either woodwork or some other scientific subject should be introduced?—Both for boys and girls; I would restrict the woodwork to boys, but girls could learn the scientific subject just as well as boys.

24335. And you mentioned gardening as one of the subjects?—Yes, for either girls or boys.

24336. Do you think together with gardening they should be taught elementary botany?—Botany would be one of the sciences that might be taken up specially by itself, but in the case of gardening, elementary botany would have to be taught, and in the junior classes I would like to see that taught as object lessons.

24337. Would you approve of teaching botany alone?—Without doubt I regard botany as one of the most interesting and practical of sciences for school work. You can only have about one or two of these in any school, and if the teacher had a great liking for botany, that is a subject I should like to see introduced into the school and recognised as the science subject for developing the observing powers of the children.

24338. And elementary chemistry?—Elementary chemistry or magnetism, but only one other science subject should be taken in addition to the manual instruction, which I think might go on simultaneously with the other.

24339. You would not approve of practical gardening without scientific instruction?—Undoubtedly not.

24340. What sized garden would be sufficient?—A comparatively small one. I have seen a number of school gardens of half a rood, or even less, that in my opinion would do all that is wanted.

24341. That would be quite sufficient?—I should think so.

24387. What subjects of physical science did you take up to lecture at Marlborough-street College?—They might be grouped under the heads of mechanical physics and experimental physics, including sound, light, heat, magnetism, and electricity; all of these not being taken up during the same session; one session, heat, and another magnetism, &c. We carried out the mechanical laws of solids and liquids in every course.

24388. At present you are professor in experimental science and the art of teaching?—Yes.

24389. You mentioned that you always had the important subject of general science?—Quite so.

24390. What subjects come under that denomination?—The natural properties of air and water, experiments showing the pressure of the air, pumps and their structure, simple experiments illustrating combustion, leading up to the subject of respiration and ventilation.

24391. Would you be in favour of a return to that system of circulating instructors in physical science, visiting certain centres throughout the country, grouping the teachers of the locality together, and giving them instruction at those centres?—I would recommend that course in the case of drawing and in the case of this elementary manual instruction, or hand and eye training; and then, when you had those subjects fairly taught to the teachers, I think science teachers might be sent round.

24392. You referred a while ago to object lessons; how did these object lessons differ from what was years ago familiarly known as history of common things?—They are practically the same thing: if by common things would be understood natural phenomena. Combustion, for instance, I would call an object lesson. The candle would be the object.

24393. In connexion with Marlborough-street, have you any chemical laboratory?—No.

24394. In the case of the teachers who took up the subject of chemistry, was all their information of a theoretical kind?—We never took up chemistry as a subject.

24395. But it was open to them to take up chemistry?—It was; but we never took it up as a subject of instruction. I never lectured on it.

24396. No instruction in your experience within a quarter of a century has been given in chemistry?—No; except the simple chemical experiments to illustrate the principles underlying respiration.

24397. What is the difficulty about carrying out these object lessons throughout the country?—None at all, in my opinion; and I would like to see them introduced into every National school in the country—made compulsory.

24398. Rev. Dr. Evans.—You are in favour of hand and eye training being introduced into all our schools?—I am strongly in favour of it.

24399. Have you any provision for preparing the teachers to teach in that subject in the training college?—No; but with the permission of the Board we will introduce it into our training college, and for the future all our students will be turned out, we hope, able to give instruction in the subject.

24400. But it is not done at present?—It is not done at present.

24401. Is drawing compulsory on all the students in the training college?—Yes; male and female.

24402. Have you ever found it impossible to teach some one or other—that is, that some Queen's Scholar is not naturally capable of learning drawing?—No doubt some find great difficulty in learning the subject, and in a few cases fail at the examination. Such cases have occurred.

Dublin. [illegible]

Professor [illegible], M.A.

24417. Therefore, without asking you to say anything to magnify your office, would you not consider that a professor of method really is one of the most important officials in the training college?—I regard him as absolutely essential in a training college. The great object of the training college is not to teach any subject so much as to teach students how to teach the subject, and that can only be done by having a man whose whole time and attention is devoted to the science and art of teaching, and I think that, without boasting, in our college at Marlborough-street we do as much or more than is done in any other college.

24418. Most Rev. Dr. Walsh.—Will you kindly explain to the Commissioners what the actual practice is in reference to these model lessons that we have heard about, in connection with the examination of the students in the training colleges, especially in reference to those known as impromptu lessons?—As has been mentioned, everyone of our students selects three subjects, and prepares notes of lessons on these three subjects; and presents these notes to the head inspector.

24419. How long before the examination does the student present these three subjects?—Only on the day of the examination; he has prepared them months before.

24420. That is, on the day of the examination he gives his list of these subjects to the inspector, and then, as I understand it, the inspector calls on him then and there to give a lesson on some one of the three?—Yes.

24421. And, in addition to that, the inspector also calls upon him to give a lesson not specially prepared?—Yes.

24422. The selection of that additional subject is absolutely in the hands of the inspector?—Yes, absolutely in the hands of the inspector.

24423. To what pupils is this lesson given?—To the same class of pupils.

24424. These are the pupils of the ordinary practising school attached to the training college?—Yes.

24425. Is not a lesson so given to the children likely to be, to some extent, a rather bungling performance?—Oh, no.

24426. We are speaking of a lesson given absolutely without preparation; is not that a wild sort of proceeding to set going in a school?—In all fairness, it is understood that the subject shall not be of a recondite nature, but a simple subject, such as is taken up in school classes.

24427. But, recondite or simple, is it desirable to set before young teachers, or candidates preparing to be teachers, the idea of giving impromptu teaching in the schools?—That is a question that has often occurred to me.

24428. I am sorry it has not been decisively answered long ago. Let me ask you now, do you think it is a desirable thing to put before the teachers, or candidate teachers in training, that, instead of preparing for the lessons which they are to give in their schools, they should give lessons to the children without preparation?—The question has often arisen in my mind, and I have come to the conclusion that it is not consistent with the principles I am constantly commending to my students, that they should make a careful preparation for each lesson.

Most Rev. Dr. Walsh.—I heard some time ago of a fairly good teacher who was decidedly injured by this feature of the training college course. Before he went to the training college he never thought of taking up any part of his school-work without preparation. The idea of giving impromptu lessons had never occurred to him. But from that out, he took to the system. He seemed to have taken up the idea that by giving impromptu lessons he could show that he was a trained teacher. So gradually he became very careless about his work, and it ended badly for him.

24429. Mr. [illegible].—How much preparation is there for these impromptu lessons?—None, the students have to begin at a moment's notice. The late Head Inspector [illegible] told me he had come to the conclusion that in all fairness a certain time for preparation should be allowed.

24430. Most Rev. Dr. Walsh.—Now, if these impromptu lessons, as they are called, are to be continued, should not something like that be arranged—is it fair to ask you for your opinion on the point?—I would like to see a quarter of an hour given for preparation.

34442. You have a large practising school attached to the Drumcondra Training College?—We have.

34443. And to the college in Baggot-street also there is attached a very large practising school?—Yes, your Grace.

34444. Do the students and teachers in training practise in those schools the art of teaching?—They do.

34445. Do they practise it under any special supervision?—They practise it under the supervision of the professor of method.

34446. Does he superintend their teaching in all the subjects of the school course?—I think he does.

34447. He does not confine his instruction in method to those particular subjects which he teaches himself?—By no means.

34448. Your professor of method is, I believe, the teacher also of some particular subject?—He professes arithmetic and mensuration.

34449. But in dealing with the subject of method, he does not confine himself to the method of teaching arithmetic and mensuration?—Most certainly not, he deals with the method of teaching in general.

34450. Do you think that this system which we have, the system of having the students of the training colleges practising on the children of the school, is a very satisfactory one as regards the educational work of the school: do you think the children suffer?—I don't think the children suffer, because the teachers that go down there are very earnest, and as they are under the eye, not merely of the professor of method, but of the principal of the school, who also takes notice of what goes on, they feel themselves under the necessity of doing their very best.

34451. I believe the National Education Board now give special advantages, in the way of better salaries, to teachers in the practising school?—They do.

34452. And in that way the practising school is able to command the services of better teachers, and this, I suppose, makes up for any little drawback that there may be, if there is any drawback, from the introduction of the training college students?—Yes, your Grace.

34453. Do you think it would be an improvement to the system if each professor was made, at least to some extent, a professor of method in his own particular department, whilst retaining the services of a special professor of method for the work of teaching generally?—I think it would be very beneficial.

34454. Do you not think that this would have the effect of emphasising the importance of method?—Certainly.

34455. It would emphasise the idea that the first work of the training college is, as the name implies, the work of training persons to teach?—It would certainly.

34456. A training college must, of course, teach such subjects as history, arithmetic, algebra, and that, but you do not consider that to be the primary work of a training college?—Properly speaking, it ought not to be.

34457. It is not the primary work of the training college to prepare a person for the work of teaching?—Certainly.

any work left for the college to do?—Very little in the way of teaching.

34461. But there would be the work of teaching them how to teach these subjects?—There would be work to remove wrong impressions perhaps.

34462. There would be the work of training them to teach, which you regard as the essential work of the training college?—Yes.

34463. And in so far as the other work, the work of teaching the subjects, has to be done, it has to be done because people come in not sufficiently prepared to enable the college to dispense with it?—Yes.

34464. The better they are prepared, the less work the college would have to do in that respect?—Yes.

34465. I believe the training diploma is not given for sometime after the teacher leaves the college?—They must spend two years teaching, and satisfactorily teaching.

34466. I have heard it stated as more or less of a grievance in connection with the training colleges—the statement was made to me, but I don't think it is correct—that under the National Education Board's new programme for the promotion of teachers, untrained candidates who go in for promotion have an advantage over other candidates, I think it is in the case of the 2nd Division of First Class, that whereas a trained candidate can only get this classification after two years' subsequent teaching and after passing an examination, an untrained candidate can get it simply by passing the examination?—That is not quite correct. The untrained teachers who can get promotion to 2nd of First must be themselves 1st of Second, and they must have been persons exempted from training under one of the rules of the Board.

34467. They are persons treated as having preserved privileges?—Certainly, they have been teaching for the last ten years.

34468. A complaint has been made about the working of the new programme, that the introduction of it had in some way killed the teaching of natural science in the training colleges; now as to your training college, was natural science taught there previous to the introduction of the new programme?—It was.

34469. Is it taught there now?—Not since the introduction of the new programme.

34470. Who determines whether a subject which is in the programme is to be taught or not?—We must follow the programme, and if the programme leaves certain subjects optional——.

34471. Natural science is in the programme as optional?—Yes.

34472. Who decides then whether it is to be taught in the college or not?—The students themselves choose that it is not to be taught; that is, their general feeling is obtained, and then the authorities of the college decide on taking something else.

34473. That is, the students represent their views to you, and you are influenced by that?—Yes.

34474. I believe the subject that is now taught in place of natural science is trigonometry?—Yes.

34475. Each of these is an optional subject at present?—Yes.

Dublin.

Jan. 13, 1897.

Rev. George Campbell, S.J.

be trained?—That may be in other colleges, but it is not so with us.

24517. I have totted up the figures from the National Education Board's Report; they seem to me to show that there were not more than ten per cent. of the students in the training colleges actually teachers?—With us last year we had about sixty going in for one year's course, and every one of these was a teacher.

24518. That is to say, almost one-third of your entire number?—One third of the entire number.

24519. Is there any other observation you wish to make?—I would merely wish to say that some of these teachers that apply are of the third class. We had some of these examined beforehand to find out whether they would be capable of going through the one year's course, and a good number of them failed.

24520. The one year's course is practically the only course for those who are actually teachers?—Yes.

24521. And a large number of those who presented themselves for it failed at your test examination?—Yes.

24522. So that, whilst you have a large proportion of actual teachers, it is not your fault that you have not more?—Certainly not. We would take in as many as would pass the examination.

24523. I know that an entrance examination is held for the training colleges in the case of persons who are not yet teachers; it is held by the National Education Board. Is there any examination held officially by the Board for candidate teachers who apply for admission?—There is no such examination.

24524. Do you think it would be a good thing if there was some such examination?—Yes.

24525. I believe it has been done in some cases?—It was done on application from the college, and that examination does not at all interfere with the classification of these teachers.

24526. But you think it would be a useful thing if it was provided that all teachers applying for entrance to the training college should be examined by the Education Board as a matter of course?—I think it would.

24527. I believe you are guided very much by the percentage of answering at the entrance examination?—I might say altogether.

24528. Of course everyone can understand that a college would not be conducted if you were obliged to admit absolutely on a mere percentage of passes. You have to make inquiries about character?—Yes, and various things of that kind.

24529. Can you tell me what was the lowest percentage at which anyone was admitted to your college this year?—The lowest percentage was 67 per cent.

24530. A person, no matter what influence he might have brought to bear on you in his favour, could not go in if he was below 67 per cent.?—No.

24531. I believe I am right in saying that the corresponding percentage for admission to the Baggot-street Training College this year was even higher—70 per cent.?—Yes.

24532. Absolutely no candidate was admitted there this year who did not get 70 per cent. at the entrance examination?—No.

24533. Mr. REDINGTON.—If you had an examination now for one year's students, in what column of the programme would you examine them?—In column 2.

24534. So as to let them enter the college at the same level, as it were, as those who were going in for the two years' course?—As those who were going to begin the second year of the two years' course.

24535. Would not that be a little hard on the very class you want to see trained, those who have been rather backward and are not conducting their schools with efficiency?—It might be, but I don't see how you can remedy that, unless you put those who are third-class, or those who have been conducting schools for some time, or are backward, in for a two years'

24536. What would be the objection to letting them come in for a one year's course at a lower examination?—They would not be able to follow the class and fall in with those who were better prepared.

24537. At present the college gets a bonus for all the diplomas gained by the students after two years' efficient service?—Yes.

24538. These candidates must have passed the final College Examination?—Yes; they cannot have a special diploma unless they have passed.

24539. If a diploma were given to all who passed in methods of teaching alone, would that induce the college authorities to devote more attention to that side of the college work?—I don't think that we could be induced to give more attention than we do—we give all the attention we can.

24540. But the students are very anxious to pass their examination?—They are, most certainly.

24541. And it is necessary also for the college that they should do so; but supposing the necessity of passing in all subjects were done away with?—I think we would be just as we are—we would work as hard as we could.

24542. Have you formed an opinion about the teaching of agriculture?—No; we have a professor of agriculture in the college, who gives lectures twice a week but we have no practical agriculture.

24544. Do you think is a good thing to have theoretical teaching of agriculture without practical experiments?—It would be of course better if you had the practical experiments, but I think even that the mere theoretical knowledge is a benefit.

24545. You are familiar with the new edition of the "Introduction to Practical Farming?"—I have not seen it.

24546. Do many of your students take up vocal music?—A very large number, we have sixty per cent. or seventy per cent. of the entire house.

24547. Do you think it desirable that they should all take it up?—As many of them, of course, as are capable of being trained to sing, many of them have no ear, no capability of learning the chant in that way. It would require more than a two years' course to train them.

24548. Mr. MOLLOY.—If I mistake not St. Patrick's College has been in connection with the National Board for thirteen years, since 1883?—Yes.

24549. I see by an official return here published, by the National Board, that as many as 1,310 Queen's Scholars have been trained at St. Patrick's College, between 1883 and 1896?—That is true.

24550. Have you had accounts of their system of teaching throughout the schools to which they went later on?—In a general way, we have had from managers.

24551. Were those accounts satisfactory?—In almost every case.

24552. And since 1891, when the bonuses were established and certificates based thereon, have many bonuses been lost, so to say, to the college?—Very few, some were in consequence of death, or something of the kind preventing them giving the two years' service.

24553. That would indicate that methods of teaching had been practically attended to?—As far as we can judge.

24554. You represent Baggot-street College also, if I mistake not; I find that as many as 1,103 Queen's Scholars were trained in that college in the corresponding period?—Yes.

24555. Are you aware whether the accounts of their subsequent progress was satisfactory or not in the schools?—I have got no report of that.

24556. Is there any record kept in St. Patrick's College of the schools to which the teachers go?—Yes.

24557. Are communications kept up?—We require that every teacher when he changes from his school sends us notice of it and that is entered in our register

Dublin. — Dec. [illegible] — Rev. George Campbell, [illegible]

college?—They send a letter to inquire whether or not they would be permitted to enter, we send forms necessary, these forms are filled up, then they have a recommendation from the Bishop and a letter from the manager—he is usually a parish priest, and when we get all these we send the names to the Board and the Board sends us a return of those candidates who are eligible.

24559. Then you must depend on your own action in order to ensure students for your college?—Yes, or on the action of the managers of the country.

24560. Do the Commissioners of National Education co-operate with you in any way in supplying students for your college?—In no way.

24561. They do that, however, in the case of Marlborough-street, the Inspectors furnish the names of students throughout the various districts of Ireland?—That is not the case with us, they do nothing for us in that way at all.

24562. In connection with St. Patrick's Training College have you had students who have served previously as pupil teachers in the model school?—No, we have monitors and ex-monitors of the ordinary schools but no ex-pupil teachers.

24563. Who have already been classed and under [illegible] for the office of teacher, for two years?—No.

24564. They have that in Marlborough-street. On the point of classification—if classification were not so important a point to aim at, do you think the teachers would come up simply to acquire a superior method of teaching?—I don't think so by any means.

24565. But now that the colleges have been thirteen years in operation, do you think the time has come when that classification idea might be dispensed with, and they might, on a separate and independent curriculum, be admitted to the training college?—I think the time has come when some change should be made.

24566. That would secure the presence of a number of persons who perhaps think themselves too old to begin a course of study with a view to improved classification?—Probably.

24567. Might I inquire the maximum limit of age for admission to your college, St. Patrick's?—We put it down at thirty-two, sometimes we go beyond that.

24568. The average age very likely is about twenty-five?—About that.

24569. All along since 1883-4 when your college was established you admitted teachers for a one year's course, that is teachers actually in charge of schools?—From the very beginning.

24570. And in connexion with the last course, that terminated in July, you had a number of those teachers coming forward for such high classification as second Division of First?—Yes, a great number, I think there were forty-five or fifty.

24571. Have they succeeded in obtaining that on the new programme?—On the old programme; this is the first year of the new.

24572. Rev. Dr. Evans.—Coming to the matter of model lessons given by the Queen's Scholars in July before the head inspector, the principal and vice-principal of your college, I suppose, will be present?—Oh, yes, always.

24573. Anyone else?—Two of the professors generally also, the professor of literature and the professor of science.

24574. Now, then, in the presence of the two head inspectors, would it be possible, do you think, for any training college to limit itself to three subjects without those head inspectors immediately detecting it?—I am sure they would detect it.

24575. Immediately?—They could not but detect.

24576. With regard to the subject that is given to the teachers to teach an impromptu lesson on, is not the reason for giving that lesson to prevent such a thing as has just been mentioned, that is a college, or students themselves, training themselves to do three subjects?—Well, I don't know what the object was, but I know this, that if they gave them, say, half an hour to prepare beforehand it would effect the same purpose.

24577. The principal, and the vice-principal, and the professors are present, they see, do they not, when this impromptu lesson is given, any defects there may have been in the teaching of the Queen's Scholars individually.

24578. And would have an opportunity therefore of knowing elsewhere for the improvement of the teaching in the next session?—I don't think they derive any advantage of that kind from it, or that they turn it to any account.

24579. But they would have the opportunity?—Yes, if they liked to use it.

24580. Do your students select drawing as one of the three subjects?—I have never seen it selected, but I have been only these four years altogether, but during all that time I never saw it even once proposed.

24581. Mr. Molloy asked you about the part that the Inspectors [illegible] in regard to candidates for the Marlborough-street Training College; do you think in the case of a denominational training college that the Inspector's action in that way would be admissible?—I would prefer that the Inspectors took no action for any college.

24582. Rev. Dr. Wilson.—Are your training colleges full?—We have the full number, 155.

24583. Chairman.—In both?—Yes, in both Drumcondra and Baggot-street.

24584. Most Rev. Dr. Walsh.—A very large number of candidates apply for admission?—We had any number of applications that we were obliged to put aside, in consequence of the fact that they did not come up to the percentage, although they passed the examination of the National Education Board; 50 per cent. is sufficient for that.

24585. Rev. Dr. Wilson.—What would you say is the main object of bringing up these young men to Dublin, is it to give them information or to train them how to teach?—The main object of a training college is to train them how to teach.

24586. Have you a professor for that?—We have.

---

distances, not having the natural turn for Dublin.

What do you say about the training colleges now in classification?—The teachers come Nov. [illegible]

Mr. Stephen Fitzpatrick.

[illegible]

in the present

Dublin.
Nov. [illegible], 1897.
Br. [illegible]

24667. They are only optional in the colleges?—But then the colleges have them. The colleges have enough to do.

24668. Most Rev. Dr. Walsh.—They must take one optional subject?—Yes.

24669. Mr. Redington.—You would have no optional subjects taught in the colleges, that are outside the ordinary curriculum of the school?—I would not. I would have the training college do school work, and nothing else, or very little beyond it.

24670. Mr. Molloy.—In your opening statement you mentioned that five-sixths of the time now devoted to the training course was given up to preparing pupils in the programme for classification?—The matter of the other programme.

24671. You would advocate the propriety, then, of doing away with that?—One half of their time they should be learning how to teach.

24672. Would you advocate the propriety of doing away with classification carrying with it a money value later on?—I would.

24673. Do you think the time has now come, these colleges having been so many years in existence, that that course might be pursued?—I think so, and the teachers should come up for training knowing that on their success in teaching afterwards their promotion would depend.

24674. Chairman.—I think you said that so many would not want to come as at present?—They would want to come because the promotion could not be obtained in any other way. He must be a trained teacher and capable of teaching well, and show by his school that he is teaching well, and then only promotion would come.

24675. Mr. Molloy.—Have you compared the course under the English and Scotch Departments with our Irish course with a view to see whether they are on all-fours for admission to the training college?—I think the tests are pretty much the same.

24676. If you look into your own subject, arithmetic, I think you will find that our programme is decidedly higher?—It is; our Irish teachers are very good in arithmetic as a rule.

24677. Chairman.—Is not that, on the whole, the subject that is best taught in the National schools?—I daresay it is, and our children have a wonderful aptitude for that; a few other things like that there should be no trouble in teaching them.

24678. Mr. Molloy.—You have had a good deal of experience—I am personally aware of that—in the practical work of school teaching quite independently of your position in connection with the training college?—Yes.

24679. Now from your experience would you contrast the state of education prior to the establishment of these colleges with the present time. Do you think the schools are better taught now?—They are, taken where the results system destroyed the old teaching. Under the old teaching the teacher made the school, and got his character from the school, not from individuals. In the present system you make your boys fit to pass an examination, but how you make them, what means you take, and whether you are skilled or unskilled if the boy passes that is all, and no credit is given to the teacher who taught him properly.

24680. In your opinion the old system was more intellectual if the teacher were qualified?—Yes, but we had not then many qualified.

24681. The number of trained teachers at that time happened to be very limited?—Very limited.

24682. Where did they acquire that superior method of teaching?—Often at the expense of the school, and the teachers having a natural turn for teaching.

24683. Most Rev. Dr. Walsh.—Presiding on the [illegible] many hours in the week are given to methods of teaching them, or what proportion of the entire college time for the week is devoted to methods of teaching?—We have three sections—the first section, those that come in for two years, and are now in their first year, that is the lowest, we call them the juniors; then we have those that were in last year and are now in their second year, we call them the middle division; and then those students who come in from schools for one year, looking for first class. To each division I give a model lesson of an hour's length; it may be one lesson or two, or sometimes three in the week, just one hour.

24686. Most Rev. Dr. Walsh.—One hour to each of these three divisions?—Yes, each division gets an hour's lesson; coming towards the end for the requirements of the examination by the inspectors it is necessary to increase that to two hours and very often more.

24687. Then the examinations are of some use?—It is no easy task for a man to be called upon, out of a thousand subjects, to teach this one or that one; I have generally to give lessons in 300 or 400 subjects.

24688. Mr. Molloy.—Are you quite satisfied with that number of lessons in the week?—Not at all.

24689. Perhaps those lessons do not include the time you are in the practising school?—There are special lessons given by myself for method purposes, but I never give a lesson in arithmetic or any other subject, and that the teacher should be able to go away and say that he saw any difference in the teaching of that, and the lesson I purposely give on Method. They are called in to hear a lesson on a subject, supposed to be a special one; but I am saying about what His Grace asked a moment ago about all professors, that I never teach a lesson but I go upon the lines exactly I would go upon in giving a lesson to children, which they call a model lesson, a lesson of one hour a week before each section. In all my teaching, three or four hours in the day, I never take up a subject or any part of it that I don't teach in such a way as I would teach it to a class of children, the only drawback is that I need not teach it so minutely.

24690. Chairman.—Was that what you were referring to a while ago, when you said it was not fair to practise on the children?—To learn proper methods from bad teaching.

24691. I don't understand in what way you think you practise upon them bad methods?—A teacher takes charge of a school that he is not able to teach, he sees ill results, and day by day he begins to improve, he sees there is something wrong in his teaching, but half a generation may go out of his school and be all the time under bad treatment.

24692. Most Rev Dr. Walsh.—Of course you are not speaking of what goes on in the practising school of the training college?—Oh no.

24693. Chairman.—That arises from the inefficiency of the teacher when he first begins?—Yes.

24694. You say he should be a more efficient teacher before he is allowed to begin?—Yes, a poor man's son might be fit for something decent if trained properly, and he goes away a labourer, owing to bad teaching.

24695. Mr. Molloy.—You mentioned the disadvantages under which your college laboured from teachers coming up who were rusty and not able to pursue the course with younger men, was it not always in the power of the college authorities to subject those teachers to an examination on entrance?—It is in the power of the college, but it is felt to be a grievance to a teacher to bring him up from a school where he has appointed a substitute, and then after [illegible]

Dublin. Jan. [illegible], 18[illegible]. Mr. Stephen Fitzgerald.

who suggested that they should be subjected to an examination.

24697. It was also the practice for some years in connexion especially with St. Patrick's, that the reports of each candidate's school underwent consideration by the principal of the college?—Always, he is very particular.

24698. He had an opportunity of seeing for three years the opinion expressed by the inspectors how [illegible] conducted their schools?—He is very particular about it, takes it down.

24699. With regard to the inspectors' test applied prior to the July examination, within your experience was not the test confined exclusively to elementary subjects?—As a rule, very seldom a departure from it, and I think that if an inspector [illegible] was a departure he would change the moment the teacher appeared to look as if he did not like the subject.

24700. And if a teacher happened to fail in that particular [illegible]?—I don't think it had much weight against him.

24701. Did he not get a further opportunity?—Sometimes.

24702. But your experience was that really the tests were applicable exclusively to elementary subjects?—School subjects. It was a little unfair towards our two years students who had never charge of schools, but those who had had charge of schools ought to be able to teach what they were called upon to teach.

24703. You mention that a great many managers were not aware of the essential difference between the [illegible] and [illegible] training diploma?—No.

24704. Don't you think steps ought to be taken by the college authorities to inform the managers, applying for teachers that "So and so holds a first-class diploma?"—I think someone should make it known; but there is a wrong in that, that if you get a second-class certificate it is impossible for you ever afterwards to get a [illegible]—that is very wrong. A man may fail in being a good teacher and in a year or two become a good teacher. It is a pity to keep him down with a second-class certificate.

24705. A second-class teacher may have a first-class diploma, and a first-class man may have only a second-class diploma, he ought to be afforded an opportunity of taking a first-class diploma by improving his method of teaching in the school?—Yes, but he is scarcely concerned about it, because no one knows of or values it.

24706. You think it ought to be by some authority made more generally known than it is at present?—Yes.

24707. Rev. Dr. EVANS.—Are there criticism lessons given at all by your Queen's Scholars?—Yes, an hour a week is given, a quarter of an hour for each lesson, from a quarter to half an hour by the students. All the teachers in the college are in the [illegible] at this time, and I myself see that they all have their criticism books. The teacher [illegible] with his notes of the lesson and hands it to me. I look at it while he is teaching and the teachers are listening and writing down in their criticism books their opinion on his teaching. When he has done teaching I call upon one or two to give their opinion upon it and when they have given it, I generally wind up myself.

24708. And the teacher that gives the criticism lesson in this particular case is one of the critics in another case?—He may be called upon to-morrow to give a criticism of the lesson.

24709. So that they criticise one another and help one another to practical and good methods of teaching?—By quite friendly criticism.

[illegible]

24712. Have you not a register in your training college in which the different opinions are entered?—No, I have a criticism book myself, you know, and the name of each teacher is put down and the subject he is teaching, and then my own opinion and some little reference to the criticism given by the teachers called upon.

24713. They have such a book in Marlborough street, and you will find the vice-principals in both cases, male and female, Miss [illegible] and so on, supplying in writing their comments, and these are recorded in a book which can be looked at any time in the training college?—I have my criticism book, of course, and the students keep theirs.

24714. But then there is no handing of it over to the principal to have it further recorded in any other book?—If the principal wishes to see the result of any particular teaching by the student on such a day, or criticism by a teacher, he can refer to me.

24715. In criticism lessons do you ever have drawing as one of them?—Sometimes. Father Campbell told you that never in the school was it asked for, and I think not, but with me the teacher is free to take what he pleases—the only thing I ask is that, "three or four may come in for this day and see that you four have different subjects."

24716. As a matter of fact are you able to say that any did take drawing?—Oh yes, but they would be very odd cases.

24717. Not often?—Not often, because drawing is not well taught, we don't know much about it.

24718. Is it not obligatory now?—It is and a poor hand is made of it; it is a shame to call it drawing at all, there is no drawing in the country.

24719. Do you think the drawing-master would agree with you in that?—I think he would. My idea of drawing is that a teacher should be able to take the chalk and go to the blackboard and illustrate for his pupils, let their eye take in something that their mind might not take in easily. A boy is put to draw and he rubs out with indiarubber and after a time he gets a straight line—it is a labour to him and he will never take to it afterwards. If you look at those who have been a [illegible] at drawing you will find they had a readiness in sketching and were not [illegible] because the line was not straight.

24720. Rev. Dr. WILSON.—You say the programme puts you in a false position as regards methods of training, for five-sixths of your time is taken up in other subjects?—Yes, instructing in subjects rather than teaching them how to teach.

24721. Could you curtail those literary subjects?—You cannot either curtail them or extend the course.

24722. But you think you could curtail them without injury to the literary subjects?—Many of these things, taught to the extent they are taught, will never be used by the teachers in their schools afterwards.

24723. You say the teachers come up to be trained solely to be classified; you would not mean that as an argument why training colleges should be dispensed with?—No, it is impossible to have teachers unless they are trained—teaching is too difficult a matter to be taken up haphazard by anyone. We have too many at it who are unfitted for it, no matter what their ability as scholars.

24724. Do you think that, suppose classification was not the reward of being trained, they would come in such numbers?—I would have it the reward, but I would only have it the first step toward classification. I would have them trained properly, and if they show the result of training in after life, promote them, but don't have them classified because they passed their course in some fashion.

Dublin. — Jan. 22, 18[illegible]. — [illegible]

to teach. *Have you as many persons qualified as you have schools, as far as you know, taking all Ireland?* —Oh, no.

24726. Or have you more qualified teachers than you have schools?—If we are to speak of those who are trained, and have gone through a course of training, as fairly prepared for teaching, we have to besitate about the large number who have not undergone any course of training—there must certainly be a limitation, they cannot be fit for it, unless those who have given ten or twelve years to it, and learned it from some master or other. We should turn out 400 or 500 teachers a year to meet all the requirements.

24727. Rev. Dr. Evans.—Just with regard to that, a Catholic bishop told me very recently that there are a very large number of teachers unemployed?—There may be. You have been told of some 2,000 monitors with a little smattering of knowledge, and a little knowledge of teaching, getting schools, but I am referring now to qualified teachers going into schools. We would want to be turning out 300 or 400 teachers a year in order to supply the schools. Of course that is the Commissioners' fault that such boys leave the school after three or four years as monitors; the Commissioners have very little knowledge of what training the monitor goes through; it is enough that they have been four or five years under the name of monitor, and passed this examination, and into a school they are put—the manager has power to do it, and does it.

24728. Most Rev. Dr. Walsh.—There is an important matter upon which I should wish to have your opinion—it is about the system of the promotion and payment of the teachers; the best course is for me to state first my own view. It comprises, practically, three points, and when I have stated them, I shall ask your opinion upon each, to see how far you may be disposed to agree with me. In the first place, I would have a qualifying examination, as at present, as the first step for getting into the teaching profession. So far there is nothing new. But my next point is a revolutionary one. From that out, there should, I think, with one exception, be no other examinations for the teacher. I would have an opportunity of getting trained given to every teacher, young or old, who might wish for it, and I would have a special rate of salary for the trained as distinct from the untrained teacher. By training I mean, of course, not mere preparation to pass examinations in certain subjects, but the acquisition of skill in the art of teaching; this, probably, would have to be tested by examination. But, with that one exception, I would have no more examinations after the one that admitted a man or woman to be a teacher; thus I would set the teachers free from the work of preparing for the series of examinations which at present they have to pass, from year to year, if they wish to get on; and I would leave them free, as teachers are in England, to give their time to their proper work—the work of teaching in their schools—and of improving themselves as schoolmasters and schoolmistresses. Then, finally, I would have a system of promotion, or rather advancement, for the teachers of each of the two classes, the trained and the untrained; that is to say, I would give them increments of salaries, improved status as to pensions, and so forth, on the basis of length of service and good work done in their schools. Now let us take all this, point by point. First, as to the qualifying examination; this we have at present, and I assume it should be retained?—Oh, of course.

24729. Then I would have a system of training, available for all who had passed the qualifying examination, including, as far as possible, the untrained teachers now in charge of schools, and then from the outset, and all along the line, I would pay the trained teachers better than the untrained?—Yes, I agree with that.

24730. And what I mean by a trained teacher is, not one who has merely passed an examination in certain subjects, but one who is certified by competent authorities—the officials of the National Education Board—to have acquired sufficient skill in the art of teaching; teachers so certified should have a claim to payment on a higher scale?—They deserve better payment.

24731. The third point then is that I would do away with all other examinations in reference to the promotion or advancement of the teachers, and make that depend on their length of service and their work in their schools?—It would not be a bad system at all; the only objection I see to it is that it might give them a suggestion, which they would too readily take up, that they had learned enough, and it might lead them to give up their proper reading; I think a teacher must always read to keep up his knowledge; I would be afraid of that.

24732. Then you would have a subsequent examination or examinations?—Yes, but not a severe one.

24733. But take the medical profession or the bar. When a man goes to the medical profession he has to get qualified, and for this he must pass certain examinations, but then, when he has got into the profession, once he has got qualified, his advancement is not made to depend upon his passing a number of other examinations; it will depend on his practice, and for that he has to depend upon his skill, his fitness for his work, and the way in which he does his work. It is the same with the lawyer. No one thinks of worrying either doctors or lawyers with examinations on the plea that if they are not kept up to it by examinations they will give up their reading and fall away. Why should it be thought that a teacher under my system, if I may call it so, would give up study?—Well, the one who does not study will get as much salary as the one who does.

24734. No; that is what happens at present, once a man has got his promotion; my idea is that they would get their annual or periodic advancement, increments of salary, and so forth, only on condition of their doing and continuing to do their work well. I want to set them free from the work of cramming for examinations, and to leave them free to attend to their proper work; if they don't keep up their reading as a teacher always should, their work in the school is bound to suffer, and they will lose in the end?—Yes, there is a great deal to be said for that.

24735. Of course each teacher should have the opportunity of knowing from year to year how he stood. I don't think that one year's falling off, unless the case was a really bad one, should tell very much against a teacher. But in any case an adverse report should be subject to revision on appeal. I may say to you again that this whole plan that I am sketching out is altogether my own. I know that it is as yet rather crude. But suppose that we had it well thought out, and had a good machinery provided for the working of it, would you approve of it?—Oh, fully.

24736. It would be necessary, of course, to provide for the teaching of special subjects, outside the ordinary all-round work of the school, and I suppose there might be some system of giving special certificates of fitness to teach these; and it has been suggested that the training colleges should deal only with the real work of the school, and that anything outside of that might be provided for by the holding of examinations, qualifying examinations, in order to the giving of certificates in those special subjects?—Quite so, it would relieve the training colleges seriously.

FIFTY-THIRD PUBLIC SITTING.—THURSDAY, NOVEMBER 11, 1897.

AT 11 O'CLOCK, A.M.,

At the Antient Concert Rooms, Dublin.

PRESENT:—THE RIGHT HON. THE EARL OF BELMORE, G.C.M.G., in the Chair; HIS GRACE THE MOST REV. WILLIAM J. WALSH, D.D.; THE RIGHT HON. C. T. REDINGTON, M.A.; THE RIGHT REV. MONSIGNOR MOLLOY, D.D., D.Sc.; THE REV. HENRY EVANS, D.D.; THE REV. HAMILTON WILSON, D.D.; and W. R. J. MOLLOY, Esq.;

with J. D. DALY, Esq., M.A., Secretary.

Professor GEORGE PEYTON, LL.B., Marlborough-street Training College, Dublin, examined.

24737. CHAIRMAN.—You are a Professor in the Marlborough-street Training College?—Yes, my lord.

24738. What are you professor of?—English.

24739. I believe you have some suggestions to make with regard to kindergarten occupations in National schools?—I would suggest that the kindergarten occupations, which at present are carried on only in infant schools, should be extended to the first and second, and, possibly, third classes of the ordinary National schools. A child in the first or second class in an infant school, spends a certain amount of time at these kindergarten occupations; in an ordinary school a child of the same class does not spend any time at kindergarten work. My suggestion is that the pupil in the ordinary school should spend some time at kindergarten occupations.

24740. In the same way as the child does in an infant school?—In the very same way.

24741. Coming to drawing, in what respect do you think the present programme is incomplete?—It is incomplete first with regard to its extent. We have no programme for drawing in the ordinary school in the first and second classes. The drawing begins only in the third class, and a pupil who does not attend at an infant school, receives no instruction in drawing until he or she comes to the third class. That is too late to begin the teaching of drawing.

24742. What suggestions do you make for revising the programme or the method of examination?—Then I would wish to include in the programme for drawing, mechanical drawing, in the first and second classes, that is, drawing with a ruler and measuring with a ruler.

24743. From the very beginning?—From the very beginning. I have experience of that in schools; I have tried it myself. It is very simple; there is no difficulty about it. Then with regard to the examination in drawing in the junior class, I would suggest that the present system of examination should be changed to something like what I have seen in other places—examining the schools in sections. One section of the class is examined in mechanical drawing, and in addition to merely drawing these figures upon slate or paper, the pupils are questioned upon the figures. They should know the names of the figures drawn, such as square and rectangle and diagonal, even at a very early stage. I have been present at an examination held by one of the Science and Art Inspectors, in England. He examined a very junior class in this way, and I think it is a very good system of examination.

24744. Do you think that the present teachers are qualified to teach drawing as a rule?—Every teacher is sufficiently qualified to teach drawing, as a rule, up to third or fourth class.

24745. Whether they have a certificate or not?—Whether they have a certificate or not.

24746. Now with regard to object lessons, do you think that elementary science should be taught experimentally?—Object lessons and elementary science should be taught experimentally. I think object lessons ought to be made compulsory in all schools. Every teacher who is able to teach, can teach object lessons, and the materials required for object lessons are such as are within the reach of every teacher.

24747. First of all, tell me what you mean by elementary science exactly; what range?—There seems to be some difference of opinion as to what should be called elementary science and object lessons in the books on the subject.

24748. Are you confining it to chemistry?—Not necessarily.

24749. Then will you tell me what should be taught experimentally?—Any science taken up ought to be taught by the teacher by actual demonstration and by calling upon the children to make experiments, and not taught from books. I have taught science classes under the Science and Art Department, and the method of teaching for the Science and Art Department would be too advanced for our schools. In these classes a great amount of time and energy is devoted to teaching the pupils how to write answers to questions; that is not what we want in the National schools, but to make experiments and ask the pupils to make experiments.

24750. Have you taught them to make experiments in the way of measuring and weighing substances?—Not to any great extent.

24751. That is what I had in my mind when I asked you that question, because I have seen it done in English schools. Do you think that it should be made compulsory?—Object lessons should be made compulsory in all schools at once.

24752. And what time should be devoted to those lessons?—One object lesson per week for each pupil would be the minimum.

24753. What arrangement do you think would be suitable for small schools with one teacher?—I would group the children into junior and senior divisions, and teach one object lesson to the junior class, and another object lesson to the senior class.

24754. Now will you tell me the nature of such lessons as regards either of these groups?—As regards the junior children, the object lessons would be very simple, they would be upon objects with which the children are more or less familiar, such as fruit or vegetables, simple objects, or they might be simple lessons upon phenomena.

24755. With regard to the higher group?—They might be upon weights or measures, or what we call more particularly elementary science, some of the facts of elementary science treated experimentally; they might be upon any article that is manufactured in the locality. They should be arranged, in my opinion, so as to suit the children, and therefore the teacher ought to have the privilege of making out his own set of object lessons, and submitting it to the Inspector.

24756. How many lessons do you think should

would carry it on through?—

the programme in drawing is

34807. As a rule there are infants to be found in every school?—Yes.

34808. And your proposition is to extend the Kindergarten instruction to the ordinary schools, not

was offered by the parents [illegible]
an active interest.—The pupils
to instruction carried on a

is carried on under [illegible]
difficulty in keeping the [illegible]
ahead, for the rest [illegible]
tion lessons in needlework [illegible]
ly known as needlework drill
ible to see the classes taught,
pupils, by a teacher taking [illegible]
terial to be practised; there is [illegible]
which we have in our schools,
and which has been introduced
a number of pieces of material
The teacher [illegible]
[illegible] before a large class
four times the length of [illegible]
coloured thread, which enables
thread is worked in and [illegible]
All the work of [illegible]
a whole class.
[illegible] advocate the use of the
[illegible] with that [illegible]—
the same method, but is [illegible]
blackboard.
[illegible] used. The
the blackboard, and [illegible]

of drawing; it is, perhaps, the simplest [illegible] making the practical application of draw-

[illegible] you see cookery courses in oper[illegible] [illegible]—Yes, I saw the cookery classes in Liverpool, and in London.

[illegible] some of those cities cookery is taught in [illegible] other places it is taught in the school [illegible].

Which would you think the best course? [illegible] to keep the children of one school in [illegible]; the other system works well under [illegible] Board, but it would not work well here, I

[illegible] you see any rural schools in England? [illegible] small school in the Barrow district, [illegible]

What manual occupations had they there? [illegible] all the manual occupations except—— [illegible] Except woodwork?—I was going to say [illegible] the pupils go to the centre school at [illegible] this instruction.

[illegible] Monsignor Molloy.—They have basket[illegible] That is an industry pure and simple; I [illegible] how far we are concerned with industries [illegible] education, I have a small basket which [illegible] young children in that school.

Mr. Redington.—In that rural school was [illegible] objection to these manual occupations?—I

[illegible] Do you think, therefore, they might be intro[illegible] our rural schools?—I think they might, if [illegible] were able to teach them.

You said you would be in favour of making [illegible] and work a compulsory subject?—Oh, yes, I [illegible] in favour of making it a compulsory subject [illegible] were able to teach it; but I know the [illegible] could not at present teach the subject. If [illegible] competent to teach it I would be in favour [illegible] it compulsory.

If science teaching were developed in our [illegible] would there be great difficulty in providing [illegible]?—I would not consider it a great difficulty: [illegible] difficulty in providing apparatus for the [illegible] lessons in different science subjects of the [illegible]. The cost of providing apparatus for [illegible] appears to me to be much less than that [illegible] the apparatus for a general course, but [illegible] he could do this cardboard work would be [illegible] most of the apparatus required.

You don't think that the cost of the apparatus [illegible] be a bar to the teaching of elementary [illegible]—I don't think so at all.

With regard to agriculture, you said it [illegible] taught by object lessons in the fourth [illegible] would you teach it in the higher classes?—[illegible] disposed to make it practical for rural [illegible] have the subject taught in the gardens.

If there were no gardens how would you [illegible]—I would be disposed not to teach it

Then you don't think our present system is [illegible] one?—It is all book-learning and word-

Dublin.

Nov. [illegible], 1897.

Professor George [illegible], M.A.

Dublin.
Jan. 1[illegible], 18[illegible].
Professor [illegible] [illegible], M.A.

24898. Mr. Redington.—Is it not a fact that in order to understand the papers which are written on scientific agriculture some elementary knowledge of chemistry is necessary?—It is very desirable. With regard to the practical teaching in the garden, I would just like to say that if the teacher is to give the instruction in agriculture in the garden then the junior pupils cannot be looked after, and I would suggest there be an arrangement somewhat similar to the arrangement that might be carried out in the case of working in wood in town schools—viz., to send away the junior pupils at two o'clock on one day in the week.

24899. Most Rev. Dr. Walsh.—In connection with one of the special occupations that you mentioned (basket making), you made an important distinction between industrial and educational work. I take it that you do not consider that industries, as such, are at all in place in a primary school?—I do not.

24900. Such a thing as basketmaking you view simply as an industry. When you speak of woodwork as a desirable subject to introduce into the schools, do you advocate the introduction of it with the view of preparing the boys to be carpenters?—Oh, no, decidedly not.

24901. And so, I assume, that when you advocate the teaching of gardening, you do not advocate it with a view of preparing the boys to be gardeners?—Oh, no.

24902. Now, let me ask you about agriculture; when the teaching of agriculture is brought into our primary schools, is there not some reason to think that this is done because the boys are to be taught to be farmers?—The teaching of agriculture in the advanced classes appears to me to be done with that view.

24903. I take it for granted that you do not think that anything of that kind is a natural or proper object for even a portion of the energies of the teacher of a primary school to be directed to?—I do not think so, your Grace.

24904. There is no more reason why boys should be trained in a primary school to become farmers, than there is to have them trained to become carpenters, or tailors, or shoemakers, and although manual and practical instruction may have, as undoubtedly it has, an advantage in laying a foundation for special instruction that may afterwards come on in reference to these occupations, such instruction is in place in a primary school only in so far as it is educational in its tendency?—That is my view.

24905. Then you would draw a broad line of distinction between the kind of manual and practical educational work that you advocate, and the teaching of a trade?—Oh, yes. I don't think the teaching of woodwork, in so far as it is a branch of schoolwork, could possibly be called the teaching of a trade.

24906. But you are aware that there is a good deal of confusion in this matter, not only in the public mind, but in the minds of many of our National school teachers?—I am.

24907. Of course they are not to be blamed for it: the feeling is stirred up for a purpose, and unfortunately they are easily misled. You are quite clear as to the essential distinction between the work of manual

24908. It is desirable, is it not, t
matter what occupation in life he is t
should acquire certain habits of neat
any of us may have occasion to put
of things on a table to illustrate some
it is well to have the idea of putting
symmetrical or orderly way, and I sa
arranged system of manual and pract
in the primary school is likely to
instilling ideas of order and neatness
of children; that, I take it, is
kind of instruction a place in the pr
That is my opinion.

24910. Now let us take another p
asked about the cost of the apparat
these practical branches, did I underst
that there would not be much difficulty
necessary apparatus?—For science
much, but for woodwork there would

24911. Please tell us the schools wh
experience of up to this?—The schools
cerned, are Trim Model School, I
School, the Model School in Dun
Enniscorthy, and a National school i

24912. Now as to these schools, wh
there was in them, how was it provid
answer you about Trim. I provi
portion out of my own pocket.

24913. So the locality did not rise
way of providing funds?—They formed
me and I was very much obliged to th
interest they took in the welfare of

24914. Passing committees to p
other people who are willing to put
their pockets and pay for the
popular form of so called philanthrop
number of people in Ireland. Be
as the hard facts of the case,
there would be a considerable diff
the public in Ireland to put their
pockets to subscribe any substan
any really educational work, in th
the word, such as this manual
instruction that we are talking
present I think there would be.

24915. Yet the want of it is a sub
clamour all over the country.
advocates of this kind of instruction,
to you that when we were in Edinburg
the city raised £20,000 a year by
taxing the citizens to that amount
way in which the city of Edinburgh
vide for these various branches of ed
think that there is even the most r
of the city of Dublin raising £20,0
city rate for this or for any other educ
—If they were allowed the control
decency they might.

24916. You think that if the Do
were allowed to add to their pow
duties, the management of all the Na
Dublin, they would levy a subs
is levied in Edinburgh? I think
our aldermen and town council
unreasonable to think of such a thing.

24917. What do you understand kindergarten to be?—It is a method of teaching children, teaching them to observe, to use their hands, and to talk properly about things.

24918. To use their eyes, to use their hands, to observe accurately, and to express themselves accurately, we mean, of course, with such accuracy as can be expected from very young children?—Yes, your Grace.

24919. According to Froebel's idea, kindergarten was a system of instruction specially suited for children up to six or seven years of age, is not that so?—I believe that is the limit.

24920. Now, according to Froebel's idea, was the kindergarten a part of the school, or rather did he not make an express distinction between the two things; he held, I think, that children below six or seven years of age should not be let into school at all: that they should be kept in the kindergarten, the nursery as it were, is not that so?—Yes, your Grace.

24921. Did Froebel not also say that the children who were not at school, but in the kindergarten, should not be allowed to learn the use of letters, or to learn reading or anything that was afterwards to be a portion of the school course; that, I think, was his view, so that in a country like Germany, where kindergarten is taken in the strict sense of the term, there would be an absurdity in looking for kindergarten in a school?—That is so.

24922. When we speak of kindergarten in these countries, we are, of course, not speaking of kindergarten in the strict sense of Froebel's system, or in the sense in which kindergarten work is done, as of course you are aware that it is done in Germany, not in the schools, but in establishments distinct from the schools?—Yes.

24923. Then, let me ask you, in what sense do we in Ireland take the word kindergarten; this is a very important matter, and I should wish you to explain it fully for us?—Kindergarten teaching, as we have it, consists of a series of occupations, which the children are taught to process with the object of making them observe things and use their hands.

24924. But this is only, as it were, the mechanical aspect of the case; all this that you refer to is the outcome of a principle, and a highly excellent one; the child's natural powers are to be drawn out, materials and opportunities are to be supplied to the child, not to put the child merely to do a number of set exercises, but to set the child thinking and working for itself?—That is the object of the kindergarten system.

24925. And then the school is made attractive and pleasant, instead of irksome, ideas are associated with it; all this has a very useful effect?—Yes, your Grace.

24926. Here in Ireland we have not the kindergarten system, at least in our public, I mean our National schools; we have a modification of it, that is, the work of our infants' schools is largely influenced by the kindergarten idea, that, I think, is what it comes to?—Yes, your Grace.

24927. And this is the sense in which we speak of kindergarten whenever it is spoken of in connection with our public system of primary education in Ireland, I think, was his idea, so that even where schools might be supported at the public expense, this particular kindergarten work should be provided for by the family, and not by the State?—Yes.

24931. There is one other point, drawing. I believe that, up to this, drawing is not recognised by the National Education Board as a branch of school work before the third class?—It is not on the programme.

24932. But do you not think that it ought to be on the programme?—Oh, yes.

24933. You have said, I think, that every National school teacher in Ireland is qualified to teach drawing, at all events to teach what might be required up to the third class?—I should say up to above them.

24934. Now, when you say that, is it that you know, as a matter of fact, that there is no teacher at present teaching in a National school in Ireland who is not qualified to teach drawing—excuse me for putting the question; I know what you mean, but it is necessary to put this question to avoid misconception—do you mean, then, that, as a matter of fact, there is no teacher in our Irish National schools who is not able to teach this elementary drawing, or do you mean that no teacher is really fit to be in a primary school unless he is able to teach drawing?—I mean the latter; any teacher who is able to teach anything ought to be able to teach drawing.

24935. That is, if a person is fit to be a teacher, he ought to be able to teach this elementary drawing, and if he is not able to teach it he ought not to be left as a teacher in the school at all; that is your view?—That is my view.

24936. But of course you do not take it on yourself to say that everyone of the 10,000 National school teachers in Ireland is qualified to teach drawing?—Oh, no.

24937. Perhaps you can clear up for us a point that seems to be a good deal confused; can you give us the distinction between object lessons and elementary science?—Not clearly.

24938. Let me read this for you—in last year's Code of the English Education Department, where provision is made for object lessons, an express instruction is given to the inspectors, in the official instructions issued to them, that object lessons are to be carefully distinguished from elementary science. Here are the words:—"It is important that, if, for example, object lessons are given on plant life, no attempt should be made to treat them as a systematic introduction to the study of botany, or, if the lessons relate to animal life, as an introduction to the study of zoology." Before I ask you any question about this passage, I should wish to say that when we were in England I questioned one or more of the English school inspectors on the point, and they told me that they did not act on that letter of instruction. At Kendal I called the attention of a very eminent man, Dr. Gladstone, to it, and he did not at all accept the view that object lessons should be distinguished from instruction in natural science. What he said was that the object lesson was "the first stage" in it, and again, "the first step towards systematic science." Are you inclined to agree with that view of the case?—I consider object lessons are the beginning of science work.

24942. How is that; the new programme recognises natural science just as it recognised any other subject?—The programme is too extensive.

24943. There are certain optional subjects allowed by the new programme—elementary science is one, trigonometry is another; now, what optional subject do your students in the Marlborough-street Training College take up?—Trigonometry.

24944. Do you think that is a wise choice, when the programme of the National Education Board makes provision for the students who take up elementary science, just as for those who take up trigonometry?—From the point of view of the pupils whom they have to teach afterwards, it certainly is not.

24945. The report of the National Education Board shows that trigonometry was taught in only two National schools in Ireland last year, and that the total number of pupils examined in it was two—apparently one from each school; how, then, could it be a subject of real utility for the Queen's Scholars to take up in the training college?—It is a good mental training for the Queen's Scholars.

24946. Do you think it is from that point of view that the students regard it when they say they will have trigonometry in preference to elementary science?—I am sure they regard it as the easier to learn, and as the one in which they will get higher marks at the examination.

24947. Do you not think that in the present system for the promotion of teachers that view enters largely into the calculation of Queen's Scholars in our training colleges, that instead of looking to the benefit they may derive there in learning how to teach things afterwards in their schools, they are looking rather to how they can most easily get the marks that will get them through at their final examination in the college?—I think the Queen's Scholars attend largely to the final examination.

24948. Don't you think that this is a result of the plan upon which the system of the training colleges, and of their work, is at present constructed?—I do.

24949. Have you ever thought how that difficulty could be remedied?—If there were no final examination for classification it would do away with striving for marks in various subjects.

24950. It was suggested here yesterday, and some of us thought that there might be something in the suggestion, that the training colleges, as regards teaching, should confine themselves to what is really the proper all-round work of our National schools, and not spend time, as at present, in teaching these more or less out-of-the-way subjects, such as trigonometry, and the like; don't you think that the teaching of these subjects is calculated to put before the students the idea that the college is a place for teaching them certain subjects, rather than a place for training them in the work of a National teacher?—It does keep that idea before the minds of the students, certainly.

24951. The dropping of the teaching of such subjects would have the effect of concentrating attention more on what ought to be the primary work of the training college?—It would.

24952. At present there is no time to do everything, and questions arise as to what is to be dropped?—In the new programme we have not very many optional subjects, the number has been restricted considerably.

24953. Suppose trigonometry was taken out, would not that be an improvement as far as it went?—It would.

24954. Do you think that natural science should be made compulsory?—Science ought to be made compulsory in the training colleges.

24955. You are aware that it was compulsory until recently, and the Commissioners of National Education were bombarded with criticisms for making a thing compulsory in Ireland that was not compulsory in England; the Board then gave way to some extent to that kind of criticism, and now we are bombarded with tenfold vigour for having made the subject optional?—I think object lessons and elementary science lessons ought to be made compulsory.

25001. And should provide teachers in cookery for a great many other schools throughout the country as well?—Yes.

25002. Mr. Harrington.—Of course to do that would cost a great deal of money. Did it strike you that it would be better to instruct the ordinary teachers in cookery, so that they might give lessons continuously in their schools?—That would be a very desirable thing, but I was speaking to my principal, and she said if we got another assistant we should look out for a lady who could give instruction, but she said her time will be all required in the school during school hours.

25003. How are you able now to give two hours out of the day for this cookery instruction?—It was not in charge of one of the teachers of the school, but of this lady who came from Kildare-street.

25004. But the teachers were able to afford to lose two hours during the week?—Only one hour, the class worked from two to four.

25005. Chairman.—Could you not arrange merely to drop a lesson for an hour?—That is what we did in this case.

25006. I mean drop a lesson as regards the teacher as well as regards the girls?—It might be arranged; I have not looked into it yet, for we have not got the assistant.

25007. A teacher could not be in two places at once, and if she was teaching cookery she must drop her ordinary work?—Yes.

25008. Mr. Redington.—Have you any experience of country schools?—No, not any.

25009. You think the kind of cookery instruction given was practical?—Very practical.

25010. It was simple enough?—The children were not only interested in it, but practised it at home, and the parents told me how very much delighted they were with the results of the instruction.

25011. Would you make drawing compulsory for girls?—Yes; I think they should have a hand and eye training just as well as boys.

25012. Most Rev. Dr. Walsh.—Don't you think that boys should have some manual and practical instruction as well as girls?—I think they should, but I have nothing to do with boys.

Dublin.
Jan. [illegible]
Rev. J. H. [illegible]

would work well in Ireland; first, would it not have this advantage, that the initial expense of setting up a cookery class, instead of being thrown as at present upon one school, such as yours on the [illegible]-road, or on the school of your neighbour, Canon Fricker, at Rathmines, would be spread over a number of schools? —I think it would be an advantage; of course there was a considerable expense in the case of my school, but the children contributed to it.

[illegible]. There is, of course, an aspect of the case that we cannot shut our eyes to in this country. We wish to have—each religious denomination wishes to have—schools of its own. You would not wish the children of your congregation to go to Canon Fricker's school, nor would Canon Fricker or his Catholic parishioners like the Catholic children to go to your school. But is there any reason why there might not be a centre that would supply everything required for the teaching of cookery in all the schools of a neighbourhood; your children could go there, say, on Friday; it would not be a good day for Canon Fricker's young charges, but they could go on Thursday; and the children from some other school in the neighbourhood on Monday; and so on. Would not the establishment of such a centre facilitate the teaching of cookery and of all such work?—The only objection I would see to the centre is taking the children along the streets any great distance; the children that come to my school come from a very short distance around.

[illegible]. That, no doubt, is a difficulty; but there are cases where it would not be severely felt. Within a very short radius in and near Dublin there may be a number of schools for which such a system could be worked; but, at all events, apart from that question of distance, you think that the system would work well?—I think it would.

[illegible] referred to, and the answer from [illegible] with 1,329 pupils was "Yes." [illegible] twenty-three schools with 1,130 and the answer from thirty-eight [illegible] was "No."

[illegible] did they say about local resources [illegible] a purpose?—We asked them had [illegible] resources available; nine schools with [illegible] "Yes." Eighty-three schools with [illegible] "No." Two schools with 203 [illegible] no reply.

[illegible] reply did you receive to your question [illegible] drawing compulsory?—Thirty-eight [illegible] pupils answered "Yes." Thirty- [illegible] with 1,116 pupils answered "No." Six [illegible] pupils sent no reply.

[illegible] you ask them whether they would be [illegible] making needlework for girls essential [illegible] the Results examinations?—We did. [illegible] pupils answered "Yes." Thirteen [illegible] pupils answered "No."

[illegible] you ask them whether they would be [illegible] the present programme of the [illegible], in compulsory subjects, to any ex- [illegible]

[illegible] making any subject optional?— [illegible] three or four queries, the first [illegible] making any subject optional, [illegible] answered "Yes," sixty-one schools with [illegible] no reply. A few of the managers [illegible] sufficient data to form a correct [illegible] twenty-seven schools with 1,800 pupils [illegible] with regard to particular subjects, [illegible] to English grammar and geography. [illegible] you ask whether they would make the [illegible] in any school or schools in which [illegible]?—We did, five schools with 408 [illegible] "Yes," nine with 475 pupils said [illegible] with 639 pupils said "higher [illegible] with 308 pupils answered "No." [illegible] with 2,857 pupils sent no reply, the

[illegible] hand, and eye training. [illegible] preparation of all the work which [illegible] work—general training merely from [illegible], which is the primary [illegible] the Sloyd system was introduced.

25004. Would you be in favour [illegible] fourth class cardboard work; and in [illegible] going beyond cardboard work where [illegible] had appliances for woodwork?—Most [illegible] of opinion that in some very small [illegible] not possibly or practically introduce [illegible]

25005. You would not introduce [illegible] the fifth standard?—Not before the [illegible]

25006. Would you be in favour [illegible] literary work to get more time for [illegible] you have indicated?—I should. I think [illegible] school education, English and literary [illegible] devoted to too great an extent, and I [illegible] in favour of curtailing the literary [illegible] a great many subjects optional, which [illegible] pulsory, although at the same time [illegible] is absolutely necessary that for the [illegible] general training we should do so. [illegible] perience in England is that although [illegible] has been introduced the literary [illegible] greatly curtailed.

25007. Have you any ideas as to [illegible] of preparing teachers for this work?— [illegible] it would be desirable that we should [illegible] the time at present given to higher [illegible] training colleges to manual instruction [illegible] there are no fewer than seventeen [illegible] in our training colleges, and a great [illegible] jects that are taught in our training [illegible] students are very often taught [illegible] rather than to teach afterwards. I [illegible] could be prepared in the training college [illegible] these higher and more advanced [illegible]

25008. How many subjects do you [illegible] dropped out of the programme?—[illegible] for an expert, but I certainly think [illegible] advanced Euclid and trigonometry [illegible]

23100. What would be your own view with regard to the establishment of an advising body of that kind? —Well, our Diocesan Board of Education is supposed to be the recognised Church machinery for that purpose, but it does not consist exclusively of school managers. It consists in part of laymen, none of whom, with one exception, is a school manager, and some of the clerical members are not school managers. I think the diocese has sufficient confidence in the Diocesan Board of Education to regard it as representing largely the views of managers, though not so exclusively as some would like.

23101. So substantially there is a managerial body? —Substantially there is; but I daresay a great many would desire the body you speak of.

23102. With regard to the training colleges, are you representing the views of the authorities, in any observations you make, of Kildare-place?—Not at all.

23103. But your own view is that manual training might be established in the training colleges? —Certainly.

23104. Some of the advanced subjects—higher arithmetic, trigonometry, and subjects of that kind—might be toned down, and the time so obtained devoted to instruction in manual work?—Quite so.

23105. With regard to the results system, you said the results fees—perhaps you meant something else—were injurious to primary education?—It was the results system I meant.

23106. As a matter of fact, there is a sum of about £350,000 distributed annually amongst the teachers in results fees. I presume that grant is not reprobated by anybody?—I daresay not, but you could distribute it on some other basis.

23107. You have had a great experience as inspector of schools. Would you be in favour, instead of the individual examination, of having pupils examined by classes, and all the pupils, so to say, on the rolls, or least all as far as possible, brought into attendance on the day of examination?—I should mean decidedly. Class examination generally or by specimens taken haphazard.

23108. What is called the sample system?—Yes.

23109. You decidedly prefer that to the mere mechanical individual examination at present?—Very much.

23110. From your experience as inspector do you find that the school hours are extensive enough during the ordinary week days?—I would rather redistribute the time. I think four and a-half hours would be short enough time to give to secular knowledge, independently of religious knowledge, instead of four hours as at present.

23111. That would not include the recreation time?—No.

23112. What is your view about utilising Saturdays. At present generally Saturdays are not very much used in our schools?—I should like to carry the teachers with me in everything we do, and if I utilised Saturdays I think I should be inclined to give extra results for it. I think it would be desirable that Saturdays should be utilised, at first, at all events, by the teachers going to centres to learn the principles of manual training.

23113. Such a subject as manual training could be carried on on Saturdays, and, perhaps, payments made in connection with it?—I think so.

23114. You referred to the alternative scheme. From your visiting so many schools in the country in connection with the Diocesan Board, may I ask, what is the view entertained about that scheme?—It is not looked upon as a particularly wise scheme by a great many teachers, particularly with respect to needlework, making dresses for school children?—The view is favourable to them.

23118. Is it your experience that object lessons receive much attention throughout the schools?—Not very much.

23119. You would be in favour of the introduction of object lessons?—I should as part of the course training.

23120. You would not confine the extra instruction to be given to manual work alone. You would also have science classes?—Elementary science classes.

23121. Monsignor Molloy.—Can you give the Commission any general idea as to the size of your schools; I mean the number of pupils attending them?—I can. We publish a report, which I shall be happy to place the Commission in possession of. Our schools vary from schools with an average attendance in three departments of 380 down to an average attendance of eight.

23122. Is there any considerable number in which the average attendance is, say, under thirty? —A very large number; particularly in the country districts.

23123. Under your scheme your Board has power to establish what are called district schools by the amalgamation of endowments?—We have.

23124. Has that power been practically exercised? —Well, it has not been exercised, owing to the rather delicate nature of the machinery that the scheme specifies as necessary to set in motion. Before we close any school for the purpose of amalgamation we must have the consent of the Synod, and the consent of the Synod is difficult to obtain; and we must also have the cooperation of the managers. We have not tried to close any schools.

23125. It would have been difficult to get the scheme through, unless these conditions were put in? —I should say so.

23126. Have you in any case amalgamated endowments for the purpose of establishing a district school of a more advanced character?—We have established a district school in Dublin of a more advanced character, but not by the amalgamation of schools. It is established in the old Ralph Macklin School in Molesworth street. We call it the Diocesan and Commercial School. The National school there has ceased to exist.

23127. The Ralph Macklin School was in existence before you put your scheme?—It was in existence before our scheme, as a National school.

23128. I meant to ask if your Board has established any district schools as centres for more advanced primary education?—Not any.

23129. Then you have not put into operation the provision for establishing scholarships?—We have not. But we have invited the parishes, with our co-operation, to establish free scholarships in the Diocesan School in Molesworth-street, of which some of the parishes have taken advantage, and sent their better boys from the parochial schools to the school.

23130. And in that way the Ralph Macklin School serves as a sort of centre to which their best boys are drafted?—Yes.

23131. Should you think it desirable to carry out that plan on a larger scale?—Most desirable. I wish we had a similar school on the north side of Dublin, and also a similar school or two similar schools for girls.

23132. Most Rev. Dr. Walsh.—You said, Dr. Trimmer, that you had authority to speak as a representative up to a certain point in your evidence?—Quite so.

Dublin. Nov. 12, 1887. Rev. J. W. Tristram, B.D.

think it is at all generally understood, that when we speak of drawing, what we have in view is not artistic work, but drawing of a totally different character, suited to elementary schools?—Well, I should say most of our managers have a clear perception as to what is meant.

25162. If a manager thought it was artistic drawing that was in question, he would naturally say no?—Certainly, as unnecessary and wasteful of time.

25163. About manual instruction, most of your managers said they were in favour of the introduction of it, but not to any such extent that it would introduce the teaching of trades; do you think there is any general idea amongst your friends that when manual instruction in woodwork is talked of, there is any reference to the teaching of trades?—I do think there is such an idea, because it was at first not known as manual instruction. It was known as technical instruction, and the expression technical instruction leads to a great deal of misunderstanding.

25164. You know that in connection with this Commission we have from the beginning done everything possible to keep those two terms perfectly distinct?—So I saw by the evidence.

25165. The word "technical" does not occur in the warrant of our Commission: by technical instruction, in the sense in which you very properly object to its being brought into a primary school, you probably mean instruction directed to the work of a particular trade?—Yes.

25166. By manual and practical instruction you mean that kind of training of the hand and eye, and of the faculties generally, which would be of use to a person in after-life, no matter what particular trade he may go to, or even if he does not go to any trade at all: for instance, you would probably think it might be of use to clergymen, or doctors, or lawyers?—Quite so, as strengthening mental training.

25167. And it does this, in addition to giving people habits of neatness, of order, and of accuracy, which are useful in every walk of life, and are unfortunately now sadly needed in most walks of life in this country?—Yes.

25168. You know something of the work of the training colleges?—I do, a great deal.

25169. Have you formed any idea as to whether our training college work is going on right lines—I am not, of course, speaking specially of the training college of your church, the college in Kildare-place, but of the general system: do you think that the system as it is worked out in the training colleges, of which the Kildare-place college is one, is likely to put before the minds of the Queen's Scholars under training, that they have come up to the college to be taught a certain number of subjects, rather than that they come there to be shown how to teach the children in their schools?—I think I expressed that in my reply to the Chairman; I said that unfortunately the training colleges were at present places rather for preparing for an examination than for preparing for teaching, and they are looked upon to a certain extent as a modified university.

25170. You would be anxious to see that system totally changed?—Entirely changed.

25171. I may tell you that one of Her Majesty's [illegible]

many subjects, is all wrong?—Oh, yes primary subjects are too many.

25172. You mentioned that agricul in a number of your schools; you are that under the rules of the National ture, or what is called agriculture, i rural schools?—Agriculture from bo

25173. There is no reason to think taken up in schools where they were or not?—I am very much afraid it mean it was taken up for the results

25174. This subject may be taught —Yes, just as well as in the country ing to the present system.

25175. And, being what it is, it ca hugh almost as suitably here, in the of Dublin, as in the country?—Quite

25176. Now, as to handicraft, I training college in Kildare-place is places in Ireland where the subject craft is taught?—Yes.

25177. Have you observed any part of the teachers who were trained to introduce this subject afterwards in —In two or three instances only gained diplomas perhaps about sixty trained in Kildare-place, and out of the I have not observed, on the part of than half a dozen, any attempt to tea

25178. Have you looked into the handicraft course as formulated in the gramme?—I have thought a little on read a good deal.

25179. You know something of the I know its leading principles.

25180. Comparing the National E present system of handicraft with Slo think represents the proper system schools?—Unquestionably Sloyd from effect.

25181. You agree the present hand the Board is not really educational?

25182. Don't you think, moreover, lated to set the public mind agains question of woodwork in schools, and fact, done a great deal of mischief to it has created a great deal of prejudice parents and others which it will take y

25183. It is not wanting in almost of an educational course of woodwork side by side with drawing?—No.

25184. They made a mistake, I be requirement even in freedom, but clear of it now; but even apart from the absence of all connection with dra of woodwork, the system that we are educational system?—No, there is no up to it, and it does not lead up to is not taught on a practical principle.

25185. You said, I think, that you recommending that a fee should be even though the teacher had not thought it might be so.

25186. When you see all our pu you will find pretty plain proof that

23190. CHAIRMAN.—What, in your opinion, is the chief difficulty in the way of extending manual instruction and training in connexion with the National system of education?—I think it would be the unpreparedness of the present teachers, and of course they are naturally reluctant to take up fresh subjects, if they could avoid it.

23191. You think, I believe, that whilst the feeling and interest of the teachers must not be allowed to stand in the way of necessary improvements, it will be desirable to make some of the changes gradually, in order to introduce manual instruction and matters of that sort. In what way do you think that could be done; what concession should be made to the teachers?—I think it ought to be made as easy for the present teachers as possible, and I think we ought to go as far as possible to meet them. They ought to get facilities for acquiring certificates in special subjects.

23192. In what way?—That is a matter of detail on which I could hardly give an opinion, whether by local classes under special teachers. I think they ought to be allowed to attend short courses of instruction. I am aware that already, under the Science and Art Department, teachers were allowed to go to London for a short time, and their expenses were paid, if I mistake not, to get a short course in the laboratory there, and it occurred to me a similar course might be adopted if any special subject was to be worked up; they might in the Easter holidays or Midsummer holidays get a short course of training in Dublin or Belfast or Cork.

23193. Where in Dublin could the means be found of giving them such instruction as you have in your mind?—I suppose the College of Science would do.

23194. It would do for certain things, but not for the training in woodwork?—We have technical schools here which might be available, and if the thing is worth doing it is worth the while of the State to expend what is needful to get it done; but the technical schools here, which are not availed of quite to the extent they might be, are very efficient in that respect. I was thinking partly of teachers, for instance, who had not had Kindergarten training and who might get, not at their own expense if necessary, a grounding in Kindergarten, and so those who had never learned drawing sufficiently enough to teach it might get further instruction in drawing; that would facilitate its introduction into some schools where the teachers at present are not quite ready to do it.

23195. Have you any suggestions to offer with regard to payment to teachers for these special subjects?—Well, I suppose you don't want to increase the proportion that depends upon results examinations. I see that has been suggested in some portions of the evidence. It was suggested that results fees should be increased; but I think no larger proportion of the teachers' salary ought to depend on results fees than at present. If you give them more subjects to teach I think you will have to give them assistants for a smaller average. That is one difficulty that will meet you at once. The average of seventy with a variety of classes in a school at present is very hard work for a teacher, and if you introduce Kindergarten to the extent that I think it ought to be introduced you will probably find it necessary to allow an assistant at an early stage.

23196. That is more a matter for the Treasury than the National Board, I understand. Do you think that anything could be done in the way of finding time, by dismissing the junior classes while the higher classes are getting instruction in either manual or scientific work?—That might be done, but I don't think you could well shorten the hours for any except infants. I don't know that they are too long for the stages above that.

23197. Supposing the shortening consisted of only

... to what ought to be accomplished in ... needlework, and just because they have to ... do that little grudgingly. I believe ... the time is robbed from the sewing for

... result of the evidence we have taken ... Scotland is that they already give less ... work there than you do here, and yet ... to be enough; three hours a week is ... standard?—I certainly would not like to ... for six half hours. I think few of our ... well enough to take an interest in ... to me as if they were dragged up to a ... rather reluctantly on the part of the

23312. Would you pay them accordingly?—I would make that part of the regular system, but I would have lady inspectors and have a distinct day.

23313. Where would you obtain the ladies from?—That is a question for the Board, and not for me.

23314. Can you not suggest; could you get volunteers?—I don't see why they should do voluntary work for the State in such an important matter.

23315. Your idea is that you should have lady inspectors, who should only take needlework, to be in the same position as the ordinary inspectors, going about the country, having each a district?—Certainly.

23316. Salaried officers?—Certainly; I am ...

in the infant schools, and the teachers of a large portion of that percentage may be said to be masters, do you not think that in the training colleges they ought to extend the instruction in kindergarten to the masters as well as the mistresses?—I believe it would be a training that would be most valuable.

25244. And kindergarten drawing would lead up to other kinds of drawing more advanced in the senior classes?—Yes. With regard to that question, I hardly know why the Board do not go more in the direction of providing assistants, and a little less in the direction of monitresses. I imagine that without serious increase of expense, assistants might in many cases be substituted for monitresses with great advantage; there is a rather over-production of monitresses, there is an excessive eagerness among our girls to become teachers, numbers of them never can be, and you will have to kill them off by examinations. You should have a larger number of assistants and fewer monitresses.

25245. Perhaps you are not aware that the National Board for some years have put that view forward to the Treasury and repeated it over and over again without much success?—The Treasury seem to hinder every improvement.

25246. You remark that drawing is as necessary as writing?—I do.

25247. Consequently you would have it taught in every National School throughout the country, and with regard to the teachers in charge of schools, who are not qualified, what steps would you take?—You would have to deal gently with them, I daresay many of them have a sort of knowledge of drawing, and perhaps some of them have not got encouragement to do it. But if it were made compulsory, and they got this short course in the art of teaching drawing, it would come easier.

25248. You advance in the case of needlework two standards, have you looked into the requirements of the present programme?—Yes, I read them over.

25249. Have you also looked at the alternative scheme for sixth class girls?—I have not, that means two hours a day, that is too long a course. I always thought that was quite an excessive time to be given to the subject.

25250. You reject the alternative scheme, which is really a higher standard, on the ground of excess of time?—Yes, and I hold a higher standard can be reached if your present time is properly utilised. You as yet have teachers who know how to teach needlework; there is much more pains taken now to see that the teachers know how to teach needlework, but formerly it was not so. I think the mistresses ought to be in advance of the other people.

25251. Of course you are aware now that needlework is an essential qualification for recognition at the end of the [illegible] course?—Yes, I know it is.

25252. And in that way a vast improvement has been brought about?—That is a great improvement.

25253. The Chairman asked you how many hours for needlework you would have; did you say five hours was too much?—It is not too much really, according to the importance of the subject, but I think that in three hours, not divided into half [illegible] against for needlework back to the level of the child who can hardly thread a needle.

25254. But the requirements of the highest class where one hour a day only is given to needlework are "to be able to cut out a man's shirt, and any article of female apparel, and to exhibit satisfactory proficiency in the different branches of plain sewing and knitting." Is not that a very high standard?—You might add something else to it in the way of special branches. I think if you want them really to do these things well they ought to have to learn to do something else beyond that.

25255. Something else beyond, that the National Board thought might be met by the special industrial programme, such as lacemaking, Mountmellick work, and art needlework. That branch, however, has turned out not to be so successful; it has been previously abandoned, and under the alternative scheme dressmaking comes in and underclothing, knitting, and general repairing of garments; you would class that portion of it, would you not, in the higher standard of needlework—the general repairing of garments?—I suppose that ought to be included in the ordinary course.

25256. Dr. Wilson has already referred to this point, that if cookery and laundry and needlework were more extensively carried out, that might lead to the appointment of ladies to supervise these branches?—I think that would be desirable; the inspection should not take place at results examination; there should be an interval of time between the two.

25257. In the case of cookery at present under the four teachers who have been trained by the Association in Kildare-street, the examination is held at the end of the two months course; you would suggest something like that in the case of needlework?—I would.

25258. Would you also suggest that the needlework should be regularly carried on by the teacher of the school?—Yes, I would not at all release the ordinary teacher from her full responsibility.

25259. Perhaps you are not aware that under the existing requirements the infants may be dismissed prior to the termination of the ordinary school time?—I know that, but for the reason mentioned we do not do that. But where I have established an infant school separately apart from the others I have made the time a little earlier. What is the shortest time?

25260. It is not absolutely defined?—I know you are allowed to count the playtime.

25261. Most Rev. Dr. Walsh.—You can count the playtime in the four hours for all the children?—It seems hardly wise to count it in the case of the older ones.

25262. Mr. Molloy.—Some educationists call the playground the uncovered schoolroom. Pending the appointment of these lady inspectors, would you think it advisable to extend what the Commissioners have at present, organising teachers of schools; we have two lady organisers who go round the schools and give instruction to the teachers?—I doubt if very much will come of that. In the first place the teachers don't always welcome the aid of those who come in to propose changes. I would send the [illegible]

Dublin.
Dec. 11, 1897.
Rev. G. Mahaffy, A.M.

25365. You were familiar with the mode of examination prior to the establishment of results; that was a class examination; contrasting that with the present mode, which would you prefer—which did more good for the teachers and pupils?—I suppose there was more educational value in the class examination; this other perhaps makes the teacher do his work more thoroughly. I think that the system of examining classes for results would work fairly by sampling classes. I remember a Scotch teacher of a Glasgow school describing to me the inspector's mode there. He introduced him to a large class. "Now," said the inspector, "pick out the twelve best boys in the class." The teacher did. "Now pick out the twelve worst." So he did. "Now pick out the medium twelve. Now I will examine the rest," the inspector said.

25366. The Chairman asked you a question whether under the existing result system dull pupils got more or less attention from the teacher than the bright pupils?—That depends very much on the conscience of the teacher.

25367. Is it not the interest of the teacher rather to work up the dull pupils, and assume that the bright boys will earn the results fees for him without any attention?—That is a very interesting mathematical question, but I don't know the figures. The teachers go into these questions more closely than I would do. I had one teacher who had not a single failure in his school for five or six years; that was the case of a teacher conscientiously working up every boy, but then there would have been schools where it was not possible to do that.

25368. A specialist in drawing also?—Yes, and I think his teaching of drawing favourably affected the whole work of the school.

25369. Your teacher, who was so successful, did he take up many extra branches?—Scarcely any; he was too conscientious to do that; he felt it was his duty to work up the ordinary subjects well. I never went into a calculation whether he made more or less money that way; he satisfied his conscience.

25370. You are disposed to say that the taking up of a great number of extra subjects may interfere with the teaching of the ordinary subjects?—Yes, and I have known a teacher to take up extra branches, not from a desire of making money, but because a neighbouring school had a number of extra branches, and he could not afford to have it said that his school was taking up less.

25371. Would you advocate the propriety of the National Board limiting the number of extras?—I would.

25372. Would not that interfere with the managerial freedom of the schools; a manager who wished to take up a number of subjects might take offence at our restricting the work?—I don't think any manager has a right to exact that the primary system should be made an intermediate system.

25373. Some approach in the direction of your view has already been made by the National Board and the inspection staff by repeatedly suggesting the propriety of not having more than two extras?—I think it should be a standard on the efficiency with which the primary subjects are taught; if they were not taught thoroughly well I would put a very firm brake on the extras. I wonder the Board have not taken more care hitherto in training teachers in the art of teaching; it strikes me as a curious thing that we should get teachers with first-class certificates, which certificates only certify that they have passed in a number of subjects, and do not certify that they are first-class teachers of these subjects. I hope more prominence will be given to the art of teaching itself. The two greatest failures I saw in a boys' school were men who had come out of the training college with first-class certificates; they were the most inefficient teachers I ever saw in a school.

part of the person who has been trained, in order that he may get a diploma?—Yes.

25375. And the diplomas are of two classes, first and second; so that a manager could ask for teachers with a first-class diploma?—You cannot get that in the case of a teacher just coming out, there is great reluctance to refuse to a man who has passed first class his first-class diploma at the end of two years. I think the test of a person's teaching power should be applied at an earlier stage; the residential course is a fair test where a teacher continues through the whole five years, but not a great number enter by examination only. I have known some of these turn out very well, because nature gifted them so, but I have known some that were merely teaching machines.

25376. We had a professor of a college yesterday who said five-sixths of the time of the students was devoted to subjects bearing on examination, leaving a very short time for the teaching of method—you would not approve of that?—No.

25377. Most Rev. Dr. Walsh.—Are you at all familiar with the working of the training colleges?—Just the very slightest, except what I know from the teachers.

25378. Well, you are in a position to judge of the results?—Yes.

25379. And you do not think that they are satisfactory?—I think they are by accident better than they really deserved to be.

25380. You consider that the idea of the training college being a place where people come to learn how to teach is not sufficiently prominently before the minds of the students in the training colleges?—I am sure it is not.

25381. The idea that the training college is primarily a place, as its name indicates, for training persons in the art of teaching?—I can assure your Grace, it is not kept sufficiently before them.

25382. Has it ever struck you that the colleges, most of them at least, are not doing very much for the existing teachers in the way of training?—They are merely grinding establishments, for the most part, preparing them for their class examinations.

25383. Not merely in the matter of grinding, but I find in one college, where there are 102 students, only 6 of them are teachers, the 96 being persons who have come in from outside. Now, is that a satisfactory state of things in one of the colleges set up to train the teachers of the country, over 5,800 of whom, a decided majority of the entire number, are still untrained?—Very unsatisfactory.

25384. In another of the colleges, where there are 117 students, only 18 of them are teachers, and in a larger one where there are 218 students, only 31 of them are teachers. In fact, in these three colleges, out of 437 Queen's Scholars, only 62 are teachers, less than one-seventh of the entire number in these colleges, and 375, that is, six-sevenths of the whole, are students who have not yet entered the service of the Board?—I think it is very unsatisfactory.

25385. Many of these may have been monitors, but they are not yet teachers, and while that is going on, there are over 6,000 National teachers in Ireland absolutely untrained?—I think in many cases the normal monitor would be the teacher who had just completed five years, and passed the third class examination; are these included?

25386. Yes. What I put to you is this, is it not unsatisfactory that in a country like Ireland, where, from there having been only one training college until a comparatively few years ago, there are over 6,000 untrained teachers in our National schools, there should be such a small proportion of teachers getting the advantages of training in the training colleges?—I think it is very undesirable to go on training new ones until the old ones are brought up and trained, if possible.

the introduction of manual and practical instruction into our schools, from the reluctance of teachers to undertake this work; do you think that there is any very serious difficulty of that kind?—I am afraid there is—managers for one thing would be slow to force a teacher.

35788. But why do you use the word force; why do you think the teachers require to be forced? I know just one case in this diocese where there happens to be a local fund available for the work of practical education of some kind in the school, it is our Catholic school in [illegible], and so far from there being any reluctance on the teacher's part to take up the work, the teacher of that school has taken it up with the greatest eagerness, and I might even say, enthusiasm; he was a witness before this Commission. Have you any tangible reason for supposing that the teachers as a body are really reluctant to undertake work that comes before them with a sufficient guarantee that it is really useful work—work for the good of the school?—Nothing, but that I have heard that teachers were opposed to it, individual teachers.

35789. Yes; some of course object, but I am speaking of the teachers as a body?—I suppose they don't like to change their ways.

35790. My experience of teachers is that they are very ready to take up anything that is put before them in a proper way, provided they can be personally satisfied, as of course they ought to be, that it is a good thing for the school. Is your difficulty about the teachers a matter of mere vague apprehension?—Chiefly so, that they would not like to be put out of their way. I think if they are treated with consideration in some of the ways I have suggested that difficulty will disappear.

35791. I quite agree with you. Suppose there were facilities given to them to enable them to qualify themselves to teach some of the new subjects; I have seen numbers of resolutions—you probably have seen them also—passed by bodies of teachers objecting to any of these subjects being introduced unless such facilities were afforded; my reason for putting the question to you was that I feared the inference might afterwards be drawn from your evidence, that you had reason to know there would be reluctance on the part of the teachers?—It was just a general idea that they were unready.

35792. In reference to drawing, you are decidedly of opinion that it is of general utility in the school, that it is of help to the work of the school all round?—Yes, it benefits every other subject.

35793. You are also quite clear as to the educational value of kindergarten work in the school?—I

Dublin. Jan. 12, 1897. Rev. [illegible]

25312. But I hope you do not ascribe the good results of it to the particular form in which we have it, a system of fees based on the results of the examination of each individual pupil in each individual subject?—I do not; I think a class examination might be really of a higher educational value.

25313. You are aware that in England, as a result of sufficient experience, a results system, such as our present system, was long ago abandoned; your remarks in favour of a results system, apply rather to the general principle that the grant should depend on the nature of the work done, than to our present particular system of individual examination?—Yes, the grant should depend on a close scrutiny of the work of the school, and whether that is carried out by individual examination or a careful examination of the class, it is a matter of indifference.

25314. You recognise that the present system is capable of being largely improved?—Yes, but not abandoned altogether.

25315. Rev. Dr. Evans.—May I understand you to say you are strongly in favour of the appointment of female inspectors in needlework?—Most strongly.

25316. Are there such people in the world as tailors?—Yes.

25317. And if I wanted a suit of clothes would you recommend me to go to a dressmaker or to a tailor?—To a tailor by all means.

25318. If a tailor is a good man at cutting-out and sewing and making gentlemen's clothes, wherein is the male sex lacking, the inherent incapacity or unfitness to be an inspector of needlework?—For one thing I consider if the examination is to be of educational value the inspector ought to be able to indicate, not only that the work is weak, but the direction in which it is weak, and I don't think an inspector of the Board has served sufficient time at needlework to be able efficiently to point that out.

25319. Are you aware that in many establishments they will advertise tailor-made dresses for ladies, as having some superiority over those made by ladies themselves?—I am quite aware of that, but it does not alter my opinion that the inspectors of the Board are not the most efficient inspectors of needlework.

25320. Is there anything in the male nature that unfits or makes a man less fit for the duty of inspector in needlework?—I suppose he fails to some extent his ungainliness himself.

25321. You are not officially connected with any training college?—I am not.

25322. Are you aware that the teachers in schools already always get the preference for coming in for training over other candidates?—I believe they do, but I don't know whether that is very effective under the present system. Are there a certain number of places kept vacant for teachers already elected?

25323. Are you aware that if a teacher would come into the training college for training he has to appoint a substitute at his school, and the absence from his school for a year involves so much detriment to his interests that he would rather do without training than run the risk of losing his school?—I am sure that it has hindered them in some cases, but I am not sure that they are entirely welcome in the training college—they are often not the best material for them to get for showing results upon in the training college.

25324. Are you aware that pupil teachers get the second preference for admission to the training colleges?—I believe they do.

25325. And monitors the third?—But that is not very easily carried out in some of these under the system now where all are submitted to examination.

25326. And as regards those particular teachers and pupil teachers and monitors that make application for admission to the training colleges, the greatest difficulty is with clergymen throughout the country, who have favourites of their own in their several parishes, each one urging on the authorities of the training college to take in his candidate?—I am sure that is a difficulty.

Mr. Edward MacCreanor, J.P., formerly an Inspector of National Schools, examined.

Mr. Edward MacCreanor

25327. Chairman.—I believe that you were formerly an Inspector of Schools in Ireland?—I was.

25328. When were you appointed and when did you retire?—I was appointed in April, 1850, and retired at the end of 1891.

25329. Then you had experience of schools before the result system and after the result system?—Oh, considerable.

25330. Will you tell us first of all, what was the state of the schools when you first became an inspector?—I was first appointed to a district in the West of Ireland; the centre was Westport, and my district had a coast line from Sligo Bay to Galway Bay, including the islands. Many of the schools when I first saw them were closed; they were vested schools, and they were unsatisfactory in some parties. But, however, there were no teachers, and very little plant except the corner posts that could not be broken. Most of those schools on the property of the Marquis of Sligo and Sir Richard O'Donel had no teachers, and we had scanty opportunity of making teachers, although I had my heart more or less in the work. There was a convent in Westport, and there were some grown-up pupils in it who could write and read nicely, and were well taught in needlework, and we managed to get some additional assistance for teaching arithmetic, and it was in that way we got over the difficulty at first of supplying teachers.

25331. That was in 1850 or a few years after?—This is my note-book for 1851, 1852, 1853. In my time the schools that had been closed were reopened, and I believe I left fifty-three or fifty-four new National schools besides a very few schools closed.

25332. Were those schools in good order before the result system; after you got them opened, were they working well?—They were in a poor state, because the teachers were appointed just as soon as they could be. Some were from the back of Croagh-patrick, where they were extremely smart children. I watched the schools about Louisburgh, as I was very anxious about the matter, and I liked the children also, and it was wonderful how we got teachers made out of the material.

25333. But I wanted to know about the state of the schools?—They were very low: it was the opening of the system almost there. On my first inspection the numbers I found present were 1,870, of which number 710 were in first class, 546 in second, 320 in third, and 94 in the fourth; that is about 62½ per cent. in first, 26 per cent. in second, 18 per cent. in third, and 5½ per cent. above third. In arithmetic, also, there were, nominally at least, 420 in simple rules, and 120 in compound rules.

25334. I want to get information from you as to what was the system of inspection of schools when you first became an inspector; what was the method of inspection?—The year was divided into three terms, each of four months, and you were supposed to go round the schools of the district once in each term.

25335. What did you do when you got to the school; did you examine the children individually?—Oh, not individually, partly individually and partly in class, and listened to the teacher, also, for I thought the best thing I could do was to try and give a little assistance to the teacher, and teach him also. I had never been in a National school as a pupil myself, for there were none in my part of the country. I set to to organise in my own way, to help to arrange the furniture and establish a starting point. I arranged order, and system, and gave practical hints respecting the training of pupils, and their promotion, and the instruments I used for that purpose were the reading tablets. I divided the school, generally speaking, into two divisions, and we carried out the same principle as far as possible.

25336. What means had you in those days, before the results system was introduced, of passing the intelligent children, and deciding upon their promotion from one class to another, examining their reading and spelling and writing and arithmetic in the classes—you took a child here and there?—Oh, I took the children all together. I took a draft which was generally the class if it was not large—a large class might contain different drafts—and I then promoted on what I found there. And I made suggestions to the teachers.

25337. Before you ceased to be an inspector the present system of examination for results was introduced?—Yes, in 1872.

25338. Did you find any raising of the standard of education when that was done?—Decidedly, my own opinion is that it had an enormous advantage in inducing promotion.

25339. Mr. Molloy.—That is promotion of pupils?—Yes. In inducing the promotion of pupils and reducing the labour, and consequently in ensuring improved answering in the schools.

25340. Do you think it improved the teachers?—It must have improved the teachers. First, it would make them, I presume, read a little more for the purpose of securing better results, and it could not do them an injury by making them read more, and work harder.

25341. Rev. Dr. Evans.—Are you acquainted with the books that were in use when you became an inspector?—Oh, yes.

25342. As compared with those of the present day, what is your opinion now with regard to the change in the school books; has it been for the better or worse?—I would be very slow about saying it was for the worse, and I am scarcely prepared to give a very close idea of the relative values, but there was in the old school books some very valuable matter, quite as valuable as there is in the present ones.

25343. You are not certain, but the improvement in the school books may have had to do with the improvement in the schools?—I would not take the books as the sole cause of the improvement.

25344. But you think that in your latter period, as an inspector, the inspection work was better done than in the earlier period?—The inspection work was so arranged that it must be done according to a certain rule, whether that was the inspector's intention or aim or view or not, he had to work according to a certain programme. He had a heavy day's work in order to produce the matter required in the Education Office.

25345. There were fewer trained teachers when you began your career as an inspector than when you closed?—Very much fewer.

25346. Might not the large number of trained teachers have contributed greatly to the improvement of the schools?—It should, necessarily.

25347. What I want to show is that there were other causes at work to improve the schools besides results, and we must not give credit to results for what was done by improved teachers and improved books?—The training of teachers should improve them. I don't see how it could be otherwise, and as the books are an improvement on the whole, those would be contributory to the improvement of the schools.

25348. And there are improved methods of teaching?—Oh, yes. Here is an old note I found in this book, that "many of the teachers had no knowledge of drawing up a timetable with a rational distribution by which he could work better than he did before. The organisation of the school was arranged, the children were divided into two divisions, and some fair distribution of them in classes. And I am satisfied, as I do still, that true organisation simplifies the school business, and takes away a great deal of annoyance from the poor little children when starting. If a beginner has a fixed place, when he gets up to the head of a draft, he has got promotion; that is one of the first things it will call where he goes home, and take a delight in. The children were set in a higgledy-piggledy way, here to-day and somewhere else to-morrow, until they began to cry and get unhappy. I take that in connection with the answering of your question, I think it has something to do with it. Here is a document that I carried since the year 1855 constantly when inspecting schools.

25349. Mr. Molloy.—I think you were engaged in other districts than Westport—you had experience of Clonmel and Newry?—Yes, from the extreme west I was sent to the extreme east to Wicklow, and from that to Clonmel, Clonmel to Cavan, Cavan to Dungannon, then to Ballymena, and eventually to Newry.

25350. Now, in connection with the state of the schools prior to the introduction of the result system, did you not find an overwhelming number in the junior classes, and very few in the senior?—Oh, yes.

25351. Would you think it too much to say that 90 per cent. of the pupils were kept in the junior classes, and it was very rare to find even half a dozen pupils in the senior classes?—That was the case very often.

25352. That was prior to 1872?—Yes.

25353. May I read for you the figures lately published by the Commissioners for 1891–96; they say they now have 30 per cent. of the pupils in the senior division—fourth, fifth, and sixth, and of these about 10 per cent. may be said to be in the senior class?—Yes.

25354. That is a very marked improvement?—A very marked improvement. I happen to have a paper here for about forty or fifty schools; there were about 6 per cent. above the third class, and only 2 per cent. of girls when I first went to Clonmel in 1855. I was surprised to find Clonmel district so low.

25355. In view of that, was not the introduction of some system, such as has brought about an improvement of 30 per cent. in the senior pupils, very necessary at the time, in 1872?—It was very necessary. The whole force impinged upon the inspector, and I didn't very unfairly, for urging and securing promotion.

25356. Prior to 1872 was there any organised system of promoting pupils from one class to another?—Oh, no, there was not.

25357. What check did the inspectors exercise over the promotion of pupils?—I pointed out to the teacher that these children were in the same class in which they were the year before, and if I could induce the manager to come to the school and see the examination I did so.

25358. So it was only the personal influence of the inspector that brought about the promotion of pupils?—That is so.

25359. Was it not the interest of the teachers to a certain extent to allow the pupils to remain a long time in the same class and present them to the inspector, and get favourable reports without promoting the pupils?—Yes, but with an inspector who looked closely into the matter it would scarcely pass.

25360. At the present time the sixth is our highest standard, and we have three years in the sixth class. What was the highest standard before the introduction of the result system?—Scarcely anybody beyond fourth class, and even a small number in the fourth.

25361. And two or three in the fifth class?—Very

fourth class that it was wonderful how well they were up.

23363. At the time you ceased to act as inspector what would you regard as the value of stopping at fourth class; how long would the school instruction prove effectual to later on?—I don't say it was a stopping point except in the case of [illegible] children.

23364. Supposing a boy left at the end of fourth class, would you say he was likely to derive much benefit from the previous instruction?—Oh, no.

23365. Prior to the result system when the fourth was the highest, the state of information of a boy was almost nil?—It would stick to him as much as to a good fourth class boy at present.

23366. Consequently 50 per cent. now in the senior division is a vast improvement?—Yes, compared with 6 per cent. for boys and 3 per cent. for girls.

23367. It was chiefly in the way of more rapidly promoting the pupils that the result system operated shortly after its introduction?—Yes, and took away a great deal of labour in the school by improved attendance.

23368. Do you think the time has now come when there might be a change in another direction?—I subscribe to this—that results has got a bad name occasionally in places, and I think it is unjustly blamed; it is not the system that is so much to blame as the style of examination under it.

23369. That is the individual examination of pupils with a view to fees?—It is not the individual examination alone. Take arithmetic—a comparatively bad teacher may earn as much as a good teacher, because a child can be drummed up to do a card of questions during the year like the one set the year before, or during the year.

23370. Would not that be an argument for changing the present form?—For changing the style of examination under it; to take away results entirely would be injudicious, it would leave the matter personally on mere individuals.

23371. Have you directed your attention to any modification of the result system that you think would be more appropriate?—Latterly I have not been thinking much about the matter, but the matter is easily worked out with regard to examination under the result system—the child should know something of what it was talking about, and grammar and arithmetic should be better taught.

23372. CHAIRMAN.—Don't you think that arithmetic is well taught now—is it not about the best taught subject in the schools?—I don't know that it is.

23373. MR. MOLLOY.—In your later days did you find the theory of arithmetic attended to?—Not sufficiently. I was pleased to an arrangement of my own —blackboard demonstrations I called it for want of a better term—it was a safety valve in the school; any subject that was behind could be worked up with the aid of the blackboard demonstrations.

23374. Have you thought of any modification by which the present system could be altered for the better?—I have not thought it out sufficiently.

23375. Have you directed your attention to the introduction of manual work in schools?—Yes, I have.

23376. Are you in favour of that?—Oh, decidedly. But I think the children's tastes and habits and tendencies should be studied. It is no use trying to teach all of them the same work.

23377. You would not have any objection to the introduction of manual work in suitable places?—No, but it cannot be done in individual schools, I think. I heard something mentioned about a central point; the idea was in my own mind that where there were five or six schools that could be grouped and it would not be too far for the children to go one school for such instruction, where there was a teacher who had a taste for it—some may have a taste for shoemaking, others for saddlery or carpentry or woodwork—and above all things teach the child to sharpen tools, and to

Dublin. Jan. 12, 1897. Mr. Edward MacDermott.

it was a wrong thing in the interests of education to introduce any results system when it was introduced thirty years ago, because people recognise that it requires reconstruction now?—A free agent would scarcely state such a thing.

25392. But it is very frequently stated. I am seeing it in newspapers every week in my life; you at all events are very far from saying it; you distinguish between the two things, and you say that the fact of its being capable of improvement, even need of improvement now, has nothing whatever to do with the wisdom or unwisdom of introducing it when it was introduced; and you say moreover that when it was introduced it was a most useful and even necessary change?—I think so.

25393. Before the results system was introduced you were an inspector?—Yes.

25394. And you have described your practice in inspection. You said you were able to pay three visits a year to a school, and on the occasion of those visits you were able to give the teachers useful directions?—Well, I tried.

25395. Do you not think it is impossible for the inspectors to do that important educational work under the system that we have now?—Under the present system it is impossible they could do it, for this reason, they have a heavy day's work independently of that.

25396. In other words, the inspector's time is now so completely taken up with examining everybody and everything, putting down marks, and calculating percentages, and filling up returns, that it is quite impossible for him to do that useful, and I would say necessary, work that you used to do?—Quite impossible.

25397. Of course you recognise that it would be a decided advantage to set the inspector free to do that work again?—As free as possible.

25398. Apart from examining, you object to what is sometimes called class examination, and I think you used the word in the sense of having the children singing out an answer all together in a sort of chorus?—Yes.

25399. I suppose there is very little room for difference of opinion as to that; but what would you say to class examination in another sense, as I understand the term; to bring out the point I will put a question to you that I put to Sir Joshua Fitch when we were in London. Suppose that, instead of examining every child in every subject, the examination was so conducted that every child would be examined in some subject—one set of children in arithmetic, another set in reading, another in geography, and so on, would not that enable the inspector really to test how the different subjects were being taught in the school?—I think it would unless the children were manipulated.

25400. But suppose they were not manipulated; take it in this way—let us say there are six subjects, then, instead of the inspectors spending two or three days worrying himself and everybody else by examining every child in each of those subjects, he divided the children into six batches, and examined one batch in reading, another in arithmetic, and so on, and then if his report were satisfactory the teacher would get recognition for the teaching of all the children in the six subjects?—Yes, if it was carefully done.

25401. And as it could be done in one-sixth of the time, or say one-fourth of the time, it would enable the inspector to give useful help educationally to the teacher of the school?—Yes.

25402. The inspector now is so planned in his work that the teachers of the district are almost always enabled to know precisely where he is and where he is not, and that may not be an unmixed advantage?—No, and I think it would be useful to have incidental visits more frequently paid.

25403. What I suggest would set him free to pay incidental visits?—Not himself only but his assistants also; I think their visits should be taken after consulting with the district inspector, and they should make the visit while the school is in operation; no honest teacher will have any objection to it.

25404. But at present everybody's time is taken up with all this work of examination and tabulation of results and making up statistical returns. I suppose the inspector's assistants would be likely to be of use to the teacher in giving directions as to methods of teaching?—The inspector's assistants also know the business thoroughly.

25405. I believe they have had practical experience as teachers in the schools?—Yes.

25406. You would strongly recommend a change to be made that would enable these visits to be paid?—I would.

FIFTY-FOURTH PUBLIC SITTING—FRIDAY, NOVEMBER 19TH, 1897.

Dublin.
Nov. 19, 1897.

AT 11 O'CLOCK A.M.,

At the Antient Concert Rooms, Dublin.

Present:—THE RIGHT HON. THE EARL OF BELMORE, G.C.M.G., in the Chair; HIS GRACE THE MOST REV. WILLIAM J. WALSH, D.D.; THE RIGHT HON. C. T. REDINGTON, M.A.; THE RIGHT REV. MONSIGNOR MOLLOY, D.D., D.SC.; REV. HENRY EVANS, D.D.; REV. HAMILTON WILSON, D.D.; and W. R. J. MOLLOY, ESQ.;

with J. D. DALY, ESQ., M.A., Secretary.

Rev. H. KINGSMILL MOORE, M.A., Principal, Church of Ireland Training College, Kildare-place, Dublin, examined.

Rev. H. Kingsmill Moore, M.A.

25407. CHAIRMAN.—You are the Principal of the Church of Ireland Training College in Kildare-place?—Yes, my lord.

25408. That college is under local management, but in connexion with the National Education Board?—Yes.

25409. You consider that certain subjects should be made compulsory in our system of education, which at present are not compulsory. Kindly state what the subjects are, the introduction of which as compulsory subjects you think would be desirable?—I think, my lord, that drawing might very well be made compulsory, because from the standpoint of the schools, for reasons which I could give if questioned on the subject, that I think might fairly be made compulsory, and on the other side, from the point of view of the object of this Commission, it appears to me to be one of the most necessary subjects for manual and practical training.

25410. When you say that you think drawing should be made compulsory, you have in view the general system—the school programme—of the National schools throughout Ireland indiscriminately.

25411. Do you think that elementary science should be made compulsory, or, if not, what would you say about it?—I suggest in the memorandum which I sent in, that it might be made compulsory as soon as preliminaries could be arranged;—that is a rather important exception.

25412. Will you tell us what the preliminaries are?—The preliminaries would fall under three heads—the first is a proper syllabus from the National Board; next, encouragement for the training colleges to teach it; and the third, is training for the inspectors to examine in it. All these things would require a great deal of thought.

25413. Would you not add to that, means being found of acquiring the apparatus necessary?—Your lordship means, I suppose, financial means?

25414. I have more in my mind—laboratory apparatus where chemistry is taught?—These would, of course, come under the necessary preliminaries. And the idea I had in my mind in speaking of a proper syllabus would be a syllabus that could be worked, and that would be one of the essential points.

25415. It is a very important detail for us to inquire into, where the means of purchasing apparatus is to come from?—I was not contemplating a thorough knowledge of elementary science, but there is a great deal—for instance measurement, which forms so important a part in England—a great deal which could be done without much apparatus, and I should be sorry that such a subject should be postponed, because it could not be done all at once perfectly.

25416. What are your views upon the subject of school gardens?—I think that school gardens might be almost indefinitely extended. I became to be familiar with a great many schools in the diocese of Cork. A very large number of them had some land attached to them, quite enough for a garden, though certainly not enough for a farm, and I think nothing but good could come from cultivating the intelligence of the children with reference to horticulture. I remember one school garden, which was a subject of great delight to all who had to do with it, it is near Dunmanway. Sometimes in Kildare-place, where we suffer very great drawbacks, being in the middle of the city, one tries to do something in the way of imparting a knowledge of plants and plant life. All these things might be worked out with great ease and little cost—fruit growing, vegetable culture, and things of that kind. It is one of the simplest subjects to introduce, if the teacher only gets training and encouragement.

25417. As regards agriculture, at present agriculture is only taught out of books as a rule?—That is practically so.

25418. There are, I believe, eighty-one school farms through all Ireland, which is, of course, a poor percentage. Do you think that the present system of teaching agriculture out of books is of any practical use, if it is not followed up by something more definite in practical instruction?—I should be very sorry to say it was of no practical use. One illustration came under my notice quite recently—such a matter as a haybarn. I believe haybarns have been advocated in the book, and they have been largely introduced into the country, and I should think the book had something to do with it. All my life I have had an interest in horticulture, but I knew absolutely nothing about crops; what little I did learn was from the agriculture book, when I was an inspector in the diocese of Cork. I found the book gave me great help, and it is a step, although I don't think it goes a long way. The book could be made of very much more value if the examination was of a different kind. It is one of the many ways in which the whole system suffers from the results system. The inspectors examine in a cut and dried way from the book. If, instead of doing that, they were to examine practically, there is nothing in the world to prevent the teacher having specimens of potatoes, turnips, mangolds, and corn present on the day of the examination; nothing to prevent certain kinds of manures—such as would not be offensive—nothing to prevent them being required by the inspector, and a practical examination given, even with the present limited resources. I think the system of examination is a good deal to blame for the subject not being more practical.

25419. As regards the hand and eye training, you think that that should be encouraged in the junior and middle classes of the school?—Yes, certainly, I do.

25420. Kindergarten, I believe, is now only carried on in the infant schools or infant department of schools?—So far as I know, only there.

25421. Would you be in favour of extending that sort of thing under the head of occupations to the third and fourth classes?—Yes; I certainly should.

25422. So that there may be no gap between that and any manual work in the fifth and sixth classes? —Certainly.

25423. Would you be in favour of encouraging where possible, not as a compulsory matter—that probably would be very difficult—but as an optional subject, the introduction of woodwork in fifth and sixth classes?—Certainly, in favour of encouraging it. It is a subject with which I see great difficulties connected. The question of plant comes in there at once in a very emphatic way.

25424. And also the question of suitable teachers?—Suitable teachers, of course, is another difficulty.

25425. But where it could be done, and the teacher wished to take it up, or the manager and teacher jointly wished to take it up, would you be in favour of encouragement being given for its introduction?—Yes, certainly.

25426. I believe that you think that there are three necessary factors required in connection with the introduction of manual instruction, and these other subjects you have mentioned—one connected with the Education Office, one connected with the training colleges, and one connected with the system of inspection. Taking these heads in the order I have given, will you tell us what your views are?—I think that at the bottom of all these subjects must be the directions laid down by the Education Office, and in accordance as they are wise and workable, must, to a very large extent, be the success of any scheme that is introduced. I took the liberty of putting down in my memorandum some examples to the contrary.

25427. You say a well-known? In speaking about the regulations of the National Board, I trust I may do so without being suspected of a desire to criticise Mr. Redington, whom I have always found most considerate and kind; I should not have entered on the subject if I thought it would have annoyed him. One of my examples was the industrial programme. I am under the impression that needlework had been a good deal neglected when that industrial programme was introduced; it seemed to me to be just the opposite swing of the pendulum; it put the needlework on in such a way as to provoke a rebellion. I know that the witnesses generally have attacked that programme, so that probably there is no necessity for saying more on it.

25428. The trend of evidence, I don't say in Ireland, but certainly in England, is that the time for needlework should be reduced?—Two hours a day is quite too much. The new programme, which has been at work this year for the first time, is a subject on which in Kildare-place we have felt a little.

25429. Mr. Molloy.—That is the teachers' programme?—Yes, the teachers' programme, there is a great deal in the programme with which we have agreed very cordially and we welcome its introduction, but there are certain ways in which it is applied which have hurt us very considerably, and which I think will hurt all who come gradually to work it. It has been worked this year at Marlborough-street and Kildare-place, I am not sure whether it was worked at De la Salle. The first point that comes out strikingly in connection with it is this. Our college was opened in 1884, and from 1884 to 1898 we presented over a thousand students for examination, but we only had fourteen failures in all those years. This year we presented our students as usual, and in the one year, even after some consideration being shown in the matter, we have had [illegible]

25436. You would advocate a system analogous to the English system?—Yes, in the existing colleges most certainly.

25437. I believe that in the training colleges you are willing to co-operate in introducing such subjects as cookery, dressmaking, kindergarten and handiwork?—I gave them at an [illegible] of subjects in which we do co-operate very willingly already. I believe, speaking for Kildare-place, and I think the same applies to all the Irish training colleges, that we are very willing to follow any lead given by the National Board, and to introduce any subjects that may be thought good.

25438. With regard to defects in the present system of training colleges, what do you say as regards their being places of acquiring knowledge in contradistinction to places where persons are trained how to teach what they know already?—What I have to say with reference to that is, that, owing to the nature of the conditions laid down, which I have to a certain extent detailed, they must do a great deal of work, which is solely a preparation for an examination. Of course I should be very sorry to convey the idea that we have not laid very great stress in Kildare-place upon preparation for teaching, even long before it had anything to do with the certificate examination, which I am glad to say it has now. That is one of the great advantages of the new programme. But even before that there was very heavy stress laid by us on this preparation of teachers in the most practical way. I may mention that I have been in the habit of drawing up, with the help of the master and [illegible] of method, at the end of the year a list of students in order of merit. That order of merit has nothing to do with their examination results, either at entrance or the first year, it is based solely upon the work they do in the schools and criticism lessons; and in the patronage, which it is my duty to exercise in appointing them to schools, that is the list by which I am guided.

25439. You exercise that patronage upon what you consider to be their ability to teach, and not upon their personal knowledge?—Not upon their personal knowledge; but of course, as I said, we have to do more in the way of grinding for an examination in subjects than we like.

25440. Could you give us any idea how much time you devote to teaching the knowledge which they have to acquire as compared with the time given to teaching them how to teach?—It would not be possible to answer that question precisely, I can, of course, say the regulations of the training college for the definite teaching work, but I cannot say what each professor in his class-room gives to teaching work as distinguished from mere grinding work.

25441. Has he discretion to a certain extent?—In his own hour each professor has discretion as to what he does.

25442. What do you say upon the subject of handicraft and drawing?—The present handicraft course is not educational, it is a valuable practical course, which our students have taken up and have passed in large numbers. Since we commenced it in 1887, which I think was very nearly the commencement of the drawing up of the syllabus at the Education Office, we have had in our college 175 male students, a number of whom we could not present, but altogether we have got ninety-four certificates for handicraft. The course is in no sense an educational course, it merely requires them to do certain mechanical operations, and the questions set in the paper are altogether of a practical kind.

25443. Your handicraft consists of woodwork?—Yes.

25444. Is it done in connection with drawing?—No, that was one of the things I was going to speak about.

25445. Don't you think that that is the weak point of it?—Most certainly.

25446. Do you think that woodwork, as we saw it in one school in the North of Ireland, done without the slightest connection with drawing, is likely to be anything but a failure?—It fails in its chief educational object. I may mention that I saw those schools at Westminster, which the Commission visited, and I did my best to master the outline of the system. Afterwards I entered into communication with the authorities, and persuaded them to make for me a set of models illustrating their system and drawings to accompany the models. I got them over in the hope of introducing them at Kildare-street, but I found in face of the present programme it was no use. It is just an illustration of the want of a sympathetic syllabus.

25447. What do you say about drawing?—Drawing in the same way is examined in a manner which is not likely to make the teachers think how to teach it; they are simply asked to copy either a model or a a specimen of freehand, which is set before them, no questions are ever asked with regard to the method of teaching. By the introduction into the course of some questions of that kind with reference to such a book as Mr. Taylor's there would be a very great improvement.

25448. Do the inspectors ever ask the students when examining them, to use the blackboard and show how they would teach with reference to drawing?—Never with reference to drawing, with regard to other subjects the blackboard is used continually.

25449. Do you think that the inspectors are sufficiently in touch with the colleges?—No, I don't think that there is any sign of the inspectors as a body in touch with the colleges, and it is no use for a college to do good work unless the inspectors are in touch with them.

25450. In what way do you think they should carry out a different system to what they are doing?—I am speaking from a certain point of view, I know the inspectors are an exceedingly hard-worked body of public servants, but for a year or two after they begin they may not have such a large amount of work. I think they ought to visit the colleges, see the criticism lessons, and have conversations with the masters and mistresses of method. We might gain something from visits of that kind, and the inspectors may gain something themselves. If they mastered such systems as are good at the training colleges, it would help them to improve the schools, so that the system, if good at the training colleges, might make the schools better.

25451. Is your method of teaching measurements, geography, grammar, and [illegible], a different one to what is practised in the schools?—Yes, I think with regard to all these subjects we have been trying to do better than the level of the schools and have failed to a large extent, because while they were with us the students had a knowledge that they would not be questioned on these subjects afterwards, and when they went out they dropped them at once, because nobody ever made any allusion to them. What I mean by measurements is training the eye to know heights and breadths and lengths, it is one of the first stages in an [illegible] course to teach careful measurement. We have in nearly all our rooms the height of the rooms marked, and in some signals as to the area of the rooms. In our criticism lessons we accustom our students to apply these practically, and we urge our students when they go out into their schools to carry out the system. It is one only by putting the measurements up on a slate in a corner of the room. I have some cases where our advice had been taken, but in the majority of cases the advice has been forgotten.

25452. Now as regards geography?—That was a subject that I often felt great regret was not treated in a more intelligent way in the examination of the schools. The methods now recommended are no new discovery; Mr. Robinson, whose book is on the Board's list, lays it down in that book, published as far back as 1860, that the proper way to teach geography is to begin by dealing with the locality, and getting the locality mastered in a practical and interesting way. It is a rule with us at Kildare-place that every female student must draw a map of her surroundings. They draw a map of the schoolroom and then a map of Kildare-place, and in its surroundings in the neighbourhood. We endeavour to impress on them the importance of that, and to carry out the same system in their schools. But it is plain that if the inspector only examines in a cut and dried way, "How many counties in Ireland?" and "How many towns?" and still more [illegible], the lengths of rivers and heights of mountains, it is quite plain that it is not their fault if they don't carry out that system. Something might be done by the Commissioners publishing better maps. It is allowable for a teacher to take up the geography of a county, but the maps are so indifferent that they don't serve as an encouragement.

25453. Are there not good and useful maps of the Irish counties to be had on a sufficient scale to be really instructive?—I don't know of any, and I think it is extremely improbable, because I find when I come to study maps drawn up by the very best English houses, they show a lofty contempt for all things Irish, and even a railway that may have been established for two or three years will not be marked on the latest English map. I have some knowledge of this, through my Depository in Kildare-place, and when I occasionally take the liberty of pointing out the shortcomings of these gentlemen with regard to Ireland, they say there is no demand and it does not pay to be up to date.

25454. How do you teach grammar?—We always try to impress on students the importance of teaching grammar on the inductive method, we get them to examine sentences. Suppose the lesson was on adverbs, they select sentences in which there are adverbs, and working from the sentences, they are taught to lead up to the definition of an adverb; and we try to carry that right through our grammar, but I don't think it ever passes beyond the walls of Kildare-place. As regards calisthenics, that is a minor point, since the schools were founded by Lancaster, from 1810 onwards, drill and calisthenics have always been our speciality there, and personally I believe in them. I think they are the keynote for order and discipline in the school, so we insist on all our teachers mastering a system of calisthenics with the view of improving their discipline.

25455. Do you find they do not follow that up afterwards?—A great many do, that is more followed than any of the other matters, because it is attractive and is appreciated by the parents.

25456. It amuses the children?—Yes, but I don't think the inspectors take any notice of it.

25457. Most Rev. Dr. Walsh.—Are you aware that in the Scottish system a school cannot get the highest grant for organization unless attention is paid to drill, and drill, I suppose, corresponds pretty nearly with calisthenics?—I did not know about the Scottish system, but I knew it was so in England.

25458. Don't you think that it would be a very useful arrangement to make in Ireland?—It would.

25460. Take it in this way; suppose that our present system of paying out the grants to the schools was changed, and that a special grant was to be given for general organization, discipline, general good tone of the school, that is to say, having the school on a way he would not on any account let a text-book on grammar into the hands of a child. Then he was asked how he would teach grammar, and he said he would teach it by taking up sentences from their reading books. That seems to me a very rational system. Does it correspond with your system?—Yes, your Grace.

25462. In reference to geography, you say that the absence of county maps of Ireland is a drawback, and I think you said that the maps published by the Commissioners of National Education are not everything they ought to be; now I am not at all likely to champion the Commissioners of National Education over everything they did in the past, but we must be fair; remember that there are no maps published by the Commissioners?—I did not mean to any published by the Commissioners, because I don't think they are published by the Commissioners.

25463. There are maps on the Commissioners' list of school requisites, and they supply them on requisition, but there are no maps published by the Commissioners themselves; is not that so?—Yes.

25464. Mr. Molloy.—And the price of the maps Mr. Moore refers to is three halfpence each.

Most Rev. Dr. Walsh.—Possibly you may think it would be an advantage to have such maps published by the Commissioners, or at all events, if not by them, then by some other body?—Most certainly it would be a great advantage to have them published.

25465. The Commissioners, as you know, have published a large number of books, and many of them are not exactly such as you or I would regard as models of what school books ought to be?—That is so.

25466. And consequently a number of those books have almost dropped out of use in the schools?—Yes.

25467. I understand you to say that you approve of the system of beginning geography with the geography, or perhaps it is better to call it the topography, of the place that the children know, and first of all with the schoolroom?—Yes.

25468. There is a system generally adopted in some of the German schools, we saw it in England also; first, they have a plan of the schoolroom, then a plan or map of the place immediately adjoining the school, and of course including it, then perhaps the town or city, say, Dublin, as a whole, then the city and suburbs, next the County Dublin, and then Ireland and so on, until in the end they have got on, step by step, to those two hemispheres that our unfortunate children are set to puzzle themselves over in the very beginning?—May I mention in that connection that some of our most useful evidence lessons are on the spots from which the students come and its surroundings, and another lesson is on the Dodder, and many of them will walk along the Dodder to study it.

25469. A very experienced inspector told us here that he sometimes asked the Dublin children had they ever seen the Liffey, and they said they never had, they were then asked to point out the Liffey on the map of Ireland, and they pointed it out at once, then he asked had they not sometimes been on one of the bridges in Dublin and had they not seen the Liffey there, and they said so, and when he asked them what they had seen, they said "the river." You are not surprised at that?—I could quite understand that from the ordinary teaching of geography.

25470. I tell you that we found the very same thing in a certain place in England?—I am very glad to hear it.

be recognised in the schools, and that, being recognised in the schools, they ought to be prepared for in the training colleges?—Certainly.

25474. There is, it seems to me, there is a slight inconsistency in what you say; correct me if I am wrong. You began, I think, by objecting that there was not a sufficient number of subjects for examination in the training colleges, now this recommendation seems to go towards introducing an examination in other subjects; is that so?—Geography is a subject, grammar is a subject and drill and calisthenics would be so much a habit that an experienced inspector would see in two minutes whether it was done.

25475. But that would be of no use unless it was followed up by something in the way of regulating the grant?—No use, certainly.

25476. Then do you think that these things should be taken into account in regulating the grant?—Yes.

25477. Take geography, for instance, you would require, in addition to all the things required at present, or at all events in addition to some of them, that the children should be taught the topography of their own locality?—I think I was careful to imply that I would not care how little they knew about such matters as rivers in Asia or in Europe, or even almost the rivers of England, except in a general way.

25478. What you mean then is that they would get a real grasp of the meaning of geographical terms if they began by having those terms applied to places and things that they were seeing every day of their lives?—That is my view.

25479. You also think that the inspectors ought to be more in touch with the schools, and, of course, I quite agree with you, but do you think it is physically possible for the inspectors at present to be really in touch with any school in the country, seeing that so much of their time is taken up with all the routine work they have to do over the details of the results system as we have it, at its present form?—Your Grace is touching on a subject I did not touch on, but on which I am quite prepared to answer. It was in the training colleges I said the inspector ought to know what is going on.

25480. But I would ask whether in the present state of affairs you think it possible for the inspectors to be in touch either with the schools or colleges?—I don't think it is.

25481. You regard this as one of the evils of the results system in its present form?—Yes.

25482. We heard yesterday from an ex-inspector that when he first became an inspector, he visited, and was obliged to visit, every school in his district three or four times a year, and when he was asked what he did on those occasions, he said he conferred with the teachers, observing their method of teaching and made suggestions and so on; you regard all that, I am sure, as very important?—Yes.

25483. But unfortunately it is work that can hardly be done at present, indeed I may say that cannot possibly be done at present, owing to the way in which the time of the inspectors is occupied, with making out figures about the answering of the pupils in connection with the results examinations?—That is so.

25484. Now in reference to drawing: in the examination in drawing, you say, the teachers are merely tested as to whether they can draw, and not at all as to whether they can teach drawing?—That is so.

25485. The blackboard, I think you said, is not used in the teaching of drawing?—I did not say that, your Grace. I said I did not think the blackboard was ever used in examining in drawing.

25486. Then it is used in the classroom in the teaching of drawing?—Certainly.

25487. You consider that it ought to be used also in the examination in drawing. Is there, so far as you know, any test required by the Board of National Education—any test that would ascertain whether the candidate knows how to teach drawing?—Nothing that I know of, your Grace, in the examinations.

25488. I am not speaking now of voluntary tests. I understand from some questions I have heard put here, that any teacher who wishes can give in the subject of drawing as one of the three extra honours that he is prepared to submit himself to the inspectors to be tested on; but that is voluntary. He needn't not put that subject in at all if he does not like?—No.

25489. Therefore there is really no test, in the proper sense of the word, imposed by the National Education Board to ascertain whether a person, whom the Board is going to certify as a teacher of drawing, can teach drawing at all?—No test.

25490. The Board gives certificates of capacity to teach drawing without doing anything to ascertain whether the person whom it is going to certify has any capacity whatever to teach drawing; that obviously is a great defect?—I think it is.

25491. Now as to another subject, handicraft; in handicraft your difficulty is that the present programme or syllabus of the National Education Board is not, I think you said, sympathetic?—I quoted that as an illustration of why the present handicraft instruction, such as it is, and as we try to work it, is not educational in the sense in which the phrase is used with reference to manual training in England.

25492. I don't quite like the word sympathetic; it is apt to convey an idea which I don't think you meant at all to convey; I am sure you do not think of suggesting that there is want of sympathy with those very remarkable views of yours at the Board of National Education?—Certainly I did not mean to convey that.

25493. You mean that the present programme of the Board is not really educational?—Yes.

25494. It is worked practically without a connection with drawing, which is an obvious radical defect; the whole object appears to be industrial rather than educational?—Yes.

25495. You are acquainted, I assume, with the Sloyd system?—Yes.

25496. I suppose you would say that the present handicraft programme of the National Education Board has no connection whatever with Sloyd, and in fact no relation to it?—None whatever.

25497. I need hardly ask you which of the two do you think the more appropriate in a school?—The Sloyd, beyond all question.

25498. You speak of the Sloyd, I take it, only in a general way?—Yes, I have seen it taught and know the principles.

25499. It is capable of adaptation to the needs of different countries; you don't of course mean exclusively Swedish Sloyd as worked in Sweden?—No.

25500. But you mean a system of woodwork constructed on really educational lines, as the Swedish Sloyd system undoubtedly is, and as the variously constructed system of the National Education Board undoubtedly is not?—Yes.

25501. As to the special work of the training colleges. You were asked by Lord Belmore about the time that is given to each of the two branches of work of the training college, that is, on the one hand, the teaching of certain subjects to the students, and, on the other, the training of the students in the art of teaching; you said, I think, that you could not exactly define the amount of time given to each?—I said I could give the principles upon which we work.

25502. Don't you think that the whole system embodied in the programme of the National Education Board obliges you to give an undue amount of time to the work of teaching the students, as distinct from the work of training them in the art of teaching?—Beyond question.

Dublin.
[illegible]
Rev. H. Kingsmill Moore, M.A.

Dublin.
Nov. 22, 1897.
Rev. H. Kingsmill Moore, M.A.

25503. And don't you think that the whole system, as it exists in all the training colleges, taking years of course only as a specimen, is calculated to put before the students in these colleges a wrong idea of the function of a training college, to suggest, I mean, that the college is a place to which students come to be prepared for passing examinations, examinations by passing which they can improve their classification, and so get a better salary?—I think the system has that tendency, but if I may speak for my own college there is nothing they are told there so often as that mere examination work is not the object of the college.

25504. Still the system is such that it is put upon the college to make a special effort to counteract what is undoubtedly the natural result of the system itself?—Yes.

25505. But as all this is, we have to remember for our comfort, if it is any comfort to us, that in this respect the programmes in other countries labour under exactly the same defects; the programme in the English and Scotch training colleges, I have been assured by inspectors of great experience in England and Scotland, raises exactly the same difficulty that we complain of here?—That is so, I think, to perhaps a lesser extent; but it is so.

25506. At all events you recognise, I am sure, that the Commissioners of National Education deserve some credit for moving of their own accord in all this matter with a view to ascertain the defects of the existing system?—I should be very sorry to appear as an unfriendly critic of the Commissioners of National Education.

25507. You recognise that the National Education Board of the present day has a thoroughly open mind on all these subjects, and we, the members of this Commission, such of us as are also members of the Board, have come here for the one purpose of getting every useful suggestion that persons of experience such as you can give us?—Undoubtedly.

25508. As to the results system, you said that you had to work to a certain extent under it in the training college, but not in its pecuniary aspect—that you only suffer in prestige?—We suffer in prestige, of course, if we don't pass our students.

25509. But there is no reason why you should not pass your students any more than the people in other training colleges: if the cause of failure is that there is anything wrong in the programme, then it tells all round, and if everybody suffers all round there is no particular loss of prestige anywhere?—I am not complaining as compared with the other colleges.

25510. But there is point in your complaint: all the training colleges may suffer in the eyes of untrained teachers. If they see the students failing, they will think it is because the colleges are not what they ought to be?—Certainly.

25511. But as to the results system, have you not to work under it in the training colleges, even in its pecuniary aspect?—To some extent, yes.

25512. I should certainly think so, and hence I was surprised at your limiting it to a question of prestige: there is a bonus given to the college on condition that the trained teacher who goes out from it subsequently fulfils a number of requirements—he has to satisfy all the tests of the National Education Board that he has taught satisfactorily for two years?—Yes, £14 and £20.

25513. No matter how well the training college has done its work, still if the teacher does not actually fulfil those conditions, the training college does not get the money it has done its best to earn?—No.

25514. Just as if an eminent doctor had done his best for a patient, but was to get no fee because the patient was not perfectly cured: that, as we know, is the aspect of the results system in the schools that is so generally complained of by the teachers: they say that when they do their work, and do it honestly and thoroughly, so far as in them lies, they ought to get paid for it?—Yes, your Grace.

25515. We know, of course, we cannot but that the bonus to be paid to the training college may be calculated on the principle that it is impossible that every candidate going out from the college should comply with the prescribed conditions, so that the bonus should be fixed at such a figure as will secure the college getting what it is entitled to, allowance being made in the computation for the fair average percentage of failures?—That is so.

25516. And it is quite possible that the bonus is really struck at the particular figure at which it stands, in order to make all due payments to the college for doing its work as well as a college can be expected to do it, allowing for the usual inevitable percentage of failures: if this is really so, and, for all I know, it may be, the college in the net result would get all it ought to get?—That is really the reason I said we should not suffer pecuniarily.

25517. Possibly it is so: so that if, instead of a bonus on the successful students, an extra payment was to be made for every student, in addition to the £50 a year now paid, then the extra payment would have to be struck at a lower figure than at present?—Yes.

25518. Perhaps that may be the correct view, and, if so, it may possibly apply to the case of the teachers and their results fees as well. Still it has the look of a hardship about it. I suppose we cannot clear it up. There is just one other matter. You have given us some very valuable criticisms about the new programme of the National Education Board for the examination of teachers and of students of training colleges, but, let me ask you, comparing the new programme with the old, which would you prefer?—The new programme certainly, as a whole, and on its merits.

25519. The Commissioners of National Education, as I think you know, took considerable pains to ascertain the view of the heads of the training colleges and of other persons interested in this matter, before they drew up this new programme: did they not?—Yes, your Grace.

25520. May I ask you then did you, when you were consulted on the new programme, make the suggestions that you are making now?—I thought that that question might come up, and I took some pains to see where the difference lay. We made suggestions, but of course they were only suggestions, and we were not finally consulted as to the programme.

25521. I take it that this is how the case stands: from the practical working out of the programme you have come to see these defects that you have told us about, and it is quite possible that the National Education Board itself did not foresee all the consequences that you say have resulted in practice; you did not foresee them, and perhaps some of us did not foresee them either?—Yes.

25522. My reason for asking these questions is that in an official report since published we were told:—"The Commissioners' new programme for teachers has been favourably received by the colleges, and all the Queen's Scholars who have entered this year for a two years' course are now studying according to the new programme"?—That is so; we were very much pleased with the new programme as a whole.

25523. But you have found out in the course of actual working that there are some drawbacks?—I don't wish to convey either that all the suggestions we made were adopted, or that the non-adoption of them has led to this difficulty. There was mensuration, for instance.

25524. In the old programme, geometry and mensuration formed a combined subject, failure in which combined subject would be fatal to the chance of the candidate passing?—That is so.

Dublin.
Nov. [illegible]
Rev. H. Kingsmill Moore, M.A.

25625. But if a candidate got sufficient marks in geometry to amount to 30 per cent. of the whole number assigned to both geometry and mensuration, combined, then the candidate would pass?—That is so.

25626. And this, even if he answered nothing in mensuration?—Yes.

25627. But under the new programme, as it at present stands, he must get 30 per cent. of the marks assigned to geometry, and also 30 per cent. of those assigned to mensuration, failure to secure both these percentages being fatal to him?—That is so.

25628. In reference to drawing, you advocate the making of it compulsory?—Yes.

25629. You say that elementary science also should be made compulsory, but you recommend this to be done only as soon as certain preliminaries have been arranged; of drawing you say that it ought to be made compulsory apparently at once; you intended to make that distinction?—Yes, I did.

25630. And do you think that drawing can be made compulsory without waiting for preliminary arrangements; if so, who is to teach it?—I thought of that in drawing up my suggestions; it would depend on the way in which the Commissioners expected the drawing to be done at first; anything of that kind introduced for the first time should be treated very gently.

25631. To use your own word, treated sympathetically?—Yes. There is a saying, which is a very old one, I find in a report of one of the inspectors of Kildare-place in 1820, that everybody who can be taught to write can be taught to draw.

25632. We were told yesterday by a person of a good deal of experience that anyone who is fit to be a teacher at all is really capable of teaching drawing for elementary purposes?—I think that is the case for elementary purposes.

25633. Of course, it could not be introduced in the higher classes without some steps being taken to secure the competence of the teachers; don't you think it would be advisable all round that the teachers should not be, as it were, let loose on this subject of drawing without some means being first taken to enable them to qualify themselves?—I think that would be advisable.

25634. You are aware that the way some teachers at present teach it, according to the information before us, is that they simply give out a number of copies to the children, and set the children to copy them,—that sort of thing might go on to a large extent if the subject were made compulsory; hence I think it would be well, and I trust you will agree with me, that, in the first instance, something should be done to show them how to teach?—Certainly, I do.

25635. Have you thought how that could be done?—I have read the different evidence given. I think there are a great many ways in which it could be done; first of all, a very simple treatise on the subject would be a very great help to start with.

25636. It would be better than nothing?—Yes; secondly, very simple requirements laid down clearly, with definite instructions to the inspectors what they are to ask for; then, of course, there are all those valuable suggestions about gathering teachers together for lectures—those are more difficult.

25637. Don't you think it would be well to instruct the inspectors in the beginning that what they had to look to was not to mark the drawing done by the pupils so the method of teaching adopted by the teachers?—That would be most important.

25638. And in that way an inspector observing a defect could give some useful suggestions to the teacher?—Certainly.

25639. School gardens you spoke of with approval; I think you spoke of the special difficulty of schools in towns—that they cannot always have gardens?—It would be more difficult for them.

25640. Someone suggested to us that window gardening could be introduced?—It could; we have it at Kildare-place, in spite of a chimney that sends its smoke.

25641. So that in places where a school garden was not available, some use could be made of a window garden?—Yes.

25642. And I believe that even school gardening can be worked out on a very small plot of ground?—Certainly.

25643. I don't know whether you read the evidence that we had here about the Benlissane school?—No; I did not.

25644. As regards agriculture in the full sense of the word, you don't contemplate, I suppose, that the National Education Board should undertake to teach boys how to farm?—No; I do not.

25645. Any more than we should teach boys in towns how to become carpenters, or tailors, or shoemakers?—No.

25646. But suppose you consider that the scientific principles should be taught that underlie agricultural operations?—Those would be most important.

25647. And then, as far as possible, experiments in connection with those principles should come in?—I don't see how those could come into ordinary schools myself; but if made possible, they would be very valuable.

25648. But supposing that some simple experiments could be made?—Yes.

25649. We have had suggestions about the forming of collections of natural objects; what do you think of that?—I think it ought to be encouraged in every school.

25650. Especially if those collections were made by the pupils themselves?—Yes.

25651. It was suggested that it would be a useful thing to introduce some system of experiments, perhaps, in connection with gardening, with a view of getting the notion out of the minds of a large section of the population of this country the idea that people are to go on doing certain things simply because their fathers and grandfathers had done them before them?—Yes.

25652. I understand that this idea unfortunately prevails to a large extent in some of the agricultural districts of Ireland?—Yes.

25653. Don't you think that introducing some little experimental work in connection with gardening would do something to eradicate that idea?—I think so.

25654. And those experiments could easily be made in connection with horticulture?—Possibly.

25655. Here again, your object in dealing with horticulture would not be to train the boys to become gardeners as a profession?—Certainly not.

25656. Has it ever occurred to you as a means of getting over the difficulty of the outfit for the instruction in woodwork, that a system of centres might be conveniently adopted. Let us suppose that in this neighbourhood, for instance, where we are now met, some convenient place could be found, not far from your Kildare-place schools, not far from the Rev. Mr. Robinson's new school in Westland-row, and not far from Father Murphy's new school in Brunswick-street, and that, for a couple of hours, once a week, that centre might be used by the pupils from one or other of these different schools—would not a plan like that help us in getting over the cost of providing the necessary plant for a number of schools; it is a plan that we found working very well in London?—I know it is done, and I don't see any reason why it should not work here; I have often heard it discussed, and the question argued at different educational boards, but it has not come to anything.

25657. You don't think it would interfere in any way with the denominational distinction of our Dublin schools?—I don't see any reason why it should.

Dublin.
Jan. [illegible]
Rev. E. [illegible] [illegible], M.A.

25558. You made some reference to the difficulties of the new programme of the National Education Board as experienced by the students of your college this year at the examinations, but I was glad to hear you say that certain important concessions were afterwards made by the National Education Board, particularly glad for I was not there myself, so that even if they were not sympathetic on the occasion I should not have come in for any of the blame?—The Commissioners always are very sympathetic.

25559. Mr. Redington.—In reference to your criticism of the new programme, I should like to ask you whether some of the subjects that have been introduced into it meet with your approval; do you approve of reading being included as one of the subjects that carry marks?—Certainly.

25560. You are aware that was not the case formerly?—Yes.

25561. In the same way penmanship; do you think that ought to count?—It certainly ought to count.

25562. You are aware it does count in the English programme?—I know it does.

25563. As regards those two subjects, I wish to point out that making them carry marks is certainly an advantage to the teachers?—Yes, we take no objection to that. When I said seventeen subjects I summed up all that were there.

25564. Yes, but perhaps it gives a false impression, two of these subjects not being very difficult. Then there are marks for English composition?—I strongly approve of it.

25565. I suppose you think the course of English literature is better than the old subject "lesson books"?—There is no question about that.

25566. Also that giving marks for a practical test in teaching is an improvement?—It is, perhaps, the best feature in the whole programme.

25567. I take it that what you object to is that so many of the mathematical subjects are compulsory—algebra, geometry, and mensuration?—That and the fact that arithmetic is required in the second year; we, I think, were rather in favour of the mathematical programme as it is, provided arithmetic might be omitted the second year.

25568. Do I understand that the suggestion you would make is that algebra, geometry, and mensuration should not be compulsory subjects?—Yes, I think that would be a very great relief.

25569. What do you think of book-keeping; would you make that optional too?—Book-keeping is a subject of which I know little, but it seems to me unwise to make it compulsory.

25570. Then we come to the question of geography and agriculture; geography does not occur among the compulsory subjects in England; do you think it might be dropped?—After the first year I think the new programme does allow us to drop it, and we like that very much, but I should not like to drop it altogether.

25571. In order to reduce the seventeen you must drop some subject?—It is not necessary, I think, to drop a subject altogether; it is one thing to drop a subject and another to make a student fail if he gets under 20 per cent. marks.

25572. I mean to make it cease to be compulsory?—Could there not be another plan, which I think is the English plan—take the subject of drawing, which we approve of being made compulsory, but it be a requirement that candidates shall get 50 per cent. in the whole examination, yet, although they may fall below 20 per cent. in drawing, or in some difficult subject, still let them go through their examination as a whole; that is the English system.

25573. You compel them to take it up, but you do not make failure in it entail loss of the examination?—Yes.

25574. Is that what you would suggest as regards these mathematical subjects?—Yes.

25575. As regards agriculture, would you still have it a compulsory subject or omit it altogether?—I should be sorry to see it dropped, I would like the method of examination altered.

25576. Then I take it your idea is to make a failure in only a certain number of subjects fatal?—That is my view.

25577. That applies, I suppose, to the examination when your students are leaving college, or would it also apply to the entrance examination?—Not to the entrance, for of course when candidates are coming up to the college it is a fair time to reject those who are not qualified; but when they have been admitted after an entrance examination which is a real test, nobody has much right to complain of failures; and I don't think we should complain except for the startling figure of the failures last year as compared with fourteen in all the previous years.

25578. I take it that as long as geography is compulsory in schools, it would be right to exact the minimum knowledge of it from every teacher who gets classification, therefore it must remain in scheme I?—Yes.

25579. I think I am right in saying that some of the subjects in the English Training College course, include two of our subjects—does not "English" in the English code mean what we call grammar and literature combined?—English composition is a separate subject.

25580. In the first year's syllabus "English" includes "general knowledge of the history and grammatical structure of the language," and also "an intelligent acquaintance with the language, style and subject matter of a 'Selection from Tennyson,' and Addison's Sir Roger de Coverley." That would cover grammar and literature. In the second year it is "an intelligent acquaintance with the language, style and subject matter of Tennyson's 'The Coming of Arthur' and 'The Passing of Arthur,' &c., &c."—that would also include grammar and literature?—It ought to be made to do so.

25581. Monsignor Molloy.—I find in your prospectus that you have a professor of experimental physics in the training college in Kildare-place?—That subject has disappeared with the new programme.

25582. But you have a professor?—He has disappeared also.

25583. So the new programme has not only killed science but killed the professor. The new programme came in and experimental physics went out, and with experimental physics the professor disappeared?—Yes.

25584. You are in favour of teaching the elements of physical science in primary schools?—Yes.

25585. Would you agree with me in saying that the teaching should be more simple and elementary?—Oh, certainly.

25586. That is to say, it should consist very largely of explanation of common things and of simple scientific principles, and be illustrated with objects and with simple experiments?—Experiments done by the pupils is a very important part of it I should think.

25587. Up to the present, any programme of physical science under which it could be taught in the schools, sets forth a long list and rather a high sounding list of great branches of physical science. I find mechanics, hydrostatics, pneumatics, light, sound, heat and the steam engine, physical geography, magnetism and electricity, inorganic chemistry. Now does it seem to you that that is the sort of programme under which such a course as you think desirable in primary schools could be most efficiently taught?—Certainly not, but Course H in the English course seems to me a workable programme.

Dublin. Jan. 12, 1898. Rev. [illegible] Marsh, M.A.

25589. Would you agree with me then in saying that a much better method would be to draw up an outline of the common things to be explained, and the simple principles of science that are to be illustrated, and set that before the teachers as what they are to teach in the primary schools?—That, I think, would be the right way to do it.

25590. Provided always that that syllabus would be a sympathetic syllabus?—Yes.

25591. Now in order to introduce the subject of physical science into primary schools, you say certain preliminaries would be necessary, and one of these preliminaries would, I suppose, be that these subjects should be taught in the training colleges?—Yes.

25592. Which might lead to, perhaps, a revival of the professors of that subject. Would you think also that the course taught in the training college should be framed with a view to what the teachers have to teach afterwards in the schools?—Certainly, but I don't know that it should be limited to it.

25593. But you agree it should be framed with a view to that. You think it ought not to be strictly limited to it?—The teacher wants to know something more than he has to teach.

25594. A teacher should know his subject more thoroughly and widely than a pupil is expected to know it?—Yes.

25595. And therefore, while the course taught in the training colleges should be framed with a view to the programme of the primary schools, it should be wider and deeper?—Yes.

25596. And the course should be compulsory?—Yes.

25597. Because if it is not compulsory in the training colleges, it cannot be possible in the primary schools?—Certainly, it should be compulsory in the training colleges.

25598. Mr. Molloy.—I notice by the last published report of the Commissioners that you had thirty-four men and sixty-one women in the training session of 1896–98. How can you account for the disproportion between men and women, is it that you had not accommodation for the men?—There are two ways of accounting for it—one is that we have always until this year found a difficulty in getting men. We got sufficient male candidates this year for the first time. We had qualified male candidates, twice as many as we required. We always had enough male candidates for the July examinations, that is to say, they came up, but they did not come up sufficiently well prepared to pass.

25599. What course do you adopt in order to get candidates?—We have to advertise in all the papers and circulate our report ourselves. We have addressed all the clergy of our church.

25600. Do the Board's inspectors, upwards of sixty in number, cooperate in securing candidates for your college as they do for Marlborough-street?—Certainly not, the officials to some extent—this relates rather to former years, when our work was not so well known—discouraged students from coming to Kildare-place. That has now disappeared, and I am glad to say the contrary is now just as often the case.

25601. Most Rev. Dr. Walsh.—They have become more sympathetic?—More sympathetic.

25602. Mr. Molloy.—In connection with Marlborough-street College the inspectors are called upon to fill up a form expressing an opinion of the candidates; is there any form similar to that in operation in the interests of your college or any other college except Marlborough-street?—None that I know of.

25603. So that in that respect, although the colleges are everywhere on an equality, there is an advantage of one college over the others?—Certainly.

25604. And that leads to the necessity of expensive advertising on your part, and communication with the clergy throughout the country, with a view to securing candidates?—Yes.

25605. Looking to your College staff, as published in the last report of the Commissioners, I don't observe any training assistants, have you such an office?—No, we have no training assistants, so-called. We have one master of method, who is master of the boys' school, and then the mistresses of the girls' school and infant school work in connection with him, and in addition we have a lady superintendent, who also works in connection with him—they assist in training.

25606. They have all that in Marlborough-street College, and over and above that they have specialists called training assistants, who assist the students in training in the course of their studies in the evening, looking after them during the daytime in a general way. You have not got officers of that kind?—We have not.

25607. There is a pretty large staff of that kind in connection with Marlborough-street College?—I believe there is.

25608. Are there any members of your professoriate pensionable by the Treasury on the termination of their course, or at any time?—Not that I know of.

25609. Has the introduction of a pension ever been thought of? I believe as a matter of fact, in the case of Marlborough-street some members of the professoriate are pensionable?—So I believe.

25610. It was at one time, if I mistake not, under consideration in connection with your college, and indeed, some of the other colleges, to look after the interests of the untrained teachers now in charge of schools of a suitable age?—Yes.

25611. On your side, I believe the number was 167 ascertained to be then in charge of schools who were untrained, and who by age would be regarded as fairly suitable to be brought up for improvement in methods of teaching?—It is a matter of memory with me, but I think it is about that figure.

25612. Would you advocate that course now, that was suggested some two or three years ago?—Yes, I should.

25613. The 167, if I mistake not, were persons generally suitable for training?—Yes.

25614. And training them, even in a short course, would qualify, so to say, nearly all the teachers of your schools throughout the country to rank as trained teachers?—It would.

25615. Would there be any difficulty in carrying out that system in connection with your college?—It could be done, of course it would mean extra work, and giving up vacations and things of that kind. I don't think we could be expected to do it without some additional State aid.

25616. Obviously, not without additional State aid?—It could be done, certainly.

25617. There is no intrinsic difficulty in having it carried out under the supervision of the authorities in your college?—There is none.

25618. You referred to the point that you would be glad to see inspectors visiting your college more frequently. You don't mean merely those inspectors who are officially in charge of the college?—Certainly not, we welcome their visits at all times.

25619. I understand you to mean the general body of inspectors and above all newly-appointed inspectors?—Yes.

25620. I would regard that as a matter of very great importance. They would have an opportunity of conferring with the authorities of the college, seeing the students in training, the reference libraries, the methods of teaching, the museum (such as you have in your college), and being in touch, so to say, with the work done?—We could draw their attention to any special points to which we attached importance and which had not hitherto been recognised.

25621. It would be a sort of mutual education?—Yes.

25622. As a matter of fact, in connection with the early appointment of inspectors under the National Board, that was one of the conditions of the appointment. At that time there was only one normal college, and it was a *sine qua non* that an inspector, on his

Dublin. [illegible]

appointment, and as often as he came to Dublin subsequently, should visit that training college, confer with the professors and heads of the primary schools in connexion with it, and spend some time there?—I know it was the custom in the old Kildare-place society. In 1839–[illegible] the inspectors had to come to the normal schools.

25623. So that harmonises with your suggestion now?—Yes.

25624. And benefit would accrue to the inspectors from it?—And benefit would accrue to the college, too; we should both be helped. They might point out if our plans were difficult to apply; they might modify them from their experience. It would help us all.

25625. You have a system of [illegible] and [illegible] (delineated) in your class course and study halls?—Yes.

25626. Would not that be largely taken into account in the tests applied to the students by the inspectors who examine at the end of the session?—It would come in in this way: very often in the lessons sent up to the inspectors there are allusions to [illegible] and practical things of that kind.

25627. And the fact of having those practically before the students would certainly be appreciated by the inspectors?—I think so; for instance, in a lesson on architecture, if 10 feet or 13 feet was mentioned, they would refer to the room, and so make it a concrete reality.

25628. I see that since the establishment of your college in 1884 up to 1896, as many as 593—close upon 600—Queen's Scholars passed through your college and obtained certificates with a view to teaching?—Yes.

25629. Now, all these, you explain, underwent examination with a view to classification at the end of their course?—Yes.

25630. Do you think so many would have applied for entrance to your college if there were not that object prominently before them at that time?—I am quite certain they would not.

25631. Are you of opinion that the time has come when that might be largely dispensed with, and you might restrict your instruction in the colleges mainly to the art of teaching?—That would be a very radical change. I want to see something in that direction, but I would not be prepared to say without consideration whether we were to go the whole distance or not; certainly we would be better able to do it now when training has been made compulsory. If it was merely a training place, and training was not made compulsory, a very large number of teachers would never dream of coming to it.

25632. Do you think the managers of your schools throughout the country appreciate the training diploma in the art of teaching alone—a certificate that a man has obtained a first-class diploma in teaching as distinct from proficiency in literary subjects?—That has not been made at all a sufficient reality yet. I am always glad, in recommending trained teachers, to call attention to the grade of their diploma, and it has weight that way, but a great deal more importance should be attached to that diploma.

25633. By whom ought steps to be taken to make that diploma better known?—The first thing that is wanted is a little more connexion between the Commissioners and the training college authorities. The rule is that when a student has taught well for two years the diploma is to be issued, provided two satisfactory reports have been given. In England the two satisfactory reports are sometimes issued under two years; in our case they are never issued until two years have passed, and frequently they are not issued until after a number of years—in one case it was only issued after ten years. I don't complain of that if the teaching has not been right; but for the most part we have no complaint from the Commissioners that teachers are not doing good work, so we cannot understand why the diplomas do not come. I have sometimes applied five times without receiving any information as to why they are not issued. It happens very frequently that, in the case of female teachers, the girls know nothing of this blank. They have been teaching for four or five years, and they get married, [illegible] we have no claim upon them. Then I go to the Education Office to make personal inquiries as to the cause of the delay, and there I, perhaps, find for the first time there are four or five unsatisfactory reports.

25634. That delay you complain of would, perhaps, arise from too much sympathy on the part of the Education Office with the training college—not wishing to convey the unwelcome intelligence that your candidate had failed, and wishing, perhaps, to give a further chance?—I think it has arisen largely from kindly motives, but I don't see why the fact of their telling us that someone was in danger might not help that teacher to get on finally, for, naturally, from the patronage that comes to the head of a training college his communication to a teacher would have a stimulating effect.

25635. Do you think it would help you if a report was made from the office to you on these teachers, just as it is sent to the managers?—Yes, it would help us greatly.

25636. Or we might allow you to see the reports?—It would be quite enough for my purpose if we were told that such and such a teacher's report was not satisfactory.

25637. What year did you introduce the instruction in manual work? I think you called it carpentry, straight off?—It is carpentry. In 1887–88.

25638. What teacher did you employ for that?—It was a carpenter. We have a very clever carpenter, who does a great deal of work for us. He is a man quite out of the common with regard to his creative capacities and skill as an artisan; he is a builder and contractor.

25639. In that manual instruction course is drawing taught to scale?—No; it is mere carpentry.

25640. Now, with regard to the museum that I have often seen in your practising school, the pupils, I believe, collect the objects?—Yes. The master, Mr. Hanley, is the guiding spirit, and the pupils bring in the specimens.

25641. Does he take them out into the country and let them pick up anything of a special kind?—He does that occasionally.

25642. Rev. Dr. Evans.—In the earlier part of your evidence did you intend to convey that the Board of Education has no test of the ability of Queen's Scholars to teach drawing, as distinguished from their knowledge of drawing?—Yes. So far as I am aware, all that is asked of the teachers is to copy either a model or a drawing from the flat.

25643. But it is your opinion that they make no test of the abilities of the Queen's Scholars to teach drawing, as distinguished from their knowledge of drawing?—That is my opinion.

25644. Does the Board of Education make any distinction of the same kind in regard to any other subject—that is to say, has it a test of the ability of the Queen's Scholars to teach arithmetic, as distinguished from the test of the knowledge of arithmetic?—I should think that the introduction of theoretical questions would tend in that direction, but more might be done all along the subjects with advantage.

25645. Is there a single case in which the Board tests the ability of the candidate to teach, as distinguished from testing the knowledge of the subject?—I don't think there is any case in which that is distinguished, but there are papers—as, for instance, the theoretical part of arithmetic—in which the idea comes in, but, as I said, not sufficiently. Of course there is inspection by the inspectors, which is the most valuable part of the system, but I take it you are questioning solely with reference to the paper work.

25646. Now, in regard to practical tests, does th[e]

Dublin.
Dec. 12, 1897.
Rev. H. [illegible] Henry, M.A.

Board require Queen's Scholars to go through practical tests in providing schools?—Yes.

25647. Has the Board anywhere excluded drawing from these tests? Nowhere.

25648. Therefore it does not follow that drawing is in any exceptional way at a disadvantage?—No, I did not mean to convey that it was.

25649. Then you must mean that you want to see something more done for drawing than for any other subject?—Yes, I think so, on account of the comparative absence of drawing from the schools, the subject has been neglected very largely, and if it is to be made compulsory, you require to draw the teacher's attention pointedly to the way way he is to teach it.

25650. In the admission of Queen's Scholars to the training college, have you ever found any difficulty in getting candidates who were competent in drawing at that stage?—We have always found a difficulty.

25651. Have you ever rejected anyone because there seemed to be an inability to learn the subject of drawing?—No, because we had hitherto no means of testing; but I may mention that although drawing is optional in the new programme, in colleges 1, we have this year at Kildare-place, made it compulsory for female students, that, of course, will give us an opportunity of rejecting them.

25652. I am glad to hear you are in favour of introducing elementary science into the schools; if elementary science is to be introduced into the schools, does it not follow that it must be taught in the training colleges?—Certainly.

25653. And if it follows that it must be taught in the training colleges, then the training colleges must be teaching places?—I have been careful, I hope all along, to say that the training colleges must be teaching places, teaching a subject, and teaching how to teach it, there is no opposition between these positions.

25654. I agree, but we cannot ever, I suppose, hope to eliminate the teaching of subjects from the training colleges, and restrict these institutions entirely to the task of teaching how to teach?—I don't see how it is to be done. I was asked the question as to whether I would be in favour altogether of giving up the examination of teachers in connection with the training colleges for classes, and I said I could not see my way to such a radical change as that; the line of thought of your question suggested that answer.

25655. You always have a larger number of female candidates?—Yes, but we have now as many male candidates as we desire.

25656. Do the clergy throughout the country ever write to you in favour of certain candidates in whom they may be naturally interested?—Almost invariably, in fact we require something of that kind from the clergyman, some testimonial as to character.

25657. Is your training college at any disadvantage because you had not some sort of list of eligible candidates from the inspectors throughout Ireland?—I think there is a certain disadvantage; the inspectors are the officers of the State, and the colleges are colleges of the State, and I think the inspectors ought to be absolutely impartial at any rate.

25658. And you would be in favour in the case of a denominational training college, of having the same practice carried out that was in existence in the undenominational training colleges; I don't wish to be understood as moving in the matter, because we seem to be pretty right about the male candidates now?—Perhaps if I was asked the question five or ten years ago, I would say yes, and as a matter of equality, I think it would be right, but I don't wish to be understood now as complaining.

25659. Rev. Dr. Whelan.—You prefer, I think I have heard you say, the new programme to the old one?—Yes.

25660. Were you under the old programme from 1884 to 1896?—Yes.

25661. And during that time you had only fourteen failures out of some thousand students?—Yes.

25662. In 1897 you have had ten failures out of 115 students?—Yes.

25663. How is it you failed more on your own preferred programme than on the old one?—That question is very easily answered, but it is rather a long subject to go over; the mathematical papers this time, in which the chief failures occurred, were supposed to be given to a second class, and they were really first class papers, this we are prepared to prove; it is a very simple proof and does not involve any knowledge of mathematics, because questions on the B new paper were, in many cases, identical with questions on the old A paper, and questions on the C paper were identical with the old B, so that there was an increase of the standard in mathematics, for which we were not prepared, and could not be prepared.

25664. So that such a large proportion of failures may not occur again, what remedy would you suggest?—There is one practical remedy, that is a return to the old system of setting papers in former years. In former years half the questions were easy and half the questions were difficult; this year for the first time, all the questions were made of equal difficulty. The old plan seemed to me the proper one; for a student who was weak upon a subject, would take up the easy questions and get low marks, it is true, but still qualifying marks. The removal of that condition has been disastrous.

25665. You complain that our inspectors have not visited your training colleges often enough?—I don't make that particular complaint, it is a suggestion for the improvement of our work.

25666. What practical benefit would you expect to derive from their more frequent visits?—The advantage which we would derive would be a knowledge of how our teachers were working in their district. On the occasion of the July examinations, the Board send certain inspectors to superintend the examinations, and it is always a great pleasure to me to hear how the teachers from Kildare-place are doing. That would be one of the advantages of the colleges being in touch with the inspectors. If we found they were failing in certain lines we should consider the question, and try to do all we could to anticipate such failure.

25667. Is not the National system of education an undenominational system?—Theoretically.

25668. And is not yours a denominational college?—Yes.

25669. What claim have you on the visits of an inspector at all?—I am not making any claim.

25670. Then if we were consistent as a Board, we would not send them to you?—I suppose if you were consistent you would not have a denominational college.

25671. Dr. Evans has stated you should get the same advantage as any other college, I don't think so, as long as your Church maintains a denominational college. I don't think you have the same claim on our inspectors as an undenominational college, what have you to say to that?—I say the Government appears to think otherwise. In Mr. Balfour's letter, the duty of putting colleges on an equality was fully recognised, and we could take our stand upon the way in which the Government administers the system apart from any theories; but I should be sorry that my remark in reference to the inspectors was spoken of as a claim; I suppose it would be a great deal more trouble to me as an individual if they did come there. I should be glad to see them, but it would take up a good deal of my time, nevertheless for the good of the education of the country, I would welcome their presence; the connection between our college and Drumcondra and Baggot-street with the inspectors, would greatly help education in the country.

25672. Most Rev. Dr. Walsh.—You wish to have

some communication from the National Board in reference to the teaching of your former pupils after they have gone out as teachers?—In cases where they are not supposed to be teaching well.

25673. Would it meet your views if there was a report each year, for a certain number of years, stating whether or not the teacher's work for the year in question was satisfactory, in the cases in which the Board has to satisfy itself that the work is satisfactory before assenting to it for the granting of the training diploma to the teacher, or for the payment of the bonus to the training college?—Certainly.

25674. There must be two years' satisfactory teaching in order to entitle the teacher to the diploma and the college to the bonus; a report coming to you for a certain number of years stating whether the year's work of the teacher was in that sense satisfactory, would satisfy you?—Yes.

25675. You seem to think it is a hardship that there are so many subjects in our programme, failure in any of which would disqualify a student at a teacher for passing; would you approve of an arrangement in which failure to pass in certain subjects could be made up for by some superior merit in others?—Yes.

25676. So that if a student failed in one or two subjects, a certain amount of failure could be made up for by a certain amount of superior answering in others?—Yes.

25677. I find that since the introduction of the new programme experimental physics has disappeared from Kildare-place, as it has disappeared from other training colleges; in Kildare-place what subject has been taken up in place of it?—The men take trigonometry.

25678. Whatever may be wrong in this, how is the defect to be ascribed to the new programme; the new programme gives an option between these two subjects, and gives precisely the same number of marks to each; why did the people who had previously been teaching experimental physics give it up and take to teaching trigonometry?—The scheme laid down here is wholly and entirely out of the question.

25679. So that if they exercised their option of taking experimental science instead of trigonometry, they should do so at a considerable risk of their failing?—Failure would be absolutely certain.

Mr. Alfred Purser, Head Inspector of National Schools, further examined.

25682. Chairman.—You are one of the Head Inspectors of National schools?—Yes.

25683. You were examined at considerable length on the subject of our inquiry?—Yes.

25684. On looking at your paper I see that you give some general suggestions and also some special suggestions about manual training. First of all, with regard to manual training, it is your opinion that it would be well to require all colleges to provide facilities for the Queen's Scholars to obtain practical knowledge of hand and eye training?—Yes, I think it would. I think in the practising schools the Queen's Scholars should have an opportunity of seeing kindergarten carried on, in all the practising schools, not only those for women, but for men also.

25685. Further, you would encourage the introduction into all schools in the country, outside the ordinary school hours, by a grant of additional salary?—Yes.

25686. Does that apply only to such things as Sloyd and woodwork, or does it apply to cardboard work?—It would apply to cardboard work as well.

25687. You think that that could not be introduced into the ordinary school hours?—Not very conveniently, I think; if we have only one or two teachers in a school it would be very hard to introduce it.

25688. You are not in favour of tying teachers strictly down to the programme?—No, I would lay down general principles they were to follow, and let them draw up their own programme, which, of course, should be submitted and approved of.

25689. What is your opinion about garden plots?—I think there is very often land round a school that might be utilised to some extent for that purpose. The ground in the first instance was probably given for a playground, and therefore they are not allowed to use it for any other purpose, but certain parts of the ground might yet be used for garden beds—it would not be agriculture, but floriculture, or a basic horti-

should be the explanation of the common phenomena which children observe every day of their lives.

25694. That is, it should be of a general rather than a particular character; you are aware that one result of the introduction of the new programme has been that the teaching of physical science has been dropped altogether in the training colleges?—Yes, practically it has.

25695. Do you not look upon that as an unfortunate result?—Most unfortunate.

25696. What remedy do you suggest?—I think it should be a compulsory subject.

25697. But our programme has been already criticised on the ground that we have too many compulsory subjects?—You should have not more, I suppose.

25698. Then which subjects should we leave out?—So many are optional in one column and obligatory in another, it is hard to say; and some of the subjects that are put down as separate are not really so—reading, penmanship, spelling, English grammar, and English composition should be grouped.

25699. And you would make failure in the whole group, not failure in each individual branch, a disqualification?—Yes.

25700. Do you think it is fair to require a student to pass in both geometry and mensuration?—I should not as such of a student teacher, but I don't think it is. I think the two should be combined and the geometry should be less Euclid and more practical geometry.

25701. What do you think of the suggestion you have just heard me make to Mr. Kingsmill Moore that something of failure in one subject might be made up for by special merit in others?—Yes, I think failure in some subjects should not disqualify.

25702. Then the subject would cease to be an obligatory subject; a student would think it foolish to take up a subject which it is not necessary for him to pass in?—I would not quite agree with you, if you make it obligatory to teach it in the college he

sum of marks in order to pass; but besides that he must actually pass in a certain number of specified subjects; now, the subjects in which it is not absolutely necessary he should pass will still be most useful to him to obtain the necessary minimum of marks? —Yes.

25706. Most Rev. Dr. Walsh.—You know the principle that was adopted this year by the Commissioners, out of consideration for candidates working for the first time under the new programme, that subjects which in theory were obligatory were not finally treated as obligatory?—I did not know that.

25707. That was the case certainly in drawing?—I was not informed of anything of that sort.

25708. Would it be a desirable permanent arrangement in reference to a subject such as drawing?—I don't see any objection to the falling in a couple of subjects if you have a very large number.

25709. At all events it would be a safeguard to require that a certain amount of failure in some subjects should be made up for by superior excellence in others?—You make that up by requiring them to get a certain percentage.

25710. What I wished to ascertain is whether you would approve of that being done; I take it that you would?—Yes.

25711. I observe that in the programme of the English Education Department there is a partial option given between languages and science, but the arrangements are such that 100 marks are given to the languages and 75 marks are given to the science; do you think a system of that sort would work advantageously in this country. What would the result of it be as regards the subjects taken up?—They would still take up science here.

25712. But they have not taken it up when it came into conflict with trigonometry?—Trigonometry is a science, too.

25713. I am speaking of physical science?—Trigonometry is more easily made up, and a language would take a long time to make up, and most candidates would have nothing of language before coming up.

25714. Do you not think that the examination system largely determines the choice of subjects taken up in the colleges?—Of course it does.

25715. The choice is determined by the requirements of the examination programme rather than by any consideration of the utility of these subjects in school work afterwards?—It is decidedly made entirely by the examination, they must pass their students or they would lose part of their grant and the teachers won't get classification.

25716. Mr. Redington.—If manual work were introduced into a school where there is only one teacher, would it be possible for him to give instruction in it?—During school hours it would be very difficult.

25717. Would you be in favour of some modification of the programme by which fewer classes would be recognised in small schools?—Certainly.

25718. That would give a teacher more time for extra subjects?—I would not care for him to have extra subjects during school hours at all; he would have quite enough to do to teach three or four classes.

25719. Would you consider drawing an extra subject, to be taught outside school hours?—No, I would make it an ordinary subject, to be taught in every school.

25720. Cardboard work or woodwork?—That is an two hours?—Oh, yes, I think it can; a practical lesson in two hours, and then there is a theoretical lesson, one lesson a week for three hours.

25724. Would you be in favour of Saturday being used as a school day?—Certainly, if you can get the children to come in.

25725. Would you recognise it as a school day?—Yes, I see no objection if the roll was called the same as usual.

25726. Most Rev. Dr. Walsh.—But remember that the attendance would be lower, and that would be hard on the teacher?—Yes, I say if you get the children to attend.

25727. Mr. Redington.—From your experience do you think the attendance would be lower?—Certainly, because the people have got out of the habit of attending on Saturday.

25728. What do the children do on Saturdays?—Nothing at all but playing about.

25729. Why should they not go to school?—The teachers don't go to school—they like to have the day, too.

25730. Do you think the standard of the entrance examination for the training colleges should be raised?—I think it should.

25731. That would mean that the standard of classification all through the country would be raised?—Certainly, I think in certain things you ask perhaps too much, but in the way of English you ought to ask more.

25732. You mean English literature and grammar?—I mean composition, too, and reading.

25733. You approve of the change that has been made in the last couple of years in that direction?—I do, but I think it should go further; I think you ask too little.

25734. What would you leave out in case you brought in more English?—That would be hard to say straight off.

25735. You heard the evidence upon our programme that the students at the end of the second year had to take up seventeen subjects?—Yes; that includes five subjects that I would put down as one under the head of English, for instance.

25736. Are there subjects, now compulsory, that you would make optional; what would you think of making algebra optional?—No, I would make it obligatory.

25737. Do you see your way to making any of the seventeen subjects optional?—I think book-keeping might be optional, but I would not mind their failing in a certain number of subjects. I would insist on their passing in certain subjects and allow them to fail in others.

25738. Most Rev. Dr. Walsh.—Something like the English plan?—And the Continental plan, too.

25739. Mr. Redington.—Do you think the number of workmistresses should be increased?—It would depend upon whether you would amalgamate the small schools or not.

25740. Assuming no change is made and workmistresses are only employed where there is a male teacher and a certain number of girls, would you be in favour of reducing the average number of girls that would justify the employment of a workmistress?—I don't think so; I think you give liberal terms at present.

Dublin. Jan. 11, 1898. Mr. Alfred Purser.

Dublin. Nov. 12, 1897. Mr. Alfred Purser.

25782. And when you came to examine a school, if you found the drawing satisfactorily done you would be in favour of a payment to the teachers who produced those results?—I am not in favour of these results payments at all.

25783. Until we get rid of them, which I hope is coming?—I would pay the teacher a fixed salary for doing his work, and that should be part of his work to teach drawing as well as he could.

25784. You think the entrance examination should be raised to a higher grade in the training colleges?—Yes.

25785. You would do that by making a corresponding increase in difficulty in the monitors' examination?—Yes.

25786. Would you bring that to bear at the end of the monitor's work, or from year to year throughout the monitorial course?—Each year from year to year.

25787. Because it is very important, I think, to bring them up to the higher grade from year to year?—That is what I meant.

25788. You would do the same thing with regard to pupil teachers?—Certainly, except that a pupil teacher would in the one year have to make up the full standard, because at the end of the first year they are eligible for admission to the college; you would have to raise the standard of admission as a pupil teacher; no person should become a pupil teacher, as easily as he does at present; the standard for that would have to be slightly raised.

25789. You would also be in favour of increasing the staff in training colleges?—Yes.

25790. Could you indicate how?—You should appoint more professors. Take the Board's own college in Marlborough-street; there are but four professors, and two of them also enjoy the title, I don't know whether it is anything more, of principals. The number of students in training in that college has gone up from 100 to 200, yet there is no corresponding change in the staff.

25791. It is not so easy to lecture fifty as to lecture twenty?—Not so efficiently; you cannot give the same attention to each. At present each of them will have so many to lecture and teach which, I think, is altogether too many. The Commissioners and managers all complain that one teacher for every thirty-five is not enough to give.

25792. You would be in favour of laying more stress at the examination on ability to teach and testing that more?—Yes.

25793. How would you do that?—Instead of asking questions that merely involve mere memory work, the questions the teacher should get should be rather how they would teach certain things; give them a problem in arithmetic, the question should not be "work out the answer to that," but "show us how you would teach a class that."

25794. Rev. Dr. Whitaker.—Do you recommend that female teachers should resign on being married?—Yes.

25795. That has never been our rule; I hope you would not propose a rigid enforcement of that new regulation?—It would be a very desirable thing; it is a general rule in Dublin, I think, at least among Roman Catholic teachers; there is no fixed rule.

25796. Most Rev. Dr. Walsh.—There is no rule, certainly?—No, but there is a general understanding in Dublin that if a female teacher gets married she leaves her school.

25797. Rev. Dr. Whitaker.—I would not be a party to enforcing it?—A married woman is much better employed minding her family.

25798. If she has no family she would be all the better to be employed?—That would be a very exceptional case.

Mr. Samuel E. Stronge, A.B., Head Inspector of National Schools, further examined.

Mr. Samuel E. Stronge, A.B.

25799. Chairman.—You are one of the head inspectors of National Schools, and you have been already examined?—Yes, my lord, at the beginning of the inquiry.

25800. I see by your memorandum that you are in favour of shortening the hours in infant schools and in junior classes in other schools; is that with a view of introducing some form of hand and eye training more generally?—That is to give the opportunity to the teacher of teaching the senior classes afterwards; at present the infant and first and second classes in the school can learn quite as much in three hours as children of that age are capable of taking in.

25801. You think that, irrespective of any question of introducing hand and eye training, it would be in itself an advantage to shorten the hours of the junior classes?—Yes.

25802. And it would be no disadvantage if it was decided that hand and eye training in some form should be introduced, that those hours should be shortened for the junior classes?—Yes, they could do the hand and eye training as well as their ordinary work within the three hours without any detriment.

25803. Do you think that the hours of attendance in the senior classes are long enough at present?—If I shortened the hours of the junior classes I would lengthen the seniors to four and a-half or five hours a day for secular instruction, giving them a half holiday on Saturdays and Wednesdays.

25804. You would have four whole school days and two half school days?—Quite so.

25805. What would you do on the Wednesday and Saturday afternoons?—That I would reserve in the girls' school for cookery and branches of that kind, and in the boys' school for manual training, or if there was no manual training, an extra lesson in drawing.

25806. Would you call that half-holiday work?—Yes.

25807. How long do you think a lesson in drawing should last for the senior classes?—An hour.

25808. And for the junior classes?—From forty to forty-five minutes; you see you lose a great deal of time in giving out the drawing books and pencils if you take only half an hour, and then take them up again; children's hands have not got into the way of using the pencil well when you are calling in the copybooks.

25809. Would you be in favour of continuing the examination in practical subjects in the hands of the present examiners; or would you be in favour of special examiners being appointed for that purpose?—I prefer expert examiners.

25810. Would you go so far as somebody did yesterday, as to say there ought to be lady inspectors of needlework?—It takes an inspector five years practice in the schools before he would know good needlework if he saw it, unless he came into the service with some special qualification on the subject.

25811. Do you think that the present programme ought to be reduced and recast?—That is the present programme for schools. Yes, I think it ought to be.

25812. In what way?—Reduced in the amount, and then recast, that is, by cutting out results altogether.

25813. Most Rev. Dr. Walsh.—In reference to this important point of the system of payment to teachers, you consider that the present system ought to be altered?—Yes, I do.

25814. Do you think that each teacher should have a fixed salary, which should be paid to him to the full amount, neither more or less, irrespective of

[illegible]
particular qualities put

system he [illegible] his choice

d advantage for persons

Dublin.
Nov. 19, 1897.
Mr. Samuel E. [illegible]

25585. Prior to the establishment of the new system of examination—that is, unlimiting candidates by numbers—were you ever called upon to revise teachers' papers?—You don't mean simply first marking and remarking.

25586. Where it was found the teachers failed in certain subjects?—Yes; I have looked through a lot of them.

25587. Was that revision by you of a special character confined exclusively to training college students? Did you ever get papers of ordinary teachers throughout the country?—Only occasionally. The ones from the training college all came up, but it was only some of the country teachers, where a question arose, that were brought. Where a question was raised by the manager, or possibly by the teacher, as to his marks.

25588. Or raised by the Education Office authorities on seeing that a teacher, say, in Kerry failed in grammar, but answered on the whole remarkably well, and scored a high percentage. Would not the paper of such a man be subjected to re-examination as well as if he had been a student in a training college?—Oh, yes.

25589. Rev. Dr. Evans.—You are in favour of employing experts as examiners in art and practical subjects?—Yes.

25590. Is that in the schools?—Yes.

25591. Would you be in favour of the same mode of examining teachers?—Certainly.

25592. For their classification and promotion?—Yes. That is, of course, in the particular subjects—the ones you have mentioned there. I should be in favour always of those being examined by experts.

25593. Have we not on our inspection staff men who are as competent to examine in music as could be found?—That is so, but you don't make those men examine alone in music, you pay a man specially for doing it, Mr. Goodman.

25594. Is no part of that work done by any inspector?—No, you have a specialist there.

25595. Do you know our old fifth class book—the one before the one we recently revised?—Yes, I remember that.

25596. There was a good deal of elementary science in that class book?—I don't remember any science in the old fifth book. It is in the fifth book that Monsignor Molloy's papers were.

25597. There was an old fifth book a good many years ago, full of lessons on scientific subjects?—There was one upon the agriculture of Ireland, industrial resources of Ireland, and so on.

Rev. Dr. Evans.—At all events, I wanted just to have your opinion as to how far it might be suitable for our present purpose if we introduced elementary science.

25598. Rev. Dr. Wilson.—His Grace brought before you the question of payment of teachers. I presume from what you said that you would be in favour of the English and Scotch system of giving teachers a higher salary than they get, and doing away with the results fees?—That is what I would be in favour of.

25599. You think on the whole it would contribute to improve education in Ireland?—Yes, you would get superior work done than at present.

25600. As to the question of shortening the hours for infant and junior classes, I quite agree with you, and I think that should be emphasised. I met a teacher lately who complained that she had to keep her little children too long, and I said to her, as Mr. Molloy suggested, that the manager had power to dismiss them earlier. "Well," she said, "I would be very much afraid to meet the inspector if I had them dismissed." I think it should be emphasised that the teacher or manager have the power to allow infant children to go home early. Do you think it does great harm to the small children's health, and does not contribute to their education?—Certainly, after one o'clock in the day children under seven or eight years of age will learn very little. They are tired out with the heat of the schoolroom and the work they have done, and they are restless and disturb the other classes.

Nov. 19, 1897.

FIFTY-FIFTH PUBLIC SITTING.—FRIDAY, NOVEMBER 19, 1897,

AT 2 O'CLOCK, P.M.,

At the Antient Concert Rooms, Dublin.

Present:—His Grace the Most Rev. William J. Walsh, D.D., in the Chair; The Right Hon. C. Palles, LL.D., Lord Chief Baron of the Exchequer; The Right Hon. O. T. Redington, M.A.; His Honor Judge Shaw, Q.C., LL.D.; The Right Rev. Monsignor Molloy, D.D., D.Sc.; Rev. Henry Evans, D.D.; Rev. Hamilton Wilson, D.D.; Professor G. F. FitzGerald, F.T.C.D.; Stanley Harrington, Esq., B.A.; W. R. J. Molloy, Esq.; Captain T. B. Shaw, and J. Struthers, Esq., LL.D.;

with J. D. Daly, Esq., M.A., Secretary.

Dublin.

[illegible]

Professor T. Johnson, [illegible]

general facilities which it possesses, it has been done; but compared with the London College of Science, and with the University Colleges which have sprung up almost all over the country, it is not, I should say, getting fair play; at any rate it has not been developed all along the line. I hold that opinion very strongly.

25908. In speaking of University Colleges which have since sprung up all over the country, you are evidently speaking not of Ireland but of England?—Yes, I am speaking of the Royal College of Science, London; University College, Liverpool; Owens College, Manchester, and the Yorkshire College, Leeds, and so on. All these Colleges have government subsidies in order to enable teachers to get a training in them, and so far as the Dublin College is concerned, no attempt has been made to develop it in that direction.

25909. Do you think it desirable that the Dublin College of Science should be utilised in that direction?—The members of the Council are, I know, most anxious to do it, and they have sent in recommendations which have never been acted upon.

25910. To whom did you send those recommendations?—We did it through the official channels—through the head office in London—and they are most anxious to help in the matter, but nothing has been done.

25911. As a matter of fact, then, it has not gone further?—It has not gone further.

25912. You seem to have done your part—you sent them the recommendations, and the recommendations have not been acted upon?—Yes. I had been accustomed to the training of teachers when I was in the Royal College of Science in London. I was demonstrator there from 1885 to 1890, and then I came to Ireland. I was so much delighted with the work of aiding the teachers there that I offered three years ago on an indication that the teachers of Ireland would come to our College if they got a chance, to give a course of lectures in the month of July. I sent an official letter saying, "If you will allow me I will give a course of lectures in July to the teachers without fee, to prove that the teachers would come for instruction if they got an opportunity." The Department itself, so far as I can speak of its policy, seemed to be quite willing to let the teachers come, but nothing came of the suggestion.

25913. To whom was the suggestion made?—It went from the Council to the head quarters in London.

25914. That is the Science and Art Department?—Yes. It was the inadequacy of the College itself—that the building was not suitable for the existing requirements of the College—that partly stopped the matter.

25915. I believe the Royal College of Science in England has made arrangements to enable a certain number of science teachers to attend a course of instruction at the College in South Kensington in July?—That is so.

25916. And the teachers selected to attend any of these courses receive their railway fare, and a sum not exceeding £3 towards their expenses while attending the College?—Yes.

25917. Is there any corresponding regulation here in Dublin?—No.

25918. Captain Shaw.—That London arrangement applies to Ireland?—Yes. I had one or two from the Belfast district nearly ten years ago when I was in the College, but I think most Irish teachers would prefer to be trained in Dublin and not in London.

25919. Mr. Molloy.—You would prefer it?—Yes.

25920. Chairman.—In looking over the reports for the current year I see that 150 offered themselves for this course, but that only 250 were admitted?—Yes. I think at least 600 teachers apply in London College every year, and of the 600 only 250 are admitted, so that there is a big demand for instruction.

25921. Then, again, in the London College of Science arrangements are also made for a limited number of science teachers, and of students in science classes who intend to become science teachers, to be admitted free for a term or a session to the complete courses of instruction in the College?—Yes, that is so, in many cases for three or four years each.

25922. And while under instruction they receive a maintenance allowance at the rate of 21s. a week, and their railway fare is paid for one journey to and from each session between the home of the teacher or student and the College?—That is so.

25923. Is there any corresponding arrangement to that in Ireland?—No; I may give you an illustration more or less bearing upon that matter. Quite recently, about two years ago, I found a man in the Botanical Department in the museum, seeking botanical information to help him to obtain a Royal Exhibition in the London College. I saw he was working on the wrong lines altogether, and I told him what he should do, seeing that he was ready and fit for competition for an exhibition. He was a student from the agricultural farm in Glasnevin; he is now in London in his second year of training as a teacher in science. One of his chief recommendations in getting into the College was that he was going to teach in Ireland. I told him that he ought to apply as the English teachers apply, and ask the Department in making the selection to take into consideration the demands of the district, and that teachers in science were few in it. That was one of his strongest recommendations.

25924. I find that another arrangement in the London College of Science is that any bona fide teacher who is qualified to earn payments on results, and who is actually engaged or who has actually taught approved science classes under the Science and Art Department, may be permitted to attend without payment any course of lectures in the College; and that arrangement seems to hold both for London and for Dublin?—That is so.

25925. The only provision made therefore for Irish teachers is that they will have a right to attend the lectures, but there is no provision made to pay their railway fare, or to pay for their maintenance whilst they are attending the lectures?—No.

25926. Over and above the privilege which they get by gaining an exhibition in competition with English teachers trained in the English colleges, the Irish College of Science gives the teachers no assistance of the kind I have mentioned?—Nothing of that kind.

25927.—There are, I believe, Royal exhibitions and National scholarships?—Yes.

25928. There are twenty-one Royal exhibitions I understand?—I cannot say the exact number for the whole of the United Kingdom.

25929. There seem to be seven open for competition each year, four of these are to be held in London and three in Dublin?—There are three for Dublin.

25930. I find that during the present year there are twelve exhibitions held in connection with the London College?—We have three here each year. We have nine exhibitioners altogether, three each year, each staying three years.

25931. These exhibitions are of £50 a year, and they include the privilege of free admission to lectures and also the use of the laboratory?—Yes.

25932. Besides these, there are thirty-six National scholarships?—Yes.

25933. And twenty-two of these are open for competition each year?—Yes.

25934. These scholarships entitle the holders to free attendance at lectures, and to free access to the [illegible] there is a maintenance allowance of [illegible] a session of forty weeks?—Yes.

[illegible] comes to £50 for the session. Thus [illegible] to be more valuable than the exhibi- [illegible]

[illegible] holders of these scholarships get also [illegible]?—Yes.

[illegible] persons who obtain the scholarships [illegible] of attending either the London or [illegible] College?—Yes.

[illegible] addition to all this, there are eighteen [illegible]?—Yes.

[illegible] these entitle the holders to free

I think there are two things to be considered—one is that the College should be on a broader basis than it is at present. The college at present is very inadequate. We have the case of an exhibitioner who left the College rather than hold it in our College, and we have a case of Irish persons who went over to London to be trained, because of the facilities that exist there.

[illegible]. The amount of knowledge necessary for an exhibition is very much greater than would be required for an ordinary teacher teaching in a National school?—Yes, the competition is so much keener.

25664. Does not paragraph "D" page 41, in the report apply to the College of Science here—"And is granted to a limited number of teachers engaged in science teaching who are selected to attend provincial science colleges"?—No, it does not apply to us at all.

25665. I think it includes the College in Dublin?—It may be applicable; it has, however, never been acted upon.

25666. Mr. HARRINGTON.—From what class of schools do the Royal College of Science students come?—They come from the schools generally, and places where they help themselves at evening classes of instruction.

Dublin.

Professor

Dublin.
Jan. 13, 1887.
Professor W. N. Hartley, F.R.S., F.C.S.

course be more advisable or more suitable?—You must remember that the College staff is very hard worked, and it would be scarcely fair to ask all the professors to come back in the evening and give lectures after doing the day's work.

26007. Professor FITZGERALD.—Some of the assistants could help?—Yes; some of the assistants do help. We have assistants in the Kevin-street school and in the Kingstown school.

26008. Isn't it from the intermediate rather than the primary school that the students come?—Probably.

26009. And the increase in the training in the National schools would probably make not much difference at the present time?—It would gradually. The elementary school boy would be trained gradually.

26010. Teachers to attend the College would have to reside in Dublin or near Dublin?—Yes.

26011. Don't you think that they could be well trained in science teaching in their own colleges?—I should say without any disrespect to the men in the training colleges, that with the apparatus of our College we could give the course of instruction better there.

26012. Take the training college at Drumcondra, would it not be a long way off for the classes to come to Stephen's-green? Wouldn't that make a great difference?—If you compare the distance that is covered with the greater facility for teaching in the College of Science—the much greater facility than in a local training college—it would not make a difference.

26013. CHAIRMAN.—But has the Royal College of Science this greater facility?—In apparatus, certainly. I don't know, of course, what the accommodation in point of apparatus and diagrams in the training college may be, but certainly the facilities must be greater in the College of Science or it would be a discredit to the College, having regard to the money it gets.

26014. Professor FITZGERALD.—They have to reside in the training college in Dublin while under training, and wouldn't it be desirable that they should be instructed there rather than in some other college?—I don't know quite enough of the training colleges, but if the tuition could be given there, it would be the better system.

26015. There are two classes of teachers we have to deal with, the teachers in training and the existing teachers, for whom you would intend the summer course; and as regards the teachers in training, you propose that they should be trained, not in the training college, but in classes in the College of Science?—I think it might be done in the training college, but you have not the necessary apparatus and specimens in the college.

26016. CHAIRMAN.—Are you aware that there are 160 students in training in the Drumcondra Training College?—I don't know the exact number.

26017. Well that is the number: now supposing there are 160 students in that one college, and, say, 100 in Marlborough-street, making 260 in all, what accommodation have you for them?—The largest lecture theatre holds about 150.

26018. I merely wish to know what exactly you propose. Supposing that there are 260 students to be trained as teachers of elementary science, what do you suggest can be done by your College in that way?—It might not be necessary to take the whole of them in the same subject at the same time.

26019. Professor FITZGERALD.—Do you know how they manage the training in England?—I do not know how they manage it generally there, but I know most of them go to the University colleges, the college. I think they were trained in my own College. In Liverpool, they are trained in the University College.

26020. Captain SHAW.—Yes, the students go in from Edge Hill.

26021. Professor FITZGERALD.—Now, the teachers who are being trained to teach science, don't you think they should have practice classes, where they would see and learn what they are taught?—Yes, I think it is much better that every teacher in training should not only know the subject, but that he should be able to supervise the teaching of it, and be able to give object lessons on the subject to a class of students.

26022. In London in the training of teachers they don't provide anything of that kind?—No.

26023. Don't you think it would be a great deal better if they did?—Yes.

26024. Do you think in a college where teachers are being trained there should be a practising school attached to the college?—I think so.

26025. A centre for science; a centre, say, for woodwork?—Subject to the supervision, of course, of a person who would be really able to supervise it.

26026. The best arrangement, then, for a training college where teachers are being taught is that there should be a practising school in some way attached to it, so that the teachers in training could have an opportunity of seeing how the work is done, and doing the work themselves?—Yes; and have their methods criticised and their faults corrected.

26027. One thing, it would have a powerful effect on the teaching of agriculture, and prevent it being taught out of mere books. Do you agree that agriculture should be taught in primary schools?—The principles of botany should be taught. There should be practical illustrations of the principles underlying the growth of plants.

26028. Do you think it a desirable thing that the teachers should be taught the way they should teach that subject to children?—Yes.

26029. Could that be done in the College of Science?—Certainly.

26030. Do you think it could be done with some sort of economy?—My own impression here is that the facilities for teaching botany here are much better than in London. We can go out to the Botanical Gardens.

26031. Then you propose that the students should go out to the Botanical Gardens as a practising ground?—Yes. It is a Government institution.

26032. Look at the distance. Would not a great deal of time be spent going backwards and forwards?—I think not. I think it would be time spent in exercise; two hours' exercise and instruction.

26033. You think that, instead of the present system of teaching agriculture out of books, it would be most important in Ireland that the teachers should teach the principles of botany underlying agriculture?—Yes. There should be practical illustrations of the subject, and men should see as much as possible the thing they are reading about.

26034. Do you say that boys who are to plough and sow should know the way plants germinate?—Yes; and know something of the history of the plant itself. May I mention one point? Any Irish boy may understand the principles of the formation of hybrids in a few minutes if the subject is taught with the aid of specimens.

26035. Would they want to know how the hybrids are actually produced?—Students could do that for themselves.

26036. Monsignor MOLLOY.—I think you said the supply of material is very poor in the College of Science?—It is the material of the student himself is

Dublin.
Nov. 11, 1897.
Professor T. Johnson, D.Sc., F.L.S.

number, 110 students. Twenty of these are not Irish, but the rest are Irish, or resident in Ireland.

26041. Then you have many Irish students?—At present we have.

26041a. Is that for the day course?—Yes.

26042. Professor FITZGERALD.—How many of the ninety take up the full course in the college?—I think about thirty.

26043. Monsignor MOLLOY.—What are the remaining eighty students doing?—They are taking out special courses.

26044. What courses do they chiefly take?—Last year in botany there were twenty-six, some of them teachers.

26045. Professor FITZGERALD.—How many are going to the Royal University?—Very few, indeed; perhaps two. Certainly not more than three or four.

26046. Monsignor MOLLOY.—Then the great majority, though reading the regular course, were taking up only particular subjects?—Yes, they take some special subjects, but thirty take the full associate course.

26047. Professor FITZGERALD.—Are not the majority of those thirty who take the full course assisted, but the others are not assisted in the same way?—Many of the thirty will be exhibitioners or have scholarships.

26048. Monsignor MOLLOY.—How do you account for the fact that so many fail to take the full associate course?—I think the school system in Ireland is wrong, and that the boys get no encouragement to study science.

26049. Do you think it is desirable that there should be some elementary science taught in primary schools?—I do.

26050. Do you think it would be desirable that the children should be taught the rudimentary principles of science generally rather than that they should be taught particular branches of science?—Yes, I think they should be taught the foundations of science first.

26051. Do you think that if elementary science were introduced in a more advanced form, into the intermediate schools, there would be a larger supply of students to take advantage of the College of Science?—I think it would have that effect.

26052. In reference to the summer course, I take it that you contemplate a summer course for those who are already masters of schools, not for teachers in training?—I don't see why the students should not come also.

26053. But if they were in training colleges, going through a regular course, there would be no necessity for them to come to the College of Science?—That would be better, of course.

26054. For those masters who had never got a science training, and who were engaged in teaching in schools, the summer course at the College of Science would be a great advantage?—I think it would be.

26055. Many of these teachers have studied science out of books; and a few weeks summer course in practical work would make their knowledge more exact and thorough?—Yes, a summer course is a holiday course, and no man would come unless he was anxious to receive information, and he would naturally learn something of the subject before he came.

Professor GRENVILLE A. J. COLE, F.G.S., Professor of Geology, Royal College of Science, Dublin, examined.

Professor Grenville A. J. Cole, F.G.S.

26056. CHAIRMAN.—You are a Professor of Geology in the Dublin Royal College of Science?—Yes.

26057. You are in a position to give us information as to the training of teachers in the Royal College of Science in London?—I will tell you my own experience there. The teachers brought up in the London College are of two classes. Some are brought up for the whole course and trained from the beginning in science, and some are brought up for the summer course. The latter class have generally already undertaken the teaching of schools.

26058. The first class, I assume, are those who intend to become teachers?—Most of these are young men who are beginning their careers, and they enter upon a course of science which they are pledged to apply in teaching, and as far as there is room the courses are open to them.

26059. Then they can go for any particular branch?—Yes, they apply at their own time, but the Department has the choice. These men have passed certain of the Departmental Examinations.

26060. Is it from the training colleges that the teachers come in?—These persons are not trained in the training colleges. They are taken from the country at large and from technical or other schools.

26061. Do any teachers or students in training in the English training colleges go to the London College of Science to learn scientific principles?—That I am not aware of.

26062. As far as your experience goes?—As far as my experience goes they were not actually engaged in the training colleges.

26063. Well, as to the other branch of the work, the summer work?—The summer work is for men already engaged in teaching for the Department. They were known by the results of their teaching, and even where those results were excellent, they might not have been sufficiently trained in certain branches of a subject or there might be some other elements against their future success, and they are brought up for a special course in a subject which they may have already taught, or which they may not have taught up to that time.

26064. Can you say how many teachers for the summer course were brought over from Ireland?—Not many in the subjects of geology and physiography—three or four each year.

26065. Were any of these Irish National school teachers?—I think from the addresses they gave that they usually were.

26066. Three would be the whole number for the year?—In that particular branch.

26067. That would be a very small proportion?—There would be six or seven such courses going on at the time and that number would have to be multiplied.

26068. What do you think as to the possibility of the College of Science in Dublin being utilised for the instruction of teachers of elementary schools, whether throughout the year, or by means of a summer course?—I imagine if the teachers offered themselves, who proposed to teach in the elementary schools, they could be trained side by side with the students in the college.

26069. You are speaking now, not of actual teachers, but of candidate teachers?—Yes.

26070. That is, persons who as yet are only preparing for the office of teachers?—Yes.

26071. Do you really think the College has sufficient accommodation for the teaching of the students in the training colleges?—I think it could offer in its present condition considerable facilities in the way of apparatus and materials for the improvement of the training of those who go to the training colleges.

26072. But have you room in the College for the students from the training colleges in addition to your present students?—They could be taken at separate hours.

26073. But remember that, as I have pointed out to Professor Johnson, they are to be coached by the

Dublin.

Nov. 23, 1887.

Professor Grenville A. J. Cole, F.G.S.

hundred?—In that case an enlargement of the College would first be necessary.

26074. Does it come then to this, that taking the College as it stands, with its existing buildings, it is not possible for it to do any substantial work there for the training of our teachers?—With the existing buildings it could not.

26075. Next then, as to the summer courses that have been suggested, is the College in a position to do anything substantial in that direction?—I should say it could.

26076. Are the professors willing to take up all this extra work during the summer, without receiving extra payment for it?—I think that under the circumstances they would not be willing to take up the additional work for the salaries they now receive.

26077. So then, taking the College as it stands, with its existing buildings and its existing grant, it is not really in a position to do very much for us either in the work of teaching throughout the year, or in the work of summer courses?—No. I may say for this work extra employment was given in the London College many years ago.

26078. Now, let us look at the case in another way; supposing that anything could be done for us by the College, what branch of science should be taught?—I think the present physiography course, which has been arranged by the Department of Science and Art, with modifications in favour of the elements of agricultural teaching and some of the elements of zoology and botany.

26079. That is, botany and the sciences that underlie agriculture, with special reference to the teaching of agriculture?—Yes.

26080. The course would be on the existing lines of the physiography course, with modifications having regard to the fact that it was to be taught by teachers in country schools?—Yes.

26081. Would it not be useful that it should be modified also in view of the fact that it is to be taught not only to boys but to girls?—I don't think so to any extent.

26082. In reference, for instance, to cookery, as there are branches of science that underlie cookery, would it not be useful to have the course modified in the interests of girls?—I did not contemplate cookery as a branch of physiography.

26083. But of course there are certain natural laws that come into play in cookery?—I think that relates more to chemistry and physics.

26084. Is there not something of chemistry in the physiography course?—Yes.

26085. And could you not, in teaching girls the elementary principles of chemistry, bring into special prominence some of those principles that relate to the operation of cookery?—Yes.

26086. Is there any general observation that you wish to make?—I think the schools should have a course of physiography, including the elements of physics, and the fundamental things in chemistry. With regard to Irish schools, a certain amount of zoology and botany should also be considered fundamental subjects.

26087. You are of opinion that in elementary schools there should be a course of a general nature in science, rather than a course in any particular branch of science?—Yes, the first year's course in scientific instruction should be of a very general character.

26088. Captain Shaw.—Do you say the children should have some practice on the materials?—Yes.

26089. Is there a practice by the teacher or the children?—By the children in every case.

26090. Professor Fitzgerald.—Are not the teachers trained in the South Kensington School mainly from the organised secondary and technical schools rather than those from the primary schools?—I can't tell you that matter numerically, but I know the summer courses there are largely engaged in the Board schools and teach evening classes in science.

26091. But don't they come from the organised science schools through the country rather than from the elementary schools?—I think the summer course always draws largely from the teachers of the general schools, the Board schools.

26092. Some of the teachers in the Board schools and in the science schools have evening classes?—Yes.

26093. There is very little of that in Ireland?—Less than there used to be.

26094. Do we not require teachers in advanced science for teaching in the technical schools?—Yes.

26095. Is not that more the direction in which the College of Science ought to devote itself?—I think the College of Science would gain greatly in influence by having the teachers in the elementary schools side by side with the other students.

26096. In order to teach the children to do experiments, would it not be essential that there should be practising classes for the teachers?—I regard that as work for the training colleges. In the College of Science they would have the example of our own teachers.

26097. But you cannot teach children in the same way as grown-up people?—I think the training college should undertake that duty; that is a branch of pedagogy which might be supplied in the training colleges.

26098. Don't you think in the training colleges a teacher in training should see a teacher teaching children?—I think the scientific instructor of the teachers might not be the most suitable person to teach. He might be a very clever person, and yet he might not be capable of teaching boys.

26099. Mr. Molloy.—Do you think it would be possible to teach in the primary schools natural history by means of object lessons?—Yes.

26100. Do you think that would be desirable?—I think it would in a country such as Ireland.

26101. Do you think it would be desirable to encourage collections of minerals and plants in schools?—Most desirable.

26102. That would not involve any great difficulty?—Provided the master knew where to look for them.

26103. But you would suppose that the master was trained in a training college?—Yes. He should be taught where to look for them.

26104. With regard to the fundamental principles of physics and chemistry, there might be experiments to illustrate them?—These experiments are incorporated in the course of the *Science and Art Department*.

26105. Such a course in physiography as that might be the course in the training colleges, but there should be something more simple for the training of children in schools?—Something slightly simpler.

Professor W. F. Barrett, F.R.S.E.

Professor W. F. Barrett, F.R.S.E., *Professor of Physics, Royal College of Science, Dublin, examined.*

26106. Chairman.—You are a Professor of Experimental Physics in the Royal College of Science, Dublin?—Yes.

26107. I remember that you gave evidence before the Royal Commission on Technical Instruction in 1883?—I did, your Grace.

26108. And you delivered an important address to the Congress of National School Teachers in 1870?—I do not know if it were "important," but I gave an address.

26109. It has been printed and forms a very interesting pamphlet; I have the pamphlet here, and

Dublin.
[illegible]
Professor W. F. Barrett, F.R.S.E.

a great deal of what you say in it seems to bear upon the subject of this Commission's inquiry. First, you are strongly of opinion that elementary science should be an essential part of the ordinary school curriculum?—I am.

26110. And that it should not at all be confined to the higher classes?—Yes.

26111. You are aware that on the existing programme for the National schools, science only comes in as an extra subject, and even that, only in the higher classes?—Yes, I am aware of that.

26112. But I am sure you don't approve of it; you consider that, as far as possible, science should begin in the lower classes, in the form of object lessons?—It should begin in the kindergarten.

26113. That will be at least a foundation for it, and then it should go on without a break through the whole course?—Yes.

26114. Unfortunately it has to be recognised that in the past the Board of National Education, as you remark, has not done very much for the teaching of science in the schools in Ireland?—True, and I am not the only person who has regretted this.

26115. Well, I trust it is by this sufficiently well-known that the National Education Board are now quite as anxious as you yourself could be to do anything that can possibly be done in that particular Department?—I am very glad to hear it.

26116. As a result of the grants from the Science and Art Department, something has been done for the teaching of science in such schools?—It has, I believe.

26117. And in your address in 1883 you spoke of a change having been then made in the arrangement of the Science and Art Department's grants, and you said that, as a result of the new arrangements, even this small achievement, which was then to the credit of the Science and Art Department, was likely to be destroyed?—It was probable.

26118. There was a diminution of the grant on account of the increased difficulty in passing the new standard of examination, and the lower grade pass was altogether abolished?—Yes.

26119. And you appeared to think that the change practically meant the extinction even of the small amount of scientific instruction then given in the primary schools?—Yes, so far as that depended on the Science and Art Department.

26120. I believe the event fully justified your prediction?—I do not know officially, but I believe it has.

26121. You consider at all events that the change then made was a very unfortunate one?—Yes.

26122. Now turning from the past to the present, you consider that something effective should be done for the training of teachers at the Royal College of Science?—Certainly, I am very strongly of that opinion.

26123. In your pamphlet you advocate an increase of the existing accommodation in the College, and an enlargement of the staff, all involving, of course, an increase of the grant to enable this work to be done. Does it come to this that nothing can be done by the College with its existing grant, its existing staff, and its existing building?—I think I mentioned in that address that it would be absolutely necessary to increase the grants, as the funds remain the same as they were a quarter of a century ago, although the number of students has quadrupled in the same time.

26124. But it is not very easy to get such grants increased; at all events we are dealing with facts, and taking the College with the existing grant, the existing staff, and everything as it stands, the College does not appear to be in a position to do very much in the way of training teachers in elementary science?—I am not sure of that.

26125. Then what can it do?—The teachers can now enter at a merely nominal fee.

26126. Is there room for them?—There is room for a certain number.

26127. A large number or a small number?—Not a very large number.

26128. That is precisely the point I had in view. The College then is not in a position to do very much in the matter?—Not very much without enlargement.

26129. Taking things as they stand, taking the number of teachers in training in Dublin, say 500 or 600, with that large number, the College is not in a position to do very much for the teachers in training in the way of teaching them elementary science?—If they came all at once, it would be impossible to accommodate them, but they might come in batches.

26130. Even as regards the halls for the delivery of lectures, has the College accommodation for them, no matter how they might come?—Not for so many.

26131. And as to your special branch, for the laboratory or experimental work, it would be out of the question?—Yes.

26132. Of course you consider that it is a serious defect in the teaching of science if it be confined to lectures?—Yes; books are mere channels of knowledge; not knowledge itself.

26133. Do you agree that the science to be taught in the elementary schools should be on general lines, science on the lines of physiography as laid down in the programme of the Science and Art Department?—That very much depends on the capacity of the teacher. The education should be like physiography or be even more elementary, mere object lessons, and then pass on to elementary lessons in science in the higher classes.

26134. You must remember that there is the important limitation of time. Do you think it is really possible to teach any one branch of science in any useful way in an elementary school, having regard to the question of time?—I think there would be abundance of time, if time were economised by dropping some of the subjects taught at present.

26135. If they gave up teaching grammar for instance?—Yes, and I pointed out the observations of the president of the English Union of Teachers on the subject of their adopting the metric system.

26136. I think you said in your address that one of the main advantages of scientific teaching in elementary schools, is that it conduces to accuracy?—Yes.

26137. And leads to the formation of habits of observation and of precision in thought and in action?—Yes.

26138. And that it cultivates judgment?—Yes.

26139. And you quote Professor Fowler in support of that view; you also say that it cultivates truthfulness and cleanliness?—Yes.

26140. What you have to say about kindergarten teaching applies chiefly to the object lessons to be given as a part of the kindergarten training?—Quite so.

26141. This would be the most elementary teaching?—Yes, to the youngest classes.

26142. You express views also as to the importance of manual training?—Yes.

26143. You regard it as a very useful branch of school work?—Absolutely essential.

26144. Well, unfortunately it may not be possible to have it in many schools. For instance, where there is only one teacher, and perhaps only one room in which all the work of the school has to be carried on, it would not be possible to have manual training in those circumstances?—With proper arrangements and with a capable teacher it might be done, even under such circumstances.

26145. Do you consider that manual training would have an injurious effect as regards other branches of school work?—No. On the contrary, I think it would stimulate it. The experience in Clifton College was to that effect.

...m ever heard an unfavourable
...le of manual training in schools
... had practical experience of its
...o the contrary, I believe it is a
...ration.
...consider that manual work in the
... for instance, should be based on
...ically; drawing underlies good
...wledge, and I think it would be
... with it.
... aware that drawing is now only
...n our Irish National schools?—
...
...d it is not very long since it was
... England?—Yes.
... optional in Scotland?—I do not
...
...it to be made obligatory here?—
...
...as well as for boys?—Yes.
...ime should be given to it?—I
...xpress an opinion on that subject.
...pprove of the teaching of science
...ks, or by means of lectures?—It
...accompanied by demonstrations
...ler experiments, by actual experiment-
...dents themselves?—Yes.
...uld not merely look on at the ex-
...y should take part in the making
...A great many years ago, in 1876,
... school teachers were invited over
...d a course of instruction, I gave
...s to the teachers. I have here the
...ade at the time by the teachers of
...s, and amongst them there were
...h.
... no objection to having some of
...ur notes as specimens?—Not the
...ticularly at your service, I believe
...he earliest printed lessons on prac-
...gland.
...ider that whilst the teaching, for
...ork, in our primary schools is to be
...d, the schools should do nothing in
...aching trades?—No. I would not
...of trades.
...ld simply teach woodwork for the
...agree that the teaching of it ceases?
...
...lvergan.—You say manual work
... Are there not other species of
... work which have their value, such
...k?—I am not an expert on that
...
...tach great value to this kind of
...
...e to the instruction in elementary
...—I do.
...think it would be possible to have
... the regular programme?—I think
...
...Yes. Elementary science and also
...s, or manual instruction, including
...
... say what time could be given to
...they might run concurrently. I

have object lessons and elementary instruction in drawing objects, and some other easy manual instruction.

26168. And after that the course might be made more definite?—Yes.

26169. But before eleven you would have drawing, object lessons and simple manual instruction?—Yes.

26170. Professor Fitzgerald.—Have you considered the system of Mr. Heller?—No.

26171. That is the elementary course in science the boys are required to make experiments themselves?—It comes very good, but I consider this the aim of every good science teacher.

26172. From your experience, can persons teach others to make experiments without having some experience in doing them themselves?—In teaching children if the teachers themselves can make experiments I think they can teach the children to make them.

26173. The pedagogy of making experiments is very different from the pedagogy of teaching. The pedagogy of managing a class that are making experiments is entirely different from the pedagogy of managing a class which you are teaching out of a book?—Very different.

26174. Therefore instruction and experience in teaching classes out of a book would not enable a teacher to manage a class making experiments?—No.

26175. Don't you think that unless the teacher is trained to make the experiments that the work of teaching would fail?—It is useful, I would say most important, that the teacher himself should be able to make every experiment.

26176. Wouldn't it be necessary that the teacher should be well trained if he has to teach a class to make experiments?—It would, certainly.

26177. Monsignor Molloy.—You said that it would be a great saving of time if the metric system was taught?—Yes.

26178. Would you be in favour of teaching the metric system only, and not teaching the English system?—That would now be a different matter, and it would take time.

26179. But if you do not teach the English system, then the children will not know the weights and measures in use in this country?—They would not have to spend so much time in mental gymnastics.

26179a. It is not the misfortune of our present [illegible] that we have to learn two systems: the English system for the common business of life, and the metric system for scientific purposes?—Yes.

26180. Mr. Molloy.—Is there not a certain amount of elementary science in the kindergarten system?—In well taught kindergarten there is. In some of the schools in England no doubt there is.

26181. I understand that you think that experiments in chemistry and the teaching of the principles of chemistry should be deferred till the higher classes were reached. Do you think it important that the children when learning lessons should be taught from the earliest infancy to take an intelligent interest in the objects round about them?—Yes.

with in that way becomes a mere matter of books, like history.

24183. And, of course, you would not have it so. Then here was the next question (reading)—

"Suppose, however, that our contemplated system was to be one in which the result of the teaching, or so-called teaching, of science was to be tested only by an examination conducted exclusively in writing, and conducted so such lines that a boy might get the highest possible marks who had never performed an experiment, or seen an experiment performed, or had never seen any scientific apparatus, even of the most rudimentary kind"?—

It would be perfectly worthless.

24184. And again (reading)—

"And you would probably add that the less there was of it be a country the better in the interests of science"?—Yes; I quite agree with Dr. Gladstone. Perhaps I may mention a instance to illustrate that. I knew a gentleman who took a high degree as a Doctor of Science, and he afterwards entered a laboratory for the first time in his life, and he saw there a concave and convex mirror. He asked me what they were, and when I told him he said he always thought the convex was the concave, and when I drew a section of them he thought the pictures represented portions of cylinders.

Rev. FRANCIS RYAN, P.P., St. Joseph's, Dublin, examined.

24185. CHAIRMAN.—You have had some interesting experience in the matter of evening schools and night schools in the city of Dublin?—Yes, your Grace, I have been experimenting in the matter for some time.

24186. Tell us the result of some of your experiments?—I tried a night school first, thirty years ago in the village of Maynooth, and as long as I stayed there it was a very considerable success. The boys attended regularly and a great deal of good was done, but I don't know what its fate has been since I left the place. I had not much opportunity of doing anything in the matter afterwards until I got charge of my present parish in the city here in 1890.

24187. You established a night school shortly after you were appointed parish priest?—Yes, in September, 1890.

24188. I believe the school was not particularly attractive, as regards either its internal fittings and equipment, or the school buildings generally?—It was certainly an extraordinary place. We were lodged in a hay-loft for four and a half years, a hay-loft over a stable, in the lane at the back of Eccles-street.

24189. Notwithstanding the unattractive character of the school building, did you find the poor children willing to come to it?—Yes; the very first night we were able to get 120 boys of a rough class, though we didn't promise to give them anything, except to examine them and give them a slate and a pencil.

24190. You found then that these poor boys were quite willing to learn?—Yes; during the four years there, and up to the present time in our new school, we found they were only too willing to learn.

24191. What were the ages of the boys?—From twelve to seventeen years. At first we had a difficulty to get teachers. Of course the National Board refused to recognise a school in a hay loft, and then the poor fellow I had as a teacher, though he was exceedingly good in many ways, did not seem to be quite right in his head, and he fell out with the people.

24192. I believe he was not sufficiently skilled in pugilism to be able to hold his own with one or two of them?—That is so. Sir Patrick Keenan, when he saw the eagerness of the boys to come to the school, sent an inspector to the place, and offered to stretch a point to have the school recognised, and it was recognised in January, 1891.

24193. How many boys had the school then on its roll?—That year the exact number on the roll was eighty; the average nightly attendance was thirty.

24194. Things have greatly improved since then?—Yes.

24195. You have moved out of the hay loft?—Yes; we have a decent school now. In the new building in Dorset-street we opened a night school last year, and the number on the roll has increased.

24196. The school where the boys are now taught in the evening is in the fine school building in Dorset-street where you have an ordinary National School in the daytime?—Yes.

24197. Do you still find that the boys are ready and willing to come to the night school?—Yes. In the quarter ending April, 1897, we had 114 on the roll, and in the quarter ending June last we had 310. Some people appear to think that it would be better to have the boys attending the day school, and that these night schools interfere with the day school, but that is a mistake. We have a strict rule on the subject, which is carried out by personal communication, and the moment we discover that a boy is there who is able to attend day school—though we might, of course, stretch a point in some very exceptional cases—we insist that he shall leave the room at once. We have at present a nightly attendance of ninety boys, and I must say their diligence is most remarkable. I have been singularly fortunate in my teachers. Even the poor fellow I had at the start was a most excellent man, and he managed the boys for a time very well. Only for the help I got from the teacher, Mr. Healy, who was the first regular appointment when the school was placed under the National Board, and the self-sacrificing spirit he showed, I could not have got on at all. He was the principal in the day school, and after his hard day's work in that school with such a crowd of poor boys, he came in the evening and taught in the night school for a mere pittance. The salary given by the Board is, of course, wholly inadequate.

24198. Only for help of that sort you would not have been able to carry on the good work at all?—No. I don't blame the National Board, but I must say that with only the Board's existing arrangements for night schools, the thing would be impossible to carry on.

24199. And probably the teachers who would come to you for the pittance that has up to this been allowed by the Board—which, I think, is as low as £1 a month—would not be of a class you would desire to have in charge of this specially trying kind of work?—Unless a man is almost starving he would not come.

24200. What is paid for a night school?—The regular pay is £1 a month for each twenty-five pupils, and if one of the pupils missed even a day in the month, and you had only twenty-four, the teacher would get no pay at all. There has been an instance where we had an attendance of forty-eight, and as we didn't bring it up to fifty the teacher got only £1.

24201. The standard is £1 per month for each twenty-five pupils?—Yes.

24202. In addition there are the results fees, but of course in such schools, from the necessarily irregular attendance and other causes, the results fees do not come to much?—No, the results fees are not much. A boy must make fifty attendances in order to entitle the teacher to get any results fees for him, and what between irregular attendance, and the necessary dulness of the boys, the results fees never can come to

ue of boy is mostly of wild habits, and ady for an examination; put the very

be available for the grown children?—I think for the teaching of kindergarten and time to influence [illegible]

Dublin. Dec. 16, 1897. Rev. Francis Ryan, P.P.

26227. I may say down in Cork the St. Vincent de Paul Society have to contribute to their night-schools, out of their own funds, money that should be more properly payable by the National Board?—I hope they will kindly do the same here.

CHAIRMAN.—I should rather see it done by the National Education Board.

26228. MR. HARRINGTON.—Are there any other night schools in the city besides yours?—There is a very successful one in Churchstreet-street, and there was a very old-established one in North Anne-street twenty years ago, and that one had since undergone, I think.

26229. CHAIRMAN.—You used to attend there when you were a curate in the district?—I used to spend my evenings there.

26230. CHAIRMAN.—There is also one in Lower-street, in charge of the nuns; it is doing excellent work, but it has no connection with the National Education Board.

26231. MR. MOLLOY.—I believe in answer to his Grace you summarised the Board's restrictions on the night schools which required a remedy as being the fact that the remuneration of the teachers is inadequate, and that there is the difficulty about the presentation of pupils for results fees; also that the teachers had not a free hand regarding the general course?—The hardest thing is the money.

26232. Isn't that owing to the fact that the school having been recently opened, the children were not sufficiently qualified in the short time that elapsed from the opening?—In the summer evenings, owing to the rough element who attend, the night school is quite a failure, as the boys would not come in.

26233. Is it your opinion that the restrictions of the Board is responsible for the fact that there are virtually no night schools in Dublin, except the ones in Dorset-street and Churchstreet-street?—The nuns have one in Lower-street in connection with the convent. There are no restrictions of that nature that would prevent the actual extension of night schools.

26234. Your idea is that instead of an afternoon session there should be an evening school?—Yes, I don't think there would be any difficulty if the system is changed, and if you were to go in for morning and evening schools. Coming home after the morning school the boys could go of messages, and then they could go back from 8 to 9 o'clock. Let the morning session be over at 12 or 12.30, and have the roll called at half past nine o'clock, and it would not be a hardship on the teacher to attend again in the evening, for he would have three or four hours in the middle of the day, if he is paid as he ought to be paid.

26235. What kind of work should be done at the day school?—I am only dealing with one boy, and that is the lad of the evening school—you have to make special arrangements for him. You can call it technical education and teach manual work.

CHAIRMAN.—It is better to speak of manual instruction, not technical education; the word technical is misleading, especially from the loose way in which it is used.

26236. MR. MOLLOY.—Have you considered how long the morning session should be?—There should be a short morning session. The greater number of these boys do not attend school at all, and the excuse they make is that they have to go on messages—to go with their father's dinner, generally, and it is often really so. If the boy were allowed off at 12 or 12.30 then he could go for these messages, and he would be encouraged to come back and use the evening school, if that arrangement were made for him. In Belfast there is an arrangement made for factory and working boys and girls.

26237. Half times, with two hundred days for results fees?—You could make it 150 days for results in such schools. Another great advantage of the morning school would be that the little children, the boys and girls, would go home to dinner at the hour when the dinner takes place in their homes, and it would do something to encourage home life.

26238. Your experience is that there is no practical difficulty in getting the pupils to come earlier?—Yes.

26239. This could be done better in a town school than in a country school?—I don't know. In the country the children are in bed early, and often the farther they have to come the earlier they are. The children two miles away come early, and those next the school take their time.

26240. You attribute the success of your night school to some extent to the co-operation of the members of the St. Vincent de Paul Society?—They have begun well, and I have every hope they will continue so.

26241. And there are similar good results under that society in connection with the Churchstreet-street night school?—Yes.

FIFTY-SIXTH PUBLIC SITTING.—FRIDAY, DECEMBER 17, 1897,

Dec. 17, 1897.

AT 3 O'CLOCK, P.M.,

At the Antient Concert Rooms, Dublin.

PRESENT:—THE RIGHT HON. THE EARL OF BELMORE, G.C.M.G., in the Chair; HIS GRACE THE MOST REV. WILLIAM J. WALSH, D.D.; THE RIGHT HON. C. T. REDINGTON, M.A.; HIS HONOUR JUDGE SHAW, Q.C., LL.D.; THE RIGHT REV. MONSIGNOR MOLLOY, D.D., D.SC.; REV. HENRY EVANS, D.D.; REV. HAMILTON WILSON, D.D.; PROFESSOR G. F. FITZGERALD, F.T.C.D.; STANLEY HARRINGTON, ESQ., B.A.; W. R. J. MOLLOY, ESQ.; CAPTAIN T. B. SHAW; and J. STRUTHERS, ESQ., B.A.;

with J. D. DALY, ESQ., M.A., Secretary.

Dublin.

Professor W. N. Hartley, F.R.S.

confined to any one branch of science, and is, therefore, not what I think could be carried out entirely by the College of Science, but some arrangement might be made for a course of instruction like that, and a syllabus could be drawn up.

26769. What we have had before us chiefly in reference to that matter is the Schedule II of the Elementary Education Department in England;—I don't know whether you are familiar with that?—I am not familiar with it at all. I only know it from discussions that have taken place from time to time, in which one or two of my friends have been interested. I may mention Dr. Gladstone and Dr. Armstrong.

26770. Have you read any of the evidence that has been given by these gentlemen?—Last night or the night before I glanced through the evidence they gave before the Commission, and, to a great extent, I agree with it; but I think the kind of work has been pushed too far; in some cases it has gone beyond what is really intended.

26771. I don't understand exactly what you mean?—I meant to say that so far as I can gather from the evidence of Dr. Gladstone the work which was carried out under the syllabus originally drawn up by Professor Armstrong has been greatly improved upon, because he drew it up on lines which were more strictly those on which a chemist would draw it up, and those who were engaged in the instruction under him subsequently developed it by making the facts more general—the information obtained was of a more general nature.

26772. Less specialised?—Yes.

26773. Do you think that is an advantage for the schools?—That, I think, is decidedly an advantage. I think that is what should be aimed at. I think it should not be at all confined to any one branch of science.

26774. And don't you think that the kind of teaching—teaching children to observe phenomena—to give an accurate account of what they do observe, without going into scientific explanations or theories, don't you think that is the best sort of introduction to scientific teaching?—Oh, decidedly; it is what I call common information.

26775. The common information is the basis of all science?—Exactly.

26776. As a matter of fact, I understand that at the College of Science you have trained some of the most successful of these organisers of science who have gone to England and Scotland?—Yes.

26777. Could you tell us who they are, any of them?—There is Dr. Reilly, at Hull, the director of the technical schools there; I am sorry to say I have not brought a calendar with me; there is one at Manchester, and another at Bradford, and there are

person taught in this way, or taught these subjects in this way, do you think he would be easily trained to teach?—Well, I think in nine cases out of ten he could not be trusted to teach efficiently in this manner. It is very difficult to train a master who has already been accustomed to instruction of another kind. In some cases where they have had a little instruction in science, or have read, as a matter of interest, scientific books, it might be possible, but I think in nine cases out of ten it would be extremely difficult, if not impossible.

26282. I suppose you don't consider that this instruction would be of much use if it was not given by a thoroughly qualified and enlightened teacher?—No, it would be, in most cases, worse than useless; it would be injurious.

26283. Rev. Dr. Evans.—You think that your College might be able to aid us in training teachers to teach elementary science in our schools?—Yes.

26284. Do you draw a distinction between training teachers to teach and instructing teachers in the knowledge of science itself?—I don't quite understand your question.

26284a. I want to get at what you mean by training. Do you understand by training instructing persons in science, or teaching people who already know something of science how to teach it?—No, I take it that scientific training is training both by lectures and practical work, and this work is carried on as all scientific research is carried on, and when a student has been trained in this way he is capable of teaching. In some cases he may not be capable of teaching, because it is not every scientific man who can teach, but we can always make a selection of those who are the best and most competent of those trained with us, and who are eventually good teachers—there is a weeding-out process year by year—and it is only those capable who receive certificates or diplomas.

26285. Do you believe that elementary science can be usefully taught in the primary schools?—Well, I would put it at the fifth class, for instance. I believe in the syllabus of the Board at the present time—the Board of National Education—in the fifth class there is chemistry prescribed, and that is the proper time to prescribe a course of elementary physics and chemistry, both taught practically as well as by lectures.

26286. Have you any experience as to the capacity of these Irish teachers?—None whatever. I have never come in contact with them.

26287. So that you could scarcely now form an opinion as to whether they would be suitable men to come in to you for training as a body?—No, I can't sort at all express an opinion on that matter.

26288. Rev. Dr. Wilson.—Do any students in your classes contemplate becoming teachers in the higher schools?—Yes, I think that a good many of them so frame their course, or rather pursue such a course of studies in the College, that they may be either teachers or take up some professional course as engineers or officials under the Board of Works or in the Valuation Office, but if a good opportunity occurs, and they can get the necessary recommendations from their professors, they take up teaching as their aim in life.

26289. Do any of these contemplate taking part in the manufacturing industries of the country?—Oh, yes, most of those that come to me.

26290. You consider chemistry a most important branch of study for these manufacturing industries?—Undoubtedly.

26291. Is the spread, do you think, of the study of chemistry proportionate to the spread of the manufactures of the country?—Yes.

26292. Is it increasing?—Yes.

26293. Mr. Harrington.—Have a large proportion of the students who come to the College of

26294. So I should say that the College here in Ireland suffers a great disadvantage, as compared with similar institutions in England and elsewhere, where science is taught in the elementary schools?—Oh, certainly, they are all at a disadvantage; all our students on that account.

26295. Is there a considerable proportion of English students in the Royal College of Science?—No, last year we had only five; this year I don't exactly know how many there may be, but I should think not more than, at the outside, nine students from England. I cannot say whether those who are resident in Dublin are English or not.—I think they are probably not. At any rate, we have only, so far as I am aware, about nine in the College at the present time, and they nearly all pass through my laboratory and lecture room, so I am pretty well acquainted with the students as a body.

26296. Professor Fitzgerald.—As I understand from the abstract that we have been given, the College of Science is specially devoting itself to training people who would be teachers in more advanced schools than primary schools?—Oh, certainly, yes.

26297. Do you think that the College of Science could help us much in providing teachers in primary schools with science instruction suitable to them?—That is a question which I think I have dealt with. If what I understand is the course contemplated for primary schools, it is not exactly what I call science; it is common information on ordinary facts imparted to the pupils by way of object lessons and by simple experiments which they carry out themselves, but it is not an instruction in any one branch of science or the elements of two or three branches; it is not exactly scientific instruction.

26298. You object to its being exactly scientific instruction?—It is not exact.

26299. Why should it not be exact?—The way in which it is carried out, the operation of such teaching is this:—Supposing you have a teacher with a number of common objects, such as salt, and lime, and chalk and coal, or salt, chalk, coal, and something else, any other stone or a piece of wood; he shows these to the boys, and asks them to make experiments on them—say, for instance, by burning, and they having carried out the experiments and got certain results, note them in their own little note-books in their own language; in nine cases out of ten it is very satisfactory; they have informed themselves of certain facts, but there is generally one bright, intelligent boy in such a class, and that boy will bother his teacher to know why these things are different, and it is there where the system breaks down, because the teacher who is not a scientific man fails to explain them, and I draw a marked distinction between the teaching of science and the teaching of common information by experiments and objects which are experimented upon.

26300. But supposing the teaching takes this form—you give them a piece of paper and ask them to determine the amount of ash by accurate weighing, would not that be an exact determination?—But what does it lead to?

26301. It leads them to observe that there are different constituents in the paper, some of which can be burned and some of which cannot?—That is common information; it is not science.

26302. If you show them that the part that is burned away is the same substance as comes by acting on chalk with a certain acid, would not that be leading them to scientific generalisation?—I don't take it that way at all, it is simply common information obtained by an experiment, which you may say necessitates the use of scientific instruments—the balance.

to that by means of
a different class;
schools.
of that kind can be
on all?—Teaching
I think, is a very
ary school.
children could frame
them in a primary
uld have a distinct
comes later on.
uming of hypotheses
to be introduced into
an at that stage; it
of decisive branches
d physics. But that
discussing is useful
those who are not
ematics.
gone long beyond
resolve to fluorescence
capable of solving

I think they might

t science instruction
? Certainly.
uld provide us with
uld give that instruc-
tion.
derstand you to say
capable of directing
ose that they were
n give the scientific
might look for?—
impress upon Pro-
ment.
say that a bright
ing for and seeking
that the teacher could

might be fairly well
phenomena that had

I should like to know
ition, as elementary
ements of science.
hat there is such a
Yes, I think there can
science —
encourage to study
that there is a
?—There is.
h a beginning can be
epends entirely upon

be a beginning in the

be made in primary

dvisable it should be
desirable.
h a beginning made
the people to profit
in more advanced
l technical education
necessarily a special

at that beginning of
ave in your mind to
dy science. Would
to primary schools, as
would it be a help to
gained is to profit by
afterwards?—Yes;
education, which is the

education have been greatly hampered by the want of such a beginning in the primary schools?—I do.

Dublin.
Jan. 21, 1897.
Professor W. N. Hartley, F.R.S.

26325. Most Rev. Dr. Walsh.—You object to the use of the term "elementary science"?—Yes, I do object to it. I can understand "elements of science," but not exactly "elementary science."

26326. Do you think it makes any practical difference whether that branch of school work be called the elements of science or elementary science?—Well, I think it does. I think there is a difference. The information that is conveyed to the people by the course of instruction which we have been discussing I don't look upon exactly as even elementary science.

26327. Is the term "elementary science" not a recognised one amongst scientific men?—It may or may not be; I cannot say—I am just giving my own views.

26328. So that you are now stating only a personal objection of your own?—Yes, my own personal views.

26329. Now, let me ask you this. You were asked some questions about Course H in the English Education Code. You said, I think, that this course was drawn up by Professor Armstrong?—Yes; I am not acquainted with the Code. I have had personal discussions with him from time to time.

26330. May we take it that it was probably drawn up by Professor Armstrong?—I believe it was.

26331. Now kindly look at the page of the English Code where that Course H is contained (handing book to witness). You see the heading of it there?—Yes, "Elementary science."

26332. So that this branch of school teaching that we are now speaking of is officially known in England by the very name that you find fault with us for using, "elementary science"?—This is for the Board schools.

26333. Oh no, it is for all the primary schools?—Not all primary schools, but the Board schools.

26334. Excuse me, I am very well acquainted with the publication. It is the official Code issued by the English Education Department, and it is not at all exclusively for the Board schools, but for all the primary schools receiving aid from the English Educational Department?—Oh, I beg your pardon; I did not see the title. Then I don't think that was drawn up by Dr. Armstrong.

26335. But you see that it is the official publication from the Education Department in England—it is the official English Education Code?—Yes, I see that.

26336. And do you see that in that official document the official designation given to this branch of schoolwork is "elementary science"?—I do.

26337. So that it is plain, not only that your objection is merely a personal objection, but that your view is at variance with the view officially taken in England?—Certainly.

26338. Have you any experience in the work of primary schools?—I have none. I have never been a teacher, neither have I drawn up a syllabus for primary schools.

26339. You have experience in connection with secondary schools and with colleges?—Yes.

26340. And with universities?—Yes, the University of Wales and at the Royal University.

26341. But, so far as you know, the students whom you may have examined in connection with those various bodies were not students of primary schools?—They may or may not be; I have no evidence as to what they are. The Science and Art schools may be schools, for instance, here under the Intermediate Board, or they may be under the National Board. I have nothing before me to show to what they belong.

26342. You were asked, I think, whether your College could give the kind of training that would be suitable for teachers in our primary schools?—Yes.

26344. But at the same time you say you have no experience of the work of any primary school?—No, but I am explaining that it is the science teaching, the special branches of science which are taught in various schools throughout the country that we train teachers for.

26345. Do you think that the teaching of special branches of science is suitable work for a primary school?—In the fifth class yes.

26346. But not until we come to the fifth class?—No.

26347. I think you said that it is exceedingly difficult to train teachers for teaching this branch of school work?—I should imagine so.

26348. You said, I think, that nine out of ten teachers could not be trained for it at all?—Not if they had been the general run teachers for some time.

26349. Then do you consider that the nine who cannot be trained should be allowed to teach this subject?—Well, that is a question I cannot offer an opinion upon; I should think it depended very much upon the natural aptitude of the teacher.

26350. Let me understand you; I thought I understood you to say that nine out of every ten teachers could not be prepared for this work?—Exactly.

26351. Then is it a desirable thing in the interests of science that teachers who cannot be prepared for teaching it, though a course of instruction is provided for them, should be allowed to teach it?—Well, I should say no; but I cannot say that a hard and fast line could be drawn, because they might be able to teach to a certain extent and not be able to teach with complete advantage to the schools. They might be able to teach a very young class but not an advanced class, say, boys of ten or twelve years of age, though they might be able to teach infants.

26352. You said, I think, that the course of training that the College of Science could give would be a course that would require two years' work?—Yes.

26353. And during these two years special attention should be given to two special branches of science?—Two special branches.

26354. And that is the kind of assistance that the Royal College of Science in Dublin could give us if it was asked to give assistance at all?—Yes.

26355. Monsignor Molloy.—I think you have just mentioned that you were acquainted with the working of the Science and Art system in England?—Yes.

26356. I dare say you have been an examiner under that system?—I have been an examiner for the last six years.

26357. Coming back to the question between us about elementary science, I am not sure whether you consider that there is such a thing as an elementary course in science?—Yes, there are elementary courses in special subjects.

26358. Then, your only difficulty is about the phrase "elementary science"?—Exactly.

26359. But you do admit that there is an elementary course in science?—Yes.

26360. And you think such a course might be advantageously taught in primary schools?—I do.

End of Minutes of Evidence.

INDEX TO EVIDENCE.

[Note.—*The figures refer to the Numbers of the Questions.*]

A

Printed for Her Majesty's Stationery Office,
By Alex. Thom & Co. (Limited), 87, 88, & 89, Abbey-street, Dublin.
The Queen's Printing Office.

www.ingramcontent.com/pod-product-compliance
Lightning Source LLC
Chambersburg PA
CBHW031049110726
47900CB00003B/869

* 9 7 8 3 7 4 2 8 0 5 3 8 6 *